PENGUIN BOOKS

THE STORIES OF WILLIAM TREVOR

William Trevor was born in Mitchelstown, Co. Cork, in 1928, and spent his childhood in provincial Ireland. He attended a number of Irish schools and later Trinity College, Dublin. He is a member of the Irish Academy of Letters.

Among his books are *The Old Boys* (1964), winner of the Hawthornden Prize, *The Boarding House* (1965), *The Love Department* (1966), *The Day We Got Drunk on Cake* (1967), *Mrs Eckdorf in O'Neill's Hotel* (1969), *Miss Gomez and the Brethren* (1971), *The Ballroom of Romance* (1972), *Elizabeth Alone* (1973), *Angels at the Ritz* (1975), winner of the Royal Society of Literature Award, *The Children of Dynmouth* (1976), winner of the Whitbread Award, *Lovers of Their Time* (1978), *The Distant Past* (1979), *Other People's Worlds* (1980), *Beyond the Pale* (1981), *Fools of Fortune* (1983), winner of the Whitbread Award, *A Writer's Ireland* (1984), *The News from Ireland* (1986), *The Silence in the Garden* (1989), winner of the *Yorkshire Post* Book of the Year Award and *Family Sins and Other Stories* (1989). He is the editor of *The Oxford Book of Irish Short Stories* (1989), and has also written many plays for the stage, and for radio and television. Several of his television plays have been based on his short stories. Many of his books are published in Penguin. In 1976 Mr Trevor received the Allied Irish Banks' Prize, and in 1977 was awarded an honorary CBE in recognition of his valuable services to literature.

The Stories of
WILLIAM TREVOR

PENGUIN BOOKS

PENGUIN BOOKS

Published by the Penguin Group
Penguin Books Ltd, 27 Wrights Lane, London W8 5TZ, England
Viking Penguin, a division of Penguin Books USA Inc.
375 Hudson Street, New York, New York 10014, USA
Penguin Books Australia Ltd, Ringwood, Victoria, Australia
Penguin Books Canada Ltd, 2801 John Street, Markham, Ontario, Canada L3R 1B4
Penguin Books (NZ) Ltd, 182–190 Wairau Road, Auckland 10, New Zealand

Penguin Books Ltd, Registered Offices: Harmondsworth, Middlesex, England

The Day We Got Drunk on Cake and Other Stories first published by
The Bodley Head 1967
Published in Penguin Books 1969
Copyright © William Trevor, 1967

The Ballroom of Romance and Other Stories first published by
The Bodley Head 1972
Published in Penguin Books 1976
Copyright © William Trevor, 1972

Angels at the Ritz and Other Stories first published by
The Bodley Head 1975
Published in Penguin Books 1979
Copyright © William Trevor, 1975

Lovers of Their Time and Other Stories first published by
The Bodley Head 1978
Published in Penguin Books 1980
Copyright © William Trevor, 1978

Beyond the Pale and Other Stories first published by The Bodley Head 1981
Copyright © William Trevor, 1981

This collection published under the title *The Stories of William Trevor* in
Penguin Books 1983
10 9

Copyright © William Trevor, 1983
All rights reserved

Printed in England by Clays Ltd, St Ives plc
Set in VIP Times

Contents

Acknowledgements

These stories first appeared in the following publications: *Antaeus, Antioch Review, Best Irish Stories 2, A Book of Contemporary Nightmares, The Eighth Ghost Book, Encounter, Irish Ghost Stories, Irish Press, Listener, Literary Review, London Magazine, New Review, New Yorker, Nova, Observer, Penguin Modern Short Stories, The Real Thing: Seven Stories of Love* (The Bodley Head), *Redbook, Spectator, The Times, Town, Transatlantic Review, Voices 2* (Michael Joseph), *Winter's Tales* (Macmillan, London), *Winter's Tales from Ireland.*

'Going Home' and 'Attracta' first appeared as radio plays on BBC Radio Three.

Grateful acknowledgement is made to A T V Music Group for permission to quote from 'Yesterday' by John Lennon and Paul McCartney. Copyright © Maclen Music, Inc., 1965. ATV Music Corp., 6255 Sunset Boulevard, Los Angeles, California 90028, for the U.S.A., Canada, Mexico, and the Philippines. Northern Songs Limited for the rest of the world. Used by permission. All rights reserved.

The Day We Got Drunk on Cake
and Other Stories

The Table

In a public library, looking through the appropriate columns in a businesslike way, Mr Jeffs came across the Hammonds' advertisement in *The Times*. It contained a telephone number which he noted down on a scrap of paper and which he telephoned later that same day.

'Yes,' said Mrs Hammond vaguely, 'I think this table is still for sale. Let me just go and look.'

Mr Jeffs saw her in his mind's eye going to look. He visualized a fattish, middle-aged woman with light-blue hair, and shapely legs coming out of narrow shoes.

'It is my husband's affair, really,' explained Mrs Hammond. 'Or I suppose it is. Although strictly speaking the table is my property. Left to me by my grandmother. Yes, it's still there. No one, I'm sure, has yet made an offer for this table.'

'In that case –' said Mr Jeffs.

'It was foolish of me to imagine that my husband might have had an offer, or that he might have sold it. He would naturally not have done so without consultation between us. It being my table, really. Although he worded the advertisement and saw to putting it in the paper. I have a daughter at the toddling stage, Mr Jeffs. I'm often too exhausted to think about the composition of advertisements.'

'A little daughter. Well, that is nice,' said Mr Jeffs, looking at the ceiling and not smiling. 'You're kept busy, eh?'

'Why not come round if the table interests? It's completely genuine and is often commented upon.'

'I will do that,' announced Mr Jeffs, naming an hour.

Replacing the receiver, Mr Jeffs, a small man, a dealer in furniture, considered the voice of Mrs Hammond. He wondered if the voice belonged to a woman who knew her p's and q's where antique furniture was concerned. He had been wrong, quite clearly, to have seen her as middle-aged and plumpish. She was younger if she had a toddling child, and because she had spoken of exhaustion he visualized her again, this time in soft slippers, with a strand of hair across her forehead. 'It's a cultured voice,' said Mr Jeffs to himself, and went on to believe that there was money in the Hammond house, and probably a maid or two, in spite of the protest about exhaustion. Mr Jeffs, who had made his small fortune through his attention to such nagging details, walked on the bare boards of his Victorian house, sniffing the air and considering afresh. All about him furniture was stacked, just purchased, waiting to be sold again.

Mrs Hammond forgot about Mr Jeffs almost as soon as his voice ceased to echo in her consciousness. Nothing about Mr Jeffs remained with her because as she had conversed with him no image had formed in her mind, as one had in his. She thought of Mr Jeffs as a shop person, as a voice that might interrupt a grocery order or a voice in the jewellery department of Liberty's. When her *au pair* girl announced the presence of Mr Jeffs at the appointed hour, Mrs Hammond frowned and said: 'My dear Ursula, you've certainly got this name wrong.' But the girl insisted. She stood with firmness in front of her mistress repeating that a Mr Jeffs had called by appointment. 'Heavens!' cried Mrs Hammond eventually. 'How extraordinarily stupid of me! This is the new man for the windows. Tell him to go at them immediately. The kitchen ones first so that he gets them over with while he's still mellow. They're as black as your boot.'

So it was that Mr Jeffs was led into the Hammonds' kitchen by a girl from central Switzerland and told abruptly, though not intentionally so, to clean the windows.

'What?' said Mr Jeffs.

'Start with the kitchen, Mrs Hammond says, since they have most filth on them. There is hot water in the tap.'

'No,' said Mr Jeffs. 'I've come to see a table.'

'I myself have scrubbed the table. You may stand on it if you place a newspaper underneath your feet.'

Ursula left Mr Jeffs at this juncture, although he had already begun to speak again. She felt she could not stand there talking to a window-cleaner, since she was not employed in the house to do that.

'He is a funny man,' she reported to Mrs Hammond. 'He wanted to wash the table too.'

'My name is Jeffs,' said Mr Jeffs, standing at the door, holding his stiff black hat. 'I have come about the console table.'

'How odd!' murmured Mrs Hammond, and was about to add that here indeed was a coincidence since at that very moment a man called Jeffs was cleaning her kitchen windows. 'Oh my God!' she cried instead. 'Oh, Mr Jeffs, what a terrible thing!'

It was this confusion, this silly error that Mrs Hammond quite admitted was all her fault, that persuaded her to let Mr Jeffs have the table. Mr Jeffs, standing with his hat, had recognized a certain psychological advantage and had pressed it imperceptibly home. He saw that Mrs Hammond, beneath the exterior of her manner, was concerned lest he might have felt himself slighted. She is a nice woman, he thought, in the way in which a person buying meat decides that a piece is succulent. She is a nice person, he assured himself, and will therefore be the easier and the quicker to deal with. He was correct in his surmise. There was a prick of guilt in Mrs

Hammond's face: he saw it arrive there as the explanation dawned on her and as she registered that he was a dealer in antiques, one with the features and the accents of a London Jew. She is afraid I am thinking her anti-Semitic, thought Mr Jeffs, well pleased with himself. He named a low price which was immediately accepted.

'I've been clever,' said Mrs Hammond to her husband. 'I have sold the console table to a little man called Mr Jeffs whom Ursula and I at first mistook for a window-cleaner.' Mr Jeffs put a chalk mark on the table and made a note of it in a notebook. He sat in the kitchen of his large house, eating kippers that he had cooked in a plastic bag. His jaws moved slowly and slightly, pulping the fish as a machine might. He didn't pay much attention to the taste in his mouth: he was thinking that if he sold the table to Sir Andrew Charles he could probably rely on a hundred per cent profit, or even more.

'An everyday story of country folk,' said a voice on Mr Jeffs' old wireless, and Mr Jeffs rose and carried the plate from which he had eaten to the sink. He wiped his hands on a tea-cloth and climbed the stairs to the telephone.

Sir Andrew was in Africa, a woman said, and might not be back for a month. It was far from certain when he would return, but it would be a month at least. Mr Jeffs said nothing more. He nodded to himself, but the woman in Sir Andrew Charles' house, unaware of this confirmation, reflected that the man was ill-mannered not to acknowledge what she was saying.

Mr Jeffs made a further note in his notebook, a reminder to telephone Sir Andrew in six weeks' time. As it happened, however, this note was unnecessary, because three days later Mr Jeffs received a telephone call from Mrs Hammond's husband, who asked him if he still had the table. Mr Jeffs made a pretence of looking, and replied after a moment that he rather thought he had.

'In that case,' said Mrs Hammond's husband, 'I rather think I would like to buy it back.'

Mr Hammond announced his intention of coming round. He contradicted himself by saying that it was really a friend of his who wanted the table and that he would bring his friend round too, if that was all right with Mr Jeffs.

'Bring whomsoever you wish,' said Mr Jeffs. He felt awkward in advance: he would have to say to Mr Hammond or to Mr Hammond's friend that the price of the table had doubled itself in three days. He could not put it like that, but Mr Hammond would recognize that that was what it amounted to.

Mr Jeffs was in the kitchen, drinking tea, when they called. He blew at the mug of tea, not wishing to leave it there, for he disapproved of waste. He drank most of it and wiped his lips with the tea-cloth. The door-bell sounded again and Mr Jeffs hastened to answer it.

'I am the nigger in the woodpile,' said a Mrs Youghal who was standing with Hammond. 'It is I who cause all this nonsense over a table.'

'Mrs Youghal hasn't ever seen it,' Hammond explained. 'She, too, answered our advertisement, but you, alas, had snaffled the treasure up.'

'Come into the house,' said Mr Jeffs, leading the way to the room with the table in it. He turned to Mrs Youghal, pointing with one hand. 'There it is, Mrs Youghal. You are quite at liberty to purchase it, though I had earmarked it for another, a client in Africa who has been looking for that very thing and who would pay an exceedingly handsome price. I am just warning you of that. It seems only fair.'

But when Mr Jeffs named the figure he had in mind neither Mrs Youghal nor Hammond turned a hair. Hammond drew out a cheque-book and at once inscribed a cheque. 'Can you deliver it?' he asked.

'Oh yes,' said Mr Jeffs, 'provided it is not too far away. There will be a small delivery charge to cover everything, insurance in transit, et cetera. Four pounds four.'

Mr Jeffs drove his Austin van to the address that Hammond had given him. On the way, he reckoned what his profit on this journey would be: a quarter of a gallon of petrol would come to one and three; subtracting that from four guineas, he was left with four pounds two and ninepence. Mr Jeffs did not count his time: he considered it of little value. He would have spent three-quarters of an hour standing about in his large house, or moving himself to keep his circulation going. It was not a bad profit, he decided, and he began to think of Mrs Youghal and Hammond, and of Mrs Hammond who had mistaken him for a window-cleaner. He guessed that Hammond and Mrs Youghal were up to something, but it was a funny way in which to be up to something, buying antique tables and having them delivered.

'They are conducting an affair,' said Mr Jeffs to himself. 'They met because the table was up for sale and are now romantic over it.' He saw the scene clearly: the beautiful Mrs Youghal arriving at the Hammonds' house, explaining that she had come about the table. Perhaps she had made a bit of a scene, reminding the Hammonds that she had previously telephoned and had been told to come. 'And now I find the table is already disposed of,' said Mrs Youghal in Mr Jeffs's imagination. 'You should have telephoned me back, for God's sake. I am a busy creature.'

'Come straight in, Mrs Youghal, and have a glass of brandy,' cried Hammond in Mr Jeffs's mind. 'How can we make amends?'

'It is all my fault,' explained Mrs Hammond. 'I've been quite hopelessly scatty, placing our beautiful table in the hands of a Jewish trader. A Mr Jeffs whom Ursula in her foreign ignorance ordered to wash down the kitchen windows.'

'The table has brought nothing but embarrassment,' said Hammond, pouring out a fair quantity of brandy. 'Have this, Mrs Youghal. And have a nut or two. Do.'

'I had quite set my heart on that table,' said Mrs Youghal in Mr Jeffs's mind. 'I am disappointed unto tears.'

'A table for Mrs Youghal,' said Mr Jeffs to a woman with a shopping basket who was leaving the blocks of flats.

'Oh yes?' said the woman.

'Which floor, please? I have been given this address.'

'No one of that name at all,' said the woman. 'I never heard of no Youghal.'

'She may be new here. Is there an empty flat? It tells you nothing on these bells.'

'I'm not at liberty,' said the woman, her voice striking a high pitch. 'I'm not at liberty to give out information about the tenants in these flats. Not to a man in a closed van. I don't know you from Adam.'

Mr Jeffs recognized the woman as a charwoman and thereafter ignored her, although she stood on the steps, close to him, watching his movements. He rang one of the bells and a middle-aged woman opened the door and said, when Mr Jeffs had inquired, that everyone was new in the flats, the flats themselves being new. She advised him quite pleasantly to ring the top bell, the one that connected apparently with two small attic rooms.

'Ah, Mr Jeffs,' said the beautiful Mrs Youghal a moment later. 'So you got here.'

Mr Jeffs unloaded the table from the van and carried it up the steps. The charwoman was still about. She was saying to Mrs Youghal that she would clean out the place for six shillings an hour whenever it was suitable or desired.

Mr Jeffs placed the table in the smaller of the two attic rooms. The room was empty except for some rolled-up carpeting and a standard lamp. The door of the second room was closed: he imagined it contained a bed and a wardrobe and two brandy glasses on a bedside table. In time, Mr Jeffs imagined, the whole place would be extremely luxurious. 'A love-nest,' he said to himself.

'Well, thank you, Mr Jeffs,' said Mrs Youghal.

'I must charge you an extra pound. You are probably unaware, Mrs Youghal, that it is obligatory and according to the antique dealers' association to charge one pound when goods have to be moved up a staircase. I could be struck off if I did not make this small charge.'

'A pound? I thought Mr Hammond had –'

'It is to do with the stairs. I must honour the rules of the antique dealers' association. For myself, I would easily waive it, but I have, you understand, my biennial returns to make.'

Mrs Youghal found her handbag and handed him a five-pound note. He gave her back three pounds and sixteen shillings, all the change he claimed to have.

'Imagine it!' exclaimed Mrs Youghal. 'I thought that cleaning woman must be your wife come to help you carry the thing. I couldn't understand why she was suddenly talking about six shillings an hour. She's just what I'm looking for.'

Mr Jeffs thought that it was rather like Mrs Hammond's *au pair* girl making the mistake about the window-cleaner. He thought that but he did not say it. He imagined Mrs Youghal recounting the details of the episode at some later hour, recounting them to Hammond as they lay in the other room, smoking cigarettes or involved with one another's flesh. 'I thought she was the little Jew's wife. I thought it was a family business, the way these people often have. I was surprised beyond measure when she mentioned about cleaning.'

Naturally enough, Mr Jeffs thought that he had seen the end of the matter. A Louis Seize console table, once the property of Mrs Hammond's grandmother, was now the property of her husband's mistress, or the joint property of husband and mistress, Mr Jeffs was not sure. It was all quite interesting, Mr Jeffs supposed, but he had other matters to concern him: he had further furniture to accumulate and to sell at the right moment; he had a living to make, he assured himself.

But a day or two after the day on which he had delivered the table to Mrs Youghal he received a telephone call from Mrs Hammond.

'Am I speaking to Mr Jeffs?' said Mrs Hammond.

'Yes, this is he. Jeffs here.'

'This is Mrs Hammond. I wonder if you remember, I sold you a table.'

'I remember you perfectly, Mrs Hammond. We were amused at an error.' Mr Jeffs made a noise that he trusted would sound like laughter. He was looking at the ceiling, without smiling.

'The thing is,' said Mrs Hammond, 'are you by any chance still in possession of that table? Because if you are I think perhaps I had better come round and see you.'

There rushed into Mr Jeffs's mind the vision of further attic rooms, of Mrs Hammond furnishing them with the table and anything else she could lay her hands on. He saw Mrs Hammond walking down a street, looking at beds and carpets in shop windows, her elbow grasped by a man who was not her husband.

'Hullo, Mr Jeffs,' said Mrs Hammond. 'Are you there?'

'Yes, I am here,' said Mr Jeffs. 'I am standing here listening to you, madam.'

'Well?' said Mrs Hammond.

'I'm sorry to disappoint you about the table.'

'You mean it's sold? Already?'

'I'm afraid that is the case.'

'Oh God in heaven!'

'I have other tables here. In excellent condition and keenly priced You might not find a visit here a waste of time.'

'No, no.'

'I do not as a rule conduct my business in that way: customers coming into my house and that. But in your case, since we are known to one another –'

'It wouldn't do. I mean, it's only the table I sold you I am possibly interested in. Mr Jeffs, can you quickly give me the name and address of the person who bought it?'

This question caught Mr Jeffs off his guard, so he at once replaced the telephone receiver. Mrs Hammond came through again a moment or so later, after he had had time to think. He said:

'We were cut off, Mrs Hammond. There is something the matter with the line. Sir Andrew Charles was twice cut off this morning, phoning from Nigeria. I do apologize.'

'I was saying, Mr Jeffs, that I would like to have the name and address of the person who bought the table.'

'I cannot divulge that, Mrs Hammond. I'm afraid divulgences of that nature are very much against the rules of the antique dealers' association. I could be struck off for such a misdemeanour.'

'Oh dear. Oh dear, Mr Jeffs. Then what am I to do? Whatever is the answer?'

'Is this important? There are ways and means. I could, for instance, act as your agent. I could approach the owner of the table in that guise and attempt to do my best.'

'Would you, Mr Jeffs? That is most kind.'

'I would have to charge the customary agent's fee. I am sorry about that, Mrs Hammond, but the association does not permit otherwise.'

'Yes, yes, of course.'

'Shall I tell you about that fee, how it's worked out and what it may amount to? It's not much, a percentage.'

'We can fix that up afterwards.'

'Well, fine,' said Mr Jeffs, who meant when he spoke of a percentage thirty-three and a third.

'Please go up to twice the price you paid me. If it seems to be going higher I'd be grateful if you'd telephone for instructions.'

'That's the usual thing, Mrs Hammond.'

'But do please try and keep the price down. Naturally.'

'I'll be in touch, Mrs Hammond.'

Walking about his house, shaking his body to keep his circulation in trim, Mr Jeffs wondered if tables nowadays had a part to play in lovers' fantasies. It was in his interest to find out, he decided, since he could accumulate tables of the correct kind and advertise them astutely. He thought for a while longer and then entered his van. He drove it to Mrs Youghal's attic room, taking a chance on finding her there.

'Why, Mr Jeffs,' said Mrs Youghal.

'Yes,' said Mr Jeffs.

She led him upstairs, trailing her curiosity behind her. She is thinking, he thought, that I have come to sell her another thing or two, but she does not care to order me out in case she is wrong, in case I have come to blackmail her.

'Well, Mr Jeffs, what can I do for you?'

'I have had a handsome offer for the Louis Seize table. Or a fairly handsome offer. Or an offer that might be turned into an exceedingly handsome offer. Do you take my meaning?'

'But the table is mine. Are you telling me you wish to buy it back?'

'I am saying something of the kind. I received a hint of this offer and thought I should let you know at once. "I will act as Mrs Youghal's agent," I said to myself, "in case she is at all tempted to dispose of the article at one and a half times what she paid for it." '

'Oh, but no, Mr Jeffs.'

'You are not interested?'

'Not at all, I'm afraid.'

'Suppose my client goes up to twice the price? How would you feel about that? Or how would Mr Hammond feel about that?'

'Mr Hammond?'

'Well, I am not quite certain who owns the article. That is why I mention the gentleman. Perhaps I should have contacted him. It was Mr Hammond who gave me the cheque.'

'The table is mine. A gift. I would rather you didn't contact Mr Hammond.'

'Well, that is that, then. But since I have acted in your interest in this matter, Mrs Youghal, thinking that I should report the offer to you without delay and involving myself in travelling expenses et cetera, I'm afraid I shall have to charge you the usual agent's fee. It is the ruling of the antique dealers' association that a fee be charged on such occasions. I feel you understand?'

Mrs Youghal said she did understand. She gave him some money, and Mr Jeffs took his leave.

In his house Mr Jeffs considered for a further hour. Eventually he thought it wise to telephone Mrs Hammond and ascertain her husband's office telephone number. He went out on to the street with a piece of paper in his hand which stated that he was deaf and dumb and wished urgently to have a telephone call made for him. He handed this to an elderly woman, pointing to a telephone booth.

'May I know your husband's office telephone number?' said the woman to Mrs Hammond. 'It's a matter of urgency.'

'But who are you?'

'I am a Mrs Lacey, and I am phoning you on behalf of Sir Andrew Charles of Africa.'

'I've heard that name before,' said Mrs Hammond, and gave the telephone number of her husband's office.

'You say you have been to see Mrs Youghal,' said Hammond. 'And what did she say?'

'I don't believe she fully understood what was at stake. I don't think she got the message.'

'The table was a gift from me to Mrs Youghal. I can hardly ask for it back.'

'This is an excellent offer, Mr Hammond.'

'Oh, I don't dispute that.'

'I was wondering if you could use your influence with Mrs Youghal, that's all. If you happen to be seeing her, that is.'

'I'll ring you back, Mr Jeffs.'

Mr Jeffs said thank you and then telephoned Mrs Hammond. 'Negotiations are under way,' he said.

But two days later negotiations broke down. Hammond telephoned Mr Jeffs to say that the table was to remain the property of Mrs Youghal. Mr Jeffs, sorrowfully, decided to drive round to tell Mrs Hammond, so that he could collect what little was owing him. He would tell her, he decided, and that would surely now be the end of the matter.

'I'm afraid I have come up against a stone wall,' he reported. 'I'm sorry, Mrs Hammond, about that, and I would trouble you now only for what is owing.'

He mentioned the sum, but Mrs Hammond seemed not to hear clearly. Tears rolled down her cheeks and left marks on the powder on her face. She took no notice of Mr Jeffs. She sobbed and shook, and further tears dropped from her eyes.

In the end Mrs Hammond left the room. Mr Jeffs remained because he had, of course, to wait for the money owing to him. He sat there examining the furniture and thinking it odd of Mrs Hammond to have cried so passionately and for so long. The *au pair* girl came in with a tray of tea for him, blushing as she arranged it, remembering, he imagined, the orders she had given him as regards the windows. He poured himself some tea and ate two pieces of shortbread. It was very quiet in the room, as though a funeral had taken place.

'Whoever are you?' said a child, a small girl of five.

Mr Jeffs looked at her and endeavoured to smile, forcing his lips back from his teeth.

'My name is Mr Jeffs. What is your name?'

'My name is Emma Hammond. Why are you having tea in our house?'

'Because it was kindly brought to me.'

'What is the matter with your mouth?'

'That is how my mouth is made. Are you a good little girl?'

'But why are you waiting here?'

'Because I have to collect something that your mother has arranged to give me. A little money.'

'A little money? Are you poor?'

'It is money owing to me.'

'Run along, Emma,' said Mrs Hammond from the door, and when the child had gone she said:

'I apologize, Mr Jeffs.'

She wrote him a cheque. He watched her, thinking of Hammond and Mrs Youghal and the table, all together in the attic rooms at the top of the big block of flats. He wondered what was going to happen. He supposed Mrs Hammond would be left with the child. Perhaps Mrs Youghal would marry Hammond then; perhaps they would come to this house and bring the table back with them, since Mrs Youghal was so attached to it, and perhaps they would take on the same *au pair* girl, and perhaps Mrs Hammond and the child would go to live in the attic rooms. They were all of a kind, Mr Jeffs decided: even the child seemed tarred with her elders' sophistication. But if sides were to be taken, he liked Mrs Hammond best. He had heard of women going berserk in such circumstances, taking their lives even. He hoped Mrs Hammond would not do that.

'Let me tell you, Mr Jeffs,' said Mrs Hammond.

'Oh now, it doesn't matter.'

'The table belonged to my grandmother, who died and left it to me in her will.'

'Do not fret, Mrs Hammond. It's all perfectly all right.'

'We thought it ugly, my husband and I, so we decided to be rid of it.'

'Your husband thought it was ugly?'

'Well, yes. But I more than he. He doesn't notice things so much.'

Mr Jeffs thought that he had noticed Mrs Youghal all right when Mrs Youghal had walked into this house. Mrs Hammond was lying her head off, he said to himself, because she was trying to save face: she knew quite well where the table was, she had known all along. She had wept because she could not bear the thought of it, her grandmother's ugly table in the abode of sin.

'So we put in an advertisement. We had only two replies. You and a woman.'

Mr Jeffs stood up, preparatory to going.

'You see,' said Mrs Hammond, 'we don't have room in a place like this for a table like that. It doesn't fit in. Well, you can see for yourself.'

Mr Jeffs looked hard at her, not into her eyes or even at her face: he looked hard and seriously at the green wool of her dress. The woman said:

'But almost as soon as it had gone I regretted everything. I remember the table all my life. My grandmother had left it to me as an act of affection as well as generosity.'

Mr Jeffs reckoned that the table had stood in the grandmother's hall. He reckoned that Mrs Hammond as a child had been banished from rooms and had been bidden to stand by the table in the hall, crying and moaning. The table had mocked her childhood and it was mocking her again, with silent watching in an attic room. He could see the two of them, Mrs

Youghal and Hammond, placing their big bulbous brandy glasses on the table and marching towards one another for a slick kiss.

'Once I had sold it to you I couldn't get it out of my mind. I remembered that my grandmother had always promised it to me. She was the only one who was kind to me as a child, Mr Jeffs. I felt that truly I had thrown all her love back at her. Every night since I sold it to you I've had wretched dreams. So you see why I was so very upset.'

The grandmother was cruel, thought Mr Jeffs. The grandmother punished the child every hour of the day, and left the table as a reminder of her autocratic soul. Why could not Mrs Hammond speak the truth? Why could she not say that the spirit of the old dead grandmother had passed into the table and that the spirit and the table were laughing their heads off in Mrs Youghal's room? Imagine, thought Mr Jeffs, a woman going to such lengths, and a woman whom he had passingly respected.

'I'm sorry I've burdened you with all this, Mr Jeffs. I'm sorry it's been such a bother. You have a kindly face.'

'I am a Jewish dealer, madam. I have a Jewish nose; I am not handsome; I cannot smile.'

He was angry because he thought that she was patronizing him. She was lying still, and all of a sudden she was including him in her lies. She was insulting him with her talk of his face. Did she know his faults, his weaknesses? How dare she speak so?

'The table should have passed from me to my daughter. It should have stayed in the family. I didn't think.'

Mr Jeffs allowed himself to close his eyes. She can sit there telling those lies, he thought, one after another, while her own child plays innocently in the next room. The child will become a liar too. The child in her time will grow to be a woman who must cover up the humiliations she has suffered, who must put a face on things, and make the situation respectable with falsehoods.

With his eyes closed and his voice speaking in his mind, Mr Jeffs saw the figure of himself standing alone in his large Victorian house. Nothing was permanent in the house, not a stick of furniture remained there month by month. He sold and bought again. He laid no carpets, nor would he ever. He owned only the old wireless set because someone once had told him it was worthless.

'Why are you telling me lies?' shouted Mr Jeffs. 'Why can't you say the truth?'

He heard his voice shouting those words at Mrs Hammond and he saw the image of himself, standing quietly on the bare boards of his house. It was not his way to go shouting at people, or becoming involved, or wishing for lies to cease. These people were a law unto themselves; they did not concern him. He cooked his own food; he did not bother people.

'Your grandmother is dead and buried,' said Mr Jeffs to his amazement. 'It is Mrs Youghal who is alive. She takes her clothes off, Mrs Hammond, and in comes your husband and takes off his. And the table sees. The table you have always known. Your childhood table sees it all and you cannot bear it. Why not be honest, Mrs Hammond? Why not say straight out to me: "Jew man, bargain with this Mrs Youghal and let me have my childhood table back." I understand you, Mrs Hammond. I understand all that. I will trade anything on God's earth, Mrs Hammond, but I understand that.'

There was a silence again in the room, and in it Mr Jeffs moved his eyes around until their gaze alighted on the face of Mrs Hammond. He saw the face sway, gently, from side to side, for Mrs Hammond was shaking her head. 'I did not know any of that,' Mrs Hammond was saying. Her head ceased to shake: she seemed like a statue.

Mr Jeffs rose and walked through the deep silence to the door. He turned then, and walked back again, for he had left behind him Mrs Hammond's cheque. She seemed not to notice his movements and he considered it wiser in the circumstances not to utter the sounds of farewell. He left the house and started up the engine of his Austin van.

He saw the scene differently as he drove away: Mrs Hammond hanging her head and he himself saying that the lies were understandable. He might have brought Mrs Hammond a crumb of comfort, a word or two, a subtle shrug of the shoulder. Instead, in his clumsiness, he had brought her a shock that had struck her a blow. She would sit there, he imagined, just as he had left her, her face white, her body crouched over her sorrow; she would sit like that until her husband breezily arrived. And she would look at him in his breeziness and say: 'The Jewish dealer has been and gone. He was there in that chair and he told me that Mrs Youghal has opened up a love-nest for you.'

Mr Jeffs drove on, aware of a sadness but aware as well that his mind was slowly emptying itself of Mrs Hammond and her husband and the beautiful Mrs Youghal. 'I cook my own food,' said Mr Jeffs aloud. 'I am a good trader, and I do not bother anyone.' He had no right to hope that he might have offered comfort. He had no business to take such things upon himself, to imagine that a passage of sympathy might have developed between himself and Mrs Hammond.

'I cook my own food,' said Mr Jeffs again. 'I do not bother anyone.' He drove in silence after that, thinking of nothing at all. The chill of sadness had left him, and the mistake he had made appeared to him as a fact that could not be remedied. He noticed that dusk was falling; and he returned to the house where he had never lit a fire, where the furniture loomed and did not smile at him, where nobody wept and nobody told a lie.

The General's Day

General Suffolk pulled on two grey knitted socks and stood upright. Humming a marching air, he walked to the bathroom, intent upon his morning shave. The grey socks were his only apparel and he noticed as he passed the mirror of his wardrobe the white spare body of an elderly man reflected without flattery. He voiced no comment nor did he ponder, even in passing, upon this pictured nakedness. He was used to the sight; and had, over the years, accepted the changes as they came. Still humming, he half filled the wash-basin with water. It felt keenly warm on his fingers, a circumstance he inwardly congratulated himself on.

With deft strokes the General cleared his face of lather and whisker, savouring the crisp rasp of razor upon flesh. He used a cut-throat article and when shorn to his satisfaction wiped it on a small absorbent pad, one of a series he had collected from the bedrooms of foreign hotels. He washed, dressed, set his moustache as he liked to sport it, and descended to his kitchen.

The General's breakfast was simple: an egg poached lightly, two slices of toast and a pot of tea. It took him ten minutes to prepare and ten to consume. As he finished he heard the footsteps of the woman who daily came to work for him. They were slow, dragging footsteps, implying the bulk they gracelessly shifted. The latch of the door rose and fell and Mrs Hinch, string bags and hairnet, cigarette cocked from the corner of her mouth, stood grinning before him. 'Hullo,' this woman said, adding as she often did, 'my dear.'

'Good morning, Mrs Hinch.'

Mrs Hinch stripped herself of bags, coat and cigarette with a single complicated gesture. She grinned again at the General, replaced her cigarette and set to clearing the table.

'I shall walk to the village this morning,' General Suffolk informed her. 'It seems a pleasant morning to dawdle through. I shall take coffee at the brown café and try my luck at picking up some suitable matron.'

Mrs Hinch was accustomed to her employer's turn of speech. She laughed shrilly at this sally, pleased that the man would be away for the morning. 'Ah, General, you'll be the death of us,' she cried; and planned for his absence a number of trunk calls on his telephone, a leisurely bath and the imbibing of as much South African sherry as she considered discreet.

'It is Saturday if I am not mistaken,' the General went on. 'A good morning for my plans. Is it not a fact that there are stout matrons in and out of the brown café by the score on a Saturday morning?'

'Why, sure, General,' said Mrs Hinch, anxious to place no barrier in his way. 'Why, half the county goes to the brown café of a Saturday morning. You are certain to be successful this time.'

'Cheering words, Mrs Hinch, cheering words. It is one thing to walk through the cowparsleyed lanes on a June morning, but quite another to do so with an objective one is sanguine of achieving.'

'This is your day, General. I feel it in my bones. I said it to Hobson as I left. "This is a day for the General," I said. "The General will do well today," I said.'

'And Hobson, Mrs Hinch? Hobson replied?'

Again Mrs Hinch, like a child's toy designed for the purpose, shrilled her merriment.

'General, General, Hobson's my little bird.'

The General, rising from the table, frowned. 'Do you imagine I am unaware of that? Since for six years you have daily informed me of the fact. And why, pray, since the bird is a parrot, should the powers of speech be beyond it? It is not so with other parrots.'

'Hobson's silent, General. You know Hobson's silent.'

'Due to your lethargy, Mrs Hinch. No bird of his nature need be silent: God does not intend it. He has taken some pains to equip the parrot with the instruments of speech. It is up to you to pursue the matter in a practical way by training the animal. A child, Mrs Hinch, does not remain ignorant of self-expression. Nor of the ability to feed and clean itself. The mother teaches, Mrs Hinch. It is part of nature. So with your parrot.'

Enthusiastic in her own defence, Mrs Hinch said: 'I have brought up seven children. Four girls and three boys.'

'Maybe. Maybe. I am in no position to question this. But indubitably with your parrot you are flying in the face of nature.'

'Oh, General, never. Hobson's silent and that's that.'

The General regarded his adversary closely. 'You miss my point,' he said drily; and repeating the remark twice he left the room.

In his time General Suffolk had been a man of more than ordinary importance. As a leader and a strategist in two great wars he had risen rapidly to the heights implied by the title he bore. He had held in his hands the lives of many thousands of men; his decisions had more than once set the boundaries of nations. Steely intelligence and physical prowess had led him, in their different ways, to glories that few experience. At Roeux and Monchy-le-Preux he had come close to death. Besides all that, there was about the General a quality that is rare in the ultimate leaders of his army: he was to the last a rake, and for this humanity a popular figure. He had cared for women, for money, for alcohol of every sort; but in the end he had found himself with none of these commodities. In his modest cottage he was an elderly man with a violent past; with neither wife nor riches nor cellar to help him on his way.

Mrs Hinch had said he would thrive today. That the day should be agreeable was all he asked. He did not seek merriness or reality or some moment of truth. He had lived for long enough to forgo excitement; he had had his share; he wished only that the day, and his life in it, should go the way he wished.

In the kitchen Mrs Hinch scoured the dishes briskly. She was not one to do things by halves; hot water and detergent in generous quantities was her way.

'Careful with the cup handles,' the General admonished her. 'Adhesive for the repair of such a fracture has apparently not yet been perfected. And the cups themselves are valuable.'

'Oh they're flimsy, General. So flimsy you can't wash them. Declare to God, I shall be glad to see the last of them!'

'But not I, Mrs Hinch. I like those cups. Tea tastes better from fine china. I would take it kindly if you washed and dried with care.'

'Hoity-toity, General! Your beauties are safe with me. I treat them as babies.'

'Babies? Hardly a happy analogy, Mrs Hinch – since five of the set are lost for ever.'

'Six,' said Mrs Hinch, snapping beneath the water the handle from the cup. 'You are better without the bother of them. I shall bring you a coronation mug.'

'You fat old bitch,' shouted the General. 'Six makes the set. It was my last remaining link with the gracious life.'

Mrs Hinch, understanding and wishing to spite the General further, laughed. 'Cheery-bye, General,' she called as she heard him rattling among his walking sticks. He banged the front door and stepped out into the heat of the day. Mrs Hinch turned on the wireless.

'*I walked entranced,*' intoned the General, '*through a land of morn. The sun in wondrous excess of light . . .*' He was seventy-eight: his memory faltered over the quotation. His stick, weapon of his irritation, thrashed through the cowparsley, covering the road with broken blooms. Grasshoppers clicked; bees darted, paused, humming in flight, silent in labour. The road was brown with dust, dry and hot in the sunlight. It was a day, thought the General, to be successfully in love; and he mourned that the ecstasy of love on a hot summer's day was so far behind him. Not that he had gone without it; which gave him his yardstick and saddened him the more.

Early in his retirement General Suffolk had tried his hand in many directions. He had been, to start with, the secretary of a golf club; though in a matter of months his temper relieved him of the task. He was given to disagreement and did not bandy words. He strode away from the golf club, red in the face, the air behind him stinging with insults. He lent his talents to the business world and to a military academy: both were dull and in both he failed. He bought his cottage, agreeing with himself that retirement was retirement and meant what it suggested. Only once since moving to the country had he involved himself with salaried work: as a tennis coach in a girls' school. Despite his age he was active still on his legs and managed well enough. Too well, his grim and beady-eyed headmistress avowed, objecting to his method of instructing her virgins in the various stances by which they might achieve success with the serve. The General paused only to level at the headmistress a battery of expressions well known to him but new to her. He went on his way, his cheque in his wallet, his pockets bulging with small articles from her study. The girls he had taught pursued him, pressing upon him packets of cheap cigarettes, sweets and flowers.

The General walked on, his thoughts rambling. He thought of the past; of specific days, of moments of shame or pride in his life. The past was his hunting ground; from it came his pleasure and a good deal of everything else. Yet he was not proof against the moment he lived in. The present could snarl at him; could drown his memories so completely that when they surfaced again they were like the burnt tips of matches floating on a puddle, finished and done with. He walked through the summery day, puzzled that all this should be so.

The brown café, called 'The Cuppa', was, as General Suffolk and Mrs Hinch had anticipated, bustling with mid-morning traffic. Old men and their wives sat listening to the talk about them, exchanging by the way a hard comment on their fellows. Middle-aged women, outsize in linen dresses, were huddled three or four to a table, their great legs battling for room in inadequate space, their feet hot and unhappy in unwise shoes. Mothers passed unsuitable edibles towards the searching mouths of their young. Men with girls sipped at the pale creamy coffee, thinking only of the girls. Crumbs were everywhere; and the babel buzzed like a clockwork wind.

The General entered, surveyed the scene with distaste, and sat at a table already occupied by a youth engrossed in a weekly magazine. The youth, a fat bespotted lad, looked up and immediately grinned. General Suffolk replied in kind, stretching the flesh of his face to display his teeth in a smile designed to promote goodwill between them, for the pair were old friends.

'Good morning, Basil. And how is youth and vigour today?'

'Oh well, not so bad, General. My mum is in the family way again.'

'A cause for joy,' murmured General Suffolk, ordering coffee with Devonshire cream and the fruit pie he favoured. 'Your mother is a great one for babies, is she not?'

'My dad says the same. He don't understand it neither. Worried, is Dad. Anyone can see that.'

'I see.'

'Well, it is a bit fishy, General. Dad's not the man to be careless. It's just about as fishy as hell.'

'Basil, your mother needs all the support she can get at a time like this. Talk about fishiness is scarcely going to help her in her ordeal.'

'Mum's had five. Drops 'em like hot bricks so she says. Thing is, if this one's fishy what about the others?'

The General placed a portion of pie in his mouth. Crumbs of pastry and other matter lingered on his moustache. 'You are thinking of yourself, Basil.'

'Wouldn't you? I mean to say.'

'I would attach no importance to such a doubt, I do assure you. Basil, what do you say we spend this afternoon at some local fête? It is just an afternoon for a fête. I will stand you lunch.'

The plumpness of Basil's face sharpened into suspicion. He moved his large hams uneasily on his chair and avoided his companion's gaze. 'It's Mum really, General. I've got to tend her a bit, like you say it's a hard time for her. And with Dad so snappish and the kids all over the place I don't think she'd take it kindly if I was to go going off to fêtes and that. Not at a time like this like.'

'Ah, filial duty. I trust your mother appreciates your sacrifices.'

But Basil, not anxious to prolong the conversation in this direction, was on his feet, his right hand hovering for the General's grasp. And then, the handshake completed, he moved himself clumsily between the tables and passed through the open doorway.

General Suffolk stirred sugar into his coffee and looked about him. A lanky schoolmistress from the school he had taught tennis at sat alone at a corner table. She was a woman of forty or so, the General imagined; and he recalled having seen her by chance once, through an open window, in her underclothes. Since then he had often considered her in terms of sex, though now when he might have explored the possibility he found himself unable to remember her name. He watched her, trying to catch her glance, but either she did not recognize him or did not wish to associate with so reprobate a character. He dismissed her mentally and surveyed the room again. There was no one with whom he could fall into casual conversation, except perhaps a certain Mrs Consitine, known in her youth as Jumbo Consitine because of her size, and whose freakish appearance repelled him always to the point of physical sickness. He dodged the lady's predatory stare and left the café.

It was a quarter to twelve. If the General walked through the village he would be just in time for a morning drink with Frobisher. Frobisher always drank – sometimes considerably – before lunch. On a day like this a drink was emphatically in order.

Mrs Hinch, the General reflected, would be settling down to his South African sherry about now. 'You thieving old bitch,' he said aloud. 'Fifty years in Their Majesties' service and I end up with Mrs bloody Hinch.' A man carrying a coil of garden hose tripped and fell across his path. This man, a week-end visitor to the district, known to the General by sight and disliked by him, uttered as he dropped to the ground a series of expletives of a blasphemous and violent nature. The General, since the man's weight lay on his shoes, stooped to assist him. 'Oh, buzz off,' ordered the man, his face close to the General's. So the General left him, conscious not so much of his dismissal as of the form of words it had taken. The sun warmed his forehead and drops of sweat glistened on his nose and chin.

The Frobishers' house was small and vaguely Georgian. From the outside it had the feeling of a town house placed by some error in the country. There were pillars on either side of the front door, which was itself dressed in a grey and white canvas cover as a protection against the sun. Door and cover swung inwards and Mrs Frobisher, squat and old, spoke from the hall.

'It's General Suffolk,' she said.

'Yes,' said the General. 'That old soldier.'

'You've come to see Frob. Come in a minute and I'll fetch him. What a lovely day.'

The General stepped into the hall. It was cool and smelt rather pleasantly of floor polish. Daggers, swords, Eastern rugs, knick-knacks and novelties hung in profusion everywhere. 'Frob! Frob!' Mrs Frobisher called, climbing the stairs. There had been a day, a terrible sultry day in India all of fifty years ago, when the General – though then not yet a general – had fought a duel with a certain Major Service. They had walked together quietly to a selected spot, their seconds, carrying a pair of *kukris*, trailing behind them. It had been a quarrel that involved, surprisingly, neither man's honour. In retrospect General Suffolk could scarcely remember the cause: some insult directed against some woman, though by whom and in what manner completely escaped him. He had struck Major Service on the left forearm drawing a considerable quantity of blood, and the duel was reckoned complete. An excuse was made for the wound sustained by the Major and the affair was successfully hushed up. It was the nearest that General Suffolk had ever come to being court-martialled. He was put in mind of the occasion by the presence of a *kukri* on the Frobishers' wall. A nasty weapon, he reflected, and considered it odd that he should once have wielded one so casually. After all, Major Service might easily have lost his arm or, come to that, his life.

'Frob! Frob! Where are you?' cried Mrs Frobisher. 'General Suffolk's here to see you.'

'Suffolk?' Frobisher's voice called from another direction. 'Oh my dear, can't you tell him I'm out?'

The General, hearing the words, left the house.

In the saloon bar of the public house General Suffolk asked the barman about the local fêtes.

'Don't think so, sir. Not today. Not that I've heard of.'

'There's a fête at Marmount,' a man at the bar said. 'Conservative fête, same Saturday every year.'

'Ah certainly,' said the barman, 'but Marmount's fifteen miles away. General Suffolk means a *local* fête. The General doesn't have a car.'

'Of course, of course,' said the man. 'Marmount's not an easy spot to reach. Even if you did have a car, sir.'

'I will have a sandwich, Jock,' said General Suffolk. 'Chop me a cheese sandwich like a good man.' He was beginning to feel low; the day was not good; the day was getting out of control. Fear filled his mind and the tepid beer was little comfort. He began to pray inwardly, but he had little faith now in this communication. 'Never mind,' he said aloud. 'It is just that it seems like a day for a fête. I won a half guinea at a summer fête last year. One never knows one's luck.' He caught sight of a card advertising the weekly films at the cinema of the near-by town.

'Have you seen *The Guns of Navarone*?' he questioned the barman.

'I have, sir, and very good it is.'

The General nodded. 'A powerful epic by the sound of it.'

'That's the word, General. As the saying goes, it had me riveted.'

'Well, hurry the sandwiches then. I can catch the one-ten bus and achieve the first performance.'

'Funny thing, sir,' said the barman. 'I can never take the cinema of an afternoon. Not that it isn't a time that suits me, the hours being what they are. No, I go generally on my night off. Can't seem to settle down in the afternoon or something. Specially in the good weather. To me, sir, it seems unnatural.'

'That is an interesting point of view, Jock. It is indeed. And may well be shared by many – for I have noticed that the cinemas are often almost empty in the afternoon.'

'I like to be outside on a good afternoon. Taking a stroll by a trout stream or in a copse.'

'A change is as good as a cure, or whatever the adage is. After all, you are inside a good deal in your work. To be alone must be quite delightful after the idle chatter you have to endure.'

'If you don't mind my saying it, General, I don't know how you do it. It would kill me to sit at the pictures on an afternoon like this. I would feel – as it were, sir – guilty.'

'Guilty, Jock?'

'Looking the Great Gift Horse in the mouth, sir.'

'The –? Are you referring to the Deity, Jock?'

'Surely, sir. I would feel it like an unclean action.'

'Maybe, Jock. Though I doubt that God would care to hear you describe Him as a horse.'

'Oh but, General –'

'You mean no disrespect. It is taken as read, Jock. But you cannot be too careful.'

'Guilt is my problem, sir.'

'I am sorry to hear it. Guilt can often be quite a burden.'

'I am never free of it, sir. If it's not one thing it's another.'

'I know too well, Jock.'

'It was not presumptuous of me to mention that thing about the cinema? I was casting no stone at you, sir.'

'Quite, quite. It may even be that I would prefer to attend an evening house. But beggars, you know, cannot be choosers.'

'I would not like to offend you, General.'

'Good boy, Jock. In any case I am not offended. I enjoy a chat.'

'Thank you, sir.'

'Not at all. But now I must be on my way. Consider your problem closely: you may discover some simple solution. There are uncharted regions in the human mind.'

'Sir?'

'You are a good fellow, Jock. We old soldiers must stick together.'

'Ha, ha,' said Jock, taking the remark as a joke, since he was in the first place a young man still, and had never been in the Army.

'Well, cheerio then.'

'Cheerio, sir.'

How extraordinary, thought the General, that the man should feel like that: guilty about daytime cinema attendance. As Mrs Hinch would have it, it takes all sorts.

The thought of Mrs Hinch depressed the General further and drove him straight to a telephone booth. He often telephoned his cottage at this time of day as a check on her time-keeping. She was due to remain at work for a further hour, but generally the telephone rang unanswered. Today he got the engaged signal. As he boarded his bus, he wondered how much it was costing him.

Taurus. April 21st to May 20th. Financial affairs straighten themselves out. Do not make decisions this afternoon: your judgement is not at its best.

The General peeped around the edge of the newspaper at the woman who shared his table. She was a thin, middle-aged person with a face like a faded photograph. Her hair was inadequately dyed a shade of brown, her face touched briefly with lipstick and powder. She wore a cream-coloured blouse and a small string of green beads which the General assumed, correctly, to be jade. Her skirt, which the General could not see, was of fine tweed.

'How thoughtless of me,' said the General. 'I have picked up your paper. It was on the chair and I did it quite automatically. I am so sorry.'

He knew the newspaper was not hers. No one places a newspaper on the other chair at a restaurant table when the other chair is so well out of reach. Unless, that is, one wishes to reserve the place, which the lady, since she made no protest at his occupying it, was clearly not interested in doing. He made the pretence of offering the paper across the tea-table, leaning forward and sideways to catch a glimpse of her legs.

'Oh but,' said the lady, 'it is not my newspaper at all.'

Beautiful legs. Really beautiful legs. Shimmering in silk or nylon, with fine firm knees and intoxicating calves.

'Are you sure? In that case it must have been left by the last people. I was reading the stars. I am to have an indecisive afternoon.' She belongs to the upper classes, General Suffolk said to himself; the upper classes are still well-bred in the leg.

The lady tinkled with laughter. I am away, the General thought. 'When is your birthday?' he asked daringly. 'And I will tell you what to expect for the rest of today.'

'Oh, I'm Libra, I think.'

'It is a good moment for fresh associations,' lied the General, pretending to read from the paper. 'A new regime is on its way.'

'You can't believe a thing they say.'

'Fighting words,' said the General and they laughed and changed the subject of conversation.

In the interval at the cinema, when the lights had gone up and the girls with ice cream began their sales stroll, the General had seen, two or three rows from the screen, the fat unhealthy figure of his friend Basil. The youth was accompanied by a girl, and it distressed General Suffolk that Basil should have made so feeble an excuse when earlier he had proposed an excursion to a fête. The explanation that Basil wished to indulge in carnal pleasures in the gloom of a picture house would naturally have touched the General's sympathy. Basil was an untrustworthy lad. It was odd, the General reflected, that some people are like that: so addicted to the lie that to avoid one, when the truth is in order, seems almost a sin.

'General Suffolk,' explained the General. 'Retired, of course.'

'We live in Bradoak,' said the lady. 'My name actually is Mrs Hope-Kingley.'

'Retired?'

'Ha, ha. Though in a way it's true. My husband is not alive now.'

'Ah,' said the General, delighted. 'I'm sorry.'

'I am quite over it, thank you. It is all of fifteen years since last I saw him. We had been divorced some time before his death.'

'Divorce and death, divorce and death. You hear it all the time. May I be personal now and say I am surprised you did not remarry?'

'Oh, General Suffolk, Mr Right never came along!'

'*Attention! Les étoiles!*'

'Ha, ha.' And to her own surprise, Mrs Hope-Kingley proceeded to reveal to this elderly stranger the story of her marriage.

As he listened, General Suffolk considered how best to play his cards. It was a situation he had found himself in many times before, but as always the game must vary in detail. He felt mentally a little tired as he thought about it; and the fear that, in this, as in almost everything else, age had taken too great a toll struck at him with familiar ruthlessness. In his thirties he had played superbly, as good at love as he was at tennis. Now arrogant, now innocent, he had swooped and struck, captured and killed; and smiled over many a breakfast at the beauty that had been his prize.

They finished their tea. 'I am slipping along to the County for a drink,' said the General. 'Do join me for a quick one.'

'How kind of you. I must not delay though. My sister will expect me.' And they climbed into Mrs Hope-Kingley's small car and drove to the hotel. Over their gins the General spoke of his early days in the Army and touched upon his present life, naming Mrs Hinch.

'What a frightful woman! You must sack her.'

'But who would do for me? I need my bed made and the place kept clean. Women are not easy to find in the country.'

'I know a Mrs Gall who lives in your district. She has the reputation of being particularly reliable. My friends the Boddingtons use her.'

'Well, that is certainly a thought. D'you know, I had become quite reconciled to Hinch. I never thought to change her really. What a breath of life you are!'

After three double gins Mrs Hope-Kingley was slightly drunk. Her face was flushed with pleasure. Compliments do not come your way too often these days, thought the General; and he ambled off to the bar to clinch the matter with a further drink. How absurd to be upset by the passing details of the day! What did it all matter now that he had found this promising lady? The day and its people, so directed against him, were balanced surely by this meeting? With her there was strength; from her side he might look out on the world with power and with confidence. In a panic of enthusiasm he almost suggested marriage. His hands were shaking and he felt again a surge of the old arrogance. There is life in the old dog yet, he thought. Handing her her drink, he smiled and winked.

'After this I must go,' the lady said.

'Come, come, the night is younger than we are. It is not every day I can pick up a bundle of charms in a teashop.'

'Ha, ha, ha.' Mrs Hope-Kingley purred, thinking that for once her sister would simply have to wait, and wondering if she should dare to tell her that she had been drinking with an elderly soldier.

They were sitting at a small table in a corner. Now and again, it could have been an accident, the General's knee touched hers. He watched the level of gin lower in her glass. 'You are a pretty lady,' murmured the General, and beneath the table his hand stroked her stockinged knee and ventured a little beyond it.

'My God!' said Mrs Hope-Kingley, her face like a beetroot. The General lowered his head. He heard her snatch her handbag from the seat beside him. When he looked up she was gone.

'When were you born?' General Suffolk asked the man in the bus.

The man seemed startled. 'Well,' he said, 'nineteen-oh-three actually.'

'No, no, no. What month? When does your birthday fall?'

'Well, October the twenty-first actually.'

'Libra by a day,' the General informed him, consulting his newspaper as he spoke. 'For tomorrow, there are to be perfect conditions for enjoying yourself; though it may be a little expensive. Don't gamble.'

'I see,' said the man, glancing in embarrassment through the window.

'Patrelli is usually reliable.'

The man nodded, thinking: The old fellow is drunk. He was right: the General was drunk.

'I do not read the stars every day,' General Suffolk explained. 'It is only when I happen upon an evening paper. I must say I find Patrelli the finest augur of the lot. Do you not agree?'

The man made an effort to smile, muttering something incomprehensible.

'What's that, what's that? I cannot hear you.'

'I don't know at all. I don't know about such matters.'

'You are not interested in the stars?'

The man shook his head.

'In that case, I have been boring you.'

'No, no –'

'If you were not interested in my conversation you should have said so. It is quite simple to say it. I cannot understand you.'

'I'm sorry –'

'I do not like to offend people. I do not like to be a nuisance. You should have stopped me, sir.'

The man made a gesture, vague in its meaning.

'You have taken advantage of an old warrior.'

'I cannot see –'

'You should have halted me. It costs nothing to speak.'

'I'm sorry.'

'Think nothing of it. Think nothing of it at all. Here is my village. If you are dismounting, would you care to join me in a drink?'

'Thank you, no. I am –'

'I swear not to speak of the stars.'

'I go on a bit. This is not my stop.'

The General shook his head, as though doubting this statement. The bus stopped and, aided by the conductor, he left it.

'Did you see *The Guns*, General?' Jock shouted across the bar.

Not hearing, but understanding that the barman was addressing him, General Suffolk waved breezily. 'A large whisky, Jock. And a drop of beer for yourself.'

'Did you see *The Guns* then?'

'The guns?'

'The pictures, General. *The Guns of Navarone.*'

'That is very kind of you, Jock. But we must make it some other time. I saw that very film this afternoon.'

'General, did you like it?'

'Certainly, Jock. Certainly I liked it. It was very well done. I thought it was done very well indeed.'

'Two gins and split a bottle of tonic,' a man called out.

'I beg your pardon,' said the General, 'I think I am in your way.'

'Two gins and a split tonic,' repeated Jock.

'And something for our friend,' the man added, indicating the General.

'That is kind of you. Everyone is kind tonight. Jock here has just invited me to accompany him to the pictures. Unfortunately I have seen the film. But there will be other occasions. We shall go together again. May I ask you when you were born, the month I mean?'

The man, whose attention was taken up with the purchasing and transportation of his drinks, said: 'Some time in May, I think.'

'But exactly? When is your birthday, for instance?' But the man had returned to a small table against the wall, where a girl and several packets of unopened crisps awaited him.

'Jock, do you follow the stars?'

'D'you mean telescopes and that?'

'No, no, my boy.' The General swayed, catching at the bar to balance himself. He had had very little to eat all day: the old, he maintained, did not need it. 'No, no, I mean the augurs. Capricorn, Scorpio, Gemini, you know what I mean.'

'Lord Luck in the *Daily Express*?'

'That's it. That's the kind of thing. D'you take an interest at all?'

'Well, General, now, I don't.'

'When's your birthday, Jock?'

'August the fifteenth.'

'A Leo, by Harry! It is quite something to be a Leo, Jock. I would never have guessed it.'

Jock laughed loudly. 'After all, General, it is not my doing.'

'Fill up our glasses. Let me see what tomorrow holds for you.' But examining the paper, he found it difficult to focus. 'Here Jock, read it yourself.' And Jock read aloud:

'*You will gain a lot by mingling with friends old and new. Late evening particularly favours entry into new social circles.*'

'Hark at that then! Remember the words, my friend. Patrelli is rarely wrong. The best augur of the bunch.' The General had become dishevelled. His face was flushed and his eyelids drooped intermittently and uncontrollably. He fidgeted with his clothes, as though nervous about the positioning of his hands. 'A final whisky, Jock boy; and a half bottle to carry home.'

On the road from the village to his cottage the General felt very drunk indeed. He lurched from one grass verge to the other, grasping his half bottle of whisky and singing gently under his breath. He knocked on the Frobishers' door with his stick, and scarcely waiting for a reply knocked loudly again.

'For God's sake, man,' Frobisher demanded, 'what's the matter with you?'

'A little drink,' explained General Suffolk. 'You and me and Mrs Frob, a little drink together. I have brought some with me. In case you had run out.'

Frobisher glared at him. 'You're drunk, Suffolk. You're bloody well drunk.'

General Suffolk loosed a peal of laughter. 'Ha, ha, the old man's drunk. Let me in, Frob, and so shall you be.'

Frobisher attempted to close the door, but the General inserted his stick.

He laughed again, and then was silent. When he spoke his voice was pleading.

'One drink, Frob. Just one for you and me. Frob, when were you born?'

Frobisher began to snort with anger: he was a short-tempered man, he saw no reason to humour this unwelcome guest. He kicked sharply at the General's stick, then opening the door widely he shouted into his face: 'Get the hell off my premises, you bloody old fool! Go on, Suffolk, hop it!'

The General did not appear to understand. He smiled at Frobisher. 'Tell me the month of your birth and I shall tell you in return what the morrow holds –'

'God damn it, Suffolk –'

'One little drink, and we'll consult the stars together. They may well be of interest to Mrs –'

'Get off my premises, you fool! You've damaged my door with your damned stick. You'll pay for that, Suffolk. You'll hear from my solicitors. I promise you, if you don't go immediately I won't hesitate to call for the police.'

'One drink, Frob. Look, I'm a little lonely –'

Frobisher banged the door. 'Frob, Frob,' General Suffolk called, striking the door with his stick. 'A nightcap, my old friend. Don't refuse a drink now.' But the door remained closed against him. He spoke for a while to himself, then made his way unsteadily homewards.

'General Suffolk, are you ill?'

The General narrowed his eyes, focusing on the couple who stood before him; he did not recognize them; he was aware of feeling guilty because of it.

'We are returning home from a game of cards,' the woman of the two told him. 'It is a balmy evening for a stroll.'

The General tried to smile. Since leaving the Frobishers' house he had drunk most of the whisky. The people danced a bit before him, like outsize puppets. They moved up and down, and from side to side. They walked rapidly, silently, backwards. 'Ha, ha, ha,' laughed the General. 'What can I do for you?'

'Are you ill? You don't seem yourself.'

The General smiled at some little joke. 'I have not been myself for many years. Today is just another day.'

The people were moving away. He could hear them murmuring to each other.

'You have not asked me about the stars,' he shouted after them. 'I could tell you if you asked.' But they were already gone, and uncorking the bottle he drained the remains and threw it into a ditch.

As he passed Mrs Hinch's cottage he decided to call on her. He had it on his mind to play some joke on the woman, to say that she need not again attend to his household needs. He banged powerfully on the door and in a moment Mrs Hinch's head, rich in curling pins, appeared at a window to his right.

'Why, General dear,' said Mrs Hinch, recognizing immediately his condition. 'You've been on the razzle.'

'Mrs Hinch, when is your birthday?'

'Why, my dear? Have you a present for little Hinchie?'

'Give me the information and I will let you know what tomorrow brings.'

'April the twenty-first. I was born at two o'clock in the morning.'

But in his walk he had somewhere mislaid the newspaper and could tell her nothing. He gripped the doorstep and seemed about to fall.

'Steady now,' said Mrs Hinch. 'I'll dress myself and help you home.' The head was withdrawn and the General waited for the company of his unreliable servant.

She, in the room, slipped out of her nightdress and buttoned about her her everyday clothes. This would last her for months. 'Ho ho, my dear,' she would say, 'remember that night? Worse for wear you were. Whatever would you have done without your little Hinchie?' Chortling and crowing, she hitched up her skirts and paraded forth to meet him.

'Oh General, you're naughty! You shouldn't be allowed out.'

The General laughed. Clumsily he slapped her broad buttocks. She screamed shrilly, enjoying again the position she now held over him. 'Dirty old General! Hinchie won't carry her beauty home unless he's a good boy tonight.' She laughed her cackling laugh and the General joined in it. He dawdled a bit, and losing her patience Mrs Hinch pushed him roughly in front of her. He fell, and in picking him up she came upon his wallet and skilfully extracted two pounds ten. 'General would fancy his Hinchie tonight,' she said, shrieking merrily at the thought. But the General was silent now, seeming almost asleep as he walked. His face was gaunt and thin, with little patches of red. 'I could live for twenty years,' he whispered.

'My God Almighty, I could live for twenty years.' Tears spread on his cheeks. 'Lor' love a duck!' cried Mrs Hinch; and leaning on the arm of this stout woman the hero of Roeux and Monchy-le-Preux stumbled the last few yards to his cottage.

The Penthouse Apartment

'Flowers?' said Mr Runca into his pale blue telephone receiver. 'Shall we order flowers? What's the procedure?' He stared intently at his wife as he spoke, and his wife, eating her breakfast grape-fruit, thought that it would seem to be her husband's intention to avoid having to pay for flowers. She had become used to this element in her husband; it hardly ever embarrassed her.

'The procedure's quite simple,' said a soft voice in Mr Runca's ear. 'The magazine naturally supplies the flowers. If we can just agree between us what the flowers should be.'

'Indeed,' said Mr Runca. 'It's to be remembered that not all blooms will go with the apartment. Our fabrics must be allowed to speak for themselves, you know. Well, you've seen. You know what I mean.'

'Indeed I do, Mr Runca –'

'They came from Thailand, in fact. You might like to mention that.'

'So you said, Mr Runca. The fabrics are most beautiful.'

Mr Runca, hearing this statement, nodded. He said, because he was used to saying it when the apartment was discussed:

'It's the best-dressed apartment in London.'

'I'll come myself at three,' said the woman on the magazine. 'Will someone be there at half past two, say, so that the photographers can set up all their gear and test the light?'

'We have an Italian servant,' said Mr Runca, 'who opened the door to you before and who'll do the same thing for the photographers.'

'Till this afternoon then,' said the woman on the magazine, speaking lightly and gaily, since that was her manner.

Mr Runca carefully replaced the telephone receiver. His wife, a woman who ran a boutique, drank some coffee and heard her husband say that the magazine would pay for the flowers and would presumably not remove them from the flat after the photography had taken place. Mrs Runca nodded. The magazine was going to devote six pages to the Runcas' flat: a display in full colour of its subtleties and charm, with an article about how the Runcas had between them planned all the décor.

'I'd like to arrange the flowers myself,' said Mrs Runca. 'Are they being sent round?'

Mr Runca shook his head. The flowers, he explained, were to be brought to the house by the woman from the magazine at three o'clock, the photographers having already had time to deploy their materials in the manner they favoured.

'But how ridiculous!' cried Mrs Runca. 'It's completely hopeless, that arrangement. The photographers with their cameras poised for three o'clock and the woman arriving then with the flowers. How long does the female imagine it'll take to arrange them? Does she think it can be done in a matter of minutes?'

Mr Runca picked up the telephone and dialled the number of the magazine. He mentioned the name of the woman he had recently been speaking to. He spoke to her again. He said:

'My wife points out that the arrangement is not satisfactory. The flowers will take time to arrange, naturally. What point is there in keeping your photographers waiting? And I myself haven't got all day.'

'It shouldn't take long to arrange the flowers.'

Mrs Runca lit her first cigarette of the day, imagining that the woman on the magazine was saying something like that. She had a long, rather thin face and pale grey hair that had the glow of aluminium. Her hands were long also, hands that had grown elegant in childhood, with fingernails that now were of a fashionable length, metallically painted, a reflection of her hair. Ten years ago, on money borrowed from her husband, she had opened her boutique. She had called it St Catherine, and had watched it growing into a flourishing business with a staff of five women and a girl messenger.

'Very well then,' said the woman on the magazine, having listened further to Mr Runca. 'I'll have the flowers sent round this morning.'

'They're coming round this morning,' reported Mr Runca to his wife.

'I have to be at St Catherine at twelve,' she said, 'absolutely without fail.'

'My wife has to be at her business at midday,' said Mr Runca, and the woman on the magazine cursed silently. She promised that the flowers would be in the Runcas' penthouse apartment within three-quarters of an hour.

Mr Runca rose to his feet and stood silently for a minute. He was a rich, heavily-jowled man, the owner of three publications that appealed to those involved in the clothing trade. He was successful in much the same way as his wife was, and he felt, as she did, that efficiency and a stern outlook were good weapons in the business of accumulating wealth. Once upon a time they had both been poor and had recognized certain similar qualities in one another, and had seen the future as a more luxurious time, as in fact it had become. They were proud that once again their penthouse apartment was to be honoured by photographers and a journalist. It was the symbol of all their toil; and in a small way it had made them famous.

Mr Runca walked from the spacious room that had one side made entirely of glass, and his feet caused no sound as he crossed a white carpet of Afghanistan wool. He paused in the hall to place a hat on his head and gloves on his hands before departing for a morning's business.

At ten to ten the flowers arrived and by a quarter past eleven Mrs Runca had arranged them to her satisfaction. The Runcas' Italian maid, called

Bianca, cleaned the flat most carefully, seeking dust in an expert way, working with method and a conscience, which was why the Runcas employed her. Mrs Runca warned her to be in at half past two because the photographers were coming then. 'I must go out now then,' replied Bianca, 'for shopping. I will make these photographers coffee, I suppose?' Mrs Runca said to give the men coffee in the kitchen, or tea, if they preferred it. 'Don't let them walk about the place with cups in their hands,' she said, and went away.

In another part of the block of flats lived Miss Winton with her Cairn terrier. Her flat was different from the Runcas'; it contained many ornaments that had little artistic value, was in need of redecoration, and had a beige linoleum on the floor of the bathroom. Miss Winton did not notice her surroundings much; she considered the flat pretty in its way, and comfortable to live in. She was prepared to leave it at that.

'Well,' remarked Miss Winton to her dog in the same moment that Mrs Runca was stepping into a taxi-cab, 'what shall we do?'

The dog made no reply beyond wagging its tail. 'I have eggs to buy,' said Miss Winton, 'and honey, and butter. Shall we go and do all that?'

Miss Winton had lived in the block of flats for fifteen years. She had seen many tenants come and go. She had heard about the Runcas and the model place they had made of the penthouse. It was the talk of London, Miss Winton had been told by Mrs Neck, who kept a grocer's shop near by; the Runcas were full of taste, apparently. Miss Winton thought it odd that London should talk about a penthouse flat, but did not ever mention that to Mrs Neck, who didn't seem to think it odd at all. To Miss Winton the Runcas were like many others who had come to live in the same building: people she saw and did not know. There were no children in the building, that being a rule; but animals, within reason, were permitted.

Miss Winton left her flat and walked with her dog to Mrs Neck's shop. 'Fresh buns,' said Mrs Neck before Miss Winton had made a request. 'Just in, dear.' But Miss Winton shook her head and asked for eggs and honey and butter. 'Seven and ten,' said Mrs Neck, reckoning the cost before reaching a hand out for the articles. She said it was shocking that food should cost so much, but Miss Winton replied that in her opinion two shillings wasn't exorbitant for half a pound of butter. 'I remember it ninepence,' said Mrs Neck, 'and twice the stuff it was. I'd sooner a smear of Stork than what they're turning out today.' Miss Winton smiled, and agreed that the quality of everything had gone down a bit.

Afterwards, for very many years, Miss Winton remembered this conversation with Mrs Neck. She remembered Mrs Neck saying: 'I'd sooner a smear of Stork than what they're turning out today,' and she remembered the rather small, dark-haired girl who entered Mrs Neck's shop at that moment, who smiled at both of them in an innocent way. 'Is that so?' said the Runcas' maid, Bianca. 'Quality has gone down?'

'Lord love you, Miss Winton knows what she's talking about,' said Mrs Neck. 'Quality's gone to pieces.'

Miss Winton might have left the shop then, for her purchasing was over, but the dark-haired young girl had leaned down and was patting the head of Miss Winton's dog. She smiled while doing that. Mrs Neck said:

'Miss Winton's in the flats too.'

'Ah, yes?'

'This young lady,' explained Mrs Neck to Miss Winton, 'works for the Runcas in the penthouse we hear so much about.'

'Today they are coming to photograph,' said Bianca. 'People from a magazine. And they will write down other things about it.'

'Again?' said Mrs Neck, shaking her head in wonderment. 'What can I do for you?'

Bianca asked for coffee beans and a sliced loaf, still stroking the head of the dog.

Miss Winton smiled. 'He has taken to you,' she said to Bianca, speaking timidly because she felt shy of people, especially foreigners. 'He's very good company.'

'Pretty little dog,' said Bianca.

Miss Winton walked with Bianca back to the block of flats, and when they arrived in the large hallway Bianca said:

'Miss Winton, would you like to see the penthouse with all its fresh flowers and fruits about the place? It is at its best in the morning sunlight as Mr Runca was remarking earlier. It is ready for all the photographers.'

Miss Winton, touched that the Italian girl should display such thoughtfulness towards an elderly spinster, said that it would be a pleasure to look at the penthouse flat but added that the Runcas might not care to have her walking about their property.

'No, no,' said Bianca, who had not been long in the Runcas' employ. 'Mrs Runca would love you to see it. And him too. "Show anyone you like," they've said to me. Certainly.' Bianca was not telling the truth, but time hung heavily on her hands in the empty penthouse and she knew she would enjoy showing Miss Winton all the flowers that Mrs Runca had so tastefully arranged, and all the curtains that had been imported specially from Thailand, and the rugs and the chairs and the pictures on the walls.

'Well,' began Miss Winton.

'Yes,' said Bianca and pressed Miss Winton and her dog into the lift.

But when the lift halted at the top and Bianca opened the gates Miss Winton experienced a small shock. 'Mr Morgan is here too,' said Bianca. 'Mending the water.'

Miss Winton felt that she could not now refuse to enter the Runcas' flat, since to do so would be to offend the friendly little Italian girl, yet she really did not wish to find herself face to face with Mr Morgan in somebody else's flat. 'Look here,' she said, but Bianca and the dog were already ahead of her. 'Come on, Miss Winton,' said Bianca.

Miss Winton found herself in the Runcas' small and fastidious hall, and then in the large room that had one side made of glass. She looked around her and noted all the low furniture and the pale Afghanistan carpet and the objects scattered economically about, and the flowers that Mrs Runca had arranged. 'Have coffee,' said Bianca, going quickly off to make some, and the little dog, noting her swift movement and registering it as a form of play, gave a single bark and darted about himself, in a small circle. 'Shh,' whispered Miss Winton. 'Really,' she protested, following Bianca to the kitchen, 'don't bother about coffee.' 'No, no,' said Bianca, pretending not to understand, thinking that there was plenty of time for herself and Miss Winton to have coffee together, sitting in the kitchen, where Mrs Runca had commanded coffee was to be drunk. Miss Winton could hear a light hammering and guessed it was Mr Morgan at work on the water-pipes. She could imagine him coming out of the Runcas' bathroom and stopping quite still as soon as he saw her. He would stand there in his brown overall, large and bulky, peering at her through his spectacles, chewing, probably, a piece of his moustache. His job was to attend to the needs of the tenants when the needs were not complicated, but whenever Miss Winton telephoned down to his basement and asked for his assistance he would sigh loudly into the telephone and say that he mightn't manage to attend to the matter for a day or two.

He would come, eventually, late at night but still in his brown overall, his eyes watering, his breath rich with alcohol. He would look at whatever the trouble was and make a swift diagnosis, advising that experts should be summoned the following morning. He didn't much like her, Miss Winton thought; no doubt he considered her a poor creature, unmarried at sixty-four, thin and weak-looking, with little sign that her physical appearance had been attractive in girlhood.

'It's a lovely place,' said Miss Winton to Bianca. 'But I think perhaps we should go now. Please don't bother with coffee; and thank you most awfully.'

'No, no,' said Bianca, and while she was saying it Mr Morgan entered the kitchen in his brown overall.

One day in 1952 Miss Winton had mislaid her bicycle. It had disappeared without trace from the passage in the basement where Mr Morgan had said she might keep it. 'I have not seen it,' he had said slowly and deliberately at that time. 'I know of no cycle.' Miss Winton had reminded him that the bicycle had always had a place in the passage, since he had said she might keep it there. But Mr Morgan, thirteen years younger then, had replied that he could recall none of that. 'Stolen,' he had said. 'I dare say stolen. I should say the coke men carted it away. I cannot always be watching the place, y'know. I have me work, madam.' She had asked him to inquire of the coke men if they had in error removed her bicycle; she had spoken politely and with a smile, but Mr Morgan had repeatedly shaken his head, pointing out that he could not go suggesting that the coke men had made off with a bicycle, saying that the coke men would have the law on him. 'The wife has a cycle,' Mr Morgan had said. 'A Rudge. I could obtain it for you, madam. Fifty shillings?' Miss Winton had smiled again and had walked away, having refused this offer and given thanks for it.

'Was you wanting something, madam?' asked Mr Morgan now, his lower lip pulling a strand of his moustache into his mouth. 'This is the Runcas' flat up here.'

Miss Winton tried to smile at him. She thought that whatever she said he would be sarcastic in a disguised way. He would hide his sarcasm beneath the words he chose, implying it only with the inflection in his voice. Miss Winton said:

'Bianca kindly invited me to see the penthouse.'

'It is a different type of place from yours and mine,' replied Mr Morgan, looking about him. 'I was attending to a tap in the bathroom. Working, Miss Winton.'

'It is all to be photographed today,' said Bianca. 'Mr and Mrs Runca will return early from their businesses.'

'Was you up here doing the flowers, madam?'

He had called her madam during all the years they had known one another, pointing up the fact that she had no right to the title.

'A cup of coffee, Mr Morgan?' said Bianca, and Miss Winton hoped he would refuse.

'With two spoons of sugar in it,' said Mr Morgan, nodding his head and adding: 'D'you know what the Irish take in their coffee?' He began to laugh rumbustiously, ignoring Miss Winton and appearing to share a joke with Bianca. 'A tot of the hard stuff,' said Mr Morgan. 'Whisky.'

Bianca laughed too. She left the kitchen, and Miss Winton's dog ran after her. Mr Morgan blew at the surface of his coffee while Miss Winton, wondering what to say to him, stirred hers.

'It's certainly a beautiful flat,' said Miss Winton.

'It would be too large for you, madam. I mean to say, just you and the dog in a place like this. You'd lose one another.'

'Oh, yes, of course. No, I meant –'

'I'll speak to the authorities if you like. I'll speak on your behalf, as a tenant often asks me to do. Put a word in, y'know. I could put a word in if you like, madam.'

Miss Winton frowned, wondering what Mr Morgan was talking about. She smiled uncertainly at him. He said:

'I have a bit of influence, knowing the tenants and that. I got the left-hand ground flat for Mr McCarthy by moving the Aitchesons up to the third. I got Mrs Bloom out of the back one on the first –'

'Mr Morgan, you've misunderstood me. I wouldn't at all like to move up here.'

Mr Morgan looked at Miss Winton, sucking coffee off his moustache. His eyes were focused on hers. He said:

'You don't have to say nothing outright, madam. I understand a hint.'

Bianca returned with a bottle of whisky. She handed it to Mr Morgan, saying that he had better add it to the coffee since she didn't know how much to put in.

'Oh, a good drop,' said Mr Morgan, splashing the liquor on to his warm coffee. He approached Miss Winton with the neck of the bottle poised towards her cup. He'll be offended, she thought; and because of that she did not, as she wished to, refuse his offering. 'The Irish are heavy drinkers,' said Mr Morgan. 'Cheers.' He drank the mixture and proclaimed it good. 'D'you like that, Miss Winton?' he asked, and Miss Winton tasted it and discovered to her surprise that the beverage was pleasant. 'Yes,' she said. 'I do.'

Mr Morgan held out his cup for more coffee. 'Just a small drop,' he said, and he filled the cup with whisky. Again he inclined the neck of the bottle towards Miss Winton, who smiled and said she hadn't finished. He held the bottle in the same position, watching her drinking her coffee. She protested when Bianca poured her more, but she could sense that Bianca was enjoying this giving of hospitality, and for that reason she accepted, knowing that Mr Morgan would pour in more whisky. She felt comfortably warm from the whisky that was already in her body, and she experienced the desire to be agreeable – although she was aware, too, that she would not care for it if the Runcas unexpectedly returned.

'Fair enough,' said Mr Morgan, topping up Bianca's cup and adding a further quantity to his own. He said:

'Miss Winton is thinking of shifting up here, her being the oldest tenant in the building. She's been stuck downstairs for fifteen years.'

Bianca shook her head, saying to Miss Winton: 'What means that?'

'I'm quite happy,' said Miss Winton, 'where I am.' She spoke softly, with a smile on her face, intent upon being agreeable. Mr Morgan was sitting on the edge of the kitchen table. Bianca had turned on the wireless. Mr Morgan said:

'I came to the flats on March the twenty-first, nineteen fifty-one. Miss Winton here was already in residence. Riding about on a cycle.'

'I was six years old,' said Bianca.

'D'you remember that day, Miss Winton? March the twenty-first?'

Miss Winton shook her head. She sat down on a chair made of an ersatz material. She said:

'It's a long time ago.'

'I remember the time you lost your cycle, Miss Winton. She came down to me in the basement,' said Mr Morgan to Bianca, 'and told me to tick off the coke deliverers for thieving her bicycle. I never seen no cycle, as I said to Miss Winton. D'you understand, missy?' Bianca smiled, nodding swiftly. She hummed the tune that was coming from the wireless. 'Do you like that Irish drink?' said Mr Morgan. 'Shall we have some more?'

'I must be going,' said Miss Winton. 'It's been terribly kind of you.'

'Are you going, madam?' said Mr Morgan, and there was in his tone a hint of the belligerency that Miss Winton knew his nature was imbued with. In her mind he spoke more harshly to her, saying she was a woman who had never lived. He was saying that she might have been a nun the way she existed, not knowing anything about the world around her; she had never known a man's love, Mr Morgan was saying; she had never borne a child.

'Oh, don't go,' said Bianca. 'Please, I'll make you a cold cocktail, like Mr Runca showed me how. Cinzano with gin in it, and lemon and ice.'

'Oh, no,' said Miss Winton.

Mr Morgan sighed, implying with the intake of his breath that her protest was not unexpected. There were other women in the block of flats, Miss Winton imagined, who would have a chat with Mr Morgan now and again, who would pass the time of day with him, asking him for racing tips and suggesting that he should let them know when he heard that a flat they coveted was going to be empty. Mr Morgan was probably a man whom people tipped quite lavishly for the performance of services or favours. Miss Winton could imagine people, people like the Runcas maybe, saying to their friends: 'We greased the caretaker's palm. We gave him five pounds.' She thought she'd never be able to do that.

Bianca went away to fetch the ingredients for the drink, and again the dog went with her.

Miss Winton stood still, determined that Mr Morgan should not consider that she did not possess the nerve to receive from the Runcas' Italian maid a midday cocktail. Mr Morgan said:

'You and me have known one another a number of years.'

'Yes, we have.'

'We know what we think of a flat like this, and the type of person. Don't we, Miss Winton?'

'To tell the truth, I don't know the Runcas at all.'

'I'll admit it to you: the whisky has loosened my tongue, Miss Winton. You understand what I mean?'

Miss Winton smiled at Mr Morgan. There was sweat, she noticed, on the sides of his face. He said with vehemence: 'Ridiculous, the place being photographed. What do they want to do that for, tell me?'

'Magazines take an interest. It's a contemporary thing. Mrs Neck was saying that this flat is well known.'

'You can't trust Mrs Neck. I think it's a terrible place. I wouldn't be comfortable in a place like this.'

'Well –'

'You could report me for saying a thing like that. You could do that, Miss Winton. You could tell them I was intoxicated at twelve o'clock in the day, drinking a tenant's liquor and abusing the tenant behind his back. D'you see what I mean, madam?'

'I wouldn't report you, Mr Morgan. It's no business of mine.'

'I'd like to see you up here, madam, getting rid of all this trash and putting in a decent bit of furniture. How's about that?'

'Please, Mr Morgan, I'm perfectly happy –'

'I'll see what I can do,' said Mr Morgan.

Bianca returned with glasses and bottles. Mr Morgan said:

'I was telling Miss Winton here that she could report me to the authorities for misconduct, but she said she never would. We've known one another a longish time. We was never drinking together though.'

Bianca handed Miss Winton a glass that felt cold in Miss Winton's hand. She feared now what Mr Morgan was going to say. He said:

'I intoxicate easily.' Mr Morgan laughed, displaying darkened teeth. He swayed back and forth, looking at Miss Winton. 'I'll put in a word for you,' he said, 'no bother at all.'

She was thinking that she would finish the drink she'd been given and then go away and prepare lunch. She would buy some little present to give Bianca, and she would come up to the Runcas' flat one morning and hand it to her, thanking her for her hospitality and her thoughtfulness.

While Miss Winton was thinking that, Mr Morgan was thinking that he intended to drink at least two more of the drinks that the girl was offering, and Bianca was thinking that it was the first friendly morning she had spent in this flat since her arrival three weeks before. 'I must go to the W.C.,' said Mr Morgan, and he left the kitchen, saying he would be back. 'It's most kind of you,' said Miss Winton when he had gone. 'I do hope it's all right.' It had occurred to her that Bianca's giving people the Runcas' whisky and gin was rather different from her giving people a cup of coffee, but when she looked at Bianca she saw that she was innocently smiling. She felt light-headed, and smiled herself. She rose from her chair and thanked Bianca again and said that she must be going now. Her dog came to her, wishing to go also. 'Don't you like the drink?' said Bianca, and Miss Winton finished it. She placed the glass on the metal draining-board and as she did so a crash occurred in the Runcas' large sitting-room. 'Heavens!' said Miss Winton, and Bianca raised a hand to her mouth and kept it there. When they entered the room they saw Mr Morgan standing in the centre of it, looking at the floor.

'Heavens!' said Miss Winton, and Bianca widened her eyes and still did not take her hand away from her mouth. On the floor lay the flowers that Mrs Runca had earlier arranged. The huge vase was smashed into many pieces. Water was soaking into the Afghanistan carpet.

'I was looking at it,' explained Mr Morgan. 'I was touching a flower with my fingers. The whole thing gave way.'

'Mrs Runca's flowers,' said Bianca. 'Oh, Mother of God!'

'Mr Morgan,' said Miss Winton.

'Don't look at me, ma'am. Don't blame me for an instant. Them flowers was inadequately balanced. Ridiculous.'

Bianca, on her hands and knees, was picking up the broken stalks. She might have been more upset, Miss Winton thought, and she was glad that she was not. Bianca explained that Mrs Runca had stayed away from her boutique specially to arrange the flowers. 'They'll give me the sack,' she said, and instead of weeping she gave a small giggle.

The gravity of the situation struck Miss Winton forcibly. Hearing Bianca's giggle, Mr Morgan laughed also, and went to the kitchen, where Miss Winton heard him pouring himself some more of the Runca's gin. Miss Winton realized then that neither Bianca nor Mr Morgan had any sense of responsibility at all. Bianca was young and did not know any better; Mr Morgan was partly drunk. The Runcas would return with people from a magazine and they would find that their property had been damaged, that a vase had been broken and that a large damp patch in the centre of their Afghanistan carpet would not look good in the photographs. 'Let's have another cocktail,' said Bianca, throwing down the flowers she had collected and giggling again. 'Oh, no,' cried Miss Winton. 'Please, Bianca. We must think what's best to do.' But Bianca was already in the kitchen, and Miss Winton could hear Mr Morgan's rumbustious laugh.

'I tell you what,' said Mr Morgan, coming towards her with a glass in his hand. 'We'll say the dog done it. We'll say the dog jumped at the flowers trying to grip hold of them.'

Miss Winton regarded him with surprise. 'My dog?' she said. 'My dog was nowhere near the flowers.' Her voice was sharp, the first time it had been so that morning.

Mr Morgan sat down in an armchair, and Miss Winton, about to protest about that also, realized in time that she had, of course, no right to protest at all.

'We could say,' said Mr Morgan, 'that the dog went into a hysterical fit and attacked the flowers. How's about that?'

'But that's not true. It's not the truth.'

'I was thinking of me job, madam. And of the young missy's. It's all right for others.'

'It was an accident,' said Miss Winton, 'as you have said, Mr Morgan.'

'They'll say what was I doing touching the flowers? They'll say to the young missy what was happening at all, was you giving a party? I'll have to explain the whole thing to my wife.'

'Your wife?'

'What was I doing in the Runcas' flat with the young one? The wife will see through anything.'

'You were here to mend a water-pipe, Mr Morgan.'

'What's the matter with the water-pipes?'

'Oh really, Mr Morgan. You were repairing a pipe when I came into the flat.'

'There was nothing the matter with the pipes, ma'am. Nor never has been, which is just the point. The young missy telephones down saying the pipes is making a noise. She's anxious for company. She likes to engage in a chat.'

'I shall arrange what flowers we can salvage,' said Miss Winton, 'just as neatly as they were arranged before. And we can explain to the Runcas that you came to the flat to mend a pipe and that in passing you brushed against Mrs Runca's flowers. The only difficulty is the carpet. The best way to get that damp stain out would be to lift up the carpet and put an electric fire in front of it.'

'Take it easy,' said Mr Morgan. 'Have a drink, Miss Winton.'

'We must repair the damage –'

'Listen, madam,' said Mr Morgan, leaning forward, 'you and I know what we think of a joint like this. Tricked out like they've got it –'

'It's a question of personal taste –'

'Tell them the dog done the damage, Miss Winton, and I'll see you right. A word in the ear of the authorities and them Runcas will be out on the street in a jiffy. Upsetting the neighbours with noise, bringing the flats into disrepute. I'd say it in court, Miss Winton: I seen naked women going in and out of the penthouse. D'you see?'

'Bianca returned, and Miss Winton repeated to her what she had said already to Mr Morgan about the drying of the carpet. Between them, they moved chairs and tables and lifted the carpet from the floor, draping it across two chairs and placing an electric fire in front of it. Mr Morgan moved to a distant sofa and watched them.

'I used not to be bad with flowers,' said Miss Winton to Bianca. 'Are there other vases?' They went together to the kitchen to see what there was. 'Would you like another cocktail?' said Bianca, but Miss Winton said she thought they all had had enough to drink. 'I like these drinks,' said Bianca, sipping one. 'So cool.'

'You must explain,' said Miss Winton, 'that Mr Morgan had to come in order to repair the gurgling pipe and that he brushed against the flowers on the way across the room. You must tell the truth: that you had invited me to have a look at the beautiful flat. I'm sure they won't be angry when they know it was all an accident.'

'What means gurgling?' said Bianca.

'Hey,' shouted Mr Morgan from the other room.

'I think Mr Morgan should go now,' said Miss Winton. 'I wonder if you'd say so, Bianca? He's a very touchy man.' She imagined Mr Runca looking sternly into her face and saying he could not believe his eyes: that she, an elderly spinster, still within her wits, had played a part in the disastrous proceedings in his flat. She had allowed the caretaker to become drunk, she had egged on a young foreign girl. 'Have you no responsibility?' shouted Mr Runca at Miss Winton in her imagination. 'What's the matter with you?'

'Hey,' shouted Mr Morgan. 'That carpet's burning.'

Miss Winton and Bianca sniffed the air and smelt at once the tang of singed wool. They returned at speed to the other room and saw that the carpet was smoking and that Mr Morgan was still on the sofa, watching it. 'How's about that?' said Mr Morgan.

'The fire was too close,' said Bianca, looking at Miss Winton, who frowned and felt afraid. She didn't remember putting the fire so close to the carpet, and then she thought that she was probably as intoxicated as Mr Morgan and didn't really know what she was doing.

'Scrape off the burnt bit,' advised Mr Morgan, 'and tell them the dog ate it.'

They unplugged the fire and laid the carpet flat on the floor again. Much of the damp had disappeared, but the burnt patch, though small, was eye-catching. Miss Winton felt a weakness in her stomach, as though a quantity of jelly were turning rhythmically over and over. The situation now seemed beyond explanation, and she saw herself asking the Runcas to sit down quietly, side by side with the people from the magazine, and she heard herself trying to tell the truth, going into every detail and pleading that Bianca should not be punished. 'Blame me,' she was saying, 'if someone must be blamed, for I have nothing to lose.'

'I'll tell you what,' said Mr Morgan, 'why don't we telephone for Mrs Neck? She done a carpet for her hearth, forty different wools she told me, that she shaped with a little instrument. Ring up Mrs Neck, missy, and say there's a drink for her if she'll oblige Mr Morgan with ten minutes of her time.'

'Do no such thing,' cried Miss Winton. 'There's been enough drinking, Mr Morgan, as well you know. The trouble started with drink, when you lurched against the flowers. There's no point at all in Mrs Neck adding to the confusion.'

Mr Morgan listened to Miss Winton and then rose from the sofa. He said: ·

'You have lived in these flats longer than I have, madam. We all know that. But I will not stand here and be insulted by you, just because I am a working man. The day you came after your cycle –'

'I must go away,' cried Bianca in distress. 'I cannot be found with a burnt carpet and the flowers like that.'

'Listen,' said Mr Morgan, coming close to Miss Winton. 'I have a respect for you. I'm surprised to hear myself insulted from your lips.'

'Mr Morgan –'

'You was insulting me, madam.'

'I was not insulting you. Don't go, Bianca. I'll stay here and explain everything to the Runcas. I think, Mr Morgan, it would be best if you went off to your lunch now.'

'How can I?' shouted Mr Morgan very loudly and rudely, sticking his chin out at Miss Winton. 'How the damn hell d'you think I can go down to the wife in the condition I'm in? She'd eat the face off me.'

'Please, Mr Morgan.'

'You and your dog: I have respect for the pair of you. You and me is on the same side of the fence. D'you understand?'

Miss Winton shook her head.

'What d'you think of the Runcas, ma'am?'

'I've said, Mr Morgan: I've never met the Runcas.'

'What d'you think of the joint they've got here?'

'I think it's most impressive.'

'It's laughable. The whole caboodle is laughable. Did you ever see the like?' Mr Morgan pointed at objects in the room. 'They're two tramps,' he shouted, his face purple with rage at the thought of the Runcas. 'They're jumped-up tramps.'

Miss Winton opened her mouth in order to speak soothingly. Mr Morgan said:

'I could put a match to the place and to the Runcas too, with their bloody attitudes. I'm only a simple caretaker, madam, but I'd see their bodies in flames.' He kicked a chair, his boot thudding loudly against pale wood. 'I hate that class of person, they're as crooked as a corkscrew.'

'You're mistaken, Mr Morgan.'

'I'm bloody not mistaken,' shouted Mr Morgan. 'They're full of hate for a man like me. They'd say I was a beast.'

Miss Winton, shocked and perturbed, was also filled with amazement. She couldn't understand why Mr Morgan had said that he and she belonged on the same side of the fence, since for the past fifteen years she had noted the scorn in his eyes.

'We have a thing in common,' said Mr Morgan. 'We have no respect whatever for the jumped-up tramps who occupy this property. I'd like to see you in here, madam, with your bits and pieces. The Runcas can go where they belong.' Mr Morgan spat into the chair which he had struck with his boot.

'Oh, no,' cried Miss Winton, and Mr Morgan laughed. He walked about the room, clearing his throat and spitting carelessly. Eventually he strolled away, into the kitchen. The dog barked, sensing Miss Winton's distress. Bianca began to sob and from the kitchen came the whistling of Mr Morgan, a noise he emitted in order to cover the sound of gin being poured into his glass. Miss Winton knew what had happened: she had read of men who could not resist alcohol and who were maddened by its presence in their bloodstream. She considered that Mr Morgan had gone mad in the Runcas' flat, he was speaking like an insane person, saying he had respect for her dog.

'I am frightened of him,' said Bianca.

'No,' said Miss Winton. 'He's a harmless man, though I wish he'd go away. We can clean up a bit. We can make an effort.'

Mr Morgan returned and took no notice of them. He sat on the sofa while they set to, clearing up all the pieces of broken vase and the flowers. They placed a chair over the burnt area of carpet so that the Runcas would not notice it as soon as they entered the room. Miss Winton arranged the flowers in a vase and placed it where the other one had been placed by Mrs Runca. She surveyed the room and noticed that, apart from the presence of Mr Morgan, it wasn't so bad. Perhaps, she thought, the explanation could be unfolded gradually. She saw no reason why the room shouldn't be photographed as it was now, with the nicely-arranged flowers and the chair over the burnt patch of carpeting. The damp area, greater in size, was still a little noticeable, but she imagined that in a photograph it mightn't show up too badly.

'You have let me get into this condition,' said Mr Morgan in an aggressive way. 'It was your place to say that the Runcas' whisky shouldn't be touched, nor their gin neither. You're a fellow-tenant, Miss Winton. The girl and I are servants, madam. We was doing what came naturally.'

'I'll take the responsibility,' said Miss Winton.

'Say the dog done it,' urged Mr Morgan again. 'The other will go against the girl and myself.'

'I'll tell the truth,' said Miss Winton. 'The Runcas will understand. They're not monsters that they won't forgive an accident. Mrs Runca –'

'That thin bitch,' shouted Mr Morgan, and added more quietly: 'Runca's illegitimate.'

'Mr Morgan –'

'Tell them the bloody dog done it. Tell them the dog ran about like a mad thing. How d'you know they're not monsters? How d'you know they'll understand, may I ask? "We was all three boozing in the kitchen," are you going to say? "and Mr Morgan took more than his share of the intoxicant. All hell broke loose." Are you going to say that, Miss Winton?'

'The truth is better than lies.'

'What's the matter with saying the dog done it?'

'You would be far better off out of this flat, Mr Morgan. No good will come of you raving on like that.'

'You have always respected me, madam. You have never been familiar.'

'Well –'

'I might strike them dead. They might enter that door and I might hit them with a hammer.'

Miss Winton began to protest, but Mr Morgan waved a hand at her. He sniffed and said: 'A caretaker sees a lot, I'll tell you that. Fellows bringing women in, hypocrisy all over the place. There's those that slips me a coin, madam, and those that doesn't bother, and I'm not to know which is the worse. Some of them's miserable and some's boozing all night, having sex and laughing their heads off. The Runcas isn't human in any way whatsoever. The Runcas is saying I was a beast that might offend their eyes.' Mr Morgan ceased to speak, and glared angrily at Miss Winton.

'Come now,' she said.

'A dirty caretaker, they've said, who's not fit to be alive –'

'They've never said any such thing, Mr Morgan. I'm sure of it.'

They should have moved away from the flats if they hated the caretaker. They're a psychological case.'

There was a silence in the room, while Miss Winton trembled and tried not to show it, aware that Mr Morgan had reached a condition in which he was capable of all he mentioned.

'What I need,' he said after a time, speaking more calmly from the sofa on which he was relaxing, 'is a cold bath.'

'Mr Morgan,' said Miss Winton. She thought that he was at last about to go away, down to his basement and his angry wife, in order to immerse his large body in cold water. 'Mr Morgan, I'm sorry that you should think badly of me –'

'I'll have a quick one,' said Mr Morgan, walking towards the Runcas' bathroom. 'Who'll know the difference?'

'No,' cried Miss Winton. 'No, please, Mr Morgan.'

But with his glass in his hand Mr Morgan entered the bathroom and locked the door.

When the photographers arrived at half past two to prepare their apparatus Mr Morgan was still in the bathroom. Miss Winton waited with Bianca, reassuring her from time to time, repeating that she would not leave until she herself had explained to the Runcas what had happened. The photographers worked silently, moving none of the furniture because they had been told that the furniture was on no account to be displaced.

For an hour and twenty minutes Mr Morgan had been in the bathroom. It was clear to Miss Winton that he had thrown the vase of flowers to the ground deliberately and in anger, and that he had placed the fire closer to the carpet. In his crazy and spiteful condition Miss Winton imagined that he was capable of anything: of drowning himself in the bath maybe, so that the Runcas' penthouse might sordidly feature in the newspapers. Bianca had been concerned about his continued presence in the bathroom, but Miss Winton had explained that Mr Morgan was simply being unpleasant since he was made like that. 'It is quite disgraceful,' she said, well aware that Mr Morgan realized that she was the kind of woman who would not report him to the authorities, and was taking advantage of her nature while involving her in his own. She felt that the Runcas were the victims of circumstance, and thought that she might use that very expression when she made her explanation to them. She would speak slowly and quietly, breaking it to them in the end that Mr Morgan was still in the bathroom and had probably fallen asleep. 'It is not his fault,' she heard herself saying. 'We must try to understand.' And she felt that the Runcas would nod their heads in agreement and would know what to do next.

'Will they sack me?' said Bianca, and Miss Winton shook her head, repeating again that nothing that had happened had been Bianca's fault.

At three o'clock the Runcas arrived. They came together, having met in the hallway downstairs. 'The flowers came, did they?' Mr Runca had inquired of his wife in the lift, and she had replied that the flowers had safely been delivered and that she had arranged them to her satisfaction. 'Good,' said Mr Runca, and reported to his wife some facts about the morning he had spent.

When they entered their penthouse apartment the Runcas noted the presence of the photographers and the photographers' apparatus. They saw as well that an elderly woman with a dog was there, standing beside Bianca, that a chair had been moved, that the Afghanistan carpet was stained, and that some flowers had been loosely thrust into a vase. Mr Runca wondered about the latter because his wife had just informed him that she herself had arranged the flowers; Mrs Runca thought that something peculiar was going on. The elderly woman stepped forward to greet them, announcing that her name was Miss Winton, and at that moment a man in a brown overall whom the Runcas recognized as a Mr Morgan, caretaker and odd-job man, entered the room from the direction of the bathroom. He strode towards them and coughed.

'You had trouble with the pipes,' said Mr Morgan. He spoke urgently and it seemed to Mr and Mrs Runca that the elderly woman with the dog was affected by his speaking. Her mouth was actually open, as though she had been about to speak herself. Hearing Mr Morgan's voice, she closed it.

'What has happened here?' said Mrs Runca, moving forward from her husband's side. 'Has there been an accident?'

'I was called up to the flat,' said Mr Morgan, 'on account of noise in the pipes. Clogged pipes was on the point of bursting, a trouble I've been dealing with since eleven-thirty. You'll discover the bath is full of water. Release it, sir, at five o'clock tonight, and then I think you'll find everything O.K. Your drain-away was out of order.'

Mrs Runca removed her gaze from Mr Morgan's face and passed it on to the face of Miss Winton and then on to the bowed head of Bianca. Her husband examined the silent photographers, sensing something in the atmosphere. He said to himself that he did not yet know the full story: what, for instance, was this woman with a dog doing there? A bell rang, and Bianca moved automatically from Miss Winton's side to answer the door. She admitted the woman from the magazine, the woman who was in charge of everything and was to write the article.

'Miss Winton,' said Mr Morgan, indicating Miss Winton, 'occupies a flat lower down in the building.' Mr Morgan blew his nose. 'Miss Winton wished,' he said, 'to see the penthouse, and knowing that I was coming here she came up too and got into conversation with the maid on the doorstep. The dog dashed in, in a hysterical fit, knocking down a bowl of flowers and upsetting an electric fire on the carpet. Did you notice this?' said Mr Morgan, striding forward to display the burnt patch. 'The girl had the fire on,' added Mr Morgan, 'because she felt the cold, coming from a warmer clime.'

Miss Winton heard the words of Mr Morgan and said nothing at all. He had stood in the bathroom, she reckoned, for an hour and twenty minutes, planning to say that the girl had put on the fire because, being Italian, she had suddenly felt the cold.

'Well?' said Mr Runca, looking at Miss Winton.

She saw his eyes, dark and intent, anxious to draw a response from her, wishing to watch the opening and closing of her lips while his ears listened to the words that relayed the explanation.

'I regret the inconvenience,' she said. 'I'll pay the damage.'

'Damage?' cried Mrs Runca, moving forward and pushing the chair further away from the burnt area of carpet. 'Damage?' she said again, looking at the flowers in the vase.

'So a dog had a fit in here,' said Mr Runca.

The woman from the magazine looked from Mr Morgan to Bianca and then to Miss Winton. She surveyed the faces of Mr and Mrs Runca and glanced last of all at the passive countenances of the photographers. It seemed, she reflected, that an incident had occurred; it seemed that a dog had gone berserk. 'Well now,' she said briskly. 'Surely it's not as bad as all that? If we put that chair back who'll notice the carpet? And the flowers look most becoming.'

'The flowers are a total mess,' said Mrs Runca. 'An animal might have arranged them.'

Mr Morgan was discreetly silent, and Miss Winton's face turned scarlet.

'We had better put the whole thing off,' said Mr Runca meditatively. 'It'll take a day or two to put everything back to rights. We are sorry,' he said, addressing himself to the woman from the magazine. 'But no doubt you see that no pictures can be taken?'

The woman, swearing most violently within her mind, smiled at Mr Runca and said it was obvious, of course. Mr Morgan said:

'I'm sorry, about this.' He stood there, serious and unemotional, as though he had never suggested that Mrs Neck might be invited up to the Runcas' penthouse apartment, as though hatred and drink had not rendered him insane. 'I'm sorry, sir,' said Mr Morgan. 'I should not have permitted a dog to enter your quarters, sir. I was unaware of the dog until it was too late.'

Listening to Mr Morgan laboriously telling his lies, Miss Winton was visited by the thought that there was something else she could do. For fifteen years she had lived lonesomely in the building, her shyness causing her to keep herself to herself. She possessed enough money to exist quite comfortably; she didn't do much as the days went by.

'Excuse me,' said Miss Winton, not at all knowing how she was going to proceed. She felt her face becoming red again, and she felt the eyes of all the people on her. She wanted to explain at length, to go on talking in a manner that was quite unusual for her, weaving together the threads of an argument. It seemed to Miss Winton that she would have to remind the

Runcas of the life of Mr Morgan, how he daily climbed from his deep basement, attired invariably in his long brown overall. 'He has a right to his resentment,' was what she might say; 'he has a right to demand more of the tenants of these flats. His palm in greased, he is handed a cup of tea in exchange for a racing tip; the tenants keep him sweet.' He had come to consider that some of the tenants were absurd, or stupid, and that others were hypocritical. For Miss Winton he had reserved his scorn, for the Runcas a share of his hatred. Miss Winton had accepted the scorn, and understood why it was there; they must seek to understand the other. 'The ball is in your court,' said Miss Winton in her imagination, addressing the Runcas and pleased that she had thought of a breezy expression that they would at once appreciate.

'What about Wednesday next?' said Mr Runca to the woman from the magazine. 'All this should be sorted out by then, I imagine.'

'Wednesday would be lovely,' said the woman.

Miss Winton wanted to let Mr Morgan see that he was wrong about these people. She wanted to have it proved here and now that the Runcas were human and would understand an accident, that they, like anyone else, were capable of respecting a touchy caretaker. She wished to speak the truth, to lead the truth into the open and let it act for itself between Mr Morgan and the Runcas.

'We'll make a note of everything,' Mrs Runca said to her, 'and let you have the list of the damage and the cost of it.'

'I'd like to talk to you,' said Miss Winton. 'I'd like to explain if I may.'

'Explain?' said Mrs Runca. 'Explain?'

'Could we all sit down? I'd like you to understand. I've been in these flats for fifteen years. Mr Morgan came a year later. Perhaps I can help. It's difficult for me to explain to you.' Miss Winton paused, in some confusion.

'Is she ill?' inquired the steely voice of Mrs Runca, and Miss Winton was aware of the woman's metallic hair, and fingernails that matched it, and the four shrewd eyes of a man and a woman who were successful in all their transactions. 'I might hit them with a hammer,' said the voice of Mr Morgan in Miss Winton's memory. 'I might strike them dead.'

'We must try to understand,' cried Miss Winton, her face burning with embarrassment. 'A man like Mr Morgan and people like you and an old spinster like myself. We are all standing in this room and we must relax and attempt to understand.' Miss Winton wondered if the words that she forced from her were making sense; she was aware that she was not being eloquent. 'Don't you see?' cried Miss Winton with the businesslike stare of the Runcas fixed harshly upon her.

'What's this?' demanded Mrs Runca. 'What's all this about understanding? Understanding what?'

'Yes,' said her husband.

'Mr Morgan comes up from his basement every day of his life. The tenants grease his palm. He sees the tenants in his own way. He has a right to do that; he has a right to his touchiness –'

Mr Morgan coughed explosively, interrupting the flow of words. 'What are you talking about?' cried Mrs Runca. 'It's enough that damage has been done without all this.'

'I'm trying to begin at the beginning.' Ahead of her Miss Winton sensed a great mound of words and complication before she could lay bare the final truth: that Mr Morgan regarded the Runcas as people who had been in some way devoured. She knew that she would have to progress slowly, until they began to guess what she was trying to put to them. Accepting that they had failed the caretaker, as she had failed him too, they would understand the reason for his small revenge. They would nod their heads guiltily while she related how Mr Morgan, unhinged by alcohol, had spat at their furniture and had afterwards pretended to be drowned.

'We belong to different worlds,' said Miss Winton, wishing the ground would open beneath her, 'you and I and Mr Morgan. Mr Morgan sees your penthouse flat in a different way. What I am trying to say is that you are not just people to whom only lies can be told.'

'We have a lot to do,' said Mrs Runca, lighting a cigarette. She was smiling slightly, seeming amused.

'The bill for damage must be paid,' added Mr Runca firmly. 'You understand, Miss Winter? There can be no shelving of that responsibility.'

'I don't do much,' cried Miss Winton, moving beyond embarrassment now. 'I sit with my dog. I go to the shops. I watch the television. I don't do much, but I am trying to do something now. I am trying to promote understanding.'

The photographers began to dismantle their apparatus. Mr Runca spoke in a whisper to the woman from the magazine, making some final arrangement for the following Wednesday. He turned to Miss Winton and said more loudly: 'Perhaps you had better return to your apartment, Miss Winter. Who knows, that little dog may have another fit.'

'He didn't have a fit,' cried Miss Winton. 'He never had a fit in the whole of his life.'

There was a silence in the room then, before Mr Runca said:

'You've forgotten, Miss Winter, that your little dog had a bout of hysteria and caused a lot of trouble. Come now, Miss Winter.'

'My name is not Miss Winter. Why do you call me a name that isn't correct?'

Mr Runca threw his eyes upwards, implying that Miss Winton was getting completely out of hand and would next be denying her very existence. 'She's the Queen Mother,' whispered Mrs Runca to one of the photographers, and the photographer sniggered lightly. Miss Winton said:

'My dog did not have a fit. I am trying to tell you, but no one bothers to listen. I am trying to go back to the beginning, to the day that Mr Morgan first became caretaker of these flats –'

'Now, madam,' said Mr Morgan, stepping forward.

'I am going to tell the truth,' cried Miss Winton shrilly. Her dog began to bark, and she felt, closer to her now, the presence of Mr Morgan. 'Shall we be going, madam?' said Mr Morgan and she was aware that she was being moved towards the door. 'No,' she cried while the movement continued. 'No,' whispered Miss Winton again, but already she was on the landing and Mr Morgan was saying that there was no point whatsoever in attempting to tell people like the Runcas the truth. 'That type of person,' said Mr Morgan, descending the stairs with Miss Winton, his hand beneath her left elbow as though she required aid, 'that type of person wouldn't know the meaning of the word.'

I have failed, said Miss Winton to herself; I have failed to do something that might have been good in its small way. She found herself at the door of her flat, feeling tired, and heard Mr Morgan saying: 'Will you be all right, madam?' She reflected that he was speaking to her as though she were the one who had been mad, soothing her in his scorn. Mr Morgan began to laugh. 'Runca slipped me a quid,' he said. 'Our own Runca.' He laughed again, and Miss Winton felt wearier. She would write a cheque for the amount of the damage, and that would be that. She would often in the future pass Mr Morgan on the stairs and there would be a confused memory between them. The Runcas would tell their friends, saying there was a peculiar woman in one of the flats. 'Did you see their faces,' said Mr Morgan, 'when I mentioned about the dog in a fit?' He threw his head back, displaying all his teeth. 'It was that amusing,' said Mr Morgan. 'I nearly smiled.' He went away, and Miss Winton stood by the door of her flat, listening to his footsteps on the stairs. She heard him on the next floor, summoning the lift that would carry him smoothly to the basement, where he would tell his wife about how Miss Winton's dog had had a fit in the Runcas' penthouse, and how Miss Winton had made a ridiculous fuss that no one had bothered to listen to.

In at the Birth

Once upon a time there lived in a remote London suburb an elderly lady called Miss Efoss. Miss Efoss was a spry person, and for as long as she could control the issue she was determined to remain so. She attended the cinema and the theatre with regularity; she read at length; and she preferred the company of men and women forty years her junior. Once a year Miss Efoss still visited Athens and always on such visits she wondered why she had never settled in Greece: now, she felt, it was rather too late to make a change; in any case, she enjoyed London.

In her lifetime, nothing had passed Miss Efoss by. She had loved and been loved. She had once, even, given birth to a child. For a year or two she had known the ups and downs of early family life, although the actual legality of marriage had somehow been overlooked. Miss Efoss's baby died during a sharp attack of pneumonia; and shortly afterwards the child's father packed a suitcase one night. He said good-bye quite kindly to Miss Efoss, but she never saw him again.

In retrospect, Miss Efoss considered that she had run the gamut of human emotions. She settled down to the lively superficiality of the everyday existence she had mapped for herself. She was quite content with it. And she hardly noticed it when the Dutts entered her life.

It was Mr Dutt who telephoned. He said: 'Ah, Miss Efoss, I wonder if you can help us. We have heard that occasionally you baby-sit. We have scoured the neighbourhood for a reliable baby-sitter. Would you be interested, Miss Efoss, in giving us a try?'

'But who are you?' said Miss Efoss. 'I don't even know you. What is your name to begin with?'

'Dutt,' said Mr Dutt. 'We live only a couple of hundred yards from you. I think you would find it convenient.'

'Well –'

'Miss Efoss, come and see us. Come and have a drink. If you like the look of us perhaps we can arrange something. If not, we shan't be in the least offended.'

'That is very kind of you, Mr Dutt. If you give me your address and a time I'll certainly call. In fact, I shall be delighted to do so.'

'Good, good.' And Mr Dutt gave Miss Efoss the details, which she noted in her diary.

Mr and Mrs Dutt looked alike. They were small and thin with faces like greyhounds. 'We have had such difficulty in finding someone suitable to sit for us,' Mrs Dutt said. 'All these young girls, Miss Efoss, scarcely inspire confidence.'

'We are a nervous pair, Miss Efoss,' Mr Dutt said, laughing gently as he handed her a glass of sherry. 'We are a nervous pair and that's the truth of it.'

'There is only Mickey, you see,' explained his wife. 'I suppose we worry a bit. Though we try not to spoil him.'

Miss Efoss nodded. 'An only child is sometimes a problem.'

The Dutts agreed, staring intently at Miss Efoss, as though recognizing in her some profound quality.

'We have, as you see, the television,' Mr Dutt remarked. 'You would not be lonely here of an evening. The radio as well. Both are simple to operate and are excellent performers.'

'And Mickey has never woken up,' said Mrs Dutt. 'Our system is to leave our telephone behind. Thus you may easily contact us.'

'Ha, ha, ha.' Mr Dutt was laughing. His tiny face was screwed into an unusual shape, the skin drawn tightly over his gleaming cheek-bones.

'What an amusing thing to say, Beryl! My wife is fond of a joke, Miss Efoss.'

Unaware that a joke had been made, Miss Efoss smiled.

'It would be odd if we did *not* leave our telephone behind,' Mr Dutt went on. 'We leave the telephone *number* behind, Beryl. The telephone number of the house where we are dining. You would be surprised, Miss Efoss, to receive guests who carried with them their telephone receiver. Eh?'

'It would certainly be unusual.'

' "We have brought our own telephone, since we do not care to use another." Or: "We have brought our telephone in case anyone telephones us while we are here." Miss Efoss, will you tell me something?'

'If I can, Mr Dutt.'

'Miss Efoss, have you ever looked up the word *joke* in the *Encyclopaedia Britannica*?'

'I don't think I have.'

'You would find it rewarding. We have the full *Encyclopaedia* here, you know. It is always at your service.'

'How kind of you.'

'I will not tell you now what the *Encyclopaedia* says on the subject. I will leave you to while away a minute or two with it. I do not think you'll find it a wasted effort.'

'I'm sure I won't.'

'My husband is a great devotee of the *Encyclopaedia*,' Mrs Dutt said. 'He spends much of his time with it.'

'It is not always pleasure,' Mr Dutt said. 'The accumulation of information on many subjects is part of my work.'

'Your work, Mr Dutt?'

'Like many, nowadays, Miss Efoss, my husband works for his living.'

'You have some interesting job, Mr Dutt?'

'Interesting, eh? Yes, I suppose it is interesting. More than that I cannot reveal. That is so, eh, Beryl?'

'My husband is on the secret list. He is forbidden to speak casually about his work. Alas, even to someone to whom we trust our child. It's a paradox, isn't it?'

'I quite understand. Naturally, Mr Dutt's work is no affair of mine.'

'To speak lightly about it would mean marching orders for me,' Mr Dutt said. 'No offence, I hope?'

'Of course not.'

'Sometimes people take offence. We have had some unhappy occasions, eh, Beryl?'

'People do not always understand what it means to be on the secret list, Miss Efoss. So little is taken seriously nowadays.'

Mr Dutt hovered over Miss Efoss with his sherry decanter. He filled her glass and his wife's. He said:

'Well, Miss Efoss, what do you think of us? Can you accept the occasional evening in this room, watching our television and listening for the cry of our child?'

'Naturally, Miss Efoss, there would always be supper,' Mrs Dutt said.

'With sherry before and brandy to finish with,' Mr Dutt added.

'You are very generous. I can quite easily have something before I arrive.'

'No, no, no. It is out of the question. My wife is a good cook. And I can be relied upon to keep the decanters brimming.'

'You have made it all so pleasant I am left with no option. I should be delighted to help you out when I can manage it.'

Miss Efoss finished her sherry and rose. The Dutts rose also, smiling benignly at their satisfactory visitor.

'Well then,' Mr Dutt said in the hall, 'would Tuesday evening be a time you could arrange, Miss Efoss? We are bidden to dine with friends near by.'

'Tuesday? Yes, I think Tuesday is all right. About seven?'

Mrs Dutt held out her hand. 'Seven would be admirable. Till then, Miss Efoss.'

On Tuesday Mr Dutt opened the door to Miss Efoss and led her to the sitting-room. His wife, he explained, was still dressing. Making conversation as he poured Miss Efoss a drink, he said:

'I married my wife when she was on the point of entering a convent, Miss Efoss. What d'you think of that?'

'Well,' Miss Efoss said, settling herself comfortably before the cosy-stove, 'it is hard to know what to say, Mr Dutt. I am surprised, I suppose.'

'Most people are surprised. I often wonder if I did the right thing. Beryl would have made a fine nun. What d'you think?'

'I'm sure you both knew what you were doing at the time. It is equally certain that Mrs Dutt would have been a fine nun.'

'She had chosen a particularly severe order. That's just like Beryl, isn't it?'

'I hardly know Mrs Dutt. But if it is like her to have made that choice, I can well believe it.'

'You see my wife as a serious person, Miss Efoss? Is that what you mean?'

'In the short time I have known her, yes I think I do. Yet you also say she relishes a joke.'

'A joke, Miss Efoss?'

'So you remarked the other evening. In relation to a slip in her speech.'

'Ah yes. How right you are. You must forgive me if my memory is often faulty. My work is wearing.'

Mrs Dutt, gaily attired, entered the room. 'Here, Miss Efoss,' she said, proffering a piece of paper, 'is the telephone number of the house we are going to. If Mickey makes a sound please ring us up. I will immediately return.'

'Oh but I'm sure that's not necessary. It would be a pity to spoil your evening so. I could at least attempt to comfort him.'

'I would prefer the other arrangement. Mickey does not take easily to strangers. His room is at the top of the house, but please do not enter it. Were he to wake suddenly and catch sight of you he might be extremely frightened. He is quite a nervous child. At the slightest untoward sound do not hesitate to telephone.'

'As you wish it, Mrs Dutt. I only suggested –'

'Experience has taught me, Miss Efoss, what is best. I have laid you a tray in the kitchen. Everything is cold, but quite nice, I think.'

'Thank you.'

'Then we will be away. We should be back by eleven-fifteen.'

'Do have a good evening.'

The Dutts said they intended to have a good evening, whispered for a moment together in the hall and were on their way. Miss Efoss looked critically about her.

The room was of an ordinary kind. Utrillo prints on plain grey walls. Yellowish curtains, yellowish chair-covers, a few pieces of simple furniture on a thick grey carpet. It was warm, the sherry was good and Miss Efoss was comfortable. It was pleasant, she reflected, to have a change of scene without the obligation of conversation. In a few moments, she carried her supper tray from the kitchen to the fire. As good as his word, Mr Dutt had left some brandy. Miss Efoss began to think the Dutts were quite a find.

She had dropped off to sleep when they returned. Fortunately, she heard them in the hall and had time to compose herself.

'All well?' Mrs Dutt asked.

'Not a sound.'

'Well, I'd better change him right away. Thank you so much, Miss Efoss.'

'Thank you. I have spent a very pleasant evening.'

'I'll drive you back,' Mr Dutt offered. 'The car is still warm.'

In the car Mr Dutt said: 'A child is a great comfort. Mickey is a real joy for us. And company for Beryl. The days hang heavy when one is alone all day.'

'Yes, a child is a comfort.'

'Perhaps you think we are too careful and fussing about Mickey?'

'Oh no, it's better than erring in the other direction.'

'It is only because we are so grateful.'

'Of course.'

'We have much to be thankful for.'

'I'm sure you deserve it all.'

Mr Dutt had become quite maudlin by the time he delivered Miss Efoss at her flat. She wondered if he was drunk. He pressed her hand warmly and announced that he looked forward to their next meeting. 'Any time,' Miss Efoss said as she stepped from the car. 'Just ring me up. I am often free.'

After that, Miss Efoss baby-sat for the Dutts many times. They became more and more friendly towards her. They left her little bowls of chocolates and drew her attention to articles in magazines that they believed might be of interest to her. Mr Dutt suggested further words she might care to look up in the *Encyclopaedia* and Mrs Dutt wrote out several of her recipes.

One night, just as she was leaving, Miss Efoss said: 'You know, I think it might be a good idea for me to meet Mickey some time. Perhaps I could come in the daytime once. Then I would no longer be a stranger and could comfort him if he woke.'

'But he *doesn't* wake, Miss Efoss. He has never woken, has he? You have never had to telephone us.'

'No. That is true. But now that I have got to know you, I would like to know him as well.'

The Dutts took the compliment, smiling at one another and at Miss Efoss. Mr Dutt said: 'It is kind of you to speak like this, Miss Efoss. But Mickey is rather scared of strangers. Just at present at any rate, if you do not mind.'

'Of course not, Mr Dutt.'

'I fear he is a nervous child,' Mrs Dutt said. 'Our present arrangement is carefully devised.'

'I'm sorry,' Miss Efoss said.

'No need. No need. Let us all have a final brandy,' Mr Dutt said cheerfully.

But Miss Efoss was sorry, for she feared she had said something out of place. And then for a week or so she was worried whenever she thought of the Dutts. She felt they were mistaken in their attitude to their child; and she felt equally unable to advise them. It was not her place to speak any further on the subject, yet she was sure that to keep the child away from people just because he was nervous of them was wrong. It sounded as though there was a root to the trouble somewhere, and it sounded as though the Dutts had not attempted to discover it. She continued to baby-sit for them about once every ten days and she held her peace. Then, quite unexpectedly, something happened that puzzled Miss Efoss very much indeed.

It happened at a party given by some friends of hers. She was talking about nothing in particular to an elderly man called Summerfield. She had known him for some years but whenever they met, as on this occasion, they found themselves with little to say beyond the initial courteous greetings. Thinking that a more direct approach might yield something of interest, Miss Efoss, after the familiar lengthy silence, said: 'How are you coping with the advancing years, Mr Summerfield? I feel I can ask you, since it is a coping I have to take in my own stride.'

'Well, well, I think I am doing well enough. My life is simple since my wife died, but there is little I complain of.'

'Loneliness is a thing that sometimes strikes at us. I find one must regard it as the toothache or similar ailment, and seek a cure.'

'Ah yes. I'm often a trifle alone.'

'I baby-sit, you know. Have you ever thought of it? Do not shy off because you are a man. A responsible person is all that is required.'

'I haven't thought of baby-sitting. Not ever I think. Though I like babies and always have done.'

'I used to do quite a lot. Now I have only the Dutts, but I go there very often. I enjoy my evenings. I like to see the TV now and again and other people's houses are interesting.'

'I know the Dutts,' said Mr Summerfield. 'You mean the Dutts in Raeburn Road? A small weedy couple?'

'They live in Raeburn Road, certainly. They are small too, but you are unkind to call them weedy.'

'I don't particularly mean it unkindly. I have known Dutt a long time. One takes liberties, I suppose, in describing people.'

'Mr Dutt is an interesting person. He holds some responsible position of intriguing secrecy.'

'Dutt? 25 Raeburn Road? The man is a chartered accountant.'

'I feel sure you are mistaken –'

'I cannot be mistaken. The man was once my colleague. In a very junior capacity.'

'Oh, well . . . then I must be mistaken.'

'What surprises me is that you say you baby-sit for the Dutts. I think you must be mistaken about that too.'

'Oh no, I am completely certain about that. It is for that reason that I know them at all.'

'I cannot help being surprised. Because, Miss Efoss – and of this I am certain – the Dutts have no children.'

Miss Efoss had heard of the fantasy world with which people, as they grow old, surround themselves. Yet she could not have entirely invented the Dutts in this way because Mr Summerfield had readily agreed about their existence. Was it then for some other reason that she visited them? Did she, as soon as she entered their house, become so confused in her mind that she afterwards forgot the real purpose of her presence? Had they hired her in some other capacity altogether? A capacity she was so ashamed of that she had invented, even for herself, the euphemism of baby-sitting? Had she, she wondered, become some kind of servant to these people – imagining the warm comfortable room, the sherry, the chocolates, the brandy?

'We should be back by eleven, Miss Efoss. Here is the telephone number.' Mrs Dutt smiled at her and a moment later the front door banged gently behind her.

It is all quite real, Miss Efoss thought. There is the sherry. There is the television set. In the kitchen on a tray I shall find my supper. It is all quite real: it is old Mr Summerfield who is wandering in his mind. It was only when she had finished her supper that she had the idea of establishing her role beyond question. All she had to do was to go upstairs and peep at the child. She knew how to be quiet: there was no danger of waking him.

The first room she entered was full of suitcases and cardboard boxes. In the second she heard breathing and knew she was right. She snapped on the light and looked around her. It was brightly painted, with a wallpaper with elves on it. There was a rocking horse and a great pile of coloured bricks. In one of the far corners there was a large cot. It was very large and very high and it contained the sleeping figure of a very old man.

When the Dutts returned Miss Efoss said nothing. She was frightened and she didn't quite know why she was frightened. She was glad when she was back in her flat. The next day she telephoned her niece in Devon and asked if she might come down to stay for a bit.

Miss Efoss spoke to nobody about the Dutts. She gathered her strength in the country and returned to London at the end of a fortnight feeling refreshed and rational. She wrote a note to the Dutts saying she had decided to baby-sit no more. She gave no reason, but she said she hoped they would understand. Then, as best she could, she tried to forget all about them.

A year passed and then, one grey cold Sunday afternoon, Miss Efoss saw the Dutts in one of the local parks. They were sitting on a bench, huddled close together and seeming miserable. For a reason that she was afterwards unable to fathom Miss Efoss approached them.

'Good afternoon.'

The Dutts looked up at her, their thin, pale faces unsmiling and unhappy.

'Hello, Miss Efoss,' Mr Dutt said. 'We haven't see you for a long time, have we? How are you this nasty weather?'

'Quite well, thank you. And you? And Mrs Dutt?'

Mr Dutt rose and drew Miss Efoss a few yards away from his wife. 'Beryl has taken it badly,' he said. 'Mickey died. Beryl has not been herself since. You understand how it is?'

'Oh, I am sorry.'

'I try to cheer her up, but I'm afraid my efforts are all in vain. I have taken it hard myself too. Which doesn't make anything any easier.'

'I don't know what to say, Mr Dutt. It's a great sadness for both of you.'

Mr Dutt took Miss Efoss's arm and led her back to the seat. 'I have told Miss Efoss,' he said to his wife. Mrs Dutt nodded.

'I'm very sorry,' Miss Efoss said again.

The Dutts looked at her, their sad, intent eyes filled with a pathetic desire for comfort. There was something almost hypnotic about them.

'I must go,' Miss Efoss said. 'Good-bye.'

'They have all died, Miss Efoss,' Mr Dutt said. 'One by one they have all died.'

Miss Efoss paused in her retreat. She could think of nothing to say except that she was sorry.

'We are childless again,' Mr Dutt went on. 'It is almost unbearable to be childless again. We are so fond of them and here we are, not knowing what to do on a Sunday afternoon because we are a childless couple. The human frame, Miss Efoss, is not built to carry such misfortunes.'

'It is callous of me to say so, Mr Dutt, but the human frame is pretty resilient. It does not seem so at times like this I know, but you will find it is so in retrospect.'

'You are a wise woman, Miss Efoss, but, as you say, it is hard to accept wisdom at a moment like this. We have lost so many over the years. They are given to us and then abruptly they are taken away. It is difficult to understand God's infinite cruelty.'

'Good-bye, Mr Dutt. Good-bye, Mrs Dutt.'

They did not reply, and Miss Efoss walked quickly away.

Miss Efoss began to feel older. She walked with a stick; she found the cinema tired her eyes; she read less and discovered that she was bored by the effort of sustaining long conversations. She accepted each change quite philosophically, pleased that she could do so. She found too that there were compensations; she enjoyed, more and more, thinking about the past. Quite vividly, she re-lived the part she wished to re-live. Unlike life itself, it was pleasant to be able to pick and choose.

Again by accident, she met Mr Dutt. She was having tea one afternoon in a quiet, old-fashioned teashop, not at all the kind of place she would have associated with Mr Dutt. Yet there he was, standing in front of her. 'Hello, Miss Efoss,' he said.

'Why, Mr Dutt. How are you? How is your wife? It is some time since we met.'

Mr Dutt sat down. He ordered some tea and then he leaned forward and stared at Miss Efoss. She wondered what he was thinking about: he had the air of someone who, through politeness, makes the most of a moment but whose mind is busily occupied elsewhere. As he looked at her, his face suddenly cleared. He smiled, and when he spoke he seemed to be entirely present.

'I have great news, Miss Efoss. We are both so happy about it. Miss Efoss, Beryl is expecting a child.'

Miss Efoss blinked a little. She spread some jam on her toast and said:

'Oh, I'm so glad. How delightful for you both! Mrs Dutt will be pleased. When is it – when is it due?'

'Quite soon. Quite soon.' Mr Dutt beamed. 'Naturally Beryl is beside herself with joy. She is busy preparing all day.'

'There is a lot to see to on these occasions.'

'Indeed there is. Beryl is knitting like a mad thing. It seems as though she can't do enough.'

'It is the biggest event in a woman's life, Mr Dutt.'

'And often in a man's, Miss Efoss.'

'Yes, indeed.'

'We have quite recovered our good spirits.'

'I'm glad of that. You were so sadly low when last I saw you.'

'You gave us some wise words. You were more comfort than you think, you know.'

'Oh, I was inadequate. I always am with sorrow.'

'No, no. Beryl said so afterwards. It was a happy chance to have met you so.'

'Thank you, Mr Dutt.'

'It's not easy always to accept adversity. You helped us on our way. We shall always be grateful.'

'It is kind of you to say so.'

'The longing for a child is a strange force. To attend to its needs, to give it comfort and love – I suppose there is that in all of us. There is a streak of simple generosity that we do not easily understand.'

'The older I become, Mr Dutt, the more I realize that one understands very little. I believe one is meant not to understand. The best things are complex and mysterious. And must remain so.'

'How right you are! It is often what I say to Beryl. I shall be glad to report that you confirm my thinking.'

'On my part it is instinct rather than thinking.'

'The line between the two is less acute than many would have us believe.'

'Yes, I suppose it is.'

'Miss Efoss, may I do one thing for you?'

'What is that?'

'It is a small thing but would give me pleasure. May I pay for your tea? Beryl will be pleased if you allow me to.'

Miss Efoss laughed. 'Yes, Mr Dutt, you may pay for my tea.' And it was as she spoke this simple sentence that it dawned upon Miss Efoss just what it was she had to do.

Miss Efoss began to sell her belongings. She sold them in many directions, keeping back only a few which she wished to give away. It took her a long time, for there was much to see to. She wrote down long lists of details, finding this method the best for arranging things in her mind. She was sorry to see the familiar objects go, yet she knew that to be sentimental about them was absurd. It was for other people now to develop a sentiment for them; and she knew that the fresh associations they would in time take on would be, in the long run, as false as hers.

Her flat became bare and cheerless. In the end there was nothing left except the property of the landlord. She wrote to him, terminating her tenancy.

The Dutts were watching the television when Miss Efoss arrived. Mr Dutt turned down the sound and went to open the door. He smiled without speaking and brought her into the sitting-room.

'Welcome, Miss Efoss,' Mrs Dutt said. 'We've been expecting you.'

Miss Efoss carried a small suitcase. She said: 'Your baby, Mrs Dutt. When is your baby due? I do hope I am in time.'

'Perfect, Miss Efoss, perfect,' said Mr Dutt. 'Beryl's child is due this very night.'

The pictures flashed silently, eerily, on the television screen. A man dressed as a pirate was stroking the head of a parrot.

Miss Efoss did not sit down. 'I am rather tired,' she said. 'Do you mind if I go straight upstairs?'

'Dear Miss Efoss, please do,' Mrs Dutt smiled at her. 'You know your way, don't you?'

'Yes,' Miss Efoss said. 'I know my way.'

The Original Sins of Edward Tripp

Edward Tripp had often noticed Mrs Mayben at her sitting-room window, putting bread on the window-sills for the birds. Her hair was white and she was dressed always in the same way, in several shades of grey. She had, he considered, the kindest face in all Dunfarnham Avenue, and when she saw him she would nod at him in a dignified manner, befitting a woman of her years. He had never rung the bell of Mrs Mayben's house as he had rung the bells of the other houses; he had never held her in conversation on her doorstep, but he knew that the day would come when his sister would ask him to cross the road and speak to the old woman. Edward was notorious in Dunfarnham Avenue, yet he felt whenever he considered the fact that Mrs Mayben, who kept herself to herself and did not gossip with the other people, was perhaps – just possibly – unaware of his notoriety. He thought, too, that when the time came, when eventually he found himself face to face with Mrs Mayben, he would tell her the truth: he would speak to her bluntly, and Edward guessed that an old woman with Mrs Mayben's dignity, who was a Christian and who never forgot the birds, would listen to him and would say a word or two of comfort. He imagined how things would be after that visit, he himself passing by Mrs Mayben's house and the truth hanging between them, she nodding with a smile from her window and he giving thanks to God for her understanding heart.

On Sunday 26 August Edward Tripp's sister, Emily, spoke of Mrs Mayben and Edward knew that on this morning he would hear himself protesting in a familiar way and that in the end he would cross the road to Mrs Mayben's house.

'We have watched the neighbourhood go down,' said Emily. 'Mrs Mayben was the last who was a decent sort of person. And now she's gone too. In cold blood.'

Edward, slicing some ham that he had purchased the day before in Lipton's, had been thinking to himself that the piece of gammon was not as satisfactory as usual: there was, for instance, a certain stringiness and a confusion about the direction of the grain. Before his sister had mentioned Mrs Mayben he had been allowing his thoughts to consider the meat as once it had been, an area of living flesh on the thigh of a pig. He imagined that something might have troubled that pig, some physical disorder that caused it to wriggle and dash about its sty, banging itself against the concrete sides and causing thus the stringiness to develop in its flesh.

'In cold blood,' said Emily again.

Edward looked up and regarded her back. He stared at the blackness of the material of which her long, old-fashioned dress was composed and at the roll of her hair, neat and formal on her neck.

'No, no,' said Edward. 'Not dead, dear. Not dead.'

But his sister nodded, denying his denial, and Edward shook his head with firmness.

'I remember when she came,' said Emily. 'Fourteen years ago. Her husband with her.'

Edward agreed with that. 'Her husband,' he said, 'died in 1955.'

'Death again,' murmured Emily, and Edward sighed. His sister was standing by their dining-room window, observing through it the house of Mrs Mayben opposite. Her left hand gripped the grey curtain that had flanked the window for almost thirty years, her right hung limply by her side. Edward guessed what was in her mind and did not care to consider it, since soon, he knew, he would be obliged to consider it whether he wished to or not. Attempting to keep the workings of his sister's brain at bay, he cut deeply into the ham. The image of the living animal appeared again before him. He said:

'After lunch why don't we try to repair the sitting-room carpet? It gets worse, you know. Quite a hole has worn through. It seems a pity.'

'The carpet?' said Emily, and Edward added:

'Father used to talk about that carpet, d'you remember? About its quality. The years have proved him right.'

Emily, continuing to stare through the window, made no comment.

'It's lasted a couple of lifetimes,' Edward said quickly. 'It's a shame to let it go.' His eyes again travelled over his sister's back, moving upwards, to the roll of her hair. Emily said:

'There was a man here yesterday. Looking at Mrs Mayben's windows.'

'A robber,' suggested Edward, again slicing the ham, and in an automatic way beginning to feel sick in his stomach. He said, in a slow, low voice, that Mrs Mayben was probably now in church, or else within her house, cooking a simple lunch for herself.

'She hasn't been about,' said Emily. 'I haven't seen Mrs Mayben for four days.'

'I thought I saw her yesterday. I'm sure, you know.'

'He came,' said Emily, 'in a light-blue motor-car. The kind that's called a tourer, is it? Out of that he stepped at a quarter to four and stood on the pavement gazing up at her house – returning to his scene, God knows. He was indecently dressed, Edward: canvas shoes and light-weight trousers that matched the blue paintwork of his motor-car, and nothing at all where a shirt should have been. He was like a lunatic, I'll tell you that, walking on the edge of the pavement in the August sunshine, his eyes uplifted to the house. And I said to myself: "There's evil there." '

'Mrs Mayben's in church,' repeated Edward, 'or maybe home already, doing her Sunday chores.'

His sister shook her head. 'It's past her time for returning from church. She hasn't returned today, for I have watched at the window, being worried about her. Mrs Mayben, as well you know, Edward, is by now in two places at once.'

Edward imagined old Mrs Mayben delayed in a traffic jam in the hired car that called for her every Sunday at half past eleven to take her to church. He imagined the chauffeur, the sallow-faced man who always came, with a green peaked cap, apologizing to her about the delay, apologizing about all the traffic, since she was the kind of woman who inspired apology, he imagined. Emily said:

'You know what I mean, don't you, when I say she's in two places at once? In heaven and in some cupboard, Edward; strung to a hook.'

There was a look, Edward knew, that must be there by now in his sister's eyes as she stared through the glass, ready to inflict her punishment. He thought, as he had thought before on similar occasions, that she was like a woman entering a fit.

'Now, now,' said Edward softly.

'Read the papers,' cried his sister, turning about to face him and speaking with emotion. 'A man has killed eight nurses in Chicago.'

'Oh no,' began Edward.

'Prize fighters turn on their children. Mothers go out with the tide.'

Edward placed the ham knife on the polished mahogany of the dining-room table. Slowly, he raised his eyes to meet his sister's.

'An old woman living alone,' said Emily.

Edward watched her tongue moving over her lips, beginning at one corner and returning to it. The tip of her tongue protruded at that corner for a moment and was then withdrawn. Again he raised his eyes to hers and they looked at one another in silence for a while, a brother and a sister who had lived all their lives in this house in Dunfarnham Avenue, Number Seventeen. Edward remembered the past and he knew that his sister was remembering it too. In the past were the children they had been, two other people, a different relationship: a girl thin and tall, four years older than the brother, he a boy who had laughed and had had his way, who had grown to be a man of slight build, permitting a small moustache to accumulate on his upper lip. The house that had been the house of their parents had changed only a little over the years. Wallpaper, the colour of good oatmeal, had hung all over it for three decades, placed there one spring when Emily was fourteen. Large engravings that featured the bridges of London decorated the hall and the stairs, and in dark book-cases, dustless behind glass, were volumes by Sapper, and *The Life of a Bengal Lancer*, and poems by Austin Dobson, and the collected works of Kipling and Scott. Edward often felt strange in the house now, feeling the present dominated by the past, remembering everything. From her own private flower-bed he had pulled her pansies, roots and all, when he was five years old; and with a pair of scissors he had cut through the centre of the buds of her roses. 'I have played a trick on you,' he used to say, sidling close to her. He had given two of her books away to an old woman who came seeking alms at the door. He had lit a fire in a fireplace of her doll's house, and had been punished because it was, so they said, a dangerous thing to do. He had taken one of her guinea-pigs and put it in her bed, where by mischance it had died. 'I have played a trick on you': he had said it repeatedly, bringing out her temper and her tears and running away himself. In middle age Emily was still taller than her brother, and had a hint of beauty about her features that was not reflected in his. Edward had developed a stoop in early manhood, and the child who had been bright with darting mischief became, in his own opinion, a shrimpish creature, fond of the corners of rooms.

On that Sunday morning, 26 August, Emily continued to speak about the man who had loitered in Dunfarnham Avenue in the sunshine. She spoke of the baldness of his head and the evil that she had recognized in the pupils of his eyes. He had worn no shirt, she repeated, emphasizing the fact, and she said again that his shoes, placed over bare feet, had been of light-blue canvas, the same colour as his trousers and his car.

Listening to his sister's voice, Edward prayed in his mind. He prayed that she might turn from the window and walk away from the room, saying that she was going to the kitchen to make mustard, since mustard would be necessary with the ham. But his sister only stood before him, strange and thin as she had been as a child.

'I wish you could have seen him,' said Emily. 'I think I dreamed of him last night. The man is on my mind.'

'Why not sit down, my dear? Why not rest and try to forget?' As he spoke, Edward prayed for a day that was to come, a day that God, he felt, had promised him. His sister said:

'Perhaps on Wednesday night it was, or early on Thursday morning, that he slipped into the old woman's house to do what he had to do. And in his madness, Edward, he could not resist returning later to the scene of all the violence. I have read of this kind of thing. It has happened with other men.'

'Come along now –'

'Not at all unusual,' said Emily. 'Criminal history is not being made in Dunfarnham Avenue, if that's what you're thinking. He came and acted and returned, as others have in a similar way. D'you understand? D'you follow me?'

What was there to follow? Edward thought. What was there to understand except the facts from the past? – the quiet child of four and the son who was suddenly born in the house and allowed to go his way. The son growing up and his sport becoming the game he played with her, until her days were filled to the brim with his cunning smile and the baby tricks that everyone excused. Wasn't the simple truth that those cruelties in their thousands had fallen like a blight upon her nature in the end, wrenching some bit of it out of shape, embittering the whole?

When Edward was seventeen their parents had died, one after another within a month. He remembered still standing at his mother's funeral, the second funeral of the pair, and seeing on his sister's face the look that by now he had become familiar with, a look of reproach and sorrow. They had returned together to the dark house with the oatmeal wallpaper and Emily had said: 'There was a woman in a red coat, Edward. Did you see her? I thought it odd, you know, a woman dressed up all in red at the grave of another woman.' Edward had seen no woman in red and had said so at once, but Emily, making tea, had continued about this figure, and then had ceased to make tea and had stood quite still, gazing at him and talking at length, on and on, about the woman. 'What should we do?' she said. 'Shouldn't we try to find out a thing or two?' And then, in a moment, she had seemed to forget about the woman and had poured boiling water into a china teapot that both of them had known as a family possession all their lives. Afterwards, in the back garden, Edward all by himself had examined in detail his early sins against his sister, and he had closed his eyes and prayed to God. He prayed for forgiveness and he prayed that she in turn might forgive him and he prayed that the damage might not mark her for ever. From the garden, that day, he returned to the house, having found his duty, to live there with her, in that cool and silent place, to keep an eye on her for ever, and to atone as best he might. God had spoken harshly to Edward in the garden, and God had spoken harshly since. Every morning and evening Edward Tripp prayed at length, kneeling by his bed, and during the day he prayed as well, seeing her before him, she who never now walked out into Dunfarnham Avenue, who dressed herself in black and forgot her beauty. No longer children, they were reticent now in what they said one to another; they were polite in their relationship as their thoughts filled the rooms of the house and were not spoken. She played her game in a vengeful way, acting a madness and saying to him in silence that this was the state she should be in, warning him that her bitter nature needed his tenderness now. And Edward prayed and often wept, accepting the punishment as his due.

'There's nothing at all to worry about,' said Edward now. 'Mrs Mayben is quite all right.'

'You have a callous mind,' murmured Edward's sister, looking at him. 'You can know of a thing like this and stand there cutting ham and saying it doesn't matter that a lunatic has walked in Dunfarnham Avenue and brought an old woman to a grim full-stop. It doesn't matter what's in that house this morning, is that it? Edward, she has not come back from church because today she's never been there; because she's been dead and rotting for eighty-four hours. We have buried our parents: we know about the deceased. They're everywhere, Edward. Everywhere.'

'Please,' muttered Edward. 'Please now, my dear.'

'Death has danced through Dunfarnham Avenue and I have seen it, a man without socks or shirt, a man who shall fry in the deep fat of Hell. For you, Edward, must put a finger on him.'

'There's nothing I can do,' said Edward, feeling his size, five foot four, as his sister towered in the room with him.

'Cross the road,' said Emily, 'and go to the back of Mrs Mayben's house. Climb through some small window and walk through the rooms until you come to the woman.'

Edward sighed. He would cross the road, he knew, as he had known when first she mentioned Mrs Mayben, and he would tell Mrs Mayben the truth because she had a face that was kind. He would not stand on her doorstep and make some lame excuse, as he had with all the others. He would not today prevaricate and pretend; he would not dishonour the woman by meting out dishonest treatment to her. 'I will ease your mind,' he said to his sister. 'I'll go and see that Mrs Mayben's quite all right.'

'Carry that ham knife with you, that you may cut her down. It's wrong. I think, don't you, that we should leave her as she is?'

'Stand by the window,' said Edward, already moving to the door, 'and watch me as I cross the road to ring her bell. You'll see her appear, my dear, and if you strain your ears you may even hear her voice.'

Emily nodded. She said:

'Telephone the police when you have cut the cord. Dial 999 and ask to speak to a sergeant. Tell him the honest truth.'

Edward walked from the room and descended the stairs of the house. He opened the front door and crossed Dunfarnham Avenue, to the house of Mrs Mayben. He rang the bell, standing to one side so that his sister, from the dining-room window, would be able to see the old woman when she opened the door.

'I was trying to repair this thing,' said Mrs Mayben, holding out an electric fuse, 'with a piece of silver paper. You've been sent to me, Mr Tripp. Come in.'

Edward entered the house of Mrs Mayben, carrying the ham knife. 'I'm sorry,' he said, 'to bother you.' But Mrs Mayben seemed not to question his presence on her property. 'My husband could mend a fuse,' she said, 'with silver paper; yet I can make no hand of this.' Edward placed the ham knife on a table in the hall and took the ineffective fuse from her hand. He said there was stuff called fuse wire, and Mrs Mayben led him to a cupboard where the electric meters were and in which he discovered the wire he sought. 'I was cooking a chop,' said Mrs Mayben, a woman of eighty-two, 'when all the heat went off.'

'I was cutting ham,' said Edward, 'and I was interrupted too.' He repaired the fuse and replaced it in its socket. 'Let's go and see,' said Mrs Mayben, and led the way to her kitchen. They watched the chop for a moment, still and uninviting in the centre of a frying pan on the electric stove. In a moment a noise came from it, a spurt of sizzling that indicated to them that Edward had been successful with the fuse. 'You must take a glass of sherry,' said Mrs Mayben. 'I have one always myself, on Sundays.'

Edward followed the old woman to her sitting-room and sat down, since she wished that he should, in a comfortable arm-chair. She poured two glasses of Dry Fly sherry and then, holding hers formally in the air, she reminded Edward that she had lived in Dunfarnham Avenue for fourteen years and had never actually spoken to him before.

'I see you feeding the birds,' said Edward, 'from your sitting-room window.'

'Yes, I feed the local sparrows,' said Mrs Mayben. 'I do my bit.'

A silence fell between them, and then Mrs Mayben said:

'It is odd to have lived opposite you for all these years and yet not to have spoken. I have seen you at the windows, as you have seen me. I have seen the lady too.'

Edward felt the blood moving into his face. He felt again a sickness in his stomach and thought his hands were shivering.

'You've heard of me,' he casually said. 'I dare say you have. I am notorious in Dunfarnham Avenue.'

'I know your name is Tripp,' said Mrs Mayben. 'I know no more.'

'She is my sister, the woman you see in the house. She and I were born there, and now she never leaves it. I go out to do the shopping – well, you've seen me.'

'I have seen you, certainly,' said Mrs Mayben, 'returning from the shops with a string bag full of this and that, potatoes and tins, lettuces in season. I do not pry, Mr Tripp, but I have seen you. Have more sherry?'

Edward accepted another glass. 'I am known to every house in the road,' he said. 'Parents warn their children to cross to the other side when they see me coming. Men have approached me to issue rough warnings, using language I don't much care to hear. Women move faster when Edward Tripp's around.'

Mrs Mayben said that she was not deaf but wondered if she quite understood what Edward was talking about. 'I don't think I follow,' she said. 'I know nothing of all this. Like your sister, I don't go out much. I've heard nothing from the people of Dunfarnham Avenue about you, Mr Tripp, or how it is you have become notorious.'

Edward said he had guessed that might be so, and added that one person at least in Dunfarnham Avenue should know the truth, on this Sabbath day.

'It's very kind of you to have repaired my fuse,' said Mrs Mayben a little loudly. 'I'm most obliged to you for that.' She rose to her feet, but did not succeed in drawing her visitor to his. Edward sat on in the comfortable arm-chair, holding his sherry glass. He said:

'It is a hell for me, Dunfarnham Avenue, walking down it and feeling all eyes upon me. I have rung the bells of all the houses. I have trumped up some story on the doorsteps, even on the doorsteps that she cannot see from the dining-room window. She always knows if I have talked to someone and have been embarrassed: I come back in a peculiar state. I suffer from nerves, Mrs Mayben.'

'Thank you,' said Mrs Mayben more loudly still. 'And how nice to meet you after all these years.'

'I am going to tell you the truth,' explained Edward, 'as I have never told a soul in all my life. It is an ugly business, Mrs Mayben. Perhaps you should sit down.'

'But, Mr Tripp,' protested the old woman, greatly puzzled, 'what on earth is all this?'

'Let me tell you,' said Edward, and he told her of his sister standing at the top of the stairs while their mother broke to her the news that her two coloured story-books had been handed out to a beggar at the front door. 'He's only little,' their mother had explained to Edward's sister. 'Forgive an imp, my dear.' But Emily had not found it in her heart to forgive him and he had sniggered at the time.

'I see,' said Mrs Mayben.

'I knew you would,' cried Edward, smiling at her and nodding his head several times. 'Of course you see. You have a kindly face; you feed the birds.'

'Yes, but –' said Mrs Mayben.

'No,' said Edward. 'Listen.'

He told her about the woman in red at the funeral of their mother, the woman his sister had seen, and how he afterwards prayed in the back garden and had been sternly answered by Almighty God. He explained how he had come upon his duty then and had accepted all that was required of him.

'It has nothing to do with the present,' said Edward. 'Do not see my sister and myself as we stand today, but as two children playing in that house across the road. I sinned against my sister, Mrs Mayben, every hour of my early life. She was stamped into the ground; she was destroyed and devoured. There's nothing left of my sister except a kind of shadow.'

'I'm sorry,' said Mrs Mayben. 'I'm sorry there have been these troubles in your life. It's difficult to accept adversity and unhappiness, I know that.'

'I was cutting ham,' repeated Edward, 'when my sister turned to me and said you had been murdered by a man in canvas shoes.'

'Murdered?' repeated Mrs Mayben, opening the door of her sitting-room and appearing to be nervous.

'She's just a shadow,' said Edward. 'You understand it?'

Mrs Mayben did not reply. Instead she said:

'Mr Tripp, you have been most gallant. I wish you would now return to your home. I have my lunch to prepare and eat.'

'"I saw a dog today," my sister said, "a vicious dog abroad in Dunfarnham Avenue. Go to the houses, Edward, and tell the mothers to look to their children until the dog is captured and set to rest." She talked for seven hours, Mrs Mayben, about that dog, one day in 1951, and in the end she watched me move from house to house ringing the bells and warning people about a vicious animal.'

'This is no concern of mine. If your sister is unwell –'

'My sister is not unwell. My sister pretends, exacting her revenge. God has told me, Mrs Mayben, to play my part in her pretended fantasies. I owe her the right to punish me, I quite understand that.'

Mrs Mayben shook her head. She said in a quiet voice that she was an old woman and did not understand much of what went on in the world. She did not mind, she said, Edward ringing her doorbell, but she wished now that he would leave her house since she had much to do.

'I have never told anyone else,' said Edward. 'Years ago I said to myself that when I had to come to your house I would tell you the truth about everything. How I have grown up to be an understanding man, with the help of God. How the punishment must be shared between us – well, she has had hers. D'you see?'

Mrs Mayben shook her head and was about to speak again. Edward said:

'"There's a smell of burning," my sister said to me in 1955. "It comes from the house with the three Indian women in it." She had woken me up to tell me that, for it was half past two in the morning. "They are women from the East," she said. "They do not understand about precautions against fire as we do." In my dressing-gown, Mrs Mayben, I walked the length of Dunfarnham Avenue and rang the bell of that house. "May I use your telephone?" I said to the Indian woman who opened the door, for I could think of nothing else to say to her. But she said no, I could not; and rightly pointed out that she could not be expected to admit into her house a man in pyjamas at half past two in the morning. I have never told anyone because it seemed to be a family thing. I have never told the truth. It is all pretence and silence between my sister and myself. We play a game.'

'I must ask you to go now. I really must. An old woman like me can't be expected to take a sudden interest. You must do the best you can.'

'But I am telling you terrible things,' cried Edward. 'I killed my sister's guinea-pig, I pulled her pansies by the roots. Not an hour passed in my early childhood, Mrs Mayben, but I did not seek to torment her into madness. I don't know why I was given that role, but now I have the other since I've been guided towards it. She is quite sane, you know. She plays a part. I am rotten with guilt.'

Mrs Mayben clapped her hands sharply together. 'I cannot have you coming here,' she said, 'telling me you are rotten with guilt, Mr Tripp. You are a man I have seen about the place with a string bag. I do not know you. I do not know your sister. It's no concern of mine. Not at all.'

'You have a kind face to live up to,' said Edward, bowing and smiling in a sad way. 'I have seen you feeding the sparrows, and I've often thought you have a kind face.'

'Leave me alone, sir. Go from this house at once. You speak of madness and death, Mr Tripp; you tell me I've been murdered: I am unable to think about such things. My days are simple here.'

'Since I was seventeen, Mrs Mayben, since the day of my mother's funeral, I have lived alone with all this horror. Dunfarnham Avenue is the theatre of my embarrassment. You feed the sparrows, Mrs Mayben, yet for me it seems you have no crumb of comfort.'

'I cannot be expected –' began Mrs Mayben.

'I am forty-one this month. She is four years older. See us as children, Mrs Mayben, for it's absurd that I am here before you as a small man in a week-end suit. We are still children in that house, in our way: we have not grown up much. Surely you take an interest?'

'You come here saying you are notorious, Mr Tripp –'

'I am notorious, indeed I am, for God is a hard master. The house is dark and unchanged. Only the toys have gone. We eat the same kind of food.'

'Go away,' cried Mrs Mayben, her voice rising. 'For the sake of God, go away from me, Mr Tripp. You come here talking madly and carrying a ham knife. Leave my house.'

Edward rose to his feet and with his head bowed to his chest he walked past Mrs Mayben into her hall. He picked up the ham knife from the table and moved towards the front door.

'I'm sorry I can't interest myself in you and your sister,' said Mrs Mayben. 'I am too old, you see, to take on new subjects.'

Edward did not say anything more. He did not look at Mrs Mayben, but into his mind came the picture of her leaning from her sitting-room window putting crumbs of bread on the window-sills for the birds. He walked from her house with that picture in his mind and he heard behind him the closing of her hall-door.

Edward crossed Dunfarnham Avenue and entered the house he had always known, carrying the ham knife in his left hand. He moved slowly to the dining-room and saw that the table was neatly laid for lunch. The sliced ham had been placed by his sister on two blue and white plates. Salt and pepper were on the table, and a jar of pickles that he himself had bought, since they both relished them. She had washed a lettuce and cut up a few tomatoes and put chives and cucumber with the salad. 'I've made some mustard,' said Emily, smiling at him as he sat down, and he saw, as he expected, that the look had gone from her face. 'We might repair the sitting-room carpet this afternoon,' said Emily, 'before that hole becomes too large. We could do it together.'

He nodded and murmured, and then, although he was awake and eating his lunch, Edward dreamed. It seemed to him that he was still in Mrs Mayben's sitting-room and that she, changed in her attitude, was murmuring that of course she understood, and all the better because she was old. She placed a hand on Edward's shoulder and said most softly that he had made her feel a mother again. He told her then, once more, of the pansies plucked from the flower-bed, and Mrs Mayben nodded and said he must not mind. He must suffer a bit, she said in a gentle way, since that was his due; he must feel his guilt around him and know that it was rightly there. In Edward's dream Mrs Mayben's voice was soothing, like a cool balm in the sunshine that came prettily through her sitting-room window. 'My dear, do not weep,' said the voice. 'Do not cry, for soon there is the Kingdom of Heaven.' The birds sang while the sun illuminated the room in which Mrs Mayben stood. 'I will go now,' said Edward in his dream, 'since I have mended your fuse and had my sherry. We've had a lovely chat.' He spoke in a peculiar voice and when he rose and walked away his feet made little sound as they struck the floor. 'Come when you wish,' invited Mrs Mayben with tears in her eyes. 'Cross the road for comfort. It's all you have to do.'

Edward chewed lettuce and ham and a piece of tomato, staring over his sister's shoulder at the grey curtains that hung by the window. His eyes moved to his sister's face and then moved downwards to the table, towards the knife that lay now on the polished wood. He thought about this knife that he had carried into a neighbour's house, remembering its keen blade slicing through the flesh of a pig. He saw himself standing with the knife in his hand, and he heard a noise that might have been a cry from his sister's throat. 'I have played a trick on you,' his own voice said, tumbling back to him over the years.

'A pity if that carpet went,' said Emily.

Edward looked at her, attempting to smile. He heard her add:

'It's always been there. All our lives, Edward.' And then, without meaning to say it, Edward said:

'She was harsh in how she looked. Too old to take on new subjects: she was making excuses.'

'What?' murmured Emily and Edward sighed a little, eating more of the food she had prepared. Vaguely, he told her not to worry, and as he spoke he imagined them that afternoon, sitting on the floor of the other room stitching the carpet they had always known, not saying much except to comment perhaps upon the labour and upon the carpet. And as they worked together, he knew that he would go on praying, praying in his mind for the day to come: a day when old Mrs Mayben and all the people of Dunfarnham Avenue would see his sister walking lightly in the Kingdom of Heaven. In their presence she would smile as once she had smiled as a child, offering him her forgiveness while saying she was sorry too, and releasing in sumptuous glory all the years of imprisoned truth.

A Meeting in Middle Age

'I am Mrs da Tanka,' said Mrs da Tanka. 'Are you Mr Mileson?' The man nodded, and they walked together the length of the platform, seeking a compartment that might offer them a welcome, or failing that, and they knew the more likely, simple privacy. They carried each a small suitcase, Mrs da Tanka's of white leather or some material manufactured to resemble it, Mr Mileson's battered and black. They did not speak as they marched purposefully: they were strangers one to another, and in the noise and the bustle, examining the lighted windows of the carriages, there was little that might constructively be said.

'A ninety-nine-years' lease,' Mr Mileson's father had said, 'taken out in 1862 by my grandfather, whom of course you never knew. Expiring in your lifetime, I fear. Yet you will by then be in a sound position to accept the misfortune. To renew what has come to an end; to keep the property in the family.' The property was an expression that glorified. The house was small and useful, one of a row, one of a kind easily found; but the lease when the time came was not renewable – which released Mr Mileson of a problem. Bachelor, childless, the end of the line, what use was a house to him for a further ninety-nine years?

Mrs da Tanka, sitting opposite him, drew a magazine from an assortment she carried. Then, checking herself, said: 'We could talk. Or do you prefer to conduct the business in silence?' She was a woman who filled, but did not overflow from, a fair-sized, elegant, quite expensive tweed suit. Her hair, which was grey, did not appear so; it was tightly held to her head, a reddish gold colour. Born into another class she would have been a chirpy woman; she guarded against her chirpiness, she disliked the quality in her. There was often laughter in her eyes, and as often as she felt it there she killed it by the severity of her manner.

'You must not feel embarrassment,' Mrs da Tanka said. 'We are beyond the age of giving in to awkwardness in a situation. You surely agree?'

Mr Mileson did not know. He did not know how or what he should feel. Analysing his feelings he could come to no conclusion. He supposed he was excited but it was more difficult than it seemed to track down the emotions. He was unable, therefore, to answer Mrs da Tanka. So he just smiled.

Mrs da Tanka, who had once been Mrs Horace Spire and was not likely to forget it, considered those days. It was a logical thing for her to do, for they were days that had come to an end as these present days were coming to an end. Termination was on her mind: to escape from Mrs da Tanka into Mrs Spire was a way of softening the worry that was with her now, and a way of seeing it in proportion to a lifetime.

'If that is what you want,' Horace had said, 'then by all means have it. Who shall do the dirty work – you or I?' This was his reply to her request for a divorce. In fact, at the time of speaking, the dirty work as he called it was already done: by both of them.

'It is a shock for me,' Horace had continued. 'I thought we could jangle along for many a day. Are you seriously involved elsewhere?'

In fact she was not, but finding herself involved at all reflected the inadequacy of her married life and revealed a vacuum that once had been love.

'We are better apart,' she had said. 'It is bad to get used to the habit of being together. We must take our chances while we may, while there is still time.'

In the railway carriage she recalled the conversation with vividness, especially that last sentence, most especially the last five words of it. The chance she had taken was da Tanka, eight years ago. 'My God,' she said aloud, 'what a pompous bastard he turned out to be.'

Mr Mileson had a couple of those weekly publications for which there is no accurate term in the language: a touch of a single colour on the front – floppy, half-intellectual things, somewhere between a journal and a magazine. While she had her honest mags. *Harper's. Vogue.* Shiny and smart and rather silly. Or so thought Mr Mileson. He had opened them at dentists' and doctors', leafed his way through the ridiculous advertisements and aptly titled model girls, unreal girls in unreal poses, devoid it seemed of sex, and half the time of life. So that was the kind of woman she was.

'Who?' said Mr Mileson.

'Oh, who else, good heavens! Da Tanka I mean.'

Eight years of da Tanka's broad back, so fat it might have been padded beneath the skin. He had often presented it to her; he was that kind of man. Busy, he claimed; preoccupied.

'I shall be telling you about da Tanka,' she said. 'There are interesting facets to the man; though God knows, he is scarcely interesting in himself.'

It was a worry, in any case, owning a house. Seeing to the roof; noticing the paint cracking on the outside, and thinking about damp in mysterious places. Better off he was, in the room in Swiss Cottage; cosier in winter. They'd pulled down the old house by now, with all the others in the road. Flats were there instead: bulking up to the sky, with a million or so windows. All the gardens were gone, all the gnomes and the Snow White dwarfs, all the winter bulbs and the little paths of crazy paving; the bird-baths and bird-boxes and bird-tables; the miniature sandpits, and the metal edging, ornate, for flower-beds.

'We must move with the times,' said Mrs da Tanka, and he realized that he had been speaking to her; or speaking aloud and projecting the remarks in her direction since she was there.

His mother had made the rockery. Aubretia and sarsaparilla and pinks and Christmas roses. Her brother, his uncle Edward, bearded and queer, brought seaside stones in his motor-car. His father had shrugged his distaste for the project, as indeed for all projects of this nature, seeing the removal of stones from the seashore as being in some way disgraceful, even dishonest. Behind the rockery there were loganberries: thick, coarse, inedible fruit, never fully ripe. But nobody, certainly not Mr Mileson, had had the heart to pull away the bushes.

'Weeks would pass,' said Mrs da Tanka, 'without the exchange of a single significant sentence. We lived in the same house, ate the same meals, drove out in the same car, and all he would ever say was: "It is time the central heating was on." Or: "These windscreen-wipers aren't working."'

Mr Mileson didn't know whether she was talking about Mr da Tanka or Mr Spire. They seemed like the same man to him: shadowy, silent fellows who over the years had shared this woman with the well-tended hands.

'He will be wearing city clothes,' her friend had said, 'grey or nondescript. he is like anyone else except for his hat, which is big and black and eccentric.' An odd thing about him, the hat: like a wild oat almost.

There he had been, by the tobacco kiosk, punctual and expectant; gaunt of face, thin, fiftyish; with the old-fashioned hat and the weekly papers that somehow matched it, but did not match him.

'Now would you blame me, Mr Mileson? Would you blame me for seeking freedom from such a man?'

The hat lay now on the luggage-rack with his carefully folded overcoat. A lot of his head was bald, whitish and tender like good dripping. His eyes were sad, like those of a retriever puppy she had known in her childhood. Men are often like dogs, she thought; women more akin to cats. The train moved smoothly, with rhythm, through the night. She thought of da Tanka and Horace Spire, wondering where Spire was now. Opposite her, he thought about the ninety-nine-year lease and the two plates, one from last night's supper, the other from breakfast, that he had left unwashed in the room at Swiss Cottage.

'This seems your kind of place,' Mr Mileson said, surveying the hotel from its ornate hall.

'Gin and lemon, gin and lemon,' said Mrs da Tanka, matching the words with action: striding to the bar.

Mr Mileson had rum, feeling it a more suitable drink though he could not think why. 'My father drank rum with milk in it. An odd concoction.'

'Frightful, it sounds. Da Tanka is a whisky man. My previous liked stout. Well, well, so here we are.'

Mr Mileson looked at her. 'Dinner is next on the agenda.'

But Mrs da Tanka was not to be moved. They sat while she drank many measures of the drink; and when they rose to demand dinner they discovered that the restaurant was closed and were ushered to a grill-room.

'You organized that badly, Mr Mileson.'

'I organized nothing. I know the rules of these places. I repeated them to you. You gave me no chance to organize.'

'A chop and an egg or something. Da Tanka at least could have got us soup.'

In 1931 Mr Mileson had committed fornication with the maid in his parents' house. It was the only occasion, and he was glad that adultery was not expected of him with Mrs da Tanka. In it she would be more experienced than he, and he did not relish the implication. The grill-room was lush and vulgar. 'This seems your kind of place,' Mr Mileson repeated rudely.

'At least it is warm. And the lights don't glare. Why not order some wine?'

Her husband must remain innocent. He was a person of importance, in the public eye. Mr Mileson's friend had repeated it, the friend who knew Mrs da Tanka's solicitor. All expenses paid, the friend had said, and a little fee as well. Nowadays Mr Mileson could do with little fees. And though at the time he had rejected the suggestion downright, he had later seen that friend – acquaintance really – in the pub he went to at half past twelve on Sundays, and had agreed to take part in the drama. It wasn't just the little fee; there was something rather like prestige in the thing; his name as co-respondent – now *there* was something you'd never have guessed! The hotel bill to find its way to Mrs da Tanka's husband who would pass it to his solicitor. Breakfast in bed, and remember the face of the maid who brought it. Pass the time of day with her, and make sure she remembered yours. Oh very nice, the man in the pub said, very nice Mrs da Tanka was – or so he was led to believe. He batted his eyes at Mr Mileson; but Mr Mileson said it didn't matter, surely, about Mrs da Tanka's niceness. He knew his duties: there was nothing personal about them. He'd do it himself, the man in the pub explained, only he'd never be able to keep his hands off an attractive middle-aged woman. That was the trouble about finding someone for the job.

'I've had a hard life,' Mrs da Tanka confided. 'Tonight I need your sympathy, Mr Mileson. Tell me I have your sympathy.' Her face and neck had reddened: chirpiness was breaking through.

In the house, in a cupboard beneath the stairs, he had kept his gardening boots. Big, heavy army boots, once his father's. He had worn them at week-ends, poking about in the garden.

'The lease came to an end two years ago,' he told Mrs da Tanka. 'There I was with all that stuff, all my gardening tools, and the furniture and bric-à-brac of three generations to dispose of. I can tell you it wasn't easy to know what to throw away.'

'Mr Mileson, I don't like that waiter.'

Mr Mileson cut his steak with care: a three-cornered piece, neat and succulent. He loaded mushroom and mustard on it, added a sliver of potato and carried the lot to his mouth. He masticated and drank some wine.

'Do you know the waiter?'

Mrs da Tanka laughed unpleasantly; like ice cracking. 'Why should I know the waiter? I do not generally know waiters. Do you know the waiter?'

'I ask because you claim to dislike him.'

'May I not dislike him without an intimate knowledge of the man?'

'You may do as you please. It struck me as a premature decision, that is all.'

'What decision? What is premature? What are you talking about? Are you drunk?'

'The decision to dislike the waiter I thought to be premature. I do not know about being drunk. Probably I am a little. One has to keep one's spirits up.'

'Have you ever thought of wearing an eye-patch, Mr Mileson? I think it would suit you. You need distinction. Have you led an empty life? You give the impression of an empty life.'

'My life has been as many other lives. Empty of some things, full of others. I am in possession of all my sight, though. My eyes are real. Neither is a pretence. I see no call for an eye-patch.'

'It strikes me you see no call for anything. You have never lived, Mr Mileson.'

'I do not understand that.'

'Order us more wine.'

Mr Mileson indicated with his hand and the waiter approached. 'Some other waiter, please,' Mrs da Tanka cried. 'May we be served by another waiter?'

'Madam?' said the waiter.

'We do not take to you. Will you send another man to our table?'

'I am the only waiter on duty, madam.'

'It's quite all right,' said Mr Mileson.

'It's not quite all right. I will not have this man at our table, opening and dispensing wine.'

'Then we must go without.'

'I am the only waiter on duty, madam.'

'There are other employees of the hotel. Send us a porter or the girl at the reception.'

'It is not their duty, madam –'

'Oh nonsense, nonsense. Bring us the wine, man, and have no more to-do.'

Unruffled, the waiter moved away. Mrs da Tanka hummed a popular tune.

'Are you married, Mr Mileson? Have you in the past been married?'

'No, never married.'

'I have been married twice. I am married now. I am throwing the dice for the last time. God knows how I shall find myself. You are helping to shape my destiny. What a fuss that waiter made about the wine!'

'That is a little unfair. It was you, you know –'

'Behave like a gentleman, can't you? Be on my side since you are with me. Why must you turn on me? Have I harmed you?'

'No, no. I was merely establishing the truth.'

'Here is the man again with the wine. He is like a bird. Do you think he has wings strapped down beneath his waiter's clothes? You are like a bird,' she repeated, examining the waiter's face. 'Has some fowl played a part in your ancestry?'

'I think not, madam.'

'Though you cannot be sure. How can you be sure? How can you say you think not when you know nothing about it?'

The waiter poured the wine in silence. He was not embarrassed, Mr Mileson noted; not even angry.

'Bring coffee,' Mrs da Tanka said.

'Madam.'

'How servile waiters are! How I hate servility, Mr Mileson! I could not marry a servile man. I could not marry that waiter, not for all the tea in China.'

'I did not imagine you could. The waiter does not seem your sort.'

'He is your sort. You like him, I think. Shall I leave you to converse with him?'

'Really! What would I say to him? I know nothing about the waiter except what he is in a professional sense. I do not wish to know. It is not my habit to go about consorting with waiters after they have waited on me.'

'I am not to know that. I am not to know what your sort is, or what your personal and private habits are. How could I know? We have only just met.'

'You are clouding the issue.'

'You are as pompous as da Tanka. Da Tanka would say issue and clouding.'

'What your husband would say is no concern of mine.'

'You are meant to be my lover, Mr Mileson. Can't you act it a bit? My husband must concern you dearly. You must wish to tear him limb from limb. Do you wish it?'

'I have never met the man. I know nothing of him.'

'Well then, pretend. Pretend for the waiter's sake. Say something violent in the waiter's hearing. Break an oath. Blaspheme. Bang your fist on the table.'

'I was not told I should have to behave like that. It is against my nature.'

'What is your nature?'

'I'm shy and self-effacing.'

'You are an enemy to me. I don't understand your sort. You have not got on in the world. You take on commissions like this. Where is your self-respect?'

'Elsewhere in my character.'

'You have no personality.'

'That is a cliché. It means nothing.'

'Sweet nothings for lovers, Mr Mileson! Remember that.'

They left the grill-room and mounted the stairs in silence. In their bedroom Mrs da Tanka unpacked a dressing-gown. 'I shall undress in the bathroom. I shall be absent a matter of ten minutes.'

Mr Mileson slipped from his clothes into pyjamas. He brushed his teeth at the wash-basin, cleaned his nails and splashed a little water on his face. When Mrs da Tanka returned he was in bed.

To Mr Mileson she seemed a trifle bigger without her daytime clothes. He remembered corsets and other containing garments. He did not remark upon it.

Mrs da Tanka turned out the light and they lay without touching between the cold sheets of the double bed.

He would leave little behind, he thought. He would die and there would be the things in the room, rather a number of useless things with sentimental value only. Ornaments and ferns. Reproductions of paintings. A set of eggs, birds' eggs he had collected as a boy. They would pile all the junk together and probably try to burn it. Then perhaps they would light a couple of those fumigating candles in the room, because people are insulting when other people die.

'Why did you not get married?' Mrs da Tanka said.

'Because I do not greatly care for women.' He said it, throwing caution to the winds, waiting for her attack.

'Are you a homosexual?'

The word shocked him. 'Of course I'm not.'

'I only asked. They go in for this kind of thing.'

'That does not make me one.'

'I often thought Horace Spire was more that way than any other. For all the attention he paid to me.'

As a child she had lived in Shropshire. In those days she loved the country, though without knowing, or wishing to know, the names of flowers or plants or trees. People said she looked like Alice in Wonderland.

'Have you ever been to Shropshire, Mr Mileson?'

'No. I am very much a Londoner. I lived in the same house all my life. Now the house is no longer there. Flats replace it. I live in Swiss Cottage.'

'I thought you might. I thought you might live in Swiss Cottage.'

'Now and again I miss the garden. As a child I collected birds' eggs on the common. I have kept them all these years.'

She had kept nothing. She cut the past off every so often, remembering it when she cared to, without the aid of physical evidence.

'The hard facts of life have taken their toll of me,' said Mrs da Tanka. 'I met them first at twenty. They have been my companions since.'

'It was a hard fact the lease coming to an end. It was hard to take at the time. I did not accept it until it was well upon me. Only the spring before I had planted new delphiniums.'

'My father told me to marry a good man. To be happy and have children. Then he died. I did none of those things. I do not know why except that I did not care to. Then old Horry Spire put his arm around me and there we were. Life is as you make it, I suppose. I was thinking of homosexual in relation to that waiter you were interested in downstairs.'

'I was not interested in the waiter. He was hard done by, by you, I thought. There was no more to it than that.'

Mrs da Tanka smoked and Mr Mileson was nervous; about the situation in general, about the glow of the cigarette in the darkness. What if the woman dropped off to sleep? He had heard of fires started by careless smoking. What if in her confusion she crushed the cigarette against some part of his body? Sleep was impossible: one cannot sleep with the thought of waking up in a furnace, with the bells of fire brigades clanging a death knell.

'I will not sleep tonight,' said Mrs da Tanka, a statement which frightened Mr Mileson further. For all the dark hours the awful woman would be there, twitching and puffing beside him. *I am mad. I am out of my mind to have brought this upon myself.* He heard the words. He saw them on paper written in his handwriting. He saw them typed, and repeated again as on a telegram. The letters jolted and lost their order. The words were confused, skulking behind a fog. 'I am mad,' Mr Mileson said, to establish the thought completely, to bring it into the open. It was a habit of his; for a moment he had forgotten the reason for the thought, thinking himself alone.

'Are you telling me now you are mad?' asked Mrs da Tanka, alarmed. 'Gracious, are you worse than a homo? Are you some sexual pervert? Is that what you are doing here? Certainly that was not my plan, I do assure you. You have nothing to gain from me, Mr Mileson. If there is trouble I shall ring the bell.'

'I am mad to be here. I am mad to have agreed to all this. What came over me I do not know. I have only just realized the folly of the thing.'

'Arise then, dear Mileson, and break your agreement, your promise and your undertaking. You are an adult man, you may dress and walk from the room.'

They were all the same, she concluded: except that while others had some passing superficial recommendation, this one it seemed had none. There was something that made her sick about the thought of the stringy limbs that were stretched out beside her. What lengths a woman will go to to rid herself of a horror like da Tanka!

He had imagined it would be a simple thing. It had sounded like a simple thing: a good thing rather than a bad one. A good turn for a lady in need. That was as he had seen it. With the little fee already in his possession.

Mrs da Tanka lit another cigarette and threw the match on the floor.

'What kind of a life have you had? You had not the nerve for marriage. Nor the brains for success. The truth is you might not have lived.' She laughed in the darkness, determined to hurt him as he had hurt her in his implication that being with her was an act of madness.

Mr Mileson had not before done a thing like this. Never before had he not weighed the pros and cons and seen that danger was absent from an undertaking. The thought of it all made him sweat. He saw in the future further deeds: worse deeds, crimes and irresponsibilities.

Mrs da Tanka laughed again. But she was thinking of something else.

'You have never slept with a woman, is that it? Ah, you poor thing! What a lot you have not had the courage for!' The bed heaved with the raucous noise that was her laughter, and the bright spark of her cigarette bobbed about in the air.

She laughed, quietly now and silently, hating him as she hated da Tanka and had hated Horace Spire. Why could he not be some young man, beautiful and nicely-mannered and gay? Surely a young man would have come with her? Surely there was one amongst all the millions who would have done the chore with relish, or at least with charm?

'You are as God made you,' said Mr Mileson. 'You cannot help your shortcomings, though one would think you might by now have recognized them. To others you may be all sorts of things. To me you are a frightful woman.'

'Would you not stretch out a hand to the frightful woman? Is there no temptation for the woman's flesh? Are you a eunuch, Mr Mileson?'

'I have had the women I wanted. I am doing you a favour. Hearing of your predicament and pressed to help you, I agreed in a moment of generosity. Stranger though you were I did not say no.'

'That does not make you a gentleman.'

'And I do not claim it does. I am gentleman enough without it.'

'You are nothing without it. This is your sole experience. In all your clerkly subservience you have not paused to live. You know I am right, and as for being a gentleman – well, you are of the lower middle classes. There has never been an English gentleman born of the lower middle classes.'

She was trying to remember what she looked like; what her face was like, how the wrinkles were spread, how old she looked and what she might pass for in a crowd. Would men not be cagey now and think that she must be difficult in her ways to have parted twice from husbands? Was there a third time coming up? Third time lucky, she thought. Who would have her, though, except some loveless Mileson?

'You have had no better life than I,' said Mr Mileson. 'You are no more happy now. You have failed, and it is cruel to laugh at you.'

They talked and the hatred grew between them.

'In my childhood young men flocked about me, at dances in Shropshire that my father gave to celebrate my beauty. Had the fashion been duels, duels there would have been. Men killed and maimed for life, carrying a lock of my hair on their breast.'

'You are a creature now, with your face and your fingernails. Mutton dressed as lamb, Mrs da Tanka!'

Beyond the curtained windows the light of dawn broke into the night. A glimpse of it crept into the room, noticed and welcomed by its occupants.

'You should write your memoirs, Mr Mileson. To have seen the changes in your time and never to know a thing about them! You are like an occasional table. Or a coat-rack in the hall of a boarding-house. Who shall mourn at your grave, Mr Mileson?'

He felt her eyes upon him; and the mockery of the words sank into his heart with intended precision. He turned to her and touched her, his hands groping about her shoulders. He had meant to grasp her neck, to feel the muscles struggle beneath his fingers, to terrify the life out of her. But she, thinking the gesture was the beginning of an embrace, pushed him away, swearing at him and laughing. Surprised by the misunderstanding, he left her alone.

The train was slow. The stations crawled by, similar and ugly. She fixed her glance on him, her eyes sharpened; cold and powerful.

She had won the battle, though technically the victory was his. Long before the time arranged for their breakfast Mr Mileson had leaped from bed. He dressed and breakfasted alone in the dining-room. Shortly afterwards, after sending to the bedroom for his suitcase, he left the hotel, informing the receptionist that the lady would pay the bill. Which in time she had done, and afterwards pursued him to the train, where now, to disconcert him, she sat in the facing seat of an empty compartment.

'Well,' said Mrs da Tanka, 'you have shot your bolt. You have taken the only miserable action you could. You have put the frightful woman in her place. Have we a right,' she added, 'to expect anything better of the English lower classes?'

Mr Mileson had foolishly left his weekly magazines and the daily paper at the hotel. He was obliged to sit barefaced before her, pretending to observe the drifting landscape. In spite of everything, guilt gnawed him a bit. When he was back in his room he would borrow the vacuum cleaner and give it a good going over: the exercise would calm him. A glass of beer in the pub before lunch; lunch in the ABC; perhaps an afternoon cinema. It was Saturday today: this, more or less, was how he usually spent

Saturday. Probably from lack of sleep he would doze off in the cinema. People would nudge him to draw attention to his snoring; that had happened before, and was not pleasant.

'To give you birth,' she said, 'your mother had long hours of pain. Have you thought of that, Mr Mileson? Have you thought of that poor woman crying out, clenching her hands and twisting the sheets? Was it worth it, Mr Mileson? You tell me now, was it worth it?'

He could leave the compartment and sit with other people. But that would be too great a satisfaction for Mrs da Tanka. She would laugh loudly at his going, might even pursue him to mock in public.

'What you say about me, Mrs da Tanka, can equally be said of you.'

'Are we two peas in a pod? It's an explosive pod in that case.'

'I did not imply that. I would not wish to find myself sharing a pod with you.'

'Yet you shared a bed. And were not man enough to stick to your word. You are a worthless coward, Mr Mileson. I expect you know it.'

'I know myself, which is more than can be said in your case. Do you not think occasionally to see yourself as others see you? An ageing woman, faded and ugly, dubious in morals and personal habits. What misery you must have caused those husbands!'

'They married me, and got good value. You know that, yet dare not admit it.'

'I will scarcely lose sleep worrying the matter out.'

It was a cold morning, sunny with a clear sky. Passengers stepping from the train at the intermediate stations, muffled up against the temperature, finding it too much after the warm fug within. Women with baskets. Youths. Men with children, with dogs collected from the guard's van.

Da Tanka, she had heard, was living with another woman. Yet he refused to admit being the guilty party. It would not do for someone like da Tanka to be a public adulterer. So he had said. Pompously. Crossly. Horace Spire, to give him his due, hadn't given a damn one way or the other.

'When you die, Mr Mileson, have you a preference for the flowers on your coffin? It is a question I ask because I might send you off a wreath. That lonely wreath. From ugly, frightful Mrs da Tanka.'

'What?' said Mr Mileson, and she repeated the question.

'Oh well – cowparsley, I suppose.' He said it, taken off his guard by the image she created; because it was an image he often saw and thought about. Hearse and coffin and he within. It would not be like that probably. Anticipation was not in Mr Mileson's life. Remembering, looking back, considering events and emotions that had been at the time mundane perhaps – this kind of thing was more to his liking. For by hindsight there was pleasure in the stream of time. He could not establish his funeral in his mind; he tried often but ended up always with a funeral he had known: a repetition of his parents' passing and the accompanying convention.

'Cowparsley?' said Mrs da Tanka. Why did the man say cowparsley?

Why not roses or lilies or something in a pot? There had been cowparsley in Shropshire; cowparsley on the verges of dusty lanes; cowparsley in hot fields buzzing with bees; great white swards rolling down to the river. She had sat among it on a picnic with dolls. She had lain on it, laughing at the beautiful anaemic blue of the sky. She had walked through it by night, loving it.

'Why did you say cowparsley?'

He did not know, except that once on a rare family outing to the country he had seen it and remembered it. Yet in his garden he had grown delphiniums and wallflowers and asters and sweet-pea.

She could smell it again: a smell that was almost nothing: fields and the heat of the sun on her face, laziness and summer. There was a red door somewhere, faded and blistered, and she sat against it, crouched on a warm step, a child dressed in the fashion of the time.

'Why did you say cowparsley?'

He remembered, that day, asking the name of the white powdery growth. He had picked some and carried it home; and had often since thought of it, though he had not come across a field of cowparsley for years.

She tried to speak again, but after the night there were no words she could find that would fit. The silence stuck between them, and Mr Mileson knew by instinct all that it contained. She saw an image of herself and him, strolling together from the hotel, in this same sunshine, at this very moment, lingering on the pavement to decide their direction and agreeing to walk to the promenade. She mouthed and grimaced and the sweat broke on her body, and she looked at him once and saw words die on his lips, lost in his suspicion of her.

The train stopped for the last time. Doors banged; the throng of people passed them by on the platform outside. They collected their belongings and left the train together. A porter, interested in her legs, watched them walk down the platform. They passed through the barrier and parted, moving in their particular directions. She to her new flat where milk and mail, she hoped, awaited her. He to his room; to the two unwashed plates on the draining board and the forks with egg on the prongs; and the little fee propped up on the mantelpiece, a pink cheque for five pounds, peeping out from behind a china cat.

The Introspections of J. P. Powers

J. P. Powers, big, forty-three, his face a mass of moustache, said: 'You must depress the clutch, Miss Hobish. It is impossible to change from one gear to another without you depress the clutch.'

J. P. Powers was aware of his grammatical lapse. *It is impossible to change from one gear to another unless you depress the clutch. It is impossible to change from one gear to another without depressing the clutch.* Either variant would have done: both were within his idiom. *Without you depress* was foreign to him, the way the Irish talk. Despite the Celtic ring of his name, Justin Parke Powers was not Irish.

Miss Hobish drove the Austin in a jagged manner down Cave Crescent and into Mortimer Road. Ahead lay Putney Hill and an awkward right turn, across both streams of traffic. Powers prepared himself for the moment, feet ready for the dual controls, fingers poised to jab the starter when the engine stalled.

'Slowing down signal,' said J. P. Powers. Then: 'Change to second, hand signal, indicator. Always the old hand signal: never rely on the indicator, Miss Hobish.'

Miss Hobish edged the car forwards, aiming at a bus.

'Wait for a gap, Miss Hobish. All that traffic has the right of way.'

He had said *without you depress* just for the novelty sound of it, because he had become so used to the usual patter of words, because his tongue grew tired of forming them.

'Now, Miss Hobish.' He seized the steering wheel and swung it, giving the engine a spurt of petrol.

The Austin bore to the left at the traffic lights, along Upper Richmond Road, and later turned right, into the quiet roads of Barnes Common. Powers relaxed then, telling her to take it calmly. Miss Hobish was always happy on Barnes Common.

He lit a cigarette and lowered the window so that the smoke would be carried away. He sat in silence, watching the road. Occasionally he glanced at Miss Hobish and occasionally at parts of himself. He saw his fingernails splayed on his two thick knees. He was not a particularly clean man, and this was a fact he now thought about. He visualized his grey-brown underclothes and the tacky yellow on the underarms of his shirts. Once his wife had commented on this yellow, saying he was a dirty man, running baths for him and pushing deodorants at him. She did all this no longer, only sighing when by chance she came upon his socks, stiff like little planks, in the big cardboard carton she used as a laundry basket. A complaint had come in one summer from a fastidious man called Hopker. Roche had had him in and told him about it, with the typing girl still in the room. 'Wash out your armpits, old son. Get Lifebuoy and Odo-ro-no or Mum.' Roche was a little fellow; it was easy for Roche, there wasn't an ounce of sweat in him. Powers was fifteen stone: rolls of fat and muscle, grinding out the perspiration, secreting it in fleshy caches. To keep himself sweet he'd have to take a shower every two hours.

During his daily periods of boredom J. P. Powers was given to thought. It was thought of a depressing quality, being concerned with his uselessness. Fifty years ago there were no driving instructors in the world: what would he have done fifty years ago, how would he have made a living? The truth was he brought no skill to the job, he had no interest in it. How could one be interested in so unnecessary an occupation as teaching people to drive motor-cars? People could walk, they had legs. People could avail themselves of public transport. He gave no real service; better to be a booking clerk for British Railways. Not that people weren't grateful to him. They waved to him afterwards, implying that he had helped them on their way. But J. P. Powers was thinking of himself; there was nothing expert in what he did, anyone could teach the gears and the knack.

'Well, that was nice,' said Miss Hobish. 'I do enjoy it, Mr Powers. Now, will you take a cup of tea with me?'

Miss Hobish had been learning to drive for five years. It was an outing for her: Miss Hobish was seventy-three.

There was a job that was waiting for J. P. Powers, preserved for him by Ransome, with whom he had served in the Royal Air Force. 'Any time you're ready, J. P.,' was how Ransome put it. Ransome with an amber pint in his paw, down at the Saracen's Head on a Sunday morning. Ransome was sorry for him, remembering how he had driven a Spitfire during the war, thinking of him being driven by inept drivers now. Ransome felt he owed him something, some vague debt incurred in 1945. 'Your day's your own,' said Ransome. 'We supply the car.' The task was to sell baby requisites from door to door: gripe water and talcum powder, disinfectant and baby oil. Ransome was expanding: he'd just bought up a concern that manufactured nappies; he was taking a look at the plastic toy business. 'Let me ask you a question,' said Ransome. 'Doesn't it send you up the wall hawking these learner drivers about?' Ransome had a nice little patch keeping warm for Powers out Kingston way. 'Look at the commission,' said Ransome. 'You won't find commissions like that in your front garden.'

Justin Parke Powers, a man unclean and not entirely satisfied with himself, said yes to Miss Hobish; said yes, he would take the cup of tea, and held the car door open for her and followed her into her small house. Miss Hobish paid for her lessons in advance, by the quarter, but each lesson lasted only twenty minutes instead of the full hour: Miss Hobish at seventy-three could rarely sustain more.

Darker than the strands that crossed his scalp, softer than the bristle of moustache, was the mat of hair beneath the arms of J. P. Powers. 'A growth that traps, a growth that sours,' said Roche, referring to the twin clumps and Powers' perspiration. The hair overflowed from the armpits like stuffing from a mattress – yet his chest was naked as a girl's. Smooth and white; a suggestion of breasts; pitted, if you cared to look, with blackheads. Earlier in his life J. P. Powers had been concerned about it: a big man like him with so unmanly an expanse. He had turned his back on the company in changing rooms, whistling to cover the gesture.

In the bath on Sunday mornings he washed his body with passing diligence, watching the milky scum form on the water, lathering himself with Lifebuoy as Roche had counselled. As he bathed he could hear the cry of the radio in the kitchen and the quarrelling sounds of his two small daughters. It was a Sunday ritual, accepted by his wife who took no part in it; ritual that the geyser should snarl and the water flow, that scum should form, radio play, daughters quarrel; ritual that at midday precisely J. P. Powers should emerge from the bathroom temporarily cleansed, should leave his rented house by the back door and board a bus to the Saracen's Arms. It was ritual too that he should later return with four pints of beer in his barrel stomach and eat a lunch that had been kept for him in a low oven.

When he got going he couldn't stop himself. The images of himself, of his daily work and of his body, rose often and unbidden before him. They bloomed in Mortimer Road and Cave Crescent, among the similar houses, detached or partly so. They hovered then over conversation and instruction; they were there in the Austin, like fog. He saw houses and roads being built and wished he had the courage to join a labour gang. He saw his big hands on the steering wheel and considered afresh their function.

On Tuesday September the twenty-first, Justin Parke Powers gave Miss Hobish her two hundred and forty-first driving lesson. He sat beside her, feet and hands alerted.

'We've had no summer, Mr Powers.' She sighed, settling herself. 'One, two, three, four, up and back for reverse. Are we ready, Mr Powers?'

She drove raggedly from Cave Crescent to Amervale Avenue.

'Hand signals,' said Powers, and Miss Hobish extended a scrawny arm and waved it arbitrarily about.

He fancied the typing girl in Roche's office. When the weather was cold she wore knitted jumpers that shaped her breasts. They quivered as she typed, but there was nothing he could do about them now. Probably she'd giggled with Roche afterwards, about what fastidious Hopker had said, about Roche so bold as to recommend Odo-ro-no or Mum.

'You're forgetting those hand signals,' said Powers.

'So difficult,' murmured Miss Hobish.

'Come and have a drink,' a woman had said to him once, at the end of a lesson; and his heart had fluttered in his naked chest, for he had heard from the other men of such approaches made. Nothing had come of it though, because with the drink in his hand he had laughed and been himself, had told her a few jokes and moved around the room so that he was positioned to give her an exploratory slap on the bottom. All this the woman had not welcomed, and had requested a different tutor for future lessons.

'Slow down for the crossing,' Powers said.

'I beg your pardon?' said Miss Hobish, turning to look at him, jerking the Austin onwards, missing a woman with a pram.

'Turn right. We'll go up Mortimer Road. Hand signal, indicator. Draw out to the centre of the road.'

Excited, Miss Hobish allowed the car to stall.

'More gas, more gas,' cried J. P. Powers, apologizing to the traffic.

'Tell me about the R.A.F.,' said Miss Hobish in Mortimer Road. 'I love to hear your tales.'

'We must concentrate on our driving, Miss Hobish.'

'Shall we have a cup of coffee afterwards and shall you tell me then?'

'Yes, Miss Hobish; a coffee would be nice.'

He closed his eyes and within seconds Miss Hobish had driven the Austin into the back of a stationary van.

'Oh dear, oh dear,' said Miss Hobish.

Powers got out and examined the damage. Both wings and the radiator grill had suffered considerably. The bumper had folded like a length of cardboard.

'I'd better drive,' said Powers. 'The steering may be wonky.'

He drove in silence, reflecting upon what the incident would cost in terms of himself. Then he wondered idly, as he often did, what it would be like to be a solicitor or a bank manager. He couldn't fit himself into either role; he couldn't hear himself advising on the purchase of a house, or lending money, or retailing the details of the divorce laws. It seemed a truth that his tasks were destined to be expendable; only in war had he established himself.

'Coffee now?' Miss Hobish asked with meekness.

He looked at the front of the car again. Both headlights were smashed.

'I'm going to give you a cheque,' said Miss Hobish. She handed him coffee, and biscuits with icing on them. 'For that damage to your motor. I suppose it would be two hundred pounds?'

'Two hundred,' said Powers, falling in with the plan. 'J.P. the initials are.'

'Now we'll forget about it?' She was anxious, and he nodded, tucking the cheque away and thinking about it.

Ransome would be at the Saracen's Head at lunch-time. He'd park the Austin round at the back where Ransome wouldn't see it and wouldn't guess anything. Two hundred: he could make it last a long time, nice to have it by him, nice to be able to draw on it now and again.

'Lovely biscuits, Miss Hobish.'

'So forgiving, Mr Powers! I thought you mightn't speak to me, your beautiful motor all broken up.'

'Not at all –'

'Have some more of these biscuits, I know you like them. I get them at Sainsbury's.'

He dunked the biscuit in his coffee and sucked off the coloured icing. It was a comfortable room. The arm-chair he sat in was large and soft. Once he had fallen asleep in it. Once Miss Hobish, recognizing his fatigue, had invited him to take off his shoes.

'Good-bye, Miss Hobish.'

'More coffee? Biscuits?'

'I fear I must make my way, Miss Hobish.'

'Good-bye then, Mr Powers.' They shook hands as they always did.

It was the boredom, he thought; it was that that prevented him from being the easy extrovert he was born to be. The boredom of repeating, the boredom of talking in simple terms. Hand signals and gear changes: the boredom gave him time to think, it made him think. Powers did not employ these words in his survey of his trouble, but that was the meaning he arrived at. Thoughts ran around in his brain like hares. He didn't know how to catch them.

'I couldn't be happier,' said Ransome.

Powers examined the beer in his tankard. He nodded, smiling to display enthusiasm.

'Do you know,' queried Ransome, 'what I'm going to do next?'

In three months' time Powers knew he'd be beginning to think Ransome a swine. Ransome had the makings of another Roche; probably he was worse.

'I'm going to fire Jack Clay,' said Ransome.

It was one thing knowing the man in the Saracen's Head, talking over a beer about days in the R.A.F.; it was rather different having him in charge of one's daily life. *I'm going to fire J. P. Powers.* He could hear the man saying it, in this very bar, to some youthful figure who might make a better hand of distributing the requisites.

'I'm going to fire Jack Clay and put J. P. Powers in his car. What d'you think of that, a big Consul?'

'Fine,' said J. P. Powers. 'Fine, fine, a Consul's lovely.'

'I've got a concern making rubber sheets and hot-water bottles shaped like a bunny rabbit. I'd like to have the lot, you know; carry-cots, everything, a full service. I've got a fellow in Hoxton working on a wee-control.'

The old, tired thoughts began all over again. He couldn't see himself clearly; he couldn't see how his pattern was cut or what he was meant to do, or had ever been meant to do. He began to worry and he hated himself for it; because he didn't want to worry, because the thoughts were forced upon him.

'A pregnant woman,' Ransome was going on, 'will buy anything. Apples off a tree, old boy. Two days out and by God, you'll *know* you never had it so good.'

Powers nodded.

'Two pints,' Ransome said to the barmaid.

If he worked on the public transport he'd be a cog in a big machine, getting people to work in the morning, taking them home at night. Otherwise they'd have to walk. He'd seen them during a transport strike, walking from Regent Street to Wimbledon. You couldn't do that more than once a week.

'Will I be all right?'

'Old boy?'

'Will I fit the bill?'

'Haven't I said so? Haven't I been plaguing you to come in for years? I mean what I say, old boy.'

It occurred to him that Ransome, far from being kind, was deliberately being cruel. Ransome was pointing the moral. They had walked out of the R.A.F. together on the same day. They had gone their separate ways, he to teach learner drivers, Ransome to set up in business. And now Ransome was going to employ him. For years, all those Sunday mornings in the pub, Ransome's persuasive talk had been designed to needle him. He had been Ransome's superior in the R.A.F.

'Drink to it.'

He raised his tankard to meet Ransome's.

'Get a nice new suit,' suggested Ransome, smiling. 'Spick and span, with a polish on the shoes. They'll love you, old boy.'

He sat in the Austin, thinking about the last three hours. The pints of beer had darkened the hue of his face. He could feel them in his stomach, thick and comforting – a moat against Roche who was talking in his mind. He saw his flat mouth open and close, and the words lay between them, above Roche's tidy desk, eavesdroppings for the typing girl. So that was that: Powers must nod and understand, and go away and never return, must be forgotten by Roche, and by the typist whose breasts he had so much desired. Already he was a man of another trade, a good-hearted man who talked to the pregnant woman about what was to come, taking an interest and selling a requisite.

The sun was hot on his face as he sat in the Austin. His skin relaxed, that part of him happy in the heat. He closed his eyes and gave himself up to the tiny moment. The sun touched his hands on the steering wheel and warmed them too. Beer in his stomach, sun on his skin: he had felt such cosseting before. He had lain in bed, stretched and at peace, warmly covered. The warmth of his wife had welcomed him and given him another version of simple sensuality. Blearily, an awareness stirred in J. P. Powers. He did not think in so many words that the excuse for his life lay in moments like these: only in what he received, since he contributed nothing. He did not think it because it was absurd when it was put like that, clarified and clinical. The feeling hammered at his brain but no tendril stretched out to fashion it into thought. A cloud obscured the shaft of sunlight and the feeling evaporated, giving way to an afternoon depression. He switched on the ignition and drove the Austin for the last time, past Cave Crescent and Mortimer Road, out on to Putney Hill and into the stream of traffic.

A School Story

Every night after lights-out in the dormitory there was a ceremonial story-telling. One by one we contributed our pieces, holding the stage from the gloom for five or six minutes apiece. Many offerings were of a trite enough order: the Englishman, the Irishman and the Scotsman on a series of desert islands, and what the drunk said to the Pope. But often the stories were real: reminiscences from a short past, snippets of overheard conversation, descriptions of the naked female body in unguarded moments. Only Markham deliberately repeated himself, telling us again and again, and by unanimous demand, about the death of his mother. On a night when no one had much to say, Markham would invariably be called upon; and none of us ever expected to hear anything new. We were satisfied that it was so; because Markham told his story well and it was, to us, a fascinating one.

'It was like this, you see. One Sunday morning my father and I were walking up Tavistock Hill and I asked him to tell me about my mother. It was a good sunny morning in early May and my father looked up at the sky and started on about how beautiful she'd been. So then, when I could get a word in, I asked him about how she'd died and that. Well, he took an extra breath or two and said to prepare myself. I assured him I was well prepared, and then he told me about how they had been staying with these friends in Florence and how they had set out to the hills to do some shooting. They rode out in a great Italian shooting-brake and soon they were slaying the birds like nobody's business. But in the middle of everything there was this accident and my mother was lying in a pool of blood and all the Italians were throwing up their hands and saying "Blessed Mother of Jesus, what a terrible thing!" I said: "Did her gun go off by accident? Was she not carrying it correctly or what?" And my father said it wasn't like that at all, it was his gun that went off by accident and what a shocking thing it was to be the instrument of one's wife's slaughter. Well, sharp as a knife I could see the lie in his face and I said to myself: "Accident, forsooth! Murder more like." Or, anyway, words to that effect. You'll understand with a discovery like that fresh on the mind one is in an emotional tizzy and apt to forget the exact order of thinking. Why was I certain? I'll tell you, boys, why I was certain: because within a six-month the father had married the dead mother's sister. My stepmother to this day. And I'll tell you another thing: I have plans laid to wipe out those two with a couple of swoops of a butcher's knife. Am I not, when all's said and done, a veritable pocket Hamlet? And isn't it right that I should dream at night of the sharpening of the knife?'

Markham had a long, rather serious face; deeply set, very blue eyes; and smooth fair hair the colour of yellow terracotta. People liked him, but nobody knew him very well. His stories about his family and the threats they exposed were taken only half seriously; and when he talked in this way he seemed to be speaking outside his role. Markham was too quiet, too pleasant, too attractive to be mixed up in this way. There was something wrong, not so much with what he said – which we quite understood, whether we thought of it as fact or not – as with Markham's saying it. That at least is how it appears in retrospect, to me and to the others with whom I have since discussed it. Then, we scarcely analysed our feelings; after all, we were only fifteen at the time of the Markham affair.

'I've got some bread from Dining Hall,' Williams said. 'Let's toast it in the boiler-house.' He drew from beneath his jacket four rounds of hard-looking bread and a couple of pieces of straightened wire. His small red-rimmed eyes darted about my face as though seeking some minute, mislaid article. He held out a piece of wire and I took it from him, already recognizing its utter uselessness for the task in hand. One had to open the top of the boiler and toast from above, guiding the bread far into the bowels of the ironwork until it was poised neatly above the glowing coke. It was a business of expertise, and a single length of wire in place of an expanding toasting fork indicated rudimentary disaster.

It was mid-afternoon and, recovering from a cold, I was 'off games'. Williams, who suffered from asthma, was rarely seen on the games field. He disliked any form of physical exercise and he used his disability as an excuse to spend solitary afternoons hanging around the classrooms or enjoying a read and a smoke in the lavatories. He was despised for his laziness, his unprepossessing appearance, and his passion for deception. I said I would join him on his expedition to the boiler-house.

'I've snitched some jam,' he said, 'and a pat or two of butter.'

We walked in silence, Williams occasionally glancing over his shoulder in his customary furtive manner. In the boiler-house he laid the bread on the seat of the boilerman's chair and extracted the jam and butter from the depths of his clothes. They were separately wrapped in two sheets of paper torn from an exercise book. The jam was raspberry and contact with the paper had caused the ruled lines to run. Fearing the effects of this, I said at once that as far as I was concerned the addition of butter was quite sufficient.

The toast was badly burnt and tasted of smoke. Williams ate his ravenously, wiping his fingers on his trouser pockets. I nibbled at mine and eventually threw it into the corner. At this Williams expostulated, picked up the discarded piece, wiped it and smeared on the remains of the jam. He made a crunching noise as he ate, and explained that his inordinate appetite was due to the presence of worms in his body.

There was a footfall on the steps outside and a moment later a figure appeared, sharply silhouetted in the doorway. We could not at first establish its identity, and Williams, speaking loudly, said to me: 'It has been well worth while. The knowledge we have gained of our school's heating system will stand us in good stead. It is well to put a use to one's time in this way.' The figure advanced, and Williams, seeing that it was not the headmaster, sniggered. 'It's only bloody Markham,' he said. 'I thought it was Bodger at least.'

'I have come to smoke,' Markham announced, offering each of us a small, thin cigar.

'When I am fully grown and equipped for life,' Williams said, 'I intend to pursue a legal career. As well, I shall smoke only the most expensive cigars. One can well afford such a policy if one makes a success of the law.'

Markham and I, concerned with the lighting of our tobacco, heard this pronouncement in silence.

'It may be,' Williams went on, 'that I shall learn in time to roll the leaves together myself. The female thigh, I understand, is just the instrument for such a chore.'

'Williams will make an excellent lawyer,' Markham remarked.

'Certainly he will be splendid beneath his wig,' I said.

'And what,' Williams asked, 'do you intend to do with your years, Markham?'

'Oh, they are well numbered. I shall hang quite soon for the slaughter of my father.'

'Would you not wait a while that I might defend you?'

'It is not an action you could readily defend surely? I am guilty already. I would prefer not to die, but I would not wish to dissociate myself from my crime.'

Williams, puffing hard and with the cigar clamped in the centre of his teeth, said:

'Markham's a bloody madman, eh?'

'Damn it, isn't it correct that I should be hatching schemes of vengeance? Wasn't it my own mother? Would you do less, Mr Williams? Answer me now, would you do less?'

'Ah Markham, I wouldn't go about with the noose around my neck before it was time for it. I'd hold my peace on that account.'

'Puny, Williams, puny.'

'But wise, nonetheless.' He kicked a piece of coke across the floor, following it with his glance. He said: 'Anyway, Markham will never do it. Markham's all talk.'

'This is a good cigar,' Markham said. 'May we enjoy many another.'

'Yes,' said Williams agreeably enough. 'A fine drag.'

We smoked in silence. Looking back on it, it seems certain that it all began that afternoon in the boiler-house. Had I not met Williams on the way to his toasting session, had Markham not later shared his cigars with us, how different the course of events might have been. My friendship with Markham might never have come about; Williams might never have been transformed from a cunning nonentity into a figure of mystery and power; and Markham, somehow, might have dodged the snare he had already set for himself.

Becoming friends with Markham was an odd thing. Markham was so silent, so unforthcoming on any subject except the death of his mother. Yet he was sunny rather than sullen; thoughtful rather than brooding. We walked together on the hills behind the school, often without exchanging more than a dozen words. In spite of this, our friendship grew. I discovered that Markham's father and stepmother were now in Kenya. Markham saw them only once a year, during the summer holidays; he spent Easter and Christmas with a grandmother on the south coast.

The other odd aspect of this new relationship between Markham and me was the attitude of Williams. He hung around us. Often, uninvited, he accompanied us on our walks. He took to sidling up to us and whispering: 'Markham will never do it. Markham's just a madman, eh?' Markham rarely replied. He stared at Williams with a puzzled expression and smiled.

When he came on walks with us Williams would ask Markham to tell us about the shooting accident in Florence, and this of course Markham never tired of doing. He didn't seem to resent Williams. I think he was more generous than the rest of us about people like Williams. Certainly he was more generous than I was. Frankly, Williams used to set my teeth on edge. I found him alone one day and asked him bluntly what he was up to. He sniffed at me and asked me what I meant.

'Why do you follow Markham and me around?' I said. 'Why don't you leave Markham alone?'

Williams laughed. 'Markham's an interesting bird.'

'What are you up to, Williams?'

But he wouldn't tell me. He said: 'I'm an unhealthy personage.' He laughed again and walked away.

This exchange had no effect on Williams. He still haunted our movements, chattering of his future in the legal world or retailing the fruits of an hour's eavesdropping. When we were alone together Markham no longer repeated his famous story or made any allusion to this particular aspect of life. I came to realize that although he truly hated his father it had become a joke with him to talk about it. I was the first close friend Markham had known, and he was quite unused to the communication that such a relationship involved. It was only very gradually that new topics of conversation developed between us.

But there was always Williams, devotedly determined, it seemed, to wrap Markham and his story closer and closer together. We formed, I suppose, an odd kind of triangle.

*

At the beginning of the autumn term the headmaster, Bodger, addressed us at length about this and that, announcing the names of the new prefects and supplying us with fresh items of school routine. When he had finished this part of his peroration he paused for a suitable moment and then he said:

'There are times, boys, in the lives of us all when we must display the ultimate bravery. When we must face the slings and arrows with a fortitude we may perhaps have never had call to employ before. Such a fearful moment has come to one of our number. I would ask you to show him kindness and understanding. I would ask you this term to help him on his way; to make that way as easy as you may. For us it is a test as it is for him. A test of our humanity. A test of our Christian witness. It is with the greatest grief, boys, that I must report to you the sudden and violent death of Ian Markham's father and stepmother.'

Markham had not yet returned. During the fortnight of his absence speculation and rumour ran high. Neither Bodger nor his henchmen seemed to know about the threats he had been wont to issue. Only we who were in their care questioned the accuracy of the facts as they had been presented to us: that a Mau Mau marauder armed with a heavy knife had run berserk through the Markham farm in Kenya. Was not the coincidence too great? Was it not more likely that Markham had finally implemented his words with action?

'Markham's a madman, eh?' Williams said to me.

When he did return, Markham was changed. He no longer smiled. Waiting expectantly in the dormitory for a new and gory story, his companions received only silence from Markham's bed. He spoke no more of his mother; and when anyone sympathized with him on his more recent loss he seemed not to know what was being spoken of. He faded into the background and became quite unremarkable. Pointedly rejecting my companionship, he ended our brief friendship. Instead, he and Williams became inseparable.

It was, I remember, a particularly beautiful autumn. Red, dead leaves gleamed all day in the soft sunlight. On warm afternoons I walked alone through the gorse-covered hills. I did not make friends easily; and I missed the company of Markham.

As the weeks passed it became clear that the murder of Markham's parents by Mau Mau was now generally accepted. It might be thought that against a background of Markham's stories and avowed intentions a certain fear would have developed; an uneasiness about sharing one's daily existence with such a character. It was not so. Markham seemed almost dead himself; he was certainly not a figure to inspire terror. The more one noticed him the more unlikely it appeared that he could possibly have had any hand in the events in Kenya, although he had been in the house at the time and had himself escaped undamaged.

I thought that only I must have been aware of the ominous nature of Markham's association with Williams. Williams, I knew, was up to no good. He whispered constantly to Markham, grinning slyly, his small eyes drilling into Markham's face. I didn't like it and I didn't know what to do.

One afternoon I walked into the town with a boy called Block. We went to a café with the intention of passing an hour over tea and cakes and, if the coast seemed clear, a surreptitious smoke.

'This is an uncivilized place,' Block remarked as we sat down. 'I cannot imagine why we came here.'

'There is nowhere else.'

'It is at least too revolting for the Bodger or any of his band. Look, there's our dreaded Williams. With Markham.'

They were sitting at a table in an alcove. Williams, talking as usual, was fiddling with the spots on his face. As I watched him, he picked a brightly coloured cake from the plate between them. It looked an uninviting article, indeed scarcely edible. He nibbled at one corner and replaced it on the plate.

'Whatever does Markham see in him?' Block asked.

I shook my head. Block was a simple person, but when he next spoke he revealed a depth I had not before had evidence of. He cocked his head to one side and said: 'Williams hates Markham. You can see it easily enough. And I believe Markham's terrified of him. You used to know Markham rather well. D'you know why?'

Again I shook my head. But there was no doubt about it, Block was quite right.

The nub of the relationship was Williams's hatred. It was as though hatred of some kind was essential to Markham; as though, since he had no father to hate now, he was feeding on this unexplained hatred of himself. It all seemed a bit crazy, but I felt that something of the kind must be true.

'I feel I should do something about it all,' I said. 'Williams is a horribly untrustworthy fellow. God knows what his intentions are.'

Did Williams know something that we others were ignorant of? Something of the double death in Kenya?

'What can you do?' Block said, lighting the butt of a cigarette.

'I wonder if I should talk to Pinshow?'

Block laughed. Pinshow was a fat, middle-aged master who welcomed the personal problems of his pupils. He was also a bit of an intellectual. It was enough to tell Mr Pinshow that one had an ambition to become a writer or an actor to ensure endless mugs of black coffee in Mr Pinshow's room.

'I often wonder if we don't underestimate Pinshow,' I said. 'There's lots of goodwill in the man. And good ideas quite often originate in unexpected quarters. He just might be able to suggest something.'

'Perhaps. You know more about Markham than I do. I mean, you probably know more about what the matter is. He doesn't seem much good at anything any more, does he?'

I looked across the room at his sad, lost-looking face. 'No, I'm afraid he doesn't.'

Block suddenly began to laugh. 'Have you heard Butler's one about the sick budgerigar?'

I said I didn't think I had, and he leaned forward and told me. Listening to this obscene account of invalid bird-life, I made up my mind to see Pinshow as soon as possible.

The evening light faded and Mr Pinshow continued to talk. I tried in the gloom to take some biscuits without his observing my action. He pushed the box closer to me, oblivious, or so I hoped, of my deceit. 'Out of the slimy mud of words,' said Mr Pinshow, 'out of the sleet and hail of verbal imprecision, come approximate thoughts and feelings, words that have taken the place of thoughts and feelings, and the beauty of incantation.' Mr Pinshow often said this. I think it may have been his favourite quotation. I drained my coffee mug, filling my mouth with bitter sediment as I did so.

I said: 'There is a land of the living and a land of the dead and the bridge is love.'

'Ah, Wilder.' Mr Pinshow drew a large coloured handkerchief from his trouser pocket and blew his nose.

'The only survival,' I added, 'the only meaning.'

Mr Pinshow replaced his handkerchief. He scratched a match along the side of its box and held the flame to his pipe. 'Love,' he said, puffing, 'or love? One sort or the other sort?'

'The other sort, sir?'

'You question such a division? Good. Good.'

I said: 'I wanted to speak to you, sir.'

'Quite right. Fire away, then.'

'In confidence, sir, I think Williams is a bad influence on Markham.'

'Ah.'

'I think Markham may be very upset about his parents' death, sir. Williams is the last person . . .'

'Come now, in what way a bad influence? Speak freely, my friend. We must straightway establish the facts of the case.'

I knew then that the whole thing was going to be useless. It had been a mistake to come to Pinshow. I could not reveal to him the evidence on which my fears were based. I said nothing, hoping he would not press me.

'I see,' he said.

'Perhaps I am making a mountain out of a molehill, sir.'

Mr Pinshow, however, did not think so at all. 'This is a serious business,' he said. 'Though it is unusual in these matters, I am glad you came to me.'

Clearly, I had given the man a completely false impression. I attempted to rectify this, but Mr Pinshow waved me to silence.

'Say no more, my friend. Leave the matter with me. You can rely on me to speak with discretion in the right directions.'

'Sir, I hope I have not misled you.'

'No, no, no.'

'It is not a *serious* thing, sir. It is just that Markham was once a friend of mine and I am sure that now he . . .'

Mr Pinshow held up his hand. He smiled. 'You are a good fellow. Do not despair. All will be well.'

God knows, I thought, what damage I have done.

'Mind your own bloody business,' Williams muttered to me. 'Any more of this kind of stuff to Pinshow and I'll have you for slander. Don't you know that man's a menace?'

'Go to hell, Williams.' And Williams, seeming a fit candidate for such a destination, shuffled angrily away.

After that, I decided to forget about Markham and Williams. After all, it had nothing to do with me; and in any case I appeared to have no option. I settled down to concentrating a little harder on my work and then, when I really had forgotten all about this strange alliance, I was summoned from class one day by the headmaster.

He stood by the window of his study, a terrible, sickly figure of immense height. He remained with his back to me when I entered the room and spoke to me throughout the interview from this position. 'You will tell me what you know about Markham and the boy Williams,' he said. 'Do not lie, boy. I know a lie. I feel a lie on its utterance. Likewise, do not exaggerate. You will repeat to me simply and honestly all that is apposite. Unburden yourself, boy, that you may leave the room with your duty well done.'

I did not intend to lie. To conceal three-quarters of the story was not to lie. I said: 'The whole truth, sir, is that . . .' I paused not knowing how to go on. The headmaster said:

'Well, boy, let us have haste with the whole truth.'

'I can tell you nothing, sir.'

'Nothing?'

'Yes, sir. I know nothing of Markham and Williams.'

'They are boys in this school. You know that, I presume? You have associated with them. You have spoken to Mr Pinshow of these boys. If their relationship is an illicit one I wish to know it. You will achieve little by reticence.'

'There is nothing illicit, sir, in their friendship. I spoke to Mr Pinshow merely because I felt Williams to be the wrong sort of friend for Markham at this particular time.'

'That is a presumptuous decision for you to make, boy.'

'Yes, sir.'

'Why, then, did you so perversely make it?'

'I like Markham, sir.'

'Why, then, did you not see to it that his days were made easier by persuading him personally against an ill influence?'

'Markham no longer wished for my companionship, sir.'

'You had harmed him in some manner?'

'No, sir. At least not that I know of.'

'Yes or no, boy? Do not leave yourself a cowardly loophole.'

'No, sir. I had not harmed him.'

'Well then, why did he not wish to converse with you?'

'I'm afraid I don't know.'

'You do not know. It is unnecessary to be afraid as well.'

'Yes, sir.'

'You see, boy, that you have placed me in an intolerable position with your wild irresponsibilities? I am the fount of authority in this school. You have made me uneasy in my mind. You have forced me to pursue a course I see no good reason for pursuing. Yet because there may be one tittle of reality in your guarded suspicions I must act as I do not wish to act. Have you ever placed yourself in a headmaster's shoes?'

'No, sir.'

'No, sir. I had sensed as much. They are shoes that pinch, boy. It is well to remember that.'

'Yes, sir.'

'Walk forward to my desk, boy, and press the bell you see there. We will order this affair one way or the other.'

Markham and Williams were summoned. When they entered, the headmaster turned from the window and faced us. He said to them:

'Your friendship is in dispute. Your accuser stands beside you. Do not lie, boys. I know a lie. I can feel a lie on its utterance. Have you reason for shame?'

Williams, whose eyes were fastened on the legs of the headmaster's desk, shook his head. Markham replied that he had no cause to be ashamed.

'On what then is your relationship based? Have you like interests? Of what do you speak together?'

'Of many things, sir,' Williams said. 'Politics and affairs of state. Of our ambitions, sir. And our academic progress as the term passes.'

'We talk of one subject only, sir,' Markham said. 'The death of my father and stepmother.'

'Yet you, boy,' the headmaster said to Williams, 'would claim a wider conversational field. The air is blackened with the lie. Which boy are we to believe?'

'Markham is ill, sir. He is not at all himself. I give him what help I can. He does not recall the full extent of our conversation.'

'We speak of one subject,' Markham repeated.

'Why, boy, do you speak of this subject to the exclusion of all others?'

'Because I killed my father, sir. And my stepmother too.'

'Markham is ill, sir. He . . .'

'Leave the room, you boys. Markham, you shall remain.'

Neither Williams nor I spoke as we walked away from the headmaster's door. Then, as our ways were about to divide, I said:

'You know he didn't. You know it is not true.'

Williams did not look at me. He said: 'That's right. Why didn't you tell Bodger that?'

'You've made him believe he did it, Williams.'

'Markham's all talk. Markham's a madman, eh?'

'You're an evil bastard, Williams.'

'That's right. I'm an unhealthy personage.'

He went on his way and I stood where he had left me, looking back at the closed door of the headmaster's study. The little red light which indicated that for no reason whatsoever should the headmaster be disturbed gleamed above it. Within, I guessed that the curtains were by now closely drawn, since to do so was the headmaster's practice on all grave occasions.

Suddenly I had the absurd notion of returning to this darkened room and demanding to be heard, since now I was free to speak. I felt for the moment that I could put his case more clearly, more satisfactorily than Markham himself. I felt that I knew everything: the horror of the thought that had leapt in Markham's mind when first his father told him of the accident in Florence; the game he had made of it, and the later fears that Williams had insidiously played upon. But as I paused in doubt I heard the urgent chiming of a bell, and, like the object of some remote control, I answered the familiar summons.

That same evening Markham was driven away. He was seen briefly in the headmaster's hall, standing about in his overcoat, seeming much as usual.

'They've sent him up to Derbyshire,' said Mr Pinshow when later I attempted to elicit information. 'Poor lad; so healthy in the body, too.' He would say no more, but I knew what he was thinking; and often since I have thought of Markham, still healthy in his body, growing up and getting older in the place they had found for him in Derbyshire. I have thought of Williams too, similarly growing older though in other circumstances, marrying perhaps and begetting children, and becoming in the end the man he had said he would one day be.

The Day We Got Drunk on Cake

Garbed in a crushed tweed suit, fingering the ragged end of a tie that might well have already done a year's service about his waist, Swann de Courcey uttered a convivial obscenity in the four hundred cubic feet of air they euphemistically called my office. I had not seen him for some years: he is the kind of person who is often, for no reason one can deduce, out of the country. In passing, one may assume that his lengthy absences are due in some way to the element of disaster that features so commandingly in his make-up.

I should have known when I saw him standing there that I must instantly be on my guard. In my prevailing condition of emotional delicacy I could not hope to cope with whatever entertainment Swann had in mind for me. For, to give him his due, Swann never came empty-handed. Swann was a great one for getting the best out of life; and he offered one, invariably, a generous part of his well-laid plans. This time, he explained, he was offering me an attractive afternoon. In turn, I explained that I did not feel like an attractive afternoon, that I was too busy to gild the hours in the manner he was suggesting. But Swann was sitting down, well entrenched; and in the end he talked me into it.

I wrote a note and put it on my typewriter: *Tuesday p.m. Am under surgeon's knife.* Then I made a telephone call.

'Lucy?'

'Hullo, Mike.'

'How are you?'

'Very well, Mike. How are you?'

'Very well, too. Just thought I'd ring –'

'Thank you, Mike.'

'We must meet again soon.'

'Yes, we must.'

'I'd invite you to lunch only an old and valued friend has just transpired.'

'That's nice for you.'

'Well, yes.'

'Thanks for ringing, Mike.'

'Good-bye, Lucy.'

'Good-bye, Mike.'

Swann was drawing designs on the varnish of my desk with a straightened-out paper-clip.

'That wasn't your wife,' he said.

'Wife? Far from it.'

'You haven't married or anything?'

'No.'

'Good. I've got a couple in a hostelry. They tell me they know you.' We sauntered out into the September sun to meet them.

I thought I might cheat a little here. I have always wanted to invent pert shorthand typists with good figures and pretty lips whose heads may easily be turned by the crisp jingle of money, puritan maids who have done the stint at Pitman's and do not believe in anticipating marriage. It might quite easily have been such girls with whom we found ourselves wasting away that afternoon. As it happened, it was Margo and Jo, a smart pair who drew pictures for the glossy magazines.

'When I was eleven,' Jo told me, 'I wrote this children's book and drew all the pictures. Somebody published it, and that of course made me terribly unpopular with everyone.'

'You must have been hugely clever.'

'No, honestly. It was terribly bad, as you can imagine. Just chance that it got published.'

'Words,' said Margo, 'mean a lot to Jo. She has a real sense.'

'She's bonkers,' said Swann.

'For God's sake, Swann,' said Margo.

Jo and Swann moved together. Swann was bored and he began to tell Jo a joke. Margo said, specifically to me: 'Jo is the most talented person I've ever met.' I nodded, not caring one way or the other. The bar was full of uniformed men: dark grey suits, waistcoats, white shirts, striped ties of some club or school.

'Have a drink, Margo?'

Margo said that was a good idea and I squeezed through to the wet counter and floated a ten-shilling note on a pool of beer. When I returned to her Margo said:

'Tell me straight, what do you think of Nigel?'

Nigel? Playing for time I sipped my beer, wondering why I drank the stuff since I disliked it so much. I said:

'Oh, I like Nigel.'

'Do you *really*?'

'Well, he's all right. I mean –'

'Sometimes, Mike, I think Nigel is the most God-awful bore I ever met.'

I remembered. Nigel was plump and talkative. Nigel would tell you anything you might ever wish to know. When Nigel got going there was, in truth, no stopping Nigel. Nigel was Margo's husband.

I drank some more beer. It was cold and tasteless. I said nothing.

'Nigel and I had a barney last night.'

'Oh God!'

Margo told me about the barney. I listened dejectedly. Then I bought some more drink, and this time I made mine whisky. As I've said, Nigel was Margo's husband. She and Jo had one apiece. Both marriages were, as the saying goes, on the rocks.

Suddenly Margo stopped about Nigel. She leered at me and said something I didn't catch. From the next few sentences, I realized she was telling me I'd make a good husband.

'I suppose I would,' I said.

'I'm not in love with you or anything,' Margo said, swaying.

'Of course not.'

After the pub we went off to have some lunch. All the way in the taxi I thought about Lucy.

We went to an Italian place in Soho that was too expensive and not particularly good. Swann told us the history of his life and ate only series of cassatas. I found a telephone on the stairs and rang up Lucy.

'Hullo, Lucy. What are you doing?'

'What d'you mean, what am I doing? I'm standing here talking to you on the telephone.'

'I'm getting drunk with people in Soho.'

'Well, that's nice for you.'

'Is it? Wish you were here.'

Lucy would be bored by this. 'I've been reading *Adam Bede*,' she said.

'A good story.'

'Yes.'

'Have you had lunch?'

'I couldn't find anything. I had some chocolate.'

'I telephoned to see how you were.'

'I'm fine thanks.'

'I wanted to hear your voice.'

'Oh come off it. It's just a voice.'

'Shall I tell you about it?'

'I'd rather you didn't. I don't know why.'

'Shall we meet some time?'

'I'm sure we shall.'

'I'll ring you when I'm sober.'

'Do that. I must get back to *Adam Bede*.'

'Good-bye.'

'Good-bye.'

I replaced the receiver and stood there looking down the steep stairs. Then I descended them.

'What on earth shall we do now?' Swann said. 'It's four o'clock.'

'I want to talk to Mike,' Margo announced. 'Nobody's to listen.'

I sat beside her and she began to speak in a limping whisper. 'I want your advice about Nigel, Mike.'

'Honestly, I scarcely know him.'

'Doesn't matter. Look, I think there's something the matter with Nigel.'

I asked her to be specific. Instead she turned her assertion into a question. 'Mike, do *you* think there's something wrong with Nigel?'

'Well –'

'Be frank now.'

'I tell you, I don't know him. For all I know he may have an artificial stomach.'

'Nigel hasn't an artificial stomach, actually.'

'Good.'

'I don't know why you should think that about him. He doesn't even have trouble with his stomach.'

'Well, then, what's the matter with the man?'

'I think he's probably mental.'

'Well, for God's sake get him attended to, Margo.'

'You think I should?'

'Certainly I do. Unless you like his being mental.'

Margo giggled. 'Well, actually, you know, I rather do.'

'In that case you've got no problem, have you?'

'Old Nigel's become funny.'

'How jolly for you, Margo.'

'He's taken to doing such odd things. I mean, I don't know where this is going to stop.'

'Odd things like what?'

'Like bringing home elderly women. He comes in with these women, explaining that he has been attending some meeting with them and has brought them back for coffee. It's quite alarming – Nigel with four or five old ladies trailing behind him. They stay for ages – sometimes weeks. I've no idea where he gets them from. I think he imagines he's being kind.'

'What does Nigel say?'

'He says they haven't finished their meeting. They all sit round writing little notes. Nobody *says* anything.'

'I think it's all very interesting. I'm sure there's some quite simple explanation. I don't think you've really investigated the matter, Margo.'

'Let's leave this place,' Swann said.

We went to another place, called the Blue Goat. It was one of these clubs where you can drink in the afternoon without having to watch striptease. Margo tried to go on about Nigel, but I said firmly that I didn't want to hear anything more about Nigel. I talked to Jo.

'Jo,' I said, 'do you know a girl called Lucy Anstruth?'

'Small, plump, balding a little?'

'No. Lucy is a very beautiful person.'

'Not the same girl.'

'Tall, fair, very blue eyes. Moves like a cat.'

'Don't know her.'

'She says unexpected things. She's half Swedish or something.'

'Mike, would you guess I was half Welsh?'

'No. I want to ask you about Lucy –'

'But I don't know her.'

'I don't know what to do about Lucy.'

'You sound like Margo. Margo doesn't know what to do about Nigel. Nobody knows what to do about anyone else. God! May I have some more vodka?'

'Yes. As I say –'

'I want a triple vodka.'

I ordered the vodka. Beside us, Swann and Margo were sitting in preoccupied silence; they weren't even listening to what we were saying. Margo caught my eye and opened her mouth to speak. I turned my back and handed Jo her drink.

'Something's the matter with Margo's husband,' Jo said. 'Poor old Margo's terribly worried.'

'Yes, I know all about it. Margo has been telling me. In detail.'

'I like Nigel, you know.'

'Perhaps you can help him straighten himself out. We were talking about something else. I was telling you –'

'Seems Nigel brings women home.'

'Yes I know, Jo.'

'Bit rough on Margo.'

Margo heard this. She shouted: 'What's rough on Margo?' and then the conversation became general. I went away to telephone Lucy.

'Lucy?'

'Hullo. Is that Mike?'

'Yes.'

'Hullo, Mike.'

'Hullo, Lucy.'

'How are you?'

'I'm feeling funny. But Lucy?'

'Yes?'

'I'm not trying to be funny. I'm not being amusing.'

'Where are you?'

'In the Blue Goat.'

'Wherever's that?'

'It's lined with leopard skin. Jo and Margo and Swann are here too.'

'Who are they?'

'Just other people.'

'Nice of you to ring, Mike.'

'Margo's husband Nigel brings women home. I wondered perhaps if you had a word of advice I could give her. She's worried about the women. They're elderly and they come in groups.'

'Oh Mike, I don't know about things like that. I wouldn't know what to do. Honestly.'

'Sorry, Lucy; I just thought you might.'

'The doorbell's ringing. Good-bye, Mike. If I were you I'd go home.'

Swann said he wanted tea. We left the Blue Goat and walked in dazzling sunshine towards Floris.

Margo began again about Nigel.

Swann said he knew a man who would do Nigel a world of good. He couldn't remember the treatment this man offered, but he said it was highly thought of.

I went away to telephone Lucy.

'Lucy?'

A man's voice answered. I said: 'May I speak to Lucy? Is that the right number?'

The man didn't reply and in a moment Lucy came on. 'Is that Mike again?'

'Hullo, Lucy. How are you?'

'I'm fine, Mike.'

'Good.'

'Mike, you telephoned me at four-fifteen. Do you know what time it is now?'

'What time is it now?'

'Four-thirty-five.'

'Am I being a nuisance, is that it?'

'No, no. Just, is there anything I can do for you? I mean, do you want something and feel unable to express yourself?'

'I'm bored. I'm with these people. Lucy.'

'Yes?'

'Who's that in your flat?'

'A friend called Frank. You don't know him.'

'What's he doing there?'

'What d'you mean, what's he doing?'

'Well –'

'Look, I'll ask him. Frank, what are you doing?'

'What's he say?'

'He says he's making a cup of tea.'

'I'm having tea too. In Floris. I wish you were here.'

'Good-bye, Mike.'

'Don't go, Lucy.'

'Good-bye, Mike.'

'Good-bye, Lucy.'

When I got back to the others I found them laughing in an uproarious manner. Swann said the cake they were eating was making them drunk. 'Smell it,' he said. It smelt of rum. I tasted some: it tasted of rum too. We all ate a lot of the cake, laughing at the thought of getting drunk on cake. We ordered some more, and told the waitress it was delicious. When the enthusiasm had melted a bit Swann said:

'Mike, we want your advice about Margo's husband.'

'I've told Margo –'

'No, Mike – seriously now. You know about these things.'

'Why do you think I know about these things? Quite emphatically, I do not know about these things.'

'All right, Mike, I'll tell you. Margo's husband Nigel keeps turning up with groups of old females. Margo's worried in case the thing develops a bit – you know, tramps, grocers, one-legged soldiers. What d'you think she should do?'

'I don't know what Margo should do. Margo, I don't know what you should do. Except perhaps ask Nigel what he's up to. In the meantime, have some more cake.'

'Now there's an idea,' Swann shouted excitedly. 'Margo love, why don't you ask old Nigel what he's up to?'

Jo hacked affectionately at my face with her great spiked fingers. I guessed it was an expression of admiration rather than attack because she smiled as she did so.

'But all Nigel says,' Margo said, 'is that they haven't finished their meeting.'

'Ah yes,' said Swann, 'but you don't press him. You don't say: "What meeting?" You don't indicate that you are in the dark as to the nub of their business. Nigel may well imagine that you accept the whole state of affairs without question and expect little else of married life. When you were at the Gents,' Swann said to me, 'Margo confessed she was worried.'

'She had previously confessed as much to me. I wasn't at the Gents. I was making a telephone call.'

'Shall *I* do that?' Margo said. 'Shall I ring up Nigel and ask him to explain everything?'

We all nodded. Margo rose, hesitated, and sat down again. She said she couldn't. She explained she was too shy to telephone her husband in this way. She turned to me.

'Mike, would you do it?'

'Me?'

'Mike, would you telephone?'

'Are you asking me to telephone your husband and inquire about his relationship with some elderly women who are entirely unknown to me?'

'Mike, for my sake.'

'Think of the explanations it would involve me in. Think of the confusion. Nigel imagining I was the husband of one of these women. Nigel imagining I was the police. Nigel asking me question after question. For goodness' sake, how do you think I would get some kind of answer out of *him*?'

Swann said: 'All you have to do is to say: "Is that Nigel? Now look here, Nigel, what's all this I hear about these women who come to your house at all hours of the day and night?" Say you represent the Ministry of Pensions.'

'I can't address the man as Nigel and then say I'm from the Ministry of Pensions.'

'Mike, Margo's husband's name *is* Nigel. He'll be expecting you to address him as Nigel. If you don't address him as Nigel, he'll simply tell you to go to hell. He'll say you've got a wrong number.'

'So I say: "Hullo, Nigel, this is the Ministry of Pensions." The man'll think I'm crazy.'

Margo said: 'Mike, you just do it your own way. Take no notice of Swann. Swann's been eating too much cake. Come on, you know where the telephone is.' She gave me a piece of paper with a number on it.

'Oh God,' I said; and unable to bear it any longer I borrowed fourpence and marched off to the telephone.

'Hullo?' said the voice at the other end.

'Hullo. Can I speak to Lucy? Please.'

'Hullo,' Lucy said.

'Hullo, Lucy.'

'Well?' said Lucy.

'It's Mike.'

'I know it's Mike.'

'They wanted me to telephone this man I was telling you about, but I can't go telephoning people in this way–'

'Why don't you go home to bed?'

'Because I wouldn't sleep. Remember the man with the elderly women? Well, they wanted me to telephone him and ask him what he's up to. Lucy, I can't do that, can I?'

'No, quite honestly I don't believe you can.'

'They told me to pose as the Ministry of Pensions.'

'Good-bye, Mike.'

'Just a – Lucy?'

'Yes?'

'Isn't that man still there?'

'Which man is this?'

'The man in your flat.'

'Frank. He's still here.'

'Who is he, Lucy?'

'He's called Frank.'

'Yes, but what does he do?'

'I don't know what he does. Frank, what do you do? For a living? He says he's a – what, Frank? A freight agent, Mike.'

'A freight agent.'

'Good-bye.'

'Good-bye, Lucy.'

When I arrived back at the tea-table everyone was very gay. Nobody asked me what Nigel had said. Swann paid the bill and said he was anxious to show us a display of Eastern horrors somewhere in Euston and would afterwards take us to a party. In the taxi Margo said:

'What did Nigel say?'

'He was out.'

'Was there no reply?'

'A woman answered. She said I was interrupting the meeting. I said "What meeting?" but she wanted to know who I was before she would answer that. I said I was the Ministry of Pensions and she said "Oh my God" and rang off.'

We were hours early for the party, but nobody seemed to mind. I helped a woman in slacks to pour bottles of wine into a crock. Swann, Margo and Jo played with a tape recorder, and after a time the woman's husband arrived and we all went out to eat.

About eight, people began to arrive. The place filled with tobacco smoke, music and fumes; and the party began to swing along at a merry enough pace. A girl in ringlets talked to me earnestly about love. I think she must have been feeling much the same as I was, but I didn't fancy her as a soul-mate, not even a temporary one. She said: 'It seems to me that everyone has a quality that can get the better of love. Is stronger, you see. Like pride. Or honesty. Or moral, even intellectual, even emotional integrity. Take two people in love. The only thing that can really upset things is this personal quality in one of them. Other people don't come into it at all. Except in a roundabout way – as instruments of jealousy, for instance. Don't you agree?'

I wasn't sure about anything, but I said yes.

'Another thing about love,' the girl with the ringlets said, 'is its extraordinary infection. Has it ever occurred to you that when you're in love with someone you're really wanting to be loved yourself? Because that, of course, is the law. I mean, it would be odd if every time one person loved another person the first person wasn't loved in return. There's only a very tiny percentage of that kind of thing.'

An aggressive young man, overhearing these remarks, began to laugh. He went on laughing, looking at the girl in ringlets and looking at me.

I went away and filled my glass from the crock, and asked a pretty middle-aged woman what she did. Her answer was coy; I smiled and passed on. Margo caught my arm and dragged me off to a corner. 'Mike, you'll ring Nigel again?'

'I've been thinking about that,' I said. 'Honestly, I don't think I can interfere.'

'Oh but, dear, you promised.'

'Promised? I didn't promise anything.'

'Oh Mike.'

'Really, the whole affair – oh all right.'

'Now, Mike?'

'All right. Now.'

'Lucy?'
'Is that Mike?'
'Who else?'
'Who indeed? Where are you now?'
'I'm at a party.'
'A good party?'
'Yes, I suppose so. Why don't you come along?'
'I can't, Mike. I'm doing things.'
'With the bloody freight agent, I suppose.'
'The what agent?'
'Freight. Your friend the freight agent. Frank.'
'He's not a freight agent. He's in publishing.'
'What'd he say he was a freight agent for?'

A lengthy explanation followed. Calling himself a freight agent was a sample of Frank's humour. I thought about this as I made my way back to Margo.

'What'd he say, Mike?'
'A woman said Nigel wasn't in.'
'Is that all?'
'I said the house was being watched. I said the local authorities weren't at all happy.'
'What'd she say?'
'She began to moan, so I said "I mean it," and rang off.'
'Thank you, Mike.'
'That's all right. Any time.'

Swann joined us and Margo said: 'Mike's been on to Nigel again. Mike's being wonderful.'

Swann patted me on the back and said: 'Any joy?'

Margo started to tell him. I went away.

Jo was pretending to listen to a couple of men who were between them retailing a complicated story. She said to me in a low voice: 'Don't worry about Margo. I'll see she comes through the other side.'

I stared at her, wondering why she should imagine I was worried about Margo. 'I'm sure you will, Jo,' I said.

'Trust Jo,' she whispered.

I said I considered her a trustworthy person. I began to elaborate on the thought. One of the men said: 'D'you mind, old boy?'

I shrugged and pushed a path back to the telephone. I dialled three times to be certain, but on each occasion there was no reply.

A ragged form of dancing was now taking place. Pausing by the crock, I found myself once again in the company of the girl with the ringlets. She smiled at me and in a boring way I said: 'Do you know a girl called Lucy Anstruth?'

The girl with the ringlets shook her head. 'Should I?'

'I suppose not,' I said. The girl examined me closely and passed on.

I went upstairs and discovered a quiet room with a bed in it. A lamp on a dressing-table gave out a weak light. The bed, which looked comfortable, was almost in darkness. I stretched out on it, welcoming the gloom. In a few moments I dropped off to sleep. When I awoke the luminous dial of my watch indicated that I had been asleep for two hours. Two girls were tidying their faces at the dressing-table. They drew head-scarves with horses on them from their handbags and placed them about their heads. They spoke in a whisper and left the room. I lay there considering the events of the day and wondering how I was going to feel about them at breakfast. How one feels at breakfast about the preceding day has always seemed to be important to me.

A man with a glass in his hand entered the room and placed himself before the mirror on the dressing-table. He combed his hair and tightened his tie. Then he took a handkerchief from his pocket and wrapped it around his right forefinger. He inserted this into each ear, twisting his forefinger back and forth. He remarked to himself on the outcome of this operation, examining his handkerchief. I closed my eyes; when I opened them he was gone. I lit a cigarette and set off to the telephone again.

'What is it?' a voice said. It was the publishing man. I asked to speak to Lucy.

'Hullo, Lucy.'

'Oh Mike, really –'

'Lucy, that man's there again.'

'I know, Mike.'

'It's two o'clock in the morning.'

'Two o'clock in the morning. I'm sorry, Mike.' Her voice was so gentle that I said:

'Stop trying not to hurt me.'

'I think I'd better ring off.'

'I'll ring off, damn it.'

I stood by the telephone, considering, and feeling sick. I felt something between my fingers and looked down at the piece of paper with Nigel's telephone number on it. I lifted the receiver and dialled it.

I waited almost a minute and then a woman's voice said: 'Yes? Who is that please?'

I think I said: 'I want to know what's going on.'

The woman said quickly: 'Who is that speaking? You haf the wrong number.'

'I do not,' I retaliated briskly. 'Please bring Nigel to the phone.'

'Nigel is in the Chair. You are interrupting our meeting with this demand. There is much on the agenda. I cannot attend to you, sir.'

'This is the Ministry of Pensions,' I said, and I heard the woman breathing laboriously. Then she cut me off.

I walked back through the party and looked for the front door. I was thinking that everything had been more or less resolved. Margo's grievance had had its airing; she felt the better for it, and all anyone had to do now was to ask Nigel what he was up to and press the point until a satisfactory answer was achieved. After that, it was up to the relevant experts. As for me, time would heal and time would cure. I knew it, and it was the worst thing of all. I didn't want to be cured. I wanted the madness of my love for Lucy to go on lurching at me from dreams; to mock at me from half-empty glasses; to leap at me unexpectedly. In time Lucy's face would fade to a pin-point; in time I would see her on the street and greet her with casualness, and sit with her over coffee, quietly discussing the flow beneath the bridges since last we met. Today – not even that, for already it was tomorrow – would slide away like all the other days. Not a red letter day. Not the day of my desperate bidding. Not the day on which the love of my life was snaffled away from me. I opened the front door and looked out into the night. It was cold and uncomforting. I liked it like that. I hated the moment, yet I loved it because in it I still loved Lucy. Deliberately I swung the door and shut away the darkness and drizzle. As I went back to the party the sadness of all the forgetting stung me. Even already, I thought, time is at work; time is ticking her away; time is destroying her, killing all there was between us. And with time on my side I would look back on the day without bitterness and without emotion. I would remember it only as a flash on the brittle surface of nothing, as a day that was rather funny, as the day we got drunk on cake.

Raymond Bamber and Mrs Fitch

For fifteen years, ever since he was twenty-seven, Raymond Bamber had attended the Tamberleys' autumn cocktail party. It was a function to which the Tamberleys inclined to invite their acquaintances rather than their friends, so that every year the faces changed a bit: no one except Raymond had been going along to the house in Eaton Square for as long as fifteen years. Raymond, the Tamberleys felt, was a special case, for they had known him since he was a boy, having been close friends of his father's.

Raymond was a tall man, six foot two inches, with spectacles and a small moustache. He was neat in all he did, and he lived what he himself referred to as a tidy life.

'I come here every year,' said Raymond at the Tamberleys', to a woman he had not met before, a woman who was tall too, with a white lean face and lips that were noticeably scarlet. 'It is an occasion for me almost, like Christmas or Easter. To some extent, I guide my life by the Tamberleys' autumn party, remembering on each occasion what has happened in the year gone by.'

'My name is Mrs Fitch,' said the woman, poking a hand out for a drink. 'Is that vermouth and gin?' she inquired of the Tamberleys' Maltese maid, and the maid agreed that it was. 'Good,' said Mrs Fitch.

'Raymond, Raymond,' cried the voice of Mrs Tamberley as Mrs Tamberley materialized suddenly beside them. 'How's Nanny Wilkinson?'

'She died,' murmured Raymond.

'Of course she did,' exclaimed Mrs Tamberley. 'How silly of me!'

'Oh no –'

'You put that sweet notice in *The Times*. His old nurse,' explained Mrs Tamberley to Mrs Fitch. 'Poor Nanny Wilkinson,' she said, and smiled and bustled off.

'What was all that?' asked Mrs Fitch.

'It's one of the things that happened to me during the year. The other was –'

'What's your name, anyway?' the woman interrupted. 'I don't think I ever caught it.'

Raymond told her his name. He saw that she was wearing a black dress with touches of white on it. Her shoulders were bare and bony; she had, Raymond said to himself, an aquiline face.

'The other thing was that an uncle died and left me a business in his will. That happened, actually, before the death of Nanny Wilkinson and to tell you the truth, Mrs Fitch, I just didn't know what to do. "What could I do with a business?" I said to myself. So I made my way to Streatham where the old lady lived. "Run a business, Raymond? You couldn't run a bath," she said.' Raymond laughed, and Mrs Fitch smiled frostily, looking about her for another drink. 'It rankled, that, as you may imagine. Why couldn't I run a business? I thought. And then, less than a week later, I heard that she had died in Streatham. I went to her funeral, and discovered that she'd left me a prayer-book in her will. All that happened in the last year. You see, Mrs Fitch?'

Mrs Fitch, her eyes on her husband, who was talking to a woman in yellow in a distant corner of the room, said vaguely:

'What about the business?'

'I sold the business. I live alone, Mrs Fitch, in a flat in Bayswater; I'm forty-two. I'm telling you that simply because I felt that I could never manage anything like taking on a business so suddenly. That's what I thought when I had considered the matter carefully. No good being emotional, I said to myself.'

'No,' said Mrs Fitch. She watched the woman move quite close to her husband and engage him in speech that had all the air of confidential talk. The woman wasn't young, Mrs Fitch noticed, but had succeeded in giving the impression of youth. She was probably forty-four, she reckoned; she looked thirty.

So Mrs Tamberley had seen the notice in *The Times*, Raymond thought. He had worded it simply and had stated in a straightforward manner the service that Nanny Wilkinson had given over the years to his family. He had felt it her due, a notice in *The Times*, and there was of course only he who might do it. He remembered her sitting regally in his nursery teaching him his tidiness. Orderliness was the most important thing in life, she said, after a belief in the Almighty.

'Get me a drink, dear,' said Mrs Fitch suddenly, holding out an empty glass and causing Raymond to note that this woman was consuming the Tamberleys' liquor at a faster rate than he.

'Gin and vermouth,' ordered Mrs Fitch. 'Dry,' she added. 'Not that red stuff.'

Raymond smiled and took her glass while Mrs Fitch observed that her husband was listening with rapt care to what the woman in yellow was saying to him. In the taxi-cab on the way to the Tamberleys', he had remarked as usual that he was fatigued after his day's work. 'An early night,' he had suggested. And now he was listening carefully to a female: he wouldn't leave this party for another two hours at least.

'It was quite a blow to me,' said Raymond, handing Mrs Fitch a glass of gin and vermouth, 'hearing that she was dead. Having known her, you see, all my life –'

'Who's dead now?' asked Mrs Fitch, still watching her husband.

'Sorry,' said Raymond. 'How silly of me! No, I meant, you see, this old lady whom I had known as Nanny Wilkinson. I was saying it was a blow to me when she died, although of course I didn't see much of her these last few years. But the memories are there, if you see what I mean; and you cannot of course erase them.'

'No,' said Mrs Fitch.

'I was a particularly tall child, with my spectacles of course, and a longish upper lip. "When you're a big man," I remember her saying to me, "you'll have to grow a little moustache to cover up all that lip." And declare, Mrs Fitch, I did.'

'I never had a nanny,' said Mrs Fitch.

' "He'll be a tennis-player," people used to say – because of my height, you see. But in fact I turned out to be not much good on a tennis court.'

Mrs Fitch nodded. Raymond began to say something else, but Mrs Fitch, her eyes still fixed on her husband, interrupted him. She said:

'Interesting about your uncle's business.'

'I think I was right. I've thought of it often since, of sitting down in an office and ordering people to do this and that, instead of remaining quietly in my flat in Bayswater. I do all my own cooking, actually, and cleaning and washing up. Well, you can't get people, you know. I couldn't even get a simple char, Mrs Fitch, not for love nor money. Of course it's easy having no coal fires to cope with: the flat is all-electric, which is what, really, I prefer.'

'It was quite a blow to me,' said Raymond, having observed that Mrs Fitch was, for the first time since their conversation had commenced, regarding him closely. She was looking into his face, at his nose and his moustache and his spectacles. Her eyes passed up to his forehead and down the line of his right cheek, down his neck until they arrived at Raymond's Adam's apple. He continued to speak to her, telling of the manner in which his flat in Bayswater was furnished, how he had visited the Sanderson showrooms in Berners Street to select materials for chair-covers and curtains. 'She made them for me,' said Raymond. 'She was almost ninety then.'

'What's that?' said Mrs Fitch. 'Your nurse made them?'

'I measured up for her and wrote everything down just as she had directed. Then I travelled out to Streatham with my scrap of paper.'

'On a bicycle.'

Raymond shook his head. He thought it odd of Mrs Fitch to suggest, for no logical reason, that he had cycled from Bayswater to Streatham. 'On a bus, actually,' he explained. He paused, and then added: 'I could have had them made professionally, of course, but I preferred the other. I thought it would give her an interest, you see.'

'Instead of which it killed her.'

'No, no. No, you've got it confused. It was in 1964 that she made the curtains and the covers for me. As I was saying, she died only a matter of months ago.'

Raymond noticed that Mrs Fitch had ceased her perusal of his features and was again looking vacantly into the distance. He was glad that she had ceased to examine him because had she continued he would have felt obliged to move away from her, being a person who was embarrassed by such intent attention. He said, to make it quite clear about the covers and the curtains:

'She died in fact of pneumonia.'

'Stop,' said Mrs Fitch to the Tamberleys' Maltese maid who happened to be passing with a tray of drinks. She lifted a glass to her lips and consumed its contents while reaching out a hand for another. She repeated the procedure, drinking two glasses of the Tamberleys' liquor in a gulping way and retaining a third in her left hand.

'Nobody tells the truth,' said Mrs Fitch after all that. 'We come to these parties and everything's a sham.'

'What?' said Raymond.

'You know what I mean.'

Raymond laughed, thinking that Mrs Fitch was making some kind of joke. 'Of course,' he said, and laughed again, a noise that was more of a cough.

'You told me you were forty-two,' said Mrs Fitch. 'I in fact am fifty-one, and have been taken for sixty-five.'

Raymond thought he would move away from this woman in a moment. He had a feeling she might be drunk. She had listened pleasantly enough while he told her a thing or two about himself, yet here she was now speaking most peculiarly. He smiled at her and heard her say:

'Look over there, Mr Bamber. That man with the woman in yellow is my husband. We were born in the same year and in the same month, January 1915. Yet he could be in his thirties. That's what he's up to now; pretending the thirties with the female he's talking to. He's praying I'll not approach and give the game away. D'you see, Mr Bamber?'

'That's Mrs Anstey,' said Raymond. 'I've met her here before. The lady in yellow.'

'My husband has eternal youth,' said Mrs Fitch. She took a mouthful of her drink and reached out a hand to pick a fresh one from a passing tray. 'It's hard to bear.'

'You don't look fifty-one,' said Raymond. 'Not at all.'

'Are you mocking me?' cried Mrs Fitch. 'I do not look fifty-one. I've told you so: I've been taken for sixty-five.'

'I didn't mean that. I meant –'

'You were telling a lie, as well you know. My husband is telling lies too. He's all sweetness to that woman, yet it isn't his nature. My husband cares nothing for people, except when they're of use to him. Why do you think, Mr Bamber, he goes to cocktail parties?'

'Well –'

'So that he may make arrangements with other women. He desires their flesh and tells them so by looking at it.'

Raymond looked serious, frowning, thinking that that was expected of him.

'We look ridiculous together, my husband and I. Yet once we were a handsome couple. I am like an old crow while all he has is laughter lines about his eyes. It's an obsession with me.'

Raymond pursed his lips, sighing slightly.

'He's after women in this room,' said Mrs Fitch, eyeing her husband again.

'Oh, no, now –'

'Why not? How can you know better than I, Mr Bamber? I have had plenty of time to think about this matter. Why shouldn't he want to graze where the grass grows greener, or appears to grow greener? That Anstey woman is a walking confidence trick.'

'I think,' said Raymond, 'that I had best be moving on. I have friends to talk to.' He made a motion to go, but Mrs Fitch grasped part of his jacket in her right hand.

'What I say is true,' she said. 'He is practically a maniac. He has propositioned women in this very room before this. I've heard him at it.'

'I'm sure –'

'When I was a raving beauty he looked at me with his gleaming eye. Now he gleams for all the others. I'll tell you something, Mr Bamber.' Mrs Fitch paused. Raymond noticed that her eyes were staring over his shoulder, as though she had no interest in him beyond his being a person to talk at. 'I've gone down on my bended knees, Mr Bamber, in order to have this situation cleared up: I've prayed that that man might look again with tenderness on his elderly wife. But God has gone on,' said Mrs Fitch bitterly, 'in His mysterious way, not bothering Himself.'

Raymond did not reply to these observations. He said instead that he hadn't liked to mention it before but was Mrs Fitch aware that she was clutching in her right hand part of his clothes?

'He shall get to know your Anstey woman,' said Mrs Fitch. 'He shall come to know that her father was a bear-like man with a generous heart and that her mother, still alive in Guildford, is difficult to get on with. My husband shall come to know all the details about your Anstey woman: the plaster chipping in her bathroom, the way she cooks an egg. He shall know what her handbags look like, and how their clasps work – while I continue to wither away in the house we share.'

Raymond asked Mrs Fitch if she knew the Griegons, who were, he said, most pleasant people. He added that the Griegons were present tonight and that, in fact, he would like to introduce them to her.

'You are trying to avoid the truth. What have the Griegons to recommend them that we should move in their direction and end this conversation? Don't you see the situation, Mr Bamber? I am a woman who is obsessed because of the state of her marriage, how I have aged while he has not. I am obsessed by the fact that he is now incapable of love or tenderness. I have failed to keep all that alive because I lost my beauty. There are lines on my body too, Mr Bamber: I would show you if we were somewhere else.'

Raymond protested again, and felt tired of protesting. But Mrs Fitch, hearing him speak and thinking that he was not yet clear in his mind about the situation, supplied him with further details about her marriage and the manner in which, at cocktail parties, her husband made arrangements for the seduction of younger women, or women who on the face of it seemed younger. 'Obsessions are a disease,' said Mrs Fitch, drinking deeply from her glass.

Raymond explained then that he knew nothing whatsoever about marriage difficulties, to which Mrs Fitch replied that she was only telling him the truth. 'I do not for a moment imagine,' she said, 'that you are an angel come from God, Mr Bamber, in order to settle the unfortunateness. I didn't mean to imply that when I said I had prayed. Did you think I thought you were a messenger?' Mrs Fitch, still holding Raymond's jacket and glancing still at her husband and the woman in yellow, laughed shrilly. Raymond said:

'People are looking at us, the way you are pulling at my clothes. I'm a shy man –'

'Tell me about yourself. You know about me by now: how everything that once seemed rosy has worked out miserably.'

'Oh, come now,' said Raymond, causing Mrs Fitch to repeat her laughter and to call out for a further drink. The Tamberleys' maid hastened towards her. 'Now then,' said Mrs Fitch. 'Tell me.'

'What can I tell you?' asked Raymond.

'I drink a lot these days,' said Mrs Fitch, 'to help matters along. Cheers, Mr Bamber.'

'Actually I've told you quite a bit, you know. One thing and another –'

'You told me nothing except some nonsense about an old creature in Streatham. Who wants to hear that, for Christ's sake? Or is it relevant?'

'Well, I mean, it's true, Mrs Fitch. Relevant to what?'

'I remember you, believe it or not, in this very room on this same occasion last year. "Who's that man?" I said to the Tamberley woman and she replied that you were a bore. You were invited, year by year, so the woman said, because of some friendship between the Tamberleys and your father. In the distant past.'

'Look here,' said Raymond, glancing about him and noting to his relief that no one appeared to have heard what Mrs Fitch in her cups had said.

'What's the matter?' demanded Mrs Fitch. Her eyes were again upon her husband and Mrs Anstey. She saw them laugh together and felt her unhappiness being added to as though it were a commodity within her body. 'Oh yes,' she said to Raymond, attempting to pass a bit of the unhappiness on. 'A grinding bore. Those were the words of Mrs Tamberley.'

Raymond shook his head. 'I've known Mrs Tamberley since I was a child,' he said.

'So the woman said. You were invited because of the old friendship: the Tamberleys and your father. I cannot tell a lie, Mr Bamber: she said you were a pathetic case. She said you hadn't learned how to grow up. I dare say you're a pervert.'

'My God!'

'I'm sorry I cannot tell lies,' said Mrs Fitch, and Raymond felt her grip tighten on his jacket. 'It's something that happens to you when you've been through what I've been through. That man up to his tricks with women while the beauty drains from my face. What's it like, d'you think?'

'I don't know,' said Raymond. 'How on earth could I know? Mrs Fitch, let's get one thing clear: I am not a pervert.'

'Not? Are you sure? They may think you are, you know,' said Mrs Fitch, glancing again at her husband. 'Mrs Tamberley has probably suggested that very thing to everyone in this room. Crueller, though, I would have thought, to say you were a grinding bore.'

'I am not a pervert –'

'I can see them sniggering over that all right. Unmentionable happenings between yourself and others. Elderly newspaper-vendors –'

'Stop!' cried Raymond. 'For God's sake, woman –'

'You're not a Jew, are you?'

Raymond did not reply. He stood beside Mrs Fitch, thinking that the woman appeared to be both drunk and not of her right mind. He did not wish to create a scene in the Tamberleys' drawing-room, and yet he recognized that by the look of her she intended to hold on to his jacket for the remainder of the evening. If he attempted to pull it away from her, she would not let go: she did not, somehow, seem to be the kind of woman who would. She wouldn't mind a scene at all.

'Why,' said Mrs Fitch, 'did you all of a sudden begin to tell me about that woman in Streatham, Mr Bamber, and the details about your chair-covers and curtains? Why did you tell me about your uncle dying and trying to leave you a business and your feeling that in your perverted condition you were unfit to run a business?'

Raymond's hands began to shake. He could feel an extra tug on his jacket, as though Mrs Fitch was now insisting that he stand closer to her. He pressed his teeth together, grinding his molars one upon another, and then opened his mouth and felt his teeth and his lips quivering. He knew that his voice would sound strange when he spoke. He said:

'You are being extremely offensive to me, Mrs Fitch. You are a woman who is a total stranger to me, yet you have seen fit to drive me into a corner at a cocktail party and hold me here by force. I must insist that you let go my jacket and allow me to walk away.'

'What about me, Mr Bamber? What about my husband and your Anstey woman? Already they are immoral on a narrow bed somewhere; in a fifth-class hotel near King's Cross station.'

'Your husband is still in this room, Mrs Fitch. As well you know. What your husband does is not my business.'

'Your business is your flat in Bayswater, is it? And curtains and covers from the Sanderson showrooms in Berners Street. Your world is people dying and leaving you stuff in wills – money and prayer-books, and valuable jewellery that you wear when you dress yourself up in nurse's uniform.'

'I must ask you to stop, Mrs Fitch.'

'I could let you have a few pairs of old stockings if they interest you. Or garments of my husband's.'

Mrs Fitch saw Raymond close his eyes. She watched the flesh on his face redden further and watched it twitch in answer to a pulse that throbbed in his neck. There was sweat on his forehead. Her husband, a moment before, had reached out a hand and placed it briefly on the female's arm.

'So your nanny was a guide to you,' said Mrs Fitch. 'You hung on all her words, I dare say?'

Raymond did not reply. He turned his head away, trying to control the twitching in his face. The sweat poured freely now. Eventually he said, quietly and with the suspicion of a stammer:

'She was a good woman. She was kind in every way.'

'She taught you neatness.'

Raymond was aware, as Mrs Fitch spoke that sentence, that she had moved appreciably closer to him. He could feel her knee pressing against his. He felt a second knee, and felt next that his leg had been cleverly caught by her, between her own legs.

'Look here,' said Raymond.

'Yes?'

'Mrs Fitch, what are you trying to do?'

Mrs Fitch increased the pressure of her knees. Her right hand moved into Raymond's jacket pocket. 'I am a little the worse for wear,' she said, 'but I can still tell the truth.'

'You are embarrassing me.'

'What are your perversions? Tell me, Mr Bamber.'

'I have no perversions of any kind. I live a normal life.'

'Shall I come to you with a pram? I'm an unhappy woman, Mr Bamber. I'll wear black woollen stockings. I'll show you those lines on my body.'

'Please,' said Raymond, thinking he would cry in a moment.

Already people were glancing at Mrs Fitch's legs gripping his so strongly. Her white face and her scarlet lips were close to his eyes. He could see the lines on her cheeks, but he turned his glance away from them in case she mentioned again the lines on her body. She is a mad, drunken nymphomaniac, said Raymond to himself, and thought that never in all his life had anything so upsetting happened to him.

'Embrace me,' said Mrs Fitch.

'Please, I beg you,' said Raymond.

'You are a homosexual. A queer. I had forgotten that.'

'I'm not a homosexual,' shouted Raymond, aware that his voice was piercingly shrill. Heads turned and he felt the eyes of the Tamberleys' guests. He had been heard to cry that he was not a homosexual, and people had wished to see for themselves.

'Excuse me,' said a voice. 'I'm sorry about this.'

Raymond turned his head and saw Mrs Fitch's husband standing behind him. 'Come along now, Adelaide,' said Mrs Fitch's husband. 'I'm sorry,' he said again to Raymond. 'I didn't realize she'd had a tankful before she got here.'

'I've been telling him the truth,' said Mrs Fitch. 'We've exchanged life-stories.'

Raymond felt her legs slip away, and he felt her hand withdraw itself from the pocket of his jacket. He nodded in a worldly way at her husband and said in a low voice that he understood how it was.

'He's a most understanding chap,' said Mrs Fitch. 'He has a dead woman in Streatham.'

'Come along now,' ordered her husband in a rough voice, and Raymond saw that the man's hand gripped her arm in a stern manner.

'I was telling that man the truth,' said Mrs Fitch again, seeming to be all of a sudden in an ever greater state of inebriation. Very slowly she said: 'I was telling him what I am and what you are, and what the Tamberleys think about him. It has been home-truths corner here, for the woman with an elderly face and for the chap who likes to dress himself out as a children's nurse and go with women in chauffeur's garb. Actually, my dear, he's a homosexual.'

'Come along now,' said Mrs Fitch's husband. 'I'm truly sorry,' he added to Raymond. 'It's a problem.'

Raymond saw that it was all being conducted in a most civilized manner. Nobody shouted in the Tamberleys' drawing-room, nobody noticed the three of them talking quite quietly in a corner. The Maltese maid in fact, not guessing for a moment that anything was amiss, came up with her tray of drinks and before anyone could prevent it, Mrs Fitch had lifted one to her lips. '*In vino veritas*,' she remarked.

Raymond felt his body cooling down. His shirt was damp with sweat, and he realized that he was panting slightly and he wondered how long that had been going on. He watched Mrs Fitch being aided through the room by her husband. No wonder, he thought, the man had been a little severe with her, if she put up a performance like that very often; no wonder he treated her like an infant. She was little more than an infant, Raymond considered, saying the first thing that came into her head, and going on about sex. He saw her lean form briefly again, through an opening in the crowded room, and he realized without knowing it that he had craned his neck for a last glimpse. She saw him too, as she smiled and bowed at Mrs Tamberley, appearing to be sober and collected. She shook her head at him, deploring him or suggesting, even, that he had been the one who had misbehaved. Her husband raised a hand in the air, thanking Raymond for his understanding.

Raymond edged his way through all the people and went to find a bathroom. He washed his face, taking his spectacles off and placing them beside a piece of lime-green soap. He was thinking that her husband was probably just like any other man at a cocktail party. How could the husband help it, Raymond thought, if he had not aged and if other women found him pleasant to talk to? Did she expect him to have all his hair plucked out and have an expert come to line his face?

Leaning against the wall of the bathroom, Raymond thought about Mrs Fitch. He thought at first that she was a fantastic woman given to fantastic statements, and then he embroidered on the thought and saw her as being more subtle than that. 'By heavens!' said Raymond aloud to himself. She was a woman, he saw, who was pathetic in what she did, transferring the truth about herself to other people. She it was, he guessed, who was the grinding bore, so well known for the fact that she had come to hear the opinion herself and in her unbalanced way sought to pretend that others were bores in order to push the thing away from her. She was probably even, he thought, a little perverted the way in which she had behaved with her knees, and sought to imbue others with this characteristic too, so that she, for the moment, might feel rid of it: Mrs Fitch was clearly a case for a psychiatrist. She had said that her husband was a maniac where women were concerned; she had said that he had taken Mrs Anstey to a bed in King's Cross when Mrs Anstey was standing only yards away, in front of her eyes. *In vino veritas*, she had said, for no reason at all.

One morning, Raymond imagined, poor Mr Fitch had woken up to find his wife gabbling in that utterly crazy manner about her age and her hair and the lines on her body. Probably the woman was a nuisance with people who came to the door, the deliverers of coal and groceries, the milkman and the postman. He imagined the Express Dairy on the telephone to Mrs Fitch's husband, complaining that the entire milk round was daily being disorganized because of the antics of Mrs Fitch, who was a bore with everyone.

It accounted for everything, Raymond thought, the simple fact that the woman was a psychological case. He closed his eyes and sighed with relief, and remembered then that he had read in newspapers about women like Mrs Fitch. He opened his eyes again and looked at himself in the mirror of the Tamberleys' smallest bathroom. He touched his neat moustache with his fingers and smiled at himself to ascertain that his teeth were not carrying a piece of cocktail food. 'You have a tea-leaf on your tooth,' said the voice of Nanny Wilkinson, and Raymond smiled, remembering her.

Raymond returned to the party and stood alone watching the people talking and laughing. His eyes passed from face to face, many of which were familiar to him. He looked for the Griegons with whom last year he had spent quite some time, interesting them in a small sideboard that he had just had french polished, having been left the sideboard in the will of a godmother. The man, a Mr French amusingly enough, had come to Raymond's flat to do the job there in the evenings, having explained that he had no real facilities or premises, being a postman during the day. 'Not that he wasn't an expert polisher,' Raymond had said. 'He did a most beautiful job. I heard of him through Mrs Adams who lives in the flat below. I thought it was reasonable, you know: seven guineas plus expenses. The sideboard came up wonderfully.'

'Hullo,' said Raymond to the Griegons.

'How d'you do?' said Mrs Griegon, a pleasant, smiling woman, not at all like Mrs Fitch. Her husband nodded at Raymond, and turned to a man who was talking busily.

'Our name is Griegon,' said Mrs Griegon. 'This is my husband, and this is Dr Oath.'

'I know,' said Raymond, surprised that Mrs Griegon should say who she was since they had all met so pleasantly a year ago. 'How do you do, Dr Oath?' he said, stretching out a hand.

'Yes,' said Dr Oath, shaking the hand rapidly while continuing his conversation.

Mrs Griegon said: 'You haven't told us your name.'

Raymond, puzzled and looking puzzled, said that his name was Raymond Bamber. 'But surely you remember our nice talk last year?' he said. 'I recall it all distinctly: I was telling you about Mr French who came to polish a sideboard, and how he charged only seven guineas.'

'Most reasonable,' said Mrs Griegon. '*Most* reasonable.'

'We stood over there,' explained Raymond, pointing. 'You and I and Mr Griegon. I remember I gave you my address and telephone number in case if you were ever in Bayswater you might like to pop in to see the sideboard. You said to your husband at the time, Mrs Griegon, that you had one or two pieces that could do with stripping down and polishing, and Mr French, who'll travel anywhere in the evenings, and being, as you say, so reasonable –'

'Of course,' cried Mrs Griegon. 'Of course I remember you perfectly, and I'm sure Archie does too.' She looked at her husband, but her husband was listening carefully to Dr Oath.

Raymond smiled. 'It looks even better now that the initial shine has gone. I'm terribly pleased with it.' As he spoke, he saw the figure of Mrs Fitch's husband entering the room. He watched him glance about and saw him smile at someone he'd seen. Following the direction of this smile, Raymond saw Mrs Anstey smiling back at Mrs Fitch's husband, who at once made his way to her side.

'French polishing's an art,' said Mrs Griegon.

What on earth, Raymond wondered, was the man doing back at the Tamberleys' party? And where was Mrs Fitch? Nervously, Raymond glanced about the crowded room, looking for the black and white dress and the lean aquiline features of the woman who had tormented him. But although, among all the brightly-coloured garments that the women wore there were a few that were black and white, none of them contained Mrs Fitch. 'We come to these parties and everything's a sham,' her voice seemed to say, close to him. 'Nobody tells the truth.' The voice came to him in just the same way as Nanny Wilkinson's had a quarter of an hour ago, when she'd been telling him that he had a tea-leaf on his tooth.

'Such jolly parties,' said Mrs Griegon. 'The Tamberleys are wonderful.'

'Do you know a woman called Mrs Fitch?' said Raymond. 'She was here tonight.'

'Mrs Fitch!' exclaimed Mrs Griegon with a laugh.

'D'you know her?'

'She's married to that man there,' said Mrs Griegon. She pointed at Mr Fitch and sniffed.

'Yes,' said Raymond. 'He's talking to Mrs Anstey.'

He was about to add that Mr Fitch was probably of a social inclination. He was thinking already that Mr Fitch probably had a perfectly sound reason for returning to the Tamberleys'. Probably he lived quite near and having seen his wife home had decided to return in order to say good-bye properly to his hosts. Mrs Anstey, Raymond had suddenly thought, was for all he knew Mr Fitch's sister: in her mentally depressed condition it would have been quite like Mrs Fitch to pretend that the woman in yellow was no relation whatsoever, to have invented a fantasy that was greater even than it appeared to be.

'He's always up to that kind of carry on,' said Mrs Griegon. 'That man's famous for it.'

'Sorry?' said Raymond.

'Fitch. With women.'

'Oh but surely –'

'Really,' said Mrs Griegon.

'I was talking to Mrs Fitch earlier on and she persisted in speaking about her husband. Well, I felt she was going on rather. Exaggerating, you know. A bit of a bore.'

'He has said things to me, Mr Bamber, that would turn your stomach.'

'She has a funny way with her, Mrs Fitch has. She too said the oddest things –'

'She has a reputation,' said Mrs Griegon, 'for getting drunk and coming out with awkward truths. I've heard it said.'

'Not the truth,' Raymond corrected. 'She says things about herself, you see, and pretends she's talking about another person.'

'What?' said Mrs Griegon.

'Like maybe, you see, she was saying that she herself is a bore the way she goes on – well, Mrs Fitch wouldn't say it just like that. What Mrs Fitch would do is pretend some other person is the bore, the person she might be talking to. D'you see? She would transfer all her own qualities to the person she's talking to.'

Mrs Griegon raised her thin eyebrows and inclined her head. She said that what Raymond was saying sounded most interesting.

'An example is,' said Raymond, 'that Mrs Fitch might find herself unsteady on her feet through drink. Instead of saying that she was unsteady she'd say that you, Mrs Griegon, were the unsteady one. There's a name for it, actually. A medical name.'

'Medical?' said Mrs Griegon.

Glancing across the room, Raymond saw that Mr Fitch's right hand gripped Mrs Anstey's elbow. Mr Fitch murmured in her ear and together the two left the room. Raymond saw them wave at Mrs Tamberley, implying thanks with the gesture, implying that they had enjoyed themselves.

'I can't think what it is now,' said Raymond to Mrs Griegon, 'when people transfer the truth about themselves to others. It's some name beginning with an R, I think.'

'How nice of you,' said Mrs Tamberley, gushing up, 'to put that notice in *The Times*.' She turned to Mrs Griegon and said that, as Raymond had probably told her, a lifelong friend of his, old Nanny Wilkinson, had died a few months ago. 'Every year,' said Mrs Tamberley, 'Raymond told us all how she was bearing up. But now, alas, she's died.'

'Indeed,' said Mrs Griegon, and smiled and moved away.

Without any bidding, there arrived in Raymond's mind a picture of Mrs Fitch sitting alone in her house, refilling a glass from a bottle of Gordon's gin. '*In vino veritas*,' said Mrs Fitch, and began to weep.

'I was telling Mrs Griegon that I'd been chatting with Mrs Fitch,' said Raymond, and then he remembered that Mrs Tamberley had very briefly joined in that chat. 'I found her strange,' he added.

'Married to that man,' cried Mrs Tamberley. 'He drove her to it.'

'Her condition?' said Raymond, nodding.

'She ladles it into herself,' said Mrs Tamberley, 'and then tells you what she thinks of you. It can be disconcerting.'

'She really says anything that comes into her head,' said Raymond, and gave a light laugh.

'Not actually,' said Mrs Tamberley. 'She tells the truth.'

'Well, no, you see –'

'You haven't a drink,' cried Mrs Tamberley in alarm, and moved at speed towards her Maltese maid to direct the girl's attention to Raymond's empty glass.

Again the image of Mrs Fitch arrived in Raymond's mind. She sat as before, alone in a room, while her husband made off with a woman in yellow. She drank some gin.

'Sherry, sir?' said the Maltese maid, and Raymond smiled and thanked her, and then, in an eccentric way and entirely on an impulse, he said in a low voice:

'Do you know a woman called Mrs Fitch?'

The girl said that Mrs Fitch had been at the party earlier in the evening, and reminded Raymond that he had in fact been talking to her.

'She has a peculiar way with her,' explained Raymond. 'I just wondered if ever you had talked to her, or had listened to what she herself had to say.' But the Maltese maid shook her head, appearing not to understand.

'Mrs Fitch's a shocker,' said a voice behind Raymond's back, and added: 'That poor man.'

There was a crackle of laughter as a response, and Raymond, sipping his sherry, turned about and moved towards the group that had caused it. The person who had spoken was a small man with shiny grey hair. 'I'm Raymond Bamber,' said Raymond, smiling at him. 'By the sound of things, you saw my predicament earlier on.' He laughed, imitating the laughter that had come from the group. 'Extremely awkward.'

'She gets tight,' said the small man. 'She's liable to tell a home truth or two.' He began to laugh again. '*In vino veritas*,' he said.

Raymond looked at the people and opened his mouth to say that it wasn't quite so simple, the malaise of Mrs Fitch. 'It's all within her,' he wished to say. 'Everything she says is part of Mrs Fitch, since she's unhappy in her marriage and has lost her beauty.' But Raymond checked that speech, uttering in fact not a word of it. The people looked expectantly at him, and after a long pause the small man said:

'Mrs Fitch can be most embarrassing.'

Raymond heard the people laugh again with the same sharpness and saw their teeth for a moment harshly bared and noted that their eyes were like polished ice. They would not understand, he thought, the facts about Mrs Fitch, any more than Mrs Griegon had seemed to understand, or Mrs Tamberley. It surprised Raymond, and saddened him, that neither Mrs Griegon nor Mrs Tamberley had cared to accept the truth about the woman. It was, he told himself, something of a revelation that Mrs Griegon, who had seemed so pleasant the year before, and Mrs Tamberley whom he had known almost all his life, should turn out to be no better than this group of hard-eyed people. Raymond murmured and walked away, still thinking of Mrs Griegon and Mrs Tamberley. He imagined them laughing with their husbands over Mrs Fitch, repeating that she was a bore and a drunk. Laughter was apparently the thing, a commodity that reflected the shallowness of minds too lazy to establish correctly the facts about people. And they were minds, as had been proved to Raymond, that didn't even bother to survey properly the simple explanations of eccentric conduct – as though even that constituted too much trouble.

Soon afterwards, Raymond left the party and walked through the autumn evening, considering everything. The air was cool on his face as he strode towards Bayswater, thinking that as he continued to live his quiet life Mrs Fitch would be attending parties that were similar to the Tamberleys', and she'd be telling the people she met there that they were grinding bores. The people might be offended, Raymond thought, if they didn't pause to think about it, if they didn't understand that everything was confused in poor Mrs Fitch's mind. And it would serve them right, he reflected, to be offended – a just reward for allowing their minds to become lazy and untidy in this modern manner. 'Orderliness,' said the voice of Nanny Wilkinson, and Raymond paused and smiled, and then walked on.

The Hotel of the Idle Moon

The woman called Mrs Dankers placed a rose-tipped cigarette between her lips and lit it from the lighter on the dashboard. The brief spurt of light revealed a long, handsome face with a sharpness about it that might often have been reminiscent of the edge of a chisel. In the darkness a double funnel of smoke streamed from her nostrils, and she gave a tiny gasp of satisfaction. On a grass verge two hundred miles north of London the car was stationary except for the gentle rocking imposed by the wind. Above the persistent lashing of the rain the radio played a popular tune of the Thirties, quietly and without emotion. It was two minutes to midnight.

'Well?'

The car door banged and Dankers was again beside her. He smelt of rain; it dripped from him on to her warm knees.

'Well?' Mrs Dankers repeated.

He started the engine. The car crept on to the narrow highway, its wipers slashing at the rain, its powerful headlights drawing the streaming foliage startlingly near. He cleared the windscreen with his arm. 'It'll do,' he murmured. He drove on slowly, and the sound of the engine was lost in a medley of wind and rain and the murmur of music and the swish of the wipers.

'It'll do?' said Mrs Dankers. 'Is it the right house?'

He twisted the car this way and that along the lane. The lights caught an image of pillars and gates, closed in upon them and lost them as the car swung up the avenue.

'Yes,' he murmured. 'It's the right house.'

Within that house, an old man lying stiffly in bed heard the jangle of the bell at the hall-door and frowned over this unaccustomed sound. At first he imagined that the noise had been caused by the wind, but then the bell rang again, sharply and in a peremptory manner. The old man, called Cronin, the only servant in the house, rose from his bed and dragged an overcoat on to his body, over his pyjamas. He descended the stairs, sighing to himself.

The pair outside saw a light go on in the hall, and then they heard the tread of Cronin's feet and the sound of a bar being pulled back on the door. Dankers threw a cigarette away and prepared an expression for his face. His wife shivered in the rain.

'It's so late,' the old man in pyjamas said when the travellers had told him their tale. 'I must wake the Marstons for guidance, sir. I can't do this on my own responsibility.'

'It's wet and cold as well,' Dankers murmured, smiling at the man through his widely-spread moustache. 'No night to be abroad, really. You must understand our predicament.'

'No night to be standing on a step,' added Mrs Dankers. 'At least may we come in?'

They entered the house and were led to a large drawing-room. 'Please wait,' the man invited. 'The fire is not entirely out. I'll question the Marstons as you warm yourselves.'

The Dankerses did not speak. They stood where the man had left them, staring about the room. Their manner one to the other had an edge of hostility to it, as though they were as suspicious in this relationship as they were of the world beyond it.

'I am Sir Giles Marston,' said another old man. 'You've sustained some travelling difficulty?'

'Our car has let us down – due, I suppose, to some penetration of the weather. We left it by your gates. Sir Giles, we're at your mercy. Dankers the name is. The lady is my good wife.' Dankers stretched his arm towards his host in a manner that might have suggested to an onlooker that he, and not Sir Giles, was the welcomer.

'Our need is simple,' said Mrs Dankers. 'A roof over our heads.'

'Some outhouse maybe,' Dankers hazarded, overplaying his part. He laughed. 'Anywhere we can curl up for an hour or two. We cannot be choosers.'

'I'd prefer a chair,' his wife interceded sharply. 'A chair and a rug would suit me nicely.'

'I'm sure we can do better than that. Prepare two beds, Cronin; and light our guests a fire in their room.'

Sir Giles Marston moved into the centre of the room and in the greater light the Dankerses saw a small, hunched man, with a face like leather that has been stretched for a lifetime and is suddenly slackened; as lined as a map.

'Oh, really,' Dankers protested in his soft voice, 'you mustn't go to such trouble. It's imposition enough to rouse you like this.'

'Are there sheets?' Cronin asked. 'Sheets and bedding: God knows where I shall find them, sir.'

'Brandy,' Sir Giles suggested. 'Am I right, Mrs Dankers, in thinking that strong refreshment would partly answer the situation?'

Cronin left the room, speaking to himself. Sir Giles poured the brandy. 'I'm ninety years of age,' he told his guests, 'but yet aware that inhospitality is a sin to be ashamed of. I bid you good night.'

'Who are they?' Lady Marston asked in the morning, having heard the tale from her husband.

'My dear, they are simply people. They bear some unpleasant name. More than that I do not really wish to know.'

'It's a sunny day by the look of it. Your guests will have breakfasted and gone by now. I'm sorry in a way, for I would welcome fresh faces and a different point of view. We live too quiet a life, Giles. We are too much thrown in upon each other. It's hardly a healthy manner in which to prepare for our dying.'

Sir Giles, who was engaged in the drawing up of his trousers, smiled. 'Had you seen these two, my dear, you would not have said they are the kind to make our going any easier. The man has a moustache of great proportions, the woman you would describe as smart.'

'You're intolerant, love. And so high-handed that you didn't even discover the reason for this visit.'

'They came because they could move in neither direction. Trouble with their motor-car.'

'They've probably left with all our little bits and pieces. You're a sitting bird for a confidence trick. Oh, Giles, Giles!'

Sir Giles departed, and in the breakfast-room below discovered the pair called Dankers still at table.

'Your man has been most generous,' Dankers said. 'He's fed us like trenchermen: porridge, coffee, bacon and eggs. Two for me, one for my good wife. And toast and marmalade. And this delicious butter.'

'Are you trying to say that an essential commodity was lacking? If so, I fear you must be more precise. In this house we are now past subtlety.'

'You've made a fool of yourself,' Mrs Dankers said to her husband. 'Who wishes to know what two strangers have recently digested?'

'Pardon, pardon,' murmured Dankers. 'Sir Giles, forgive a rough diamond!'

'Certainly. If you have finished, please don't delay on my account. Doubtless you are anxious to be on your way.'

'My husband will attend to the car. Probably it's necessary to send for help to a garage. In the meantime I'll keep you company if I may.'

Dankers left the room, passing on the threshold an elderly lady whom he did not address, wishing to appear uncertain in his mind as to her identity.

'This is the woman who came in the night,' Sir Giles said to his wife. 'Her husband is seeing to their motor-car so that they may shortly be on their way. Mrs Dankers, my wife, Lady Marston.'

'We're more than grateful, Lady Marston. It looked as though we were in for a nasty night.'

'I hope Cronin made you comfortable. I fear I slept through everything. "My dear, we have two guests," my husband said to me this morning. You may imagine my surprise.'

Cronin entered and placed plates of food before Sir Giles and Lady Marston.

Conversationally, Mrs Dankers said: 'You have a fine place here.'

'It's cold and big,' Sir Giles replied.

The Marstons set about their breakfast, and Mrs Dankers, unable to think of something to say, sat in silence. The smoke from her cigarette was an irritation to her hosts, but they did not remark on it, since they accepted its presence as part of the woman herself. When he returned Dankers sat beside his wife again. He poured some coffee and said: 'I am no mechanic, Sir Giles. I would like to use your phone to summon help.'

'We are not on the telephone.'

'Not?' murmured Dankers in simulated surprise, for he knew the fact already. 'How far in that case is the nearest village? And does it boast a garage?'

'Three miles. As to the presence of a garage, I have had no cause to establish that point. But I imagine there is a telephone.'

'Giles, introduce me please. Is this man Mrs Dankers' husband?'

'He claims it. Mr Dankers, my wife, Lady Marston.'

'How d'you do?' Dankers said, rising to shake the offered hand. 'I'm afraid we're in a pickle.'

'You should walk it in an hour,' Sir Giles reminded him.

'There's no way of forwarding a message?'

'No.'

'The postman?'

'He hardly ever comes. And then brings only a circular or two.'

'Perhaps your man?'

'Cronin's days as Hermes are over. You must see that surely for yourself?'

'In that case there's nothing for it but a tramp.'

This conclusion of Dankers' was received in silence.

'Walk, Mr Dankers,' Lady Marston said eventually, and added to her husband's dismay, 'and return for lunch. Afterwards you can leave us at your leisure.'

'How kind of you,' the Dankerses said together. They smiled in unison too. They rose and left the room.

Cronin watched and listened to everything. 'Prepare two beds,' his master had said, and from that same moment Cronin had been on his guard. He had given them breakfast the following morning, and had hoped that once they had consumed it they would be on their way. He took them to be commercial travellers, since they had the air of people who were used to moving about and spending nights in places. 'You have a fine place here,' Mrs Dankers had said to the Marstons, and Cronin had narrowed his eyes, wondering why she had said it, wondering why she was sitting there, smoking a cigarette while the Marstons breakfasted. He had examined their motor-car and had thought it somehow typical of the people. They were people, thought Cronin, who would know what to do with all the knobs and gadgets on the motor-car's dashboard; they would take to that dashboard like ducks to water.

For forty-eight years Cronin had lived in the house, serving the Marstons.

Once, there had been other servants, and in his time he had watched over them and over the house itself. Now he contented himself with watching over the Marstons. 'Some outhouse maybe,' Dankers had said, and Cronin had thought that Dankers was not a man who knew much about outhouses. He saw Dankers and Mrs Dankers sitting together in a café connected with a cinema, a place such as he had himself visited twenty-odd years ago and had not cared for. He heard Dankers asking the woman what she would take to eat, adding that he himself would have a mixed grill with chips, and a pot of strong tea, and sliced bread and butter. Cronin observed these people closely and memorized much of what they said.

'Clearly,' Dankers remarked at lunch, 'we're not in training. Or perhaps it was the fascination of your magnificent orchard.'

'Are you saying you didn't walk to the village?' Sir Giles inquired, a trifle impatiently.

'Forgive these city folk,' cried Dankers loudly. 'Quite frankly, we got no distance at all.'

'What are you to do then? Shall you try again this afternoon? There are, of course, various houses on the route. One of them may have a telephone.'

'Your orchard has greatly excited us. I've never seen such trees.'

'They're the finest in England.'

'A pity,' said Mrs Dankers, nibbling at fish on a fork, 'to see it in such rack and ruin.'

Dankers blew upwards into his moustache and ended the activity with a smile. 'It is worth some money, that orchard,' he said.

Sir Giles eyed him coolly. 'Yes, sir; it is worth some money. But time is passing and we are wasting it in conversation. You must see to the affair of your motor-car.'

The storm had brought the apples down. They lay in their thousands in the long grass, damp and glistening, like immense unusual jewels in the afternoon sun. The Dankerses examined them closely, strolling through the orchard, noting the various trees and assessing their yield. For the purpose they had fetched Wellington boots from their car and had covered themselves in waterproof coats of an opaque plastic material. They did not speak, but occasionally, coming across a tree that pleased them, they nodded.

'A lot could be done, you know,' Dankers explained at dinner. 'It is a great orchard and in a mere matter of weeks it could be set on the road to profit and glory.'

'It has had its glory,' replied Sir Giles, 'and probably its profit to. Now it must accept its fate. I cannot keep it up.'

'Oh, it's a shame! A terrible shame to see it as it is. Why, you could make a fortune, Sir Giles.'

'You didn't get to the village?' Lady Marston asked.

'We could not pass the orchard!'

'Which means,' Sir Giles said, 'that you'll be with us for another night.'

'Could you bear it?' Mrs Dankers smiled a thin smile. 'Could you bear to have us all over again?'

'Of course, of course,' said Lady Marston. 'Perhaps tomorrow you'll feel a little stronger. I understand your lethargy. It's natural after an unpleasant experience.'

'They have been through neither flood nor fire,' her husband reminded her. 'And the village will be no nearer tomorrow.'

'Perhaps,' Dankers began gently, 'the postman will call in the morning –'

'We have no living relatives,' Sir Giles cut in, 'and most of our friends are gone. The circulars come once a month or so.'

'The groceries then?'

'I have inquired of Cronin about the groceries. They came yesterday. They will come again next week.'

'The daily milk is left at the foot of the avenue,' Lady Marston suggested. 'Cronin walks to fetch it. You could leave a message there. It is the arrangement we have for emergencies, such as summoning the doctor.'

'The doctor? But surely by the time he got here –?'

'In greater emergency one of the three of us would walk to the nearest house. We do not,' Sir Giles added, 'find it so difficult to pass one leg before the other. Senior though we may be.'

'Perhaps the milk is an idea,' Lady Marston said.

'Oh no, we could never put anyone to so much trouble. It would be too absurd. No, tomorrow we shall have found our feet.'

But tomorrow when it came was a different kind of day, because with something that disagreed with him in his stomach Sir Giles died in the night. His heart was taxed by sharp little spasms of pain and in the end they were too much for it.

'We're going to see to you for a bit,' Mrs Dankers said after the funeral. 'We'll pop you in your room, dear, and Cronin shall attend to all your needs. You can't be left to suffer your loss alone; you've been so kind to us.'

Lady Marston moved her head up and down. The funeral had been rather much for her. Mrs Dankers led her by the arm to her room.

'Well,' said Dankers, speaking to Cronin with whom he was left, 'so that's that.'

'I was his servant for forty-eight years, sir.'

'Indeed, indeed. And you have Lady Marston, to whom you may devote your whole attention. Meals in her room, Cronin, and pause now and then for the occasional chat. The old lady'll be lonely.'

'I'll be lonely myself, sir.'

'Indeed. Then all the more reason to be good company. And you, more than I, understand the business of being elderly. You know by instinct what to say, how best to seem soothing.'

'Your car is repaired, sir? At least it moved today. You'll be on your way? Shall I pack some sandwiches?'

'Come, come, Cronin, how could we leave two lonely people so easily in the lurch? Chance has sent us to your side in this hour of need: we'll stay to do what we can. Besides, there are Sir Giles's wishes.'

What's this? thought Cronin, examining the eyes of the man who had come in the night and had stayed to see his master buried. They were eyes he would not care to possess himself, for fear of what went with them. He said:

'His wishes, sir?'

'That his orchard should again be put in use. The trees repaired and pruned. The fruit sold for its true value. All old man's dying wish won't go unheeded.'

'But, sir, there's so much work in it. The trees run into many hundreds –'

'Quite right, Cronin. That's observant of you. Many men are needed to straighten the confusion and waste. There's much to do.'

'Sir Giles wished this, sir?' said Cronin, playing a part, knowing that Sir Giles would never have passed on to Dankers his dying wish. 'It's unlike him, sir, to think about his orchard. He watched it dying.'

'He wished it, Cronin. He wished it, and a great deal else. You who have seen some changes in your time are in for a couple more. And now, my lad, a glass of that good brandy would not go down amiss. At a time like this one must try to keep one's spirits up.'

Dankers sat by the fire in the drawing-room, sipping his brandy and writing industriously in a notebook. He was shortly joined by his wife, to whom he handed from time to time a leaf from this book so that she might share his plans. When midnight had passed they rose and walked through the house, measuring the rooms with a practised eye and noting their details on paper. They examined the kitchens and outhouses, and in the moonlight they walked the length of the gardens. Cronin watched them, peeping at them in all their activity.

'There's a pretty little room next to Cronin's that is so much sunnier,' Mrs Dankers said. 'Cosier and warmer, dear. We'll have your things moved there, I think. This one is dreary with memories. And you and Cronin will be company for one another.'

Lady Marston nodded, then changing her mind said: 'I like this room. It's big and beautiful and with a view. I've become used to it.'

'Now, now, my dear, we mustn't be morbid, must we? And we don't always quite know what's best. It's good to be happy, dear, and you'll be happier there.'

'I'll be happier, Mrs Dankers? Happier away from all my odds and ends, and Giles's too?'

'My dear, we'll move them with you. Come, now, look on the bright side. There's the future too, as well as the past.'

Cronin came, and the things were moved. Not quite everything though, because the bed and the wardrobe and the heavy dressing-table would not fit into the new setting.

In the orchard half a dozen men set about creating order out of chaos. The trees were trimmed and then treated, paths restored, broken walls rebuilt. The sheds were cleared and filled with fruit-boxes in readiness for next year's harvest.

'There's a wickedness here,' Cronin reported to Lady Marston. 'There's a cook in the kitchen, and a man who waits on them. My only task, they tell me, is to carry your food and keep your room in order.'

'And to see to yourself, Cronin, to take it easy and to watch your rheumatics. Fetch a pack of cards.'

Cronin recalled the house as it once had been, a place that was lively with week-end guests and was regularly wall-papered. Then there had been the years of decline and the drifting towards decay, and now there was a liveliness of a different order; while the days passed by, the liveliness established itself like a season. Mrs Dankers bustled from room to room, in tune with the altered world. Dankers said: 'It's good to see you seeming so sprightly, Cronin. The weather suits you, eh? And now that we've made these few little changes life is easier, I think.' Cronin replied that it was certainly true that he had less to do. 'So you should have less to do,' said Dankers. 'Face the facts: you cannot hope to undertake a young chap's work.' He smiled, to release the remark of its barb.

Cronin was worried about the passive attitude of Lady Marston. She had gone like a lamb to the small room, which now served as her sitting-room and bedroom combined. She had not stirred from the top of the house since the day of the move; she knew nothing save what he told her of all that was happening.

'The builders are here,' he had said; but quite often, midway through a game of cards, she would pause with her head a little to one side, listening to the distant sound of hammering. 'It is the noise of the builders,' he would remind her; and she would place a card on the table and say: 'I did not know that Sir Giles had ordered the builders.' In the morning she was well aware of things, but as the day passed on she spoke more often of Sir Giles; of Sir Giles's plans for the orchard and the house. Cronin feared that, day by day, Lady Marston was sinking into her dotage; the morning hours of her clarity were shrinking even as he thought about it.

One afternoon, walking to the foot of the avenue to stretch his legs, Cronin found a small, elegantly painted board secured to one of the pillars. It faced the road, inviting those who passed to read the words it bore. He read them himself and expostulated angrily, muttering the words, repeating them as he made his way back to the house.

'M'lady, this cannot happen. They've turned your house into an hotel.'

Lady Marston looked at Cronin, whom she had known for so many years, who had seen with her and her husband a thousand details of change and reconstruction. He was upset now, she could see it. His white, sparse hair seemed uncombed, which was unusual for Cronin. There was a blush of temper on his cheeks; and in his eyes a wildness one did not associate with so well-trained a servant.

'What is it, Cronin?'

'There's a notice at the gate announcing "The Hotel of the Idle Moon".'

'Well?'

'The Dankerses –'

'Ah, the Dankerses. You talk so much about the Dankerses, Cronin. Yet as I remember them they are surely not worth it. Sir Giles said the man had repeated to him every mouthful of his breakfast. In the end he had to make short shrift of the pair.'

'No, no –'

'Yes, Cronin: they tried his patience. He gave them their marching orders, reminding them that the night was fine and the moon was full. There was a coolness between us, for I believed he had gone too far.'

'No, no. You must remember: the Dankerses are still here. They've tidied up the orchard and now have turned your house into an hotel.'

Lady Marston made her impatient little shaking of the head. 'Of course, of course. Cronin, I apologize. You must find me very trying.'

'It has no meaning: The Hotel of the Idle Moon. Yet I fear, m'lady, it may in time mean much to us.'

Lady Marston laughed quite gaily. 'Few things have meaning, Cronin. It is rather much to expect a meaning for everything.'

They played three games of cards, and the matter was not again referred to. But in the night Lady Marston came to Cronin's bedside and shook him by the shoulder. 'I'm upset,' she said, 'by what you tell me. This isn't right at all. Cronin, listen carefully: tomorrow you must inform Sir Giles. Tell him of our fears. Beg him to reconsider. I'm far too old to act. I must leave it all to you.'

The house was busy then with visitors, and cars up and down the avenue. It thrived as the orchard thrived; it had a comfortable and sumptuous feel, and Cronin thought again of the past.

'Ah, Cronin,' Mrs Dankers said, pausing on the back stairs one day. 'Tell me, how is poor Lady Marston? She does not come down at all, and we're so on the go here that it's hard to find time to make the journey to the top of the house.'

'Lady Marston is well, madam.'

'She's welcome in the lounges. Always welcome. Would you be good enough to tell her, Cronin?'

'Yes, madam.'

'But keep an eye on her, like a good man. I would not like her upsetting the guests. You understand?'

'Yes, madam. I understand. I don't think Lady Marston is likely to make use of the lounges.'

'She would find the climb up and down too much, I dare say.'

'Yes, madam. She would find it too much.'

Cronin made many plans. He thought that one day when Dankers was away he would approach the orchard with Sir Giles's rifle and order the men to cut down the trees. That at least would bring one part of the sadness to an end. He saw the scene quite clearly: the trees toppling one against the other, their branches webbed as they hung in the air above the fresh stumps. But when he searched for the rifle he could not find it. He thought that he might wreak great damage in the house, burning carpets and opening up the upholstery. But for this he found neither opportunity nor the strength it demanded. Stropping his razor one morning, he hit upon the best plan of all: to creep into the Dankerses' bedroom and cut their throats. It had once been his master's bedroom and now it was theirs; which made revenge the sweeter. Every day for forty-eight years he had carried to the room a tray of teacups and a pot of Earl Grey tea. Now he would carry his sharpened razor; and for the rest of his life he would continue his shaving with it, relishing every scrape. The idea delighted him. Sir Giles would have wished to see the last of them, to see the last of all these people who strayed about the house and grounds, and to see the orchard settle down again to being the orchard he had left behind. And was not he, Cronin, the living agent of the dead Sir Giles? Was he not now companion to his wife? And did she not, in an occasional moment of failure, address him as she had her husband? Yet when he shared his plans with Lady Marston she did not at all endorse them.

'Take the will for the deed, Cronin. Leave these people be.'

'But they are guilty. They may have killed Sir Giles.'

'They may have. And does it matter this way or that – to chop off a few dwindling years?'

Cronin saw no reason in her words. He pitied her, and hardened himself in his resolve.

'I am sorry to speak to you like this, Cronin,' Dankers said, 'but I cannot, you know, have you wandering about the house in this manner. There have been complaints from the guests. You have your room, with Lady Marston to talk with; why not keep more to the region we have set aside for you?'

'Yes, sir.'

'Of late, Cronin, you've become untidy in your appearance. You have a dishevelled look and often seem – well, frankly, Cronin, dirty. It's not good for business. Not good at all.'

The moon shall not be idle, Cronin thought. The moon shall be agog to see. The moon shall clear the sky of clouds that the stars may ponder on the pillows full of blood.

'Mr Dankers, sir, why is this place called the Idle Moon?'

Dankers laughed. 'A foible of my good wife's. She liked the sound of it. Quite telling, don't you think?'

'Yes, sir.' The moon shall like the sound of her. A shriek in a severed throat, a howl of pain.

'See to it, Cronin, eh?'

'Yes, sir.'

So Cronin kept to his room, descending the back stairs only for his food and Lady Marston's. The weeks passed, and more and more he sat entranced with the duty he had set himself. Sometimes, as though drunk with it, he found himself a little uncertain as to its exactitudes. That was when he felt tired; when he dropped off into a doze as he sat by his small window, staring at the sky and listening to the faraway hum from the house below.

Then one morning Cronin discovered that Lady Marston had died in her sleep. They carried her off, and he put away the pack of cards.

'It's a sad day for us all,' Dankers said, and in the distance Cronin could hear Mrs Dankers giving some brisk order to a servant. He returned to his room and for a moment there was an oddness in his mind and he imagined that it was Sir Giles who had said that the day was sad. Then he remembered that Sir Giles was dead too and that he was the only one left.

In the months that followed he spoke to no one but himself, for he was concentrating on the details of his plan. They kept slipping away, and increasingly he had a struggle to keep them straight.

When the razor was there the faces on the pillows were vague and empty, and he could not remember whose he had planned they should be. There was the pattern of moonlight, and the red stain on the bed-clothes, but Cronin could not often now see what any of it meant. It made him tired, thinking the trouble out. And when, in the end, the shreds of his plan came floating back to him he smiled in some astonishment, seeing only how absurd it had been that late in his life he should have imagined himself a match for the world and its conquerors.

Miss Smith

One day Miss Smith asked James what a baby horse was called and James couldn't remember. He blinked and shook his head. He knew, he explained, but he just couldn't remember. Miss Smith said:

'Well, well, James Machen doesn't know what a baby horse is called.'

She said it loudly so that everyone in the classroom heard. James became very confused. He blinked and said:

'Pony, Miss Smith?'

'Pony! James Machen says a baby horse is a pony! Hands up everyone who knows what a baby horse is.'

All the right arms in the room, except James's and Miss Smith's, shot upwards. Miss Smith smiled at James.

'Everyone knows,' she said. 'Everyone knows what a baby horse is called except James.'

James thought: 'I'll run away. I'll join the tinkers and live in a tent.'

'What's a baby horse called?' Miss Smith asked the class and the class shouted:

'Foal, Miss Smith.'

'A foal, James,' Miss Smith repeated. 'A baby horse is a foal, James dear.'

'I knew, Miss Smith. I knew but –'

Miss Smith laughed and the class laughed, and afterwards nobody would play with James because he was so silly to think that a baby horse was a pony.

James was an optimist about Miss Smith. He thought it might be different when the class went on the summer picnic or sat tightly together at the Christmas party, eating cake and biscuits and having their mugs filled from big enamel jugs. But it never was different. James got left behind when everyone was racing across the fields at the picnic and Miss Smith had to wait impatiently, telling the class that James would have to have his legs stretched. And at the party she heaped his plate with seed-cake because she imagined, so she said, that he was the kind of child who enjoyed such fare.

Once James found himself alone with Miss Smith in the classroom. She was sitting at her desk correcting some homework. James was staring in front of him, admiring a fountain pen that the day before his mother had bought for him. It was a small fountain pen, coloured purple and black and white. James believed it to be elegant.

It was very quiet in the classroom. Soundlessly Miss Smith's red pencil ticked and crossed and underlined. Without looking up, she said: 'Why don't you go out and play?'

'Yes, Miss Smith,' said James. He walked to the door, clipping his pen into his pocket. As he turned the handle he heard Miss Smith utter a sound of irritation. He turned and saw that the point of her pencil had broken. 'Miss Smith, you may borrow my pen. You can fill it with red ink. It's quite a good pen.'

James crossed the room and held out his pen. Miss Smith unscrewed the cap and prodded at the paper with the nib. 'What a funny pen, James!' she said. 'Look, it can't write.'

'There's no ink in it,' James explained. 'You've got to fill it with red ink, Miss Smith.'

But Miss Smith smiled and handed the pen back. 'What a silly boy you are to waste your money on such a poor pen!'

'But I didn't –'

'Come along now, James, aren't you going to lend me your pencil-sharpener?'

'I haven't got a pencil-sharpener, Miss Smith.'

'No pencil-sharpener? Oh James, James, you haven't got anything, have you?'

When Miss Smith married she stopped teaching, and James imagined he had escaped her for ever. But the town they lived in was a small one and they often met in the street or in a shop. And Miss Smith, who at first found marriage rather boring, visited the school quite regularly. 'How's James?' she would say, smiling alarmingly at him. 'How's my droopy old James?'

When Miss Smith had been married for about a year she gave birth to a son, which occupied her a bit. He was a fine child, eight pounds six ounces, with a good long head and blue eyes. Miss Smith was delighted with him, and her husband, a solicitor, complimented her sweetly and bought cigars and drinks for all his friends. In time, mother and son were seen daily taking the air: Miss Smith on her trim little legs and the baby in his frilly pram. James, meeting the two, said: 'Miss Smith, may I see the baby?' But Miss Smith laughed and said that she was not Miss Smith any more. She wheeled the pram rapidly away, as though the child within it might be affected by the proximity of the other.

'What a dreadful little boy that James Machen is,' Miss Smith reported to her husband. 'I feel so sorry for the parents.'

'Do I know him? What does the child look like?'

'Small, dear, like a weasel wearing glasses. He quite gives me the creeps.'

Almost without knowing it, James developed a compulsion about Miss Smith. At first it was quite a simple compulsion: just that James had to talk to God about Miss Smith every night before he went to sleep, and try to find out from God what it was about him that Miss Smith so despised.

Every night he lay in bed and had his conversation, and if once he forgot it James knew that the next time he met Miss Smith she would probably say something that might make him drop down dead.

After about a month of conversation with God James discovered he had found the solution. It was so simple that he marvelled he had never thought of it before. He began to get up very early in the morning and pick bunches of flowers. He would carry them down the street to Miss Smith's house and place them on a window-sill. He was careful not to be seen, by Miss Smith or by anyone else. He knew that if anyone saw him the plan couldn't work. When he had picked all the flowers in his own garden he started to pick them from other people's gardens. He became rather clever at moving silently through the gardens, picking flowers for Miss Smith.

Unfortunately, though, on the day that James carried his thirty-first bunch of blooms to the house of Miss Smith he was observed. He saw the curtains move as he reached up to lay the flowers on the window-sill. A moment later Miss Smith, in her dressing-gown, had caught him by the shoulder and pulled him into the house.

'James Machen! It would be James Machen, wouldn't it? Flowers from the creature, if you please! What are you up to, you dozy James?'

James said nothing. He looked at Miss Smith's dressing-gown and thought it was particularly pretty: blue and woolly, with an edging of silk.

'You've been trying to get us into trouble,' cried Miss Smith. 'You've been stealing flowers all over the town and putting them at our house. You're an underhand child, James.'

James stared at her and then ran away.

After that, James thought of Miss Smith almost all the time. He thought of her face when she had caught him with the flowers, and how she had afterwards told his father and nearly everyone else in the town. He thought of how his father had had to say he was sorry to Miss Smith, and how his mother and father had quarrelled about the affair. He counted up all the things Miss Smith had ever said to him, and all the things she had ever done to him, like giving him seed-cake at the Christmas party. He hadn't meant to harm Miss Smith, as she said he had. Giving people flowers wasn't unkind; it was to show them you liked them and wanted them to like you.

'When somebody hurts you,' James said to the man who came to cut the grass, 'what do you do about it?'

'Well,' said the man, 'I suppose you hurt them back.'

'Supposing you can't,' James argued.

'Oh, but you always can. It's easy to hurt people.'

'It's not, really,' James said.

'Look,' said the man, 'all I've got to do is to reach out and give you a clip on the ear. That'd hurt you.'

'But I couldn't do that to you because you're too big. How d'you hurt someone who's bigger than you?'

'It's easier to hurt people who are weaker. People who are weaker are always the ones who get hurt.'

'Can't you hurt someone who is stronger?'

The grass-cutter thought for a time. 'You have to be cunning to do that. You've got to find the weak spot. Everyone has a weak spot.'

'Have you got a weak spot?'

'I suppose so.'

'Could I hurt you on your weak spot?'

'You don't want to hurt me, James.'

'No, but just could I?'

'Yes, I suppose you could.'

'Well then?'

'My little daughter's smaller than you. If you hurt her, you see, you'd be hurting me. It'd be the same, you see.'

'I see,' said James.

All was not well with Miss Smith. Life, which had been so happy when her baby was born, seemed now to be directed against her. Perhaps it was that the child was becoming difficult, going through a teething phase that was pleasant for no one; or perhaps it was that Miss Smith recognized in him some trait she disliked and knew that she would be obliged to watch it develop, powerless to intervene. Whatever the reason, she felt depressed. She often thought of her teaching days, of the big square schoolroom with the children's models on the shelves and the pictures of kings on the walls. Nostalgically, she recalled the feel of frosty air on her face as she rode her bicycle through the town, her mind already practising the first lesson of the day. She had loved those winter days: the children stamping their feet in the playground, the stove groaning and crackling, so red and so fierce that it had to be penned off for safety's sake. It had been good to feel tired, good to bicycle home, shopping a bit on the way, home to tea and the wireless and an evening of reading by the fire. It wasn't that she regretted anything; it was just that now and again, for a day or two, she felt she would like to return to the past.

'My dear,' Miss Smith's husband said, 'you really will have to be more careful.'

'But I am. Truly I am. I'm just as careful as anyone can be.'

'Of course you are. But it's a difficult age. Perhaps, you know, you need a holiday.'

'But I've had difficult ages to deal with for years –'

'Now now, my dear, it's not quite the same, teaching a class of kids.'

'But it shouldn't be as difficult. I don't know –'

'You're tired. Tied to a child all day long, every day of the week, it's no joke. We'll take an early holiday.'

Miss Smith did feel tired, but she knew that it wasn't tiredness that was really the trouble. Her baby was almost three, and for two years she knew she had been making mistakes with him. Yet somehow she felt that they weren't her mistakes: it was as though some other person occasionally possessed her: a negligent, worthless kind of person who was cruel, almost criminal, in her carelessness. Once she had discovered the child crawling on the pavement beside his pram: she had forgotten apparently to attach his harness to the pram hooks. Once there had been beads in his pram, hundreds of them, small and red and made of glass. A woman had drawn her attention to the danger, regarding curiously the supplier of so unsuitable a plaything. 'In his nose he was putting one, dear. And may have swallowed a dozen already. It could kill a mite, you know.' The beads were hers, but how the child had got them she could not fathom. Earlier, when he had been only a couple of months, she had come into his nursery to find an excited cat scratching at the clothes of his cot; and on another occasion she had found him eating a turnip. She wondered if she might be suffering from some kind of serious absent-mindedness, or blackouts. Her doctor told her, uncomfortingly, that she was a little run down.

'I'm a bad mother,' said Miss Smith to herself; and she cried as she looked at her child, warm and pretty in his sleep.

But her carelessness continued and people remarked that it was funny in a teacher. Her husband was upset and unhappy, and finally suggested that they should employ someone to look after the child. 'Someone else?' said Miss Smith. 'Someone *else*? Am I then incapable? Am I so wretched and stupid that I cannot look after my own child? You speak to me as though I were half crazy.' She felt confused and sick and miserable. The marriage teetered beneath the tension, and there was no question of further children.

Then there were two months without incident. Miss Smith began to feel better; she was getting the hang of things; once again she was in control of her daily life. Her child grew and flourished. He trotted nimbly beside her, he spoke his own language, he was wayward and irresponsible, and to Miss Smith and her husband he was intelligent and full of charm. Every day Miss Smith saved up the sayings and doings of this child and duly reported them to her husband. 'He is quite intrepid,' Miss Smith said, and she told her husband how the child would tumble about the room, trying to stand on his head. 'He has an aptitude for athletics,' her husband remarked. They laughed that they, so unathletic in their ways, should have produced so physically lively an offspring.

'And how has our little monster been today?' Miss Smith's husband asked, entering the house one evening at his usual time.

Miss Smith smiled, happy after a good, quiet day. 'Like gold,' she said.

Her husband smiled too, glad that the child had not been a nuisance to her and glad that his son, for his own sake, was capable of adequate behaviour. 'I'll just take a peep at him,' he announced, and he ambled off to the nursery.

He sighed with relief as he climbed the stairs, thankful that all was once again well in the house. He was still sighing when he opened the nursery door and smelt gas. It hissed insidiously from the unlit fire. The room was sweet with it. The child, sleeping, sucked it into his lungs.

The child's face was blue. They carried him from the room, both of them helpless and inadequate in the situation. And then they waited, without speaking, while his life was recovered, until the moment when the doctor, white-coated and stern, explained that it had been a nearer thing than he would wish again to handle.

'This is too serious,' Miss Smith's husband said. 'We cannot continue like this. Something must be done.'

'I cannot understand –'

'It happens too often. The strain is too much for me, dear.'

Every precaution had been taken with the gas-fire in the nursery. The knob that controlled the gas pressure was a key and the key was removable. Certainly, the control point was within the child's reach but one turned it on or off, slipped the key out of its socket and placed it on the mantelpiece. That was the simple rule.

'You forgot to take out the key,' Miss Smith's husband said. In his mind an idea took on a shape that frightened him. He shied away, watching it advance, knowing that he possessed neither the emotional nor mental equipment to fight it.

'No, no, no,' Miss Smith said. 'I never forget it. I turned the fire off and put the key on the mantelpiece. I remember distinctly.'

He stared at her, drilling his eyes into hers, hopelessly seeking the truth. When he spoke his voice was dry and weary.

'The facts speak for themselves. You cannot suggest there's another solution?'

'But it's absurd. It means he got out of his cot, turned the key, returned to bed and went to sleep.'

'Or that you turned off the fire and idly turned it on again.'

'I couldn't have; how could I?'

Miss Smith's husband didn't know. His imagination, like a pair of calipers, grasped the ugly thought and held it before him. The facts were on its side, he could not ignore them: his wife was deranged in her mind. Consciously or otherwise she was trying to kill their child.

'The window,' Miss Smith said. 'It was open when I left it. It always is, for air. Yet you found it closed.'

'The child certainly could not have done that. I cannot see what you are suggesting.'

'I don't know. I don't know what I'm suggesting. Except that I don't understand.'

'He is too much for you, dear, and that's all there is to it. You must have help.'

'We can't afford it.'

'Be that as it may, we must. We have the child to think of, if not ourselves.'

'But one child! One child cannot be too much for anyone. Look, I'll be extra careful in future. After all, it is the first thing like this that has happened for ages.'

'I'm sorry, dear. We must advertise for a woman.'

'Please –'

'Darling, I'm sorry. It's no use talking. We have talked enough and it has got us nowhere. This is something to be sensible about.'

'Please let's try again.'

'And in the meanwhile? In the meanwhile our child's life must be casually risked, day in, day out?'

'No, no.'

Miss Smith pleaded, but her husband said nothing further. He pulled hard on his pipe, biting it between his jaws, unhappy and confused in his mind.

Miss Smith's husband did indeed advertise for a woman to see to the needs of their child, but it was, in fact, unnecessary in the long run to employ one. Because on his third birthday, late in the afternoon, the child disappeared. Miss Smith had put him in the garden. It was a perfectly safe garden: he played there often. Yet when she called him in for his tea he did not come; and when she looked for the reason she found that he was not there. The small gate that led to the fields at the back of the house was open. She had not opened it; she rarely used it. Distractedly, she thought he must have managed to release the catch himself. 'That is quite impossible,' her husband said. 'It's too high and too stiff.' He looked at her oddly, confirmed in his mind that she wished to be rid of her child. Together they tramped the fields with the police, but although they covered a great area and were out for most of the night they were unsuccessful.

When the search continued in the light of the morning it was a search without hope, and the hopelessness in time turned into the fear of what discovery would reveal. 'We must accept the facts,' Miss Smith's husband said, but she alone continued to hope. She dragged her legs over the wide countryside, seeking a miracle but finding neither trace nor word of her child's wanderings.

A small boy, so quiet she scarcely noticed him, stopped her once by a sawmill. He spoke some shy salutation, and when she blinked her eyes at his face she saw that he was James Machen. She passed him by, thinking only that she envied him his life, that for him to live and her child to die was proof indeed of a mocking Providence. She prayed to this Providence, promising a score of resolutions if only all would be well.

But nothing was well, and Miss Smith brooded on the thought that her husband had not voiced. *I released the gate myself. For some reason I have not wanted this child. God knows I loved him, and surely it wasn't too weak a love? Is it that I've loved so many other children that I have none left that is real enough for my own?* Pathetic, baseless theories flooded into Miss Smith's mind. Her thoughts floundered and collapsed into wretched chaos.

'Miss Smith,' James said, 'would you like to see your baby?'

He stood at her kitchen door, and Miss Smith, hearing the words, was incapable immediately of grasping their meaning. The sun, reflected in the kitchen, was mirrored again in the child's glasses. He smiled at her, more confidently than she remembered, revealing a silvery wire stretched across his teeth.

'What did you say?' Miss Smith asked.

'I said, would you like to see your baby?'

Miss Smith had not slept for a long time. She was afraid to sleep because of the nightmares. Her hair hung lank about her shoulders, her eyes were dead and seemed to have fallen back deeper into her skull. She stood listening to this child, nodding her head up and down, very slowly, in a mechanical way. Her left hand moved gently back and forth on the smooth surface of her kitchen table.

'My baby?' Miss Smith said. 'My baby?'

'You have lost your baby,' James reminded her.

Miss Smith nodded a little faster.

'I will show you,' James said.

He caught her hand and led her from the house, through the garden and through the gate into the fields. Hand in hand they walked through the grass, over the canal bridge and across the warm, ripe meadows.

'I will pick you flowers,' James said and he ran to gather poppies and cowparsley and blue, beautiful corn-flowers.

'You give people flowers,' James said, 'because you like them and you want them to like you.'

She carried the flowers and James skipped and danced beside her, hurrying her along. She heard him laughing; she looked at him and saw his small weasel face twisted into a merriment that frightened her.

The sun was fierce on Miss Smith's neck and shoulders. Sweat gathered on her forehead and ran down her cheeks. She felt it on her body, tightening her clothes to her back and thighs. Only the child's hand was cool, and beneath her fingers she assessed its strength, wondering about its history. Again the child laughed.

On the heavy air his laughter rose and fell; it quivered through his body and twitched lightly in his hand. It came as a giggle, then a breathless spasm; it rose like a storm from him; it rippled to gentleness; and it pounded again like the firing of guns in her ear. It would not stop. She knew it would not stop. As they walked together on this summer's day the laughter would continue until they arrived at the horror, until the horror was complete.

*The Ballroom of Romance
and Other Stories*

Access to the Children

Malcolmson, a fair, tallish man in a green tweed suit that required pressing, banged the driver's door of his ten-year-old Volvo and walked quickly away from the car, jangling the keys. He entered a block of flats that was titled – gold engraved letters on a granite slab – The Quadrant.

It was a Sunday afternoon in late October. Yellow-brown leaves patterned grass that was not for walking on. Some scurried on the steps that led to the building's glass entrance doors. Rain was about, Malcolmson considered.

At three o'clock precisely he rang the bell of his ex-wife's flat on the third floor. In response he heard at once the voices of his children and the sound of their running in the hall. 'Hullo,' he said when one of them, Deirdre, opened the door. 'Ready?'

They went with him, two little girls, Deirdre seven and Susie five. In the lift they told him that a foreign person, the day before, had been trapped in the lift from eleven o'clock in the morning until teatime. Food and cups of tea had been poked through a grating to this person, a Japanese businessman who occupied a flat at the top of the block. 'He didn't get the hang of an English lift,' said Deirdre. 'He could have died there,' said Susie.

In the Volvo he asked them if they'd like to go to the Zoo and they shook their heads firmly. On the last two Sundays he'd taken them to the Zoo, Susie reminded him in her specially polite, very quiet voice: you got tired of the Zoo, walking round and round, looking at all the same animals. She smiled at him to show she wasn't being ungrateful. She suggested that in a little while, after a month or so, they could go to the Zoo again, because there might be some new animals. Deirdre said that there wouldn't be, not after a month or so: why should there be? 'Some old animals might have died,' said Susie.

Malcolmson drove down the Edgware Road, with Hyde Park in mind.

'What have you done?' he asked.

'Only school,' said Susie.

'And the news cinema,' said Deirdre. 'Mummy took us to a news cinema. We saw a film about how they make wire.'

'A man kept talking to Mummy. He said she had nice hair.'

'The usherette told him to be quiet. He bought us ice-creams, but Mummy said we couldn't accept them.'

'He wanted to take Mummy to a dance.'

'We had to move to other seats.'

'What else have you done?'

'Only school,' said Susie. 'A boy was sick on Miss Bawden's desk.'

'After school stew.'

'It's raining,' said Susie.

He turned the windscreen-wipers on. He wondered if he should simply bring the girls to his flat and spend the afternoon watching television. He tried to remember what the Sunday film was. There often was something suitable for children on Sunday afternoons, old films with Deanna Durbin or Nelson Eddy and Jeanette MacDonald.

'Where're we going?' Susie asked.

'Where d'you want to go?'

'*A Hundred and One Dalmatians.*'

'Oh, please,' said Susie.

'But we've seen it. We've seen it five times.'

'Please, Daddy.'

He stopped the Volvo and bought a *What's On*. While he leafed through it they sat quietly, willing him to discover a cinema, anywhere in London, that was showing the film. He shook his head and started the Volvo again.

'Nothing else?' Deirdre asked.

'Nothing suitable.'

At Speakers' Corner they listened to a Jehovah's Witness and then to a woman talking about vivisection. 'How horrid,' said Deirdre. 'Is that true, Daddy?' He made a face. 'I suppose so,' he said.

In the drizzle they played a game among the trees, hiding and chasing one another. Once when they'd been playing this game a woman had brought a policeman up to him. She'd seen him approaching the girls, she said; the girls had been playing alone and he'd joined in. 'He's our daddy,' Susie had said, but the woman had still argued, claiming that he'd given them sweets so that they'd say that. 'Look at him,' the woman had insultingly said. 'He needs a shave.' Then she'd gone away, and the policeman had apologized.

'The boy who was sick was Nicholas Barnet,' Susie said. 'I think he could have died.'

A year and a half ago Malcolmson's wife, Elizabeth, had said he must choose between her and Diana. For weeks they had talked about it; she knowing that he was in love with Diana and was having some kind of an affair with her, he caught between the two of them, attempting the impossible in his effort not to hurt anyone. She had given him a chance to get over Diana, as she put it, but she couldn't go on for ever giving him a chance, no woman could. In the end, after the shock and the tears and the period of reasonableness, she became bitter. He didn't blame her: they'd been in the middle of a happy marriage, nothing was wrong, nothing was lacking.

He'd met Diana on a train; he'd sat with her, talking for a long time, and after that his marriage didn't seem the same. In her bitterness Elizabeth said he was stupidly infatuated: he was behaving like a murderer: there was neither dignity nor humanity left in him. Diana she described as a flat-chested American nymphomaniac and predator, the worst type of woman in the world. She was beautiful herself, more beautiful than Diana, more gracious, warmer, and funnier: there was a sting of truth in what she said; he couldn't understand himself. In the very end, after they'd been morosely drinking gin and lime-juice, she'd suddenly shouted at him that he'd better pack his bags. He sat unhappily, gazing at the green bottle of Gordon's gin on the carpet between his chair and hers. She screamed; tears poured in a torrent from her eyes. 'For God's sake go away,' she cried, on her feet, turning away from him. She shook her head in a wild gesture, causing her long fair hair to move like a horse's mane. Her hands, clenched into fists, beat at his cheeks, making bruises that Diana afterwards tended.

For months after that he saw neither Elizabeth nor his children. He tried not to think about them. He and Diana took a flat in Barnes, near the river, and in time he became used to the absence of the children's noise in the mornings, and to Diana's cooking and her quick efficiency in little things, and the way she always remembered to pass on telephone messages, which was something that Elizabeth had always forgotten to do.

Then one day, a week or so before the divorce was due, Diana said she didn't think there was anything left between them. It hadn't worked, she said; nothing was quite right. Amazed and bewildered, he argued with her. He frowned at her, his eyes screwed up as though he couldn't properly see her. She was very poised, in a black dress, with a necklace at her throat, her hair pulled smooth and neatly tied. She'd met a man called Abbotforth, she said, and she went on talking about that, still standing.

'We could go to the Natural History Museum,' Deirdre said.

'Would you like to, Susie?'

'Certainly not,' said Susie.

They were sitting on a bench, watching a bird that Susie said was a yellow-hammer. Deirdre disagreed: at this time of year, she said, there were no yellow-hammers in England, she'd read it in a book. 'It's a little baby yellow-hammer,' said Susie. 'Miss Bawden said you see lots of them.'

The bird flew away. A man in a raincoat was approaching them, singing quietly. They began to giggle. 'Sure, maybe some day I'll go back to Ireland,' sang the man, 'if it's only at the closing of my day.' He stopped, noticing that they were watching him.

'Were you ever in Ireland?' he asked. The girls, still giggling, shook their heads. 'It's a great place,' said the man. He took a bottle of VP wine from his raincoat pocket and drank from it.

'Would you care for a swig, sir?' he said to Malcolmson, and Malcolmson thanked him and said he wouldn't. 'It would do the little misses no harm,' suggested the man. 'It's good, pure stuff.' Malcolmson shook his head. 'I was born in County Clare,' said the man, 'in 1928, the year of the Big

Strike.' The girls, red in the face from containing their laughter, poked at one another with their elbows. 'Aren't they the great little misses?' said the man. 'Aren't they the fine credit to you, sir?'

In the Volvo on the way to Barnes they kept repeating that he was the funniest man they'd ever met. He was nicer than the man in the news cinema, Susie said. He was quite like him, though, Deirdre maintained: he was looking for company in just the same way, you could see it in his eyes. 'He was staggering,' Susie said. 'I thought he was going to die.'

Before the divorce he had telephoned Elizabeth, telling her that Diana had gone. She hadn't said anything, and she'd put the receiver down before he could say anything else. Then the divorce came through and the arrangement was that the children should remain with Elizabeth and that he should have reasonable access to them. It was an extraordinary expression, he considered: reasonable access.

The Sunday afternoons had begun then, the ringing of a doorbell that had once been his own doorbell, the children in the hall, the lift, the Volvo, tea in the flat where he and Diana had lived and where now he lived on his own. Sometimes, when he was collecting them, Elizabeth spoke to him, saying in a matter-of-fact way that Susie had a cold and should not be outside too much, or that Deirdre was being bad about practising her clarinet and would he please speak to her. He loved Elizabeth again; he said to himself that he had never not loved her; he wanted to say to her that she'd been right about Diana. But he didn't say anything, knowing that wounds had to heal.

Every week he longed more for Sunday to arrive. Occasionally he invented reasons for talking to her at the door of the flat, after the children had gone in. He asked questions about their progress at school, he wondered if there were ways in which he could help. It seemed unfair, he said, that she should have to bring them up single-handed like this; he made her promise to telephone him if a difficulty arose; and if ever she wanted to go out in the evenings and couldn't find a baby-sitter, he'd willingly drive over. He always hoped that if he talked for long enough the girls would become so noisy in their room that she'd be forced to ask him in so that she could quieten them, but the ploy never worked.

In the lift on the way down every Sunday evening he thought she was more beautiful than any woman he'd ever seen, and he thought it was amazing that once she should have been his wife and should have borne him children, that once they had lain together and loved, and that he had let her go. Three weeks ago she had smiled at him in a way that was like the old way. He'd been sure of it, positive, in the lift on the way down.

He drove over Hammersmith Bridge, along Castelnau and into Barnes High Street. No one was about on the pavements; buses crept sluggishly through the damp afternoon.

'Miss Bawden's got a black boy-friend,' Susie said, 'called Eric Mantilla.'

'You should see Miss Bawden,' murmured Deirdre. 'She hasn't any breasts.'

'She has lovely breasts,' shouted Susie, 'and lovely jumpers and lovely skirts. She has a pair of earrings that once belonged to an Egyptian empress.'

'As flat as a pancake,' said Deirdre.

After Diana had gone he'd found it hard to concentrate. The managing director of the firm where he worked, a man with a stout red face called Sir Gerald Travers, had been sympathetic. He'd told him not to worry. Personal troubles, Sir Gerald had said, must naturally affect professional life; no one would be human if that didn't happen. But six months later, to Malcolmson's surprise, Sir Gerald had suddenly suggested to him that perhaps it would be better if he made a move. 'It's often so,' Sir Gerald had said, a soft smile gleaming between chubby cheeks. 'Professional life can be affected by the private side of things. You understand me, Malcolmson?' They valued him immensely, Sir Gerald said, and they'd be generous when the moment of departure came. A change was a tonic; Sir Gerald advised a little jaunt somewhere.

In reply to all that Malcolmson said that the upset in his private life was now over; nor did he feel, he added, in need of recuperation. 'You'll easily find another berth,' Sir Gerald Travers replied, with a wide, confident smile. 'I think it would be better.'

Malcolmson had sought about for another job, but had not been immediately successful: there was a recession, people said. Soon it would be better, they added, and because of Sir Gerald's promised generosity Malcolmson found himself in a position to wait until things seemed brighter. It was always better, in any case, not to seem in a hurry.

He spent the mornings in the Red Lion, in Barnes, playing dominoes with an old-age pensioner, and when the pensioner didn't turn up owing to bronchial trouble Malcolmson would borrow a newspaper from the landlord. He slept in the afternoons and returned to the Red Lion later. Occasionally when he'd had a few drinks he'd find himself thinking about his children and their mother. He always found it pleasant then, thinking of them with a couple of drinks inside him.

'It's *The Last of the Mohicans*,' said Deirdre in the flat, and he guessed that she must have looked at the *Radio Times* earlier in the day. She'd known they'd end up like that, watching television. Were they bored on Sundays? he often wondered.

'Can't we have *The Golden Shot*?' demanded Susie, and Deirdre pointed out that it wasn't on yet. He left them watching Randolph Scott and Binnie Barnes, and went to prepare their tea in the kitchen.

On Saturdays he bought meringues and brandy-snaps in Frith's Patisserie. The elderly assistant smiled at him in a way that made him wonder if she knew what he wanted them for; it occurred to him once that she felt sorry for him. On Sunday mornings, listening to the omnibus edition of *The Archers*, he made Marmite sandwiches with brown bread and tomato sandwiches with white. They loved sandwiches, which was something he remembered from the past. He remembered parties, Deirdre's friends sitting around a table, small and silent, eating crisps and cheese puffs and leaving all the cake.

When *The Last of the Mohicans* came to an end they watched *Going for a Song* for five minutes before changing the channel for *The Golden Shot*. Then Deirdre turned the television off and they went to the kitchen to have tea. 'Wash your hands,' said Susie, and he heard her add that if a germ got into your food you could easily die. 'She kept referring to death,' he would say to Elizabeth when he left them back. 'D'you think she's worried about anything?' He imagined Elizabeth giving the smile she had given three weeks ago and then saying he'd better come in to discuss the matter.

'Goody,' said Susie, sitting down.

'I'd like to marry a man like that man in the park,' said Deirdre. 'It'd be much more interesting, married to a bloke like that.'

'He'd be always drunk.'

'He wasn't drunk, Susie. That's not being drunk.'

'He was drinking out of a bottle –'

'He was putting on a bit of flash, drinking out of a bottle and singing his little song. No harm in that, Susie.'

'I'd like to be married to Daddy.'

'You couldn't be married to Daddy.'

'Well, Richard then.'

'Ribena, Daddy. Please.'

He poured drops of Ribena into two mugs and filled them up with warm water. He had a definite feeling that today she'd ask him in, both of them pretending a worry over Susie's obsession with death. They'd sit together while the children splashed about in the bathroom; she'd offer him gin and lime-juice, their favourite drink, a drink known as a Gimlet, as once he'd told her. They'd drink it out of green glasses that they'd bought, years ago, in Italy. The girls would dry themselves and come and say good night. They'd go to bed. He might tell them a story, or she would. 'Stay to supper,' she would say, and while she made risotto he would go to her and kiss her hair.

'I like his eyes,' said Susie. 'One's higher than another.'

'It couldn't be.'

'It is.'

'He couldn't see, Susie, if his eyes were like that. Everyone's eyes are –'

'He isn't always drunk like the man in the park.'

'Who?' he asked.

'Richard,' they said together, and Susie added: 'Irishmen are always drunk.'

'Daddy's an Irishman and Daddy's not always –'

'Who's Richard?'

'He's Susie's boy-friend.'

'I don't mind,' said Susie. 'I like him.'

'If he's there tonight, Susie, you're not to climb all over him.'

He left the kitchen and in the sitting-room he poured himself some whisky. He sat with the glass cold between his hands, staring at the grey television screen. 'Sure, maybe some day I'll go back to Ireland,' Deirdre sang in the kitchen, and Susie laughed shrilly.

He imagined a dark-haired man, a cheerful man, intelligent and subtle, a man who came often to the flat, whom his children knew well and were already fond of. He imagined him as he had imagined himself ten minutes before, sitting with Elizabeth, drinking Gimlets from the green Italian glasses. 'Say good night to Richard,' Elizabeth would say, and the girls would go to him and kiss him good night.

'Who's Richard?' he asked, standing in the kitchen doorway.

'A friend,' said Deirdre, 'of Mummy's.'

'A nice friend?'

'Oh, yes.'

'I love him,' said Susie.

He returned to the sitting-room and quickly poured himself more whisky. Both of his hands were shaking. He drank quickly, and then poured and drank some more. On the pale carpet, close to the television set, there was a stain where Diana had spilt a cup of coffee. He hated now this memory of her, he hated her voice when it came back to him, and the memory of her body and her mind. And yet once he had been rendered lunatic with the passion of his love for her. He had loved her more than Elizabeth, and in his madness he had spoilt everything.

'Wash your hands,' said Susie, close to him. He hadn't heard them come into the room. He asked them, mechanically, if they'd had enough to eat. 'She hasn't washed her hands,' Susie said. 'I washed mine in the sink.'

He turned the television on. It was the girl ventriloquist Shari Lewis, with Lamb Chop and Charley Horse.

Well, he thought under the influence of the whisky, he had had his fling. He had played the pins with a flat-chested American nymphomaniac and predator, and he had lost all there was to lose. Now it was Elizabeth's turn: why shouldn't she have, for a time, the dark-haired Richard who took another man's children on to his knee and kissed them good night? Wasn't it better that the score should be even before they all came together again?

He sat on the floor with his daughters on either side of him, his arms about them. In front of him was his glass of whisky. They laughed at Lamb Chop and Charley Horse, and when the programme came to an end and the news came on he didn't want to let his daughters go. An electric fire glowed cosily. Wind blew the rain against the windows, the autumn evening was dark already.

He turned the television off. He finished the whisky in his glass and poured some more. 'Shall I tell you,' he said, 'about when Mummy and I were married?'

They listened while he did so. He told them about meeting Elizabeth in the first place, at somebody else's wedding, and of the days they had spent walking about together, and about the wet, cold afternoon on which they'd been married.

'February the twenty-fourth,' Deirdre said.

'Yes.'

'I'm going to be married in summer-time,' Susie said, 'when the cow-parsley's out.'

His birthday and Elizabeth's were on the same day, 21 April. He reminded the girls of that; he told them of the time he and Elizabeth had discovered they shared the date, a date shared also with Hitler and the Queen. They listened quite politely, but somehow didn't seem much interested.

They watched *What's in a Game?* He drank more. He wouldn't be able to drive them back. He'd pretend he couldn't start the Volvo and then he'd telephone for a taxi. It had happened once before that in a depression he'd began to drink when they were with him on a Sunday afternoon. They'd been to Madame Tussaud's and the Planetarium, which Susie had said frightened her. In the flat, just as this time, while they were eating their sandwiches, he'd been overcome with the longing that they should all be together again. He'd begun to drink and in the end, while they watched television, he'd drunk quite a lot. When the time came to go he'd said that he couldn't find the keys of the Volvo and that they'd have to have a taxi. He'd spent five minutes brushing his teeth so that Elizabeth wouldn't smell the alcohol when she opened the door. He'd smiled at her with his well-brushed teeth but she, not then being over her bitterness, hadn't smiled back.

The girls put their coats on. Deirdre drank some Ribena; he had another small tot of whisky. And then, as they were leaving the flat, he suddenly felt he couldn't go through the farce of walking to the Volvo, putting the girls into it and then pretending he couldn't start it. 'I'm tired,' he said instead. 'Let's have a taxi.'

They watched the Penrhyn Male Voice Choir in *Songs of Praise* while they waited for it to arrive. He poured himself another drink, drank it slowly, and then went to the bathroom to brush his teeth. He remembered the time Deirdre had been born, in a maternity home in the country because they'd lived in the country then. Elizabeth had been concerned because she'd thought one of Deirdre's fingers was bent and had kept showing it to nurses who said they couldn't see anything the matter. He hadn't been able to see anything the matter either, nor had the doctor. 'She'll never be as beautiful as you,' he'd said and quite soon after that she'd stopped talking about the finger and had said he was nice to her. Susie had been born at home, very quickly, very easily.

The taxi arrived. 'Soon be Christmas,' said the taxman. 'You chaps looking forward to Santa Claus?' They giggled because he had called them chaps. 'Fifty-six more days,' said Susie.

He imagined them on Christmas Day, with the dark-haired Richard explaining the rules of a game he'd bought them. He imagined all four of them sitting down at Christmas dinner, and Richard asking the girls which they liked, the white or the brown of the turkey, and then cutting them small slices. He'd have brought, perhaps, champagne, because he was that kind of person. Deirdre would sip from his glass, not liking the taste. Susie would love it.

He counted in his mind: if Richard had been visiting the flat for, say, six weeks already and assuming that his love affair with Elizabeth had begun two weeks before his first visit, that left another four months to go, allowing the affair ran an average course of six months. It would therefore come to an end at the beginning of March. His own affair with Diana had lasted from April until September. 'Oh darling,' said Diana, suddenly in his mind, and his own voice replied to her, caressing her with words. He remembered the first time they had made love and the guilt that had hammered at him and the passion there had been between them. He imagined Elizabeth naked in Richard's arms, her eyes open, looking at him, her fingers touching the side of his face, her lips slightly smiling. He reached forward and pulled down the glass shutter. 'I need cigarettes,' he said. 'There's a pub in Shepherd's Bush Road, the Laurie Arms.'

He drank two large measures of whisky. He bought cigarettes and lit one, rolling the smoke around in his mouth to disguise the smell of the alcohol. As he returned to the taxi, he slipped on the wet pavement and almost lost his balance. He felt very drunk all of a sudden. Deirdre and Susie were telling the taxi-man about the man in Hyde Park.

He was aware that he walked unsteadily when they left the taxi and moved across the forecourt of the block of flats. In the hall, before they got into the lift, he lit another cigarette, rolling the smoke about his mouth. 'That poor Japanese man,' said Deirdre.

He rang the bell, and when Elizabeth opened the door the girls turned to him and thanked him. He took the cigarette from his mouth and kissed them. Elizabeth was smiling: if only she'd ask him in and give him a drink he wouldn't have to worry about the alcohol on his breath. He swore to himself that she was smiling as she'd smiled three weeks ago. 'Can I come in?' he asked, unable to keep the words back.

'In?' The smile was still there. She was looking at him quite closely. He released the smoke from his mouth. He tried to remember what it was he'd planned to say, and then it came to him.

'I'm worried about Susie,' he said in a quiet voice. 'She talked about death all the time.'

'Death?'

'Yes.'

'There's someone here actually,' she said, stepping back into the hall. 'But come in, certainly.'

In the sitting-room she introduced him to Richard who was, as he'd imagined, a dark-haired man. The sitting-room was much the same as it always had been. 'Have a drink,' Richard offered.

'D'you mind if we talk about Susie?' Elizabeth asked Richard. He said he'd put them to bed if she liked. She nodded. Richard went away.

'Well?'

He stood with the familiar green glass in his hand, gazing at her. He said:

'I haven't had gin and lime-juice since –'

'Yes. Look, I shouldn't worry about Susie. Children of that age often say odd things, you know –'

'I don't mind about Richard, Elizabeth, I think it's your due. I worked it out in the taxi. It's the end of October now –'

'My due?'

'Assuming your affair has been going on already for six weeks –'

'You're drunk.'

He closed one eye, focusing. He felt his body swaying and he said to himself that he must not fall now, that no matter what his body did his feet must remain firm on the carpet. He sipped from the green glass. She wasn't, he noticed, smiling any more.

'I'm actually not drunk,' he said. 'I'm actually sober. By the time our birthday comes round, Elizabeth, it'll all be over. On April the twenty-first we could have family tea.'

'What the hell are you talking about?'

'The future, Elizabeth. Of you and me and our children.'

'How much have you had to drink?'

'We tried to go to *A Hundred and One Dalmatians*, but it wasn't on anywhere.'

'So you drank instead. While the children –'

'We came here in a taxi-cab. They've had their usual tea, they've watched a bit of *The Last of the Mohicans* and a bit of *Going for a Song* and all of *The Golden Shot* and *The Shari Lewis Show* and –'

'You see them for a few hours and you have to go and get drunk –'

'I am not drunk, Elizabeth.'

He crossed the room as steadily as he could. He looked aggressively at her. He poured gin and lime-juice. He said:

'You have a right to your affair with Richard, I recognize that.'

'A *right*?'

'I love you, Elizabeth.'

'You loved Diana.'

'I have never not loved you. Diana was nothing – nothing, nothing at all.'

'She broke our marriage up.'

'No.'

'We're divorced.'

'I love you, Elizabeth.'

'Now listen to me –'

'I live from Sunday to Sunday. We're a family, Elizabeth; you and me and them. It's ridiculous, all this. It's ridiculous making Marmite sandwiches with brown bread and tomato sandwiches with white. It's ridiculous buying meringues and going five times to *A Hundred and One Dalmatians* and going up the Post Office Tower until we're sick of the sight of it, and watching drunks in Hyde Park and poking about at the Zoo –'

'You have reasonable access –'

'Reasonable access, my God!' His voice rose. He felt sweat on his forehead. Reasonable access, he shouted, was utterly no good to him; reasonable access was meaningless and stupid; a day would come when they wouldn't want to go with him on Sunday afternoons, when there was nowhere left in London that wasn't an unholy bore. What about reasonable access then?

'Please be quiet.'

He sat down in the armchair that he had always sat in. She said:

'You might marry again. And have other children.'

'I don't want other children. I have children already. I want us all to live together as we used to –'

'Please listen to me –'

'I get a pain in my stomach in the middle of the night. Then I wake up and can't go back to sleep. The children will grow up and I'll grow old. I couldn't begin a whole new thing all over again: I haven't the courage. Not after Diana. A mistake like that alters everything.'

'I'm going to marry Richard.'

'Three weeks ago,' he said, as though he hadn't heard her, 'you smiled at me.'

'Smiled?'

'Like you used to, Elizabeth. Before –'

'You made a mistake,' she said, softly. 'I'm sorry.'

'I'm not saying don't go on with your affair with this man. I'm not saying that, because I think in the circumstances it'd be a cheek. D'you understand me, Elizabeth?'

'Yes, I do. And I think you and I can be perfectly good friends. I don't feel sour about it any more: perhaps that's what you saw in my smile.'

'Have a six-month affair –'

'I'm in love with Richard.'

'That'll all pass into the atmosphere. It'll be nothing at all in a year's time –'

'No.'

'I love you, Elizabeth.'

They stood facing one another, not close. His body was still swaying. The liquid in his glass moved gently, slurping to the rim and then settling back again. Her eyes were on his face: it was thinner, she was thinking. Her fingers played with the edge of a cushion on the back of the sofa.

'On Saturdays,' he said, 'I buy the meringues and the brandy-snaps in Frith's Patisserie. On Sunday morning I make the sandwiches. Then I cook sausages and potatoes for my lunch, and after that I come over here.'

'Yes, yes –'

'I look forward all week to Sunday.'

'The children enjoy their outings, too.'

'Will you think about it?'

'About what?'

'About all being together again.'

'Oh, for heaven's sake.' She turned away from him. 'I wish you'd go now,' she said.

'Will you come out with me on our birthday?'

'I've told you.' Her voice was loud and angry, her cheeks were flushed. 'Can't you understand? I'm going to marry Richard. We'll be married within a month, when the girls have had time to get to know him a little better. By Christmas we'll be married.'

He shook his head in a way that annoyed her, seeming in his drunkenness to deny the truth of what she was saying. He tried to light a cigarette; matches dropped to the floor at his feet. He left them there.

It enraged her that he was sitting in an armchair in her flat with his eyelids drooping through drink and an unlighted cigarette in his hand and his matches spilt all over the floor. They were his children, but she wasn't his wife: he'd destroyed her as a wife, he'd insulted her, he'd left her to bleed and she had called him a murderer.

'Our birthday,' he said, smiling at her as though already she had agreed to join him on that day. 'And Hitler's and the Queen's.'

'On our birthday if I go out with anyone it'll be Richard.'

'Our birthday is beyond the time –'

'For God's sake, there is no beyond the time. I'm in love with another man –'

'No.'

'On our birthday,' she shouted at him, 'on the night of our birthday Richard will make love to me in the bed you slept in for nine years. You have access to the children. You can demand no more.'

He bent down and picked up a match. He struck it on the side of the empty box. The cigarette was bent. He lit it with a wobbling flame and dropped the used match on to the carpet. The dark-haired man, he saw, was in the room again. He'd come in, hearing her shouting like that. He was asking her if she was all right. She told him to go away. Her face was hard; bitterness was there again. She said, not looking at him:

'Everything was so happy. We had a happy marriage. For nine years we had a perfectly happy marriage.'

'We could –'

'Not ever.'

Again he shook his head in disagreement. Cigarette ash fell on to the green tweed of his suit. His eyes were narrowed, watching her, seemingly suspicious.

'We had a happy marriage,' she repeated, whispering the words, speaking to herself, still not looking at him. 'You met a woman on a train and that was that: you murdered our marriage. You left me to plead, as I am leaving you now. You have your Sunday access. There is that legality between us. Nothing more.'

'Please, Elizabeth –'

'Oh for God's sake, stop.' Her rage was all in her face now. Her lips quivered as though in the effort to hold back words that would not be denied. They came from her, more quietly but with greater bitterness. Her eyes roved over the green tweed suit of the man who once had been her husband, over his thin face and his hair that seemed, that day, not to have been brushed.

'You've gone to seed,' she said, hating herself for saying that, unable to prevent herself. 'You've gone to seed because you've lost your self-respect. I've watched you, week by week. The woman you met on a train took her toll of you and now in your seediness you want to creep back. Don't you know you're not the man I married?'

'Elizabeth –'

'You didn't have cigarette burns all over your clothes. You didn't smell of toothpaste when you should have smelt of drink. You stand there, pathetically, Sunday after Sunday, trying to keep a conversation going. D'you know what I feel?'

'I love –'

'I feel sorry for you.'

He shook his head. There was no need to feel sorry for him, he said, remembering suddenly the elderly assistant in Frith's Patisserie and remembering also, for some reason, the woman in Hyde Park who peculiarly had said that he wasn't shaved. He looked down at his clothes and saw the burn marks she had mentioned. 'We think it would be better,' said the voice of Sir Gerald Travers unexpectedly in his mind.

'I'll make some coffee,' said Elizabeth.

She left him. He had been cruel, and then Diana had been cruel, and now Elizabeth was cruel because it was her right and her instinct to be so. He recalled with vividness Diana's face in those first moments on the train, her eyes looking at him, her voice. 'You have lost all dignity,' Elizabeth had whispered, in the darkness, at night. 'I despise you for that.' He tried to stand up but found the effort beyond him. He raised the green glass to his lips. His eyes closed and when he opened them again he thought for a drunken moment that he was back in the past, in the middle of his happy marriage. He wiped at his face with a handkerchief.

He saw across the room the bottle of Gordon's gin so nicely matching the green glasses, and the lime-juice, a lighter shade of green. He made the journey, his legs striking the arms of chairs. There wasn't much gin in the bottle. He poured it all out; he added lime-juice, and drank it.

In the hall he could hear voices in the bathroom, Elizabeth and the man speaking quietly in the kitchen. 'Poor wretch,' Elizabeth was saying. He left the flat and descended to the ground floor.

The rain was falling heavily. He walked through it, thinking that it was better to go, quietly and without fuss. It would all work out; he knew it; he felt it definitely in his bones. He'd arrive on Sunday, a month or so before their birthday, and something in Elizabeth's face would tell him that the dark-haired man had gone for ever, as Diana had gone. By then he'd be established again, with better prospects than the red-faced Sir Gerald Travers had ever offered him. On their birthday they'd both apologize to one another, wiping the slate clean: they'd start again. As he crossed the Edgware Road to the public house in which he always spent an hour or so on Sunday nights, he heard his own voice murmuring that it was understandable that she should have taken it out on him, that she should have tried to hurt him by saying he'd gone to seed. Naturally, she'd say a thing like that; who could blame her after all she'd been through? At night in the flat in Barnes he watched television until the programmes closed down. He usually had a few drinks, and as often as not he dropped off to sleep with a cigarette between his fingers: that was how the burns occurred on his clothes.

He nodded to himself as he entered the saloon bar, thinking he'd been wise not to mention any of that to Elizabeth. It would only have annoyed her, having to listen to a lot of stuff about late-night television and cigarettes. Monday, Tuesday, Wednesday, he thought, Thursday, Friday. On Saturday he'd buy the meringues and brandy-snaps, and then it would be Sunday. He'd make the sandwiches listening to *The Archers*, and at three o'clock he'd ring the bell of the flat. He smiled in the saloon bar, thinking of that, seeing in his mind the faces of his children and the beautiful face of their mother. He'd planted an idea in Elizabeth's mind and even though she'd been a bit shirty she'd see when she thought about it that it was what she wanted, too.

He went on drinking gin and lime-juice, quietly laughing over being so upset when the children had first mentioned the dark-haired man who took them on to his knee. Gin and lime-juice was a Gimlet, he told the barmaid. She smiled at him. He was celebrating, he said, a day that was to come. It was ridiculous, he told her, that a woman casually met on a train should have created havoc, that now, at the end of it, he should week by week butter bread for Marmite and tomato sandwiches. 'D'you understand me?' he drunkenly asked the barmaid. 'It's *too* ridiculous to be true – that man will go because none of it makes sense the way it is.' The barmaid smiled again and nodded. He bought her a glass of beer, which was something he did every Sunday night. He wept as he paid for it, and touched his cheeks with the tips of his fingers to wipe away the tears. Every Sunday he wept, at the end of the day, after he'd had his access. The barmaid raised her glass, as always she did. They drank to the day that was to come, when the error he had made would be wiped away, when the happy marriage could continue. 'Ridiculous,' he said. 'Of course it is.'

Nice Day at School

Eleanor lay awake, thinking in advance about the day. The face of Miss Whitehead came into her mind, the rather pointed nose, eyes set wide apart, a mouth that turned up at the corners and gave the impression that Miss Whitehead was constantly smiling, although it was a widely held view among the girls whom she taught that Miss Whitehead had little to smile over, having missed out. The face of Liz Jones came into Eleanor's mind also, a pretty, wild face with eyes that were almost black, and black hair hanging prettily down on either side of it, and full lips. Liz Jones claimed to have gipsy blood in her, and another girl, Mavis Temple, had once remarked to Eleanor that she thought Liz Jones's lips were negroid. 'A touch of the tar brush,' Mavis Temple had said. 'A seaman done her mum.' She'd said it three years ago, when the girls had all been eleven, in Miss Homber's class. Everything had been different then.

In the early morning gloom Eleanor considered the difference, regretting, as always, that it had come about. It had been nice in Miss Homber's class, the girls' first year at Springfield Comprehensive: they'd all had a crush on Miss Homber because Miss Homber, who'd since become Mrs George Spaxton and a mother, had been truly beautiful and intelligent. Miss Homber told them it was important to wash all the parts of the body once per day, including you knew where. Four girls brought letters of complaint after that and Miss Homber read them out to the class, commenting on the grammar and the spelling errors and causing the girls to become less carefree about what they repeated to their mums. 'Remember, you can give birth at thirteen,' Miss Homber warned, and she added that if a boy ever said he was too embarrassed to go into a chemist's for preventatives he could always get them in a slot machine that was situated in the Gents at Barclay's filling station on the Portsmouth Road, which was something her own boy-friend had told her.

It had been nice in those days because Eleanor didn't believe that any boy would try stuff like that on when she was thirteen, and the girls of the first year all agreed that it sounded disgusting, a boy putting his thing up you. Even Liz Jones did, although she was constantly hanging about the boys of the estate and twice had had her knickers taken down in the middle of the estate playground. There were no boys at Springfield Comprehensive, which was just as well, Eleanor had always considered, because boys roughened up a school so.

But in spite of their physical absence boys had somehow penetrated and increasingly, as Eleanor passed up through the school, references to them infiltrated all conversation. At thirteen, in Miss Croft's class, Liz Jones confessed that a boy called Gareth Swayles had done her in the corner of the estate playground, at eleven o'clock one night. She'd been done standing up, she reported, leaning against the paling that surrounded the playground. She said it was fantastic.

Lying in bed, Eleanor remembered Liz Jones saying that and saying a few months later that a boy called Rogo Pollini was twice as good as Gareth Swayles, and later that a boy called Tich Ayling made Rogo Pollini seem totally laughable. Another girl, Susie Crumm, said that Rogo Pollini had told her that he'd never enjoyed it with Liz Jones because Liz Jones put him off with all her wriggling and pinching. Susie Crumm, at the time, had just been done by Rogo Pollini.

By the time they reached Class 2 it had become the fashion to have been done and most of the girls, even quiet Mavis Temple, had succumbed to it. Many had not cared for the experience and had not repeated it, but Liz Jones said that this was because they had got it from someone like Gareth Swayles, who was no better on the job than a dead horse. Eleanor hadn't ever been done nor did she wish to be, by Gareth Swayles or anyone else. Some of the girls said it had hurt them: she knew it would hurt her. And she'd heard that even if Gareth Swayles, or whoever it was, went to the slot machine in Barclay's filling station it sometimes happened that the preventative came asunder, a disaster that would be followed by weeks of worry. That, she knew, would be her fate too.

'Eleanor's prissy,' Liz Jones said every day now. 'Eleanor's prissy like poor prissy Whitehead.' Liz Jones went on about it all the time, hating Eleanor because she still had everything in store for her. Liz Jones had made everyone else think that Eleanor would grow into a Miss Whitehead, who was terrified of men, so Liz Jones said. Miss Whitehead had hairs on her chin and her upper lip that she didn't bother to do anything about. Quite often her breath wasn't fresh, which was unpleasant if she was leaning over you, explaining something.

Eleanor, who lived on the estate with her parents, hated being identified with Miss Whitehead and yet she felt, especially when she lay awake in the early morning, that there was something in Liz Jones's taunting. 'Eleanor's waiting for Mr Right,' Liz Jones would say. 'Whitehead waited forever.' Miss Whitehead, Liz Jones said, 'left solitary like that: you grow hairs on your face; herself wholly and in this day and age a girl had to be sensible and natural over a matter like that. Everyone agreed that this was probably so because there was no doubt about it that in her time Miss Whitehead had been pretty. 'It happens to you,' Liz Jones said, 'left solitary like that: you grow hairs on your face; you get stomach trouble that makes your breath bad. Nervous frustration, see.'

Eleanor gazed across her small bedroom, moving her eyes from the pink of the wall to her school uniform, grey and purple, hanging over the back of a chair. In the room there was a teddy-bear she'd had since she was three, and a gramophone, and records by the New Seekers and the Pioneers and Diana Ross, and photographs of such performers. In her vague, uninterested manner her mother said she thought it awful that Eleanor should waste her money on these possessions, but Eleanor explained that everyone at Springfield Comprehensive did so and that she herself did not consider it a waste of money.

'You up?' Eleanor heard her mother calling now, and she replied that she was. She got out of bed and looked at herself in a looking-glass on her dressing-table. Her night-dress was white with small sprigs of violets on it. Her hair had a reddish tinge, her face was long and thin and was not afflicted with spots, as were a few of the faces of her companions at Springfield Comprehensive. Her prettiness was delicate, and she thought as she examined it now that Liz Jones was definitely right in her insinuations: it was a prettiness that could easily disappear overnight. Hairs would appear on her chin and her upper lip, a soft down at first, later becoming harsher. 'Your sight, you know,' an oculist would worriedly remark to her, and tell her she must wear glasses. Her teeth would lose their gleam. She'd have trouble with dandruff.

Eleanor slipped her night-dress over her head and looked at her naked body. She didn't herself see much beauty in it, but she knew that the breasts were the right size for the hips, that arms and legs nicely complemented each other. She dressed and went into the kitchen, where her father was making tea and her mother was reading the *Daily Express*. Her father hadn't been to bed all night. He slept during the day, being employed by night as a doorman in a night-club called Margo's, in Shepherd Market. Once upon a time her father had been a wrestler, but in 1961 he'd injured his back in a bout with a Japanese and had since been unfit for the ring. Being a doorman of a night-club kept him in touch, so he claimed, with the glamorous world he'd been used to in the past. He often saw familiar faces, he reported, going in and out of Margo's, faces that once had been his audience. Eleanor felt embarrassed when he talked like that, being unable to believe much of what he said.

'You're in for a scorcher,' he said now, placing a pot of tea on the blue formica of the table. 'No end to the heatwave, they can't see.'

He was a large, red-faced man with closely cut grey hair and no lobe to his right ear. He'd put on weight since he'd left the wrestling ring and although he moved slowly now, as though in some way compensating for years of nimbleness on the taut canvas, he was still, in a physical sense, a formidable opponent, as occasional trouble-makers at the night-club had painfully discovered.

Eleanor knocked Special K into a dish and added milk and sugar.

'That's a lovely young girl,' her father said. 'Mia Farrow. She was in last night, Eleanor.'

His breakfast-time conversation was always the same. Princess Margaret had shaken him by the hand and Anthony Armstrong-Jones had asked him if he might take his photograph for a book about London he was doing. The Burtons came regularly, and Rex Harrison, and the Canadian Prime Minister whenever he was in London. Her father had a way of looking at Eleanor when he made such statements, his eyes screwed up, almost lost in the puffed red flesh of his face: he stared unblinkingly and beadily, as if defying her to reply that she didn't for a moment accept that Princess Margaret's hand had ever lain in his or that Anthony Armstrong-Jones had addressed him.

'Faceful of innocence,' he said. 'Just a faceful of innocence, Eleanor. "Good night, Miss Farrow," I said, and she turned the little face to me and said to call her Mia.'

Eleanor nodded. Her mother's eyes were fixed on the *Daily Express*, moving from news item to news item, her lips occasionally moving also as she read. 'Liz Jones,' Eleanor wanted to say. 'Could you complain to the school about Liz Jones?' She wanted to tell them about the fashion in Class 2, about Miss Whitehead, and how everyone was afraid of Liz Jones. She imagined her voice speaking across the breakfast table, to her father who was still in his doorman's uniform and her mother who mightn't even hear her. There'd be embarrassment as her father listened, her own face would be as hot as fire. He'd turn his head away in the end, like the time she'd had to ask him for money to buy sanitary towels.

'Lovely little fingers,' he said, 'like a baby's fingers, Eleanor. Little wisps of things. She touched me with the tips.'

'Who?' demanded her mother, suddenly sharp, looking up. 'Eh, then?'

'Mia Farrow,' he said. 'She was down in Margo's last night. Sweetest thing; sweetest little face.'

'Ah, yes, Peyton Place,' her mother said, and Eleanor's father nodded.

Her mother had spectacles with swept-up, elaborately bejewelled frames. The jewels were made of glass, but they glittered, especially in strong sunlight, just like what Eleanor imagined diamonds must glitter like. Her mother, constantly smoking, had hair which she dyed so that it appeared to be black. She was a thin woman with bones that stuck out awkwardly at the joints, seeming as though they might at any moment break through the surface of taut, anaemic skin. In Eleanor's opinion her mother had suffered, and once she had a dream in which her mother was fat and married to someone else, a man, as far as Eleanor could make out, who ran a vegetable shop.

Her mother always had breakfast in her night-dress and an old fawn-coloured dressing-gown, her ankles below it as white as paper, her feet stuck into tattered slippers. After breakfast, she would return to bed with Eleanor's father, obliging him, Eleanor knew, as she had obliged him all her life. During the school holidays, and on Saturdays and Sundays when Eleanor was still in the flat, her mother continued to oblige him: in the bedroom he made the same kind of noise as he'd made in the wrestling ring. The Prince of Hackney he'd been known as.

Her mother was a shadow. Married to a man who ran a vegetable shop or to any other kind of man except the one she'd chosen, Eleanor believed she'd have been different: she'd have had more children, she'd have been a proper person with proper flesh on her bones, a person you could feel for. As she was, you could hardly take her seriously. She sat there in her night-clothes, waiting for the man she'd married to rise from the table and go into their bedroom so that she might follow. Afterwards she cleared up the breakfast things and washed them, while he slept. She shopped in the Express Dairy Supermarket, dropping cigarette ash over tins of soup and peas and packets of crisps, and at half past eleven she sat in the corner of the downstairs lounge of the Northumberland Arms and drank a measure of gin and water, sometimes two.

'Listen to this,' her mother said in her wheezy voice. She quoted a piece about a fifty-five-year-old woman, a Miss Margaret Sugden, who had been trapped in a bath for two days and three nights. '*It ended*,' read Eleanor's mother, '*with two burly policemen – eyes carefully averted – lifting her out. It took them half an hour of gentle levering, for Miss Sugden, a well-rounded sixteen stone, was helplessly stuck.*'

He laughed. Her mother stubbed her cigarette out on her saucer and lit a fresh one. Her mother never ate anything at breakfast-time. She drank three cups of tea and smoked the same number of cigarettes. He liked a large breakfast, eggs and bacon, fried bread, a chop sometimes.

'*History's longest soak*,' her mother said, still quoting from the *Daily Express*. Her father laughed again.

Eleanor rose and carried the dish she'd eaten her Special K out of to the sink, with her cup and her saucer. She rinsed them under the hot tap and stacked them on the red, plastic-covered rack to dry. Her mother spoke in amazed tones when she read pieces out of the newspaper, surprised by the activities of people and animals, never amused by them. Some part of her had been smashed to pieces.

She said good-bye to both of them. Her mother kissed her as she always did. Winking, her father told her not to take any wooden dollars, an advice that was as regular and as mechanical as her mother's embrace.

'Netball is it?' her mother vaguely asked, not looking up from the newspaper. There wasn't netball, Eleanor explained, as she'd explained before, in the summer term: she wouldn't be late back.

She left the flat and descended three flights of concrete stairs. She passed the garages and then the estate's playground, where Liz Jones had first of all been done. 'Good morning, Eleanor,' a woman said to her, an Irish woman called Mrs Breen. 'Isn't it a great day?'

Eleanor smiled. The weather was lovely, she said. Mrs Breen was a lackadaisical woman, middle-aged and fat, the mother of eight children. On the estate it was said that she was no better than she should be, that one of her sons, who had a dark tinge in his pallor, was the child of a West Indian railway porter. Another of Mrs Breen's children and suspect also, a girl of Eleanor's age called Dolly, was reputed to be the daughter of Susie Crumm's father. In the dream Eleanor had had in which her own mother was fat rather than thin it had seemed that her mother had somehow become Mrs Breen, because in spite of everything Mrs Breen was a happy woman. Her husband had a look of happiness about him also, as did all the Breen children, no matter where they'd come from. They regularly went to Mass, all together in a family outing, and even if Mrs Breen occasionally obliged Susie Crumm's father and others it hadn't taken the same toll of her as the obliging of Eleanor's father by her mother had. For years, ever since she'd listened to Liz Jones telling the class the full facts of life, Eleanor had been puzzled by the form the facts apparently took when different people were involved. She'd accepted quite easily the stories about Mrs Breen and had thought no less of the woman, but when Dolly Breen had said, about a month ago, that she'd been done by Rogo Pollini, Eleanor had felt upset, not caring to imagine the occasion, as she didn't care to imagine the occasion that took place every morning after breakfast in her parents' bedroom. Mrs Breen didn't matter because she was somehow remote, like one of the people her mother read about in the *Daily Express* or one of the celebrities her father told lies about: Mrs Breen didn't concern her, but Dolly Breen and Rogo Pollini did because they were close to her, being the same as she was and of the same generation. And her parents concerned her because they were close to her also. You could no longer avoid any of it when you thought of Dolly Breen and Rogo Pollini, or your parents.

She passed a row of shops, Len Parrish the baker, a dry cleaner's, the Express Dairy Supermarket, the newsagent's and post office, the off-licence attached to the Northumberland Arms. Girls in the grey and purple uniform of Springfield Comprehensive alighted in numbers from a bus. A youth whistled at her. 'Hi, Eleanor,' said Gareth Swayles, coming up behind her. In a friendly manner he put his hand on her back, low down, so that as though by accident he could in a moment slip it over her buttocks.

There's a new boy in Grimes the butcher's, Liz Jones wrote on a piece of paper. *He's not on the estate at all.* She folded the paper and addressed it to Eleanor. She passed it along the row of desks.

'*Je l'ai vu qui travaillait dans la cour,*' said Miss Whitehead.

I saw him in Grimes, Eleanor wrote. *Funny-looking fish.* She passed the note back and Liz Jones read it and showed it to her neighbour, Thelma Joseph. *Typical Eleanor,* Liz Jones wrote and Thelma Joseph giggled slightly.

'*Un anglais qui passait ses vacances en France,*' said Miss Whitehead.

Miss Whitehead lived in Esher, in a bed-sitting-room. Girls had sometimes visited her there and those who had done so described for others what Miss Whitehead's residence was like. It was very clean and comfortable and neat. White paint shone on the window ledges and the skirting-boards, lace curtains hung close to sparkling glass. On the mantelpiece there were ornaments in delicate ceramic, Highland sheep and cockerels, and a chimney sweep with his brushes on his back. A clock ticked on the mantelpiece, and in the fireplace – no longer used – Miss Whitehead had stood a vase of dried flowers. Her bed was in a recess, not at all obtrusive in the room, a narrow divan covered in cheerful chintz.

'*Le pêcheur*,' said Miss Whitehead, '*est un homme qui* . . . Eleanor?'

'*Pêche?*'

'*Très bien. Et la blanchisseuse est une femme qui* . . .?'

'*Lave le linge.*'

Liz Jones said it must be extraordinary to be Miss Whitehead, never to have felt a man's hand on you. *Gareth Swayles said he'd give it to her*, she'd written on one of the notes she was constantly passing round the class. *Imagine Swayles in bed with Whitehead!*

'*La mère n'aime pas le fromage*,' said Miss Whitehead, and Liz Jones passed another note to Eleanor. *The new boy in Grimes is called Denny Price*, it said. *He wants to do you.*

'Eleanor,' said Miss Whitehead.

She looked up from the elaborately looped handwriting of Liz Jones. In their bedroom her father would be making the noises he used to make in the wrestling ring. Her mother would be lying there. Once, when she was small, she'd gone in by mistake and her father had been standing without his clothes on. Her mother had pulled a sheet up to cover her own nakedness.

'Why are you writing notes, Eleanor?'

'She didn't, Miss Whitehead,' Liz Jones said. 'I sent her –'

'Thank you, Elizabeth. Eleanor?'

'I'm sorry, Miss Whitehead.'

'Were you writing notes, Eleanor?'

'No, I –'

'I sent her the note, Miss Whitehead. It's a private matter –'

'Not private in *my* class, Elizabeth. Pass me the note, Eleanor.'

Liz Jones was sniggering: Eleanor knew that she'd wanted this to happen. Miss Whitehead would read the note out, which was her rule when a note was found.

'The new boy in Grimes is called Denny Price,' Miss Whitehead said. 'He wants to do you.'

The class laughed, a muffled sound because the girls' heads were bent over their desks.

'He wants to have sexual relations with Eleanor,' Liz Jones explained, giggling more openly. 'Eleanor's a –'

'Thank you, Elizabeth. The future tense, Elizabeth: *s'asseoir.*'

Her voice grated in the classroom. Her voice had become unattractive also, Eleanor thought, because she'd never let herself be loved. In her clean bed-sitting-room she might weep tonight, recalling the insolence of Liz Jones. She'd punish Liz Jones when the bell went, the way she always inflicted punishment. She'd call her name out and while the others left the room she'd keep the girl longer than was necessary, setting her a piece of poetry to write out ten times and explaining, as if talking to an infant, that notes and conversation about sexual matters were not permitted in her classroom. She'd imply that she didn't believe that the boy in Grimes had said what Liz Jones had reported he'd said. She'd pretend it was all a fantasy, that no girl from Springfield Comprehensive had ever been done in the playground of the estate or anywhere else. It was easy for Miss Whitehead, Eleanor thought, escaping to her bed-sitting-room in Esher.

'It's your bloody fault,' Liz Jones said afterwards in the washroom. 'If you weren't such a curate's bitch –'

'Oh, for heaven's sake, shut up about it!' Eleanor cried.

'Denny Price wants to give you his nine inches –'

'I don't want his bloody nine inches. I don't want anything to do with him.'

'You're under-sexed, Eleanor. What's wrong with Denny Price?'

'He's peculiar-looking. There's something the matter with his head.'

'Will you listen to this!' Liz Jones cried, and the girls who'd gathered round tittered. 'What's his head got to do with it for God's sake? It's not his head that's going to –' She broke off, laughing, and all the girls laughed also, even though several of them didn't at all care for Liz Jones.

'You'll end like Whitehead,' Liz Jones said. 'Doing yourself in Esher.' The likes of Whitehead, she added, gave you a sickness in your kidneys. Eleanor had the same way of walking as Whitehead had, which was a way that dried-up virgins acquired because they were afraid to walk any other way in case a man touched their dried-up bottoms.

Eleanor went away, moving through the girls of other classes, across the washroom.

'Liz Jones is a nasty little tit,' a girl called Eileen Reid whispered, and Joan Moate, a fair-haired girl with a hint of acne, agreed. But Liz Jones couldn't hear them. Liz Jones was still laughing, leaning against a wash-basin with a cigarette in her mouth.

For lunch that day at Springfield Comprehensive there was stew and processed potatoes and carrots, with blancmange afterwards, chocolate and strawberry.

'Don't take no notice,' Susie Crumm said to Eleanor. The way Liz went on, she added, it wouldn't surprise her to hear that she'd contracted syphilis.

'What's it like, Susie?' Eleanor asked.

'Syphilis? You get lesions. If you're a girl you can't tell sometimes. Fellas get them all over their equipment –'

'No, I mean what's it like being done?'

' 'Sall right. Nice really. But not like Jones goes for it. Not all the bloody time.'

They ate spoonfuls of blancmange, sucking it through their teeth.

' 'Sall right,' Susie Crumm repeated when she'd finished. ' 'Sall right for an occasion.'

Eleanor nodded. She wanted to say that she'd prefer to keep it for her wedding night, but she knew that if she said that she'd lose Susie Crumm's sympathy. She wanted it to be special, not just a woman lying down waiting for a man to finish taking his clothes off; not just fumbling in the dark of the estate playground, or something behind the Northumberland Arms, where Eileen Reid had been done.

'My dad said he'd gut any fella that laid a finger on me,' Susie Crumm said.

'Jones's said the same.'

'He done Mrs Breen. Jones's dad.'

'They've all done Mrs Breen.' For a moment she wanted to tell the truth: to add that Susie Crumm's dad had done Mrs Breen also, that Dolly Breen was Susie's half-sister.

'You've got a moustache growing on you,' Liz Jones said, coming up behind her and whispering into her hair.

The afternoon of that day passed without incident at Springfield Comprehensive, while on the estate Eleanor's father slept. He dreamed that he was wrestling again. Between his knees he could feel the ribs of Eddie Rodriguez; the crowd was calling out, urging him to give Eddie Rodriguez the final works. Two yards away, in the kitchen, Eleanor's mother prepared a meal. She cut cod into pieces, and sliced potatoes for chips. He liked a crisply fried meal at half past six before watching a bit of television. She liked cod and chips herself, with tinned peas, and maybe a tin of pears. She'd bought a tin of pears in the Express Dairy: they might as well have them with a tin of Carnation cream. She'd get everything ready and then she'd run an iron over his uniform, sponging off any spots there were. She thought about *Crossroads* on the television, wondering what would happen in the episode today.

'I'd remind you that the school photographs will be taken on Tuesday,' Miss Whitehead said. 'Clean white blouses, please.'

They would all be there: Eleanor, Liz Jones, Susie Crumm, Eileen Reid, Joan Moate, Mavis Temple, and all the others: forty smiling faces, and Miss Whitehead standing at the end of the middle row. If you kept the photograph it would be a memory for ever, another record of the days at Springfield Comprehensive. 'Who's that with the bow legs?' her father had asked a few years ago, pointing at Miss Homber.

'Anyone incorrectly dressed on Tuesday,' Miss Whitehead said, 'will forfeit her place in the photo.'

The bell rang for the end of school. 'Forfeit her bloody knickers,' said Liz Jones just before Miss Whitehead left the classroom.

The girls dispersed, going off in twos and threes, swinging the brief-cases that contained their school books.

'Walk with you?' Susie Crumm suggested to Eleanor, and together they left the classrooms and the school. 'Baking, i'n' it?' Susie Crumm remarked.

They walked slowly, past concrete buildings, the Eagle Star Insurance Company, Barclays Bank, the Halifax Building Society. Windows were open, the air was chalky dry. Two girls in front of them had taken off their shoes but now, finding the pavement too hot to walk on, had paused to put them on again. The two girls shrieked, leaning on one another. Women pushed prams around them, irritation in their faces.

'I want to get fixed in a Saxone,' Susie Crumm said. 'Can't wait to leave that bloody place.'

An *Evening Standard* van swerved in front of a bus, causing the bus-driver to shout and blow his horn. In the cab of the van the driver's mate raised two fingers in a gesture of disdain.

'I fancy selling shoes,' Susie Crumm said. 'Fashion shoes type of thing. You get them at cost if you work in a Saxone.'

Eleanor imagined the slow preparation of the evening meal in her parents' flat, and the awakening of her father. He'd get up and shave himself, standing in the bathroom in his vest, braces hanging down, his flies half open. Her mother spent ages getting the evening meal, breaking off to see to his uniform and then returning to the food. He couldn't bear not being a wrestler any more.

'What you going to do, Eleanor?'

She shook her head. She didn't know what she was going to do. All she wanted was to get away from the estate and from Springfield Comprehensive. She wondered what it would be like to work in the Eagle Star Insurance Company, but at the moment that didn't seem important. What was important was the exact present, the afternoon of a certain day, a day that was like others except for the extreme heat. She'd go back and there the two of them would be, and in her mind there'd be the face of Miss Whitehead and the voice of Liz Jones. She'd do her homework and then there'd be *Crossroads* on the TV and then the fried meal and the washing-up and more TV and then he'd go, saying it was time she was in bed. 'See you in the morning,' he'd say and soon after he'd gone they'd both go to bed, and she'd lie there thinking of being married in white lace in a church, to a delicate man who wouldn't hurt her, who'd love the virginal innocence that had been kept all these years for him alone. She'd go away in a two-piece suit on an autumn afternoon when the leaves in London were yellow-brown. She'd fly with a man whose fingers were long and thin and gentle, who'd hold her hand in the aeroplane, Air France to Biarritz. And afterwards she'd come back to a flat where the curtains were the colour of lavender, the same as the walls, where gas fires glowed and there were rugs on natural-wood floors, and the telephone was pale blue.

'What's matter?' Susie Crumm asked.

'Nothing.'

They walked past Len Parrish the baker, the dry cleaner's, the Express Dairy Supermarket, the newsagent's and post office, the off-licence attached to the Northumberland Arms.

'There's that fella,' Susie Crumm said. 'Denny Price.'

His head was awkwardly placed on his neck, cocked to one side. His hair was red and long, his face small in the midst of it. He had brown eyes and thick, blubbery lips.

'Hullo,' he said.

Susie Crumm giggled.

'Like a fag?' he said, holding out a packet of Anchor. 'Smoke, do you, girls?'

Susie Crumm giggled again, and then abruptly ceased. 'Oh God!' she said, her hand stretched out for a cigarette. She was looking over Denny Price's shoulder at a man in blue denim overalls. The man, seeing her in that moment, sharply called at her to come to him.

'Stuff him,' she said before she smiled and obeyed.

'Her dad,' said Denny Price, pleased that she had gone. 'You want a fag, Eleanor?'

She shook her head, walking on. He dropped into step with her.

'I know your name,' he said. 'I asked Liz Jones.'

'Yes.'

'I'm Denny Price. I work in Grimes.'

'Yes.'

'You're at the Comprehensive.'

'Yes.'

She felt his fingers on her arm, squeezing it just above the elbow. 'Let's go for a walk,' he said. 'Come down by the river, Eleanor.'

She shook her head again and then, quite suddenly, she didn't care what happened. What harm was there in walking by the river with a boy from Grimes'? She looked at the fingers that were still caressing her arm. All day long they had handled meat; the fingernails were bitten away, the flesh was red from scouring. Wasn't it silly, like an advertisement, to imagine that a man would come one day to marry her in white lace in a church and take her, Air France, to Biarritz?

'We'll take a bus to the bridge,' he said. 'A thirty-seven.'

He sat close to her, paying her fare, pressing a cigarette on her. She took it and he lit it for her. His eyes were foxy, she noticed; she could see the desire in them.

'I saw you a week back,' he said.

They walked by the river, away from the bridge, along the tow-path. He put his arm around her, squeezing a handful of underclothes and flesh. 'Let's sit down here,' he said.

They sat on the grass, watching barges going by and schoolboys rowing. In the distance traffic moved, gleaming, on the bridge they'd walked from. 'God,' he said, 'you have fantastic breasts.'

His hands were on them and he was pushing her back on to the grass. She felt his lips on her face, and his teeth and his tongue, and saliva. One hand moved down her body. She felt it under her skirt, on the bare flesh of her thigh, and then on her stomach. It was like an animal, a rat gnawing at her, prodding her and poking. There was no one about; he was muttering, his voice thickly slurred. 'Take down your knickers,' he said.

She pushed at him and for a moment he released his hold, imagining she was about to undo some of her clothing. Instead she ran away, tearing along the tow-path, saying to herself that if he caught up with her she'd hit him with the brief-case that contained her school books.

But he didn't follow her and when she looked back he was lying where she had left him, stretched out as though wounded on the grass.

Her father talked of who might come that night to Margo's. He mentioned Princess Margaret. Princess Margaret had seen him wrestling, or if it hadn't been Princess Margaret it had been a face almost identical to hers. The Burtons might come tonight; you never knew when the Burtons were going to pop in.

Her mother placed the fried fish, with chips and peas, in front of him. She never really listened to him when he went on about the night-club because her mind was full of what had happened on *Crossroads*. She put her cigarette on a saucer on the draining-board, not extinguishing it. She remembered the news items she'd read at breakfast-time and wondered about them all over again.

Tomorrow would be worse, Eleanor thought. Even at this very moment Denny Price's blubber lips might be relating the incident to Liz Jones, how Eleanor had almost let him and then had drawn back. 'I went down by the river with a boy,' she wanted to say. 'I wanted to get done because it's the Class 2 fashion. I'm tired of being mocked by Liz Jones.' She could say it with her eyes cast down, her fork fiddling with a piece of cod on her plate. She wouldn't have to see the embarrassment in her father's face, like she'd seen it when she'd asked for money for sanitary towels. Her mother wouldn't hear at first, but she'd go on saying it, repeating herself until her mother did hear. She longed for the facts to be there in the room, how it disgusted her to imagine her father taking off his uniform in the mornings, and Rogo Pollini doing Dolly Breen. She wanted to say she'd been disgusted when Denny Price had told her to take down her knickers.

'Extraordinary, that woman,' her mother said. 'Fancy two days stuck in a bath.'

Her father laughed. It could be exaggerated, he said: you couldn't believe everything you read, not even in the newspapers.

'Extraordinary,' her mother murmured.

Her mother was trapped, married to him, obliging him so that she'd receive housekeeping money out of which she could save for her morning glass of gin. He was trapped himself, going out every night in a doorman's uniform, the Prince of Hackney with a bad back. He crushed her mother because he'd been crushed himself. How could either of them be expected to bother if she spoke of being mocked, and then asked them questions, seeking reassurance?

They wouldn't know what to say – even if she helped them by explaining that she knew there was no man with delicate hands who'd take her away when the leaves in London were yellow-brown, that there were only the blubber lips of Denny Price and the smell of meat that came off him, and Susie Crumm's father doing Mrs Breen, and Liz Jones's father doing her also, and the West Indian railway porter, and Mr Breen not aware of a thing. They wouldn't know what she was talking about if she said that Miss Whitehead had divorced herself from all of it by lying solitary at night in a room in Esher where everything was clean and neat. It was better to be Miss Whitehead than a woman who was a victim of a man's bad back. In her gleaming room Miss Whitehead was more successful in her pretence than either of them was in theirs. Miss Whitehead was complete and alone, having discarded what she wished to discard, accepting now that there was no Mr Right.

'Nice day at school?' her mother inquired suddenly in her vague manner, as though mistily aware of a duty.

Eleanor looked up from her fish and regarded both of them at once. She smiled, forcing herself to, feeling sorry for them because they were trapped by each other; because for them it was too late to escape to a room in which everything was clean.

The Ballroom of Romance

On Sundays, or on Mondays if he couldn't make it and often he couldn't, Sunday being his busy day, Canon O'Connell arrived at the farm in order to hold a private service with Bridie's father, who couldn't get about any more, having had a leg amputated after gangrene had set in. They'd had a pony and cart then and Bridie's mother had been alive: it hadn't been difficult for the two of them to help her father on to the cart in order to make the journey to Mass. But two years later the pony had gone lame and eventually had to be destroyed; not long after that her mother had died. 'Don't worry about it at all,' Canon O'Connell had said, referring to the difficulty of transporting her father to Mass. 'I'll slip up by the week, Bridie.'

The milk lorry called daily for the single churn of milk, Mr Driscoll delivered groceries and meal in his van, and took away the eggs that Bridie had collected during the week. Since Canon O'Connell had made his offer, in 1953, Bridie's father hadn't left the farm.

As well as Mass on Sundays and her weekly visits to a wayside dance-hall Bridie went shopping once every month, cycling to the town early on a Friday afternoon. She bought things for herself, material for a dress, knitting wool, stockings, a newspaper, and paper-backed Wild West novels for her father. She talked in the shops to some of the girls she'd been at school with, girls who had married shop-assistants or shop-keepers, or had become assistants themselves. Most of them had families of their own by now. 'You're lucky to be peaceful in the hills,' they said to Bridie, 'instead of stuck in a hole like this.' They had a tired look, most of them, from pregnancies and their efforts to organize and control their large families.

As she cycled back to the hills on a Friday Bridie often felt that they truly envied her her life, and she found it surprising that they should do so. If it hadn't been for her father she'd have wanted to work in the town also, in the tinned meat factory maybe, or in a shop. The town had a cinema called the Electric, and a fish-and-chip shop where people met at night, eating chips out of newspaper on the pavement outside. In the evenings, sitting in the farmhouse with her father, she often thought about the town, imagining the shop-windows lit up to display their goods and the sweet-shops still open so that people could purchase chocolates or fruit to take with them to the Electric cinema. But the town was eleven miles away, which was too far to cycle, there and back, for an evening's entertainment.

'It's a terrible thing for you, girl,' her father used to say, genuinely troubled, 'tied up to a one-legged man.' He would sigh heavily, hobbling back from the fields, where he managed as best he could. 'If your mother hadn't died,' he'd say, not finishing the sentence.

If her mother hadn't died her mother could have looked after him and the scant acres he owned, her mother could somehow have lifted the milk-churn on to the collection platform and attended to the few hens and the cows. 'I'd be dead without the girl to assist me,' she'd heard her father saying to Canon O'Connell, and Canon O'Connell replied that he was certainly lucky to have her.

'Amn't I as happy here as anywhere?' she'd say herself, but her father knew she was pretending and was saddened because the weight of circumstances had so harshly interfered with her life.

Although her father still called her a girl, Bridie was thirty-six. She was tall and strong: the skin of her fingers and her palms were stained, and harsh to touch. The labour they'd experienced had found its way into them, as though juices had come out of vegetation and pigment out of soil: since childhood she'd torn away the rough scotch grass that grew each spring among her father's mangolds and sugar beet; since childhood she'd harvested potatoes in August, her hands daily rooting in the ground she loosened and turned. Wind had toughened the flesh of her face, sun had browned it; her neck and nose were lean, her lips touched with early wrinkles.

But on Saturday nights Bridie forgot the scotch grass and the soil. In different dresses she cycled to the dance-hall, encouraged to make the journey by her father. 'Doesn't it do you good, girl?' he'd say, as though he imagined she begrudged herself the pleasure. 'Why wouldn't you enjoy yourself?' She'd cook him his tea and then he'd settle down with the wireless, or maybe a Wild West novel. In time, while still she danced, he'd stoke the fire up and hobble his way upstairs to bed.

The dance-hall, owned by Mr Justin Dwyer, was miles from anywhere, a lone building by the roadside with treeless boglands all around and a gravel expanse in front of it. On pink pebbled cement its title was painted in an azure blue that matched the depth of the background shade yet stood out well, unfussily proclaiming *The Ballroom of Romance*. Above these letters four coloured bulbs – in red, green, orange and mauve – were lit at appropriate times, an indication that the evening rendezvous was open for business. Only the façade of the building was pink, the other walls being a more ordinary grey. And inside, except for pink swing-doors, everything was blue.

On Saturday nights Mr Justin Dwyer, a small, thin man, unlocked the metal grid that protected his property and drew it back, creating an open mouth from which music would later pour. He helped his wife to carry crates of lemonade and packets of biscuits from their car, and then took up a position in the tiny vestibule between the drawn-back grid and the pink swing-doors. He sat at a card-table, with money and tickets spread out before him. He'd made a fortune, people said: he owned other ballrooms also.

People came on bicycles or in old motor-cars, country people like Bridie from remote hill farms and villages. People who did not often see other people met there, girls and boys, men and women. They paid Mr Dwyer and passed into his dance-hall, where shadows were cast on pale-blue walls and light from a crystal bowl was dim. The band, known as the Romantic Jazz Band, was composed of clarinet, drums and piano. The drummer sometimes sang.

Bridie had been going to the dance-hall since first she left the Presentation Nuns, before her mother's death. She didn't mind the journey, which was seven miles there and seven miles back: she'd travelled as far every day to the Presentation Nuns on the same bicycle, which had once been the property of her mother, an old Rudge purchased originally in 1936. On Sundays she cycled six miles to Mass, but she never minded either: she'd grown quite used to all that.

'How're you, Bridie?' inquired Mr Justin Dwyer when she arrived in a new scarlet dress one autumn evening in 1971. She said she was all right and in reply to Mr Dwyer's second query she said that her father was all right also. 'I'll go up one of these days,' promised Mr Dwyer, which was a promise he'd been making for twenty years.

She paid the entrance fee and passed through the pink swing-doors. The Romantic Jazz Band was playing a familiar melody of the past, 'The Destiny Waltz'. In spite of the band's title, jazz was not ever played in the ballroom: Mr Dwyer did not personally care for that kind of music, nor had he cared for various dance movements that had come and gone over the years. Jiving, rock and roll, twisting, and other such variations had all been resisted by Mr Dwyer, who believed that a ballroom should be, as much as possible, a dignified place. The Romantic Jazz Band consisted of Mr Maloney, Mr Swanton, and Dano Ryan on drums. They were three middle-aged men who drove out from the town in Mr Maloney's car, amateur performers who were employed otherwise by the tinned-meat factory, the Electricity Supply Board, and the County Council.

'How're you, Bridie?' inquired Dano Ryan as she passed him on her way to the cloakroom. He was idle for a moment with his drums, 'The Destiny Waltz' not calling for much attention from him.

'I'm all right, Dano,' she said. 'Are you fit yourself? Are the eyes better?' The week before he'd told her that he'd developed a watering of the eyes that must have been some kind of cold or other. He'd woken up with it in the morning and it had persisted until the afternoon: it was a new experience, he'd told her, adding that he'd never had a day's illness or discomfort in his life.

'I think I need glasses,' he said now, and as she passed into the cloakroom she imagined him in glasses, repairing the roads, as he was employed to do by the County Council. You hardly ever saw a road-mender with glasses, she reflected, and she wondered if all the dust that was inherent in his work had perhaps affected his eyes.

'How're you, Bridie?' a girl called Eenie Mackie said in the cloakroom, a girl who'd left the Presentation Nuns only a year ago.

'That's a lovely dress, Eenie,' Bridie said. 'Is it nylon, that?'

'Tricel actually. Drip-dry.'

Bridie took off her coat and hung it on a hook. There was a small wash-basin in the cloakroom above which hung a discoloured oval mirror. Used tissues and pieces of cotton-wool, cigarette-butts and matches covered the concrete floor. Lengths of green-painted timber partitioned off a lavatory in a corner.

'Jeez, you're looking great, Bridie,' Madge Dowding remarked, waiting for her turn at the mirror. She moved towards it as she spoke, taking off a pair of spectacles before endeavouring to apply make-up to the lashes of her eye. She stared myopically into the oval mirror, humming while the other girls became restive.

'Will you hurry up, for God's sake!' shouted Eenie Mackie. 'We're standing here all night, Madge.'

Madge Dowding was the only one who was older than Bridie. She was thirty-nine, although often she said she was younger. The girls sniggered about that, saying that Madge Dowding should accept her condition – her age and her squint and her poor complexion – and not make herself ridiculous going out after men. What man would be bothered with the like of her anyway? Madge Dowding would do better to give herself over to do Saturday-night work for the Legion of Mary: wasn't Canon O'Connell always looking for aid?

'Is that fellow there?' she asked now, moving away from the mirror. 'The guy with the long arms. Did anyone see him outside?'

'He's dancing with Cat Bolger,' one of the girls replied. 'She has herself glued to him.'

'Lover boy,' remarked Patty Byrne, and everyone laughed because the person referred to was hardly a boy any more, being over fifty it was said, a bachelor who came only occasionally to the dance-hall.

Madge Dowding left the cloakroom rapidly, not bothering to pretend she wasn't anxious about the conjunction of Cat Bolger and the man with the long arms. Two sharp spots of red had come into her cheeks, and when she stumbled in her haste the girls in the cloakroom laughed. A younger girl would have pretended to be casual.

Bridie chatted, waiting for the mirror. Some girls, not wishing to be delayed, used the mirrors of their compacts. Then in twos and threes, occasionally singly, they left the cloakroom and took their places on upright wooden chairs at one end of the dance-hall, waiting to be asked to dance. Mr Maloney, Mr Swanton and Dano Ryan played 'Harvest Moon' and 'I Wonder Who's Kissing Her Now' and 'I'll Be Around'.

Bridie danced. Her father would be falling asleep by the fire; the wireless, tuned in to Radio Eireann, would be murmuring in the background. Already he'd have listened to *Faith and Order* and *Spot the Talent*. His Wild West novel, *Three Rode Fast* by Jake Matall, would have dropped from his single knee on to the flagged floor. He would wake with a jerk as he did every night and, forgetting what night it was, might be surprised not to see her, for usually she was sitting there at the table, mending clothes or washing eggs. 'Is it time for the News?' he'd automatically say.

Dust and cigarette smoke formed a haze beneath the crystal bowl, feet thudded, girls shrieked and laughed, some of them dancing together for want of a male partner. The music was loud, the musicians had taken off their jackets. Vigorously they played a number of tunes from *State Fair* and then, more romantically, 'Just One Of Those Things'. The tempo increased for a Paul Jones, after which Bridie found herself with a youth who told her he was saving up to emigrate, the nation in his opinion being finished. 'I'm up in the hills with the uncle,' he said, 'labouring fourteen hours a day. Is it any life for a young fellow?' She knew his uncle, a hill farmer whose stony acres were separated from her father's by one other farm only. 'He has me gutted with work,' the youth told her. 'Is there sense in it at all, Bridie?'

At ten o'clock there was a stir, occasioned by the arrival of three middle-aged bachelors who'd cycled over from Carey's public house. They shouted and whistled, greeting other people across the dancing area. They smelt of stout and sweat and whiskey.

Every Saturday at just this time they arrived, and, having sold them their tickets, Mr Dwyer folded up his card-table and locked the tin box that held the evening's takings: his ballroom was complete.

'How're you, Bridie?' one of the bachelors, known as Bowser Egan, inquired. Another one, Tim Daly, asked Patty Byrne how she was. 'Will we take the floor?' Eyes Horgan suggested to Madge Dowding, already pressing the front of his navy-blue suit against the net of her dress. Bridie danced with Bowser Egan, who said she was looking great.

The bachelors would never marry, the girls of the dance-hall considered: they were wedded already, to stout and whiskey and laziness, to three old mothers somewhere up in the hills. The man with the long arms didn't drink but he was the same in all other ways: he had the same look of a bachelor, a quality in his face.

'Great,' Bowser Egan said, feather-stepping in an inaccurate and inebriated manner. 'You're a great little dancer, Bridie.'

'Will you lay off that!' cried Madge Dowding, her voice shrill above the sound of the music. Eyes Horgan had slipped two fingers into the back of her dress and was now pretending they'd got there by accident. He smiled blearily, his huge red face streaming with perspiration, the eyes which gave him his nickname protuberant and bloodshot.

'Watch your step with that one,' Bowser Egan called out, laughing so that spittle sprayed on to Bridie's face. Eenie Mackie, who was also dancing near the incident, laughed also and winked at Bridie. Dano Ryan left his drums and sang. 'Oh, how I miss your gentle kiss,' he crooned, 'and long to hold you tight.'

Nobody knew the name of the man with the long arms. The only words he'd ever been known to speak in the Ballroom of Romance were the words that formed his invitation to dance. He was a shy man who stood alone when he wasn't performing on the dance-floor. He rode away on his bicycle afterwards, not saying good night to anyone.

'Cat has your man leppin' tonight,' Tim Daly remarked to Patty Byrne, for the liveliness that Cat Bolger had introduced into foxtrot and waltz was noticeable.

'I think of you only,' sang Dano Ryan. 'Only wishing, wishing you were by my side.'

Dano Ryan would have done, Bridie often thought, because he was a different kind of bachelor: he had a lonely look about him, as if he'd become tired of being on his own. Every week she thought he would have done, and during the week her mind regularly returned to that thought. Dano Ryan would have done because she felt he wouldn't mind coming to live in the farmhouse while her one-legged father was still about the place. Three could live as cheaply as two where Dano Ryan was concerned because giving up the wages he earned as a road-worker would be balanced by the saving made on what he paid for lodgings. Once, at the end of an evening, she'd pretended that there was a puncture in the back wheel of her bicycle and he'd concerned himself with it while Mr Maloney and Mr Swanton waited for him in Mr Maloney's car. He'd blown the tyre up with the car pump and had said he thought it would hold.

It was well known in the dance-hall that she fancied her chances with Dano Ryan. But it was well known also that Dano Ryan had got into a set way of life and had remained in it for quite some years. He lodged with a widow called Mrs Griffin and Mrs Griffin's mentally affected son, in a cottage on the outskirts of the town. He was said to be good to the affected child, buying him sweets and taking him out for rides on the cross-bar of his bicycle. He gave an hour or two of his time every week to the Church of Our Lady Queen of Heaven, and he was loyal to Mr Dwyer. He performed in the two other rural dance-halls that Mr Dwyer owned, rejecting advances from the town's more sophisticated dance-hall, even though it was more conveniently situated for him and the fee was more substantial than that paid by Mr Dwyer. But Mr Dwyer had discovered Dano Ryan and Dano had not forgotten it, just as Mr Maloney and Mr Swanton had not forgotten their discovery by Mr Dwyer either.

'Would we take a lemonade?' Bowser Egan suggested. 'And a packet of biscuits, Bridie?'

No alcoholic liquor was ever served in the Ballroom of Romance, the premises not being licensed for this added stimulant. Mr Dwyer in fact had never sought a licence for any of his premises, knowing that romance and alcohol were difficult commodities to mix, especially in a dignified ballroom. Behind where the girls sat on the wooden chairs Mr Dwyer's wife, a small stout woman, served the bottles of lemonade, with straws, and the biscuits and the crisps. She talked busily while doing so, mainly about the turkeys she kept. She'd once told Bridie that she thought of them as children.

'Thanks,' Bridie said, and Bowser Egan led her to the trestle table. Soon it would be the intermission: soon the three members of the band would cross the floor also for refreshment. She thought up questions to ask Dano Ryan.

When first she'd danced in the Ballroom of Romance, when she was just sixteen, Dano Ryan had been there also, four years older than she was, playing the drums for Mr Maloney as he played them now. She'd hardly noticed him then because of his not being one of the dancers: he was part of the ballroom's scenery, like the trestle table and the lemonade bottles, and Mrs Dwyer and Mr Dwyer. The youths who'd danced with her then in their Saturday-night blue suits had later disappeared into the town, or to Dublin or Britain, leaving behind them those who became the middle-aged bachelors of the hills. There'd been a boy called Patrick Grady whom she had loved in those days. Week after week she'd ridden away from the Ballroom of Romance with the image of his face in her mind, a thin face, pale beneath black hair. It had been different, dancing with Patrick Grady, and she'd felt that he found it different dancing with her, although he'd never said so. At night she'd dreamed of him and in the daytime too, while she helped her mother in the kitchen or her father with the cows. Week by week she'd returned to the ballroom, smiling on its pink façade and dancing then in the arms of Patrick Grady. Often they'd stood together drinking lemonade, not saying anything, not knowing what to say. She knew he loved her, and she believed then that he would lead her one day from the dim, romantic ballroom, from its blueness and its pinkness and its crystal bowl of light and its music. She believed he would lead her into sunshine, to the town and the Church of Our Lady Queen of Heaven, to marriage and smiling faces. But someone else had got Patrick Grady, a girl from the town who'd never danced in the wayside ballroom. She'd scooped up Patrick Grady when he didn't have a chance.

Bridie had wept, hearing that. By night she'd lain in her bed in the farmhouse, quietly crying, the tears rolling into her hair and making the pillow damp. When she woke in the early morning the thought was still naggingly with her and it remained with her by day, replacing her daytime dreams of happiness. Someone told her later on that he'd crossed to Britain, to Wolverhampton, with the girl he'd married, and she imagined him there, in a place she wasn't able properly to visualize, labouring in a factory, his children being born and acquiring the accent of the area. The Ballroom of Romance wasn't the same without him, and when no one else stood out for her particularly over the years and when no one offered her marriage, she found herself wondering about Dano Ryan. If you couldn't have love, the next best thing was surely a decent man.

Bowser Egan hardly fell into that category, nor did Tim Daly. And it was plain to everyone that Cat Bolger and Madge Dowding were wasting their time over the man with the long arms. Madge Dowding was already a figure of fun in the ballroom, the way she ran after the bachelors; Cat Bolger would end up the same if she wasn't careful. One way or another it wasn't difficult to be a figure of fun in the ballroom, and you didn't have to be as old as Madge Dowding: a girl who'd just left the Presentation Nuns had once asked Eyes Horgan what he had in his trouser pocket and he told her it was a penknife. She'd repeated this afterwards in the cloakroom, how she'd requested Eyes Horgan not to dance so close to her because his penknife was sticking into her. 'Jeez, aren't you the right baby!' Patty Byrne had shouted delightedly: everyone had laughed, knowing that Eyes Horgan only came to the ballroom for stuff like that. He was no use to any girl.

'Two lemonades, Mrs Dwyer,' Bowser Egan said, 'and two packets of Kerry Creams. Is Kerry Creams all right, Bridie?'

She nodded, smiling. Kerry Creams would be fine, she said.

'Well, Bridie, isn't that the great outfit you have!' Mrs Dwyer remarked. 'Doesn't the red suit her, Bowser?'

By the swing-doors stood Mr Dwyer, smoking a cigarette that he held cupped in his left hand. His small eyes noted all developments. He had been aware of Madge Dowding's anxiety when Eyes Horgan had inserted two fingers into the back opening of her dress. He had looked away, not caring for the incident, but had it developed further he would have spoken to Eyes Horgan, as he had on other occasions. Some of the younger lads didn't know any better and would dance very close to their partners, who generally were too embarrassed to do anything about it, being young themselves But that, in Mr Dwyer's opinion, was a different kettle of fish altogether because they were decent young lads who'd in no time at all be doing a steady line with a girl and would end up as he had himself with Mrs Dwyer, in the same house with her, sleeping in a bed with her, firmly married. It was the middle-aged bachelors who required the watching: they came down from the hills like mountain goats, released from their mammies and from the smell of animals and soil. Mr Dwyer continued to watch Eyes Horgan, wondering how drunk he was.

Dano Ryan's song came to an end, Mr Swanton laid down his clarinet, Mr Maloney rose from the piano. Dano Ryan wiped sweat from his face and the three men slowly moved towards Mrs Dwyer's trestle table.

'Jeez, you have powerful legs,' Eyes Horgan whispered to Madge Dowding, but Madge Dowding's attention was on the man with the long arms, who had left Cat Bolger's side and was proceeding in the direction of the men's lavatory. He never took refreshments. She moved, herself, towards the men's lavatory, to take up a position outside it, but Eyes

Horgan followed her. 'Would you take a lemonade, Madge?' he asked. He had a small bottle of whiskey on him: if they went into a corner they could add a drop of it to the lemonade. She didn't drink spirits, she reminded him, and he went away.

'Excuse me a minute,' Bowser Egan said, putting down his bottle of lemonade. He crossed the floor to the lavatory. He too, Bridie knew, would have a small bottle of whiskey on him. She watched while Dano Ryan, listening to a story Mr Maloney was telling, paused in the centre of the ballroom, his head bent to hear what was being said. He was a big man, heavily made, with black hair that was slightly touched with grey, and big hands. He laughed when Mr Maloney came to the end of his story and then bent his head again, in order to listen to a story told by Mr Swanton.

'Are you on your own, Bridie?' Cat Bolger asked, and Bridie said she was waiting for Bowser Egan. 'I think I'll have a lemonade,' Cat Bolger said.

Younger boys and girls stood with their arms still around one another, queueing up for refreshments. Boys who hadn't danced at all, being nervous because they didn't know any steps, stood in groups, smoking and making jokes. Girls who hadn't been danced with yet talked to one another, their eyes wandering. Some of them sucked at straws in lemonade bottles.

Bridie, still watching Dano Ryan, imagined him wearing the glasses he'd referred to, sitting in the farmhouse kitchen, reading one of her father's Wild West novels. She imagined the three of them eating a meal she'd prepared, fried eggs and rashers and fried potato-cakes and tea and bread and butter and jam, brown bread and soda and shop bread. She imagined Dano Ryan leaving the kitchen in the morning to go out to the fields in order to weed the mangolds, and her father hobbling off behind him, and the two men working together. She saw hay being cut, Dano Ryan with the scythe that she'd learned to use herself, her father using a rake as best he could. She saw herself, because of the extra help, being able to attend to things in the farmhouse, things she'd never had time for because of the cows and the hens and the fields. There were bedroom curtains that needed repairing where the net had ripped, and wallpaper that had become loose and needed to be stuck up with flour paste. The scullery required whitewashing.

The night he'd blown up the tyre of her bicycle she'd thought he was going to kiss her. He'd crouched on the ground in the darkness with his ear to the tyre, listening for escaping air. When he could hear none he'd straightened up and said he thought she'd be all right on the bicycle. His face had been quite close to hers and she'd smiled at him. At that moment, unfortunately, Mr Maloney had blown an impatient blast on the horn of his motor-car.

Often she'd been kissed by Bowser Egan, on the nights when he insisted on riding part of the way home with her. They had to dismount in order to push their bicycles up a hill and the first time he'd accompanied her he'd contrived to fall against her, steadying himself by putting a hand on her shoulder. The next thing she was aware of was the moist quality of his lips and the sound of his bicycle as it clattered noisily on the road. He'd suggested then, regaining his breath, that they should go into a field.

That was nine years ago. In the intervening passage of time she'd been kissed as well, in similar circumstances, by Eyes Horgan and Tim Daly. She'd gone into fields with them and permitted them to put their arms about her while heavily they breathed. At one time or another she had imagined marriage with one or other of them, seeing them in the farmhouse with her father, even though the fantasies were unlikely.

Bridie stood with Cat Bolger, knowing that it would be some time before Bowser Egan came out of the lavatory. Mr Maloney, Mr Swanton and Dano Ryan approached, Mr Maloney insisting that he would fetch three bottles of lemonade from the trestle table.

'You sang the last one beautifully,' Bridie said to Dano Ryan. 'Isn't it a beautiful song?'

Mr Swanton said it was the finest song ever written, and Cat Bolger said she preferred 'Danny Boy', which in her opinion was the finest song ever written.

'Take a suck of that,' said Mr Maloney, handing Dano Ryan and Mr Swanton bottles of lemonade. 'How's Bridie tonight? Is your father well, Bridie?'

Her father was all right, she said.

'I hear they're starting a cement factory,' said Mr Maloney. 'Did anyone hear talk of that? They're after striking some commodity in the earth that makes good cement. Ten feet down, over at Kilmalough.'

'It'll bring employment,' said Mr Swanton. 'It's employment that's necessary in this area.'

'Canon O'Connell was on about it,' Mr Maloney said. 'There's Yankee money involved.'

'Will the Yanks come over?' inquired Cat Bolger. 'Will they run it themselves, Mr Maloney?'

Mr Maloney, intent on his lemonade, didn't hear the questions and Cat Bolger didn't repeat them.

'There's stuff called Optrex,' Bridie said quietly to Dano Ryan, 'that my father took the time he had a cold in his eyes. Maybe Optrex would settle the watering, Dano.'

'Ah sure, it doesn't worry me that much –'

'It's terrible, anything wrong with the eyes. You wouldn't want to take a chance. You'd get Optrex in a chemist, Dano, and a little bowl with it so that you can bathe the eyes.'

Her father's eyes had become red-rimmed and unsightly to look at. She'd gone into Riordan's Medical Hall in the town and had explained what the trouble was, and Mr Riordan had recommended Optrex. She told this to Dano Ryan, adding that her father had had no trouble with his eyes since. Dano Ryan nodded.

'Did you hear that, Mrs Dwyer?' Mr Maloney called out. 'A cement factory for Kilmalough.'

Mrs Dwyer wagged her head, placing empty bottles in a crate. She'd heard references to the cement factory, she said: it was the best news for a long time.

'Kilmalough'll never know itself,' her husband commented, joining her in her task with the empty lemonade bottles.

' 'Twill bring prosperity certainly,' said Mr Swanton. 'I was saying just there, Justin, that employment's what's necessary.'

'Sure, won't the Yanks –' began Cat Bolger, but Mr Maloney interrupted her.

'The Yanks'll be in at the top, Cat, or maybe not here at all – maybe only inserting money into it. It'll be local labour entirely.'

'You'll not marry a Yank, Cat,' said Mr Swanton, loudly laughing. 'You can't catch those fellows.'

'Haven't you plenty of homemade bachelors?' suggested Mr Maloney. He laughed also, throwing away the straw he was sucking through and tipping the bottle into his mouth. Cat Bolger told him to get on with himself. She moved towards the men's lavatory and took up a position outside it, not speaking to Madge Dowding, who was still standing there.

'Keep a watch on Eyes Horgan,' Mrs Dwyer warned her husband, which was advice she gave him at this time every Saturday night, knowing that Eyes Horgan was drinking in the lavatory. When he was drunk Eyes Horgan was the most difficult of the bachelors.

'I have a drop of it left, Dano,' Bridie said quietly. 'I could bring it over on Saturday. The eye stuff.'

'Ah, don't worry yourself, Bridie –'

'No trouble at all. Honestly now –'

'Mrs Griffin has me fixed up for a test with Dr Cready. The old eyes are no worry, only when I'm reading the paper or at the pictures. Mrs Griffin says I'm only straining them due to lack of glasses.'

He looked away while he said that, and she knew at once that Mrs Griffin was arranging to marry him. She felt it instinctively: Mrs Griffin was going to marry him because she was afraid that if he moved away from her cottage, to get married to someone else, she'd find it hard to replace him with another lodger who'd be good to her affected son. He'd become a father to Mrs Griffin's affected son, to whom already he was kind. It was a natural outcome, for Mrs Griffin had all the chances, seeing him every night and morning and not having to make do with weekly encounters in a ballroom.

She thought of Patrick Grady, seeing in her mind his pale, thin face. She might be the mother of four of his children now, or seven or eight maybe.

She might be living in Wolverhampton, going out to the pictures in the evenings, instead of looking after a one-legged man. If the weight of circumstances hadn't intervened she wouldn't be standing in a wayside ballroom, mourning the marriage of a road-mender she didn't love. For a moment she thought she might cry, standing there thinking of Patrick Grady in Wolverhampton. In her life, on the farm and in the house, there was no place for tears. Tears were a luxury, like flowers would be in the fields where the mangolds grew, or fresh whitewash in the scullery. It wouldn't have been fair ever to have wept in the kitchen while her father sat listening to *Spot the Talent*: her father had more right to weep, having lost a leg. He suffered in a greater way, yet he remained kind and concerned for her.

In the Ballroom of Romance she felt behind her eyes the tears that it would have been improper to release in the presence of her father. She wanted to let them go, to feel them streaming on her cheeks, to receive the sympathy of Dano Ryan and of everyone else. She wanted them all to listen to her while she told them about Patrick Grady who was now in Wolverhampton and about the death of her mother and her own life since. She wanted Dano Ryan to put his arm around her so that she could lean her head against it. She wanted him to look at her in his decent way and to stroke with his road-mender's fingers the backs of her hands. She might wake in a bed with him and imagine for a moment that he was Patrick Grady. She might bathe his eyes and pretend.

'Back to business,' said Mr Maloney, leading his band across the floor to their instruments.

'Tell your father I was asking for him,' Dano Ryan said. She smiled and she promised, as though nothing had happened, that she would tell her father that.

She danced with Tim Daly and then again with the youth who'd said he intended to emigrate. She saw Madge Dowding moving swiftly towards the man with the long arms as he came out of the lavatory, moving faster than Cat Bolger. Eyes Horgan approached Cat Bolger. Dancing with her, he spoke earnestly, attempting to persuade her to permit him to ride part of the way home with her. He was unaware of the jealousy that was coming from her as she watched Madge Dowding holding close to her the man with the long arms while they performed a quickstep. Cat Bolger was in her thirties too.

'Get away out of that,' said Bowser Egan, cutting in on the youth who was dancing with Bridie. 'Go home to your mammy, boy.' He took her into his arms, saying again that she was looking great tonight. 'Did you hear about the cement factory?' he said. 'Isn't it great for Kilmalough?'

She agreed. She said what Mr Swanton and Mr Maloney had said: that the cement factory would bring employment to the neighbourhood.

'Will I ride home with you a bit, Bridie?' Bowser Egan suggested, and she pretended not to hear him. 'Aren't you my girl, Bridie, and always have been?' he said, a statement that made no sense at all.

His voice went on whispering at her, saying he would marry her tomorrow only his mother wouldn't permit another woman in the house. She knew what it was like herself, he reminded her, having a parent to look after: you couldn't leave them to rot, you had to honour your father and your mother.

She danced to 'The Bells Are Ringing', moving her legs in time with Bowser Egan's while over his shoulder she watched Dano Ryan softly striking one of his smaller drums. Mrs Griffin had got him even though she was nearly fifty, with no looks at all, a lumpish woman with lumpish legs and arms. Mrs Griffin had got him just as the girl had got Patrick Grady.

The music ceased, Bowser Egan held her hard against him, trying to touch her face with his. Around them, people whistled and clapped: the evening had come to an end. She walked away from Bowser Egan, knowing that not ever again would she dance in the Ballroom of Romance. She'd been a figure of fun, trying to promote a relationship with a middle-aged County Council labourer, as ridiculous as Madge Dowding dancing on beyond her time.

'I'm waiting outside for you, Cat,' Eyes Horgan called out, lighting a cigarette as he made for the swing-doors.

Already the man with the long arms – made long, so they said, from carrying rocks off his land – had left the ballroom. Others were moving briskly. Mr Dwyer was tidying the chairs.

In the cloakroom the girls put on their coats and said they'd see one another at Mass the next day. Madge Dowding hurried. 'Are you O.K., Bridie?' Patty Byrne asked and Bridie said she was. She smiled at little Patty Byrne, wondering if a day would come for the younger girl also, if one day she'd decide that she was a figure of fun in a wayside ballroom.

'Good night so,' Bridie said, leaving the cloakroom, and the girls who were still chatting there wished her good night. Outside the cloakroom she paused for a moment. Mr Dwyer was still tidying the chairs, picking up empty lemonade bottles from the floor, setting the chairs in a neat row. His wife was sweeping the floor. 'Good night, Bridie,' Mr Dwyer said. 'Good night, Bridie,' his wife said.

Extra lights had been switched on so that the Dwyers could see what they were doing. In the glare the blue walls of the ballroom seemed tatty, marked with hair-oil where men had leaned against them, inscribed with names and initials and hearts with arrows through them. The crystal bowl gave out a light that was ineffective in the glare; the bowl was broken here and there, which wasn't noticeable when the other lights weren't on.

'Good night so,' Bridie said to the Dwyers. She passed through the swing-doors and descended the three concrete steps on the gravel expanse in front of the ballroom. People were gathered on the gravel, talking in groups, standing with their bicycles. She saw Madge Dowding going off with Tim Daly. A youth rode away with a girl on the cross-bar of his bicycle. The engines of motor-cars started.

'Good night, Bridie,' Dano Ryan said.

'Good night, Dano,' she said.

She walked across the gravel towards her bicycle, hearing Mr Maloney, somewhere behind her, repeating that no matter how you looked at it the cement factory would be a great thing for Kilmalough. She heard the bang of a car-door and knew it was Mr Swanton banging the door of Mr Maloney's car because he always gave it the same loud bang. Two other doors banged as she reached her bicycle and then the engine started up and the headlights went on. She touched the two tyres of the bicycle to make certain she hadn't a puncture. The wheels of Mr Maloney's car traversed the gravel and were silent when they reached the road.

'Good night, Bridie,' someone called, and she replied, pushing her bicycle towards the road.

'Will I ride a little way with you?' Bowser Egan asked.

They rode together and when they arrived at the hill for which it was necessary to dismount she looked back and saw in the distance the four coloured bulbs that decorated the façade of the Ballroom of Romance. As she watched the lights went out, and she imagined Mr Dwyer pulling the metal grid across the front of his property and locking the two padlocks that secured it. His wife would be waiting with the evening's takings, sitting in the front of their car.

'D'you know what it is, Bridie,' said Bowser Egan, 'you were never looking better than tonight.' He took from a pocket of his suit the small bottle of whiskey he had. He uncorked it and drank some and then handed it to her. She took it and drank. 'Sure, why wouldn't you?' he said, surprised to see her drinking because she never had in his company before. It was an unpleasant taste, she considered, a taste she'd experienced only twice before, when she'd taken whiskey as a remedy for toothache. 'What harm would it do you?' Bowser Egan said as she raised the bottle again to her lips. He reached out a hand for it, though, suddenly concerned lest she should consume a greater share than he wished her to.

She watched him drinking more expertly than she had. He would always be drinking, she thought. He'd be lazy and useless, sitting in the kitchen with the *Irish Press*. He'd waste money buying a second-hand motor-car in order to drive into the town to go to the public houses on fair-days.

'She's shook these days,' he said, referring to his mother. 'She'll hardly last two years, I'm thinking.' He threw the empty whiskey bottle into the ditch and lit a cigarette. They pushed their bicycles. He said:

'When she goes, Bridie, I'll sell the bloody place up. I'll sell the pigs and the whole damn one and twopence worth.' He paused in order to raise the cigarette to his lips. He drew in smoke and exhaled it. 'With the cash that I'll get I could improve some place else, Bridie.'

They reached a gate on the left-hand side of the road and automatically they pushed their bicycles towards it and leaned them against it. He climbed over the gate into the field and she climbed after him. 'Will we sit down here, Bridie?' he said, offering the suggestion as one that had just occurred to him, as though they'd entered the field for some other purpose.

'We could improve a place like your own one,' he said, putting his right arm around her shoulders. 'Have you a kiss in you, Bridie?' He kissed her, exerting pressure with his teeth. When his mother died he would sell his farm and spend the money in the town. After that he would think of getting married because he'd have nowhere to go, because he'd want a fire to sit at and a woman to cook food for him. He kissed her again, his lips hot, the sweat on his cheeks sticking to her. 'God, you're great at kissing,' he said.

She rose, saying it was time to go, and they climbed over the gate again. 'There's nothing like a Saturday,' he said. 'Good night to you so, Bridie.'

He mounted his bicycle and rode down the hill, and she pushed hers to the top and then mounted it also. She rode through the night as on Saturday nights for years she had ridden and never would ride again because she'd reached a certain age. She would wait now and in time Bowser Egan would seek her out because his mother would have died. Her father would probably have died also by then. She would marry Bowser Egan because it would be lonesome being by herself in the farmhouse.

The Forty-seventh Saturday

Mavie awoke and remembered at once that it was Saturday. She lay for a while, alone with that thought, considering it and relishing it. Then she thought of details: the ingredients of a lunch, the cleaning of the kitchen floor, the tidying of her bedroom. She rose and reached for her dressing-gown. In the kitchen she found a small pad of paper and wrote in pencil these words: *mackerel, parmesan cheese, garlic.* Then she drew back the curtains, placed a filled kettle over a gas jet and shook cornflakes on to a plate.

Some hours later, about midday, Mr McCarthy stood thoughtfully in a wine-shop. He sighed, and then said:

'*Vin rosé.* The larger size. Is it a litre? I don't know what it's called.'

'Jumbo *vin rosé*,' the assistant murmured, ignoring the demands of the accented word. 'Fourteen and seven.'

It was not a wine-shop in which Mr McCarthy had ever before made a purchase. He paused, his hand inside his jacket, the tips of his fingers touching the leather of his wallet.

'Fourteen and seven?'

The assistant, perceiving clearly that Mr McCarthy had arrested the action with which he had planned to draw money from within his clothes, took no notice. He blew on the glass of the bottle because the bottle was dusty. Whistling thickly with tongue and lips, he tore a piece of brown paper and proceeded to wrap with it. He placed the parcel in a carrier bag.

'I thought it was ten shillings that size,' Mr McCarthy said. 'I have got it in another place for ten shillings.'

The assistant stared at him, incredulous.

'I buy a lot of *vin rosé*,' Mr McCarthy explained.

The assistant, a man of thirty-five with a face that was pock-marked, spoke no word but stared on. In his mind he was already retailing the incident to his superior when, an hour or so later, that person should return. He scrutinized Mr McCarthy, so that when the time came he might lend authority to his tale with an accurate description of the man who had demanded *vin rosé* and then had argued about the charged price. He saw before him a middle-aged man of medium height, with a hat and spectacles and a moustache.

'Well, I haven't time to argue.' Mr McCarthy handed the man a pound note and received his change. 'Threepence short, that is,' he said; and the assistant explained:

'The carrier bag. It's necessary nowadays to charge. You understand?'

But Mr McCarthy lifted the wine out of the bag, saying that the brown paper wrapping was quite sufficient, and the assistant handed him a threepenny piece.

'I take a taxi,' Mr McCarthy explained. 'It's no hardship to carry.'

In the flat Mavie laid two mackerel on the smoking fat of the frying-pan and sniffed the air. A plastic apron covered her navy-blue, rather old-fashioned suit. Her fair hair, recently released from curling-pins, quivered splendidly about her head; her bosom heaved as she drew the tasty air into her lungs. She walked from the stove to the kitchen table, seeking a glass of medium dry sherry that a minute or two previously she had poured and placed somewhere.

'Ta-ra-ta-ta-ta-ta-ta-ta, ta-ta-ta-ta-ta-ta,' tuned Mr McCarthy in his taxi-cab, trying to put from his mind the extra four and sevenpence that he had been obliged to spend on the wine. 'A basement place,' he called to the driver. 'You'll know it by a motor-cycle and side-car parked outside.' The driver made no response.

'Motor-bike and side-car,' repeated Mr McCarthy. 'Parked by a lamp-post, number twenty-one. D'you understand?'

'Twenty-one, Roeway Road,' said the driver. 'We'll endeavour.'

Mr McCarthy closed his eyes and stretched his legs stiffly in front of him. He thought of Mavie, as was suitable at that moment. He saw her standing by the edge of the kitchen table, with a cigarette protruding from the left-hand extremity of her mouth and the thumb and forefinger of her right hand grasping a glass which contained sherry and which bore, painted around it on the outside, two thin lines, one in red, the other in gold. It was the forty-seventh time that Mr McCarthy had made this mid-day journey, in a taxi-cab with a bottle of wine.

'Doesn't he want you to dress up?' the girls had asked when first she had told them. 'Pith helmets, chukka boots?' Mavie had found that funny. She had laughed and said: 'Dress up? Rather the opposite!' But that was at the very beginning of the affair, before she had fallen so deeply in love with him.

'Hullo.' Mavie, holding the sherry glass before her, struck a pose in the basement kitchen. She had taken off her plastic apron.

'Hullo, Mavie.' He held out the bottle, his hat still upon his head, his soft raincoat creased and seeming unclean. 'I've brought some wine. A little wine. I thought it would cheer us up.' He had let himself in, for the door was always on the latch. He had clicked the Yale catch behind him, as he had long since learned she liked him to do, so that no disturbances might later take place. 'I don't care for disturbances,' Mavie had said on the fifth occasion: an embarrassing time, when a coal-heaver, mistaking the basement for the basement next door, had walked into her bedroom with a sack on his back to find Mr McCarthy and herself playing about on the covers of her bed.

'My, my, you're looking sweet.' He removed his hat and overcoat and cast his eye about for a corkscrew. It was his policy on these visits to prime himself beforehand with two measures of brandy and, having made his entry, to take an immediate glass of *vin rosé*. He did not care for Mavie's sherry. *British sherry* was how the label described it; a qualification that put Mr McCarthy off.

'I love that costume.' He had said this before, referring to Mavie's navy-blue coat and skirt. In reply she had once or twice pointed out that it had been, originally, the property of her sister Linda.

Mr McCarthy could smell the fish. He could sense the atmosphere rich with mackerel and the perfumed mist with which Mavie had sprayed the room.

'I'm doing a nice fresh mackerel in a custard sauce,' Mavie announced, moving towards the stove. She had been closely embraced by Mr McCarthy, who was now a little shaken, caught between the promise of the embrace and the thought of mackerel in a sauce. He imagined he must have heard incorrectly: he could not believe that the sauce was a custard one. 'Custard!' he said. 'Custard?'

Mavie stirred the contents of a bowl. She remembered the first time: she had made an omelette; the mushrooms with which she had filled it had not cooked properly and Mr McCarthy had remarked upon the fact. She could have wept, watching him move the mushrooms to the side of his plate. 'Have them on toast,' she had cried. 'I'll cook them a bit more, love, and you can have them on a nice piece of toast.' But he had shaken his head, and then, to show that all was well, he had taken her into his arms and had at once begun to unzip her skirt.

'Custard?' said Mr McCarthy again, aware of some revulsion in his bowels.

'A garlic custard sauce. I read it in that column.'

'My dear, I'd as soon have a lightly boiled egg. This wretched old trouble again.'

'Oh, you poor thing. But fish is as easy to digest. A small helping. I'd have steamed had I known. You poor soul. Sit down, for heaven's sake.'

He was thinking that he would vomit if he had to lift a single forkful of mackerel and garlic custard sauce to his lips. He would feel a retching at the back of his throat and before another second passed there would be an accident.

'Love, I should have told you: I am off fish in any shape or form. The latest thing, I am on a diet of soft-boiled eggs. I'm a terrible trouble to you, Mavie love.'

She came to where he was sitting, drinking his way through the wine, and kissed him. She said not to worry about anything.

Mr McCarthy had told Mavie more lies than he had ever told anyone else. He had invented trouble with his stomach so that he could insist upon simple food, even though Mavie, forgetfully or hopefully, always cooked more elaborately. He had invented a Saturday appointment at four o'clock every week so that no dawdling would be required of him after he had exacted what he had come to look upon as his due. He had invented a wife and two children so that Mavie might not get ideas above her station.

'Brush your teeth, Mavie, like a good girl.' Mr McCarthy was being practical, fearful of the garlic. He spoke with confidence, knowing that Mavie would see it as reasonable that she should brush her teeth before the moments of love.

While she was in the bathroom he hummed a tune and reflected on his continuing good fortune. He drank more wine and when Mavie returned bade her drink some, too. It could only happen on Saturdays because the girl whom Mavie shared the flat with, Eithne, went away for the weekends.

'Well, this is pleasant,' said Mr McCarthy, sitting her on his knee, stroking her navy-blue clothes. She sat there, a little heavy for him, swinging her legs until her shoes slipped off.

This Saturday was Mavie's birthday. Today she was twenty-seven, while Mr McCarthy remained at fifty-two. She had, the night before and for several other nights and days, considered the fact, wondering whether or not to make anything of it, wondering whether or not to let Mr McCarthy know. She had thought, the Saturday before, that it might seem a little pushing to say that it was her birthday in a week; it might seem that her words contained the suggestion that Mr McCarthy should arm himself with a present or should contrive to transform the day into a special occasion. She thought ecstatically of his arriving at the house with a wrapped box and sitting down and saying: 'What lovely mackerel!' and putting it to her then that since this was her twenty-seventh birthday he would arrange to spend the whole afternoon and the night as well. 'We shall take to the West End later on,' Mr McCarthy had said in Mavie's mind, 'and shall go to a show, that thing at the Palladium. I have the tickets in my wallet.'

'What terrible old weather it is,' said Mr McCarthy. 'You wouldn't know whether you're coming or going.'

Mavie made a noise of agreement. She remembered other birthdays: a year she had been given a kite, the time that her cake, its flavour chosen by her, had not succeeded in the oven and had come to the table lumpy and grey, disguised with hundreds and thousands. She had cried, and her mother had picked up a teaspoon and rapped her knuckles. 'After the show,' said Mr McCarthy, 'what about a spot of dinner in a little place I've heard of? And then liqueurs before we return in style to your little nest.' As he spoke Mr McCarthy nuzzled her neck, and Mavie realized that he was, in fact, nuzzling her neck, though he was not speaking.

'Today is a special day,' said Mavie. 'It's a very special November day.'

Mr McCarthy laughed. 'Every Saturday is a special day for me. Every Saturday is outlined in red on my heart.' And he initiated some horseplay which prevented Mavie from explaining.

Born beneath the sign of Scorpio, she was meant to be strong, fearless and enterprising. As a child she had often been in trouble, not because of naughtiness but because she had been dreamy about her work. She dreamed now, dominated by an image of Mr McCarthy rushing out of a sudden for flowers. She saw him returning, blooms everywhere, saying he had telephoned to put off his Saturday appointment and had telephoned his home to say he had been called away on vital business. She felt his hands seeking the outline of her ribs, a thing he liked to do. They lay in silence for a while, and increasingly she felt low and sad.

'How lovely you are,' murmured Mr McCarthy. 'Oh, Mavie, Mavie.'

She squeezed the length of pale flesh that was Mr McCarthy's arm. She thought suddenly of the day the coal-heaver had arrived and felt her neck going red at the memory. She remembered the first day, rolling down her stockings and seeing her lover watching her, he already naked, standing still and seeming puzzled, near the electric fire. She had not been a virgin that day, but in the meanwhile she had not once been unfaithful to him.

'Tell me you love me,' Mavie cried, forgetting about her birthday, abruptly caught up in a new emotion. 'Tell me now; it worries me sometimes.'

'Of course it does. Of course I do. I'm all for you, Mavie, as I've said a thousand times.'

'It's not that I doubt you, honey, only sometimes between one Saturday and another I feel a depression. It's impossible to say. I mean, it's hard to put into words. Have you got a fag?'

Mr McCarthy shook his head on the pillow. She knew he did not smoke: why then did she ask? It was like the custard sauce all over again. When he went to the trouble of inventing stomach trouble, you'd think she'd take the trouble to remember it.

'You don't smoke. I always ask and you always don't say anything and I always remember then. Am I very irritating to you, honey? Tell me you love me. Tell me I'm not irritating to you.'

'Mavie.'

'You don't like me today. I feel it. Jesus, I'm sorry about the mackerel. Tell the truth now, you don't like me today.'

'Oh yes, I do. I love you. I love you.'

'You don't like me.' She spoke as though she had not heard his protestations; she spaced the words carefully, giving the same emphasis to each.

'I love you,' said Mr McCarthy. 'Indeed I do.'

She shook her head, and rose and walked to the kitchen, where she found cigarettes and matches.

'My Mavie,' said Mr McCarthy from the bed, assuring himself that he was not finished yet, that he had not fully exacted his pleasurable due. 'Mavie, my young heart,' he murmured, and he began to laugh, thinking that merriment in the atmosphere would cheer matters up. 'Shall I do a little dance for you?'

Mavie, cigarette aglow, pulled the sheets around her as Mr McCarthy vacated the bed and stood, his arms outstretched, on the centre of the floor. He began to dance, as on many occasions before he had danced, swaying about without much tempo. When first he had performed in this way for her he had explained that his dance was an expression of his passion, representing, so he said, roses and presents of jewellery and lamé gowns. Once Mr McCarthy had asked Mavie to take the braces off his trousers and strike him with them while he acted out his dance. He was guilty, he said, because in their life together there were neither roses nor jewels nor restaurant dinners. But Mavie, shocked that he should feel like that, had refused his request, saying there was no cause for punishment. Sulkily, he had maintained otherwise, though he had not ever again suggested chastisement.

'How's that?' said Mr McCarthy, ending with a gesture. Mavie said nothing. She threw back the bed-clothes and Mr McCarthy strode jauntily towards her, a smile shaping beneath his moustache.

'I often wonder about her,' Mavie said a moment later. 'It's only natural. You can't help that.'

Mr McCarthy said: 'My wife's a hard case. She's well able to take care of herself. I'm on a leash where the wife is concerned.'

'I don't even know her name.'

'Oh, Mavie, Mavie. Isn't Mrs McCarthy enough?'

'I'm jealous. I'm sorry, honey.'

'No bother, Mavie. No bother, love.'

'I see her as a black-haired woman. Tall and sturdy. Would you rather we didn't speak of her?'

'It would be easier, certainly.'

'I'm sorry, honey.'

'No bother.'

'It's only jealousy. The green-eyed monster.'

'No need to be jealous, Mavie. No need at all. There's no love lost between Mrs McCarthy and myself. We never go together nowadays.'

'What sign is she under?'

'Sign, love?'

'Sagittarius? Leo? When's her birthday?'

Mr McCarthy's small eyes screwed up.

He looked through the lashes. He said:

'The twenty-ninth of March.'

'You make an occasion of it, do you? In the home, with the children around? You all give her presents, I suppose. Is there a special cake?'

'The wife likes a jam-roll. She buys one at Lyons.'

'And the children get her little gifts? Things from Woolworth's?'

'Something like that.'

'When I was little I used to buy presents in Woolworth's. My dad used to take me by the hand. I suppose you did, too. And your wife.'

'Yes, love, I suppose so.'

'I often think of your wife. I can't help it. I see her in my mind's eye.'

'She's a big woman,' said Mr McCarthy meditatively. 'Bigger than you, Mavie. A big dark woman – more than that I won't say.'

'Oh, honey, I never meant to pry.'

'It's not prying I mind, Mavie. No, you're not prying. It's just that I don't wish to soil the hour.'

When Mr McCarthy had said that, he heard the words echoing in his mind as words occasionally do. *I don't wish to soil the hour.* Mavie was silent, feeling the words to be beautiful. *I don't wish to soil the hour,* she thought. She drew her finger-nails along the taut skin of Mr McCarthy's thigh. 'Oh God,' said Mr McCarthy.

She knew that when he left, at twenty to four, she would sit alone in her dressing-gown and weep. She would wash the dirty dishes from lunch and she would wash his lovingly: she would wash and dry his egg-cup and be aware that it was his. She knew that that was absurd, but she knew that it would happen because it had happened before. She did not think it odd, as Mr McCarthy had often thought, that she, so pretty and still young, should love so passionately a man of fifty-two. She adored every shred of him; she longed for his presence and the touch of his hand. 'Oh, my honey, my honey,' cried Mavie, throwing her body on the body of Mr McCarthy and wrapping him up in her plump limbs.

At half past three Mr McCarthy, who had dropped into a light doze, woke to the awareness of a parched throat and a desire for tea. He sighed and caressed the fair hair that lay on the pillow beside him.

'I'll make a cup of tea,' said Mavie.

'*Merci*,' whispered Mr McCarthy.

They drank tea in the kitchen while Mr McCarthy buttoned his waistcoat and drew on his socks. 'I've bought a bow tie,' he confided, 'though I'm still a little shy in it. Maybe next week I'll try it out on you.'

'You could ask me anything under the sun and I'd do it for you. You could ask me anything, I love you that much.'

Hearing this, Mr McCarthy paused in the lacing of a boot. He thought of his braces, taut now about his shoulders; he thought of a foot fetish he had read about in the public library.

'I love you that much,' whispered Mavie.

'And I you,' said Mr McCarthy.

'I dream of you at nights.'

'I dream of you, my dear.'

Mavie sighed and looked over her shoulder, ill at ease. 'I cannot think of you dreaming of me.'

'I dream of you in my narrow twin bed, with the dark-haired woman in the twin beside it.'

'Don't speak like that. Don't talk to me of the bedroom.'

'I'm sorry.'

'I can't bear the thought of the twin beds in that room. I've told you before, honey.'

'Oh, Mavie, Mavie, if we could be together.'

'I love you that much.'

For a moment there was silence in the kitchen. Then, having tilted his cup to drain it of tea, Mr McCarthy rose to go.

As he crossed the floor his eyes fell on a birthday card propped up on the mantelshelf. It registered with him at once that the day was Mavie's birthday, and for a moment he considered remarking on that fact. Then he remembered the time and he kissed her on the head, his usual form of farewell. 'The forty-seventh time,' he murmured. 'Today was the forty-seventh.'

She walked with him along the passage to the door of the flat. She watched him mount the basement steps and watched his legs move briskly by the railings above. His footsteps died away and she returned to the kitchen and poured herself a cup of tea. She thought of him keeping his Saturday appointment, a business appointment he had always called it, and afterwards returning on a bus to his suburb. She saw him entering a door, opening it with a latchkey, being greeted by a dog and two children and the big, dark woman who was his wife. The dog barked loudly and the woman shrilled abuse, upbraiding her husband for a misdemeanour or some piece of forgetfulness or some small deceit discovered. She could feel his tiredness as he stood in his own hall, the latchkey still poised between his fingers, like a man at bay. Her eyes closed as she held that image in her mind; tears slipped from beneath their lids.

The bus let Mr McCarthy down at an Odeon cinema. He moved rapidly, checking his watch against a brightly lit clock that hung out over a shop. He was reckoning as he walked that there was time to have another cup of tea, with a Danish pastry perhaps, because he felt quite peckish. Afterwards, as always on a Saturday, he'd go to the pictures.

A Happy Family

On the evening of Tuesday, 24 May 1962, I returned home in the usual way. I remember sitting in the number 73 bus, thinking of the day as I had spent it and thinking of the house I was about to enter. It was a fine evening, warm and mellow, the air heavy with the smell of London. The bus crossed Hammersmith Bridge, moving quite quickly towards the leafy avenues beyond. The houses of the suburbs were gayer in that evening's sunshine, pleasanter abodes than often they seemed.

'Hullo,' I said in the hall of ours, speaking to my daughter Bridget, a child of one, who happened to be loitering there. She was wearing her night-dress, and she didn't look sleepy. 'Aren't you going to bed?' I said, and Bridget looked at me as if she had forgotten that I was closely related to her. I could hear Anna and Christopher in the bathroom, talking loudly and rapidly, and I could hear Elizabeth's voice urging them to wash themselves properly and be quick about it. 'She's fourteen stone, Miss MacAdam is,' Christopher was saying. 'Isn't she, Anna?' Miss MacAdam was a woman who taught at their school, a woman about whom we had come to know a lot. 'She can't swim,' said Anna.

Looking back now, such exchanges come easily to my mind. Bits of conversations float to the surface without much of a continuing pattern and without any significance that I can see. I suppose we were a happy family: someone examining us might possibly have written that down on a report sheet, the way these things are done. Yet what I recall most vividly now when I think of us as a family are images and occasions that for Elizabeth and me were neither happy nor unhappy. I remember animals at the Zoo coming forward for the offerings of our children, smelling of confinement rather than the jungle, seeming fierce and hard-done-by. I remember birthday parties on warm afternoons, the figures of children moving swiftly from the garden to the house, creatures who might have been bored, with paper hats on their heads or in their hands, seeking adventure in forbidden rooms. I remember dawdling walks, arguments that came to involve all of us, and other days when everything went well.

I used to leave the house at half past eight every morning, and often during the day I imagined what my wife's day must be like. She told me, of course. She told me about how ill-tempered our children had been, or how tractable; about how the time had passed in other ways, whom she had met and spoken to, who had come to tea or whom she had visited. I imagined her in summer having lunch in the garden when it was warm, dozing afterwards and being woken up by Bridget. In turn, she would ask me how the hours had gone for me and I would say a thing or two about their passing, about the people who had filled them. 'Miss Madden is leaving us,' I can hear myself saying. 'Off to Buenos Aires for some reason.' In my memory of this, I seem to be repeating the information. 'Off to Buenos Aires,' I appear to be saying. 'Off to Buenos Aires. Miss Madden.' And a little later I am saying it again, adding that Miss Madden would be missed. Elizabeth's head is nodding, agreeing that that will indeed be so. 'I fell asleep in the garden,' Elizabeth is murmuring in this small vision. 'Bridget woke me up.'

My wife was pretty when I married her, and as the years passed it seemed to me that she took on a greater beauty. I believed that this was some reflection of her contentment, and she may even have believed it herself. Had she suddenly said otherwise, I'd have been puzzled; as puzzled as I was, and as she was, on the evening of 24 May, when she told me about Mr Higgs. She sat before me then, sipping at a glass of sherry that I'd poured her and remembering all the details: all that Mr Higgs had said and all that she had said in reply.

She had been listening to a story on the radio and making coffee. Christopher and Anna were at school; in the garden Bridget was asleep in her pram. When the telephone rang Elizabeth walked towards it slowly, still listening to the wireless. When she said 'Hullo' she heard the coins drop at the other end and a man's voice said: 'Mrs Farrel?'

Elizabeth said yes, she was Mrs Farrel, and the man said: 'My name is Higgs.'

His voice was ordinary, a little uneducated, the kind of voice that is always drifting over the telephone.

'A very good friend,' said Mr Higgs.

'Good morning,' said Elizabeth in her matter-of-fact way. 'Are you selling something, Mr Higgs?'

'In a sense, Mrs Farrel, in a sense. You might call it selling. Do I peddle salvation?'

'Oh, I am not religious in the least –'

'It may be your trouble, Mrs Farrel.'

'Yes, well –'

'You are Elizabeth Farrel. You have three children.'

'Mr Higgs –'

'Your father was a Captain Maugham. Born 1892, died 1959. He lost a leg in action and never forgave himself for it. You attended his funeral, but were glad that he was dead, since he had a way of upsetting your children. Your mother, seventy-four a week ago, lives near St Albans and is unhappy. You have two sisters and a brother.'

'Mr Higgs, what do you want?'

'Nothing. I don't want anything. What do you want, Mrs Farrel?'

'Look here, Mr Higgs –'

'D'you remember your tenth birthday? D'you remember what it felt like being a little girl of ten, in a white dress spotted with forget-me-not, and a blue ribbon tying back your hair? You were taken on a picnic. "You're ten years old," your father said. "Now tell us what you're going to do with yourself." "She must cut the chocolate cake first," your mother cried, and so you cut the cake and then stood up and announced the trend of your ambitions. Your brother Ralph laughed and was scolded by your father. D'you remember at all?'

Elizabeth did remember. She remembered playing hide-and-seek with her sisters after tea; she remembered Ralph climbing a tree and finding himself unable to get down again; she remembered her parents quarrelling, as they invariably did, all the way home.

'Do I know you, Mr Higgs? How do you manage to have these details of my childhood?'

Mr Higgs laughed. It wasn't a nasty laugh. It sounded even reassuring, as if Mr Higgs meant no harm.

On the evening of 24 May we sat for a long time wondering who the odd individual could be and what he was after. Elizabeth seemed nervously elated and naturally more than a little intrigued. I, on the other hand, was rather upset by this Mr Higgs and his deep mine of information. 'If he rings again,' I said, 'threaten him with the police.'

'Good morning, Mrs Farrel.'

'Mr Higgs?.'

'My dear.'

'Well then, Mr Higgs, explain.'

'Ho, ho, Mrs Farrel, there's a sharpness for you. Explain? Why, if I explained I'd be out of business in no time at all. "So that's it," you'd say, and ring off, just like I was a salesman or a Jehovah's Witness.'

'Mr Higgs –'

'You was a little girl of ten, Mrs Farrel. You was out on a picnic. Remember?'

'How did you know all that?'

'Why shouldn't I know, for heaven's sake? Listen now, Mrs Farrel. Did you think then what you would be today? Did you see yourself married to a man and mothering his children? Have you come to a sticky end, or otherwise?'

'A sticky end?'

'You clean his house, you prepare his meals, you take his opinions. You hear on the radio some news of passing importance, some bomb exploded, some army recalled. Who does the thinking, Mr Farrel? You react as he does. You've lost your identity. Did you think of that that day when you were ten? Your children will be ten one day. They'll stand before you at ten years of age, first the girl, then the boy. What of their futures, Mrs Farrel? Shall they make something of themselves? Shall they fail and be miserable? Shall they be unnatural and unhappy, or sick in some way, or perhaps too stupid? Or shall they all three of them be richly successful? Are you successful, Mrs Farrel? You are your husband's instrument. You were different at ten, Mrs Farrel. How about your children? Soon it'll be your turn to take on the talking. I'll listen like I was paid for it.'

I was aware of considerable pique when Elizabeth reported all this to me. I protested that I was not given to forcing my opinions on others, and Elizabeth said I wasn't either. 'Clearly, he's queer in the head,' I said. I paused, thinking about that, then said: 'Could he be someone like a window-cleaner to whom you once perhaps talked of your childhood? Although I can't see you doing it.'

Elizabeth shook her head; she said she didn't remember talking to a window-cleaner about her childhood, or about anything very much. We'd had the same window-cleaners for almost seven years, she reminded me: two honest, respectable men who arrived at the house every six weeks in a Ford motor-car. 'Well, he must be someone,' I said. 'Someone you've talked to. I mean, it's not guesswork.'

'Maybe he's wicked,' said Elizabeth. 'Maybe he's a small wicked man with very white skin, driven by some force he doesn't understand. Perhaps he's one of those painters who came last year to paint the hall. There was a little man –'

'That little man's name was Mr Gipe. I remember that well. "Gipe," he said, walking into the hall and saying it would be a long job. "Gipe, sir; an unusual name." '

'He could be calling himself Higgs. He could have read through my letters. And my old diaries. Perhaps Mr Gipe expected a tip.'

'The hall cost ninety pounds.'

'I know, but it didn't all go to Mr Gipe. Perhaps nobody tips poor Mr Gipe and perhaps now he's telephoning all the wives, having read through their letters and their private diaries. He telephones to taunt them and to cause trouble, being an evil man. Perhaps Mr Gipe is possessed of a devil.'

I frowned and shook my head. 'Not at all,' I said. 'It's a voice from the past. It's someone who really did know you when you were ten, and knows all that's happened since.'

'More likely Mr Gipe,' said Elizabeth, 'guided from Hell.'

'Daddy, am I asleep?'

I looked at her wide eyes, big and blue and clear, perfect replicas of her mother's. I loved Anna best of all of them; I suppose because she reminded me so much of Elizabeth.

'No, darling, you're not asleep. If you were asleep you couldn't be talking to me, now could you?'

'I could be dreaming, Daddy. Couldn't I be dreaming?'

'Yes, I suppose you could.'

'But I'm not, am I?'

I shook my head. 'No, Anna, you're not dreaming.'

She sighed. 'I'm glad. I wouldn't like to be dreaming. I wouldn't like to suddenly wake up.'

It was Sunday afternoon and we had driven into the country. We did it almost every Sunday when the weather was fine and warm. The children enjoyed it and so in a way did we, even though the woods we went to were rather tatty, too near London to seem real, too untidy with sweet-papers to be attractive. Still, it was a way of entertaining them.

'Elizabeth.'

She was sitting on a tree-stump, her eyes half-closed. On a rug at her feet Bridget was playing with some wooden beads. I sat beside her and put my arm about her shoulders.

'Elizabeth.'

She jumped a little. 'Hullo, darling. I was almost asleep.'

'You were thinking about Mr Higgs.'

'Oh, I wasn't. My mind was a blank; I was about to drop off. I can do it now, sitting upright like this.'

'Anna asked me if she was dreaming.'

'Where is she?'

'Playing with Christopher.'

'They'll begin to fight. They don't play any more. Why do they perpetually fight?'

I said it was just a phase, but Elizabeth said she thought they would always fight now. The scratching and snarling would turn to argument as they grew older and when they became adults they wouldn't ever see one another. They would say that they had nothing in common, and would admit to others that they really rather disliked one another and always had. Elizabeth said she could see them: Christopher married to an unsuitable woman, and Anna as a girl who lived promiscuously and did not marry at all. Anna would become a heavy drinker of whisky and would smoke slim cigars at forty.

'Heavens,' I said, staring at her, and then looking at the small figure of Anna. 'Why on earth are you saying all that?'

'Well, it's true. I mean, it's what I imagine. I can see Anna in a harsh red suit, getting drunk at a cocktail party. I can see Christopher being miserable –'

'This is your Mr Higgs again. Look, the police can arrange to have the telephone tapped. It's sheer nonsense that some raving lunatic should be allowed to go on like that.'

'Mr Higgs! Mr Higgs! What's Mr Higgs got to do with it? You've got him on the brain.'

Elizabeth walked away. She left me sitting there with her frightening images of our children. Out of the corner of my eye I saw that Bridget was eating a piece of wood. I took it from her. Anna was saying: 'Daddy, Christopher hurt me.'

'Why?'

'I don't know. He just hurt me.'

'How did he hurt you?'

'He pushed me and I fell.' She began to cry, so I comforted her. I called Christopher and told him he mustn't push Anna. They ran off to play again and a moment later Anna was saying: 'Daddy, Christopher pushed me.'

'Christopher, you mustn't push Anna. And you shouldn't have to be told everything twice.'

'I didn't push her. She fell.'

Anna put her thumb in her mouth. I glanced through the trees to see where Elizabeth had got to, but there was no sign of her. I made the children sit on the rug and told them a story. They didn't like it much. They never did like my stories: Elizabeth's were so much better.

'I'm sorry.' She stood looking down on us, as tall and beautiful as a goddess.

'You look like a goddess,' I said.

'What's a goddess?' Anna asked, and Christopher said: 'Why's Mummy sorry?'

'A goddess is a beautiful lady. Mummy's sorry because she left me to look after you. And it's time to go home.'

'Oh, oh, oh, I must find Mambi first,' Anna cried anxiously. Mambi was a faithful friend who accompanied her everywhere she went, but who was, at the moment of departure, almost always lost.

We walked to the car. Anna said: 'Mambi was at the top of an old tree. Mambi's a goddess too. Daddy, do you *have* to be beautiful to be a goddess?'

'I suppose so.'

'Then Mambi can't be.'

'Isn't Mambi beautiful?'

'Usually she is. Only she's not now.'

'Why isn't she now?'

'Because all her hair came off in the tree.'

The car heaved and wobbled all the way home as Christopher and Anna banged about in the back. When they fought we shouted at them, and then they sulked and there was a mile or so of peace. Anna began to cry as I turned into the garage. Mambi, she said, was cold without her hair. Elizabeth explained about wigs.

I woke up in the middle of that night, thinking about Mr Higgs. I kept seeing the man as a shrimpish little thing, like the manager of the shop where we hired our television set. He had a black moustache, like a length of thread stuck across his upper lip. I knew it was wrong, I knew this wasn't Mr Higgs at all; and then, all of a sudden, I began to think about Elizabeth's brother, Ralph.

A generation ago Ralph would have been called a remittance man. Just about the time we were married old Captain Maugham had packed him off to a farm in Kenya after an incident with a hotel receptionist and the hotel's account books. But caring for nothing in Kenya, Ralph had made his way to Cairo, and from Cairo on the long-distance telephone he had greeted the Captain with a request for financial aid. He didn't get it, and then the war broke out and Ralph disappeared. Whenever we thought of him we imagined that he was up to the most reprehensible racket he could lay his hands on. If he was, we never found out about it. All we did know was that after the war he again telephoned the Captain, and the odd thing was that he was still in Cairo. 'I have lost an arm,' Captain Maugham told him testily. 'And I,' said Ralph, 'have lost the empire of my soul.' He was given to this kind of decorated statement; it interfered so much with his conversation that most of the time you didn't know what he was talking about. But the Captain sent him some money and an agreement was drawn up by which Ralph, on receipt of a monthly cheque, promised not to return to England during his father's lifetime. Then the Captain died and Ralph was back. I gave him fifty pounds and in all he probably cleaned up quite well. Ralph wasn't the sort of person to write letters; we had no idea where he was now. As a schoolboy, and even later, he was a great one for playing practical jokes. He was certainly a good enough mimic to create a Mr Higgs. Just for fun, I wondered? Or in some kind of bitterness? Or did he in some ingenious way hope to extract money?

The following morning I telephoned Elizabeth's sisters. Daphne knew nothing about where Ralph was, what he was doing or anything about him. She said she hoped he wasn't coming back to England because it had cost her fifty pounds the last time. Margaret, however, knew a lot. She didn't want to talk about it on the telephone, so I met her for lunch.

'What's all this?' she said.

I told her about Mr Higgs and the vague theory that was beginning to crystallize in my mind. She was intrigued by the Higgs thing. 'I don't know why,' she said, 'but it rings a queer sort of bell. But you're quite wrong about Ralph.' Ralph, it appeared, was being paid by Margaret and her husband in much the same way as he had been paid by the Captain; for the same reason and with the same stipulation. 'Only for the time being,' Margaret said a little bitterly. 'When Mother dies Ralph can do what he damn well likes. But it was quite a serious business and the news of it would clearly finish her. One doesn't like to think of an old woman dying in that particular kind of misery.'

'But whatever it was, she'd probably never find out.'

'Oh yes, she would. She reads the papers. In any case, Ralph is quite capable of dropping her a little note. But at the moment I can assure you that Ralph is safe in Africa. He's not the type to take any chances with his gift horses.'

So that was that. It made me feel even worse about Mr Higgs that my simple explanation had been so easily exploded.

*

'Well,' I said, 'and what did he have to say today?'

'What did who say?'

'Higgs.'

'Nothing much. He's becoming a bore.'

She wasn't going to tell me any more. She wasn't going to talk about Mr Higgs because she didn't trust me. She thought I'd put the police on him, and she didn't want that, so she said, because she had come to feel sorry for the poor crazed creature or whatever it was he happened to be. In fact, I thought to myself, my wife has become in some way fascinated by this man.

I worked at home one day, waiting for the telephone call. There was a ring at eleven-fifteen. I heard Elizabeth answer it. She said: 'No, I'm sorry; I'm afraid you've got the wrong number.' I didn't ask her about Mr Higgs. When I looked at her she seemed a long way away and her voice was measured and polite. There was some awful shaft between us and I didn't know what to do about it.

In the afternoon I took the children for a walk in the park.

'Mambi's gone to stay in the country,' Anna said. 'I'm lonely without her.'

'Well, she's coming back tonight, isn't she?'

'Daddy,' Christopher said, 'what's the matter with Mummy?'

I'm not very sure when it was that I first noticed everything was in rather a mess. I remember coming in one night and stumbling over lots of wooden toys in the hall. Quite often the cornflakes packet and the marmalade were still on the kitchen table from breakfast. Or if they weren't on the table the children had got them on the floor and Bridget had covered most of the house with their mixed contents. Elizabeth didn't seem to notice. She sat in a dream, silent and alone, forgetting to cook the supper. The children began to do all the things they had ever wanted to do and which Elizabeth had patiently prevented, like scribbling on the walls and playing in the coal-cellar. I tried to discuss it with Elizabeth, but all she did was to smile sweetly and say she was tired.

'Why don't you see a doctor?'

She stared at me. 'A doctor?'

'Perhaps you need a tonic.' And at that point she would smile again and go to bed.

I knew that Elizabeth was still having her conversations with Mr Higgs even though she no longer mentioned them. When I asked her she used to laugh and say: 'Poor Mr Higgs was just some old fanatic.'

'Yes, but how did he –'

'Darling, you worry too much.'

I went to St Albans to see old Mrs Maugham, without very much hope. I don't know what I expected of her since she was obviously too deaf and too senile to offer me anything at all. She lived with a woman called Miss

Awpit who was employed by the old woman's children to look after her. Miss Awpit made us tea and did the interpreting.

'Mr Farrel wants to know how you are, dear,' Miss Awpit said. 'Quite well, really,' Miss Awpit said to me. 'All things being equal.'

Mrs Maugham knew who I was and all that. She asked after Elizabeth and the children. She said something to Miss Awpit and Miss Awpit said: 'She wants you to bring them to her.'

'Yes, yes,' I shouted, nodding hard. 'We shall come and see you soon. They often,' I lied, 'ask about Granny.'

'Hark at that,' shouted Miss Awpit, nudging the old lady, who snappishly told her to leave off.

I didn't quite know how to put it. I said: 'Ask her if she knows a Mr Higgs.'

Miss Awpit, imagining, I suppose, that I was making conversation, shouted: 'Mr Farrel wants to know if you know Mr Higgs.' Mrs Maugham smiled at us. 'Higgs,' Miss Awpit repeated. 'Do you know Mr Higgs at all, dear?'

'Never,' said Mrs Maugham.

'Have you ever known a Mr Higgs?' I shouted.

'Higgs?' said Mrs Maugham.

'Do you know him?' Miss Awpit asked. 'Do you know a Mr Higgs?'

'I do not,' said Mrs Maugham, suddenly in command of herself, 'know anyone of such a name. Nor would I wish to.'

'Look, Mrs Maugham,' I pursued, 'does the name mean anything at all to you?'

'I have told you, I do not know your friend. How can I be expected to know your friends, an old woman like me, stuck out here in St Albans with no one to look after me?'

'Come, come,' said Miss Awpit, 'you've got me, dear.'

But Mrs Maugham only laughed.

A week or two passed, and then one afternoon as I was sitting in the office filing my nails the telephone rang and a voice I didn't recognize said: 'Mr Farrel?'

I said 'Yes', and the voice said: 'This is Miss Awpit. You know, Mrs Maugham's Miss Awpit.'

'Of course. Good afternoon, Miss Awpit. How are you?'

'Very well, thank you. I'm ringing to tell you something about Mrs Maugham.'

'Yes?'

'Well, you know when you came here the other week you were asking about a Mr Higgs?'

'Yes, I remember.'

'Well, as you sounded rather anxious about him I just thought I'd tell you. I thought about it and then I decided. I'll ring Mr Farrel, I said, just to tell him what she said.'

'Yes, Miss Awpit?'

'I hope I'm doing the right thing.'

'What did Mrs Maugham say?'

'Well, it's funny in a way. I hope you won't think I'm being very stupid or anything.'

I had the odd feeling that Miss Awpit was going to die as she was speaking, before she could tell me. I said:

'I assure you, you are doing the right thing. What did Mrs Maugham say?'

'Well, it was at breakfast one morning. She hadn't had a good night at all. So she said, but you know what it's like with old people. I mean, quite frankly I had to get up myself in the night and I heard her sleeping as deep and sweet as you'd wish. Honestly, Mr Farrel, I often wish I had her constitution myself –'

'You were telling me about Mr Higgs.'

'I'm sorry?'

'You were telling me about Mr Higgs.'

'Well, it's nothing really. You'll probably laugh when you hear. Quite honestly I was in two minds whether or not to bother you. You see, all Mrs Maugham said was: "It's funny that man suddenly talking about Mr Higgs like that. You know, Ethel, I haven't heard Mr Higgs mentioned for almost thirty years." So I said "Yes," leading her on, you see. "And who was Mr Higgs, dear, thirty years ago?" And she said: "Oh nobody at all. He was just Elizabeth's little friend"!'

'Elizabeth's?'

'Just what I said, Mr Farrel. She got quite impatient with me. "Just someone Elizabeth used to talk to," she said, "when she was three. You know the way children invent things." '

'Like Mambi,' I said, not meaning to say it, since Miss Awpit wouldn't understand.

'Oh dear, Mr Farrel,' said Miss Awpit, 'I knew you'd laugh.'

I left the office and took a taxi all the way home. Elizabeth was in the garden. I sat beside her and I held her hands. 'Look,' I said. 'Let's have a holiday. Let's go away, just the two of us. We need a rest.'

'You're spying on me,' Elizabeth said. 'Which isn't new, I suppose. You've got so mean, darling, ever since you became jealous of poor Mr Higgs. How could you be jealous of a man like Mr Higgs?'

'Elizabeth, I know who Mr Higgs is. I can tell you –'

'There's nothing to be jealous about. All the poor creature does is to ring me up and tell me all the things he read in my diaries the time he came to paint the hall. And then he tries to comfort me about the children. He tells me not to worry about Bridget. But I can't help worrying because I know she's going to have this hard time. She's going to grow big and lumpy, poor little Bridget, and she's not going to be ever able to pass an exam, and in the end she'll go and work in a post office. But Mr Higgs –'

'Let me tell you about Mr Higgs. Let me just remind you.'

'You don't know him, darling. You've never spoken to him. Mr Higgs is very patient, you know. First of all, he did all the talking, and now, you see, he kindly allows me to. Poor Mr Higgs is an inmate of a home. He's an institutionalized person, darling. There's no need to be jealous at all.'

I said nothing. I sat there holding her two hands and looking at her. Her face was just the same; even her eyes betrayed no hint of the confusion that held her. She smiled when she spoke of Mr Higgs. She made a joke, laughing, calling him the housewife's friend.

'It was funny,' she said, 'the first time I saw Christopher as an adult, sitting in a room with that awful woman. She was leaning back in a chair, staring at him and attempting to torture him with words. And then there was Anna, half a mile away across London, in a house in a square. All the lights were on because of the party, and Anna was in that red suit, and she was laughing and saying how she hated Christopher, how she had hated him from the first moment she saw him. And when she said that, I couldn't remember what moment she meant. I couldn't quite remember where it was that Anna and Christopher had met. Well, it goes to show.' Elizabeth paused. 'Well, doesn't it?' she said. 'I mean, imagine my thinking that poor Mr Higgs was evil! The kindest, most long-suffering man that ever walked on two legs. I mean, all I had to do was to remind Mr Higgs that I'd forgotten and Mr Higgs could tell me. "They met in a garden," he could say, "at an ordinary little tea-party." And Bridget was operated on several times, and counted the words in telegrams.'

Elizabeth talked on of the children and of Mr Higgs. I rang up our doctor, and he came, and then a little later my wife was taken from the house. I sat alone with Bridget on my knee until it was time to go and fetch Christopher and Anna.

'Mummy's ill,' I said in the car. 'She's had to go away for a little.' I would tell them the story gradually, and one day perhaps we might visit her and she might still understand who we were. 'Ill?' they said. 'But Mummy's never ill.' I stopped the car by our house, thinking that only death could make the house seem so empty, and thinking too that death was easier to understand. We made tea, I remember, the children and I, not saying very much more.

Going Home

'Mulligatawny soup,' Carruthers said in the dining-car. 'Roast beef, roast potatoes, Yorkshire pudding, mixed vegetables.'

'And madam?' murmured the waiter.

Miss Fanshawe said she'd have the same. The waiter thanked her. Carruthers said:

'Miss Fanshawe'll take a medium dry sherry. Pale ale for me, please.'

The waiter paused. He glanced at Miss Fanshawe, shaping his lips.

'I'm sixteen and a half,' Carruthers said. 'Oh, and a bottle of Beaune. 1962.'

It was the highlight of every term and every holiday for Carruthers, coming like a no-man's-land between the two: the journey with Miss Fanshawe to their different homes. Not once had she officially complained, either to his mother or to the school. She wouldn't do that; it wasn't in Miss Fanshawe to complain officially. And as for him, he couldn't help himself.

'Always Beaune on a train,' he said now, 'because of all the burgundies it travels happiest.'

'Thank you, sir,' the waiter said.

'Thank *you*, old chap.'

The waiter went, moving swiftly in the empty dining-car. The train slowed and then gathered speed again. The fields it passed through were bright with sunshine; the water of a stream glittered in the distance.

'You shouldn't lie about your age,' Miss Fanshawe reproved, smiling to show she hadn't been upset by the lie. But lies like that, she explained, could get a waiter into trouble.

Carruthers, a sharp-faced boy of thirteen, laughed a familiar harsh laugh. He said he didn't like the waiter, a remark that Miss Fanshawe ignored.

'What weather!' she remarked instead. 'Just look at those weeping willows!' She hadn't ever noticed them before, she added, but Carruthers contradicted that, reminding her that she had often before remarked on those weeping willows. She smiled, with false vagueness in her face, slightly shaking her head. 'Perhaps it's just that everything looks so different this lovely summer. What will you do, Carruthers? Your mother took you to Greece last year, didn't she? It's almost a shame to leave England, I always think, when the weather's like this. So green in the long warm days –'

'Miss Fanshawe, why are you pretending nothing has happened?'

'Happened? My dear, what has happened?'

Carruthers laughed again, and looked through the window at cows resting in the shade of an oak-tree. He said, still watching the cows, craning his neck to keep them in view:

'Your mind is thinking about what has happened and all the time you're attempting to make ridiculous conversation about the long warm days. Your heart is beating fast, Miss Fanshawe; your hands are trembling. There are two little dabs of red high up on your cheeks, just beneath your spectacles. There's a pink flush all over your neck. If you were alone, Miss Fanshawe, you'd be crying your heart out.'

Miss Fanshawe, who was thirty-eight, fair-haired and untouched by beauty, said that she hadn't the foggiest idea what Carruthers was talking about. He shook his head, implying that she lied. He said:

'Why are we being served by a man whom neither of us likes when we should be served by someone else? Just look at those weeping willows, you say.'

'Don't be silly, Carruthers.'

'What has become, Miss Fanshawe, of the other waiter?'

'Now please don't start any nonsense. I'm tired and –'

'It was he who gave me a taste for pale ale, d'you remember that? In your company, Miss Fanshawe, on this train. It was he who told us that Beaune travels best. Have a cig, Miss Fanshawe?'

'No, and I wish you wouldn't either.'

'Actually Mrs Carruthers allows me the odd smoke these days. Ever since my thirteenth birthday, May the twenty-sixth. How can she stop me, she says, when day and night she's at it like a factory chimney herself?'

'Your birthday's May the twenty-sixth? I never knew. Mine's two days later.' She spoke hastily, and with an eagerness that was as false as the vague expression her face had borne a moment ago.

'Gemini, Miss Fanshawe.'

'Yes: Gemini. Queen Victoria –'

'The sign of passion. Here comes the interloper.'

The waiter placed sherry before Miss Fanshawe and beer in front of Carruthers. He murmured deferentially, inclining his head.

'We've just been saying,' Carruthers remarked, 'that you're a new one on this line.'

'Newish, sir. A month – no, tell a lie, three weeks yesterday.'

'We knew your predecessor.'

'Oh yes, sir?'

'He used to say this line was as dead as a doornail. Actually, he enjoyed not having anything to do. Remember, Miss Fanshawe?'

Miss Fanshawe shook her head. She sipped her sherry, hoping the waiter would have the sense to go away. Carruthers said:

'In all the time Miss Fanshawe and I have been travelling together there hasn't been a solitary soul beside ourselves in this dining-car.'

The waiter said it hardly surprised him. You didn't get many, he agreed, and added, smoothing the table-cloth, that it would just be a minute before the soup was ready.

'Your predecessor,' Carruthers said, 'was a most extraordinary man.'

'Oh yes, sir?'

'He had the gift of tongues. He was covered in freckles.'

'I see, sir.'

'Miss Fanshawe here had a passion for him.'

The waiter laughed. He lingered for a moment and then, since Carruthers was silent, went away.

'Now look here, Carruthers,' Miss Fanshawe began.

'Don't you think Mrs Carruthers is the most vulgar woman you've ever met?'

'I wasn't thinking of your mother. I will not have you talking like this to the waiter. Please now.'

'She wears a scent called "In Love", by Norman Hartnell. A woman of fifty, as thin as fuse wire. My God!'

'Your mother –'

'My mother doesn't concern you – oh, I agree. Still you don't want to deliver me to the female smelling of drink and tobacco smoke. I always brush my teeth in the lavatory, you know. For your sake, Miss Fanshawe.'

'Please don't engage the waiter in conversation. And please don't tell lies about the waiter who was here before. It's ridiculous the way you go on –'

'You're tired, Miss Fanshawe.'

'I'm always tired at the end of term.'

'That waiter used to say –'

'Oh, for heaven's sake, stop about that waiter!'

'I'm sorry.' He seemed to mean it, but she knew he didn't. And even when he spoke again, when his voice was softer, she knew that he was still pretending. 'What shall we talk about?' he asked, and with a weary cheerfulness she reminded him that she'd wondered what he was going to do in the holidays. He didn't reply. His head was bent. She knew that he was smiling.

'I'll walk beside her,' he said. 'In Rimini and Venice. In Zürich may be. By Lake Lugano. Or the Black Sea. New faces will greet her in an American Bar in Copenhagen. Or near the Spanish Steps – in Babbington's English Tea-Rooms. Or in Bandol or Cassis, the Ritz, the Hotel Excelsior in old Madrid. What shall we talk about, Miss Fanshawe?'

'You could tell me more. Last year in Greece –'

'I remember once we talked about guinea-pigs. I told you how I killed a guinea-pig that Mrs Carruthers gave me. Another time we talked about Rider Minor. D'you remember that?'

'Yes, but let's not –'

'McGullam was unpleasant to Rider Minor in the changing-room. McGullam and Travers went after Rider Minor with a little piece of wood.'

'You told me, Carruthers.'

He laughed.

'When I first arrived at Ashleigh Court the only person who spoke to me was Rider Minor. And of course the Sergeant-Major. The Sergeant-Major told me never to take to cigs. He described the lungs of a friend of his.'

'He was quite right.'

'Yes, he was. Cigs can give you a nasty disease.'

'I wish you wouldn't smoke.'

'I like your hat.'

'Soup, madam,' the waiter murmured. 'Sir.'

'Don't you like Miss Fanshawe's hat?' Carruthers smiled, pointing at Miss Fanshawe, and when the waiter said that the hat was very nice Carruthers asked him his name.

Miss Fanshawe dipped a spoon into her soup. The waiter offered her a roll. His name, he said, was Atkins.

'Are you wondering about us, Mr Atkins?'

'Sir?'

'Everyone has a natural curiosity, you know.'

'I see a lot of people in my work, sir.'

'Miss Fanshawe's an undermatron at Ashleigh Court Preparatory School for Boys. They use her disgracefully at the end of term – patching up clothes so that the mothers won't complain, packing trunks, sorting out laundry. From dawn till midnight Miss Fanshawe's on the trot. That's why she's tired.'

Miss Fanshawe laughed. 'Take no notice of him,' she said. She broke her roll and buttered a piece of it. She pointed at wheat ripening in a field. The harvest would be good this year, she said.

'At the end of each term,' Carruthers went on, 'she has to sit with me on this train because we travel in the same direction. I'm out of her authority really, since the term is over. Still, she has to keep an eye.'

The waiter, busy with the wine, said he understood. He raised his eyebrows at Miss Fanshawe and winked, but she did not encourage this, pretending not to notice it.

'Imagine, Mr Atkins,' Carruthers said, 'a country house in the mock Tudor style, with bits built on to it: a rackety old gym and an art-room, and changing-rooms that smell of perspiration. There are a hundred and three boys at Ashleigh Court, in narrow iron beds with blue rugs on them, which Miss Fanshawe has to see are all kept tidy. She does other things as well: she wears a white overall and gives out medicines. She pours out cocoa in the dining-hall and at eleven o'clock every morning she hands each boy four *petit beurre* biscuits. She isn't allowed to say Grace. It has to be a master who says Grace: "For what we're about to receive . . ." Or the

Reverend T. L. Edwards, who owns and runs the place, T.L.E., known to generations as a pervert. He pays boys, actually.'

The waiter, having meticulously removed a covering of red foil from the top of the wine-bottle, wiped the cork with a napkin before attempting to draw it. He glanced quickly at Miss Fanshawe to see if he could catch her eye in order to put her at her ease with an understanding gesture, but she appeared to be wholly engaged with her soup.

'The Reverend Edwards is a law unto himself,' Carruthers said. 'Your predecessor was intrigued by him.'

'Please take no notice of him.' She tried to sound bracing, looking up suddenly and smiling at the waiter.

'The headmaster accompanied you on the train, did he, sir?'

'No, no, no, no. The Reverend Edwards was never on this train in his life. No, it was simply that your predecessor was interested in life at Ashleigh Court. He would stand there happily listening while we told him the details: you could say he was fascinated.'

At this Miss Fanshawe made a noise that was somewhere between a laugh and a denial.

'You could pour the Beaune now, Mr Atkins,' Carruthers suggested.

The waiter did so, pausing for a moment, in doubt as to which of the two he should offer a little of the wine to taste. Carruthers nodded to him, indicating that it should be he. The waiter complied and when Carruthers had given his approval he filled both their glasses and lifted from before them their empty soup-plates.

'I've asked you not to behave like that,' she said when the waiter had gone.

'Like what, Miss Fanshawe?'

'You know, Carruthers.'

'The waiter and I were having a general conversation. As before, Miss Fanshawe, with the other waiter. Don't you remember? Don't you remember my telling him how I took forty of Hornsby's football cards? And drank the communion wine in the Reverend's cupboard?'

'I don't believe –'

'And I'll tell you another thing. I excused myself into Rider Minor's gum-boots.'

'Please leave the waiter alone. Please let's have no scenes this time, Carruthers.'

'There weren't any scenes with the other waiter. He enjoyed everything we said to him. You could see him quite clearly trying to visualize Ashleigh Court, and Mrs Carruthers in her awful clothes.'

'He visualized nothing of the sort. You gave him drink that I had to pay for. He was obliged to listen to your fantasies.'

'He enjoyed our conversation, Miss Fanshawe. Why is it that people like you and I are so unpopular?'

She didn't answer, but sighed instead. He would go on and on, she knew; and there was nothing she could do. She always meant not to protest, but when it came to the point she found it hard to sit silent, mile after mile.

'You know what I mean, Miss Fanshawe? At Ashleigh Court they say you have an awkward way of walking. And I've got no charm: I think that's why they don't much like me. But how for God's sake could any child of Mrs Carruthers have charm?'

'Please don't speak of your mother like that –'

'And yet men fancy her. Awful men arrive at week-ends, as keen for sex as the Reverend Edwards is. "Your mother's a most elegant woman," a hard-eyed lecher remarked to me last summer, in the Palm Court of a Greek hotel.'

'Don't drink too much of that wine. The last time –'

' "You're staggering," she said the last time. I told her I had 'flu. She's beautiful, I dare say, in her thin way. D'you think she's beautiful?'

'Yes, she is.'

'She has men all over the place. Love flows like honey while you make do with waiters on a train.'

'Oh, don't be so *silly*, Carruthers.'

'She snaps her fingers and people come to comfort her with lust. A woman like that's never alone. While you –'

'Will you please stop talking about me!'

'You have a heart in your breast like anyone else, Miss Fanshawe.'

The waiter, arrived again, coughed. He leaned across the table and placed a warm plate in front of Miss Fanshawe and a similar one in front of Carruthers. There was a silence while he offered Miss Fanshawe a silver-plated platter with slices of roast beef on it and square pieces of Yorkshire pudding. In the silence she selected what she wanted, a small portion, for her appetite on journeys with Carruthers was never great. Carruthers took the rest. The waiter offered vegetables.

'Miss Fanshawe ironed that blouse at a quarter to five this morning,' Carruthers said. 'She'd have ironed it last night if she hadn't been so tired.'

'A taste more carrots, sir?'

'I don't like carrots, Mr Atkins.'

'Peas, sir?'

'Thank you. She got up from her small bed, Mr Atkins, and her feet were chilly on the linoleum. She shivered, Mr Atkins, as she slipped her night-dress off. She stood there naked, thinking of another person. What became of your predecessor?'

'I don't know, sir. I never knew the man at all. All right for you, madam?'

'Yes, thank you.'

'He used to go back to the kitchen, Mr Atkins, and tell the cook that the couple from Ashleigh Court were on the train again. He'd lean against the sink while the cook poked about among his pieces of meat, trying to find us something to eat. Your predecessor would suck at the butt of a cig and occasionally he'd lift a can of beer to his lips. When the cook asked him what the matter was he'd say it was fascinating, a place like Ashleigh Court with boys running about in grey uniforms and an undermatron watching her life go by.'

'Excuse me, sir.'

The waiter went. Carruthers said:

' "She makes her own clothes," the other waiter told the cook. "She couldn't give a dinner party the way the young lad's mother could. She couldn't chat to this person and that, moving about among *décolletée* women and outshining every one of them." Why is she an undermatron at Ashleigh Court Preparatory School for Boys, owned and run by the Reverend T. L. Edwards, known to generations as a pervert?'

Miss Fanshawe, with an effort, laughed. 'Because she's qualified for nothing else,' she lightly said.

'I think that freckled waiter was sacked because he interfered with the passengers. "Vegetables?" he suggested, and before he could help himself he put the dish of cauliflowers on the table and put his arms around a woman. "All tickets please," cried the ticket-collector and then he saw the waiter and the woman on the floor. You can't run a railway company like that.'

'Carruthers –'

'Was it something like that, Miss Fanshawe? D'you think?'

'Of course it wasn't.'

'Why not?'

'Because you've just made it up. The man was a perfectly ordinary waiter on this train.'

'That's not true.'

'Of course it is.'

'I love this train, Miss Fanshawe.'

'It's a perfectly ordinary –'

'Of course it isn't.'

Carruthers laughed gaily, waiting for the waiter to come back, eating in silence until it was time again for their plates to be cleared away.

'Trifle, madam?' the waiter said. 'Cheese and biscuits?'

'Just coffee, please.'

'Sit down, why don't you, Mr Atkins? Join us for a while.'

'Ah no, sir, no.'

'Miss Fanshawe and I don't have to keep up appearances on your train. D'you understand that? We've been keeping up appearances for three long months at Ashleigh Court and it's time we stopped. Shall I tell you about my mother, Mr Atkins?'

'Your mother, sir?'

'Carruthers –'

'In 1960, when I was three, my father left her for another woman: she found it hard to bear. She had a lover at the time, a Mr Tennyson, but even so she found it hard to forgive my father for taking himself off.'

'I see, sir.'

'It was my father's intention that I should accompany him to his new life with the other woman, but when it came to the point the other woman decided against that. Why should she be burdened with my mother's child? she wanted to know: you can see her argument, Mr Atkins.'

'I must be getting on now, sir.'

'So my father arranged to pay my mother an annual sum, in return for which she agreed to give me house room. I go with her when she goes on holiday to a smart resort. My father's a thing of the past. What d'you think of all that, Mr Atkins? Can you visualize Mrs Carruthers at a resort? She's not at all like Miss Fanshawe.'

'I'm sure she's not –'

'Not at all.'

'Please let go my sleeve, sir.'

'We want you to sit down.'

'It's not my place, sir, to sit down with the passengers in the dining-car.'

'We want to ask you if you think it's fair that Mrs Carruthers should round up all the men she wants while Miss Fanshawe has only the furtive memory of a waiter on a train, a man who came to a sticky end, God knows.'

'Stop it!' cried Miss Fanshawe. 'Stop it! Stop it! Let go his jacket and let him go away –'

'I have things to do, sir.'

'He smelt of fried eggs, a smell that still comes back to her at night.'

'You're damaging my jacket. I must ask you to release me at once.'

'Are you married, Mr Atkins?'

'Carruthers!' Her face was crimson and her neck blotched with a flushing that Carruthers had seen before. 'Carruthers, for heaven's sake behave yourself!'

'The Reverend Edwards isn't married, as you might guess, Mr Atkins.'

The waiter tried to pull his sleeve out of Carruthers's grasp, panting a little from embarrassment and from the effort. 'Let go my jacket!' he shouted. 'Will you let me go!'

Carruthers laughed, but did not release his grasp. There was a sound of ripping as the jacket tore.

'Miss Fanshawe'll stitch it for you,' Carruthers said at once, and added more sharply when the waiter raised a hand to strike him: 'Don't do that, please. Don't threaten a passenger, Mr Atkins.'

'You've ruined this jacket. You bloody little –'

'Don't use language in front of the lady.' He spoke quietly, and to a stranger entering the dining-car at that moment it might have seemed that the waiter was in the wrong, that the torn sleeve of his jacket was the just result of some attempted insolence on his part.

'You're mad,' the waiter shouted at Carruthers, his face red and sweating in his anger. 'That child's a raving lunatic,' he shouted as noisily at Miss Fanshawe.

Carruthers was humming a hymn. 'Lord, dismiss us,' he softly sang, 'with Thy blessing.'

'Put any expenses on my bill,' whispered Miss Fanshawe. 'I'm very sorry.'

'Ashleigh Court'll pay,' Carruthers said, not smiling now, his face all of a sudden as sombre as the faces of the other two.

No one spoke again in the dining-car. The waiter brought coffee, and later presented a bill.

The train stopped at a small station. Three people got out as Miss Fanshawe and Carruthers moved down the corridor to their compartment. They walked in silence, Miss Fanshawe in front of Carruthers, he drawing his right hand along the glass of the windows. There'd been an elderly man in their compartment when they'd left it: to Miss Fanshawe's relief he was no longer there. Carruthers slid the door across. She found her book and opened it at once.

'I'm sorry,' he said when she'd read a page.

She turned the page, not looking up, not speaking.

'I'm sorry I tormented you,' he said after another pause.

She still did not look up, but spoke while moving her eyes along a line of print. 'You're always sorry,' she said.

Her face and neck were still hot. Her fingers tightly held the paperbacked volume. She felt taut and rigid, as though the unpleasantness in the dining-car had coiled some part of her up. On other journeys she'd experienced a similar feeling, though never as unnervingly as she experienced it now. He had never before torn a waiter's clothing.

'Miss Fanshawe?'

'I want to read.'

'I'm not going back to Ashleigh Court.'

She went on reading and then, when he'd repeated the statement, she slowly raised her head. She looked at him and thought, as she always did when she looked at him, that he was in need of care. There was a barrenness in his sharp face; his eyes reflected the tang of a bitter truth.

'I took the Reverend Edwards's cigarette-lighter. He's told me he won't have me back.'

'That isn't true, Carruthers –'

'At half past eleven yesterday morning I walked into the Reverend's study and lifted it from his desk. Unfortunately he met me on the way out. Ashleigh Court, he said, was no place for a thief.'

'But why? Why did you do such a silly thing?'

'I don't know. I don't know why I do a lot of things. I don't know why I pretend you were in love with a waiter. This is the last horrid journey for you, Miss Fanshawe.'

'So you won't be coming back –'

'The first time I met you I was crying in a dormitory. D'you remember that? Do you, Miss Fanshawe?'

'Yes, I remember.'

' "Are you missing your mummy?" you asked me, and I said no. I was crying because I'd thought I'd like Ashleigh Court. I'd thought it would be heaven, a place without Mrs Carruthers. I didn't say that; not then.'

'No.'

'You brought me to your room and gave me liquorice allsorts. You made me blow my nose. You told me not to cry because the other boys would laugh at me. And yet I went on crying.'

In the fields men were making hay. Children in one field waved at the passing train. The last horrid journey, she thought; she would never see the sharp face again, nor the bitterness reflected in the eyes. He'd wept, as others occasionally had to; she'd been, for a moment, a mother to him. His own mother didn't like him, he'd later said – on a journey – because his features reminded her of his father's features.

'I don't know why I'm so unpleasant, Miss Fanshawe. The Reverend stared at me last night and said he had a feeling in his bones that I'd end up badly. He said I was a useless sort of person, a boy he couldn't ever rely on. I'd let him down, he said, thieving and lying like a common criminal. "I'm chalking you up as a failure for Ashleigh," he said. "I never had much faith in you, Carruthers." '

'He's a most revolting man.' She said it without meaning to, and yet the words came easily from her. She said it because it didn't matter any more, because he wasn't going to return to Ashleigh Court to repeat her words.

'You were kind to me that first day,' Carruthers said. 'I liked that holy picture in your room. You told me to look at it, I remember. Your white overall made a noise when you walked.'

She wanted to say that once she had told lies too, that at St Monica's School for Girls she'd said the King, the late George VI, had spoken to her when she stood in the crowd. She wanted to say that she'd stolen two rubbers from Elsie Grantham and poured ink all over the face of a clock, and had never been found out.

She closed her eyes, longing to speak, longing above all things in the world to fill the compartment with the words that had begun, since he'd told her, to pound in her brain. All he'd ever done on the train was to speak a kind of truth about his mother and the school, to speak in their no-man's-land, as now and then he'd called it. Tormenting her was incidental; she knew it was. Tormenting her was just by chance, a thing that happened.

His face was like a flint. No love had ever smoothed his face, and while she looked at it she felt, unbearably now, the urge to speak as he had spoken, so many times. He smiled at her. 'Yes,' he said. 'The Reverend's a most revolting man.'

'I'm thirty-eight,' she said and saw him nod as though, precisely, he'd guessed her age a long time ago. 'Tonight we'll sit together in the bungalow by the sea where my parents live and they'll ask me about the term at Ashleigh. "Begin at the beginning, Beryl," my mother'll say and my father'll set his deaf-aid. "The first day? What happened the first day, Beryl?" And I shall tell them. "Speak up," they'll say, and in a louder voice I'll tell them about the new boys, and the new members of staff. Tomorrow night I'll tell some more, and on and on until the holidays and the term are over. "Wherever are you going?" my mother'll say when I want to go out for a walk. "Funny time," she'll say, "to go for a walk." No matter what time it is.'

He turned his head away, gazing through the window as earlier she had gazed through the window of the dining-car, in awkwardness.

'I didn't fall in love with a freckled waiter,' he heard her say, 'but God knows the freckled waiter would have done.'

He looked at her again. 'I didn't mean, Miss Fanshawe –'

'If he had suddenly murmured while offering me the vegetables I'd have closed my eyes with joy. To be desired, to be desired in any way at all . . .'

'Miss Fanshawe –'

'Born beneath Gemini, the sign of passion, you said. Yet who wants to know about passion in the heart of an ugly undermatron? Different for your mother, Carruthers: your mother might weep and tear away her hair, and others would weep in pity because of all her beauty. D'you see, Carruthers? D'you understand me?'

'No, Miss Fanshawe. No, I don't think I do. I'm not as –'

'There was a time one Christmas, after a party in the staff-room, when a man who taught algebra took me up to a loft, the place where the Wolf Cubs meet. We lay down on an old tent, and then suddenly this man was sick. That was in 1954. I didn't tell them that in the bungalow: I've never told them the truth. I'll not say tonight, eating cooked ham and salad, that the boy I travelled with created a scene in the dining-car, or that I was obliged to pay for damage to a waiter's clothes.'

'Shall we read now, Miss Fanshawe?'

'How can we read, for God's sake, when we have other things to say? What was it like, d'you think, on all the journeys to see you so unhappy? Yes, you'll probably go to the bad. He's right: you have the look of a boy who'll end like that. The unhappy often do.'

'Unhappy, Miss Fanshawe? Do I seem unhappy?'

'Oh, for God's sake, tell the truth! The truth's been there between us on all our journeys. We've looked at one another and seen it, over and over again.'

'Miss Fanshawe, I don't understand you. I promise you, I don't understand –'

'How could I ever say in that bungalow that the algebra teacher laid me down on a tent and then was sick? Yet I can say it now to you, a thing I've never told another soul.'

The door slid open and a woman wearing a blue hat, a smiling, red-faced woman, asked if the vacant seats were taken. In a voice that amazed Carruthers further Miss Fanshawe told her to go away.

'Well, really!' said the woman.

'Leave us in peace, for God's sake!' shrieked Miss Fanshawe, and the woman, her smile all gone, backed into the corridor. Miss Fanshawe rose and shut the door again.

'It's different in that bungalow by the sea,' she then quite quietly remarked, as though no red-faced woman had backed away astonished. 'Not like an American Bar in Copenhagen or the Hotel Excelsior in Madrid. Along the walls the coloured geese stretch out their necks, the brass is polished and in its place. Inch by inch oppression fills the air. On the chintz covers in the sitting-room there's a pattern of small wild roses, the stair-carpet's full of fading lupins. *To W. J. Fanshawe on the occasion of his retirement*, says the plaque on the clock on the sitting-room mantelpiece, *from his friends in the Prudential*. The clock has a gold-coloured face and four black pillars of ersatz material: it hasn't chimed since 1958. At night, not far away, the sea tumbles about, seeming too real to be true. The seagulls shriek when I walk on the beach, and when I look at them I think they're crying out with happiness.'

He began to speak, only to speak her name, for there was nothing else he could think of to say. He changed his mind and said nothing at all.

'Who would take me from it now? Who, Carruthers? What freckled waiter or teacher of algebra? What assistant in a shop, what bank-clerk, postman, salesman of cosmetics? They see a figure walking in the wind, discs of thick glass on her eyes, breasts as flat as paper. Her movements awkward, they say, and when she's close enough they raise their hats and turn away: they mean no harm.'

'I see,' he said.

'In the bungalow I'm frightened of both of them: all my life I've been afraid of them. When I was small and wasn't pretty they made the best of things, and longed that I should be clever instead. "Read to us, Beryl," my father would say, rubbing his hands together when he came in from his office. And I would try to read. "Spell *merchant*," my father would urge as though his life depended upon it, and the letters would become jumbled in my mind. Can you see it, Carruthers, a child with glasses and an awkward way of walking and two angry figures, like vultures, unforgiving? They'd exchange a glance, turning their eyes away from me as though in shame. "Not bright," they'd think. "Not bright, to make up for the other." '

'How horrid, Miss Fanshawe.'

'No, no. After all, was it nice for them that their single child should be a gawky creature who blushed when people spoke? How could they help themselves, any more than your mother can?'

'Still, my mother –'

' "Going to the pictures?" he said the last time I was home. "What on earth are you doing that for?" And then she got the newspaper which gave the programme that was showing *Tarzan and the Apemen*, she read out. "My dear, at your age!" I wanted to sit in the dark for an hour or two, not having to talk about the term at Ashleigh Court. But how could I say that to them? I felt the redness coming in my face. "For children surely," my father said, "a film like that." And then he laughed. "Beryl's made a mistake," my mother explained, and she laughed too.'

'And did you go, Miss Fanshawe?'

'Go?'

'To *Tarzan and the Apemen*?'

'No, I didn't go. I don't possess courage like that: as soon as I enter the door of the bungalow I can feel their disappointment all round me and I'm terrified all over again. I've thought of not going back but I haven't even the courage for that: they've sucked everything out of me. D'you understand?'

'Well –'

'Why is God so cruel that we leave the ugly school and travel together to a greater ugliness when we could travel to something nice?'

'Nice, Miss Fanshawe? *Nice?*'

'You know what I mean, Carruthers.'

He shook his head. Again he turned it away from her, looking at the window, wretchedly now.

'Of course you do,' her voice said, 'if you think about it.'

'I really –'

'Funny our birthdays being close together!' Her mood was gayer suddenly. He turned to look at her and saw she was smiling. He smiled also.

'I've dreamed this train went on forever,' she said, 'on and on until at last you stopped engaging passengers and waiters in fantastic conversation. "I'm better now," you said, and then you went to sleep. And when you woke I gave you liquorice allsorts. "I understand," I said: "it doesn't matter." '

'I know I've been very bad to you, Miss Fanshawe. I'm sorry –'

'I've dreamed of us together in my parents' bungalow, of my parents dead and buried and your thin mother gone too, and Ashleigh Court a thing of the nightmare past. I've seen us walking over the beaches together, you growing up, me cooking for you and mending your clothes and knitting you pullovers. I've brought you fresh brown eggs and made you apple dumplings. I've watched you smile over crispy chops.'

'Miss Fanshawe –'

'I'm telling you about a dream in which ordinary things are marvellous. Tea tastes nicer and the green of the grass is a fresher green than you've ever noticed before, and the air is rosy, and happiness runs about. I would take you to a cinema on a Saturday afternoon and we would buy chips on the way home and no one would mind. We'd sit by the fire and say whatever we liked to one another. And you would no longer steal things or tell lies, because you'd have no need to. Nor would you mock an unpretty undermatron.'

'Miss Fanshawe, I – I'm feeling tired. I think I'd like to read.'

'Why should they have a child and then destroy it? Why should your mother not love you because your face is like your father's face?'

'My mother –'

'Your mother's a disgrace,' she cried in sudden, new emotion. 'What life is it for a child to drag around hotels and lovers, a piece of extra luggage, alone, unloved?'

'It's not too bad. I get quite used to it –'

'Why can He not strike them dead?' she whispered. 'Why can't He make it possible? By some small miracle, surely to God?'

He wasn't looking at her. He heard her weeping and listened to the sound, not knowing what to do.

'You're a sorrowful mess, Carruthers,' she whispered. 'Yet you need not be.'

'Please. Please. Miss Fanshawe –'

'You'd be a different kind of person and so would I. You'd have my love, I'd care about the damage that's been done to you. You wouldn't come to a bad end: I'd see to that.'

He didn't want to turn his head again. He didn't want to see her, but in spite of that he found himself looking at her. She, too, was gazing at him, tears streaming on her cheeks. He spoke slowly and with as much firmness as he could gather together.

'What you're saying doesn't make any sense, Miss Fanshawe.'

'The waiter said that you were mad. Am I crazy too? Can people go mad like that, for a little while, on a train? Out of loneliness and locked-up love? Or desperation?'

'I'm sure it has nothing to do with madness, Miss Fanshawe –'

'The sand blows on to my face, and sometimes into my eyes. In my bedroom I shake it from my sandals. I murmur in the sitting-room. "Really, Beryl," my mother says, and my father sucks his breath in. On Sunday mornings we walk to church, all three of us. I go again, on my own, to Evensong: I find that nice. And yet I'm glad when it's time to go back to Ashleigh Court. Are you ever glad, Carruthers?'

'Sometimes I have been. But not always. Not always at all. I –'

' "Let's go for a stroll," the algebra teacher said. His clothes were stained with beer. "Let's go up there," he said. "It's nice up there." And in the pitch dark we climbed to the loft where the Wolf Cubs meet. He lit his cigarette-lighter and spread the tent out. I don't mind what happens, I thought. Anything is better than nothing happening all my life. And then the man was sick.'

'You told me that, Miss Fanshawe.'

' "You're getting fat," my mother might have said. "Look at Beryl, Dad, getting fat." And I would try to laugh. "A drunk has made me pregnant," I might have whispered in the bungalow, suddenly finding the courage for it. And they would look at me and see that I was happy, and I would kneel by my bed and pour my thanks out to God, every night of my life, while waiting for my child.' She paused and gave a little laugh. 'They are waiting for us, those people, Carruthers.'

'Yes.'

'The clock on the mantelpiece still will not chime, "Cocoa," my mother'll say at half past nine. And when they die it'll be too late.'

He could feel the train slowing, and sighed within him, a gesture of thanksgiving. In a moment he would walk away from her: he would never see her again. It didn't matter what had taken place, because he wouldn't ever see her again. It didn't matter, all she had said, or all he had earlier said himself.

He felt sick in his stomach after the beer and the wine and the images she'd created of a life with her in a seaside bungalow. The food she'd raved about would be appalling; she'd never let him smoke. And yet, in the compartment now, while they were still alone, he was unable to prevent himself from feeling sorry for her. She was right when she spoke of her craziness: she wasn't quite sane beneath the surface, she was all twisted up and unwell.

'I'd better go and brush my teeth,' he said. He rose and lifted his overnight case from the rack.

'Don't go,' she whispered.

His hand, within the suitcase, had already grasped a blue sponge-bag. He released it and closed the case. He stood, not wishing to sit down again. She didn't speak. She wasn't looking at him now.

'Will you be all right, Miss Fanshawe?' he said at last, and repeated the question when she didn't reply. 'Miss Fanshawe?'

'I'm sorry you're not coming back to Ashleigh, Carruthers. I hope you have a pleasant holiday abroad.'

'Miss Fanshawe, will you –'

'I'll stay in England, as I always do.'

'We'll be there in a moment,' he said.

'I hope you won't go to the bad, Carruthers.'

They passed by houses now; the backs of houses, suburban gardens. Posters advertised beer and cigarettes and furniture. *Geo. Small. Seeds*, one said.

'I hope not, too,' he said.

'Your mother's on the platform. Where she always stands.'

'Good-bye, Miss Fanshawe.'

'Good-bye, Carruthers. Good-bye.'

Porters stood waiting. Mail-bags were on a trolley. A voice called out, speaking of the train they were on.

She didn't look at him. She wouldn't lift her head: he knew the tears were pouring on her cheeks now, more than before, and he wanted to say, again, that he was sorry. He shivered standing in the doorway, looking at her, and then he closed the door and went away.

She saw his mother greet him, smiling, in red as always she was. They went together to collect his luggage from the van, out of her sight, and when the train pulled away from the station she saw them once again, the mother speaking and Carruthers just as he always was, laughing his harsh laugh.

An Evening with John Joe Dempsey

In Keogh's one evening Mr Lynch talked about the Piccadilly tarts, and John Joe Dempsey on his fifteenth birthday closed his eyes and travelled into a world he did not know. 'Big and little,' said Mr Lynch, 'winking their eyes at you and enticing you up to them. Wetting their lips,' said Mr Lynch, 'with the ends of their tongues.'

John Joe Dempsey had walked through the small town that darkening autumn evening, from the far end of North Street where he and his mother lived, past the cement building that was the Coliseum Cinema, past Kelly's Atlantic Hotel and a number of shops that were now closed for the day. 'Go to Keogh's like a good boy,' his mother had requested, for as well as refreshments and stimulants Keogh's public house sold a variety of groceries: it was for a pound of rashers that Mrs Dempsey had sent her son.

'Who is there?' Mr Lynch had called out from the licensed area of the premises, hearing John Joe rapping with a coin to draw attention to his presence. A wooden partition with panes of glass in the top half of it rose to a height of eight feet between the grocery and the bar. 'I'm here for rashers,' John Joe explained through the pebbly glass. 'Isn't it a stormy evening, Mr Lynch? I'm fifteen today, Mr Lynch.'

There was a silence before a door in the partition opened and Mr Lynch appeared. 'Fifteen?' he said. 'Step in here, boy, and have a bottle of stout.'

John Joe protested that he was too young to drink a bottle of stout and then said that his mother required the rashers immediately. 'Mrs Keogh's gone out to Confession,' Mr Lynch said. 'I'm in charge till her ladyship returns.'

John Joe, knowing that Mr Lynch would not be prepared to set the bacon machine in action, stepped into the bar to await the return of Mrs Keogh, and Mr Lynch darted behind the counter for two bottles of stout. Having opened and poured them, he began about the Piccadilly tarts.

'You've got to an age,' Mr Lynch said, 'when you would have to be advised. Did you ever think in terms of emigration to Britain?'

'I did not, Mr Lynch.'

'I would say you were right to leave it alone, John Joe. Is that the first bottle of stout you ever had?'

'It is, Mr Lynch.'

'A bottle of stout is an acquired taste. You have to have had a dozen bottles or maybe more before you do get an urge for it. With the other matter it's different.'

Mr Lynch, now a large, fresh-faced man of fifty-five who was never seen without a brown hat on his head, had fought for the British Army during the Second World War, which was why one day in 1947 he had found himself, with companions, in Piccadilly Circus. As he listened, John Joe recalled that he'd heard boys at the Christian Brothers' referring to some special story that Mr Lynch confidentially told to those whom he believed would benefit from it. He had heard boys sniggering over this story, but he had never sought to discover its content, not knowing it had to do with Piccadilly tarts.

'There was a fellow by the name of Baker,' said Mr Lynch, 'who'd been telling us that he knew the ropes. Baker was a London man. He knew the places, he was saying, where he could find the glory girls, but when it came to the point of the matter, John Joe, we hardly needed a guide.'

Because, explained Mr Lynch, the tarts were everywhere. They stood in the doorways of shops showing off the stature of their legs. Some would speak to you, Mr Lynch said, addressing you fondly and stating their availability. Some had their bosoms cocked out so that maybe they'd strike a passing soldier and entice him away from his companions. 'I'm telling you this, John Joe, on account of your daddy being dead. Are you fancying that stout?'

John Joe nodded his head. Thirteen years ago his father had fallen to his death from a scaffold, having been by trade a builder. John Joe could not remember him, although he knew what he had looked like from a photograph that was always on view on the kitchen dresser. He had often wondered what it would be like to have that bulky man about the house, and more often still he listened to his mother talking about him. But John Joe didn't think about his father now, in spite of Mr Lynch's reference to him: keen to hear more about the women of Piccadilly, he asked what had happened when Mr Lynch and his companions finished examining them in the doorways.

'I saw terrible things in Belgium,' replied Mr Lynch meditatively. 'I saw a Belgian woman held down on the floor while four men satisfied themselves on her. No woman could be the same after that. Combat brings out the brute in a man.'

'Isn't it shocking what they'd do, Mr Lynch? Wouldn't it make you sick?'

'If your daddy was alive today, he would be telling you a thing or two in order to prepare you for your manhood and the temptations in another country. Your mother wouldn't know how to tackle a matter like that, nor would Father Ryan, nor the Christian Brothers. Your daddy might have sat you down in this bar and given you your first bottle of stout. He might have told you about the facts of life.'

'Did one of the glory girls entice yourself, Mr Lynch?'

'Listen to me, John Joe.' Mr Lynch regarded his companion through small blue eyes, both of which were slightly bloodshot. He lit a cigarette and drew on it before continuing. Then he said: 'Baker had the soldiers worked up with his talk of the glory girls taking off their togs. He used to describe the motion of their haunches. He used to lie there at night in the dug-out describing the private areas of the women's bodies. When the time came we went out with Baker and Baker went up to the third one he saw and said could the six of us make arrangements with her. He was keen to strike a bargain because we had only limited means on account of having remained in a public house for four hours. Myself included, we were in an intoxicated condition.'

'What happened, Mr Lynch?'

'I would not have agreed to an arrangement like that if it hadn't been for drink. I was a virgin boy, John Joe. Like yourself.'

'I'm that way, certainly, Mr Lynch.'

'We marched in behind the glory girl, down a side-street. "Bedad, you're fine men," she said. We had bottles of beer in our pockets. "We'll drink that first," she said, "before we get down to business." '

John Joe laughed. He lifted the glass of stout to his lips and took a mouthful in a nonchalant manner, as though he'd been drinking stout for half a lifetime and couldn't do without it.

'Aren't you the hard man, Mr Lynch!' he said.

'You've got the wrong end of the stick,' replied Mr Lynch sharply. 'What happened was, I had a vision on the street. Amn't I saying to you those girls are no good to any man? I had a vision of the Virgin when we were walking along.'

'How d'you mean, Mr Lynch?'

'There was a little statue of the Holy Mother in my bedroom at home, a little special one my mother gave me at the occasion of my First Communion. It came into my mind, John Joe, when the six of us were with the glory girl. As soon as the glory girl said we'd drink the beer before we got down to business I saw the statue of the Holy Mother, as clear as if it was in front of me.'

John Joe, who had been anticipating an account of the soldiers' pleasuring, displayed disappointment. Mr Lynch shook his head at him.

'I was telling you a moral story,' he said reprovingly. 'The facts of life is one thing, John Joe, but keep away from dirty women.'

John Joe was a slight youth, pale of visage, as his father had been, and with large, awkward hands that bulged in his trouser pockets. He had no friends at the Christian Brothers' School he attended, being regarded there, because of his private nature and lack of interest in either scholastic or sporting matters, as something of an oddity – an opinion that was strengthened by his association with an old, simple-minded dwarf called Quigley, with whom he was regularly to be seen collecting minnows in a jam-jar or walking along the country roads. In class at the Christian

Brothers' John Joe would drift into a meditative state and could not easily be reached. 'Where've you gone, boy?' Brother Leahy would whisper, standing above him. His fingers would reach out for a twist of John Joe's scalp, and John Joe would rise from the ground with the Brother's thumb and forefinger tightening the short hairs of his neck, yet seeming not to feel the pain. It was only when the other hand of Brother Leahy gripped one of his ears that he would return to the classroom with a cry of anguish, and the boys and Brother Leahy would laugh. 'What'll we make of you?' Brother Leahy would murmur, returning to the blackboard while John Joe rubbed his head and his ear.

'There is many a time in the years afterwards,' said Mr Lynch ponderously, 'when I have gone through in my mind that moment in my life. I was tempted in bad company: I was two minutes off damnation.'

'I see what you mean, Mr Lynch.'

'When I came back to West Cork my mother asked me was I all right. Well, I was, I said. "I had a bad dream about you," my mother said. "I had a dream one night your legs were on fire." She looked at my legs, John Joe, and to tell you the truth of it she made me slip down my britches. "There's no harm there," she said. 'Twas only afterwards I worked it out: she had that dream in the very minute I was standing on the street seeing the vision in my brain. What my mother dreamed, John Joe, was that I was licked by the flames of Hell. She was warned that time, and from her dream she sent out a message that I was to receive a visit from the little statue. I'm an older man now, John Joe, but that's an account I tell to every boy in this town that hasn't got a father. That little story is an introduction to life and manhood. Did you enjoy the stout?'

'The stout's great stuff, Mr Lynch.'

'No drink you can take, John Joe, will injure you the way a dirty woman would. You might go to twenty million Confessions and you wouldn't relieve your heart and soul of a dirty woman. I didn't marry myself, out of shame for the memory of listening to Baker making that bargain. Will we have another bottle?'

John Joe, wishing to hear in further detail the bargain that Baker had made, said he could do with another drop. Mr Lynch directed him to a crate behind the counter. 'You're acquiring the taste,' he said.

John Joe opened and poured the bottles. Mr Lynch offered him a cigarette, which he accepted. In the Coliseum Cinema he had seen Piccadilly Circus, and in one particular film there had been Piccadilly tarts, just as Mr Lynch described, loitering in doorways provocatively. As always, coming out of the Coliseum, it had been a little strange to find himself again among small shops that sold clothes and hardware and meat, among vegetable shops and tiny confectioners' and tobacconists' and public houses. For a few minutes after the Coliseum's programme was over the three streets of the town were busy with people going home, walking or riding on bicycles, or driving cars to distant farms, or going towards the chip-shop. When he was alone, John Joe usually leaned against the window of a shop to watch the activity before returning home himself; when his mother accompanied him to the pictures they naturally went home at once, his mother chatting on about the film they'd seen.

'The simple thing is, John Joe, keep a certain type of thought out of your mind.'

'Thought, Mr Lynch?'

'Of a certain order.'

'Ah, yes. Ah, definitely, Mr Lynch. A young fellow has no time for that class of thing.'

'Live a healthy life.'

'That's what I'm saying, Mr Lynch.'

'If I hadn't had a certain type of thought I wouldn't have found myself on the street that night. It was Baker who called them the glory girls. It's a peculiar way of referring to the sort they are.'

'Excuse me, Mr Lynch, but what kind of an age would they be?'

'They were all ages, boy. There were nippers and a few more of them had wrinkles on the flesh of their faces. There were some who must have weighed fourteen stone and others you could put in your pocket.'

'And was the one Baker made the bargain with a big one or a little one?'

'She was medium-sized, boy.'

'And had she black hair, Mr Lynch?'

'As black as your boot. She had a hat on her head that was a disgrace to the nation, and black gloves on her hands. She was carrying a little umbrella.'

'And, Mr Lynch, when your comrades met up with you again, did they tell you a thing at all?'

Mr Lynch lifted the glass to his lips. He filled his mouth with stout and savoured the liquid before allowing it to pass into his stomach. He turned his small eyes on the youth and regarded him in silence.

'You have pimples on your chin,' said Mr Lynch in the end. 'I hope you're living a clean life, now.'

'A healthy life, Mr Lynch.'

'It is a question your daddy would ask you. You know what I mean? There's some lads can't leave it alone.'

'They go mad in the end, Mr Lynch.'

'There was fellows in the British Army that couldn't leave it alone.'

'They're a heathen crowd, Mr Lynch. Isn't there terrible reports in the British papers?'

'The body is God-given. There's no need to abuse it.'

'I've never done that thing, Mr Lynch.'

'I couldn't repeat,' said Mr Lynch, 'what the glory girl said when I walked away.'

John Joe, whose classroom meditations led him towards the naked bodies of women whom he had seen only clothed and whose conversations with the town's idiot, Quigley, were of an obscene nature, said it was understandable that Mr Lynch could not repeat what the girl had said to him. A girl like that, he added, wasn't fit to be encountered by a decent man.

'Go behind the counter,' said Mr Lynch, 'and lift out two more bottles.'

John Joe walked to the crate of stout bottles. 'I looked in at a window one time,' Quigley had said to him, 'and I saw Mrs Nugent resisting her husband. Nugent took no notice of her at all; he had the clothes from her body like you'd shell a pod of peas.'

'I don't think Baker lived,' said Mr Lynch. 'He'd be dead of disease.'

'I feel sick to think of Baker, Mr Lynch.'

'He was like an animal.'

All the women of the town – and most especially Mrs Taggart, the wife of a postman – John Joe had kept company with in his imagination. Mrs Taggart was a well-built woman, a foot taller than himself, a woman with whom he had seen himself walking in the fields on the Ballydehob road. She had found him alone and had said that she was crossing the fields to where her husband had fallen into a bog-hole, and would he be able to come with her? She had a heavy, chunky face and a wide neck on which the fat lay in encircling folds, like a fleshy necklace. Her hair was grey and black, done up in hairpins. 'I was only codding you,' she said when they reached the side of a secluded hillock. 'You're a good-looking fellow, Dempsey.' On the side of the hillock, beneath a tree, Mrs Taggart commenced to rid herself of her outer garments, remarking that it was hot. 'Slip out of that little jersey,' she urged. 'Wouldn't it bake you today?' Sitting beside him in her underclothes, Mrs Taggart asked him if he liked sunbathing. She drew her petticoat up so that the sun might reach the tops of her legs. She asked him to put his hand on one of her legs so that he could feel the muscles; she was a strong woman, she said, and added that the strongest muscles she possessed were the muscles of her stomach. 'Wait till I show you,' said Mrs Taggart.

On other occasions he found himself placed differently with Mrs Taggart: once, his mother had sent him round to her house to inquire if she had any eggs for sale and after she had put a dozen eggs in a basket Mrs Taggart asked him if he'd take a look at a thorn in the back of her leg. Another time he was passing her house and he heard her crying out for help. When he went inside he discovered that she had jammed the door of the bathroom and couldn't get out. He managed to release the door and when he entered the bathroom he discovered that Mrs Taggart was standing up in the bath, seeming to have forgotten that she hadn't her clothes on.

Mrs Keefe, the wife of a railway official, another statuesque woman, featured as regularly in John Joe's imagination, as did a Mrs O'Brien, a Mrs Summers, and a Mrs Power. Mrs Power kept a bread-shop, and a very pleasant way of passing the time when Brother Leahy was talking was to walk into Mrs Power's shop and hear her saying that she'd have to slip into the bakery for a small pan loaf and would he like to accompany her? Mrs Power wore a green overall with a belt that was tied in a knot at the front. In the bakery, while they were chatting, she would attempt to untie the belt but always found it difficult. 'Can you aid me?' Mrs Power would ask and John Joe would endeavour to loose the knot that lay tight against Mrs Power's stout stomach. 'Where've you gone, boy?' Brother Leahy's voice would whisper over and over again like a familiar incantation and John Joe would suddenly shout, realizing he was in pain.

'It was the end of the war,' said Mr Lynch. 'The following morning myself and a gang of the other lads got a train up to Liverpool, and then we crossed back to Dublin. There was a priest on the train and I spoke to him about the whole thing. Every man was made like that, he said to me, only I was lucky to be rescued in the nick of time. If I'd have taken his name I'd have sent him the information about my mother's dream. I think that would have interested him, John Joe. Wouldn't you think so?'

'Ah, it would of course.'

'Isn't it a great story, John Joe?'

'It is, Mr Lynch.'

'Don't forget it ever, boy. No man is clear of temptations. You don't have to go to Britain to get temptations.'

'I understand you, Mr Lynch.'

Quigley had said that one night he looked through a window and saw the Protestant clergyman, the Reverend Johnson, lying on the floor with his wife. There was another time, he said, that he observed Hickey the chemist being coaxed from an arm-chair by certain activities on the part of Mrs Hickey. Quigley had climbed up on the roof of a shed and had seen Mrs Swanton being helped out of her stockings by Swanton, the builder and decorator. Quigley's voice might continue for an hour and a half, for there was hardly a man and his wife in the town whom he didn't claim to have observed in intimate circumstances. John Joe did not ever ask how, when there was no convenient shed to climb on to, the dwarf managed to make his way to so many exposed upstairs windows. Such a question would have been wholly irrelevant.

At Mass, when John Joe saw the calves of women's legs stuck out from the kneeling position, he experienced an excitement that later bred new fantasies within him. 'That Mrs Dwyer,' he would say to the old dwarf, and the dwarf would reply that one night in February he had observed Mrs Dwyer preparing herself for the return of her husband from a County Council meeting in Cork. From the powdered body of Mrs Dwyer, as described by Quigley, John Joe would move to an image that included himself. He saw himself pushing open the hall-door of the Dwyers' house, having been sent to the house with a message from his mother, and hearing Mrs Dwyer's voice calling out, asking him to come upstairs. He stood on a landing and Mrs Dwyer came to him with a red coat wrapped round her to cover herself up. He could smell the powder on her body; the coat kept slipping from her shoulders. 'I have some magazines for your mother,' she said. 'They're inside the bedroom.' He went and sat on the bed while she collected a pile of magazines. She sat beside him then, drawing his attention to a story here and there that might be of particular interest to his mother. Her knee was pressed against his, and in a moment she put her arm round his shoulders and said he was a good-looking lad. The red coat fell back on to the bed when Mrs Dwyer took one of John Joe's large hands and placed it on her stomach. She then suggested, the evening being hot, that he should take off his jersey and his shirt.

Mrs Keogh, the owner of the public house, had featured also in John Joe's imagination and in the conversation of the old dwarf. Quigley had seen her, he said, a week before her husband died, hitting her husband with a length of wire because he would not oblige her with his attentions. 'Come down to the cellar,' said Mrs Keogh while Brother Leahy scribbled on the blackboard. 'Come down to the cellar, John Joe, and help me with a barrel.' He descended the cellar steps in front of her and when he looked back he saw her legs under her dark mourning skirt. 'I'm lost these days,' she said, 'since Mr Keogh went on.' They moved the barrel together and then Mrs Keogh said it was hot work and it would be better if they took off their jerseys. 'Haven't you the lovely arms!' she said as they rolled the barrel from one corner of the cellar to another. 'Will we lie down here for a rest?'

'We'll chance another bottle,' suggested Mr Lynch. 'Is it going down you all right?'

'My mother'll be waiting for the rashers, Mr Lynch.'

'No rasher can be cut, boy, till Mrs Keogh returns. You could slice your hand off on an old machine like that.'

'We'll have one more so.'

At the Christian Brothers', jokes were passed about that concerned grisly developments in the beds of freshly wedded couples, or centred around heroes who carried by chance strings of sausages in their pockets and committed unfortunate errors when it came to cutting one off for the pan. Such yarns, succeeding generally, failed with John Joe, for they seemed to him to be lacking in quality.

'How's your mammy?' Mr Lynch asked, watching John Joe pouring the stout.

'Ah, she's all right. I'm only worried she's waiting on the rashers –'

'There's honour due to a mother.'

John Joe nodded. He held the glass at an angle to receive dark foaming liquid, as Mr Lynch had shown him. Mr Lynch's mother, now seventy-nine, was still alive. They lived together in a house which Mr Lynch left every morning in order to work in the office of a meal business and which he left every evening in order to drink bottles of stout in Keogh's. The bachelor state of Mr Lynch was one which John Joe wondered if he himself would one day share. Certainly, he saw little attraction in the notion of marriage, apart from the immediate physical advantage. Yet Mr Lynch's life did not seem enviable either. Often on Sunday afternoons he observed the meal clerk walking slowly with his mother on his arm, seeming as lost in gloom as the married men who walked beside women pushing prams. Quigley, a bachelor also, was a happier man than Mr Lynch. He lived in what amounted to a shed at the bottom of his niece's garden. Food was carried to him, but there were few, with the exception of John Joe, who lingered in his company. On Sundays, a day which John Joe, like Mr Lynch, spent with his mother, Quigley walked alone.

'When'll you be leaving the Brothers?' Mr Lynch asked.

'In June.'

'And you'll be looking out for employment, John Joe?'

'I was thinking I'd go into the sawmills.'

Mr Lynch nodded approvingly. 'There's a good future in the sawmills,' he said. 'Is the job fixed up?'

'Not yet, Mr Lynch. They might give me a trial.'

Mr Lynch nodded again, and for a moment the two sat in silence. John Joe could see from the thoughtful way Mr Lynch was regarding his stout that there was something on his mind. Hoping to hear more about the Piccadilly tarts, John Joe patiently waited.

'If your daddy was alive,' said Mr Lynch eventually, 'he might mention this to you, boy.'

He drank more stout and wiped the foam from his lips with the back of his hand. 'I often see you out with Quigley. Is it a good thing to be spending your hours with a performer like that? Quigley's away in the head.'

'You'd be sorry for the poor creature, Mr Lynch.'

Mr Lynch said there was no need to feel sorry for Quigley, since that was the way Quigley was made. He lit another cigarette. He said:

'Maybe they would say to themselves up at the sawmills that you were the same way as Quigley. If he keeps company with Quigley, they might say, aren't they two of a kind?'

'Ah, I don't think they'd bother themselves, Mr Lynch. Sure, if you do the work well what would they have to complain of?'

'Has the manager up there seen you out with Quigley and the jam-jars?'

'I don't know, Mr Lynch.'

'Everything I'm saying to you is for your own good in the future. Do you understand that? If I were in your shoes I'd let Quigley look after himself.'

For years his mother had been saying the same to him. Brother Leahy had drawn him aside one day and had pointed out that an elderly dwarf wasn't a suitable companion for a young lad, especially since the dwarf was not sane. 'I see you took no notice of me,' Brother Leahy said six months later. 'Tell me this, young fellow-me-lad, what kind of a conversation do you have with old Quigley?' They talked, John Joe said, about trees and the flowers in the hedgerows. He liked to listen to Quigley, he said, because

Quigley had acquired a knowledge of such matters. 'Don't tell me lies,' snapped Brother Leahy, and did not say anything else.

Mrs Keogh returned from Confession. She came breathlessly into the bar, with pink cheeks, her ungloved hands the colour of meat. She was a woman of advanced middle age, a rotund woman who approached the proportions that John Joe most admired. She wore spectacles and had grey hair that was now a bit windswept. Her hat had blown off on the street, she said: she'd nearly gone mad trying to catch it. 'Glory be to God,' she cried when she saw John Joe. 'What's that fellow doing with a bottle of stout?'

'We had a man-to-man talk,' explained Mr Lynch. 'I started him off on the pleasures of the bottle.'

'Are you mad?' shouted Mrs Keogh with a loud laugh. 'He's under age.'

'I came for rashers,' said John Joe. 'A pound of green rashers, Mrs Keogh. The middle cut.'

'You're a shocking man,' said Mrs Keogh to Mr Lynch. She threw off her coat and hat. 'Will you pour me a bottle,' she asked, 'while I attend to this lad? Finish up that now, Mr Dempsey.'

She laughed again. She went away and they heard from the grocery the sound of the bacon machine.

John Joe finished his stout and stood up.

'Good night, Mr Lynch.'

'Remember about Quigley like a good fellow. When the day will come that you'll want to find a girl to marry, she might be saying you were the same type as Quigley. D'you understand me, John Joe?'

'I do, Mr Lynch.'

He passed through the door in the partition and watched Mrs Keogh slicing the bacon. He imagined her, as Quigley had said he'd seen her, belabouring her late husband with a length of wire. He imagined her as he had seen her himself, taking off her jersey because it was hot in the cellar, and then unzipping her green tweed skirt.

'I've sliced it thin,' she said. 'It tastes better thin, I think.'

'It does surely, Mrs Keogh.'

'Are you better after your stout? Don't go telling your mammy now.' Mrs Keogh laughed again, revealing long, crowded teeth. She weighed the bacon and wrapped it, munching a small piece of lean. 'If there's parsley in your mammy's garden,' she advised, 'chew a bit to get the smell of the stout away, in case she'd be cross with Mr Lynch. Or a teaspoon of tea-leaves.'

'There's no parsley, Mrs Keogh.'

'Wait till I get you the tea then.'

She opened a packet of tea and poured some on to the palm of his hand. She told him to chew it slowly and thoroughly and to let the leaves get into all the crevices of his mouth. She fastened the packet again, saying that no one would miss the little she'd taken from it. 'Four and two for the rashers,' she said.

He paid the money, with his mouth full of dry tea-leaves. He imagined Mrs Keogh leaning on her elbows on the counter and asking him if he had a kiss for her at all, calling him Mr Dempsey. He imagined her face stuck out towards his and her mouth open, displaying the big teeth, and her tongue damping her lips as the tongues of the Piccadilly tarts did, according to Mr Lynch. With the dryness in his own mouth and a gathering uneasiness in his stomach, his lips would go out to hers and he would taste her saliva.

'Good night so, Mrs Keogh.'

'Good night, Mr Dempsey. Tell your mother I was asking for her.'

He left the public house. The wind which had dislodged Mrs Keogh's hat felt fresh and cold on his face. The pink wash on a house across the street seemed pinker than it had seemed before, the ground moved beneath his feet, the street lighting seemed brighter. Youths and girls stood outside the illuminated windows of the small sweet-shops, waiting for the Coliseum to open. Four farmers left Regan's public house and mounted four bicycles and rode away, talking loudly. *Your Murphy Dealer* announced a large coloured sign in the window of a radio shop. Two boys that he had known at school came out of a shop eating biscuits from a paper bag. 'How're you, John Joe?' one of them said. 'How's Quigley these days?' They had left the school now: one of them worked in Kilmartin's the hardware's, the other in the Courthouse. They were wearing blue serge suits; their hair had been combed with care, and greased to remain tidy. They would go to the Coliseum, John Joe guessed, and sit behind two girls, giggling and whispering during the programme. Afterwards they would follow the girls for a little while, pretending to have no interest in them; they would buy chips in the chip-shop before they went home.

Thursday, Friday, Saturday, announced the sign outside the Coliseum: *The Rains Came.* As John Joe read them, the heavy black letters shifted, moving about on green paper that flapped in the wind, fixed with drawing-pins to an unpainted board. Mr Daly, the owner of the grey Coliseum, arrived on his bicycle and unlocked his property. *Sunday Only: Spencer Tracy in Boom Town.* In spite of the sickness in his stomach and the unpleasant taste of tea-leaves in his mouth, John Joe felt happy and was aware of an inclination to loiter for a long time outside the cinema instead of returning to his mother.

'It's great tonight, John Joe,' Mr Daly said. 'Are you coming in?'

John Joe shook his head. 'I have to bring rashers home to my mother,' he said. He saw Mrs Daly approaching with a torch, for the small cinema was a family business. Every night and twice on Sundays, Mr Daly sold the tickets while his wife showed the customers to their seats. 'I looked in a window one time,' Quigley had said, 'and she was trying to put on her .derclothes. Daly was standing in his socks.'

A man and a girl came out of a sweet-shop next to the cinema, the girl with a box of Urney chocolates in her hand. She was thanking the man for them, saying they were lovely. 'It's a great show tonight, John Joe,' Mrs

Daly said, repeating the statement of her husband, repeating what she and he said every day of their lives. John Joe wagged his head at her. It looked a great show definitely, he said. He imagined her putting on her under-clothes. He imagined her one night, unable because of a cold to show the customers to their seats, remaining at home in bed while her husband managed as best he could. 'I made a bit of bread for Mrs Daly,' his mother said. 'Will you carry it down to her, John Joe?' He rang the bell and waited until she came to the door with a coat over her night-dress. He handed her the bread wrapped in creased brown paper and she asked him to step into the hall out of the wind. 'Will you take a bottle, John Joe?' Mrs Daly said. He followed her into the kitchen, where she poured them each a glass of stout. 'Isn't it shocking hot in here?' she said. She took off her coat and sat at the kitchen table in her night-dress. 'You're a fine young fellow,' she said, touching his hand with her fingers.

John Joe walked on, past Riordan's the draper's and Kelly's Atlantic Hotel. A number of men were idling outside the entrance to the bar, smoking cigarettes, one of them leaning on a bicycle. 'There's a dance in Clonakilty,' a tall man said. 'Will we drive over to that?' The others took no notice of this suggestion. They were talking about the price of turkeys.

'How're you, John Joe?' shouted a red-haired youth who worked in the sawmills. 'Quigley was looking for you.'

'I was up in Keogh's for my mother.'

'You're a decent man,' said the youth from the sawmills, going into the bar of Kelly's Hotel.

At the far end of North Street, near the small house where he lived with his mother, he saw Quigley waiting for him. Once he had gone to the Coliseum with Quigley, telling his mother he was going with Kinsella, the boy who occupied the desk next to his at the Christian Brothers'. The occasion, the first and only time that Quigley had visited the Coliseum, had not been a success. Quigley hadn't understood what was happening and had become frightened. He'd begun to mutter and kick the seats in front of him. 'Take him off out of here,' Mr Daly had whispered, flashing his wife's torch. 'He'll bring the house down.' They had left the cinema after only a few minutes and had gone instead to the chip-shop.

'I looked in a window last night,' said Quigley now, hurrying to his friend's side, 'and, God, I saw a great thing.'

'I was drinking stout with Mr Lynch in Keogh's,' said John Joe. He might tell Quigley about the glory girls that Mr Lynch had advised him against, and about Baker who had struck a bargain with one of them, but it wouldn't be any use because Quigley never listened. No one held a conversation with Quigley: Quigley just talked.

'It was one o'clock in the morning,' said Quigley. His voice continued while John Joe opened the door of his mother's house and closed it behind him. Quigley would wait for him in the street and later on they'd perhaps go down to the chip-shop together.

'John Joe, where've you been?' demanded his mother, coming into the narrow hall from the kitchen. Her face was red from sitting too close to the range, her eyes had anger in them. 'What kept you, John Joe?'

'Mrs Keogh was at Confession.'

'What's that on your teeth?'

'What?'

'You've got dirt on your teeth.'

'I'll brush them then.'

He handed her the rashers. They went together to the kitchen, which was a small, low room with a flagged floor and a dresser that reached to the ceiling. On this, among plates and dishes, was the framed photograph of John Joe's father.

'Were you out with Quigley?' she asked, not believing that Mrs Keogh had kept him waiting for more than an hour.

He shook his head, brushing his teeth at the sink. His back was to her, and he imagined her distrustfully regarding him, her dark eyes gleaming with a kind of jealousy, her small wiry body poised as if to spring on any lie he should utter. Often he felt when he spoke to her that for her the words came physically from his lips, that they were things she could examine after he'd ejected them, in order to assess their truth.

'I talked to Mr Lynch,' he said. 'He was looking after the shop.'

'Is his mother well?'

'He didn't say.'

'He's very good to her.'

She unwrapped the bacon and dropped four rashers on to a pan that was warming on the range. John Joe sat down at the kitchen table. The feeling of euphoria that had possessed him outside the Coliseum was with him no longer; the floor was steady beneath his chair.

'They're good rashers,' his mother said.

'Mrs Keogh cut them thin.'

'They're best thin. They have a nicer taste.'

'Mrs Keogh said that.'

'What did Mr Lynch say to you? Didn't he mention the old mother?'

'He was talking about the war he was in.'

'It nearly broke her heart when he went to join it.'

'It was funny all right.'

'We were a neutral country.'

Mr Lynch would be still sitting in the bar of Keogh's. Every night of his life he sat there with his hat on his head, drinking bottles of stout. Other men would come into the bar and he would discuss matters with them and with Mrs Keogh. He would be drunk at the end of the evening. John Joe wondered if he chewed tea so that the smell of stout would not be detected by his mother when he returned to her. He would return and tell her some lies about where he had been. He had joined the British Army in order to get away from her for a time, only she'd reached out to him from a dream.

'Lay the table, John Joe.'

He put a knife and a fork for each of them on the table, and found butter and salt and pepper. His mother cut four pieces of griddle bread and placed them to fry on the pan. 'I looked in a window one time,' said the voice of Quigley, 'and Mrs Sullivan was caressing Sullivan's legs.'

'We're hours late with the tea,' his mother said. 'Are you starving, pet?'

'Ah, I am, definitely.'

'I have nice fresh eggs for you.'

It was difficult for her sometimes to make ends meet. He knew it was, yet neither of them had ever said anything. When he went to work in the sawmills it would naturally be easier, with a sum each week to add to the pension.

She fried the eggs, two for him and one for herself. He watched her basting them in her expert way, intent upon what she was doing. Her anger was gone, now that he was safely in the kitchen, waiting for the food she cooked. Mr Lynch would have had his tea earlier in the evening, before he went down to Keogh's. 'I'm going out for a long walk,' he probably said to his mother, every evening after he'd wiped the egg from around his mouth.

'Did he tell you an experience he had in the war?' his mother asked, placing the plate of rashers, eggs and fried bread in front of him. She poured boiling water into a brown enamel tea-pot and left it on the range to draw.

'He told me about a time they were attacked by the Germans,' John Joe said. 'Mr Lynch was nearly killed.'

'She thought he'd never come back.'

'Oh, he came back all right.'

'He's very good to her now.'

When Brother Leahy twisted the short hairs on his neck and asked him what he'd been dreaming about he usually said he'd been working something out in his mind, like a long division sum. Once he said he'd been trying to translate a sentence into Irish, and another time he'd said he'd been solving a puzzle that had appeared in the *Sunday Independent*. Recalling Brother Leahy's face, he ate the fried food. His mother repeated that the eggs were fresh. She poured him a cup of tea.

'Have you homework to do?'

He shook his head, silently registering that lie, knowing that there was homework to be done, but wishing instead to accompany Quigley to the chip-shop.

'Then we can listen to the wireless,' she said.

'I thought maybe I'd go out for a walk.'

Again the anger appeared in her eyes. Her mouth tightened, she laid down her knife and fork.

'I thought you'd stop in, John Joe,' she said, 'on your birthday.'

'Ah, well now –'

'I have a little surprise for you.'

She was telling him lies, he thought, just as he had told her lies. She began to eat again, and he could see in her face a reflection of the busyness that had developed in her mind. What could she find to produce as a surprise? She had given him that morning a green shirt that she knew he'd like because he liked the colour. There was a cake that she'd made, some of which they'd have when they'd eaten what was in front of them now. He knew about this birthday cake because he had watched her decorating it with hundreds and thousands: she couldn't suddenly say it was a surprise.

'When I've washed the dishes,' she said, 'we'll listen to the wireless and we'll look at that little thing I have.'

'All right,' he said.

He buttered bread and put a little sugar on the butter, which was a mixture he liked. She brought the cake to the table and cut them each a slice. She said she thought the margarine you got nowadays was not as good as margarine in the past. She turned the wireless on. A woman was singing.

'Try the cake now,' she said. 'You're growing up, John Joe.'

'Fifteen.'

'I know, pet.'

Only Quigley told the truth, he thought. Only Quigley was honest and straightforward and said what was in his mind. Other people told Quigley to keep that kind of talk to himself because they knew it was the truth, because they knew they wanted to think the thoughts that Quigley thought. 'I looked in a window,' Quigley had said to him when he was nine years old, the first time he had spoken to him, 'I saw a man and woman without their clothes on.' Brother Leahy would wish to imagine as Quigley imagined, and as John Joe imagined too. And what did Mr Lynch think about when he walked in gloom with his mother on a Sunday? Did he dream of the medium-sized glory girl he had turned away from because his mother had sent him a Virgin Mary from her dreams? Mr Lynch was not an honest man. It was a lie when he said that shame had kept him from marrying. It was his mother who prevented that, with her dreams of legs on fire and her First Communion statues. Mr Lynch had chosen the easiest course: bachelors might be gloomy on occasion, but they were untroubled men in some respects, just as men who kept away from the glory girls were.

'Isn't it nice cake?'

'Yes,' he said.

'This time next year you'll be in the sawmills.'

'I will.'

'Yes.'

'It's good there's work for you.'

They ate the two pieces of cake and then she cleared away the dishes and put them in the sink. He sat on a chair by the range. The men who'd been loitering outside Kelly's Hotel might have driven over to Clonakilty by now, he thought. They'd be dancing with girls and later they'd go back to their wives and say they'd been somewhere else, playing cards together in Kelly's maybe. Within the grey cement of the Coliseum the girl who'd brought the box of chocolates would be eating them, and the man who was with her would be wanting to put his hands on her.

Why couldn't he say to his mother that he'd drunk three bottles of stout in Keogh's? Why couldn't he say he could see the naked body of Mrs Taggart? Why hadn't he said to Mr Lynch that he should tell the truth about what was in his mind, like Quigley told the truth? Mr Lynch spent his life returning to the scenes that obsessed him, to the Belgian woman on the ground and the tarts of Piccadilly Circus. Yet he spoke of them only to ′fatherless boys, because it was the only excuse for mentioning them that he'd been able to think up.

'I have this for you,' she said.

She held towards him an old fountain-pen that had belonged to his father, a pen he had seen before. She had taken it from a drawer of the dresser, where it was always kept.

'I thought you could have it on your fifteenth birthday,' she said.

He took it from her, a black and white pen that hadn't been filled with ink for thirteen years. In the drawer of the dresser there was a pipe of his father's, and a tie-pin and a bunch of keys and a pair of bicycle clips. She had washed and dried the dishes, he guessed, racking her mind to think of something she might offer him as the surprise she'd invented. The pen was the most suitable thing; she could hardly offer him the bicycle clips.

'Wait till I get you the ink,' she said, 'and you can try it out.' From the wireless came the voice of a man advertising household products. 'Bird's Custard,' urged the voice gently, 'and Bird's Jelly De Luxe.'

He filled the pen from the bottle of ink she handed him. He sat down at the kitchen table again and tried the nib out on the piece of brown paper that Mrs Keogh had wrapped round the rashers and which his mother had neatly folded away for further use.

'Isn't it great it works still?' she said. 'It must be a good pen.'

It's hot in here, he wrote. *Wouldn't you take off your jersey?*

'That's a funny thing to write,' his mother said.

'It came into my head.'

They didn't like him being with Quigley because they knew what Quigley talked about when he spoke the truth. They were jealous because there was no pretence between Quigley and himself. Even though it was only Quigley who talked, there was an understanding between them: being with Quigley was like being alone.

'I want you to promise me a thing,' she said, 'now that you're fifteen.'

He put the cap on the pen and bundled up the paper that had contained the rashers. He opened the top of the range and dropped the paper into it. She would ask him to promise not to hang about with the town's idiot any more. He was a big boy now, he was big enough to own his father's fountain-pen and it wasn't right that he should be going out getting minnows in a jam-jar with an elderly affected creature. It would go against his chances in the sawmills.

He listened to her saying what he had anticipated she would say. She went on talking, telling him about his father and the goodness there had been in his father before he fell from the scaffold. She took from the dresser the framed photograph that was so familiar to him and she put it into his hands, telling him to look closely at it. It would have made no difference, he thought, if his father had lived. His father would have been like the others; if ever he'd have dared to mention the nakedness of Mrs Taggart his father would have beaten him with a belt.

'I am asking you for his sake,' she said, 'as much as for my own and for yours, John Joe.'

He didn't understand what she meant by that, and he didn't inquire. He would say what she wished to hear him say, and he would keep his promise to her because it would be the easiest thing to do. Quigley wasn't hard to push away, you could tell him to get away like you'd tell a dog. It was funny that they should think that it would make much difference to him now, at this stage, not having Quigley to listen to.

'All right,' he said.

'You're a good boy, John Joe. Do you like the pen?'

'It's a lovely pen.'

'You might write better with that one.'

She turned up the volume of the wireless and together they sat by the range, listening to the music. To live in a shed like Quigley did would not be too bad: to have his food carried down through a garden by a niece, to go about the town in that special way, alone with his thoughts. Quigley did not have to pretend to the niece who fed him. He didn't have to say he'd been for a walk when he'd been drinking in Keogh's or that he'd been playing cards with men when he'd been dancing in Clonakilty. Quigley didn't have to chew tea and keep quiet. Quigley talked; he said the words he wanted to say. Quigley was lucky being how he was.

'I will go to bed now,' he said eventually.

They said good night to one another, and he climbed the stairs to his room. She would rouse him in good time, she called after him. 'Have a good sleep,' she said.

He closed the door of his room and looked with affection at his bed, for in the end there was only that. It was a bed that, sagging, held him in its centre and wrapped him warmly. There was ornamental brass-work at the head but not at the foot, and on the web of interlocking wire the hair mattress was thin. John Joe shed his clothes, shedding also the small town and his mother and Mr Lynch and the fact that he, on his fifteenth birthday, had drunk his first stout and had chewed tea. He entered his iron bed and the face of Mr Lynch passed from his mind and the voices of boys telling stories about freshly married couples faded away also. No one said to him now that he must not keep company with a crazed dwarf. In his iron bed, staring into the darkness, he made of the town what he wished to make of it, knowing that he would not be drawn away from his dreams by the tormenting fingers of a Christian Brother. In his iron bed he heard again only the voice of the town's idiot and then that voice, too, was there no more. He travelled alone, visiting in his way the women of the town, adored and adoring, more alive in his bed than ever he was at the Christian Brothers' School, or in the grey Coliseum, or in the chip-shop, or Keogh's public house, or his mother's kitchen, more alive than ever he would be at the sawmills. In his bed he entered a paradise: it was grand being alone.

The Mark-2 Wife

Standing alone at the Lowhrs' party, Anna Mackintosh thought about her husband Edward, establishing him clearly for this purpose in her mind's eye. He was a thin man, forty-one years of age, with fair hair that was often untidy. In the seventeen years they'd been married he had changed very little: he was still nervous with other people, and smiled in the same abashed way, and his face was still almost boyish. She believed she had failed him because he had wished for children and she had not been able to supply any. She had, over the years, developed a nervous condition about this fact and in the end, quite some time ago now, she had consulted a psychiatrist, a Dr Abbatt, at Edward's pleading.

In the Lowhrs' rich drawing-room, its walls and ceiling gleaming with a metallic surface of ersatz gold, Anna listened to dance music coming from a tape-recorder and continued to think about her husband. In a moment he would be at the party too, since they had agreed to meet there, although by now it was three quarters of an hour later than the time he had stipulated. The Lowhrs were people he knew in a business way, and he had said he thought it wise that he and Anna should attend this gathering of theirs. She had never met them before, which made it more difficult for her, having to wait about, not knowing a soul in the room. When she thought about it she felt hard done by, for although Edward was kind to her and always had been, it was far from considerate to be as late as this. Because of her nervous condition she felt afraid and had developed a sickness in her stomach. She looked at her watch and sighed.

People arrived, some of them kissing the Lowhrs, others nodding and smiling. Two dark-skinned maids carried trays of drinks among the guests, offering them graciously and murmuring thanks when a glass was accepted. 'I'll be there by half past nine,' Edward had said that morning. 'If you don't turn up till ten you won't have to be alone at all.' He had kissed her after that, and had left the house. I'll wear the blue, she thought, for she liked the colour better than any other: it suggested serenity to her, and the idea of serenity, especially as a quality in herself, was something she valued. She had said as much to Dr Abbatt, who had agreed that serenity was something that should be important in her life.

An elderly couple, tall twig-like creatures of seventy-five, a General Ritchie and his wife, observed the lone state of Anna Mackintosh and reacted in different ways. 'That woman seems out of things,' said Mrs Ritchie. 'We should go and talk to her.'

But the General gave it as his opinion that there was something the matter with this woman who was on her own. 'Now, don't let's get involved,' he rather tetchily begged. 'In any case she doesn't look in the mood for chat.'

His wife shook her head. 'Our name is Ritchie,' she said to Anna, and Anna, who had been looking at the whisky in her glass, lifted her head and saw a thin old woman who was as straight as a needle, and behind her a man who was thin also but who stooped a bit and seemed to be cross. 'He's an old soldier,' said Mrs Ritchie. 'A general that was.'

Strands of white hair trailed across the pale dome of the old man's head. He had sharp eyes, like a terrier's, and a grey moustache. 'It's not a party I care to be at,' he muttered, holding out a bony hand. 'My wife's the one for this.'

Anna said who she was and added that her husband was late and that she didn't know the Lowhrs.

'We thought it might be something like that,' said Mrs Ritchie. 'We don't know anyone either, but at least we have one another to talk to.' The Lowhrs, she added, were an awfully nice, generous couple.

'We met them on a train in Switzerland,' the General murmured quietly.

Anna glanced across the crowded room at the people they spoke of. The Lowhrs were wholly different in appearance from the Ritchies. They were small and excessively fat, and they both wore glasses and smiled a lot. Like two balls, she thought.

'My husband knows them in a business way,' she said. She looked again at her watch: the time was half past ten. There was a silence, and then Mrs Ritchie said:

'They invited us to two other parties in the past. It's very kind, for we don't give parties ourselves any more. We live a quiet sort of life now.' She went on talking, saying among other things that it was pleasant to see the younger set at play. When she stopped, the General added:

'The Lowhrs feel sorry for us, actually.'

'They're very kind,' his wife repeated.

Anna had been aware of a feeling of uneasiness the moment she'd entered the golden room, and had Edward been with her she'd have wanted to say that they should turn round and go away again. The uneasiness had increased whenever she'd noted the time, and for some reason these old people for whom the Lowhrs were sorry had added to it even more. She would certainly talk this over with Dr Abbatt, she decided, and then, quite absurdly, she felt an urge to telephone Dr Abbatt and tell him at once about the feeling she had. She closed her eyes, thinking that she would keep them like that for only the slightest moment so that the Ritchies wouldn't notice and think it odd. While they were still closed she heard Mrs Ritchie say:

'Are you all right, Mrs Mackintosh?'

She opened her eyes and saw General Ritchie and his wife were examining her face with interest. She imagined them wondering about her, a woman of forty whose husband was an hour late. They'd be thinking, she thought, that the absent husband didn't have much of a feeling for his wife to be as careless as that. And yet, they'd probably think, he must have had a feeling for her once since he had married her in the first place.

'It's just,' said Mrs Ritchie, 'that I had the notion you were going to faint.'

The voice of Petula Clark came powerfully from the tape-recorder. At one end of the room people were beginning to dance in a casual way, some still holding their glasses in their hands.

'The heat could have affected you,' said the General, bending forward so that his words would reach her.

Anna shook her head. She tried to smile, but the smile failed to materialize. She said:

'I never faint, actually.'

She could feel a part of herself attempting to bar from her mind the entry of unwelcome thoughts. Hastily she said, unable to think of anything better:

'My husband's really frightfully late.'

'You know,' said General Ritchie, 'it seems to me we met your husband here.' He turned to his wife. 'A fair-haired man – he said his name was Mackintosh. Is your husband fair, Mrs Mackintosh?'

'Of course,' cried Mrs Ritchie. 'Awfully nice.'

Anna said that Edward was fair. Mrs Ritchie smiled at her husband and handed him her empty glass. He reached out for Anna's. She said:

'Whisky, please. By itself.'

'He's probably held up in bloody traffic,' said the General before moving off.

'Yes, probably that,' Mrs Ritchie said. 'I do remember him well, you know.'

'Edward did come here before. I had a cold.'

'Completely charming. We said so afterwards.'

One of the dark-skinned maids paused with a tray of drinks. Mrs Ritchie explained that her husband was fetching some. 'Thank you, madam,' said the dark-skinned maid, and the General returned.

'It isn't the traffic,' Anna said rather suddenly and loudly. 'Edward's not held up like that at all.'

The Ritchies sipped their drinks. They can sense I'm going to be a nuisance, Anna thought. 'I'm afraid it'll be boring,' he had said. 'We'll slip away at eleven and have dinner in Charlotte Street.' She heard him saying it now, quite distinctly. She saw him smiling at her.

'I get nervous about things,' she said to the Ritchies. 'I worry unnecessarily. I try not to.'

Mrs Ritchie inclined her head in a sympathetic manner; the General coughed. There was a silence and then Mrs Ritchie spoke about episodes in their past. Anna looked at her watch and saw that it was five to eleven. 'Oh God,' she said.

The Ritchies asked her again if she was all right. She began to say she was but she faltered before the sentence was complete, and in that moment she gave up the struggle. What was the point, she thought, of exhausting oneself being polite and making idle conversation when all the time one was in a frightful state?

'He's going to be married again,' she said quietly and evenly. 'His Mark-2 wife.'

She felt better at once. The sickness left her stomach; she drank a little whisky and found its harsh taste a comfort.

'Oh, I'm terribly sorry,' said Mrs Ritchie.

Anna had often dreamed of the girl. She had seen her, dressed all in purple, with slim hips and a purple bow in her black hair. She had seen the two of them together in a speedboat, the beautiful young creature laughing her head off like a figure in an advertisement. She had talked for many hours to Dr Abbatt about her, and Dr Abbatt had made the point that the girl was simply an obsession. 'It's just a little nonsense,' he had said to her kindly, more than once. Anna knew in her calmer moments that it was just a little nonsense, for Edward was always kind and had never ceased to say he loved her. But in bad moments she argued against that conclusion, reminding herself that other kind men who said they loved their wives often made off with something new. Her own marriage being childless would make the whole operation simpler.

'I hadn't thought it would happen at a party,' Anna said to the Ritchies. 'Edward has always been decent and considerate. I imagined he would tell me quietly at home, and comfort me. I imagined he would be decent to the end.'

'You and your husband are not yet separated then?' Mrs Ritchie inquired.

'This is the way it is happening,' Anna repeated. 'D'you understand? Edward is delayed by his Mark-2 wife because she insists on delaying him. She's demanding that he should make his decision and afterwards that he and she should come to tell me, so that I won't have to wait any more. You understand,' she repeated, looking closely from one face to the other, 'that this isn't Edward's doing?'

'But, Mrs Mackintosh –'

'I have a woman's intuition about it. I have felt my woman's intuition at work since the moment I entered this room. I know precisely what's going to happen.'

Often, ever since the obsession had begun, she had wondered if she had any rights at all. Had she rights in the matter, she had asked herself, since she was running to fat and could supply no children? The girl would repeatedly give birth and everyone would be happy, for birth was a happy business. She had suggested to Dr Abbatt that she probably hadn't any rights, and for once he had spoken to her sternly. She said it now to the Ritchies, because it didn't seem to matter any more what words were spoken. On other occasions, when she was at home, Edward had been late and she had sat and waited for him, pretending it was a natural thing for him to be late. And when he arrived her fears had seemed absurd.

'You understand?' she said to the Ritchies.

The Ritchies nodded their thin heads, the General embarrassed, his wife concerned. They waited for Anna to speak. She said:

'The Lowhrs will feel sorry for me, as they do for you. "This poor woman," they'll cry, "left all in the lurch at our party! What a ghastly thing!" I should go home, you know, but I haven't even the courage for that.'

'Could we help at all?' asked Mrs Ritchie.

'You've been married all this time and not come asunder. Have you had children, Mrs Ritchie?'

Mrs Ritchie replied that she had had two boys and a girl. They were well grown up by now, she explained, and among them had provided her and the General with a dozen grandchildren.

'What did you think of my husband?'

'Charming, Mrs Mackintosh, as I said.'

'Not the sort of man who'd mess a thing like this up? You thought the opposite, I'm sure: that with bad news to break he'd choose the moment elegantly. Once he would have.'

'I don't understand,' protested Mrs Ritchie gently, and the General lent his support to that with a gesture.

'Look at me,' said Anna. 'I've worn well enough. Neither I nor Edward would deny it. A few lines and flushes, fatter and coarser. No one can escape all that. Did you never feel like a change, General?'

'A change?'

'I have to be rational. I have to say that it's no reflection on me. D'you understand that?'

'Of course it's no reflection.'

'It's like gadgets in shops. You buy a gadget and you develop an affection for it, having decided on it in the first place because you thought it was attractive. But all of a sudden there are newer and better gadgets in the shops. More up-to-date models.' She paused. She found a handkerchief and blew her nose. She said:

'You must excuse me: I am not myself tonight.'

'You mustn't get upset. Please don't,' Mrs Ritchie said.

Anna drank all the whisky in her glass and lifted another glass from a passing tray. 'There are too many people in this room,' she complained. 'There's not enough ventilation. It's ideal for tragedy.'

Mrs Ritchie shook her head. She put her hand on Anna's arm. 'Would you like us to go home with you and see you safely in?'

'I have to stay here.'

'Mrs Mackintosh, your husband would never act like that.'

'People in love are cruel. They think of themselves: why should they bother to honour the feelings of a discarded wife?'

'Oh, come now,' said Mrs Ritchie.

At that moment a bald man came up to Anna and took her glass from her hand and led her, without a word, on to the dancing area. As he danced with her, she thought that something else might have happened. Edward was not with anyone, she said to herself: Edward was dead. A telephone had rung in the Lowhrs' house and a voice had said that, en route to their party, a man had dropped dead on the pavement. A maid had taken the message and, not quite understanding it, had done nothing about it.

'I think we should definitely go home now,' General Ritchie said to his wife. 'We could be back for *A Book at Bedtime.*'

'We cannot leave her as easily as that. Just look at the poor creature.'

'That woman is utterly no concern of ours.'

'Just look at her.'

The General sighed and swore and did as he was bidden.

'My husband was meant to turn up,' Anna said to the bald man. 'I've just thought he may have died.' She laughed to indicate that she did not really believe this, in case the man became upset. But the man seemed not to be interested. She could feel his lips playing with a strand of her hair. Death, she thought, she could have accepted.

Anna could see the Ritchies watching her. Their faces were grave, but it came to her suddenly that the gravity was artificial. What, after all, was she to them that they should bother? She was a wretched woman at a party, a woman in a state, who was making an unnecessary fuss because her husband was about to give her her marching orders. Had the Ritchies been mocking her, she wondered, he quite directly, she in some special, subtle way of her own?

'Do you know those people I was talking to?' she said to her partner, but with a portion of her hair still in his mouth he made no effort at reply. Passing near to her, she noticed the thick, square fingers of Mr Lowhr embedded in the flesh of his wife's shoulder. The couple danced by, seeing her and smiling, and it seemed to Anna that their smiles were as empty as the Ritchies' sympathy.

'My husband is leaving me for a younger woman,' she said to the bald man, a statement that caused him to shrug. He had pressed himself close to her, his knees on her thighs, forcing her legs this way and that. His hands were low on her body now, advancing on her buttocks. He was eating her hair.

'I'm sorry,' Anna said. 'I'd rather you didn't do that.'

He released her where they stood and smiled agreeably: she could see pieces of her hair on his teeth. He walked away, and she turned and went in the opposite direction.

'We're really most concerned,' said Mrs Ritchie. She and her husband were standing where Anna had left them, as though waiting for her. General Ritchie held out her glass to her.

'Why should you be concerned? That bald man ate my hair. That's what people do to used-up women like me. They eat your hair and force their bodies on you. You know, General.'

'Certainly, I don't. Not at all.'

'That man knew all about me. D'you think he'd have taken his liberties if he hadn't? A man like that can guess.'

'Nonsense,' said Mrs Ritchie firmly. She stared hard at Anna, endeavouring to impress upon her the errors in her logic.

'If you want to know, that man's a drunk,' said the General. 'He was far gone when he arrived here and he's more so now.'

'Why are you saying that?' Anna cried shrilly. 'Why are you telling me lies and mocking me?'

'Lies?' demanded the General, snapping the word out. 'Lies?'

'My dear, we're not mocking you at all,' murmured Mrs Ritchie.

'You and those Lowhrs and everyone else, God knows. The big event at this party is that Edward Mackintosh will reject his wife for another.'

'Oh now, Mrs Mackintosh –'

'Second marriages are often happier, you know. No reason why they shouldn't be.'

'We would like to help if we could,' Mrs Ritchie said.

'Help? In God's name, how can I be helped? How can two elderly strangers help me when my husband gives me up? What kind of help? Would you give me money – an income, say? Or offer me some other husband? Would you come to visit me and talk to me so that I shouldn't be lonely? Or strike down my husband, General, to show your disapproval? Would you scratch out that little girl's eyes for me, Mrs Ritchie? Would you slap her brazen face?'

'We simply thought we might help in some way,' Mrs Ritchie said. 'Just because we're old and pretty useless doesn't mean we can't make an effort.'

'We are all God's creatures, you are saying. We should offer aid to one another at all opportunities, when marriages get broken and decent husbands are made cruel. Hold my hands then, and let us wait for Edward and his Mark-2 wife. Let's all three speak together and tell them what we think.'

She held out her hands, but the Ritchies did not take them.

'We don't mean to mock you, as you seem to think,' the General said. 'I must insist on that, madam.'

'You're mocking me with your talk about helping. The world is not like that. You like to listen to me for my entertainment value: I'm a good bit of gossip for you. I'm a woman going on about her husband and then getting insulted by a man and seeing the Lowhrs smiling over it. Tell your little grandchildren that sometime.'

Mrs Ritchie said that the Lowhrs, she was sure, had not smiled at any predicament that Anna had found herself in, and the General impatiently repeated that the man was drunk.

'The Lowhrs smiled,' Anna said, 'and you have mocked me too. Though perhaps you don't even know it.'

As she pushed a passage through the people, she felt the sweat running on her face and her body. There was a fog of smoke in the room by now, and the voices of the people, struggling to be heard above the music, were louder than before. The man she had danced with was sitting in a corner with his shoes off, and a woman in a crimson dress was trying to persuade him to put them on again. At the door of the room she found Mr Lowhr. 'Shall we dance?' he said.

She shook her head, feeling calmer all of a sudden. Mr Lowhr suggested a drink.

'May I telephone?' she said. 'Quietly somewhere?'

'Upstairs,' said Mr Lowhr, smiling immensely at her. 'Up two flights, the door ahead of you: a tiny guest-room. Take a glass with you.'

She nodded, saying she'd like a little whisky.

'Let me give you a tip,' Mr Lowhr said as he poured her some from a nearby bottle. 'Always buy Haig whisky. It's distilled by a special method.'

'You're never going so soon?' said Mrs Lowhr, appearing at her husband's side.

'Just to telephone,' said Mr Lowhr. He held out his hand with the glass of whisky in it. Anna took it, and as she did so she caught a glimpse of the Ritchies watching her from the other end of the room. Her calmness vanished. The Lowhrs, she noticed, were looking at her too, and smiling. She wanted to ask them why they were smiling, but she knew if she did that they'd simply make some polite reply. Instead she said:

'You shouldn't expose your guests to men who eat hair. Even unimportant guests.'

She turned her back on them and passed from the room. She crossed the hall, sensing that she was being watched. 'Mrs Mackintosh,' Mr Lowhr called after her.

His plumpness filled the doorway. He hovered, seeming uncertain about pursuing her. His face was bewildered and apparently upset.

'Has something disagreeable happened?' he said in a low voice across the distance between them.

'You saw. You and your wife thought fit to laugh, Mr Lowhr.'

'I do assure you, Mrs Mackintosh, I've no idea what you're talking about.'

'It's fascinating, I suppose. Your friends the Ritchies find it fascinating too.'

'Look here, Mrs Mackintosh –'

'Oh, don't blame them. They've nothing left but to watch and mock, at

an age like that. The point is, there's a lot of hypocrisy going on tonight.'
She nodded at Mr Lowhr to emphasize that last remark, and then went
swiftly upstairs.

'I imagine the woman's gone off home,' the General said. 'I dare say her
husband's drinking in a pub.'

'I worried once,' replied Mrs Ritchie, speaking quietly, for she didn't
wish the confidence to be heard by others. 'That female, Mrs Flynn.'

The General roared with laughter. 'Trixie Flynn,' he shouted. 'Good
God, she was a free-for-all!'

'Oh, do be quiet.'

'Dear girl, you didn't ever think –'

'I didn't know what to think, if you want to know.'

Greatly amused, the General seized what he hoped would be his final
drink. He placed it behind a green plant on a table. 'Shall we dance one
dance,' he said, 'just to amuse them? And then when I've had that drink
to revive me we can thankfully make our way.'

But he found himself talking to nobody, for when he had turned from
his wife to secrete his drink she had moved away. He followed her to
where she was questioning Mrs Lowhr.

'Some little tiff,' Mrs Lowhr was saying as he approached.

'Hardly a tiff,' corrected Mrs Ritchie. 'The woman's terribly upset.' She
turned to her husband, obliging him to speak.

'Upset,' he said.

'Oh, there now,' cried Mrs Lowhr, taking each of the Ritchies by an arm.
'Why don't you take the floor and forget it?'

They both of them recognized from her tone that she was thinking that
the elderly exaggerated things and didn't always understand the ways of
marriage in the modern world. The General especially resented the
insinuation. He said:

'Has the woman gone away?'

'She's upstairs telephoning. Some silly chap upset her apparently, during
a dance. That's all it is, you know.'

'You've got the wrong end of the stick entirely,' said the General angrily,
'and you're trying to say we have. The woman believes her husband may
arrive here with the girl he's chosen as his second wife.'

'But that's ridiculous!' cried Mrs Lowhr with a tinkling laugh.

'It is what the woman thinks,' said the General loudly, 'whether it's
ridiculous or not.' More quietly, Mrs Ritchie added:

'She thinks she has a powerful intuition when all it is is a disease.'

'I'm cross with this Mrs Mackintosh for upsetting you two dear people!'
cried Mrs Lowhr with a shrillness that matched her roundness and her
glasses. 'I really and truly am.'

A big man came up as she spoke and lifted her into his arms, preparatory
to dancing with her. 'What could anyone do?' she called back at the

Ritchies as the man rotated her away. 'What can you do for a nervy woman like that?'

There was dark wallpaper on the walls of the room: black and brown with little smears of muted yellow. The curtains matched it; so did the bedspread on the low single bed, and the covering on the padded headboard. The carpet ran from wall to wall and was black and thick. There was a narrow wardrobe with a door of padded black leather and brass studs and an ornamental brass handle. The dressing-table and the stool in front of it reflected this general motif in different ways. Two shelves, part of the bed, attached to it on either side of the pillows, served as bedside tables: on each there was a lamp and a book, and on one of them a white telephone.

As Anna closed and locked the door, she felt that in a dream she had been in a dark room in a house where there was a party, waiting for Edward to bring her terrible news. She drank a little whisky and moved towards the telephone. She dialled a number and when a voice answered her call she said:

'Dr Abbatt? It's Anna Mackintosh.'

His voice, as always, was so soft she could hardly hear it. 'Ah, Mrs Mackintosh,' he said.

'I want to talk to you.'

'Of course, Mrs Mackintosh, of course. Tell me now.'

'I'm at a party given by people called Lowhr. Edward was to be here but he didn't turn up. I was all alone and then two old people like scarecrows talked to me. They said their name was Ritchie. And a man ate my hair when we were dancing. The Lowhrs smiled at that.'

'I see. Yes?'

'I'm in a room at the top of the house. I've locked the door.'

'Tell me about the room, Mrs Mackintosh.'

'There's black leather on the wardrobe and the dressing table. Curtains and things match. Dr Abbatt?'

'Yes?'

'The Ritchies are people who injure other people, I think. Intentionally or unintentionally, it never matters.'

'They are strangers to you, these Ritchies?'

'They attempted to mock me. People know at this party, Dr Abbatt; they sense what's going to happen because of how I look.'

Watching for her to come downstairs, the Ritchies stood in the hall and talked to one another.

'I'm sorry,' said Mrs Ritchie. 'I know it would be nicer to go home.'

'What can we do, old sticks like us? We know not a thing about such women. It's quite absurd.'

'The woman's on my mind, dear. And on yours too. You know it.'

'I think she'll be more on our minds if we come across her again. She'll turn nasty, I'll tell you that.'

'Yes, but it would please me to wait a little.'

'To be insulted,' said the General.

'Oh, do stop being so cross, dear.'

'The woman's a stranger to us. She should regulate her life and have done with it. She has no right to bother people.'

'She is a human being in great distress. No, don't say anything, please, if it isn't pleasant.'

The General went into a sulk, and at the end of it he said grudgingly:

'Trixie Flynn was nothing.'

'Oh, I know. Trixie Flynn is dead and done for years ago. I didn't worry like this woman if that's what's on your mind.'

'It wasn't,' lied the General. 'The woman worries ridiculously.'

'I think you know, we may yet be of use to her: I have a feeling about that.'

'For God's sake, leave the feelings to her. We've had enough of that for one day.'

'As I said to her, we're not entirely useless. No one ever can be.'

'You feel you're being attacked again, Mrs Mackintosh. Are you calm? You haven't been drinking too much?'

'A little.'

'I see.'

'I am being replaced by a younger person.'

'You say you're in a bedroom. Is it possible for you to lie on the bed and talk to me at the same time? Would it be comfortable?'

Anna placed the receiver on the bed and settled herself. She picked it up again and said:

'If he died, there would be a funeral and I'd never forget his kindness to me. I can't do that if he has another wife.'

'We have actually been over this ground,' said Dr Abbatt more softly than ever. 'But we can of course go over it again.'

'Any time, you said.'

'Of course.'

'What has happened is perfectly simple. Edward is with the girl. He is about to arrive here to tell me to clear off. She's insisting on that. It's not Edward, you know.'

'Mrs Mackintosh, I'm going to speak firmly now. We've agreed between us that there's no young girl in your husband's life. You have an obsession, Mrs Mackintosh, about the fact that you have never had children and that men sometimes marry twice –'

'There's such a thing as the Mark-2 wife,' Anna cried. 'You know there is. A girl of nineteen who'll delightedly give birth to Edward's sons.'

'No, no –'

'I had imagined Edward telling me. I had imagined him pushing back his hair and lighting a cigarette in his untidy way. "I'm terribly sorry," he would say, and leave me nothing to add to that. Instead it's like this: a nightmare.'

'It is not a nightmare, Mrs Mackintosh.'

'This party is a nightmare. People are vultures here.'

'Mrs Mackintosh, I must tell you that I believe you're seeing the people at this party in a most exaggerated light.'

'A man –'

'A man nibbled your hair. Worse things can happen. This is not a nightmare, Mrs Mackintosh. Your husband has been delayed. Husbands are always being delayed. D'you see? You and I and your husband are all together trying to rid you of this perfectly normal obsession you've developed. We mustn't complicate matters, now must we?'

'I didn't run away, Dr Abbatt. I said to myself I mustn't run away from this party. I must wait and face whatever was to happen. You told me to face things.'

'I didn't tell you, my dear. We agreed between us. We talked it out, the difficulty about facing things, and we saw the wisdom of it. Now I want you to go back to the party and wait for your husband.'

'He's more than two hours late.'

'My dear Mrs Mackintosh, an hour or so is absolutely nothing these days. Now listen to me please.'

She listened to the soft voice as it reminded her of all that between them they had agreed. Dr Abbatt went over the ground, from the time she had first consulted him to the present moment. He charted her obsession until it seemed once again, as he said, a perfectly normal thing for a woman of forty to have.

After she had said good-bye, Anna sat on the bed feeling very calm. She had read the message behind Dr Abbatt's words: that it was ridiculous, her perpetually going on in this lunatic manner. She had come to a party and in no time at all she'd been behaving in a way that was, she supposed, mildly crazy. It always happened, she knew, and it would as long as the trouble remained: in her mind, when she began to worry, everything became jumbled and unreal, turning her into an impossible person. How could Edward, for heaven's sake, be expected to live with her fears and her suppositions? Edward would crack as others would, tormented by an impossible person. He'd become an alcoholic or he'd have some love affair with a woman just as old as she was, and the irony of that would be too great. She knew, as she sat there, that she couldn't help herself and that as long as she lived with Edward she wouldn't be able to do any better. 'I have lost touch with reality,' she said. 'I shall let him go, as a bird is released. In my state how can I have rights?'

She left the room and slowly descended the stairs. There were framed prints of old motor-cars on the wall and she paused now and again to examine one, emphasizing to herself her own continued calmness. She was thinking that she'd get herself a job. She might even tell Edward that Dr Abbatt had suggested that their marriage should end since she wasn't able to live with her thoughts any more. She'd insist on a divorce at once. She didn't mind the thought of it now, because of course it would be different: she was doing what she guessed Dr Abbatt had been willing her to do for quite a long time really: she was taking matters into her own hands, she was acting positively – rejecting, not being rejected herself. Her marriage was ending cleanly and correctly.

She found her coat and thanked the dark-skinned maid who held it for her. Edward was probably at the party by now, but in the new circumstances that was neither here nor there. She'd go home in a taxi and pack a suitcase and then telephone for another taxi. She'd leave a note for Edward and go to a hotel, without telling him where.

'Good night,' she said to the maid. She stepped towards the hall-door as the maid opened it for her, and as she did so she felt a hand touch her shoulder. 'No, Edward,' she said. 'I must go now.' But when she turned she saw that the hand belonged to Mrs Ritchie. Behind her, looking tired, stood the General. For a moment there was a silence. Then Anna, speaking to both of them, said:

'I'm extremely sorry. Please forgive me.'

'We were worried about you,' said Mrs Ritchie. 'Will you be all right, my dear?'

'The fear is worse than the reality, Mrs Ritchie. I can no longer live with the fear.'

'We understand.'

'It's strange,' Anna said, passing through the doorway and standing at the top of the steps that led to the street. 'Strange, coming to a party like this, given by people I didn't know and meeting you and being so rude. Please don't tell me if my husband is here or not. It doesn't concern me now. I'm quite calm.'

The Ritchies watched her descend the steps and call out to a passing taxi-cab. They watched the taxi drive away.

'Calm!' said General Ritchie.

'She's still in a state, poor thing,' agreed his wife. 'I do feel sorry.'

They stood on the steps of the Lowhrs' house, thinking about the brief glance they had had of another person's life, bewildered by it and saddened, for they themselves, though often edgy on the surface, had had a happy marriage.

'At least she's standing on her own feet now,' Mrs Ritchie said. 'I think it'll save her.'

A taxi drew up at the house and the Ritchies watched it, thinking for a moment that Anna Mackintosh, weak in her resolve, had returned in search of her husband. But it was a man who emerged and ran up the steps in a manner which suggested that, like the man who had earlier misbehaved on the dance-floor, he was not entirely sober. He passed the Ritchies and entered the house. 'That is Edward Mackintosh,' said Mrs Ritchie.

The girl who was paying the taxi-driver paused in what she was doing to see where her companion had dashed away to and observed two thin figures staring at her from the lighted doorway, murmuring to one another.

'Cruel,' said the General. 'The woman said so: we must give her that.'

'He's a kind man,' replied Mrs Ritchie. 'He'll listen to us.'

'To us, for heaven's sake?'

'We have a thing to do, as I said we might have.'

'The woman has gone. I'm not saying I'm not sorry for her –'

'And who shall ask for mercy for the woman, since she cannot ask herself? There is a little to be saved, you know: she has made a gesture, poor thing. It must be honoured.'

'My dear, we don't know these people; we met the woman quite in passing.'

The girl came up the steps, settling her purse into its right place in her handbag. She smiled at the Ritchies, and they thought that the smile had a hint of triumph about it, as though it was her first smile since the victory that Anna Mackintosh had said some girl was winning that night.

'Even if he'd listen,' muttered the General when the girl had passed by, 'I doubt that she would.'

'It's just that a little time should be allowed to go by,' his wife reminded him. 'That's all that's required. Until the woman's found her feet again and feels she has a voice in her own life.'

'We're interfering,' said the General, and his wife said nothing. They looked at one another, remembering vividly the dread in Anna Mackintosh's face and the confusion that all her conversation had revealed.

The General shook his head. 'We are hardly the happiest choice,' he said, in a gentler mood at last, 'but I dare say we must try.'

He closed the door of the house and they paused for a moment in the hall, talking again of the woman who had told them her troubles. They drew a little strength from that, and felt armed to face once more the Lowhrs' noisy party. Together they moved towards it and through it, in search of a man they had met once before on a similar occasion. 'We are sorry for interfering,' they would quietly say; and making it seem as natural as they could, they would ask him to honour, above all else and in spite of love, the gesture of a woman who no longer interested him.

'A tall order,' protested the General, pausing in his forward motion, doubtful again.

'When the wrong people do things,' replied his wife, 'it sometimes works.' She pulled him on until they stood before Edward Mackintosh and the girl he'd chosen as his Mark-2 wife. They smiled at Edward Mackintosh and shook hands with him, and then there was a silence before the General said that it was odd, in a way, what they had to request.

The Grass Widows

The headmaster of a great English public school visited every summer a
village in County Galway for the sake of the fishing in a number of nearby rivers. For more than forty years this stern, successful man had brought
his wife to the Slieve Gashal Hotel, a place, so he said, he had come to
love. A smiling man called Mr Doyle had been for all the headmaster's
experience of the hotel its obliging proprietor: Mr Doyle had related
stories to the headmaster late at night in the hotel bar, after the
headmaster's wife had retired to bed; they had discussed together the
fruitfulness of the local rivers, although in truth Mr Doyle had never held
a rod in his life. 'You feel another person,' the headmaster had told
generations of his pupils, 'among blue mountains, in the quiet little hotel.'
On walks through the school grounds with a senior boy on either side of
him he had spoken of the soft peace of the riverside and of the unrivalled
glory of being alone with one's mind. He talked to his boys of Mr Doyle
and his unassuming ways, and of the little village that was a one-horse
place and none the worse for that, and of the good plain food that came
from the Slieve Gashal's kitchen.

To Jackson Major the headmaster enthused during all the year that
Jackson Major was head boy of the famous school, and Jackson Major did
not ever forget the paradise that then had formed in his mind. 'I know a
place,' he said to his fiancée long after he had left the school, 'that's perfect
for our honeymoon.' He told her about the heathery hills that the
headmaster had recalled for him, and the lakes and rivers and the one-
horse little village in which, near a bridge, stood the ivy-covered bulk of
the Slieve Gashal Hotel. 'Lovely, darling,' murmured the bride-to-be of
Jackson Major, thinking at the time of a clock in the shape of a human
hand that someone had given them and which would naturally have to be
changed for something else. She'd been hoping that he would suggest
Majorca for their honeymoon, but if he wished to go to this other place she
didn't intend to make a fuss. 'Idyllic for a honeymoon,' the headmaster
had once remarked to Jackson Major, and Jackson Major had not
forgotten. *Steady but unimaginative* were words that had been written of
him on a school report.

The headmaster, a square, bald man with a head that might have
been carved from oak, a man who wore rimless spectacles and whose
name was Angusthorpe, discovered when he arrived at the Slieve Gashal
Hotel in the summer of 1968 that in the intervening year a tragedy had

occurred. It had become the custom of Mr Angusthorpe to book his fortnight's holiday by saying simply to Mr Doyle: 'Till next year then,' an anticipation that Mr Doyle would translate into commercial terms, reserving the same room for the headmaster and his wife in twelve months' time. No letters changed hands during the year, no confirmation of the booking was ever necessary: Mr Angusthorpe and his wife arrived each summer after the trials of the school term, knowing that their room would be waiting for them, with sweet-peas in a vase in the window, and Mr Doyle full of welcome in the hall. 'He died in Woolworth's in Galway,' said Mr Doyle's son in the summer of 1968. 'He was buying a shirt at the time.'

Afterwards, Mr Angusthorpe said to his wife that when Mr Doyle's son spoke those words he knew that nothing was ever going to be the same again. Mr Doyle's son, known locally as Scut Doyle, went on speaking while the headmaster and his small wife, grey-haired, and bespectacled also, stood in the hall. He told them that he had inherited the Slieve Gashal and that for all his adult life he had been employed in the accounts department of a paper-mill in Dublin. 'I thought at first I'd sell the place up,' he informed the Angusthorpes, 'and then I thought maybe I'd attempt to make a go of it. "Will we have a shot at it?" I said to the wife, and, God bless her, she said why wouldn't I?' While he spoke, the subject of his last remarks appeared behind him in the hall, a woman whose appearance did not at all impress Mr Angusthorpe. She was pale-faced and fat and, so Mr Angusthorpe afterwards suggested to his wife, sullen. She stood silently by her husband, whose appearance did not impress Mr Angusthorpe either, since the new proprietor of the Slieve Gashal, a man with shaking hands and cocky black moustache, did not appear to have shaved himself that day. 'One or other of them, if not both,' said Mr Angusthorpe afterwards, 'smelt of drink.'

The Angusthorpes were led to their room by a girl whose age Mr Angusthorpe estimated to be thirteen. 'What's become of Joseph?' he asked her as they mounted the stairs, referring to an old porter who had always in the past been spick and span in a uniform, but the child seemed not to understand the question, for she offered it no reply. In the room there were no sweet-peas, and although they had entered by a door that was familiar to them, the room itself was greatly altered: it was, to begin with, only half the size it had been before. 'Great heavens!' exclaimed Mr Angusthorpe, striking a wall with his fist and finding it to be a partition. 'He had the carpenters in,' the child said.

Mr Angusthorpe, in a natural fury, descended the stairs and shouted in the hall. 'Mr Doyle!' he called out in his peremptory headmaster's voice. 'Mr Doyle! Mr Doyle!'

Doyle emerged from the back regions of the hotel, with a cigarette in his mouth. There were feathers on his clothes, and he held in his right hand a half-plucked chicken. In explanation he said that he had been giving his wife a hand. She was not herself, he confided to Mr Angusthorpe, on account of it being her bad time of the month.

'Our room,' protested Mr Angusthorpe. 'We can't possibly sleep in a tiny space like that. You've cut the room in half, Mr Doyle.'

Doyle nodded. All the bedrooms in the hotel, he told Mr Angusthorpe, had been divided, since they were uneconomical otherwise. He had spent four hundred and ten pounds having new doorways made and putting on new wallpaper. He began to go into the details of this expense, plucking feathers from the chicken as he stood there. Mr Angusthorpe coldly remarked that he had not booked a room in which you couldn't swing a cat.

'Excuse me, sir,' interrupted Doyle. 'You booked a room a year ago: you did not reserve a specific room. D'you know what I mean, Mr Angusthorpe? I have no note that you specified with my father to have the exact room again.'

'It was an understood thing between us –'

'My father unfortunately died.'

Mr Angusthorpe regarded the man, disliking him intensely. It occurred to him that he had never in his life carried on a conversation with a hotel proprietor who held in his right hand a half-plucked chicken and whose clothes had feathers on them. His inclination was to turn on his heel and march with his wife from the unsatisfactory hotel, telling, if need be, this unprepossessing individual to go to hell. Mr Angusthorpe thought of doing that, but then he wondered where he and his wife could go. Hotels in the area were notoriously full at this time of year, in the middle of the fishing season.

'I must get on with this for the dinner,' said Doyle, 'or the wife will be having me guts for garters.' He winked at Mr Angusthorpe, flicking a quantity of cigarette ash from the pale flesh of the chicken. He left Mr Angusthorpe standing there.

The child had remained with Mrs Angusthorpe while the headmaster had sought an explanation downstairs. She had stood silently by the door until Mrs Angusthorpe, fearing a violent reaction on the part of her husband if he discovered the child present when he returned, suggested that she should go away. But the child had taken no notice of that and Mrs Angusthorpe, being unable to think of anything else to say, had asked her at what time of year old Mr Doyle had died. 'The funeral was ten miles long, missus,' replied the child. 'Me father wasn't sober till the Monday.' Mr Angusthorpe, returning, asked the child sharply why she was lingering and the child explained that she was waiting to be tipped. Mr Angusthorpe gave her a threepenny-piece.

In the partitioned room, which now had a pink wallpaper on the walls and an elaborate frieze from which flowers of different colours cascaded down the four corners, the Angusthorpes surveyed their predicament. Mr Angusthorpe told his wife the details of his interview with Doyle, and when he had talked for twenty minutes he came more definitely to the conclusion that the best thing they could do would be to remain for the moment. The rivers could hardly have altered, he was thinking, and that the hotel was now more than inadequate was a consequence that would affect his wife more than it would affect him. In the past she had been wont to spend her days going for a brief walk in the morning and returning to the pleasant little dining-room for a solitary lunch, and then sleeping or reading until it was time for a cup of tea, after which she would again take a brief walk. She was usually sitting by the fire in the lounge when he returned from his day's excursion. Perhaps all that would be less attractive now, Mr Angusthorpe thought, but there was little he could do about it and it was naturally only fair that they should at least remain for a day or two.

That night the dinner was well below the standard of the dinners they had in the past enjoyed in the Slieve Gashal. Mrs Angusthorpe was unable to consume her soup because there were quite large pieces of bone and gristle in it. The headmaster laughed over his prawn cocktail because, he said, it tasted of absolutely nothing at all. He had recovered from his initial shock and was now determined that the hotel must be regarded as a joke. He eyed his wife's plate of untouched soup, saying it was better to make the best of things. Chicken and potatoes and mashed turnip were placed before them by a nervous woman in the uniform of a waitress. Turnip made Mrs Angusthorpe sick in the stomach, even the sight of it: at another time in their life her husband might have remembered and ordered the vegetable from the table, but what he was more intent upon now was discovering if the Slieve Gashal still possessed a passable hock, which surprisingly it did. After a few glasses, he said:

'We'll not come next year, of course. While I'm out with the rod, my dear, you might scout around for another hotel.'

They never brought their car with them, the headmaster's theory being that the car was something they wished to escape from. Often she had thought it might be nice to have a car at the Slieve Gashal so that she could drive around the countryside during the day, but she saw his argument and had never pressed her view. Now, it seemed, he was suggesting that she should scout about for another hotel on foot.

'No, no,' he said. 'There is an excellent bus service in Ireland.' He spoke with a trace of sarcasm, as though she should have known that no matter what else he expected of her, he did not expect her to tramp about the roads looking for another hotel. He gave a little laugh, leaving the matter vaguely with her, his eyes like the eyes of a fish behind his rimless spectacles. Boys had feared him and disliked him too, some even had hated him; yet others had been full of respect that seemed at times like adoration. As she struggled with her watery turnips she could sense that his mind was quite made up: he intended to remain for the full fortnight in the changed hotel because the lure of the riverside possessed him too strongly to consider an alternative.

'I might find a place we could move to,' she said. 'I mean, in a day or so.'

'They'll be all full, my dear.' He laughed without humour in his laugh, not amused by anything. 'We must simply grin and bear it. The chicken,' he added, 'might well have been worse.'

'Excuse me,' Mrs Angusthorpe said, and quickly rose from the table and left the dining-room. From a tape-recorder somewhere dance music began to play.

'Is the wife all right?' Doyle asked Mr Angusthorpe, coming up and sitting down in the chair she had vacated. He had read in a hotelier's journal that tourists enjoyed a friendly atmosphere and the personal attention of the proprietor.

'We've had a long day,' responded the headmaster genially enough.

'Ah well, of course you have.'

The dining-room was full, indicating that business was still brisk in the hotel. Mr Angusthorpe had noted a familiar face or two and had made dignified salutations. These people would surely have walked out if the hotel was impossible in all respects.

'At her time of the month,' Doyle was saying, 'the wife gets as fatigued as an old horse. Like your own one, she's gone up to her bed already.'

'My wife –'

'Ah, I wasn't suggesting Mrs Angusthorpe was that way at all. They have fatigue in common tonight, sir, that's all I meant.'

Doyle appeared to be drunk. There was a bleariness about his eyes that suggested inebriation to Mr Angusthorpe and his shaking hands might well be taken as a sign of repeated over-indulgence.

'She wakes up at two a.m. as lively as a bird,' said Doyle. 'She's keen for a hug and a pat –'

'Quite so,' interrupted Mr Angusthorpe quickly. He looked unpleasantly at his unwelcome companion. He allowed his full opinion of the man to pervade his glance.

'Well, I'll be seeing you,' said Doyle, rising and seeming to be undismayed. 'I'll tell the wife you were asking for her,' he added with a billowing laugh, before moving on to another table.

Shortly after that, Mr Angusthorpe left the dining-room, having resolved that he would not relate this conversation to his wife. He would avoid Doyle in the future, he promised himself, and when by chance they did meet he would make it clear that he did not care to hear his comments on any subject. It was a pity that the old man had died and that all this nastiness had grown up in his place, but there was nothing whatsoever that might be done about it and at least the weather looked good. He entered the bar and dropped into conversation with a man he had met several times before, a solicitor from Dublin, a bachelor called Gorman.

'I was caught the same way,' Mr Gorman said, 'only everywhere else is full. It's the end of the Slieve Gashal, you know: the food's inedible.'

He went on to relate a series of dishes that had already been served during his stay, the most memorable of which appeared to be a rabbit stew that had had a smell of ammonia. 'There's margarine every time instead of butter, and some queer type of marmalade in the morning: it has a taste of tin to it. The same mashed turnip,' said Gorman, 'is the only vegetable he offers.'

The headmaster changed the subject, asking how the rivers were. The fishing was better than ever he'd known it, Mr Gorman reported, and he retailed experiences to prove the claim. 'Isn't it all that matters in the long run?' suggested Mr Gorman, and Mr Angusthorpe readily agreed that it was. He would refrain from repeating to his wife the information about the marmalade that tasted of tin, or the absence of variation where vegetables were concerned. He left the bar at nine o'clock, determined to slip quietly into bed without disturbing her.

In the middle of that night, at midnight precisely, the Angusthorpes were awakened simultaneously by a noise from the room beyond the new partition.

'Put a pillow down, darling,' a male voice was saying as clearly as if its possessor stood in the room beside the Angusthorpes' bed.

'Couldn't we wait until another time?' a woman pleaded in reply. 'I don't see what good a pillow will do.'

'It'll lift you up a bit,' the man explained. 'It said in the book to put a pillow down if there was difficulty.'

'I don't see –'

'It'll make entry easier,' said the man. 'It's a well-known thing.'

Mrs Angusthorpe switched on her bedside light and saw that her husband was pretending to be asleep. 'I'm going to rap on the wall,' she whispered. 'It's disgusting, listening to this.'

'I think I'm going down,' said the man.

'My God,' whispered Mr Angusthorpe, opening his eyes. 'It's Jackson Major.'

At breakfast, Mrs Angusthorpe ate margarine on her toast and the marmalade that had a taste of tin. She did not say anything. She watched her husband cutting into a fried egg on a plate that bore the marks of the waitress's two thumbs. Eventually he placed his knife and fork together on the plate and left them there.

For hours they had lain awake, listening to the conversation beyond the inadequate partition. The newly wed wife of Jackson Major had wept and said that Jackson had better divorce her at once. She had designated the hotel they were in as a frightful place, fit only for Irish tinkers. 'That filthy meal!' the wife of Jackson Major had cried emotionally. 'That awful drunk man!' And Jackson Major had apologized and had mentioned Mr Angusthorpe by name, wondering what on earth his old headmaster could ever have seen in such an establishment. 'Let's try again,' he had suggested, and the Angusthorpes had listened to a repetition of Mrs Jackson's unhappy tears. 'How can you rap on the wall?' Mr Angusthorpe had angrily whispered. 'How can we even admit that conversation can be heard? Jackson was head boy.'

'In the circumstances,' said Mrs Angusthorpe at breakfast, breaking the long silence, 'it would be better to leave.'

He knew it would be. He knew that on top of everything else the unfortunate fact that Jackson Major was in the room beyond the partition and would sooner or later discover that the partition was far from soundproof could be exceedingly embarrassing in view of what had taken place during the night. There was, as well, the fact that he had enthused so eloquently to Jackson Major about the hotel that Jackson Major had clearly, on his word alone, brought his bride there. He had even said, he recalled, that the Slieve Gashal would be ideal for a honeymoon. Mr Angusthorpe considered all that yet could not forget his forty years' experience of the surrounding rivers, or the information of Mr Gorman that the rivers this year were better than ever.

'We could whisper,' he suggested in what was itself a whisper. 'We could whisper in our room so that they wouldn't know you can hear.'

'Whisper?' she said. She shook her head.

She remembered days in the rain, walking about the one-horse village with nothing whatsoever to do except to walk about, or lie on her bed reading detective stories. She remembered listening to his reports of his day and feeling sleepy listening to them. She remembered thinking, once or twice, that it had never occurred to him that what was just a change and a rest for her could not at all be compared to the excitements he derived from his days on the river-bank, alone with his mind. He was a great, successful man, big and square and commanding, with the cold eyes of the fish he sought in mountain rivers. He had made a firm impression on generations of boys, and on parents and governors, and often on a more general public, yet he had never been able to give her children. She had needed children because she was, compared with him, an unimportant kind of person.

She thought of him in Chapel, gesturing at six hundred boys from the pulpit, in his surplice and red academic hood, releasing words from his throat that were as cold as ice and cleverly made sense. She thought of a time he had expelled two boys, when he had sat with her in their drawing-room waiting for a bell to ring. When the chiming had ceased he had risen and gone without a word from the room, his oaken face pale with suppressed emotion. She knew he saw in the crime of the two boys a failure on his part, yet he never mentioned it to her. He had expelled the boys in public, castigating them with bitterness in his tone, hating them and hating himself, yet rising above his shame at having failed with them: dignity was his greatest ally.

She sat with him once a week at the high table in the dining-hall, surrounded by his prefects, who politely chatted to her. She remembered Jackson Major, a tall boy with short black hair who would endlessly discuss with her husband a web of school affairs. 'The best head boy I remember,' her husband's voice said again, coming back to her over a number of years: 'I made no mistake with Jackson.' Jackson Major had set a half-mile record that remained unbroken to this day. There had been a complaint from some child's mother, she recalled, who claimed that her son had been, by Jackson Major, too severely caned. *We must not forget*, her husband had written to that mother, *that your son almost caused another boy to lose an eye. It was for that carelessness that he was punished. He bears no resentment: boys seldom do.*

Yet now this revered, feared, and clever man was suggesting that they should whisper for a fortnight in their bedroom, so that the couple next door might not feel embarrassment, so that he himself might remain in a particularly uncomfortable hotel in order to fish. It seemed to Mrs Angusthorpe that there were limits to the role he had laid down for her and which for all her married life she had ungrudgingly accepted. She hadn't minded being bored for this fortnight every year, but now he was asking more than that she should continue to feel bored; he was asking her to endure food that made her sick, and to conduct absurd conversations in their bedroom.

'No,' she said, 'we could not whisper.'

'I meant it only for kindness. Kindness to them, you see –'

'You have compensations here. I have none, you know.'

He looked sharply at her, as at an erring new boy who had not yet learnt the ways of school.

'I think we should leave at once,' she said. 'After breakfast.'

That suggestion, he pointed out to her, was nonsensical. They had booked a room in the hotel: they were obliged to pay for it. He was exhausted, he added, after a particularly trying term.

'It's what I'd like,' she said.

He spread margarine on his toast and added to it some of the marmalade. 'We must not be selfish,' he said, suggesting that both of them were on the point of being selfish and that together they must prevent themselves.

'I'd be happier,' she began, but he swiftly interrupted her, reminding her that his holiday had been spoilt enough already and that he for his part was intent on making the best of things. 'Let's simply enjoy what we can,' he said, 'without making a fuss about it.'

At that moment Jackson Major and his wife, a pretty, pale-haired girl called Daphne, entered the dining-room. They stood at the door, endeavouring to catch the eye of a waitress, not sure about where to sit. Mrs Jackson indicated a table that was occupied by two men, reminding her husband that they had sat at it last night for dinner. Jackson Major looked towards it and looked impatiently away, seeming annoyed with his wife for bothering to draw his attention to a table at which they clearly could not sit. It was then, while still annoyed, that he noticed the Angusthorpes.

Mrs Angusthorpe saw him murmuring to his wife. He led the way to their table, and Mrs Angusthorpe observed that his wife moved less eagerly than he.

'How marvellous, sir,' Jackson Major said, shaking his headmaster by the hand. Except for a neat moustache, he had changed hardly at all, Mrs Angusthorpe noticed; a little fatter in the face, perhaps, and the small pimples that had marked his chin as a schoolboy had now cleared up completely. He introduced his wife to the headmaster, and then he turned to Mrs Angusthorpe and asked her how she was. Forgetfully, he omitted to introduce his wife to her, but she, in spite of that, smiled and nodded at his wife.

'I'm afraid it's gone down awfully, Jackson,' Mr Angusthorpe said. 'The hotel's changed hands, you know. We weren't aware ourselves.'

'It seems quite comfortable, sir,' Jackson Major said, sitting down and indicating that his wife should do the same.

'The food was nice before,' said Mrs Angusthorpe. 'It's really awful now.'

'Oh, I wouldn't say awful, dear,' Mr Angusthorpe corrected her. 'One becomes used to a hotel,' he explained to Jackson Major. 'Any change is rather noticeable.'

'We had a perfectly ghastly dinner,' Daphne Jackson said.

'Still,' said Mr Angusthorpe, as though she had not spoken, 'we'll not return another year. My wife is going to scout around for a better place. You've brought your rod, Jackson?'

'Well, yes, I did. I thought that maybe if Daphne felt tired I might once or twice try out your famous rivers, sir.'

Mrs Angusthorpe saw Mrs Jackson glance in surprise at her new husband, and she deduced that Mrs Jackson hadn't been aware that a fishing-rod had comprised part of her husband's luggage.

'Capital,' cried Mr Angusthorpe, while the waitress took the Jacksons' order for breakfast. 'You could scout round together,' he said, addressing the two women at once, 'while I show Jackson what's what.'

'It's most kind of you, sir,' Jackson Major said, 'but I think, you know –'

'Capital,' cried Mr Angusthorpe again, his eyes swivelling from face to face, forbidding defiance. He laughed his humourless laugh and he poured himself more tea. 'I told you, dear,' he said to Mrs Angusthorpe. 'There's always a silver lining.'

In the hall of the Slieve Gashal Doyle took a metal stand from beneath the reception desk and busied himself arranging picture postcards on it.

His wife had bought the stand in Galway, getting it at a reduced price because it was broken. He was at the moment offended with his wife because of her attitude when he had entered the hotel kitchen an hour ago with a number of ribs of beef. 'Did you drop that meat?' she had said in a hard voice, looking up from the table where she was making bread. 'Is that dirt on the suet?' He had replied that he'd been obliged to cross the village street hurriedly, to avoid a man on a bicycle. 'You dropped the meat on the road,' she accused. 'D'you want to poison the bloody lot of them?' Feeling hard done by, he had left the kitchen.

While he continued to work with the postcards, Mr Angusthorpe and Jackson Major passed before him with their fishing-rods. 'We'll be frying tonight,' he observed jollily, wagging his head at their two rods. They did not reply: weren't they the queer-looking eejits, he thought, with their sporty clothes and the two tweed hats covered with artificial flies. 'I'll bring it up, sir,' Jackson Major was saying, 'at the Old Boys' Dinner in the autumn.' It was ridiculous, Doyle reflected, going to all that trouble to catch a few fish when all you had to do was to go out at night and shine a torch into the water. 'Would you be interested in postcards, gentlemen?' he inquired, but so absorbed were Mr Angusthorpe and Jackson Major in their conversation that again neither of them made a reply.

Some time later, Daphne Jackson descended the stairs of the hotel. Doyle watched her, admiring her slender legs and the flowered dress she was wearing. A light blue cardigan hung casually from her shoulders, its sleeves not occupied by her arms. Wouldn't it be great, he thought, to be married to a young body like that? He imagined her in a bedroom, taking off her cardigan and then her dress. She stood in her underclothes; swiftly she lifted them from her body.

'Would you be interested in postcards at all?' inquired Doyle. 'I have the local views here.'

Daphne smiled at him. Without much interest, she examined the cards on the stand, and then she moved towards the entrance door.

'There's a lovely dinner we have for you today,' said Doyle. 'Ribs of beef that I'm just handing over to the wife. As tender as an infant.'

He held the door open for her, talking all the time, since he knew they liked to be talked to. He asked her if she was going for a walk and told her that a walk would give her a healthy appetite. The day would keep good, he promised; he had read it in the paper.

'Thank you,' she said.

She walked through a sunny morning that did little to raise her spirits. Outside the hotel there was a large expanse of green grass, bounded on one side by the short village street. She crossed an area of the grass and then passed the butcher's shop in which earlier Doyle had purchased the ribs of beef. She glanced in and the butcher smiled and waved at her, as though he knew her well. She smiled shyly back. Outside a small public house a man was mending a bicycle, which was upturned on the pavement:

a child pushing a pram spoke to the man and he spoke to her. Farther on, past a row of cottages, a woman pumped water into a bucket from a green pump at the road's edge, and beyond it, coming towards her slowly, she recognized the figure of Mrs Angusthorpe.

'So we are grass widows,' said Mrs Angusthorpe when she had arrived at a point at which it was suitable to speak.

'Yes.'

'I'm afraid it's our fault, for being here. My husband's, I mean, and mine.'

'My husband could have declined to go fishing.'

The words were sour. They were sour and icy, Mrs Angusthorpe thought, matching her own mood. On her brief walk she had that morning disliked her husband more than ever she had disliked him before, and there was venom in her now. Once upon a time he might at least have heard her desires with what could even have been taken for understanding. He would not have acted upon her desires, since it was not in his nature to do so, but he would not have been guilty, either, of announcing in so obviously false a way that they should enjoy what they could and not make a fuss. There had been a semblance of chivalry in the attitude from which, at the beginning of their marriage, he had briefly regarded her; but forty-seven years had efficiently disposed of that garnish of politeness. A week or so ago a boy at the school had been casual with her, but the headmaster, hearing her report of the matter, had denied that what she stated could ever have occurred: he had moulded the boy in question, he pointed out, he had taken a special interest in the boy because he recognized in him qualities that were admirable: she was touchy, the headmaster said, increasingly touchy these days. She remembered in the first year of their marriage a way he had of patiently leaning back in his chair, puffing at the pipe he affected in those days and listening to her, seeming actually to weigh her arguments against his own. It was a long time now since he had weighed an argument of hers, or even devoted a moment of passing consideration to it. It was a long time since he could possibly have been concerned as to whether or not she found the food in a hotel unpalatable. She was angry when she thought of it this morning, not because she was unused to these circumstances of her life but because, quite suddenly, she had seen her state of resignation as an insult to the woman she once, too long ago, had been.

'I would really like to talk to you,' Mrs Angusthorpe said, to Daphne Jackson's surprise. 'It might be worth your while to stroll back to that hotel with me.'

On her short, angry walk she had realized, too, that once she had greatly disliked Jackson Major because he reminded her in some ways of her husband. A priggish youth, she had recalled, a tedious bore of a boy who had shown her husband a ridiculous respect while also fearing and resembling him. On her walk she had remembered the day he had broken the half-mile record, standing in the sports field in his running clothes, deprecating his effort because he knew his headmaster would wish him to act like that. What good was winning a half-mile race if he upset his wife the first time he found himself in a bedroom with her?

'I remember your husband as a boy,' said Mrs Angusthorpe. 'He set an athletic record which has not yet been broken.'

'Yes, he told me.'

'He had trouble with his chin. Pimples that wouldn't go away. I see all that's been overcome.'

'Well, yes –'

'And trouble also because he beat a boy too hard. The mother wrote, enclosing the opinion of a doctor.'

Daphne frowned. She ceased to walk. She stared at Mrs Angusthorpe.

'Oh yes,' said Mrs Angusthorpe.

They passed the butcher's shop, from the doorway of which the butcher now addressed them. The weather was good, the butcher said: it was a suitable time for a holiday. Mrs Angusthorpe smiled at him and bowed. Daphne, frowning still, passed on.

'You're right,' Mrs Angusthorpe said next, 'when you say that your husband could have declined to go fishing.'

'I think he felt –'

'Odd, I thought, to have a fishing-rod with him in the first place. Odd on a honeymoon.'

They entered the hotel. Doyle came forward to meet them. 'Ah, so you've palled up?' he said. 'Isn't that grand?'

'We could have sherry,' Mrs Angusthorpe suggested, 'in the bar.'

'Of course you could,' said Doyle. 'Won't your two husbands be pegging away at the old fish for the entire day?'

'They promised to be back for lunch,' Daphne said quickly, her voice seeming to herself to be unduly weak. She cleared her throat and remarked to Doyle that the village was pretty. She didn't really wish to sit in the hotel bar drinking sherry with the wife of her husband's headmaster. It was all ridiculous, she thought, on a honeymoon.

'Go down into the bar,' said Doyle, 'and I'll be down myself in a minute.'

Mrs Angusthorpe seized with the fingers of her left hand the flowered material of Daphne's dress. 'The bar's down here,' she said, leading the way without releasing her hold.

They sat at a table on which there were a number of absorbent mats which advertised brands of beer. Doyle brought them two glasses of sherry, which Mrs Angusthorpe ordered him to put down on her husband's account. 'Shout out when you're in need of a refill,' he invited. 'I'll be up in the hall.'

'The partition between our bedrooms is far from soundproof,' said Mrs Angusthorpe when Doyle had gone. 'We were awakened in the night.'

'Awakened?'

'As if you were in the room beside us, we heard a conversation.'
'My God!'
'Yes.'
Blood rushed to Daphne Jackson's face. She was aware of an unpleasant sensation in her stomach. She turned her head away. Mrs Angusthorpe said:
'People don't speak out. All my married life, for instance, I haven't spoken out. My dear, you're far too good for Jackson Major.'
It seemed to Daphne, who had been Daphne Jackson for less than twenty-four hours, that the wife of her husband's headmaster was insane. She gulped at the glass of sherry before her, unable to prevent herself from vividly recalling the awfulness of the night before in the small bedroom. He had come at her as she was taking off her blouse. His right hand had shot beneath her underclothes, pressing at her and gripping her. All during their inedible dinner he had been urging her to drink whisky and wine, and drinking quantities of both himself. In bed he had suddenly become calmer, remembering instructions read in a book.
'Pack a suitcase,' said Mrs Angusthorpe, 'and go.'
The words belonged to a nightmare and Daphne was aware of wishing that she was asleep and dreaming. The memory of tension on her wedding day, and of guests standing around in sunshine in a London garden, and then the flight by plane, were elements that confused her mind as she listened to this small woman. The tension had been with her as she walked towards the altar and had been with her, too, in her parents' garden. Nor had it eased when she escaped with her husband on a Viscount: it might even have increased on the flight and on the train to Galway, and then in the hired car that had carried her to the small village. It had certainly increased while she attempted to eat stringy chicken at a late hour in the dining-room, while her husband smiled at her and talked about intoxicants. The reason he had talked so much about whisky and wine, she now concluded, was because he'd been aware of the tension that was coiled within her.
'You have made a mistake,' came the voice of Mrs Angusthorpe, 'but even now it is not too late to rectify it. Do not accept it, reject your error, Mrs Jackson.'
Doyle came into the bar and brought to them, without their demanding it, more sherry in two new glasses. Daphne heard him remarking that the brand of sherry was very popular in these parts. It was Spanish sherry, he said, since he would stock nothing else. He talked about Spain and Spaniards, saying that at the time of the Spanish Armada Spanish sailors had been wrecked around the nearby coast.
'I love my husband,' Daphne said when Doyle had gone again.
She had met her husband in the Hurlingham Club. He had partnered her in tennis and they had danced together at a charity dance. She'd listened while he talked one evening, telling her that the one thing he regretted was

that he hadn't played golf as a child. Golf was a game, he'd said, that must be started when young if one was ever to achieve championship distinction. With tennis that wasn't quite so important but it was, of course, as well to start tennis early also. She had thought he was rather nice. There was something about his distant manner that attracted her; there was a touch of arrogance in the way he didn't look at her when he spoke. She'd make him look at her, she vowed.

'My dear,' said Mrs Angusthorpe, 'I've seen the seamy side of Jackson Major. The more I think of him the more I can recall. He forced his way up that school, snatching at chances that weren't his to take, putting himself first, like he did in the half-mile race. There was cruelty in Jackson Major's eye, and ruthlessness and dullness. Like my husband, he has no sense of humour.'

'Mrs Angusthorpe, I really can't listen to all this. I was married yesterday to a man I'm in love with. It'll be all right –'

'Why will it be all right?'

'Because,' snapped Daphne Jackson with sudden spirit, 'I shall ask my husband as soon as he returns to take me at once from this horrible hotel. My marriage does not at all concern you, Mrs Angusthorpe.'

'They are talking now on a riverside, whispering maybe so as not to disturb their prey. They are murmuring about the past, of achievements on the sports field and marches undertaken by a cadet force. While you and I are having a different kind of talk.'

'What our husbands are saying to one another, Mrs Angusthorpe, may well make more sense.'

'What they are not saying is that two women in the bar of this hotel are unhappy. They have forgotten about the two women: they are more relaxed and contented than ever they are with us.'

Mrs Angusthorpe, beady-eyed as she spoke, saw the effect of her words reflected in the uneasy face of the woman beside her. She felt herself carried away by this small triumph, she experienced a headiness that was blissful. She saw in her mind another scene, imagining herself, over lunch, telling her husband about the simple thing that had happened. She would watch him sitting there in all his dignity: she would wait until he was about to pass a forkful of food to his mouth and then she would say: 'Jackson Major's wife has left him already.' And she would smile at him.

'You walked across the dining-room at breakfast,' said Mrs Angusthorpe. 'An instinct warned me then that you'd made an error.'

'I haven't made an error. I've told you, Mrs Angusthorpe –'

'Time will erode the polish of politeness. One day soon you'll see amusement in his eyes when you offer an opinion.'

'Please stop, Mrs Angusthorpe. I must go away if you continue like this –'

' "This man's a bore," you'll suddenly say to yourself, and look at him amazed.'

'Mrs Angusthorpe –'

'Amazed that you could ever have let it happen.'

'Oh God, please stop,' cried Daphne, tears coming suddenly from her eyes, her hands rushing to her cheeks.

'Don't be a silly girl,' whispered Mrs Angusthorpe, grasping the arm of her companion and tightening her fingers on it until Daphne felt pain. She thought as she felt it that Mrs Angusthorpe was a poisonous woman. She struggled to keep back further tears, she tried to wrench her arm away.

'I'll tell the man Doyle to order you a car,' said Mrs Angusthorpe. 'It'll take you into Galway. I'll lend you money, Mrs Jackson. By one o'clock tonight you could be sitting in your bed at home, eating from a tray that your mother brought you. A divorce will come through and one day you'll meet a man who'll love you with a tenderness.'

'My husband loves me, Mrs Angusthorpe –'

'Your husband should marry a woman who's keen on horses or golf, a woman who might take a whip to him, being ten years older than himself. My dear, you're like me: you're a delicate person.'

'Please let go my arm. You've no right to talk to me like this –'

'He is my husband's creature, my husband moulded him. The best head boy he'd ever known, he said to me.'

Daphne, calmer now, did not say anything. She felt the pressure on her arm being removed. She stared ahead of her, at a round mat on the table that advertised Celebration Ale. Without wishing to and perhaps, she thought, because she was so upset, she saw herself suddenly as Mrs Angusthorpe had suggested, sitting up in her own bedroom with a tray of food on her knees and her mother standing beside her, saying it was all right. 'I suddenly realized,' she heard herself saying. 'He took me to this awful hotel, where his old headmaster was. He gave me wine and whisky, and then in bed I thought I might be sick.' Her mother replied to her, telling her that it wasn't a disgrace, and her father came in later and told her not to worry. It was better not to be unhappy, her father said: it was better to have courage now.

'Let me tell Doyle to order a car at once.' Mrs Angusthorpe was on her feet, eagerness in her eyes and voice. Her cheeks were flushed from sherry and excitement.

'You're quite outrageous,' said Daphne Jackson.

She left the bar and in the hall Doyle again desired her as she passed. He spoke to her, telling her he'd already ordered a few more bottles of that sherry so that she and Mrs Angusthorpe could sip a little as often as they liked. It was sherry, he repeated, that was very popular in the locality. She nodded and mounted the stairs, not hearing much of what he said, feeling that as she pushed one leg in front of another her whole body would open and tears would gush from everywhere. Why did she have to put up with talk like that on the first morning of her honeymoon? Why had he casually gone out fishing with his old headmaster? Why had he brought her to this terrible place and then made her drink so that the tension would leave her body? She sobbed on the stairs, causing Doyle to frown and feel concerned for her.

'Are you all right?' Jackson Major asked, standing in the doorway of their room, looking to where she sat, by the window. He closed the door and went to her. 'You've been all right?' he said.

She nodded, smiling a little. She spoke in a low voice: she said she thought it possible that conversations might be heard through the partition wall. She pointed to the wall she spoke of. 'It's only a partition,' she said.

He touched it and agreed, but gave it as his opinion that little could be heard through it since they themselves had not heard the people on the other side of it. Partitions nowadays, he pronounced, were constructed always of soundproof material.

'Let's have a drink before lunch,' she said.

In the hour that had elapsed since she had left Mrs Angusthorpe in the bar she had changed her stockings and her dress. She had washed her face in cold water and had put lipstick and powder on it. She had brushed her suede shoes with a rubber brush.

'All right,' he said. 'We'll have a little drink.'

He kissed her. On the way downstairs he told her about the morning's fishing and the conversations he had had with his old headmaster. Not asking her what she'd like, he ordered both of them gin and tonic in the bar.

'I know her better than you do, sir,' Doyle said, bringing her a glass of sherry, but Jackson Major didn't appear to realize what had happened, being still engrossed in the retailing of the conversations he had had with his old headmaster.

'I want to leave this hotel,' she said. 'At once, darling, after lunch.'

'Daphne –'

'I do.'

She didn't say that Mrs Angusthorpe had urged her to leave him, nor that the Angusthorpes had lain awake during the night, hearing what there was to hear. She simply said she didn't at all like the idea of spending her honeymoon in a hotel which also contained his late headmaster and the headmaster's wife. 'They remember you as a boy,' she said. 'For some reason it makes me edgy. And anyway it's such a nasty hotel.'

She leaned back after that speech, glad that she'd been able to make it as she'd planned to make it. They would move on after lunch, paying whatever money must necessarily be paid. They would find a pleasant room in a pleasant hotel and the tension inside her would gradually relax. In the Hurlingham Club she had made this tall man look at her when he spoke to her, she had made him regard her and find her attractive, as she found him. They had said to one another that they had fallen in love, he had asked her to marry him, and she had happily agreed: there was nothing the matter.

'My dear, it would be quite impossible,' he said.

'Impossible?'

'At this time of year, in the middle of the season? Hotel rooms are gold dust, my dear. Angusthorpe was saying as much. His wife's a good sort, you know –'

'I want to leave here.'

He laughed good-humouredly. He gestured with his hands, suggesting his helplessness.

'I cannot stay here,' she said.

'You're tired, Daphne.'

'I cannot stay here for a fortnight with the Angusthorpes. She's a woman who goes on all the time; there's something the matter with her. While you go fishing –'

'Darling, I had to go this morning. I felt it polite to go. If you like, I'll not go out again at all.'

'I've told you what I'd like.'

'Oh, for God's sake!' He turned away from her. She said:

'I thought you would say yes at once.'

'How the hell can I say yes when we've booked a room for the next fortnight and we're duty-bound to pay for it? Do you really think we can just walk up to that man and say we don't like his hotel and the people he has staying here?'

'We could make some excuse. We could pretend –'

'Pretend? Pretend, Daphne?'

'Some illness. We could say my mother's ill,' she hurriedly said. 'Or some aunt who doesn't even exist. We could hire a car and drive around the coast –'

'Daphne –'

'Why not?'

'For a start, I haven't my driving licence with me.'

'I have.'

'I doubt it, Daphne.'

She thought, and then she agreed that she hadn't. 'We could go to Dublin,' she said with a fresh burst of urgency. 'Dublin's a lovely place, people say. We could stay in Dublin and –'

'My dear, this is a tourist country. Millions of tourists come here every summer. Do you really believe we'd find decent accommodation in Dublin in the middle of the season?'

'It wouldn't have to be decent. Some little clean hotel –'

'Added to which, Daphne, I must honestly tell you that I have no wish to go gallivanting on my honeymoon. Nor do I care for the notion of telling lies about the illness of people who are not ill, or do not even exist.'

'I'll tell the lies. I'll talk to Mr Doyle directly after lunch. I'll talk to him now.' She stood up. He shook his head, reaching for the hand that was nearer to him.

'What's the matter?' he asked.

Slowly she sat down again.

'Oh, darling,' she said.

'We must be sensible, Daphne. We can't just go gallivanting off –'

'Why do you keep on about gallivanting? What's it matter whether we're gallivanting or not so long as we're enjoying ourselves?'

'Daphne –'

'I'm asking you to do something to please me.'

Jackson Major, about to reply, changed his mind. He smiled at his bride. After a pause, he said:

'If you really want to, Daphne –'

'Well, I do. I think perhaps it'll be awkward here with the Angusthorpes. And it's not what we expected.'

'It's just a question,' said Jackson Major, 'of what we could possibly do. I've asked for my mail to be forwarded here and, as I say, I really believe it would be a case of out of the frying-pan into nothing at all. It might prove horribly difficult.'

She closed her eyes and sat for a moment in silence. Then she opened them and, being unable to think of anything else to say, she said:

'I'm sorry.'

He sighed, shrugging his shoulders slightly. He took her hand again. 'You do see, darling?' Before she could reply he added: 'I'm sorry I was angry with you. I didn't mean to be: I'm very sorry.'

He kissed her on the cheek that was near to him. He took her hand. 'Now tell me,' he said, 'about everything that's worrying you.'

She repeated without more detail, what she had said already, but this time the sentences she spoke did not sound like complaints. He listened to her, sitting back and not interrupting, and then they conversed about all she had said. He agreed that it was a pity about the hotel and explained to her that what had happened, apparently, was that the old proprietor had died during the previous year. It was unfortunate too, he quite agreed, that the Angusthorpes should be here at the same time as they were because it would, of course, have been so much nicer to have been on their own. If she was worried about the partition in their room he would ask that their room should be changed for another one. He hadn't known when she'd mentioned the partition before that it was the Angusthorpes who were on the other side of it. It would be better, really, not to be in the next room to the Angusthorpes since Angusthorpe had once been his headmaster, and he was certain that Doyle would understand a thing like that and agree to change them over, even if it meant greasing Doyle's palm. 'I imagine he'd fall in with anything,' said Jackson Major, 'for a bob or two.'

They finished their drinks and she followed him to the dining-room.

There were no thoughts in her mind: no voice, neither her own nor Mrs Angusthorpe's, spoke. For a reason she could not understand and didn't want to bother to understand, the tension within her had snapped and was no longer there. The desire she had felt for tears when she'd walked away from Mrs Angusthorpe was far from her now; she felt a weariness, as though an ordeal was over and she had survived it. She didn't know why she felt like that. All she knew was that he had listened to her: he had been patient and understanding, allowing her to say all that was in her mind and then being reassuring. It was not his fault that the hotel had turned out so unfortunately. Nor was it his fault that a bullying old man had sought him out as a fishing companion. He couldn't help it if his desire for her brought out a clumsiness in him. He was a man, she thought: he was not the same as she was: she must meet him half-way. He had said he was sorry for being angry with her.

In the hall they met the Angusthorpes on their way to the dining-room also.

'I'm sorry if I upset you,' Mrs Angusthorpe said to her, touching her arm to hold her back for a moment. 'I'm afraid my temper ran away with me.'

The two men went ahead, involved in a new conversation. 'We might try that little tributary this afternoon,' the headmaster was suggesting.

'I sat there afterwards, seeing how horrid it must have been for you,' Mrs Angusthorpe said. 'I was only angry at the prospect of an unpleasant fortnight. I took it out on you.'

'Don't worry about it.'

'One should keep one's anger to oneself. I feel embarrassed now,' said Mrs Angusthorpe. 'I'm not the sort of person –'

'Please don't worry,' murmured Daphne, trying hard to keep the tiredness that possessed her out of her voice. She could sleep, she was thinking, for a week.

'I don't know why I talked like that.'

'You were angry –'

'Yes,' said Mrs Angusthorpe.

She stood still, not looking at Daphne and seeming not to wish to enter the dining-room. Some people went by, talking and laughing. Mr Gorman, the solicitor from Dublin, addressed her, but she did not acknowledge his greeting.

'I think we must go in now, Mrs Angusthorpe,' Daphne said.

In her weariness she smiled at Mrs Angusthorpe, suddenly sorry for her because she had so wretched a marriage that it caused her to become emotional with strangers.

'It was just,' said Mrs Angusthorpe, pausing uncertainly in the middle of r sentence and then continuing, 'I felt that perhaps I should say something. I felt, Mrs Jackson –'

'Let's just forget it,' interrupted Daphne, sensing with alarm that Mrs Angusthorpe was about to begin all over again, in spite of her protestations.

'What?'

'I think we must forget it all.'

Daphne smiled again, to reassure the woman who'd been outrageous because her temper had run away with her. She wanted to tell her that just now in the bar she herself had had a small outburst and that in the end she had seen the absurdity of certain suggestions she had made. She wanted to say that her husband had asked her what the matter was and then had said he was sorry. She wanted to explain, presumptuously perhaps, that there must be give and take in marriage, that a bed of roses was something that couldn't be shared. She wanted to say that the tension she'd felt was no longer there, but she couldn't find the energy for saying it.

'Forget it?' said Mrs Angusthorpe. 'Yes, I suppose so. There are things that shouldn't be talked about.'

'It's not that really,' objected Daphne softly. 'It's just that I think you jumped to a lot of wrong conclusions.'

'I had an instinct,' began Mrs Angusthorpe with all her previous eagerness and urgency. 'I saw you at breakfast time, an innocent girl. I couldn't help remembering.'

'It's different for us,' said Daphne, feeling embarrassed to have to converse again in this intimate vein. 'At heart my husband's patient with me. And understanding too: he listens to me.'

'Of course,' agreed Mrs Angusthorpe, slowly nodding her head and moving at last towards the dining-room.

A Choice of Butchers

The upper landing of our house had brown linoleum on it and outside each of the bedroom doors there was a small black mat. From this square landing with its three mats and its window overlooking the backyard there rose a flight of uncarpeted steps that led to the attic room where Bridget, who was our maid, slept. The stairs that descended to the lower landing, where the bathroom and lavatory were and where my mother and father slept, were carpeted with a pattern of red flowers which continued downwards to a hall that also had brown linoleum on its floor. There was a hall-stand in the hall and beside it a high green plant in a brass pot, and a figure of the Holy Mother on a table, all by itself. The walls of the landing, and of the hall and the staircase, were papered gloomily in an oatmeal shade that had no pattern, only a pebbly roughness that was fashionable in my childhood in our West Cork town. On this hung two brown pictures, one of oxen dragging a plough over rough ground at sunrise, the other of a farmer leading a working horse towards a farmyard at the end of the day. It was against a background of the oatmeal shade and the oxen in the dawn that I, through the rails of the banisters on the upper landing, saw my father kissing Bridget at the end of one summer holiday.

I had come from my room on that warm September evening to watch for Henry Dukelow, who came up every night to say good night to me. I had knelt down by the banisters, with my face against them, pressing hard so that I might be marked, so that Mr Dukelow would laugh when he saw me. 'God, you're tip-top,' my father said in a whisper that travelled easily up to me, and then he put his arms around her shoulders and roughly hugged her, with his lips pressed on to her lips.

I was seven years of age, the afterthought of the family, as my father called me. My brothers and sisters were all grown up, but I didn't feel then, not yet, that my parents had given so much to them that there wasn't a lot left to give me. Once upon a time they had all been a family like any other family: the children in turn had left home, and then, when my mother should have been resting and my father finding life less demanding, I had arrived. I did not ever doubt my parents' concern for me, but for the six months that he was in our house I felt that Mr Dukelow loved me as much as they did. 'Say good night to him for me,' I often heard my mother calling out to him as he mounted the stairs to tell me my night-time story, and I grew up thinking of my mother as a tired person because that was what she was. Her hair was going grey and her face bore a fatigued look: Mr Dukelow said she probably didn't sleep well. There were a lot of people who didn't sleep well, he told me, sitting on my bed one night when I was seven, and I remember he went on talking about that until I must have fallen asleep myself.

Mr Dukelow, who occupied the room next to mine, taught me to play marbles on the rough surface of our backyard. He made me an aeroplane out of heavy pieces of wood he found lying about and he explained to me that although a star could fall through the sky it would never land on the earth. He told me stories about Columbus and Vasco da Gama, and about the great emperors of Europe and the Battle of the Yellow Ford. He had a good memory for what had interested him at school, but he had forgotten as easily the rest: he had been a poor scholar, he said. He told me the plots of films he'd seen and of a play called *Paddy the Next Best Thing*. He spoke very quietly and he always answered my questions: a small man, as thin as a willow, bony and pale-faced and supposed to be delicate, different from my father. He was fifty-seven; my father was fifty-nine.

In the middle of the night that my father kissed Bridget Mr Dukelow came to my room again. He switched the light on and stood there in grey-striped pyjamas that were badly torn.

'I could hear you crying,' he said. 'What's the trouble with you?'

He wore spectacles with fine wire rims, and all his face seemed to have gone into his nose, which was thin and tapering. His greased hair was black, his hands were like a skeleton's. The first night Mr Dukelow arrived in our house my father brought him into the kitchen, where my mother was reading the *Irish Press* at the table and Bridget was darning one of her black stockings. 'I've employed this man,' my father said, and as he stepped to one side of the doorway the bent figure of Mr Dukelow appeared suddenly and silently, and my father gestured in the manner of a ringmaster introducing a circus act. Mr Dukelow was carrying a cardboard suitcase that had too many clothes in it. I remember seeing the flannel material of a shirt protruding, for the case was not fastened as it was meant to be.

'What are you crying for?' he asked me on that later occasion. 'What's up with you?'

'Go away, Mr Dukelow.'

A frown appeared on his white forehead. He went away, leaving the light on, and he returned within a minute carrying a packet of cigarettes and a cigarette-lighter I'd bought in Woolworth's in Cork and given him the Christmas before. He always smoked Craven A, claiming that they were manufactured from a superior kind of tobacco. He lit one and sat on my bed. He talked, as often he did, about the moment of his arrival at our house and how he had paused for a moment outside it.

Looking at our house from the street, you saw the brown hall door, its paintwork grained to make it seem like mahogany. There was a brass knocker and a letter-box that every morning except Sunday were cleaned with Brasso by Bridget. To the right of the hall door, and dwarfing it, were the windows of my father's butcher shop, with its sides of mutton hanging from hooks, tripe on a white enamel dish, and beef and sausages and mince and suet.

Afterwards, when he became my friend, Mr Dukelow said that he had stood on the street outside the shop, having just got off the Bantry bus. With his suitcase weighing him down, he had gazed at the windows, wondering about the shop and the house, and about my father. He had not come all the way from Bantry but from a house in the hills somewhere, where he had been employed as some kind of manservant. He had walked to a crossroads and had stood there waiting for the bus: there had been dust on his shoes that night when first he came into our kitchen. 'I looked at the meat in the window,' he told me afterwards, 'and I thought I'd rather go away again.' But my father, expecting him, had come out of the shop and had told him to come on in. My father was a big man; beside Mr Dukelow he looked like a giant.

Mr Dukelow sat on my bed, smoking his Craven A. He began to talk about the advertisement my father had placed in the *Cork Examiner* for an assistant. He repeated the words my father had employed in the advertisement and he said he'd been nervous even to look at them. 'I had no qualifications,' Mr Dukelow said. 'I was afraid.'

That night, six months before, there'd been that kind of fear in his face. 'Sit down, Mr Dukelow,' my mother had said. 'Have you had your tea?' He shook hands with my mother and myself and with Bridget, making a great thing of it, covering up his shyness. He said he'd had tea, although he confessed to me afterwards that he hadn't. 'You'll take a cup, anyway,' my mother offered, 'and a piece of fruit-cake I made?' Bridget took a kettle from the range and poured boiling water into a teapot to warm it. 'Errah, maybe he wants something stronger,' my father said, giving a great gusty laugh. 'Will we go down to Keogh's, Henry?' But my mother insisted that, first of all, before strong drink was taken, before even Mr Dukelow was led to his room, he should have a cup of tea and a slice of fruit-cake. 'He's hardly inside the door,' she said chidingly to my father, 'before you're lifting him out again.' My father, who laughed easily, laughed again. 'Doesn't he have to get to know the people of the town?' he demanded. 'It's a great little town,' he informed Mr Dukelow. 'There's tip-top business here.' My father had only seven fingers and one thumb: being a clumsy man, he had lost the others at different moments, when engaged in his trade. When he had no fingers left he would retire, he used to say, and he would laugh in his roaring way, and add that the sight of a butcher with no fingers would be more than customers could tolerate.

'I often think back,' said Mr Dukelow, 'to the kindness of your mother that first time.'

'He kissed Bridget in the hall,' I said. 'He said she was looking great.'

'Ah, no.'

'I saw him through the banisters.'

'Is it a nightmare you had? Will I get your mammy up?'

I said it wasn't a nightmare I had had: I said I didn't want my mother. My mother was sleeping beside him in their bed and she didn't know that he'd been kissing the maid.

'She'd go away,' I said. 'My mother would go away.'

'Ah no, no.'

'He was kissing Bridget.'

Once, saying good night to me, Mr Dukelow had unexpectedly given me a kiss, but it was a kiss that wasn't at all like the kiss I had observed in the hall. Mr Dukelow had kissed me because my mother was too tired to climb the stairs; he had kissed me in case I felt neglected. Another time, just as unexpectedly, he had taken a florin from his waistcoat pocket and had put it under my pillow, telling me to buy sweets with it. 'Where d'you get that from?' my father had demanded the next day, and when I told him he hit the side of his leg with his fist, becoming angry in a way that puzzled me. Afterwards I heard him shouting at my mother that Henry Dukelow had given me a two-bob bit and had she anything to say to that? My father was sometimes so peculiar in his behaviour that I couldn't make him out. My mother's quietness was always more noticeable when he was present; I loved her for her quietness.

'He had a few jars in tonight.'

'Was he drunk, Mr Dukelow?'

'I think he was.'

'My mother –'

'Will I tell you a story?'

'No, no.'

I imagined Bridget, as I had been imagining her while I lay awake, thinking to herself that she'd give my mother her marching orders. I imagined, suddenly, my mother doing Bridget's work in the kitchen and Bridget standing at the door watching her. She was a plump girl, red-cheeked, with black curly hair. She had fat arms and legs, and she wasn't as tall as my mother. She must have been about twenty-five at the time; Mr Dukelow had told me that my mother was fifty-one. Bridget used to bring me the green glass balls that fishermen use for floating their nets, because she lived by the sea and often found them washed up on the strand. She didn't tell me stories like Mr Dukelow did, but sometimes she'd read to me out of one of the romances she borrowed from a library that the nuns ran. All the books had brown paper covers on them to keep them from getting dirty, with the titles written in ink on the front. I couldn't remember a time that Bridget hadn't been in the house, with those brown-covered volumes, cycling back from her Sunday afternoon off with fish and vegetables in a basket. I had always liked her, but she was different from my mother: I was fonder of my mother.

'If my mother died,' I said, 'he would be married to Bridget. She didn't mind it when he kissed her.'

Mr Dukelow shook his head. She might have been taken unawares, he pointed out: she might have minded it and not been able to protest owing to surprise. Maybe she'd protested, he suggested, after I'd run back to bed.

'She's going out with the porter in the Munster and Leinster Bank,' he said. 'She's keen on that fellow.'

'My father's got more money.'

'Don't worry about your father now. A little thing like that can happen and that's the end of it. Your father's a decent man.'

It was typical of Mr Dukelow to say that my father was a decent man, even though he knew my father didn't like him. In the shop Mr Dukelow outclassed him: after he'd recovered from his initial nervousness, he'd become neater with the meat than my father was, and it was impossible to imagine Mr Dukelow banging through his thin fingers with the cleaver, or letting a knife slip into his flesh. My father said Mr Dukelow had a lot to learn, but it was my father really who had a lot to learn, since he hadn't been able to learn properly in the first place. Once, a woman called Mrs Tighe had returned a piece of meat to the shop, complaining that it had a smell. 'Will you watch that, Henry?' my father expostulated after Mrs Tighe had left the shop, but Mrs Tighe hadn't said it was Mr Dukelow who had sold her the meat. I was there myself at the time and I knew from the expression on Mr Dukelow's face that it was my father who had sold the bad meat to Mrs Tighe. 'Any stuff like that,' my father said to me, 'mince up in the machine.' I could see Mr Dukelow deciding that he intended to do no such thing: it would go against his sensitivity to mince up odorous meat, not because of the dishonesty of the action but because he had become a more prideful butcher than my father, even though he was only an assistant. Mr Dukelow would throw such a piece of meat away, hiding it beneath offal so that my father couldn't accuse him of wasting anything.

In my bedroom, which had a yellow distemper on the walls and a chest of drawers painted white, with a cupboard and washstand to match, Mr Dukelow told me not to worry. There was a little crucifix on the wall above my bed, placed there by my mother, and there was a sacred picture opposite the bed so that I could see the face of Our Lady from where I lay. 'Say a prayer,' urged Mr Dukelow, indicating with a thin hand the two reminders of my Faith. 'I would address St Agnes on a question like that.' Slowly he selected and lit another cigarette. 'Your father's a decent man,' he repeated, and then he must have gone away because when I woke up the light had been switched off. It was half past seven and the first thing I thought was that the day was the last day of the summer holidays. Then I remembered my father kissing Bridget and Mr Dukelow talking to me in the night.

We all had our breakfast together in the kitchen, my mother at one end of the table, my father at the other, Bridget next to me, and Mr Dukelow opposite us. We always sat like that, for all meals, but what I hadn't paid any attention to before was that Bridget was next to my father.

'Two dozen chops,' he said, sitting there with blood on his hands. 'Did I tell you that, Henry? To go over to Mrs Ashe in the hotel.'

'I'll cut them so,' promised Mr Dukelow in his quiet way.

My father laughed. 'Errah, man, haven't I cut them myself?' He laughed again. He watched while Bridget knelt down to open the iron door of the oven. 'There's nothing like cutting chops,' he said, 'to give you an appetite for your breakfast, Bridget.'

My eyes were on a piece of fried bread on my plate. I didn't lift them, but I could feel Mr Dukelow looking at me. He knew I felt jealous because my father had addressed Bridget instead of my mother. I was jealous on my mother's behalf, because she couldn't be jealous herself, because she didn't know. Mr Dukelow sensed everything, as though there was an extra dimension to him. The chops for Mrs Ashe would have been more elegantly cut if he had cut them himself; they'd have been more cleverly cut, with less waste and in half the time.

'Ah, that's great,' said my father as Bridget placed a plate of rashers and sausages in front of him. She sat down quietly beside me. Neither she nor my mother had said anything since I'd entered the kitchen.

'Is there no potato cakes?' my father demanded, and my mother said she'd be making fresh ones today.

'The last ones were lumpy.'

'A little,' agreed my mother. 'There were a few little lumps.'

He held his knife and fork awkwardly because of the injuries to his hands. Often he put too much on his fork and pieces of bacon would fall off. Mr Dukelow, when he was eating, had a certain style.

'Well, mister-me-buck,' said my father, addressing me, 'it's the final day of your holidays.'

'Yes.'

'When I was the age you are I had to work in my holidays. I was delivering meat at six and a half years.'

'Yes.'

'Don't the times change, Bridget?'

Bridget said that times did change. My father asked Mr Dukelow if he had worked during the holidays as a child and Mr Dukelow replied that he had worked in the fields in the summer-time, weeding, harvesting potatoes, and making hay.

'They have an easy time of it these days,' my father pronounced. He had addressed all of us except my mother. He pushed his cup towards Bridget and she passed it to my mother for more tea.

'An easy time of it,' repeated my father.

I could see him eyeing Mr Dukelow's hands as if he was thinking to himself that they didn't look as if they would be much use for harvesting potatoes. And I thought to myself that my father was wrong in this estimation: Mr Dukelow would collect the potatoes speedily, having dug them himself in a methodical way; he would toss them into sacks with a flick of the wrist, a craftsman even in that.

The postman, called Mr Dicey, who was small and inquisitive and had squinting eyes, came into the kitchen from the yard. When he had a letter for the household he delivered it in this manner, while we sat at breakfast. He would stand while the letter was opened, drinking a cup of tea.

'That's a fine morning,' said Mr Dicey. 'We'll have a fine day of it.'

'Unless it rains.' My father laughed until he was red in the face, and then abruptly ceased because no one was laughing with him. 'How're you, Dicey?' he more calmly inquired.

'I have an ache in my back,' replied Mr Dicey, handing my mother a letter.

Mr Dukelow nodded at him, greeting him in that way. Sometimes Mr Dukelow was so quiet in the kitchen that my father asked him if there was something awry with him.

'I was saying to the bucko here,' said my father, 'that when I was his age I used to deliver meat from the shop. Haven't times changed, Dicey?'

'They have not remained the same,' agreed Mr Dicey. 'You could not expect it.'

Bridget handed him a cup of tea. He stirred sugar into it, remarking to Bridget that he'd seen her out last night. It was said that Mr Dicey's curiosity was so great that he often steamed open a letter and delivered it a day late. He was interested in everyone in the town and was keen to know of fresh developments in people's lives.

'You didn't see me at all,' he said to Bridget. He paused, drinking his tea. 'You were engaged at the same time,' he said, 'with another person.'

'Oh, Bridie has her admirers all right,' said my father.

'From the Munster and Leinster Bank.' Mr Dicey laughed. 'There's a letter from your daughter,' he said to my mother. 'I know her little round-shaped writing.'

My mother, concerned with the letter, nodded.

'Bridie could claim the best,' said my father.

I looked at him and saw that he was glancing down the length of the table at my mother.

'Bridie could claim the best,' he repeated in a notably loud voice. 'Wouldn't you say that, Dicey? Isn't she a great-looking girl?'

'She is, of course,' said Mr Dicey. 'Why shouldn't she be?'

'It's a wonder she never claimed Henry Dukelow.' My father coughed and laughed. 'Amn't I right she could claim the best, Henry? Couldn't Bridie have any husband she put her eye on?'

'I'll carry over the chops to Mrs Ashe,' said Mr Dukelow, getting up from the table.

My father laughed. 'Henry Dukelow wouldn't be interested,' he said. 'D'you understand me, Dicey?'

'Oh, now, why wouldn't Henry be interested?' inquired Mr Dicey, interested himself.

Mr Dukelow washed his hands at the sink. He dried them on a towel that hung on the back of the kitchen door, a special towel that only he and my father used.

'He's not a marrying man,' said my father. 'Amn't I right, Henry?'

Mr Dukelow smiled at my father and left the kitchen without speaking. Mr Dicey began to say something, but my father interrupted him.

'He's not a marrying man,' he repeated. He pressed a piece of bread into the grease on his plate. He cleaned the plate with it, and then ate it and drank some tea. Mr Dicey put his cup and saucer on to the table, telling Bridget she was a marvel at making tea. There wasn't better tea in the town, Mr Dicey said, than the tea he drank in this kitchen. He wanted to remain, to hang around in case something happened: he was aware of a heavy atmosphere that morning and he was as puzzled as I was.

My mother was still reading the letter, my father was still staring at her head. Was he trying to hurt her? I wondered: was he attempting to upset her by saying that Bridget could have anyone she wanted as a husband?

She handed the letter to me, indicating that I should pass it on to him. I saw that it was from my sister Sheila, who had married, two Christmases before, a salesman of stationery. I gave it to my father and I watched him reading.

'Bedad,' he said. 'She's due for a baby.'

When I heard my father saying that I thought for only a moment about what the words signified. Bridget exclaimed appropriately, and then there was a silence while my father looked at my mother. She smiled at him in a half-hearted way, obliged by duty to do that, reluctant to share any greater emotion with him.

'Is it Sheila herself?' cried Mr Dicey in simulated excitement. 'God, you wouldn't believe it!' From the way he spoke it was evident that he had known the details of the letter. He went on to say that it seemed only yesterday that my sister was an infant herself. He continued to talk, his squinting eyes moving rapidly over all of us, and I could sense his interest in the calm way my mother had taken the news, not saying a word. There was a damper on the natural excitement, which no one could have failed to be aware of.

My father tried to make up for the lack of commotion by shouting out that for the first time in his life he would be a grandfather. My mother smiled again at him and then, like Mr Dukelow, she rose and left the kitchen. Reluctantly, Mr Dicey took his leave of us also.

Bridget collected the dishes from the table and conveyed them to the sink. My father lit a cigarette. He poured himself a cup of tea, humming a melody that often, tunelessly, he did hum. 'You're as quiet as Henry

Dukelow this morning,' he said to me, and I wanted to reply that we were all quiet except himself, but I didn't say anything. Sometimes when he looked at me I remembered the time he'd said to me that he wondered when I was grown up if I'd take over his shop and be a butcher like he was. 'Your brothers didn't care for that,' he'd said, speaking without rancour but with a certain sorrow in his voice. 'They didn't fancy the trade.' He had smiled at me coaxingly, saying that he was a happy man and that he had built up the business and wouldn't want to see it die away. At the time I felt revulsion at the thought of cutting up dead animals all day long, knifing off slices of red steak and poking for kidneys. I had often watched him at work since he encouraged me to do that, even offering me the experience as a treat. 'Well, mister-me-buck,' he would shout at me, bustling about in his white apron, 'is there a nice piece of liver there for Mrs Bourke?' He would talk to his customers about me as he weighed their orders, remarking that I was growing well and was a good boy when I remembered to be. 'Will you be a butcher like your daddy?' a woman often asked me and I could feel the tension in him without at the time understanding it. It wasn't until I saw Mr Dukelow going about the business in his stylish way that I began to say to the women that I might be a butcher one day. Mr Dukelow didn't make me feel that he was cutting up dead animals at all: Mr Dukelow made it all seem civilized.

I didn't leave the kitchen that morning until my father had finished his cup of tea and was ready to go also, in case he'd kiss Bridget when they were alone together. He told me to hurry up and go and help my mother, but I delayed deliberately and in the end I shamed him into going before me. Bridget went on cleaning the dishes in the sink, standing there silently, as if she didn't know what was happening.

I went to my parents' bedroom, where my mother was making their bed. She asked me to take the end of a sheet and to pull it up so that she wouldn't have to walk around the bed and do it herself. She had taught me how to help her. I seized the end of the sheet and then the end of a blanket. I said:

'If you go away I will go with you.'

She looked at me. She asked me what I'd said and I said it again. She didn't reply. We went on making the bed together and when it was finished, she said:

'It isn't me who's going away, love.'

'Is it Bridget?'

'There's no need for Bridget –'

'I saw him –'

'He didn't mean any harm.'

'Did you see him too?'

'It doesn't matter at all. Sheila's going to have a little baby. Isn't that grand?'

I couldn't understand why she was suddenly talking about my sister having a baby since it had nothing to do with my father kissing Bridget.

296 · A CHOICE OF BUTCHERS

'It's not he who's going away?' I asked, knowing that for my father to go away would be the most unlikely development of all.

'Bridget was telling me yesterday,' my mother said, 'she's going to marry the porter at the Munster and Leinster Bank. It's a secret Bridget has: don't tell your father or Mr Dicey or anyone like that.'

'Mr Dukelow –'

'It is Mr Dukelow who will be going away.'

She covered the big bed with a candlewick bedspread. She pointed a finger at the side of the bedspread that was near me, indicating that I should aid her with it.

'Mr Dukelow?' I said. 'Why would –'

'He moves around from one place to another. He does different kinds of work.'

'Does he get the sack?'

My mother shrugged her shoulders. I went on asking questions, but she told me to be quiet. I followed her to the kitchen and watched her making potato cakes, while Bridget went in and out. Occasionally they spoke, but they weren't unfriendly: it wasn't between them that there was anything wrong. I remembered Bridget saying to me one time that my mother was always very good to her, better than her own mother had ever been. She had a great fondness for my mother, she said, and I sensed it between them that morning because somehow it seemed greater than it had been in the past, even though the night before my father had been kissing Bridget in the hall. I kept looking at my mother, wanting her to explain whatever there was to explain to me, to tell me why Mr Dukelow, who'd said he never wanted to leave my father's shop, was going to leave now, after only six months. I couldn't imagine the house without Mr Dukelow. I couldn't imagine lying in my bed without anyone to come and tell me about Vasco da Gama. I couldn't imagine not seeing him lighting a Craven A cigarette from the little lighter I'd bought him.

'Well, isn't that terrible?' said my father when we were all sitting down again at the kitchen table for our dinner. 'Henry Dukelow's shifting on.'

Mr Dukelow looked nervous. He glanced from me to my mother, not knowing that my mother had guessed he would be going, not knowing she'd suggested it to me.

'We thought he might be,' my mother said. 'He's learnt the business.'

My father pressed potatoes into his mouth and remarked on the stew we were eating. His mood was wholly different now: he wagged his head at my mother, saying she'd cooked the meat well. There wasn't a woman in the country, he tediously continued, who could cook stew like my mother. He asked me if I agreed with that, and I said I did. 'You'll be back at school tomorrow,' he said, and I agreed with that also. 'Tell them they'll have an uncle in the class,' he advised, 'and give the teach a few smiles.'

Releasing an obstreperous laugh, he pushed his plate away from him with the stumps of two fingers. 'Will we go down to Keogh's,' he suggested to Mr Dukelow, 'and have a talk about what you will do?'

'You can talk here,' said my mother with severity. I could see her saying to herself that it was the half-day and if my father entered Keogh's he'd remain there for the afternoon.

'Hurry up, Henry,' said my father, scraping his chair as he pushed it back on the flagged floor. 'A tip-top stew,' he repeated. He made a noise in his mouth, sucking through his teeth, a noise that was familiar to all of us. He told Mr Dukelow he'd be waiting for him in Keogh's.

'Keep an eye on him,' my mother murmured when he'd gone, and Mr Dukelow nodded.

'I would have told you that tonight,' he said to me. 'I didn't want to say a thing until I'd mentioned it to your father first.'

'Mr Dukelow'll be here a month yet.' My mother smiled at me. 'He can tell you a good few stories in that time.'

But Mr Dukelow in fact did not remain in our house for another month. When he returned with my father later that day, my father, in a better mood than ever, said:

'We've come to a good agreement. Henry's going to pack his traps. He'll catch the half seven bus.'

But Mr Dukelow didn't say anything. He walked from the kitchen without swaying like my father was swaying.

My father had his hat on and he didn't take it off. He took his turnip watch from his waistcoat pocket and examined it. 'I can't see without my glasses,' he said to me. 'Will you take a gander at it, boy?'

He never wore glasses, but he often made the joke when he'd been down to Keogh's for a while. I told him it was twenty past six. He put the stumps of two fingers on my head and said I was a great boy. Did I know, he asked me, that in six months' time I'd be an uncle? He had a way of touching me with his stumps instead of with the fingers that remained with him, just as he had a way of pushing from him a plate from which he'd eaten a meal. 'Don't forget to tell the teacher,' he said. 'It's not every day he has an uncle to instruct.'

My mother took a barm brack from a tin and began to butter it for Mr Dukelow before he went. Bridget moved a kettle on to the hot areas of the stove. It boiled at once. 'Will I fry him something?' she asked my mother.

'There's rashers there,' said my mother, 'and a bit of black pudding. Do him eggs, Bridget, and a few potato cakes.'

'He's going,' repeated my father. His face, redder than usually it was, had sweat on the sides of it. 'He's going,' he said again.

I was sitting at the end of the table with a comic spread out in front of me. While I gazed at my father half my vision retained the confused mass of cartoon characters.

'Well, that's that,' said my father.

He stood there swaying, his feet rooted to the kitchen floor, like a statue about to topple in a wind. He was wearing the blue-striped suit that he always wore on the half-day; his hands were hanging by his sides.

'You should be bloody ashamed of yourself,' he said suddenly, and I thought he was talking to me. He wasn't looking at any of us; his eyes were turned upwards, regarding a corner of the ceiling. 'A chancer like that,' he said, 'that gives a young fellow two-bob pieces.' Instinctively I knew then that he was speaking to my mother, even though she did not acknowledge his remarks.

'Sent up from Satan,' he said. 'Sent up to make wickedness. I'm sorry about that thing, Bridget.'

Bridget shook her head, implying that it didn't matter, and I knew they were referring to what had happened in the hall last night.

'Tell Henry Dukelow I'll see him at the bus.' He moved to the back door, adding that he was returning to Keogh's until it was time to say good-bye to Mr Dukelow. 'He'll never make a butcher,' he said, 'or any other bloody thing either.'

I closed the comic and watched my mother and Bridget preparing Mr Dukelow's last meal in our house. They didn't speak and I was afraid to, now. I still couldn't understand why this series of events was taking place. I tried to connect one occurrence with another, but I failed. I felt forgotten in the house: I might have been dead at the table for all they considered me: they were assuming I had no mind.

Mr Dukelow came into the silence, carrying the suitcase he had first carried into the kitchen six months ago, bound up with what looked like the same piece of string. He ate in silence, and Bridget and my mother sat at the table, not saying anything either. I pretended to read the comic, but all the time I was thinking that I'd rather have Mr Dukelow for my father. I couldn't help thinking it and I began to imagine my father sitting on the Bantry bus and Mr Dukelow staying where he was, running the shop better than my father had ever run it, cutting the meat better. I thought of Mr Dukelow in the big bed with my mother, lying asleep beside her. I saw his hands on the white sheets, the thin clever hands instead of hands that made you turn your head away. I saw Mr Dukelow and my mother and myself going out for a walk together on a Sunday afternoon, and Mr Dukelow telling us about Vasco da Gama and Columbus. Mr Dukelow could spend the afternoon in Keogh's and not sway and lurch when he came back. There was no need for Mr Dukelow to go kissing the maid.

'I'm sorry I upset him,' said Mr Dukelow suddenly. 'He's a decent man.'

'It has nothing to do with anything,' said my mother. 'He's in a bad way with drink.'

'Yes,' said Mr Dukelow.

As out of a fog the truth came in pieces to me, and some of the pieces as yet were missing. In six months Mr Dukelow had become a better butcher than my father and my father was jealous of that. Jealousy had caused him to see Mr Dukelow as a monster; jealousy had spread from him in different directions until it wrapped my mother and myself, and tortured my father's pride until he felt he must get his own back and prove himself in some way.

'I'll say good-bye,' said Mr Dukelow, and I hated my father then for his silly pettiness. I wanted Mr Dukelow to go to my mother and kiss her as my father had kissed Bridget. I wanted him to kiss Bridget too, in a way more elegant than the way of my father.

But none of that happened, nor did I ask why, in the face of everything, my father was being described as a decent man. Mr Dukelow left the kitchen, having shaken hands with the three of us. I sat down again at the table while my mother and Bridget prepared the tea. They did not say anything, but I thought to myself that I could see in Bridget's flushed face a reflection of what was passing in her mind: that Mr Dukelow was a nicer man than the porter at the Munster and Leinster Bank. My mother's face was expressionless, but I thought to myself that I knew what expression would be there if my mother cared to permit its presence.

Again I pretended I was reading the comic, but all the time I was thinking about what had silently occurred in our house and how for no sensible reason at all my father's rumbustiousness had spoilt everything. No one but my father could not love Mr Dukelow: no one in the wide world, I thought, except that red-faced man with stumps on his hands, who fell over chairs when he'd been down in Keogh's, who swayed and couldn't read the time. I thought about the ugliness of my father's jealous nature and the gentleness it had taken exception to. 'Sent up from Satan,' his stumbling voice had ridiculously announced. 'Sent up to make wickedness.' How could it be, I wondered, that I was the child of one instead of the other?

'Well, mister-me-buck,' said my father, returning to the kitchen after a time. When I looked at him I began to cry and my mother took me up to bed, saying I was tired.

Kinkies

'Look,' said Mr Belhatchet in the office one Thursday afternoon, 'want you back in Trilby Mews.'

'Me, Mr Belhatchet?'

'Whole stack new designs. Sort them out.'

A year ago, when Eleanor had applied for the position at Sweetawear, he'd walked into Mr Syatt's office, a young man with a dark bush of hair. She'd been expecting someone much older, about the age of Mr Syatt himself: Mr Belhatchet, a smiling, graceful figure, was in his mid-twenties. 'Happy to know you,' he'd said in an American manner but without any trace of an American accent. He'd been sharply dressed, in a dark grey suit that contained both a blue and a white pin-stripe. He wore a discreetly jewelled ring on the little finger of his left hand. 'Mr Belhatchet,' Mr Syatt had explained, 'will be your immediate boss. Sweetawear, of which he is in command, is one small part of our whole organization. There is, as well, Lisney and Company, Harraps, Tass and Grady Designs, Swiftway Designs, Dress-U, et cetera, et cetera.' There was a canteen in the basement, Mr Syatt had added; the Christmas bonus was notably generous. Mr Syatt spoke in a precise, rather old-fashioned manner, punctuating his sentences carefully. 'Use these?' Mr Belhatchet had more casually offered, holding out a packet of Greek cigarettes, and she, wearing that day a high-necked blouse frilled with lace, had smilingly replied that she didn't smoke.

'All righty, Eleanor?' pursued Mr Belhatchet a year later, referring to his suggestion that she should help him sort out dress designs in Trilby Mews. 'Okayie?'

'Yes, of course, Mr Belhatchet.'

Trilby Mews was where Mr Belhatchet lived. He'd often mentioned it and Eleanor had often imagined it, seeing his flat and the mews itself as being rather glamorous. Occasionally he telephoned from there, saying he was in bed or in the bath. He couldn't bear a room that did not contain a telephone.

They left the office at a quarter past six, having finished off what work there was. Eleanor was wearing a pale blue suit in tweed so fine that it might have been linen, and a pale blue blouse. Around her neck there was a double row of small cultured pearls. Her shoes, in darker blue, were square-toed, as current fashion decreed.

That evening she was due to attend the night-school where, once a week, she learned Spanish. It wouldn't matter missing a class because she never had in the past. Several of the other girls missed classes regularly and it never seemed to matter much. They'd be surprised not to see her all the same.

In the taxi Mr Belhatchet lit a Greek cigarette and remarked that he was exhausted. He'd had an exhausting week, she agreed, which was true, because he'd had to fly to Rome in order to look at designs, and then to Germany. In the taxi he said he'd spent all of Tuesday night examining the Italian designs, discussing them with Signor Martelli.

'Dog's Head,' he suddenly ordered the taxi-driver, and the taxi-driver, who appeared to know Mr Belhatchet personally, nodded.

'Join us, Bill?' Mr Belhatchet invited as he paid the fare, but the taxi-driver, addressing Mr Belhatchet with equal familiarity, declined to do so on the grounds that the delay would cost him some trade.

'Two gin, tonic,' Mr Belhatchet ordered in the Dog's Head. 'Large, Dorrie,' he said to the plump barmaid. 'How keeping?'

The barmaid smiled at Eleanor even though the bar was full and she was busy. She was keeping well, she told Mr Belhatchet, whom she addressed, as the taxi-driver had, as Andy.

A Mr Logan, who taught golf at the night-school, had asked Eleanor to have a drink a few times and he'd taken her to a place that wasn't unlike the Dog's Head. She'd quite liked Mr Logan at first, even though he was nearly thirty years older than she was. On the third occasion he'd held her hand as they sat in a corner of a lounge-bar, stroking the back of it. He'd confessed then that he was married – to a woman who'd once dropped, deliberately, a seven-pound weight on his foot. He wanted to leave her, he said, and had then suggested that Eleanor might like to accompany him to Bury St Edmunds the following Saturday. They could stay in a hotel called the Queen's Arms, he suggested, which he'd often stayed in before and which was comfortable and quiet, with excellent food. Eleanor declined, and had since only seen Mr Logan hurrying through the corridors of the night-school. He hadn't invited her to have another drink with him.

Mr Belhatchet consumed his gin and tonic very quickly. He spoke to a few people in the bar and at one point, while speaking to a man with a moustache, he put his arm round Eleanor's shoulders and said that Eleanor was his secretary. He didn't introduce her to any of the others, and he didn't reveal her name to the man with the moustache.

'Feel better,' he said when he'd finished his drink. He looked at hers and she drank the remainder of it as quickly as she could, finding it difficult because the ice made her teeth cold. She wanted to say to Mr Belhatchet that she was just an ordinary girl – in case, later on, there should be any misunderstanding. But although she formed a sentence to that effect and commenced to utter it, Mr Belhatchet didn't appear to be interested.

'I just thought –' she said, smiling.

'You're fantastic,' said Mr Belhatchet.

They walked to Trilby Mews, Mr Belhatchet addressing familiarly a newsvendor on the way. The flat was much as she had imagined it, a small, luxuriously furnished apartment with green blinds half drawn against the glare of the evening sun. The sitting-room was full of small pieces of Victorian furniture and there was a large sofa in purple velvet, fashionably buttoned. The walls were covered with framed pictures, but in the green gloom Eleanor couldn't see what any of them were of.

'Want loo?' suggested Mr Belhatchet, leading her down a short passage, the walls of which also bore framed pictures that couldn't be properly seen. ' 'Nother drink,' he said, opening the lavatory door and ushering her into it. She said she'd better not have another drink, not really if she was to keep a clear head. She laughed while she spoke, realizing that her head was far from clear already. 'Fix you one,' said Mr Belhatchet, closing the door on her.

The lavatory had a telephone in a nook in the wall and the seat was covered in brown and white fur. There were framed picture postcards on the walls, seaside cards with suggestive messages. They didn't seem the kind of thing that should be so expensively framed, Eleanor considered, and was surprised to see them there, especially in such numbers. One or two, she noticed, were in German.

'Same 'gain,' said Mr Belhatchet in the sitting-room. 'Sit yourself, Ellie.'

She couldn't see the designs he'd spoken of: she'd imagined they'd be spread all over the place, propped up on chairs, even on the walls, because that was the way he liked to surround himself with designs when he was making a selection in the office. She couldn't even see a pile anywhere, but she put this down to the gloom that pervaded the sitting-room. It surprised her, though, that he'd addressed her as Ellie, which he'd never done before. Nobody, in fact, had ever called her Ellie before.

'Know Nick's?' asked Mr Belhatchet. 'Nick's Diner? Okayie?'

He smiled at her, blowing out Greek cigarette smoke.

'What about the designs?' she asked, smiling at him also.

'Eat first,' he said, and he picked up a green telephone and dialled a number. 'Belhatchet,' he said. 'Andy. Table two, nine-thirty. All righty?'

She said it was very kind of him to invite her to dinner, thinking that it couldn't be more than half past seven and that for almost two hours apparently they were going to sit in Trilby Mews drinking gin and tonic. She hoped it was going to be all right.

Besides Mr Logan, many men – most of them much younger than Mr Logan – had taken Eleanor out. One called Robert had repeatedly driven her in his yellow sports car to a country club on the London–Guildford road called The Spurs. At half past three one morning he'd suggested that they should walk in the wood behind the country club: Eleanor had declined. Earlier that evening he'd said he loved her, but he never even telephoned her again, not after she declined to walk in the woods with him.

Other men spoke of love to her also. They kissed her and pressed themselves against her. Occasionally she felt the warm tip of a tongue exploring one of her ears and she was naturally obliged to wriggle away from it, hastily putting on lipstick as a sign that the interlude was over. She was beautiful, they said, men she met at the night-school or men employed in Sweetawear or Lisney and Company or Dress-U. But when she resisted their ultimate advances they didn't again say she was beautiful; more often than not they didn't say anything further to her at all. She'd explained a few times that she didn't want to anticipate marriage because she believed that marriage was special. But when it came to the point, although stating that they loved her, not one of them proposed marriage to her. Not that any of them had ever been right, which was something she felt most strongly after they'd made their ultimate advances.

'Use grass?' inquired Mr Belhatchet and for a moment, because of his economical manner of speech, she didn't know what he was talking about: use grass for what? she wondered, and shook her head.

'Mind?' asked Mr Belhatchet, breaking open a fresh cigarette and poking what looked like another kind of tobacco among the leaves that were already there. He fiddled around for some time, adding and taking away, and then placed the untidy-looking cigarette between his lips. She asked again about the designs, but he didn't seem to hear her.

Eleanor didn't enjoy the next two hours, sipping at her drink while Mr Belhatchet smoked and drank and asked her a series of economically-framed questions about herself. Later, while they waited for a taxi, he said he felt marvellous. He put his arm round her shoulders and told her that the first day he saw her he'd thought she was fabulous.

'Fabulous,' he said in Nick's Diner, referring to a bowl of *crudités* that had been placed in front of them. He asked her then if she liked him, smiling at her again, smoking another Greek cigarette.

'Well, of course, Mr Belhatchet.'

'Andy. What like 'bout me?'

'Well –'

'Ha, ha, ha,' said Belhatchet, hitting the table with the palm of his left hand. He was smiling so much now that the smile seemed to Eleanor to be unnatural. Nevertheless, she tried to keep smiling herself. None of the girls at Sweetawear had ever told her that there was anything the matter with Mr Belhatchet. She'd never thought herself that there might be something the matter with him: apart from his mode of speech he'd always seemed totally normal. His mother had set him up in Sweetawear, people said, occasionally adding that he'd certainly made a go of it.

'Fabulous,' said Mr Belhatchet when a waiter served them with fillet steak encased in pastry.

They drank a red wine that she liked the taste of. She said, making conversation, that it was a lovely restaurant, and when he didn't reply she said it was the best restaurant she'd ever been in.

'Fabulous,' said Mr Belhatchet.

At eleven o'clock she suggested that perhaps they should return to Trilby Mews to examine the designs. She knew, even while she spoke, that she shouldn't be going anywhere that night with Mr Belhatchet. She knew that if he was anyone else she'd have smiled and said she must go home now because she had to get up in the morning. But Mr Belhatchet, being her office boss, was different. It was all going to be much harder with Mr Belhatchet.

'Age you now, Ellie?' he asked in the taxi, and she told him she'd become twenty-seven the previous Tuesday, while he'd been in Rome.

'Lovely,' he said. 'Fabulous.'

He was still smiling and she thought he must be drunk except that his speech was in no way slurred.

'It's really so late,' she said as the taxi paused in traffic. 'Perhaps we should leave the designs for tonight, Mr Belhatchet?'

'Andy.'

'Perhaps, Andy –'

'Take morning off, Ellie.'

As they entered the flat he asked her again if she'd like to use the lavatory and reminded her where it was. While she was in there the telephone in the nook beside her rang, causing her to jump. It rang for only a moment, before he picked up one of the other extensions. When she entered the sitting-room he was speaking into the receiver, apparently to Signor Martelli in Rome. 'Fabulous,' he was saying. 'No, truly.'

He'd turned several lights on and pulled the green blinds fully down. The pictures that crowded the walls were more conventional than those in the lavatory, reproductions of drawings mainly, limbs and bones and heads scattered over a single sheet, all of them belonging to the past.

' 'vederci,' said Mr Belhatchet, replacing his green telephone.

In the room there was no pile of designs and she said to herself that in a moment Mr Belhatchet would make a suggestion. She would deal with it as best she could; if the worst came to the worst she would naturally have to leave Sweetawear.

'Fancy drop brandy?' offered Mr Belhatchet.

'Thanks awfully, but I really think I'd better –'

'Just get designs,' he said, leaving the sitting-room.

He returned with a stack of designs which he arrayed around the room just as he would have done in the office. He asked her to assess them while he poured both of them some orange juice.

'Oh, lovely,' she said, because she really felt like orange juice.

The designs were of trouser-suits, a selection of ideas from four different designers. One would be chosen in the end and Sweetawear would manufacture it on a large scale and in a variety of colours.

'Fancy that,' he said, returning with the orange juice and pointing at a drawing with the point of his right foot.

'Yes. And that, the waistcoat effect.'

'Right.'

She sipped her juice and he sipped his. They discussed the designs in detail, taking into consideration the fact that some would obviously be more economical to mass-produce than others. They whittled them down to three, taking about half an hour over that. He'd come to a final decision, he said, some time tomorrow, and the way he said it made her think that he'd come to it on his own, and that his choice might even be one of the rejected designs.

She sat down on the buttoned sofa, feeling suddenly strange, wondering if she'd drunk too much. Mr Belhatchet, she saw, had pushed a few of the designs off an embroidered arm-chair and was sitting down also. He had taken the jacket of his suit off and was slowly loosening his tie.

'Okayie?' he inquired, and leaned his head back and closed his eyes.

She stood up. The floor was peculiar beneath her feet, seeming closer to her, as though her feet had become directly attached to her knees. It moved, like the deck of a ship. She sat down again.

'Fantastic,' said Mr Belhatchet.

'I'm afraid I've had a little too much to drink.'

'God, those days,' said Mr Belhatchet. 'Never 'gain. Know something, Ellie?'

'Mr Belhatchet —'

'Mother loved me, Ellie. Like I was her sweetheart, Mother loved me.'

'Mr Belhatchet, what's happening?'

She heard her own voice, as shrill as a bird's, in the bright, crowded room. She didn't want to move from the sofa. She wanted to put her feet up but she felt she might not be able to move them and was frightened to try in case she couldn't. She closed her eyes and felt herself moving upwards, floating in the room, with a kaleidoscope in each eyelid. 'Mr Belhatchet!' she cried out. 'Mr Belhatchet! Mr Belhatchet!'

She opened her eyes and saw that he had risen from his chair and was standing above her. He was smiling; his face was different.

'I feel,' she cried, but he interrupted her before she could say what she felt.

'Love,' he murmured.

He lifted her legs and placed them on the sofa. He took her shoes off and then returned to the chair he'd occupied before.

'You made us drunk,' she heard her own voice crying, shrill again, shrieking almost in the room. Yet in another way she felt quite tranquil.

'We're going high,' he murmured. 'All righty? We had it in our orange juice.'

She cried out again with part of her. She was floating above the room, she said. The colours of the trouser-suits that were all around her were vivid. They came at her garishly from the paper; the drawn heads of the girls were strange, like real people. The purple of the buttoned sofa was vivid also, and the green of the blinds. All over the walls the pictures of limbs and bones were like glass cases containing what the pictures contained, startling on a soft background. Bottles gleamed, and silver here and there, and brass. There was polished ebony in the room, and ivory.

'You're riding high, Ellie,' Mr Belhatchet said and his voice seemed a long way away, although when she looked at him he seemed nearer and more beautiful than before. He was insane, she thought: there was beauty in his insanity. She never wanted to leave the vivid room above which and through which she floated, depending on the moment. She closed her eyes and there were coloured orchids.

Eleanor slept, or seemed to sleep, and all through her dreams Mr Belhatchet's voice came to her, speaking about his mother. At the same time she herself was back at school, at Springfield Comprehensive, where Miss Whitehead was teaching Class 2 French. The clothes of Miss Whitehead were beautiful and the hairs on her face were as beautiful as the hair on her head, and the odour of her breath was sweet.

'Mother died,' said Mr Belhatchet. 'She left me, Ellie.'

He talked about a house. His voice described a house situated among hills, a large house, remote and rich, with an exotic garden where his mother walked in a white dress, wearing dark glasses because of the sunshine.

'She left me the little business,' he said. 'The pretty little business. Flair: she had flair, Ellie.'

He said he could remember being in his mother's womb. She'd taught him to remember, he said. They read novels together. His mother's hand took his and stroked the flesh of her arm with it.

He took off his shirt and sat in the embroidered chair with the upper half of his body naked. His feet, she saw, were naked also.

'I loved her too,' he said. 'She's back with me now. I can taste her milk, Ellie.'

He was like a god in the embroidered chair, his bushy hair wild on his head, his pale flesh gleaming. His eyes seemed far back in his skull, gazing at her from the depths of caverns. Time did not seem to be passing.

In the house among the hills there were parties, he said, and afterwards quiet servants gathered glasses from the lawns. Cars moved on gravel early in the morning, driving away. Couples were found asleep beneath trees.

She wanted to take some of her own clothes off as Mr Belhatchet had, but her arms were heavy and in time, she guessed, he would take them off for her and that would be beautiful too. His eyes were a rare blue, his flesh was like the flesh of flowers. The room was saturated with colours that were different now, subtly changing: the colours of the trouser-suits and the purple of the sofa and the coloured threads of the embroidered chair and the green blinds and telephone. The colours were liquid in the room, gently flowing, one into another. People stood on banks of foliage, people at Mrs Belhatchet's parties. Mrs Belhatchet stood with her son.

She would like to have children, Eleanor said, she would like to be married. She'd noticed a house once, in Gwendolyn Avenue in Putney, not far from where her bed-sitting-room was: she described it, saying she'd once dreamed she lived there, married to a man with delicate hands.

'I love you,' she said, knowing that she was speaking to that man, a man she had always imagined, who would marry her in a church and take her afterwards to Biarritz for a honeymoon.

'I love you,' she said again, with her eyes closed. 'I've waited all my life.'

She wanted him to come to her, to lie beside her on the sofa and gently to take her clothes off. In the room they would anticipate marriage because marriage was certain between them, because there was perfection in their relationship, because in every detail and in every way they understood each other. They were part of one another; only death could part them now.

'Come to me,' she said with her eyes still closed. 'Oh, come to me now.'

'Mother,' he said.

'No, no –'

'Up here you can be anyone, Ellie. Up here where everything is as we wish it.'

He went on speaking, but she couldn't hear what he said, and it didn't matter. She murmured, but she didn't hear her own words either. And then, a long time later it seemed, she heard a voice more clearly.

'The truth is in this room,' Mr Belhatchet was saying. 'I couldn't ravish anyone, Mother.'

She opened her eyes and saw Mr Belhatchet with his bushy hair, still looking like a god.

'My friend,' she said, closing her eyes again.

She spoke of her bed-sitting-room in East Putney and the posters she'd bought to decorate its walls, and the two lamps with pretty jade-coloured shades that she'd bought in the British Home Stores. She'd said to her landlady that she was determined to make a home of her bed-sitting-room and the landlady said that that sounded a first-class idea. Her landlady gave her a brass gong she didn't want.

In the room their two voices spoke together.

'I put my arms around her,' he said. 'With my arms around her and hers round me, it is beautiful.'

'It is beautiful here,' she said. 'The foliage, the leaves. It is beautiful in the garden of your mother's house.'

'Yes,' he said.

'I am waiting here for a tender man who wouldn't ever hurt me.'

'That's beautiful too,' he said. 'Your clothes are beautiful. Your blue clothes and the pearls at your neck, and your shoes. We are happy in this present moment.'

'Yes.'

'We have floated away.'

They ceased to speak. Time, of which as they dreamed and imagined neither of them was aware, passed normally in the room. At half past six Eleanor, still feeling happy but by now more in control of her limbs, slowly pushed herself from the sofa and stood up. The floor swayed less beneath her feet; the colours in the room, though vivid still, were less so than they had been. Mr Belhatchet was asleep.

Eleanor went to the lavatory and when she returned to the sitting-room she did not lie down on the sofa again. She stood instead in the centre of the room, gazing around it, at Mr Belhatchet with bare feet and a bare chest, asleep in his embroidered chair, at the designs of trouser-suits and the pictures of limbs and bones. 'Mother,' murmured Mr Belhatchet in his sleep, in a voice that was a whisper.

She left the flat, moving slowly and gently closing the door behind her. She descended the stairs and stepped out into Trilby Mews, into fresh early-morning air.

Police Constable Edwin Lloyd found Eleanor an hour later. She was lying on the pavement outside a betting-shop in Garrad Street, W.1. He saw the still body from a distance and hurried towards it, believing he had a death on his hands. 'I fell down,' Eleanor explained as he helped her to rise again. 'I'm tired.'

'Drugs,' said Police Constable Lloyd in Garrad Street police station, and another officer, a desk sergeant, sighed. 'Cup of tea, miss?' Constable Lloyd offered. 'Nice hot tea?'

A middle-aged policewoman searched Eleanor's clothing in case there were further drugs on her person.

'Pretty thing like you,' the woman said. 'Shame, dear.'

They brought her tea and Eleanor drank it, spilling some over her pale blue suit because her hands were shaking. Constable Lloyd, returning to his beat, paused by the door.

'Will she be O.K.?' he asked, and his two colleagues said that they considered she would be.

In the police station the colours were harsh and ugly, not at all like the colours there'd been in Mr Belhatchet's flat. And the faces of the desk sergeant and the policewoman were unpleasant also: the pores of their skin were large, like the cells of a honeycomb. There was something the matter with their mouths and their hands, and the uniforms they wore, and the place they occupied. The wooden seat was uncomfortable, the pages of a book in front of the desk sergeant were torn and grubby, the air stank of stale cigarette smoke. The man and the woman were regarding her as skeletons might, their teeth bared at her, their fingers predatory, like animals' claws. She hated their eyes. She couldn't drink the tea they'd given her because it caused nausea in her stomach.

The noise in the room, a distant fuzziness, was her voice. It spoke of what her mind was full of: Mrs Belhatchet and her son in the garden he had described. Servants collected glasses that were broken and jagged; their hands had blood on them. Couples were found dead beneath trees. The garden was all as ugly as the room she was in now, as dirty and as unpleasant.

And then it was different. In the garden they came at her, Mr Logan of the night-school, Robert in his yellow sports car, and all the others. The touch of their hands was hard, like metal; she moaned in distress at their nakedness. They laughed because of that, pressing her apart, grunting with the passion of beasts. Through blood she screamed, and the voices of the men said that her tortured face was ecstasy to them. They longed for her cries of pain. They longed to wrap her in the filth of their sweat.

Their voices ceased and she heard the fuzziness again, and then it ceased also.

'Eh now,' murmured the desk sergeant soothingly.

'I can't help it,' she said weeping. 'I'm frightened of it, and disgusted. I can't help it; I don't know why I'm like this.'

'Just drink your tea and stop quiet, dear,' the policewoman suggested. 'Best to stop quiet, dear.'

Eleanor shook her head and for a moment her vision was blurred. She closed her eyes and forgot where she was. She opened them and found that her vision had cleared: she saw that she was in a grimy police station with two ugly people. Tea was spilt over her suit and there were drops of tea on her shoes. Her office boss had given her a drug in orange juice: she had experienced certain dreams and fantasies and had conducted with him a formless conversation. She'd never be able to return to the offices of Sweetawear.

'He floats away,' she heard a voice crying out and realized that it was her own. 'He lies there entranced, floating away from his fear and his disgust. "The truth's in this room," he says – when what he means is the opposite. Poor wretched thing!'

She wept and the policewoman went to her and tried to help her, but Eleanor struck at her, shrieking obscenities. 'Everywhere there's ugliness,' she cried. 'His mother loved him with a perverted passion. He floats away from that.'

Tears fell from her eyes, dripping on to her clothes and on the floor by her feet. She wanted to be dead, she whispered, to float away for ever from the groping hands. She wanted to be dead, she said again.

They took her to a cell; she went with them quietly. She lay down and slept immediately, and the desk sergeant and the policewoman returned to their duties. 'Worse than drink,' the woman said. 'The filth that comes out of them; worse than a navvy.'

'She's hooked, you know,' the desk sergeant remarked. 'She's hooked on that floating business. That floating away.'

The policewoman sighed and nodded. They sounded like two of a kind, she commented: the girl and the chap she'd been with.

'Kinkies,' said the desk sergeant. 'Extraordinary, people getting like that.'

'Bloody disgraceful,' said the policewoman.

O Fat White Woman

Relaxing in the garden of her husband's boarding-school, Mrs Digby-Hunter could not help thinking that it was good to be alive. On the short grass of the lawn, tucked out of sight beneath her deck-chair, was a small box of Terry's All Gold chocolates, and on her lap, open at page eight, lay a paper-backed novel by her second-favourite writer of historical fiction. In the garden there was the pleasant sound of insects, and occasionally the buzzing of bees. No sound came from the house: the boys, beneath the alert tutelage of her husband and Mr Kelly, were obediently labouring, the maids, Dympna and Barbara, were, Mrs Digby-Hunter hoped, washing themselves.

Not for the moment in the mood for reading, she surveyed the large, tidy garden that was her husband's pride, even though he never had a moment to work in it. Against high stone walls forsythia grew, and honeysuckle and little pear-trees, and beneath them in rich, herbaceous borders the garden flowers of summer blossomed now in colourful variety. Four beech-trees shaded patches of the lawn and roses grew, and geraniums, in round beds symmetrically arranged. On either side of an archway in the wall ahead of Mrs Digby-Hunter were two yew-trees and beyond the archway, in a wilder part, she could see the blooms of rhododendrons. She could see as well, near one of the yew-trees, the bent figure of Sergeant Wall, an ex-policeman employed on a part-time basis by her husband. He was weeding, his movements slow in the heat of that June afternoon, a stained white hat on his hairless head. It was pleasant to sit in the shade of a beech-tree watching someone else working, having worked oneself all morning in a steamy kitchen. Although she always considered herself an easy-going woman, she had been very angry that morning because one of the girls had quite clearly omitted to make use of the deodorant she was at such pains to supply them with. She had accused each in turn and had got nowhere whatsoever, which didn't entirely surprise her. Dympna was just fifteen and Barbara only a month or two older; hardly the age at which to expect responsibility and truthfulness. Yet it was her duty to train them, as it was her husband's duty to train the boys. 'You'll strip wash, both of you,' she'd commanded snappishly in the end, 'immediately you've done the lunch dishes. From top to toe, please, every inch of you.' They had both, naturally, turned sulky.

Mrs Digby-Hunter, wearing that day a blue cotton dress with a pattern of pinkish lupins on it, was fifty-one. She had married her husband twenty-nine years ago, at a time when he'd been at the beginning of a career in the army. Her father, well-to-do and stern, had given her away and she'd been quite happy about his gesture, for love had then possessed her fully. Determined at all costs to make a success of her marriage and to come up to scratch as a wife, she had pursued a policy of agreeableness: she smiled instead of making a fuss, in her easy-going way she accepted what there was to accept, placing her faith in her husband as she believed a good wife should. In her own opinion she was not a clever person, but at least she could offer loyalty and devotion, instead of nagging and arguing. In a bedroom of a Welsh hotel she had disguised, on her wedding night, her puzzled disappointment when her husband had abruptly left her side, having lain there for only a matter of minutes.

Thus a pattern began in their marriage and as a result of it Mrs Digby-Hunter had never borne children although she had, gradually and at an increasing rate, put on weight. At first she had minded about this and had attempted to diet. She had deprived herself of what she most enjoyed until it occurred to her that caring in this way was making her bad-tempered and miserable: it didn't suit her, all the worrying about calories and extra ounces. She weighed now, although she didn't know it, thirteen stone.

Her husband was leaner, a tall man with bony fingers and smooth black hair and eyes that stared at other people's eyes as if to imply shrewdness. He had a gaunt face and on it a well-kept though not extensive moustache. Shortly after their marriage he had abandoned his career in the army because, he said, he could see no future in it. Mrs Digby-Hunter was surprised but assumed that what was apparent to her husband was not apparent to her. She smiled and did not argue.

After the army her husband became involved with a firm that manufactured a new type of all-purpose, metal step-ladder. He explained to her the mechanism of this article, but it was complicated and she failed to understand: she smiled and nodded, murmuring that the ladder was indeed an ingenious one. Her husband, briskly businesslike in a herring-bone suit, became a director of the step-ladder company on the day before the company ran into financial difficulties and was obliged to cease all production.

'Your father could help,' he murmured, having imparted to her the unfortunate news, but her father, when invited to save the step-ladder firm, closed his eyes in boredom.

'I'm sorry,' she said, rather miserably, feeling she had failed to come up to scratch as a wife. He said it didn't matter, and a few days later he told her he'd become a vending-machine operator. He would have an area, he said, in which he would daily visit schools and swimming-pools, launderettes, factories, offices, wherever the company's vending-machines were sited. He would examine the machines to see that they were in good trim and would fill them full of powdered coffee and powdered milk and a form of tea, and minerals and biscuits and chocolate. She thought the work odd for an ex-army officer, but she did not say so. Instead, she listened while he told her that there was an expanding market for vending-machines, and that in the end they would make a considerable amount of money. His voice went on, quoting percentages and conversion rates. She was knitting him a blue pullover at the time. He held his arms up while she fitted it about his chest; she nodded while he spoke.

Then her father died and left her a sum of money.

'We could buy a country house,' her husband said, 'and open it up as a smart little hotel.' She agreed that that would be nice. She felt that perhaps neither of them was qualified to run an hotel, but it didn't seem worth making a fuss about that, especially since her husband had, without qualifications, joined a step-ladder firm and then, equally unskilled, had gone into the vending-machine business. In fact, their abilities as hoteliers were never put to the test because all of a sudden her husband had a better idea. Idling one evening in a saloon bar, he dropped into conversation with a man who was in a state of depression because his son appeared to be a dunce.

'If I was starting again,' said the man, 'I'd go into the cramming business. My God, you could coin it.' The man talked on, speaking of parents like himself who couldn't hold their heads up because their children's poor performance in the Common Entrance examination deprived them of an association with one of the great public schools of England. The next day Mrs Digby-Hunter's husband scrutinized bound volumes of the Common Entrance examination papers.

'A small boarding-school,' he later said to her, 'for temporarily backward boys; we might do quite nicely.' Mrs Digby-Hunter, who did not immediately take to the notion of being surrounded day and night by temporarily backward boys, said that the idea sounded an interesting one. 'There's a place for sale in Gloucestershire,' her husband said.

The school, begun as a small one, remained so because, as her husband explained, any school of this nature must be small. The turn-over in boys was rapid, and it soon became part of the educational policy of Milton Grange to accept not more than twenty boys at any one time, the wisdom of which was reflected in results that parents and headmasters agreed were remarkable: the sons who had idled at the back of their preparatory school classrooms passed into the great public schools of England, and their parents paid the high fees of Milton Grange most gratefully.

At Milton Grange, part ivy-clad, turreted and baronial, Mrs Digby-Hunter was happy. She did not understand the ins and outs of the Common Entrance examination, for her province was the kitchen and the dormitories, but certainly life at Milton Grange as the headmaster's wife was much more like it than occupying half the ground floor of a semi-detached villa in Croydon, as the wife of a vending-machine operator.

'Christ, what a time we're having with that boy for Harrow,' her husband would say, and she would make a sighing noise to match the annoyance he felt, and smile to cheer him up. It was extraordinary what he had achieved with the dullards he took on, and she now and again wondered if one day he might even receive a small recognition, an OBE maybe. As for her, Milton Grange was recognition enough: an apt reward, she felt, for her marital agreeableness, for not being a nuisance, and coming up to scratch as a wife.

Just occasionally Mrs Digby-Hunter wondered what life would have been like if she'd married someone else. She wondered what it would have been like to have had children of her own and to have engaged in the activity that caused, eventually, children to be born. She imagined, once a year or so, as she lay alone in her room in the darkness, what it would be like to share a double bed night after night. She imagined a faceless man, a pale naked body beside hers, hands caressing flesh. She imagined, occasionally, being married to a clergyman she'd known as a girl, a man who had once embraced her with intense passion, suddenly, after a dance in a church hall. She had experienced the pressure of his body against hers and she could recall still the smell of his clothes and the dampness of his mouth.

But Milton Grange was where she belonged now: she had chosen a man and married him and had ended up, for better or worse, in a turreted house in Gloucestershire. There was give and take in marriage, as always she had known, and where she was concerned there was everything to be thankful for. Once a year, on the last Saturday in July, the gardens of the school were given over to a Conservative fête, and more regularly she and her husband drove to other country houses, for dinner or cocktails. A local Boy Scout group once asked her to present trophies at a sports because she was her husband's wife and he was well regarded. She had enjoyed the occasion and had bought new clothes specially for it.

In winter she put down bulbs, and in spring she watched the birds collecting twigs and straw for nests. She loved the gardens and often repeated to the maids in the kitchen that one was 'nearer God's Heart in a garden than anywhere else on earth'. It was a beautiful sentiment, she said, and very true.

On that June afternoon, while Mrs Digby-Hunter dropped into a doze beneath the beech-trees and Sergeant Wall removed the weeds from a herbaceous border, the bearded Mr Kelly walked between two rows of desks in a bare attic room. Six boys bent over the desks, writing speedily. In the room next door six other boys wrote also. They would not be idling, Mr Kelly knew, any more than the boys in the room across the corridor would be idling.

'*Amavero, amaveris, amaverit*,' he said softly, his haired lips close to the ear of a boy called Timpson, '*Amaverimus*, Timpson, *amaveritis, amaverint*.' A thumb and forefinger of Mr Kelly's seized and turned the flesh on the back of Timpson's left hand. '*Amaveritis*,' he said again, '*amaverint*.' While the flesh was twisted this way and that and while Timpson moaned in the quiet manner that Mr Kelly preferred, Dympna and Barbara surveyed the sleeping form of Mrs Digby-Hunter in the garden. They had not washed themselves. They stood in the bedroom they shared, gazing through an open, diamond-paned window, smoking two Embassy tipped cigarettes. 'White fat slug,' said Barbara. 'Look at her.'

They looked a moment longer. Sergeant Wall in the far distance pushed himself from his knees on to his feet. 'He's coming in for his tea,' said Barbara. She held cigarette smoke in her mouth and then released it in short puffs. 'She can't think,' said Dympna. 'She's incapable of mental activity.' 'She's a dead white slug,' said Barbara.

They cupped their cigarettes in their hands for the journey down the back stairs to the kitchen. They both were thinking that the kettle would be boiling on the Aga: it would be pleasant to sit in the cool, big kitchen drinking tea with old Sergeant Wall, who gossiped about the village he lived in. It was Dympna's turn to make his sandwich, turkey paste left over from yesterday, the easy-to-spread margarine that Mrs Digby-Hunter said was better for you than butter. 'Dead white slug,' repeated Barbara, laughing on the stairs. 'Was she human once?'

Sergeant Wall passed by the sleeping Mrs Digby-Hunter and heard, just perceptibly, a soft snoring coming from her partially open mouth. She was tired, he thought; heat made women tired, he'd often heard. He removed his hat and wiped an accumulation of sweat from the crown of his head. He moved towards the house for his tea.

In his study Digby-Hunter sat with one boy, Marshalsea, listening while Marshalsea repeated recently acquired information about triangles.

'Then DEF,' said Marshalsea, 'must be equal in all respects to –'

'Why?' inquired Digby-Hunter.

His voice was dry and slightly high. His bony hands, on the desk between himself and Marshalsea, had minute finger-nails.

'Because DEF –'

'Because the triangle DEF, Marshalsea.'

'Because the triangle DEF –'

'Yes, Marshalsea?'

'Because the triangle DEF has the two angles at the base and two sides equal to the two angles at the base and two sides of the triangle ABC –'

'You're talking bloody nonsense,' said Digby-Hunter quietly. 'Think about it, boy.'

He rose from his position behind his desk and crossed the room to the window. He moved quietly, a man with a slight stoop because of his height, a man who went well with the room he occupied, with shelves of text books, and an empty mantelpiece, and bare, pale walls. It was simple sense, as he often pointed out to parents, that in rooms where teaching took place there should be no diversions for the roving eyes of students.

Glancing from the window, Digby-Hunter observed his wife in her deck-chair beneath the beeches. He reflected that in their seventeen years at

Milton Grange she had become expert at making shepherd's pie. Her bridge, on the other hand, had not improved and she still made tiresome remarks to parents. Once, briefly, he had loved her, a love that had begun to die in the bedroom of a Welsh hotel, on the night of their wedding day. Her nakedness, which he had daily imagined in lush anticipation, had strangely repelled him. 'I'm sorry,' he'd murmured, and had slipped into the other twin bed, knowing then that this side of marriage was something he was not going to be able to manage. She had not said anything, and between them the matter had never been mentioned again.

It was extraordinary, he thought now, watching her in the garden, that she should lie in a deck-chair like that, unfastidiously asleep. Once at a dinner-party she had described a dream she'd had, and afterwards, in the car on the way back to Milton Grange, he'd had to tell her that no one had been interested in her dream. People had quietly sighed, he'd had to say, because that was the truth.

There was a knock on the door and Digby-Hunter moved from the window and called out peremptorily. A youth with spectacles and long, uncared-for hair entered the sombre room. He was thin, with a slight, thin mouth and a fragile nose; his eyes, magnified behind the tortoiseshell-rimmed discs, were palely nondescript, the colour of water in which vegetables have been boiled. His lengthy hair was lustreless.

'Wraggett,' said Digby-Hunter at once, as though challenging the youth to disclaim this title.

'Sir,' replied Wraggett.

'Why are you moving your head about like that?' Digby-Hunter demanded.

He turned to the other boy. 'Well?' he said.

'If the two angles at the base of D E F,' said Marshalsea, 'are equal to the two angles at the base of –'

'Open the book,' said Digby-Hunter. 'Learn it.'

He left the window and returned to his desk. He sat down. 'What d'you want, Wraggett?' he said.

'I think I'd better go to bed, sir.'

'Bed? What's the matter with you?'

'There's a pain in my neck, sir. At the back, sir. I can't seem to see properly.'

Digby-Hunter regarded Wraggett with irritation and dislike. He made a noise with his lips. He stared at Wraggett. He said:

'So you have lost your sight, Wraggett?'

'No, sir.'

'Why the damn hell are you bellyaching, then?'

'I keep seeing double, sir. I feel a bit sick, sir.'

'Are you malingering, Wraggett?'

'No, sir.'

'Then why are you saying you can't see?'

'Sir –'

'If you're not malingering, get on with the work you've been set, boy. The French verb to drink, the future conditional tense?'

'*Je boive* –'

'You're a cretin,' shouted Digby-Hunter. 'Get out of here at once.'

'I've a pain, sir –'

'Take your pain out with you, for God's sake. Get down to some honest work, Wraggett. Marshalsea?'

'If the two angles at the base of DEF,' said Marshalsea, 'are equal to the two angles at the base of ABC it means that the sides opposite the angles –'

His voice ceased abruptly. He closed his eyes. He felt the small fingers of Digby-Hunter briefly on his scalp before they grasped a clump of hair.

'Open your eyes,' said Digby-Hunter.

Marshalsea did so and saw pleasure in Digby-Hunter's face.

'You haven't listened,' said Digby-Hunter. His left hand pulled the hair, causing the boy to rise from his seat. His right hand moved slowly and then suddenly shot out, completing its journey, striking at Marshalsea's jaw-bone. Digby-Hunter always used the side of his hand, Mr Kelly the ball of the thumb.

'Take two triangles, ABC and DEF,' said Digby-Hunter. Again the edge of his right hand struck Marshalsea's face and then, clenched into a fist, the hand struck repeatedly at Marshalsea's stomach.

'Take two triangles,' whispered Marshalsea, 'ABC and DEF.'

'In which the angle ABC equals the angle DEF.'

'In which the angle ABC equals the angle DEF.'

In her sleep Mrs Digby-Hunter heard a voice. She opened her eyes and saw a figure that might have been part of a dream. She closed her eyes again.

'Mrs Digby-Hunter.'

A boy whose name escaped her stood looking down at her. There were so many boys coming and going for a term or two, then passing on: this one was thin and tall, with spectacles. He had an unhealthy look, she thought, and then she remembered his mother, who had an unhealthy look also, a Mrs Wraggett.

'Mrs Digby-Hunter, I have a pain at the back of my neck.'

She blinked, looking at the boy. They'd do anything, her husband often said, in order to escape their studies, and although she sometimes felt sorry for them she quite understood that their studies must be completed since that was the reason for their presence at Milton Grange. Still, the amount of work they had to do and their excessively long hours, half past eight until seven at night, caused her just occasionally to consider that she herself had been lucky to escape such pressures in her childhood. Every afternoon, immediately after lunch, all the boys set out with Mr Kelly for a brisk walk, which was meant to be, in her husband's parlance, twenty minutes of freshening up. There was naturally no time for games.

'Mrs Digby-Hunter.'

The boy's head was moving about in an eccentric manner. She tried to remember if she had noticed it doing that before, and decided she hadn't. She'd have certainly noticed, for the movement made her dizzy. She reached beneath the deck-chair for the box of All Gold. She smiled at the boy. She said:

'Would you like a chocolate, Wraggett?'

'I feel sick, Mrs Digby-Hunter. I keep seeing double. I can't seem to keep my head steady.'

'You'd better tell the headmaster, old chap.'

He wasn't a boy she'd ever cared for, any more than she'd ever cared for his mother. She smiled at him again, trying to make up for being unable to like either himself or his mother. Again she pushed the box of chocolates at him, nudging a coconut caramel out of its rectangular bed. She always left the coconut caramels and the blackcurrant boats: the boy was more than welcome to them.

'I've told the headmaster, Mrs Digby-Hunter.'

'Have you been studying too hard?'

'No, Mrs Digby-Hunter.'

She withdrew her offer of chocolates, wondering how long he'd stand there waggling his head in the sunshine. He'd get into trouble if the loitering went on too long. She could say that she'd made him remain with her in order to hear further details about his pain, but there was naturally a limit to the amount of time he could hope to waste. She said:

'I think, you know, you should buzz along now, Wraggett –'

'Mrs Digby-Hunter –'

'There's a rule, you know: the headmaster must be informed when a boy is feeling under the weather. The headmaster comes to his own conclusions about who's malingering and who's not. When I was in charge of that side of things, Wraggett, the boys used to pull the wool over my eyes like nobody's business. Well, I didn't blame them, I'd have done the same myself. But the headmaster took another point of view. With a school like Milton Grange, every single second has a value of its own. Naturally, time can't be wasted.'

'They pull the hair out of your head,' Wraggett cried, his voice suddenly shrill. 'They hit you in a special way, so that it doesn't bruise you. They drive their fists into your stomach.'

'I think you should return to your classroom –'

'They enjoy it,' shouted Wraggett.

'Go along now, old chap.'

'Your husband half murdered me, Mrs Digby-Hunter.'

'Now that simply isn't true, Wraggett.'

'Mr Kelly hit Malcolmson in the groin. With a ruler. He poked the end of the ruler –'

'Be quiet, Wraggett.'

'Mrs Digby-Hunter –'

'Go along now, Wraggett.' She spoke for the first time sharply, but when the boy began to move she changed her mind about her command and called him back. He and all the other boys, she explained with less sharpness in her voice, were at Milton Grange for a purpose. They came because they had idled at their preparatory schools, playing noughts and crosses in the back row of a classroom, giggling and disturbing everyone. They came to Milton Grange so that, after the skilled teaching of the headmaster and Mr Kelly, they might succeed at an examination that would lead them to one of England's great public schools. Corporal punishment was part of the curriculum at Milton Grange, and all parents were apprised of that fact. If boys continued to idle as they had idled in the past they would suffer corporal punishment so that, beneath its influence, they might reconsider their behaviour. 'You understand, Wraggett?' said Mrs Digby-Hunter in the end.

Wraggett went away, and Mrs Digby-Hunter felt pleased. The little speech she had made to him was one she had heard her husband making on other occasions. 'We rap the occasional knuckle,' he said to prospective parents. 'Quite simply, we stand no nonsense.'

She was glad that it had come so easily to her to quote her husband, once again to come up to scratch as a wife. Boys who were malingering must naturally receive the occasional rap on the knuckles and her husband, over seventeen years, had proved that his ways were best. She remembered one time a woman coming and taking her son away on the grounds that the pace was too strenuous for him. As it happened, she had opened the door in answer to the woman's summons and had heard the woman say she'd had a letter from her son and thought it better that he should be taken away. It turned out that the child had written hysterically. He had said that Milton Grange was run by lunatics and criminals. Mrs Digby-Hunter, hearing that, had smiled and had quietly inquired if she herself resembled either a lunatic or a criminal. The woman shook her head, but the boy, who had been placed in Milton Grange so that he might pass on to the King's School in Canterbury, was taken away. 'To stagnate,' her husband had predicted and she, knitting another pullover for him, had without much difficulty agreed.

Mrs Digby-Hunter selected a raspberry and honey cream. She returned the chocolate-box to the grass beneath her deck-chair and closed her eyes.

'What's the matter, son?' inquired Sergeant Wall on his way back to his weeding.

Wraggett said he had a pain at the back of his neck. He couldn't keep his head still, he said; he kept seeing double; he felt sick in the stomach.

'God almighty,' said Sergeant Wall. He led the boy back to the kitchen, which was the only interior part of Milton Grange that he knew. 'Here,' he said to the two maids, who were still sitting at the kitchen table, drinking tea. 'Here,' said Sergeant Wall, 'have a look at this.'

Wraggett sat down and took off his spectacles. As though seeking to control its wobbling motion, he attempted to shake his head, but the effort, so Barbara and Dympna afterwards said, appeared to be too much for him. His shoulders slipped forward, the side of his face struck the scrubbed surface of the kitchen table, and when the three of them settled him back on his chair in order to give him water in a cup they discovered that he was dead.

When Mrs Digby-Hunter entered the kitchen half an hour later she blinked her eyes several times because the glaring sunshine had affected them. 'Prick the sausages,' she automatically commanded, for today being a Tuesday it would be sausages for tea, a fact of which both Barbara and Dympna would, as always, have to be reminded. She was then aware that something was the matter.

She blinked again. The kitchen contained people other than Barbara and Dympna. Mr Kelly, a man who rarely addressed her, was standing by the Aga, Sergeant Wall was endeavouring to comfort Barbara, who was noisily weeping.

'What's the matter, Barbara?' inquired Mrs Digby-Hunter, and she noticed as she spoke that Mr Kelly turned more of his back to her. There was a smell of tobacco smoke in the air: Dympna, to Mrs Digby-Hunter's astonishment, was smoking a cigarette.

'There's been a tragedy, Mrs Digby-Hunter,' said Sergeant Wall. 'Young Wraggett.'

'What's the matter with Wraggett?'

'He's dead,' said Dympna. She released smoke through her nose, staring hard at Mrs Digby-Hunter. Barbara, who had looked up on hearing Mrs Digby-Hunter's voice, sobbed more quietly, gazing also, through tears, at Mrs Digby-Hunter.

'Dead?' As she spoke, her husband entered the kitchen. He addressed Mr Kelly, who turned to face him. He said he had put the body of Wraggett on a bed in a bedroom that was never used. There was no doubt about it, he said, the boy was dead.

'Dead?' said Mrs Digby-Hunter again. '*Dead*?'

Mr Kelly was mumbling by the Aga, asking her husband where Wraggett's parents lived. Barbara was wiping the tears from her face with a handkerchief. Beside her, Sergeant Wall, upright and serious, stood like a statue. 'In Worcestershire,' Mrs Digby-Hunter's husband said. 'A village called Pine.' She was aware that the two maids were still looking at her. She wanted to tell Dympna to stop smoking at once, but the words wouldn't come from her. She was asleep in the garden, she thought: Wraggett had come and stood by her chair, she had offered him a chocolate, now she was dreaming that he was dead, it was all ridiculous.

Her husband's voice was quiet, still talking about the village called Pine and about Wraggett's mother and father.

Mr Kelly asked a question that she couldn't hear: her husband replied that he didn't think they were that kind of people. He had sent for the school doctor, he told Mr Kelly, since the cause of death had naturally to be ascertained as soon as possible.

'A heart attack,' said Mr Kelly.

'Dead?' said Mrs Digby-Hunter for the fourth time.

Dympna held towards Barbara her packet of cigarettes. Barbara accepted one, and the eyes of the two girls ceased their observation of Mrs Digby-Hunter's face. Dympna struck a match. Wraggett had been all right earlier, Mr Kelly said. Her husband's lips were pursed in a way that was familiar to her; there was anxiety in his eyes.

The kitchen was flagged, large grey flags that made it cool in summer and which sometimes sweated in damp weather. The boys' crockery, of hardened primrose-coloured plastic, was piled on a dresser that almost reached the ceiling. Through huge, barred windows Mrs Digby-Hunter could see shrubs and a brick wall and an expanse of gravel. Everything was familiar and yet seemed not to be. 'So sudden,' her husband said. 'So wretchedly out of the blue.' He added that after the doctor had given the cause of death he himself would motor over to the village in Worcestershire and break the awful news to the parents.

She moved, and felt again the eyes of the maids following her. She would sack them, she thought, when all this was over. She filled a kettle at the sink, running water into it from the hot tap. Mr Kelly remained where he was standing when she approached the Aga, appearing to be unaware that he was in her way. Her husband moved. She wanted to say that soon, at least, there'd be a cup of tea, but again the words failed to come from her. She heard Sergeant Wall asking her husband if there was anything he could do, and then her husband's voice said that he'd like Sergeant Wall to remain in the house until the doctor arrived so that he could repeat to the doctor what Wraggett had said about suddenly feeling unwell. Mr Kelly spoke again, muttering to her husband that Wraggett in any case would never have passed into Lancing. 'I shouldn't mention that,' her husband said.

She sat down to wait for the kettle to boil, and Sergeant Wall and the girls sat down also, on chairs near to where they were standing, between the two windows. Her husband spoke in a low voice to Mr Kelly, instructing him, it seemed: she couldn't hear the words he spoke. And then, without warning, Barbara cried out loudly. She threw her burning cigarette on the floor and jumped up from her chair. Tears were on her face, her teeth were widely revealed, though not in a smile. 'You're a fat white slug,' she shouted at Mrs Digby-Hunter.

Sergeant Wall attempted to quieten the girl, but her finger-nails scratched at his face and her fingers gripped and tore at the beard of Mr Kelly, who had come to Sergeant Wall's aid. Dympna did not move from her chair. She was looking at Mrs Digby-Hunter, smoking quietly, as though nothing at all was happening.

'It'll be in the newspapers,' shouted Barbara.

She was taken from the kitchen, and the Digby-Hunters could hear her sobbing in the passage and on the back stairs. 'She'll sell the story,' said Dympna.

Digby-Hunter looked at her. He attempted to smile at her, to suggest by his smile that he had a fondness for her. 'What story?' he said.

'The way the boys are beaten up.'

'Now look here, Dympna, you know nothing whatsoever about it. The boys at Milton Grange are here for a special purpose. They undergo special education –'

'You killed one, Mr Digby-Hunter.' Still puffing at her cigarette, Dympna left the kitchen, and Mrs Digby-Hunter spoke.

'My God,' she said.

'They're upset by death,' said her husband tetchily. 'Naturally enough. They'll both calm down.'

But Mr Kelly, hearing those remarks as he returned to the kitchen, said that it was the end of Milton Grange. The girls would definitely pass on their falsehoods to a newspaper. They were telling Sergeant Wall now, he said. They were reminding him of lies they had apparently told him before, and of which he had taken no notice.

'What in the name of heaven,' Digby-Hunter angrily asked his wife, 'did you have to go engaging creatures like that for?'

They hated her, she thought: two girls who day by day had worked beside her in the kitchen, to whom she had taught useful skills. A boy had come and stood beside her in the sunshine and she had offered him a chocolate. He had complained of a pain, and she had pointed out that he must make his complaint to the headmaster, since that was the rule. She had explained as well that corporal punishment was part of the curriculum at Milton Grange. The boy was dead. The girls who hated her would drag her husband's boarding-school through the mud.

She heard the voice of Sergeant Wall saying that the girls, one of them hysterical but calming down, the other insolent, were out to make trouble. He'd tried to reason with them, but they hadn't even listened.

The girls had been in Milton Grange for two and a half months. She remembered the day they had arrived together, carrying cardboard suitcases. They'd come before that to be interviewed, and she'd walked them round the house, explaining about the school. She remembered saying in passing that once a year, at the end of every July, a Conservative fête was held, traditionally now, in the gardens. They hadn't seemed much interested.

'I've built this place up,' she heard her husband say. 'Month by month, year by year. It was a chicken farm when I bought it, Kelly, and now I suppose it'll be a chicken farm again.'

She left the kitchen and walked along the kitchen passage and up the uncarpeted back stairs. She knocked on the door of their room. They called out together, saying she should come in. They were both packing their belongings into their cardboard suitcases, smoking fresh cigarettes. Barbara appeared to have recovered.

She tried to explain to them. No one knew yet, she said, why Wraggett had died. He'd had a heart attack most probably, like Mr Kelly said. It was a terrible thing to have happened.

The girls continued to pack, not listening to her. They folded garments or pressed them, unfolded, into their suitcases.

'My husband's built the place up. Month by month, year by year, for seventeen years he has built it up.'

'The boys are waiting for their tea,' said Dympna. 'Mrs Digby-Hunter, you'd better prick the sausages.'

'Forget our wages,' said Barbara, and laughed in a way that was not hysterical.

'My husband –'

'Your husband,' said Dympna, 'derives sexual pleasure from inflicting pain on children. So does Kelly. They are queer men.'

'Your husband,' said Barbara, 'will be jailed. He'll go to prison with a sack over his head so that he won't have to see the disgust on people's faces. Isn't that true, Mrs Digby-Hunter?'

'My husband –'

'Filth,' said Dympna.

She sat down on the edge of a bed and watched the two girls packing. She imagined the dead body in the bedroom that was never used, and then she imagined Sergeant Wall and Mr Kelly and her husband in the kitchen, waiting for the school doctor to arrive, knowing that it didn't much matter what cause he offered for the death if these two girls were allowed to have their way.

'Why do you hate me?' she asked, quite calmly.

Neither replied. They went on packing and while they packed she talked, in desperation. She tried to speak the truth about Milton Grange, as she saw the truth, but they kept interrupting her. The bruises didn't show on the boys because the bruises were inflicted in an expert way, but sometimes hair was actually pulled out of the boys' scalps, small bunches of hair, she must have noticed that. She had noticed no such thing. 'Corporal punishment,' she began to say, but Barbara held out hairs that had been wrenched from the head of a boy called Bridle. She had found them in a wastepaper basket; Bridle had said they were his and had shown her the place they'd come from. She returned the hairs to a plastic bag that once had contained stockings. The hairs would be photographed, Barbara said, they would appear on the front page of a Sunday newspaper. They'd be side by side with the ex-headmaster, his head hidden beneath a sack, and Mr Kelly skulking behind his beard. Milton Grange, turreted, baronial, part ivy-clad, would be examined by Sunday readers as a torture chamber. And in the garden, beneath the beech-trees, a man would photograph the deck-chair where a woman had slept while violence and death occurred. She and her husband might one day appear in a waxworks, and Mr Kelly, too; a man who, like her husband, derived sexual pleasure from inflicting pain on children.

'You are doing this for profit,' she protested, trying to smile, to win them from the error of their ways.

'Yes,' they said together, and then confessed, sharing the conversation, that they had often considered telephoning a Sunday newspaper to say they had a story to tell. They had kept the hairs in the plastic bag because they'd had that in mind; in every detail they knew what they were going to say.

'You're making money out of –'

'Yes,' said Dympna. 'You've kept us short, Mrs Digby-Hunter.'

She saw their hatred of her in their faces and heard it in both their voices; like a vapour, it hung about the room.

'Why do you hate me?' she asked again.

They laughed, not answering, as though an answer wasn't necessary.

She remembered, although just now she didn't wish to, the clergyman who had kissed her with passion after a dance in a church hall, the dampness of his lips, his body pressed into hers. The smell of his clothes came back to her, across thirty years, seeming familiar because it had come before. She might have borne his children in some rectory somewhere. Would they have hated her then?

Underclothes, dresses, lipsticks, Woolworth's jewellery, unframed photographs of male singing stars were jumbled together in the two cardboard suitcases. The girls moved about the room, picking up their belongings, while Mrs Digby-Hunter, in greater misery than she had ever before experienced, watched them from the edge of the bed. How could human creatures be so cruel? How could they speak to her about being a figure in a waxworks tableau when she had done nothing at all? How could they so callously propose to tell lies to a newspaper about her husband and Mr Kelly when the boy who had so tragically died was still warm with the memory of life?

She watched them, two girls so young that they were not yet fully developed. They had talked about her. In this room, night after night, they had wondered about her, and in the end had hated her. Had they said in their nightly gossiping that since the day of her marriage she had lived like a statue with another statue?

It was all her fault, she suddenly thought: Milton Grange would be a chicken farm again, her husband would be examined by a psychiatrist in a prison, she would live in a single room. It was all her fault. In twenty-nine years it had taken violence and death to make sense of facts that were as terrible.

The girls were saying they'd catch a bus on the main road. Without looking at her or addressing her again they left the bedroom they had shared. She heard their footsteps on the back stairs, and Dympna's voice asking Barbara if she was all right now and Barbara saying she was. A white slug, the girl had called her, a fat white slug.

She did not leave the room. She remained sitting on the edge of the bed, unable to think. Her husband's face appeared in her mind, with its well-kept moustache and shrewd-seeming, dark eyes, a face in the bedroom of a Welsh hotel on the night of her wedding day. She saw herself weeping, as she had not wept then. In a confused way she saw herself on that occasion and on others, protesting, shaking her head, not smiling.

'I'm leaving the army for a step-ladder firm,' he said to her, and she struck his face with her hands, tormented by the absurdity of what he said. She cried out in anger that she had married an army officer, not a step-ladder salesman who was after her father's money. She wept again when ridiculously he told her that he intended to spend his days filling machines full of powdered coffee. He had failed her, she shrilled at him, that night in the Welsh hotel and he had failed her ever since. In front of boys, she accused him of ill-treating those who had been placed in his care. If ever it happened again, she threatened, the police would be sent for. She turned to the boys and ordered them to run about the gardens for a while. It was ludicrous that they should be cooped up while the sun shone, it was ludicrous that they should strive so painfully simply to pass an examination into some school or other. She banged a desk with her hand after the boys had gone, she spat out words at him: they'd all be in the Sunday papers, she said, if he wasn't careful, and she added that she herself would leave Milton Grange for ever unless he pursued a gentler course with the boys who were sent to him, unless he at once dismissed the ill-mannered Mr Kelly, who was clearly a sinister man.

In the room that had been the maids' room Mrs Digby-Hunter wept as her mind went back through the years of her marriage and then, still weeping, she left the room and descended the back stairs to the kitchen. To her husband she said that it was all her fault, she said she was sorry. She had knitted and put down bulbs, she said, and in the end a boy had died. Two girls had hated her because in her easy-going way she had held her peace, not wanting to know. Loyalty and devotion, said Mrs Digby-Hunter, and now a boy was dead, and her husband with a sack over his head would be taken from Milton Grange and later would have sessions with a prison psychiatrist. It was all her fault. She would say so to the reporters when they came. She would explain and take the blame, she would come up to scratch as a wife.

Her husband and Sergeant Wall and Mr Kelly looked at Mrs Digby-Hunter. She stood in the centre of the kitchen, one hand on the table, a stout woman in a blue and pink dress, weeping. The tragedy had temporarily unhinged her, Sergeant Wall thought, and Mr Kelly in irritation thought that if she could see herself she'd go somewhere else, and her husband thought that it was typical of her to be tiresomely stupid at a time like this.

She went on talking: you couldn't blame them for hating her, she said, for she might have prevented death and hadn't bothered herself. In a bedroom in Wales she should have wept, she said, or packed a suitcase and gone away. Her voice continued in the kitchen, the words poured from it, repetitiously and in a hurry. The three men sighed and looked away, all of them thinking the same thing now, that she made no sense at all, with her talk about putting down bulbs and coming up to scratch.

Angels at the Ritz
and Other Stories

In Isfahan

They met in the most casual way, in the upstairs office of Chaharbagh Tours Inc. In the downstairs office a boy asked Normanton to go upstairs and wait: the tour would start a little later because they were having trouble with the engine of the minibus.

The upstairs office was more like a tiny waiting-room than an office, with chairs lined against two walls. The chairs were rudimentary: metal frames, and red plastic over foam rubber. There was a counter stacked with free guides to Isfahan in French and German, and guides to Shiraz and Persepolis in English as well. The walls had posters on them, issued by the Iranian Tourist Board: Mount Damavand, the Chalus road, native dancers from the Southern tribes, club-swinging, the Apadana Palace at Persepolis, the Theological School in Isfahan. The fees and conditions of Chaharbagh Tours were clearly stated: *Tours by De Lux microbus. Each Person Rls. 375 ($5). Tours in French and English language. Microbus comes to Hotel otherwise you'll come to Office. All Entrance Fees. No Shopping. Chaharbagh Tours Inc. wishes you the best.*

She was writing an air-mail letter with a ballpoint pen, leaning on a brochure which she'd spread out on her handbag. It was an awkward arrangement, but she didn't seem to mind. She wrote steadily, not looking up when he entered, not pausing to think about what each sentence might contain. There was no one else in the upstairs office.

He took some leaflets from the racks on the counter. *Isfahan était capitale de l'Iran sous les Seldjoukides et les Safavides. Sous le règne de ces deux dynasties l'art islamique de l'Iran avait atteint son apogée.*

'Are you going on the tour?'

He turned to look at her, surprised that she was English. She was thin and would probably not be very tall when she stood up, a woman in her thirties, without a wedding ring. In a pale face her eyes were hidden behind huge round sunglasses. Her mouth was sensuous, the lips rather thick, her hair soft and black. She was wearing a pink dress and white high-heeled sandals. Nothing about her was smart.

In turn she saw a man who seemed to her to be typically English. He was middle-aged and greying, dressed in a linen suit and carrying a linen hat that matched it. There were lines and wrinkles in his face, about the eyes especially, and the mouth. When he smiled more lines and wrinkles gathered. His skin was tanned, but with the look of skin that usually wasn't: he'd been in Persia only a few weeks, she reckoned.

'Yes, I'm going on the tour,' he said. 'They're having trouble with the minibus.'

'Are we the only two?'

He said he thought not. The minibus would go round the hotels collecting the people who'd bought tickets for the tour. He pointed at the notice on the wall.

She took her dark glasses off. Her eyes were her startling feature: brown, beautiful orbs, with endless depth, mysterious in her more ordinary face. Without the dark glasses she had an Indian look: lips, hair and eyes combined to give her that. But her voice was purely English, made uglier than it might have been by attempts to disguise a Cockney twang.

'I've been writing to my mother,' she said.

He smiled at her and nodded. She put her dark glasses on again and licked the edges of the air-mail letter-form.

'Microbus ready,' the boy from downstairs said. He was a smiling youth of about fifteen with black-rimmed spectacles and very white teeth. He wore a white shirt with tidily rolled-up sleeves, and brown cotton trousers. 'Tour commence please,' he said. 'I am Guide Hafiz.'

He led them to the minibus. 'You German two?' he enquired, and when they replied that they were English he said that not many English came to Persia. 'American,' he said. 'French. German people often.'

They got into the minibus. The driver turned his head to nod and smile at them. He spoke in Persian to Hafiz, and laughed.

'He commence a joke,' Hafiz said. 'He wish me the best. This is the first tour I make. Excuse me, please.' He perused leaflets and guide-books, uneasily licking his lips.

'My name's Iris Smith,' she said.

His, he revealed, was Normanton.

They drove through blue Isfahan, past domes and minarets, and tourist shops in the Avenue Chaharbagh, and blue mosaic on surfaces everywhere, and blue taxi-cabs. Trees and grass had a precious look because of the arid earth. The sky was pale with the promise of heat.

The minibus called at the Park Hotel and at the Inter-continental and the Shah Abbas, where Normanton was staying. It didn't call at the Old Atlantic, which Iris Smith had been told at Teheran Airport was cheap and clean. It collected a French party and a German couple who were having trouble with sunburn, and two wholesome-faced American girls. Hafiz continued to speak in English, explaining that it was the only foreign language he knew. 'Ladies-gentlemen, I am a student from Teheran,' he announced with pride, and then confessed: 'I do not know Isfahan well.'

The leader of the French party, a testy-looking man whom Normanton put down as a university professor, had already protested at their guide's inability to speak French. He protested again when Hafiz said he didn't know Isfahan well, complaining that he had been considerably deceived.

'No, no,' Hafiz replied. 'That is not my fault, sir, I am poor Persian student, sir. Last night I arrive in Isfahan the first time only. It is impossible my father send me to Isfahan before.' He smiled at the testy Frenchman. 'So listen please, ladies-gentlemen. This morning we commence happy tour, we see many curious scenes.' Again his smile flashed. He read in English from an Iran Air leaflet: '*Isfahan is the showpiece of Islamic Persia, but founded at least two thousand years ago!* Here we are, ladies-gentlemen, at the Chehel Sotun. This is pavilion of lyric beauty, palace of forty columns where Shah Abbas II entertain all royal guests. All please leave microbus.'

Normanton wandered alone among the forty columns of the palace. The American girls took photographs and the German couple did the same. A member of the French party operated a moving camera, although only tourists and their guides were moving. The girl called Iris Smith seemed out of place, Normanton thought, teetering on her high-heeled sandals.

'So now Masjed-e-Shah,' Hafiz cried, clapping his hands to collect his party together. The testy Frenchman continued to expostulate, complaining that time had been wasted in the Chehel Sotun. Hafiz smiled at him.

'*Masjed-e-Shah*,' he read from a leaflet as the minibus began again, '*is most outstanding and impressive mosque built by Shah Abbas the Great in early seventeenth century*.'

But when the minibus drew up outside the Masjed-e-Shah it was discovered that the Masjed-e-Shah was closed to tourists because of renovations. So, unfortunately, was the Sheikh Lotfollah.

'So commence to carpet-weaving,' Hafiz said, smiling and shaking his head at the protestations of the French professor.

The cameras moved among the carpet-weavers, women of all ages, producing at speed Isfahan carpets for export. 'Look now at once,' Hafiz commanded, pointing at a carpet that incorporated the features of the late President Kennedy. 'Look please on this skill, ladies-gentlemen.'

In the minibus he announced that the tour was now on its way to the Masjed-e-Jamé, the Friday Mosque. This, he reported after a consultation of his leaflets, displayed Persian architecture of the ninth to the eighteenth century. '*Oldest and largest in Isfahan*,' he read. '*Don't miss it! Many minarets in narrow lanes!* All leave microbus, ladies-gentlemen. All return to microbus in one hour.'

At this there was chatter from the French party. The tour was scheduled to be conducted, points of interest were scheduled to be indicated. The tour was costing three hundred and seventy-five rials.

'O.K., ladies-gentlemen,' Hafiz said. 'Ladies-gentlemen come by me to commence informations. Other ladies-gentlemen come to microbus in one hour.'

An hour was a long time in the Friday Mosque. Normanton wandered away from it, through dusty crowded lanes, into market-places where letter-writers slept on their stools, waiting for illiterates with troubles. In hot, bright sunshine peasants with produce to sell bargained with deft-witted shopkeepers. Crouched on the dust, cobblers made shoes: on a wooden chair a man was shaved beneath a tree. Other men drank sherbet, arguing as vigorously as the heat allowed. Veiled women hurried, pausing to prod entrails at butchers' stalls or to finger rice.

'You're off the tourist track, Mr Normanton.'

Her white high-heeled sandals were covered with dust. She looked tired.

'So are you,' he said.

'I'm glad I ran into you. I wanted to ask how much that dress was.'

She pointed at a limp blue dress hanging on a stall. It was difficult when a woman on her own asked the price of something in this part of the world, she explained. She knew about that from living in Bombay.

He asked the stall-holder how much the dress was, but it turned out to be too expensive, although to Normanton it seemed cheap. The stall-holder followed them along the street offering to reduce the price, saying he had other goods, bags, lengths of cotton, pictures on ivory, all beautiful workmanship, all cheap bargains. Normanton told him to go away.

'Do you live in Bombay?' He wondered if she perhaps was Indian, brought up in London, or half-caste.

'Yes, I live in Bombay. And sometimes in England.'

It was the statement of a woman not at all like Iris Smith: it suggested a grandeur, a certain style, beauty, and some riches.

'I've never been in Bombay,' he said.

'Life can be good enough there. The social life's not bad.'

They had arrived back at the Friday Mosque.

'You've seen all this?' He gestured towards it.

She said she had, but he had the feeling that she hadn't bothered much with the mosque. He couldn't think what had drawn her to Isfahan.

'I love travelling,' she said.

The French party were already established again in the minibus, all except the man with the moving camera. They were talking loudly among themselves, complaining about Hafiz and Chaharbagh Tours. The German couple arrived, their sunburn pinker after their excursions. Hafiz arrived with the two American girls. He was laughing, beginning to flirt with them.

'So,' he said in the minibus, 'we commence the Shaking Minarets. *Two minarets able to shake,*' he read, '*eight kilometres outside the city.* Very famous, ladies-gentlemen, very curious.'

The driver started the bus, but the French party shrilly protested, declaring that the man with the moving camera had been left behind. '*Où est-ce qu'il est?*' a woman in red cried.

'I will tell you a Persian joke,' Hafiz said to the American girls. 'A Persian student commences at a party –'

'*Attention!*' the woman in red cried.

'*Imbécile!*' the professor shouted at Hafiz.

Hafiz smiled at them. He did not understand their trouble, he said, while

IN ISFAHAN · 333

they continued to shout at him. Slowly he took his spectacles off and wiped a sheen of dust from them. 'So a Persian student commences at a party,' he began again.

'I think you've left someone behind,' Normanton said. 'The man with the moving camera.'

The driver of the minibus laughed and then Hafiz, realizing his error, laughed also. He sat down on a seat beside the American girls and laughed unrestrainedly, beating his knees with a fist and flashing his very white teeth. The driver reversed the minibus, with his finger on the horn. 'Bad man!' Hafiz said to the Frenchman when he climbed into the bus, laughing again. 'Heh, heh, heh,' he cried, and the driver and the American girls laughed also.

'*Il est fou!*' one of the French party muttered crossly. '*Incroyable!*'

Normanton glanced across the minibus and discovered that Iris Smith, amused by all this foreign emotion, was already glancing at him. He smiled at her and she smiled back.

Hafiz paid two men to climb into the shaking minarets and shake them. The Frenchman took moving pictures of this motion. Hafiz announced that the mausoleum of a hermit was located near by. He pointed at the view from the roof where they stood. He read slowly from one of the leaflets, informing them that the view was fantastic. 'At the party,' he said to the American girls, 'the student watches an aeroplane on the breast of a beautiful girl. "Why watch you my aeroplane?" the girl commences. "Is it you like my aeroplane?" "It is not the aeroplane which I like," the student commences. "It is the aeroplane's airport which I like." That is a Persian joke.'

It was excessively hot on the roof with the shaking minarets. Normanton had put on his linen hat. Iris Smith tied a black chiffon scarf around her head.

'We commence to offices,' Hafiz said. 'This afternoon we visit Vank Church. Also curious Fire Temple.' He consulted his leaflets. 'An Armenian Museum. *Here you can see a nice collection of old manuscripts and paintings.*'

When the minibus drew up outside the offices of Chaharbagh Tours Hafiz said it was important for everyone to come inside. He led the way, through the downstairs office and up to the upstairs office. Tea was served. Hafiz handed round a basket of sweets, wrapped pieces of candy locally manufactured, very curious taste, he said. Several men in lightweight suits, the principals of Chaharbagh Tours, drank tea also. When the French professor complained that the tour was not satisfactory, the men smiled, denying that they understood either French or English and in no way betraying that they could recognize any difference when the professor changed from one language to the other. It was likely, Normanton guessed, that they were fluent in both.

'Shall you continue after lunch?' he asked Iris Smith. 'The Vank Church, an Armenian museum? There's also the Theological School, which really is the most beautiful of all. No tour is complete without that.'

'You've been on the tour before?'

'I've walked about. I've got to know Isfahan.'

'Then why –'

'It's something to do. Tours are always rewarding. For a start, there are the other people on them.'

'I shall rest this afternoon.'

'The Theological School is easy to find. It's not far from the Shah Abbas Hotel.'

'Are you staying there?'

'Yes.'

She was curious about him. He could see it in her eyes, for she'd taken off her dark glasses. Yet he couldn't believe that he presented as puzzling an exterior as she did herself.

'I've heard it's beautiful,' she said. 'The hotel.'

'Yes, it is.'

'I think everything in Isfahan is beautiful.'

'Are you staying here for long?'

'Until tomorrow morning, the five o'clock bus back to Teheran. I came last night.'

'From London?'

'Yes.'

The tea-party came to an end. The men in the lightweight suits bowed. Hafiz told the American girls that he was looking forward to seeing them in the afternoon, at two o'clock. In the evening, if they were doing nothing else, they might meet again. He smiled at everyone else. They would continue to have a happy tour, he promised, at two o'clock. He would be honoured to give them the informations they desired.

Normanton said goodbye to Iris Smith. He wouldn't, he said, be on the afternoon tour either. The people of a morning tour, he did not add, were never amusing in the afternoon: it wouldn't be funny if the Frenchman with the moving camera got left behind again, the professor's testiness and Hafiz's pidgin English might easily become wearisome as the day wore on.

He advised her again not to miss the Theological School. There was a tourist bazaar beside it, with boutiques, where she might find a dress. But prices would be higher there. She shook her head: she liked collecting bargains.

He walked to the Shah Abbas. He forgot about Iris Smith.

She took a mild sleeping-pill and slept on her bed in the Old Atlantic. When she awoke it was a quarter to seven.

The room was almost dark because she'd pulled over the curtains. She'd taken off her pink dress and hung it up. She lay in her petticoat, staring sleepily at a ceiling she couldn't see. For a few moments before she'd slept her eyes had traversed its network of cracks and flaking paint. There'd been enough light then, even though the curtains had been drawn.

She slipped from the bed and crossed to the window. It was twilight outside, a light that seemed more than ordinarily different from the bright sunshine of the afternoon. Last night, at midnight when she'd arrived, it had been sharply different too: as black as pitch, totally silent in Isfahan.

It wasn't silent now. The blue taxis raced their motors as they paused in a traffic-jam outside the Old Atlantic. Tourists chattered in different languages. Bunches of children, returning from afternoon school, called out to one another on the pavements. Policemen blew their traffic whistles.

Neon lights were winking in the twilight, and in the far distance she could see the massive illuminated dome of the Theological School, a fat blue jewel that dominated everything.

She washed herself and dressed, opening a suitcase to find a black and white dress her mother had made her and a black frilled shawl that went with it. She rubbed the dust from her high-heeled sandals with a Kleenex tissue. It would be nicer to wear a different pair of shoes, more suitable for the evening, but that would mean more unpacking and anyway who was there to notice? She took some medicine because for months she'd had a nagging little cough, which usually came on in the evenings. It was always the same: whenever she returned to England she got a cough.

In his room he read that the Shah was in Moscow, negotiating a deal with the Russians. He closed his eyes, letting the newspaper fall on to the carpet.

At seven o'clock he would go downstairs and sit in the bar and watch the tourist parties. They knew him in the bar now. As soon as he entered one of the barmen would raise a finger and nod. A moment later he would receive his vodka lime, with crushed ice. 'You have good day, sir?' the barman would say to him, whichever barman it was.

Since the Chaharbagh tour of the morning he had eaten a chicken sandwich and walked, he estimated, ten miles. Exhausted, he had had a bath, delighting in the flow of warm water over his body, becoming drowsy until the water cooled and began to chill him. He'd stretched himself on his bed and then had slowly dressed, in a different linen suit.

His room in the Shah Abbas Hotel was enormous, with a balcony and blown-up photographs of domes and minarets, and a double bed as big as a nightclub dance-floor. Ever since he'd first seen it he'd kept thinking that his bed was as big as a dance-floor. The room itself was large enough for a quite substantial family to live in.

He went downstairs at seven o'clock, using the staircase because he hated lifts and because, in any case, it was pleasant to walk through the luxurious hotel. In the hall a group of forty or so Swiss had arrived. He stood by a pillar for a moment, watching them. Their leader made arrangements at the desk, porters carried their luggage from the airport bus. Their faces looked happier when the luggage was identified. Swiss archaeologists, Normanton conjectured, a group tour of some Geneva society. And then, instead of going straight to the bar, he walked out of the hotel into the dusk.

They met in the tourist bazaar. She had bought a brooch, a square of coloured cotton, a canvas carrier-bag. When he saw her, he knew at once that he'd gone to the tourist bazaar because she might be there. They walked together, comparing the prices of ivory miniatures, the traditional polo-playing scene, variously interpreted. It was curiosity, nothing else, that made him want to renew their acquaintanceship.

'The Theological School is closed,' she said.

'You can get in.'

He led her from the bazaar and rang a bell outside the school. He gave the porter a few rials. He said they wouldn't be long.

She marvelled at the peace, the silence of the open courtyards, the blue mosaic walls, the blue water, men silently praying. She called it a grotto of heaven. She heard a sound which she said was a nightingale, and he said it might have been, although Shiraz was where the nightingales were. 'Wine and roses and nightingales,' he said because he knew it would please her. Shiraz was beautiful, too, but not as beautiful as Isfahan. The grass in the courtyards of the Theological School was not like ordinary grass, she said. Even the paving stones and the water gained a dimension in all the blueness. Blue was the colour of holiness: you could feel the holiness here.

'It's nicer than the Taj Mahal. It's pure enchantment.'

'Would you like a drink, Miss Smith? I could show you the enchantments of the Shah Abbas Hotel.'

'I'd love a drink.'

She wasn't wearing her dark glasses. The nasal twang of her voice continued to grate on him whenever she spoke, but her eyes seemed even more sumptuous than they'd been in the bright light of day. It was a shame he couldn't say to her that her eyes were just as beautiful as the architecture of the Theological School, but such a remark would naturally be misunderstood.

'What would you like?' he asked in the bar of the hotel. All around them the Swiss party spoke in French. A group of Texan oilmen and their wives, who had been in the bar the night before, were there again, occupying the same corner. The sunburnt German couple of the Chaharbagh tour were there, with other Germans they'd made friends with.

'I'd like some whisky,' she said. 'With soda. It's very kind of you.'

When their drinks came he suggested that he should bring her on a conducted tour of the hotel. They could drink their way around it, he said 'I shall be Guide Hafiz.'

He enjoyed showing her because all the time she made marvelling noises, catching her breath in marble corridors and fingering the endless mosaic of the walls, sinking her high-heeled sandals into the pile of carpets.

Everything made it enchantment, she said: the gleam of gold and mirror-glass among the blues and reds of the mosaic, the beautifully finished furniture, the staircase, the chandeliers.

'This is my room,' he said, turning the key in the lock of a polished mahogany door.

'Gosh!'

'Sit down, Miss Smith.'

They sat and sipped at their drinks. They talked about the room. She walked out on to the balcony and then came and sat down again. It had become quite cold, she remarked, shivering a little. She coughed.

'You've a cold.'

'England always gives me a cold.'

They sat in two dark, tweed-covered armchairs with a glass-topped table between them. A maid had been to turn down the bed. His green pyjamas lay ready for him on the pillow.

They talked about the people on the tour, Hafiz and the testy professor, and the Frenchman with the moving camera. She had seen Hafiz and the American girls in the tourist bazaar, in the teashop. The minibus had broken down that afternoon: he'd seen it outside the Armenian Museum, the driver and Hafiz examining its plugs.

'My mother would love that place,' she said.

'The Theological School?'

'My mother would feel its spirit. And its holiness.'

'Your mother is in England?'

'In Bournemouth.'

'And you yourself –'

'I have been on holiday with her. I came for six weeks and stayed a year. My husband is in Bombay.'

He glanced at her left hand, thinking he'd made a mistake.

'I haven't been wearing my wedding ring. I shall again, in Bombay.'

'Would you like to have dinner?'

She hesitated. She began to shake her head, then changed her mind. 'Are you sure?' she said. 'Here, in the hotel?'

'The food is the least impressive part.'

He'd asked her because, quite suddenly, he didn't like being in this enormous bedroom with her. It was pleasant showing her around, but he didn't want misunderstandings.

'Let's go downstairs,' he said.

In the bar they had another drink. The Swiss party had gone, so had the Germans. The Texans were noisier than they had been. 'Again, please,' he requested the barman, tapping their two glasses.

In Bournemouth she had worked as a shorthand typist for the year. In the past she had been a shorthand typist when she and her mother lived in London, before her marriage. 'My married name is Mrs Azann,' she said.

'When I saw you first I thought you had an Indian look.'

'Perhaps you get that when you marry an Indian.'

'And you're entirely English?'

'I've always felt drawn to the East. It's a spiritual affinity.'

Her conversation was like the conversation in a novelette. There was that and her voice, and her unsuitable shoes, and her cough, and not wearing enough for the chilly evening air: all of it went together, only her eyes remained different. And the more she talked about herself, the more her eyes appeared to belong to another person.

'I admire my husband very much,' she said. 'He's very fine. He's most intelligent. He's twenty-two years older than I am.'

She told the story then, while they were still in the bar. She had, although she did not say it, married for money. And though she clearly spoke the truth when she said she admired her husband, the marriage was not entirely happy. She could not, for one thing, have children, which neither of them had known at the time of the wedding and which displeased her husband when it was established as a fact. She had been displeased herself to discover that her husband was not as rich as he had appeared to be. He owned a furniture business, he'd said in the Regent Palace Hotel, where they'd met by chance when she was waiting for someone else: this was true, but he had omitted to add that the furniture business was doing badly. She had also been displeased to discover on the first night of her marriage that she disliked being touched by him. And there was yet another problem: in their bungalow in Bombay there lived, as well as her husband and herself, his mother and an aunt, his brother and his business manager. For a girl not used to such communal life, it was difficult in the bungalow in Bombay.

'It sounds more than difficult.'

'Sometimes.'

'He married you because you have an Indian look, while being the opposite of Indian in other ways. Your pale English skin. Your – your English voice.'

'In Bombay I give elocution lessons.'

He blinked, and then smiled to cover the rudeness that might have shown in his face.

'To Indian women,' she said, 'who come to the Club. My husband and I belong to a club. It's the best part of Bombay life, the social side.'

'It's strange to think of you in Bombay.'

'I thought I mightn't return. I thought I'd maybe stay on with my mother. But there's nothing much in England now.'

'I'm fond of England.'

'I thought you might be.' She coughed again, and took her medicine from her handbag and poured a little into her whisky. She drank a mouthful of the mixture, and then apologized, saying she wasn't being very ladylike. Such behaviour would be frowned upon in the Club.

IN ISFAHAN · 339

'You should wear a cardigan with that cough.' He gestured at the barman and ordered further drinks.

'I'll be drunk,' she said, giggling.

He felt he'd been right to be curious. Her story was strange. He imagined the Indian women of the Club speaking English with her nasal intonation, twisting their lips to form the distorted sounds, dropping 'h's' because it was the thing to do. He imagined her in the bungalow, with her elderly husband who wasn't rich, and his relations and his business manager. It was a sour little fairy-story, a tale of Cinderella and a prince who wasn't a prince, and the carriage turned into an ice-cold pumpkin. Uneasiness overtook his curiosity, and he wondered again why she had come to Isfahan.

'Let's have dinner now,' he suggested in a slightly hasty voice.

But Mrs Azann, looking at him with her sumptuous eyes, said she couldn't eat a thing.

He would be married, she speculated. There was pain in the lines of his face, even though he smiled a lot and seemed lighthearted. She wondered if he'd once had a serious illness. When he'd brought her into his bedroom she wondered as they sat there if he was going to make a pass at her. But she knew a bit about people making passes, and he didn't seem the type. He was too attractive to have to make a pass. His manners were too elegant; he was too nice.

'I'll watch you having dinner,' she said. 'I don't mind in the least watching you if you're hungry. I couldn't deprive you of your dinner.'

'Well, I am rather hungry.'

His mouth curved when he said things like that, because of his smile. She wondered if he could be an architect. From the moment she'd had the idea of coming to Isfahan she'd known that it wasn't just an idea. She believed in destiny and always had.

They went to the restaurant, which was huge and luxurious like everywhere else in the hotel, dimly lit, with oil lamps on each table. She liked the way he explained to the waiters that she didn't wish to eat anything. For himself, he ordered a chicken kebab and salad.

'You'd like some wine?' he suggested, smiling in the same way. 'Persian wine's very pleasant.'

'I'd love a glass.'

He ordered the wine. She said:

'Do you always travel alone?'

'Yes.'

'But you're married?'

'Yes, I am.'

'And your wife's a home bird?'

'It's a *modus vivendi*.'

She imagined him in a house in a village, near Midhurst possibly, or

Sevenoaks. She imagined his wife, a capable woman, good in the garden and on committees. She saw his wife quite clearly, a little on the heavy side but nice, cutting sweet-peas.

'You've told me nothing about yourself,' she said.

'There's very little to tell. I'm afraid I haven't a story like yours.'

'Why are you in Isfahan?'

'On holiday.'

'Is it always on your own?'

'I like being on my own. I like hotels. I like looking at people and walking about.'

'You're like me. You like travel.'

'Yes, I do.'

'I imagine you in a village house, in the Home Counties somewhere.'

'That's clever of you.'

'I can clearly see your wife.' She described the woman she could clearly see, without mentioning about her being on the heavy side. He nodded. She had second sight, he said with his smile.

'People have said I'm a little psychic. I'm glad I met you.'

'It's been a pleasure meeting you. Stories like yours are rare enough.'

'It's all true. Every word.'

'Oh, I know it is.'

'Are you an architect?'

'You're quite remarkable,' he said.

He finished his meal and between them they finished the wine. They had coffee and then she asked if he would kindly order more. The Swiss party had left the restaurant, and so had the German couple and their friends. Other diners had been and gone. The Texans were leaving just as Mrs Azann suggested more coffee. No other table was occupied.

'Of course,' he said.

He wished she'd go now. They had killed an evening together. Not for a long time would he forget either her ugly voice or her beautiful eyes. Nor would he easily forget the fairy-story that had gone sour on her. But that was that: the evening was over now.

The waiter brought their coffee, seeming greatly fatigued by the chore.

'D'you think,' she said, 'we should have another drink? D'you think they have cigarettes here?'

He had brandy and she more whisky. The waiter brought her American cigarettes.

'I don't really want to go back to Bombay,' she said.

'I'm sorry about that.'

'I'd like to stay in Isfahan for ever.'

'You'd be very bored. There's no club. No social life of any kind for an English person, I should think.'

'I do like a little social life.' She smiled at him, broadening her sensuous mouth. 'My father was a counter-hand,' she said. 'In a co-op. You wouldn't think it, would you?'

'Not at all,' he lied.

'It's my little secret. If I told the women in the Club that, or my husband's mother or his aunt, they'd have a fit. I've never even told my husband. Only my mother and I share that secret.'

'I see.'

'And now you.'

'Secrets are safe with strangers.'

'Why do you think I told you that secret?'

'Because we are ships that pass in the night.'

'Because you are sympathetic.'

The waiter hovered close and then approached them boldly. The bar was open for as long as they wished it to be. There were lots of other drinks in the bar. Cleverly, he removed the coffee-pot and their cups.

'He's like a magician,' she said. 'Everything in Isfahan is magical.'

'You're glad you came?'

'It's where I met you.'

He rose. He had to stand for a moment because she continued to sit there, her handbag on the table, her black frilled shawl on top of it. She hadn't finished her whisky but he expected that she'd lift the glass to her lips and drink what she wanted of it, or just leave it there. She rose and walked with him from the restaurant, taking her glass with her. Her other hand slipped beneath his arm.

'There's a discotheque downstairs,' she said.

'Oh, I'm afraid that's not really me.'

'Nor me, neither. Let's go back to our bar.'

She handed him her glass, saying she had to pay a visit. She'd love another whisky and soda, she said, even though she hadn't quite finished the one in her glass. Without ice, she said.

The bar was empty except for a single barman. Normanton ordered more brandy for himself and whisky for Mrs Azann. He much preferred her as Iris Smith, in her tatty pink dress and the dark glasses that hid her eyes: she could have been any little typist except that she'd married Mr Azann and had a story to tell.

'It's nice in spite of things,' she explained as she sat down. 'It's nice in spite of him wanting to you-know-what, and the women in the bungalow, and his brother and the business manager. They all disapprove because I'm English, especially his mother and his aunt. He doesn't disapprove because he's mad about me. The business manager doesn't much mind, I suppose. The dogs don't mind. D'you understand? In spite of everything, it's nice to have someone mad about you. And the Club, the social life. Even though we're short of the ready, it's better than England for a woman. There's servants, for a start.'

The whisky was affecting the way she put things. An hour ago she wouldn't have said 'wanting to you-know-what' or 'short of the ready'. It was odd that she had an awareness in this direction and yet could not hear the twang in her voice which instantly gave her away.

'But you don't love your husband.'

'I respect him. It's only that I hate having to you-know-what with him. I really do hate that. I've never actually loved him.'

He regretted saying she didn't love her husband: the remark had slipped out, and it was regrettable because it involved him in the conversation in a way he didn't wish to be.

'Maybe things will work out better when you get back.'

'I know what I'm going back to.' She paused, searching for his eyes with hers. 'I'll never till I die forget Isfahan.'

'It's very beautiful.'

'I'll never forget the Chaharbagh Tours, or Hafiz. I'll never forget that place you brought me to. Or the Shah Abbas Hotel.'

'I think it's time I saw you back to your own hotel.'

'I could sit in this bar for ever.'

'I'm afraid I'm not at all one for night-life.'

ł 'I shall visualize you when I'm back in Bombay. I shall think of you in your village, with your wife, happy in England. I shall think of you working at your architectural plans. I shall often wonder about you travelling alone because your wife doesn't care for it. Your *modus*.'

'I hope it's better in Bombay. Sometimes things are, when you least expect them to be.'

'It's been like a tonic. You've made me very happy.'

'It's kind of you to say that.'

'There's much that's unsaid between us. Will you remember me?'

'Oh yes, of course.'

Reluctantly, she drank the dregs of her whisky. She took her medicine from her handbag and poured a little into the glass and drank that, too. It helped the tickle in her throat, she said. She always had a tickle when the wretched cough came.

'Shall we walk back?'

They left the bar. She clung to him again, walking very slowly between the mosaiced columns. All the way back to the Old Atlantic Hotel she talked about the evening they had spent and how delightful it had been. Not for the world would she have missed Isfahan, she repeated several times.

When they said goodbye she kissed his cheek. Her beautiful eyes swallowed him up, and for a moment he had a feeling that her eyes were the real thing about her, reflecting her as she should be.

He woke at half-past two and could not sleep. Dawn was already beginning to break. He lay there, watching the light increase in the gap he'd left between the curtains so that there'd be fresh air in the room. Another day had passed: he went through it piece by piece, from his early-morning walk to the moment when he'd put his green pyjamas on and got into bed. It was a regular night-time exercise with him. He closed his eyes, remembering in detail.

He turned again into the offices of Chaharbagh Tours and was told by Hafiz to go to the upstairs office. He saw her sitting there writing to her mother, and heard her voice asking him if he was going on the tour. He saw again the sunburnt faces of the German couple and the wholesome faces of the American girls and faces in the French party. He went again on his afternoon walk, and after that there was his bath. She came towards him in the bazaar, with her dark glasses and her small purchases. There was her story as she had told it.

For his part, he had told her nothing. He had agreed with her novelette picture of him, living in a Home Counties village, a well-to-do architect married to a wife who gardened. Architects had become as romantic as doctors, there'd been no reason to disillusion her. She would for ever imagine him travelling to exotic places, on his own because he enjoyed it, because his wife was a home bird.

Why could he not have told her? Why could he not have exchanged one story for another? She had made a mess of things and did not seek to hide it. Life had let her down, she'd let herself down. Ridiculously, she gave elocution lessons to Indian women and did not see it as ridiculous. She had told him her secret, and he knew it was true that he shared it only with her mother and herself.

The hours went by. He should be lying with her in this bed, the size of a dance-floor. In the dawn he should be staring into her sumptuous eyes, in love with the mystery there. He should be telling her and asking for her sympathy, as she had asked for his. He should be telling her that he had walked into a room, not in a Home Counties village, but in harsh, ugly Hampstead, to find his second wife, as once he had found his first, in his bed with another man. He should in humility have asked her why it was that he was naturally a cuckold, why two women of different temperaments and characters had been inspired to have lovers at his expense. He should be telling her, with the warmth of her body warming his, that his second wife had confessed to greater sexual pleasure when she remembered that she was deceiving him.

It was a story no better than hers, certainly as unpleasant. Yet he hadn't had the courage to tell it because it cast him in a certain light. He travelled easily, moving over surfaces and revealing only surfaces himself. He was acceptable as a stranger: in two marriages he had not been forgiven for turning out to be different from what he seemed. To be a cuckold once was the luck of the game, but his double cuckoldry had a whiff of revenge about it. In all humility he might have asked her about that.

At half-past four he stood by the window, looking out at the empty street below. She would be on her way to the bus station, to catch the five o'clock bus to Teheran. He could dress, he could even shave and still be

344 · IN ISFAHAN

there in time. He could pay, on her behalf, the extra air fare that would accrue. He could tell her his story and they could spend a few days. They could go together to Shiraz, city of wine and roses and nightingales.

He stood by the window, watching nothing happening in the street, knowing that if he stood there for ever he wouldn't find the courage. She had met a sympathetic man, more marvellous to her than all the marvels of Isfahan. She would carry that memory to the bungalow in Bombay, knowing nothing about a pettiness which brought out cruelty in people. And he would remember a woman who possessed, deep beneath her unprepossessing surface, the distinction that her eyes mysteriously claimed for her. In different circumstances, with a less unfortunate story to tell, it would have emerged. But in the early morning there was another truth, too. He was the stuff of fantasy. She had quality, he had none.

The Distant Past

In the town and beyond it they were regarded as harmlessly peculiar. Odd, people said, and in time this reference took on a burnish of affection.

They had always been thin, silent with one another, and similar in appearance: a brother and sister who shared a family face. It was a bony countenance, with pale blue eyes and a sharp, well-shaped nose and high cheek-bones. Their father had had it too, but unlike them their father had been an irresponsible and careless man, with red flecks in his cheeks that they didn't have at all. The Middletons of Carraveagh the family had once been known as, but now the brother and sister were just the Middletons, for Carraveagh didn't count any more, except to them.

They owned four Herefords, a number of hens, and the house itself, three miles outside the town. It was a large house, built in the reign of George II, a monument that reflected in its glory and later decay the fortunes of a family. As the brother and sister aged, its roof increasingly ceased to afford protection, rust ate at its gutters, grass thrived in two thick channels all along its avenue. Their father had mortgaged his inherited estate, so local rumour claimed, in order to keep a Catholic Dublin woman in brandy and jewels. When he died, in 1924, his two children discovered that they possessed only a dozen acres. It was locally said also that this adversity hardened their will and that because of it they came to love the remains of Carraveagh more than they could ever have loved a husband or a wife. They blamed for their ill-fortune the Catholic Dublin woman whom they'd never met and they blamed as well the new national regime, contriving in their eccentric way to relate the two. In the days of the Union Jack such women would have known their place: wasn't it all part and parcel?

Twice a week, on Fridays and Sundays, the Middletons journeyed into the town, first of all in a trap and later in a Ford Anglia car. In the shops and elsewhere they made, quite gently, no secret of their continuing loyalty to the past. They attended on Sundays St Patrick's Protestant Church, a place that matched their mood, for prayers were still said there for the King whose sovereignty their country had denied. The revolutionary regime would not last, they quietly informed the Reverend Packham: what sense was there in green-painted pillar-boxes and a language that nobody understood?

On Fridays, when they took seven or eight dozen eggs to the town, they dressed in pressed tweeds and were accompanied over the years by a series of red setters, the breed there had always been at Carraveagh. They sold the eggs in Keogh's grocery and then had a drink with Mrs Keogh in the part of her shop that was devoted to the consumption of refreshment. Mr Middleton had whiskey and his sister Tio Pepe. They enjoyed the occasion, for they liked Mrs Keogh and were liked by her in return. Afterwards they shopped, chatting to the shopkeepers about whatever news there was, and then they went to Healy's Hotel for a few more drinks before driving home.

Drink was their pleasure and it was through it that they built up, in spite of their loyalty to the past, such convivial relationships with the people of the town. Fat Driscoll, who kept the butcher's shop, used even to joke about the past when he stood with them in Healy's Hotel or stood behind his own counter cutting their slender chops or thinly slicing their liver. 'Will you ever forget it, Mr Middleton? I'd ha' run like a rabbit if you'd lifted a finger at me.' Fat Driscoll would laugh then, rocking back on his heels with a glass of stout in his hand or banging their meat on to his weighing-scales. Mr Middleton would smile. 'There was alarm in your eyes, Mr Driscoll,' Miss Middleton would murmur, smiling also at the memory of the distant occasion.

Fat Driscoll, with a farmer called Maguire and another called Breen, had stood in the hall of Carraveagh, each of them in charge of a shot-gun. The Middletons, children then, had been locked with their mother and father and an aunt into an upstairs room. Nothing else had happened: the expected British soldiers had not, after all, arrived and the men in the hall had eventually relaxed their vigil. 'A massacre they wanted,' the Middletons' father said after they'd gone. 'Damn bloody ruffians.'

The Second World War took place. Two Germans, a man and his wife called Winkelmann who ran a glove factory in the town, were suspected by the Middletons of being spies for the Third Reich. People laughed, for they knew the Winkelmanns well and could lend no credence to the Middletons' latest fantasy: typical of them, they explained to the Winkelmanns, who had been worried. Soon after the War the Reverend Packham died and was replaced by the Reverend Bradshaw, a younger man who laughed also and regarded the Middletons as an anachronism. They protested when prayers were no longer said for the Royal Family in St Patrick's, but the Reverend Bradshaw considered that their protests were as absurd as the prayers themselves had been. Why pray for the monarchy of a neighbouring island when their own island had its chosen President now? The Middletons didn't reply to that argument. In the Reverend Bradshaw's presence they rose to their feet when the BBC played 'God Save the King', and on the day of the coronation of Queen Elizabeth II they drove into the town with a small Union Jack propped up in the back window of their Ford Anglia. 'Bedad, you're a holy terror, Mr Middleton!' Fat Driscoll laughingly exclaimed, noticing the flag as he lifted a tray of pork-steaks from his display shelf. The Middletons smiled. It was a great day for the Commonwealth of Nations, they replied, a remark which further amused Fat Driscoll and which he later repeated in Phelan's public house. 'Her Britannic Majesty,' guffawed his friend Mr Breen.

Situated in a valley that was noted for its beauty and with convenient access to rich rivers and bogs over which game-birds flew, the town benefited from post-war tourism. Healy's Hotel changed its title and became, overnight, the New Ormonde. Shopkeepers had their shop-fronts painted and Mr Healy organized an annual Salmon Festival. Even Canon Kelly, who had at first commented severely on the habits of the tourists, and in particular on the summertime dress of the women, was in the end obliged to confess that the morals of his flock remained unaffected. 'God and good sense,' he proclaimed, meaning God and his own teaching. In time he even derived pride from the fact that people with other values came briefly to the town and that the values esteemed by his parishioners were in no way diminished.

The town's grocers now stocked foreign cheeses, brie and camembert and Port Salut, and wines were available to go with them. The plush Cocktail Room of the New Ormonde set a standard: the wife of a solicitor, a Mrs O'Brien, began to give six o'clock parties once or twice a year, obliging her husband to mix gin and Martini in glass jugs and herself handing round a selection of nuts and small Japanese crackers. Canon Kelly looked in as a rule and satisfied himself that all was above board. He rejected, though, the mixture in the jugs, retaining his taste for a glass of John Jameson.

From the windows of their convent the Loretto nuns observed the long, sleek cars with G.B. plates; English and American accents drifted on the breeze to them. Mothers cleaned up their children and sent them to the Golf Club to seek employment as caddies. Sweet shops sold holiday mementoes. The brown, soda and currant breads of Murphy-Flood's bakery were declared to be delicious. Mr Healy doubled the number of local girls who served as waitresses in his dining-room, and in the winter of 1961 he had the builders in again, working on an extension for which the Munster and Leinster Bank had lent him twenty-two thousand pounds.

But as the town increased its prosperity Carraveagh continued its decline. The Middletons were in their middle-sixties now and were reconciled to a life that became more uncomfortable with every passing year. Together they roved the vast lofts of their house, placing old paint tins and flower-pot saucers beneath the drips from the roof. At night they sat over their thin chops in a dining-room that had once been gracious and which in a way was gracious still, except for the faded appearance of furniture that was dry from lack of polish and of a wallpaper that time had rendered colourless. In the hall their father gazed down at them, framed in ebony and gilt, in the uniform of the Irish Guards. He had conversed with Queen Victoria, and even in their middle-sixties they could still hear him saying that God and Empire and Queen formed a trinity unique in any worthy soldier's heart. In the hall hung the family crest, and on ancient Irish linen the Cross of St George.

The dog that accompanied the Middletons now was called Turloch, an animal whose death they dreaded for they felt they couldn't manage the antics of another pup. Turloch, being thirteen, moved slowly and was blind and a little deaf. He was a reminder to them of their own advancing years and of the effort it had become to tend the Herefords and collect the weekly eggs. More and more they looked forward to Fridays, to the warm companionship of Mrs Keogh and Mr Healy's chatter in the hotel. They stayed longer now with Mrs Keogh and in the hotel, and idled longer in the shops, and drove home more slowly. Dimly, but with no less loyalty, they still recalled the distant past and were listened to without ill-feeling when they spoke of it and of Carraveagh as it had been, and of the Queen whose company their careless father had known.

The visitors who came to the town heard about the Middletons and were impressed. It was a pleasant wonder, more than one of them remarked, that old wounds could heal so completely, that the Middletons continued in their loyalty to the past and that, in spite of it, they were respected in the town. When Miss Middleton had been ill with a form of pneumonia in 1958 Canon Kelly had driven out to Carraveagh twice a week with pullets and young ducks that his housekeeper had dressed. 'An upright couple,' was the Canon's public opinion of the Middletons, and he had been known to add that eccentric views would hurt you less than malice. 'We can disagree without guns in this town,' Mr Healy pronounced in his Cocktail Room, and his visitors usually replied that as far as they could see that was the result of living in a Christian country. That the Middletons bought their meat from a man who had once locked them into an upstairs room and had then waited to shoot soldiers in their hall was a fact that amazed the seasonal visitors. You lived and learned, they remarked to Mr Healy.

The Middletons, privately, often considered that they led a strange life. Alone in their two beds at night they now and again wondered why they hadn't just sold Carraveagh forty-eight years ago when their father had died: why had the tie been so strong and why had they in perversity encouraged it? They didn't fully know, nor did they attempt to discuss the matter in any way. Instinctively they had remained at Carraveagh, instinctively feeling that it would have been cowardly to go. Yet often it seemed to them now to be no more than a game they played, this worship of the distant past. And at other times it seemed as real and as important as the remaining acres of land, and the house itself.

'Isn't that shocking?' Mr Healy said one day in 1967. 'Did you hear about that, Mr Middleton, blowing up them post offices in Belfast?'

Mr Healy, red-faced and short-haired, spoke casually in his Cocktail Room, making midday conversation. He had commented in much the same way at breakfast-time, looking up from the *Irish Independent*.

Everyone in the town had said it too: that the blowing up of sub-post offices in Belfast was a shocking matter.

'A bad business,' Fat Driscoll remarked, wrapping the Middletons' meat. 'We don't want that old stuff all over again.'

'We didn't want it in the first place,' Miss Middleton reminded him. He laughed, and she laughed, and so did her brother. Yes, it was a game, she thought: how could any of it be as real or as important as the afflictions and problems of the old butcher himself, his rheumatism and his reluctance to retire? Did her brother, she wondered, privately think so too?

'Come on, old Turloch,' he said, stroking the flank of the red setter with the point of his shoe, and she reflected that you could never tell what he was thinking. Certainly it wasn't the kind of thing you wanted to talk about.

'I've put him in a bit of mince,' Fat Driscoll said, which was something he often did these days, pretending the mince would otherwise be thrown away. There'd been a red setter about the place that night when he waited in the hall for the soldiers: Breen and Maguire had pushed it down into a cellar, frightened of it.

'There's a heart of gold in you, Mr Driscoll,' Miss Middleton murmured, nodding and smiling at him. He was the same age as she was, sixty-six: he should have shut up shop years ago. He would have, he'd once told them, if there'd been a son to leave the business to. As it was, he'd have to sell it and when it came to the point he found it hard to make the necessary arrangements. 'Like us and Carraveagh,' she'd said, even though on the face of it it didn't seem the same at all.

Every evening they sat in the big old kitchen, hearing the news. It was only in Belfast and Derry, the wireless said; outside Belfast and Derry you wouldn't know anything was happening at all. On Fridays they listened to the talk in Mrs Keogh's bar and in the hotel. 'Well, thank God it has nothing to do with the South,' Mr Healy said often, usually repeating the statement.

The first British soldiers landed in the North of Ireland, and soon people didn't so often say that outside Belfast and Derry you wouldn't know anything was happening. There were incidents in Fermanagh and Armagh, in Border villages and towns. One Prime Minister resigned and then another one. The troops were unpopular, the newspapers said; internment became part of the machinery of government. In the town, in St Patrick's Protestant Church and in the Church of the Holy Assumption, prayers for peace were offered, but no peace came.

'We're hit, Mr Middleton,' Mr Healy said one Friday morning. 'If there's a dozen visitors this summer it'll be God's own stroke of luck for us.'

'Luck?'

'Sure, who wants to come to a country with all that malarkey in it?'

'But it's only in the North.'

'Tell that to your tourists, Mr Middleton.'

The town's prosperity ebbed. The Border was more than sixty miles away, but over that distance had spread some wisps of the fog of war. As anger rose in the town at the loss of fortune so there rose also the kind of talk there had been in the distant past. There was talk of atrocities and counter-atrocities, and of guns and gelignite and the rights of people. There was bitterness suddenly in Mrs Keogh's bar because of the lack of trade, and in the empty hotel there was bitterness also.

On Fridays, only sometimes at first, there was a silence when the Middletons appeared. It was as though, going back nearly twenty years, people remembered the Union Jack in the window of their car and saw it now in a different light. It wasn't something to laugh at any more, nor were certain words that the Middletons had gently spoken, nor were they themselves just an old, peculiar couple. Slowly the change crept about, all around them in the town, until Fat Driscoll didn't wish it to be remembered that he had ever given them mince for their dog. He had stood with a gun in the enemy's house, waiting for soldiers so that soldiers might be killed: it was better that people should remember that.

One day Canon Kelly looked the other way when he saw the Middletons' car coming and they noticed this movement of his head, although he hadn't wished them to. And on another day Mrs O'Brien, who had always been keen to talk to them in the hotel, didn't reply when they addressed her.

The Middletons naturally didn't discuss these rebuffs but they each of them privately knew that there was no conversation they could have at this time with the people of the town. The stand they had taken and kept to for so many years no longer seemed ridiculous in the town. Had they driven with a Union Jack now they would, astoundingly, have been shot.

'It will never cease.' He spoke disconsolately one night, standing by the dresser where the wireless was.

She washed the dishes they'd eaten from, and the cutlery. 'Not in our time,' she said.

'It is worse than before.'

'Yes, it is worse than before.'

They took from the walls of the hall the portrait of their father in the uniform of the Irish Guards because it seemed wrong to them that at this time it should hang there. They took down also the crest of their family and the Cross of St George, and from a vase on the drawing-room mantelpiece they removed the small Union Jack that had been there since the Coronation of Queen Elizabeth II. They did not remove these articles in fear but in mourning for the *modus vivendi* that had existed for so long between them and the people of the town. They had given their custom to a butcher who had planned to shoot down soldiers in their hall and he, in turn, had given them mince for their dog. For fifty years they had experienced, after suspicion had seeped away, a tolerance that never again in the years that were left to them would they know.

One November night their dog died and he said to her after he had buried it that they must not be depressed by all that was happening. They would die themselves and the house would become a ruin because there was no one to inherit it, and the distant past would be set to rest. But she disagreed: the *modus vivendi* had been easy for them, she pointed out, because they hadn't really minded the dwindling of their fortunes while the town prospered. It had given them a life, and a kind of dignity: you could take a pride out of living in peace.

He did not say anything and then, because of the emotion that both of them felt over the death of their dog, he said in a rushing way that they could no longer at their age hope to make a living out of the remains of Carraveagh. They must sell the hens and the four Herefords. As he spoke, he watched her nodding, agreeing with the sense of it. Now and again, he thought, he would drive slowly into the town, to buy groceries and meat with the money they had saved, and to face the silence that would sourly thicken as their own two deaths came closer and death increased in another part of their island. She felt him thinking that and she knew that he was right. Because of the distant past they would die friendless. It was worse than being murdered in their beds.

Angels at the Ritz

The game was played when the party, whichever party it happened to be, had thinned out. Those who stayed on beyond a certain point – beyond, usually, about one o'clock – knew that the game was on the cards and in fact had stayed for that reason. Often, as one o'clock approached, there were marital disagreements about whether or not to go home.

The game of swapping wives and husbands, with chance rather than choice dictating the formations, had been practised in this outer suburb since the mid-1950s. The swinging wives and husbands of that time were now passing into the first years of elderliness, but their party game continued. In the outer suburb it was most popular when the early struggles of marriage were over, after children had been born and were established at school, when there were signs of marital wilting that gin and tonic did not cure.

'I think it's awfully silly,' Polly Dillard pronounced, addressing her husband on the evening of the Ryders' party.

Her husband, whose first name was Gavin, pointed out that they'd known for years that the practice was prevalent at Saturday-night parties in the outer suburb. There'd been, he reminded her, the moment at the Meacocks' when they'd realized they'd stayed too late, when the remaining men threw their car-keys on to the Meacocks' carpet and Sylvia Meacock began to tie scarves over the eyes of the wives.

'I mean, it's silly Sue and Malcolm going in for it. All of a sudden, out of the blue like that.'

'They're just shuffling along with it, I suppose.'

Polly shook her head. Quietly, she said that in the past Sue and Malcolm Ryder hadn't been the kind to shuffle along with things. Sue had sounded like a silly schoolgirl, embarrassed and not looking her in the eye when she told her.

Gavin could see she was upset, but one of the things about Polly since she'd had their two children and had come to live in the outer suburb was that she was able to deal with being upset. She dealt with it now, keeping calm, not raising her voice. She'd have been the same when Sue Ryder averted her eyes and said that she and Malcolm had decided to go in, too, for the outer suburb's most popular party game. Polly would have been astonished and would have said so, and then she'd have attempted to become reconciled to the development. Before this evening came to an end she really would be reconciled, philosophically accepting the development as part of the Ryders' middle age, while denying that it could ever be part of hers.

'I suppose,' Gavin said, 'it's like a schoolgirl deciding to let herself be kissed for the first time. Don't you remember sounding silly then, Polly?'

She said it wasn't at all like that. Imagine, she suggested, finding yourself teamed up with a sweaty creature like Tim Gruffydd. Imagine any schoolgirl in her senses letting Tim Gruffydd within two million miles of her. She still couldn't believe that Sue and Malcolm Ryder were going in for stuff like that. What on earth happened to people? she asked Gavin, and Gavin said he didn't know.

Polly Dillard was thirty-six, her husband two years older. Her short fair hair had streaks of grey in it now. Her thin, rather long face wasn't pretty but did occasionally seem beautiful, the eyes deep blue, the mouth wide, becoming slanted when she smiled. She herself considered that nothing matched properly in her face and that her body was too lanky and her breasts too slight. But after thirty-six years she'd become used to all that, and other women envied her her figure and her looks.

On the evening of the Ryders' party she surveyed the features that did not in her opinion match, applying eye-shadow in her bedroom looking-glass and now and again glancing at the reflection of her husband, who was changing from his Saturday clothes into clothes more suitable for Saturday night at the Ryders': a blue corduroy suit, pink shirt and pinkish tie. Of medium height, fattening on lunches and alcohol, he was dark-haired and still handsome, for his chunky features were only just beginning to trail signs of this telltale plumpness. By profession Gavin Dillard was a director of promotional films for television, mainly in the soap and detergent field.

The hall-door bell rang as Polly rose from the chair in front of her looking-glass.

'I'll go,' he said, adding that it would be Estrella, their babysitter.

'Estrella couldn't come, I had to ring Problem. Some Irish-sounding girl it'll be.'

'Hannah McCarthy,' a round-faced girl at the door said. 'Are you Mr Dillard, sir?'

He smiled at her and said he was. He closed the door and took her coat. He led her through a white, spacious hall into a sitting-room that was spacious also, with pale blue walls and curtains. One child was already in bed, he told her, the other was still in his bath. Two boys, he explained: Paul and David. His wife would introduce her to them.

'Would you like a drink, Hannah?'

'Well, I wouldn't say no to that, Mr Dillard.' She smiled an extensive smile at him. 'A little sherry if you have it, sir.'

'And how's the old country, Hannah?' He spoke lightly, trying to be friendly, handing her a glass of sherry. He turned away and poured himself some gin and tonic, adding a sliver of lemon. 'Cheers, Hannah!'

'Cheers, sir! Ireland, d'you mean, sir? Oh, Ireland doesn't change.'

'You go back, do you?'

'Every holidays. I'm in teacher training, Mr Dillard.'

'I was at the Cork Film Festival once. A right old time we had.'

'I don't know Cork, actually. I'm from Listowel myself. Are you in films yourself, sir? You're not an actor, Mr Dillard?'

'Actually I'm a director.'

Polly entered the room. She said she was Mrs Dillard. She smiled, endeavouring to be as friendly as Gavin had been, in case the girl didn't feel at home. She thanked her for coming at such short notice and presumably so far. She was wearing a skirt that Gavin had helped her to buy in Fenwick's only last week, and a white lace blouse she'd had for years, and her jade beads. The skirt, made of velvet, was the same green as the jade. She took the babysitter away to introduce her to the two children.

Gavin stood with his back to the fire, sipping at his gin and tonic. He didn't find it puzzling that Polly should feel so strongly about the fact that Sue and Malcolm Ryder had reached a certain stage in their marriage. The Ryders were their oldest and closest friends. Polly and Sue had known one another since they'd gone together to the Misses Summers' nursery school in Putney. Perhaps it was this depth in the relationship that caused Polly to feel so disturbed by a new development in her friend's life. In his own view, being offered a free hand with an unselected woman in return for agreeing that some man should maul his wife about wasn't an attractive proposition. It surprised him that the Ryders had decided to go in for this particular party game, and it surprised him even more that Malcolm Ryder had never mentioned it to him. But it didn't upset him.

'All right?' Polly enquired from the doorway, with her coat on. The coat was brown and fur-trimmed and expensive: she looked beautiful in it, Gavin thought, calm and collected. Once, a long time ago, she had thrown a milk-jug across a room at him. At one time she had wept a lot, deploring her lankiness and her flat breasts. All that seemed strangely out of character now.

He finished his drink and put the glass down on the mantelpiece. He put the sherry bottle beside the babysitter's glass in case she should feel like some more, and then changed his mind and returned the bottle to the cabinet, remembering that they didn't know the girl: a drunk babysitter – an experience they'd once endured – was a great deal worse than no babysitter at all.

'She seems very nice,' Polly said in the car. 'She said she'd read to them for an hour.'

'An hour? The poor girl!'

'She loves children.'

It was dark, half-past eight on a night in November. It was raining just enough to make it necessary to use the windscreen-wipers. Automatically, Gavin turned the car radio on: there was something pleasantly cosy about the glow of a car radio at night when it was raining, with the background whirr of the windscreen-wipers and the wave of warmth from the heater.

'Let's not stay long,' he said.

It pleased her that he said that. She wondered if they were dull not to wish to stay, but he said that was nonsense.

He drove through the sprawl of their outer suburb, all of it new, disguised now by the night. Orange street lighting made the façades of the carefully-designed houses seem different, changing the colours, but the feeling of space remained, and the uncluttered effect of the unfenced front gardens. Roomy Volvo estate-cars went nicely with the detached houses. So did Vauxhall Victors, and big bus-like Volkswagens. Families were packed into such vehicles on summer Saturday mornings, for journeys to cottages in the Welsh hills or in Hampshire or Herts. The Dillards' cottage was in the New Forest.

Gavin parked the car in Sandiway Crescent, several doors away from the Ryders' house because other cars were already parked closer to it. He'd have much preferred to be going out to dinner in Tonino's with Malcolm and Sue, lasagne and peperonata and a carafe of Chianti Christina, a lazy kind of evening that would remind all of them of other lazy evenings. Ten years ago they'd all four gone regularly to Tonino's trattoria in Greek Street, and the branch that had opened in their outer suburb was very like the original, even down to the framed colour photographs of A.C. Milan.

'Come on *in*!' Sue cried jollily at Number Four Sandiway Crescent. Her face was flushed with party excitement, her large brown eyes flashed adventurously with party spirit. Her eyes were the only outsize thing about her: she was tiny and black-haired, as pretty as a rose-bud.

'Gin?' Malcolm shouted at them from the depths of the crowded hall. 'Sherry, Polly? Burgundy?'

Gavin kissed the dimpled cheek that Sue Ryder pressed up to him. She was in red, a long red dress that suited her, with a red band in her hair and red shoes.

'Yes, wine please, Malcolm,' Polly said, and when she was close enough she slid her face towards his for the same kind of embrace as her husband had given his wife.

'You're looking edible, my love,' he said, a compliment he'd been paying her for seventeen years.

He was an enormous man, made to seem more so by the smallness of his wife. His features had a mushy look. His head, like a pink sponge, was perched jauntily on shoulders that had once been a force to reckon with in rugby scrums. Although he was exactly the same age as Gavin, his hair had balded away to almost nothing, a rim of fluff not quite encircling the sponge.

'You're looking very smart yourself,' Polly said, a statement that might or might not have been true: she couldn't see him properly because he was so big and she was so close to him, and she hadn't looked when she'd been further away. He was wearing a grey suit of some kind and a blue-striped shirt and the tie of the Harlequins' Rugby Club. Usually he looked smart: he probably did now.

'I'm feeling great,' he said. 'Nice little party we're having, Poll.'

It wasn't really little. Sixty or so people were in the Ryders' house, which was similar to the Dillards' house, well-designed and spacious. Most of the downstairs rooms, and the hall, had coffee-coloured walls, an experiment of Sue's which she believed had been successful. For the party, the bulkier furniture had been taken out of the coffee-coloured sitting-room, and all the rugs had been lifted from the parquet floor. Music came from a tape-recorder, but no one was dancing yet. People stood in small groups, smoking and talking and drinking. No one, so far, appeared to be drunk.

All the usual people were there: the Stubbses, the Burgesses, the Pedlars, the Thompsons, the Stevensons, Sylvia and Jack Meacock, Philip and June Mulally, Oliver and Olive Gramsmith, Tim and Mary-Ann Gruffydd and dozens of others. Not all of them lived in the outer suburb; and some were older, some younger, than the Ryders and the Dillards. But there was otherwise a similarity about the people at the party: they were men who had succeeded or were in the process of succeeding, and women who had kept pace with their husbands' advance. No one looked poor at the Ryders' party.

At ten o'clock there was food, smoked salmon rolled up and speared with cocktail sticks, chicken *vol-au-vent* or beef Stroganoff with rice, salads of different kinds, stilton and brie and Port Salut, and meringues. Wine flowed generously, white burgundy and red. Uncorked bottles were distributed on all convenient surfaces.

The dancing began when the first guests had eaten. To 'Love of the Loved', Polly danced with a man whose name she didn't know, who told her he was an estate agent with an office in Jermyn Street. He held her rather close for a man whose name she didn't know. He was older than Polly, about fifty, she reckoned, and smaller. He had a foxy moustache and foxy hair, and a round stomach, like a ball, which kept making itself felt. So did his knees.

In the room where the food was Gavin sat on the floor with Sylvia and Jack Meacock, and a woman in an orange trouser suit, with orange lips.

'Ralphie wouldn't come,' this woman said, balancing food in the hollow of a fork. 'He got cross with me last night.'

Gavin ate from his fingers a *vol-au-vent* full of chicken and mushrooms that had gone a little cold. Jack Meacock said nothing would hold him back from a party given by the Ryders. Or any party, he added, guffawing, given by anyone. Provided there was refreshment, his wife stipulated. Well naturally, Jack Meacock said.

'He wouldn't come,' the orange woman explained, 'because he thought I misbehaved in Olive Gramsmith's kitchen. A fortnight ago, for God's sake!'

Gavin calculated he'd had four glasses of gin and tonic. He corrected himself, remembering the one he'd had with the babysitter. He drank some wine. He wasn't entirely drunk, he said to himself, he hadn't turned a certain corner, but the corner was the next thing there was.

'If you want to kiss someone you kiss him,' the orange woman said. 'I mean, for God's sake, he'd no damn right to walk into Olive Gramsmith's kitchen. I didn't see you,' she said, looking closely at Gavin. 'You weren't there, were you?'

'We couldn't go.'

'You were there,' she said to the Meacocks. 'All over the place.'

'We certainly were!' Jack Meacock guffawed through his beef Stroganoff, scattering rice on to the coffee-coloured carpet.

'Hello,' their hostess said, and sat down on the carpet beside Gavin, with a plate of cheese.

'You mean you've been married twelve years?' the estate agent said to Polly. 'You don't look it.'

'I'm thirty-six.'

'What's your better half in? Is here, is he?'

'He directs films. Advertisements for TV. Yes, he's here.'

'That's mine.' He indicated with his head a woman who wasn't dancing, in lime-green. She was going through a bad patch, he said: depressions.

They danced to 'Sunporch Cha-Cha-Cha', Simon and Garfunkel.

'Feeling O.K.?' the estate agent enquired, and Polly said yes, not understanding what he meant. He propelled her towards the mantelpiece and took from it the glass of white burgundy Polly had left there. He offered it to her and when she'd taken a mouthful he drank some from it himself. They danced again. He clutched her more tightly with his arms and flattened a cheek against one of hers, rasping her with his moustache. With dead eyes, the woman in lime-green watched.

At other outer-suburb parties Polly had been through it all before. She escaped from the estate agent and was caught by Tim Gruffydd, who had already begun to sweat. After that another man whose name she didn't know danced with her, and then Malcolm Ryder did.

'You're edible tonight,' he whispered, the warm mush of his lips damping her ear. 'You're really edible, my love.'

'Share my cheese,' Sue offered in the other room, pressing brie on Gavin.

'I need more wine,' the woman in orange said, and Jack Meacock pushed himself up from the carpet. They all needed more wine, he pointed out. The orange woman predicted that the next day she'd have a hangover and Sylvia Meacock, a masculine-looking woman, said she'd never had a hangover in forty-eight years of steady drinking.

'You going to stay a while?' Sue said to Gavin. 'You and Polly going to stay?' She laughed, taking one of his hands because it was near to her. Since they'd known one another for such a long time it was quite in order for her to do that.

'Our babysitter's unknown,' Gavin explained. 'From the bogs of Ireland.'
The orange woman said the Irish were bloody.

'Jack's Irish, actually,' Sylvia Meacock said.

She went on talking about that, about her husband's childhood in County
Down, about an uncle of his who used to drink a bottle and a half of
whiskey a day – on top of four glasses of stout, with porridge and bread,
for his breakfast. If you drank at all you should drink steadily, she
said.

Gavin felt uneasy, because all the time Sylvia Meacock was talking
about the drinking habits of her husband's uncle in County Down Sue
clung on to his hand. She held it lightly, moving her fingers in a caress that
seemed to stray outside the realm of their long friendship. He was in love
with Polly: he thought that deliberately, arraying the sentiment in his mind
as a statement, seeing it suspended there. There was no one he'd ever
known whom he'd been fonder of than Polly, or whom he respected more,
or whom it would upset him more to hurt. Seventeen years ago he'd met
her in the kitchens of the Hotel Belvedere, Penzance, where they had both
gone to work for the summer. Five years later, having lived with one
another in a flat in the cheaper part of Maida Vale, they'd got married
because Polly wanted to have children. They'd moved to the outer suburb
because the children needed space and fresh air, and because the Ryders,
who'd lived on the floor above theirs in Maida Vale, had moved there a
year before.

'She'll be all right,' Sue said, returning to the subject of the Irish
babysitter. 'She could probably stay the night. She'd probably be delighted.'

'Oh, I don't think so, Sue.'

He imagined without difficulty the hands of men at the party unbuttoning
Polly's lace blouse, the hands of Jack Meacock or the sweaty hands of Tim
Gruffydd. He imagined Polly's clothes falling on to a bedroom carpet and
then her thin, lanky nakedness, her small breasts and the faint mark of her
appendix scar. 'Oh, I say!' she said in a way that wasn't like her when the
man, whoever he was, took off his own clothes. Without difficulty either,
Gavin imagined being in a room himself for the same purpose, with the
orange woman or Sylvia Meacock. He'd walk out again if he found himself
in a room with Sylvia Meacock and he'd rather be in a room with Sue than
with the orange woman. Because he wasn't quite sober, he had a flash of
panic when he thought of what might be revealed when the orange trouser-
suit fell to the floor: for a brief, disturbing moment he felt it was actually
happening, that in the bonhomie of drunkenness he'd somehow agreed to
the situation.

'Why don't we dance?' Sue suggested, and Gavin agreed.

'I think I'd like a drink,' Polly said to Philip Mulally, an executive with
Wolsey Menswear. He was a grey shadow of a man, not at all the kind to
permit himself or his wife to be a party to sexual games. He nodded
seriously when Polly interrupted their dance to say she'd like a drink. It

was time in any case, he revealed, that he and June were making a move homewards.

'I love you in that lace thing,' Malcolm Ryder whispered boringly as soon as Polly stopped dancing with Philip Mulally. He was standing waiting for her.

'I was saying to Philip I'd like a drink.'

'Of course you must have a drink. Come and quaff a brandy with me, Poll.' He took her by the hand and led her away from the dancers. The brandy was in his den, he said.

She shook her head, following him because she had no option. Above the noise of Cilla Black singing 'Anyone Who Had a Heart' she shouted at him that she'd prefer some more white burgundy, that she was actually feeling thirsty. But he didn't hear her, or didn't wish to. 'Ain't misbehaving,' the foxy estate agent mouthed at her as they passed him, standing on his own in the hall. It was an expression that was often used, without much significance attaching to it, at parties in the outer suburb.

'Evening, all,' Malcolm said in the room he called his den, closing the door behind Polly. The only light in the room was from a desk-lamp. In the shadows, stretched on a mock-leather sofa, a man and a woman were kissing one another. They parted in some embarrassment at their host's jocular greeting, revealing themselves, predictably, as a husband and another husband's wife.

'Carry on, folks,' Malcolm said.

He poured Polly some brandy even though she had again said that what she wanted was a glass of burgundy. The couple on the sofa got up and went away, giggling. The man told Malcolm he was an old bastard.

'Here you are,' Malcolm said, and then to Polly's distaste he placed his mushy lips on hers and exerted some pressure. The brandy glass was in her right hand, between them: had it not been there, she knew the embrace would have been more intimate. As it was, it was possible for both of them to pretend that what had occurred was purely an expression of Malcolm Ryder's friendship for her, a special little detour to show that for all these years it hadn't been just a case of two wives being friends and the husbands tagging along. Once, in 1965, they'd all gone to the Italian Adriatic together and quite often Malcolm had given her a kiss and a hug while telling her how edible she was. But somehow – perhaps because his lips hadn't been so mushy in the past – it was different now.

'Cheers!' he said, smiling at her in the dimness. For an unpleasant moment she thought he might lock the door. What on earth did you do if an old friend tried to rape you on a sofa in his den?

With every step they made together, the orange woman increased her entwinement of Oliver Gramsmith. The estate agent was dancing with June Mulally, both of them ignoring the gestures of June Mulally's husband, Philip, who was still anxious to move homewards. The

Thompsons, the Pedlars, the Stevensons, the Suttons, the Heeresmas and the Fultons were all maritally separated. Tim Gruffydd was clammily tightening his grasp of Olive Gramsmith, Sylvia Meacock's head lolled on the shoulder of a man called Thistlewine.

'Remember the Ritz?' Sue said to Gavin.

He did remember. It was a long time ago, years before they'd all gone together to the Italian Adriatic, when they'd just begun to live in Maida Vale, one flat above the other, none of them married. They'd gone to the Ritz because they couldn't afford it. The excuse had been Polly's birthday.

'March the twenty-fifth,' he said. '1961.' He could feel her breasts, like spikes because of the neat control of her brassière. He'd become too flabby, he thought, since March 25th, 1961.

'What fun it was!' With her dark, petite head on one side, she smiled up at him. 'Remember it all, Gavin?'

'Yes, I remember.'

'I wanted to sing that song and no one would let me. Polly was horrified.'

'Well, it was Polly's birthday.'

'And of course we couldn't have spoiled that.' She was still smiling up at him, her eyes twinkling, the tone of her voice as light as a feather. Yet the words sounded like a criticism, as though she were saying now – fourteen years later – that Polly had been a spoilsport, which at the time hadn't seemed so in the least. Her arms tightened around his waist. Her face disappeared as she sank her head against his chest. All he could see was the red band in her hair and the hair itself. She smelt of some pleasant scent. He liked the sharpness of her breasts. He wanted to stroke her head.

'Sue fancies old Gavin, you know,' Malcolm said in his den.

Polly laughed. He had put a hand on her thigh and the fingers were now slightly massaging the green velvet of her skirt and the flesh beneath it. To have asked him to take his hand away or to have pushed it away herself would have been too positive, too much a reflection of his serious mood rather than her own determinedly casual one. A thickness had crept into his voice. He looked much older than thirty-eight; he'd worn less well than Gavin.

'Let's go back to the party, Malcolm.' She stood up, dislodging his hand as though by accident.

'Let's have another drink.'

He was a solicitor now, with Parker, Hille and Harper. He had been, in fact, a solicitor when they'd all lived in the cheaper part of Maida Vale. He'd still played rugby for the Harlequins then. She and Gavin and Sue used to watch him on Saturday afternoons, in matches against the London clubs, Rosslyn Park and Blackheath, Richmond, London Welsh, London Irish, and all the others. Malcolm had been a towering wing three-quarter, with a turn of speed that was surprising in so large a man: people repeatedly said, even newspaper commentators, that he should play for England.

Polly was aware that it was a cliché to compare Malcolm as he had been with the blubbery, rather tedious Malcolm beside whom it was unwise to sit on a sofa. Naturally he wasn't the same. It was probably a tedious life being a solicitor with Parker, Hille and Harper day after day. He probably did his best to combat the blubberiness, and no man could help being bald. When he was completely sober, and wasn't at a party, he could still be quite funny and nice, hardly tedious at all.

'I've always fancied you, Poll,' he said. 'You know that.'

'Oh, nonsense, Malcolm!'

She took the brandy glass from him, holding it between them in case he should make another lurch. He began to talk about sex. He asked her if she'd read, a few years ago, about a couple in an aeroplane, total strangers, who had performed the sexual act in full view of the other passengers. He told her a story about Mick Jagger on an aeroplane, at the time when Mick Jagger was making journeys with Marianne Faithfull. He said the springing system of Green Line buses had the same kind of effect on him. Sylvia Meacock was lesbian, he said. Olive Gramsmith was a slapparat. Philip Mulally had once been seen hanging about Shepherd Market, looking at the tarts. He hadn't been faithful to Sue, he said, but Sue knew about it and now they were going to approach all that side of things in a different way. Polly knew about it, too, because Sue had told her: a woman in Parker, Hille and Harper had wanted Malcolm to divorce Sue, and there'd been, as well, less serious relationships between Malcolm and other women.

'*Since you went away the days grow long,*' sang Nat King Cole in the coffee-coloured sitting-room, '*and soon I'll hear ole winter's song.*' Some guests, in conversation, raised their voices above the voice of Nat King Cole. Others swayed to his rhythm. In the sitting-room and the hall and the room where the food had been laid out there was a fog of cigarette smoke and the warm smell of burgundy. Men sat together on the stairs, talking about the election of Margaret Thatcher as leader of the Conservative party. Women had gathered in the kitchen and seemed quite happy there, with glasses of burgundy in their hands. In a bedroom the couple who had been surprised in Malcolm's den continued their embrace.

'So very good we were,' Sue said on the parquet dance-floor. She broke away from Gavin, seizing him by the hand as she did so. She led him across the room to a teak-faced cabinet that contained gramophone records. On top of it there was a gramophone and the tape-recorder that was relaying the music.

'Don't dare move,' she warned Gavin, releasing his hand in order to poke among the records. She found what she wanted and placed it on the turn-table of the gramophone. The music began just before she turned the tape-recorder off. A cracked female voice sang: '*That certain night, the night we met, there was magic abroad in the air . . .*'

'Listen to it,' Sue said, taking Gavin's hand again and drawing him on to the dancing area.

'*There were angels dining at the Ritz, and a nightingale sang in Berkeley Square.*'

The other dancers, who'd been taken aback by the abrupt change of tempo, slipped into the new rhythm. The two spiky breasts again depressed Gavin's stomach.

'Angels of a kind we were,' Sue said. 'And fallen angels now, Gavin? D'you think we've fallen?'

Once in New York and once in Liverpool he'd made love since his marriage, to other girls. Chance encounters they'd been, irrelevant and unimportant at the time and more so now. He had suffered from guilt immediately afterwards, but the guilt had faded, with both girls' names. He could remember their names if he tried: he once had, when suffering from a bout of indigestion in the night. He had remembered precisely their faces and their naked bodies and what each encounter had been like, but memories that required such effort hadn't seemed quite real. It would, of course, be different with Sue.

'Fancy Sue playing that,' her husband said, pausing outside the den with Polly. 'They've been talking about the Ritz, Poll.'

'Goodness!' With a vividness that was a welcome antidote to Malcolm's disclosure about the sex-life of his guests, the occasion at the Ritz returned to her. Malcolm said:

'It was my idea, you know. Old Gavin and I were boozing in the Hoop and he suddenly said, "It's Polly's birthday next week," and I said, "For God's sake! Let's all go down to the Ritz." '

'You had oysters, I remember.' She smiled at him, feeling better because they were no longer in the den, and stronger because of the brandy. Malcolm would have realized by now how she felt, he wouldn't pursue the matter.

'We weren't much more than kids.' He seized her hand in a way that might have been purely sentimental, as though he was inspired by the memory.

'My twenty-second birthday. What an extraordinary thing it was to do!'

In fact, it had been more than that. Sitting in the restaurant with people she liked, she'd thought it was the nicest thing that had ever happened to her on her birthday. It was absurd because none of them could afford it. It was absurd to go to the Ritz for a birthday treat: martinis in the Rivoli Bar because Malcolm said it was the thing, the gilt chairs and the ferns. But the absurdity hadn't mattered because in those days nothing much did. It was fun, they enjoyed being together, they had a lot to be happy about. Malcolm might yet play rugby for England. Gavin was about to make his breakthrough into films. Sue was pretty, and Polly that night felt beautiful. They had sat there carelessly laughing, while deferential waiters simulated the gaiety of their mood. They had drunk champagne because Malcolm said they must.

With Malcolm still holding her hand, she crossed the spacious hall of

Number Four Sandiway Crescent. People were beginning to leave. Malcolm released his hold of her in order to bid them goodbye.

She stood in the doorway of the sitting-room watching Gavin and Sue dancing. She lifted her brandy glass to her lips and drank from it calmly. Her oldest friend was attempting to seduce her husband, and for the first time in her life she disliked her. Had they still been at the Misses Summers' nursery school she would have run at her and hit her with her fists. Had they still been in Maida Vale or on holiday on the Italian Adriatic she would have shouted and made a fuss. Had they been laughing in the Ritz she'd have got up and walked out.

They saw her standing there, both of them almost in the same moment. Sue smiled at her and called across the coffee-coloured sitting-room, as though nothing untoward were happening, 'D'you think we've fallen, Polly?' Her voice was full of laughter, just like it had been that night. Her eyes still had their party gleam, which probably had been there too.

'Let's dance, Poll,' Malcolm said, putting his arms around her waist from behind.

It made it worse when he did that because she knew by the way he touched her that she was wrong: he didn't realize. He probably thought she'd enjoyed hearing all that stuff about Philip Mulally hanging about after prostitutes and Olive Gramsmith being a slapparat, whatever a slapparat was.

She finished the brandy in her glass and moved with him on to the parquet. What had happened was that the Ryders had had a conversation about all this. They'd said to one another that this was how they wished – since it was the first time – to make a sexual swap. Polly and Gavin were to be of assistance to their friends because a woman in Parker, Hille and Harper had wanted Malcolm to get a divorce and because there'd been other relationships. Malcolm and Sue were approaching all that side of things in a different way now, following the fashion in the outer suburb since the fashion worked wonders with wilting marriages.

'Estrella babysitting, is she?' Malcolm asked. 'All right if you're late, is she? You're not going to buzz off, Poll?'

'Estrella couldn't come. We had to get a girl from Problem.'

He suggested, as though the arrangement were a natural one and had been practised before, that he should drive her home when she wanted to go. He'd drive the babysitter from Problem home also. 'Old Gavin won't want to go,' he pronounced, trying to make it all sound like part of his duties as host. To Polly it sounded preposterous, but she didn't say so. She just smiled as she danced with him.

They'd made these plans quite soberly presumably, over breakfast or when there was nothing to watch on television, or in bed at night. They'd discussed the game that people played with car-keys or playing cards, or by drawing lots in other ways. They'd agreed that neither of them cared for the idea of taking a chance. 'Different,' Malcolm had probably quite casually said, 'if we got the Dillards.' Sue wouldn't have said anything then. She might have laughed, or got up to make tea if they were watching the television, or turned over and gone to sleep. On some other occasion she might have drifted the conversation towards the subject again and Malcolm would have known that she was interested. They would then have worked out a way of interesting their oldest friends. Dancing with Malcolm, Polly watched while Gavin's mouth descended to touch the top of Sue's head. He and Sue were hardly moving on the dance-floor.

'Well, that's fixed up then,' Malcolm said. He didn't want to dance any more. He wanted to know that it was fixed up, that he could return to his party for an hour or so, with something to look forward to. He would drive her home and Gavin would remain. At half-past one or two, when the men threw their car-keys on to the carpet and the blind-folded women each picked one out, Gavin and Sue would simply watch, not taking part. And when everyone went away Gavin and Sue would be alone with all the mess and the empty glasses. And she would be alone with Malcolm.

Polly smiled at him again, hoping he'd take the smile to mean that everything was fixed because she didn't want to go on dancing with him. If one of them had said, that night in the Ritz, that for a couple of hours after dinner they should change partners there'd have been a most unpleasant silence.

Malcolm patted her possessively on the hip. He squeezed her forearm and went away, murmuring that people might be short of drink. A man whom she didn't know, excessively drunk, took her over, informing her that he loved her. As she swayed around the room with him, she wanted to say to Sue and Malcolm and Gavin that yes, they had fallen. Of course Malcolm hadn't done his best to combat his blubberiness, of course he didn't make efforts. Malcolm was awful, and Sue was treacherous. When people asked Gavin if he made films why didn't he ever reply that the films he made were television commercials? She must have fallen herself, for it was clearly in the nature of things, but she couldn't see how.

'It's time we went home, Sue,' Gavin said.

'Of course it isn't, Gavin.'

'Polly –'

'You're nice, Gavin.'

He shook his head. He whispered to her, explaining that Polly wouldn't ever be a party to what was being suggested. He said that perhaps they could meet some time, for a drink or for lunch. He would like to, he said; he wanted to.

She smiled. That night in the Ritz, she murmured, she hadn't wanted to be a blooming angel. 'I wanted you,' she murmured.

'That isn't true.' He said it harshly. He pushed her away from him, wrenching himself free of her arms. It shocked him that she had gone so far, spoiling the past when there wasn't any need to. 'You shouldn't have said that, Sue.'

'You're sentimental.'

He looked around for Polly and saw her dancing with a man who could hardly stand up. Some of the lights in the room had been switched off and the volume of the tape-recorder had been turned down. Simon and Garfunkel were whispering about Mrs Robinson. A woman laughed shrilly, kicking her shoes across the parquet.

Sue wasn't smiling any more. The face that looked up at him through the gloom was hard and accusing. Lines that weren't laughter-lines had developed round the eyes: lines of tension and probably fury, Gavin reckoned. He could see her thinking: he had led her on, he had kissed the top of her head. Now he was suggesting lunch some time, dealing out the future to her when the present was what mattered. He felt he'd been rude.

'I'm sorry, Sue.'

They were standing in the other dancers' way. He wanted to dance again himself, to feel the warmth of her small body, to feel her hands, and to smell her hair, and to bend down and touch it again with his lips. He turned away and extricated Polly from the grasp of the drunk who had claimed to love her. 'It's time to go home,' he said angrily.

'You're never going, old Gavin,' Malcolm protested in the hall. 'I'll run Poll home, you know.'

'I'll run her home myself.'

In the car Polly asked what had happened, but he didn't tell her the truth. He said he'd been rude to Sue because Sue had said something appalling about one of her guests and that for some silly reason he'd taken exception to it.

Polly did not believe him. He was making an excuse, but it didn't matter. He had rejected the game the Ryders had wanted to play and he had rejected it for her sake. He had stood by her and shown his respect for her, even though he had wanted to play the game himself. In the car she laid her head against the side of his shoulder. She thanked him, without specifying what she was grateful for.

'I feel terrible about being rude to Sue,' he said.

He stopped the car outside their house. The light was burning in the sitting-room window. The babysitter would be half asleep. Everything was as it should be.

'I'd no right to be rude,' Gavin said, still in the car.

'Sue'll understand.'

'I don't know that she will.'

She let the silence gather, hoping he'd break it by sighing or saying he'd telephone and apologize tomorrow, or simply saying he'd wait in the car for the babysitter. But he didn't sigh and he didn't speak.

'You could go back,' she said calmly, in the end, 'and say you're sorry. When you've driven the babysitter home.'

He didn't reply. He sat gloomily staring at the steering-wheel. She thought he began to shake his head, but she wasn't sure. Then he said:

'Yes, perhaps I should.'

They left the car and walked together on the short paved path that led to their hall-door. She said that what she felt like was a cup of tea, and then thought how dull that sounded.

'Am I dull, Gavin?' she asked, whispering in case the words somehow carried in to the babysitter. Her calmness deserted her for a moment. 'Am I?' she repeated, not whispering any more, not caring about the babysitter.

'Of course you're not dull. Darling, of course you aren't.'

'Not to want to stay? Not to want to go darting into beds with people?'

'Oh, don't be silly, Polly. They're all dull except you, darling. Every single one of them.'

He put his arms around her and kissed her, and she knew that he believed what he was saying. He believed she hadn't fallen as he and the Ryders had, that middle age had dealt no awful blows. In a way that seemed true to Polly, for it had often occurred to her that she, more than the other three, had survived the outer suburb. She was aware of pretences but could not pretend herself. She knew every time they walked into the local Tonino's that the local Tonino's was just an Italian joke, a sham compared with the reality of the original in Greek Street. She knew the party they'd just been to was a squalid little mess. She knew that when Gavin enthused about a fifteen-second commercial for soap his enthusiasm was no cause for celebration. She knew the suburb for what it was, its Volvos and Vauxhalls, its paved paths in unfenced front gardens, its crescents and avenues and immature trees, and the games its people played.

'All right, Polly?' he said, his arms still about her, with tenderness in his voice.

'Yes, of course.' She wanted to thank him again, and to explain that she was thanking him because he had respected her feelings and stood by her. She wanted to ask him not to go back and apologize, but she couldn't bring herself to do that because the request seemed fussy. 'Yes, of course I'm all right,' she said.

In the sitting-room the babysitter woke up and reported that the children had been as good as gold. 'Not a blink out of either of them, Mrs Dillard.'

'I'll run you home,' Gavin said.

'Oh, it's miles and miles.'

'It's our fault for living in such a godforsaken suburb.'

'Well, it's terribly nice of you, sir.'

Polly paid her and asked her again what her name was because she'd forgotten. The girl repeated that it was Hannah McCarthy. She gave Polly her telephone number in case Estrella shouldn't be available on another occasion. She didn't at all mind coming out so far, she said.

When they'd gone Polly made tea in the kitchen. She placed the tea-pot and a cup and saucer on a tray and carried the tray upstairs to their bedroom. She was still the same as she'd always been, they would say to one another, lying there, her husband and her friend. They'd admire her for that, they'd share their guilt and their remorse. But they'd be wrong to say she was the same.

She took her clothes off and got into bed. The outer suburb was what it was, so was the shell of middle age: she didn't complain because it would be silly to complain when you were fed and clothed and comfortable, when your children were cared for and warm, when you were loved and respected. You couldn't forever weep with anger, or loudly deplore yourself and other people. You couldn't hit out with your fists as though you were back at the Misses Summers' nursery school in Putney. You couldn't forever laugh among the waiters at the Ritz just because it was fun to be there.

In bed she poured herself a cup of tea, telling herself that what had happened tonight – and what was probably happening now – was reasonable and even fair. She had rejected what was distasteful to her, he had stood by her and had respected her feelings: his unfaithfulness seemed his due. In her middle-age calmness that was how she felt. She couldn't help it.

It was how she had fallen, she said to herself, but all that sounded silly now.

Mrs Silly

Michael couldn't remember a time when his father had been there. There'd always been the flat where he and his mother lived, poky and cluttered even though his mother tried so. Every Saturday his father came to collect him. He remembered a blue car and then a greenish one. The latest one was white, an Alfa-Romeo.

Saturday with his father was the highlight of the week. Unlike his mother's flat, his father's house was spacious and nicely carpeted. There was Gillian, his father's wife, who never seemed in a hurry, who smiled and didn't waste time. Her smile was cool, which matched the way she dressed. Her voice was quiet and reliable: Michael couldn't imagine it ever becoming shrill or weepy or furious, or in any other way getting out of control. It was a nice voice, as nice as Gillian herself.

His father and Gillian had two little girls, twins of six, two years younger than Michael. They lived near Haslemere, in a half-timbered house in pretty wooded countryside. On Saturday mornings the drive from London took over an hour, but Michael never minded and on the way back he usually fell asleep. There was a room in the house that his father and Gillian had made his own, which the twins weren't allowed to enter in his absence. He had his Triang train circuit there, on a table that had been specially built into the wall for it.

It was in this house, one Saturday afternoon, that Michael's father brought up the subject of Elton Grange. 'You're nearly nine, you know,' his father said. 'It's high time, really, old chap.'

Elton Grange was a preparatory school in Wiltshire, which Michael's father had gone to himself. He'd mentioned it many times before and so had Michael's mother, but in Michael's mind it was a place that belonged to the distant future – with Radley, where his father had gone, also. He certainly knew that he wasn't going to stay at the primary school in Hammersmith for ever, and had always taken it for granted that he would move away from it when the rest of his class moved, at eleven. He felt, without actually being able to recall the relevant conversation, that his mother had quite definitely implied this. But it didn't work out like that. 'You should go in September,' his father said, and that was that.

'Oh, darling,' his mother murmured when the arrangements had all been made. 'Oh, Michael, I'll miss you.'

His father would pay the fees and his father would in future give him pocket money, over and above what his mother gave him. He'd like it at Elton Grange, his father promised. 'Oh yes, you'll like it,' his mother said too.

She was a woman of medium height, five foot four, with a round, plump face and plump arms and legs. There was a soft prettiness about her, about her light-blue eyes and her wide, simple mouth and her fair, rather fluffy hair. Her hands were always warm, as if expressing the warmth of her nature. She wept easily and often said she was silly to weep so. She talked a lot, getting carried away when she didn't watch herself: for this failing, too, she regularly said she was silly. 'Mrs Silly', she used to say when Michael was younger, condemning herself playfully for the two small follies she found it hard to control.

She worked as a secretary for an Indian, a Mr Ashaf, who had an office-stationery business. There was the shop – more of a warehouse, really – with stacks of swivel chairs and filing-cabinets on top of one another and green metal desks, and cartons containing continuation paper and top-copy foolscap and flimsy, and printed invoices. There were other cartons full of envelopes, and packets of paper-clips, drawing-pins and staples. The carbon-paper supplies were kept in the office behind the shop, where Michael's mother sat in front of a typewriter, typing invoices mainly. Mr Ashaf, a small wiry man, was always on his feet, moving between the shop and the office, keeping an eye on Michael's mother and on Dolores Welsh who looked after the retail side. Before she'd married, Michael's mother had been a secretary in the Wedgwood Centre, but returning to work at the time of her divorce she'd found it more convenient to work for Mr Ashaf since his premises were only five minutes away from where she and Michael lived. Mr Ashaf was happy to employ her on the kind of part-time basis that meant she could be at home every afternoon by the time Michael got in from school. During the holidays Mr Ashaf permitted her to take the typewriter to her flat, to come in every morning to collect what work there was and hand over what she'd done the day before. When this arrangement wasn't convenient, due to the nature of the work, Michael accompanied her to Mr Ashaf's premises and sat in the office with her or with Dolores Welsh in the shop. Mr Ashaf used occasionally to give him a sweet.

'Perhaps I'll change my job,' Michael's mother said brightly, a week before he was due to become a boarder at Elton Grange. 'I could maybe go back to the West End. Nice to have a few more pennies.' She was cheering herself up – he could tell by the way she looked at him. She packed his belongings carefully, giving him many instructions about looking after himself, about keeping himself warm and changing any clothes that got wet. 'Oh, darling,' she said at Paddington on the afternoon of his departure. 'Oh, darling, I'll miss you so!'

He would miss her, too. Although his father and Gillian were in every way more fun than his mother, it was his mother he loved. Although she fussed and was a nuisance sometimes, there was always the warmth, the cosiness of climbing into her bed on Sunday mornings or watching Magic Roundabout together. He was too big for Magic Roundabout now, or so he considered, and he rather thought he was too big to go on climbing into her bed. But the memories of all this cosiness had become part of his relationship with her.

She wept as they stood together on the platform. She held him close to her, pressing his head against her breast. 'Oh, darling!' she said. 'Oh, my darling.'

Her tears damped his face. She sniffed and sobbed, whispering that she didn't know what she'd do. 'Poor thing!' someone passing said. She blew her nose. She apologized to Michael, trying to smile. 'Remember where your envelopes are,' she said. She'd addressed and stamped a dozen envelopes for him so that he could write to her. She wanted him to write at once, just to say he'd arrived safely.

'And don't be homesick now,' she said, her own voice trembling again. 'Big boy, Michael.'

The train left her behind. He waved from the corridor window, and she gestured at him, indicating that he shouldn't lean out. But because of the distances between them he couldn't understand what the gesture meant. When the train stopped at Reading he found his writing-paper and envelopes in his overnight bag and began to write to her.

At Elton Grange he was in the lowest form, Miss Brooks's form. Miss Brooks, grey-haired at sixty, was the only woman on the teaching staff. She did not share the men's common-room but sat instead in the matrons' room, where she smoked Senior Service cigarettes between lessons. There was pale tobacco-tinged hair on her face and on Tuesday and Friday afternoons she wore jodhpurs, being in charge of the school's riding. Brookie she was known as.

The other women at Elton Grange were Sister, and the undermatron Miss Trenchard, the headmaster's wife Mrs Lyng, the lady cook Miss Arland, and the maids. Mrs Lyng was a stout woman, known among the boys as Outsize Dorothy, and Sister was thin and brisk. Miss Trenchard and Miss Arland were both under twenty-three, Miss Arland was pretty and Miss Trenchard wasn't. Miss Arland went about a lot with the history and geography master, Cocky Marshall, and Miss Trenchard was occasionally seen with the P.T. instructor, a Welshman, who was also in charge of the carpentry shop. Among the older boys Miss Trenchard was sometimes known as Tampax.

Twice a week Michael wrote to his mother, and on Sundays he wrote to his father as well. He told them that the headmaster was known to everyone as A.J.L. and he told them about the rules, how no boy in the three lower forms was permitted to be seen with his hands in his pockets and how no boy was permitted to run through A.J.L.'s garden. He said the food was awful because that was what everyone else said, although he quite liked it really.

At half-term his father and Gillian came. They stayed in the Grand, and Michael had lunch and tea there on the Saturday and on the Sunday, and just lunch on the Monday because they had to leave in the afternoon. He told them about his friends, Carson and Tichbourne, and his father suggested that next half-term Carson and Tichbourne might like to have lunch or tea at the Grand. 'Or maybe Swagger Thompson,' Michael said. Thompson's people lived in Kenya and his grandmother, with whom he spent the holidays, wasn't able to come at half-term. 'Hard up,' Michael said.

Tichbourne and Carson were in Michael's dormitory, and one other boy, called Andrews: they were all aged eight. At night, after lights out, they talked about most things: about their families and the houses they lived in and the other schools they'd been at. Carson told about the time he'd put stink-bombs under the chair-legs when people were coming to play bridge, and Andrews about the time he'd been caught, by a policeman, stealing strawberries.

'What's it like?' Andrews asked in the dormitory one night. 'What's it like, a divorce?'

'D'you see your mother?' Tichbourne asked, and Michael explained that it was his mother he lived with, not his father.

'Often wondered what it's like for the kids,' Andrews said. 'There's a woman in our village who's divorced. She ran off with another bloke, only the next thing was he ran off with someone else.'

'Who'd your mum run off with?' Carson asked.

'No one.'

'Your dad run off then?'

'Yes.'

His mother had told him that his father left her because they didn't get on any more. He hadn't left her because he knew Gillian. He hadn't met Gillian for years after that.

'D'you like her?' Andrews asked. 'Gillian?'

'She's all right. They've got twins now, my dad and Gillian. Girls.'

'I'd hate it if my mum and dad got divorced,' Tichbourne said.

'Mine quarrelled all last holidays,' Carson said, 'about having a room decorated.'

'Can't stand it when they quarrel,' Andrews said.

Intrigued by a situation that was strange to them, the other boys often asked after that about the divorce. How badly did people have to quarrel before they decided on one? Was Gillian different from Michael's mother? Did Michael's mother hate her? Did she hate his father?

'They never see one another,' Michael said. 'She's not like Gillian at all.'

At the end of the term the staff put on a show called Staff Laughs. Cocky Marshall was incarcerated all during one sketch in a wooden container that was meant to be a steam bath. Something had gone wrong with it. The steam was too hot and the catch had become jammed. Cocky Marshall was red in the face and nobody knew if he was putting it on or not until the end of the sketch, when he stepped out of the container in his underclothes. Mr Waydelin had to wear a kilt in another sketch and Miss Arland and Miss Trenchard were dressed up in rugby togs, with Cocky Marshall's and Mr Brine's scrum caps. The Reverend Green – mathematics and divinity – was enthusiastically applauded in his Mrs Wagstaffe sketch. A.J.L. did his magic, and as a grand finale the whole staff, including Miss Brooks, sang together, arm-in-arm, on the small stage. 'We're going home,' they sang. 'We're going home. We're on the way that leads to home. We've seen the good things and the bad and now we're absolutely mad. We're g-o-i-n-g home.' All the boys joined in the chorus, and that night in Michael's dormitory they ate Crunchie, Galaxy and Mars Bars and didn't wash their teeth afterwards. At half-past twelve the next day Michael's mother was waiting for him at Paddington.

At home, nothing was different. On Saturdays his father came and drove him away to the house near Haslemere. His mother talked about Dolores Welsh and Mr Ashaf. She hadn't returned to work in the West End. It was quite nice really, she said, at Mr Ashaf's.

Christmas came and went. His father gave him a new Triang locomotive and Gillian gave him a pogo-stick and the twins a magnet and a set of felt-pens. His mother decorated the flat and put fairy-lights on a small Christmas tree. She filled his stocking on Christmas Eve when he was asleep and the next day, after they'd had their Christmas dinner, she gave him a football and a glove puppet and a jigsaw of Windsor Castle. He gave her a brooch he'd bought in Woolworth's. On 14 January he returned to Elton Grange.

Nothing was different at Elton Grange either, except that Cocky Marshall had left. Nobody had known he was going to leave, and some boys said he had been sacked. But others denied that, claiming that he'd gone of his own accord, without giving the required term's notice. They said A.J.L. was livid.

Three weeks passed and then one morning Michael received a letter from his father saying that neither he nor Gillian would be able to come at half-term because he had to go to Tunisia on business and wanted to take Gillian with him. He sent some money to make up for the disappointment.

In a letter to his mother, not knowing what to say because nothing much was happening, Michael revealed that his father wouldn't be there at half-term. *Then I shall come*, his mother wrote back.

She stayed, not in the Grand, but in a boarding-house called Sans Souci, which had coloured gnomes fishing in a pond in the front garden, and a black gate with one hinge broken. They weren't able to have lunch there on the Saturday because the woman who ran it, Mrs Malone, didn't do lunches. They had lunch in the Copper Kettle, and since Mrs Malone didn't do teas either they had tea in the Copper Kettle as well. They walked around the town between lunch and tea, and after tea they sat together in his mother's bedroom until it was time to catch the bus back to school.

The next day she said she'd like to see over the school, so he brought her into the chapel, which once had been the gate-lodge, and into the classrooms and the gymnasium and the art-room and the changing-rooms. In the carpentry shop the P.T. instructor was making a cupboard. 'Who's that boy?' his mother whispered, unfortunately just loud enough for the P.T. instructor to hear. He smiled. Swagger Thompson, who was standing about doing nothing, giggled.

'But how could he be a boy?' Michael asked dismally, leading the way on the cinder path that ran around the cricket pitch. 'Boys at Elton only go up to thirteen and a half.'

'Oh dear, of course,' his mother said. She began to talk of other things. She spoke quickly. Dolores Welsh, she thought, was going to get married, Mr Ashaf had wrenched his arm. She'd spoken to the landlord about the damp that kept coming in the bathroom, but the landlord had said that to cure it would mean a major upheaval for them.

All the time she was speaking, while they walked slowly on the cinder path, he kept thinking about the P.T. instructor, unable to understand how his mother could ever have mistaken him for a boy. It was a cold morning and rather damp, not raining heavily, not even drizzling, but misty in a particularly wetting kind of way. He wondered where they were going to go for lunch, since the woman in the Copper Kettle had said yesterday that the café didn't open on Sundays.

'Perhaps we could go and look at the dormitories?' his mother suggested when they came to the end of the cinder path.

He didn't want to, but for some reason he felt shy about saying so. If he said he didn't want to show her the dormitories, she'd ask him why and he wouldn't know what to say because he didn't know himself.

'All right,' he said.

They walked through the dank mist, back to the school buildings, which were mostly of red brick, some with a straggle of Virginia creeper on them. The new classrooms, presented a year ago by the father of a boy who had left, were of pinker brick than the rest. The old classrooms had been nicer, Michael's father said: they'd once been the stables.

There were several entrances to the house itself. The main one, approached from the cricket pitch by crossing A.J.L.'s lawns and then crossing a large, almost circular gravel expanse, was grandiose in the early Victorian style. Stone pillars supported a wide gothic arch through which, in a sizeable vestibule, further pillars framed a heavy oak front door. There were croquet mallets and hoops in a wooden box in this vestibule, and deck-chairs and two coloured golfing umbrellas. There was an elaborate wrought-iron scraper and a revolving brush for taking the mud from shoes and boots. On either side of the large hall-door there was a round window, composed of circular, lead-encased panes. 'Well, at least they haven't got rid of those,' Michael's father had said, for these circular windows were a feature that boys who had been to Elton Grange often recalled with affection.

The other entrances to the house were at the back and it was through one of these, leading her in from the quadrangle and the squat new classrooms, past the kitchens and the staff lavatory, that Michael directed his mother on their way to the dormitories. All the other places they'd visited had been outside the house itself – the gymnasium and the changing-rooms were converted outbuildings, the carpentry shop was a wooden shed tucked neatly out of the way beside the garages, the art-room was an old conservatory, and the classroom block stood on its own, forming two sides of the quadrangle.

'What a nice smell!' Michael's mother whispered as they passed the kitchens, as Michael pressed himself against the wall to let Miss Brooks, in her jodhpurs, go by. Miss Brooks was carrying a riding stick and had a cigarette going. She didn't smile at Michael, nor at Michael's mother.

They went up the back stairs and Michael hoped they wouldn't meet anyone else. All the boys, except the ones like Swagger Thompson whose people lived abroad, were out with their parents and usually the staff went away at half-term, if they possibly could. But A.J.L. and Outsize Dorothy never went away, nor did Sister, and Miss Trenchard had been there at prayers.

'How ever do you find your way through all these passages?' his mother whispered as he led her expertly towards his dormitory. He explained, in a low voice also, that you got used to the passages.

'Here it is,' he said, relieved to find that neither Sister nor Miss Trenchard was laying out clean towels. He closed the door behind them. 'That's my bed there,' he said.

He stood against the door with his ear cocked while she went to the bed and looked at it. She turned and smiled at him, her head a little on one side. She opened a locker and looked inside, but he explained that the locker she was looking in was Carson's. 'Where'd that nice rug come from?' she asked, and he said that he'd written to Gillian to say he'd been cold once or twice at night, and she'd sent him the rug immediately. 'Oh,' his mother said dispiritedly. 'Well, that was nice of Gillian,' she added.

She crossed to one of the windows and looked down over A.J.L.'s lawns to the chestnut trees that surrounded the playing-fields. It really was a beautiful place, she said.

She smiled at him again and he thought, what he'd never thought before, that her clothes were cheap-looking. Gillian's clothes were clothes you somehow didn't notice: it didn't occur to you to think they were cheap-looking or expensive. The women of Elton Grange all dressed differently, Outsize Dorothy in woollen things, Miss Brooks in suits, with a tie, and Sister and Miss Trenchard and Miss Arland always had white coats. The maids wore blue overalls most of the time but sometimes you saw them going home in the evenings in their ordinary clothes, which you never really thought about and certainly you never thought were cheap-looking.

'Really beautiful,' she said, still smiling, still at the window. She was wearing a headscarf and a maroon coat and another scarf at her neck. Her handbag was maroon also, but it was old, with something broken on one of the buckles: it was the handbag, he said to himself, that made you think she was cheaply dressed.

He left the door and went to her, taking her arm. He felt ashamed that he'd thought her clothes were cheap-looking. She'd been upset when he'd told her that the rug had been sent by Gillian. She'd been upset and he hadn't bothered.

'Oh, Mummy,' he said.

She hugged him to her, and when he looked up into her face he saw the mark of a tear on one of her cheeks. Her fluffy hair was sticking out a bit beneath the headscarf, her round, plump face was forcing itself to smile.

'I'm sorry,' he said.

'Sorry? Darling, there's no need.'

'I'm sorry you're left all alone there, Mummy.'

'Oh, but I'm not at all. I've got the office every day, and one of these days I really will see about going back to the West End. We've been awfully busy at the office, actually, masses to do.'

The sympathy he'd showed caused her to talk. Up to now – ever since they'd met the day before – she'd quite deliberately held herself back in this respect, knowing that to chatter on wouldn't be the thing at all. Yesterday she'd waited until she'd returned to Sans Souci before relaxing. She'd had a nice long chat with Mrs Malone on the landing, which unfortunately had been spoiled by a man in one of Mrs Malone's upper rooms poking his head out and asking for a bit of peace. 'Sorry about that,' she'd heard Mrs Malone saying to him later. 'Couldn't really stop her.' – a statement that had spoiled things even more. 'I'm ever so sorry,' she'd said quietly to Mrs Malone at breakfast.

'Let's go down now,' Michael said.

But his mother didn't hear this remark, engaged as she was upon making a series of remarks herself. She was no longer discreetly whispering, but chattering on with more abandon than she had even displayed on Mrs Malone's stairs the night before. A flush had spread over her cheeks and around her mouth and on the portion of her neck which could be seen above her scarf. Michael could see she was happy.

'We'll have to go to Dolores' wedding,' she said. 'On the eighth. The eighth of May, a Thursday I think it is. They're coming round actually,

Dolores and her young chap, Brian Haskins he's called. Mr Ashaf says he wouldn't trust him, but actually Dolores is no fool.'

'Let's go down now, Mum.'

She said she'd like to see the other dormitories. She'd like to see the senior dormitories, into one of which Michael would eventually be moving. She began to talk about Dolores Welsh and Brian Haskins again and then about Mrs Malone, and then about a woman Michael had never heard of before, a person called Peggy Urch.

He pointed out that the dormitories were called after imperial heroes. His was Drake, others were Raleigh, Nelson, Wellington, Marlborough and Clive. 'I think I'll be moving to Nelson,' Michael said. 'Or Marlborough. Depends.' But he knew she wasn't listening, he knew she hadn't taken in the fact that the dormitories were named like that. She was talking about Peggy Urch when he led her into Marlborough. Outsize Dorothy was there with Miss Trenchard, taking stuff out of Verschoyle's locker because Verschoyle had just gone to the sanatorium.

'Very nice person,' Michael's mother was saying. 'She's taken on the Redmans' flat – the one above us, you know.'

It seemed to Michael that his mother didn't see Outsize Dorothy and Miss Trenchard. It seemed to him for a moment that his mother didn't quite know where she was.

'Looking for me?' Outsize Dorothy said. She smiled and waddled towards them. She looked at Michael, waiting for him to explain who this visitor was. Miss Trenchard looked, too.

'It's my mother,' he said, aware that these words were inept and inelegant.

'I'm Mrs Lyng,' Outsize Dorothy said. She held out her hand and Michael's mother took it.

'The Matron,' she said. 'I've heard of you, Mrs Lyng.'

'Well actually,' Outsize Dorothy contradicted with a laugh, 'I'm the headmaster's wife.' All the flesh on her body wobbled when she laughed. Tichbourne said he knew for a fact she was twenty stone.

'What a lovely place you have, Mrs Lyng. I was just saying to Michael. What a view from the windows!'

Outsize Dorothy told Miss Trenchard to go on getting Verschoyle's things together, in a voice that implied that Miss Trenchard wasn't paid to stand about doing nothing in the dormitories. All the women staff – the maids and Sister and Miss Arland and Miss Trenchard – hated Outsize Dorothy because she'd expect them, even Sister, to go on rooting in a locker while she talked to a parent. She wouldn't in a million years say: 'This is Miss Trenchard, the undermatron.'

'Oh, I'm afraid we don't have much time for views at Elton,' Outsize Dorothy said. She was looking puzzled, and Michael imagined she was thinking that his mother was surely another woman, a thinner, smarter, quieter person. But then Outsize Dorothy wasn't clever, as she often light-heartedly said herself, and was probably saying to herself that she must be confusing one boy's mother with another.

'Dorothy!' a voice called out, a voice which Michael instantly and to his horror recognized as A.J.L.'s.

'We had such a view at home!' Michael's mother said. 'Such a gorgeous view!' She was referring to her own home, a rectory in Somerset somewhere. She'd often told Michael about the rectory and the view, and her parents, both dead now. Her father had received the call to the Church late in life: he'd been in the Customs and Excise before that.

'Here, dear,' Outsize Dorothy called out. 'In Marlborough.'

Michael knew he'd gone red in the face. His stomach felt hot also, the palms of his hands were clammy. He could hear the clatter of the headmaster's footsteps on the uncarpeted back stairs. He began to pray, asking for something to happen, anything at all, anything God could think of.

His mother was more animated than before. More fluffy hair had slipped out from beneath her headscarf, the flush had spread over a greater area of her face. She was talking about the lack of view from the flat where she and Michael lived in Hammersmith, and about Peggy Urch who'd come to live in the flat directly above them and whose view was better because she could see over the poplars.

'Hullo,' A.J.L. said, a stringy, sandy man, the opposite of Outsize Dorothy and in many ways the perfect complement. Tichbourne said he often imagined them naked in bed, A.J.L. winding his stringiness around her explosive bulk.

Hands were shaken again. 'Having a look round?' A.J.L. said. 'Staying at the Grand?'

Michael's mother said she wasn't staying at the Grand but at Sans Souci, did he know it? They'd been talking about views, she said, it was lovely to have a room with a view, she hoped Michael wasn't giving trouble, her husband of course – well, ex-husband now – had been to this school in his time, before going on to Radley. Michael would probably go to Radley too.

'Well, we hope so,' A.J.L. said, seizing the back of Michael's neck. 'Shown her the new classrooms, eh?'

'Yes, sir.'

'Shown her where we're going to have our swimming-pool?'

'Not yet, sir.'

'Well, then.'

His mother spoke of various diseases Michael had had, measles and whooping cough and chicken-pox, and of diseases he hadn't had, mumps in particular. Miss Trenchard was like a ghost, all in white, still sorting out the junk in Verschoyle's locker, not daring to say a word. She was crouched there, with her head inside the locker, listening to everything.

'Well, we mustn't keep you,' A.J.L. said, shaking hands again with Michael's mother. 'Always feel free to come.'

There was such finality about these statements, more in the headmaster's tone than in the words themselves, that Michael's mother was immediately silent. The statements had a physical effect on her, as though quite violently they had struck her across the face. When she spoke again it was in the whisper she had earlier employed.

'I'm sorry,' she said. 'I'm ever so sorry for going on so.'

A.J.L. and Outsize Dorothy laughed, pretending not to understand what she meant. Miss Trenchard would tell Miss Arland. Sister would hear and so would Brookie, and the P.T. Instructor would say that this same woman had imagined him to be one of the boys. Mr Waydelin would hear, and Square-jaw Simpson – Cocky Marshall's successor – and Mr Brine and the Reverend Green.

'I have enjoyed it,' Michael's mother whispered. 'So nice to meet you.'

He went before her down the back stairs. His face was still red. They passed by the staff lavatory and the kitchens, out on to the concrete quadrangle. It was still misty and cold.

'I bought things for lunch,' she said, and for an awful moment he thought that she'd want to eat them somewhere in the school or in the grounds – in the art-room or the cricket pavilion. 'We could have a picnic in my room,' she said.

They walked down the short drive, past the chapel that once had been the gate-lodge. They caught a bus after a wait of half an hour, during which she began to talk again, telling him more about Peggy Urch, who reminded her of another friend she'd had once, a Margy Bassett. In her room in Sans Souci she went on talking, spreading out on the bed triangles of cheese and tomatoes and rolls and biscuits and oranges. They sat in her room when they'd finished, eating Rollo. At six o'clock they caught a bus back to Elton Grange. She wept a little when she said goodbye.

Michael's mother did not, as it happened, ever arrive at Elton Grange at half-term again. There was no need for her to do so because his father and Gillian were always able to come themselves. For several terms he felt embarrassed in the presence of A.J.L. and Outsize Dorothy and Miss Trenchard, but no one at school mentioned the unfortunate visit, not even Swagger Thompson, who had so delightedly overheard her assuming the P.T. Instructor to be one of the boys. School continued as before and so did the holidays, Saturdays in Haslemere and the rest of the week in Hammersmith, news of Mr Ashaf and Dolores Welsh, now Dolores Haskins. Peggy Urch, the woman in the flat upstairs, often came down for a chat.

Often, too, Michael and his mother would sit together in the evenings on the sofa in front of the electric fire. She'd tell him about the rectory in Somerset and her father who had received the call to the Church late in his life, who'd been in the Customs and Excise. She'd tell him about her own childhood, and even about the early days of her marriage.

Sometimes she wept a little, hardly at all, and he would take her arm on the sofa and she would smile and laugh. When they sat together on the sofa or went out together, to the cinema, or for a walk by the river or to the teashop called the Maids of Honour near Kew Gardens, Michael felt that he would never want to marry because he'd prefer to be with his mother. Even when she chatted on to some stranger in the Maids of Honour he felt he loved her: everything was different from the time she'd come to Elton Grange because away from Elton Grange things didn't matter in the same way.

Then something unpleasant threatened. During his last term at Elton Grange Michael was to be confirmed. 'Oh, but of course I must come,' his mother said.

It promised to be worse than the previous occasion. After the service you were meant to bring your parents in to tea in the Great Hall and see that they had a cup of tea and sandwiches and cakes. You had to introduce them to the Bishop of Bath and Wells. Michael imagined all that. In bed at night he imagined his father and Gillian looking very smart, his father chatting easily to Mr Brine, Gillian smiling at Outsize Dorothy, and his mother's hair fluffing out from beneath her headscarf. He imagined his mother and his father and Gillian having to sit together in a pew in chapel, as naturally they'd be expected to, being members of the same party.

'There's no need to,' he said in the flat in Hammersmith. 'There's really no need to, Mum.'

She didn't mention his father and Gillian, although he'd repeatedly said that they'd be there. It was as if she didn't want to think about them, as if she was deliberately pretending that they'd decided not to attend. She'd stay in Sans Souci again, she said. They'd have a picnic in her room, since the newly confirmed were to be excused school tea on the evening of the service. 'Dinner at the Grand, old chap,' his father said. 'Bring Tichbourne if you want to.'

Michael returned to Elton Grange at the end of the Easter holidays, leaving his mother in a state of high excitement at Paddington Station because she'd be seeing him again within five weeks. He thought he might invent an illness a day or two before the confirmation, or say at the last moment that he had doubts. In fact, he did hint to the Reverend Green that he wasn't certain about being quite ready for the occasion, but the Reverend Green sharply told him not to be silly. Every time he went down on his knees at the end of a session with the Reverend Green he prayed that God might come to his rescue. But God did not, and all during the night before the confirmation service he lay awake. It wasn't just because she was weepy and embarrassing, he thought: it was because she dressed in that cheap way, it was because she was common, with a common voice that wasn't at all like Gillian's or Mrs Tichbourne's or Mrs Carson's or even Outsize Dorothy's. He couldn't prevent these thoughts from occurring. Why couldn't she do something about her fluffy hair? Why did she have to gabble like that? 'I think I have a temperature,' he said in the morning, but when Sister took it it was only 98.

Before the service the other candidates waited outside the chapel to greet their parents and godparents, but Michael went into the chapel early and took up a devout position. Through his fingers he saw the Reverend Green lighting the candles and preparing the altar. Occasionally, the Reverend Green glanced at Michael, somewhat suspiciously.

'Defend, O Lord, this Thy child,' said the Bishop of Bath and Wells, and when Michael walked back to his seat he kept his head down, not wanting to see his parents and Gillian. They sang Hymn 459. 'My God, accept,' sang Michael, 'my heart this day.'

He walked with Swagger Thompson down the aisle, still with his eyes down. 'Fantastic,' said Swagger Thompson outside the chapel, for want of anything better to say. 'Bloody fantastic.' They waited for the congregation to come out.

Michael had godparents, but his father had said that they wouldn't be able to attend. His godmother had sent him a prayer-book.

'Well done,' his father said. 'Well done, Mike.'

'What lovely singing!' Gillian murmured. She was wearing a white dress with a collar that was slightly turned up, and a white wide-rimmed hat. On the gravel outside the chapel she put on dark glasses against the afternoon sun.

'Your mother's here somewhere,' his father said. 'You'd better see to her, Mike.' He spoke quietly, with a hand resting for a moment on Michael's shoulder. 'We'll be all right,' he added.

Michael turned. She was standing alone, as he knew she would be. Unable to prevent himself, he wished she wouldn't always wear head-scarves. 'Oh, darling,' she said.

She took his hands and pulled him towards her. She kissed him, apologizing for the embrace but saying that it was a special occasion. She wished her father were alive, she said.

'Tea in the Great Hall,' A.J.L. was booming, and Outsize Dorothy was waddling about in flowered yellow, smiling at the faces of parents and godparents. 'Do come and have tea,' she gushed.

'Oh, I'd love a cup of tea,' Michael's mother whispered.

The crowd was moving through the sunshine, suited men, the Reverend Green in his cassock, the Bishop in crimson, women in their garden-party finery. They walked up the short drive from the chapel. They passed through the wide gothic arch that heralded the front door, through the vestibule where the croquet set was tidily in place and the deck-chairs neat against a wall. They entered what A.J.L. had years ago christened the Great Hall, where buttered buns and sandwiches and cakes and sausage-rolls were laid out on trestle tables. Miss Trenchard and Miss Arland were in charge of two silver-plated tea-urns.

'I'll get you something to eat,' Michael said to his mother, leaving her although he knew she didn't want to be left. 'Seems no time since I was getting done myself,' he heard his father saying to A.J.L.

Miss Arland poured a cup of tea for his mother and told him to offer her something to eat. He chose a plate of sausage-rolls. She smiled at him. 'Don't go away again,' she whispered.

But he had to go away again because he couldn't stand there holding the sausage-rolls. He darted back to the table and left the plate there, taking one for himself. When he returned to his mother she'd been joined by the Reverend Green and the Bishop.

The Bishop shook Michael's hand and said it had been a very great pleasure to confirm him.

'My father was in the Church,' Michael's mother said, and Michael knew that she wasn't going to stop now. He watched her struggling to hold the words back, crumbling the pastry of her sausage-roll beneath her fingers. The flush had come into her cheeks, there was a brightness in her eyes. The Bishop's face was kind: she couldn't help herself, when kindness like that was there.

'We really must be moving,' the Reverend Green said, but the Bishop only smiled, and on and on she went about her father and the call he'd received so late in life. 'I'm sure you knew him, my lord,' was one suggestion she made, and the Bishop kindly agreed that he probably had.

'Mrs Grainer would like to meet the Bishop,' Outsize Dorothy murmured to the Reverend Green. She looked at Michael's mother and Michael could see her remembering her and not caring for her.

'Well, if you'll excuse us,' the Reverend Green said, seizing the Bishop's arm.

'Oh Michael dear, isn't that a coincidence!'

There was happiness all over her face, bursting from her eyes, in her smile and her flushed cheeks and her fluffy hair. She turned to Mr and Mrs Tichbourne, who were talking to Mrs Carson, and said the Bishop had know her father, apparently quite well. She hadn't even been aware that it was to be this particular bishop today, it hadn't even occurred to her while she'd been at the confirmation service that such a coincidence could be possible. Her father had passed away fifteen years ago, he'd have been a contemporary of the Bishop's. 'He was in the Customs and Excise,' she said, 'before he received the call.'

They didn't turn away from her. They listened, putting in a word or two, about coincidences and the niceness of the Bishop. Tichbourne and Carson stood eating sandwiches, offering them to one another. Michael's face felt like a bonfire.

'We'll probably see you later,' Mr Tichbourne said, eventually edging his wife away. 'We're staying at the Grand.'

'Oh no, I'm at Sans Souci. Couldn't ever afford the Grand!' She laughed.

'Don't think we know the Sans Souci,' Mrs Tichbourne said.

'Darling, I'd love another cup of tea,' his mother said to Michael, and he went away to get her one, leaving her with Mrs Carson. When he returned she was referring to Peggy Urch.

It was then, while talking to Mrs Carson, that Michael's mother fell. Afterwards she said that she'd felt something slimy under one of her heels and had moved to rid herself of it. The next thing she knew she was lying on her back on the floor, soaked in tea.

Mrs Carson helped her to her feet. A.J.L. hovered solicitously. Outsize Dorothy picked up the cup and saucer.

'I'm quite all right,' Michael's mother kept repeating. 'There was something slippy on the floor, I'm quite all right.'

She was led to a chair by A.J.L. 'I think we'd best call on Sister,' he said. 'Just to be sure.'

But she insisted that she was all right, that there was no need to go bothering Sister. She was as white as a sheet.

Michael's father and Gillian came up to her and said they were sorry. Michael could see Tichbourne and Carson nudging one another, giggling. For a moment he thought of running away, hiding in the attics or something. Half a buttered bun had got stuck to the sleeve of his mother's maroon coat when she'd fallen. Her left leg was saturated with tea.

'We'll drive you into town,' his father said. 'Horrible thing to happen.'

'It's just my elbow,' his mother whispered. 'I came down on my elbow.'

Carson and Tichbourne would imitate it because Carson and Tichbourne imitated everything. They'd stand there, pretending to be holding a cup of tea, and suddenly they'd be lying flat on their backs. 'I think we'd best call on Sister,' Carson would say, imitating A.J.L.

His father and Gillian said goodbye to Outsize Dorothy and to A.J.L. His mother, reduced to humble silence again, seemed only to want to get away. In the car she didn't say anything at all and when they reached Sans Souci she didn't seem to expect Michael to go in with her. She left the car, whispering her thanks, a little colour gathering in her face again.

That evening Michael had dinner with Gillian and his father in the Grand. Tichbourne was there also, and Carson, and several other boys, all with their parents. 'I can drive a few of them back,' his father said, 'save everyone getting a car out.' He crossed the dining-room floor and spoke to Mr Tichbourne and Mr Carson and the father of a boy called Mallabedeely. Michael ate minestrone soup and chicken with peas and roast potatoes. Gillian told him what the twins had been up to and said his father was going to have a swimming-pool put in. His father returned to the table and announced that he'd arranged to drive everyone back at nine o'clock.

Eating his chicken, he imagined his mother at Sans Souci, sitting on the edge of the bed, probably having a cry. He imagined her bringing back to London the stuff she'd bought for a picnic in her room. She'd never refer to any of that, she'd never upbraid him for going to the Grand for dinner when she'd wanted him to be with her. She'd consider it just that she should be punished.

As they got into the car, his father said he'd drive round by Sans Souci so that Michael could run in for a minute. 'We're meant to be back by a quarter past,' Michael said quickly. 'I've said goodbye to her,' he added, which wasn't quite true.

It would perhaps have been different if Tichbourne and Carson hadn't been in the car. He'd have gone in and paused with her for a minute because he felt pity for her. But the unattractive façade of Sans Souci, the broken gate of the small front garden and the fishermen gnomes would have caused further nudging and giggling in his father's white Alfa-Romeo.

'You're sure now?' his father said. 'I'll get you there by a quarter past.'

'No, it's all right.'

She wouldn't be expecting him. She wouldn't even have unpacked the picnic she'd brought.

'Hey, was that your godmother?' Tichbourne asked in the dormitory. 'The one who copped it on the floor?'

He began to shake his head and then he paused and went on shaking it. An aunt, he said, some kind of aunt, he wasn't sure what the relationship was. He hadn't thought of saying that before, yet it seemed so simple, and so right and so natural, that a distant aunt should come to a confirmation service and not stay, like everyone else, in the Grand. 'God, it was funny,' Carson said, and Tichbourne did his imitation, and Michael laughed with his friends. He was grateful to them for assuming that such a person could not be his mother. A.J.L. and Outsize Dorothy and Miss Trenchard knew she was his mother, and so did the Reverend Green, but for the remainder of his time at Elton Grange none of these people would have cause to refer to the fact in public. And if by chance A.J.L. did happen to say in class tomorrow that he hoped his mother was all right after her fall, Michael would say afterwards that A.J.L. had got it all wrong.

In the dark, he whispered to her in his mind. He said he was sorry, he said he loved her better than anyone.

A Complicated Nature

At a party once Attridge overheard a woman saying he gave her the shivers. 'Vicious-tongued,' this woman, a Mrs de Paul, had said. 'Forked like a serpent's.'

It was true, and he admitted it to himself without apology, though 'sharp' was how he preferred to describe the quality the woman had referred to. He couldn't help it if his quick eye had a way of rooting out other people's defects and didn't particularly bother to search for virtues.

Sharp about other people, he was sharp about himself as well: confessing his own defects, he found his virtues tedious. He was kind and generous to the people he chose as his friends, and took it for granted that he should be. He was a tidy man, but took no credit for that since being tidy was part of his nature. He was meticulous about his dress, and he was cultured, being particularly keen on opera – especially the operas of Wagner – and on Velasquez. He had developed his own good taste, and was proud of the job he had made of it.

A man of fifty, with hair that had greyed and spectacles with fine, colourless rims, he was given to slimming, for the weight he had gained in middle age rounded his face and made it pinker than he cared for: vanity was a weakness in him.

Attridge had once been married. In 1952 his parents had died, his father in February and his mother in November. Attridge had been their only child and had always lived with them. Disliking – or so he then considered – the solitude their death left him in, he married in 1953 a girl called Bernice Golder, but this most unfortunate conjunction had lasted only three months. 'Nasty dry old thing,' his ex-wife had screamed at him on their honeymoon in Siena, and he had enraged her further by pointing out that nasty and dry he might be but old he wasn't. 'You were never young,' she had replied more calmly than before. 'Even as a child you must have been like dust.' That wasn't so, he tried to explain; the truth was that he had a complicated nature. But she didn't listen to him.

Attridge lived alone now, existing comfortably on profits from the shares his parents had left him. He occupied a flat in a block, doing all his own cooking and taking pride in the small dinner parties he gave. His flat was just as his good taste wished it to be. The bathroom was tiled with blue Italian tiles, his bedroom severe and male, the hall warmly rust. His sitting-room, he privately judged, reflected a part of himself that did not come into the open, a mysterious element that even he knew little about and could only guess at. He'd saved up for the Egyptian rugs, scarlet and black and brown, on the waxed oak boards. He'd bought the first one in 1959 and each year subsequently had contrived to put aside his January and February Anglo-American Telegraph dividends until the floor was covered. He'd bought the last one a year ago.

On the walls of the room there was pale blue hessian, a background for his four tiny Velasquez drawings, and for the Toulouse-Lautrec drawing and the Degas, and the two brown charcoal studies, school of Michelangelo. There was a sofa and a sofa-table, authenticated Sheraton, and a Regency table in marble and gold that he had almost made up his mind to get rid of, and some Staffordshire figures. There was drama in the decoration and arrangement of the room, a quite flamboyant drama that Attridge felt was related to the latent element in himself, part of his complicated nature.

'I'm hopeless in an emergency,' he said in this room one afternoon, speaking with off-putting asperity into his ivory-coloured telephone. A woman called Mrs Matara, who lived in the flat above his, appeared not to hear him. 'Something has gone wrong, you see,' she explained in an upset voice, adding that she'd have to come down. She then abruptly replaced the receiver.

It was an afternoon in late November. It was raining, and already – at half-past three – twilight had settled in. From a window of his sitting-room Attridge had been gazing at all this when his telephone rang. He'd been looking at the rain dismally falling and lights going on in other windows and at a man, five storeys down, sweeping sodden leaves from the concrete forecourt of the block of flats. When the phone rang he'd thought it might be his friend, old Mrs Harcourt-Egan. He and Mrs Harcourt-Egan were to go together to Persepolis in a fortnight's time and there were still some minor arrangements to be made, although the essential booking had naturally been completed long since. It had been a considerable surprise to hear himself addressed by name in a voice he had been quite unable to place. He'd greeted Mrs Matara once or twice in the lift and that was all: she and her husband had moved into the flats only a year ago.

'I do so apologize,' Mrs Matara said when he opened the door to her. Against his will he welcomed her into the hall and she, knowing the geography of the flat since it was the same as her own, made for the sitting-room. 'It's really terrible of me,' she said, 'only I honestly don't know where to turn.' She spoke in a rushed and agitated manner, and he sighed as he followed her, resolving to point out when she revealed what her trouble was that Chamberlain, the janitor, was employed to deal with tenants' difficulties. She was just the kind of woman to make a nuisance of herself with a neighbour, you could tell that by looking at her. It irritated him that he hadn't sized her up better when he'd met her in the lift.

She was a woman of about the same age as himself, he guessed, small and thin and black-haired, though the hair, he also guessed, was almost certainly dyed. He wondered if she might be Jewish, which would account for her emotional condition: she had a Jewish look, and the name was presumably foreign. Her husband, whom he had also only met in the lift, had a look about the eyes which Attridge now said to himself might well have been developed in the clothing business. Of Austrian origin, he hazarded, or possibly even Polish. Mrs Matara had an accent of some kind, although her English appeared otherwise to be perfect. She was not out of the top drawer, but then people of the Jewish race rarely were. His own ex-wife, Jewish also, had most certainly not been.

Mrs Matara sat on the edge of a chair he had bought for ninety guineas fifteen years ago. It was also certainly Sheraton, a high-back chair with slim arms in inlaid walnut. He'd had it resprung and upholstered and covered in striped pink, four different shades.

'A really ghastly thing,' Mrs Matara said, 'a terrible thing has happened in my flat, Mr Attridge.'

She'd fused the whole place. She couldn't turn a tap off. The garbage disposal unit had failed. His ex-wife had made a ridiculous fuss when, because of her own stupidity, she'd broken her electric hair-curling apparatus on their honeymoon. Grotesque she'd looked with the plastic objects in her hair; he'd been relieved that they didn't work.

'I really can't mend anything,' he said. 'Chamberlain is there for that, you know.'

She shook her head. She was like a small bird sitting there, a wren or an undersized sparrow. A Jewish sparrow, he said to himself, pleased with this analogy. She had a handkerchief between her fingers, a small piece of material, which she now raised to her face. She touched her eyes with it, one after the other. When she spoke again she said that a man had died in her flat.

'Good heavens!'

'It's terrible!' Mrs Matara cried. 'Oh, my God!'

He poured brandy from a Georgian decanter that Mrs Harcourt-Egan had given him three Christmases ago, after their trip to Sicily. She'd given him a pair, in appreciation of what she called his kindness on that holiday. The gesture had been far too generous: the decanters were family heirlooms, and he'd done so little for her in Sicily apart from reading *Northanger Abbey* aloud when she'd had her stomach upset.

The man, he guessed, was not Mr Matara. No woman would say that a man had died, meaning her husband. Attridge imagined that a window-cleaner had fallen off a step-ladder. Quite clearly, he saw in his mind's eye a step-ladder standing at a window and the body of a man in white overalls huddled on the ground. He even saw Mrs Matara bending over the body, attempting to establish its condition.

'Drink it all,' he said, placing the brandy glass in Mrs Matara's right hand, hoping as he did so that she wasn't going to drop it.

She didn't drop it. She drank the brandy and then, to Attridge's surprise, held out the glass in a clear request for more.

'Oh, if only you would,' she said as he poured it, and he realized that while he'd been pouring the first glass, while his mind had been wandering back to the occasion in Sicily and the gift of the decanters, his guest had made some demand of him.

'You could say he was a friend,' Mrs Matara said.

She went on talking. The man who had died had died of a heart attack. The presence of his body in her flat was an embarrassment. She told a story of a love affair that had begun six years ago. She went into details: she had met the man at a party given by people called Morton, the man had been married, what point was there in hurting a dead man's wife? what point was there in upsetting her own husband, when he need never know? She rose and crossed the room to the brandy decanter. The man, she said, had died in the bed that was her husband's as well as hers.

'I wouldn't have come here – oh God, I wouldn't have come here if I hadn't been desperate.' Her voice was shrill. She was nearly hysterical. The brandy had brought out two patches of brightness in her cheeks. Her eyes were watering again, but she did not now touch them with the handkerchief. The water ran, over the bright patches, trailing mascara and other make-up with it.

'I sat for hours,' she cried. 'Well, it seemed like hours. I sat there looking at him. We were both without a stitch, Mr Attridge.'

'Good heavens!'

'I didn't feel anything at all. I didn't love him, you know. All I felt was, Oh God, what a thing to happen!'

Attridge poured himself some brandy, feeling the need for it. She reminded him quite strongly of his ex-wife, not just because of the Jewish thing or the nuisance she was making of herself but because of the way she had so casually said they'd been without a stitch. In Siena on their honeymoon his ex-wife had constantly been flaunting her nakedness, striding about their bedroom. 'The trouble with you,' she'd said, 'you like your nudes on canvas.'

'You could say he was a friend,' Mrs Matara said again. She wanted him to come with her to her flat. She wanted him to help her dress the man. In the name of humanity, she was suggesting, they should falsify the location of death.

He shook his head, outraged and considerably repelled. The images in his mind were most unpleasant. There was the naked male body, dead on a bed. There was Mrs Matara and himself pulling the man's clothes on to his body, struggling because *rigor mortis* was setting in.

'Oh God, what can I do?' cried Mrs Matara.

'I think you should telephone a doctor, Mrs Matara.'

'Oh, what use is a doctor, for God's sake? The man's dead.'

'It's usual –'

'Look, one minute we're having lunch – an omelette, just as usual, and salad and Pouilly Fuissé – and the next minute the poor man's dead.'

'I thought you said –'

'Oh, you know what I mean. "Lovely, oh darling, lovely," he said, and then he collapsed. Well, I didn't know he'd collapsed. I mean, I didn't know he was dead. He collapsed just like he always collapses. Post-coital–'

'I'd rather not hear –'

'Oh, for Jesus' sake!' She was shouting. She was on her feet, again approaching the decanter. Her hair had fallen out of the pins that held it and was now dishevelled. Her lipstick was blurred, some of it even smeared her chin. She looked most unattractive, he considered.

'I cannot help you in this matter, Mrs Matara,' he said as firmly as he could. 'I can telephone a doctor –'

'Will you for God's sake stop about a doctor!'

'I cannot assist you with your friend, Mrs Matara.'

'All I want you to do is to help me put his clothes back on. He's too heavy, I can't do it myself –'

'I'm very sorry, Mrs Matara.'

'And slip him down here. The lift is only a few yards –'

'That's quite impossible.'

She went close to him, with her glass considerably replenished. She pushed her face at his in a way that he considered predatory. He was aware of the smell of her scent, and of another smell that he couldn't prevent himself from thinking must be the smell of sexual intercourse: he had read of this odour in a book by Ernest Hemingway.

'My husband and I are a contentedly married couple,' she said, with her lips so near to his that they almost touched. 'That man upstairs has a wife who doesn't know a thing, an innocent woman. Don't you understand such things, Mr Attridge? Don't you see what will happen if the dead body of my lover is discovered in my husband's bed? Can't you visualize the pain it'll cause?'

He moved away. It was a long time since he had felt so angry and yet he was determined to control his anger. The woman knew nothing of civilized behaviour or she wouldn't have come bursting into the privacy of a stranger like this, with preposterous and unlawful suggestions. The woman, for all he knew, was unbalanced.

'I'm sorry,' he said in what he hoped was an icy voice. 'I'm sorry, but for a start I do not see how you and your husband could possibly be a contentedly married couple.'

'I'm telling you we are. I'm telling you my lover was contentedly married also. Listen, Mr Attridge.' She approached him again, closing in on him like an animal. 'Listen, Mr Attridge; we met for physical reasons, once a week at lunchtime. For five years, ever since the Mortons' party, we've been meeting once a week, for an omelette and Pouilly Fuissé, and sex. It had nothing to do with our two marriages. But it will now: that woman will see her marriage as a failure now. She'll mourn it for the rest of her days, when she should be mourning her husband. I'll be divorced.'

'You should have thought of that –'

She hit him with her left hand. She hit him on the face, the palm of her hand stinging the pink, plump flesh.

'Mrs Matara!'

He had meant to shout her name, but instead his protest came from him in a shrill whisper. Since his honeymoon no one had struck him, and he recalled the fear he'd felt when he'd been struck then, in the bedroom in Siena. 'I could kill you,' his ex-wife had shouted at him. 'I'd kill you if you weren't dead already.'

'I must ask you to go, Mrs Matara,' he said in the same shrill whisper. He cleared his throat. 'At once,' he said, in a more successful voice.

She shook her head. She said he had no right to tell her what she should have thought of. She was upset as few women can ever be upset: in all decency and humanity it wasn't fair to say she should have thought of that. She cried out noisily in his sitting-room and he felt that he was in a nightmare. It had all the horror and absurdity and violence of a nightmare: the woman standing in front of him with water coming out of her eyes, drinking his brandy and hitting him.

She spoke softly then, not in her violent way. She placed the brandy glass on the marble surface of the Regency table and stood there with her head down. He knew she was still weeping even though he couldn't see her face and couldn't hear any noise coming from her. She whispered that she was sorry.

'Please forgive me, Mr Attridge. I'm very sorry.'

He nodded, implying that he accepted this apology. It was all very nasty, but for the woman it was naturally an upsetting thing to happen. He imagined, when a little time had passed, telling the story to Mrs Harcourt-Egan and to others, relating how a woman, to all intents and purposes a stranger to him, had telephoned him to say she was in need of assistance and then had come down from her flat with this awful tragedy to relate. He imagined himself describing Mrs Matara, how at first she'd seemed quite smart and then had become dishevelled, how she'd helped herself to his brandy and had suddenly struck him. He imagined Mrs Harcourt-Egan and others gasping when he said that. He seemed to see his own slight smile as he went on to say that the woman could not be blamed. He heard himself saying that the end of the matter was that Mrs Matara just went away.

But in fact Mrs Matara did not go away. Mrs Matara continued to stand, weeping quietly.

'I'm sorry too,' he said, feeling that the words, with the finality he'd slipped into them, would cause her to move to the door of the sitting-room.

'If you'd just help me,' she said, with her head still bent. 'Just to get his clothes on.'

He began to reply. He made a noise in his throat.

'I can't manage,' she said, 'on my own.'

She raised her head and looked across the room at him. Her face was blotched all over now, with make-up and tears. Her hair had fallen down a little more, and from where he stood Attridge thought he could see quite large areas of grey beneath the black. A rash of some kind, or it might have been flushing, had appeared on her neck.

'I wouldn't bother you,' she said, 'if I could manage on my own.' She would have telephoned a friend, she said, except there wouldn't be time for a friend to get to the block of flats. 'There's very little time, you see,' she said.

It was then, while she spoke those words, that Attridge felt the first hint of excitement. It was the same kind of excitement that he experienced just before the final curtain of *Tannhäuser*, or whenever, in the Uffizi, he looked upon Credi's Annunciation. Mrs Matara was a wretched, unattractive creature who had been conducting a typical hole-in-corner affair and had received her just rewards. It was hard to feel sorry for her, and yet for some reason it was harder not to. The man who had died had got off scot-free, leaving her to face the music miserably on her own. 'You're inhuman,' his ex-wife had said in Siena. 'You're incapable of love. Or sympathy, or anything else.' She'd stood there in her underclothes, taunting him.

'I'll manage,' Mrs Matara said, moving towards the door.

He did not move himself. She'd been so impatient, all the time in Siena. She didn't even want to sit in the square and watch the people. She'd been lethargic in the cathedral. All she'd ever wanted was to try again in bed. 'You don't like women,' she'd said, sitting up with a glass of Brolio in her hand, smoking a cigarette.

He followed Mrs Matara into the hall, and an image entered his mind of the dead man's wife. He saw her as Mrs Matara had described her, as an innocent woman who believed herself faithfully loved. He saw her as a woman with fair hair, in a garden, simply dressed. She had borne the children of the man who now lay obscenely dead, she had made a home for him and had entertained his tedious business friends, and now she was destined to suffer. It was a lie to say he didn't like women, it was absurd to say he was incapable of sympathy.

Once more he felt a hint of excitement. It was a confused feeling now, belonging as much in his body as in his mind. In a dim kind of way he seemed again to be telling the story to Mrs Harcourt-Egan or to someone else. Telling it, his voice was quiet. It spoke of the compassion he had suddenly felt for the small unattractive Jewish woman and for another woman, a total stranger whom he'd never even seen. 'A moment of truth,' his voice explained to Mrs Harcourt-Egan and others. 'I could not pass these women by.'

He knew it was true. The excitement he felt had to do with sympathy, and the compassion that had been engendered in it. His complicated nature worked in that way: there had to be drama, like the drama of a man dead in a bed, and the beauty of being unable to pass the women by, as real as the beauty of the Madonna of the Meadow. With her cigarette and her Brolio, his ex-wife wouldn't have understood that in a million years. In their bedroom in Siena she had expected something ordinary to take place, an act that rats performed.

Never in his entire life had Attridge felt as he felt now. It was the most extraordinary, and for all he knew the most important, occasion in his life. As though watching a play, he saw himself assisting the dead, naked man into his clothes. It would be enough to put his clothes on, no need to move the body from one flat to another, enough to move it from the bedroom. 'We put it in the lift and left it there,' his voice said, still telling the story. ' "No need," I said to her, "to involve my flat at all." She agreed; she had no option. The man became a man who'd had a heart attack in a lift. A travelling salesman, God knows who he was.'

The story was beautiful. It was extravagant and flamboyant, incredible almost, like all good art. Who really believed in the Madonna of the Meadow, until jolted by the genius of Bellini? *The Magic Flute* was an impossible occasion, until Mozart's music charged you like an electric current.

'Yes, Mr Attridge?'

He moved towards her, fearing to speak lest his voice emerged from him in the shrill whisper that had possessed it before. He nodded at Mrs Matara, agreeing in this way to assist her.

Hurrying through the hall and hurrying up the stairs because one flight of stairs was quicker than the lift, he felt the excitement continuing in his body. Actually it would be many months before he could tell Mrs Harcourt-Egan or anyone else about any of it. It seemed, for the moment at least, to be entirely private.

'What was he?' he asked on the stairs in a whisper.

'Was?'

'Professionally.' He was impatient, more urgent now than she. 'Salesman or something, was he?'

She shook her head. Her friend had been a dealer in antiques, she said.

Another Jew, he thought. But he was pleased because the man could have been on his way to see him, since dealers in antiques did sometimes visit him. Mrs Matara might have said to the man, at another party given by the Mortons or anywhere else you liked, that Mr Attridge, a collector of pictures and Staffordshire china, lived in the flat below hers. She could have said to Attridge that she knew a man who might have stuff that would interest him and then the man might have telephoned him, and he'd have said come round one afternoon. And in the lift the man collapsed and died.

She had her latchkey in her hand, about to insert it into the lock of her flat door. Her hand was shaking. Surprising himself, he gripped her arm, preventing it from completing the action with the key.

'Will you promise me,' he said, 'to move away from these flats? As soon as you conveniently can?'

'Of course, of course! How could I stay?'

'I'd find it awkward, meeting you about the place, Mrs Matara. Is that a bargain?'

'Yes, yes.'

She turned the key in the lock. They entered a hall that was of the exact proportions of Attridge's but different in other ways. It was a most unpleasant hall, he considered, with bell chimes in it, and two oil paintings that appeared to be the work of some emergent African, one being of negro children playing on crimson sand, the other of a negro girl with a baby at her breast.

'Oh, God!' Mrs Matara cried, turning suddenly, unable to proceed. She pushed herself at him, her sharp head embedding itself in his chest, her hands grasping the jacket of his grey suit.

'Don't worry,' he said, dragging his eyes away from the painting of the children on the crimson sand. One of her hands had ceased to grasp his jacket and had fallen into one of his. It was cold and had a fleshless feel.

'We have to do it,' he said, and for a second he saw himself again as he would see himself in retrospect: standing with the Jewish woman in her hall, holding her hand to comfort her.

While they still stood there, just as he was about to propel her forward, there was a noise.

'My God!' whispered Mrs Matara.

He knew she was thinking that her husband had returned, and he thought the same himself. Her husband had come back sooner than he usually did. He had found a corpse and was about to find his wife holding hands with a neighbour in the hall.

'Hey!' a voice said.

'Oh no!' cried Mrs Matara, rushing forward into the room that Attridge knew was her sitting-room.

There was the mumble of another voice, and then the sound of Mrs Matara's tears. It was a man's voice, but the man was not her husband: the atmosphere which came from the scene wasn't right for that.

'There now,' the other voice was saying in the sitting-room. 'There now, there now.'

The noise of Mrs Matara's weeping continued, and the man appeared at the door of the sitting-room. He was fully dressed, a sallow man, tall and black-haired, with a beard. He'd guessed what had happened, he said, as soon as he heard voices in the hall: he'd guessed that Mrs Matara had gone to get help. In an extremely casual way he said he was really quite all right, just a little groggy due to the silly blackout he'd had. Mrs Matara was a customer of his, he explained, he was in the antique business. 'I just passed out,' he said. He smiled at Attridge. He'd had a few silly blackouts recently and despite what his doctor said about there being nothing to worry about he'd have to be more careful. Really embarrassing, it was, plopping out in a client's sitting-room.

Mrs Matara appeared in the sitting-room doorway. She leaned against it, as though requiring its support. She giggled through her tears and the man spoke sharply to her, forgetting she was meant to be his client. He warned her against becoming hysterical.

'My God, you'd be hysterical,' Mrs Matara cried, 'if you'd been through all that kerfuffle.'

'Now, now –'

'For Christ's sake, I thought you were a goner. Didn't I?' she cried, addressing Attridge without looking at him and not waiting for him to reply. 'I rushed downstairs to this man here. I was in a frightful state. Wasn't I?'

'Yes.'

'We were going to put your clothes on and dump you in his flat.'

Attridge shook his head, endeavouring to imply that that was not accurate, that he'd never have agreed to the use of his flat for this purpose. But neither of them was paying any attention to him. The man was looking embarrassed, Mrs Matara was grim.

'You should damn well have told me if you were having blackouts.'

'I'm sorry,' the man said. 'I'm sorry you were troubled,' he said to Attridge. 'Please forgive Mrs Matara.'

'Forgive *you*, you mean!' she cried. 'Forgive you for being such a damn fool!'

'Do try to pull yourself together, Miriam.'

'I tell you, I thought you were dead.'

'Well, I'm not. I had a little blackout –'

'Oh, for Christ's sake, stop about your wretched blackout!'

The way she said that reminded Attridge very much of his ex-wife. He'd had a headache once, he remembered, and she'd protested in just the same impatient tone of voice, employing almost the same words. She'd married again, of course – a man called Saunders in ICI.

'At least be civil,' the man said to Mrs Matara.

They were two of the most unpleasant people Attridge had ever come across. It was a pity the man hadn't died. He'd run to fat and was oily, there was a shower of dandruff on his jacket. You could see his stomach straining his shirt, one of the shirt-buttons had actually given way.

'Well, thank you,' Mrs Matara said, approaching Attridge with her right hand held out. She said it gracelessly, as a duty. The same hand had struck him on the face and later had slipped for comfort into one of his. It was hard and cold when he shook it, with the same fleshless feel as before. 'We still have a secret,' Mrs Matara said. She smiled at him in her dutiful way, without displaying interest in him.

The man had opened the hall-door of the flat. He stood by it, smiling also, anxious for Attridge to go.

'This afternoon's a secret,' Mrs Matara murmured, dropping her eyes in a girlish pretence. 'All this,' she said, indicating her friend. 'I'm sorry I hit you.'

'Hit him?'

'When we were upset. Downstairs. I hit him.' She giggled, apparently unable to help herself.

'Great God!' The man giggled also.

'It doesn't matter,' Attridge said.

But it did matter. The secret she spoke of wasn't worth having because it was sordid and nothing else. It was hardly the kind of thing he'd wish to mull over in private, and certainly not the kind he'd wish to tell Mrs Harcourt-Egan or anyone else. Yet the other story might even have reached his ex-wife, it was not impossible. He imagined her hearing it, and her amazement that a man whom she'd once likened to dust had in the cause of compassion falsified the circumstances of a death. He couldn't imagine the man his ex-wife had married doing such a thing, or Mrs Matara's husband, or the dandruffy man who now stood by the door of the flat. Such men would have been frightened out of their wits.

'Goodbye,' she said.

'Goodbye,' the man said, smiling at the door.

Attridge wanted to say something. He wanted to linger for a moment longer and to mention his ex-wife. He wanted to tell them what he had never told another soul, that his ex-wife had done terrible things to him. He disliked all Jewish people, he wanted to say, because of his ex-wife and her lack of understanding. Marriage repelled him because of her. It was she who had made him vicious-tongued. It was she who had embittered him.

He looked from one face to the other. They would not understand and they would not be capable of making an effort, as he had when faced with the woman's predicament. He had always been a little on the cold side, he knew that well. But his ex-wife might have drawn on the other aspects of his nature and dispelled the coldness. Instead of displaying all that impatience, she might have cosseted him and accepted his complications. The love she sought would have come in its own good time, as sympathy and compassion had eventually come that afternoon. Warmth was buried deep in some people, he wanted to say to the two faces in the hall, but he knew that, like his ex-wife, the faces would not understand.

As he went he heard the click of the door behind him and imagined a hushed giggling in the hall. He would be feeling like a prince if the man had really died.

Teresa's Wedding

The remains of the wedding-cake was on top of the piano in Swanton's lounge-bar, beneath a framed advertisement for Power's whiskey. Chas Flynn, the best man, had opened two packets of confetti: it lay thickly on the remains of the wedding-cake, on the surface of the bar and the piano, on the table and the two small chairs that the lounge-bar contained, and on the tattered green and red linoleum.

The wedding guests, themselves covered in confetti, stood in groups. Father Hogan, who had conducted the service in the Church of the Immaculate Conception, stood with Mrs Atty, the mother of the bride, and Mrs Cornish, the mother of the bridegroom, and Mrs Tracy, a sister of Mrs Atty's.

Mrs Tracy was the stoutest of the three women, a farmer's widow who lived eight miles from the town. In spite of the jubilant nature of the occasion, she was dressed in black, a colour she had affected since the death of her husband three years ago. Mrs Atty, bespectacled, with her grey hair in a bun, wore a flowered dress – small yellow and blue blooms that blended easily with the confetti. Mrs Cornish was in pink, with a pink hat. Father Hogan, a big red-complexioned man, held a tumbler containing whiskey and water in equal measures; his companions sipped Winter's Tale sherry.

Artie Cornish, the bridegroom, drank stout with his friends Eddie Boland and Chas Flynn, who worked in the town's bacon factory, and Screw Doyle, so called because he served behind the counter in Phelan's hardware shop. Artie, who worked in a shop himself – Driscoll's Provisions and Bar – was a freckled man of twenty-eight, six years older than his bride. He was heavily built, his bulk encased now in a suit of navy-blue serge, similar to the suits that all the other men were wearing that morning in Swanton's lounge-bar. In the opinion of Mr Driscoll, his employer, he was a conscientious shopman, with a good memory for where commodities were kept on the shelves. Customers occasionally found him slow.

The fathers of the bride and bridegroom, Mr Atty and Mr Cornish, were talking about greyhounds, keeping close to the bar. They shared a feeling of unease, caused by being in the lounge-bar of Swanton's, with women present, on a Saturday morning. 'Bring us two more big ones,' Mr Cornish requested of Kevin, a youth behind the bar, hoping that this addition to his consumption of whiskey would relax matters. They wore white carnations in the button-holes of their suits, and stiff white collars which were reddening their necks. Unknown to one another, they shared the same thought: a wish that the bride and groom would soon decide to bring the occasion to an end by going to prepare themselves for their journey to Cork on the half-one bus. Mr Atty and Mr Cornish, bald-headed men of fifty-three and fifty-five, had it in mind to spend the remainder of the day in Swanton's lounge-bar, celebrating in their particular way the union of their children.

The bride, who had been Teresa Atty and was now Teresa Cornish, had a round, pretty face and black, pretty hair, and was a month and a half pregnant. She stood in the corner of the lounge with her friends, Philomena Morrissey and Kitty Roche, both of whom had been bridesmaids. All three of them were attired in their wedding finery, dresses they had feverishly worked on to get finished in time for the wedding. They planned to alter the dresses and have them dyed so that later on they could go to parties in them, even though parties were rare in the town.

'I hope you'll be happy, Teresa,' Kitty Roche whispered. 'I hope you'll be all right.' She couldn't help giggling, even though she didn't want to. She giggled because she'd drunk a glass of gin and Kia-Ora orange, which Screw Doyle had said would steady her. She'd been nervous in the church. She'd tripped twice on the walk down the aisle.

'You'll be marrying yourself one of these days,' Teresa whispered, her cheeks still glowing after the excitement of the ceremony. 'I hope you'll be happy too, Kit.'

But Kitty Roche, who was asthmatic, did not believe she'd ever marry. She'd be like Miss Levis, the Protestant woman on the Cork road, who'd never got married because of tuberculosis. Or old Hannah Flood, who had a bad hip. And it wasn't just that no one would want to be saddled with a diseased wife: there was also the fact that the asthma caused a recurrent skin complaint on her face and neck and hands.

Teresa and Philomena drank glasses of Babycham, and Kitty drank Kia-Ora with water instead of gin in it. They'd known each other all their lives. They'd been to the Presentation Nuns together, they'd taken First Communion together. Even when they'd left the Nuns, when Teresa had gone to work in the Medical Hall and Kitty Roche and Philomena in Keane's drapery, they'd continued to see each other almost every day.

'We'll think of you, Teresa,' Philomena said. 'We'll pray for you.' Philomena, plump and pale-haired, had every hope of marrying and had even planned her dress, in light lemony lace, with a Limerick veil. Twice in the last month she'd gone out with Des Foley the vet, and even if he was a few years older than he might be and had a car that smelt of cattle disinfectant, there was more to be said for Des Foley than for many another.

Teresa's two sisters, much older than Teresa, stood by the piano and the framed Power's advertisement, between the two windows of the lounge-bar. Agnes, in smart powder-blue, was tall and thin, the older of the two; Loretta, in brown, was small. Their own two marriages, eleven and nine years ago, had been consecrated by Father Hogan in the Church of the Immaculate Conception and celebrated afterwards in this same lounge-bar. Loretta had married a man who was no longer mentioned because he'd gone to England and had never come back. Agnes had married George Tobin, who was at present sitting outside the lounge-bar in a Ford Prefect, in charge of his and Agnes's three small children. The Tobins lived in Cork now, George being the manager of a shoe-shop there. Loretta lived with her parents, like an unmarried daughter again.

'Sickens you,' Agnes said. 'She's only a kid, marrying a goop like that. She'll be stuck in this dump of a town for ever.'

Loretta didn't say anything. It was well known that Agnes's own marriage had turned out well: George Tobin was a teetotaller and had no interest in either horses or greyhounds. From where she stood Loretta could see him through the window, sitting patiently in the Ford Prefect, reading a comic to his children. Loretta's marriage had not been consummated.

'Well, though I've said it before I'll say it again,' said Father Hogan. 'It's a great day for a mother.'

Mrs Atty and Mrs Cornish politely agreed, without speaking. Mrs Tracy smiled.

'And for an aunt too, Mrs Tracy. Naturally enough.'

Mrs Tracy smiled again. 'A great day,' she said.

'Ah, I'm happy for Teresa,' Father Hogan said. 'And for Artie, too, Mrs Cornish; naturally enough. Aren't they as fine a couple as ever stepped out of this town?'

'Are they leaving the town?' Mrs Tracy asked, confusion breaking in her face. 'I thought Artie was fixed in Driscoll's.'

'It's a manner of speaking, Mrs Tracy,' Father Hogan explained. 'It's a way of putting the thing. When I was marrying them this morning I looked down at their two faces and I said to myself, "Isn't it great God gave them life?" '

The three women looked across the lounge, at Teresa standing with her friends Philomena and Kitty Roche, and then at Artie, with Screw Doyle, Eddie Boland and Chas Flynn.

'He has a great career in front of him in Driscoll's,' Father Hogan pronounced. 'Will Teresa remain on in the Medical Hall, Mrs Atty?'

Mrs Atty replied that her daughter would remain for a while in the Medical Hall. It was Father Hogan who had persuaded Artie of his duty when Artie had hesitated. Mrs Atty and Teresa had gone to him for advice, he'd spoken to Artie and to Mr and Mrs Cornish, and the matter had naturally not been mentioned on either side since.

'Will I get you another glassful, Father?' enquired Mrs Tracy, holding out her hand for the priest's tumbler.

'Well, it isn't every day I'm honoured,' said Father Hogan with his smile, putting the tumbler into Mrs Tracy's hand.

At the bar Mr Atty and Mr Cornish drank steadily on. In their corner Teresa and her bridesmaids talked about weddings that had taken place in the Church of the Immaculate Conception in the past, how they had stood by the railings of the church when they were children, excited by the finery and the men in serge suits. Teresa's sisters whispered, Agnes continuing about the inadequacy of the man Teresa had just married. Loretta whispered without actually forming words. She wished her sister wouldn't go on so because she didn't want to think about any of it, about what had happened to Teresa, and what would happen to her again tonight, in a hotel in Cork. She'd fainted when it had happened to herself, when he'd come at her like a farm animal. She'd fought like a mad thing.

It was noisier in the lounge-bar than it had been. The voices of the bridegroom's friends were raised; behind the bar young Kevin had switched on the wireless. *Take my hand*, cooed a soft male voice, *take my whole life too.*

'Bedad, there'll be no holding you tonight, Artie,' Eddie Boland whispered thickly into the bridegroom's ear. He nudged Artie in the stomach with his elbow, spilling some Guinness. He laughed uproariously.

'We're following you in two cars,' Screw Doyle said. 'We'll be waiting in the double bed for you.' Screw Doyle laughed also, striking the floor repeatedly with his left foot, which was a habit of his when excited. At a late hour the night before he'd told Artie that once, after a dance, he'd spent an hour in a field with the girl whom Artie had agreed to marry. 'I had a great bloody ride of her,' he'd confided.

'I'll have a word with Teresa,' said Father Hogan, moving away from Teresa's mother, her aunt and Mrs Cornish. He did not, however, cross the lounge immediately, but paused by the bar, where Mr Cornish and Mr Atty were. He put his empty tumbler on the bar itself, and Mr Atty pushed it towards young Kevin, who at once refilled it.

'Well, it's a great day for a father,' said Father Hogan. 'Aren't they a tip-top credit to each other?'

'Who's that, Father?' enquired Mr Cornish, his eyes a little bleary, sweat hanging from his cheeks.

Father Hogan laughed. He put his tumbler on the bar again, and Mr Cornish pushed it towards young Kevin for another refill.

In their corner Philomena confided to Teresa and Kitty Roche that she wouldn't mind marrying Des Foley the vet. She'd had four glasses of Babycham. If he asked her this minute, she said, she'd probably say yes. 'Is Chas Flynn nice?' Kitty Roche asked, squinting across at him.

On the wireless Petula Clark was singing 'Downtown'. Eddie Boland was whistling 'Mother Macree'. 'Listen, Screw,' Artie said, keeping his voice low although it wasn't necessary. 'Is that true? Did you go into a field with Teresa?'

Loretta watched while George Tobin in his Ford Prefect turned a page of the comic he was reading to his children. Her sister's voice continued in its abuse of the town and its people, in particular the shopman who had got Teresa pregnant. Agnes hated the town and always had. She'd met George Tobin at a dance in Cork and had said to Loretta that in six months' time she'd be gone from the town for ever. Which was precisely what had happened, except that marriage had made her less nice that she'd been. She'd hated the town in a jolly way once, laughing over it. Now she hardly laughed at all.

'Look at him,' she was saying. 'I doubt he knows how to hold a knife and fork.'

Loretta ceased her observation of her sister's husband through the window and regarded Artie Cornish instead. She looked away from him immediately because his face, so quickly replacing the face of George Tobin, had caused in her mind a double image which now brutally persisted. She felt a sickness in her stomach, and closed her eyes and prayed. But the double image remained: George Tobin and Artie Cornish coming at her sisters like two farmyard animals and her sisters fighting to get away. 'Dear Jesus,' she whispered to herself. 'Dear Jesus, help me.'

'Sure it was only a bit of gas,' Screw Doyle assured Artie. 'Sure there was no harm done, Artie.'

In no way did Teresa love him. She had been aware of that when Father Hogan had arranged the marriage, and even before that, when she'd told her mother that she thought she was pregnant and had then mentioned Artie Cornish's name. Artie Cornish was much the same as his friends: you could be walking along a road with Screw Doyle or Artie Cornish and you could hardly tell the difference. There was nothing special about Artie Cornish, except that he always added up the figures twice when he was serving you in Driscoll's. There was nothing bad about him either, any more than there was anything bad about Eddie Boland or Chas Flynn or even Screw Doyle. She'd said privately to Father Hogan that she didn't love him or feel anything for him one way or the other: Father Hogan had replied that in the circumstances all that line of talk was irrelevant.

When she was at the Presentation Convent Teresa had imagined her wedding, and even the celebration in this very lounge-bar. She had imagined everything that had happened that morning, and the things that were happening still. She had imagined herself standing with her brides-maids as she was standing now, her mother and her aunt drinking sherry, Agnes and Loretta being there too, and other people, and music. Only the bridegroom had been mysterious, some faceless, bodiless presence, beyond imagination. From conversations she had had with Philomena and Kitty Roche, and with her sisters, she knew that they had imagined in a similar way. Yet Agnes had settled for George Tobin because George

Tobin was employed in Cork and could take her away from the town. Loretta, who had been married for a matter of weeks, was going to become a nun.

Artie ordered more bottles of stout from young Kevin. He didn't want to catch the half-one bus and have to sit beside her all the way to Cork. He didn't want to go to the Lee Hotel when they could just as easily have remained in the town, when he could just as easily have gone in to Driscoll's tomorrow and continued as before. It would have been different if Screw Doyle hadn't said he'd been in a field with her: you could pretend a bit on the bus, and in the hotel, just to make the whole thing go. You could pretend like you'd been pretending ever since Father Hogan had laid down the law, you could make the best of it like Father Hogan had said.

He handed a bottle of stout to Chas Flynn and one to Screw Doyle and another to Eddie Boland. He'd ask her about it on the bus. He'd repeat what Screw Doyle had said and ask her if it was true. For all he knew the child she was carrying was Screw Doyle's child and would be born with Screw Doyle's thin nose, and everyone in the town would know when they looked at it. His mother had told him when he was sixteen never to trust a girl, never to get involved, because he'd be caught in the end. He'd get caught because he was easy-going, because he didn't possess the smartness of Screw Doyle and some of the others. 'Sure, you might as well marry Teresa as anyone else,' his father had said after Father Hogan had called to see them about the matter. His mother had said things would never be the same between them again.

Eddie Boland sat down at the piano and played 'Mother Macree', causing Agnes and Loretta to move to the other side of the lounge-bar. In the motor-car outside the Tobin children asked their father what the music was for.

'God go with you, girl,' Father Hogan said to Teresa, motioning Kitty Roche and Philomena away. 'Isn't it a grand thing that's happened, Teresa?' His red-skinned face, with the shiny false teeth so evenly arrayed in it, was close to hers. For a moment she thought he might kiss her, which of course was ridiculous, Father Hogan kissing anyone, even at a wedding celebration.

'It's a great day for all of us, girl.'

When she'd told her mother, her mother said it made her feel sick in her stomach. Her father hit her on the side of the face. Agnes came down specially from Cork to try and sort the matter out. It was then that Loretta had first mentioned becoming a nun.

'I want to say two words,' said Father Hogan, still standing beside her, but now addressing everyone in the lounge-bar. 'Come over here alongside us, Artie. Is there a drop in everyone's glass?'

Artie moved across the lounge-bar, with his glass of stout. Mr Cornish told young Kevin to pour out a few more measures. Eddie Boland stopped playing the piano.

'It's only this,' said Father Hogan. 'I want us all to lift our glasses to Artie and Teresa. May God go with you, the pair of you,' he said, lifting his own glass.

'Health, wealth and happiness,' proclaimed Mr Cornish from the bar.

'And an early night,' shouted Screw Doyle. 'Don't forget to draw the curtains, Artie.'

They stood awkwardly, not holding hands, not even touching. Teresa watched while her mother drank the remains of her sherry, and while her aunt drank and Mrs Cornish drank. Agnes's face was disdainful, a calculated reply to the coarseness of Screw Doyle's remarks. Loretta was staring ahead of her, concentrating her mind on her novitiate. A quick flush passed over the roughened countenance of Kitty Roche. Philomena laughed, and all the men in the lounge-bar, except Father Hogan, laughed.

'That's sufficient of that talk,' Father Hogan said with contrived severity. 'May you meet happiness halfway,' he added, suitably altering his intonation. 'The pair of you, Artie and Teresa.'

Noise broke out again after that. Father Hogan shook hands with Teresa and then with Artie. He had a funeral at half-past three, he said: he'd better go and get his dinner inside him.

'Goodbye, Father,' Artie said. 'Thanks for doing the job.'

'God bless the pair of you,' said Father Hogan, and went away.

'We should be going for the bus,' Artie said to her. 'It wouldn't do to miss the old bus.'

'No, it wouldn't.'

'I'll see you down there. You'll have to change your clothes.'

'Yes.'

'I'll come the way I am.'

'You're fine the way you are, Artie.'

He looked at the stout in his glass and didn't raise his eyes from it when he spoke again. 'Did Screw Doyle take you into a field, Teresa?'

He hadn't meant to say it then. It was wrong to come out with it like that, in the lounge-bar, with the wedding-cake still there on the piano, and Teresa still in her wedding-dress, and confetti everywhere. He knew it was wrong even before the words came out; he knew that the stout had angered and befuddled him.

'Sorry,' he said. 'Sorry, Teresa.'

She shook her head. It didn't matter: it was only to be expected that a man you didn't love and who didn't love you would ask a question like that at your wedding celebration.

'Yes,' she said. 'Yes, he did.'

'He told me. I thought he was codding. I wanted to know.'

'It's your baby, Artie. The other thing was years ago.'

He looked at her. Her face was flushed, her eyes had tears in them.

'I had too much stout,' he said.

They stood where Father Hogan had left them, drawn away from their wedding guests. Not knowing where else to look, they looked together at Father Hogan's black back as he left the lounge-bar, and then at the perspiring, naked heads of Mr Cornish and Mr Atty by the bar.

At least they had no illusions, she thought. Nothing worse could happen than what had happened already, after Father Hogan had laid down the law. She wasn't going to get a shock like Loretta had got. She wasn't going to go sour like Agnes had gone when she'd discovered that it wasn't enough just to marry a man for a purpose, in order to escape from a town. Philomena was convincing herself that she'd fallen in love with an elderly vet, and if she got any encouragement Kitty Roche would convince herself that she was mad about anyone at all.

For a moment as Teresa stood there, the last moment before she left the lounge-bar, she felt that she and Artie might make some kind of marriage together because there was nothing that could be destroyed, no magic or anything else. He could ask her the question he had asked, while she stood there in her wedding dress: he could ask her and she could truthfully reply, because there was nothing special about the occasion, or the lounge-bar all covered in confetti.

Office Romances

'Oh no, I couldn't,' Angela said in the outer office. 'Really, Mr Spelle. Thank you, though.'

'Don't you drink then, Miss Hosford? Nary a drop at all?' He laughed at his own way of putting it. He thought of winking at her as he laughed, but decided against it: girls like this were sometimes scared out of their wits by a wink.

'No, it's not that, Mr Spelle –'

'It's just that it's a way of getting to know people. Everyone else'll be down in the Arms, you know.'

Hearing that, she changed her mind and quite eagerly put the grey plastic cover on her Remington International. She'd refused his invitation to have a drink because she'd been flustered when he'd come into the outer office with his right hand poked out for her to shake, introducing himself as Gordon Spelle. He hadn't said anything about the other people from the office being there: in a matter of seconds he'd made the whole thing sound romantic, a tête-à-tête with a total stranger. Any girl's reaction would be to say she couldn't.

'Won't be a moment, Mr Spelle,' she said. She picked up her handbag from the floor beside her chair and walked with it from the office. Behind her, she heard the office silence broken by a soft whistling: Gordon Spelle essaying 'Smoke Gets in Your Eyes'.

Angela had started at C.S. & E. at half-past nine that morning, having been interviewed a month ago by Miss Ivygale, her immediate employer. Miss Ivygale was a slender woman of fifty or thereabouts, her face meticulously made up. Her blue-grey hair was worked on daily by a hairdresser, a Mr Patric, whom twice that day she'd mentioned to Angela, deploring the fact that next March he was planning to leave the Elizabeth Salon. At C.S. & E. Miss Ivygale occupied an inner office that was more luxuriously appointed than the outer one where Angela sat with her filing cabinets and her Remington International. On the windowsill of the outer office Miss Ivygale's last secretary, whom she referred to as Sue, had left a Busy Lizzie in a blue-glazed pot. There was a calendar that showed Saturdays and Sundays in red, presented by the Michelin Tyre Company.

In a small lavatory Angela examined her face in the mirror over the wash-basin. She sighed at her complexion. Her eyes had a bulgy look because of her contact lenses. The optician had said the bulgy look would go when the lids became used to the contact lenses, but as far as she was concerned it never had. 'No, no, you're imagining it, Miss Hosford,' the optician had said when she'd gone back after a month to complain that the look was still there.

In the lavatory she touched one or two places on her cheeks with Pure Magic and powdered over it. She rubbed lipstick into her lips and then pressed a tissue between them. She ran a comb through her hair, which was fair, and fluffy because she'd washed it the night before: it was her best feature, she considered, a pretty shade, soft and naturally curly.

'I like your dress, Miss Hosford,' he said when she returned to the outer office. 'Fresh as a flower it looks.' He laughed at his own description of the blue-and-white dress she was wearing. The blue parts were flowers of a kind, he supposed, a type of blue geranium they appeared to be, with blue leaves sprouting out of blue stems. Extraordinary, the tasteless stuff a girl like this would sometimes wear.

'Thank you,' she said.

'We don't bother much with surnames at C.S. & E.,' he told her as they walked along a green-carpeted corridor to a lift. 'All right to call you Angela, Miss Hosford?'

'Oh, yes, of course.'

He closed the lift doors. He smiled at her. He was a tall, sleek man who had something the matter with his left eye, a kind of droop in the upper lid and a glazed look in the eye itself, a suggestion of blindness. Another oddness about him, she thought in the lift, was his rather old-fashioned suit. It was a pepper-coloured suit with a waistcoat, cut in an Edwardian style. His manners were old-fashioned too, and the way he spoke had a pedantic air to it that recalled the past: Edwardian again perhaps, she didn't know. It seemed right that he had whistled 'Smoke Gets in Your Eyes' rather than a current pop song.

'I suppose it's your first job, Angela?'

'Oh, heavens, no!'

'I'd say you were twenty.'

'Twenty-six, actually.'

He laughed. 'I'm thirty-eight myself.'

They left the lift and walked together through the elegant reception area of C.S. & E. When she'd walked through it for her interview Angela had been reminded of the lounge of a large, new hotel: there were sofas and armchairs covered in white ersatz leather, and steel-framed reproductions of paintings by Paul Klee on rust-coloured walls, and magazines on steel-topped tables. When Angela had come for her interview, and again when she'd arrived at C.S. & E. that morning, there'd been a beautiful black-haired girl sitting at the large reception desk, which was upholstered here and there in the same ersatz leather as the sofas and the armchairs. But at this time of the evening, five to six, the beautiful black-haired girl was not there.

'I'd really have said it was your first job,' he said when they reached the street. He smiled at her. 'Something about you.'

She knew what he meant. She was often taken to be younger than she was, it had something to do with being small: five foot one she was, with thin, small arms that she particularly disliked. And of course there was her complexion, which was a schoolgirl complexion in the real sense, since schoolgirls rather than adults tended to be bothered with pimples. 'Attack them from inside, Miss Hosford,' her doctor had advised. 'Avoid all sweets and chocolate, avoid cakes and biscuits with your coffee. Lots of lemon juice, fresh fruit, salads.' She ate lots of fruit and salads anyway, just in case she'd get fat, which would have been the last straw. She naturally never ate sweet things.

'Horrid being new,' he said. 'Like your first day at school.'

The street, fashionably situated just off Grosvenor Square, was busy with people impatient to be home: it was a cold night in November, not a night for loitering. Girls in suede boots or platform shoes had turned up the collars of their coats. Some carried bundles of letters which had been signed too late to catch the afternoon dispatch boys. In the harsh artificial light their faces were pale, sometimes garish with make-up: the light drew the worst out of girls who were pretty, and killed the subtleties of carefully-chosen lipstick and make-up shades. God alone knew, Angela said to herself, what it did to her. She sighed, experiencing the familiar feeling of her inferiority complex getting the upper hand.

'Hullo, Gordon,' a man in a black overcoat said to Gordon Spelle. The man had been walking behind them for some time, while Angela had been listening to Gordon Spelle going on about the first day he'd spent at school. Miserable beyond measure he'd been.

'God, it's chilly,' the man said, dropping into step with them and smiling at Angela.

'Angela Hosford,' Gordon Spelle said. 'She's come to work for Pam Ivygale.'

'Oh, Pam, dear Pam!' the man said. He laughed in much the same way as Gordon Spelle was given to laughing, or so it seemed to Angela. His black overcoat had a little rim of black fur on its collar. His hair was black also. His face in the distorting street-light had a purple tinge, and Angela guessed that in normal circumstances it was a reddish face.

'Tommy Blyth,' Gordon Spelle said.

They entered a public house at the corner of a street. It was warm there, and crowded, and quite attractively noisy. Fairy lights were draped on a Christmas tree just inside the door because Christmas was less than six weeks away. Men like Tommy Blyth, in overcoats with furred collars and with reddish faces, were standing by a coal fire with glasses in their hands. One of them had his right arm round the waist of C.S. & E.'s black-haired reception-ist

'What's your poison, Angela?' Gordon Spelle asked, and she said she'd like some sherry.

'Dry?'

'Oh, it doesn't matter – well, medium, actually.'

He didn't approach the bar but led her into a far corner and sat her down at a table. It was less crowded there and rather dimly lit. He said he wouldn't be a minute.

People were standing at the bar, animatedly talking. Some of the men had taken off their overcoats. All of them were wearing suits, most of them grey or blue but a few of a more extravagant shade, like Gordon Spelle's. Occasionally a particular man, older and stouter than his companions, laughed raucously, swaying backwards on his heels. On a bar-stool to this man's right, in a red wool dress with a chiffon scarf at her throat, sat Miss Ivygale. The red wool coat that had been hanging just inside the outer office door all day hung on the arm of the raucous man: Miss Ivygale, Angela deduced, was intent on staying a while, or at least as long as the man was agreeable to looking after her coat for her. 'You'll find it friendly at C.S. & E.,' Miss Ivygale had said. 'A generous firm.' Miss Ivygale looked as though she'd sat on her bar-stool every night for the past twenty-three years, which was the length of time she'd been at C.S. & E.

'Alec Hemp,' Gordon Spelle said, indicating the man who had Miss Ivygale's coat on his arm.

The name occurred on C.S. & E.'s stationery: *A. R. Hemp.* It was there with other names, all of them in discreet italics, strung out along the bottom of the writing paper that had *C.S. & E.* and the address at the top: *S. P. Bakewell, T. P. Cooke, N. N. E. Govier, I. D. Jackson, A. F. Norris, P. Onniman, A. R. Hemp,* the directors of the C.S. & E. board.

'That's been going on for years,' Gordon Spelle said. He handed her her sherry and placed on the table in front of him a glass of gin and Britvic orange juice. His droopy eye had closed, as if tired. His other, all on its own, looked a little beady.

'Sorry?'

'Pam Ivygale and Alec Hemp.'

'Oh.'

'It's why she never married anyone else.'

'I see.'

Miss Ivygale's brisk manner in the office and her efficient probing when she'd interviewed Angela had given Angela the impression that she lived entirely for her work. There was no hint of a private life about Miss Ivygale, and certainly no hint of any love affair beyond a love affair with C.S. & E.

'Alec,' Gordon Spelle said, 'has a wife and four children in Brighton.'

'I see.'

'Office romance.' His droopy eye opened and gazed bleakly at her, contrasting oddly with the busyness of the other eye. He said it was disgraceful that all this should be so, that a woman should be messed up the way Mr Hemp for twenty-three years had messed up Miss Ivygale. Everyone knew, he said, that Alec Hemp had no intention of divorcing his wife: he was stringing Miss Ivygale along. 'Mind you, though,' he added, 'she's tricky.'

'She seems very nice –'

'Oh, Pam's all right. Now, tell me all about yourself.'

Angela lived in a flat with two other girls, a ground-floor flat in what had once been a private house in Putney. She'd lived there for three years, and before that she'd lived in a similar flat in another part of Putney, and before that in a hostel. Every six or seven weeks she went home for the weekend, to her parents in Exeter, Number 4 Carhampton Road. When she'd qualified as a shorthand typist at the City Commercial College in Exeter the College had found her a position in the offices of a firm that manufactured laminates. Three years later, after some months' discussion and argument with her parents, she'd moved to London, to the offices of a firm that imported and marketed German wine. From there, she'd moved to the firm called C.S. & E.

'You can hear it in your voice,' Gordon Spelle said. 'Exeter and all that.'

She laughed. 'I thought I'd lost it.'

'It's nice, a touch of the West Countries.'

The laminates firm had been a dull one, or at least a dull one for a girl to work in. But her parents hadn't understood that. Her parents, whom she liked and respected very much, had been frightened by the idea of her going to London, where there was loose living, so other parents had told them, and drinking and drugs, and girls spending every penny they had on clothes and rarely eating a decent meal. The German wine firm had turned out to be a dull place for a girl to work in too, or so at least it seemed after a few years. Often, though, while finding it dull, Angela had felt that it suited her. With her poor complexion and her bulging contact lenses and her small, thin arms, it was a place to crouch away in. Besides herself, two elderly women were employed in the office, and there was Mr Franklin and Mr Snyder, elderly also. Economy was practised in the office, the windows seemed always to be dusty, electric-light bulbs were of a low wattage. On the mornings when a new pimple cruelly erupted on her neck or one of her cheeks, Angela had hurried from bus to tube and was glad when she reached the dingy office of the wine firm and lost herself in its shadows. Then a girl in the flat introduced her to Pure Magic, so good at disguising imperfections of the skin. But although it did not, as in an advertisement, change Angela's life and could do nothing at all for her thin arms, it did enough to draw her from the dinginess of the wine firm. A girl in the flat heard of the vacancy with Miss Ivygale at C.S. & E. and, not feeling like a change herself, persuaded Angela to apply for it. The shared opinion of the girls in the flat was that Angela needed drawing out. They liked her and were sorry for her: no joke at all, they often said to one another, to have an inferiority complex like Angela's. The inferiority complex caused nerviness in her, one of them diagnosed, and the nerviness caused her bad complexion. In actual fact, her figure and her arms were perfectly all right, and her hair was really pretty the way it curled. Now that she'd at last stopped wearing spectacles she really looked quite presentable, even if her eyes did tend to bulge a little.

'Oh, you'll like it at C.S. & E.,' Gordon Spelle said. 'It's really friendly, you know. Sincerely so.'

He insisted on buying her another drink and while he was at the bar she wondered when, or if, she was going to meet the people he'd mentioned, the other employees of C.S. & E. Miss Ivygale had narrowed her eyes in her direction and then had looked away, as if she couldn't quite place her. The black-haired receptionist had naturally not remembered her face when she'd come into the bar with the two men. The only person Gordon Spelle had so far introduced her to was the man called Tommy Blyth, who had joined the group around the fire and was holding the hand of a girl.

'It's the C.S. & E. pub,' Gordon Spelle said when he returned with the drinks. 'There isn't a soul here who isn't on the strength.' He smiled at her, his bad eye twitching. 'I like you, you know.' She smiled back at him, not knowing how to reply. He picked up her left hand and briefly squeezed it.

'Don't trust that man, Angela,' Miss Ivygale said, passing their table on her way to the Ladies. She stroked the back of Gordon Spelle's neck. 'Terrible man,' she said.

Angela was pleased that Miss Ivygale had recognized her and had spoken to her. It occurred to her that her immediate employer was probably shortsighted and had seen no more than the outline of a familiar face when she'd peered across the bar at her.

'Come on, have a drink with us,' Miss Ivygale insisted on her way back from the Ladies.

'Oh, it's all right, Pam,' Gordon Spelle said quickly, but Miss Ivygale stood there, waiting for them to get up and accompany her. 'You watch your step, my boy,' she said to Gordon Spelle as they all three made their way together. Gordon Spelle told her she was drunk.

'This is my secretary, Alec,' Miss Ivygale said at the bar. 'Replacing Sue. Angela Hosford.'

Mr Hemp shook Angela's hand. He had folded Miss Ivygale's red coat and placed it on a bar-stool. He asked Angela what she was drinking and while she was murmuring that she wouldn't have another one Gordon Spelle said a medium sherry and a gin and Britvic orange for himself. Gordon Spelle was looking cross, Angela noticed. His bad eye closed again. He was glaring at Miss Ivygale with the other one.

'Cheers, Angela,' Mr Hemp said. 'Welcome to C.S. & E.'

'Thank you, Mr Hemp.'

People were leaving the bar, waving or calling out good-night to the group she was with. A man paused to say something to Mr Hemp and then stayed to have another drink. By the fire the receptionist and another girl listened while Tommy Blyth told them about car radios, advising which kind to buy if they ever had to.

'I brought her in here to have a simple drink,' Gordon Spelle was protesting to Miss Ivygate, unsuccessfully attempting to keep his voice low. 'So's the poor girl could meet a few people.'

Miss Ivygale looked at Angela and Angela smiled at her uneasily, embarrassed because they were talking about her. Miss Ivygale didn't smile back, and it couldn't have been that Miss Ivygale didn't see her properly this time because the distance between them was less than a yard.

'You watch your little step, my boy,' Miss Ivygale warned again, and this time Gordon Spelle leaned forward and kissed her on the cheek. 'All right, my love?' he said.

Miss Ivygale ordered Mr Hemp another Bell's whisky and one for herself, reminding the barman that the measures they were drinking were double measures. 'What're you on, Dil?' she asked the man who was talking to Mr Hemp. 'No, no, must go,' he said.

'Bell's I think he's on,' the barman said, pouring a third large whisky.

'And a gin and Britvic for Gordon,' Miss Ivygale said. 'And a medium sherry.'

'Oh, really,' murmured Angela.

'Nonsense,' Miss Ivygale said.

In the lavatory Gordon Spelle swore as he urinated. Typical of bloody Pam Ivygale to go nosing in like that. He wouldn't have brought the girl to the Arms at all if he'd thought Ivygale would be soaked to the gills, hurling abuse about like bloody snowballs. God alone knew what kind of a type the girl thought he was now. Girls like that had a way of thinking you a sexual maniac if you so much as took their arm to cross a street. There'd been one he'd known before who'd come from the same kind of area, Plymouth or Bristol or somewhere. Bigger girl actually, five foot ten she must have been, fattish. 'Touch of the West Countries,' he'd said when she'd opened her mouth, the first time he'd used the expression. Tamar Dymond she'd been called, messy bloody creature.

Gordon Spelle combed his hair and then decided that his tie needed to be reknotted. He removed his pepper-coloured jacket and his waistcoat and took the tie off, cocking up the collar of his striped blue shirt in order to make the operation easier. His wife, Peggy, would probably be reading a story to the younger of their two children, since she generally did so at about seven o'clock. As he reknotted his tie, he imagined his wife sitting by the child's bed reading a Topsy and Tim book.

*

'Oh, say you're going to Luton,' Miss Ivygale said. 'Tell her it's all just cropped up in the last fifteen minutes.'

Mr Hemp shook his head. He pointed out that rather often recently he'd telephoned his wife at seven o'clock to say that what had cropped up in the last fifteen minutes was the fact that unexpectedly he had to go to Luton. Mr Hemp had moved away from the man called Dil, closer to Miss Ivygale. They were speaking privately, Mr Hemp in a lower voice than Miss Ivygale. The man called Dil was talking to another man.

Standing by herself and not being spoken to by anyone, Angela was feeling happy. It didn't matter that no one was speaking to her, or paying her any other kind of attention. She felt warm and friendly, quite happy to be on her own while Gordon Spelle was in the Gents and Mr Hemp and Miss Ivygale talked to each other privately. She liked him, she thought as she stood there: she liked his old-fashioned manners and the way he'd whistled 'Smoke Gets in Your Eyes', and his sympathy over her being new. She smiled at him when he returned from the Gents. It was all much nicer than the German wine firm, or the laminates firm.

'Hello,' he said in a whisper, staring at her.

'It was nice of you to bring me here,' she said, whispering also.

'Nice for me, too,' said Gordon Spelle.

Mr Hemp went away to telephone his wife. The telephone was behind Angela, in a little booth against the wall. The booth was shaped like a sedan chair, except that it didn't have any shafts to carry it by. Angela had noticed it when she'd been sitting down with Gordon Spelle. She hadn't known then that it contained a telephone and had wondered at the presence of a sedan chair in a bar. But several times since then people had entered it and each time a light had come on, revealing a telephone and a pile of directories.

'Because they only told me ten minutes ago,' Mr Hemp was saying. 'Because the bloody fools couldn't make their minds up, if you can call them minds.'

Gordon Spelle squeezed her hand and Angela squeezed back because it seemed a friendly thing to do. She felt sorry for him because he had only one good eye. It was the single defect in his handsome face. It gave him a tired look, and suggested suffering.

'I wish you'd see it my way,' Mr Hemp was saying crossly in the sedan chair. 'God damn it, I don't *want* to go to the bloody place.'

'I really must go,' Angela murmured, but Gordon Spelle continued to hold her hand. She didn't want to go. 'I really must,' she said again.

In the Terrazza, where the waiters wore striped blue-and-white jerseys and looked like sailors at a regatta, Mr Hemp and Miss Ivygale were well known. So was Gordon Spelle. The striped waiters greeted them affectionately, and a man in a dark suit addressed all three of them by name. He bowed at Angela. 'How d'you do?' he said, handing her a menu.

'*Petto di pollo sorpresa*,' Gordon Spelle recommended. 'Chicken with garlic in it.'

'Garlic? Oh –'

'He always has it,' Miss Ivygale said, pointing with the menu at Gordon Spelle. 'You'll be all right, dear.'

'What're you having, darling?' Mr Hemp asked Miss Ivygale. In the taxi on the way to the Terrazza he had sat with his arm around her and once, as though they were in private, he'd kissed her on the mouth, making quite a lot of noise about it. Angela had been embarrassed and so, she imagined, had Gordon Spelle.

'*Gamberone al spiedo*,' Miss Ivygale ordered.

'Cheers,' Mr Hemp said, lifting a glass of white wine into the air.

'I think I'm a bit drunk,' Angela said to Gordon Spelle and he wagged his head approvingly. Mr Hemp said he was a bit drunk himself, and Miss Ivygale said she was drunk, and Gordon Spelle pointed out that you only live once.

'Welcome to C.S. & E.,' Mr Hemp said, lifting his glass again.

The next morning, in the flat in Putney, Angela told her flatmates about the delicious food at the Terrazza and how she couldn't really remember much else. There'd certainly been a conversation at the restaurant table, and in a taxi afterwards she remembered Gordon Spelle humming and then Gordon Spelle had kissed her. She seemed to remember him saying that he'd always wanted to be a dance-band leader, although she wasn't sure if she'd got that right. There were other memories of Gordon Spelle in the taxi, which she didn't relate to her flat-mates. There'd been, abruptly, his cold hand on the flesh of one of her thighs, and her surprise that the hand could have got there without her noticing. At another point there'd been his cold hand on the flesh of her stomach. 'Look, you're not married or anything?' she remembered herself saying in sudden alarm. She remembered the noise of Gordon Spelle's breathing and his tongue penetrating her ear. 'Married?' he'd said at some other point, and had laughed.

Feeling unwell but not unhappy, Angela vividly recalled the face and clothes of Gordon Spelle. She recalled his hands, which tapered and were thin, and his sleek hair and droopy eye. She wondered how on earth she was going to face him after what had happened in the taxi, or how she was going to face Miss Ivygale because Miss Ivygale, she faintly remembered, had fallen against a table on their way out of the restaurant, upsetting plates of soup and a bottle of wine. When Angela had tried to help her to stand up again she'd used unpleasant language. Yet the dim memories didn't worry Angela in any real way, not like her poor complexion sometimes worried her, or her contact lenses. Even though she was feeling unwell, she only wanted to smile that morning. She wanted to write a letter to her parents in Carhampton Road, Exeter, and tell them she'd made a marvellous decision when she'd decided to leave the German wine business and go to C.S. & E. She should have done it years ago, she wanted to tell them, because everyone at C.S. & E. was so friendly and because you only lived once. She wanted to tell them about Gordon Spelle, who had said in the taxi that he thought he was falling in love with her, which was of course an exaggeration.

She drank half a cup of Nescafé and caught a thirty-seven bus. Sitting beside an Indian on the lower deck, she thought about Gordon Spelle. On the tube to Earl's Court she thought of him again, and on the Piccadilly line between Earl's Court and Green Park she went on thinking about him. When she closed her eyes, as she once or twice did, she seemed to be with him in some anonymous place, stroking his face and comforting him because of his bad eye. She walked from the tube station, past the Rootes' Group car showrooms and Thos Cook's in Berkeley Street, along Lansdowne Row with its pet shops and card shop and coffee shops, past the Gresham Arms, the C.S. & E. pub. It was a cold morning, but the cold air was pleasant. Pigeons waddled on the pavements, cars drew up at parking-meters. Fresh-faced and shaven, the men of the night before hurried to their offices. She wouldn't have recognized Tommy Blyth, she thought, or the man called Dil, or even Mr Hemp. Girls in suede boots hurried, also looking different in the morning light. She was being silly, she said to herself in Carlos Place: he probably said that to dozens of girls.

In Angela's life there had been a few other men. At the age of twelve she had been attracted by a youth who worked in a newsagent's. She'd liked him because he'd always been ready to chat to her and smile at her, two or three years older he'd been. At fourteen she'd developed a passion for an American actor called Don Ameche whom she'd seen in an old film on television. For several weeks he'd carried with her the memory of his face and had lain in bed at night imagining a life with him in a cliff-top house she'd invented, in California. She'd seen herself and Don Ameche running into the sea together, as he had run with an actress in the film. She'd seen them eating breakfast together, out in the open, on a sunny morning. But Don Ameche, she'd suddenly realized, was sixty or seventy now.

When Angela had first come to London a man who'd briefly been employed in the German wine business used occasionally to invite her to have a cup of coffee with him at the end of the day, just as Gordon Spelle had invited her to have a drink. But being with this man wasn't like being with Gordon Spelle: the man was a shabby person who was employed in some lowly capacity, who seemed to Angela, after the third time they'd had coffee together, to be mentally deficient. One Monday morning he didn't turn up for work, and was never heard of again.

There'd been another man, more briefly, in Angela's life, a young man called Ted Apwell whom she'd met at a Saturday-night party given by a friend of one of her flat-mates. She and Ted Apwell had paired off when the party, more or less at an end, had become uninhibited. At half-past three in the morning she'd allowed herself to be driven home by Ted Apwell, knowing that it was to his home rather than hers they were going. He'd taken her clothes off and in a half-hearted, inebriated way had put an end to her virginity, on a hearth-rug in front of a gas fire. He'd driven her on to her flat, promising – too often, she realized afterwards – that he'd telephone her on Monday. She'd found him hard to forget at first, not because she'd developed any great fondness for him but because of his nakedness and her own on the hearth-rug, the first time all that had happened. There hadn't, so far, been a second time.

Miss Ivygale did not come in that morning. Angela sat alone in the outer office, with nothing to do because there were no letters to type. A tea-lady arrived at a quarter-past ten and poured milky coffee on to two lumps of sugar in a cup she'd earlier placed on Angela's desk. 'Pam not in this morning?' she said, and Angela said no, Miss Ivygale wasn't.

At ten-past twelve Gordon Spelle entered the outer office. 'Red roses,' he lilted, 'for a blue lady. Oh, Mr Florist, please . . .' He laughed, standing by the door. He closed the door and crossed to her desk and kissed her. If anyone had asked her in that moment she'd have said that her inferiority complex was a thing of the past. She felt pretty when Gordon Spelle kissed her, not knowing what everyone else knew, that Gordon Spelle was notorious.

They had lunch in a place called the Coffee Bean, more modest than the Terrazza. Gordon Spelle told her about his childhood, which had not been happy. He told her about coming to C.S. & E. nine years ago, and about his earlier ambition to be a dance-band leader. 'Look,' he said when they'd drunk a carafe of Sicilian wine. 'I want to tell you, Angela: I'm actually married.'

She felt a coldness in her stomach, as though ice had somehow become lodged there. The coldness began to hurt her, like indigestion. All the warmth of her body had moved into her face and neck. She hated the flush that had come to her face and neck because she knew it made her look awful.

'Married?' she said.

He'd only laughed last night in the taxi, she remembered: he hadn't actually said he wasn't married, not that she could swear to it. He'd laughed and given the impression that married was the last thing he was, so that she'd woken up that morning with the firmly-established thought that Gordon Spelle, a bachelor, had said he loved her and had embraced her with more passion than she'd ever permitted in another man or youth. In the moments of waking she'd even been aware of thinking that one day she and Gordon Spelle might be married, and had imagined her parents in their best clothes, her father awkward, giving her away. It was all amazing; incredible that Gordon Spelle should have picked her out when all around him, in C.S. & E. and in the other offices, there were beautiful girls.

'I didn't dare tell you,' he said. 'I tried to, Angela. All last night I tried to, but I couldn't. In case you'd go away.'

They left the Coffee Bean and walked about Grosvenor Square in bitter November sunshine. Men were tidying the flowerbeds. The people who had hurried from their offices last night and had hurried into them this morning, and out of them for lunch, were hurrying back to them again.

'I'm in love with you, Angela,' he said, and again she felt it was incredible. She might be dreaming, she thought, but knew she was not.

They walked hand in hand, and she suddenly remembered Mr Hemp telephoning in the sedan chair, cross and untruthful with his wife. She imagined Gordon Spelle's wife and saw her as a hard-faced woman who was particular about her house, who didn't let him smoke in certain rooms, who'd somehow prevented him from becoming a dance-band leader. She seemed to be older than Gordon Spelle, with hair that was quite grey and a face that Angela remembered from a book her father used to read her as a child, the face of a farmyard rat.

'She's a bit of an invalid, actually,' Gordon Spelle said. 'She isn't well most of the time and she's a ball of nerves anyway. She couldn't stand a separation, Angela, or anything like that: I wouldn't want to mislead you, Angela, like Alec Hemp –'

'Oh, Gordon.'

He looked away from her and with his face still averted he said he wasn't much of a person. It was all wrong, being in love with her like this, with a wife and children at home. He would never want her to go on waiting for him, as Pam Ivygale had waited for twenty-three years.

'Oh, love,' she said.

The ice had gone from her stomach, and her face had cooled again. He put his arms around her, one hand on her hair, the other pressing her body into his. He whispered, but she couldn't hear what he said and the words didn't seem important. The hurrying people glanced at them, surprised to witness a leisurely embrace, in daylight on a path in Grosvenor Square.

'Oh, love,' she said again.

The cold had brought out the defects on her face: beneath heavily-applied make-up he noticed that the skin was pimply and pitted. Affected by the cold also, her eyes were red-rimmed. She reminded him of Dolores Birkett, a girl who'd been at C.S. & E. three years ago.

They returned to the office. He released her hand and took her arm instead. He'd see her at half-past five, he said in the lift. He kissed her in the lift because there was no one else in it. His mouth was moist and open. No one ever before had kissed her like he did, as though far more than kisses were involved, as though his whole being was passionate for hers. 'I love you terribly,' he said.

All afternoon, with no real work to do, she thought about it, continuing to be amazed. It was a mystery, a gorgeous mystery that became more gorgeous the more she surveyed the facts. The facts were gorgeous themselves: nicer, she considered, than any of the other facts of her life. In prettily coloured clothes the girls of C.S. & E. walked the green-carpeted corridors from office to office, their fingernails gleaming, their skins like porcelain, apparently without pores. In their suede boots or their platform shoes they queued for lunchtime tables in the Coffee Bean, or stood at five-past six in the warm bar of the Gresham Arms. Their faces were nicer than her face, their bodies more lissom, their legs and arms more suavely elegant. Yet she had been chosen.

She leafed through files, acquainting herself further with the affairs of Miss Ivygale's office. She examined without interest the carbon copies of letters in buff-coloured folders. The faint, blurred type made no sense to her and the letters themselves seemed as unimportant as the flimsy paper they were duplicated on. In a daydream that was delicious his tapering hands again caressed her. 'I love you terribly, too,' she said.

At four o'clock Miss Ivygale arrived. She'd been working all day in her flat, she said, making notes for the letters she now wished to dictate. Her manner was businesslike, she didn't mention the evening before. 'Dear Sir,' she said. 'Further to yours of the twenty-ninth .   '

Angela made shorthand notes and then typed Miss Ivygale's letters. He did not love his wife; he had hinted that he did not love his wife; no one surely could kiss you like that, no one could put his arms around you in the broad daylight in Grosvenor Square, and still love a wife somewhere. She imagined being in a room with him, a room with an electric fire built into the wall, and two chintz-covered armchairs and a sofa covered in the same material, with pictures they had chosen together, and ornaments on the mantelpiece. 'No, I don't love her,' his voice said. 'Marry me, Angela,' his voice said.

'No, no, that's really badly done,' Miss Ivygale said. 'Type it again, please.'

You couldn't blame Miss Ivygale. Naturally Miss Ivygale was cross, having just had her share of Mr Hemp, one night out of so many empty ones. She smiled at Miss Ivygale when she handed her the retyped letter. Feeling generous and euphoric, she wanted to tell Miss Ivygale that she was still attractive at fifty, but naturally she could not do that.

'See they catch the post,' Miss Ivygale sourly ordered, handing her back the letters she'd signed.

'Yes, yes, of course, Miss Ivygale –'

'You'll need to hurry up.'

She took the letters to the dispatch-room in the basement and when she returned to the outer office she found that Miss Ivygale had already left the inner one. She put the grey plastic cover on her Remington International and went to the lavatory to put Pure Magic on her face. 'I wonder who's kissing her now,' Gordon Spelle was murmuring when she entered the outer office again. 'I wonder who's showing her how.'

He put his arms around her. His tongue crept between her teeth, his hands caressed the outline of her buttocks. He led her into Miss Ivygale's office, an arm around her waist, his lips damply on her right ear. He was whispering something about Miss Ivygale having left for the Gresham Arms and about having to lock the door because the cleaners would be coming round. She heard the door being locked. The light went out and the office was dark except for the glow of the street lamps coming through two uncurtained windows. His mouth was working on hers again, his fingers undid the zip at the side of her skirt. She closed her eyes, saturated by the gorgeousness of the mystery.

Take it easy, he said to himself when he had her on the floor, remembering the way Dolores Birkett had suddenly shouted out, in discomfort apparently, although at the time he'd assumed it to be pleasure. A Nigerian cleaner had come knocking at the door when she'd shouted out the third or fourth time. 'Oh, God, I love you,' he whispered to Angela Hosford.

She had vodka and lime in the Gresham Arms because she felt she needed pulling together and one of the girls in the flat had said that vodka was great for that. It had been very painful on the floor of Miss Ivygale's office, and not even momentarily pleasurable, not once. It had been less painful the other time, with Ted Apwell on the hearth-rug. She wished it didn't always have to be on a floor, but even so it didn't matter – nor did the pain, nor the apprehension about doing it in Miss Ivygale's office. All the time he'd kept saying he loved her, and as often as she could manage it she'd said she loved him too.

'Must go,' he said now with sudden, awful abruptness. He buttoned the jacket of his pepper-coloured suit. He kissed her on the lips, in full view of everyone in the Gresham Arms. She wanted to go with him but felt she shouldn't because the drink he'd just bought her was scarcely touched. He'd drunk his own gin and Britvic in a couple of gulps.

'Sorry for being so grumpy,' Miss Ivygale said.

The Gresham Arms was warm and noisy, but somehow not the same at all. The men who'd been there last night were there again: Tommy Blyth and the man called Dil and all the other men – and the black-haired receptionist and all the other girls. Mr Hemp was not. Mr Hemp was hurrying back to his wife, and so was Gordon Spelle.

'What're you drinking?' Miss Ivygale asked her.

'Oh no, no. I haven't even started this one, thanks.'

But Miss Ivygale, whose own glass required refilling, insisted. 'Sit down, why don't you?' Miss Ivygale suggested, indicating the bar-stool next to hers. 'Take off your coat. It's like a furnace in here.'

Slowly Angela took off her coat. She sat beside her immediate employer, still feeling painful and in other ways aware of what had occurred on Miss Ivygale's office floor. They drank together and in time they both became a little drunk. Angela felt sorry for Miss Ivygale then, and Miss Ivygale felt sorry for Angela, but neither of them said so. And in the end, when Angela asked Miss Ivygale why it was that Gordon Spelle had picked her out, Miss Ivygale replied that it was because Gordon Spelle loved her. What else could she say? Miss Ivygale asked herself. How could she say that everyone knew that Gordon Spelle chose girls who were unattractive because he believed such girls, deprived of sex for long periods at a time, were an easier bet? Gordon Spelle was notorious, but Miss Ivygale naturally couldn't say it, any more than she'd been able to say it to Dolores Birkett or Tamar Dymond or Sue, or any of the others.

'Oh, it's beautiful!' Angela cried suddenly, having drunk a little more. She was referring, not to her own situation, but to the fact that Miss Ivygale had wasted half a lifetime on a hopeless love. Feeling happy herself, she wanted Miss Ivygale to feel happy also.

Miss Ivygale did not say anything in reply. She was fifty and Angela was twenty-six: that made a difference where knowing what was beautiful was concerned. The thing about Gordon Spelle was that with the worst possible motives he performed an act of charity for the girls who were his victims. He gave them self-esteem, and memories to fall back on – for the truth was too devious for those closest to it to guess, and too cruel for other people ever to reveal to them. The victims of Gordon Spelle left C.S. & E. in the end because they believed the passion of his love for them put him under a strain, he being married to a wife who was ill. As soon as each had gone he looked around for someone else.

'And beautiful for you too, my dear,' Miss Ivygale murmured, thinking that in a way it was, compared with what she had herself. She'd been aware for twenty-three years of being used by the man she loved: self-esteem and memories were better than knowing that, no matter how falsely they came.

'Let's have two for the road,' murmured Miss Ivygale, and ordered further drinks.

Mr McNamara

'How was he?' my mother asked on the morning of my thirteenth birthday.

She spoke while pouring tea into my father's extra-large breakfast cup, the last remaining piece of a flowered set, *Ville de Lyon* clematis on a leafy ground. My father had a special knife and fork as well, the knife another relic of the past, the fork more ordinary, extra-strong because my father was always breaking forks.

'Oh, he's well enough,' he said on the morning of my thirteenth birthday, while I sat patiently. 'The old aunt's kicking up again.'

My mother, passing him his tea, nodded. She remarked that in her opinion Mr McNamara's aunt should be placed in an asylum, which was what she always said when the subject of Mr McNamara's aunt, reputedly alcoholic, cropped up.

My mother was tallish and slender, but softly so. There was nothing sharp or angular about my mother, nothing wiry or hard. She had misty blue eyes and she seemed always to be on the point of smiling. My father, in contrast, was bulky, a man with a brown face and a brown forehead stretching back where hair once had been, with heavy brown-backed hands and eyes the same shade of blue mist as my mother's. They were gentle with one another in a way that was similar also, and when they disagreed or argued their voices weren't ever raised. They could be angry with us, but not with one another. They meted out punishments for us jointly, sharing disapproval or disappointment. We felt doubly ashamed when our misdemeanours were uncovered.

'The train was like a Frigidaire,' my father said. 'Two hours late at the halt. Poor Flannagan nearly had pneumonia waiting.' The whole country had ivy growing over it, he said, like ivy on a gravestone. Eating bacon and sausages with his special knife and fork, he nodded in agreement with himself. 'Ivy-clad Ireland,' he said when his mouth was momentarily empty of food. 'Anthracite motor-cars, refrigerators on the Great Southern Railway. Another thing, Molly: it's the opinion in Dublin that six months' time will see foreign soldiers parading themselves on O'Connell Street. German or English, take your pick, and there's damn all Dev can do about it.'

My mother smiled at him and sighed. Then, as though to cheer us all up, my father told a story that Mr McNamara had told him, about a coal merchant whom Mr McNamara had apparently known in his youth. The story had to do with the ill-fitting nature of the coal merchant's artificial teeth, and the loss of the teeth when he'd once been swimming at Ringsend. Whenever my father returned from a meeting with Mr McNamara he brought us back such stories, as well as the current opinion of Mr McNamara on the state of the nation and the likelihood of the nation becoming involved in the war. 'The opinion in Dublin' was the opinion of Mr McNamara, as we all knew. Mr McNamara drove a motor-car powered by gas because there wasn't much petrol to be had. The gas, so my father said, was manufactured by anthracite in a burner stuck on to the back of Mr McNamara's Ford V-8.

Returning each time from Dublin, my father bore messages and gifts from Mr McNamara, a tin of Jacob's biscuits or bars of chocolate. He was a man who'd never married and who lived on inherited means, in a house in Palmerston Road, with members of his family – the elderly alcoholic aunt who should have been in an asylum, a sister and a brother-in-law. The sister, now Mrs Matchette, had earlier had theatrical ambitions, but her husband, employed in the National Bank, had persuaded her away from them. My father had never actually met Mr McNamara's insane aunt or Mrs Matchette or her husband: they lived through Mr McNamara for him, at second hand, and for us they lived through my father, at a further remove. We had a vivid image of all of them, Mrs Matchette thin as a blade of grass, endlessly smoking and playing patience, her husband small and solemn, neatly moustached, with dark neat hair combed straight back from what Mr McNamara had called a 'squashed forehead'. Mr McNamara himself we imagined as something of a presence: prematurely white-haired, portly, ponderous in speech and motion. Mr McNamara used to frequent the bar of a hotel called Fleming's, an old-fashioned place where you could get snuff as well as tobacco, and tea, coffee and Bovril as well as alcoholic drinks. It was here that my father met him on his visits to Dublin. It was a comfort to go there, my father said, when his business for the day was done, to sit in a leather chair and listen to the chit-chat of his old companion. The bar would fill with smoke from their Sweet Afton cigarettes, while my father listened to the latest about the people in the house in Palmerston Road, and the dog they had, a spaniel called Wolfe Tone, and a maid called Trixie O'Shea, from Skibbereen. There was ritual about it, my father smoking and listening, just as a day or so later he'd smoke and we'd listen ourselves, at breakfast-time in our house in the country.

There were my three sisters and myself: I was the oldest, the only boy. We lived in a house that had been in the family for several generations, three miles from Curransbridge, where the Dublin train halted if anyone wanted it to, and where my father's granary and mill were. Because of the shortage of petrol, my father used to walk the three miles there and back every day. Sometimes he'd persuade Flannagan, who worked in the garden for us, to collect him in the dog-cart in the evening, and always when he went to Dublin he arranged for Flannagan to meet the train he returned on. In the early hours of the morning I'd sometimes hear the rattle of the dog-cart on the avenue and then the wheels on the gravel outside the front of the house. At breakfast-time the next morning my father would say he was glad to be back again, and kiss my mother with the rest of us. The whole thing occurred once every month or so, the going away in the first place, the small packed suitcase in the hall, my father in his best tweed suit, Flannagan and the dog-cart. And the returning a few days later: breakfast with Mr McNamara, my sister Charlotte used to say.

As a family we belonged to the past. We were Protestants in what had become Catholic Ireland. We'd once been part of an ascendancy, but now it was not so. Now there was the income from the granary and the mill, and the house we lived in: we sold grain and flour, we wielded no power. 'Proddy-woddy green-guts,' the Catholic children cried at us in Currans-bridge. 'Catty, Catty, going to mass,' we whispered back, 'riding on the devil's ass.' They were as good as we were. It had not always been assumed so, and it sometimes seemed part of all the changing and the shifting of this and that, that Mr McNamara, so honoured in our house, was a Catholic himself. 'A liberal, tolerant man,' my father used to say. 'No trace of the bigot in him.' In time, my father used to say, religious differences in Ireland wouldn't exist. The war would sort the whole matter out, even though as yet Ireland wasn't involved in it. When the war was over, and whether there was involvement or not, there wouldn't be any patience with religious differences. So, at least, Mr McNamara appeared to argue.

Childhood was all that: my sisters, Charlotte, Amelia, and Frances, and my parents gentle with each other, and Flannagan in the garden and Bridget our maid, and the avuncular spirit of Mr McNamara. There was Miss Ryan as well, who arrived every morning on an old Raleigh bicycle, to teach the four of us, since the school at Curransbridge was not highly thought of by my parents.

The house itself was a Georgian rectangle when you looked straight at it, spaciously set against lawns which ran back to the curved brick of the kitchen-garden wall, with a gravel sweep in front, and an avenue running straight as a die for a mile and a half through fields where sheep grazed. My sisters had some world of their own which I knew I could not properly share. Charlotte, the oldest of them, was five years younger than I was, Amelia was six and Frances five.

'Ah, he was in great form,' my father said on the morning of my thirteenth birthday. 'After a day listening to rubbish it's a pleasure to take a ball of malt with him.'

Frances giggled. When my father called a glass of whiskey a ball of malt Frances always giggled, and besides it was a giggly occasion. All my presents were sitting there on the sideboard, waiting for my father to finish his breakfast and to finish telling us about Mr McNamara. But my father naturally took precedence: after all, he'd been away from the house for three days, he'd been cold and delayed on the train home, and attending to business in Dublin was something he disliked in any case. This time, though, as well as his business and the visit to Fleming's Hotel to see Mr McNamara, I knew he'd bought the birthday present that he and my mother would jointly give me. Twenty minutes ago he'd walked into the dining-room with the wrapped parcel under his arm. 'Happy birthday, boy,' he'd said, placing the parcel on the sideboard beside the other three, from my sisters. It was the tradition in our house – a rule of my father's – that breakfast must be over and done with, every scrap eaten, before anyone opened a birthday present or a Christmas present.

'It was McNamara said that,' my father continued. 'Ivy-clad Ireland. It's the neutral condition of us.'

It was my father's opinion, though not my mother's, that Ireland should have acceded to Winston Churchill's desire to man the Irish ports with English soldiers in case the Germans got in there first. Hitler had sent a telegram to de Valera apologizing for the accidental bombing of a creamery, which was a suspicious gesture in itself. Mr McNamara, who also believed that de Valera should hand over the ports to Churchill, said that any gentlemanly gesture on the part of the German Führer was invariably followed by an act of savagery. Mr McNamara, in spite of being a Catholic, was a keen admirer of the House of Windsor and of the English people. There was no aristocracy in the world to touch the English, he used to say, and no people, intent on elegance, succeeded as the English upper classes did. Class-consciousness in England was no bad thing, Mr McNamara used to argue.

My father took from the side pocket of his jacket a small wrapped object. As he did so, my sisters rose from the breakfast table and marched to the sideboard. One by one my presents were placed before me, my parents' brought from the sideboard by my mother. It was a package about two and a half feet long, a few inches in width. It felt like a bundle of twigs and was in fact the various parts of a box-kite. Charlotte had bought me a book called *Dickon the Impossible*, Amelia a kaleidoscope. 'Open mine exceedingly carefully,' Frances said. I did, and at first I thought it was a pot of jam. It was a goldfish in a jar.

'From Mr McNamara,' my father said, pointing at the smallest package. I'd forgotten it, because already the people who normally gave me presents were accounted for. 'I happened to mention,' my father said, 'that today was a certain day.'

It was so heavy that I thought it might be a lead soldier, or a horseman. In fact it was a dragon. It was tiny and complicated, and it appeared to be made of gold, but my father assured me it was brass. It had two green eyes that Frances said were emeralds, and small pieces let into its back which she said looked like rubies. 'Priceless,' she whispered jealously. My father laughed and shook his head. The eyes and the pieces in the brass back were glass, he said.

I had never owned so beautiful an object. I watched it being passed from hand to hand around the breakfast table, impatient to feel it again myself. 'You must write at once to Mr McNamara,' my mother said. 'It's far too generous of him,' she added, regarding my father with some slight disapproval, as though implying that my father shouldn't have accepted the gift. He vaguely shook his head, lighting a Sweet Afton. 'Give me the letter when you've done it,' he said. 'I have to go up again in a fortnight.'

I showed the dragon to Flannagan, who was thinning beetroot in the garden. I showed it to Bridget, our maid. 'Aren't you the lucky young hero?' Flannagan said, taking the dragon in a soil-caked hand. 'You'd get a five-pound note for that fellow, anywhere you cared to try.' Bridget polished it with Brasso for me.

That day I had a chocolate birthday cake, and sardine sandwiches, which were my favourite, and brown bread and greengage jam, a favourite also. After tea all the family watched while my father and I tried to fly the kite, running with it from one end of a lawn to the other. It was Flannagan who got it up for us in the end, and I remember the excitement of the string tugging at my fingers, and Bridget crying out that she'd never seen a thing like that before, wanting to know what it was for. 'Don't forget, dear, to write to Mr McNamara first thing in the morning,' my mother reminded me when she kissed me goodnight. I wouldn't forget, I promised, and didn't add that of all my presents, including the beautiful green and yellow kite, I liked the dragon best.

But I never did write to Mr McNamara. The next day was a different kind of day, a grim nightmare of a day during all of which someone in the house was weeping, and often several of us together. My father, so affectionate towards all of us, was no longer alive.

The war continued and Ireland continued to play no part in it. Further accidental German bombs were dropped and further apologies were sent to de Valera by the German Führer. Winston Churchill continued to fulminate about the ports, but the prophecy of Mr McNamara that foreign soldiers would parade in O'Connell Street did not come true.

Knitting or sewing, my mother listened to the BBC news with a sadness in her eyes, unhappy that elsewhere death was occurring also. It was no help to any of us to be reminded that people in Britain and Europe were dying all the time now, with the same sudden awfulness as my father had.

Everything was different after my father died. My mother and I began to go for walks together. I'd take her arm, and sometimes her hand, knowing she was lonely. She talked about him to me, telling me about their honeymoon in Venice, the huge square where they'd sat drinking chocolate, listening to the bands that played there. She told me about my own birth, and how my father had given her a ring set with amber which he'd bought in Louis Wine's in Dublin. She would smile at me on our walks and tell me that even though I was only thirteen I was already taking his place. One day the house would be mine, she pointed out, and the granary and the mill. I'd marry, she said, and have children of my own, but I didn't want even to think about that. I didn't want to marry; I wanted my mother always to be there with me, going on walks and telling me about the person we all missed so much. We were still a family, my sisters and my mother and myself, Flannagan in the garden, and Bridget. I didn't want anything to change.

After the death of my father Mr McNamara lived on, though in a different kind of way. The house in Palmerston Road, with Mr McNamara's aunt drinking in an upstairs room, and the paper-thin Mrs Matchette playing patience instead of being successful in the theatre, and Mr Matchette with his squashed forehead, and Trixie O'Shea from Skibbereen, and the spaniel called Wolfe Tone: all of them remained quite vividly alive after my father's death, as part of our memory of him. Fleming's Hotel remained also, and all the talk there'd been there of the eccentric household in Palmerston Road. For almost as long as I could remember, and certainly as long as my sisters could remember, our own household had regularly been invaded by the other one, and after my father's death my sisters and I often recalled specific incidents retailed in Fleming's Hotel and later at our breakfast table. There'd been the time when Mr McNamara's aunt had sold the house to a man she'd met outside a public house. And the time when Mrs Matchette appeared to have fallen in love with Garda Molloy, who used to call in at the kitchen for Trixie O'Shea every night. And the time the spaniel was run over by a van and didn't die. All of it was preserved, with Mr McNamara himself, white-haired and portly in the smoke-brown bar of Fleming's Hotel, where snuff could be bought, and Bovril as well as whiskey.

A few months after the death my mother remarked one breakfast-time that no doubt Mr McNamara had seen the obituary notice in the *Irish Times*. 'Oh, but you should write,' my sister Frances cried out in her excitable manner. My mother shook her head. My father and Mr McNamara had been bar-room friends, she pointed out: letters in either direction would not be in order. Charlotte and Amelia agreed with this opinion, but Frances still protested. I couldn't see that it mattered. 'He gave us all that chocolate,' Frances cried, 'and the biscuits.' My mother said again that Mr McNamara was not the kind of man to write to about a death, nor the kind who would write himself. The letter that I was to have written thanking him for the dragon was not mentioned. Disliking the writing of letters, I didn't raise the subject myself.

At the end of that year I was sent to a boarding-school in the Dublin mountains. Miss Ryan continued to come to the house on her Raleigh to teach my sisters, and I'd have far preferred to have remained at home with her. It could not be: the boarding-school in the Dublin mountains, a renowned Protestant monument, had been my father's chosen destiny for me and that was that. If he hadn't died, leaving home might perhaps have been more painful, but the death had brought with it practical complica-

424 · MR MCNAMARA

tions and troubles, mainly concerned with the running of the granary and the mill: going away to school was slight compared with all that, or so my mother convinced me.

The headmaster of the renowned school was a small, red-skinned English cleric. With other new boys, I had tea with him and his wife in the drawing-room some days after term began. We ate small ham-paste sandwiches and Battenburg cake. The headmaster's wife, a cold woman in grey, asked me what I intended to do – 'in life', as she put it. I said I'd run a granary and a mill at Curransbridge; she didn't seem interested. The headmaster told us he was in *Who's Who*. Otherwise the talk was of the war.

Miss Ryan had not prepared me well. 'Dear boy, whoever taught you French?' a man with a pipe asked me, and did not stay to hear my answer. 'Your Latin, really!' another man exclaimed, and the man who taught me mathematics warned me never to set my sights on a profession that involved an understanding of figures. I sat in the back row of the class with other boys who had been ill-prepared for the renowned school.

I don't know when it was – a year, perhaps, or eighteen months after my first term – that I developed an inquisitiveness about my father. Had he, I wondered, been as bad at everything as I was? Had some other man with a pipe scorned his inadequacy when it came to French? Had he felt, as I did, a kind of desperation when faced with algebra? You'd *have* to know a bit about figures, I used, almost miserably, to say to myself: you'd have to if you hoped to run a granary and a mill. Had he been good at mathematics?

I asked my mother these questions, and other questions like them. But my mother was vague in her replies and said she believed, although perhaps she was wrong, that my father had not been good at mathematics. She laughed when I asked the questions. She told me to do my best.

But the more I thought about the future, and about myself in terms of the man whose place I was to take, the more curious I became about him. In the holidays my mother and I still went on our walks together, through the garden and then into the fields that stretched behind it, along the banks of the river that flowed through Curransbridge. But my mother spoke less and less about my father because increasingly there was less to say, except with repetition. I imagined the huge square in Venice and the cathedral and the bands playing outside the cafés. I imagined hundreds of other scenes, her own varied memories of their relationship and their marriage. We often walked in silence now, or I talked more myself, drawing her into a world of cross-country runs, and odorous changing-rooms, and the small headmaster's repeated claim that the food we ate had a high calorific value. School was ordinarily dreary: I told her how we smoked wartime American cigarettes in mud huts specially constructed for the purpose and how we relished the bizarre when, now and again, it broke the monotony. There was a master called Mr Dingle, whose practice it was to enquire of new boys the colour and nature of their mother's night-dresses. In the oak-panelled dining-hall that smelt of mince and the butter that generations had flicked on to the ceiling, Mr Dingle's eye would glaze as he sat at the end of a Junior House table while one boy after another fuelled him with the stuff of fantasies. On occasions when parents visited the school he would observe through cigarette smoke the mothers of these new boys, stripping them of their skirts and blouses in favour of the night clothes that their sons had described for him. There was another master, known as Buller Achen, who was reputed to take a sensual interest in the sheep that roamed the mountainsides, and a boy called Testane-Hackett who was possessed of the conviction that he was the second son of God. In the dining-hall a gaunt black-clad figure, a butler called Tripp, hovered about the high table where the headmaster and the prefects sat, assisted by a maid, said to be his daughter, who was known to us as the Bicycle. There was Fisher Major, who never washed, and Strapping, who disastrously attempted to treat some kind of foot ailment with mild acid. My mother listened appreciatively, and I often saw in her eyes the same look that had been there at breakfast-time when my father spoke of Fleming's Hotel and Mr McNamara. 'How like him you are!' she now and again murmured, smiling at me.

At Curransbridge I stood in his office above the mill, a tiny room now occupied by the man my mother had chosen to look after things, a Mr Devereux. In the house I rooted through the belongings he'd left behind; I stared at photographs of him. With Flannagan and my sisters I flew the kite he'd bought me that last time he'd been to Dublin. I polished the small brass dragon that his bar-room companion had given him to give to me. 'It's the boy's birthday,' I imagined him saying in the brown bar of Fleming's Hotel, and I imagined the slow movement of Mr McNamara's hand as he drew the dragon from his pocket. It was inevitable, I suppose, that sooner or later I should seek out Fleming's Hotel.

'An uncle,' I said to the small headmaster. 'Passing through Dublin, sir.'

'Passing? Passing?' He had a Home Counties accent and a hard nasal intonation. 'Passing?' he said again, giving the word an extra vowel sound.

'On his way to Galway, sir. He's in the R.A.F., sir. I think he'd like to see me, sir, because my father –'

'Ah, yes, yes. Back in time for Chapel, please.'

Fleming's Hotel, it said in the telephone directory, *21 Wheeler Street*. As I cycled down from the mountains, I didn't know what I was going to do when I got there.

It was a narrow, four-storey building in a terrace with others, a bleak-looking stone façade. The white woodwork of the windows needed a coat of paint, the glass portico over the entrance doors had a dusty look. It was on this dusty glass that the name *Fleming's Hotel* was picked out in white enamel letters stuck to the glass itself. I cycled past the hotel twice, glancing at the windows – a dozen of them, the four at the top much smaller than the others – and at the entrance doors. No one left or entered. I propped the bicycle against the edge of the pavement some distance away from the hotel, outside what seemed to be the street's only shop, a greengrocer's. There were pears in the window. I went in and bought one.

I wheeled the bicycle away from the shop and came, at the end of the street, to a canal. Slowly I ate the pear, and then I took my red and green school cap from my head and wheeled my bicycle slowly back to Fleming's Hotel. I pushed open one of the entrance doors and for a split second I heard my father's voice again, describing what I now saw: the smokiness of the low-ceilinged hall, a coal fire burning, and a high reception counter with the hotel's register open on it, and a brass bell beside the register. There were brown leather armchairs in the hall and a brown leather bench running along one wall. Gas lamps were lit but even so, and in spite of the fact that it was four o'clock in the afternoon, the hall was dim. It was empty of other people and quiet. A tall grandfather clock ticked, the fire occasionally hissed. There was a smell of some kind of soup. It was the nicest, most comfortable hall I'd ever been in.

Beyond it, I could see another coal fire, through an archway. That was the bar where they used to sit, where for all I knew Mr McNamara was sitting now. I imagined my father crossing the hall as I crossed it myself. The bar was the same as the hall, with the same kind of leather chairs, and a leather bench and gas lamps and a low ceiling. There were net curtains pulled across the two windows, and one wall was taken up with a counter, with bottles on shelves behind it, and leather-topped stools in front of it. There was a woman sitting by the fire drinking orange-coloured liquid from a small glass. Behind the bar a man in a white jacket was reading the *Irish Independent*.

I paused in the archway that divided the bar from the hall. I was under age. I had no right to take a further step and I didn't know what to do or to say if I did. I didn't know what drink to order. I didn't know if in the dim gaslight I looked a child.

I went to the bar and stood there. The man didn't look up from his newspaper. *Smithwick's Ale* were words on the labels of bottles: I would ask for a Smithwick's Ale. All I wanted was to be allowed to remain, to sit down with the beer and to think about my father. If Mr McNamara did not come today he'd come another day. Frances had been right: he should have been written to. I should have written to him myself, to thank my father's friend for his present.

'Good evening,' the barman said.

'Smithwick's, please,' I said as casually as I could. Not knowing how much the drink might be, I placed a ten-shilling note on the bar.

'Drop of lime in it, sir?'

'Lime? Oh, yes. Yes, please. Thanks very much.'

'Choppy kind of day,' the barman said.

I took the glass and my change, and sat down as far as possible from where the woman was sitting. I sat so that I was facing both the bar and the archway, so that if Mr McNamara came in I'd see him at once. I'd have to leave at six o'clock in order to be safely back for Chapel at seven.

I finished the beer. I took an envelope out of my pocket and drew pieces of holly on the back of it, a simple art-form that Miss Ryan had taught all of us. I took my glass to the bar and asked for another Smithwick's. The barman had a pale, unhealthy-seeming face, and wire-rimmed glasses, and a very thin neck. 'You do want the best, don't you?' he said in a joky kind of voice, imitating someone. 'Bird's Custard,' he said in the same joky way, 'and Bird's Jelly de Luxe.' My father had mentioned this barman: he was repeating the advertisements of Radio Eireann. 'You do want the best, don't you?' he said again, pushing the glass of beer towards me. By the fire, the woman made a noise, a slight, tired titter of amusement. I laughed myself, politely too.

When I returned to my armchair I found the woman was looking at me. I wondered if she could be a prostitute, alone in a hotel bar like that. A boy at school called Yeats claimed that prostitutes hung about railway stations mostly, and on quays. But there was of course no reason why you shouldn't come across one in a bar.

Yet she seemed too quietly dressed to be a prostitute. She was wearing a green suit and a green hat, and there was a coat made of some kind of fur draped over a chair near the chair she sat on. She was a dark-haired woman with an oval face. I'd no idea what age she was: somewhere between thirty and forty, I imagined: I wasn't good at guessing people's ages.

The Smithwick's Ale was having an effect on me. I wanted to giggle. How extraordinary it would be, I thought, if a prostitute tried to sell herself to me in my father's and Mr McNamara's hotel. After all, there was no reason at all why some prostitutes shouldn't be quietly-dressed, probably the more expensive ones were. I could feel myself smiling, holding back the giggle. Naturally enough, I thought, my father hadn't mentioned the presence of prostitutes in Fleming's Hotel. And then I thought that perhaps, if he'd lived, he would have told me one day, when my sisters and my mother weren't in the room. It was the kind of thing, surely, that fathers did tell sons.

I took the envelope I'd drawn the holly on out of my pocket and read the letter it contained. They were managing, my mother said. Miss Ryan had had a dose of 'flu, Charlotte and Amelia wanted to breed horses, Frances didn't know what she wanted to do. His rheumatics were slowing Flannagan down a bit in the garden. Bridget was insisting on sweeping the drawing-room chimney. *It'll be lovely at Christmas*, she wrote. *So nice being all together again.*

The oval-faced woman put on her fur coat, and on her way from the bar she passed close to where I was sitting. She looked down and smiled at me.

*

'Hills of the North, rejoice!' we sang in chapel that night. 'Valley and lowland, sing!'

I smelt of Smithwick's Ale. I knew I did because as we'd stood in line in Cloisters several other boys had remarked on it. As I sang, I knew I was puffing the smell all over everyone else. 'Like a bloody brewery,' Gahan Minor said afterwards.

'. . . this night,' intoned the small headmaster nasally, 'and for ever more.'

'Amen,' we all replied.

Saturday night was a pleasant time. After Chapel there were two and a half hours during which you could do more or less what you liked, provided the master on duty knew where you were. You could work in the Printing Shop or read in the Library, or take part in a debate, such as that this school is an outpost of the British Empire, or play billiards or do carpentry, or go to the model railway club or the music-rooms. At half-past nine there was some even freer time, during which the master on duty didn't have to know where you were. Most boys went for a smoke then.

After Chapel on the Saturday night after I'd visited Fleming's Hotel I read in the Library. I read *Jane Eyre*, but all the time the oval face of the woman in the hotel kept appearing in my mind. It would stay there for a few seconds and then fade, and then return. Again and again, as I read *Jane Eyre*, she passed close to my chair in the bar of Fleming's Hotel, and looked down and smiled at me.

The end of that term came. The Sixth Form and Remove did *Macbeth* on the last two nights, A. McC. P. Jackson giving what was generally regarded as a fine performance as Banquo. Someone stole the secondhand Penguin I'd bought from Grace Major to read on the train, *Why Didn't They Ask Evans?* Aitcheson and Montgomery were found conversing in the shower-room in the middle of the night.

On the journey home I was unable to stop thinking about Fleming's Hotel. A man in the carriage lent me a copy of *Barrack Variety*, but the jokes didn't seem funny. It was at moments like these that the truth most harshly mocked me. Ever since I'd found the hotel, ever since the woman had stared at me, it had been a part of every day, and for whole nights in my long, cheerless dormitory I had been unable to sleep. My father's voice had returned to me there, telling again the stories of his friend, and reminding me of his friend's opinions. My father had disagreed with my mother in her view that de Valera should not hand over the ports to Churchill, preferring to share the view of his friend. At school and on the train, and most of all when I returned home, the truth made me feel ill, as though I had 'flu.

That Christmas morning we handed each other our presents, after we'd eaten, still observing my father's rule. We thought of him then, they in one way, I in another. 'Oh, my dear, how lovely!' my mother whispered over some ornament I'd bought her in a Dublin shop. I had thrown the dragon with the green glass eyes far into a lake near the school, unable to understand how my father had ever brought it to the house, or brought bars of chocolate or tins of Jacob's biscuits. To pass to his children beneath my mother's eyes the gifts of another woman seemed as awful a sin as any father could commit, yet somehow it was not as great as the sin of sharing with all of us this other woman's eccentric household, her sister and her sister's husband, her alcoholic aunt, a maid and a dog. 'That's Norah McNamara,' the barman's voice seemed to say again at our breakfast table, and I imagined them sitting there, my father and she, in that comfortable bar, and my father listening to her talk of the house in Palmerston Road and of how she admired the English aristocracy. I watched my mother smile that Christmas morning, and I wanted to tell the truth because the truth was neat and without hypocrisy: I wanted carefully to say that I was glad my father was dead.

Instead I left the breakfast table and went to my bedroom. I wept there, and then washed my face in cold water from the jug on my wash-stand. I hated the memory of him and how he would have been that Christmas morning; I hated him for destroying everything. It was no consolation to me then that he had tried to share with us a person he loved in a way that was different from the way he loved us. I could neither forgive nor understand. I felt only bitterness that I, who had taken his place, must now continue his deception, and keep the secret of his lies and his hypocrisy.

Afternoon Dancing

Every summer since the war the two couples had gone to Southend in September, staying in Mr Roope's Prospect Hotel. They'd known each other since childhood: Poppy and Albert, Alice and Lenny. They'd been to the same schools, they'd all been married in the summer of 1938. They rented houses in the same street, Paper Street, S.E.4., Poppy and Albert Number 10, and Alice and Lenny Number 41. They were all in their mid-fifties now, and except for Poppy they'd all run to fat a bit. Len was a printer, Albert was employed by the London Electricity Board, as a cable-layer. Every night the two men had a few drinks together in the Cardinal Wolsey in Northbert Road, round the corner from Paper Street. Twice a week, on Wednesdays and Fridays, the wives went to Bingo. Alice's children – Beryl and Ron – were now married and had children of their own. Poppy's son, George, married also, had gone to Canada in 1969.

Poppy was very different from Alice. Alice was timid, she'd never had Poppy's confidence. In middle age Poppy was a small, wiry woman with glasses, the worrying kind you might think to look at her, only Poppy didn't worry at all. Poppy was always laughing, nudging Alice when they were together on a bus, drawing attention to some person who amused her. 'Poppy Edwards, you're a holy terror!' Miss Curry of Tatterall Elementary School had pronounced forty years ago, and in lots of ways Poppy was a holy terror still. She'd been a slap-happy mother and was a slap-happy wife, not caring much what people thought if her child wasn't as meticulously turned out as other children, or if Albert's sandwiches were carelessly made. Once, back in 1941 when Albert was in the army, she'd begun to keep company with a man who was an air-raid warden, whose bad health had prevented him from joining one of the armed forces. When the war came to an end she was still involved with this man and it had seemed likely then that she and Albert would not continue to live together. Alice had been worried about it all, but then, a month before Albert was due to be demobbed, the man had been knocked down by an army truck in Holborn and had instantly died. Albert remained in ignorance of everything, even though most people in Paper Street knew just what had been going on and how close Albert had come to finding himself wifeless. In those days Poppy had been a slim, small girl in her twenties, with yellow hair that looked as though it had been peroxided but which in fact hadn't, and light-blue mischievous eyes. Alice had been plumper, dark-haired and reliable-looking, pretty in her nice-girl way. Beryl and Ron had not been born yet.

During the war, with their two husbands serving in Italy and Africa together, Poppy had repeatedly urged Alice to let her hair down a bit, as she herself was doing with the air-raid warden. They were all going to be blown up, she argued, and if Alice thought that Lenny and Albert weren't chancing their arms with the local talent in Italy and Africa then Alice definitely had another think coming. But Alice, even after Lenny confessed that he'd once chanced his arm through physical desperation, couldn't bring herself to emulate the easy attitudes of her friend. The air-raid warden was always producing friends for her, men whose health wasn't good either, but Alice chatted politely to each of them and made it clear that she didn't wish for a closer relationship. With peace and the death of the air-raid warden, Poppy calmed down a bit, and the birth of her child eighteen months later calmed her down further.

But even so she was still the same Poppy, and in late middle age when she suggested that she and Alice should take up dancing again the idea seemed to Alice to be just like all the other ideas Poppy had had in the past: when they were seven, to take Mrs Grounds' washing off her line and peg it up on Mrs Bond's; when they were ten, to go to Woolworth's with Davie Rickard and slip packets of carrots from the counter into the pockets of his jacket; at fifteen, to write anonymous letters to every teacher who'd ever had anything to do with them; at sixteen, to cut the hair of people in the row in front of them in the Regal Cinema. 'Dancing?' Alice said. 'Oh, Poppy, whatever would they say?'

Whatever would the two husbands say, she meant, and the other wives of Paper Street and Beryl and Ron? Going to Bingo was one thing and quite accepted. Going dancing at fifty-four was a different kettle of fish altogether. Before their marriages they had often gone dancing: they had been taken to dance-halls on Saturday nights by the men they later married, and by other men. Every June, all four of them went dancing once or twice in Southend, even though the husbands increasingly complained that it made them feel ridiculous. But what Poppy had in mind now wasn't the Grand Palais in Southend or the humbler floors of thirty years ago, or embarrassed husbands, or youths treading over your feet: what Poppy had in mind was afternoon dancing in a place in the West End, without the husbands or anyone else knowing a thing about it. 'Tea-time foxtrots,' Poppy said. 'The Tottenham Court Dance-Rooms. All the rage, they are.' And in the end Alice agreed.

They went quite regularly to the Tottenham Court Dance-Rooms, almost every Tuesday. They dressed up as they used to dress up years ago; with discretion they applied rouge and eye-shadow. Alice put on a peach-coloured corset in an effort to trim down her figure a bit, and curled the hair that had once been fair and now was grey. It looked a bit frizzy when she curled it now, the way it had never done when she was a girl, but although the sight of it sometimes depressed her she accepted the middle-aged frizziness because there was nothing she could do about it. Poppy's hair had become rather thin on the top of her head, but she didn't seem to notice and Alice naturally didn't mention the fact. In middle age Poppy always kept her grey hair dyed a brightish shade of chestnut, and when Alice once read in a magazine that excessive dyeing eventually caused a degree of baldness she didn't mention it either, fearing that in Poppy's case the damage was already done. On their dancing afternoons they put on headscarves and pulled their coats carefully about them, to hide the finery beneath. Poppy wore spectacles with gold-coloured trim on the orange frames, her special-occasion spectacles she called them. They always walked quickly away from Paper Street.

In the dance-rooms they had tea on the balcony as soon as they arrived, at about a quarter-to-three. There was a lot of scarlet plush on the balcony, and scarlet lights. There were little round tables with paper covers on them, for convenience. When they'd had tea and Danish pastries and a few slices of Swiss roll they descended one of the staircases that led to the dance-floor and stood chatting by a pillar. Sometimes men came up to them and asked if one or other would like to dance. They didn't mind if men came up or not, or at least they didn't mind particularly. What they enjoyed was the band, usually Leo Ritz and his Band, and looking at the other dancers and the scarlet plush and having tea. Years ago they'd have danced together, just for the fun of it, but somehow they felt too old for that, at fifty-four. An elderly man with rather long grey hair once danced too intimately with Alice and she'd had to ask him to release her. Another time a middle-aged man, not quite sober, kept following them about, trying to buy them Coca-Cola. He was from Birmingham, he told them; he was in London on business and had had lunch with people who were making a cartoon film for his firm. He described the film so that they could look out for it on their television screens: it was an advertisement for wallpaper paste, which was what his firm manufactured. They were glad when this man didn't appear the following Tuesday.

Other men were nicer. There was one who said his name was Sidney, who was lonely because his wife had left him for a younger man; and another who was delicate, a Mr Hawke. There was a silent, bald-headed man whom they both liked dancing with because he was so good at it, and there was Grantly Palmer, who was said to have won awards for dancing in the West Indies.

Grantly Palmer was a Jamaican, a man whom neither of them had agreed to dance with when he'd first asked them because of his colour. He worked as a barman in a club, he told them later, and because of that he rarely had the opportunity to dance at night. He'd often thought of changing his job since dancing meant so much to him, but bar work was all he knew. In the end they became quite friendly with Grantly Palmer, so much so that whenever they entered the dance-rooms he'd hurry up to them smiling, neat as a new pin. He'd dance with one and then the other. Tea had to wait, and when eventually they sat down to it he sat with them and insisted on paying. He was always attentive, pressing Swiss roll on both of them and getting them cigarettes from the coin machine. He talked about the club where he worked, the Rumba Rendezvous in Notting Hill Gate, and often tried to persuade them to give it a try. They giggled quite girlishly at that, wondering what their husbands would say about their attending the Rumba Rendezvous, a West Indian Club. Their husbands would have been astonished enough if they knew they went afternoon tea-dancing in the Tottenham Court Dance-Rooms.

Grantly Palmer was a man of forty-two who had never married, who lived alone in a room in Maida Vale. He was a born bachelor, he told the two wives, and would not have appreciated home life, with children and all that it otherwise implied. In his youth he had played the pins, he informed them with an elaborate, white smile, meaning by this that he'd had romantic associations. He would laugh loudly when he said it. He'd been naughty in his time, he said.

Whenever he talked like that, with his eyes blazing excitedly and his teeth flashing, Alice couldn't help thinking that Grantly Palmer was a holy terror just like Poppy had been and still in a way was, the male equivalent. She once said this to Poppy and immediately regretted it, fearing that Poppy would take offence at being likened to a black man, but Poppy hadn't minded at all. Poppy had puffed at a tipped Embassy and had made Alice blush all over her neck by saying that in her opinion Grantly Palmer fancied her. 'Skin and bone he'd think me,' Poppy said. 'Blacks like a girl they can get their teeth into.' They were on the upper deck of a bus at the time and Poppy had laughed shrilly into her cigarette smoke, causing people to glance amusedly at her. She peered through her gold-trimmed spectacles at the people who looked at her, smiling at them. 'My friend has a fella in love with her,' she said to the conductor, shouting after him as he clattered down the stairs. 'A holy terror she says he is.'

He was cheeky, Alice said, the way he always insisted on walking off the dance-floor hand in hand with you, the way he'd pinch your arm sometimes. But her complaints were half-hearted because the liberties Grantly Palmer took were never offensive: it wasn't at all the same as having a drunk pulling you too close to him and slobbering into your hair. 'You'll lose him, Alice,' Poppy cried now and again in shrill mock-alarm as they watched him paying attentions to some woman who was new to the dance-rooms. Once he'd referred to such a person, asking them if they'd noticed her, a stout woman in pink, an unmarried shorthand typist he said she was. 'My, my,' he said in his Jamaican drawl, shaking his head. 'My, my.' They never saw the unmarried shorthand typist again, but Poppy said he'd definitely been implying something, that he'd probably enticed her to his room in Maida Vale. 'Making you jealous,' Poppy said.

The men whom Alice and Poppy had married weren't at all like Grantly

Palmer. They were quiet men, rather similar in appearance and certainly similar in outlook. Both were of medium build, getting rather bald in their fifties, Alice's Lenny with a moustache, Poppy's Albert without. They were keen supporters of Crystal Palace Football Club, and neither of them, according to Poppy, knew anything about women. The air-raid warden had known about women, Poppy said, and so did Grantly Palmer. 'He wants you to go out with him,' she said to Alice. 'You can see it in his eyes.' One afternoon when he was dancing with Alice he asked her if she'd consider having a drink on her own with him, some evening when she wasn't doing anything better. She shook her head when he said that, and he didn't ever bring the subject up again. 'He's mad for you,' Poppy said when she told her of this invitation. 'He's head over heels, love.' But Alice laughed, unable to believe that Grantly Palmer could possibly be mad for a corseted grandmother of fifty-four with unmanageable grey hair.

Without much warning, Poppy died. During a summer holiday at Mrs Roope's Prospect Hotel she'd complained of pains, though not much, because that was not her way. 'First day back you'll see Dr Pace,' Albert commanded. Two months later she died one night, without waking up.

After the death Alice was at a loss. For almost fifty years Poppy had been her friend. The affection between them had increased as they'd watched one another age and as their companionship yielded more memories they could share. Their children – Alice's Beryl and Ron, and Poppy's George – had played together. There'd been the business of George's emigration to Canada, and Alice's comforting of Poppy because of it. There'd been the marriage of Ron and then of Beryl, and Poppy's expression of Alice's unspoken thought, that Ron's Hilda wasn't good enough for him, too bossy for any man really, and Poppy's approval of Beryl's Tony, an approval that Alice shared.

Alice had missed her children when they'd gone, just as Poppy had missed George. 'Oh Lord, I know, dear!' Poppy cried when Alice wept the day after Beryl's wedding. Beryl had lived at home until then, as Ron had until his marriage. It was a help, being able to talk to Poppy about it, and Poppy so accurately understanding what Alice felt.

After Poppy's death the silence she'd prevented when Alice's children had grown up fell with a vengeance. It icily surrounded Alice and she found it hard to adapt herself to a life that was greyer and quieter, to days going by without Poppy dropping in or she herself dropping in on Poppy, without the cups of Maxwell House coffee they'd had together, and the cups of tea, and the biscuits and raspberry-jam sandwich cake, which Poppy had been fond of. Once, awake in the middle of the night, she found herself thinking that if Lenny had died she mightn't have missed him so much. She hated that thought and tried, unsuccessfully, to dispel it from her mind. It was because she and Poppy had told one another everything, she kept saying to herself, the way you couldn't really tell Lenny. But all this sounded rather lame, and when she said to herself instead that it was because she and Poppy had known one another all their lives it didn't sound much better: she and Lenny had known one another all their lives, too. For six months after the death she didn't go to Bingo, unable to face going on her own. It didn't even occur to her to go afternoon dancing.

The first summer after the death, Alice and Lenny and Albert went as usual to the Prospect Hotel in Southend. There seemed to the two men to be no good reason why they shouldn't, although when they arrived there Albert was suddenly silent and Alice could see that he was more upset than he'd imagined he would be. But after a day he was quite himself again, and when it wasn't necessary to cheer him up any more she began to feel miserable herself. It wasn't so much because of the death, but because she felt superfluous without Poppy. She realized gradually, and the two men realized even more gradually, that on previous holidays there had been no conversation that was general to all four of them: the men had talked to each other and so had their wives. The men did their best now to include Alice, but it was difficult and awkward.

She took to going for walks by herself, along the front and down the piers, out to the sea and back again. It was then, that summer at Southend, that Alice began to think about Grantly Palmer. It had never occurred to her before that he didn't even know that Poppy had died, even though they'd all three been such good friends on Tuesday afternoons at the Tottenham Court Dance-Rooms. She wondered what he thought, if he'd been puzzled by their sudden absence, or if he still attended the dance-rooms himself. One night in the Prospect Hotel, listening to the throaty breathing of her husband, she suddenly and quite urgently wanted to tell Grantly Palmer about Poppy's death. She suddenly felt that it was his due, that she'd been unkind not ever to have informed him. Poppy would wish him to know, she said to herself; it was bad that she'd let down her friends in this small way. In the middle of that night, while still listening to Lenny's breathing, she resolved to return to the Tottenham Court Dance-Rooms and found herself wondering if Leo Ritz and his Band would still be playing there.

'Breakfasts've gone down a bit,' Albert said on the way back to London, and Lenny reminded him that Mrs Roope had had a bit of family trouble. 'Dropped Charlie Cooke, I see,' Lenny said, referring to a Crystal Palace player. He handed Albert the *Daily Mirror*, open at the sports page. 'Dare say they'll be back to normal next year,' Albert said, still referring to the breakfasts.

In Paper Street, a week after their return, she put on her peach-coloured corset and the dress she'd worn the first time they'd gone afternoon dancing – blue-green satin, with a small array of sequins at the shoulders and the breast. It felt more silent than ever in the house in Paper Street, because in the past Poppy used to chat and giggle in just the same way as she had as a girl, lavishly spraying scent on herself, a habit she'd always had also. Alice closed the door of Number 41 behind her and walked quickly in Paper Street, feeling guiltier than she had when the guilt could be shared. She'd tell some lie if someone she knew said she was looking smart. She'd probably say she was going to Bingo, which was what they'd both said once when Mrs Tedman had looked them up and down, as though suspecting the finery beneath. You could see that Mrs Tedman hadn't believed that they were going to Bingo, but Poppy said it didn't matter what Mrs Tedman thought. It was all a bit frightening without Poppy, but then everything was something else without Poppy, dull or silent or frightening. Alice caught a bus, and at a quarter-to-three she entered the dance-rooms.

'Well, well!' Grantly Palmer said, smiling his bright smile. 'Well, well, stranger lady!'

'Hullo, Mr Palmer.'

'Oh, child, child!'

'Hullo, Grantly.'

It had always been a joke, the business of Christian names between the three of them. 'Alice and Poppy!' he'd said the first time they'd had tea together. 'My, my, what charmin' names!' They'd just begun to use his own Christian name when Poppy had died. 'Funny name, Grantly,' Poppy had remarked on the bus after he'd first told them, but soon it had become impossible to think of him as anything else.

'Where's Poppy, dear?'

'Poppy died, Grantly.'

She told him all about it, about last year's holiday at Southend and the development of the illness and then the funeral. 'My God!' he said, staring into her eyes. 'My God, Alice.'

The band was playing 'Lullaby of Broadway': middle-aged women, in twos or on their own, stood about, sizing up the men who approached them, in the same expert way as she and Poppy had sized men up in their time. 'Let's have a cup of tea,' Grantly Palmer said.

They had tea and Swiss roll slices and Danish pastries. They talked about Poppy. 'Was she happy?' he asked. And Alice said her friend had been happy enough.

In silence on the balcony they watched the dancers rotating below them. He wasn't going to dance with her, she thought, because Poppy had died, because the occasion was a solemn one. She was aware of disappointment. Poppy had been dead for more than a year, after all.

'It's a horrible thing,' he said. 'A friend dying. In the prime of her life.'

'I miss her.'

'Of course, Alice.'

He reached across the tea-table and seized one of her hands. He held it for a moment and then let it go. It was a gesture that reminded her of being a girl. On television men touched girls' hands in that way. How nice, she suddenly thought, the chap called Ashley was in *Gone with the Wind*.

She'd seen the film with Poppy, revived a few years back, Leslie Howard playing Ashley.

He went away and returned with another pot of tea and a plate of Swiss roll slices. Leo Ritz and his Band were playing 'September Love'.

'I thought I'd never lay eyes on you again, Alice.'

He regarded her solemnly. He didn't smile when he said that the very first time he'd met her he'd considered her a very nice person. He was wearing a suit made of fine, black corduroy. His two grey hands were gripping his tea-cup, nursing it.

'I came back to tell you about Poppy, Grantly.'

'I kept on hoping you'd come back. I kept on thinking about you.' He nodded, lending emphasis to this statement. Without drinking from it, he placed his tea-cup on the table and pulled his chair in a bit, nearer to hers. She could feel some part of his legs, an ankle-bone it felt like. Then she felt one of his hands, beneath the table, touching her right knee and then touching the left one.

She didn't move. She gazed ahead of her, feeling through the material of her dress the warmth of his flesh. The first time they'd had tea with him he'd told a joke about three Jamaican clergymen on a desert island and she and Poppy had laughed their heads off. Even when it had become clear to Poppy and herself that what he was after was sex and not love, Poppy had still insisted that she could chance her arm with him. It was as though Poppy wanted her to go out with Grantly Palmer because she herself had gone out with the air-raid warden.

His hand remained on her left knee. She imagined it there, the thin grey hand on the blue satin material of her dress. It moved, pushing back the satin, the palm caressing, the tip of the thumb pressing into her thigh.

She withdrew her leg, smiling to cover the unfriendliness of this decision. She could feel warmth all over her neck and her cheeks and around her eyes. She could feel her eyes beginning to water. On her back and high up on her forehead, beneath the grey frizz of her hair, she felt the moisture of sweat.

He looked away from her. 'I always liked you, Alice,' he said. 'You know? I liked you better than Poppy, even though I liked Poppy too.'

It was different, a man putting his hand on your knee: it was different altogether from the natural intimacy of dancing, when anything might have been accidental. She wanted to go away now; she didn't want him to ask her to dance with him. She imagined him with the pink woman, fondling her knees under a table before taking her to Maida Vale. She saw herself in the room in Maida Vale, a room in which there were lilies growing in pots, although she couldn't remember that he'd ever said he had lilies. There was a thing like a bedspread hanging on one of the walls, brightly coloured, red and blue and yellow. There was a gas fire glowing and a standard lamp such as she'd seen in the British Home Stores, and a bed with a similar brightly-coloured cloth covering it, and a table and two upright chairs, and a tattered green screen behind which there'd be a sink and a cooking stove. In the room he came to her and took her coat off and then undid the buttons of her dress. He lifted her petticoat over her head and unhooked her peach-coloured corset and her brassière.

'Will you dance with me, Alice?'

She shook her head. Her clothes were sticking to her now. Her armpits were clammy.

'Won't you dance, dear?'

She said she'd rather not, not today. Her voice shivered and drily crackled. She'd just come to tell him about Poppy, she said again.

'I'd like to be friends with you, Alice. Now that Poppy has –'

'I have to go home, Grantly. I have to.'

'Don't go, darling.'

His hands had crossed the table again. They held her wrists; his teeth and his eyes flashed at her, though not in a smiling way. She shouldn't have come, her own voice kept protesting in the depths of her mind, like an echo. It had all been different when there were three of them, all harmless flirtation, with Poppy giggling and pretending, just fun.

There was excitement in his face. He released her wrists, and again, beneath the table, she felt one of his legs against hers. He pushed his chair closer to the table, a hand moved on her thigh again.

'No, no,' she said.

'I looked for you. I don't know your other name, you know. I didn't know Poppy's either. I didn't know where you lived. But I looked for you, Alice.'

He didn't say how he'd looked for her, but repeated that he had, nodding emphatically.

'I thought if I found you we'd maybe have a drink one night. I have records in my room I'd like you to hear, Alice. I'd like to have your opinion.'

'I couldn't go to your room –'

'It would be just like sitting here, Alice. It would be quite all right.'

'I couldn't ever, Grantly.'

What would Beryl and Ron say if they could see her now, if they could hear the conversation she was having, and see his hand on her leg? She remembered them suddenly as children, Beryl on the greedy side yet refusing to eat fish in any shape or form, Ron having his nails painted with Nail-Gro because he bit them. She remembered the birth of Ron and how it had been touch and go because he'd weighed so little. She remembered the time Beryl scalded herself on the electric kettle and how Lenny had rung 999 because he said it would be the quickest way to get attention. She remembered the first night she'd been married to Lenny, taking her clothes off under a wrap her mother had given her because she'd always been shy about everything. All she had to do, she said to herself, was to stand up and go.

His hands weren't touching her any more. He moved his body away from hers, and she looked at him and saw that the excitement had gone from his face. His eyes had a dead look. His mouth had a melancholy twist to it.

'I'm sorry,' she said.

'I fancied you that first day, Alice. I always fancied you, Alice.'

He was speaking the truth to her and it was strange to think of it as the truth, even though she had known that in some purely physical way he desired her. It was different from being mad for a person, and yet she felt that his desiring her was just as strange as being mad for her. If he didn't desire her she'd have been able to return to the dance-rooms, they'd have been able to sit here on the balcony, again and again, she telling him more about Poppy and he telling her more about himself, making one another laugh. Yet if he didn't desire her he wouldn't want to be bothered with any of that.

'Can't fancy black girls,' he said, with his head turned well away from her. 'White women, over sixty if it's possible. Thirteen stone or so. That's why I go to the dance-rooms.' He turned to face her and gazed morosely at her eyes. 'I'm queer that way,' he said. 'I'm a nasty kind of black man.'

She could feel sickness in her stomach, and the skin of her back, which had been so damp with sweat, was now cold. She picked up her handbag and held it awkwardly for a moment, not knowing what to say. 'I must go,' she said eventually, and her legs felt shaky when she stood on them.

He remained at the table, all his politeness gone. He looked bitter and angry and truculent. She thought he might insult her. She thought he might shout loudly at her in the dance-rooms, calling her names and abusing her. But he didn't. He didn't say anything at all to her. He sat there in the dim, tinted light, seeming to slump from one degree of disappointment to a deeper one. He looked crude and pathetic. He looked another person.

Again, as she stood there awkwardly, she thought about the room in Maida Vale, which she'd furnished with lilies and brightly-coloured cloths. Again his grey hands undid her corset and her brassière, and just for a moment it seemed that there wouldn't have been much wrong in letting him admire her in whatever way he wanted to. It was something that would disgust people if they knew; Beryl and Ron would be disgusted, and Lenny and Albert naturally enough. Grantly Palmer would disgust them, and she herself, a grandmother, would disgust them for permitting his attentions. There was something wrong with Grantly Palmer, they'd all say: he was sick and dirty, as he even admitted himself. Yet there were always things wrong with people, things you didn't much care for and even were disgusted by, like Beryl being greedy and Ron biting his nails, like the way Lenny would sometimes blow his nose without using a handkerchief or a tissue. Even Poppy hadn't been perfect: on a bus it had sometimes been too much, her shrillness and her rushy ways, so clearly distasteful to other people sitting there.

Alice wanted to tell Grantly Palmer all that. Desperately she tried to form an argument in her mind, a conversation with herself that had as its elements the greediness of her daughter and her son's bitten nails and her husband clearing the mucus from his nose at the sink, and she herself agreeing to be the object of perversion. But the elements would not connect, and she felt instinctively that she could not transform them into coherent argument. The elements spun dizzily in her mind, the sense she sought from them did not materialize.

'Goodbye,' she said, knowing he would not answer. He was ashamed of himself; he wanted her to go. 'Goodbye,' she said again. 'Goodbye, Grantly.'

She moved away from him, forcing herself to think about the house in Paper Street, about entering it and changing her clothes before Lenny returned. She'd bought two chops that morning and there was part of a packet of frozen beans in the fridge. She saw herself peeling potatoes at the sink, but at the same time she could feel Grantly Palmer behind her, still sitting at the table, ashamed when he need not be. She felt ashamed herself for having tea with him, for going to see him when she shouldn't, just because Poppy was dead and there was no one else who was fun to be with.

Leo Ritz and his Band were playing 'Scatterbrain' as she left the dance-rooms. The middle-aged dancers smiled as they danced, some of them humming the tune.

Last Wishes

In the neighbourhood Mrs Abercrombie was a talking point. Strangers who asked at Miss Dobbs' Post Office and Village Stores or at the Royal Oak were told that the wide entrance gates on the Castle Cary road were the gates to Rews Manor, where Mrs Abercrombie lived in the past, with servants. No one from the village except old Dr Ripley and a window-cleaner had seen her since 1947, the year of her husband's death. According to Dr Ripley, she'd become a hypochondriac.

But even if she had, and in spite of her desire to live as a recluse, Mrs Abercrombie continued to foster the grandeur that made Rews Manor, nowadays, seem old-fashioned. Strangers were told that the interior of the house had to be seen to be believed. The staircase alone, in white rose-veined marble, was reckoned to be worth thousands; the faded carpets had come from Persia; all the furniture had been in the Abercrombie family for four or five generations. On every second Sunday in the summer the garden was open to visitors and the admission charges went to the Nurses.

Once a week Plunkett, the most important of Mrs Abercrombie's servants, being her butler, drove into the village and bought stamps and cigarettes in the post office and stores. It was a gesture more than anything else, Miss Dobbs considered, because the bulk of the Rews Manor shopping was done in one or other of the nearby towns. Plunkett was about fifty, a man with a sandy appearance who drove a pre-war Wolseley and had a pleasant, easy-going smile. The window-cleaner reported that there was a Mrs Plunkett, a uniformed housemaid, but old Dr Ripley said the uniformed maid was a person called Tindall. There were five servants at Rews Manor, Dr Ripley said, if you counted the two gardeners, Mr Apse and Miss Bell, and all of them were happy. He often repeated that Mrs Abercrombie's servants were happy, as though making a point: they were pleasant people to know, he said, because of their contentment. Those who had met Plunkett in the village agreed, and strangers who had come across Mr Apse and Miss Bell in the gardens of Rews Manor found them pleasant also, and often envied them their dispositions.

In the village it was told how there'd always been Abercrombies at Rews Manor, how the present Mrs Abercrombie's husband had lived there alone when he'd inherited it – until he married at forty-one, having previously not intended to marry at all because he suffered from a blood disease that had killed his father and his grandfather early in their lives. It was told how the marriage had been a brief and a happy one, and how there'd been no children. Mrs Abercrombie's husband had died within five years and had been buried in the grounds of Rews Manor, near the azaleas.

'So beautifully kept, the garden,' visitors to the neighbourhood would marvel. 'That gravel in front, not a stone out of place! Those lawns and rose-bushes!' And then, intrigued by the old-fashioned quality of the place, they'd hear the story of this woman whose husband had inopportunely died, who existed now only in the world of her house and gardens, who lived in the past because she did not care for the present. People wove fantasies around this house and its people; to those who were outside it, it touched on fantasy itself. It was real because it was there and you could see it, because you could see the man called Plunkett buying stamps in the post office, but its reality was strange, as exotic as a coloured orchid. In the nineteen-sixties and -seventies, when life often had a grey look, the story of Rews Manor cheered people up, both those who told it and those who listened. It created images in minds and it affected imaginations. The holidaymakers who walked through the beautifully-kept garden, through beds of begonias and roses, among blue hydrangeas and potentilla and witch-hazel and fuchsia, were grateful. They were grateful for the garden and for the story that went with them, and later they told the story themselves, with conjectured variations.

At closer quarters, Rews Manor was very much a world of its own. In 1948, at the time of Mr Abercrombie's death, Mr Apse, the gardener, worked under the eighty-year-old Mr Marriott, and when Mr Marriott died Mrs Abercrombie promoted Mr Apse and advertised for an assistant. There seemed no reason why a woman should not be as suitable as a man and so Miss Bell, being the only applicant, was given the post. Plunkett had also been advertised for when his predecessor, Stubbins, had become too old to carry on. The housemaid, Tindall, had been employed a few years after the arrival of Plunkett, as had Mrs Pope, who cooked.

The servants all lived in, Mr Apse where he had always lived, in a room over the garage, Miss Bell next door to him. The other three had rooms in a wing of the house which servants, in the days when servants were more the thing, had entirely occupied. They met for meals in the kitchen and sometimes they would sit there in the evenings. The room which once had been the servants' sitting-room had a dreariness about it: in 1956 Plunkett moved the television set into the kitchen.

Mr Apse was sixty-three now and Miss Bell was forty-five. Mrs Pope was fifty-nine, Tindall forty-three. Plunkett, reckoned in the village to be about fifty, was in fact precisely that. Plunkett, who had authority over the indoor servants and over Mr Apse and Miss Bell when they were in the kitchen, had at the time of Mrs Abercrombie's advertisement held a position in a *nouveau riche* household in Warwickshire. He might slowly have climbed the ladder and found himself, when death or age had made a gap for him, in charge of its servants. He might have married and had children. He might have found himself for the rest of his life in the butler's bungalow, tucked out of sight on the grounds, growing vegetables in his spare time. But for Plunkett these prospects hadn't seemed quite right. He didn't want to marry, nor did he wish to father children. He wanted to continue being a servant because being a servant made him happy, yet the stuffiness of some households was more than he could bear and he didn't like having to wait for years before being in charge. He looked around, and as soon as he set foot in Rews Manor he knew it was exactly what he wanted, a small world in which he had only himself to blame if the food and wine weren't more than up to scratch. He assisted Mrs Abercrombie in her choosing of Mrs Pope as cook, recognizing in Mrs Pope the long-latent talents of a woman who sought the opportunity to make food her religion. He also assisted in the employing of Tindall, a fact he had often recalled since, on the nights he spent in her bed.

Mrs Pope had cooked in a YWCA until she answered the advertisement. The raw materials she was provided with had offered her little opportunity for the culinary experiments she would have liked to attempt. For twenty years she had remained in the kitchens of the YWCA because her husband, now dead, had been the janitor. In the flat attached to the place she had brought up two children, a boy and a girl, both of them now married. She'd wanted to move to somewhere nicer when Winnie, the girl, had married a traveller in stationery, but her husband had refused point-blank, claiming that the YWCA had become his home. When he died, she hadn't hesitated.

Miss Bell had been a teacher of geography, but had been advised for health considerations to take on outdoor work. Having always enjoyed gardening and knowing quite a bit about it, she'd answered Mrs Abercrombie's advertisement in *The Times*. She'd become used to living in, in a succession of boarding-schools, so that living in somewhere else suited her quite well. Mr Apse was a silent individual, which suited her also. For long hours they would work side by side in the vegetable garden or among the blue hydrangeas and azaleas that formed a shrubbery around the house, neither of them saying anything at all.

Tindall had worked as a packer in a frozen-foods factory. There'd been trouble in her life in that the man she'd been engaged to when she was twenty-two, another employee in the factory, had made her pregnant and had then, without warning, disappeared. He was a man called Bert Fask, considerate in every possible way, quiet and seemingly reliable. Everyone said she was lucky to be engaged to Bert Fask and she had imagined quite a happy future. 'Don't matter a thing,' he said when she told him she was pregnant, and he fixed it that they could get married six months sooner than they'd intended. Then he disappeared. She'd later heard that he'd done the same thing with other girls, and when it became clear that he didn't intend to return she began to feel bitter. Her only consolation was the baby, which she still intended to have even though she didn't know how on earth she was going to manage. She loved her unborn child and she longed for its birth so that she herself could feel loved again. But the child, two months premature, lived for only sixteen hours. That blow was a terrible one, and it was when endeavouring to get over it that she'd come across Mrs Abercrombie's advertisement, on a page of a newspaper that a greengrocer had wrapped a beetroot in. That chance led her to a contentment she hadn't known before, to a happiness that was different only in detail from the happinesses of the other servants.

On the morning of July 12th, 1974, a Friday, Tindall knocked on Mrs Abercrombie's bedroom door at her usual time of eight forty-five. She carried into the room Mrs Abercrombie's breakfast tray and the morning mail, and placed the tray on the Queen Anne table just inside the door. She pulled back the bedroom's six curtains. 'A cloudy day,' she said.

Mrs Abercrombie, who had been reading Butler's *Lives of the Saints*, extinguished her bedside light. She remarked that the wireless the night before had predicted that the weather would be unsettled: rain would do the garden good.

Tindall carried the tray to the bed, placed it on the mahogany bed-table and settled the bed-table into position. Mrs Abercrombie picked up her letters. Tindall left the room.

Letters were usually bills, which were later passed to Plunkett to deal with. Plunkett had a housekeeping account, into which a sum of money was automatically transferred once a month. Mrs Abercrombie's personal requirements were purchased from this same account, negligible since she had ceased to buy clothes. It was Tindall who noticed when she needed a lipstick refill or lavender water or more hairpins. Tindall made a list and handed it to Plunkett. For years Mrs Abercrombie herself hadn't had the bother of having to remember, or having to sign a cheque.

This morning there was the monthly account from the International Stores and one from the South-Western Electricity Board. The pale brown envelopes were identification enough: she put them aside unopened. The third envelope contained a letter from her solicitors about her will.

In the kitchen, over breakfast, the talk turned to white raspberries. Mr Apse said that in the old days white raspberries had been specially cultivated in the garden. Tindall, who had never heard of white raspberries before, remarked that the very idea of them gave her the creeps. 'More flavour really,' Miss Bell said quietly.

Plunkett, engrossed in the *Daily Telegraph*, did not say anything. Mrs Pope said she'd never had white raspberries and would like to try them. She'd be more than grateful, she added, if Mr Apse could see his way to putting in a few canes. But Mr Apse had relapsed into his more familiar mood of silence. He was a big man, slow of movement, with a brown bald head and tufts of grey hair about his ears. He ate bacon and mushrooms and an egg in a slow and careful manner, occasionally between mouthfuls drinking tea. Miss Bell nodded at Mrs Pope, an indication that Mr Apse had heard the request about the raspberries and would act upon it.

'Like slugs they sound,' Tindall said.

Miss Bell, who had small tortoiseshell glasses and was small herself, with a weather-beaten face, said that they did not taste like slugs. Her father had grown white raspberries, her mother had made a delicious dish with them, mixing them with loganberries and baking them with a meringue top. Mrs Pope nodded. She'd read a recipe like that once, in Mrs Beeton it might have been; she'd like to try it out.

In the *Daily Telegraph* Plunkett read that there was a strike of television technicians and a strike of petrol hauliers. The sugar shortage was to continue and there was likely to be a shortage of bread. He sighed without making a sound. Staring at print he didn't feel like reading, he recalled the warmth of Tindall's body the night before. He glanced round the edge of the newspaper at her: there was a brightness in her eyes, which was always there the morning after he'd visited her in bed. She'd wept twice during the four hours he'd spent: tears of fulfilment he'd learnt they were, but all the same he could never prevent himself from comforting her. Few words passed between them when they came together in the night; his comforting consisted of stroking her hair and kissing her damp cheeks. She had narrow cheeks, and jet-black hair which she wore done up in a knot during the day but which tumbled all over the pillows when she was in bed. Her body was bony, which he appreciated. He didn't know about the tragedy in her life because she'd never told him; in his eyes she was a good and efficient servant and a generous woman, very different from the sorrowful creature who'd come looking for employment eighteen years ago. She had never once hinted at marriage, leaving him to deduce that for her their arrangement was as satisfactory as it was for him.

'Moussaka for dinner,' Mrs Pope said, rising from the breakfast table. 'She asked for it special.'

'No wonder, after your last one,' Miss Bell murmured. The food at the schools where she'd taught geography had always been appalling: grey-coloured mince and soup that smelt, huge sausage-rolls for Sunday tea, cold scrambled egg.

'Secret is, cook it gently,' Mrs Pope said, piling dishes into the sink. 'That's all there's to it if you ask me.'

'Oh no, no,' Miss Bell murmured, implying that there was a great deal more to moussaka than that. She carried her own dishes to the sink. Mrs Pope had a way with moussaka, she added in her same quiet way, which was why Mrs Abercrombie had asked for it again.

Tindall chewed her last corner of toast and marmalade. She felt just slightly sore, pleasantly so, as she always did after a visit from Plunkett. Quite remarkable he sometimes was in the middle of the night, yet who'd have thought he'd know a thing about any of it?

Mr Apse left the kitchen and Miss Bell followed him. Tindall carried her dishes to the sink and assisted Mrs Pope with the washing up. At the table Plunkett lit his first cigarette of the day, lingering over a last cup of tea.

As she did every morning after breakfast, Mrs Abercrombie recalled her husband's death. It had taken place on a fine day in March, a day with a frost in the early morning and afterwards becoming sunny, though still cold. He'd had a touch of 'flu but was almost better; Dr Ripley had suggested his getting up in time for lunch. But by lunch-time he was dead, with the awful suddenness that had marked the deaths of his father and his grandfather, nothing to do with 'flu at all. She'd come into their bedroom, with the clothes she'd aired for him to get up into.

Mrs Abercrombie was sixty-one now; she'd been thirty-four at the time of the death. Her life for twenty-seven years had been a memorial to her brief marriage, but death had not cast unduly gloomy shadows, for after the passion of her sorrow there was some joy at least in her sentimental memories. Her own death preoccupied her now: she was going to die because with every day that passed she felt more weary. She felt herself slipping away and even experienced slight pains in her body, as if some ailment had developed in order to hurry her along. She'd told Dr Ripley, wondering if her gallstones were playing up, but Dr Ripley said there was nothing the matter with her. It didn't comfort her that he said it because she didn't in the least mind dying. She had a belief that after death she would meet again the man who had himself died so abruptly, that the interrupted marriage would somehow continue. For twenty-seven years this hope had been the consolation that kept her going. That and the fact that she had provided a home for Mr Apse and Miss Bell, and Mrs Pope and Tindall and Plunkett, all of whom had grown older with her and had shared with her the beauty of her husband's house.

'I shall not get up today,' she murmured on the morning of July 12th. She did not, and in fact did not ever again get up.

They were thrown into confusion. They stood in the kitchen looking at one another, only Plunkett looking elsewhere, at the Aga that for so long now had been Mrs Pope's delight. No one had expected Mrs Abercrombie to die, having been repeatedly assured by Dr Ripley that there was nothing the matter with her. The way she lived, so carefully and so well looked after, there had seemed no reason why she shouldn't last for another twenty years at the very least, into her eighties. In bed at night, on the occasions when he didn't visit Tindall's bed, Plunkett had worked out that if Mrs Abercrombie lived until she was eighty, Miss Bell would be seventy-four and Mrs Pope seventy-eight. Tindall, at sixty-two, would presumably be beyond the age of desire, as he himself no doubt would be at sixty-nine. Mr Apse, so grizzled and healthy did he sometimes seem, might still b able to be useful in the garden, at eighty-two. It seemed absurd to Plunkett on the morning of July 12th that Mrs Abercrombie had died twenty years too soon. It also seemed unfair.

It seemed particularly unfair because, according to the letter which Mrs Abercrombie had that morning received from her solicitors, she had been in the process of altering her will. Mrs Abercrombie had once revealed to Plunkett that it had been her husband's wish, in view of the fact that there were no children, that Rews Manor should eventually pass into the possession of a body which was engaged in the study of rare grasses. It was a subject that had interested him and which he had studied in considerable detail himself. 'There'll be legacies of course,' Mrs Abercrombie had reassured Plunkett, 'for all of you.' She'd smiled when she'd said that and Plunkett had bowed and murmured in a way that, years ago, he'd picked up from Hollywood films that featured English butlers.

But in the last few weeks Mrs Abercrombie had apparently had second thoughts. Reading between the lines of the letter from her solicitors, it was clear to Plunkett that she'd come to consider that legacies for her servants weren't enough. *We assume your wish to be*, the letter read, *that after your death your servants should remain in Rews Manor, retaining the house as it is and keeping the gardens open to the public. That this should be so until such time as Mr Plunkett should have reached retirement age, i.e. sixty-five years or, in the event of Mr Plunkett's previous death, that this arrangement should continue until the year 1990. At either time, the house and gardens should be disposed of as in your current will and the servants remaining should receive the legacies as previously laid down. We would be grateful if you would confirm at your convenience that we are correct in this interpretation of your wishes: in which case we will draw up at once the necessary papers.* But her convenience had never come because she had left it all too late. With the typewritten sheet in his hand, Plunkett had felt a shiver of bitterness. He'd felt it again, with anger, when he'd looked at her dead face.

'Grass,' he said in the kitchen. 'They'll be studying grass here.'

The others knew what he was talking about. They, like he, believing that Mrs Abercrombie would live for a long time yet, had never paused to visualize Rews Manor in that far-off future. They did so now, since the future was bewilderingly at hand. Contemporary life closed in upon the house and garden that had belonged to the past. They saw the house without its furniture since such furniture would be unsuitable in a centre for the studying of grasses. They saw, in a vague way, men in shirtsleeves, smoking pipes and carrying papers. Tindall saw grasses laid out for examination on a long trestle table in the hall. Mr Apse saw roses uprooted from the garden, the blue hydrangeas disposed of, and small seed-beds neatly laid out, for the cultivation of special grass. Miss Bell had a vision of men with a bulldozer, but she could not establish their activity with more precision. Mrs Pope saw caterers' packs on the kitchen table and in the cold room and the store cupboards: transparent plastic bags containing powdered potatoes in enormous quantities, fourteen-pound tins of instant coffee, dried mushrooms and dried all-purpose soup. Plunkett saw a laboratory in the drawing-room.

'I must telephone Dr Ripley,' Plunkett said, and the others thought, but did not say it, that it was too late for Dr Ripley to be of use.

'You have to,' Plunkett said, 'when a person dies.'

He left the kitchen, and Mrs Pope began to make coffee. The others sat down at the table, even though it was half-past eleven in the morning. There were other houses, Tindall said to herself, other country houses where life would be quiet and more agreeable than life in a frozen-foods firm. And yet other houses would not have him coming to her bedroom, for she could never imagine his suggesting that they should go somewhere together. That wasn't his way; it would be too binding, too formal, like a proposal of marriage. And she wouldn't have cared to be Mrs Plunkett, for she didn't in the least love him.

'Poor thing,' Mrs Pope said, pouring her boiling water on to the coffee she had ground, and for a moment Tindall thought the reference was to her.

'Yes,' Miss Bell whispered, 'poor old thing.' She spoke in a kind way, but her words, sincerely meant, did not sound so in the kitchen. Somewhere in the atmosphere that the death had engendered there was resentment, a reflection of the bitterness it had engendered in Plunkett. There was a feeling that Mrs Abercrombie, so considerate in her lifetime, had let them down by dying. Even while she called her a poor old thing, Miss Bell wondered what she should do now. Many employers might consider the idea of a woman gardener eccentric, and certainly other men, more set in their ways than Mr Apse, mightn't welcome a female assistant.

Mrs Pope thought along similar lines. You became used to a place, she was reflecting as she poured the coffee into cups, and there'd be few other places where you could cook so grandly for a single palate, where you were appreciated every day of your life. 'Bloody inedible,' she'd heard a girl exclaim in a corridor of the YWCA, referring to carefully poached haddock in a cream sauce.

'The doctor'll be here at twelve,' Plunkett sombrely announced, re-entering the kitchen from the back hall. 'I left a message; I didn't say she'd died.'

He sat down at the table and waited while Mrs Pope filled his coffee-cup. Tindall placed the jug of hot milk beside him and for a moment the image of her fingers on the flowered surface of the china caused him to remember the caressing of those fingers the night before. He added two lumps of sugar and poured the milk. He felt quite urgent about Tindall, which he never usually did at half-past eleven on a morning after. He put it down to the upset of the death, and the fact that he was idle when normally on a Friday morning he'd be going through the stores with Mrs Pope.

'Doctor'll sign a death warrant,' Mrs Pope said. 'There'll be the funeral.'

Plunkett nodded. Mrs Abercrombie had a cousin in Lincolnshire and another in London, two old men who once, twelve years ago, had spent a weekend in Rews Manor. Mrs Abercrombie hadn't corresponded with them after that, not caring for them, Plunkett imagined. The chances were they were dead by now.

'No one much to tell,' Mrs Pope said, and Miss Bell mentioned the two cousins. He'd see if they were alive, Plunkett said.

It was while saying that, and realizing as he said it the pointlessness of summoning these two ancient men to a funeral, that he had his idea: why should not Mrs Abercrombie's last wishes be honoured, even if she hadn't managed to make them legal? The idea occurred quickly and vividly to him, and immediately he regretted his telephoning of Dr Ripley. But as soon as he regretted it he realized that the telephoning had been essential. Dr Ripley was a line of communication with the outside world and had been one for so long that it would seem strange to other people if a woman, designated a hypochondriac, failed to demand as regularly as before the attentions of her doctor. It would seem stranger still to Dr Ripley.

Yet there was no reason why Mrs Abercrombie should not be quietly buried beside the husband she had loved, where she was scheduled to be buried anyway. There was no reason that Plunkett could see why the household should not then proceed as it had in the past. The curtains of the drawing-room would be drawn when next the window-cleaner came, Dr Ripley would play his part because he'd have no option.

'I see no harm in it,' Plunkett said.

'In what?' Mrs Pope enquired, and then, speaking slowly to break the shock of his idea, he told them. He told them about the letter Mrs Abercrombie had received that morning from her solicitors. He took it from an inside pocket and showed it to them. They at first thought it strange that he should be carrying Mrs Abercrombie's correspondence on his person, but as the letter passed among them, they understood.

'Oh no,' Miss Bell murmured, her small brown face screwed up in distaste. Mrs Pope shook her head and said she couldn't be a party to deception. Mr Apse did not say anything. Tindall half shook her head.

'It was what she clearly wished,' Plunkett explained. 'She had no intention of dying until she'd made this stipulation.'

'Death waits for no one's wishes,' Mr Apse pointed out in a ponderous voice.

'All we are doing,' Plunkett said, 'is to make it wait.'

'But there's Dr Ripley,' Tindall said, and Mrs Pope added that a doctor couldn't ever lend himself to anything shady. It surprised Mrs Pope that Plunkett had made such an extraordinary suggestion, just as it surprised Miss Bell. Tindall and Mr Apse were surprised also, but more at themselves for thinking that what Plunkett was suggesting was only a postponement of the facts, not a suppression.

'But, Plunkett, what exactly are you wanting to do?' Mrs Pope cried out, suddenly shrill.

'She must be buried as she said. She spoke to us all of it, that she wished to be laid down by Mr Abercrombie in the garden.'

'But you have to inform the authorities,' Miss Bell whispered, and Mrs Pope, still shrill, said there had to be a coffin and a funeral.

'I'd make a coffin,' Plunkett replied swiftly. 'There's the timber left over from the drawing-room floorboards. Beautiful oak, plenty of it.'

They knew he could. They'd seen him making other things, a step-ladder and bird-boxes, and shelves for the store-room.

'I was with her one day,' Plunkett said, not telling the truth now. 'We were standing in the garage looking at the timber. "You could make a coffin out of that," she said. "I don't suppose you've ever made a coffin, Plunkett." Those were her exact words. Then she turned and went away: I knew what she meant.'

They believed this lie because to their knowledge he had never lied before. They believed that Mrs Abercrombie had spoken of a coffin, but Miss Bell and Mrs Pope considered that she had only spoken in passing, without significance. Mr Apse and Tindall, wishing to believe that the old woman had been giving a hint to Plunkett, saw no reason to doubt that she had.

'I really couldn't,' Miss Bell said, 'be a party to anything like that.'

For the first time in their association Plunkett disliked Miss Bell. He'd always thought her a little field-mouse of a thing, all brown creases he imagined her body would be, like her face. Mrs Abercrombie had asked him what he'd thought when Miss Bell had answered the advertisement for an assistant gardener. 'She's been a teacher,' Mrs Abercrombie had said, handing him Miss Bell's letter, in which it was stated that Miss Bell was qualified to teach geography but had been medically advised to seek outdoor work. 'No harm in seeing her,' he'd said, and had promised to give Mrs Abercrombie his own opinion after he'd opened the hall-door to the applicant and received her into the hall.

'You would not be here, Miss Bell,' he said now, 'if I hadn't urged Mrs Abercrombie that it wasn't peculiar to employ a woman in the garden. She was dead against it.'

'But that's no reason to go against the law,' Mrs Pope cried, shrill again. 'Just because she took a woman into the garden doesn't mean anything.'

'You would not be here yourself, Mrs Pope. She was extremely reluctant to have a woman whose only experience in the cooking line was in a hostel. It was I who had an instinct about your letter, Mrs Pope.'

'There's still Dr Ripley,' Miss Bell said, feeling that all the protestation and argument were anyway in vain because Dr Ripley was shortly due in the house and would put an end to all this absurdity. Dr Ripley would issue a death certificate and would probably himself inform a firm of undertakers. The death of Mrs Abercrombie had temporarily affected

Plunkett, Miss Bell considered. She'd once read in the *Daily Telegraph* of a woman who'd wished to keep the dead body of her husband under glass.

'Of course there's Dr Ripley,' Mrs Pope said. She spoke sharply and with a trace of disdain in her voice. If Mrs Abercrombie had let them down by dying before her time, then Plunkett was letting them down even more. Plunkett had always been in charge, taking decisions about everything, never at a loss. It was ironic that he should be the one to lose his head now.

'It is Dr Ripley I'm thinking about,' Plunkett said. 'People will say he neglected her.'

There was a silence then in the kitchen. Mrs Pope had begun to lick her lips, a habit with her when she was about to speak. She changed her mind and somehow, because of what had been said about Dr Ripley, found herself less angry. Everyone liked the old doctor, even though they'd often agreed in the kitchen that he was beyond it.

When Plunkett said that Dr Ripley might have neglected Mrs Abercrombie, guilt nibbled at Miss Bell. There was a time two years ago when she'd cut her hand on a piece of metal embedded in soil. She'd gone to Dr Ripley with it and although he'd chatted to her and been extremely kind his treatment hadn't been successful. A week later her whole arm had swelled up and Plunkett had insisted on driving her to the out-patients' department of a hospital. She was lucky to keep the arm, an Indian doctor had pronounced, adding that someone had been careless.

Mrs Pope recalled the affair of Miss Bell's hand, and Mr Apse recalled the occasion, and so did Tindall. In the snow once Dr Ripley's old Vauxhall had skidded on the drive and Mr Apse had had to put gravel under the back wheels to get it out of the ditch. It had puzzled Mr Apse that the skid had occurred because, as far as he could see, there'd been no cause for Dr Ripley to apply his brakes. It had occurred to him afterwards that the doctor hadn't quite known what he was doing.

'It's a terrible thing for a doctor to be disgraced,' Plunkett said. 'She thought the world of him, you know.'

The confusion in the kitchen was now considerable. The shock of the death still lingered and with it, though less than before, the feeling of resentment. There was the varying reaction to Plunkett's proposal that Mrs Abercrombie's remains should be quietly disposed of. There was concern for Dr Ripley, and a mounting uneasiness that caused the concern to give way to a more complicated emotion: it wasn't simply that the negligence of Dr Ripley had brought about a patient's death, it seemed that his negligence must be shared, since they had known he wasn't up to it and had not spoken out.

'Her death will cause unhappiness all round,' Plunkett said. 'Which she didn't wish at all. He'd be struck off.'

Dr Ripley had attended Miss Bell on a previous occasion, a few months after her arrival in Rews Manor. She'd come out in spots which Dr Ripley

452 · LAST WISHES

had diagnosed as German measles. He had been called in when Tindall
had influenza in 1960. He'd been considerate and efficient about a tiresome
complaint of Mrs Pope's.

The two images of Dr Ripley hovered in the kitchen: a man firm of
purpose and skilful in his heyday, moustached and smart but always
sympathetic, a saviour who had become a medical menace.

'She died of gallstones,' Plunkett said, 'which for eight or nine years she
suffered from, a fact he always denied. She'd be still alive if he'd treated
her.'

'We don't know it was gallstones,' Miss Bell protested quietly.

'We would have to say. We would have to say that she complained of
gallstones.' Plunkett looked severe. 'If he puts down pneumonia on the
death certificate we would have to disagree. After all,' he continued, his
severity increasing with each word, 'he could kill other people too.'

He looked from one face to another and saw that the mind behind each
was lost in the confusion he had created. He, though, could see his way
through the murk of it. Out of the necessary chaos he could already see
the order he desired, and it seemed to him now that everything else he had
ever experienced paled beside the excitement of the idea he'd been visited
by.

'We must bargain with Dr Ripley,' he said, 'for his own sake. She would
not have wished him to be punished for his negligence, any more than she
would wish us to suffer through her unnecessary death. We must put it all
to Dr Ripley. He must sign a death certificate in her room this morning
and forget to hand it in. I would be satisfied with that.'

'Forget?' Miss Bell repeated, aghast and totally astonished.

'Or leave it behind here and forget that he has left it behind. Any elderly
behaviour like that, it's all of a piece. I'm sure there's no law that says she
can't be quietly put away in the garden, and the poor old chap'll be long
since dead before anyone thinks to ask a question. We would have saved
his bacon for him and be looked after ourselves, just as she wished. No one
would bother about any of it in a few years' time, and we'd have done no
wrong by burying her where she wished to be. Only the old chap would be
a bit amiss by keeping quiet about a death, but he'd be safely out of
business by then.'

Mr Apse remembered a lifetime's association with the garden of Rews
Manor, and Mrs Pope recalled the cheerless kitchens of the YWCA, and
Miss Bell saw herself kneeling in a flower-bed on an autumn evening,
taking begonia tubers from the earth. There could be no other garden for
Mr Apse, and for Miss Bell no other garden either, and no other kitchen
for Mrs Pope. Plunkett might propose to her, Tindall said to herself, just
in order to go on sharing beds with her, but the marriage would not be
happy because it was not what they wanted.

'There's the will,' Miss Bell said, whispering so low that her words were
almost incomprehensible. 'There's the will she has signed.'

'In time,' Plunkett said, 'the will shall naturally come into its own. That is what she intended. We should all be properly looked after, and then the grass merchants will take over, as laid down. When the place is no longer of use to us.' He added that he felt he had been visited, that the idea had quite definitely come from outside himself rather than from within. Regretful in death, he said, Mrs Abercrombie had expressed herself to him because she was cross with herself, because she was worried for her servants and for the old doctor.

'He let her die of neglected gallstones,' Plunkett repeated with firm conviction. 'A most obvious complaint.'

In the hall the doorbell rang, a clanging sound, for the bell was of an old-fashioned kind.

'Well?' Plunkett said, looking from one face to another.

'We don't know that it was gallstones,' Miss Bell protested again. 'She only mentioned gallstones. Dr Ripley said –'

'Oh, for heaven's sake, Miss Bell!'

He glared at Miss Bell with dislike in his face. They'd been through all that, he said: gallstones or something else, what did it matter? The woman was dead.

'It's perfectly clear to all of us, Miss Bell, that Mrs Abercrombie would not have wished her death to cause all this fuss. That's the only point I'm making. In my opinion, apparently not shared by you, Mrs Abercrombie was a woman of remarkable sensitivity. And kindness, Miss Bell. Do you really believe that she would have wished to inflict this misery on a harmless old doctor?' He paused, staring at Miss Bell, aware that the dislike in his face was upsetting her. 'Do you really believe she wished to deprive us of our home? Do you believe that Mrs Abercrombie was unkind?'

Miss Bell did not say anything, and in the silence the doorbell pealed again. Mrs Pope was aware that her head had begun to ache. Mr Apse took his pipe from his pocket and put it on the table. He cut slivers from a plug of tobacco and rubbed them together in the palm of his left hand. Tindall watched him, thinking that she had never seen him preparing his pipe in the kitchen before.

'You're mad!' Miss Bell suddenly cried. 'The whole thing has affected you, Plunkett. It's ridiculous what you're saying.' The blood had gone to her face and neck, and showed in dark blotches beneath her weathered skin. Her eyes, usually so tranquil, shone fierily in her anger. She didn't move, but continued to stand at the corner of the kitchen table, just behind Mr Apse, who was looking up at her, astonished.

'How can we possibly do such a thing?' Miss Bell shrieked. 'It's a disgusting, filthy kind of thing to suggest. Her body's still warm and you can stand there saying that everything should be falsified. You don't care tuppence for Dr Ripley, it's not Dr Ripley who matters to you. They could hang him for murder –'

'I did not say Dr Ripley would be hanged.'

'You implied it. You implied the most terrible things.'

The power left her voice as she uttered the last three words. Her eyes closed for a moment and when she opened them again she was weeping.

'Now, now, my dear,' Mrs Pope said, going to her and putting a hand on her arm.

'I am only thinking of Mrs Abercrombie's wishes,' Plunkett said, unmoved and still severe. 'Her wishes didn't say the old doctor should be hounded.'

Mrs Pope continued to murmur consolation. She sat Miss Bell down at the table. Tindall went to a drawer in the dresser and took from it a number of household tissues which she placed in front of Miss Bell. Mr Apse pressed the shredded tobacco into his pipe.

'I see no reason at all not to have a private household funeral,' Plunkett said. He spoke slowly, emphasizing the repetition in his statement, summing everything up. What right had the stupid little creature to create a ridiculous fuss when the other three would easily now have left everything in his hands? It wasn't she who mattered, or she who had the casting vote: it was old Ripley, still standing on the doorstep.

'No,' Miss Bell whispered. 'No, no.'

It was a nightmare. It was a nightmare to be crouched over the kitchen table, with Mrs Pope's hand on her shoulder and tissues laid out in front of her. It was a nightmare to think that Mr Apse wouldn't have cared what they did with Mrs Abercrombie, that Tindall wouldn't have cared, that Mrs Pope was coming round to Plunkett's horrible suggestions. It was a nightmare to think of the doctor being blackmailed by Plunkett's oily tongue. Plunkett was like an animal, some creature out of which a devil of hell had come.

'Best maybe to have a chat with the doctor,' Miss Bell heard Mrs Pope's voice say, and heard the agreement of Tindall, soothing, like a murmur. She was aware of Mr Apse nodding his head. Plunkett said:

'I think that's fair.'

'No. No, no,' Miss Bell cried.

'Then what is fair, Miss Bell?' Mrs Pope, quite sharply, asked.

'Mrs Abercrombie is dead. It must be reported.'

'That's the doctor's job,' Plunkett pointed out. 'It don't concern us.'

'The doctor'll know,' Tindall said, considering it odd that Plunkett had all of a sudden used bad grammar, a lapse she had never before heard from him.

Without saying anything else, Plunkett left the kitchen.

Dr Ripley, who had pulled the bell four times, was pulling it again when Plunkett opened the hall-door. The butler, Dr Ripley thought, was looking dishevelled and somewhat flushed. Blood pressure, he automatically said to himself, while commenting on the weather.

'She died,' Plunkett said. 'I wanted to tell you in person, Doctor.'

They stood for a moment while Plunkett explained the circumstances, giving the time of death as nine-thirty or thereabouts.

'I'm really sorry,' Dr Ripley said. 'Poor dear.'

He mounted the stairs, with Plunkett behind him. Never again would he do so, he said to himself, since he, too, knew that the house was to pass into the possession of an organization which studied grasses. In the bedroom he examined the body and noted that death was due to simple heart failure, a brief little attack, he reckoned, judging by her countenance and the unflustered arrangement of her body. He sighed over the corpse, although he was used to corpses. It seemed a lifetime, and indeed it was, since he had attended her for a throat infection when she was a bride.

'Heart,' Dr Ripley said on the landing outside the bedroom. 'She was very beautiful, you know. In her day, Plunkett.'

Plunkett nodded. He stood aside to allow the doctor to precede him downstairs.

'She'll be happy,' Dr Ripley said. 'Being still in love with her husband.'

Again Plunkett nodded, even though the doctor couldn't see him. 'We wondered what best to do,' he said.

'Do?'

'You'll be issuing a certificate?'

'Well yes, of course.'

'It was that we were wondering about. The others and myself.'

'Wondering?'

'I'd like a chat with you, Doctor.'

Dr Ripley, who hadn't turned his head while having this conversation, reached the hall. Plunkett stepped round him and led the way to the drawing-room.

'A glass of sherry?' Plunkett suggested.

'Well, that's most kind of you, Plunkett. In the circumstances –'

'I think she'd have wished you to have one, sir.'

'Yes, maybe she would.'

Plunkett poured from a decanter and handed Dr Ripley the glass. He waited for the doctor to sip before he spoke.

'She sent a message to you, Doctor. Late last night she rang her bell and asked for me. She said she had a feeling she might die in the night. "If I do," she said, "I don't want him blamed." '

'Blamed? Who blamed? I don't understand you, Plunkett.'

'I asked her that myself. "Who blamed?" I said, and she said: "Dr Ripley." '

Plunkett watched while a mouthful of sherry was consumed. He moved to the decanter and carried it to Dr Ripley's glass. Mrs Abercrombie had had a heart attack, Dr Ripley said. He couldn't have saved her even if he'd been called in time.

'Naturally, we didn't send for you last night, sir, even though she said that. On account of your attitude, Doctor.'

'Attitude?'

'You considered her a hypochondriac, sir.'

'Mrs Abercrombie was.'

'No, sir. She was a sick woman.'

Dr Ripley finished his second glass of sherry and crossed the drawing-room to the decanter. He poured some more, filling the glass to the brim.

'I'm afraid,' he said, 'I've no idea what you're talking about, Plunkett.'

In the kitchen they did not speak. Mrs Pope made more coffee and put pieces of shortbread on a plate. No one ate the shortbread, and Miss Bell shook her head when Mrs Pope began to refill her coffee-cup.

'Bovril, dear?' Mrs Pope suggested, but Miss Bell rejected Bovril also.

The garden had an atmosphere, different scents came out at different times of year, varying also from season to season. It was in the garden that she'd realized how unhappy she'd been, for eleven years, teaching geography. Yet even if the garden were Paradise itself you couldn't just bury a dead woman in it and pretend she hadn't died. Every day of your life you'd pass the mound, your whole existence would be a lie.

'I'll go away,' Miss Bell said shakily, in a whisper. 'I'll pack and go. I promise you, I'll never tell a thing.'

To Dr Ripley's astonishment, Mrs Abercrombie's butler accused him of negligence and added that it would have been Mrs Abercrombie's desire to hush the matter up. He said that Mrs Abercrombie would never have wished to disgrace an old man.

'What I'm suggesting,' Plunkett said, 'is that you give the cause of death to suit yourself and then become forgetful.'

'Forgetful?'

'Leave the certificate behind you, sir, as if in error.'

'But it has to be handed in, Plunkett. Look here, there's no disgrace involved, or negligence or anything else. You haven't been drinking, have you?'

'It's a decision we came to in the kitchen, Doctor. We're all agreed.'

'But for heaven's sake, man –'

'Mrs Abercrombie's wish was that her body should be buried in the shrubbery, beside her husband's. That can be quietly done. Your good name would continue, Doctor, without a stain. Whether or not you take on further patients is your own affair.'

Dr Ripley sat down. He stared through wire-rimmed spectacles at a man he had always considered pleasant. Yet this same man was now clearly implying that he was more of an undertaker than a doctor.

'What I am saying, sir, is that Rews Manor shall continue as Mrs Abercrombie wished it to. What I am saying is that you and we shall enter into the small conspiracy that Mrs Abercrombie is guiding us towards.'

'Guiding?'

'Since her death she has been making herself felt all over the house. Read that, sir.'

He handed Dr Ripley the letter from Mrs Abercrombie's solicitors, which Dr Ripley slowly read and handed back. Plunkett said:

'It would be disgraceful to go against the wishes of the recently dead, especially those of a person like Mrs Abercrombie, who was kindness itself – to all of us, and to you, sir.'

'You're suggesting that her death should be suppressed, Plunkett? So that you and the others may remain here?'

'So that you may not face charges, sir.'

'But, for the Lord's sake, man, I'd face no charges. I've done nothing at all.'

'A doctor can be in trouble for doing nothing, when he should be doing everything, when he should be prolonging life instead of saying his patients are imagining things.'

'But Mrs Abercrombie did –'

'In the kitchen we're all agreed, sir. We remember, Doctor. We remember Miss Bell's hand a few years ago, that she nearly died of. Criminal neglect, they said in the out-patients'. Another thing, we remember the time we had to get your car out of the ditch.'

'I skidded. There was ice –'

'I have seen you drunk, Doctor,' Plunkett said, 'at half-past ten in the morning.'

Dr Ripley stared harder at Plunkett, believing him now to be insane. He didn't say anything for a moment and then, recovering from his bewilderment, he spoke quietly and slowly. There was a perfectly good explanation for the skid on the icy snow of the drive: he'd braked to avoid a blackbird that was limping about in front of him. He'd never in his life been drunk at half-past ten in the morning.

'You know as well as I do,' Plunkett continued, as though he were deaf or as though the doctor hadn't spoken, 'you know as well as I do that Mrs Abercrombie wouldn't rest if she was responsible for getting you into the Sunday papers.'

In the kitchen they did not reply when Miss Bell said she'd pack and go. They didn't look at her, and she knew they were thinking that she wouldn't be able to keep her word. They were thinking she was hysterical and frightened, and that the weight of so eccentric a secret would prove too much for her.

'It's just that Mrs Abercrombie wanted to change her will, dear,' Mrs Pope said.

'Yes,' said Mr Apse.

They spoke gently, in soft tones like Miss Bell's own. They looked at her in a gentle way, and Tindall smiled at her, gently also. They'd be going against Mrs Abercrombie as soon as she was dead, Tindall said, speaking

as softly as the others had spoken. They must abide by what had been in
Mrs Abercrombie's heart, Mr Apse said.

Again Miss Bell wondered what she would do when she left the garden,
and wondered then if she had the right to plunge these people into
unhappiness. With their faces so gently disposed before her, and with
Plunkett out of the room, she saw for the first time their point of view. She
said to herself that Plunkett would return to normal, since all her other
knowledge of him seemed to prove that he was not a wicked man. Certainly
there was no wickedness in Mrs Pope or Mr Apse, or in Tindall; and was
it really so terrible, she found herself wondering then, to take from Mrs
Abercrombie what she had wished to give? Did it make sense to quibble
now when you had never quibbled over Dr Ripley's diagnosis of hypo-
chondria?

Miss Bell imagined the mound in the shrubbery beside the other mound,
and meals in the kitchen, the same as ever, and visitors in the garden on a
Sunday, and the admission charges still passed on to the Nurses. She
imagined, as often she had, growing quite old in the setting she had come
to love.

'A quiet little funeral,' Mrs Pope said. 'She'd have wanted that.'

'Yes,' Mr Apse said.

In her quiet voice, not looking at anyone, Miss Bell apologized for
making a fuss.

To Dr Ripley's surprise, Plunkett took a packet of cigarettes from his
pocket and lit one. He blew out smoke. He said:

'Neglected gallstones: don't wriggle out of it, Doctor.' His voice was
cool and ungracious. He regarded Dr Ripley contemptuously. 'What about
Bell's hand? That woman near died as well.'

For a moment Dr Ripley felt incapable of a reply. He remembered the
scratch on Miss Bell's hand, a perfectly clean little wound. He'd put some
iodine on it and a sticking-plaster dressing. He'd told her on no account to
go poking it into her flower-beds, but of course she'd taken no notice.

'Miss Bell was extremely foolish,' he said at length, speaking quietly.
'She should have returned to me the moment the complication began.'

'You weren't to be found, Doctor. You were in the bar of the Clarence
Hotel or down in the Royal Oak, or the Rogues' Arms –'

'I am not a drunkard, Plunkett. I was not negligent in the matter of Miss
Bell's hand. Nor was I negligent over Mrs Abercrombie. Mrs Abercrombie
suffered in no way whatsoever from gallstone trouble. Her heart was a
little tired; she had a will to die and she died.'

'That isn't true, Doctor. She had a will to live, as this letter proves. She
had a will to get matters sorted out –'

'If I were you, Plunkett, I'd go and lie down for a while.'

Dr Ripley spoke firmly. The astonishment that the butler had caused in
him had vanished, leaving him unflustered and professional. His eyes

behind their spectacles stared steadily into Plunkett's. He didn't seem at all beyond the work he did.

'Your car skidded,' Plunkett said, though without his previous confidence. 'You were whistled to the gills on Christmas booze that day –'

'That's offensive and untrue, Plunkett.'

'All I'm saying, sir, is that it'd be better for all concerned –'

'I'd be obliged if you didn't speak to me in that manner, Plunkett.'

To Plunkett's horror, Dr Ripley began to go. He placed his empty sherry glass on the table beside the decanter. He buttoned his jacket.

'Please, sir,' Plunkett said, changing his tone a little and hastening towards the sherry decanter. 'Have another glassful, sir.'

Dr Ripley ignored the invitation. 'I would just like to speak to the others,' he said, 'before I go.'

'Of course. Of course, sir.'

It was, Dr Ripley recognized afterwards, curiosity that caused him to make that request. Were the others in the same state as Plunkett? Had they, too, changed in a matter of hours from being agreeable people to being creatures you could neither like nor respect nor even take seriously? Would they, too, accuse him to his face of negligence and drunkenness?

In the kitchen the others rose to their feet when he entered.

'Doctor's here to have a word,' Plunkett said. He added that Dr Ripley had come to see their point of view, a statement that Dr Ripley didn't contradict immediately. He said instead that he was sorry that Mrs Abercrombie had died.

'Oh, so are we, sir,' Mrs Pope cried. 'We're sorry and shaken, sir.'

But in the kitchen Dr Ripley didn't feel their sorrow, any more than he had felt sorrow emanating from Plunkett in the drawing-room. In the kitchen there appeared to be fear in the eyes of quiet Mr Apse and in the eyes of Mrs Pope and the softly-spoken Miss Bell, and in the eyes of Tindall. It was fear, Dr Ripley suddenly realized, that had distorted Plunkett and continued to distort him, though differently now. Fear had bred greed in them, fear had made them desperate, and had turned them into fools.

'Dr Ripley'll see us through,' Plunkett said.

When he told the truth, they didn't say anything at all. Not even Plunkett spoke, and for a moment the only sound in the kitchen was the soft weeping of Miss Bell.

'Her wishes were clear,' Dr Ripley said. 'She died when she knew she'd made them so, when she received the letter this morning. Her wishes would have been honoured in law, even though they weren't in a will.'

They stood like statues in the kitchen. The weeping of Miss Bell ceased; there was no sound at all. They would none of them remain in the house now, Dr Ripley thought, because of their exposure one to another. In guilt and deception they had imagined they would remain, held together by their aberration. But now, with the memory of their greed and the irony of their error, there would be hatred and shame among them.

He wanted to comfort them, but could not. He wanted to say that they should forget what had taken place since Mrs Abercrombie's death, that they should attempt to carry out her wishes. But he knew it was too late for any of that. He turned and went away, leaving them still standing like statues. It was strange, he thought as he made his way through the house, that a happiness which had been so rich should have trailed such a snare behind it. And yet it seemed cruelly fitting that the loss of so much should wreak such damage in pleasant, harmless people.

Mrs Acland's Ghosts

Mr Mockler was a tailor. He carried on his business in a house that after twenty-five years of mortgage arrangements had finally become his: 22 Juniper Street, S.W.17. He had never married and since he was now sixty-three it seemed likely that he never would. In an old public house, the Charles the First, he had a drink every evening with his friends Mr Uprichard and Mr Tile, who were tailors also. He lived in his house in Juniper Street with his cat Sam, and did his own cooking and washing and cleaning: he was not unhappy.

On the morning of October 19th, 1972, Mr Mockler received a letter that astonished him. It was neatly written in a pleasantly rounded script that wasn't difficult to decipher. It did not address him as 'Dear Mr Mockler', nor was it signed, nor conventionally concluded. But his name was used repeatedly, and from its contents it seemed to Mr Mockler that the author of the letter was a Mrs Acland. He read the letter in amazement and then read it again and then, more slowly, a third time.

Dr Scott-Rowe is dead, Mr Mockler. I know he is dead because a new man is here, a smaller, younger man, called Dr Friendman. He looks at us, smiling, with his unblinking eyes. Miss Acheson says you can tell at a glance that he has practised hypnosis.

They're so sure of themselves, Mr Mockler: beyond the limits of their white-coated world they can accept nothing. I am a woman imprisoned because I once saw ghosts. I am paid for by the man who was my husband, who writes out monthly cheques for the peaches they bring to my room, and the beef olives and the *marrons glacés*. 'She must above all things be happy,' I can imagine the stout man who was my husband saying, walking with Dr Scott-Rowe over the sunny lawns and among the rosebeds. In this house there are twenty disturbed people in private rooms, cosseted by luxury because other people feel guilty. And when we walk ourselves on the lawns and among the rosebeds we murmur at the folly of those who have so expensively committed us, and at the greater folly of the medical profession: you can be disturbed without being mad. Is this the letter of a lunatic, Mr Mockler?

I said this afternoon to Miss Acheson that Dr Scott-Rowe was dead. She said she knew. All of us would have Dr Friendman now, she said, with his smile and his tape recorders. 'May Dr Scott-Rowe rest in peace,' said Miss Acheson: it was better to be dead than to be like Dr Friendman. Miss

Acheson is a very old lady, twice my age exactly: I am thirty-nine and she is seventy-eight. She was committed when she was eighteen, in 1913, a year before the First World War. Miss Acheson was disturbed by visions of St Olaf of Norway and she still is. Such visions were an embarrassment to Miss Acheson's family in 1913 and so they quietly slipped her away. No one comes to see her now, no one has since 1927.

'You must write it all down,' Miss Acheson said to me when I told her, years ago, that I'd been committed because I'd seen ghosts and that I could prove the ghosts were real because the Rachels had seen them too. The Rachels are living some normal existence somewhere, yet they were terrified half out of their wits at the time and I wasn't frightened at all. The trouble nowadays, Miss Acheson says and I quite agree, is that if you like having ghosts near you people think you're round the bend.

I was talking to Miss Acheson about all this yesterday and she said why didn't I do what Sarah Crookham used to do? There's nothing the matter with Sarah Crookham, any more than there is with Miss Acheson or myself: all that Sarah Crookham suffers from is a broken heart. 'You must write it all down,' Miss Acheson said to her when she first came here, weeping, poor thing, every minute of the day. So she wrote it down and posted it to A. J. Rawson, a person she found in the telephone directory. But Mr Rawson never came, nor another person Sarah Crookham wrote to. I have looked you up in the telephone directory, Mr Mockler. It is nice to have a visitor.

'You must begin at the beginning,' Miss Acheson says, and so I am doing that. The beginning is back a bit, in January 1949, when I was fifteen. We lived in Richmond then, my parents and one brother, George, and my sisters Alice and Isabel. On Sundays, after lunch, we used to walk all together in Richmond Park with our dog, a Dalmatian called Salmon. I was the oldest and Alice was next, two years younger, and George was eleven and Isabel eight. It was lovely walking together in Richmond Park and then going home to Sunday tea. I remember the autumns and winters best, the cosiness of the coal fire, hot sponge cake and special Sunday sandwiches, and little buns that Alice and I always helped to make on Sunday mornings. We played Monopoly by the fire, and George would always have the ship and Anna the hat and Isabel the racing-car and Mummy the dog. Daddy and I would share the old boot. I really loved it.

I loved the house: 17 Lorelei Avenue, an ordinary suburban house built some time in the early nineteen-twenties, when Miss Acheson was still quite young. There were bits of stained glass on either side of the hall-door and a single stained-glass pane, Moses in the bulrushes, in one of the landing windows. At Christmas especially it was lovely: we'd have the Christmas tree in the hall and always on Christmas Eve, as long as I can remember, there'd be a party. I can remember the parties quite vividly. There'd be people standing round drinking punch and all the children would play hide-and-seek upstairs, and nobody could ever find George.

It's George, Mr Mockler, that all this is about. And Alice, of course, and Isabel.

When I first described them to Dr Scott-Rowe he said they sounded marvellous, and I said I thought they probably were, but I suppose a person can be prejudiced in family matters of that kind. Because they were, after all, my brother and my two sisters and because, of course, they're dead now. I mean, they were probably ordinary children, just like any children. Well, you can see what you think, Mr Mockler.

George was small for his age, very wiry, dark-haired, a darting kind of boy who was always laughing, who had often to be reprimanded by my father because his teachers said he was the most mischievous boy in his class. Alice, being two years older, was just the opposite: demure and silent, but happy in her quiet way, and beautiful, far more beautiful than I was. Isabel wasn't beautiful at all. She was all freckles, with long pale plaits and long legs that sometimes could run as fast as George's. She and George were as close as two persons can get, but in a way we were all close: there was a lot of love in 17 Lorelei Avenue.

I had a cold the day it happened, a Saturday it was. I was cross because they all kept worrying about leaving me in the house on my own. They'd bring me back Black Magic chocolates, they said, and my mother said she'd buy a bunch of daffodils if she saw any. I heard the car crunching over the gravel outside the garage, and then their voices telling Salmon not to put his paws on the upholstery. My father blew the horn, saying goodbye to me, and after that the silence began. I must have known even then, long before it happened, that nothing would be the same again.

When I was twenty-two, Mr Mockler, I married a man called Acland, who helped me to get over the tragedy. George would have been eighteen, and Anna twenty and Isabel fifteen. They would have liked my husband because he was a good-humoured and generous man. He was very plump, many years older than I was, with a fondness for all food. 'You're like a child,' I used to say to him and we'd laugh together. Cheese in particular he liked, and ham and all kinds of root vegetables, parsnips, turnips, celeriac, carrots, leeks, potatoes. He used to come back to the house and take four or five pounds of gammon from the car, and chops, and blocks of ice-cream, and biscuits, and two or even three McVitie's fruitcakes. He was very partial to McVitie's fruitcakes. At night, at nine or ten o'clock, he'd make cocoa for both of us and we'd have it while we were watching the television, with a slice or two of fruitcake. He was such a kind man in those days. I got quite fat myself, which might surprise you, Mr Mockler, because I'm on the thin side now.

My husband was, and still is, both clever and rich. One led to the other: he made a fortune designing metal fasteners for the aeroplane industry. Once, in May 1960, he drove me to a house in Worcestershire. 'I wanted it to be a surprise,' he said, stopping his mustard-coloured Alfa-Romeo in front of this quite extensive Victorian façade. 'There,' he said, embracing me, reminding me that it was my birthday. Two months later we went to live there.

We had no children. In the large Victorian house I made my life with the man I'd married and once again, as in 17 Lorelei Avenue, I was happy. The house was near a village but otherwise remote. My husband went away from it by day, to the place where his aeroplane fasteners were manufactured and tested. There were – and still are – aeroplanes in the air which would have fallen to pieces if they hadn't been securely fastened by the genius of my husband.

The house had many rooms. There was a large square drawing-room with a metal ceiling – beaten tin, I believe it was. It had patterns like wedding-cake icing on it. It was painted white and blue and gave, as well as the impression of a wedding-cake, a Wedgwood effect. People remarked on this ceiling and my husband used to explain that metal ceilings had once been very popular, especially in the large houses of Australia. Well-to-do Australians, apparently, would have them shipped from Birmingham in colonial imitation of an English fashion. My husband and I, arm in arm, would lead people about the house, pointing out the ceiling or the green wallpaper in our bedroom or the portraits that hung on the stairs.

The lighting was bad in the house. The long first-floor landing was a gloomy place by day and lit by a single wall-light at night. At the end of this landing another flight of stairs, less grand than the stairs that led from the hall, wound upwards to the small rooms that had once upon a time been servants' quarters, and another flight continued above them to attics and store-rooms. The bathroom was on the first floor, tiled in green Victorian tiles, and there was a lavatory next door to it, encased in mahogany.

In the small rooms that had once been the servants' quarters lived Mr and Mrs Rachels. My husband had had a kitchen and a bathroom put in for them so that their rooms were quite self-contained. Mr Rachels worked in the garden and his wife cleaned the house. It wasn't really necessary to have them at all: I could have cleaned the house myself and even done the gardening, but my husband insisted in his generous way. At night I could hear the Rachels moving about above me. I didn't like this and my husband asked them to move more quietly.

In 1962 my husband was asked to go to Germany, to explain his aeroplane fasteners to the German aircraft industry. It was to be a prolonged trip, three months at least, and I was naturally unhappy when he told me. He was unhappy himself, but on March 4th he flew to Hamburg, leaving me with the Rachels.

They were a pleasant enough couple, somewhere in their fifties I would think, he rather silent, she inclined to talk. The only thing that worried me about them was the way they used to move about at night above my head. After my husband had gone to Germany I gave Mrs Rachels money to buy slippers, but I don't think she ever did because the sounds continued just as before. I naturally didn't make a fuss about it.

On the night of March 7th I was awakened by a band playing in the house. The tune was an old tune of the fifties called, I believe, 'Looking for Henry Lee'. The noise was very loud in my bedroom and I lay there frightened, not knowing why this noise should be coming to me like this, Victor Silvester in strict dance tempo. Then a voice spoke, a long babble of French, and I realized that I was listening to a radio programme. The wireless was across the room, on a table by the windows. I put on my bedside light and got up and switched it off. I drank some orange juice and went back to sleep. It didn't even occur to me to wonder who had turned the wireless on.

The next day I told Mrs Rachels about it, and it was she, in fact, who made me think that it was all rather stranger than it seemed. I definitely remembered turning the wireless off myself before going to bed, and in any case I was not in the habit of listening to French stations, so that even if the wireless had somehow come on of its own accord it should not have been tuned in to a French station.

Two days later I found the bath half-filled with water and the towels all rumpled and damp, thrown about on the floor. The water in the bath was tepid and dirty: someone, an hour or so ago, had had a bath.

I climbed the stairs to the Rachels' flat and knocked on their door. 'Is your bathroom out of order?' I said when Mr Rachels came to the door, not wearing the slippers I'd given them money for. I said I didn't at all mind their using mine, only I'd be grateful if they'd remember to let the water out and to bring down their own towels. Mr Rachels looked at me in the way people have sometimes, as though you're insane. He called his wife and all three of us went down to look at my bathroom. They denied emphatically that either of them had had a bath.

When I came downstairs the next morning, having slept badly, I found the kitchen table had been laid for four. There was a table-cloth on the table, which was something I never bothered about, and a kettle was boiling on the Aga. Beside it, a large brown teapot, not the one I normally used, was heating. I made some tea and sat down, thinking about the Rachels. Why should they behave like this? Why should they creep into my bedroom in the middle of the night and turn the wireless on? Why should they have a bath in my bathroom and deny it? Why should they lay the breakfast table as though we had overnight guests? I left the table just as it was. Butter had been rolled into pats. Marmalade had been placed in two china dishes. A silver toast-rack that an aunt of my husband had given us as a wedding present was waiting for toast.

'Thank you for laying the table,' I said to Mrs Rachels when she entered the kitchen an hour later.

She shook her head. She began to say that she hadn't laid the table but then she changed her mind. I could see from her face that she and her husband had been discussing the matter of the bath the night before. She could hardly wait to tell him about the breakfast table. I smiled at her.

'A funny thing happened the other night,' I said. 'I woke up to find Victor Silvester playing a tune called "Looking for Henry Lee".'

'Henry Lee?' Mrs Rachels said, turning around from the sink. Her face, usually blotched with pink, like the skin of an apple, was white.

'It's an old song of the fifties.'

It was while saying that that I realized what was happening in the house. I naturally didn't say anything to Mrs Rachels, and I at once began to regret that I'd said anything in the first place. It had frightened me, finding the bathroom like that, and clearly it must have frightened the Rachels. I didn't want them to be frightened because naturally there was nothing to be frightened about. George and Alice and Isabel wouldn't hurt anyone, not unless death had changed them enormously. But even so I knew I couldn't ever explain that to the Rachels.

'Well, I suppose I'm just getting absentminded,' I said. 'People do, so they say, when they live alone.' I laughed to show I wasn't worried or frightened, to make it all seem ordinary.

'You mean, you laid the table yourself?' Mrs Rachels said. 'And had a bath?'

'And didn't turn the wireless off properly. Funny,' I said, 'how these things go in threes. Funny, how there's always an explanation.' I laughed again and Mrs Rachels had to laugh too.

After that it was lovely, just like being back in 17 Lorelei Avenue. I bought Black Magic chocolates and bars of Fry's and Cadbury's Milk, all the things we'd liked. I often found bathwater left in and the towels crumpled, and now and again I came down in the morning to find the breakfast table laid. On the first-floor landing, on the evening of March 11th, I caught a glimpse of George, and in the garden, three days later, I saw Isabel and Alice.

On March 15th the Rachels left. I hadn't said a word to them about finding the bathroom used again or the breakfast laid or actually seeing the children. I'd been cheerful and smiling whenever I met them. I'd talked about how Brasso wasn't as good as it used to be to Mrs Rachels, and had asked her husband about the best kinds of soil for bulbs.

'We can't stay a minute more,' Mrs Rachels said, her face all white and tight in the hall, and then to my astonishment they attempted to persuade me to go also.

'The house isn't fit to live in,' Mr Rachels said.

'Oh now, that's nonsense,' I began to say, but they both shook their heads.

'There's children here,' Mrs Rachels said. 'There's three children appearing all over the place.'

'Come right up to you,' Mr Rachels said. 'Laugh at you sometimes.'

They were trembling, both of them. They were so terrified I thought they might die, that their hearts would give out there in the hall and they'd just drop down. But they didn't. They walked out of the hall-door with their three suitcases, down the drive to catch a bus. I never saw them again.

I suppose, Mr Mockler, you have to be frightened of ghosts: I suppose that's their way of communicating. I mean, it's no good being like me, delighting in it all, being happy because I wasn't lonely in that house any more. You have to be like the Rachels, terrified half out of your wits. I think I knew that as I watched the Rachels go: I think I knew that George and Isabel and Alice would go with them, that I was only a kind of go-between, and the Rachels were what George and Isabel and Alice could really have fun with. I almost ran after the Rachels, but I knew it would be no good.

Without the Rachels and my brother and my two sisters, I was frightened myself in that big house. I moved everything into the kitchen: the television set and the plants I kept in the drawing-room, and a camp-bed to sleep on. I was there, asleep in the camp-bed, when my husband returned from Germany; he had changed completely. He raved at me, not listening to a word I said. There were cups of tea all over the house, he said, and bits of bread and biscuits and cake and chocolates. There were notes in envelopes, and messages scrawled in my handwriting on the wallpaper in various rooms. Everywhere was dusty. Where, he wanted to know, were the Rachels?

He stood there with a canvas bag in his left hand, an airline bag that had the word *Lufthansa* on it. He'd put on at least a stone, I remember thinking, and his hair was shorter than before.

'Listen,' I said, 'I would like to tell you.' And I tried to tell him, as I've told you, Mr Mockler, about George and Isabel and Alice in 17 Lorelei Avenue and how we all went together for a walk with our dog, every Sunday afternoon in Richmond Park, and how on Christmas Eve my mother always gave a party. I told him about the stained-glass pane in the window, Moses in the bulrushes, and the hide-and-seek we played, and how my father and I always shared the old boot in Monopoly. I told him about the day of the accident, how the tyre on the lorry suddenly exploded and how the lorry went whizzing around on the road and then just tumbled over on top of them. I'd put out cups of tea, I said, and biscuits and cake and the little messages, just in case they came back again – not for them to eat or to read particularly, but just as a sign. They'd given me a sign first, I explained: George had turned on my wireless in the middle of the night and Isabel had had baths and Alice had laid the breakfast table. But then they'd gone because they'd been more interested in annoying the Rachels than in comforting me. I began to weep, telling him how lonely I'd been without them, how lonely I'd been ever since the day of the accident, how the silence had been everywhere. I couldn't control myself: tears came out of my eyes as though they'd never stop. I felt sickness all over my body, paining me in my head and my chest, sour in my stomach. I wanted to die because the loneliness was too much. Loneliness was the worst thing in the world, I said, gasping out words, with spit and tears going cold on my face. People were only shadows, I tried to explain, when you had loneliness and silence like that, like a shroud around you. You couldn't reach out of the shroud sometimes, you couldn't connect because shadows are hard to connect with and it's frightening when you try because everyone is looking at you. But it was lovely, I whispered, when the children came back to annoy the Rachels. My husband replied by telling me I was insane.

The letter finished there, and Mr Mockler was more astonished each time he read it. He had never in his life received such a document before, nor did he in fact very often receive letters of any kind, apart from bills and, if he was fortunate, cheques in settlement. He shook his head over the letter and placed it in the inside pocket of his jacket.

That day, as he stitched and measured, he imagined the place Mrs Acland wrote of, the secluded house with twenty female inmates, and the lawn and the rosebeds. He imagined the other house, 17 Lorelei Avenue in Richmond, and the third house, the Victorian residence in the Worcestershire countryside. He imagined Mrs Acland's obese husband with his short hair and his aeroplane fasteners, and the children who had been killed in a motor-car accident, and Mr and Mrs Rachels whom they had haunted. All day long the faces of these people flitted through Mr Mockler's mind, with old Miss Acheson and Sarah Crookham and Dr Scott-Rowe and Dr Friendman. In the evening, when he met his friends Mr Tile and Mr Uprichard in the Charles the First, he showed them the letter before even ordering them drinks.

'Well, I'm beggared,' remarked Mr Uprichard, a man known locally for his gentle nature. 'That poor creature.'

Mr Tile, who was not given to expressing himself, shook his head.

Mr Mockler asked Mr Uprichard if he should visit this Mrs Acland. 'Poor creature,' Mr Uprichard said again, and added that without a doubt Mrs Acland had written to a stranger because of the loneliness she mentioned, the loneliness like a shroud around her.

Some weeks later Mr Mockler, having given the matter further thought and continuing to be affected by the contents of the letter, took a Green Line bus out of London to the address that Mrs Acland had given him. He made enquiries, feeling quite adventurous, and was told that the house was three-quarters of a mile from where the bus had dropped him, down a side road. He found it without further difficulty. It was a house surrounded by a high brick wall in which large, black wrought-iron gates were backed with sheets of tin so that no one could look through the ornamental scroll-work. The gates were locked. Mr Mockler rang a bell in the wall.

'Yes?' a man said, opening the gate that was on Mr Mockler's left.

'Well,' said Mr Mockler and found it difficult to proceed.

'Yes?' the man said.

'Well, I've had a letter. Asking me to come, I think. My name's Mockler.'

The man opened the gate a little more and Mr Mockler stepped through. The man walked ahead of him and Mr Mockler saw the lawns that had been described, and the rosebeds. The house he considered most attractive: a high Georgian building with beautiful windows. An old woman was walking slowly by herself with the assistance of a stick: Miss Acheson, Mr Mockler guessed. In the distance he saw other women, walking slowly on leaf-strewn paths.

Autumn was Mr Mockler's favourite season and he was glad to be in the country on this pleasantly autumnal day. He thought of remarking on this to the man who led him towards the house, but since the man did not incline towards conversation he did not do so.

In the yellow waiting-room there were no magazines and no pictures on the walls and no flowers. It was not a room in which Mr Mockler would have cared to wait for long, and in fact he did not have to. A woman dressed as a nurse except that she wore a green cardigan came in. She smiled briskly at him and said that Dr Friendman would see him. She asked Mr Mockler to follow her.

'How very good of you to come,' Dr Friendman said, smiling at Mr Mockler in the way that Mrs Acland had described in her letter. 'How very humane,' said Dr Friendman.

'I had a letter, from a Mrs Acland.'

'Quite so, Mr Mockler. Mr Mockler, could I press you towards a glass of sherry?'

Mr Mockler, surprised at this line of talk, accepted the sherry, saying it was good of Dr Friendman. He drank the sherry while Dr Friendman read the letter. When he'd finished, Dr Friendman crossed to the window of the room and pulled aside a curtain and asked Mr Mockler if he'd mind looking out.

There was a courtyard, small and cobbled, in which a gardener was sweeping leaves into a pile. At the far end of it, sitting on a tapestry-backed dining-chair in the autumn sunshine, was a woman in a blue dress. 'Try these,' said Dr Friendman and handed Mr Mockler a pair of binoculars.

It was a beautiful face, thin and seeming fragile, with large blue eyes and lips that were now slightly parted, smiling in the sunshine. Hair the colour of corn was simply arranged, hanging on either side of the face and curling in around it. The hair shone in the sunlight, as though it was for ever being brushed.

'I find them useful,' Dr Friendman said, taking the binoculars from Mr Mockler's hands. 'You have to keep an eye, you know.'

'That's Mrs Acland?' Mr Mockler asked.

'That's the lady who wrote to you: the letter's a bit inaccurate, Mr Mockler. It wasn't quite like that in 17 Lorelei Avenue.'

'Not quite like it?'

'She cannot forget Lorelei Avenue. I'm afraid she never will. That beautiful woman, Mr Mockler, was a beautiful girl, yet she married the first man who asked her, a widower thirty years older than her, a fat designer of aircraft fasteners. He pays her bills just as she says in her letter, and even when he's dead they'll go on being paid. He used to visit her at first, but he found it too painful. He stood in this very room one day, Mr Mockler, and said to Dr Scott-Rowe that no man had ever been appreciated by a woman as much as he had by her. And all because he'd been kind to her in the most ordinary ways.'

Mr Mockler said he was afraid that he didn't know what Dr Friendman was talking about. As though he hadn't heard this quiet protest, Dr Friendman smiled and said:

'But it was, unfortunately, too late for kindness. 17 Lorelei Avenue had done its damage, like a cancer in her mind: she could not forget her childhood.'

'Yes, she says in her letter. George and Alice and Isabel –'

'All her childhood, Mr Mockler, her parents did not speak to one another. They didn't quarrel, they didn't address each other in any way whatsoever. When she was five they'd come to an agreement: that they should both remain in 17 Lorelei Avenue because neither would ever have agreed to give up an inch of the child they'd between them caused to be born. In the house there was nothing, Mr Mockler, for all her childhood years: nothing except silence.'

'But there was George and Alice and Isabel –'

'No, Mr Mockler. There was no George and no Alice and no Isabel. No hide-and-seek or parties on Christmas Eve, no Monopoly on Sundays by the fire. Can you imagine 17 Lorelei Avenue, Mr Mockler, as she is now incapable of imagining it? Two people so cruel to one another that they knew that either of them could be parted from the child in some divorce court. A woman bitterly hating the man whom once she'd loved, and he returning each evening, hurrying back from an office in case his wife and the child were having a conversation. She would sit, Mr Mockler, in a room with them, with the silence heavy in the air, and their hatred for one another. All three of them would sit down to a meal and no one would speak. No other children came to that house, no other people. She used to hide on the way back from school: she'd go down the area steps of other houses and crouch beside dustbins.'

'Dustbins?' repeated Mr Mockler, more astonished than ever. '*Dustbins?*'

'Other children didn't take to her. She couldn't talk to them. She'd never learned to talk to anyone. He was a patient man, Mr Acland, when he came along, a good and patient man.'

Mr Mockler said that the child's parents must have been monsters, but Dr Friendman shook his head. No one was a monster, Dr Friendman said in a professional manner, and in the circumstances Mr Mockler didn't feel he could argue with him. But the people called Rachels were real, he did point out, as real as the fat designer of aircraft fasteners. Had they left the house, he asked, as it said in the letter? And if they had, what had they been frightened of?

Dr Friendman smiled again. 'I don't believe in ghosts,' he said, and he explained at great length to Mr Mockler that it was Mrs Acland herself who had frightened the Rachels, turning on a wireless in the middle of the night and running baths and laying tables for people who weren't there. Mr Mockler listened and was interested to note that Dr Friendman used words that were not easy to understand, and quoted from experts who were in Dr Friendman's line of business but whose names meant nothing to Mr Mockler.

Mr Mockler, listening to all of it, nodded but was not convinced. The Rachels had left the house, just as the letter said: he knew that, he felt it in his bones and it felt like the truth. The Rachels had been frightened of Mrs Acland's ghosts even though they'd been artificial ghosts. They'd been real to her, and they'd been real to the Rachels because she'd made them so. Shadows had stepped out of her mind because in her loneliness she'd wished them to. They'd laughed and played, and frightened the Rachels half out of their wits.

'There's always an explanation,' said Dr Friendman.

Mr Mockler nodded, profoundly disagreeing.

'She'll think you're Mr Rachels,' said Dr Friendman, 'come to say he saw the ghosts. If you wouldn't mind saying you did, it keeps her happy.'

'But it's the truth,' Mr Mockler cried with passion in his voice. 'Of course it's the truth: there can be ghosts like that, just as there can be in any other way.'

'Oh, come now,' murmured Dr Friendman with his sad, humane smile.

Mr Mockler followed Dr Friendman from the room. They crossed a landing and descended a back staircase, passing near a kitchen in which a chef with a tall chef's hat was beating pieces of meat. 'Ah, Wiener Schnitzel,' said Dr Friendman.

In the cobbled courtyard the gardener had finished sweeping up the leaves and was wheeling them away in a wheelbarrow. The woman was still sitting on the tapestry-backed chair, still smiling in the autumn sunshine.

'Look,' said Dr Friendman, 'a visitor.'

A woman rose and went close to Mr Mockler. 'They didn't mean to frighten you,' she said, 'even though it's the only way ghosts can communicate. They were only having fun, Mr Rachels.'

'I think Mr Rachels realizes that now,' Dr Friendman said.

'Yes, of course,' said Mr Mockler.

'No one ever believed me, and I kept on saying, "When the Rachels come back, they'll tell the truth about poor George and Alice and Isabel." You saw them, didn't you, Mr Rachels?'

'Yes,' Mr Mockler said. 'We saw them.'

She turned and walked away, leaving the tapestry-backed chair behind her.

'You're a humane person,' Dr Friendman said, holding out his right hand, which Mr Mockler shook. The same man led him back through the lawns and the rosebeds, to the gates.

It was an experience that Mr Mockler found impossible to forget. He measured and stitched, and talked to his friends Mr Uprichard and Mr Tile in the Charles the First; he went for a walk morning and evening, and no day passed during which he did not think of the woman whom people looked at through binoculars. Somewhere in England, or at least somewhere in the world, the Rachels were probably still alive, and had Mr Mockler been a younger man he might even have set about looking for them. He would have liked to bring them to the secluded house where the woman now lived, to have been there himself when they told the truth to Dr Friendman. It seemed a sadness, as he once remarked to Mr Uprichard, that on top of everything else a woman's artificial ghosts should not be honoured, since she had brought them into being and given them life, as other women give other children life.

*Lovers of Their Time
and Other Stories*

Broken Homes

'I really think you're marvellous,' the man said.

He was small and plump, with a plump face that had a greyness about it where he shaved; his hair was grey also, falling into a fringe on his forehead. He was untidily dressed, a turtle-necked red jersey beneath a jacket that had a ballpoint pen and a pencil sticking out of the breast pocket. When he stood up his black corduroy trousers developed concertina creases. Nowadays you saw a lot of men like this, Mrs Malby said to herself.

'We're trying to help them,' he said, 'and of course we're trying to help you. The policy is to foster a deeper understanding.' He smiled, displaying small evenly-arranged teeth. 'Between the generations,' he added.

'Well, of course it's very kind,' Mrs Malby said.

He shook his head. He sipped the instant coffee she'd made for him and nibbled the edge of a pink wafer biscuit. As if driven by a compulsion, he dipped the biscuit into the coffee. He said:

'What age actually are you, Mrs Malby?'

'I'm eighty-seven.'

'You really are splendid for eighty-seven.'

He went on talking. He said he hoped he'd be as good himself at eighty-seven. He hoped he'd even be in the land of the living. 'Which I doubt,' he said with a laugh. 'Knowing me.'

Mrs Malby didn't know what he meant by that. She was sure she'd heard him quite correctly, but she could recall nothing he'd previously stated which indicated ill-health. She thought carefully while he continued to sip at his coffee and attend to the mush of biscuit. What he had said suggested that a knowledge of him would cause you to doubt that he'd live to old age. Had he already supplied further knowledge of himself which, due to her slight deafness, she had not heard? If he hadn't, why had he left everything hanging in the air like that? It was difficult to know how best to react, whether to smile or to display concern.

'So what I thought,' he said, 'was that we could send the kids on Tuesday. Say start the job Tuesday morning, eh, Mrs Malby?'

'It's extremely kind of you.'

'They're good kids.'

He stood up. He remarked on her two budgerigars and the geraniums on her window-sill. Her sitting-room was as warm as toast, he said; it was freezing outside.

'It's just that I wondered,' she said, having made up her mind to say it, 'if you could possibly have come to the wrong house?'

'Wrong? *Wrong*? You're Mrs Malby, aren't you?' He raised his voice. 'You're Mrs Malby, love?'

'Oh, yes, it's just that my kitchen isn't really in need of decoration.'

He nodded. His head moved slowly and when it stopped his dark eyes stared at her from beneath his grey fringe. He said, quite softly, what she'd dreaded he might say: that she hadn't understood.

'I'm thinking of the community, Mrs Malby. I'm thinking of you here on your own above a greengrocer's shop with your two budgies. You can benefit my kids, Mrs Malby; they can benefit you. There's no charge of any kind whatsoever. Put it like this, Mrs Malby: it's an experiment in community relations.' He paused. He reminded her of a picture there'd been in a history book, a long time ago, History with Miss Deacon, a picture of a Roundhead. 'So you see, Mrs Malby,' he said, having said something else while he was reminding her of a Roundhead.

'It's just that my kitchen is really quite nice.'

'Let's have a little look, shall we?'

She led the way. He glanced at the kitchen's shell-pink walls, and at the white paintwork. It would cost her nearly a hundred pounds to have it done, he said; and then, to her horror, he began all over again, as if she hadn't heard a thing he'd been saying. He repeated that he was a teacher, from the school called the Tite Comprehensive. He appeared to assume that she wouldn't know the Tite Comprehensive, but she did: an ugly sprawl of glass and concrete buildings, children swinging along the pavements, shouting obscenities. The man repeated what he had said before about these children: that some of them came from broken homes. The ones he wished to send to her on Tuesday morning came from broken homes, which was no joke for them. He felt, he repeated, that we all had a special duty where such children were concerned.

Mrs Malby again agreed that broken homes were to be deplored. It was just, she explained, that she was thinking of the cost of decorating a kitchen which didn't need decorating. Paint and brushes were expensive, she pointed out.

'Freshen it over for you,' the man said, raising his voice. 'First thing Tuesday, Mrs Malby.'

He went away, and she realized that he hadn't told her his name. Thinking she might be wrong about that, she went over their encounter in her mind, going back to the moment when her doorbell had sounded. 'I'm from Tite Comprehensive,' was what he'd said. No name had been mentioned, of that she was positive.

In her elderliness Mrs Malby liked to be sure of such details. You had to work quite hard sometimes at eighty-seven, straining to hear, concentrating carefully in order to be sure of things. You had to make it clear you understood because people often imagined you didn't. Communication was what it was called nowadays, rather than conversation.

Mrs Malby was wearing a blue dress with a pattern of darker blue flowers on it. She was a woman who had been tall but had shrunk a little with age and had become slightly bent. Scant white hair crowned a face that was touched with elderly freckling. Large brown eyes, once her most striking feature, were quieter than they had been, tired behind spectacles now. Her husband, George, the owner of the greengrocer's shop over which she lived, had died five years ago; her two sons, Eric and Roy, had been killed in the same month – June 1942 – in the same desert retreat.

The greengrocer's shop was unpretentious, in an unpretentious street in Fulham called Agnes Street. The people who owned it now, Jewish people called King, kept an eye on Mrs Malby. They watched for her coming and going and if they missed her one day they'd ring her doorbell to see that she was all right. She had a niece in Ealing who looked in twice a year, and another niece in Islington, who was crippled with arthritis. Once a week Mrs Grove and Mrs Halbert came round with Meals on Wheels. A social worker, Miss Tingle, called; and the Reverend Bush called. Men came to read the meters.

In her elderliness, living where she'd lived since her marriage in 1920, Mrs Malby was happy. The tragedy in her life – the death of her sons – was no longer a nightmare, and the time that had passed since her husband's death had allowed her to come to terms with being on her own. All she wished for was to continue in these same circumstances until she died, and she did not fear death. She did not believe she would be re-united with her sons and her husband, not at least in a specific sense, but she could not believe, either, that she would entirely cease to exist the moment she ceased to breathe. Having thought about death, it seemed likely to Mrs Malby that after it came she'd dream, as in sleep. Heaven and hell were surely no more than flickers of such pleasant dreaming, or flickers of a nightmare from which there was no waking release. No loving omnipotent God, in Mrs Malby's view, doled out punishments and reward: human conscience, the last survivor, did that. The idea of a God, which had puzzled Mrs Malby for most of her life, made sense when she thought of it in terms like these, when she forgot about the mystic qualities claimed for a Church and for Jesus Christ. Yet fearful of offending the Reverend Bush, she kept such conclusions to herself when he came to see her.

All Mrs Malby dreaded now was becoming senile and being forced to enter the Sunset Home in Richmond, of which the Reverend Bush and Miss Tingle warmly spoke. The thought of a communal existence, surrounded by other elderly people, with sing-songs and card-games, was anathema to her. All her life she had hated anything that smacked of communal jolliness, refusing even to go on coach trips. She loved the house above the greengrocer's shop. She loved walking down the stairs and out on to the street, nodding at the Kings as she went by the shop, buying birdseed and eggs and fire-lighters, and fresh bread from Len Skipps, a man of sixty-two whom she'd remembered being born.

The dread of having to leave Agnes Street ordered her life. With all her visitors she was careful, constantly on the look-out for signs in their eyes which might mean they were diagnosing her as senile. It was for this reason that she listened so intently to all that was said to her, that she concentrated, determined to let nothing slip by. It was for this reason that she smiled and endeavoured to appear agreeable and co-operative at all times. She was well aware that it wasn't going to be up to her to state that she was senile, or to argue that she wasn't, when the moment came.

After the teacher from Tite Comprehensive School had left, Mrs Malby continued to worry. The visit from this grey-haired man had bewildered her from the start. There was the oddity of his not giving his name, and then the way he'd placed a cigarette in his mouth and had taken it out again, putting it back in the packet. Had he imagined cigarette smoke would offend her? He could have asked, but in fact he hadn't even referred to the cigarette. Nor had he said where he'd heard about her: he hadn't mentioned the Reverend Bush, for instance, or Mrs Grove and Mrs Halbert, or Miss Tingle. He might have been a customer in the green-grocer's shop, but he hadn't given any indication that that was so. Added to which, and most of all, there was the consideration that her kitchen wasn't in the least in need of attention. She went to look at it again, beginning to wonder if there were things about it she couldn't see. She went over in her mind what the man had said about community relations. It was difficult to resist men like that, you had to go on repeating yourself and after a while you had to assess if you were sounding senile or not. There was also the consideration that the man was trying to do good, helping children from broken homes.

'Hi,' a boy with long blond hair said to her on the Tuesday morning. There were two other boys with him, one with a fuzz of dark curls all round his head, the other red-haired, a greased shock that hung to his shoulders. There was a girl as well, thin and beaky-faced, chewing something. Between them they carried tins of paint, brushes, cloths, a blue plastic bucket, and a transistor radio. 'We come to do your kitchen out,' the blond boy said. 'You Mrs Wheeler then?'

'No, no. I'm Mrs Malby.'

'That's right, Billo,' the girl said. 'Malby.'

'I thought he says Wheeler.'

'Wheeler's the geyser in the paint shop,' the fuzzy-haired boy said.

'Typical Billo,' the girl said.

She let them in, saying it was very kind of them. She led them to the kitchen, remarking on the way that strictly speaking it wasn't in need of decoration, as they could see for themselves. She'd been thinking it over, she added: she wondered if they'd just like to wash the walls down, which was a task she found difficult to do herself?

They'd do whatever she wanted, they said, no problem. They put their paint tins on the table. The red-haired boy turned on the radio. 'Welcome back to Open House,' a cheery voice said and then reminded its listeners that it was the voice of Pete Murray. It said that a record was about to be played for someone in Upminster.

'Would you like some coffee?' Mrs Malby suggested above the noise of the transistor.

'Great,' the blond boy said.

They all wore blue jeans with patches on them. The girl had a T-shirt with the words *I Lay Down With Jesus* on it. The others wore T-shirts of different colours, the blond boy's orange, the fuzzy one's light blue, the red haired one's red. *Hot Jam-roll* a badge on the chest of the blond boy said; *Jaws* and *Bay City Rollers* other badges said.

Mrs Malby made them Nescafé while they listened to the music. They lit cigarettes, leaning about against the electric stove and against the edge of the table and against a wall. They didn't say anything because they were listening. 'That's a load of crap,' the red-haired boy pronounced eventually, and the others agreed. Even so they went on listening. 'Pete Murray's crappy,' the girl said.

Mrs Malby handed them the cups of coffee, drawing their attention to the sugar she'd put out for them on the table, and to the milk. She smiled at the girl. She said again that it was a job she couldn't manage any more, washing walls.

'Get that, Billo?' the fuzzy-haired boy said. 'Washing walls.'

'Who loves ya, baby?' Billo replied.

Mrs Malby closed the kitchen door on them, hoping they wouldn't take too long because the noise of the transistor was so loud. She listened to it for a quarter of an hour and then she decided to go out and do her shopping.

In Len Skipps' she said that four children from the Tite Comprehensive had arrived in her house and were at present washing her kitchen walls. She said it again to the man in the fish shop and the man was surprised. It suddenly occurred to her that of course they couldn't have done any painting because she hadn't discussed colours with the teacher. She thought it odd that the teacher hadn't mentioned colours and wondered what colour the paint tins contained. It worried her a little that all that hadn't occurred to her before.

'Hi, Mrs Wheeler,' the boy called Billo said to her in her hall. He was standing there combing his hair, looking at himself in the mirror of the hall-stand. Music was coming from upstairs.

There were yellowish smears on the stair-carpet, which upset Mrs Malby very much. There were similar smears on the landing carpet. 'Oh, but please,' Mrs Malby cried, standing in the kitchen doorway. 'Oh, please, no!' she cried.

Yellow emulsion paint partially covered the shell-pink of one wall. Some had spilt from the tin on to the black-and-white vinyl of the floor and had been walked through. The boy with fuzzy hair was standing on a draining-board applying the same paint to the ceiling. He was the only person in the kitchen.

He smiled at Mrs Malby, looking down at her. 'Hi, Mrs Wheeler,' he said.

'But I said only to wash them,' she cried.

She felt tired, saying that. The upset of finding the smears on the carpets and of seeing the hideous yellow plastered over the quiet shell-pink had already taken a toll. Her emotional outburst had caused her face and neck to become warm. She felt she'd like to lie down.

'Eh, Mrs Wheeler?' The boy smiled at her again, continuing to slap paint on to the ceiling. A lot of it dripped back on top of him, on to the draining-board and on to cups and saucers and cutlery, and on to the floor. 'D'you fancy the colour, Mrs Wheeler?' he asked her.

All the time the transistor continued to blare, a voice inexpertly singing, a tuneless twanging. The boy referred to this sound, pointing at the transistor with his paint-brush, saying it was great. Unsteadily she crossed the kitchen and turned the transistor off. 'Hey, sod it, missus,' the boy protested angrily.

'I said to wash the walls. I didn't even choose that colour.'

The boy, still annoyed because she'd turned off the radio, was gesturing crossly with the brush. There was paint in the fuzz of his hair and on his T-shirt and his face. Every time he moved the brush about paint flew off it. It speckled the windows, and the small dresser, and the electric stove and the taps and the sink.

'Where's the sound gone?' the boy called Billo demanded, coming into the kitchen and going straight to the transistor.

'I didn't want the kitchen painted,' Mrs Malby said again. 'I told you.'

The singing from the transistor recommenced, louder than before. On the draining-board the fuzzy-haired boy began to sway, throwing his body and his head about.

'Please stop him painting,' Mrs Malby shouted as shrilly as she could.

'Here,' the boy called Billo said, bundling her out on to the landing and closing the kitchen door. 'Can't hear myself think in there.'

'I don't want it painted.'

'What's that, Mrs Wheeler?'

'My name isn't Wheeler. I don't want my kitchen painted. I told you.'

'Are we in the wrong house? Only we was told –'

'Will you please wash that paint off?'

'If we come to the wrong house –'

'You haven't come to the wrong house. Please tell that boy to wash off the paint he's put on.'

'Did a bloke from the Comp come in to see you, Mrs Wheeler? Fat bloke?'

'Yes, yes, he did.'

'Only he give instructions –'

'Please would you tell that boy?'

'Whatever you say, Mrs Wheeler.'

'And wipe up the paint where it's spilt on the floor. It's been trampled out, all over my carpets.'

'No problem, Mrs Wheeler.'

Not wishing to return to the kitchen herself, she ran the hot tap in the bathroom on to the sponge-cloth she kept for cleaning the bath. She found that if she rubbed hard enough at the paint on the stair-carpet and on the landing carpet it began to disappear. But the rubbing tired her. As she put away the sponge-cloth, Mrs Malby had a feeling of not quite knowing what was what. Everything that had happened in the last few hours felt like a dream; it also had the feeling of plays she had seen on television; the one thing it wasn't like was reality. As she paused in her bathroom, having placed the sponge-cloth on a ledge under the hand-basin, Mrs Malby saw herself standing there, as she often did in a dream: she saw her body hunched within the same blue dress she'd been wearing when the teacher called, and two touches of red in her pale face, and her white hair tidy on her head, and her fingers seeming fragile. In a dream anything could happen next: she might suddenly find herself forty years younger, Eric and Roy might be alive. She might be even younger; Dr Ramsey might be telling her she was pregnant. In a television play it would be different: the children who had come to her house might kill her. What she hoped for from reality was that order would be restored in her kitchen, that all the paint would be washed away from her walls as she had wiped it from her carpets, that the misunderstanding would be over. For an instant she saw herself in her kitchen, making tea for the children, saying it didn't matter. She even heard herself adding that in a life as long as hers you became used to everything.

She left the bathroom; the blare of the transistor still persisted. She didn't want to sit in her sitting-room, having to listen to it. She climbed the stairs to her bedroom, imagining the coolness there, and the quietness.

'Hey,' the girl protested when Mrs Malby opened her bedroom door.

'Sod off, you guys,' the boy with the red hair ordered.

They were in her bed. Their clothes were all over the floor. Her two budgerigars were flying about the room. Protruding from sheets and blankets she could see the boy's naked shoulders and the back of his head. The girl poked her face up from under him. She gazed at Mrs Malby. 'It's not them,' she whispered to the boy. 'It's the woman.'

'Hi there, missus.' The boy twisted his head round. From the kitchen, still loudly, came the noise of the transistor.

'Sorry,' the girl said.

'Why are they up here? Why have you let my birds out? You've no right to behave like this.'

'We needed sex,' the girl explained.

The budgerigars were perched on the looking-glass on the dressing-table, beadily surveying the scene.

'They're really great, them budgies,' the boy said.

Mrs Malby stepped through their garments. The budgerigars remained where they were. They fluttered when she seized them but they didn't offer any resistance. She returned with them to the door.

'You had no right,' she began to say to the two in her bed, but her voice had become weak. It quivered into a useless whisper, and once more she thought that what was happening couldn't be happening. She saw herself again, standing unhappily with the budgerigars.

In her sitting-room she wept. She returned the budgerigars to their cage and sat in an armchair by the window that looked out over Agnes Street. She sat in sunshine, feeling its warmth but not, as she might have done, delighting in it. She wept because she had intensely disliked finding the boy and girl in her bed. Images from the bedroom remained vivid in her mind. On the floor the boy's boots were heavy and black, composed of leather that did not shine. The girl's shoes were green, with huge heels and soles. The girl's underclothes were purple, the boy's dirty. There'd been an unpleasant smell of sweat in her bedroom.

Mrs Malby waited, her head beginning to ache. She dried away her tears, wiping at her eyes and cheeks with a handkerchief. In Agnes Street people passed by on bicycles, girls from the polish factory returning home to lunch, men from the brickworks. People came out of the greengrocer's with leeks and cabbages in baskets, some carrying paper bags. Watching these people in Agnes Street made her feel better, even though her headache was becoming worse. She felt more composed, and more in control of herself.

'We're sorry,' the girl said again, suddenly appearing, teetering on her clumsy shoes. 'We didn't think you'd come up to the bedroom.'

She tried to smile at the girl, but found it hard to do so. She nodded instead.

'The others put the birds in,' the girl said. 'Meant to be a joke, that was.'

She nodded again. She couldn't see how it could be a joke to take two budgerigars from their cage, but she didn't say that.

'We're getting on with the painting now,' the girl said. 'Sorry about that.'

She went away and Mrs Malby continued to watch the people in Agnes Street. The girl had made a mistake when she'd said they were getting on with the painting: what she'd meant was that they were getting on with washing it off. The girl had come straight downstairs to say she was sorry; she hadn't been told by the boys in the kitchen that the paint had been applied in error. When they'd gone, Mrs Malby said to herself, she'd open her bedroom window wide in order to get rid of the odour of sweat. She'd put clean sheets on her bed.

From the kitchen, above the noise of the transistor, came the clatter of raised voices. There was laughter and a crash, and then louder laughter. Singing began, attaching itself to the singing from the transistor.

She sat for twenty minutes and then she went and knocked on the kitchen door, not wishing to push the door open in case it knocked someone off a chair. There was no reply. She opened the door gingerly.

More yellow paint had been applied. The whole wall around the window was covered with it, and most of the wall behind the sink. Half of the ceiling had it on it; the woodwork that had been white was now a glossy dark blue. All four of the children were working with brushes. A tin of paint had been upset on the floor.

She wept again, standing there watching them, unable to prevent her tears. She felt them running warmly on her cheeks and then becoming cold. It was in this kitchen that she had cried first of all when the two telegrams had come in 1942, believing when the second one arrived that she would never cease to cry. It would have seemed ridiculous at the time, to cry just because her kitchen was all yellow.

They didn't see her standing there. They went on singing, slapping the paint-brushes back and forth. There'd been neat straight lines where the shell-pink met the white of the woodwork, but now the lines were any old how. The boy with the red hair was applying the dark-blue gloss.

Again the feeling that it wasn't happening possessed Mrs Malby. She'd had a dream a week ago, a particularly vivid dream in which the Prime Minister had stated on television that the Germans had been invited to invade England since England couldn't manage to look after herself any more. That dream had been most troublesome because when she'd woken up in the morning she'd thought it was something she'd seen on television, that she'd actually been sitting in her sitting-room the night before listening to the Prime Minister saying that he and the Leader of the Opposition had decided the best for Britain was invasion. After thinking about it, she'd established that of course it hadn't been true; but even so she'd glanced at the headlines of newspapers when she went out shopping.

'How d'you fancy it?' the boy called Billo called out to her, smiling across the kitchen at her, not noticing that she was upset. 'Neat, Mrs Wheeler?'

She didn't answer. She went downstairs and walked out of her hall-door, into Agnes Street and into the greengrocer's that had been her husband's. It never closed in the middle of the day; it never had. She waited and Mr King appeared, wiping his mouth. 'Well then, Mrs Malby?' he said.

He was a big man with a well-kept black moustache and Jewish eyes. He didn't smile much because smiling wasn't his way, but he was in no way morose, rather the opposite.

'So what can I do for you?' he said.

She told him. He shook his head and repeatedly frowned as he listened. His expressive eyes widened. He called his wife.

While the three of them hurried along the pavement to Mrs Malby's open hall-door it seemed to her that the Kings doubted her. She could feel them thinking that she must have got it all wrong, that she'd somehow imagined all this stuff about yellow paint and pop music on a radio, and her birds flying around her bedroom while two children were lying in her bed. She didn't blame them; she knew exactly how they felt. But when they entered her house the noise from the transistor could at once be heard.

The carpet of the landing was smeared again with the paint. Yellow footprints led to her sitting-room and out again, back to the kitchen.

'You bloody young hooligans,' Mr King shouted at them. He snapped the switch on the transistor. He told them to stop applying the paint immediately. 'What the hell d'you think you're up to?' he demanded furiously.

'We come to paint out the old ma's kitchen,' the boy called Billo explained, unruffled by Mr King's tone. 'We was carrying out instructions, mister.'

'So it was instructions to spill the blooming paint all over the floor? So it was instructions to cover the windows with it and every knife and fork in the place? So it was instructions to frighten the life out of a poor woman by messing about in her bedroom?'

'No one frightens her, mister.'

'You know what I mean, son.'

Mrs Malby returned with Mrs King and sat in the cubbyhole behind the shop, leaving Mr King to do his best. At three o'clock he arrived back, saying that the children had gone. He telephoned the school and after a delay was put in touch with the teacher who'd been to see Mrs Malby. He made this telephone call in the shop but Mrs Malby could hear him saying that what had happened was a disgrace. 'A woman of eighty-seven,' Mr King protested, 'thrown into a state of misery. There'll be something to pay on this, you know.'

There was some further discussion on the telephone, and then Mr King replaced the receiver. He put his head into the cubbyhole and announced that the teacher was coming round immediately to inspect the damage. 'What can I entice you to?' Mrs Malby heard him asking a customer, and a woman's voice replied that she needed tomatoes, a cauliflower, potatoes and Bramleys. She heard Mr King telling the woman what had happened, saying that it had wasted two hours of his time.

She drank the sweet milky tea which Mrs King had poured her. She tried not to think of the yellow paint and the dark-blue gloss. She tried not to remember the scene in the bedroom and the smell there'd been, and the new marks that had appeared on her carpets after she'd wiped off the original ones. She wanted to ask Mr King if these marks had been washed out before the paint had had a chance to dry, but she didn't like to ask this because Mr King had been so kind and it might seem like pressing him.

'Kids nowadays,' Mrs King said. 'I just don't know.'

'Birched they should be,' Mr King said, coming into the cubbyhole and picking up a mug of the milky tea. 'I'd birch the bottoms off them.'

Someone arrived in the shop. Mr King hastened from the cubbyhole. 'What can I entice you to, sir?' Mrs Malby heard him politely enquiring and the voice of the teacher who'd been to see her replied. He said who he was and Mr King wasn't polite any more. An experience like that, Mr King declared thunderously, could have killed an eighty-seven-year-old stone dead.

Mrs Malby stood up and Mrs King came promptly forward to place a hand under her elbow. They went into the shop like that. 'Three and a half p,' Mr King was saying to a woman who'd asked the price of oranges. 'The larger ones at four.'

Mr King gave the woman four of the smaller size and accepted her money. He called out to a youth who was passing by on a bicycle, about to start an afternoon paper round. He was a youth who occasionally assisted him on Saturday mornings: Mr King asked him now if he would mind the shop for ten minutes since an emergency had arisen. Just for once, Mr King argued, it wouldn't matter if the evening papers were a little late.

'Well, you can't say they haven't brightened the place up, Mrs Malby,' the teacher said in her kitchen. He regarded her from beneath his grey fringe. He touched one of the walls with the tip of a finger. He nodded to himself, appearing to be satisfied.

The painting had been completed, the yellow and the dark-blue gloss. Where the colours met there were untidily jagged lines. All the paint that had been spilt on the floor had been wiped away, but the black-and-white vinyl had become dull and grubby in the process. The paint had also been wiped from the windows and from other surfaces, leaving them smeared. The dresser had been wiped down and was smeary also. The cutlery and the taps and the cups and saucers had all been washed or wiped.

'Well, you wouldn't believe it!' Mrs King exclaimed. She turned to her husband. However had he managed it all? she asked him. 'You should have seen the place!' she said to the teacher.

'It's just the carpets,' Mr King said. He led the way from the kitchen to the sitting-room, pointing at the yellow on the landing carpet and on the sitting-room one. 'The blooming stuff dried,' he explained, 'before we could get to it. That's where compensation comes in.' He spoke sternly, addressing the teacher. 'I'd say she has a bob or two owing.'

Mrs King nudged Mrs Malby, drawing attention to the fact that Mr King was doing his best for her. The nudge suggested that all would be well because a sum of money would be paid, possibly even a larger sum than was merited. It suggested also that Mrs Malby in the end might find herself doing rather well.

'Compensation?' the teacher said, bending down and scratching at the paint on the sitting-room carpet. 'I'm afraid compensation's out of the question.'

'She's had her carpets ruined,' Mr King snapped quickly. 'This woman's been put about, you know.'

'She got her kitchen done free,' the teacher snapped back at him.

'They released her pets. They got up to tricks in a bed. You'd no damn right –'

'These kids come from broken homes, sir. I'll do my best with your carpets, Mrs Malby.'

'But what about my kitchen?' she whispered. She cleared her throat because her whispering could hardly be heard. 'My kitchen?' she whispered again.

'What about it, Mrs Malby?'

'I didn't want it painted.'

'Oh, don't be silly now.'

The teacher took his jacket off and threw it impatiently on to a chair. He left the sitting-room. Mrs Malby heard him running a tap in the kitchen.

'It was best to finish the painting, Mrs Malby,' Mr King said. 'Otherwise the kitchen would have driven you mad, half done like that. I stood over them till they finished it.'

'You can't take paint off, dear,' Mrs King said, 'once it's on. You've done wonders, Leo,' she said to her husband. 'Young devils.'

'We'd best be getting back,' Mr King said.

'It's quite nice, you know,' his wife added. 'Your kitchen's quite cheerful, dear.'

The Kings went away and the teacher rubbed at the yellow on the carpets with her washing-up brush. The landing carpet was marked anyway, he pointed out, poking a finger at the stains left behind by the paint she'd removed herself with the sponge-cloth from the bathroom. She must be delighted with the kitchen, he said.

She knew she mustn't speak. She'd known she mustn't when the Kings had been there; she knew she mustn't now. She might have reminded the Kings that she'd chosen the original colours in the kitchen herself. She might have complained to the man as he rubbed at her carpets that the carpets would never be the same again. She watched him, not saying anything, not wishing to be regarded as a nuisance. The Kings would have considered her a nuisance too, agreeing to let children into her kitchen to paint it and then making a fuss. If she became a nuisance the teacher and the Kings would drift on to the same side, and the Reverend Bush would somehow be on that side also, and Miss Tingle, and even Mrs Grove and Mrs Halbert. They would agree among themselves that what had happened had to do with her elderliness, with her not understanding that children who brought paint into a kitchen were naturally going to use it.

'I defy anyone to notice that,' the teacher said, standing up, gesturing at the yellow blurs that remained on her carpets. He put his jacket on. He left the washing-up brush and the bowl of water he'd been using on the floor of her sitting-room. 'All's well that ends well,' he said. 'Thanks for your co-operation, Mrs Malby.'

She thought of her two sons, Eric and Roy, not knowing quite why she thought of them now. She descended the stairs with the teacher, who was cheerfully talking about community relations. You had to make allowances, he said, for kids like that; you had to try and understand; you couldn't just walk away.

Quite suddenly she wanted to tell him about Eric and Roy. In the desire to talk about them she imagined their bodies, as she used to in the past, soon after they'd been killed. They lay on desert sand, desert birds swooped down on them. Their four eyes were gone. She wanted to explain to the teacher that they'd been happy, a contented family in Agnes Street, until the war came and smashed everything to pieces. Nothing had been the same afterwards. It hadn't been easy to continue with nothing to continue for. Each room in the house had contained different memories of the two boys growing up. Cooking and cleaning had seemed pointless. The shop which would have been theirs would have to pass to someone else.

And yet time had soothed the awful double wound. The horror of the emptiness had been lived with, and if having the Kings in the shop now wasn't the same as having your sons there at least the Kings were kind. Thirty-four years after the destruction of your family you were happy in your elderliness because time had been merciful. She wanted to tell the teacher that also, she didn't know why, except that in some way it seemed relevant. But she didn't tell him because it would have been difficult to begin, because in the effort there'd be the danger of seeming senile. Instead she said goodbye, concentrating on that. She said she was sorry, saying it just to show she was aware that she hadn't made herself clear to the children. Conversation had broken down between the children and herself, she wanted him to know she knew it had.

He nodded vaguely, not listening to her. He was trying to make the world a better place, he said. 'For kids like that, Mrs Malby. Victims of broken homes.'

Another Christmas

You always looked back, she thought. You looked back at other years, other Christmas cards arriving, the children younger. There was the year Patrick had cried, disliking the holly she was decorating the living-room with. There was the year Bridget had got a speck of coke in her eye on Christmas Eve and had to be taken to the hospital at Hammersmith in the middle of the night. There was the first year of their marriage, when she and Dermot were still in Waterford. And ever since they'd come to London there was the presence on Christmas Day of their landlord, Mr Joyce, a man whom they had watched becoming elderly.

She was middle-aged now, with touches of grey in her fluffy jet-black hair, a woman known for her cheerfulness, running a bit to fat. Her husband was the opposite: thin and seeming ascetic, with more than a hint of the priest in him, a good man. 'Will we get married, Norah?' he'd said one night in the Tara Ballroom in Waterford, November 6th, 1953. The proposal had astonished her: it was his brother Ned, bulky and fresh-faced, a different kettle of fish altogether, whom she'd been expecting to make it.

Patiently he held a chair for her while she strung paper-chains across the room, from one picture-rail to another. He warned her to be careful about attaching anything to the electric light. He still held the chair while she put sprigs of holly behind the pictures. He was cautious by nature and alarmed by little things, particularly anxious in case she fell off chairs. He'd never mount a chair himself, to put up decorations or anything else: he'd be useless at it in his opinion and it was his opinion that mattered. He'd never been able to do a thing about the house but it didn't matter because since the boys had grown up they'd attended to whatever she couldn't manage herself. You wouldn't dream of remarking on it: he was the way he was, considerate and thoughtful in what he did do, teetotal, clever, full of fondness for herself and for the family they'd reared, full of respect for her also.

'Isn't it remarkable how quick it comes round, Norah?' he said while he held the chair. 'Isn't it no time since last year?'

'No time at all.'

'Though a lot happened in the year, Norah.'

'An awful lot happened.'

Two of the pictures she decorated were scenes of Waterford: the quays and a man driving sheep past the Bank of Ireland. Her mother had given them to her, taking them down from the hall of the farm-house.

There was a picture of the Virgin and Child, and other, smaller pictures. She placed her last sprig of holly, a piece with berries on it, above the Virgin's halo.

'I'll make a cup of tea,' she said, descending from the chair and smiling at him.

'A cup of tea'd be great, Norah.'

The living-room, containing three brown armchairs and a table with upright chairs around it, and a sideboard with a television set on it, was crowded by this furniture and seemed even smaller than it was because of the decorations that had been added. On the mantelpiece, above a built-in gas fire, Christmas cards were arrayed on either side of an ornate green clock.

The house was in a terrace in Fulham. It had always been too small for the family, but now that Patrick and Brendan no longer lived there things were easier. Patrick had married a girl called Pearl six months ago, almost as soon as his period of training with the Midland Bank had ended. Brendan was training in Liverpool, with a firm of computer manufacturers. The three remaining children were still at school, Bridget at the nearby convent, Cathal and Tom at the Sacred Heart Primary. When Patrick and Brendan had moved out the room they'd always shared had become Bridget's. Until then Bridget had slept in her parents' room and she'd have to return there this Christmas because Brendan would be back for three nights. Patrick and Pearl would just come for Christmas Day. They'd be going to Pearl's people, in Croydon, on Boxing Day – St Stephen's Day, as Norah and Dermot always called it, in the Irish manner.

'It'll be great, having them all,' he said. 'A family again, Norah.'

'And Pearl.'

'She's part of us now, Norah.'

'Will you have biscuits with your tea? I have a packet of Nice.'

He said he would, thanking her. He was a meter-reader with North Thames Gas, a position he had held for twenty-one years, ever since he'd emigrated. In Waterford he'd worked as a clerk in the Customs, not earning very much and not much caring for the stuffy, smoke-laden office he shared with half-a-dozen other clerks. He had come to England because Norah had thought it was a good idea, because she'd always wanted to work in a London shop. She'd been given a job in Dickins & Jones, in the household linens department, and he'd been taken on as a meter-reader, cycling from door to door, remembering the different houses and where the meters were situated in each, being agreeable to householders: all of it suited him from the start. He devoted time to thought while he rode about, and in particular to religious matters.

In her small kitchen she made the tea and carried it on a tray into the living-room. She'd been late this year with the decorations. She always liked to get them up a week in advance because they set the mood, making everyone feel right for Christmas. She'd been busy with stuff for a stall Father Malley had asked her to run for his Christmas Sale. A fashion stall he'd called it, but not quite knowing what he meant she'd just asked people for any old clothes they had, jumble really. Because of the time it had taken she hadn't had a minute to see to the decorations until this afternoon, two days before Christmas Eve. But that, as it turned out, had been all for the best. Bridget and Cathal and Tom had gone up to Putney to the pictures, Dermot didn't work on a Monday afternoon: it was convenient that they'd have an hour or two alone together because there was the matter of Mr Joyce to bring up. Not that she wanted to bring it up, but it couldn't be just left there.

'The cup that cheers,' he said, breaking a biscuit in half. Deliberately she put off raising the subject she had in mind. She watched him nibbling the biscuit and then dropping three heaped spoons of sugar into his tea and stirring it. He loved tea. The first time he'd taken her out, to the Savoy Cinema in Waterford, they'd had tea afterwards in the cinema café and they'd talked about the film and about people they knew. He'd come to live in Waterford from the country, from the farm his brother had inherited, quite close to her father's farm. He reckoned he'd settled, he told her that night: Waterford wasn't sensational, but it suited him in a lot of ways. If he hadn't married her he'd still be there, working eight hours a day in the Customs and not caring for it, yet managing to get by because he had his religion to assist him.

'Did we get a card from Father Jack yet?' he enquired, referring to a distant cousin, a priest in Chicago.

'Not yet. But it's always on the late side, Father Jack's. It was February last year.'

She sipped her tea, sitting in one of the other brown armchairs, on the other side of the gas fire. It was pleasant being there alone with him in the decorated room, the green clock ticking on the mantelpiece, the Christmas cards, dusk gathering outside. She smiled and laughed, taking another biscuit while he lit a cigarette. 'Isn't this great?' she said. 'A bit of peace for ourselves?'

Solemnly he nodded.

"Peace comes dropping slow," he said, and she knew he was quoting from some book or other. Quite often he said things she didn't understand. 'Peace and goodwill,' he added, and she understood that all right.

He tapped the ash from his cigarette into an ashtray which was kept for his use, beside the gas fire. All his movements were slow. He was a slow thinker, even though he was clever. He arrived at a conclusion, having thought long and carefully; he balanced everything in his mind. 'We must think about that, Norah,' he said that day, twenty-two years ago, when she'd suggested that they should move to England. A week later he'd said that if she really wanted to he'd agree.

They talked about Bridget and Cathal and Tom. When they came in from the cinema they'd only just have time to change their clothes before setting out again for the Christmas party at Bridget's convent.

'It's a big day for them. Let them lie in in the morning, Norah.'

'They could lie in for ever,' she said, laughing in case there might seem to be harshness in this recommendation. With Christmas excitement running high, the less she heard from them the better.

'Did you get Cathal the gadgets he wanted?'

'Chemistry stuff. A set in a box.'

'You're great the way you manage, Norah.'

She denied that. She poured more tea for both of them. She said, as casually as she could:

'Mr Joyce won't come. I'm not counting him in for Christmas Day.'

'He hasn't failed us yet, Norah.'

'He won't come this year.' She smiled through the gloom at him. 'I think we'd best warn the children about it.'

'Where would he go if he didn't come here? Where'd he get his dinner?'

'Lyons used to be open in the old days.'

'He'd never do that.'

'The Bulrush Café has a turkey dinner advertised. There's a lot of people go in for that now. If you have a mother doing a job she maybe hasn't the time for the cooking. They go out to a hotel or a café, three or four pounds a head –'

'Mr Joyce wouldn't go to a café. No one could go into a café on their own on Christmas Day.'

'He won't come here, dear.'

It had to be said: it was no good just pretending, laying a place for the old man on an assumption that had no basis to it. Mr Joyce would not come because Mr Joyce, last August, had ceased to visit them. Every Friday night he used to come, for a cup of tea and a chat, to watch the nine o'clock news with them. Every Christmas Day he'd brought carefully chosen presents for the children, and chocolates and nuts and cigarettes. He'd given Patrick and Pearl a radio as a wedding present.

'I think he'll come all right. I think maybe he hasn't been too well. God help him, it's a great age, Norah.'

'He hasn't been ill, Dermot.'

Every Friday Mr Joyce had sat there in the third of the brown armchairs, watching the television, his bald head inclined so that this good ear was closer to the screen. He was tallish, rather bent now, frail and bony, with a modest white moustache. In his time he'd been a builder, which was how he had come to own property in Fulham, a self-made man who'd never married. That evening in August he had been quite as usual. Bridget had kissed him good-night because for as long as she could remember she'd always done that when he came on Friday evenings. He'd asked Cathal how he was getting on with his afternoon paper round.

There had never been any difficulties over the house. They considered that he was fair in his dealings with them; they were his tenants and his friends. When the Irish bombed English people to death in Birmingham and Guildford he did not cease to arrive every Friday evening and on Christmas Day. The bombings were discussed after the News, the Tower of London bomb, the bomb in the bus, and all the others. 'Maniacs,' Mr Joyce said and nobody contradicted him.

'He would never forget the children, Norah. Not at Christmastime.'

His voice addressed her from the shadows. She felt the warmth of the gas fire reflected in her face and knew if she looked in a mirror she'd see that she was quite flushed. Dermot's face never reddened. Even though he was nervy, he never displayed emotion. On all occasions his face retained its paleness, his eyes acquired no glimmer of passion. No wife could have a better husband, yet in the matter of Mr Joyce he was so wrong it almost frightened her.

'Is it tomorrow I call in for the turkey?' he said.

She nodded, hoping he'd ask her if anything was the matter because as a rule she never just nodded in reply to a question. But he didn't say anything. He stubbed his cigarette out. He asked if there was another cup of tea in the pot.

'Dermot, would you take something round to Mr Joyce?'

'A message, is it?'

'I have a tartan tie for him.'

'Wouldn't you give it to him on the day, Norah? Like you always do.' He spoke softly, still insisting. She shook her head.

It was all her fault. If she hadn't said they should go to England, if she hadn't wanted to work in a London shop, they wouldn't be caught in the trap they'd made for themselves. Their children spoke with London accents. Patrick and Brendan worked for English firms and would make their homes in England. Patrick had married an English girl. They were Catholics and they had Irish names, yet home for them was not Waterford.

'Could you make it up with Mr Joyce, Dermot? Could you go round with the tie and say you were sorry?'

'Sorry?'

'You know what I mean.' In spite of herself her voice had acquired a trace of impatience, an edginess that was unusual in it. She did not ever speak to him like that. It was the way she occasionally spoke to the children.

'What would I say I was sorry for, Norah?'

'For what you said that night.' She smiled, calming her agitation. He lit another cigarette, the flame of the match briefly illuminating his face. Nothing had changed in his face. He said:

'I don't think Mr Joyce and I had any disagreement, Norah.'

'I know, Dermot. You didn't mean anything –'

'There was no disagreement, girl.'

There had been no disagreement, but on that evening in August something else had happened. On the nine o'clock news there had been a report of another outrage and afterwards, when Dermot had turned the television off, there'd been the familiar comment on it. He couldn't understand the mentality of people like that, Mr Joyce said yet again, killing just anyone, destroying life for no reason. Dermot had shaken his head over it, she herself had said it was uncivilized. Then Dermot had added that they mustn't of course forget what the Catholics in the North had suffered. The bombs were a crime but it didn't do to forget that the crime would not be there if generations of Catholics in the North had not been treated as animals. There'd been a silence then, a difficult kind of silence which she'd broken herself. All that was in the past, she'd said hastily, in a rush, nothing in the past or the present or anywhere else could justify the killing of innocent people. Even so, Dermot had added, it didn't do to avoid the truth. Mr Joyce had not said anything.

'I'd say there was no need to go round with the tie, Norah. I'd say he'd make the effort on Christmas Day.'

'Of course he won't.' Her voice was raised, with more than impatience in it now. But her anger was controlled. 'Of course he won't come.'

'It's a time for goodwill, Norah. Another Christmas: to remind us.'

He spoke slowly, the words prompted by some interpretation of God's voice in answer to a prayer. She recognized that in his deliberate tone.

'It isn't just another Christmas. It's an awful kind of Christmas. It's a Christmas to be ashamed, and you're making it worse, Dermot.' Her lips were trembling in a way that was uncomfortable. If she tried to calm herself she'd become jittery instead, she might even begin to cry. Mr Joyce had been generous and tactful, she said loudly. It made no difference to Mr Joyce that they were Irish people, that their children went to school with the children of I.R.A. men. Yet his generosity and his tact had been thrown back in his face. Everyone knew that the Catholics in the North had suffered, that generations of injustice had been twisted into the shape of a cause. But you couldn't say it to an old man who had hardly been outside Fulham in his life. You couldn't say it because when you did it sounded like an excuse for murder.

'You have to state the truth, Norah. It's there to be told.'

'I never yet cared for a North of Ireland person, Catholic or Protestant. Let them fight it out and not bother us.'

'You shouldn't say that, Norah.'

'It's more of your truth for you.'

He didn't reply. There was the gleam of his face for a moment as he drew on his cigarette. In all their married life they had never had a quarrel that was in any way serious, yet she felt herself now in the presence of a seriousness that was too much for her. She had told him that whenever a new bombing took place she prayed it might be the work of the Angry Brigade, or any group that wasn't Irish. She'd told him that in shops she'd begun to feel embarrassed because of her Waterford accent. He'd said she must have courage, and she realized now that he had drawn on courage himself when he'd made the remark to Mr Joyce. He would have prayed and considered before making it. He would have seen it in the end as his Catholic duty.

'He thinks you don't condemn people being killed.' She spoke quietly even though she felt a wildness inside her. She felt she should be out on the streets, shouting in her Waterford accent, violently stating that the bombers were more despicable with every breath they drew, that hatred and death were all they deserved. She saw herself on Fulham Broadway, haranguing the passers-by, her greying hair blown in the wind, her voice more passionate than it had ever been before. But none of it was the kind of thing she could do because she was not that kind of woman. She hadn't the courage, any more than she had the courage to urge her anger to explode in their living-room. For all the years of her marriage there had never been the need of such courage before: she was aware of that, but found no consolation in it.

'I think he's maybe seen it by now,' he said. 'How one thing leads to another.'

She felt insulted by the words. She willed herself the strength to shout, to pour out a torrent of fury at him, but the strength did not come. Standing up, she stumbled in the gloom and felt a piece of holly under the sole of her shoe. She turned the light on.

'I'll pray that Mr Joyce will come,' he said.

She looked at him, pale and thin, with his priestly face. For the first time since he had asked her to marry him in the Tara Ballroom she did not love him. He was cleverer than she was, yet he seemed half blind. He was good, yet he seemed hard in his goodness, as though he'd be better without it. Up to the very last moment on Christmas Day there would be the pretence that their landlord might arrive, that God would answer a prayer because His truth had been honoured. She considered it hypocrisy, unable to help herself in that opinion.

He talked but she did not listen. He spoke of keeping faith with their own, of being a Catholic. Crime begot crime, he said, God wanted it to be known that one evil led to another. She continued to look at him while he spoke, pretending to listen but wondering instead if in twelve months' time, when another Christmas came, he would still be cycling from house to house to read gas meters. Or would people have objected, requesting a meter-reader who was not Irish? An objection to a man with an Irish accent was down-to-earth and ordinary. It didn't belong in the same grand category as crime begetting crime or God wanting something to be known, or in the category of truth and conscience. In the present circumstances the objection would be understandable and fair. It seemed even right that it should be made, for it was a man with an Irish accent in whom the worst had been brought out by the troubles that had come, who was guilty of a cruelty no one would have believed him capable of. Their harmless elderly landlord might die in the course of that same year, a friendship he had valued lost, his last Christmas lonely. Grand though it might seem in one way, all of it was petty.

Once, as a girl, she might have cried, but her contented marriage had caused her to lose that habit. She cleared up the tea things, reflecting that the bombers would be pleased if they could note the victory they'd scored in a living-room in Fulham. And on Christmas Day, when a family sat down to a conventional meal, the victory would be greater. There would be crackers and chatter and excitement, the Queen and the Pope would deliver speeches. Dermot would discuss these Christmas messages with Patrick and Brendan, as he'd discussed them in the past with Mr Joyce. He would be as kind as ever. He would console Bridget and Cathal and Tom by saying that Mr Joyce hadn't been up to the journey. And whenever she looked at him she would remember the Christmases of the past. She would feel ashamed of him, and of herself.

Old Mrs Ashburton used to drive about the lanes in a governess cart drawn by a donkey she called Trot. We often met her as we cycled home from school, when my brother and my sister were at the Grammar School and I was still at Miss Pritchard's Primary. Of the three of us I was Mrs Ashburton's favourite, and I don't know why that was except that I was the youngest. 'Hullo, my Matilda,' Mrs Ashburton would whisper in her throaty, crazy-sounding way. 'Matilda,' she'd repeat, lingering over the name I so disliked, drawing each syllable away from the next. 'Dear Matilda.' She was excessively thin, rather tall, and frail-looking. We made allowances for her because she was eighty-one.

Usually when we met her she was looking for wild flowers, or if it was winter or autumn just sitting in her governess cart in some farmer's gateway, letting the donkey graze the farmer's grass. In spring she used to root out plants from the hedges with a little trowel. Most of them were weeds, my brother said; and looking back on it now, I realize that it wasn't for wild flowers, or weeds, or grazing for her donkey that she drove about the lanes. It was in order to meet us cycling back from school.

'There's a tennis court at Challacombe Manor,' she said one day in May, 1939. 'Any time you ever wanted to play, Dick.' She stared at my brother with piercing black eyes that were the colour of quality coal. She was eccentric, standing there in a long, very old and bald fur coat, stroking the ears of her donkey while he nibbled a hedge. Her hat was attached to her grey hair by a number of brass hat-pins. The hat was of faded green felt, the hat-pins had quite large knobs at the ends of them, inlaid with pieces of green glass. Green, Mrs Ashburton often remarked, was hei favourite colour, and she used to remove these hat-pins to show us the glass additions, emphasizing that they were valueless. Her bald fur coat was valueless also, she assured us, and not even in its heyday would it have fetched more than five pounds. In the same manner she remarked upon her summer hats and dresses, and her shoes, and the governess cart, and the donkey.

'I mean, Dick,' she said that day in 1939, 'it's not much of a tennis court, but it was once, of course. And there's a net stacked away in one of the out-houses. And a roller, and a marker. There's a lawnmower, too, because naturally you'll need that.'

'You mean, we could play on your court, Mrs Ashburton?' my sister Betty said.

'Of course I mean that, my dear. That's just what I mean. You know, before the war we really did have marvellous tennis parties at Challacombe. Everyone came.'

'Oh, how lovely!' Betty was fourteen and Dick was a year older, and I was nine. Betty was fair-haired like the rest of us, but much prettier than me. She had very blue eyes and a wide smiling mouth that boys at the Grammar School were always trying to kiss, and a small nose, and freckles. Her hair was smooth and long, the colour of hay. It looked quite startling sometimes, shining in the sunlight. I used to feel proud of Betty and Dick when they came to collect me every afternoon at the Primary School. Dick was to leave the Grammar School in July, and on the afternoons of that warm May, as Betty and I cycled home with him, we felt sorry that he wouldn't be there next term. But Dick said he was glad. He was big, as tall as my father, and very shy. He'd begun to smoke, a habit not approved of by my father. On the way home from school we had to stop and go into a ruined cottage so that he could have a Woodbine. He was going to work on the farm; one day the farm would be his.

'It would be lovely to play tennis,' Betty said.

'Then you must, my dear. But if you want to play this summer you'll have to get the court into trim.' Mrs Ashburton smiled at Betty in a way that made her thin, elderly face seem beautiful. Then she smiled at Dick. 'I was passing the tennis court the other day, Dick, and I suddenly thought of it. Now why shouldn't those children get it into trim? I thought. Why shouldn't they come and play, and bring their friends?'

'Yes,' Dick said.

'Why ever don't you come over to Challacombe on Saturday? Matilda, too, of course. Come for tea, all three of you.'

Mrs Ashburton smiled at each of us in turn. She nodded at us and climbed into the governess cart. 'Saturday,' she repeated.

'Honestly, Betty!' Dick glared crossly at my sister, as though she were responsible for the invitation. 'I'm not going, you know.'

He cycled off, along the narrow, dusty lane, big and red-faced and muttering. We followed him more slowly, talking about Mrs Ashburton. 'Poor old thing!' Betty said, which was what people round about often said when Mrs Ashburton was mentioned, or when she was seen in her governess cart.

The first thing I remember in all my life was my father breaking a fountain-pen. It was a large black-and-white pen, like tortoiseshell or marble. That was the fashion for fountain-pens then: two or three colours marbled together, green and black, blue and white, red and black-and-white. Conway Stewart, Waterman's, Blackbird. Propelling pencils were called Eversharp.

The day my father broke his pen I didn't know all that: I learnt it afterwards at Miss Pritchard's Primary. I was three the day he broke the pen. 'It's just a waste of blooming money!' he shouted. He smashed the pen across his knee while my mother anxiously watched. Waste of money or not, she said, it wouldn't help matters to break the thing. She fetched him the ink and a dip-pen from a drawer of the dresser. He was still angry, but after a minute or two he began to laugh. He kissed my mother, pulling her down on to the knee he'd broken the pen over. Dick, who must have been nine then, didn't even look up from his homework. Betty was there too, but I can't remember what she was doing.

The kitchen hasn't changed much. The old range has gone, but the big light-oak dresser is still there, with the same brass handles on its doors and drawers and the same Wedgwood-blue dinner-set on its shelves, and cups and jugs hanging on hooks. The ceiling is low, the kitchen itself large and rectangular, with the back stairs rising from the far end of it, and a door at the bottom of them. There are doors to the pantry and the scullery, and to the passage that leads to the rest of the house, and to the yard. There's a long narrow light-oak table, with brass handles on its drawers, like the dresser ones, and oak chairs that aren't as light as all the other oak because chairs darken with use. But the table isn't scrubbed once a week any more, and the brass doesn't gleam. I know, because now and again I visit the farm-house.

I remember the kitchen with oil-lamps, and the time, the day after my fifth birthday, when the men came to wire the house for electricity. My mother used to talk about an Aga, and often when she took us shopping with her she'd bring us to Archers', the builders' merchants, to look at big cream-coloured Agas. After a time, Mr Gray of the Aga department didn't even bother to bustle up to her when he saw her coming. She'd stand there, plump and pink-cheeked, her reddish hair neat beneath the brim of her hat, touching the display models, opening the oven doors and lifting up the two big hot-plate covers. When we returned to the farm-house my father would tease her, knowing she'd been to Archers' again. She'd blush, cutting ham at tea-time or offering round salad. My father would then forget about it. 'Well, I'm damned,' he'd say, and he'd read out an item from the weekly paper, about some neighbouring farmer or new County Council plans. My mother would listen and then both of them would nod. They were very good friends, even though my father teased her. She blushed like a rose, he said: he teased her to see it.

Once, before the electricity came, I had a nightmare. It was probably only a few months before, because when I came crying down to the kitchen my father kept comforting me with the reminder that it would soon be my fifth birthday. 'You'll never cry then, Matilda,' he whispered to me, cuddling me to him. 'Big girls of five don't cry.' I fell asleep, but it's not that that I remember now, not the fear from the nightmare going away, or the tears stopping, or my father's caressing: it's the image of my parents in the kitchen as I stumbled down the back stairs. There were two oil-lamps lit and the fire in the range was glowing red-hot behind its curved bars, and the heavy black kettle wasn't quite singing. My father was asleep with last Saturday's weekly paper on his knees, my mother was reading one of the books from the bookcase in the dining-room we never used, probably *The Garden of Allah*, which was her favourite. The two sheepdogs were asleep under the table, and when I opened the door at the top of the stairs they both barked because they knew that at that particular time no one should be opening that door. 'Oh, now, now,' my mother said, coming to me, listening to me when I said that there were cows on my bedroom wall. I remember the image of the two of them because they looked so happy sitting there, even though my mother hadn't got her Aga, even though my father was sometimes worried about the farm.

Looking back on it now, there was a lot of happiness, although perhaps not more than many families experience. Everything seems either dismal or happy in retrospect, and the happiness in the farm-house is what I think of first whenever I think now of that particular past. I remember my mother baking in the kitchen, flour all over her plump arms, and tiny beads of sweat on her forehead, because the kitchen was always hot. I remember my father's leathery skin and his smile, and the way he used to shout at the sheepdogs, and the men, Joe and Arthur, sitting on yellow stubble, drinking tea out of a bottle, on a day hay had been cut.

Our farm had once been the home-farm of Challacombe Manor, even though our farm-house was two miles away from the manor house. There'd been servants and gardeners at Challacombe Manor then, and horses in the stables, and carriages coming and going. But the estate had fallen into rack and ruin after the First World War because Mr Ashburton hadn't been able to keep it going and in the end, in 1924, he'd taken out various mortgages. When he died, in 1929, the extent of his debts was so great that Mrs Ashburton had been obliged to let Lloyd's Bank foreclose on the mortgages, which is how it came about that my father bought Challacombe Farm. It was a tragedy, people round about used to say, and the real tragedy was that Mr Ashburton had come back from the war in such a strange state that he hadn't minded about everywhere falling into rack and ruin. According to my father, Lloyd's Bank owned Challacombe Manor itself and had granted Mrs Ashburton permission to live there in her lifetime. It wouldn't surprise him, my father said, if it turned out that Lloyd's Bank owned Mrs Ashburton as well. 'He drank himself to death,' people used to say about Mr Ashburton. 'She watched him and didn't have the heart to stop him.' Yet before the First World War Mr Ashburton had been a different kind of man, energetic and sharp. The Challacombe estate had been a showpiece.

To me in particular Mrs Ashburton talked about her husband. She was lucky that he'd come back from the war, even if he hadn't been able to manage very well. His mind had been affected, she explained, but that was better than being dead. She told me about the men who'd died, gardeners at Challacombe Manor, and farm workers on the estate, and men she and her husband had known in the town. 'I thanked God,' Mrs Ashburton said, 'when he came safely back here all in one piece. Everything fell to bits around us, but it didn't matter because at least he was still alive. You understand, Matilda?'

I always nodded, although I didn't really understand. And then she'd go on about the estate as it had been, and then about her husband and the conversations they used to have. Sometimes she didn't address me directly. She smiled and just talked, always returning to the men who had been killed and how lucky she was that her husband had at least come back. She'd prayed, she said, that he'd come back, and every time another man from the estate or from the neighbourhood had been reported dead she'd felt that there was a better chance that her husband wouldn't die also. 'By the law of averages,' she explained, 'some had to come back. Some men have always come back from wars, you convince yourself.'

At this point I would always nod again, and Mrs Ashburton would say that looking back on it now she felt ashamed that she had ever applied the law of averages to the survival or death of men. Doing so was as horrible as war itself: the women who were left at home became cruel in their fear and their selfishness. Cruelty was natural in war, Mrs Ashburton said.

At the time she'd hated the Germans and she was ashamed of that too, because the Germans were just people like other people. But when she talked about them the remains of the hatred were still in her voice, and I imagined the Germans from what she told me about them: people who ate black bread and didn't laugh much, who ate raw bacon, who were dour, grey and steely. She described the helmets they wore in wartime. She told me what a bayonet was, and I used to feel sick when I thought of one going into a man's stomach and being twisted in there to make sure the man would die. She told me about poison gas, and the trenches, and soldiers being buried alive. The way she spoke I knew she was repeating, word for word, the things her husband had told her, things that had maybe been the cause of his affected mind. Even her voice sounded unusual when she talked about the war, as though she was trying to imitate her husband's voice, and the terror that had been in it. He used to cry, she said, as he walked about the gardens, unable to stop the tears once they'd begun.

Dick didn't say anything while we rode the two miles over to Challacombe Manor that Saturday. He didn't even say anything when he suddenly dismounted and leaned his bicycle against a black gate, and climbed over the gate to have a smoke behind the hedge. If my father had come by he'd have known what was happening because he would have seen Betty and myself waiting in the lane, surrounded by the cloud of smoke that Dick always managed to make with his Woodbine. Our job was to warn him if we saw my father coming, but my father didn't come that afternoon and when Dick had finished we continued on our way.

We'd often been to tea at Challacombe Manor before. Mrs Ashburton said we were the only visitors she had because most of her friends were dead, which was something that happened, she explained, if you were eighty-one. We always had tea in the kitchen, a huge room that smelt of oil, with armchairs in it and a wireless, and an oil-stove on which Mrs Ashburton cooked, not wishing to have to keep the range going. There were oatcakes for tea, and buttered white and brown bread, and pots of jam that Mrs Ashburton bought in the town, and a cake she bought also, usually a fruitcake. Afterwards we'd walk through the house with her, while she pointed out the places where the roof had given way, and the dry rot, and windows that were broken. She hadn't lived in most of the house since the war, and had lived in even less of it since her husband had died in 1929. We knew these details by heart because she'd told us so many times. In one of the out-houses there was an old motor-car with flat tyres, and the gardens were now all overgrown with grass and weeds. Rhododendrons were choked, and buddleia and kerria and hydrangeas.

The house was grey and square with two small wings, a stone Georgian house with wide stone steps leading to a front door that had pillars on either side of it and a fan-light above it. The gravel expanse in front of it was grassy now, and slippery in wet weather because of moss that had accumulated. French windows opened on to it on either side of the hall-door, from the rooms that had been the drawing-room and the dining-room. Lawns stretched around the house, with grass like a meadow on them now. The tennis court, which we'd never known about until Mrs Ashburton mentioned it, was hidden away, beyond the jungle of shrubbery.

'You see?' she said. 'You see, Dick?' She was wearing a long, old-fashioned dress and a wide-brimmed white hat, and sunglasses because the afternoon was fiercely bright.

The grass on the tennis court was a yard high, as high as the rusty iron posts that were there to support the net. 'Look,' Mrs Ashburton said.

She led us to the stable-yard, past the out-house where the motor-car was, and into a smaller out-house. There was a lawnmower there, as rusty as the tennis posts, and a marker in the same condition, and an iron roller. Tucked into the beams above our heads was a rolled-up tennis net. 'He adored tennis,' she said. 'He really loved it.'

She turned and we followed her across the stable-yard, into the kitchen by the back door. She talked about her husband while she made tea.

We ate the bought fruitcake, listening to her. We'd heard it all before, but we always considered it was worth it because of the cake and the biscuits and the buttered bread and the pots of jam. And always before we left she gave us ginger beer and pieces of chocolate broken up on a saucer. She told us about the child which might have been born to her husband and herself, six months after the beginning of the war, but which had miscarried. 'Everything went wrong,' she said. She told us about the parties there'd been at Challacombe Manor. Champagne and strawberries and cream, and parties with games that she described and fancy dress.

'No reason at all,' she said, 'why we shouldn't have a tennis party.'

Dick made a sighing sound, a soft, slight noise that Mrs Ashburton didn't hear.

'Tennis party?' Betty murmured.

'No reason, dear.'

That morning Dick and Betty had had an argument. Betty had said that of course he must go to tea with Mrs Ashburton, since he'd always gone in the past. And Dick had said that Mrs Ashburton had been cunning: all these years, he said, she'd been inviting us to tea so that when the time was ripe she could get us to clean up her old tennis court. 'Oh, don't be silly!' Betty had cried, and then had said that it would be the cruellest thing that Dick had ever done if he didn't go to tea with an old woman just because she'd mentioned her tennis court. I'd been cross with Dick myself, and none of us felt very happy because the matter of the tennis court had unattractively brought into the open the motive behind our putting up with Mrs Ashburton. I didn't like it when she called me her Matilda and put her arms around me, and said she was sure her child would have been a little girl, and that she was almost as sure that she'd have called her Matilda. I didn't like it when she went on and on about the war and her husband coming back a wreck, or about the champagne and the strawberries and cream. 'Poor Mrs Ashburton!' we'd always said, but it wasn't because she was poor Mrs Ashburton that we'd filled the emptiness of Saturday afternoons by cycling over to Challacombe Manor.

'Shall we go and have another look at it?' she said when we'd eaten all the food that was on the table. She smiled in her frail, almost beautiful way, and for a moment I wondered if Dick wasn't perhaps right about her cunning. She led the way back to the overgrown tennis court and we all four stood looking at it.

'It's quite all right to smoke, Dick,' Mrs Ashburton said, 'if you want to.'

Dick laughed because he didn't know how else to react. He'd gone as red as a sunset. He kicked at the rusty iron tennis post, and then as casually as he could he took a packet of squashed Woodbines from his pocket and began to fiddle with a box of matches. Betty poked him with her elbow, suggesting that he should offer Mrs Ashburton a cigarette.

'Would you like one, Mrs Ashburton?' Dick said, proffering the squashed packet.

'Well, you know, I think I would, Dick.' She laughed and took the cigarette, saying she hadn't smoked a cigarette since 1915. Dick lit it for her. Some of the matches fell from the matchbox on the long grass. He picked them up and replaced them, his own cigarette cocked out of the corner of his mouth. They looked rather funny, the two of them, Mrs Ashburton in her big white hat and sunglasses.

'You'd need a scythe,' Dick said.

That was the beginning of the tennis party. When Dick walked over the next Saturday with a scythe, Mrs Ashburton had a packet of twenty

Craven A waiting for him. He scythed the grass and got the old hand-mower going. The stubble was coarse and by the time he'd cut it short there were quite large patches of naked earth, but Betty and Mrs Ashburton said they didn't matter. The court would do as it was for this summer, but in the spring, Dick said, he'd put down fresh grass-seed. It rained heavily a fortnight later, which was fortunate, because Dick was able to even out some of the bumps with the roller. Betty helped him, and later on she helped him mark the court out. Mrs Ashburton and I watched, Mrs Ashburton holding my hand and often seeming to imagine that I was the child which hadn't been born to her.

We took to going to Challacombe Manor on Sunday mornings as well as Saturdays. There were always packets of Craven A, and ginger beer and pieces of chocolate. 'Of course, it's not her property,' my father said whenever anyone mentioned the tennis court, or the net that Mrs Ashburton had found rolled up in an out-house. At dinnertime on Sundays, when we all sat around the long table in the kitchen, my father would ask Dick how he'd got on with the court. He'd then point out that the tennis court and everything that went with it was the property of Lloyd's Bank. Every Sunday dinner-time we had the same: roast beef and roast potatoes and Yorkshire pudding, and carrots or brussels sprouts according to the seasonal variation, and apple-pie and cream.

Dick didn't ever say much when my father asked him about the tennis court. 'You want to be careful, lad,' my father used to say, squashing roast potatoes into gravy. 'Lloyd's is strict, you know.' My father would go on for ages, talking about Lloyd's Bank or the Aga cooker my mother wanted, and you never quite knew whether he was being serious or not. He would sit there with his jacket on the back of his chair, not smiling as he ate and talked. Farmers were like that, my mother once told Betty when Betty was upset by him. Farmers were cautious and watchful and canny. He didn't at all disapprove of what Betty and Dick and Mrs Ashburton were doing with the tennis court, my mother explained, rather the opposite; but he was right when he reminded them that everything, including the house itself, was the property of Lloyd's Bank.

Mrs Ashburton found six tennis racquets in presses, which were doubtless the property of Lloyd's Bank also. Dick examined them and said they weren't too bad. They had an antiquated look, and the varnish had worn off the frames, but only two of them had broken strings. Even those two, so Dick said, could be played with. He and Mrs Ashburton handed the racquets to one another, blowing at the dust that had accumulated on the presses and the strings. They lit up Craven A cigarettes, and Mrs Ashburton insisted on giving Dick ten shillings to buy tennis balls with.

I sat with Mrs Ashburton watching Dick and Betty playing their first game on the court. The balls bounced in a peculiar way because in spite of all the rolling there were still hollows and bumps on the surface. The grass wasn't green. It was a brownish yellow, except for the bare patches, which were ochre-coloured. Mrs Ashburton clapped every time there was a rally, and when Dick had beaten Betty 6–1, 6–4, he taught me how to hit the ball over the net, and how to volley it and keep it going. 'Marvellous, Matilda!' Mrs Ashburton cried, in her throaty voice, applauding again. 'Marvellous!'

We played all that summer, every Saturday and Sunday until the end of term, and almost every evening when the holidays came. We had to play in the evenings because at the end of term Dick began to work on the farm. 'Smoke your cigarettes if you want to,' my father said the first morning of the holidays, at breakfast. 'No point in hiding it, boy.' Friends of Dick's and Betty's used to come to Challacombe Manor to play also, because that was what Mrs Ashburton wanted: Colin Gregg and Barbara Hosell and Peggy Goss and Simon Turner and Willie Beach.

Sometimes friends of mine came, and I'd show them how to do it, standing close to the net, holding the racquet handle in the middle of the shaft. Thursday, August 31st, was the day Mrs Ashburton set for the tennis party: Thursday because it was half-day in the town.

Looking back on it now, it really does seem that for years and years she'd been working towards her tennis party. She'd hung about the lanes in her governess cart waiting for us because we were the children from the farm, the nearest children to Challacombe Manor. And when Dick looked big and strong enough and Betty of an age to be interested, she'd made her bid, easing matters along with fruitcake and Craven A. I can imagine her now, on her own in that ruin of a house, watching the grass grow on her tennis court and watching Dick and Betty growing up and dreaming of one more tennis party at Challacombe, a party like there used to be before her husband was affected in the head by the Kaiser's War.

'August 31st,' Betty reminded my parents one Sunday at dinnertime. 'You'll both come,' she said fiercely, blushing when they laughed at her.

'I hear Lloyd's is on the rampage,' my father said laboriously. 'Short of funds. Calling everything in.'

Dick and Betty didn't say anything. They ate their roast beef, pretending to concentrate on it.

'Course they're not,' my mother said.

'They'll sell Challacombe to some building fellow, now that it's all improved with tennis courts.'

'Daddy, don't be silly,' Betty said, blushing even more. All three of us used to blush. We got it from my mother. If my father blushed you wouldn't notice.

'True as I'm sitting here, my dear. Nothing like tennis courts for adding a bit of style to a place.'

Neither my mother nor my father had ever seen the tennis court. My father wouldn't have considered it the thing, to go walking over to Challacombe Manor to examine a tennis court. My mother was always busy, cooking and polishing brass. Neither my father nor my mother knew the rules of tennis. When we first began to play Betty used to draw a tennis court on a piece of paper and explain.

'Of course we'll come to the tennis party,' my mother said quietly. 'Of course, Betty.'

In the middle of the tennis party, my father persisted, a man in a hard black hat from Lloyd's Bank would walk on to the court and tell everyone to go home.

'Oh, Giles, don't be silly now,' my mother said quite sharply, and added that there was such a thing as going on too much. My father laughed and winked at her.

Mrs Ashburton asked everyone she could think of to the tennis party, people from the farms round about and shop-keepers from the town. Dick and Betty asked their friends and their friends' parents, and I asked Belle Frye and the Gorrys and the Seatons. My mother and Betty made meringues and brandy-snaps and fruitcakes and Victoria sponge cakes and scones and buns and shortbread. They made sardine sandwiches and tomato sandwiches and egg sandwiches and ham sandwiches. I buttered the bread and whipped up cream and wrapped the plates of sandwiches in damp tea-cloths. Dick cleared a place in the shrubbery beside the tennis court and built a fire to boil kettles on. Milk was poured into bottles and left to keep cool in the larder. August 31st was a fine, hot day.

At dinnertime my father pretended that the truck which was to convey all the food, and all of us too, to the tennis court had a broken carburettor. He and Joe had been working on it all morning, he said, but utterly without success. No one took any notice of him.

I remember, most of all, what they looked like. Mrs Ashburton thin as a rake in a long white dress and her wide-brimmed white hat and her sunglasses. My father in his Sunday clothes, a dark blue suit, his hair combed and his leathery brown face shining because he had shaved it and washed it specially. My mother had powder on her cheeks and her nose, and a touch of lipstick on her lips, although she didn't usually wear lipstick and must have borrowed Betty's. She was wearing a pale blue dress speckled with tiny white flowers. She'd spent a fortnight making it herself, for the occasion. Her reddish hair was soft and a little unruly, being freshly washed. My father was awkward in his Sunday suit, as he always was in it. His freckled hands lolled uneasily by his sides, or awkwardly held tea things, cup and saucer and plate. My mother blushed beneath her powder, and sometimes stammered, which she did when she was nervous.

Betty was beautiful that afternoon, in a white tennis dress that my mother had made her. Dick wore long white flannels that he'd been given by old Mr Bowe, a solicitor in the town who'd been to other tennis parties at Challacombe Manor but had no further use for white flannel trousers, being seventy-two now and too large for the trousers he'd kept for more than fifty years. My mother had made me a tennis dress, too, but I felt shy that day and didn't want to do anything except hand round plates of meringues and cake. I certainly didn't want to play, for the tennis was serious: mixed doubles, Betty and Colin Gregg against Dick and Peggy Goss, and Simon Turner and Edie Turner against Barbara Hosell and Willie Beach.

People were there whom my father said he hadn't seen for years, people who had no intention of playing tennis, any more than he had. Between them, Dick and Betty and Mrs Ashburton had cast a wide net, and my father's protests at the mounds of food that had been prepared met with their answer as car after car drew up, and dog-carts and pony-and-traps. Belle Frye and I passed around the plates of meringues, and people broke off in their conversations to ask us who we were. Mrs Ashburton had spread rugs on the grass around the court, and four white ornamental seats had been repainted by Dick the week before. 'Just like the old days,' a man called Mr Race said, a corn merchant from the town. My mother nervously fidgeted, and I could feel her thinking that perhaps my father's laborious joke would come true, that any moment now the man from Lloyd's Bank would arrive and ask people what on earth they thought they were doing, playing tennis without the Bank's permission.

But that didn't happen. The balls zipped to and fro across the net, pinging off the strings, throwing up dust towards the end of the afternoon. Voices called out in exasperation at missed shots, laughter came and went. The sun continued to shine warmly, the tennis players wiped their foreheads with increasing regularity, the rugs on the grass were in the shade. Belle Frye and I collected the balls and threw them back to the servers. Mr Bowe said that Dick had the makings of a fine player.

Mrs Ashburton walked among the guests with a packet of Craven A in her hand, talking to everyone. She kept going up to my mother and thanking her for everything she'd done. Whenever she saw me she kissed me on the hair. Mr Race said she shook hands like a duchess. The rector, Mr Throataway, laughed jollily.

At six o'clock, just as people were thinking of going, my father surprised everyone by announcing that he had a barrel of beer and a barrel of cider in the truck. I went with him and there they were, two barrels keeping cool beneath a tarpaulin, and two wooden butter-boxes full of glasses that he'd borrowed from the Heart of Oak. He drove the truck out from beneath the shade of the trees and backed it close to the tennis court. He and Dick set the barrels up and other men handed round the beer and cider, whichever anyone wanted. 'Just like him,' I heard a woman called Mrs Garland saying. 'Now, that's just like him.'

It was a quarter to ten that evening before they stopped playing tennis. You could hardly see the ball as it swayed about from racquet to racquet, looping over the net, driven out of court. My father and Mr Race went on drinking beer, and Joe and Arthur, who'd arrived after milking, stood some distance away from them, drinking beer also. Mrs Garland and my mother and Miss Sweet and Mrs Tissard made more tea, and the remains of the sandwiches and cakes were passed around by Belle Frye and myself. Joe said he reckoned it was the greatest day in Mrs Ashburton's life. 'Don't go drinking that cider now,' Joe said to Belle Frye and myself.

We all sat around in the end, smacking at midges and finishing the sandwiches and cakes. Betty and Colin Gregg had cider, and you could see from the way Colin Gregg kept looking at Betty that he was in love with her. He was holding her left hand as they sat there, thinking that no one could see because of the gloom, but Belle Frye and I saw, all right. Just before we all went home, Belle Frye and I were playing at being ghosts round at the front of the house and we came across Betty and Colin Gregg kissing behind a rhododendron bush. They were lying on the grass with their arms tightly encircling one another, kissing and kissing as though they were never going to stop. They didn't even know Belle Frye and I were there. 'Oh, Colin!' Betty kept saying. 'Oh, Colin, Colin!'

We wanted to say goodbye to Mrs Ashburton, but we couldn't find her. We ran around looking everywhere, and then Belle Frye suggested that she was probably in the house.

'Mrs Ashburton!' I called, opening the door that led from the stable-yard to the kitchen. 'Mrs Ashburton!'

It was darker in the kitchen than it was outside, almost pitch-dark because the windows were so dirty that even in daytime it was gloomy.

'Matilda,' Mrs Ashburton said. She was sitting in an armchair by the oil-stove. I knew she was because that was where her voice came from. We couldn't see her.

'We came to say goodbye, Mrs Ashburton.'

She told us to wait. She had a saucer of chocolate for us, she said, and we heard her rooting about on the table beside her. We heard the glass being removed from a lamp and then she struck a match. She lit the wick and put the glass back. In the glow of lamplight she looked exhausted. Her eyes seemed to have receded, the thinness of her face was almost sinister.

We ate our chocolate in the kitchen that smelt of oil, and Mrs Ashburton didn't speak. We said goodbye again, but she didn't say anything. She didn't even nod or shake her head. She didn't kiss me like she usually did, so I went and kissed her instead. The skin of her face felt like crinkled paper.

'I've had a very happy day,' she said when Belle Frye and I had reached the kitchen door. 'I've had a lovely day,' she said, not seeming to be talking to us but to herself. She was crying, and she smiled in the lamplight, looking straight ahead of her. 'It's all over,' she said. 'Yet again.'

We didn't know what she was talking about and presumed she meant the tennis party. 'Yet again,' Belle Frye repeated as we crossed the stable-yard. She spoke in a soppy voice because she was given to soppiness. 'Poor Mrs Ashburton!' she said, beginning to cry herself, or pretending to. 'Imagine being eighty-one,' she said. 'Imagine sitting in a kitchen and remembering all the other tennis parties, knowing you'd have to die soon. Race you,' Belle Frye said, forgetting to be soppy any more.

Going home, Joe and Arthur sat in the back of the truck with Dick and Betty. Colin Gregg had ridden off on his bicycle, and Mr Bowe had driven away with Mrs Tissard beside him and Mr Tissard and Miss Sweet in the dickey of his Morris Cowley. My mother, my father and myself were all squashed into the front of the truck, and there was so little room that my father couldn't change gear and had to drive all the way to the farm in first. In the back of the truck Joe and Arthur and Dick were singing, but Betty wasn't, and I could imagine Betty just sitting there, staring, thinking about Colin Gregg. In Betty's bedroom there were photographs of Clark Gable and Ronald Colman, and Claudette Colbert and the little Princesses. Betty was going to marry Colin, I kept saying to myself in the truck. There'd be other tennis parties and Betty would be older and would know her own mind, and Colin Gregg would ask her and she'd say yes. It was very beautiful, I thought, as the truck shuddered over the uneven back avenue of Challacombe Manor. It was as beautiful as the tennis party itself, the white dresses and Betty's long hair, and everyone sitting and watching in the sunshine, and evening slowly descending. 'Well, that's the end of that,' my father said, and he didn't seem to be talking about the tennis party because his voice was too serious for that. He repeated a conversation he'd had with Mr Bowe and one he'd had with Mr Race, but I didn't listen because his voice was so lugubrious, not at all like it had been at the tennis party. I was huddled on my mother's knees, falling asleep. I imagined my father was talking about Lloyd's Bank again, and I could hear my mother agreeing with him.

I woke up when my mother was taking off my dress in my bedroom. 'What is it?' I said. 'Is it because the tennis party's over? Why's everyone so sad?'

My mother shook her head, but I kept asking her because she was looking sorrowful herself and I wasn't sleepy any more. In the end she sat on the edge of my bed and said that people thought there was going to be another war against the Germans.

'Germans?' I said, thinking of the grey, steely people that Mrs Ashburton had so often told me about, the people who ate black bread.

It would be all right, my mother said, trying to smile. She told me that we'd have to make special curtains for the windows so that the German aeroplanes wouldn't see the lights at night. She told me there'd probably be sugar rationing.

I lay there listening to her, knowing now why Mrs Ashburton had said that yet again it was all over, and knowing what would happen next. I didn't want to think about it, but I couldn't help thinking about it: my father would go away, and Dick would go also, and Joe and Arthur and Betty's Colin Gregg. I would continue to attend Miss Pritchard's Primary and then I'd go on to the Grammar, and my father would be killed. A soldier would rush at my father with a bayonet and twist the bayonet in my father's stomach, and Dick would do the same to another soldier, and Joe and Arthur would be missing in the trenches, and Colin Gregg would be shot.

My mother kissed me and told me to say my prayers before I went to sleep. She told me to pray for the peace to continue, as she intended to do herself. There was just a chance, she said, that it might.

She went away and I lay awake, beginning to hate the Germans and not feeling ashamed of it, like Mrs Ashburton was. No German would ever have played tennis that day, I thought, no German would have stood around having tea and sandwiches and meringues, smacking away the midges when night came. No German would ever have tried to recapture the past, or would have helped an old woman to do so, like my mother and my father had done, and Mr Race and Mr Bowe and Mr Throataway and Mrs Garland and Betty and Dick and Colin Gregg. The Germans weren't like that. The Germans wouldn't see the joke when my father said that for all he knew Lloyd's Bank owned Mrs Ashburton.

I didn't pray for the peace to continue, but prayed instead that my father and Dick might come back when the war was over. I didn't pray that Joe and Arthur and Colin Gregg should come back since that would be asking too much, because some men had to be killed, according to Mrs Ashburton's law of averages. I hadn't understood her when Mrs Ashburton had said that cruelty was natural in wartime, but I understood now. I understood her law of averages and her sitting alone in her dark kitchen, crying over the past. I cried myself, thinking of the grass growing on her tennis court, and the cruelty that was natural.

My father came back twice to the farm, unexpectedly, without warning. He walked into the kitchen, the first time one Thursday morning when there was nobody there, the second time on a Thursday afternoon.

My mother told us how on the first occasion she'd been crossing the yard with four eggs, all that the hens had laid, and how she'd sensed that something was different. The sheepdogs weren't in the yard, where they usually were at this time. Vaguely she'd thought that that was unusual. Hours later, when Betty and Dick and I came in from school, our parents were sitting at the kitchen table, talking. He was still in his army uniform. The big brown tea-pot was on the table, and two cups with the dregs of tea in them, and bread on the bread-board, and butter and blackberry jam. There was a plate he'd eaten a fry from, with the marks of egg-yolk on it. Even now it seems like yesterday. He smiled a slow, teasing smile at us, as though mocking the emotion we felt at seeing him there, making a joke even of that. Then Betty ran over to him and hugged him. I hugged him too. Dick stood awkwardly.

The second time he returned he walked into the kitchen at half-past four, just after I'd come in from school. I was alone, having my tea.

'Hullo, Matilda,' he said.

I was nearly eleven then. Betty was sixteen and Dick was seventeen. Dick wasn't there that second time: he'd gone into the army himself. Betty had left the Grammar School and was helping my mother to keep the farm going. I was still at Miss Pritchard's Primary.

I was going to be pretty, people used to say, although I couldn't see it myself. My hair had a reddish tinge, like my mother's, but it was straight and uninteresting. I had freckles, which I hated, and my eyes were a shade of blue I didn't much care for either. I detested being called Matilda. Betty and Dick, I considered, were much nicer names, and Betty was beautiful now. My friend Belle Frye was getting to be beautiful also. She claimed to have Spanish blood in her, though it was never clear where it came from. Her hair was jet-black and her skin, even in the middle of winter, was almost as deeply brown as her eyes. I'd have loved to look like her and to be called Belle Frye, which I thought was a marvellous name.

I made my father tea that Thursday afternoon and I felt a bit shy because I hadn't seen him for so long. He didn't comment on my making the tea, although he might have said that I hadn't been able to before. Instead he said he hadn't had a decent cup of tea since he'd been home the last time. 'It's great to be home, Matilda,' he said.

A few weeks later my mother told me he was dead. She told me at that same time of day and on a Thursday also: a warm June afternoon that had been tiring to trudge home from school through.

'Belle Frye had to stay in for two hours,' I was saying as I came into the kitchen. My mother told me to sit down.

The repetition was extraordinary, the three Thursday afternoons. That night in bed I was aware of it, lying awake thinking about him, wondering if he'd actually been killed on a Thursday also.

All the days of the week had a special thing about them: they had different characters and even different colours. Monday was light-brown, Tuesday black, Wednesday grey, Thursday orange, Friday yellow, Saturday purplish, Sunday white. Tuesday was a day I liked because we had double History, Friday was cosy, Saturday I liked best of all. Thursday would be special now: I thought that, marking the day with my grief, unable to cry any more. And then I remembered that it had been a Thursday afternoon when old Mrs Ashburton had invited everyone for miles round to her tennis party, when I had realized for the first time that there was going to be a war against the Germans: Thursday, August 31st, 1939.

I would have liked there to be a funeral, and I kept thinking about one. I never mentioned it to my mother or to Betty, or asked them if my father had had a funeral in France. I knew he hadn't. I'd heard him saying they just had to leave you there. My mother would cry if I said anything about it.

Then Dick came back, the first time home since he'd joined the army. He'd been informed too, and time had passed, several months, so that we were all used to it by now. It was even quite like the two occasions when my father had returned, Dick telling stories about the army. We sat in the kitchen listening to him, huddled round the range, with the sheepdogs under the table, and when the time came for him to go away I felt as I'd felt when my father had gone back. I knew that Betty and my mother were thinking about Dick in that way, too: I could feel it, standing in the yard holding my mother's hand.

Colin Gregg, who'd kissed Betty at Mrs Ashburton's tennis party, came to the farm when he was home on leave. Joe and Arthur, who'd worked for my father on the farm, came also. At one time or another they all said they were sorry about my father's death, trying not to say it when I was listening, lowering their voices, speaking to my mother.

Two years went by like that. Dick still came back, and Colin Gregg and Joe and Arthur. I left Miss Pritchard's Primary and went to the Grammar School. I heard Betty confiding to my mother that she was in love with Colin Gregg, and you could see that it was Colin Gregg being in the war she thought about now, not Dick. Belle Frye's father had had his left arm amputated because of a wound, and had to stay at home after that. A boy who'd been at the Grammar School, Roger Laze, had an accident with a gun when he was shooting rabbits, losing half his left foot. People said it was a lie about the rabbit-shooting. They said his mother had shot his foot off so that he wouldn't have to go into the army.

At church on Sundays the Reverend Throataway used to pray for victory and peace, and at school there was talk about the Russians, and jokes about Hitler and Göring and most of all about Goebbels. I remembered how old Mrs Ashburton used to talk about the previous war, from which her husband had come back with some kind of shell-shock. She'd made me think of Germans as being grey and steely, and I hated them now, just as she had. Whenever I thought about them I could see their helmets, different from the helmets of English soldiers, protecting their necks as well as their heads. Whenever I thought of the time before the war I thought of Mrs Ashburton, who had died soon after she'd given her tennis party. On the way home from school I'd sometimes go into the garden of Challacombe Manor and stand there looking at the tall grass on the tennis court, remembering all the people who'd come that afternoon, and how they'd said it was just like my father to say the tennis party was a lot of nonsense and then to bring on beer and cider at the end of the day. The tennis party had been all mixed up with our family. It felt like the last thing that had happened before the war had begun. It was the end of our being as we had been in our farm-house, just as in the past, after the previous war, there must have been another end: when the farm had ceased to be the home-farm of Challacombe Manor, when the estate had been divided up after Mrs Ashburton's husband hadn't been able to run it any more.

When I wandered about the overgrown garden of Challacombe Manor I wondered what Mr Ashburton had been like before the war had affected him, but I couldn't quite see him in my mind's eye: all I could see was the person Mrs Ashburton had told me about, the silent man who'd come back, who hadn't noticed that everything was falling into rack and ruin around him. And then that image would disappear and I'd see my father instead, as he'd been in the farm-house. I remembered without an effort the brown skin of his arms and his brown, wide forehead and the way crinkles formed at the sides of his eyes. I remembered his hands on the kitchen table at mealtimes, or holding a newspaper. I remembered his voice saying there'd been frost. 'Jack Frost's been,' he used to say.

When I was twelve I began to pray a lot. I prayed that my father should be safe in Heaven and not worried about us. I prayed that Dick should be safe in the war, and that the war would soon end. In Divinity lessons the Reverend Throataway used to explain to us that God was in the weeds and the insects, not just in butterflies and flowers. God was involved in the worst things we did as well as our virtues, he said, and we drove another thorn into His beloved son's head when we were wicked. I found that difficult to understand. I looked at weeds and insects, endeavouring to imagine God's presence in them but not succeeding. I asked Belle Frye if she could, but she giggled and said God was a carpenter called Joseph, the father of Jesus Christ. Belle Frye was silly and the Reverend Throataway so vague and complicated that his arguments about the nature of God seemed to me like foolish chatter. God was neither a carpenter nor a presence in weeds and insects. God was a figure in robes, with a beard and shreds of cloud around Him. The Paradise that was mentioned in the Bible was a garden with tropical plants in it, through which people walked, Noah and Moses and Jesus Christ and old Mrs Ashburton. I could never help thinking that soon the Reverend Throataway would be there too: he was so old and frail, with chalk on the black material of his clothes, sometimes not properly shaved, as if he hadn't the energy for it. I found it was a consolation to imagine the Paradise he told us about, with my own God in it, and to imagine Hitler and Göring and Goebbels, with flames all around them, in Hell. The more I thought about it all and prayed, the closer I felt to my father. I didn't cry when I thought about him any more, and my mother's face wasn't all pulled down any more. His death was just a fact now, but I didn't ever want not to feel close to him. It was as if being close to him was being close to God also, and I wanted that so that God could answer my prayer about keeping Dick safe in the war. I remembered how Mrs Ashburton had worked it out that by the law of averages some men have to come back from a war, and I suggested to the robed figure in charge of the tropical Paradise that in all fairness our family did not deserve another tragedy. With my eyes tightly closed, in bed at night or suddenly stopping on the journey to school, I repetitiously prayed that Dick would be alive to come back when the war was over. That was all I asked for in the end because I could feel that my father was safe in the eternal life that the Reverend Throataway spoke of, and I didn't ask any more that the war should be over soon in case I was asking too much. I never told anyone about my prayers and I was never caught standing still with my eyes closed on the way to school. My father used to smile at me when I did that and I could faintly hear his voice teasing Dick about his smoking or teasing my mother about the Aga cooker she wanted, or Betty about almost anything. I felt it was all right when he smiled like that and his voice came back. I felt he was explaining to me that God had agreed to look after us now, provided I prayed properly and often and did not for a single instant doubt that God existed and was in charge. Mrs Ashburton had been doubtful about that last point and had told me so a few times, quite frightening me. But Mrs Ashburton would be in possession of the truth now, and would be forgiven.

My thoughts and my prayers seemed like a kind of world to me, a world full of God, with my father and Mrs Ashburton in their eternal lives, and the happiness that was waiting for the Reverend Throataway in his. It was a world that gradually became as important as the reality around me. It affected everything. It made me different. Belle Frye was still my friend, but I didn't like her the way I once had.

514 · MATILDA'S ENGLAND

One wet afternoon she and I clambered into Challacombe Manor through a window that someone had smashed. We hadn't been there since the night of the tennis party, when we'd found Mrs Ashburton crying and she'd given us pieces of chocolate. We'd run out into the night, whispering excitedly about an old woman crying just because a party was over. I wouldn't have believed it then if someone had said I'd ever think Belle Frye silly.

'Whoever's going to live here?' she whispered in the dank hall after we'd climbed through the window. 'D'you think it'll just fall down?'

'There's a mortgage on it. Lloyd's Bank have it.'

'What's that mean then?'

'When the war's finished they'll sell the house off to someone else.'

All the furniture in the drawing-room had been taken away, stored in the cellars until someone, some day, had time to attend to it. People had pulled off pieces of the striped red wallpaper, boys from the Grammar School probably. There were names and initials and dates scrawled on the plaster. Hearts with arrows through them had been drawn.

'Anyone could come and live here,' Belle Frye said.

'Nobody'd want to.'

We walked from room to room. The dining-room still had a sideboard in it. There was blue wallpaper on the walls: none of that had been torn off, but there were great dark blots of damp on it. There were bundled-up newspapers all over the floor, and empty cardboard boxes that would have been useless for anything because they'd gone soft due to the damp. Upstairs there was a pool of water on a landing and in one of the bedrooms half the ceiling had fallen down. Everywhere there was a musty smell.

'It's haunted,' Belle Frye said.

'Of course it isn't.'

'She died here, didn't she?'

'That doesn't make it haunted.'

'I can feel her ghost.'

I knew she couldn't. I thought she was silly to say it, pretending about ghosts just to set a bit of excitement going. She said it again and I didn't answer.

We crawled out again, through the broken window. We wandered about in the rain, looking in the out-houses and the stables. The old motor-car that used to be in one of them had been taken away. The iron roller that Dick had rolled the tennis court with was still there, beside the tennis court itself.

'Let's try in here,' Belle Frye said, opening the door of the summer-house.

All the times I'd come into the garden on my own I'd never gone into the summer-house. I'd never even looked through a window of Challacombe Manor itself, or poked about the out-houses. I'd have been a bit frightened, for even though I thought it was silly of Belle Frye to talk about ghosts it wouldn't have surprised me to see a figure moving in the empty house or to hear something in one of the stables, a tramp maybe or a prisoner escaped from the Italian prisoner-of-war camp five miles away. The Italians were small black-haired men whom we often met being marched along a road to work in the fields. They always waved and were given to laughing and singing. But even so I wouldn't have cared to meet one on his own.

In the centre of the summer-house was the table that had been covered with a white cloth, with sandwiches and cakes and the tea-urn on it, for the tennis party. The tennis marker was in a corner, placed there by Dick, I supposed, after he'd marked the court. The net was beside it, and underneath it, almost hidden by it, were two rugs, one of them brown and white, a kind of Scottish tartan pattern, the other grey. Both of these rugs belonged in our farm-house. Could they have been lying in the summer-house since the tennis party? I wondered. I couldn't remember when I'd seen them last.

Facing one another across the table were two chairs which I remembered being there on the day of the party. They were dining-room chairs with red plush seats, brought from the house with a dozen or so others and arrayed on one side of the tennis court so that people could watch the games in comfort. These two must have been left behind when the others had been returned. I was thinking that when I remembered my father hurriedly putting them into the summer-house at the end of the day. 'It'll maybe rain,' he'd said.

'Hey, look,' Belle Frye said. She was pointing at an ashtray on the table, with cigarette-butts and burnt-out matches in it. 'There's people using this place,' she said, giggling. 'Maybe an escaped prisoner,' she suggested, giggling again.

'Maybe.' I said it quickly, not wanting to pursue the subject. I knew the summer-house wasn't being used by an escaped prisoner. Our rugs hadn't been there since the day of the tennis party. They were part of something else, together with the cigarette-butts and the burnt-out matches. And then, quite abruptly, it occurred to me that the summer-house was where Betty and Colin Gregg came when Colin Gregg was on leave: they came to kiss, to cuddle one another like they'd been cuddling in the rhododendrons after the tennis party. Betty had brought the rugs specially, so that they could be warm and comfortable.

'I bet you it's an Eye-tie,' Belle Frye said. 'I bet you there's one living here.'

'Could be.'

'I'm getting out of it.'

We ran away. We ran through the overgrown garden on that wet afternoon and along the lane that led to the Fryes' farm. I should have turned in the opposite direction after we'd left the garden, but I didn't: I went with her because I didn't want her silliness to spoil everything. I thought it was romantic, Betty and Colin Gregg going to the summer-house. I remembered a film called *First Love*, which Betty had gone on about. It had Deanna Durbin in it.

'I'm going to tell,' Belle Frye said, stopping for breath before we came to the Fryes' farmyard. Her eyes jangled with excitement. There were drops of moisture in her smooth black hair.

'Let's have it a secret, Belle.'

'He could murder you, a blooming Eye-tie.'

'It's where my sister and Colin Gregg go.' I had to say it because I knew she'd never be able to keep a secret that involved an Italian prisoner of war. I knew that even if no prisoner had escaped people would go to the summer-house to see for themselves. I knew for a fact, I said, that it was where Betty and Colin Gregg went, and if she mentioned it to anyone I'd tell about going into Challacombe Manor through a broken window. She'd said as we'd clambered through it that her father would murder her if he knew. He'd specifically told her that she mustn't go anywhere near the empty house because the floor-boards were rotten and the ceilings falling down.

'But why would you tell?' she cried, furious with me. 'What d'you want to tell for?'

'It's private about the summer-house. It's a private thing of Betty's.'

She began to giggle. We could watch, she whispered. We could watch through the window to see what they got up to. She went on giggling and whispering and I listened to her, not liking her. In the last year or so she'd become like that, repeating the stories she heard from the boys at school, all to do with undressing and peeping. There were rhymes and riddles and jokes that she repeated also, none of them funny. She'd have loved peeping through the summer-house window.

'No,' I said. 'No.'

'But we could. We could wait till he was home on leave. We needn't make a sound.' Her voice had become shrill. She was cross with me again, not giggling any more. Her eyes glared at me. She said I was stupid, and then she turned and ran off. I knew she'd never peep through the summer-house window on her own because it wasn't something you could giggle over when you were alone. And I knew she wouldn't try and persuade anyone to go with her because she believed me when I said I'd tell about breaking into Challacombe Manor. Her father was a severe man; she was, fortunately, terrified of him.

I thought about the summer-house that evening when I was meant to be learning a verse of *The Lady of Shalott* and writing a composition, *The Worst Nightmare I Ever Had*. I imagined Betty and Colin Gregg walking hand in hand through the overgrown garden and then slipping into the summer-house when it became dusky. A summer's evening it was, with pink in the sky, and the garden was scented with the blossoms of its shrubs. I imagined them sitting on the two dining-chairs at the table, Colin telling her about the war while he smoked his cigarettes, and Betty crying because he would be gone in twelve hours' time and Colin comforting her, and both of them lying down on the rugs so that they could be close enough to put their arms around each other.

In the kitchen while I tried to record the details of a nightmare all I could think about was the much pleasanter subject of my sister's romance. She was in the kitchen also. She'd changed from her farm-working clothes into a navy-blue skirt and a matching jersey. I thought she was more beautiful than usual. She and my mother were sitting on either side of the range, both of them knitting, my mother reading a book by A. J. Cronin at the same time, my sister occasionally becoming lost in a reverie. I knew what she was thinking about. She was wondering if Colin Gregg was still alive.

Months went by and neither he nor Dick came back. There were letters, but there were also periods when no letters arrived and you could feel the worry, for one of them or the other. The war was going to be longer than everyone had thought. People looked gloomy sometimes, and when I caught their gloom I imagined bodies lying unburied and men in aeroplanes, with goggles on, the aeroplanes on fire and the men in goggles burning to death. Ages ago France had been beaten, and I remembered that in a casual moment in a Divinity class the Reverend Throataway had said that that could never happen, that the French would never give in. We would never give in either, Winston Churchill said, but I imagined the Germans marching on the lanes and the roads and through the fields, not like the cheerful Italians. The Germans were cruel in their helmets and their grey steeliness. They never smiled. They knew you hated them.

Belle Frye would have thought I was mad if I'd told her any of that, just like she'd have thought I was mad if I'd mentioned about praying and keeping my father vivid in my mind. She was the first friend I'd ever had, but the declining of our friendship seemed almost natural now. We still sat next to one another in class, but we didn't always walk home together. Doing that had always meant that one of us had to go the long way round and avoiding this extra journey now became an excuse. Not having had Dick and Betty to walk home with for so long, I'd enjoyed Belle Frye's company, but now I found myself pretending to be in a hurry or just slipping away when she wasn't looking. She didn't seem to mind, and we still spent days together, at the weekends or in the holidays. We'd have tea in each other's kitchen, formally invited by our mothers, who didn't realize that we weren't such friends. And that was still quite nice.

Sometimes in the evenings my mother used to go to see a woman called Mrs Latham because Mrs Latham was all alone in the Burrow Farm, three miles away. On these occasions I always hoped Betty would talk to me about Colin Gregg, that she'd even mention the summer-house. But she never did. She'd sit there knitting, or else writing a letter to him. She'd hear me say any homework I had to learn by heart, a theorem or poetry or spelling. She'd make me go to bed, just like my mother did, and then she'd turn on the wireless and listen to *Monday Night at Eight* or *Waterlogged*

Spa or *Itma*. She'd become very quiet, less impatient with me than she'd been when we were younger, more grown-up, I suppose. I often used to think about her on those nights when my mother was out, when she was left alone in the kitchen listening to the wireless. I used to feel sorry for her.

And then, in that familiar sudden way, Colin Gregg came back on leave.

That was the beginning of everything. The evening after he came back was a Saturday, an evening in May. I'd been at the Fryes' all afternoon and when we'd finished tea we played cards for an hour or so and then Mrs Frye said it was time for me to go home. Belle wanted to walk with me, even though we'd probably have walked in silence. I was glad when her father said no. It was too late and in any case he had to go out himself, to set his rabbit snares: he'd walk with me back to our farm. I said goodbye, remembering to thank Mrs Frye, and with his remaining arm Mr Frye pushed his bicycle on the road beside me. He didn't talk at all. He was completely different from my father, never making jokes or teasing. I was quite afraid of him because of his severity.

The sheepdogs barked as I ran across our yard and into the kitchen. My mother had said earlier that she intended to go over to see Mrs Latham that evening. By eight o'clock Betty and Colin Gregg were to be back from the half-past four show at the pictures, so that I wouldn't be in the house alone. It was twenty-past eight now, and they weren't there.

I ran back into the yard, wanting to tell Mr Frye, but already he'd cycled out of sight. I didn't at all like the idea of going to bed in the empty house.

I played with the dogs for a while and then I went to look at the hens, and then I decided that I'd walk along the road to meet Betty and Colin Gregg. I kept listening because at night you could always hear the voices of people cycling in the lanes. I kept saying to myself that my mother wouldn't want me to go to bed when there was no one in the farm-house. It was very still, with bits of red in the sky. I took the short cut through the garden of Challacombe Manor and I wasn't even thinking about Betty and Colin Gregg when I saw two bicycles in the shrubbery at the back of the summer-house. I didn't notice them at first because they were almost entirely hidden by rhododendron bushes. They reminded me of the rugs half hidden beneath the tennis net.

Colin Gregg was going away again on Monday. He was being sent somewhere dangerous, he didn't know where, but I'd heard Betty saying to my mother that she could feel in her bones it was dangerous. When my mother had revealed that she intended to visit Mrs Latham that evening I'd said to myself that she'd arranged the visit so that Colin Gregg and Betty could spend the evening on their own in our kitchen. But on the way back from the pictures they'd gone into the summer-house, their special place.

Even now I can't think why I behaved like Belle Frye, unable to resist something. It was silly curiosity, and yet at the time I think it may have seemed more than just that. In some vague way I wanted to have something nice to think about, not just my imagining the war, and my prayers for Dick's safety and my concern with people's eternal lives. I wanted to see Betty and Colin Gregg together. I wanted to feel their happiness, and to see it.

It was then, while I was actually thinking that, that I realized something was the matter. I realized I'd been stupid to assume they could take the short cut through the garden: you couldn't take the short cut if you were coming from the town on a bicycle because you had to go through fields. You'd come by the lanes, and if you wanted to go to the summer-house you'd have to turn back and go there specially. It seemed all wrong that they should do that when they were meant to be back in the farm-house by eight o'clock.

I should have turned and gone away. In the evening light I was unable to see the bicycles clearly, but even so I was aware that neither of them was Betty's. They passed out of my sight as I approached one of the summer-house's two small windows.

I could see nothing. Voices murmured in the summer-house, not saying anything, just quietly making sounds. Then a man's voice spoke more loudly, but I still couldn't hear what was being said. A match was struck and in a sudden vividness I saw a man's hand and a packet of Player's cigarettes on the table, and then I saw my mother's face. Her reddish hair was untidy and she was smiling. The hand that had been on the table put a cigarette between her lips and another hand held the match to it. I had never in my life seen my mother smoking a cigarette before.

The match went out and when another one was struck it lit up the face of a man who worked in Blow's drapery. My mother and he were sitting facing one another at the table, in the two chairs with the red plush seats.

Betty was frying eggs at the range when I returned to the kitchen. Colin Gregg had had a puncture in his back tyre. They hadn't even looked yet to see if I was upstairs. I said we'd all forgotten the time at the Fryes', playing cards.

In bed I kept remembering that my mother's eyes had been different, not like they'd been for a long time, two dark-blue sparks. I kept saying to myself that I should have recognized her bicycle in the bushes because its mudguards were shaped like a V, not rounded like the mudguards of modern bicycles.

I heard Colin and Betty whispering in the yard and then the sound of his bicycle as he rode away and then, almost immediately, the sound of my mother's bicycle and Betty saying something quietly and my mother quietly replying. I heard them coming to bed, Betty first and my mother twenty minutes later. I didn't sleep, and for the first time in my life I watched the sky becoming brighter when morning began to come. I heard my mother getting up and going out to do the milking.

At breakfast-time it was as though none of it had happened, as though she had never sat on the red plush chair in the summer-house, smoking cigarettes and smiling at a man from a shop. She ate porridge and brown bread, reading a book: *Victoria Four-Twenty* by Cecil Roberts. She reminded me to feed the hens and she asked Betty what time Colin Gregg was coming over. Betty said any minute now and began to do the washing up. When Colin Gregg came he mended one of the cow-house doors.

That day was horrible. Betty tried to be cheerful, upset because Colin Gregg was being sent to somewhere dangerous. But you could feel the effort of her trying and when she thought no one was looking, when my mother and Colin were talking to one another, her face became unhappy. I couldn't stop thinking about my father. Colin Gregg went back to the war.

A month went by. My mother continued to say she was going to see Mrs Latham and would leave Betty and me in the kitchen about once a week.

'Whatever's the matter with Matilda?' I heard Betty saying to her once, and later my mother asked me if I had a stomach ache. I used to sit there at the table trying to understand simultaneous equations, imagining my mother in the summer-house, the two bicycles half hidden in the bushes, the cigarettes and the ashtray.

'The capital of India,' I would say. 'Don't tell me; I know it.'

'Begins with a "D",' Betty would prompt.

He came to the kitchen one evening. He ate cabbage and baked potatoes and fish pie, chewing the cabbage so carefully you couldn't help noticing. He was thin, with one eye that was funny, dead or crooked or something, and a bony nose. His teeth were narrowly crowded, his whole face pulled out to an edge, like the head of a hatchet. His hair was jet-black, parted in the middle and oiled. His hands were clean, with tapering fingers. I was told his name but I didn't listen, not wishing to know it.

'Where'd you get the fish?' he asked my mother in a casual way. His head was cocked a little to one side. He was smiling with his narrow teeth, making my mother flustered as she used to get in the past, when my father was alive. She was even beginning to blush, not that I could see a cause for it. She said:

'Betty, where did you get the cod?'

'Timpson's,' Betty said.

Betty smiled at him and my mother said quickly that Timpson's were always worth trying in case they'd got any fish in, although of course you could never tell. It sounded silly the way she said it.

'I like fish,' he said.

'We must remember that.'

'They say it's good for you,' Betty said.

'I always liked fish,' the man said. 'From a child I've enjoyed it.'

'Eat it up now,' my mother ordered me.

'Don't you like fish, Matilda?' he said.

THE SUMMER-HOUSE · 521

Betty laughed. 'Matilda doesn't like lots of things. Fish, carrots, eggs.
Semolina. Ground rice. Custard. Baked apples, gravy, cabbage.'

He laughed, and my mother laughed. I bent my head over the plate I
was eating from. My face had gone as hot as a fire.

'Unfortunately there's a war on,' he said. 'Hard times, Matilda.'

I considered that rude. It was rude the way he'd asked where the fish
had come from. He was stupid, as well. Who wanted to hear that he liked
fish? He was a fool, like Stupid Miller, who'd been at Miss Pritchard's
Primary. He was ridiculous-looking and ugly, with his pointed face and
crushed-together teeth. He'd no right to say there was a war on since he
wasn't fighting in it.

They listened to the news on the wireless and afterwards they listened to
the national anthem of the countries which were fighting against Germany.
He offered my mother and Betty cigarettes and they both took one. I'd
never seen Betty smoking a cigarette before. He'd brought a bottle of
some kind of drink with him. They drank it sitting by the range, still
listening to the national anthems.

'Good-night, Matilda,' he said, standing up when my mother told me it
was time to go to bed. He kissed me on the cheek and I could feel his damp
teeth. I didn't move for a moment after he'd done that, standing quite
close to him. I thought I was going to bring up the fish pie and if I did I
wanted to cover his clothes with it. I wouldn't have cared. I wouldn't have
been embarrassed.

I heard Betty coming to bed and then I lay for hours, waiting for the
sound of his bicycle going away. I couldn't hear their voices downstairs,
the way I'd been able to hear voices when Betty had been there. Betty's
had become quite loud and she'd laugh repeatedly. I guessed they'd been
playing cards, finishing off the bottle of drink he'd brought. When I'd been
there Betty had suggested rummy and he'd said that not a drop of the
drink must be left. He'd kept filling up Betty's and my mother's glasses,
saying the stuff was good for you.

I crossed the landing to the top of the stairs that led straight down into
the kitchen. I thought they must have fallen asleep by the range because
when a board creaked beneath my feet no one called out. I stood at the
turn of the narrow staircase, peering through the shadows at them.

Betty had taken one of the two lamps with her as she always did. The
kitchen was dim, with only the glow from the other. On the table, close to
the lamp, was the bottle and one of the glasses they'd drunk from. The two
dogs were stretched in front of the range. My mother was huddled on the
man's knee. I could see his tapering fingers, one hand on the black material
of her dress, the other stroking her hair. While I watched he kissed her,
bending his damp mouth down to her lips and keeping it there. Her eyes
were closed but his were open, and when he finished kissing her he stared
at her face.

I went on down the stairs, shuffling my bare feet to make a noise. The dogs growled, pricking up their ears. My mother was halfway across the kitchen, tidying her hair with both hands, murmuring at me.

'Can't you sleep, love?' she said. 'Have you had a dream?'

I shook my head. I wanted to walk forward, past her to the table. I wanted to pick up the bottle he'd brought and throw it on to the flags of the floor. I wanted to shout at him that he was ugly, no more than a half-wit, no better than Stupid Miller, who hadn't been allowed in the Grammar School. I wanted to say no one was interested in his preference for fish.

My mother put her arms around me. She felt warm from sitting by the range, but I hated the warmth because it had to do with him. I pushed by her and went to the sink. I drank some water even though I wasn't thirsty. Then I turned and went upstairs again.

'She's sleepy,' I heard my mother say. 'She often gets up for a drink when she's sleepy. You'd better go, dear.'

He muttered something else and my mother said that they must have patience.

'One day,' she said. 'After it's all over.'

'It'll never end.' He spoke loudly, not muttering any more. 'This bloody thing could last for ever.'

'No, no, my dear.'

'It's all I want, to be here with you.'

'It's what I want too. But there's a lot in the way.'

'I don't care what's in the way.'

'We have to care, dear.'

'I love you,' he said.

'My own darling,' my mother said.

She was the same as usual the next day, presumably imagining that being half-asleep I hadn't noticed her sitting on the man's knees and being kissed by his mouth. In the afternoon I went into the summer-house. I looked at the two plush-seated chairs, imagining the figures of my mother and the man on them. I carried the chairs, one by one, to an out-house and up a ladder to a loft. I put the tennis net underneath some seed-boxes. I carried the two rugs to the well in the cobbled yard and dropped them down it. I returned to the summer-house, thinking of doing something else, I wasn't sure what. There was a smell of stale tobacco, coming from butts in the ashtray. On the floor I found a tie-pin with a greyhound's head on it and I thought the treacherous, ugly-looking dog suited him. I threw it into the rhododendron shrubbery.

'Poor chap,' I heard Betty saying that evening. 'It's a horrid thing to have.' She'd always noticed that he looked delicate, she added.

'He doesn't get enough to eat,' my mother said.

In spite of her sympathy, you could see that Betty wasn't much interested in the man: she was knitting and trying to listen to *Bandwagon*. As far as Betty was concerned he was just some half-sick man whom my mother felt sorry for, the way she was supposed to feel sorry for Mrs Latham of Burrow Farm. But my mother wanted to go on talking about him, with a pretended casualness. It wasn't the right work for a person who was tubercular, she said, serving in a shop.

I imagined him in Blow's, selling pins and knitting-needles and satin by the yard. I thought the work suited him like the greyhound's head tie-pin did.

'What's it mean, tubercular?' I asked Belle Frye, and she said it meant you suffered from a disease in your lungs.

'I expect you could fake it.'

'What'd you want to do that for?'

'To get out of the war. Like Mrs Laze shot off Roger Laze's foot.'

'Who's faking it then?'

'That man in Blow's.'

I couldn't help myself: I wanted it to be known that he was faking a disease in his lungs. I wanted Belle Frye to tell people, giggling at him in Blow's, pointing him out. But in fact she wasn't much interested. She nodded, and then shrugged in a jerky way she had, which meant she was impatient to be talking about something else. You could tell she didn't know the man in Blow's had become a friend of my mother's. She hadn't seen them on their bicycles; she wouldn't have wanted to change the subject if she'd looked through the summer-house window and seen them with their cigarettes. Before that I hadn't thought about her finding out, but now I wondered if perhaps she would some time, and if other people would. I imagined the giggling and the jokes made up by the boys in the Grammar School, and the severity of Mr Frye, and the astonishment of people who had liked my father.

I prayed that none of that would happen. I prayed that the man would go away, or die. I prayed that my mother would be upset again because my father had been killed in the war, that she would remember the time when he had been in the farm-house with us. I prayed that whatever happened she would never discredit him by allowing the man from Blow's to be there in the farm-house, wearing my father's clothes.

Every day I prayed in the summer-house, standing close to the table with my eyes closed, holding on to the edge of it. I went there specially, and more vividly than ever I could see my father in the tropical garden of his eternal life. I could see old Mrs Ashburton walking among the plants with her husband, happy to be with him again. I could see the bearded face of the Almighty I prayed to, not smiling but seeming kind.

'Oh, my God,' was all my mother could say, whispering it between her bursts of tears. 'Oh, my God.'

Betty was crying too, but crying would do no good. I stood there between them in the kitchen, feeling I would never cry again. The telegram was still on the table, its torn envelope beside it. It might have said that

Dick was coming home on leave, or that Colin Gregg was. It looked sinister on the table because Dick was dead.

I might have said to my mother that it was my fault as well as hers. I might have said that I'd known I should pray only for Dick to be safe and yet hadn't been able to prevent myself praying for the other too: that she'd be as she used to be, that she wouldn't ever marry the man from Blow's.

But I didn't say that. I didn't say I'd prayed about the man, I just said it was a Thursday again.

'Thursday?' my mother whispered, and when I explained she didn't understand. She hadn't even noticed that the two times my father had come home it had been a Thursday and that the tennis party had been on a Thursday and that the other telegram had come on a Thursday too. She shook her head, as if denying all this repetition, and I wanted to hurt her when she did that because the denial seemed all part and parcel of the summer-house and the man from Blow's. More deliberately than a moment ago I again didn't confess that I had ceased to concentrate on Dick's safety in my prayers. Instead I said that in a war against the Germans you couldn't afford to take chances, you couldn't go kissing a man when your husband had been killed.

'Oh, my God,' my mother said again.

Betty was staring at her, tears still coming from her eyes, bewildered because she'd never guessed about my mother and the man.

'It has nothing to do with this,' my mother whispered. 'Nothing.'

I thought Betty was going to attack my mother, maybe hammer at her face with her fists, or scratch her cheeks. But she only cried out, shrieking like some animal caught in a trap. The man was even married, she shrieked, his wife was away in the Women's Army. It was horrible, worse than ever when you thought of that. She pointed at me and said I was right: Dick's death was a judgement, things happened like that.

My mother didn't say anything. She stood there, white-faced, and then she said the fact that the man was married didn't make anything worse.

She spoke to Betty, looking at her, not at me. Her voice was quiet. She said the man intended to divorce his wife when the war came to an end. Of course what had happened wasn't a judgement.

'You won't marry him now,' Betty said, speaking as quietly.

My mother didn't reply. She stood there by the table and there was a silence. Then she said again that Dick's death and the man were two different things. It was terrible, she said, to talk as we were talking at a time like this. Dick was dead: that was the only thing that mattered.

'They used to go to the summer-house,' I said. 'They had two of our rugs there.'

My mother turned her head away, and I wanted Betty to remember as I was remembering and I believe she did. I could sense her thinking of the days when my father was alive, when Dick used to smoke cigarettes on the way home from school, when we were all together in the farm-house, not knowing we were happy. That time seemed to haunt the kitchen just then, as if my mother was thinking about it too, as if our remembering had willed it back.

'He could never come here now,' Betty said to my mother. 'You couldn't do it to Matilda.'

I didn't know why she should have particularly mentioned me since it concerned us all, and anyway I felt it was too late to bother about me. Too much had happened. I felt I'd been blown to pieces, as if I'd been in the war myself, as if I'd been defeated by it, as old Mrs Ashburton had been defeated by her war. The man would come to live in the farm-house. He would wear my father's clothes. He would sit by the range, reading the newspaper. He would eat at the table, and smile at me with his narrow teeth.

My mother left the kitchen. She went upstairs and after a few minutes we heard her sobbing in her bedroom. Sobbing would do no good, I thought, any more than crying would.

I walked by myself through the fields. Dick's death wasn't the same as my father's. There was the same emptiness and the same feeling that I never wanted to eat anything again or to drink anything again, but it was different because this was the second time. Dick was dead and we'd get used to it: that was something I knew now.

I didn't cry and I didn't pray. Praying seemed nonsense as I walked through the fields; praying was as silly as Belle Frye's thinking that God was a carpenter or the Reverend Throataway saying God was in weeds. God wasn't like that in the least. He wasn't there to listen to what you prayed for. God was something else, something harder and more awful and more frightening.

I should have known that the man from Blow's would be married, that he'd have a wife who was helping in the war while he was going on about a disease. It was somehow all of a piece with Betty wanting to hit my mother, and Mrs Laze shooting off her son's foot so that he could stay alive, and God being frightening. Facts and images rattled in my mind, senselessly jumbled, without rhyme or reason. Dick was there too, dead and unburied in his uniform, something ordinary to get used to.

I sat in the sunshine on a bank that had primroses on it. I could have returned to the farm-house and let my mother put her arms around me, but I continued to sit there, still not crying, remembering Mrs Ashburton saying that cruelty in wartime was natural. At the time I hadn't understood what she'd meant, but I could feel the cruelty she'd spoken of now. I could feel it in myself, in my wanting my mother to be more unhappy than I was. Dick's death was more bearable because she could be blamed, as Betty had blamed her in speaking of a judgement.

I am writing this in the drawing-room, in fact at Mrs Ashburton's writing-desk. I don't think of it as a story – and certainly not as a letter, for she can never read it – but as a record of what happened in her house after the war. If she hadn't talked to me so much when I was nine there would not be this record to keep, and I would not still feel her presence. I do not understand what has happened, but as I slowly move towards the age she was when she talked to me I slowly understand a little more. What she said has haunted me for thirty-nine years. It has made me old before my time, and for this I am glad. I feel like a woman of sixty; I'm only forty-eight.

In 1951 the house was bought by people called Gregary. 'Filthy rich,' my stepfather said.

My stepfather had just been made manager at Blow's drapery in the town. He used to drive off every day in a blue pre-war baby Ford, and I was always glad to see him go. I worked on the farm with Joe and Arthur, like my father had, like my brother Dick would have if he hadn't been killed in the desert offensive.

I thought it was typical of my stepfather to know that the Gregarys were rich. It was the kind of information he picked up in Blow's, conversing across his counter, the gossip enlivening his hatchet face and his funny eye. He said Mr Gregary was a businessman involved in the manufacture of motor-car components. He'd made a killing during the war: my stepfather called him a post-war tycoon.

On my twenty-first birthday my mother insisted on giving a kind of party. We had it in the farm-house kitchen. We cooked a turkey and a ham and my mother made a great fuss about the vegetables that had been my favourites when I was small: celery and parsnips and carrots, and roast potatoes. The carrots were to be in a parsley sauce, the parsnips roasted with the potatoes. We made trifle because trifle had been a childhood favourite also, and brandy-snaps. It was impossible not to recall the preparations for Mrs Ashburton's tennis party on the Thursday before the war, but of course I didn't mention that. My mother believed that I didn't want to live in the present. I often felt her looking at me and when I turned my head I could see for a moment, before she changed her expression, that she believed I dwelt far too much on times that were not our own.

Fifteen people came to my birthday party, not counting my mothe. and my stepfather and myself. My sister Betty, who had married Colin Gregg, came with her two children. Belle Frye had married Martin Draper, who'd inherited the mill at Bennett's Cross: they brought the baby that had made the marriage necessary. Mr and Mrs Frye were there, and Miss Pritchard, who'd taught us all at the Primary School. Joe and Arthur, and Joe's wife, Maudie, came; and Mrs Laze and her son Roger. The idea was, I believe, that I might one day marry Roger, but it wasn't a prospect I relished. He limped because of his foot, and he hardly ever spoke, being shy like his mother. I didn't dislike him, I just didn't want to marry him.

All the time I kept wishing my mother hadn't given this party. It made me think of my other birthdays. Not that there was any reason to avoid doing that, except that naturally the past seemed better, especially the distant past, before the war. Miss Pritchard was the only person I ever talked to about things like that. 'Come and talk to me whenever you want to, Matilda,' she'd said one day in 1944, and ever since I'd been visiting her in her tiny sitting-room, knowing she was lonely because she was retired now. In a way our conversations reminded me of my conversations with Mrs Ashburton, except that it was Mrs Ashburton, not I, who used to do the talking and half the time I hadn't understood her. It was I who'd suggested that Miss Pritchard should come to my birthday party. I'd heard my mother saying to my stepfather that she couldn't understand it: she thought it extraordinary that I didn't want to invite lots of the boys I'd been at the Grammar School with, that I didn't want to have a gramophone going and tables of whist. My stepfather said he didn't think people played whist like they used to. He stood up for me, the way he always did, even though he didn't know I was listening. He made such efforts and still I couldn't like him.

Seventeen of us sat down at the kitchen table at half-past six and my stepfather poured out cider for us, and Kia-Ora for Betty's children. Belle Frye's baby was put to sleep upstairs. I couldn't think of her as Belle Draper, and haven't ever been able to since. Martin Draper had been a silly kind of boy at school and he still was silly now.

My stepfather carved the turkey and my mother the ham. Everyone was talking about Challacombe Manor having been sold to the people called Gregary.

'The son's going to run the place,' my stepfather said. 'Tax fiddle, I dare say.'

You could see that Miss Pritchard didn't know what he was talking about, and you could see that she suspected he didn't know what he was talking about himself. In his gossipy way he was always referring to tax fiddles and how people had made a fortune and what price such and such a shop in the town would fetch. The fact that he'd mentioned income tax evasion in connection with the Gregarys didn't mean that there was any truth in the suggestion. Even so, the reference, coupled with the information that Mr Gregary was in the motor-components industry, established the Gregarys as people of a certain kind. Carving the turkey, my stepfather said that in his opinion Challacombe would be restored to its former splendour.

'They haven't the land,' Mr Frye pointed out, for he himself farmed eighty acres of what had once been the Challacombe estate.

'It couldn't never be the same,' Joe added.

Plates of turkey and ham were passed from hand to hand until everyone present was attended to. My mother said that people must take vegetables and start, else the food would get cold. A more lively chatter about the new people at Challacombe broke out as the cider was consumed. Two of the Gregary daughters were married and living in some other part of the country, a third one was at a university. The son was the apple of his parents' eye. The father owned a grey Daimler.

The old range which had been in our kitchen all during my childhood had only the week before been replaced by a cream-coloured Aga. The acquisition of an Aga had been my mother's dream for almost as long as I could remember. I think she'd grown to hate the range, lighting it every morning with sticks and paper, the struggles she'd had with it during the war, trying to burn wood instead of coal. But I'd been sorry to see it go. I tried to stop myself being like that about things, but I couldn't help it.

'To the birthday girl,' my stepfather said, raising his glass of cider. 'Many happy returns, my best.'

It was that that I didn't care for in him: I wasn't his best, my mother was. Yet he'd say it casually, wanting to pay a compliment but overdoing it so that you didn't believe him, so that you distrusted him.

'Matilda,' other people said, holding up their glasses also. 'To Matilda.'

'Oh, my love!' my mother cried out, getting up and running round the table to kiss me. 'Oh, little Matilda!' I could feel the warm dampness of tears as her cheek came into contact with mine, and the touch of her mouth, reminding me of childhood. It was a long time since my mother had kissed me.

Everyone made a fuss then, even Martin Draper and Joe and Arthur. I can still see the sunburnt face of Colin Gregg, and his pale smooth hair, his eyes seeming to laugh at me as he wished me many happy returns. For a split second he reminded me of my father.

Betty said the turkey was delicious because she could see I was embarrassed by all the attention. Belle Frye said the next thing after a twenty-first was getting married. She reminded us that she'd been married herself within a fortnight of becoming twenty-one. She giggled and Martin Draper went red because everyone knew they'd got married in a hurry. She'd been terrified at the time of what her father would say, but to her surprise he'd taken the whole thing calmly, pointing out that there were worse than Martin Draper, reminding her that he'd just inherited the Bennett's Cross mill. It was Mrs Frye who'd been upset, unable to find consolation in her son-in-law's inheritance of a mill. Belle deserved better, she'd said.

'There's that chap on the haberdashery counter,' my stepfather said, winking his good eye all round the table, resting it for a moment on Roger Laze in order to stir up rivalry. 'Keen as mustard, that chap is.'

I knew he'd say that. As soon as Belle Frye had mentioned that the next thing after a twenty-first was a wedding I knew he'd refer to the chap on the haberdashery counter, a pimpled youth with no roof to his mouth. It was typical of my stepfather that he'd notice a counter-hand's interest in me. He'd repeatedly mentioned it before. It was typical that he'd mention it now, in public, assuming I'd be pleased that everyone should know I had an admirer, not thinking to himself that no girl would want even remotely to be associated with an unattractive shop-boy. It wasn't teasing, even though he winked: it was an attempt to be kind. My father would just have teased. He'd have made me blush and I'd have been angry and would have complained to my mother afterwards. It seemed silly now that I'd ever minded.

'Delicious, this stuffing is,' Betty said. 'Eat every scrap of your ham,' she warned one of her children, with a threat in her voice.

'Tip-top ham,' my stepfather said.

'I'll always remember the day Matilda was born,' Joe said. 'I nearly got sacked for letting a heifer wander.'

'A beautiful autumn,' Miss Pritchard said quietly, '1930.'

I was six weeks early, my mother said, a fact she'd told me before. She'd been over to Bennett's Cross in the trap and had had to pull hard on the reins when the pony had taken fright at a piece of newspaper on the road. It was that that had brought me on.

'Old Ashburton's funeral the day before,' Arthur said.

'I never knew that.' I looked at him, interested at last in the conversation, for it wasn't important that I'd been six weeks early or that the autumn had been beautiful. But it did seem strange that in all my conversations with Mrs Ashburton it had never become established that the man she talked so much about had been buried the day before my birth.

'Big old funeral,' Arthur said.

Miss Pritchard nodded and I could see the memory of it in her face. She wouldn't of course have attended it because the Ashburtons and she wouldn't have been on any kind of terms, there being nothing to connect them. She'd told me that when I'd asked her once; she'd explained that to people like the Ashburtons she'd been just a schoolteacher, adding that she'd only been invited to Mrs Ashburton's tennis party because everyone else had. But she'd have drawn the blinds of the school-house and would have waited in the gloom until the funeral had gone by.

I watched her as she ate her turkey and ham. I watched her thinking and remembering, not taking part in the conversations around her. She was slight and fragile-looking, wearing a brown suit with a necklace of beads falling on to a brown jersey. She'd retired about eighteen months ago; it was impossible to believe that we'd ever considered her unfair.

'You're looking lovely, dear,' Mrs Laze whispered across the table at me, leaning and poking her head out so that no one else would hear, for she was a woman who rarely spoke. The story was still told that she'd shot off

Roger's foot during the war so that he wouldn't be called up, but now that the war was over it was increasingly difficult to visualize the scene and I began to think the rumour wasn't true. They both still said that an accident had happened when he was setting out to shoot rabbits.

'Thank you, Mrs Laze.'

I wasn't looking lovely, just ordinary in a lavender-coloured dress, my hair straight and reddish, freckles everywhere. Betty and Belle Frye were far prettier than I was, as they'd always been. And Betty's girls were prettier than I'd been at their age. My face was uninteresting, not quite plain, but too round, too lacking in special characteristics. I greatly disliked my hair and always had.

'D'you remember the day you kept us all in, Miss Pritchard?' Colin Gregg said, laughing. 'The entire top class?'

'*Long fields of barley and of rye,*' Martin Draper said, laughing also. '*An abbot on an ambling pad.*'

Miss Pritchard laughed herself. She'd taught Joe and Arthur too. Roger Laze had been a favourite of hers, she'd never liked Belle Frye. She used to shout at Martin Draper because he couldn't understand things.

'Who's else for ham?' my stepfather cried out, on his feet again, waving a carving knife about. 'Ham? Turkey? Orders taken now please. Pass up the plates, young Martin.'

'The builders moved in today,' I heard Roger Laze saying in his quiet voice, answering a question Miss Pritchard had asked him. He was referring to Challacombe Manor, and I imagined the builders shaking their heads over the place, over the broken windows and the leaking roof and the floorboards that gave way when you walked on them. 'D'you remember that day?' Belle Frye shouted down the table at me, and I smiled at her and said yes, knowing she meant the day we'd climbed in through a window.

'Go round with the cider, love,' my stepfather murmured at me because my mother and Betty were busy seeing to the vegetables.

'Oh, I'm sorry,' I whispered back at him apologetically, feeling I should have noticed that no one was attending to people's glasses.

'No matter,' he said.

I don't know what I wanted then. I don't know what birthday present I'd have awarded myself if I'd been able to, October 2nd, 1951. When I'd left the Grammar School it seemed natural to work on the farm, and I preferred it to the other occupations people suggested to me. My stepfather said he could get me into Blow's and my mother wanted me to try for a position in the accounting department of the Electricity Board because she said I was good at figures, which I wasn't. She used also to say it might be nice to be a receptionist in the Hogarth Arms Hotel. Miss Pritchard said I should become a teacher.

But I liked our farm. I liked it all the year round, the cold dairy on icy mornings, the clatter of cans and churns, driving in the cattle on a warm afternoon, working the sheepdogs. I didn't mind when the yard was thick with muck. I didn't object to the smell of silage. I even liked the hens.

Joe did all the rough work, clearing drains and the hedging and muck-spreading. My mother helped, especially at hay-making. Everyone helped then, even my stepfather; Colin Gregg and Betty came over, and the Fryes and the Lazes. More than anything else, hay-making reminded me of the past. Belle Frye and I used to run about when we were children, trying to be useful but really being a nuisance. I remembered dinnertimes, pasties and meat sandwiches in the fields, and cider and tea. My father used to eye the sky, but it always seemed to be fine then, for just long enough. 'We can laugh at it now,' he used to say when rain came and the hay was safely in.

On my twenty-first birthday I kept thinking of my mother and my stepfather becoming older in the farm-house, my stepfather retiring from Blow's and being around all during the day. It was the same resentment I'd had of him when I was a child, before he married my mother, but of course it wasn't so intense now and it wasn't so violent. Yet it felt all wrong when I contemplated remaining with them in the farm-house. It felt as if I'd married him too.

I opened my presents when we'd had our trifle, and I felt that everyone had been generous. Miss Pritchard had given me a cameo brooch which she used to wear herself and which I'd often admired. There were even little things from Betty's children. My mother and stepfather had bought me a sewing-machine and Betty a little clock for beside my bed, and Belle Frye a framed photograph of Trevor Howard, which was a joke really and typical of Belle Frye. Joe and Maudie had brought honeycombs and Mrs Laze and Roger a set of make-up and scent. There was another parcel, wrapped in red tissue paper and tied with a bow. It contained an eggcup and a matching saucer, and my stepfather said they came from the youth in Blow's. I didn't believe they did. I believed my stepfather had wrapped up the eggcup and saucer, thinking I'd be pleased if he pretended the boy had sent them. I felt awkward and embarrassed; I'd no idea what to say.

We played games with Betty's children afterwards, snap and Snakes and Ladders. Roger Laze sat next to me, too shy to say a word; I often wondered if he was in pain from his foot. At a quarter-past nine Betty and Colin Gregg had to go because it was long past their children's bedtime, and Joe and Maudie said they must be getting along also.

'So must I,' Miss Pritchard said.

She refused a lift with Colin and Betty and I said I'd like to walk with her because the night was beautiful, glaring with moonlight. I could see my mother thought I was silly to want to walk a mile and a half with an old schoolteacher who was being silly herself not to accept a lift when a lift was going. It was typical of me, my mother was thinking, like not having a more suitable twenty-first birthday party. Yet that walk through the moonlit lanes was the nicest part of it.

'Well, Matilda?' Miss Pritchard asked.

I knew what she was talking about. I said I didn't know; just stay on at the farm, I supposed.

'You'd be quite good with children, you know.'

'No.'

'Oh, well, perhaps you'll become a farmer's wife. You could do worse, I suppose.'

'I don't want to marry anyone.' The square face of Roger Laze came into my mind, and the face of the youth in Blow's. 'I really don't.'

'People often don't until someone comes along. Mr Right he's called.' Miss Pritchard laughed, and then we talked about other things, in particular about the new people at Challacombe Manor and what a difference it would make having that big old house occupied again.

Mr Gregary was a stout man and his wife was exceedingly thin. Their son was much older than I'd thought he'd be, thirty-seven as it turned out. They called him Ralphie. His brown hair was balding, and as if to make up for that he had a moustache. It was neat and not very big, like a trimmed brown hedge in the pinkness of his face. He was bulky and quite tall, rather clumsy in his movements.

All three of them came over to the farm one morning. They'd driven down from London to see how the builders were getting on and they came over to introduce themselves. Neither my mother nor I liked them.

'Cooee!' Mrs Gregary called out in our yard, standing there in unsuitable shoes and clothes. Her husband and her son were poking about the out-houses, pointing things out to one another as if they owned the place. They were dressed in tweed suits which you could see had been put on specially for the occasion; Mr Gregary carried a shooting-stick.

'Forgive the intrusion!' Mrs Gregary shouted at me when I came out of the byre. Her voice was shrill, like a bird's. A smile broke her bony face in half. Her hair was very smart; her lipstick matched the red of the suit she was wearing.

'We're the Gregarys,' her husband said. 'Challacombe Manor.'

'This was the home-farm, wasn't it?' his son asked, more modestly than his parents might have, less casually.

I said it had been and brought them into the kitchen, not knowing what on earth to do with them. I was wearing fawn corduroy trousers and a fawn jersey that was darned and dirty. My mother was covered in flour, making a cake at the kitchen table. She became as flustered as I'd ever seen her when I walked in with the three Gregarys.

They were totally unlike their predecessor at Challacombe Manor, seeming a different species from her. As my mother cleared away her cake-making stuff I kept imagining Mrs Ashburton frowning over the Gregarys, bewildered by them and their conversation. In a humble way that annoyed me my mother apologized because the sitting-room wasn't warm, giving the Gregarys to believe it just happened to be that on this one particular morning a fire hadn't been lit there. I don't ever remember a fire being lit in the sitting-room, which was a room that smelt of must. The only time I remember anyone sitting down in it was when my father entertained a man from the taxation authorities, going through papers with him and giving him whisky.

'Now please don't put yourselves out!' Mrs Gregary shrilled. 'Anything does for the Gregarys.'

'We've been pigging it up in the house all morning,' her husband added, and he and his wife laughed over this, finding it amusing. The son laughed less.

'You could do with tea, I'm sure,' my mother said. She was cross with me for bringing them into the kitchen to find her all red-faced and floury, but what could I have done? Her hair was untidy and she was wearing a pair of slippers. 'Put out the cups, Matilda,' she ordered, finding it hard to keep the displeasure out of her voice, worried in case the Gregarys thought it was directed at them.

'So you're a Matilda?' the woman said, smiling her bony smile. 'What an enchanting name!'

She'd sat down at the table. The two men were poking about the place, trying to work out what the kitchen had been like when the house had first been built. They murmured about an open fire and an oven in the wall. They glanced up the steep back stairs that led straight out of a corner of the kitchen. They even opened cupboards.

'There'd have been a wheel there,' the son said, pointing at the Aga, 'which you turned to operate the bellows.'

His father wasn't listening to him. 'Structurally in splendid nick,' he was saying. 'Not a dodgy wall, I'd say.'

'More than you could claim for the manor!' the woman cried, her sudden shrillness making my mother jump. 'My God, the damage!'

'It's been a long time empty,' my mother said.

'Dry rot, wet rot, you name it!' cried the woman. She had four rings on the fingers of her left hand and two on her right. It seemed a mistake of some kind that she was coming to live in Challacombe Manor, like an absurdity in a dream.

'We'll be interested in buying land,' Mr Gregary revealed. His head was very neat, with strands of hair brushed into its baldness. His face had a polished look, like faintly pink marble. The flesh of his chins didn't wobble, but was firm and polished too. His eyes had a flicker of amusement in them.

'It's Ralphie's venture really,' Mrs Gregary said. 'We'll only ever come on visits.'

'Oh no, no,' the son protested.

'Longish visits, darling.'

'We're all in love with Challacombe Manor actually,' Mr Gregary said. 'We can't resist it.'

I wanted to say I loved it too, just to make the statement and by making it to imply that my love was different from theirs. I wanted it to be clear that I had loved Challacombe Manor all my life, that I loved our farm, and the gardens of Challacombe and the lanes around it, and the meadow we used to walk through on the way home from school, a journey which had been boring at the time. I wanted to say that I loved the memory of the past, of the Challacombe Mrs Ashburton had told me about, as it had been before the first of the two wars, and the memory of our family as it had been before the second. I wanted to say all that to show them how silly it was to stand there in a tweed suit and to state you were in love with a house and couldn't resist it. I wanted to belittle what wasn't real.

Politely I offered them milk and sugar, not saying anything. My mother told me to get some biscuits and Mrs Gregary said not to bother, but I got them anyway. I put some on to a plate and handed them around while my mother talked about the farm-house and the farm. The Gregarys' son smiled at me when I held the plate out to him, and all of a sudden I was aware of a pattern of events. It seemed right that Challacombe Manor had stood there empty for so long, and Mrs Ashburton's voice echoed in my mind, telling me something when I was nine. I didn't know what it was, but all the same I felt that sense was being woven into the confusion. An event had occurred that morning in the kitchen, and it seemed extraordinary that I hadn't guessed it might, that I hadn't known that this was how things were meant to be.

'They think we're peasants, finding us like this,' my mother said crossly when they'd gone.

'It doesn't matter what they think.'

A long time went by, more than a year. Challacombe Manor was put to rights. The garden was cleared of the brambles that choked it; for the second time in my memory the tennis court became a tennis court again; the masonry of the summer-house was repointed. I watched it all happening. I stood in the garden and sometimes Ralphie Gregary stood beside me, as if seeking my approval for what he was doing. I walked with him through the fields; I showed him the short cut we'd taken every day from school, the walk through the meadow and then through the garden; I told him about the tennis party Mrs Ashburton had given on the Thursday afternoon before the second of the two wars.

One day we had a picnic, one Sunday morning. We had it in the garden, near a magnolia tree; there was white wine and chicken and tomatoes and chives, and then French cheese and grapes. He told me about the boarding-school he'd been to. When he left it he went into his father's motor-components business and then he had fought in the war. During the war he had slowly come to the conclusion that what he wanted to do when it was over was to live a quiet life. He had tried to return to his father's business but he hadn't cared for it in the least. 'This is what I like,' he said. I felt quite heady after the wine, wanting to lie down in the warmth of the afternoon sun. I told him how Dick and Betty and I had collected ladybirds for Mrs Ashburton so that they could eat the aphids that attacked the roses. I showed him the table in the summer-house which had been laden with food on the day of the tennis party. I smiled at him and he smiled back at me, understanding my love of the past.

'You can't make it come back, you know,' Miss Pritchard pointed out to me that same day, in her tiny sitting-room.

'I hate the present.'

We ate the macaroons she'd made, and drank tea from flowered porcelain. It was all right for Miss Pritchard. Miss Pritchard was too old to belong in the present, she didn't have to worry about it.

'You mustn't hate it.' Her pale eyes were like ice, looking into mine. For a moment she was frightening, as she used to be when you didn't know something at school. But I knew she didn't mean to frighten me. 'You should love the man you marry, Matilda.'

She didn't know, she couldn't be expected to understand. Mrs Ashburton would have known at once what was in my mind.

'He says he loves me,' I said.

'That isn't the same.'

'Mrs Ashburton –'

'Oh, for heaven's sake forget her!'

I shook my head. 'It'll be all right, Miss Pritchard.' He wasn't like his parents, I tried to explain to her; he was thoughtful and much quieter than either his father or his mother. In all sorts of ways he had been kind to me; he considered me beautiful even though I was not; there was a goodness about him.

'You're doing something wrong,' Miss Pritchard said.

I shook my head again and smiled at her. Already I had persuaded Ralphie to have the drawing-room of Challacombe Manor redecorated as it had been in Mrs Ashburton's time, with the same striped red wallpaper, and brass lamps on the walls, connected now to the electricity he'd had put in. A lot of the furniture from the drawing-room was still there, stored in the cellars, locked in after Mrs Ashburton's death so that it wouldn't be stolen. It was the kind of thing that had happened in the war, a temporary measure until everyone had time to think again. No one knew who'd put it there, and some of it had suffered so much from damp that it had to be abandoned. But there were four upright armchairs, delicately inlaid, which needed only to be re-upholstered. I had them done as I remembered them, in crimson and pink stripes that matched the walls. There were the two small round mahogany tables I'd admired, and the pictures of local landscapes in heavy gilt frames, and the brass fire-irons, and Mrs Ashburton's writing-desk and the writing-desk that had been her husband's. The pale patterned carpet came from Persia, she had told me. A corner of it had been nibbled by rats, but Ralphie said we could put a piece of furniture over the damage.

He told me he'd loved me the moment he'd seen me in our farmyard. He had closed his eyes in that moment; he had thought he was going to faint. There was no girl in England who was loved as much as I was, he said shyly, and I wondered if it would sound any different if Roger Laze had said it, or the counter-hand in Blow's. When I'd handed him the biscuits, I said I'd felt the same because there didn't seem any harm in saying that, in telling a minor lie in order to be kind. His parents didn't like what was happening, and my mother and stepfather didn't either. But none of that mattered because Ralphie and I were both grown-up, because Ralphie was getting on for forty and had a right to make a choice. And I intended to be good to him, to cook nice food for him and listen to his worries.

The wedding reception took place in the Hogarth Arms, although the Gregarys suggested the Bower House Hotel, twelve miles away, because there was more room there. They wanted to pay for everything, but my mother wouldn't agree to that. I suppose, in a way, it was all a bit awkward. You could feel the Gregarys thinking that my stepfather worked in a shop, that it was ridiculous of Ralphie to imagine he could take a girl from a farmyard and put her into Challacombe Manor.

Miss Pritchard came to the service and to the Hogarth Arms afterwards. Betty and Belle Frye were my matrons of honour and someone I'd never seen before was best man. I asked all sorts of people, the Fryes of course and Mrs Laze and Roger, and other people I'd been at school with, and Mrs Latham from Burrow Farm. I asked people from the shops in the town, and the people from the Hare and Hounds at Bennett's Cross, and the man from the artificial insemination centre, and Joe and Maudie, and Arthur. The Gregarys asked lots of people also, people like themselves.

I kept wanting to close my eyes as I stood in the lounge of the Hogarth Arms. I wanted to float away on the bubbles of the champagne I'd drunk. I couldn't understand why Miss Pritchard didn't see that everything was all right, that strictly speaking everything was perfect: I was there in my wedding-dress, married to Ralphie, who wasn't unkind; Challacombe Manor was as it used to be in its heyday, it was as Mrs Ashburton had known it as a bride also. Going to live there and watching over it seemed to make up for everything, for all the bad things that had happened, my father's death, and Dick's, and the arm that Mr Frye had had blown off, and Roger Laze's foot. The Fryes had sold their land to Ralphie because farming hadn't been easy since the losing of the arm. They'd be tenants in their farm-house now for the rest of their lives, with a couple of acres they rented back from Ralphie: the arrangement suited them because there was no son to leave the farm to and they could enter old age in comfort. With the passing of time our own farm would revert to being the home-farm again, when it became too much for my mother. I couldn't help feeling that Ralphie knew it was what I wanted, and in his thoughtful kindliness had quietly brought it all about.

'Bless you, child,' my stepfather said.

I smiled at him because it was the thing to do on my wedding-day, but when he drew away his narrow face from mine after he'd kissed me I could see in it a reflection of what Miss Pritchard had said: he believed I shouldn't have married a man I didn't love, not even Ralphie, who was good and kind. It was in my mother's face too when she kissed me, and in my sister's and Belle Frye's, but not in the Gregarys' because none of them knew me.

'I'm happy,' I kept saying, smiling.

We went away to a hotel and then we came back to Challacombe. I'd almost imagined there'd be servants waiting, but of course there weren't. Instead there were the people called Stritch, a man and his wife. I'd always known the Stritches. I remembered Belle Frye and myself singing as we went by their cottage, raising our voices in a song about a bad-tempered woman because that was what Mrs Stritch was. I didn't like finding them there when we came back from our honeymoon.

There were small, silly misunderstandings between Ralphie and myself. They didn't matter because Ralphie's goodness lapped over them, and when I think about them I can't even remember very clearly what some of them were. All I can remember was that Ralphie always listened to me: I think he believed he needed to be gentle with me because I was still almost a child. I couldn't understand why he hadn't married someone before. I asked him, but all he ever did was to smile and shake his head. I had the feeling that in his mind there was the house, and the estate, and me; that I was part of the whole; that he had fallen in love with everything. All that, of course, should have been a bond between us, because the house and the estate formed the island of common ground where both of us were happy. Our marriage had Challacombe at its heart, and I was only alarmed when Ralphie spoke about our children because I didn't see that there was a need for them. Children, it seemed to me, would be all wrong. They would distort the pattern I could so precisely sense. They felt particularly alien.

Ralphie was patient with me. 'Yes, I understand,' he had said on the evening of our marriage, standing in front of me in the bedroom of the hotel he'd brought me to. The walls of the room were papered with a pinkish paper; Ralphie was wearing a flannel suit. In the hotel restaurant, called the Elizabethan Room, we had had dinner and wine. I'd had a coupe Jacques and Ralphie some kind of apricot soufflé. 'Yes,' he said again in the pinkish bedroom, and I talked to him for ages, making him sit beside me on one of the two beds in the room, holding his hand and stroking it. 'Yes, I understand,' he said, and I really think he did; I really think he understood that there was no question of children at Challacombe. He kept saying he loved me; he would never not love me, he said.

On the evening when we returned from our honeymoon I brought up the subject of the Stritches straight away. I explained it all to Ralphie when we were having supper, but he replied that he'd told me ages ago the Stritches were going to be at Challacombe. The arrangement apparently was that Mrs Stritch would come to the house every day except Sunday, and her husband would work in the garden. Ralphie repeated most earnestly that he'd told me all this before, that he'd quite often mentioned the Stritches, and had asked my opinion of them. I knew he was mistaken, but I didn't want to say so. Ralphie had a lot on his mind, buying the Fryes' land and negotiating to buy Mrs Laze's, and wondering how to go about buying my mother's. He didn't know much about farming, but he was keenly endeavouring to learn. All of it took time: he couldn't be blamed if he made little mistakes about what he'd said to me and what he hadn't.

'You see, it's awkward, Ralphie,' I explained again one night at supper, smiling at him. 'Belle Frye and I said terrible things to her.'

'Oh, Mrs Stritch'll have forgotten. Darling, it's donkeys' years ago.'

For some reason I didn't like him using that endearment, especially when he put the word at the beginning of a sentence, as he often for some reason did. I don't know why I objected so much to that. It was how it sounded, I think, a sort of casualness that seemed out of place in the house. There was another thing: he had a way of turning the pages of a newspaper, one page and then another, until finally he pored over the obituaries and the little advertisements. I didn't like the way he did that. And I didn't like the way he sometimes drummed the surface of a table with one hand when he was thinking, as if playing the piano. Another thing was, he wore leather gaiters.

'It's just that it's embarrassing for me,' I said, still smiling. 'Having her around.'

He ate beetroot and a sardine salad I had prepared because he'd told me he liked sardines. I'd made him wait that morning in the car while I went into a shop and bought several tins. I wouldn't let him see what they were, wanting it to be a surprise. He said:

'Actually, Mrs Stritch is very nice. And he's doing wonders with the garden.'

'We called her terrible names. She'd be hanging out her washing or something and we'd deliberately raise our voices. "Worst temper in Dorset," Belle would say and then we'd giggle. "Driven her husband to drink," I'd say. "Mrs Stritch is a – very nice lady," we used to call out in sing-song voices.'

'All children call people names.'

'Oh, Betty would never have let me do that. Going home from school with Betty and Dick was different. But then they left, you see. They left the Grammar when Belle and I were just finishing at Miss Pritchard's Primary, the same time that –'

'Darling, the Stritches have to be here. We have to have help.'

'I wish you wouldn't do that, Ralphie.'

'Do what?'

THE DRAWING-ROOM · 539

'I wish you wouldn't begin a sentence like that.'

He frowned at my smile, not understanding what was in my mind even though he was an understanding person. He didn't understand when I explained that I could manage the house on my own, that I didn't need Mrs Stritch in the way. I explained to him that Mrs Stritch had once taken a pair of gloves from Blow's. 'Please let's try it,' he said, and of course I didn't want to be difficult. I wanted him to see that I was prepared to try what he wished to try.

'Yes,' I said, smiling at him.

Like a black shadow she was in the drawing-room. She leaned back in her chair, one hand stretched out to the round table in front of her. It was just a memory, not the ghost of Mrs Ashburton, nothing like that. But the memory would have been better if Mrs Stritch hadn't always been around when Ralphie wasn't. Ralphie would go off every morning in his gaiters, and then Mrs Stritch would arrive. She would dust and clean and carry buckets of soapy water about the house. Her husband would come to the kitchen to have lunch with her, and Ralphie and I would have lunch in the dining-room. All afternoon I'd continue to be aware of her in the house, making little noises as she did her work. When it was time for her to go Ralphie would be back again.

'We're buying the Lazes' land,' he said one evening, crossing the drawing-room and pouring some whisky for himself from a decanter. I could see that he was delighted. 'I think your mother'll want to sell too,' he said.

I knew she would. Joe and Arthur were getting old, my stepfather was always saying the day would come. He'd no interest in the farm himself, and my mother would be glad not to have the responsibility.

'But you'll let the Lazes stay on in the farm-house?' I said, because it worried me that they should have to move away.

He shook his head. He said they didn't want to. They wanted to go and live nearer the town, like the Fryes did.

'The Fryes? But the Fryes don't want to move away. You said they were going to farm a couple of acres –'

'They've changed their minds.'

I didn't smile at him any more because I didn't like what he was saying. He'd explained quite clearly that the Fryes would stay in the farm-house, and that the Lazes could if they wanted to. He had reassured me about that. Yet he said now:

'You wanted the estate to be all together again, Matilda.'

'I didn't want people driven off, Ralphie. Not the Fryes and the Lazes. And what about my mother? Will she go also?'

'It'll be your mother's choice, Matilda. As it was theirs.'

'You've bought them all out. You promised me one thing and –'

'We need the housing for our own men.'

I felt deceived. I imagined a discussion between Ralphie and the man he'd hired to look after the estate, a cold-faced man called Epstone. I imagined Epstone saying that if you were going to do the thing, do it properly, offer them enough and they'll go. I imagined a discussion between Ralphie and his father, Ralphie asking if he could have another loan in order to plan his estate correctly and his father agreeing.

'Well, I dare say,' I said to Ralphie, smiling at him again, determined not to be cross.

'In the old days on the Challacombe estate,' he said, 'it would have happened less humanely.'

I didn't want to hear him going on about that so I didn't ask him what he meant. Even though he was considerate, I had begun to feel I was his property. It was an odd feeling, and I think it came from the other feeling I had, that he'd married me because I was part of an idea he'd fallen in love with. I used to look at the china vases on the drawing-room mantelpiece and feel like one of them, or like the carpets and the new wallpaper. I was part of something his money had created, and I don't think he noticed that the rattling of his newspaper or the clink of the decanter against his glass had a way of interrupting my thoughts. These noises, and his footsteps in the hall or in a room, were like the noises Mrs Stritch made with her buckets and the Electrolux, but of course I never told him that.

I have forgotten a little about all that time in the house with Ralphie. He didn't always tell me what was happening on the estate; in a way he talked more readily to Mrs Stritch, for I often heard him. He also talked to himself. He would pace up and down the lawns Mr Stritch had restored, wagging his head or nodding, while I watched him from a window of the house. As time went by, it was clear that he had done what he'd wanted. As he said, the estate was all of a piece again. He had bought our farm and the farm-house, offering so much for both that it couldn't be resisted. Joe and Arthur worked for him now.

Years were passing. Sometimes I walked over to see Miss Pritchard, going by the meadow we'd gone through on our way to school. I can't quite recall what we talked about as we had tea; only bits from our conversations come back to me. There is my own cheerfulness, my smiling at Miss Pritchard, and Miss Pritchard's glumness. Now and again I walked down to our farm and sat for a while with my mother, getting up to go before my stepfather returned. I went to see Betty and Belle, but I did that less and less. I began to think that they were all a little jealous of me. I thought that because I sensed an atmosphere when I went on these visits. 'You're cruel, Matilda,' Miss Pritchard said once, seeming to be unable to control the ill-temper that had caused the remark to surface. She turned her head away from me when she'd spoken. 'Cruel,' she said again, and I laughed because of course that was nonsensical. I remember thinking it was extraordinary that Miss Pritchard should be jealous.

Ralphie, I believe, must have begun to live some kind of life of his own. He often went out in the evenings, all dressed up. He came back jovial and would come to my room to kiss me good-night, until eventually I asked him not to. When I enquired at breakfast about where he'd been the night before his answer was always the same, that he had been to a house in the neighbourhood for dinner. He always seemed surprised that I should ask the question, claiming on each occasion that he had told me these details beforehand and that I had, in fact, refused to accompany him. In all this I really do not think he can have been right.

I welcomed the occasions when Ralphie went out in the evenings. I drew the curtains in the drawing-room and sat by the fire, just happy to be there. I thought of the time when we were all together in the farm-house, my father teasing Betty about Colin Gregg, Dick going as red as a sunset because my father mentioned an empty Woodbine packet he'd found. Every Sunday morning Ralphie went to church and, since Mrs Stritch didn't come on Sundays, that was another good time. Ralphie would return and sit opposite me in the dining-room, carving the beef I'd cooked him, looking at me now and again from his pink face, his teeth like chalk beneath the trim brown hedge of his moustache. I wanted to explain to him that I was happy in the house when Mrs Stritch wasn't there and when he wasn't there. I wanted to make him understand that old Mrs Ashburton had wanted me to be in her house, that that was why she had told me so much when I was a child, that everything had to do with the two wars there'd been. He didn't know as much about war as Mrs Ashburton had, even though he'd fought in one: I wanted to explain that to him, too. But I never did because his eyes would have begun to goggle, which they had a way of doing if something he couldn't comprehend was put to him. It was easier just to cook his meals and smile at him.

There was another thing Ralphie said I had forgotten: a conversation about a party he gave. When I asked him afterwards he repeatedly assured me we'd had a conversation about it, and in all honesty I believe it must have been his own memory that was at fault. Not that it matters in the least which way round it was. What mattered at the time was that the house was suddenly full of people. I was embroidering in the drawing-room, slowly stitching the eye of a peacock, and the next thing was that Ralphie's parents were embracing me, pretending they liked me. It seemed they had come for the weekend, so that they could be at the party, which was to be on the following night. They brought other people with them in their grey Daimler, people called Absom. Mrs Absom was thin, like Mrs Gregary, but younger than Mrs Gregary. Mr Absom was stout, like Mr Gregary, but not like polished marble, and younger also.

Mrs Stritch's daughter Nellie came to help on the Saturday morning and stayed all day. Apparently Ralphie had given Mrs Stritch money to buy navy-blue overalls for both of them so that they'd stand out from the guests at the party. They bought them in Blow's, Mrs Stritch told me, and it was quite funny to think that my stepfather might have served them, even fitted them with the overalls. Mr Stritch was there on the night of the party also, organizing the parking of cars.

It all took place in the drawing-room. People stood around with drinks in their hands. Ralphie introduced them to me, but I found it hard to know what to say to them. It was his mother, really, who gave the party, moving about the drawing-room as if she owned it. I realized then why she'd come for the weekend.

'So how you like Challacombe Manor, Mrs Gregary?' a man with very short hair asked me.

Politely I replied that I was fond of the house.

'Ralphie!' the man said, gesturing around him. 'Fantastic!' He added that he enjoyed life in the country, and told me the names of his dogs. He said he liked fishing and always had.

There were fifty-two people in the drawing-room, which had begun to smell of cigarette-smoke and alcohol. It was hot because Mrs Gregary had asked Mrs Stritch to make up an enormous fire, and it was becoming noisier because as the party advanced people talked more loudly. A woman, wearing a coffee-coloured dress, appeared to be drunk. She had sleek black hair and kept dropping her cigarette on to Mrs Ashburton's Persian carpet. Once when she bent to pick it up she almost toppled over.

'Hullo,' a man said. 'You're Mrs Ralphie.'

He was younger than the short-haired man. He stood very close to me, pressing me into a corner. He told me his name but I didn't listen because listening was an effort in the noisy room.

'Ever been there?' this man shouted at me. 'Ferns magnificent, this time of year.'

He smiled at me, revealing jagged teeth. 'Ferns,' he shouted, and then he said that he, or someone, had a collection of stuffed birds. I could feel one of his knees pressing into the side of my leg. He asked me something and I shook my head again. Then he went away.

Mrs Stritch and her daughter had covered the dining-room table with food. All kinds of cold meats there were, and various salads, and tarts of different kinds, and huge bowls of whipped cream, and cheeses. They'd done it all at the direction of Mrs Gregary: just by looking at the table you could see Mrs Gregary's hand in it, Mrs Stritch wouldn't have known a thing about it. The sideboard was entirely taken up with bottles of wine and glasses. The electric light wasn't turned on: there were slender red candles everywhere, another touch of Mrs Gregary's, or even Mrs Absom's. I had crossed the hall to the dining-room in order to get away from the noise for a moment. I thought I'd sit there quietly for a little; I was surprised to see all the food and the candles.

I was alone in the dining-room, as I'd guessed I would be. But it wasn't any longer a room you could be quiet in. Everything seemed garish, the red glitter of the wine bottles, the red candles, dish after dish of different food, the cheeses. It made me angry that Mrs Gregary and Mrs Absom should have come to Challacombe Manor in order to instruct Mrs Stritch, that Mrs Gregary should strut about in the drawing-room, telling people who she was.

I jumbled the food about, dropping pieces of meat into the bowls of cream, covering the tarts with salad. I emptied two wine bottles over everything, watching the red stain spreading on the table-cloth and on the cheeses. They had no right to be in the house, their Daimler had no right to be in the garage. I had asked years ago that Mrs Stritch should not be here.

In the drawing-room someone said to me:

'I enjoy to get out after pheasants, to tramp with my dogs.'

It was the short-haired man. I hadn't noticed that he was a foreigner. I knew before he told me that he was German.

'You have dogs, Mrs Gregary?'

I smiled at him and shook my head. It seemed extraordinary that there should be a German in this drawing-room. I remembered when Mrs Ashburton used to talk to me about the First World War that I'd imagined the Germans as grey and steel-like, endlessly consuming black bread. This man didn't seem in the least like that.

'Hasenfuss,' he said. 'The name, you know.'

For a moment the room was different. People were dancing there at some other party. A man was standing near the door, waiting for someone to arrive, seeming a little anxious. It was all just a flash, as if I had fallen asleep and for a moment had had a dream.

'We are enemies and then we are friends. I advise on British beer, I enjoy your British countryside. It is my profession to advise on British beer. I would not enjoy to live in Germany today, Mrs Gregary.'

'You are the first German I have ever met.'

'Oh, I hope not the last.'

Again the drawing-room was different. There was the music and the dancing and the man by the door. The girl he was waiting for arrived. It was Mrs Ashburton, as she was in the photographs she'd showed me when I was nine. And he was the man she'd married.

'Here I am standing,' said the short-haired German, 'in the house of the people who put Mr Hitler in his place.' He laughed loudly when he'd made that remark, displaying more gold fillings than I had ever before seen in anyone's mouth. 'Your father-in-law, you know, made a lot of difference to the war.'

I didn't know what he was talking about. I was thinking of the dining-room and what would happen when everyone walked into it. It was like something Belle Frye and I might have done together, only we'd never have had the courage. It was worse than singing songs outside Mrs Stritch's cottage.

'In that I mean,' the German said, 'the manufacturing of guns.'

I hadn't known that. My stepfather had said that the Gregarys had made a killing, but I hadn't thought about it. Ralphie had never told me that his father's motor-components business had made guns during the war, that the war had made him rich. It was the war that enabled Ralphie now to buy up all the land and set the Challacombe estate to rights again. It was the war that had restored this drawing-room.

'The world is strange,' the German said.

I went upstairs and came down with Ralphie's gaiters. I remember standing at the door of the drawing-room, looking at all the people drinking, and seeing again, for an instant, the dancers of the distant past. Mrs Ashburton and her husband were among them, smiling at one another.

I moved into the room and when I reached the fire-place I threw the gaiters on to the flames. Someone noticed me, Mrs Absom, I think it was. She seemed quite terrified as she watched me.

The German was again alone. He told me he enjoyed alcohol, emphasizing this point by reaching his glass out towards Mrs Stritch, who was passing with some mixture in a jug. I told him about Mrs Ashburton's husband, how he had returned from the first of the two wars suffering from shell-shock, how the estate had fallen to bits because of that, how everything had had to be mortgaged. I was telling her story, and I was even aware that my voice was quite like hers, that I felt quite like her as well. Everything had happened all over again, I told the German, the repetition was cloying. I told him about Mrs Ashburton's law of averages, how some men always came back from a war, how you had to pray it would be the men who were closest to you, how it would have been better if her own husband had been killed.

The smell of burning leather was unpleasant in the room. People noticed it. Ralphie poked at his smouldering gaiters with a poker, wondering why they were there. I saw his mother looking at me while I talked to the German. 'Mrs Ashburton did what she could,' I said. 'There's nothing wrong with living in the past.'

I went around from person to person then, asking them to go. The party had come to an end, I explained, but Mrs Gregary tried to contradict that. 'No, no, no,' she cried. 'We've scarcely started.' She ushered people into the dining-room and then, of course, she saw that I was right.

'I would like you to go as well,' I said to Mr Gregary in the hall, while the visitors were rooting for their coats. 'I would like you to go and take the Absoms with you. I did not invite the Absoms here any more than I invited you.' I said it while smiling at him, so that he could see I wasn't being quarrelsome. 'Oh now, look here, Matilda!' he protested.

In the kitchen I told Mrs Stritch that I'd rather she didn't return to the house. I could easily manage on my own, I explained to her, trying to be kind in how I put it. 'It's just that it's embarrassing,' I said, 'having you here.'

The Gregarys and the Absoms didn't go until the following day, a Sunday. They didn't say goodbye to me, and I only knew that they had finally departed because Ralphie told me. 'Why are you doing this?' he said, sitting down on the other side of the fire in the drawing-room, where I was embroidering my peacocks. 'Why, Matilda?' he said again.

'I don't understand you.'

'Yes, you do.'

He had never spoken like that before. All his considerateness had disappeared. His eyes were fiery and yet cold. His large hands looked as though they wanted to commit some act of violence. I shook my head at him. He said:

'You're pretending to be deranged.'

I laughed. I didn't like him sitting opposite me like that, with his eyes and his hands. Everything about him had been a pretence: all he wanted was his own way, to have his mother giving parties in my drawing-room, to have Mrs Stritch forever vacuuming the stairs, to own me as he owned the land and the farms and the house. It was horrible, making money out of war.

'You don't even cook for me,' he said to my astonishment. 'Half-raw potatoes, half-raw chops –'

'Oh, Ralphie, don't be silly. You know I cook for you.'

'The only food that is edible in this house is made by Mrs Stritch. You can cook if you want to, only you can't be bothered.'

'I do my best. In every way I do my best. I want our marriage to be –'

'It isn't a marriage,' he said. 'It's never been a marriage.'

'We were married in the church.'

'Stop talking like that!' He shouted at me again, suddenly on his feet, looking down at me. His face was red with fury; I thought he might pick something up and hit me with it.

'I'm sorry,' I said.

'You're as sane as I am. For God's sake, Matilda!'

'Of course I'm sane,' I said quietly. 'I could not be sitting here if I were not. I could not live a normal life.'

'You don't live a normal life.' He was shouting again, stamping about the room like an animal. 'Every second of every day is devoted to the impression you wish to give.'

'But, Ralphie, why should I wish to give an impression?'

'To cover up your cruelty.'

I laughed again, gently so as not to anger him further. I remembered Miss Pritchard saying I was cruel, and of course there was the cruelty Mrs Ashburton had spoken of, the cruelty that was natural in wartime. I had felt it in myself when my father had been killed, and when Dick had been killed. I had felt it when I had first seen my mother embracing the man who became my stepfather, too soon after my father had died. God, if He existed, I had thought in the end, was something to be frightened of.

'The war is over,' I said, and he looked at me, startled by that remark.

'It isn't for you,' he said. 'It'll never be for you. It's all we ever hear from you, the war and that foolish old woman –'

'It wasn't over for Mrs Ashburton either. How could it be when she lived to see it all beginning again?'

'Oh, for God's sake, stop talking about her. If it hadn't been for her, if she hadn't taken advantage of a nine-year-old child with her rubbish, you would be a normal human being now.' He stood above my chair again, pushing his red face down at me and speaking slowly. 'She twisted you, she filled you full of hate. Whatever you are now, that dead woman has done to you. Millions have suffered in war,' he suddenly shouted. 'Who's asking you to dwell on it, for God's sake?'

'There are people who find it hard to pick up the pieces. Because they're made like that.'

'You'd have picked them up if she hadn't prevented you. She didn't want you to, because she couldn't herself.' Furiously he added, 'Some kind of bloody monster she was.'

I didn't reply to any of that. He said, with a bitterness in his voice which had never been there before, 'All I know is that she has destroyed Challacombe for me.'

'It was never real for you, Ralphie. I shall never forget the happiness in our farm-house. What memories of Challacombe can you have?'

But Ralphie wasn't interested in the happiness in our farm-house, or in memories he couldn't have. All he wanted to do was wildly to castigate me.

'How can I live here with you?' he demanded in a rough, hard voice, pouring at the same time a glass of whisky for himself. 'You said you loved me once. Yet everything you do is calculated to let me see your hatred. What have I done,' he shouted at me, 'that you hate me, Matilda?'

I quietly replied that he was mistaken. I protested that I did not hate him, but even as I spoke I realized that that wasn't true. I hated him for being what he was, for walking with his parents into the farmyard that morning, for thinking he had a place in the past. I might have confided in him but I did not want to. I might have said that I remembered, years ago, Miss Pritchard coming to see my mother and what Miss Pritchard had said. I had eavesdropped on the stairs that led to the kitchen, while she said she believed there was something the matter with me. It was before the death of Dick, after I'd discovered about my mother and the man who was now my stepfather. 'She dwells on her father's death,' Miss Pritchard had said and she'd gone on to say that I dwelt as well on the conversations I'd had with old Mrs Ashburton. I remembered the feeling I'd had, standing there listening: the feeling that the shell-shock of Mr Ashburton, carried back to Challacombe from the trenches in 1917, had conveyed itself in some other form to his wife, that she, as much as he, had been a victim of violence. I felt it because Miss Pritchard was saying something like it to my mother. 'There are casualties in wars,' she said, 'thousands of miles from where the fighting is.' She was speaking about me. I'd caught a mood, she said, from old Mrs Ashburton, and when my mother replied that you couldn't catch a mood like you caught the measles Miss Pritchard sharply replied that you could. '*Folie à deux* the French call it,' she insisted, an expression I welcomed and have never since forgotten. There had been *folie à deux* all over this house, and in the garden too, when he came back with his mind in pieces. She had shared the horror with him and later she had shared it with me, as if guessing that I, too, would be a casualty. As long as I lived I would honour that *folie* in their house. I would honour her and her husband, and my father and Dick, and the times they had lived in. It was right that the cruelty was there.

'Of course I don't hate you,' I said again. 'Of course not, Ralphie.'

He did not reply. He stood in the centre of the drawing-room with his glass in his hand, seeming like a beast caught in a snare: he had all the beaten qualities of such an animal. His shoulders slouched, his eyes had lost their fire.

'I don't know what to do,' he said.

'You may stay here,' I said, 'with me.' Again I smiled, wishing to make the invitation seem kind. I could feel no pity for him.

'How could I?' he shouted. 'My God, how could I? I lose count of the years in this house. I look at you every day, I look at your eyes and your hair and your face. I look at your hands and your fingernails, and the arch of your neck. I love you; every single inch of you I love. How can I live here and love you like that, Matilda? I shared a dream with you, Matilda, a dream that no one else but you would have understood. I longed for my quiet life, with you and with our children. I married you out of passion and devotion. You give me back nothing.'

'You married me because I was part of something, part of the house and the estate –'

'That isn't true. That's a rubbishy fantasy; not a word of it is true.'

'I cannot help it if I believe it.' I wasn't smiling now. I let my feelings show in my eyes because there was no point in doing otherwise any more. Not in a million years would he understand. 'Yes, I despise you,' I said. 'I have never felt affection for you.'

I said it calmly and bent my head again over my embroidery. He poured more whisky and sat down in the chair on the other side of the fire-place. I spoke while still embroidering, magenta thread in a feather of my peacock's tail.

'You must never again touch me,' I said. 'Not even in passing me by in a room. We shall live here just as we are, but do not address me with endearments. I shall cook and clean, but there shall be no parties. Your parents are not welcome. It is discourteous to me to give parties behind my back and to employ people I do not care for.'

'You were told, you know perfectly well you were told –'

'You will fatten and shamble about the rooms of this house. I shall not complain. You will drink more whisky, and perhaps lose heart in your dream. "His wife does not go out," people will say; "they have no children. He married beneath him, but it isn't that that cut him down to size." '

'Matilda, please. Please for a moment listen to me –'

'Why should I? And why should you not lose heart in your dream because isn't your dream ridiculous? If you think that your Challacombe estate is like it was, or that you in your vulgarity could ever make it so, then you're the one who is deranged.'

I had not taken my eyes from the peacock's tail. I imagined a patch of damp developing on the ceiling of an upstairs room. I imagined his lifting the heavy lead-lined hatch in the loft and stepping out on to the roof to find the missing tile. I stood with him on the roof and pointed to the tile, lodged in a gutter. I had removed it myself and slid it down the incline of the roof. He could reach it with an effort, by grasping the edge of the chimney-stack to be safe. I heard the thump of his body as it struck the cobbles below. I heard it in the drawing-room as I worked my stitches, while he drank more whisky and for a while was silent.

'Damn you,' he shouted in the end, once more on his feet and seething above me. 'Damn you to hell, Matilda.'

'No matter what you do,' I said, still sewing the magenta thread, 'I shall not leave this house.'

He sold everything he'd bought except the house and garden. He sold the land and the farm-houses, the Fryes' and the Lazes' and what had been ours. He didn't tell me about any of it until he'd done it. 'I'll be gone in a week,' he said one day, six or seven months after we'd had that quarrel, and I did not urge him to stay.

It is a long time ago now, that day. I can't quite remember Ralphie's going, even though with such vividness I remember so much else. There are new people in all the farm-houses now, whole families have grown up; again the tennis court is overgrown. Miss Pritchard died of course, and my mother and my stepfather. I never saw much of them after Ralphie went, and I never laid eyes on Ralphie or even had a line from him. But if Ralphie walked in now I would take his hand and say I was sorry for the cruelty that possessed me and would not go away, the cruelty she used to talk about, a natural thing in wartime. It lingered and I'm sorry it did, and perhaps after all this time Ralphie would understand and believe, but Ralphie, I know, will never return.

I sit here now in her drawing-room, and may perhaps become as old as she was. Sometimes I walk up to the meadow where the path to school was, but the meadow isn't there any more. There are rows of coloured caravans, and motor-cars and shacks. In the garden I can hear the voices of people drifting down to me, and the sound of music from their wireless sets. Nothing is like it was.

Torridge

Perhaps nobody ever did wonder what Torridge would be like as a man – or what Wiltshire or Mace-Hamilton or Arrowsmith would be like, come to that. Torridge at thirteen had a face with a pudding look, matching the sound of his name. He had small eyes and short hair like a mouse's. Within the collar of his grey regulation shirt the knot of his House tie was formed with care, a maroon triangle of just the right shape and bulk. His black shoes were always shiny.

Torridge was unique in some way: perhaps only because he was beyond the pale and appeared, irritatingly, to be unaware of it. He wasn't good at games and had difficulty in understanding what was being explained in the classroom. He would sit there frowning, half smiling, his head a little to one side. Occasionally he would ask some question that caused an outburst of groaning. His smile would increase then. He would glance around the classroom, not flustered or embarrassed in the least, seeming to be pleased that he had caused such a response. He was naïve to the point where it was hard to believe he wasn't pretending, but his naïveté was real and was in time universally recognized as such. A master called Buller Yeats reserved his cruellest shafts of scorn for it, sighing whenever his eyes chanced to fall on Torridge, pretending to believe his name was Porridge.

Of the same age as Torridge, but similar in no other way, were Wiltshire, Mace-Hamilton and Arrowsmith. All three of them were blond-haired and thin, with a common sharpness about their features. They wore, untidily, the same clothes as Torridge, their House ties knotted any old how, the laces in their scuffed shoes often tied in several places. They excelled at different games and were quick to sense what was what. Attractive boys, adults had more than once called them.

The friendship among the three of them developed because, in a way, Torridge was what he was. From the first time they were aware of him – on the first night of their first term – he appeared to be special. In the darkness after lights-out someone was trying not to sob and Torridge's voice was piping away, not homesick in the least. His father had a button business was what he was saying: he'd probably be going into the button business himself. In the morning he was identified, a boy in red and blue striped pyjamas, still chattering in the wash-room. 'What's your father do, Torridge?' Arrowsmith asked at breakfast, and that was the beginning. 'Dad's in the button business,' Torridge beamingly replied. 'Torridge's, you know.' But no one did know.

He didn't, as other new boys, make a particular friend. For a while he attached himself to a small gang of homesick boys who had only their malady in common, but after a time this gang broke up and Torridge found himself on his own, though it seemed quite happily so. He was often to be found in the room of the kindly housemaster of Junior House, an ageing white-haired figure called Old Frosty, who listened sympathetically to complaints of injustice at the hands of other masters, always ready to agree that the world was a hard place. 'You should hear Buller Yeats on Torridge, sir,' Wiltshire used to say in Torridge's presence. 'You'd think Torridge had no feelings, sir.' Old Frosty would reply that Buller Yeats was a frightful man. 'Take no notice, Torridge,' he'd add in his kindly voice, and Torridge would smile, making it clear that he didn't mind in the least what Buller Yeats said. 'Torridge knows true happiness,' a new young master, known as Mad Wallace, said in an unguarded moment one day, a remark which caused immediate uproar in a Geography class. It was afterwards much repeated, like 'Dad's in the button business' and 'Torridge's, you know.' The true happiness of Torridge became a joke, the particular property of Wiltshire and Mace-Hamilton and Arrowsmith. Furthering the joke, they claimed that knowing Torridge was a rare experience, that the private realm of his innocence and his happiness was even exotic. Wiltshire insisted that one day the school would be proud of him. The joke was worked to death.

At the school it was the habit of certain senior boys to 'take an interest in' juniors. This varied from glances and smiles across the dining-hall to written invitations to meet in some secluded spot at a stated time. Friendships, taking a variety of forms, were then initiated. It was flattering, and very often a temporary antidote for homesickness, when a new boy received the agreeable but bewildering attentions of an important fifth-former. A meeting behind Chapel led to the negotiating of a barbed-wire fence on a slope of gorse bushes, the older boy solicitous and knowledge-able. There were well-trodden paths and nooks among the gorse where smoking could take place with comparative safety. Farther afield, in the hills, there were crude shelters composed of stones and corrugated iron. Here, too, the emphasis was on smoking and romance.

New boys very soon became aware of the nature of older boys' interest in them. The flattery changed its shape, an adjustment was made – or the new boys retreated in panic from this area of school life. Andrews and Butler, Webb and Mace-Hamilton, Dillon and Pratt, Tothill and Goldfish Stewart, Good and Wiltshire, Sainsbury Major and Arrowsmith, Brewitt and King: the liaisons were renowned, the combinations of names sometimes seeming like a music-hall turn, a soft-shoe shuffle of entangled hearts. There was faithlessness, too: the Honourable Anthony Swain made the rounds of the senior boys, a fickle and tartish *bijou*, desired and yet despised.

Torridge's puddingy appearance did not suggest that he had *bijou* qualities, and glances did not readily come his way in the dining-hall. This was often the fate, or good fortune, of new boys and was not regarded as a sign of qualities lacking. Yet quite regularly an ill-endowed child would mysteriously become the object of fifth- and sixth-form desire. This remained a puzzle to the juniors until they themselves became fifth- or sixth-formers and desire was seen to have to do with something deeper than superficial good looks.

It was the apparent evidence of this truth that caused Torridge, first of all, to be aware of the world of *bijou* and protector. He received a note from a boy in the Upper Fifth who had previously eschewed the sexual life offered by the school. He was a big, black-haired youth with glasses and a protruding forehead, called Fisher.

'Hey, what's this mean?' Torridge enquired, finding the note under his pillow, tucked into his pyjamas. 'Here's a bloke wants to go for a walk.'

He read the invitation out: '*If you would like to come for a walk meet me by the electricity plant behind Chapel. Half-past four Tuesday afternoon. R. A. J. Fisher.*'

'Jesus Christ!' said Armstrong.

'You've got an admirer, Porridge,' Mace-Hamilton said.

'Admirer?'

'He wants you to be his *bijou*,' Wiltshire explained.

'What's it mean, *bijou*?'

'Tart, it means, Porridge.'

'Tart?'

'Friend. He wants to be your protector.'

'What's it mean, protector?'

'He loves you, Porridge.'

'I don't even know the bloke.'

'He's the one with the big forehead. He's a half-wit actually.'

'Half-wit?'

'His mother let him drop on his head. Like yours did, Porridge.'

'My mum never.'

Everyone was crowding around Torridge's bed. The note was passed from hand to hand. 'What's your dad do, Porridge?' Wiltshire suddenly asked, and Torridge automatically replied that he was in the button business.

'You've got to write a note back to Fisher, you know,' Mace-Hamilton pointed out.

'Dear Fisher,' Wiltshire prompted, 'I love you.'

'But I don't even –'

'It doesn't matter not knowing him. You've got to write a letter and put it in his pyjamas.'

Torridge didn't say anything. He placed the note in the top pocket of his jacket and slowly began to undress. The other boys drifted back to their own beds, still amused by the development. In the wash-room the next morning Torridge said:

'I think he's quite nice, that Fisher.'

'Had a dream about him, did you, Porridge?' Mace-Hamilton enquired. 'Got up to tricks, did he?'

'No harm in going for a walk.'

'No harm at all, Porridge.'

In fact, a mistake had been made. Fisher, in his haste or his excitement, had placed the note under the wrong pillow. It was Arrowsmith, still allied with Sainsbury Major, whom he wished to attract.

That this error had occurred was borne in on Torridge when he turned up at the electricity plant on the following Tuesday. He had not considered it necessary to reply to Fisher's note, but he had, across the dining-hall, essayed a smile or two in the older boy's direction: it had surprised him to meet with no response. It surprised him rather more to meet with no response by the electricity plant. Fisher just looked at him and then turned his back, pretending to whistle.

'Hullo, Fisher,' Torridge said.

'Hop it, look. I'm waiting for someone.'

'I'm Torridge, Fisher.'

'I don't care who you are.'

'You wrote me that letter.' Torridge was still smiling. 'About a walk, Fisher.'

'Walk? What walk?'

'You put the letter under my pillow, Fisher.'

'Jesus!' said Fisher.

The encounter was observed by Arrowsmith, Mace-Hamilton and Wiltshire, who had earlier taken up crouched positions behind one of the chapel buttresses. Torridge heard the familiar hoots of laughter, and because it was his way he joined in. Fisher, white-faced, strode away.

'Poor old Porridge,' Arrowsmith commiserated, gasping and pretending to be contorted with mirth. Mace-Hamilton and Wiltshire were leaning against the buttress, issuing shrill noises.

'Gosh,' Torridge said, '*I* don't care.'

He went away, still laughing a bit, and there the matter of Fisher's attempt at communication might have ended. In fact it didn't, because Fisher wrote a second time and this time he made certain that the right boy received his missive. But Arrowsmith, still firmly the property of Sainsbury Major, wished to have nothing to do with R. A. J. Fisher.

When he was told the details of Fisher's error, Torridge said he'd guessed it had been something like that. But Wiltshire, Mace-Hamilton and Arrowsmith claimed that a new sadness had overcome Torridge. Something beautiful had been going to happen to him, Wiltshire said: just as the petals of friendship were opening the flower had been crudely snatched away. Arrowsmith said Torridge reminded him of one of Picasso's sorrowful harlequins. One way or the other, it was agreed that the experience would be beneficial to Torridge's sensitivity. It was seen as his reason for turning to religion, which recently he had done, joining a band of similarly inclined boys who were inspired by the word of the chaplain, a figure known as God Harvey. God Harvey was ascetic, seeming dangerously thin, his face all edge and as pale as paper, his cassock odorous with incense. He conducted readings in his room, offering coffee and biscuits afterwards, though not himself partaking of these refreshments. 'God Harvey's linnets' his acolytes were called, for often a hymn was sung to round things off. Welcomed into this fold, Torridge regained his happiness.

R. A. J. Fisher, on the other hand, sank into greater gloom. Arrowsmith remained elusive, mockingly faithful to Sainsbury Major, haughty when Fisher glanced pleadingly, ignoring all his letters. Fisher developed a look of introspective misery. The notes that Arrowsmith delightedly showed around were full of longing, increasingly tinged with desperation. The following term, unexpectedly, Fisher did not return to the school.

There was a famous Assembly at the beginning of that term, with much speculation beforehand as to the trouble in the air. Rumour had it that once and for all an attempt was to be made to stamp out the smiles and the glances in the dining-hall, the whole business of *bijous* and protectors, even the faithless behaviour of the Honourable Anthony Swain. The school waited and then the gowned staff arrived in the Assembly Hall and waited also, in grim anticipation on a raised dais. Public beatings for past offenders were scheduled, it was whispered: the Sergeant-major – the school's boxing instructor, who had himself told tales of public beatings in the past – would inflict the punishment at the headmaster's bidding. But that did not happen. Small and bald and red-skinned, the headmaster marched to the dais unaccompanied by the Sergeant-major. Twitching with anger that many afterwards declared had been simulated, he spoke at great length of the school's traditions. He stated that for fourteen years he had been proud to be its headmaster. He spoke of decency, and then of his own dismay. The school had been dishonoured; he would wish certain practices to cease. 'I stand before you ashamed,' he added, and paused for a moment. 'Let all this cease,' he commanded. He marched away, tugging at his gown in a familiar manner.

No one understood why the Assembly had taken place at that particular time, on the first day of a summer term. Only the masters looked knowing, as though labouring beneath some secret, but pressed and pleaded with they refused to reveal anything. Even Old Frosty, usually a most reliable source on such occasions, remained awesomely tight-lipped.

But the pronounced dismay and shame of the headmaster changed nothing. That term progressed and the world of *bijous* and their protectors continued as before, the glances, the meetings, cigarettes and romance in the hillside huts. R. A. J. Fisher was soon forgotten, having never made much of a mark. But the story of his error in placing a note under Torridge's pillow passed into legend, as did the encounter by the electricity plant and Torridge's deprivation of a relationship. The story was repeated as further terms passed by; new boys heard it and viewed Torridge with greater interest, imagining what R. A. J. Fisher had been like. The liaisons of Wiltshire with Good, Mace-Hamilton with Webb, and Arrowsmith with Sainsbury Major continued until the three senior boys left the school. Wiltshire, Mace-Hamilton and Arrowsmith found fresh protectors then, and later these new liaisons came to an end in a similar manner. Later still, Wiltshire, Mace-Hamilton and Arrowsmith ceased to be *bijous* and became protectors themselves.

Torridge pursued the religious side of things. He continued to be a frequent partaker of God Harvey's biscuits and spiritual uplift, and a useful presence among the chapel pews, where he voluntarily dusted, cleaned brass, and kept the hymn-books in a state of repair with Sellotape. Wiltshire, Mace-Hamilton and Arrowsmith continued to circulate stories about him which were not true: that he was the product of virgin birth, that he possessed the gift of tongues but did not care to employ it, that he had three kidneys. In the end there emanated from them the claim that a liaison existed between Torridge and God Harvey. 'Love and the holy spirit,' Wiltshire pronounced, suggesting an ambience of chapel fustiness and God Harvey's grey boniness. The swish of his cassock took on a new significance, as did his thin, dry fingers. In a holy way the fingers pressed themselves on to Torridge, and then their holiness became a passion that could not be imagined. It was all a joke because Torridge was Torridge, but the laughter it caused wasn't malicious because no one hated him. He was a figure of fun; no one sought his downfall because there was no downfall to seek.

The friendship between Wiltshire, Mace-Hamilton and Arrowsmith continued after they left the school, after all three had married and had families. Once a year they received the Old Boys' magazine, which told of the achievements of themselves and the more successful of their school-fellows. There were Old Boys' cocktail parties and Old Boys' Day at the school every June and the Old Boys' cricket match. Some of these occasions, from time to time, they attended. Every so often they received the latest rebuilding programme, with the suggestion that they might like to contribute to the rebuilding fund. Occasionally they did.

As middle age closed in, the three friends met less often. Arrowsmith was an executive with Shell and stationed for longish periods in different countries abroad. Once every two years he brought his family back to England, which provided an opportunity for the three friends to meet. The wives met on these occasions also, and over the years the children. Often the men's distant schooldays were referred to, Buller Yeats and Old Frosty and the Sergeant-major, the little red-skinned headmaster, and above all Torridge. Within the three families, in fact, Torridge had become a myth. The joke that had begun when they were all new boys together continued, as if driven by its own impetus. In the minds of the wives and children the innocence of Torridge, his true happiness in the face of mockery and his fondness for the religious side of life all lived on. With some exactitude a physical image of the boy he'd been took root; his neatly knotted maroon House tie, his polished shoes, the hair that resembled a mouse's fur, the pudding face with two small eyes in it. 'My dad's in the button business,' Arrowsmith had only to say to cause instant laughter. 'Torridge's, you know.' The way Torridge ate, the way he ran, the way he smiled back at Buller Yeats, the rumour that he'd been dropped on his head as a baby, that he had three kidneys, all this was considerably appreciated, because Wiltshire and Mace-Hamilton and Arrowsmith related it well.

What was not related was R. A. J. Fisher's error in placing a note beneath Torridge's pillow, or the story that had laughingly been spread about concerning Torridge's relationship with God Harvey. This would have meant revelations that weren't seemly in family circles, the explanation of the world of *bijou* and protector, the romance and cigarettes in the hillside huts, the entangling of hearts. The subject had been touched upon among the three husbands and their wives in the normal course of private conversation, although not everything had been quite recalled. Listening, the wives had formed the impression that the relationships between older and younger boys at their husbands' school were similar to the platonic admiration a junior girl had so often harboured for a senior girl at their own schools. And so the subject had been left.

One evening in June, 1976, Wiltshire and Mace-Hamilton met in a bar called the Vine, in Piccadilly Place. They hadn't seen one another since the summer of 1974, the last time Arrowsmith and his family had been in England. Tonight they were to meet the Arrowsmiths again, for a family dinner in the Woodlands Hotel, Richmond. On the last occasion the three families had celebrated their reunion at the Wiltshires' house in Cobham and the time before with the Mace-Hamiltons in Ealing. Arrowsmith insisted that it was a question of turn and turn about and every third time he arranged for the family dinner to be held at his expense at the Woodlands. It was convenient because, although the Arrowsmiths spent the greater part of each biennial leave with Mrs Arrowsmith's parents in Somerset, they always stayed for a week at the Woodlands in order to see a bit of London life.

In the Vine in Piccadilly Place Wiltshire and Mace-Hamilton hurried over their second drinks. As always, they were pleased to see one another, and both were excited at the prospect of seeing Arrowsmith and his family again. They still looked faintly alike. Both had balded and run to fat. They wore inconspicuous blue suits with a discreet chalk stripe, Wiltshire's a little smarter than Mace-Hamilton's.

'We'll be late,' Wiltshire said, having just related how he'd made a small killing since the last time they'd met. Wiltshire operated in the import-export world; Mace-Hamilton was a chartered accountant.

They finished their drinks. 'Cheerio,' the barman called out to them as they slipped away. His voice was deferentially low, matching the softly-lit surroundings. 'Cheerio, Gerry,' Wiltshire said.

They drove in Wiltshire's car to Hammersmith, over the bridge and on to Barnes and Richmond. It was a Friday evening; the traffic was heavy.

'He had a bit of trouble, you know,' Mace-Hamilton said.

'Arrows?'

'She took a shine to some guy in Mombasa.'

Wiltshire nodded, poking the car between a cyclist and a taxi. He wasn't surprised. One night six years ago Arrowsmith's wife and he had committed adultery together at her suggestion. A messy business it had been, and afterwards he'd felt terrible.

In the Woodlands Hotel Arrowsmith, in a grey flannel suit, was not entirely sober. He, too, had run a bit to fat although, unlike Wiltshire and Mace-Hamilton, he hadn't lost any of his hair. Instead, it had dramatically changed colour: what Old Frosty had once called 'Arrows' blond thatch' was grey now. Beneath it his face was pinker than it had been and he had taken to wearing spectacles, heavy and black-rimmed, making him look even more different from the boy he'd been.

In the bar of the Woodlands he drank whisky on his own, smiling occasionally to himself because tonight he had a surprise for everybody. After five weeks of being cooped up with his in-laws in Somerset he was feeling good. 'Have one yourself, dear,' he invited the barmaid, a girl with an excess of lipstick on a podgy mouth. He pushed his own glass towards her while she was saying she didn't mind if she did.

His wife and his three adolescent children, two boys and a girl, entered the bar with Mrs Mace-Hamilton. 'Hi, hi, hi,' Arrowsmith called out to them in a jocular manner, causing his wife and Mrs Mace-Hamilton to note that he was drunk again. They sat down while he quickly finished the whisky that had just been poured for him. 'Put another in that for a start,' he ordered the barmaid, and crossed the floor of the bar to find out what everyone else wanted.

Mrs Wiltshire and her twins, girls of twelve, arrived while drinks were being decided about. Arrowsmith kissed her, as he had kissed Mrs Mace-Hamilton. The barmaid, deciding that the accurate conveying of such a large order was going to be beyond him, came and stood by the two tables that the party now occupied. The order was given; an animated conversation began.

The three women were different in appearance and in manner. Mrs Arrowsmith was thin as a knife, fashionably dressed in a shade of ash-grey that reflected her ash-grey hair. She smoked perpetually, unable to abandon the habit. Mrs Wiltshire was small. Shyness caused her to coil herself up in the presence of other people so that she often resembled a ball. Tonight she was in pink, a faded shade. Mrs Mace-Hamilton was carelessly plump, a large woman attired in a carelessly chosen dress that had begonias on it. She rather frightened Mrs Wiltshire. Mrs Arrowsmith found her trying.

'Oh, heavenly little drink!' Mrs Arrowsmith said, briefly drooping her blue-tinged eyelids as she sipped her gin and tonic.

'It *is* good to see you,' Mrs Mace-Hamilton gushed, beaming at everyone and vaguely raising her glass. 'And how they've all grown!' Mrs Mace-Hamilton had not had children herself.

'Their boobs have grown, by God,' the older Arrowsmith boy murmured to his brother, a reference to the Wiltshire twins. Neither of the two Arrowsmith boys went to their father's school: one was at a preparatory school in Oxford, the other at Charterhouse. Being of an age to do so, they both drank sherry and intended to drink as much of it as they possibly could. They found these family occasions tedious. Their sister, about to go to university, had determined neither to speak nor to smile for the entire evening. The Wiltshire twins were quite looking forward to the food.

Arrowsmith sat beside Mrs Wiltshire. He didn't say anything but after a moment he stretched a hand over her two knees and squeezed them in what he intended to be a brotherly way. He said without conviction that it was great to see her. He didn't look at her while he spoke. He didn't much care for hanging about with the women and children.

In turn Mrs Wiltshire didn't much care for his hand on her knees and was relieved when he drew it away. 'Hi, hi, hi,' he suddenly called out, causing her to jump. Wiltshire and Mace-Hamilton had appeared.

The physical similarity that had been so pronounced when the three men were boys and had been only faintly noticeable between Wiltshire and Mace-Hamilton in the Vine was clearly there again, as if the addition of Arrowsmith had supplied missing reflections. The men had thickened in the same way; the pinkness of Arrowsmith's countenance was a pinkness that tinged the other faces too. Only Arrowsmith's grey thatch of hair seemed out of place, all wrong beside the baldness of the other two: in their presence it might have been a wig, an impression it did not otherwise give. His grey flannel suit, beside their pinstripes, looked like something put on by mistake. 'Hi, hi, hi,' he shouted, thumping their shoulders.

Further rounds of drinks were bought and consumed. The Arrowsmith boys declared to each other that they were drunk and made further *sotto voce* observations about the forming bodies of the Wiltshire twins. Mrs Wiltshire felt the occasion becoming easier as Cinzano Bianco coursed through her bloodstream. Mrs Arrowsmith was aware of a certain familiar edginess within her body, a desire to be elsewhere, alone with a man she did not know. Mrs Mace-Hamilton spoke loudly of her garden.

In time the party moved from the bar to the dining-room. 'Bring us another round at the table,' Arrowsmith commanded the lipsticked barmaid. 'Quick as you can, dear.'

In the large dim dining-room waiters settled them around a table with little vases of carnations on it, a long table beneath the chandelier in the centre of the room. Celery soup arrived at the table, and smoked salmon and pâté, and the extra round of drinks Arrowsmith had ordered, and bottles of Nuits St Georges, and bottles of Vouvray and Anjou Rosé, and sirloin of beef, chicken à la king and veal escalope. The Arrowsmith boys laughed shrilly, openly staring at the tops of the Wiltshire twins' bodies. Potatoes, peas, spinach and carrots were served. Mrs Arrowsmith waved the vegetables away and smoked between courses. It was after this dinner six years ago that she had made her suggestion to Wiltshire, both of them being the worse for wear and it seeming not to matter because of that. 'Oh, *isn't* this jolly?' the voice of Mrs Mace-Hamilton boomed above the general hubbub.

Over Chantilly trifle and Orange Surprise the name of Torridge was heard. The name was always mentioned just about now, though sometimes sooner. 'Poor old bean,' Wiltshire said, and everybody laughed because it was the one subject they all shared. No one really wanted to hear about the Mace-Hamiltons' garden; the comments of the Arrowsmith boys were only for each other; Mrs Arrowsmith's needs could naturally not be voiced; the shyness of Mrs Wiltshire was private too. But Torridge was different. Torridge in a way was like an old friend now, existing in everyone's mind, a family subject. The Wiltshire twins were quite amused to hear of some freshly remembered evidence of Torridge's naïveté; for the Arrowsmith girl it was better at least than being questioned by Mrs Mace-Hamilton; for her brothers it was an excuse to bellow with simulated mirth. Mrs Mace-Hamilton considered that the boy sounded frightful, Mrs Arrowsmith couldn't have cared less. Only Mrs Wiltshire had doubts: she thought the three men were hard on the memory of the boy, but of course had not ever said so. Tonight, after Wiltshire had recalled the time when Torridge had been convinced by Arrowsmith that Buller Yeats had dropped dead in his bath, the younger Arrowsmith boy told of a boy at his own school who'd been convinced that his sister's dog had died.

'Listen,' Arrowsmith suddenly shouted out. 'He's going to join us. Old Torridge.'

There was laughter, no one believing that Torridge was going to arrive, Mrs Arrowsmith saying to herself that her husband was pitiful when he became as drunk as this.

'I thought it would be a gesture,' Arrowsmith said. 'Honestly. He's looking in for coffee.'

'You bloody devil, Arrows,' Wiltshire said, smacking the table with the palm of his hand.

'He's in the button business,' Arrowsmith shouted. 'Torridge's, you know.'

As far as Wiltshire and Mace-Hamilton could remember, Torridge had never featured in an Old Boys' magazine. No news of his career had been printed, and certainly no obituary. It was typical, somehow, of Arrowsmith to have winkled him out. It was part and parcel of him to want to add another dimension to the joke, to recharge its batteries. For the sight of Torridge in middle age would surely make funnier the reported anecdotes.

'After all, what's wrong,' demanded Arrowsmith noisily, 'with old school pals all meeting up? The more the merrier.'

He was a bully, Mrs Wiltshire thought: all three of them were bullies.

Torridge arrived at half-past nine. The hair that had been like a mouse's fur was still like that. It hadn't greyed any more; the scalp hadn't balded. He hadn't run to fat; in middle age he'd thinned down a bit. There was even a lankiness about him now, which was reflected in his movements. At school he had moved slowly, as though with caution. Jauntily attired in a pale linen suit, he crossed the dining-room of the Woodlands Hotel with a step as nimble as a tap dancer's.

No one recognized him. To the three men who'd been at school with him the man who approached their dinner table was a different person, quite unlike the figure that existed in the minds of the wives and children.

'My dear Arrows,' he said, smiling at Arrowsmith. The smile was different too, a brittle snap of a smile that came and went in a matter-of-fact way. The eyes that had been small didn't seem so in his thinner face. They flashed with a gleam of some kind, matching the snap of his smile.

'Good God, it's never old Porridge!' Arrowsmith's voice was slurred. His face had acquired the beginnings of an alcoholic crimson, sweat glistened on his forehead.

'Yes, it's old Porridge,' Torridge said quietly. He held his hand out towards Arrowsmith and then shook hands with Wiltshire and Mace-Hamilton. He was introduced to their wives, with whom he shook hands also. He was introduced to the children, which involved further handshaking. His hand was cool and rather bony: they felt it should have been damp.

'You're nicely in time for coffee, Mr Torridge,' Mrs Mace-Hamilton said.

'Brandy more like,' Arrowsmith suggested. 'Brandy, old chap?'

'Well, that's awfully kind of you, Arrows. Chartreuse I'd prefer, really.'

A waiter drew up a chair. Room was made for Torridge between Mrs Mace-Hamilton and the Arrowsmith boys. It was a frightful mistake, Wiltshire was thinking. It was mad of Arrowsmith.

Mace-Hamilton examined Torridge across the dinner table. The old Torridge would have said he'd rather not have anything alcoholic, that a cup of tea and a biscuit were more his line in the evenings. It was impossible to imagine this man saying his dad had a button business. There was a suavity about him that made Mace-Hamilton uneasy. Because of what had been related to his wife and the other wives and their children he felt he'd been caught out in a lie, yet in fact that wasn't the case.

The children stole glances at Torridge, trying to see him as the boy who'd been described to them, and failing to. Mrs Arrowsmith said to herself that all this stuff they'd been told over the years had clearly been rubbish. Mrs Mace-Hamilton was bewildered. Mrs Wiltshire was pleased.

'No one ever guessed,' Torridge said, 'what became of R. A. J. Fisher.' He raised the subject suddenly, without introduction.

'Oh God, Fisher,' Mace-Hamilton said.

'Who's Fisher?' the younger of the Arrowsmith boys enquired.

Torridge turned to flash his quick smile at the boy. 'He left,' he said. 'In unfortunate circumstances.'

'You've changed a lot, you know,' Arrowsmith said. 'Don't you think he's changed?' he asked Wiltshire and Mace-Hamilton.

'Out of recognition,' Wiltshire said.

Torridge laughed easily. 'I've become adventurous. I'm a late developer, I suppose.'

'What kind of unfortunate circumstances?' the younger Arrowsmith boy asked. 'Was Fisher expelled?'

'Oh no, not at all,' Mace-Hamilton said hurriedly.

'Actually,' Torridge said, 'Fisher's trouble all began with the writing of a note. Don't you remember? He put it in my pyjamas. But it wasn't for me at all.'

He smiled again. He turned to Mrs Wiltshire in a way that seemed polite, drawing her into the conversation. 'I was an innocent at school. But innocence eventually slips away. I found my way about eventually.'

'Yes, of course,' she murmured. She didn't like him, even though she was glad he wasn't as he might have been. There was malevolence in him, a ruthlessness that seemed like a work of art. He seemed like a work of art himself, as though in losing the innocence he spoke of he had recreated himself.

'I often wonder about Fisher,' he remarked.

The Wiltshire twins giggled. 'What's so great about this bloody Fisher?' the older Arrowsmith boy murmured, nudging his brother with an elbow.

'What're you doing these days?' Wiltshire asked, interrupting Mace-Hamilton, who had also begun to say something.

'I make buttons,' Torridge replied. 'You may recall my father made buttons.'

'Ah, here're the drinks,' Arrowsmith rowdily observed.

'I don't much keep up with the school,' Torridge said as the waiter placed a glass of Chartreuse in front of him. 'I don't so much as think about it except for wondering about poor old Fisher. Our headmaster was a cretin,' he informed Mrs Wiltshire.

Again the Wiltshire twins giggled. The Arrowsmith girl yawned and her brothers giggled also, amused that the name of Fisher had come up again.

'You will have coffee, Mr Torridge?' Mrs Mace-Hamilton offered, for the waiter had brought a fresh pot to the table. She held it poised above a cup. Torridge smiled at her and nodded. She said:

'Pearl buttons d'you make?'

'No, not pearl.'

'Remember those awful packet peas we used to have?' Arrowsmith enquired. Wiltshire said:

'Use plastics at all? In your buttons, Porridge?'

'No, we don't use plastics. Leathers, various leathers. And horn. We specialize.'

'How very interesting!' Mrs Mace-Hamilton exclaimed.

'No, no. It's rather ordinary really.' He paused, and then added, 'Someone once told me that Fisher went into a timber business. But of course that was far from true.'

'A chap was expelled a year ago,' the younger Arrowsmith boy said, contributing this in order to cover up a fresh outburst of sniggering. 'For stealing a transistor.'

Torridge nodded, appearing to be interested. He asked the Arrowsmith boys where they were at school. The older one said Charterhouse and his brother gave the name of his preparatory school. Torridge nodded again and asked their sister and she said she was waiting to go to university. He had quite a chat with the Wiltshire twins about their school. They considered it pleasant the way he bothered, seeming genuinely to want to know. The giggling died away.

'I imagined Fisher wanted me for his *bijou*,' he said when all that was over, still addressing the children. 'Our place was riddled with fancy larks like that. Remember?' he added, turning to Mace-Hamilton.

'*Bijou*?' one of the twins asked before Mace-Hamilton could reply.

'A male tart,' Torridge explained.

The Arrowsmith boys gaped at him, the older one with his mouth actually open. The Wiltshire twins began to giggle again. The Arrowsmith girl frowned, unable to hide her interest.

'The Honourable Anthony Swain,' Torridge said, 'was no better than a whore.'

Mrs Arrowsmith, who for some minutes had been engaged with her own thoughts, was suddenly aware that the man who was in the button business was talking about sex. She gazed diagonally across the table at him, astonished that he should be talking in this way.

'Look here, Torridge,' Wiltshire said, frowning at him and shaking his head. With an almost imperceptible motion he gestured towards the wives and children.

'Andrews and Butler. Dillon and Pratt. Tothill and Goldfish Stewart. Your dad,' Torridge said to the Arrowsmith girl, 'was always very keen. Sainsbury Major in particular.'

'Now look here,' Arrowsmith shouted, beginning to get to his feet and then changing his mind.

'My gosh, how they broke chaps' hearts, those three!'

'Please don't talk like this.' It was Mrs Wiltshire who protested, to everyone's surprise, most of all her own. 'The children are quite young, Mr Torridge.'

Her voice had become a whisper. She could feel herself reddening with embarrassment, and a little twirl of sickness occurred in her stomach. Deferentially, as though appreciating the effort she had made, Torridge apologized.

'I think you'd better go,' Arrowsmith said.

'You were right about God Harvey, Arrows. Gay as a grig he was, beneath that cassock. So was Old Frosty, as a matter of fact.'

'Really!' Mrs Mace-Hamilton cried, her bewilderment turning into outrage. She glared at her husband, demanding with her eyes that instantly something should be done. But her husband and his two friends were briefly stunned by what Torridge had claimed for God Harvey. Their schooldays leapt back at them, possessing them for a vivid moment: the dormitory, the dining-hall, the glances and the invitations, the meetings behind Chapel. It was somehow in keeping with the school's hypocrisy that God Harvey had had inclinations himself, that a rumour begun as an outrageous joke should have contained the truth.

'As a matter of fact,' Torridge went on, 'I wouldn't be what I am if it hadn't been for God Harvey. I'm what they call queer,' he explained to the children. 'I perform sexual acts with men.'

'For God's sake, Torridge,' Arrowsmith shouted, on his feet, his face the colour of ripe strawberry, his watery eyes quivering with rage.

'It was nice of you to invite me tonight, Arrows. Our *alma mater* can't be too proud of chaps like me.'

People spoke at once, Mrs Mace-Hamilton and Mrs Wiltshire, all three men. Mrs Arrowsmith sat still. What she was thinking was that she had become quietly drunk while her husband had more boisterously reached the same condition. She was thinking, as well, that by the sound of things he'd possessed as a boy a sexual urge that was a lot livelier than the one he'd once exposed her to and now hardly ever did. With boys who had grown to be men he had had a whale of a time. Old Frosty had been a kind of Mr Chips, she'd been told. She'd never ever heard of Sainsbury Major or God Harvey.

'It's quite disgusting,' Mrs Mace-Hamilton's voice cried out above the other voices. She said the police should be called. It was scandalous to have to listen to unpleasant conversation like this. She began to say the children should leave the dining-room, but changed her mind because it appeared that Torridge himself was about to go. 'You're a most horrible man,' she cried.

Confusion gathered, like a fog around the table. Mrs Wiltshire, who knew that her husband had committed adultery with Mrs Arrowsmith, felt another bout of nerves in her stomach. 'Because she was starved, that's why,' her husband had almost violently confessed when she'd discovered. 'I was putting her out of her misery.' She had wept then and he had comforted her as best he could. She had not told him that he had never succeeded in arousing in her the desire to make love: she had always assumed that to be a failing in herself, but now for some reason she was not so sure. Nothing had been directly said that might have caused this doubt, but an instinct informed Mrs Wiltshire, that the doubt should be there. The man beside her smiled his brittle, malevolent smile at her, as if in sympathy.

With his head bent over the table and his hands half hiding his face, the younger Arrowsmith boy examined his father by glancing through his fingers. There were men whom his parents warned him against, men who would sit beside you in buses or try to give you a lift in a car. This man who had come tonight, who had been such a joke up till now, was apparently one of these, not a joke at all. And the confusion was greater: at one time, it seemed, his father had been like that too.

The Arrowsmith girl considered her father also. Once she had walked into a room in Lagos to find her mother in the arms of an African clerk. Ever since she had felt sorry for her father. There'd been an unpleasant scene at the time, she'd screamed at her mother and later in a fury had told her father what she'd seen. He'd nodded, wearily seeming not to be surprised, while her mother had miserably wept. She'd put her arms around her father, comforting him; she'd felt no mercy for her mother, no sympathy or understanding. The scene formed vividly in her mind as she sat at the dinner table: it appeared to be relevant in the confusion and yet not clearly so. Her parents' marriage was messy, messier than it had looked. Across the table her mother grimly smoked, focusing her eyes with difficulty. She smiled at her daughter, a soft, inebriated smile.

The older Arrowsmith boy was also aware of the confusion. Being at a school where the practice which had been spoken of was common enough, he could easily believe the facts that had been thrown about. Against his will, he was forced to imagine what he had never imagined before: his father and his friends as schoolboys, engaged in passion with other boys. He might have been cynical about this image but he could not. Instead it made him want to gasp. It knocked away the smile that had been on his face all evening.

The Wiltshire twins unhappily stared at the white tablecloth, here and there stained with wine or gravy. They, too, found they'd lost the urge to smile and instead shakily blinked back tears.

'Yes, perhaps I'd better go,' Torridge said.

With impatience Mrs Mace-Hamilton looked at her husband, as if expecting him to hurry Torridge off or at least to say something. But Mace-Hamilton remained silent. Mrs Mace-Hamilton licked her lips, preparing to speak herself. She changed her mind.

'Fisher didn't go into a timber business,' Torridge said, 'because poor old Fisher was dead as a doornail. Which is why our cretin of a headmaster, Mrs Mace-Hamilton, had that Assembly.'

'Assembly?' she said. Her voice was weak, although she'd meant it to sound matter-of-fact and angry.

'There was an Assembly that no one understood. Poor old Fisher had strung himself up in a barn on his father's farm. I discovered that,' Torridge said, turning to Arrowsmith, 'years later: from God Harvey actually. The poor chap left a note but the parents didn't care to pass it on. I mean it was for you, Arrows.'

Arrowsmith was still standing, hanging over the table. 'Note?' he said. 'For me?'

'Another note. Why d'you think he did himself in, Arrows?'

Torridge smiled, at Arrowsmith and then around the table.

'None of that's true,' Wiltshire said.

'As a matter of fact it is.'

He went, and nobody spoke at the dinner table. A body of a schoolboy hung from a beam in a barn, a note on the straw below his dangling feet. It hung in the confusion that had been caused, increasing the confusion. Two waiters hovered by a sideboard, one passing the time by arranging sauce bottles, the other folding napkins into cone shapes. Slowly Arrowsmith sat down again. The silence continued as the conversation of Torridge continued to haunt the dinner table. He haunted it himself, with his brittle smile and his tap dancer's elegance, still faithful to the past in which he had so signally failed, triumphant in his middle age.

Then Mrs Arrowsmith quite suddenly wept and the Wiltshire twins wept and Mrs Wiltshire comforted them. The Arrowsmith girl got up and walked away, and Mrs Mace-Hamilton turned to the three men and said they should be ashamed of themselves, allowing all this to happen.

Flights of Fancy

In her middle age Sarah Machaen had developed the habit of nostalgically slipping back into her childhood. Often, on a bus or at a dinner party, she would find herself caught in a mesh of voices and events that had been real forty years ago. There were summer days in the garden of her father's rectory, her brothers building another tree-house, her father asleep in a brown-and-orange-striped deck-chair. In the cool untidy kitchen she helped her mother to make strawberry cake; she walked with the old spaniel, Dodge, to Mrs Rolleston's Post Office and Stores in the village, her shoes dusty as soon as she took a single step. On wet winter afternoons, cosy by the fire in the drawing-room, the family played consequences or card games, or listened to the wireless. The war brought black-out curtains and rationing, and two evacuees.

At forty-seven Sarah Machaen was reconciled to the fact that her plainness wasn't going to go away. As a child she had believed that growing up would put paid to the face she couldn't care for, that it would develop prettily in girlhood, as the ugly duckling had developed. 'Oh, it's quite common,' she heard a woman say to her mother. 'Many a beauty was as plain as a pikestaff to begin with.' But no beauty dawned in Sarah's face.

Her older brother became a clergyman like their father, her younger one an engineer. She herself, in 1955, found employment she enjoyed in the firm of Pollock-Brown Lighting. She became secretary to Mr Everend, who at that time was assistant to the director in charge of publicity, whom he subsequently succeeded. The office was a busy one, and although Sarah had earlier had ambitions to work in the more cultural ambience of a museum or a publishing house she soon found herself taking a genuine interest in Pollock-Brown's range of well-designed products: light fittings that were increasingly specified by architects of taste all over Britain and Europe. The leaflets that passed through the Pollock-Brown publicity department constantly drew attention to the quality and the elegance that placed Pollock-Brown ahead of the field; the photographs in trade advertisements made many of the Pollock-Brown fitments seem like works of art. Sarah could discover no reason to argue with these claims, and was content to let Pollock-Brown become her daytime world, as a museum or a publishing house might have been. Her status in the organization rose with the status of Mr Everend, who often stated that he wished to be served by no other secretary. The offices of the firm were in London, a large block of glass and concrete in Kingsway. Twenty miles away, in factories just beyond the Green Belt, the manufacture of the well-designed fitments took place.

Since 1960 Sarah had had a flat in Tufnell Park, which was quite convenient, the Northern line all the way to Tottenham Court Road, the Central on to Holborn. The brother who was a clergyman lived in Harrogate and did not often come to London; the one who was an engineer had spent his life building dams in Africa and returned to England only with reluctance. Sarah's parents, happily married for almost fifty years, had died within a month of one another in 1972, sharing a room in an old-persons' home that catered exclusively for the clergy and their wives.

But even so Sarah was not alone. She had many friends, made in Pollock-Brown and through the Bach choir in which she sang, and some that dated back to her schooldays. She was a popular choice as a godmother. She was invited to parties and went regularly to the theatre or to concerts, often with her friend Anna, whose marriage had failed six years ago. She lived on her own in the flat in Tufnell Park now: when first she'd lived there she'd shared it with a girl called Elizabeth, with whom she'd been at school. Elizabeth, a librarian, was bespectacled and rather fat, a chatterbox and a compulsive nibbler. She hadn't been all that easy to live with but Sarah knew her well and appreciated her kindness and her warmth. It had astonished her when Elizabeth began to go out with a man she'd met in her library, a man whom she later became engaged to. It seemed to Sarah that Elizabeth wasn't the kind of girl who became engaged, any more than she herself was, yet in the end Elizabeth married and went to live in Cricklewood, where she reared a family. Sarah took in another girl but this time the arrangement didn't work because the new girl, a stranger to Sarah, kept having men in her bedroom. Sarah asked her to go, and did not attempt to replace her.

Almost every weekend she made the journey to Cricklewood to see Elizabeth and her family. The children loved her and often said so. Elizabeth's husband enjoyed chatting to her, drinking gin and tonic, to which Sarah had become mildly addicted. It was a home-from-home, and it wasn't the only one. No husband disliked Sarah. No one found her a bore. She brought small presents when she visited. She struck the right note and fitted in.

Now and again these friends attempted to bring Sarah into contact with suitable men, but nothing ever came of such efforts. There'd been, while she was still at the secretarial college she'd attended, a man called George, who had taken her out, who had embraced her and had once, in his bed-sitting-room, begun to undress her. She had enjoyed these attentions even though their perpetrator was not a person she greatly cared for. She had been quite prepared to permit him to take her clothes off and then to proceed in whatever way he wished, but he had suddenly appeared to change his mind, to lose interest or to develop nerves, it wasn't clear which. She'd felt quite sick and shaky, sitting on his lap in an armchair, while his fingers fell away from the buttons he'd been undoing. Awkwardly she had nuzzled her nose into his neck, hoping this would induce him to continue, but his arms, which hung down on either side of the armchair, had remained where they were. A moment later he'd clambered to his feet and had filled a kettle for tea. As an experience, it was one that Sarah was destined never to forget. She recalled it often as she lay alone in bed at night, extending her companion's desire and sometimes changing his identity before she did so. In middle age his bed-sitting-room was still as vivid as it had ever been, and she could still recall the feel of the blood draining away from her face and the sickness that developed when he seemed suddenly to reject her.

Sarah was not obsessed by this and she made efforts not to dwell on it, but it often struck her that it was unfair that she should be deprived of a side of life which was clearly pleasant. There was an assumption that girls without much in the way of looks didn't possess the kind of desire that looks appeared to indicate, but this of course was not true. When politely dancing with men or even when just talking to them she had more than once experienced what privately she designated as a longing to be loved by them. Her expression on these occasions did not ever betray her, and her plainness trailed a modesty that prevented her from ever being forward. She learnt to live with her frustrations, wondering as she grew older if some elderly widower, no longer moved by physical desire but seeking only an agreeable companion, might not one day propose marriage to her. She might accept, she vaguely thought. She wasn't at all sure what it would be like being married to an elderly widower, but some instinct informed her that she'd prefer it to being on her own in the flat in Tufnell Park all through her middle age. Alone at night her thoughts went further, creating the widower as a blind man who could not even sense her plainness, whose fingers caressing her face felt a beauty that was not there. Other scenes took place in which the widower ended by finding a vigour he thought he'd lost. It often astonished her in the daytime that she had imagined so.

On the other hand, her friend Anna, the one whose marriage had failed, lived a rackety life with men and sometimes said she envied Sarah the quietness of hers. Now and again, having dinner together after a visit to the theatre or a concert, Anna would refer to the lovers she'd had, castigating most of them as selfish. 'How right you are,' she had a way of saying, 'to steer clear of all that.' Sarah always laughed when Anna said that, pointing out that it hadn't been her choice. 'Oh, choice or not, by God you're better off,' Anna would insist. 'I really swear.' Then Anna met a Canadian, who married her and took her off to Montreal.

That was another person to miss, as she had missed the people of her childhood, and her friend Elizabeth – for it naturally wasn't the same after Elizabeth married. She had often thought of telling Anna about her longing for a relationship with a man, but shyness had always held her back. The shyness had to do with not knowing enough, with having so little experience, the very opposite of Anna. Yet once, when they'd both had quite a lot of wine to drink, she'd almost asked her what she should do. 'Just because I'm so wretchedly plain,' she'd almost said, 'doesn't mean I can do without things.' But she hadn't said that, and now Anna was gone and there was no one else who wouldn't have been just a little shocked to hear stuff like that. Not in a million years could she have said it to Elizabeth.

And so it remained. No widower, elderly or otherwise, proposed marriage; no blind man proclaimed love. What happened was rather different from all that. Once a year, as Christmas approached, Pollock-Brown held its annual staff party at the factories beyond the Green Belt. Executive and clerical staff from the building in Kingsway met the factory workers in their huge canteen, richly decorated now with Christmas hangings. Dancing took place. There was supper, and unlimited drinks at the firm's expense. The managing director made a speech and the present chairman, Sir Robert Quinn, made a speech also, in the course of which he thanked his workers for their loyalty. A thousand Pollock-Brown employees let their hair down, typists and secretaries, directors, executives who would soon be directors, tea-women, mould-makers, van-drivers, lorry-drivers, warehousemen, finishers, polishers. In a formal manner Mr Everend always reserved the first dance for Sarah and she felt quite proud to be led on to the floor in the wake of Sir Robert and his secretary and the managing director and his secretary, a woman called Mrs Mykers. After that the Christmas spirit really got going. Paper hats were supplied to everyone, including Sir Robert Quinn, Mr Everend, and the managing director. One of the dispatch boys had once poured a little beer over Mr Everend, because Mr Everend always so entered into the spirit of things that horseplay with beer seemed quite in order. There were tales, many of them true, of sexual congress in out-of-the way corners, particularly in store rooms.

'Hullo,' a girl said, addressing Sarah in what for this one evening of the year was called the Ladies' Powder Room. *Female Staff* a painted sign more ordinarily stated, hidden now beneath the festive card that bore the grander title.

'Hullo,' Sarah replied, unable to place the girl. She was small, with short black hair that was smooth and hung severely straight on either side of her face. She was pretty: an oval face with eyes almost as black as her hair, and a mouth that slightly pouted, dimpling her cheeks. Sarah frowned as the dimples came and went. The girl smiled in a friendly way. She said her name was Sandra Pond.

'You're Everend's girl,' she added.

'Secretary,' Sarah said.

'I meant that.' She laughed and the dimples danced about. 'I didn't mean nothing suspect, Miss Machaen.'

'Suspect?'

'You know.'

She wore a black dress with lace at her neck and wrists. Her feet were neat, in shiny black shoes. Her legs were slim, black-clad also. How nice to be so attractive! Sarah thought, a familiar reflection when meeting such girls for the first time. It wouldn't even matter having a slack, lower-class accent, as this girl had. You'd give up a lot for looks like that.

'I'm in polishing,' the girl said. 'Your plastic lamp-shades.'

'You don't sound as if you like it.' Sarah laughed. She glanced at herself in the mirror above one of the two wash-basins. Hurriedly she looked away.

'It's clean,' Sandra Pond said. 'A polishing machine's quite clean to operate.'

'Yes, I suppose it would be.'

'Care for a drink at all, Miss Machaen?'

'A drink?'

'Don't you drink, Miss Machaen?'

'Well, yes, but –'

'We're meant to mix at a thing like this. The peasants and the privileged.' She gave a rasping, rather unattractive laugh. 'Come on,' she said.

Beneath the prettiness there was something hard about her. There were flashes of bitterness in the way she'd said 'the peasants and the privileged', and in the way she'd laughed and in the way she walked out of the Ladies' Powder Room. She walked impatiently, as if she disliked being at the Christmas party. She was a prickly girl, Sarah said to herself. She wasn't at all glad that she'd fallen into conversation with her.

They sat down at a small table at the edge of the dance-floor. 'What d'you drink?' the girl said, immediately getting to her feet again in an edgy way. 'Whisky?'

'I'd like a gin and tonic.'

The dimples came and went, cracking the brittleness. The smile seemed disposed to linger but did not. 'Don't go away now,' the slack voice commanded as she jerked quickly away herself.

'Someone looking after you?' Dancing with the wife of the dispatch manager, Mr Everend shouted jollily at Sarah. He wore a scarlet, cone-shaped paper hat. The wife of the dispatch manager was eyeing, over his shoulder, a sales executive called Chumm, with whom, whenever it was possible, she went to bed.

'Yes, thanks, Mr Everend,' Sarah answered, waving a hand to indicate that he mustn't feel responsible for her.

'Horrid brute, that man,' Sandra Pond said, returning with their drinks. 'Cheers,' she said, raising a glass of what looked like whisky and touching Sarah's glass with it.

'Cheers,' Sarah said, although it was a salutation she disliked.

'It began last year here,' Sandra said, pointing with her glass at the dispatch manager's wife. 'Her and Chumm.'

'I've never met her actually.'

'You didn't miss nothing. That Chumm's a villain.'

'He has that reputation.'

'He screwed her in a store-room. I walked in on top of them.'

'Oh.'

'Oh in-bloody-deed.' She laughed. 'You like gin and t, d'you? Your drink, Miss Machaen?'

'Please call me Sarah. Yes, I like it.'

'Whisky mac this is. I love booze. You like it, Sarah?'

'Yes, I do rather.'

'Birds of a feather.' She laughed, and paused. 'I seen you last year. Dancing with Everend and that. I noticed you.'

'I've been coming for a long time.'

'How long you been at P-B, then?'

'Since 1960.'

'Jesus!'

'I know.'

'I was only a nipper in 1960. What age'd you say I was, Sarah?'

'Twenty-five?'

'Thirty. Don't look it, do I?'

'No, indeed.'

'You live alone, do you, Sarah?'

'Yes, I do. In Tufnell Park.'

'Nice?'

'It is quite nice.'

Sandra Pond nodded repeatedly. Tufnell Park was very nice indeed, she said, extremely nice.

'You sit there, Sarah,' she said. 'I'm going to get you another drink.'

'Oh, no. Let me. Please.' She began to get to her feet, but Sandra Pond shot out a hand, a movement like a whip's, instantly restraining her. Her small fingers pressed into the flesh of Sarah's arm. 'Stay right where you are,' she said.

An extraordinary thought occurred to Sarah as she watched the girl moving rapidly away with their two empty glasses: Sandra Pond wanted to share her flat.

'Now, now, now,' Mr Priddy from Accounts admonished, large and perspiring, staring down at her through thick spectacles. He reached for her, seemingly unaware of her protestations. His knees pressed into hers, forcing them into waltztime.

'They do an awful lot of good, these things,' Mr Priddy confidently remarked. 'People really get a chance.' He added something else, something about people getting a chance to chew the rag. Sarah nodded. 'We've had a miracle of a year,' Mr Priddy said. 'In spite of everything.'

She could see Sandra Pond standing with two full glasses, looking furious. She tried to smile at her through the dancing couples, to make some indication with her eyes that she'd had no option about dancing with Mr Priddy. But Sandra Pond, glaring into the dancers, hadn't even noticed her yet.

'Mrs Priddy couldn't come,' Mr Priddy told her. 'Tummy trouble.'

She said she was sorry, trying to remember what Mrs Priddy looked like and failing in that.

'She gets it,' Mr Priddy said.

Sandra Pond had seen them and was looking aggrieved now, her head on one side. She sat down at the table and lit a cigarette. She crossed her thin legs.

'Thank you very much,' Sarah said, and Mr Priddy smiled graciously and went away to do his duty by some other lone woman.

'Can't stand him,' Sandra Pond said. 'Clammy blooming hands.'

Sarah drank some gin and tonic. 'I say, you know,' a man called out, 'it's a hell of a party, eh?'

He wasn't sober. He swayed, with a glass in one hand, peering down at them. He was in charge of some department or other, Sarah couldn't remember which. He spent a great deal of time in a pub near the Kingsway building, not going home until the last minute. He lived with a sister, someone had once told her.

'Hey, who's she?' he demanded, wagging his glass at Sandra. 'Who's this one, Sarah?'

'Sandra Pond,' Sarah said sharply. 'In the polishing department.'

'Polishing, eh? Nice party, Sandra?'

'If you like the type of thing.'

'The drink's good.'

'It's free, you mean.'

'That's what I mean, girlie.'

He went away. Sandra Pond laughed. She was a little drunk herself, she confessed. It took her like that, quite suddenly, after the fifth or sixth whisky mac. 'How about you, Sarah?'

'I'm just about right.'

'D'you know what I'd like to do?'

'What?'

'Oh, no.' She looked away, coyly pouting, the dimples in her cheeks working. 'No, I couldn't say,' she said. 'I couldn't tell you, Sarah.'

The notion that the girl wanted to share her flat had remained with Sarah while she'd danced with Mr Priddy and while the man had swayed in front of them, saying the party was nice. It was still there now, at the very front of her mind, beginning to dominate everything else. It seemed to be an unspoken thought between them, deliberately placed there by the girl while she'd been saying that Tufnell Park was nice.

'Actually I'm quite pissed,' the girl was saying now, giggling.

The expression grated on Sarah. She could never see why people had to converse in an obscene way. It didn't in any way whatsoever make sense for the girl to say she was urinated when she meant drunk.

'Sorry,' Sandra Pond said.

'It's all right.'

'I offended you. It showed in your face. I'm sorry, Sarah.'

'Actually, it's time for me to go home.'

'Oh, God, I've driven you away.'

'It's not that.'

'Have another drink. I've spoiled your evening.'

'No, not at all.'

'You know how it is: everything smooth and unruffled and then everything going bonk! You know, Sarah?'

Sarah frowned, shaking her head.

'Like if you looked down a well and then you dropped a stone in. Know what I mean? There'd be a disturbance. I had a friend said that to me once, we was very close. Hazel she was called.'

'Well, I do know what she meant of course –'

'D'you really, Sarah?'

'Yes, of course.'

'She was talking about people, see. What happens to people. Like you meet someone, Sarah.'

It was the kind of cliché that Sarah didn't care for, still water and someone throwing a stone. It was silly and half-baked, but typical in a way of what was said at an office party.

'She was like that,' Sandra Pond said. 'She talked like that, did Hazel.'

'I see.'

'When she met me, she meant. A disturbance.'

'Yes.'

'Merry Christmas then, Sarah.'

'Merry Christmas.'

As she edged her way around the dance-floor, she felt glad she'd escaped and was thinking that when Mr Everend collided with her almost. He always gave her a lift home after the Christmas party. He offered to now, sensing that she was ready to go. But he insisted on a last dance and while they danced he thanked her for all the work she'd done during the year, and for being patient with him, which she really hadn't had to. 'A last drink,' he said as they stepped off the dance-floor, just beside where the drinks table was. He found her a gin and tonic and had a tomato juice himself.

In the arms of a black-haired youth, Sandra Pond danced by while the band played 'Just One of Those Things'; her thin arms were around the youth's neck, her head lolled on his shoulder. Her eyes were blank, Sarah noticed in the moment it took the couple to dance by.

'Merry Christmas, Sarah,' Mr Everend said.

'Merry Christmas, Mr Everend.'

*

That night she lay in bed, feeling woozy after all the gin and tonic. Not really wishing to, and yet slowly and quite carefully, she went over everything that had happened since Sandra Pond had addressed her in the Ladies' Powder Room. She remembered the grip of the girl's fingers and the pout of her lips and her bitterness when she spoke of Pollock-Brown and even when she didn't. Had she really walked in on the dispatch manager's wife and Chumm in a store-room? It was odd the way she'd spoken to her in the Ladies' Powder Room, odd the way she'd spoken of Tufnell Park. For some minutes she imagined Sandra Pond sharing her flat with her as Elizabeth had, sharing the things in the kitchen cupboards, the Special K and the marmalade and the sugar. The girl was seventeen years younger, she didn't have the same background or presumably the same interests. Sarah smiled a little in the darkness, thinking about what people would say if she began to share her flat with a polisher of plastic lampshades. People would think she was mad, her brother and his wife in their Harrogate rectory, her other brother and his wife in Africa, the friends whose parties she went to, the Bach choir, Elizabeth, Anna in Montreal. And of course they would all be right. She was well-to-do and middle-aged and plain. Side by side with Mr Everend she had found her way to the top of the firm. She would retire one day and that would be that. It didn't make sense to share a flat with someone like Sandra Pond, but she sensed that had she stayed in Sandra Pond's company the flat would have been openly mentioned. And yet surely it must be as clear to Sandra Pond as it would be to everyone else that they'd make a most ill-assorted couple? What was in the girl's mind, that she could see the picture so differently? Thinking about it, Sarah could find only a single piece of common ground between them. It wasn't even properly real, based neither on a process of deduction or indeed of observation. It was an instinct that Sandra Pond, unlike Elizabeth or Anna, wouldn't marry. And for some reason Sarah sensed that Sandra Pond wouldn't be difficult, as the girl she'd tried to share the flat with after Elizabeth's departure had been. Her mind rebelliously wandered, throwing up flights of fancy that she considered silly almost as soon as they came to her, flights of fancy in which she educated Sandra Pond and discovered in her an intelligence that was on a par with her own, in which slowly a real friendship developed, and why should it not? Clearly there was a lot that Sandra Pond didn't know. Sarah doubted that the girl had ever been inside a theatre in her life, except maybe to see something like the Black and White Minstrel Show or a Christmas pantomime. She wondered if she ever opened a book or listened to music or went to an art gallery.

For a week, at odd moments of the day, or at night, Sarah wondered about Sandra Pond. She half expected that she might hear from her, that the slack accents would drift over her telephone, suggesting a drink. But she didn't. Instead, with the flights of fancy that she considered silly, she saw herself persevering in her patience and finally rewarded as Sandra

Pond, calling on a sensitivity that had remained unaired till now, responded. Something assured Sarah that such a sensitivity was there: increasingly unable to prevent herself, she went over the course of their conversation in search of signs of it. And then, as if rejecting the extravagances of a dream in the first moments of consciousness, she would reject the fantasies that had not required a surrender to sleep. But all of them returned.

Sarah spent Christmas that year with Elizabeth and her family in Cricklewood. She relaxed with gin and tonic, listened to Elizabeth's husband complaining about his sister, from whom he'd just bought a faulty car. She received presents and gave them, she helped to cook the Christmas dinner. Preparing stuffing for the turkey, she heard herself saying:

'It's the only thing that worries me, being alone when I'm old.'

Elizabeth, plumper than ever this Christmas, expressed surprise by wrinkling her nose, which was a habit with her.

'Oh, but you manage so well.'

'Actually the future looks a little bleak.'

'Oh, Sarah, what nonsense!'

It was, and Sarah knew it was: she had learnt how to live alone. There was nothing nicer than coming back to the flat and putting a record on, pouring herself a drink and just sitting there listening to Mozart. There was nothing nicer than not having to consider someone else. She'd only shared the flat with Elizabeth in the first place because it had been necessary financially. That period was past.

'It's just that whatever shall I do when I finish at Pollock-Brown?'

'But that's years away.'

'Not really. Thirteen years. When I'm sixty.'

'They'll keep you on, surely? If you want to stay?'

'Mr Everend will be gone. I don't think I'd want to work for anyone else. No, I'll retire at sixty. According to the book.'

'But, my dear, you'll be perfectly all right.'

'I keep thinking of the flat, alone in it.'

'You've been alone in it for years.'

'I know.'

She placed more stuffing in the turkey and pressed it down with a wooden spoon. Sandra Pond would be forty-three when she was sixty. She'd probably look much the same, a little grey in her hair perhaps; she'd never run to fat.

'How are things going?' Elizabeth's husband demanded, coming into the kitchen in a breezy mood. 'Drink for Sarah?'

She smiled at him as he took tonic bottles from the fridge. 'I think she's got the change,' she heard Elizabeth saying to him later. 'Poor thing's gone all jittery.'

Sarah didn't mention the subject of her flat again that Christmas.

*

Well Im a les and I thought you was as well, the letter said. *Im sorry Sarah I didnt' mean to ofend you I didnt' no a thing about you. Ive loved other girls but not like you not as much. I really do love you Sarah. Im going to leave bloody PB because I dont want reminding every time I walk into that bloody canteen. What I wanted was to dance with you remember when I said I wanted to do something? Thats what I ment when I said that. Sandra Pond.*

Sarah tried not to think about the letter, which both upset and shocked her. She tried to forget the whole thing, the meeting with Sandra Pond and how she'd felt herself drawn towards having a friendship with the girl. It made her shiver when she thought about all that the letter suggested, it even made her feel a little sick.

Such relationships between women had been talked about at school and often occurred in newspaper reports and in books, on the television even. Sarah had occasionally wondered if this woman or that might possibly possess lesbian tendencies but she had done so without much real interest and had certainly never wondered about such tendencies in relation to herself. But now, just as she had been unable to prevent her mind from engaging in flights of fancy after her meeting with Sandra Pond, she was unable to prevent it from straying about in directions that were inspired by the girl's letter. The man called George, who over the years had become a root of many fantasies, lost his identity to that of Sandra Pond. Yet it was all different because revulsion, not present before, seemed everywhere now. Was it curiosity of a kind, Sarah wondered, that drove her on, enslaving her to fancies she did not care for? No longer did she think of them as silly; malicious rather, certainly malign, like the stuff of nightmares. Grimly she watched while Sandra Pond crossed the floor of a room, coming closer to her, smiling at her. As the man called George had, the hands of the girl undid the buttons of her dress, and then it seemed that fear was added to revulsion. 'I really do love you, Sarah,' the slack voice said, as it had said in the letter, as no other voice had ever said. The passion had a cloying kind of headiness about it, like drunkenness. It was adoration, the girl said, whispering now: it was adoration for every inch of skin and every single hair that grew from Sarah's body and every light in her eyes, and the beauty of her plainness. The pouting lips came closer to her own, the dimples danced. And Sarah, then, would find herself weeping.

She never knew why she wept and assumed it was simply an extension of her revulsion. She felt no desire to have this kind of relationship with a person of her own sex. She didn't want a girl's lips leaving lipstick on her own, she didn't want to experience their softness or the softness of the body that went with them. She didn't want to experience a smell of scent or painted fingernails.

In rational moments Sarah said to herself that as time passed this nightmare would fog over, as other occurrences in her life had fogged over with the passing of time. She had destroyed the letter almost as soon as she'd read it. She had made enquiries: Sandra Pond, as she'd promised, had left Pollock-Brown.

Sarah visited Elizabeth and her family more frequently, she spent a weekend with her brother and his wife in Harrogate, she wrote at length to her other brother, saying they must not lose touch. She forced her mind back into childhood, to which it had regularly and naturally drifted before its invasion by Sandra Pond. It was a deliberate journey now, requiring discipline and concentration, but it was possible to make. Her father ambled into the sitting-room of the rectory, the spaniel called Dodge ambling after him. The wood fire brightly burned as indoor games were played, no one sulky or out of temper. 'And the consequences were,' her brother who was an engineer said, 'fire over England.' In the sunny garden she read about the girls of the Châlet School. Her brothers, in short trousers and flannel shirts, ran about catching wasps in jam-jars. 'The peace of God,' her father's voice murmured, drifting over his small congregation. 'Of course you'll grow up pretty,' her mother softly promised, wiping away her tears.

The passing of time did help. The face of Sandra Pond faded a little, the wording of the ill-written letter became jumbled and uncertain. She would never hear of the girl again, she said to herself, and with an effort that lessened as more months passed by she continued to conjure up the distant world of the rectory.

Then, one Saturday morning in November, nearly a year after the Christmas party, Sandra Pond was there in the flesh again. She was in the Express Dairy, where Sarah always did her Saturday-morning shopping, and as soon as she saw her Sarah knew the girl had followed her into the shop. She felt faint and sickish when Sandra Pond smiled her pouting smile and the two dimples danced. She felt the blood draining away from her face and a tightening in her throat.

'Sorry,' Sandra Pond said instead of saying hullo, just standing there.

Sarah had a tin of Crosse and Blackwell's soup in one hand and a wire shopping basket in the other. She didn't know what to say. She thought she probably couldn't say anything even if she tried.

'I just wanted to say I was sorry,' Sandra Pond said. 'I've had it on my mind, Miss Machaen.'

Sarah shook her head. She put the Crosse and Blackwell's soup back on the stack of tins.

'I shouldn't have written that letter's what I mean.'

The girl didn't look well. She seemed to have a cold. She didn't look as pretty as she had at the Christmas party. She wore a brown tweed coat which wasn't very smart. Her shoes were cheap-looking.

'I don't know why I did it, Miss Machaen.'

Sarah tried to smile because she didn't want to be unkind. She ran her tongue about the inside of her mouth, which was dry, as though she'd eaten salt. She said:

'It doesn't matter.'

'It does to me. I couldn't sleep nights.'

'It was just a misunderstanding.'

Sandra Pond didn't say anything. She let a silence gather, and Sarah realized that she was doing so deliberately. Sandra Pond had come back to see how things were, to discover if, with time, the idea appealed to Sarah now, if she'd come to terms with the strangeness of it. As she stood there with the wire basket, she was aware that Sandra Pond had waited for an answer to her letter, that even before that, at the Christmas party, she had hoped for some sign. The girl was staring down at the cream-coloured tiles of the floor, her hands awkwardly by her sides.

The flights of fancy tumbled into Sarah's mind, jogging each other for precedence. They came in flashes: she and Sandra Pond sitting down to a meal, and walking into the foyer of a theatre, and looking at the 'Madonna of the Meadow' in the National Gallery, and then a scene like the scene with the man called George occurred.

Sandra Pond looked up and at once the flights of fancy snapped out, like lights extinguished. What would people say? Sarah thought again, as she had on the night of the party. What would her brothers say to see passion thumping at their sister from the eyes of Sandra Pond? What would Elizabeth say, or Anna, or Mr Everend, or her dead father and mother? Would they cry out, amazed and yet delighted, that her plainness should inspire all this, that her plainness at last was beauty? Or would they shudder with disgust?

'I can't help being,' Sandra Pond said, 'the way I am.'

Sarah shook her head, trying to make the gesture seem sympathetic. She wanted to explain that she knew the girl had come specially back, to see what passing time had done, but she could not bring herself to. To have mentioned passing time in that way would have begun another kind of conversation. It was all ridiculous, standing here in the Express Dairy.

'I just wanted to say that and to say I was sorry. Thank you for listening, Miss Machaen.'

She was moving away, the heels of her shoes making a clicking noise on the cream-tiled floor. The smooth back of her head was outlined against packets of breakfast cereals and then against stacks of Mother's Pride bread. Something about her shoulders suggested to Sarah that she was holding back tears.

'Excuse me, dear,' a woman said, poking around Sarah to reach for oxtail soup.

'Oh, sorry.' Mechanically she smiled. She felt shaky and wondered if her face had gone pale. She couldn't imagine eating any of the food she'd selected. She couldn't imagine opening a tin or unwrapping butter without being overcome by the memory of Sandra Pond's sudden advent in the shop. Her instinct was to replace the goods on the shelves and she almost did so. But it seemed too much of a gesture, and too silly. Instead she carried the wire basket to the cashier and paid for what she'd chosen, transferring everything into her shopping-bag.

She walked away from the Express Dairy, by the newsagent's and the butcher's and the Martinez Dry Cleaners, who were offering a bargain, three garments cleaned for the normal price of one. She felt, as she had when the man called George had suddenly lost interest in her body, a pain inside her somewhere.

There was a bus-stop, but Sandra Pond was not standing by it. Nor was she on the pavements that stretched on either side of a road that was busy with Saturday-morning traffic. Nor did she emerge from the telephone box, nor from the newsagent's, nor from Walton's the fruiterer's.

Sarah waited, still looking about. Sandra Pond had been genuinely sorry; she'd meant it when she'd said she'd hated causing the upset. 'Please come and have coffee,' were the words Sarah had ready to say now. 'It's really quite all right.' But she did not say them, because Sandra Pond had not lingered. And in a million years, Sarah thought, she would not ever find her.

Death in Jerusalem

'Till then,' Father Paul said, leaning out of the train window. 'Till Jerusalem, Francis.'

'Please God, Paul.' As he spoke the Dublin train began to move and his brother waved from the window and he waved back, a modest figure on the platform. Everyone said Francis might have been a priest as well, meaning that Francis's quietness and meditative disposition had an air of the cloister about them. But Francis contented himself with the running of Daly's hardware business, which his mother had run until she was too old for it. 'Are we game for the Holy Land next year?' Father Paul had asked that July. 'Will we go together, Francis?' He had brushed aside all Francis's protestations, all attempts to explain that the shop could not be left, that their mother would be confused by the absence of Francis from the house. Rumbustiously he'd pointed out that there was their sister Kitty, who was in charge of the household of which Francis and their mother were part and whose husband, Myles, could surely be trusted to look after the shop for a single fortnight. For thirty years, ever since he was seven, Francis had wanted to go to the Holy Land. He had savings which he'd never spent a penny of: you couldn't take them with you, Father Paul had more than once stated that July.

On the platform Francis watched until the train could no longer be seen, his thoughts still with his brother. The priest's ruddy countenance smiled again behind cigarette smoke; his bulk remained impressive in his clerical clothes, the collar pinching the flesh of his neck, his black shoes scrupulously polished. There were freckles on the backs of his large, strong hands; he had a fine head of hair, grey and crinkly. In an hour and a half's time the train would creep into Dublin, and he'd take a taxi. He'd spend a night in the Gresham Hotel, probably falling in with another priest, having a drink or two, maybe playing a game of bridge after his meal. That was his brother's way and always had been – an extravagant, easy kind of way, full of smiles and good humour. It was what had taken him to America and made him successful there. In order to raise money for the church that he and Father Steigmuller intended to build before 1980 he took parties of the well-to-do from San Francisco to Rome and Florence, to Chartres and Seville and the Holy Land. He was good at raising money, not just for the church but for the boys' home of which he was president, and for the Hospital of Our Saviour, and for St Mary's Old People's Home on the west side of the city. But every July he flew back to Ireland, to the town in Co.

Tipperary where his mother and brother and sister still lived. He stayed in the house above the shop which he might have inherited himself on the death of his father, which he'd rejected in favour of the religious life. Mrs Daly was eighty now. In the shop she sat silently behind the counter, in a corner by the chicken-wire, wearing only clothes that were black. In the evenings she sat with Francis in the lace-curtained sitting-room, while the rest of the family occupied the kitchen. It was for her sake most of all that Father Paul made the journey every summer, considering it his duty.

Walking back to the town from the station, Francis was aware that he was missing his brother. Father Paul was fourteen years older and in childhood had often taken the place of their father, who had died when Francis was five. His brother had possessed an envied strength and knowledge; he'd been a hero, quite often worshipped, an example of success. In later life he had become an example of generosity as well: ten years ago he'd taken their mother to Rome, and their sister Kitty and her husband two years later; he'd paid the expenses when their sister Edna had gone to Canada; he'd assisted two nephews to make a start in America. In childhood Francis hadn't possessed his brother's healthy freckled face, just as in middle age he didn't have his ruddy complexion and his stoutness and his easiness with people. Francis was slight, his sandy hair receding, his face rather pale. His breathing was sometimes laboured because of wheeziness in the chest. In the ironmonger's shop he wore a brown cotton coat.

'Hullo, Mr Daly,' a woman said to him in the main street of the town. 'Father Paul's gone off, has he?'

'Yes, he's gone again.'

'I'll pray for his journey so,' the woman promised, and Francis thanked her.

A year went by. In San Francisco another wing of the boys' home was completed, another target was reached in Father Paul and Father Steigmuller's fund for the church they planned to have built by 1980. In the town in Co. Tipperary there were baptisms and burial services and First Communions. Old Loughlin, a farmer from Bansha, died in Flynn's grocery and bar, having gone there to celebrate a good price he'd got for a heifer. Clancy, from behind the counter in Doran's drapery, married Maureen Talbot; Mr Nolan's plasterer married Miss Driscoll; Johneen Lynch married Seamus in the chip shop, under pressure from her family to do so. A local horse, from the stables on the Limerick road, was said to be an entry for the Fairyhouse Grand National, but it turned out not to be true. Every evening of that year Francis sat with his mother in the lace-curtained sitting-room above the shop. Every weekday she sat in her corner by the chicken-wire, watching while he counted out screws and weighed staples, or advised about yard brushes or tap-washers. Occasionally, on a Saturday, he visited the three Christian Brothers who lodged with Mrs Shea and afterwards he'd tell his mother about how the authority was slipping these days from the nuns and the Christian Brothers, and how Mrs Shea's elderly maid, Agnes, couldn't see to cook the food any more. His mother would nod and hardly ever speak. When he told a joke – what young Hogan had said when he'd found a nail in his egg or how Agnes had put mint sauce into a jug with milk in it – she never laughed and looked at him in surprise when he laughed himself. But Dr Grady said it was best to keep her cheered up.

All during that year Francis talked to her about his forthcoming visit to the Holy Land, endeavouring to make her understand that for a fortnight next spring he would be away from the house and the shop. He'd been away before for odd days, but that was when she'd been younger. He used to visit an aunt in Tralee, but three years ago the aunt had died and he hadn't left the town since.

Francis and his mother had always been close. Before his birth two daughters had died in infancy, and his very survival had often struck Mrs Daly as a gift. He had always been her favourite, the one among her children whom she often considered least able to stand on his own two feet. It was just like Paul to have gone blustering off to San Francisco instead of remaining in Co. Tipperary. It was just like Kitty to have married a useless man. 'There's not a girl in the town who'd touch him,' she'd said to her daughter at the time, but Kitty had been headstrong and adamant, and there was Myles now, doing nothing whatsoever except cleaning other people's windows for a pittance and placing bets in Donovan's the turf accountant's. It was the shop and the arrangement Kitty had with Francis and her mother that kept her and the children going, three of whom had already left the town, which in Mrs Daly's opinion they mightn't have done if they'd had a better type of father. Mrs Daly often wondered what her own two babies who'd died might have grown up into, and imagined they might have been like Francis, about whom she'd never had a moment's worry. Not in a million years would he give you the feeling that he was too big for his boots, like Paul sometimes did with his lavishness and his big talk of America. He wasn't silly like Kitty, or so sinful you couldn't forgive him, like you couldn't forgive Edna, even though she was dead and buried in Toronto.

Francis understood how his mother felt about the family. She'd had a hard life, left a widow early on, trying to do the best she could for everyone. In turn he did his best to compensate for the struggles and disappointments she'd suffered, cheering her in the evenings while Kitty and Myles and the youngest of their children watched the television in the kitchen. His mother had ignored the existence of Myles for ten years, ever since the day he'd taken money out of the till to pick up the odds on Gusty Spirit at Phoenix Park. And although Francis got on well enough with Myles he quite understood that there should be a long aftermath to that day. There'd been a terrible row in the kitchen, Kitty screaming at Myles and Myles telling lies and Francis trying to keep them calm, saying they'd give the old woman a heart attack.

She didn't like upsets of any kind, so all during the year before he was to visit the Holy Land Francis read the New Testament to her in order to prepare her. He talked to her about Bethlehem and Nazareth and the miracle of the loaves and fishes and all the other miracles. She kept nodding, but he often wondered if she didn't assume he was just casually referring to episodes in the Bible. As a child he had listened to such talk himself, with awe and fascination, imagining the walking on the water and the temptation in the wilderness. He had imagined the cross carried to Calvary, and the rock rolled back from the tomb, and the rising from the dead on the third day. That he was now to walk in such places seemed extraordinary to him, and he wished his mother was younger so that she could appreciate his good fortune and share it with him when she received the postcards he intended, every day, to send her. But her eyes seemed always to tell him that he was making a mistake, that somehow he was making a fool of himself by doing such a showy thing as going to the Holy Land. *I have the entire itinerary mapped out*, his brother wrote from San Francisco. *There's nothing we'll miss.*

It was the first time Francis had been in an aeroplane. He flew by Aer Lingus from Dublin to London and then changed to an El Al flight to Tel Aviv. He was nervous and he found it exhausting. All the time he seemed to be eating, and it was strange being among so many people he didn't know. 'You will taste honey such as never before,' an Israeli businessman in the seat next to his assured him. 'And Galilean figs. Make certain to taste Galilean figs.' Make certain too, the businessman went on, to experience Jerusalem by night and in the early dawn. He urged Francis to see places he had never heard of, the Yad Va-Shem, the treasures of the Shrine of the Book. He urged him to honour the martyrs of Masada and to learn a few words of Hebrew as a token of respect. He told him of a shop where he could buy mementoes and warned him against Arab street traders.

'The hard man, how are you?' Father Paul said at Tel Aviv airport, having flown in from San Francisco the day before. Father Paul had had a drink or two and he suggested another when they arrived at the Plaza Hotel in Jerusalem. It was half-past nine in the evening. 'A quick little nightcap,' Father Paul insisted, 'and then hop into bed with you, Francis.' They sat in an enormous open lounge with low, round tables and square modern armchairs. Father Paul said it was the bar.

They had said what had to be said in the car from Tel Aviv to Jerusalem. Father Paul had asked about their mother, and Kitty and Myles. He'd asked about other people in the town, old Canon Mahon and Sergeant Malone. He and Father Steigmuller had had a great year of it, he reported: as well as everything else, the boys' home had turned out two tip-top footballers. 'We'll start on a tour at half-nine in the morning,' he said. 'I'll be sitting having breakfast at eight.'

Francis went to bed and Father Paul ordered another whisky, with ice. To his great disappointment there was no Irish whisky in the hotel so he'd had to content himself with Haig. He fell into conversation with an American couple, making them promise that if they were ever in Ireland they wouldn't miss out Co. Tipperary. At eleven o'clock the barman said he was wanted at the reception desk and when Father Paul went there and announced himself he was given a message in an envelope. It was a telegram that had come, the girl said in poor English. Then she shook her head, saying it was a telex. He opened the envelope and learnt that Mrs Daly had died.

· Francis fell asleep immediately and dreamed that he was a boy again, out fishing with a friend whom he couldn't now identify.

On the telephone Father Paul ordered whisky and ice to be brought to his room. Before drinking it he took his jacket off and knelt by his bed to pray for his mother's salvation. When he'd completed the prayers he walked slowly up and down the length of the room, occasionally sipping at his whisky. He argued with himself and finally arrived at a decision.

For breakfast they had scrambled eggs that looked like yellow ice-cream, and orange juice that was delicious. Francis wondered about bacon, but Father Paul explained that bacon was not readily available in Israel.

'Did you sleep all right?' Father Paul enquired. 'Did you have the jet-lag?'

'Jet-lag?'

'A tiredness you get after jet flights. It'd knock you out for days.'

'Ah, I slept great, Paul.'

'Good man.'

They lingered over breakfast. Father Paul reported a little more of what had happened in his parish during the year, in particular about the two young footballers from the boys' home. Francis told about the decline in the cooking at Mrs Shea's boarding-house, as related to him by the three Christian Brothers. 'I have a car laid on,' Father Paul said, and twenty minutes later they walked out into the Jerusalem sunshine.

The hired car stopped on the way to the walls of the old city. It drew into a lay-by at Father Paul's request and the two men got out and looked across a wide valley dotted with houses and olive trees. A road curled along the distant slope opposite. 'The Mount of Olives,' Father Paul said. 'And that's the road to Jericho.' He pointed more particularly. 'You see that group of eight big olives? Just off the road, where the church is?'

Francis thought he did, but was not sure. There were so many olive trees, and more than one church. He glanced at his brother's pointing finger and followed its direction with his glance.

'The Garden of Gethsemane,' Father Paul said.

Francis did not say anything. He continued to gaze at the distant church, with the clump of olive trees beside it. Wild flowers were profuse on the slopes of the valley, smears of orange and blue on land that looked poor. Two Arab women herded goats.

'Could we see it closer?' he asked, and his brother said that definitely they would. They returned to the waiting car and Father Paul ordered it to the Gate of St Stephen.

Tourists heavy with cameras thronged the Via Dolorosa. Brown, barefoot children asked for alms. Stall-keepers pressed their different wares, cotton dresses, metal-ware, mementoes, sacred goods. 'Get out of the way,' Father Paul kept saying to them, genially laughing to show he wasn't being abrupt. Francis wanted to stand still and close his eyes, to visualize for a moment the carrying of the Cross. But the ceremony of the Stations, familiar to him for as long as he could remember, was unreal. Try as he would, Christ's journey refused to enter his imagination, and his own plain church seemed closer to the heart of the matter than the noisy lane he was now being jostled on. 'God damn it, of course it's genuine,' an angry American voice proclaimed, in reply to a shriller voice which insisted that cheating had taken place. The voices argued about a piece of wood, neat beneath plastic in a little box, a sample or not of the cross that had been carried.

They arrived at the Church of the Holy Sepulchre, and at the Chapel of the Nailing to the Cross, where they prayed. They passed through the Chapel of the Angel, to the tomb of Christ. Nobody spoke in the marble cell, but when they left the church Francis overheard a quiet man with spectacles saying it was unlikely that a body would have been buried within the walls of the city. They walked to Hezekiah's Pool and out of the old city at the Jaffa Gate, where their hired car was waiting for them. 'Are you peckish?' Father Paul asked, and although Francis said he wasn't they returned to the hotel.

Delay funeral till Monday was the telegram Father Paul had sent. There was an early flight on Sunday, in time for an afternoon one from London to Dublin. With luck there'd be a late train on Sunday evening and if there wasn't they'd have to fix a car. Today was Tuesday. It would give them four and a half days. *Funeral eleven Monday* the telegram at the reception desk now confirmed. 'Ah, isn't that great?' he said to himself, bundling the telegram up.

'Will we have a small one?' he suggested in the open area that was the bar. 'Or better still a big one.' He laughed. He was in good spirits in spite of the death that had taken place. He gestured at the barman, wagging his head and smiling jovially.

His face had reddened in the morning sun; there were specks of sweat on his forehead and his nose. 'Bethlehem this afternoon,' he laid down. 'Unless the jet-lag . . . ?'

'I haven't got the jet-lag.'

In the Nativity Boutique Francis bought for his mother a small metal plate with a fish on it. He had stood for a moment, scarcely able to believe it, on the spot where the manger had been, in the Church of the Nativity. As in the Via Dolorosa it had been difficult to rid the imagination of the surroundings that now were present, of the exotic Greek Orthodox trappings, the foreign-looking priests, the oriental smell. Gold, frankincense and myrrh, he'd kept thinking, for somehow the church seemed more the church of the kings than of Joseph and Mary and their child. Afterwards they returned to Jerusalem, to the Tomb of the Virgin and the Garden of Gethsemane. 'It could have been anywhere,' he heard the quiet, bespectacled sceptic remarking in Gethsemane. 'They're only guessing.'

Father Paul rested in the late afternoon, lying down on his bed with his jacket off. He slept from half-past five until a quarter-past seven and awoke refreshed. He picked up the telephone and asked for whisky and ice to be brought up and when it arrived he undressed and had a bath, relaxing in the warm water with the drink on a ledge in the tiled wall beside him. There would be time to take in Nazareth and Galilee. He was particularly keen that his brother should see Galilee because Galilee had atmosphere and was beautiful. There wasn't, in his own opinion, very much to Nazareth but it would be a pity to miss it all the same. It was at the Sea of Galilee that he intended to tell his brother of their mother's death.

We've had a great day, Francis wrote on a postcard that showed an aerial view of Jerusalem. *The Church of the Holy Sepulchre, where Our Lord's tomb is, and Gethsemane and Bethlehem. Paul's in great form.* He addressed it to his mother, and then wrote other cards, to Kitty and Myles and to the three Christian Brothers in Mrs Shea's, and to Canon Mahon. He gave thanks that he was privileged to be in Jerusalem. He read St Mark and some of St Matthew. He said his rosary.

'Will we chance the wine?' Father Paul said at dinner, not that wine was something he went in for, but a waiter had come up and put a large padded wine-list into his hand.

'Ah, no, no,' Francis protested, but already Father Paul was running his eye down the listed bottles.

'Have you local wine?' he enquired of the waiter. 'A nice red one?'

The waiter nodded and hurried away, and Francis hoped he wouldn't get drunk, the red wine on top of the whisky he'd had in the bar before the meal. He'd only had the one whisky, not being much used to it, making it last through his brother's three.

'I heard some gurriers in the bar,' Father Paul said, 'making a great song and dance about the local red wine.'

Wine made Francis think of the Holy Communion, but he didn't say so. He said the soup was delicious and he drew his brother's attention to the

586 · DEATH IN JERUSALEM

custom there was in the hotel of a porter ringing a bell and walking about with a person's name chalked on a little blackboard on the end of a rod.

'It's a way of paging you,' Father Paul explained. 'Isn't it nicer than bellowing out some fellow's name?' He smiled his easy smile, his eyes beginning to water as a result of the few drinks he'd had. He was beginning to feel the strain: he kept thinking of their mother lying there, of what she'd say if she knew what he'd done, how she'd savagely upbraid him for keeping the fact from Francis. Out of duty and humanity he had returned each year to see her because, after all, you only had the one mother. But he had never cared for her.

Francis went for a walk after dinner. There were young soldiers with what seemed to be toy guns on the streets, but he knew the guns were real. In the shop windows there were television sets for sale, and furniture and clothes, just like anywhere else. There were advertisements for some film or other, two writhing women without a stitch on them, the kind of thing you wouldn't see in Co. Tipperary. 'You want something, sir?' a girl said, smiling at him with broken front teeth. The siren of a police car or an ambulance shrilled urgently near by. He shook his head at the girl. 'No, I don't want anything,' he said, and then realized what she had meant. She was small and very dark, no more than a child. He hurried on, praying for her.

When he returned to the hotel, he found his brother in the lounge with other people, two men and two women. Father Paul was ordering a round of drinks and called out to the barman to bring another whisky. 'Ah, no, no,' Francis protested, anxious to go to his room and to think about the day, to read the New Testament and perhaps to write a few more postcards. Music was playing, coming from speakers that could not be seen.

'My brother Francis,' Father Paul said to the people he was with, and the people all gave their names, adding that they came from New York. 'I was telling them about Tipp,' Father Paul said to his brother, offering his packet of cigarettes around.

'You like Jerusalem, Francis?' one of the American women asked him, and he replied that he hadn't been able to take it in yet. Then, feeling that that didn't sound enthusiastic enough, he added that being there was the experience of a lifetime.

Father Paul went on talking about Co. Tipperary and then spoke of his parish in San Francisco, the boys' home and the two promising footballers, the plans for the new church. The Americans listened and in a moment the conversation drifted on to the subject of their travels in England, their visit to Istanbul and Athens, an argument they'd had with the Customs at Tel Aviv. 'Well, I'm for the hay-pile,' one of the men announced eventually, standing up.

The others stood up too and so did Francis. Father Paul remained where he was, gesturing in the direction of the barman. 'Sit down for a nightcap,' he urged his brother.

'Ah, no, no –' Francis began.

'Bring us two more of those,' the priest ordered with a sudden abruptness, and the barman hurried away. 'Listen,' said Father Paul. 'I've something to tell you.'

After dinner, while Francis had been out on his walk, before he'd dropped into conversation with the Americans, Father Paul had said to himself that he couldn't stand the strain. It was the old woman stretched out above the hardware shop, as stiff as a board already, with the little lights burning in her room: he kept seeing all that, as if she wanted him to, as if she was trying to haunt him. Nice as the idea was, he didn't think he could continue with what he'd planned, with waiting until they got up to Galilee.

Francis didn't want to drink any more. He hadn't wanted the whisky his brother had ordered him earlier, nor the one the Americans had ordered for him. He didn't want the one that the barman now brought. He thought he'd just leave it there, hoping his brother wouldn't see it. He lifted the glass to his lips, but he managed not to drink any.

'A bad thing has happened,' Father Paul said.

'Bad? How d'you mean, Paul?'

'Are you ready for it?' He paused. Then he said, 'She died.'

Francis didn't know what he was talking about. He didn't know who was meant to be dead, or why his brother was behaving in an odd manner. He didn't like to think it but he had to: his brother wasn't fully sober.

'Our mother died,' Father Paul said. 'I'm after getting a telegram.'

The huge area that was the lounge of the Plaza Hotel, the endless tables and people sitting at them, the swiftly moving waiters and barmen, seemed suddenly a dream. Francis had a feeling that he was not where he appeared to be, that he wasn't sitting with his brother, who was wiping his lips with a handkerchief. For a moment he appeared in his confusion to be struggling his way up the Via Dolorosa again and then in the Nativity Boutique.

'Take it easy, boy,' his brother was saying. 'Take a mouthful of whisky.'

Francis didn't obey that injunction. He asked his brother to repeat what he had said, and Father Paul repeated that their mother had died.

Francis closed his eyes and tried as well to shut away the sounds around them. He prayed for the salvation of his mother's soul. 'Blessed Virgin, intercede,' his own voice said in his mind. 'Dear Mary, let her few small sins be forgiven.'

Having rid himself of his secret, Father Paul felt instant relief. With the best of intentions in the world it had been a foolish idea to think he could maintain the secret until they arrived in a place that was perhaps the most suitable in the world to hear about the death of a person who'd been close to you. He took a gulp of his whisky and wiped his mouth with his handkerchief again. He watched his brother, waiting for his eyes to open.

'When did it happen?' Francis asked eventually.

'Yesterday.'

'And the telegram only came –'

'It came last night, Francis. I wanted to save you the pain.'

'Save me? How could you save me? I sent her a postcard, Paul.'

'Listen to me, Francis –'

'How could you save me the pain?'

'I wanted to tell you when we got up to Galilee.'

Again Francis felt he was caught in the middle of a dream. He couldn't understand his brother: he couldn't understand what he meant by saying a telegram had come last night, why at a moment like this he was talking about Galilee. He didn't know why he was sitting in this noisy place when he should be back in Ireland.

'I fixed the funeral for Monday,' Father Paul said.

Francis nodded, not grasping the significance of this arrangement. 'We'll be back there this time tomorrow,' he said.

'No need for that, Francis. Sunday morning's time enough.'

'But she's dead –'

'We'll be there in time for the funeral.'

'We can't stay here if she's dead.'

It was this, Father Paul realized, he'd been afraid of when he'd argued with himself and made his plan. If he'd have knocked on Francis's door the night before, Francis would have wanted to return immediately without seeing a single stone of the land he had come so far to be moved by.

'We could go straight up to Galilee in the morning,' Father Paul said quietly. 'You'll find comfort in Galilee, Francis.'

But Francis shook his head. 'I want to be with her,' he said.

Father Paul lit another cigarette. He nodded at a hovering waiter, indicating his need of another drink. He said to himself that he must keep his cool, an expression he was fond of.

'Take it easy, Francis,' he said.

'Is there a plane out in the morning? Can we make arrangements now?' He looked about him as if for a member of the hotel staff who might be helpful.

'No good'll be done by tearing off home, Francis. What's wrong with Sunday?'

'I want to be with her.'

Anger swelled within Father Paul. If he began to argue his words would become slurred: he knew that from experience. He must keep his cool and speak slowly and clearly, making a few simple points. It was typical of her, he thought, to die inconveniently.

'You've come all this way,' he said as slowly as he could without sounding peculiar. 'Why cut it any shorter than we need? We'll be losing a week anyway. She wouldn't want us to go back.'

'I think she would.'

He was right in that. Her possessiveness in her lifetime would have reached out across a dozen continents for Francis. She'd known what she was doing by dying when she had.

'I shouldn't have come,' Francis said. 'She didn't want me to come.'

'You're thirty-seven years of age, Francis.'

'I did wrong to come.'

'You did no such thing.'

The time he'd taken her to Rome she'd been difficult for the whole week, complaining about the food, saying everywhere was dirty. Whenever he'd spent anything she'd disapproved. All his life, Father Paul felt, he'd done his best for her. He had told her before anyone else when he'd decided to enter the priesthood, certain that she'd be pleased. 'I thought you'd take over the shop,' she'd said instead.

'What difference could it make to wait, Francis?'

'There's nothing to wait for.'

As long as he lived Francis knew he would never forgive himself. As long as he lived he would say to himself that he hadn't been able to wait a few years, until she'd passed quietly on. He might even have been in the room with her when it happened.

'It was a terrible thing not to tell me,' he said. 'I sat down and wrote her a postcard, Paul. I bought her a plate.'

'So you said.'

'You're drinking too much of that whisky.'

'Now, Francis, don't be silly.'

'You're half drunk and she's lying there.'

'She can't be brought back no matter what we do.'

'She never hurt anyone,' Francis said.

Father Paul didn't deny that, although it wasn't true. She had hurt their sister Kitty, constantly reproaching her for marrying the man she had, long after Kitty was aware she'd made a mistake. She'd driven Edna to Canada after Edna, still unmarried, had had a miscarriage that only the family knew about. She had made a shadow out of Francis although Francis didn't know it. Failing to hold on to her other children, she had grasped her last-born to her, as if she had borne him to destroy him.

'It'll be you'll say a mass for her?' Francis said.

'Yes, of course it will.'

'You should have told me.'

Francis realized why, all day, he'd been disappointed. From the moment when the hired car had pulled into the lay-by and his brother had pointed across the valley at the Garden of Gethsemane he'd been disappointed and had not admitted it. He'd been disappointed in the Via Dolorosa and in the Church of the Holy Sepulchre and in Bethlehem. He remembered the bespectacled man who'd kept saying that you couldn't be sure about anything. All the people with cameras made it impossible to think, all the jostling and pushing was distracting. When he'd said there'd been too much to take in he'd meant something different.

'Her death got in the way,' he said.

'What d'you mean, Francis?'

'It didn't feel like Jerusalem, it didn't feel like Bethlehem.'

'But it is, Francis, it is.'

'There are soldiers with guns all over the place. And a girl came up to me on the street. There was that man with a bit of the Cross. There's you, drinking and smoking in this place –'

'Now, listen to me, Francis –'

'Nazareth would be a disappointment. And the Sea of Galilee. And the Church of the Loaves and Fishes.' His voice had risen. He lowered it again. 'I couldn't believe in the Stations this morning. I couldn't see it happening the way I do at home.'

'That's nothing to do with her death, Francis. You've got a bit of jet-lag, you'll settle yourself up in Galilee. There's an atmosphere in Galilee that nobody misses.'

'I'm not going near Galilee.' He struck the surface of the table, and Father Paul told him to contain himself. People turned their heads, aware that anger had erupted in the pale-faced man with the priest.

'Quieten up,' Father Paul commanded sharply, but Francis didn't.

'She knew I'd be better at home,' he shouted, his voice shrill and reedy. 'She knew I was making a fool of myself, a man out of a shop trying to be big –'

'Will you keep your voice down? Of course you're not making a fool of yourself.'

'Will you find out about planes tomorrow morning?'

Father Paul sat for a moment longer, not saying anything, hoping his brother would say he was sorry. Naturally it was a shock, naturally he'd be emotional and feel guilty, in a moment it would be better. But it wasn't and Francis didn't say he was sorry. Instead he began to weep.

'Let's go up to your room,' Father Paul said, 'and I'll fix about the plane.'

Francis nodded but did not move. His sobbing ceased, and then he said, 'I'll always hate the Holy Land now.'

'No need for that, Francis.'

But Francis felt there was and he felt he would hate, as well, the brother he had admired for as long as he could remember. In the lounge of the Plaza Hotel he felt mockery surfacing everywhere. His brother's deceit, and the endless whisky in his brother's glass, and his casualness after a death seemed like the scorning of a Church which honoured so steadfastly the mother of its founder. Vivid in his mind, his own mother's eyes reminded him that they'd told him he was making a mistake, and upbraided him for not heeding her. Of course there was mockery everywhere, in the splinter of wood beneath plastic, and in the soldiers with guns that were not toys, and the writhing nakedness in the Holy City. He'd become part of it himself, sending postcards to the dead. Not speaking again to his brother, he went to his room to pray.

'Eight a.m., sir,' the girl at the reception desk said, and Father Paul asked that arrangements should be made to book two seats on the plane, explaining that it was an emergency, that a death had occurred. 'It will be all right, sir,' the girl promised.

He went slowly downstairs to the bar. He sat in a corner and lit a cigarette and ordered two whiskies and ice, as if expecting a companion. He drank them both himself and ordered more. Francis would return to Co. Tipperary and after the funeral he would take up again the life she had ordained for him. In his brown cotton coat he would serve customers with nails and hinges and wire. He would regularly go to Mass and to Confession and to Men's Confraternity. He would sit alone in the lace-curtained sitting-room, lonely for the woman who had made him what he was, married forever to her memory.

Father Paul lit a fresh cigarette from the butt of the last one. He continued to order whisky in two glasses. Already he could sense the hatred that Francis had earlier felt taking root in himself. He wondered if he would ever again return in July to Co. Tipperary, and imagined he would not.

At midnight he rose to make the journey to bed and found himself unsteady on his feet. People looked at him, thinking it disgraceful for a priest to be drunk in Jerusalem, with cigarette ash all over his clerical clothes.

Attracta

Attracta read about Penelope Vade in a newspaper, an item that upset her. It caused her to wonder if all her life as a teacher she'd been saying the wrong things to the children in her care. It saddened her when she thought about the faces that had passed through her schoolroom, ever since 1937. She began to feel she should have told them about herself.

She taught in a single schoolroom that hadn't altered much since the days when she'd been a pupil in it herself. There were portraits of England's kings and queens around the walls, painted by some teacher in the past. There were other pictures, added at some later date, of Irish heroes: Niall of the Nine Hostages, Lord Edward FitzGerald, Wolfe Tone and Grattan. Maps of Europe and of Ireland and of England, Wales and Scotland hung side by side. A new blackboard, attached to the wall, had ten years ago replaced the old pedestal one. The globe had always been there in Attracta's time, but since it did not designate political boundaries it wasn't much out of date. The twenty-five wooden desks more urgently needed to be replaced.

In the schoolroom Attracta taught the sixteen Protestant children of the town. The numbers had been sometimes greater in the past, and often fewer; sixteen was an average, a number she found easy to manage when divided into the four classes that the different ages demanded. The room was large, the desks arranged in groups, discipline had never been a problem. The country children brought sandwiches for lunch, the children of the town went home at midday. Attracta went home herself, to the house in North Street which she'd inherited from her Aunt Emmeline and where now she lived alone. She possessed an old blue Morris Minor but she did not often drive it to and from her schoolroom, preferring to make the journey on foot in order to get fresh air and exercise. She was a familiar figure, the Protestant teacher with her basket of groceries or exercise-books. She had never married, though twice she'd been proposed to: by an exchange clerk in the Provincial Bank and by an English visitor who'd once spent the summer in the area with his parents. All that was a long time ago now, for Attracta was sixty-one. Her predecessor in the schoolroom, Mr Ayrie, hadn't retired until he was over seventy. She had always assumed she'd emulate him in that.

Looking back on it, Attracta didn't regret that she had not married. She hadn't much cared for either of the men who'd proposed to her and she didn't mind being alone at sixty-one in her house in North Street. She regularly went to church, she had friends among the people who had been her pupils in the past. Now and again in the holidays she drove her Morris Minor to Cork for a day's shopping and possibly a visit to the Savoy or the Pavilion, although the films they offered were not as good as they'd been in the past. Being on her own was something she'd always known, having been both an only child and an orphan. There'd been tragedy in her life but she considered that she had not suffered. People had been good to her.

English Girl's Suicide in Belfast the headline about Penelope Vade said, and below it there was a photograph, a girl with a slightly crooked smile and freckled cheeks. There was a photograph of her husband in army uniform, taken a few weeks before his death, and of the house in Belfast in which she had later rented a flat. *From the marks of blood on carpets and rugs*, the item said, *it is deduced that Mrs Vade dragged herself across the floors of two rooms. She appears repeatedly to have fainted before she reached a bottle of aspirins in a kitchen cupboard.* She had been twenty-three at the time of her death.

It was Penelope Vade's desire to make some kind of gesture, a gesture of courage and perhaps anger, that had caused her to leave her parents' home in Haslemere and to go to Belfast. Her husband, an army officer, had been murdered in Belfast; he'd been decapitated as well. His head, wrapped in cotton-wool to absorb the ooze of blood, secured within a plastic bag and packed in a biscuit-tin, had been posted to Penelope Vade. Layer by layer the parcel had been opened by her in Haslemere. She hadn't known that he was dead before his dead eyes stared into hers.

Her gesture was her mourning of him. She went to Belfast to join the Women's Peace Movement, to make the point that somehow neither he nor she had been defeated. But her gesture, publicly reported, had incensed the men who'd gone to the trouble of killing him. One after another, seven of them had committed acts of rape on her. It was after that that she had killed herself.

A fortnight after Attracta had first read the newspaper item it still upset her. It haunted her, and she knew why it did, though only imprecisely. Alone at night, almost catching her unawares, scenes from the tragedy established themselves in her mind: the opening of the biscuit-box, the smell of death, the eyes, blood turning brown. As if at a macabre slide-show, the scene would change: before people had wondered about her whereabouts Penelope Vade had been dead for four days; mice had left droppings on her body.

One afternoon, in order to think the matter over in peace and quiet, Attracta drove her Morris Minor to the sea at Cedarstrand, eight miles from the town. She clambered from the strand up to the headland and paused there, gazing down into the bay, at the solitary island it held. No one had ever lived on the island because its smallness would have made a self-supporting existence impossible. When she'd been growing up she'd often wondered what it would be like to live alone on the rocky fastness, in a wooden hut or a cottage built of stones. Not very agreeable, she'd thought, for she'd always been sociable. She thought it again as she turned abruptly from the sea and followed a path inland through wiry purple heather.

Two fishermen, approaching her on the path, recognized her as the Protestant teacher from the town eight miles away and stood aside for her to pass. She was thinking that nothing she might ever have said in her schoolroom could possibly have prevented the death of a girl in a city two hundred miles away. Yet in a way it seemed ridiculous that for so long she had been relating the details of Cromwell's desecration and the laws of Pythagoras, when she should have been talking about Mr Devereux and Geraldine Carey. And it was Mr Purce she should have recalled instead of the Battle of the Boyne.

The fishermen spoke to her as she passed them by but she didn't reply. It surprised them that she didn't, for they hadn't heard that the Protestant teacher had recently become deaf or odd. Just old, they supposed, as they watched her progressing slowly: an upright figure, spare and seeming fragile, a certain stiffness in her movement.

What made Attracta feel close to the girl in the newspaper item was the tragedy in her own life: the death of her mother and her father when she was three. Her parents had gone away, she had been told, and at first she had wept miserably and would not be comforted. But as days passed into weeks, and weeks into months, this unhappiness gradually left her. She ceased to ask about her parents and became used to living in her Aunt Emmeline's house in North Street. In time she no longer remembered the morning she'd woken up in this house in a bed that was strange to her; nor could she recollect her parents' faces. She grew up assuming they were no longer alive and when once she voiced this assumption her aunt did not contradict it. It wasn't until later in her childhood, when she was eleven, that she learnt the details of the tragedy from Mr Purce, a small man in a hard black hat, who was often to be seen on the streets of the town. He was one of the people she noticed in her childhood, like the elderly beggar-woman called Limerick Nancy and the wild-looking builder's labourer who could walk a hundred miles without stopping, who never wore a jersey or a coat over his open shirt even on the coldest winter days. There were other people too: priests going for a walk in pairs, out along the road that led to the golf-course and to Cedarstrand by the longer route. Strolling through the afternoon sunshine there were nuns in pairs also, and there was Redmond the solicitor hurrying about with his business papers, and Father Quinn on his bicycle. At night there were the red-fleshed country bachelors tipsily smiling through cigarette smoke, lips glistening in the street-light outside Keogh's public house. At all times of day, at all the town's corners, the children of the poor waited for nothing in particular.

The town was everything in Attracta's childhood, and only some of it had changed in the fifty years that had passed. Without nostalgia she remembered now the horses and carts with milk churns for the creamery, slowly progressing on narrow streets between colour-washed houses. On fair-days the pavements had been slithery with dung, and on fair-days they still were. Farmers stood by their animals, their shirts clean for the occasion, a stud at their throats, without collar or tie. Dogs slouched in a manner that was characteristic of the dogs of the town; there was a smell of stout and sawdust. In her childhood there had been O'Mara's Picture House, dour grey cement encasing the dreamland of Fred Astaire and Ginger Rogers. Built with pride in 1929, O'Mara's was a ruin now.

Within the world of the town there was for Attracta a smaller, Protestant world. Behind green railings there was Mr Ayrie's Protestant schoolroom. There was the Church of Ireland church, with its dusty flags of another age, and Archdeacon Flower's prayers for the English royal family. There were the Sunday-school classes of Mr and Mrs Bell, and the patience of her aunt, which seemed like a Protestant thing also – the Protestant duty of a woman who had never expected to find herself looking after a child. There was Mr Devereux, a Protestant who never went to church.

No one in the town, not even her aunt, was kinder to Attracta than Mr Devereux. On her birthday he came himself to the house in North Street with a present carefully wrapped, a dolls' house once, so big he'd had to ask the man next door to help him out of the dickey of his motor-car with it. At Christmas he had a Christmas tree in his house, and other children in the town, her friends from school, were invited to a party. Every Saturday she spent the afternoon with him, eating his housekeeper's delicious orange cake for tea and sticking stamps into the album he'd given her, listening to his gramophone in the room he called his office. He loved getting a huge fire going in his office, banking up the coals so that they'd glow and redden her cheeks. In summer he sat in his back garden with her, sometimes reading *Coral Island* aloud. He made her run away to the raspberry canes and come back with a punnet of fruit which they'd have at suppertime. He was different from her aunt and from Mr Ayrie and Archdeacon Flower. He smelt of the tobacco he smoked in his pipe. He wore tweed suits and a striped shirt with a white celluloid collar, and patterned brown shoes which Attracta greatly admired. His tie matched the tweed of his suit, a gold watch dangled from the lapel of his jacket into his top pocket. He was by trade a grain merchant.

His house was quiet and always a little mysterious. The drawing-room, full of looming furniture, was dark in the daytime. Behind layers of curtains that hung to the ground blue blinds obscured the greater part of the light: sunshine would damage the furniture, Mr Devereux's housekeeper used to say. On a summer's afternoon this woman would light a paraffin lamp so that she could polish the mahogany surfaces of the tables and the grand piano. Her name was Geraldine Carey: she added to the house's mystery.

Mr Devereux's smile was slow. There was a laziness about it, both in its leisurely arrival and the way it lingered. His eyes had a weary look, quite out of keeping with all the efforts he made to promote his friendship with Attracta and her aunt. Yet the efforts seemed natural to Attracta, as were the efforts of Geraldine Carey, who was the quietest person Attracta had ever met. She spoke in a voice that was often hard to hear. Her hair was as black as coal, drawn back from her face and arranged in a coiled bun at the back of her head. Her eyes were startlingly alive, seeming to be black also, often cast down. She had the kind of beauty that Attracta would like one day to possess herself, but knew she would not. Geraldine Carey was like a nun because of the dark clothes she wore, and she had a nun's piety. In the town it was said she couldn't go to mass often enough. 'Why weren't you a nun, Geraldine?' Attracta asked her once, watching her making bread in her big, cool kitchen. The habit would have suited her, she added, already imagining the housekeeper's face framed by the coif, and the black voluminous skirts. But Geraldine Carey replied that she'd never heard God calling her. 'Only the good are called,' she said.

There'd been a time, faintly remembered by Attracta, when her Aunt Emmeline hadn't been well disposed towards Mr Devereux and Geraldine Carey. There'd been suspicion of some kind, a frowning over the presents he brought, an agitation whenever Attracta was invited to tea. Because of her own excitement over the presents and the invitations Attracta hadn't paid much attention to the nature of her aunt's concern, and looking back on it years later could only speculate. Her Aunt Emmeline was a precise person, a tall woman who had never married, reputed to be delicate. Her house in North Street, very different from Mr Devereux's, reflected her: it was neat as a new pin, full of light, the windows of its small rooms invariably open at the top to let in fresh air. The fan-light above the hall-door was always gleaming, filling the hall with morning sunlight. Attracta's Aunt Emmeline had a fear of dankness, of damp clothes and wet feet, and rain falling on the head. She worried about lots of things.

Clearly she had worried about Mr Devereux. There was an occasion when Archdeacon Flower had been specially invited to tea, when Attracta had listened at the sitting-room door because she'd sensed from her aunt's flustered manner that something important was to be discussed. 'Oh, have no worry in that direction at all,' she heard the Archdeacon say. 'Gentle as a lamb that man's become.' Her aunt asked a question Attracta could not hear because of the sound of a tea-cup being replaced on a saucer. 'He's doing the best he can,' the Archdeacon continued, 'according to his lights.' Her aunt mentioned Geraldine Carey, and again the Archdeacon reassured her. 'Bygones are bygones,' he said. 'Isn't it a remarkable thing when a man gets caught in his own snare?' He commented on the quality of her aunt's fruitcake, and then said that everyone should be charitably disposed towards Mr Devereux and Geraldine Carey. He believed, he said, that that was God's wish.

After that, slowly over the years, Attracta's aunt began to think more highly of Mr Devereux, until in the end there was no one in the entire town, with the possible exception of Archdeacon Flower, whom she held in greater esteem. Once when Phelan the coal merchant insisted that she hadn't paid for half a ton of coal and she recollected perfectly giving the money to the man who'd delivered it, Mr Devereux had come to her aid. 'A right old devil, Phelan is,' Attracta heard him saying in the hall, and that was the end her aunt had ever heard of the matter. On Saturday evenings, having kept Attracta company on her walk home, Mr Devereux might remain for a little while in the house in North Street. He sometimes brought lettuces or cuttings with him, or tomatoes or strawberries. He would take a glass of sherry in the trim little sitting-room with its delicate inlaid chairs that matched the delicacy of Attracta's aunt. Often he'd still be there, taking a second glass, when Attracta came down to say good-night. Her aunt's cat, Diggory, liked to climb up on to his knees, and as if in respect of some kind Mr Devereux never lit his pipe. He and her aunt would converse in low voices and generally they'd cease when Attracta entered the room. She would kiss him good-night after she'd kissed her aunt. She imagined it was what having a father was like.

At the town's approximate centre there stood a grey woman on a pedestal, a statue of the Maid of Erin. It was here, only yards from this monument, that Mr Purce told Attracta the truth about her parents' death, when she was eleven. She'd always had the feeling that Mr Purce wanted to speak to her, even that he was waiting until she could understand what it was he had to say. He was a man people didn't much like; he'd settled in the town, having come there from somewhere else. He was a clerk in the court-house.

'There's a place I know where there's greenfinches,' he said, as if introducing himself. 'Ten nests of them, maybe twelve, maybe more. D'you understand me, Attracta? Would you like me to show you?'

She was on her way home from school. She had to get back to do her homework, she said to Mr Purce. She didn't want to go looking for greenfinches with him.

'Did Devereux tell you not to talk to Mr Purce?' he said, and she shook her head. As far as she could remember, Mr Devereux had never mentioned Mr Purce. 'I see you in church,' Mr Purce said.

She had seen him too, sitting in the front, over on the left-hand side. Her aunt had often remarked that the day Mr Purce didn't go to church it would be a miracle. It was like Geraldine Carey going to mass.

'I'll walk out with you,' he said. 'I have a half-day today for myself.'

They walked together, to her embarrassment. She glanced at shop-windows to catch a glimpse of their reflection, to see if they looked as awkward as she felt. He was only a head taller than she and part of that was made up by his hard black hat. His clerk's suit was double-breasted, navy-blue with a pale stripe in it, shiny here and there, in need of a good ironing.

He wore black leather gloves and carried a walking-stick. He always had
the gloves and the walking-stick in church, but his Sunday suit was superior
to the one he wore now. Her own fair hair, pinned up under her green-
brimmed hat, was what stood out between the two of them. The colour of
good corn, Mr Devereux used to say, and she always considered that a
compliment, coming from a grain merchant. Her face was thin and her eyes
blue, but reflected in the shop-windows there was now only a blur of flesh,
a thin shaft between her and the green coat that matched it.

'You've had misfortune, Attracta.' Solemnly he nodded, repeating the
motion of his head until she wished he'd stop. 'It was a terrible thing to be
killed by mistake.'

Attracta didn't know what he was talking about. They passed by the last
of the shops in North Street, Shannon's grocery and bar, O'Brien's bakery,
the hardware that years ago had run out of stock. The narrow street
widened a bit. Mr Purce said:

'Has she made a Catholic girl out of you, Attracta?'

'Who, Mr Purce?'

'Devereux's woman. Has she tried anything on? Has she shown you
rosary beads?'

She shook her head.

'Don't ever look at them if she does. Look away immediately if she gets
them out of her apron or anything like that. Will you promise me that,
girl?'

'I don't think she would. I don't think Mr Devereux –'

'You can never tell with that crowd. There isn't a trick in the book they
won't hop on to. Will you promise me now? Have nothing to do with
carry-on like that.'

'Yes, Mr Purce.'

As they walked he prodded at the litter on the pavement with his
walking-stick. Cigarette packets and squashed match-boxes flew into the
gutter, bits of the *Cork Examiner*, sodden paper-bags. He was known for
this activity in the town, and even when he was on his own his voice was
often heard protesting at the untidiness.

'I'm surprised they never told you, Attracta,' he said. 'What are you
now, girl?'

'I'm eleven.'

'A big girl should know things like that.'

'What things, Mr Purce?'

He nodded in his repetitious manner, and then he explained himself.
The tragedy had occurred in darkness, at night: her parents had
accidentally become involved with an ambush meant for the Black and
Tan soldiers who were in force in the area at the time. She herself had
long since been asleep at home, and as he spoke she remembered
waking up to find herself in a bed in her aunt's house, without knowing
how she got there. 'That's how they got killed, Attracta,' Mr Purce said,

and then he said an extraordinary thing. 'You've got Devereux and his woman to thank for it.'

She knew that the Black and Tan soldiers had been camped near the town; she knew there'd been fighting. She realized that the truth about the death had been counted too terrible for a child to bear. But that her parents should have been shot, and shot in error, that the whole thing had somehow been the responsibility of Mr Devereux and Geraldine Carey, seemed inconceivable to Attracta.

'They destroyed a decent Protestant pair,' Mr Purce continued, still flicking litter from the pavement. 'Half-ten at night on a public road, destroyed like pests.'

The sun, obscured by clouds while Attracta and Mr Purce had made the journey from the centre of the town, was suddenly warm on Attracta's face. A woman in a horse and cart, attired in the black hooded cloak of the locality, passed slowly by. There were sacks of meal in the cart which had probably come from Mr Devereux's mill.

'Do you understand what I'm saying to you, Attracta? Devereux was organizing resistance up in the hills. He had explosives and booby traps, he was drilling men to go and kill people. Did nobody tell you about himself and Geraldine Carey?'

She shook her head. He nodded again, as if to indicate that little better could be expected.

'Listen to me, Attracta. Geraldine Carey was brought into this town by the man she got married to, who used to work at Devereux's mill. Six months later she'd joined up with Devereux in the type of dirty behaviour I wouldn't soil myself telling you about. Not only that, Attracta, she was gun-running with him. She was fixing explosives like a man would, dressed up like a man in uniform. Devereux was as wild as a savage. There was nothing Devereux wouldn't do, there was nothing the woman wouldn't do either. They'd put booby traps down and it didn't matter who got killed. They'd ambush the British soldiers when the soldiers didn't have a chance.'

It was impossible to believe him. It was impossible to visualize the housekeeper and Mr Devereux in the role he'd given them. No one with any sense could believe that Geraldine Carey would kill people. Was everything Mr Purce said a lie? He was a peculiar man: had he some reason for stating her mother and her father had met their deaths in this way?

'Your father was a decent man, Attracta. He was never drunk in his life. There was prayers for him in the chapel, but that was only a hypocrisy of the priests. Wouldn't the priest Quinn like to see every Protestant in this town dead and buried? Wouldn't he like to see you and me six foot down with clay in our eye-sockets?'

Attracta didn't believe that, and more certainly now it seemed to her that everything Mr Purce said was untrue. Catholics were different; they crossed themselves when they passed their chapel; they went in for crosses and confession; they had masses and candles. But it was hard to accept that Father Quinn, a jovial red-haired man, would prefer it if she were dead. She'd heard her aunt's maid, Philomena, saying that Father Doran was cantankerous and that Father Martin wasn't worth his salt, but neither of them seemed to Attracta to be the kind of man who'd wish people dead. 'Proddy-woddy green-guts,' Catholic children would shout out sometimes. 'Catty-catty going to mass,' the Protestants would reply, 'riding on the Devil's ass.' But there was never much vindictiveness about any of it. The sides were unevenly matched: there were too few Protestants in the town to make a proper opposition; trouble was avoided.

'He was a traitor to his religion, Attracta. And I'll promise you this: if I was to tell you about that woman of his you wouldn't enter the house they have.' Abruptly he turned and walked away, back into the town, his walking-stick still frantically working, poking away any litter it could find.

The sun was hot now. Attracta felt sticky within her several layers of clothes. She had a chapter of her history book to read, about the Saxons coming to England. She had four long-division sums to do, and seven lines of poetry to learn. *What potions have I drunk of Syren tears*, the first one stated, a statement Attracta could make neither head nor tail of.

She didn't go straight home. Instead she turned off to the left and walked through a back street, out into the country. She passed fields of mangels and turnips, again trying to imagine the scenes Mr Purce had sketched for her, the ambush of men waiting for the soldiers, the firing of shots. It occurred to her that she had never asked anyone if her parents were buried in the Church of Ireland graveyard.

She passed by tinkers encamped on the verge of the road. A woman ran after her and asked for money, saying her husband had just died. She swore when Attracta said she hadn't any, and then her manner changed again. She developed a whine in her voice, she said she'd pray for Attracta if she'd bring her money, tomorrow or the next day.

Had Mr Purce only wished to turn her against Mr Devereux because Mr Devereux did not go to church? Was there no more to it than that? Did Mr Purce say the first thing that came into his head? As Attracta walked, the words of Archdeacon Flower came back to her: in stating that Mr Devereux was now as gentle as a lamb, was there the implication that once he hadn't been? And had her aunt, worried about Geraldine Carey, been reassured on that score also?

'It's all over now, dear,' her aunt said. She looked closely at Attracta and then put her arms round her, as if expecting tears. But tears didn't come, for Attracta was only amazed.

Fifty years later, walking through the heather by the sea, Attracta remembered vividly that moment of her childhood. She couldn't understand how Mr Devereux and Geraldine Carey had changed so. 'Maybe they bear the burden of guilt,' Archdeacon Flower had explained, summoned to the house the following day by her aunt. 'Maybe they look at you and feel responsible. It was an accident, but people can feel responsible for an accident.' What had happened was in the past, he reminded her, as her aunt had. She understood what they were implying, that it must all be forgotten, yet she couldn't help imagining Mr Devereux and his housekeeper laying booby traps on roads and drilling men in the hills. Geraldine Carey's husband had left the town, Mr Purce told her on a later occasion: he'd gone to Co. Louth and hadn't been heard of since. 'Whore,' Mr Purce said. 'No better than a whore she is.' Attracta, looking the word up in a dictionary, was astonished.

Having started, Mr Purce went on and on. Mr Devereux's house wasn't suitable for an eleven-year-old girl to visit, since it was the house of a murderer. Wasn't it a disgrace that a Protestant girl should set foot in a house where the deaths of British soldiers and the Protestant Irish had been planned? One Saturday afternoon, unable to restrain himself, he arrived at the house himself. He shouted at Mr Devereux from the open hall-door. 'Isn't it enough to have destroyed her father and mother without letting that woman steal her for the Pope?' His grey face was suffused beneath his hard hat, his walking-stick thrashed the air. Mr Devereux called him an Orange mason. 'I hate the bloody sight of you,' Mr Purce said in a quieter voice, and then in his abrupt way he walked off.

That, too, Attracta remembered as she continued her walk around the headland. Mr Devereux afterwards never referred to it, and Mr Purce never spoke to her again, as if deciding that there was nothing left to say. In the town as she grew up people would reluctantly answer her when she questioned them about her parents' tragedy in an effort to discover more than her aunt or Archdeacon Flower had revealed. But nothing new emerged, the people she asked only agreeing that Mr Devereux in those day had been as wild as Mr Purce suggested. He'd drilled the local men, he'd been assisted in every way by Geraldine Carey, whose husband had gone away to Co. Louth. But everything had been different since the night of the tragedy.

Her aunt tried to explain to her the nature of Mr Purce's hatred of Mr Devereux. Mr Purce saw things in a certain light, she said, he could not help himself. He couldn't help believing that Father Quinn would prefer the town's Protestants to be dead and buried. He couldn't help believing that immorality continued in the relationship between Mr Devereux and his housekeeper when clearly it did not. He found a spark and made a fire of it, he was a bigot and was unable to do anything about it. The Protestants of the town felt ashamed of him.

Mr Purce died, and was said to have continued in his hatred with his last remaining breaths. He mentioned the Protestant girl, his bleak, harsh voice weakening. She had been contaminated and infected, she was herself no better than the people who used her for their evil purposes. She was not fit to teach the Protestant children of the town, as she was now commencing to do. 'As I lie dying,' Mr Purce said to the clergyman who had succeeded Archdeacon Flower, 'I am telling you that, sir.' But afterwards, when the story of Mr Purce's death went round, the people of the town looked at Attracta with a certain admiration, seeming to suggest that for her the twisting of events had not been easy, neither the death of her parents nor the forgiveness asked of her by Mr Devereux, nor the bigotry of Mr Purce. She'd been caught in the middle of things, they seemed to suggest, and had survived unharmed.

Surviving, she was happy in the town. Too happy to marry the exchange clerk from the Provincial Bank or the young man who came on a holiday to Cedarstrand with his parents. *Pride goeth before destruction*, her pupils' headlines stated, and *Look before you leap*. Their fingers pressed hard on inky pens, knuckles jutting beneath the strain, tongue-tips aiding concentration. Ariadne, Finn MacCool, King Arthur's sword, Cathleen ni Houlihan: legends filled the schoolroom, with facts about the Romans and the Normans, square roots and the Gulf Stream. Children grew up and went away, returning sometimes to visit Attracta in her house in North Street. Others remained and in the town she watched them changing, grey coming into their hair, no longer moving as lithely as they had. She developed an affection for the town without knowing why, beyond the fact that it was part of her.

'Yet in all a lifetime I learnt nothing,' she said aloud to herself on the headland. 'And I taught nothing either.' She gazed out at the smooth blue Atlantic but did not see it clearly. She saw instead the brown-paper parcel that contained the biscuit-box she had read about, and the fingers of Penelope Vade undoing the string and the brown paper. She saw her lifting off the lid. She saw her frowning for a moment, before the eyes of the man she loved stared deadly into hers. Months later, all courage spent and defeated in her gesture, the body of Penelope Vade dragged itself across the floors of two different rooms. There was the bottle full of aspirins in a cupboard, and water drunk from a Wedgwood-patterned cup, like the cups Attracta drank from every day.

In her schoolroom, with its maps and printed pictures, the sixteen faces stared back at her, the older children at the back. She repeated her question.

'Now, what does anyone think of that?'

Again she read them the news item, reading it slowly because she wanted it to become as rooted in their minds as it was in hers. She lingered over the number of bullets that had been fired into the body of Penelope Vade's husband, and over the removal of his head.

'Can you see that girl? Can you imagine men putting a human head in a tin box and sending it through the post? Can you imagine her receiving it? The severed head of the man she loved?'

'Sure, isn't there stuff like that in the papers the whole time?' one of the children suggested.

She agreed that that was so. 'I've had a good life in this town,' she added, and the children looked at her as if she'd suddenly turned mad.

'I'm getting out of it,' one of them said after a pause. 'Back of beyond, miss.'

She began at the beginning. She tried to get into the children's minds an image of a baby sleeping while violence and death took place on the Cork road. She described her Aunt Emmeline's house in North Street, the neat feminine house it had been, her aunt's cat, Diggory, the small sitting-room, her aunt's maid, Philomena. She spoke of her own very fair hair and her thin face, and the heavy old-fashioned clothes she'd worn in those days. She spoke of the piety of Geraldine Carey, and the grain merchant's tired face. The friendship they offered her was like Penelope Vade proclaiming peace in a city where her husband had been killed; it was a gesture, too.

'His house would smell of roses on a summer's day. She'd carry his meals to him, coming out of the shadows of her kitchen. As if in mourning, the blue blinds darkened the drawing-room. It was they who bore the tragedy, not I.'

She described Mr Purce's face and his grating voice. She tried to make of him a figure they could see among the houses and shops that were familiar to them: the hard black hat, the walking-stick poking away litter. He had done his best to rescue her, acting according to his beliefs. He wanted her not to forget, not realizing that there was nothing for her to remember.

'But I tried to imagine,' she said, 'as I am asking you to imagine now: my mother and father shot dead on the Cork road, and Mr Devereux and Geraldine Carey as two monstrous people, and arms being blown off soldiers, and vengeance breeding vengeance.'

A child raised a hand and asked to leave the room. Attracta gave permission and awaited the child's return before proceeding. She filled the time in by describing things that had changed in the town, the falling to pieces of O'Mara's Picture House, the closing of the tannery in 1938. When the child came back she told of Mr Purce's death, how he'd said she was not fit to teach Protestant children.

'I tried to imagine a night I'd heard about,' she said, 'when Mr Devereux's men found a man in Madden's public house whom they said had betrayed them, and how they took him out to Cedarstrand and hanged him in a barn. Were they pleased after they'd done that? Did they light cigarettes, saying the man was better dead? One of those other men must have gone to a post office with the wrapped biscuit-box. He must have watched it being weighed and paid the postage. Did he say to himself he was exceptional to have hoodwinked a post-office clerk?'

Obediently listening in their rows of worn desks, the children wondered what on earth all this was about. No geography or history lesson had ever been so bewildering; those who found arithmetic difficult would have settled for attempting to understand it now. They watched the lined face of their teacher, still thin as she'd said it had been in childhood, the fair hair grey now. The mouth twitched and rapidly moved, seeming sometimes to quiver as if it struggled against tears. What on earth had this person called Penelope Vade to do with anything?

'She died believing that hell had come already. She'd lost all faith in human life, and who can blame her? She might have stayed in Haslemere, like anyone else would have. Was she right to go to the city where her husband had been murdered, to show its other victims that her spirit had not been wholly crushed?'

No one answered, and Attracta was aware of the children's startled gaze. But the startled gaze was a natural reaction. She said to herself that it didn't matter.

'My story is one with hers,' she said. 'Horror stories, with different endings only. I think of her now and I can see quite clearly the flat she lived in in Belfast. I can see the details, correctly or not I've no idea. Wallpaper with a pattern of brownish-purple flowers on it, gaunt furniture casting shadows, a tea-caddy on the hired television set. I drag my body across the floors of two rooms, over a carpet that smells of dust and cigarette ash, over rugs and cool linoleum. I reach up in the kitchen, a hand on the edge of the sink: one by one I eat the aspirins until the bottle's empty.'

There was a silence. Feet were shuffled in the schoolroom. No one spoke.

'If only she had known,' Attracta said, 'that there was still a faith she might have had, that God does not forever withhold His mercy. Will those same men who exacted that vengeance on her one day keep bees and budgerigars? Will they serve in shops, and be kind to the blind and the deaf? Will they garden in the evenings and be good fathers? It is not impossible. Oh, can't you see,' she cried, 'what happened in this town? Here, at the back of beyond. Can't you appreciate it? And can't you see her lying there, mice nibbling her dried blood?'

The children still were quiet, their faces still not registering the comment she wished to make. It was because she'd been clumsy, she thought. All she'd meant to tell them was never to despair. All she had meant to do was to prepare them for a future that looked grim. She had been happy, she said again. The conversation of Mr Purce had been full of the truth but it hadn't made sense because the years had turned the truth around.

To the children she appeared to be talking now to herself. She was old, a few of them silently considered; that was it. She didn't appear to understand that almost every day there was the kind of vengeance she spoke of reported on the television. Bloodshed was wholesale, girls were tarred and left for dead, children no older than they were armed with guns.

'I only hope,' they heard her saying, 'she knows that strangers mourn her.'

Another silence lingered awkwardly and then she nodded at a particular child and the child rose and rang a hand-bell. The children filed away, well-mannered and docile as she had taught them to be. She watched them in the playground, standing in twos and threes, talking about her. It had nothing when she'd said that people change. The gleam of hope she'd offered had been too slight to be of use, irrelevant in the horror they took for granted, as part of life. Yet she could not help still believing that it mattered when monsters did not remain monsters for ever. It wasn't much to put against the last bleak moments of Penelope Vade, but it was something for all that. She wished she could have made her point.

Twenty minutes later, when the children returned to the schoolroom, her voice no longer quivered, nor did it seem to struggle against tears. The older children learnt about agriculture in Sweden, the younger ones about the Pyrenees, the youngest that Munster had six counties. The day came to an end at three o'clock and when all the children had gone Attracta locked the schoolroom and walked to the house she had inherited in North Street.

A week later Archdeacon Flower's successor came to see her, his visit interrupting further violence on the television news. He beat about the bush while he nibbled biscuits and drank cups of tea by the fire; then he suggested that perhaps she should consider retiring one of these days. She was over sixty, he pointed out with his clerical laugh, and she replied that Mr Ayrie had gone on until seventy. Sixty, the clergyman repeated with another laugh, was the post's retirement age. Children were a handful nowadays.

She smiled, thinking of her sixteen docile charges. They had chattered to their parents, and the parents had been shocked to hear that they'd been told of a man decapitated and a girl raped seven times. School was not for that, they had angrily protested to the clergyman, and he had had no option but to agree. At the end of the summer term there'd be a presentation of Waterford glass.

'Every day in my schoolroom I should have honoured the small, remarkable thing that happened in this town. It matters that she died in despair, with no faith left in human life.'

He was brisk. For as long as most people could remember she had been a remarkable teacher; in no way had she failed. He turned the conversation to more cheerful topics, he ate more biscuits and a slice of cake. He laughed and even made a joke. He retailed a little harmless gossip.

Eventually she stood up. She walked with her visitor to the hall, shook hands with him and saw him out. In the sitting-room she piled the tea things on to a tray and placed it on a table by the door. She turned the television on again but when the screen lit up she didn't notice it. The face of Penelope Vade came into her mind, the smile a little crooked, the freckled cheeks.

Lovers of Their Time

Looking back on it, it seemed to have to do with that particular decade in London. Could it have happened, he wondered, at any other time except the 1960s? That feeling was intensified, perhaps, because the whole thing had begun on New Year's Day, 1963, long before that day became a bank holiday in England. 'That'll be two and nine,' she'd said, smiling at him across her counter, handing him toothpaste and emery boards in a bag. 'Colgate's, remember,' his wife had called out as he was leaving the flat. 'The last stuff we had tasted awful.'

His name was Norman Britt. It said so on a small plastic name-plate in front of his position in the travel agency where he worked, Travel-Wide as it was called. *Marie* a badge on her light-blue shop-coat announced. His wife, who worked at home, assembling jewellery for a firm that paid her on a production basis, was called Hilda.

Green's the Chemist's and Travel-Wide were in Vincent Street, a street that was equidistant from Paddington station and Edgware Road. The flat where Hilda worked all day was in Putney. Marie lived in Reading with her mother and her mother's friend Mrs Druk, both of them widows. She caught the 8.05 every morning to Paddington and usually the 6.30 back.

He was forty in 1963, as Hilda was; Marie was twenty-eight. He was tall and thin, with a David Niven moustache. Hilda was thin also, her dark hair beginning to grey, her sharply-featured face pale. Marie was well-covered, carefully made up, her reddish hair dyed blond. She smiled a lot, a slack half-crooked smile that made her eyes screw up and twinkle; she exuded laziness and generosity. She and her friend Mavis went dancing a lot in Reading and had a sizeable collection of men friends. 'Fellas' they called them.

Buying things from her now and again in Green's the Chemist's Norman had come to the conclusion that she was of a tartish disposition, and imagined that if ever he sat with her over a drink in the nearby Drummer Boy the occasion could easily lead to a hug on the street afterwards. He imagined her coral-coloured lips, like two tiny sausages, only softer, pressed upon his moustache and his abbreviated mouth. He imagined the warmth of her hand in his. For all that, she was a little outside reality: she was there to desire, to glow erotically in the heady atmosphere of the Drummer Boy, to light cigarettes for in a dream.

'Isn't it cold?' he said as she handed him the emery boards and the toothpaste.

'Shocking,' she agreed, and hesitated, clearly wanting to say something else. 'You're in that Travel-Wide,' she added in the end. 'Me and my friend want to go to Spain this year.'

'It's very popular. The Costa Brava?'

'That's right.' She handed him threepence change. 'In May.'

'Not too hot on the Costa in May. If you need any help –'

'Just the bookings.'

'I'd be happy to make them for you. Look in any time. Britt the name is. I'm on the counter.'

'If I may, Mr Britt. I could slip out maybe at four, or roundabout.'

'Today, you mean?'

'We want to fix it up.'

'Naturally. I'll keep an eye out for you.'

It was hard not to call her madam or miss, the way he'd normally do. He'd heard himself saying that he'd be happy to make the bookings for her, knowing that that was business jargon, knowing that the unfussy voice he'd used was a business one also. Her friend was a man, he supposed, some snazzy tough in a car. 'See you later then,' he said, but already she was serving another customer, advising about lipstick refills.

She didn't appear in Travel-Wide at four o'clock; she hadn't come when the doors closed at five-thirty. He was aware of a sense of disappointment, combined with one of anticipation: for if she'd come at four, he reflected as he left the travel agency, their bit of business would be in the past rather than the future. She'd look in some other time and he'd just have to trust to luck that if he happened to be busy with another customer she'd be able to wait. There'd be a further occasion, when she called to collect the tickets themselves.

'Ever so sorry,' she said on the street, her voice coming from behind him. 'Couldn't get away, Mr Britt.'

He turned and smiled at her, feeling the movement of his moustache as he parted his lips. He knew only too well, he said. 'Some other time then?'

'Maybe tomorrow. Maybe lunchtime.'

'I'm off myself from twelve to one. Look, you wouldn't fancy a drink? I could advise you just as easily over a drink.'

'Oh, you wouldn't have the time. No, I mustn't take advantage –'

'You're not at all. If you've got ten minutes?'

'Well, it's awfully good of you, Mr Britt. But I really feel I'm taking advantage, I really do.'

'A New Year's drink.'

He pushed open the doors of the saloon bar of the Drummer Boy, a place he didn't often enter except for office drinks at Christmas or when someone leaving the agency was being given a send-off. Ron Stocks and Mr Blackstaffe were usually there in the evenings: he hoped they'd be there now to see him in the company of the girl from Green's the Chemist's. 'What would you like?' he asked her.

'Gin and peppermint's my poison, only honestly I should pay. No, let me ask you –'

'I wouldn't dream of it. We can sit over there, look.'

The Drummer Boy, so early in the evening, wasn't full. By six o'clock the advertising executives from the firm of Dalton, Dure and Higgins, just round the corner, would have arrived, and the architects from Frine and Knight. Now there was only Mrs Gregan, old and alcoholic, known to everyone, and a red-fleshed man called Bert, with his poodle, Jimmy. It was disappointing that Ron Stocks and Mr Blackstaffe weren't there.

'You were here lunchtime Christmas Eve,' she said.

'Yes, I was.' He paused, placing her gin and peppermint on a cardboard mat that advertised Guinness. 'I saw you too.'

He drank some of his Double Diamond and carefully wiped the traces of foam from his moustache. He realized now that it would, of course, be quite impossible to give her a hug on the street outside. That had been just imagination, wishful thinking as his mother would have said. And yet he knew that when he arrived home twenty-five or so minutes late he would not tell Hilda that he'd been advising an assistant from Green's the Chemist's about a holiday on the Costa Brava. He wouldn't even say he'd been in the Drummer Boy. He'd say Blackstaffe had kept everyone late, going through the new package that Eurotours were offering in Germany and Luxembourg this summer. Hilda wouldn't in a million years suspect that he'd been sitting in a public house with a younger woman who was quite an eyeful. As a kind of joke, she quite regularly suggested that his sexual drive left something to be desired.

'We were thinking about the last two weeks in May,' Marie said. 'It's when Mavis can get off too.'

'Mavis?'

'My friend, Mr Britt.'

Hilda was watching *Z-Cars* in the sitting-room, drinking V.P. wine. His stuff was in the oven, she told him. 'Thanks,' he said.

Sometimes she was out when he returned in the evenings. She went round to friends, a Mr and Mrs Fowler, with whom she drank V.P. and played bridge. On other occasions she went to the Club, which was a place with a licence, for card-players and billiard-players. She quite liked her social life, but always said beforehand when she'd be out and always made arrangements about leaving food in the oven. Often in the daytime she'd go and make jewellery with Violet Parkes, who also went in for this occupation; and often Violet Parkes spent the day with Hilda. The jewellery-making consisted for the most part of threading plastic beads on to a string or arranging plastic pieces in the settings provided. Hilda was quick at it and earned more than she would have if she went out every day, saving the fares for a start. She was better at it than Violet Parkes.

'All right then?' she said as he carried his tray of food into the sitting-room and sat down in front of the television set. 'Want some V.P., eh?'

Her eyes continued to watch the figures on the screen as she spoke. He knew she'd prefer to be in the Fowlers' house or at the Club, although now that they'd acquired a TV set the evenings passed easier when they were alone together.

'No, thanks,' he said in reply to her offer of wine and he began to eat something that appeared to be a rissole. There were two of them, round and brown in a tin-foil container that also contained gravy. He hoped she wasn't going to be demanding in their bedroom. He eyed her, for sometimes he could tell.

'Hi,' she said, noticing the glance. 'Feeling fruity, dear?' She laughed and winked, her suggestive voice seeming odd as it issued from her thin, rather dried-up face. She was always saying things like that, for no reason that Norman could see, always talking about feeling fruity or saying she could see he was keen when he wasn't in the least. Norman considered that she was unduly demanding and often wondered what it would be like to be married to someone who was not. Now and again, fatigued after the intensity of her love-making, he lay staring at the darkness, wondering if her bedroom appetites were related in some way to the fact that she was unable to bear children, if her abandon reflected a maternal frustration. Earlier in their married life she'd gone out every day to an office where she'd been a filing clerk; in the evenings they'd often gone to the cinema.

He lay that night, after she'd gone to sleep, listening to her heavy breathing, thinking of the girl in Green's the Chemist's. He went through the whole day in his mind, seeing himself leaving the flat in Putney, hearing Hilda calling out about the emery boards and the toothpaste, seeing himself reading the *Daily Telegraph* in the Tube. Slowly he went through the morning, deliciously anticipating the moment when she handed him his change. With her smile mistily hovering, he recalled the enquiries and demands of a number of the morning's customers. 'Fix us up Newcastle and back?' a couple enquired. 'Mid-week's cheaper, is it?' A man with a squashed-up face wanted a week in Holland for himself and his sister and his sister's husband. A woman asked about Greece, another about cruises on the Nile, a third about the Scilly Isles. Then he placed the Closed sign in front of his position at the counter and went out to have lunch in Bette's Sandwiches off the Edgware Road. 'Packet of emery boards,' he said again in Green's the Chemist's, 'and a small Colgate's.' After that there was the conversation they'd had, and then the afternoon with her smile still mistily hovering, as in fact it had, and then her presence beside him in the Drummer Boy. Endlessly she lifted the glass of gin and peppermint to her lips, endlessly she smiled. When he slept he dreamed of her. They were walking in Hyde Park and her shoe fell off. 'I could tell you were a deep one,' she said, and the next thing was Hilda was having one of her early-morning appetites.

*

'I don't know what it is about that chap,' Marie confided to Mavis. 'Something though.'

'Married, is he?'

'Oh, he would be, chap like that.'

'Now, you be careful, girl.'

'He has Sinatra's eyes. That blue, you know.'

'Now, Marie –'

'I like an older fella. He's got a nice moustache.'

'So's that fella in the International.'

'Wet behind the ears. And my God, his dandruff!'

They left the train together and parted on the platform, Marie making for the Underground, Mavis hurrying for a bus. It was quite convenient, really, living in Reading and travelling to Paddington every day. It was only half an hour and chatting on the journey passed the time. They didn't travel back together in the evenings because Mavis nearly always did an hour's overtime. She was a computer programmer.

'I talked to Mavis. It's O.K. about the insurance,' Marie said in Travel-Wide at half-past eleven that morning, having slipped out when the shop seemed slack. There'd been some details about insurance which he'd raised the evening before. He always advised insurance, but he'd quite understood when she'd made the point that she'd better discuss the matter with her friend before committing herself to the extra expenditure.

'So I'll go ahead and book you,' he said. 'There'll just be the deposit.'

'Mavis wrote the cheque.' She pushed the pink slip across the counter to him. 'Payable to Travel-Wide.'

'That's quite correct.' He glanced at it and wrote her a receipt. He said:

'I looked out another brochure or two. I'd quite like to go through them with you. So you can explain what's what to your friend.'

'Oh, that's very nice, Mr Britt. But I got to get back. I mean, I shouldn't be out in the middle of the morning.'

'Any chance of lunchtime?'

His suavity astounded him. He thought of Hilda, deftly working at her jewellery, stringing orange and yellow beads, listening to the Jimmy Young programme.

'Lunchtime, Mr Britt?'

'We'd maybe talk about the brochures.'

He fancied her, she said to herself. He was making a pass, talking about brochures and lunchtime. Well, she wasn't disagreeable. She'd meant what she'd said to Mavis: she liked an older fella and she liked his moustache, so smooth it looked as if he put something on it. She liked the name Norman.

'All right then,' she said.

He couldn't suggest Bette's Sandwiches because you stood up at a shelf on the wall and ate the sandwiches off a cardboard plate.

'We could go to the Drummer Boy,' he suggested instead. 'I'm off at twelve-fifteen.'

'Say half-past, Mr Britt.'

'I'll be there with the brochures.'

Again he thought of Hilda. He thought of her wiry, pasty limbs and the way she had of snorting. Sometimes when they were watching the television she'd suddenly want to sit on his knee. She'd get worse as she grew older; she'd get scrawnier; her hair, already coarse, would get dry and grey. He enjoyed the evenings when she went out to the Club or to her friends the Fowlers. And yet he wasn't being fair because in very many ways she did her best. It was just that you didn't always feel like having someone on your knee after a day's work.

'Same?' he said in the Drummer Boy.

'Yes please, Mr Britt.' She'd meant to say that the drinks were definitely on her, after all he'd spent last night. But in her flurry she forgot. She picked up the brochures he'd left on the seat beside her. She pretended to read one, but all the time she was watching him as he stood by the bar. He smiled as he turned and came back with their drinks. He said something about it being a nice way to do business. He was drinking gin and peppermint himself.

'I meant to pay for the drinks. I meant to say I would. I'm sorry, Mr Britt.'

'Norman, my name is.' He surprised himself again by the ease with which he was managing the situation. They'd have their drinks and then he'd suggest some of the shepherd's pie, or a ham-and-salad roll if she'd prefer it. He'd buy her another gin and peppermint to get her going. Eighteen years ago he used to buy Hilda further glasses of V.P. wine with the same thought in mind.

They finished with the brochures. She told him she lived in Reading; she talked about the town. She mentioned her mother and her mother's friend Mrs Druk, who lived with them, and Mavis. She told him a lot about Mavis. No man was mentioned, no boyfriend or fiancé.

'Honestly,' she said, 'I'm not hungry.' She couldn't have touched a thing. She just wanted to go on drinking gin with him. She wanted to get slightly drunk, a thing she'd never done before in the middle of the day. She wanted to put her arm through his.

'It's been nice meeting you,' he said.

'A bit of luck.'

'I think so too, Marie.' He ran his forefinger between the bones on the back of her hand, so gently that it made her want to shiver. She didn't take her hand away, and when she continued not to he took her hand in his.

After that they had lunch together every day, always in the Drummer Boy. People saw them, Ron Stocks and Mr Blackstaffe from Travel-Wide, Mr Fineman, the pharmacist from Green's the Chemist's. Other people

612 · LOVERS OF THEIR TIME

from the travel agency and from the chemist's saw them walking about the streets, usually hand in hand. They would look together into the shop windows of Edgware Road, drawn particularly to an antique shop full of brass. In the evenings he would walk with her to Paddington station and have a drink in one of the bars. They'd embrace on the platform, as other people did.

Mavis continued to disapprove; Marie's mother and Mrs Druk remained ignorant of the affair. The holiday on the Costa Brava that June was not a success because all the time Marie kept wishing Norman Britt was with her. Occasionally, while Mavis read magazines on the beach, Marie wept and Mavis pretended not to notice. She was furious because Marie's low spirits meant that it was impossible for them to get to know fellas. For months they'd been looking forward to the holiday and now, just because of a clerk in a travel agency, it was a flop. 'I'm sorry, dear,' Marie kept saying, trying to smile; but when they returned to London the friendship declined. 'You're making a fool of yourself,' Mavis pronounced harshly, 'and it's dead boring having to hear about it.' After that they ceased to travel together in the mornings.

The affair remained unconsummated. In the hour and a quarter allotted to each of them for lunch there was nowhere they might have gone to let their passion for one another run its course. Everywhere was public: Travel-Wide and the chemist's shop, the Drummer Boy, the streets they walked. Neither could easily spend a night away from home. Her mother and Mrs Druk would guess that something untoward was in the air; Hilda, deprived of her bedroom mating, would no longer be nonchalant in front of the TV. It would all come out if they were rash, and they sensed some danger in that.

'Oh, darling,' she whispered one October evening at Paddington, huddling herself against him. It was foggy and cold. The fog was in her pale hair, tiny droplets that only he, being close to her, could see. People hurried through the lit-up station, weary faces anxious to be home.

'I know,' he said, feeling as inadequate as he always did at the station.

'I lie awake and think of you,' she whispered.

'You've made me live,' he whispered back.

'And you me. Oh, God, and you me.' She was gone before she finished speaking, swinging into the train as it moved away, her bulky red handbag the last thing he saw. It would be eighteen hours before they'd meet again.

He turned his back on her train and slowly made his way through the crowds, his reluctance to start the journey back to the flat in Putney seeming physical, like a pain, inside him. 'Oh, for God's sake!' a woman cried angrily at him, for he had been in her way and had moved in the same direction as she had in seeking to avoid her, causing a second collision. She dropped magazines on to the platform and he helped her to pick them up, vainly apologizing.

It was then, walking away from this woman, that he saw the sign. *Hotel*

Entrance it said in red neon letters, beyond the station's main bookstall. It was the back of the Great Western Royal, a short cut to its comforts for train travellers at the end of their journey. If only, he thought, they could share a room there. If only for one single night they were granted the privilege of being man and wife. People passed through the swing-doors beneath the glowing red sign, people hurrying, with newspapers or suitcases. Without quite knowing why, he passed through the swing-doors himself.

He walked up two brief flights of steps, through another set of doors, and paused in the enormous hall of the Great Western Royal Hotel. Ahead of him, to the left, was the long, curved reception counter and, to the right, the porter's desk. Small tables and armchairs were everywhere; it was carpeted underfoot. There were signs to lifts and to the bar and the restaurant. The stairway, gently rising to his left, was gracious, carpeted also.

They would sit for a moment in this hall, he imagined, as other people were sitting now, a few with drinks; others with pots of tea and plates half empty of assorted biscuits. He stood for a moment, watching these people, and then, as though he possessed a room in the hotel, he mounted the stairs, saying to himself that it must somehow be possible, that surely they could share a single night in the splendour of this place. There was a landing, made into a lounge, with armchairs and tables, as in the hall below. People conversed quietly; a foreign waiter, elderly and limping, collected silver-plated tea-pots; a Pekinese dog slept on a woman's lap.

The floor above was different. It was a long, wide corridor with bedroom doors on either side of it. Other corridors, exactly similar, led off it. Chambermaids passed him with lowered eyes; someone gently laughed in a room marked *Staff Only*; a waiter wheeled a trolley containing covered dishes, and a bottle of wine wrapped in a napkin. *Bathroom* a sign said, and he looked in, just to see what a bathroom in the Great Western Royal Hotel would be like. 'My God!' he whispered, possessed immediately with the idea that was, for him, to make the decade of the 1960s different. Looking back on it, he was for ever after unable to recall the first moment he beheld the bathroom on the second floor without experiencing the shiver of pleasure he'd experienced at the time. Slowly he entered. He locked the door and slowly sat down on the edge of the bath. The place was huge, as the bath itself was, like somewhere in a palace. The walls were marble, white veined delicately with grey. Two monstrous brass taps, the biggest bath taps he'd ever in his life seen, seemed to know already that he and Marie would come to the bathroom. They seemed almost to wink an invitation to him, to tell him that the bathroom was a comfortable place and not often in use since private bathrooms were now attached to most of the bedrooms. Sitting in his mackintosh coat on the edge of the bath, he wondered what Hilda would say if she could see him now.

*

He suggested it to Marie in the Drummer Boy. He led up to it slowly, describing the interior of the Great Western Royal Hotel and how he had wandered about it because he hadn't wanted to go home. 'Actually,' he said, 'I ended up in a bathroom.'

'You mean the toilet, dear? Taken short –'

'No, not the toilet. A bathroom on the second floor. Done out in marble, as a matter of fact.'

She replied that honestly he was a one, to go into a bathroom like that when he wasn't even staying in the place! He said:

'What I mean, Marie, it's somewhere we could go.'

'Go, dear?'

'It's empty half the time. Nearly all the time it must be. I mean, we could be there now. This minute if we wanted to.'

'But we're having our lunch, Norman.'

'That's what I mean. We could even be having it there.'

From the saloon bar's juke-box a lugubrious voice pleaded for a hand to be held. 'Take my hand,' sang Elvis Presley, 'take my whole life too.' The advertising executives from Dalton, Dure and Higgins were loudly talking about their hopes of gaining the Canadian Pacific account. Less noisily the architects from Frine and Knight complained about local planning regulations.

'In a bathroom, Norman? But we couldn't just go into a bathroom.'

'Why not?'

'Well, we couldn't. I mean, we *couldn't*.'

'What I'm saying is we could.'

'I want to marry you, Norman. I want us to be together. I don't want just going to a bathroom in some hotel.'

'I know; I want to marry you too. But we've got to work it out. You know we've got to work it out, Marie – getting married.'

'Yes, I know.'

It was a familiar topic of conversation between them. They took it for granted that one day, somehow, they would be married. They had talked about Hilda. He'd described Hilda to her, he'd drawn a picture in Marie's mind of Hilda bent over her jewellery-making in a Putney flat, or going out to drink V.P. with the Fowlers or at the Club. He hadn't presented a flattering picture of his wife, and when Marie had quite timidly said that she didn't much care for the sound of her he had agreed that naturally she wouldn't. The only aspect of Hilda he didn't touch upon was her bedroom appetite, night starvation as he privately dubbed it. He didn't mention it because he guessed it might be upsetting.

What they had to work out where Hilda was concerned were the economics of the matter. He would never, at Travel-Wide or anywhere else, earn a great deal of money. Familiar with Hilda's nature, he knew that as soon as a divorce was mooted she'd set out to claim as much alimony as she possibly could, which by law he would have to pay. She would state that she only made jewellery for pin-money and increasingly found it difficult to do so due to a developing tendency towards chilblains or arthritis, anything she could think of. She would hate him for rejecting her, for depriving her of a tame companion. Her own resentment at not being able to have children would somehow latch on to his unfaithfulness: she would see a pattern which wasn't really there, bitterness would come into her eyes.

Marie had said that she wanted to give him the children he had never had. She wanted to have children at once and she knew she could. He knew it too: having children was part of her, you'd only to look at her. Yet that would mean she'd have to give up her job, which she wanted to do when she married anyway, which in turn would mean that all three of them would have to subsist on his meagre salary. And not just all three, the children also.

It was a riddle that mocked him: he could find no answer, and yet he believed that the more he and Marie were together, the more they talked to one another and continued to be in love, the more chance there was of suddenly hitting upon a solution. Not that Marie always listened when he went on about it. She agreed they had to solve their problem, but now and again just pretended it wasn't there. She liked to forget about the existence of Hilda. For an hour or so when she was with him she liked to assume that quite soon, in July or even June, they'd be married. He always brought her back to earth.

'Look, let's just have a drink in the hotel,' he urged. 'Tonight, before the train. Instead of having one in the buffet.'

'But it's a hotel, Norman. I mean, it's for people to stay in –'

'Anyone can go into a hotel for a drink.'

That evening, after their drink in the hotel bar, he led her to the first-floor landing that was also a lounge. It was warm in the hotel. She said she'd like to sink down into one of the armchairs and fall asleep. He laughed at that; he didn't suggest an excursion to the bathroom, sensing that he shouldn't rush things. He saw her on to her train, abandoning her to her mother and Mrs Druk and Mavis. He knew that all during the journey she would be mulling over the splendours of the Great Western Royal.

December came. It was no longer foggy, but the weather was colder, with an icy wind. Every evening, before her train, they had their drink in the hotel. 'I'd love to show you that bathroom,' he said once. 'Just for fun.' He hadn't been pressing it in the least; it was the first time he'd mentioned the bathroom since he'd mentioned it originally. She giggled and said he was terrible. She said she'd miss her train if she went looking at bathrooms, but he said there'd easily be time. 'Gosh!' she whispered, standing in the doorway, looking in. He put his arm around her shoulders and drew her inside, fearful in case a chambermaid should see them loitering there. He locked the door and kissed her. In almost twelve months it was their first embrace in private.

They went to the bathroom during the lunch hour on New Year's Day, and he felt it was right that they should celebrate in this way the anniversary of their first real meeting. His early impression of her, that she was of a tartish disposition, had long since been dispelled. Voluptuous she might seem to the eye, but beneath that misleading surface she was prim and proper. It was odd that Hilda, who looked dried-up and wholly uninterested in the sensual life, should also belie her appearance. 'I've never done it before,' Marie confessed in the bathroom, and he loved her the more for that. He loved her simplicity in this matter, her desire to remain a virgin until her wedding. But since she repeatedly swore that she could marry no one else, their anticipating of their wedding night did not matter. 'Oh, God, I love you,' she whispered, naked for the first time in the bathroom. 'Oh, Norman, you're so good to me.'

After that it became a regular thing. He would saunter from the hotel bar, across the huge entrance lounge, and take a lift to the second floor. Five minutes later she would follow, with a towel brought specially from Reading in her handbag. In the bathroom they always whispered, and would sit together in a warm bath after their love-making, still murmuring about the future, holding hands beneath the surface of the water. No one ever rapped on the door to ask what was going on in there. No one ever questioned them as they returned, separately, to the bar, with the towel they'd shared damping her compact and her handkerchief.

Years instead of months began to go by. On the juke-box in the Drummer Boy the voice of Elvis Presley was no longer heard. *Why she had to go I don't know*, sang the Beatles, *she didn't say . . . I believe in yesterday*. And Eleanor Rigby entered people's lives, and Sergeant Pepper with her. The fantasies of secret agents, more fantastic than ever before, filled the screens of London's cinemas. Carnaby Street, like a jolly trash-can, overflowed with noise and colour. And in the bathroom of the Great Western Royal Hotel the love affair of Norman Britt and Marie was touched with the same preposterousness. They ate sandwiches in the bathroom; they drank wine. He whispered to her of the faraway places he knew about but had never been to: the Bahamas, Brazil, Peru, Seville at Easter, the Greek islands, the Nile, Shiraz, Persepolis, the Rocky Mountains. They should have been saving their money, not spending it on gin and peppermint in the bar of the hotel and in the Drummer Boy. They should have been racking their brains to find a solution to the problem of Hilda, but it was nicer to pretend that one day they would walk together in Venice or Tuscany. It was all so different from the activities that began with Hilda's bedroom appetites, and it was different from the coarseness that invariably surfaced when Mr Blackstaffe got going in the Drummer Boy on an evening when a Travel-Wide employee was being given a send-off. Mr Blackstaffe's great joke on such occasions was that he liked to have sexual intercourse with his wife at night and that she preferred the conjunction in the mornings. He was always going on about how difficult it was in the mornings, what with the children liable to interrupt you, and he usually went into details about certain other, more intimate preferences of his wife's. He had a powerful, waxy guffaw, which he brought regularly into play when he was engaged in this kind of conversation, allying it with a nudging motion of the elbow. Once his wife actually turned up in the Drummer Boy and Norman found it embarrassing even to look at her, knowing as he did so much about her private life. She was a stout middle-aged woman with decorated spectacles: her appearance, too, apparently belied much.

In the bathroom all such considerations, disliked equally by Norman Britt and Marie, were left behind. Romance ruled their brief sojourns, and love sanctified – or so they believed – the passion of their physical intimacy. Love excused their eccentricity, for only love could have found in them a willingness to engage in the deception of a hotel and the courage that went with it: that they believed most of all.

But afterwards, selling tickets to other people or putting Marie on her evening train, Norman sometimes felt depressed. And then gradually as more time passed, the depression increased and intensified. 'I'm so sad,' he whispered in the bathroom once, 'when I'm not with you. I don't think I can stand it.' She dried herself on the towel brought specially from Reading in her large red handbag. 'You'll have to tell her,' she said, with an edge in her voice that hadn't ever been there before. 'I don't want to leave having babies too late.' She wasn't twenty-eight any more; she was thirty-one. 'I mean, it isn't fair on me,' she said.

He knew it wasn't fair on her, but going over the whole thing yet again in Travel-Wide that afternoon he also knew that poverty would destroy them. He'd never earn much more than he earned now. The babies Marie wanted, and which he wanted too, would soak up what there was like blotting paper; they'd probably have to look for council accommodation. It made him weary to think about it, it gave him a headache. But he knew she was right: they couldn't go on for ever, living off a passing idyll, in the bathroom of a hotel. He even thought, quite seriously for a moment, of causing Hilda's death.

Instead he told her the truth, one Thursday evening after she'd been watching *The Avengers* on television. He just told her he'd met someone, a girl called Marie, he said, whom he had fallen in love with and wished to marry. 'I was hoping we could have a divorce,' he said.

Hilda turned the sound on the television set down without in any way dimming the picture, which she continued to watch. Her face did not register the hatred he had imagined in it when he rejected her; nor did bitterness suddenly enter her eyes. Instead she shook her head at him, and poured herself some more V.P. She said:

'You've gone barmy, Norman.'

'You can think that if you like.'

'Wherever'd you meet a girl, for God's sake?'

'At work. She's there in Vincent Street. In a shop.'

'And what's she think of you, may I ask?'

'She's in love with me, Hilda.'

She laughed. She told him to pull the other one, adding that it had bells on it.

'Hilda, I'm not making this up. I'm telling you the truth.'

She smiled into her V.P. She watched the screen for a moment, then she said:

'And how long's this charming stuff been going on, may I enquire?'

He didn't want to say for years. Vaguely, he said it had been going on for just a while.

'You're out of your tiny, Norman. Just because you fancy some piece in a shop doesn't mean you go getting hot under the collar. You're no tomcat, you know, old boy.'

'I didn't say I was.'

'You're no sexual mechanic.'

'Hilda –'

'All chaps fancy things in shops: didn't your mother tell you that? D'you think I haven't fancied stuff myself, the chap who came to do the blinds, that randy little postman with his rugby songs?'

'I'm telling you I want a divorce, Hilda.'

She laughed. She drank more V.P. wine. 'You're up a gum-tree,' she said, and laughed again.

'Hilda –'

'Oh, for God's sake!' All of a sudden she was angry, but more, he felt, because he was going on, not because of what he was actually demanding. She thought him ridiculous and said so. And then she added all the things he'd thought himself: that people like them didn't get divorces, that unless his girlfriend was well-heeled the whole thing would be a sheer bloody nonsense, with bloody solicitors the only ones to benefit. 'They'll send you to the cleaners, your bloody solicitors will,' she loudly pointed out, anger still trembling in her voice. 'You'd be paying them back for years.'

'I don't care,' he began, although he did. 'I don't care about anything except –'

'Of course you do, you damn fool.'

'Hilda –'

'Look, get over her. Take her into a park after dark or something. It'll make no odds to you and me.'

She turned the sound on the television up and quite quickly finished the V.P. wine. Afterwards, in their bedroom, she turned to him with an excitement that was greater than usual. 'God, that switched me on,' she whispered in the darkness, gripping him with her limbs. 'The stuff we were talking about, that girl.' When she'd finished her love-making she said, 'I had it with that postman, you know. Swear to God. In the kitchen. And since we're on the subject, Fowler looks in here the odd time.'

He lay beside her in silence, not knowing whether or not to believe what she was saying. It seemed at first that she was keeping her end up because he'd mentioned Marie, but then he wasn't so sure. 'We had a foursome once,' she said, 'the Fowlers and me and a chap that used to be in the Club.'

She began to stroke his face with her fingers, the way he hated. She always seemed to think that if she stroked his face it would excite him. She said, 'Tell me more about this piece you fancy.'

He told her to keep her quiet and to make her stop stroking his face. It didn't seem to matter now if he told her how long it had been going on, not since she'd made her revelations about Fowler and the postman. He even enjoyed telling her, about the New Year's Day when he'd bought the emery boards and the Colgate's, and how he'd got to know Marie because she and Mavis were booking a holiday on the Costa Brava.

'But you've never actually?'

'Yes, we have.'

'For God's sake where? Doorways or something? In the park?'

'We go to a hotel.'

'You old devil!'

'Listen, Hilda –'

'For God's sake go on, love. Tell me about it.'

He told her about the bathroom and she kept asking him questions, making him tell her details, asking him to describe Marie to her. Dawn was breaking when they finished talking.

'Forget about the divorce stuff,' she said quite casually at breakfast. 'I wouldn't want to hear no more of that. I wouldn't want you ruined for my sake, dear.'

He didn't want to see Marie that day, although he had to because it was arranged. In any case she knew he'd been going to tell his wife the night before; she'd want to hear the outcome.

'Well?' she said in the Drummer Boy.

He shrugged. He shook his head. He said:

'I told her.'

'And what'd she say, Norman? What'd Hilda say?'

'She said I was barmy to be talking about divorce. She said what I said to you: that we wouldn't manage with the alimony.'

They sat in silence. Eventually Marie said:

'Then can't you leave her? Can't you just not go back? We could get a flat somewhere. We could put off kiddies, darling. Just walk out, couldn't you?'

'They'd find us. They'd make me pay.'

'We could try it. If I keep on working you could pay what they want.'

'It'll never pan out, Marie.'

'Oh, darling, just walk away from her.'

Which is what, to Hilda's astonishment, he did. One evening when she was at the Club he packed his clothes and went to two rooms in Kilburn that he and Marie had found. He didn't tell Hilda where he was going. He just left a note to say he wouldn't be back.

They lived as man and wife in Kilburn, sharing a lavatory and a bathroom with fifteen other people. In time he received a court summons, and in court was informed that he had behaved meanly and despicably to the woman he'd married. He agreed to pay regular maintenance.

The two rooms in Kilburn were dirty and uncomfortable, and life in them was rather different from the life they had known together in the Drummer Boy and the Great Western Royal Hotel. They planned to find somewhere better, but at a reasonable price that wasn't easy to find. A certain melancholy descended on them, for although they were together they seemed as far away as ever from their own small house, their children, and their ordinary contentment.

'We could go to Reading,' Marie suggested.

'Reading?'

'To my mum's.'

'But your mum's nearly disowned you. Your mum's livid, you said yourself she was.'

'People come round.'

She was right. One Sunday afternoon they made the journey to Reading to have tea with Marie's mother and her friend Mrs Druk. Neither of these women addressed Norman, and once when he and Marie were in the kitchen he heard Mrs Druk saying it disgusted her, that he was old enough to be Marie's father. 'Don't think much of him,' Marie's mother replied. 'Pipsqueak really.'

Nevertheless, Marie's mother had missed her daughter's contribution to the household finances and before they returned to London that evening it was arranged that Norman and Marie should move in within a month, on the firm understanding that the very second it was feasible their marriage would take place. 'He's a boarder, mind,' Marie's mother warned. 'Nothing only a boarder in this house.' There were neighbours, Mrs Druk added, to be thought of.

Reading was worse than the two rooms in Kilburn. Marie's mother continued to make disparaging remarks about Norman, about the way he left the lavatory, or the thump of his feet on the staircarpet, or his fingermarks around the light-switches. Marie would deny these accusations and then there'd be a row, with Mrs Druk joining in because she loved a row, and Marie's mother weeping and then Marie weeping. Norman had been to see a solicitor about divorcing Hilda, quoting her unfaithfulness with a postman and with Fowler. 'You have your evidence, Mr Britt?' the solicitor enquired, and pursed his lips when Norman said he hadn't.

He knew it was all going to be too difficult. He knew his instinct had been right: he shouldn't have told Hilda, he shouldn't have just walked out. The whole thing had always been unfair on Marie; it had to be when a girl got mixed up with a married man. 'Should think of things like that,' her mother had a way of saying loudly when he was passing an open door. 'Selfish type he is,' Mrs Druk would loudly add.

Marie argued when he said none of it was going to work. But she wasn't as broken-hearted as she might have been a year or so ago, for the strain had told on Marie too, especially the strain in Reading. She naturally wept when Norman said they'd been defeated, and so for a moment did he. He asked for a transfer to another branch of Travel-Wide and was sent to Ealing, far away from the Great Western Royal Hotel.

Eighteen months later Marie married a man in a brewery. Hilda, hearing on some grapevine that Norman was on his own, wrote to him and suggested that bygones should be allowed to be bygones. Lonely in a bed-sitting-room in Ealing, he agreed to talk the situation over with her and after that he agreed to return to their flat. 'No hard feelings,' Hilda said, 'and no deception: there's been a chap from the Club in here, the Woolworth's manager.' No hard feelings, he agreed.

For Norman Britt, as the decade of the 1960s passed, it trailed behind it the marvels of his love affair with Marie. Hilda's scorn when he had confessed had not devalued them, nor had the two dirty rooms in Kilburn, nor the equally unpleasant experience in Reading. Their walk to the Great Western Royal, the drinks they could not afford in the hotel bar, their studied nonchalance as they made their way separately upstairs, seemed to Norman to be a fantasy that had miraculously become real. The second-floor bathroom belonged in it perfectly, the bathroom full of whispers and caressing, where the faraway places of his daily work acquired a hint of magic when he spoke of them to a girl as voluptuous as any of James Bond's. Sometimes on the Tube he would close his eyes and with the greatest pleasure that remained to him he would recall the delicately veined marble and the great brass taps, and the bath that was big enough for two. And now and again he heard what appeared to be the strum of distant music, and the voices of the Beatles celebrating a bathroom love, as they had celebrated Eleanor Rigby and other people of that time.

The Raising of Elvira Tremlett

My mother preferred English goods to Irish, claiming that the quality was better. In particular she had a preference for English socks and vests, and would not be denied in her point of view. Irish motor-car assemblers made a rough-and-ready job of it, my father used to say, the Austins and Morrises and Vauxhalls that came direct from British factories were twice the cars. And my father was an expert in his way, being the town's single garage-owner. *Devlin Bros*. it said on a length of painted wood, black letters on peeling white. The sign was crooked on the red corrugated iron of the garage, falling down a bit on the left-hand side.

In all other ways my parents were intensely of the country that had borne them, of the province of Munster and of the town they had always known. When she left the Presentation convent my mother had been found employment in the meat factory, working a machine that stuck labels on to tins. My father and his brother Jack, finishing at the Christian Brothers', had automatically passed into the family business. In those days the only sign on the corrugated façade had said *Raleigh Cycles*, for the business, founded by my grandfather, had once been a bicycle one. 'I think we'll make a change in that,' my father announced one day in 1933, when I was five, and six months or so later the rusty tin sheet that advertised bicycles was removed, leaving behind an island of grey in the corrugated red. 'Ah, that's grand,' my mother approved from the middle of the street, wiping her chapped hands on her apron. The new sign must have had a freshness and a gleam to it, but I don't recall that. In my memory there is only the peeling white behind the letters and the drooping down at the left-hand side where a rivet had fallen out. 'We'll paint that in and we'll be dandy,' my Uncle Jack said, referring to the island that remained, the contours of Sir Walter Raleigh's head and shoulders. But the job was never done.

We lived in a house next door to the garage, two storeys of cement that had a damp look, with green window-sashes and a green hall-door. Inside a wealth of polished brown linoleum, its pattern faded to nothing, was cheered here and there by the rugs my mother bought in Roche's Stores in Cork. The votive light of a crimson Sacred Heart gleamed day and night in the hall. Christ blessed us halfway up the stairs; on the landing the Virgin Mary was coy in garish robes. On either side of a narrow trodden carpet the staircase had been grained to make it seem like oak. In the dining-room, never used, there was a square table with six rexine-seated chairs around it, and over the mantelpiece a mirror with chromium decoration. The sitting-room smelt of must and had a picture of the Pope.

The kitchen was where everything happened. My father and Uncle Jack read the newspaper there. The old Philips wireless, the only one in the house, stood on one of the window-sills. Our two nameless cats used to crouch by the door into the scullery because one of them had once caught a mouse there. Our terrier, Tom, mooched about under my mother's feet when she was cooking at the range. There was a big scrubbed table in the middle of the kitchen, and wooden chairs, and a huge clock, like the top bit of a grandfather clock, hanging between the two windows. The dresser had keys and bits of wire and labels hanging all over it. The china it contained was never used, being hidden behind bric-à-brac: broken ornaments left there in order to be repaired with Seccotine, worn-out parts from the engines of cars which my father and uncle had brought into the kitchen to examine at their leisure, bills on spikes, letters and Christmas cards. The kitchen was always rather dusky, even in the middle of the day: it was partially a basement, light penetrating from outside only through the upper panes of its two long windows. Its concrete floor had been reddened with Cardinal polish, which was renewed once a year, in spring. Its walls and ceiling were a sooty white.

The kitchen was where we did our homework, my two sisters and two brothers and myself. I was the youngest, my brother Brian the oldest. Brian and Liam were destined for the garage when they finished at the Christian Brothers', as my father and Uncle Jack had been. My sister Effie was good at arithmetic and the nuns had once or twice mentioned accountancy. There was a commercial college in Cork she could go to, the nuns said, the same place that Miss Madden, who did the books for Bolger's Medical Hall, had attended. Everyone said my sister Kitty was pretty: my father used to take her on his knee and tell her she'd break some fellow's heart, or a dozen hearts or maybe more. She didn't know what he was talking about at first, but later she understood and used to go red in the face. My father was like that with Kitty. He embarrassed her without meaning to, hauling her on to his knee when she was much too old for it, fondling her because he liked her best. On the other hand, he was quite harsh with my brothers, constantly suspicious that they were up to no good. Every evening he asked them if they'd been to school that day, suspecting that they might have tricked the Christian Brothers and would the next day present them with a note they had written themselves, saying they'd had stomach trouble after eating bad sausages. He and my Uncle Jack had often engaged in such ploys themselves, spending a whole day in the field behind the meat factory, smoking Woodbines.

My father's attitude to my sister Effie was coloured by Effie's plainness. 'Ah, poor old Effie,' he used to say, and my mother would reprimand him. He took comfort from the fact that if the garage continued to thrive it would be necessary to have someone doing the increased book-work instead of himself and Uncle Jack trying to do it. For this reason he was in favour of Effie taking a commercial course: he saw a future in which she and my two brothers would live in the house and run the business between them. One or other of my brothers would marry and maybe move out of the house, leaving Effie and whichever one would still be a bachelor: it was my father's way of coming to terms with Effie's plainness. 'I wonder if Kitty'll end up with young Lacy?' I once heard him enquiring of my mother, the Lacy he referred to being the only child of another business in the town – Geo. Lacy and Sons, High-Class Drapers – who was about eight at the time. Kitty would do well, she'd marry whom she wanted to, and somehow or other she'd marry money: he really believed that.

For my part I fitted nowhere into my father's vision of the family's future. My performance at school was poor and there would be no place for me in the garage. I used to sit with the others at the kitchen table trying to understand algebra and Irish grammar, trying without any hope to learn verses from *Ode to the West Wind* and to improve my handwriting by copying from a headline book. 'Slow,' Brother Flynn had reported. 'Slow as a dying snail, that boy is.'

That was the family we were. My father was bulky in his grey overalls, always with marks of grease or dirt on him, his fingernails rimmed with black, like fingers in mourning, I used to think. Uncle Jack wore similar overalls but he was thin and much smaller than my father, a ferrety little man who had a way of looking at the ground when he spoke to you. He, too, was marked with grime and had the same rimmed fingernails, even at weekends. They both brought the smell of the garage into the kitchen, an oily smell that mingled with the fumes of my uncle's pipe and my father's cigarettes.

My mother was red-cheeked and stout, with waxy black hair and big arms and legs. She ruled the house, and was often cross: with my brothers when they behaved obstreperously, with my sisters and myself when her patience failed her. Sometimes my father would spend a long time on a Saturday night in Keogh's, which was the public house he favoured, and she would be cross with him also, noisily shouting in their bedroom, telling him to take off his clothes before he got into bed, telling him he was a fool. Uncle Jack was a teetotaller, a member of the Pioneer movement. He was a great help to Canon O'Keefe in the rectory and in the Church of the Holy Assumption, performing chores and repairing the electric light. Twice a year he spent a Saturday night in Cork in order to go to greyhound racing, but there was more than met the eye to these visits, for on his return there was always a great silence in the house, a fog of disapproval emanating from my father.

The first memories I have are of the garage, of watching my father and Uncle Jack at work, sparks flying from the welding apparatus, the dismantling of oil-caked engines. A car would be driven over the pit and my father or uncle would work underneath it, lit by an electric bulb in a wire casing on the end of a flex. Often, when he wasn't in the pit, my father would drift into conversation with a customer. He'd lean on the bonnet of a car, smoking continuously, talking about a hurling match that had taken place or about the dishonesties of the Government. He would also talk about his children, saying that Brian and Liam would fit easily into the business and referring to Effie's plans to study commerce and Kitty's prettiness. 'And your man here?' the customer might remark, inclining his head in my direction. To this question my father always replied in the same way. The Lord, he said, would look after me.

As I grew up I became aware that I made both my father and my mother uneasy. I assumed that this was due to my slowness at school, an opinion that was justified by a conversation I once overheard coming from their bedroom: they appeared to regard me as mentally deficient. My father repeated twice that the Lord would look after me. It was something she prayed for, my mother replied, and I imagined her praying after she'd said it, kneeling down by their bed, as she'd taught all of us to kneel by ours. I stood with my bare feet on the linoleum of the landing, believing that a plea from my mother was rising from the house at that very moment, up into the sky, where God was. I had been on my way to the kitchen for a drink of water, but I returned to the bedroom I shared with Brian and Liam and lay awake thinking of the big brown-brick mansion on the Mallow road. Once it had been owned and lived in by a local family. Now it was the town's asylum.

The town itself was small and ordinary. Part of it was on a hill, the part where the slum cottages were, where three or four shops had nothing in their windows except pasteboard advertisements for tea and Bisto. The rest of the town was flat, a single street with one or two narrow streets running off it. Where they met there was a square of a kind, with a statue of Daniel O'Connell. The Munster and Leinster Bank was here, and the Bank of Ireland, and Lacy and Sons, and Bolger's Medical Hall, and the Home and Colonial. Our garage was at one end of the main street, opposite Corrigan's Hotel. The Electric Cinema was at the other, a stark white façade not far from the Church of the Holy Assumption. The Protestant church was at the top of the hill, beyond the slums.

When I think of the town now I can see it very clearly: cattle and pigs on a fair-day, always a Monday; Mrs Driscoll's vegetable shop, Vickery's hardware, Phelan's the barber's, Kilmartin's the turf accountant's, the convent and the Christian Brothers', twenty-nine public houses. The streets are empty on a sunny afternoon, there's a smell of bread. Brass plates gleam on the way home from school: Dr Thos. Garvey M.D., R.C.S., Regan and O'Brien, Commissioners for Oaths, W. Tracy, Dental Surgeon.

But in my thoughts our house and our garage close in on everything else, shadowing and diminishing the town. The bedroom I shared with Brian and Liam had the same nondescript linoleum as the hall and the landing had. There was a dressing-table with a wash-stand in white-painted wood, and a wardrobe that matched. There was a flowery wallpaper on the walls, but the flowers had all faded to a uniform brown, except behind the bedroom's single picture, of an ox pulling a cart. Our three iron bedsteads were lined against one wall. Above the mantelpiece Christ on his cross had already given up the ghost.

I didn't in any way object to this bedroom and, familiar with no alternative, I didn't mind sharing it with my brothers. The house itself was somewhere I was used to also, accepted and taken for granted. But the garage was different. The garage was a kind of hell, its awful earth floor made black with sump oil, its huge indelicate vices, the chill of cast iron, the grunting of my father and my uncle as they heaved an engine out of a tractor, the astringent smell of petrol. It was there that my silence, my dumbness almost, must have begun. I sense that now, without being able accurately to remember. Looking back, I see myself silent in a classroom, taught first by nuns and later by Christian Brothers. In the kitchen, while the others chattered at mealtimes, I was silent too. I could take no interest in what my father and uncle reported about the difficulties they were having in getting spare parts or about some fault in a farmer's carburettor. My brothers listened to all that, and clearly found it easy to. Or they would talk about sport, or tease Uncle Jack about the money he lost on greyhounds and horses. My mother would repeat what she had heard in the shops, and Uncle Jack would listen intently because although he never himself indulged in gossip he loved to hear it. My sisters would retail news from the convent, the decline in the health of an elderly nun, or the inability of some family to buy Lacy's more expensive First Communion dresses. I often felt, listening at mealtimes, that I was scarcely there. I didn't belong and I sensed it was my fault; I felt I was a burden, being unpromising at school, unable to hold out hopes for the future. I felt I was a disgrace to them and might even become a person who was only fit to lift cans of paraffin about in the garage. I thought I could see that in my father's eyes, and in my uncle's sometimes, and in my mother's. A kind of shame it was, peering back at me.

I turned to Elvira Tremlett because everything about her was quiet. 'You great damn clown,' my mother would shout angrily at my father. He'd smile in the kitchen, smelling like a brewery, as she used to say. 'Mind that bloody tongue of yours,' he'd retort, and then he'd eye my uncle in a belligerent manner. 'Jeez, will you look at the cut of him?' he'd roar, laughing and throwing his head about. My uncle would usually be sitting in front of the range, a little to one side so as not to be in the way of my mother while she cooked. He'd been reading the *Independent* or *Ireland's Own*, or trying to mend something. 'You're the right eejit,' my father would say to him. 'And the right bloody hypocrite.'

It was always like that when he'd been in Keogh's on a Saturday evening and returned in time for his meal. My mother would slap the plates on to the table, my father would sing in order to annoy her. I used to feel that my uncle and my mother were allied on these occasions, just as she and my father were allied when my uncle spent a Saturday night in Cork after the greyhound racing. I much preferred it when my father didn't come back until some time in the middle of the night. 'Will you look at His Nibs?' he'd say in the kitchen, drawing attention to me. 'Haven't you a word in you, boy? Bedad, that fellow'll never make a lawyer.' He'd explode with laughter and then he'd tell Kitty that she was looking great and could marry the crowned King of England if she wanted to. He'd say to Effie she was getting fat with the toffees she ate; he'd tell my brothers they were lazy.

They didn't mind his talk the way I did; even Kitty's embarrassment used to evaporate quite quickly because for some reason she was fond of him. Effie was fond of my uncle, and my brothers of my mother. Yet in spite of all this family feeling, whenever there was quarrelling between our parents, or an atmosphere after my uncle had spent a night away, my brothers used to say the three of them would drive you mad. 'Wouldn't it make you sick, listening to it?' Brian would say in our bedroom, saying it to Liam. Then they'd laugh because they couldn't be bothered to concern themselves too much with other people's quarrels, or with atmospheres.

The fact was, my brothers and sisters were all part of it, whatever it was – the house, the garage, the family we were – and they could take everything in their stride. They were the same as our parents and our uncle, and Elvira Tremlett was different. She was a bit like Myrna Loy, whom I had seen in the Electric, in *Test Pilot* and *Too Hot to Handle* and *The Thin Man*. Only she was more beautiful than Myrna Loy, and her voice was nicer. Her voice, I still consider, was the nicest thing about Elvira Tremlett, next to her quietness.

'What do you want?' the sexton of the Protestant church said to me one Saturday afternoon. 'What're you doing here?'

He was an old, hunched man in black clothes. He had rheumy eyes, very red and bloody at the rims. It was said in the town that he gave his wife an awful time.

'It isn't your church,' he said.

I nodded, not wanting to speak to him. He said:

'It's a sin for you to be coming into a Protestant church. Are you wanting to be a Protestant, is that it?' He was laughing at me, even though his lips weren't smiling. He looked as if he'd never smiled in his life.

I shook my head at him, hoping he might think I was dumb.

'Stay if you want to,' he said, surprising me, even though I'd seen him coming to the conclusion that I wasn't going to commit some act of vandalism. I think he might even have decided to be pleased because a Catholic boy had chosen to wander among the pews and brasses of his church. He hobbled away to the vestry, breathing noisily because of his bent condition.

Several months before that Saturday I had wandered into the church for the first time. It was different from the Church of the Holy Assumption. It had a different smell, a smell that might have come from mothballs or from the tidy stacks of hymn-books and prayer-books, whereas the Church of the Holy Assumption smelt of people and candles. It was cosier, much smaller, with dark-coloured panelling and pews, and stained-glass windows that seemed old, and no cross on the altar. There were flags and banners that were covered with dust, all faded and in shreds, and a Bible spread out on the wings of an eagle.

The old sexton came back. I could feel him watching me as I read the tablets on the walls, moving from one to the next, pretending that each of them interested me. I might have asked him: I might have smiled at him and timidly enquired about Elvira Tremlett because I knew he was old enough to remember. But I didn't. I walked slowly up a side-aisle, away from the altar, to the back of the church. I wanted to linger there in the shadows, but I could feel his rheumy eyes on my back, wondering about me. As I slipped away from the church, down the short path that led through black iron gates to the street at the top of the hill, I knew that I would never return to the place.

'Well, it doesn't matter,' she said. 'You don't have to go back. There's nothing to go back for.'

I knew that was true. It was silly to keep on calling in at the Protestant church.

'It's curiosity that sends you there,' she said. 'You're much too curious.'

I knew I was: she had made me understand that. I was curious and my family weren't.

She smiled her slow smile, and her eyes filled with it. Her eyes were brown, the same colour as her long hair. I loved it when she smiled. I loved watching her fingers playing with the daisies in her lap, I loved her old-fashioned clothes, and her shoes and her two elaborate earrings. She laughed once when I asked her if they were gold. She'd never been rich, she said.

There was a place, a small field with boulders in it, hidden on the edge of a wood. I had gone there the first time, after I'd been in the Protestant church. What had happened was that in the church I had noticed the tablet on the wall, the left wall as you faced the altar, the last tablet on it, in dull grey marble.

> Near by this Stone
> Lies Interred the Body
> of Miss Elvira Tremlett
> Daughter of Wm. Tremlett
> of Tremlett Hall
> in the County of Dorset.
> She Departed this Life
> August 30   1873
> Aged 18.

Why should an English girl die in our town? Had she been passing through? Had she died of poisoning? Had someone shot her? Eighteen was young to die.

On that day, the first day I read her tablet, I had walked from the Protestant church to the field beside the wood. I often went there because it was a lonely place, away from the town and from people. I sat on a boulder and felt hot sun on my face and head, and on my neck and the backs of my hands. I began to imagine her, Elvira Tremlett of Tremlett Hall in the county of Dorset, England. I gave her her long hair and her smile and her elaborate earrings, and I felt I was giving her gifts. I gave her her clothes, wondering if I had got them right. Her fingers were delicate as straws, lacing together the first of her daisy-chains. Her voice hadn't the edge that Myrna Loy's had, her neck was more elegant.

'Oh, love,' she said on the Saturday after the sexton had spoken to me. 'The tablet's only a stone. It's silly to go gazing at it.'

I knew it was and yet it was hard to prevent myself. The more I gazed at it the more I felt I might learn about her: I didn't know if I was getting her right. I was afraid even to begin to imagine her death because I thought I might be doing wrong to have her dying from some cause that wasn't the correct one. It seemed insulting to her memory not to get that perfectly correct.

'You mustn't want too much,' she said to me on that Saturday afternoon. 'It's as well you've finished with the tablet on the wall. Death doesn't matter, you know.'

I never went back to the Protestant church. I remember what my mother had said about the quality of English goods, and how cars assembled in England were twice the ones assembled in Dublin. I looked at the map of England in my atlas and there was Dorset. She'd been travelling, maybe staying in a house near by, and had died somehow: she was right, it didn't matter.

Tremlett Hall was by a river in the country, with Virginia creeper all over it, with long corridors and suits of armour in the hall, and a fire-place in the hall also. In *David Copperfield*, which I had seen in the Electric, there might have been a house like Tremlett Hall, or in *A Yank at Oxford*: I couldn't quite remember. The gardens were beautiful: you walked from one garden to another, to a special rose-garden with a sundial, to a vegetable garden with high walls around it. In the house someone was always playing a piano. 'Me,' Elvira said.

My brothers went to work in the garage, first Brian and then Liam. Effie went to Cork, to the commercial college. The boys at the Christian Brothers' began to whistle at Kitty and sometimes would give me notes to pass on to her. Even when other people were there I could feel Elvira's nearness, even her breath sometimes, and certainly the warmth of her hands. When Brother Flynn hit me one day she cheered me up. When my father came back from Keogh's in time for his Saturday tea her presence made it easier. The garage I hated, where I was certain now I would one day lift paraffin cans from one corner to another, was lightened by her. She was in Mrs Driscoll's vegetable shop when I bought cabbage and potatoes for my mother. She was there while I waited for the Electric to open, and when I walked through the animals on a fair-day. In the stony field the sunshine made her earrings glitter. It danced over a brooch she had not had when first I imagined her, a brooch with a scarlet jewel, in the shape of a dragon. Mist caught in her hair, wind ruffled the skirts of her old-fashioned dress. She wore gloves when it was cold, and a green cloak that wrapped itself all around her. In spring she often carried daffodils, and once – one Sunday in June – she carried a little dog, a grey Cairn that afterwards became part of her, like her earrings and her brooch.

I grew up but she was always eighteen, as petrified as her tablet on the wall. In the bedroom which I shared with Brian and Liam I came, in time, to take her dragon's brooch from her throat and to take her earrings from her pale ears and to lift her dress from her body. Her limbs were warm, and her smile was always there. Her slender fingers traced caresses on my cheeks. I told her that I loved her, as the people told one another in the Electric.

'You know why they're afraid of you?' she said one day in the field by the wood. 'You know why they hope that God will look after you?'

I had to think about it but I could come to no conclusion on my own, without her prompting. I think I wouldn't have dared; I'd have been frightened of whatever there was.

'You know what happens,' she said, 'when your uncle stays in Cork on a Saturday night? You know what happened once when your father came back from Keogh's too late for his meal, in the middle of the night?'

I knew before she told me. I guessed, but I wouldn't have if she hadn't been there. I made her tell me, listening to her quiet voice. My Uncle Jack went after women as well as greyhounds in Cork. It was his weakness, like going to Keogh's was my father's. And the two weaknesses had once combined, one Saturday night a long time ago when my uncle hadn't gone to Cork and my father was a long time in Keogh's. I was the child of my Uncle Jack and my mother, born of his weakness and my mother's anger as she waited for the red bleariness of my father to return, footless in the middle of the night. It was why my father called my uncle a hypocrite. It was maybe why my uncle was always looking at the ground, and why he assisted Canon O'Keefe in the rectory and in the Church of the Holy Assumption. I was their sin, growing in front of them, for God to look after.

'They have made you,' Elvira said. 'The three of them have made you what you are.'

I imagined my father returning that night from Keogh's, stumbling on the stairs, and haste being made by my uncle to hide himself. In these images it was always my uncle who was anxious and in a hurry: my mother kept saying it didn't matter, pressing him back on to the pillows, wanting him to be found there.

My father was like a madman in the bedroom then, wild in his crumpled Saturday clothes. He struck at both of them, his befuddled eyes tormented while my mother screamed. She went back through all the years of their marriage, accusing him of cruelty and neglect. My uncle wept. 'I'm no more than an animal to you,' my mother screamed, half-naked between the two of them. 'I cook and clean and have children for you. You give me thanks by going out to Keogh's.' Brian was in the room, attracted by the noise. He stood by the open door, five years old, telling them to be quiet because they were waking the others.

'Don't ever tell a soul,' Brian would have said, years afterwards, retailing that scene for Liam and Effie and Kitty, letting them guess the truth. He had been sent back to bed, and my uncle had gone to his own bed, and in the morning there had begun the pretending that none of it had happened. There was confession and penance, and extra hours spent in Keogh's. There were my mother's prayers that I would not be born, and my uncle's prayers, and my father's bitterness when the prayers weren't answered.

On the evening of the day that Elvira shared all that with me I watched them as we ate in the kitchen, my father's hands still smeared with oil, his fingernails in mourning, my uncle's eyes bent over his fried eggs. My brothers and sisters talked about events that had taken place in the town; my mother listened without interest, her large round face seeming stupid to me now. It was a cause for celebration that I was outside the family circle. I was glad not to be part of the house and the garage, and not to be part of the town with its statue and its shops and its twenty-nine public houses. I belonged with a figment of my imagination to an English ghost who had acquired a dog, whose lips were soft, whose limbs were warm, Elvira Tremlett, who lay beneath the Protestant church.

'Oh, love,' I said in the kitchen, 'thank you.'

The conversation ceased, my father's head turned sharply. Brian and Liam looked at me, so did Effie and Kitty. My mother had a piece of fried bread on a fork, on the way to her mouth. She returned it to her plate. There was grease at the corner of her lips, a little shiny stream from some previous mouthful, running down to her chin. My uncle pushed his knife and fork together and stared at them.

I felt them believing with finality now, with proof, that I was not sane. I was fifteen years old, a boy who was backward in his ways, who was all of a sudden addressing someone who wasn't in the room.

My father cut himself a slice of bread, moving the bread-saw slowly through the loaf. My brothers were as valuable in the garage now as he or my uncle; Effie kept the books and sent out bills. My father took things easy, spending more time talking to his older customers. My uncle pursued the racing pages; my mother had had an operation for varicose veins, which she should have had years ago.

I could disgrace them in the town, in all the shops and public houses, in Bolger's Medical Hall, in the convent and the Christian Brothers' and the Church of the Holy Assumption. How could Brian and Liam carry on the business if they couldn't hold their heads up? How could Effie help with the petrol pumps at a busy time, standing in her Wellington boots on a wet day, for all the town to see? Who would marry Kitty now?

I had spoken by mistake, and I didn't speak again. It was the first time I had said anything at a meal in the kitchen for as long as I could remember, for years and years. I had suddenly felt that she might grow tired of coming into my mind and want to be left alone, buried beneath the Protestant church. I had wanted to reassure her.

'They're afraid of you,' she said that night. 'All of them.'

She said it again when I walked in the sunshine to our field. She kept on saying it, as if to warn me, as if to tell me to be on the look-out. 'They have made you,' she repeated. 'You're the child of all of them.'

I wanted to go away, to escape from the truth we had both instinctively felt and had shared. I walked with her through the house called Tremlett Hall, haunting other people with our footsteps. We stood and watched while guests at a party laughed among the suits of armour in the hall, while there was waltzing in a ballroom. In the gardens dahlias bloomed, and sweet-pea clung to wires against a high stone wall. Low hedges of fuchsia bounded the paths among the flower-beds, the little dog ran on in front of us. She held my hand and said she loved me; she smiled at me in the sunshine. And then, just for a moment, she seemed to be different; she wasn't wearing the right clothes; she was wearing a tennis dress and had a racquet in her hand. She was standing in a conservatory, one foot on a cane chair. She looked like another girl, Susan Peters in *Random Harvest*.

I didn't like that. It was the same kind of thing as feeling I had to speak to her even though other people were in the kitchen. It was a muddle, and somewhere in it I could sense an unhappiness I didn't understand. I couldn't tell if it was hers or mine. I tried to say I was sorry, but I didn't know what I was sorry for.

In the middle of one night I woke up screaming. Brian and Liam were standing by my bed, cross with me for waking them. My mother came, and then my father. I was still screaming, unable to stop. 'He's had some type of nightmare,' Brian said.

It wasn't a nightmare because it continued when I was awake. She was there, Elvira Tremlett, born 1855. She didn't talk or smile: I couldn't make her. Something was failing in me: it was the same as Susan Peters suddenly appearing with a tennis racquet, the same as my desperation in wanting to show gratitude when we weren't in private.

My mother sat beside my bed. My brothers returned to theirs. The light remained on. I must have whispered, I must have talked about her because I remember my mother's nodding head and her voice assuring me that it was all a dream. I slept, and when I woke up it was light in the room and my mother had gone and my brothers were getting up. Elvira Tremlett was still there, one eye half-closed in blindness, the fingers that had been delicate misshapen now. When my brothers left the room she was more vivid, a figure by the window, turning her head to look at me, a gleam of fury in her face. She did not speak but I knew what she was saying. I had used her for purposes of my own, to bring solace. What right, for God's sake, had I to blow life into her decaying bones? Born 1855, eighty-nine years of age.

I closed my eyes, trying to imagine her as I had before, willing her young girl's voice and her face and hair. But even with my eyes closed the old woman moved about the room, from the window to the foot of Liam's bed, to the wardrobe, into a corner, where she stood still.

She was on the landing with me, and on the stairs and in the kitchen. She was in the stony field by the wood, accusing me of disturbing her and yet still not speaking. She was in pain from her eye and her arthritic hands: I had brought about that. Yet she was no ghost, I knew she was no ghost. She was a figment of my imagination, drawn from her dull grey tablet by my interest. She existed within me, I told myself, but it wasn't a help.

Every night I woke up screaming. The sheets of my bed were sodden with my sweat. I would shout at my brothers and my mother, begging them to take her away from me. It wasn't I who had committed the sin, I shouted, it wasn't I who deserved the punishment. All I had done was to talk to a figment. All I'd done was to pretend, as they had.

Canon O'Keefe talked to me in the kitchen. His voice came and went, and my mother's voice spoke of the sheets sodden with sweat every morning, and my father's voice said there was terror in my eyes. All I wanted to say was that I hadn't meant any harm in raising Elvira Tremlett from the dead in order to have an imaginary friend, or in travelling with her to the house with Virginia creeper on it. She hadn't been real, she'd been no more than a flicker on the screen of the Electric Cinema: I wanted to say all that. I wanted to be listened to, to be released of the shame that I felt like a shroud around me. I knew that if I could speak my imagination would be free of the woman who haunted it now. I tried, but they were afraid of me. They were afraid of what I was going to say and between them they somehow stopped me. 'Our Father,' said Canon O'Keefe, 'Who art in heaven, Hallowed be Thy Name. . . .'

Dr Garvey came and looked at me: in Cork another man looked at me. The man in Cork tried to talk to me, telling me to lie down, to take my shoes off if I wanted to. It wasn't any good, and it wasn't fair on them, having me there in the house, a person in some kind of nightmare. I quite see now that it wasn't fair on them, I quite see that.

Because of the unfairness I was brought, one Friday morning in a Ford car my father borrowed from a customer, to this brown-brick mansion, once the property of a local family. I have been here for thirty-four years.

The clothes I wear are rough, but I have ceased to be visited by the woman who Elvira Tremlett became in my failing imagination. I ceased to be visited by her the moment I arrived here, for when that moment came I knew that this was the house she had been staying in when she died. She brought me here so that I could live in peace, even in the room that had been hers. I had disturbed her own peace so that we might come here together.

I have not told this story myself. It has been told by my weekly visitor, who has placed me at the centre of it because that, of course, is where I belong. Here, in the brown-red mansion, I have spoken without difficulty. I have spoken in the garden where I work in the daytime; I have spoken at all meals; I have spoken to my weekly visitor. I am different here. I do not need an imaginary friend, I could never again feel curious about a girl who died.

I have asked my visitor what they say in the town, and what the family say. He replies that in the bar of Corrigan's Hotel commercial travellers are told of a boy who was haunted, as a place or a house is. They are drawn across the bar to a window: Devlin Bros., the garage across the street, is pointed out to them. They listen in pleasurable astonishment to the story of nightmares, and hear the name of an English girl who died in the town in 1873, whose tablet is on the wall of the Protestant church. They are told of the final madness of the boy, which came about through his visions of this girl, Elvira Tremlett.

The story is famous in the town, the only story of its kind the town possesses. It is told as a mystery, and the strangers who hear it sometimes visit the Protestant church to look up at the tablet that commemorates a death in 1873. They leave the church in bewilderment, wondering why an uneasy spirit should have lighted on a boy so many years later. They never guess, not one of them, that the story as it happened wasn't a mystery in the least.

A Dream of Butterflies

Various people awoke with a sense of relief. Sleepily, Colin Rhodes wondered what there was to be relieved about. As he did in the moment of waking every morning, he encased with his left hand one of his wife's plump breasts and then remembered the outcome of last night's meeting. Miss Cogings, alone in her narrow bed and listening to a chorus of house-martins, remembered it with the same degree of satisfaction. So did the Poudards when their Teasmade roused them at a quarter to seven. So did the Reverend Feare, and Mr Mottershead and Mr and Mrs Tilzey, and the Blennerhassetts, who ran the Village Stores. Mrs Feare, up since dawn with an ailing child, was pleased because her husband was. There would be peace when there might have been war. A defeat had been inflicted.

The Allenbys, however, awoke in Luffnell Lodge with mixed feelings. What to do with the Lodge now that it remained unsold? How long would they have to wait for another buyer? For having made their minds up, they really wanted to move on as soon as possible. A bridging loan had been negotiated at one point but they'd decided against it because the interest was so high. They planned to buy a bungalow in a part of Cornwall that was noted for its warmth and dryness, both of which would ease Mrs Allenby's arthritis. Everything that had been said at the meeting made sense to Mr and Mrs Allenby; they quite understood the general point of view. But they wished, that morning, that things might have been different.

'That's really bizarre,' Hugh said in the Mansors' breakfast-room.
'Dreams often are.'
'But butterflies –'
'It has to do with the meeting.'
'Ah, of course, the meeting.'
He saw at once what had been happening. He traced quite easily the series of his wife's thoughts, one built upon the last, fact in the end becoming fantasy.

Emily buttered toast and reached for grapefruit marmalade. 'Silly,' she said, not believing that it was.

'A bit,' he agreed, smiling at her. He went on to talk of something else, an item in *The Times*, another airliner hi-jacked.

The sun filled their breakfast-room. It struck the bones of his narrow face; it livened his calm grey hair. It found the strawberry mark, like a tulip, on her neck; it made her spectacles glint. They were the same age, fifty-two, not yet grandparents but soon to be. He dealt in property; she'd once been a teacher of Latin and Greek. She was small and given to putting on weight if she wasn't careful: dumpy, she considered herself.

'Don't let it worry you,' Hugh said, folding *The Times* for further perusal on the train. 'It's all over now.'

He was handsome in his thin way, and she was plain. Perhaps he had married her because he had not felt up to the glamour of a beautiful woman: as a young man, unproved in the world, he had had an inferiority complex, and success in middle age had not managed to shake it off. It wouldn't have surprised him if the heights he'd scaled in his business world all of a sudden turned out to be a wasteland. He specialized in property in distant places, Jamaica, Spain, the Bahamas: some economic jolt could shatter everything. The house they lived in, on the edge of a Sussex village, was the symbol of his good fortune over the years. It was also his due, for he had worked doggedly; only his inferiority complex prevented him from taking it for granted. It puzzled him that he, so unpromising as a boy at school, had done so well; and occasionally, but not often, it puzzled him that they'd made a success of their marriage in times when the failure rate was high. Perhaps they'd made a go of it because she was modest too: more than once he'd wondered if that could be true. Could it be that Emily, so much cleverer than he, had found a level with him because her lack of beauty kept her in her place, as his inferiority complex kept him? She had said that as a girl she'd imagined she would not marry, assuming that a strawberry mark and dumpiness, and glasses too, would be too much for any man. He often thought about her as she must have been, cleverest in the class; while he was being slow on the uptake. 'You're very kind' was what most often, in the way of compliments, Emily said to him.

'Have a good day' was what she said now, forcing cheerfulness on to her face, for the dream she'd had still saddened her and the memory of the meeting worried her.

'I'll be on the five o'clock.' He touched her cheek with his lips, and then was gone, the door of the breakfast-room opening and closing, the hall-door banging. She listened to the starting of the car and the sound of the wheels on the tarmac, then the engine fading to nothing in the distance.

She felt as he did, that together they had not done badly in twenty-seven years of marriage. She'd been a Miss Forrest; becoming Mrs Mansor had seemed the nicest thing that yet had happened to her; and for all their married life – the worries during the lean years, the bringing up of their three children – she had regretted nothing, and in the end there'd been the reward of happiness in middle age. She missed their son and daughters, all of whom were now married themselves, but in compensation there was the contentment that the house and garden brought, and the unexacting life of the village. As well, there were the visits of their children and her memories of girls whom she had taught, some of whom kept up with her. It was still a pleasure to read Horace and the lesser Greek poets, to find in an experimental way a new interpretation in place of the standard, scholar's one.

Their house, in the style of Queen Anne though in fact of a later period, was hidden from the road and the surrounding fields by modest glades of silver birches. It was a compact house, easy to run and keep clean, modernized with gadgets, warm in winter. Alone in it in the mornings Emily often played Bach or Mozart on the sitting-room hi-fi system, the music drifting into the kitchen and the bedrooms and the breakfast-room, pursuing her agreeably wherever she went.

But this morning she was not in the mood for Bach or Mozart. She continued to sit as her husband had left her, saying to herself that she must come to terms with what had happened. She had raised her voice but no one had cared to listen to it. Only Golkorn had listened, his great tightly-cropped head slowly nodding, his eyes occasionally piercing hers. At the meeting her voice had faltered; her cheeks had warmed; nothing had come out as she'd meant it to.

Unladylike assortment of calumnies. In the train on the way to Waterloo he couldn't think of a nine-lettered word. As a chore, he did *The Times* crossword every day, determined to do better with practice. *There's none of the Old Adam in a cardinal* (6). He sighed and put the paper down.

It worried him that she'd been so upset. He hadn't known what to say, or to do, when she'd stood up suddenly at the meeting to make her unsuccessful speech. He'd felt himself embarrassed, in sympathy or shame, he couldn't tell which. He hadn't been quite able to agree with her and had been surprised when she'd stood up because it wasn't like her to do anything in public, even though she'd been saying she was unhappy about the thing for months. But then she was so unemphatic as a person that quite often it was hard to guess when she felt strongly.

With other suited men, some carrying as he did a brief-case and a newspaper, he stepped from the train at Waterloo. He strode along the platform with them, one in an army, it often seemed. In spite of how she felt, he really couldn't help believing that the village had been saved. Their own house and garden, and the glades of silver birches, would in no way suffer. The value of the house would continue to rise with inflation instead of quite sharply declining. There would be calm again in the village instead of angry voices and personal remarks, instead of Colin Rhodes saying to Golkorn's face that he was a foreigner. Thank God it was all over.

'There's been a telex,' Miss Brooks informed him in his office. 'That place in Gibraltar.'

In the breakfast-room Emily's thoughts had spread out, from her dream of butterflies and the meeting there had been the night before. She saw images of women as they might have been, skulking in the woods near the village, two of them sitting on the stone seat beside the horse-trough on the green, another in a lane with ragwort in her hand. They were harmless women, as Golkorn had kept insisting. It was just that their faces were strange and their movements not properly articulated; nothing, of course, that they said made sense. 'Anywhere but here,' snapped the voice of Colin Rhodes, as vividly she recalled the meeting. 'My God, you've got the world to choose from, Golkorn.'

Golkorn had smiled. Their village was beautiful, he had irritatingly stated, as if in reply. Repeatedly it had been said at the meeting last night, and at previous meetings, that the village was special because it was among the most beautiful in England. The Manor dated back to Saxon times, it had been said, and the cottages round the green were almost unique. But it was that very beauty, and the very peacefulness of the lanes and woods, that Golkorn had claimed would be a paradise for his afflicted women. It was why he had chosen Luffnell Lodge when it went up for sale. Luffnell Lodge was less impressive than the Manor, and certainly nothing like as old. It was larger and less convenient, colder and in worse repair, yet ideal apparently for Golkorn's purpose. In her dream Emily had been walking with him in a field and he had pointed at what at first she'd taken to be flowers but had turned out to be butterflies. 'You've never seen that before,' he'd said. 'Butterflies in mourning, Mrs Mansor.' They flew away as he spoke, a whole swarm of them, busily flapping their black wings.

She rose and cleared away the breakfast things. She carried them on a tray through the hall and into the kitchen. Her dog, an old Sealyham called Spratts, wagged his tail without getting out of his basket. On the window-sill in front of the sink, hot with morning sunshine, a butterfly was poised and she thought at once that that was a coincidence. Its wings were tightly closed; it might have been dead but she knew it wasn't, and when she touched it and the wings opened they were not sinister.

Of course it had been for the best when the Allenbys had realized that to sell Luffnell Lodge to Golkorn would have caused havoc: dealing with the telex about the place in Gibraltar, Hugh found himself yet again thinking that. Golkorn was a frightful person; it was Golkorn's presence rather than his sick women whom one might reasonably object to. Luffnell Lodge would put the village on the map, Golkorn had confidently promised, once it was full of his patients: in medical terms he was making a breakthrough. And Hugh knew that what he had offered the Allenbys was more than they'd get otherwise. You couldn't blame them, elderly and wanting to get rid of what they'd come to think of as a white elephant, for listening to Golkorn's adroit arguments. The Allenbys had done nothing wrong and in the end had made the sacrifice. They'd sell the Lodge eventually, it stood to reason, even if they had to wait a bit. 'You see, we don't particularly want to wait,' old Mr Allenby had said. 'That's just the trouble. We've waited two years as it is.' The Allenbys had asked Hugh's advice because they thought that being in the international property market he might know a little more than Musgrove and Carter, who after all were only country estate agents. 'Dr Golkorn is offering you a most attractive proposition,' he'd had to admit, no way around that. 'It could be a while before anyone matched it.' Mr Allenby had asked if he'd care to handle the sale, in conjunction with Musgrove and Carter, but Hugh had had to explain that property in England was outside his firm's particular field. 'Oh, dear, it's all so difficult,' Mrs Allenby had disconsolately murmured, clearly most unhappy at the prospect of having to hang on in the Lodge for another couple of years. Hugh had always liked the Allenbys. In many ways, as a friend and as an expert, he should have told them to accept immediately Golkorn's offer. But he hadn't and that was that; it was all now best forgotten.

For Hugh that day passed as days did at the office. He dictated letters and received telephone calls. He lunched with a client in the Isola Bella, quite often he thought about his wife. Emily was unhappy because of everything that had happened. She felt, but had not said so, that he had let the Allenbys down. She felt that she herself had let the inmates of Golkorn's home down. Hugh tried not to think about it; but in his mind's eye he kept seeing her again, standing up at the meeting and saying that afflicted women have to live somewhere. Like mongol children, she had said, stammering; or the blind. 'That's quite appreciated, Mrs Mansor,' the Reverend Feare had murmured, and as if to come to her assistance Golkorn had asked if he might address the meeting. He had nodded his heavy razored head at Emily; he had repeated what she'd said, that afflicted women, like mongol children and the blind, have to go somewhere. He had smiled and spread his hands out, impatient with those who were protesting and yet oilily endeavouring to hide it. A woman present, he'd even suggested, might one day need the home he proposed for Luffnell Lodge. Hugh sighed, remembering it all vividly. He would take Emily out to dinner, to the Rowan House Hotel. He was about to pick up the telephone in order to ask to be put through to her when it rang. Odd, he thought as he picked up the receiver, that she had dreamed so strangely of butterflies.

'It's a Dr Golkorn,' his secretary's voice said. 'On the other line, Mr Mansor.'

He hesitated. There was no point in speaking to Golkorn; at half-past ten last night Golkorn had lost his case; the matter was closed. Yet something – perhaps just politeness, he afterwards thought – made him pick up the other telephone. 'Yes?' he said.

'It's Golkorn,' Golkorn said. 'Look, Mr Mansor, could we talk?'

'About the Lodge? But that's all over, Dr Golkorn. The Allenbys –'

'Sir, they agreed beneath all this pressure not to let me have the house. But with respect, is that just, sir? At least agree to exchange another word or two with me, Mr Mansor.'

'It would be useless, I'm afraid.'

'Mr Mansor, do me a favour.'

'I would willingly do you a favour if I thought –'

'I ask you only for ten minutes. If I may come to see you for ten minutes, Mr Mansor, I would esteem it.'

'You mean, you want to come here?'

'I mean, sir, I would like to come to your very pleasant home. I would like to call in at seven tonight if that might be convenient. The reason I am suggesting this, Mr Mansor, is I am still in the neighbourhood of the village. I am still staying in the same hotel.'

'Well, yes, come over by all means, but I really must warn you –'

'I am used to everything, Mr Mansor.' Laughter accompanied this remark and then Golkorn said, 'I look forward to seeing you and your nice wife. I promise only to occupy ten minutes.'

Hugh telephoned Emily. 'Golkorn,' he said. 'He wants to come and see us.'

'But what for?'

'I really can't think. I couldn't say no.'

'Of course not.'

'He's coming at seven.'

She said goodbye and put the receiver down. The development astonished her. She thought that at least they had finished with Golkorn.

The telephone rang again and Hugh suggested that they should go out to dinner, to Rowan House, where they often went. She knew he was suggesting it because she'd been upset. She appreciated that, but she said she'd rather make it another night, mainly because she had a stew in the oven. 'I'm sorry about that wretched man,' Hugh said. 'He wasn't easy to choke off.' She reassured him, making a joke of Golkorn's insistence, saying that of course it didn't matter.

In the garden she picked sweet-peas. She sat for a moment in the corner where she and Hugh often had coffee together on Saturday and Sunday mornings. She put the sweet-peas on the slatted garden table and let her glance wander over lupins and delphiniums, and the tree geranium that was Hugh's particular pride. On trellises and archways which he'd made roses trailed in profusion, Mermaid and Danse du Feu. She loved the garden, as she loved the house.

At her feet the Sealyham called Spratts settled down to rest for a while, but she warned him that she didn't intend to remain long in the secluded corner. In a moment she picked up the sweet-peas and took them to the kitchen, where she arranged them in a cut-glass vase. The dog followed her when she carried it to the sitting-room. Was it unusual, she wondered, to pick flowers specially for a person you didn't like? Yet it had seemed a natural thing to do; she always picked flowers when a visitor was coming.

'Ten minutes I promised,' Golkorn said at seven o'clock, having been notably prompt, 'so ten minutes it must be.' He laughed, as if he'd made a joke of some kind. 'No, no drink for me, please.'

Hugh poured Emily a glass of sherry, Harvey's Luncheon Dry, which was what she always had. He smeared a glass with Angostura drops and added gin and water to it for himself. Perhaps there was something in the fact that he had rescued her, he thought, wanting to think about her rather than their visitor. Even though she loved the subject, she had never been entirely happy as a teacher of Classics because she was shy. Until she came to know them she was nervous of the girls she taught: her glasses and her strawberry mark and her dumpiness, the very fact that she was a teacher, seemed to put her into a certain category, at a disadvantage. And perhaps his rescuing of her, if you could so grandly call it that, had in turn given him something he'd lacked before. Perhaps their marriage was indeed built on debts to one another.

'Orange juice, Mr Golkorn?' Emily suggested, already rising to get it for him.

He waved a hand, denying his need of orange juice. 'Look,' he said, 'I don't want to beat about the bush. I want to come to the point. Luffnell Lodge, Mr Mansor. You're a man of business, you know those people wouldn't ever get that price. They'll lose a lot. You know that.'

'We've been through all of it, Dr Golkorn. The Allenbys do not wish to sell their property to you.'

'They're elderly people –'

'That has nothing to do with it.'

'With respect, Mr Mansor, it may have. Our elderly friends could be sitting there in that barracks for winter after winter. They could freeze to death. The old lady's crippled with arthritis as it is.'

'Mrs Allenby's illness cannot enter into this. The Allenbys –'

'With respect, sir, they came to you for advice.'

'That is so.'

'With respect, sir, the advice you gave them was unfortunate.'

'If they'd sold the Lodge to you they'd be hated in the village.'

'But they'd be gone, Mr Mansor. They'd have kicked the dust off their heels. They'd be imbibing the sun on some island somewhere. As their doctor advised.'

'They've lived in this village for more than fifty years. It matters to them what the village thinks of them. We've been all through this, you know. I can't help you, Dr Golkorn.'

Golkorn bent his head for a moment over clasped hands, as if praying for patience. He was slightly smiling. When eventually he looked up there was a glint in his dark, clever eyes which suggested that, despite appearances, he held the more useful cards. His black pin-striped suit was uncreased, his smooth black shoes had a glassy glow. He wore a blue shirt and a blue bow-tie with small white spots on it. The night before, at the meeting, he'd been similarly dressed except for his shirt and tie. The shirt had last night been pink and the tie a shade of deep crimson, though also with white spots.

'What do you think, Mrs Mansor?' he said in his soft, unhurried voice, still smiling a little. 'How do you see this unhappy business?' His manner suggested that they might have been his patients. Any moment now, Hugh thought, he might tell them to go out for a walk.

'I feel as my husband does,' Emily said. 'I feel the Allenbys have given you their answer.'

'I mean, madam, how do you feel about the people I wish to help? I do not mean the Allenbys, Mrs Mansor; I mean of course those who would one day be my patients in Luffnell Lodge.'

'You heard what my wife said last night, Dr Golkorn,' Hugh interjected quickly. 'She is sympathetic towards such people.'

'You would not yourself object to these patients in your village, Mrs Mansor? Did I understand you correctly when you spoke last night?'

'That is what I said. I would personally not object.'

'With respect, madam, you feel a certain guilt? Well, I assure you it is natural to feel a certain guilt. By that I mean it is natural for some people.' He laughed. 'Not Colin Rhodes of course, or Mr Mottershead, or Mr and Mrs Tilzey, or Miss Cogings. Not your clergyman, Mr Feare, even though he is keen to show his concern for the unwell. I think you're different, madam.'

'My wife –'

'Let us perhaps hear your wife, eh? Mrs Mansor, you do not believe the village would be a bear garden if a handful of unhappy women were added to it: that was what you implied last night?'

'Yes.'

'But the vote went against you.'

'No vote was taken,' Hugh said sharply. 'The meeting was simply to explain to you why the Allenbys had decided not to sell.'

'But there had been other meetings, eh? At which I naturally was not present. There have been six months of meetings, I think I'm correct in stating. You've argued back and forth among yourselves, and sides have naturally been taken. In the end, you know, the question we have to ask is should our elderly friends not be allowed to do what is best for them since they have done so much for the village in the past? The other question we have to ask is would it be the end of the universe to have a handful of mentally ill women in Luffnell Lodge? With respect, madam, you feel guilty now because you did not fight hard enough for justice and humanity. And you, sir, because in your efforts to see everyone's point of view you permitted yourself to be bulldozed by the majority and to become their tool.'

'Now look here, Dr Golkorn –'

'With respect, you misinformed the vendors, sir. They'll be in Luffnell Lodge till they die now.'

'The house will be sold to another buyer. It's only a matter of time.'

'It's what you call a white elephant, sir.'

'I think we'd rather you went, Dr Golkorn.'

Golkorn leaned back in his chair. He crossed one leg over the other. He smiled, turning his head a little so that the smile was directed first at Hugh and then at Emily. He said:

'You are both of you upset. In my profession, Mr Mansor, which has to do with the human heart as much as the human mind, I could sense last night that you were both upset. You were saying to yourself, sir, that you had made an error of judgement. Mrs Mansor was wanting to weep.'

'I admit to no error of judgement –'

'Shall we refer to it as a mistake then, sir? You have made a mistake with which you will live until the white elephant is sold. And even then, if ever it is sold in the lifetime of the vendors, the mistake will still be there because of the amount they will have forfeited. In good faith they called you in, sir, taking you to be an honest man –'

'You're being offensive, Dr Golkorn.'

'I apologize for that, sir. I was purely making a point. Let me make another one. Your wife, as long as she has breath to keep her alive, will never forgive herself.'

Emily tried not to look at him. She looked at the sweet-peas she'd arranged. Through her shoes she could feel the warmth of the Sealyham, who had a way of hugging her feet. She felt there was nothing she could say.

Hugh rose and crossed the room. He noticed that Emily hadn't touched her sherry. He shook the little bottle of Angostura bitters over his own glass, and added gin and water.

'Actually, sir,' Golkorn said, 'all I am suggesting you should do is to pick up the telephone. And you, madam, all that is necessary is to say how you feel to Mrs Allenby. She, too, has humanitarian instincts.'

His beadiness had discovered that they were the weak links in the chain. When he'd argued with the others the night before, trying to make them see his point of view, opinion had hardened immediately. And when he'd persisted, anger had developed. 'In blunt terms,' Colin Rhodes had shouted at him, 'we don't want you here. If you're going to be a blot on the landscape, we'd be obliged if you could be it somewhere else.' And Colin Rhodes would say it even more forcibly now: there'd have been no point in Golkorn's insinuating his way into the Rhodes's sitting-room, or the sitting-room of the Reverend Feare, or the sitting-room of Mr Mottershead or Miss Cogings. There'd have been no point in tackling the Poudards, or taking on the Tilzeys, or making a fuss with Mr and Mrs Blennerhassett in the Village Stores.

'My trouble is,' Golkorn said softly, laughing as if to dress the words with delicacy, 'I cannot accept no for an answer.'

She imagined telling him now that she had dreamed of butterflies in mourning. She imagined his cropped head carefully nodding, going slowly up and down in unspoken delight. Eventually he would explain the dream, relishing the terms he employed, telling her nothing she did not already know. He was a master of the obvious. He took ordinary, blunt facts and gave them a weapon's edge.

'Which comes first,' he enquired quite casually, 'the beauty of an English village, like a picture on a calendar, or the happiness of the wretched?' He went on talking, going over the same ground, mentioning again by name the Poudards and the Tilzeys and the Blennerhassetts, Mr Mottershead, Miss Cogings, Colin Rhodes and the Reverend Feare and Mrs Feare, comparing these healthy, normal people with other people who were neither. He made them seem like monsters. He mentioned the Middle Ages and referred to the people of the village as belonging to an inferno of ignorance out of which the world had hauled itself by its own bootstraps. He himself, he threw in for some kind of good measure, had been a poor man once; he had worked his way through a foreign university, details of which he gave; he was devoted to humanity, he said.

But the Poudards and the Tilzeys were not monsters. The Blennerhassetts just felt strongly, as the others, varying in degree, did also. Mr Mottershead would do anything for you; the Feares had had children from Northern Ireland to stay for two summers running; Miss Cogings cleaned old Mrs Dugdall's windows for her because naturally old Mrs Dugdall couldn't do it herself any more. Having sherry with Colin Rhodes after church on Sundays was a civilized occasion; you couldn't in a million years say that Colin Rhodes and Daphne were a pair of monsters.

'Listen, you've got this all wrong, Dr Golkorn,' Hugh said.

'I wouldn't have said so, sir.'

'Your patients would be all over the neighbourhood. You admitted that yourself. They would be free to wander in the village –'

'I see now, sir, I should have told a lie. I should have said these unhappy people would be safely behind bars; I should have said that no suffering face would ever disturb the peace of your picture-postcard village.'

'Why didn't you?' Emily asked, unable to restrain curiosity.

'Because with respect, madam, it is not in my life-style to tell lies.'

They had to agree with that. In all he had said to the Allenbys and at the meeting last night he had been open and straightforward about what he had intended to do with Luffnell Lodge. He might easily have kept quiet and simply bought the place. It was almost as if he had wished to fight his battle according to the rules he laid down himself, for if lies were not his style deviousness made up for their absence. He knew that if they approached the Allenbys with the second thoughts he was proposing the Allenbys would not hesitate. Deliberately he had let the rowdier opposition burn itself out in righteous fury, and had accepted defeat while seeing victory in sight. His eyes had not strayed once to Emily's tulip-shaped birth-mark, nor lingered on her spectacles or her dumpiness, as such eyes might so easily have done. He had not sought to humiliate Hugh with argument too fast and clever.

'I think,' he said, 'all three of us know. You are decent people. You cannot turn your backs.'

In Luffnell Lodge the women would be comforted, some even cured. Emily knew that. She knew he was not pretending, or claiming too much for himself. She knew his treatment of such women was successful. He was right when he said you could not turn your back. You could not build a wall around a pretty village and say that nothing unpleasant should be permitted within it. No wonder she had dreamed of butterflies mourning the human race. And yet she hated Golkorn. She hated his arrogance in assuming that because his cause was good no one could object. She hated his deviousness far more than the few simple lies he might have told. If he'd told a lie or two to the Allenbys all this might have been avoided.

Hugh only wanted him to go. He didn't need Golkorn to tell him he had misled the Allenbys. In misleading them he had acted out of instincts that were not dishonourable, but Golkorn would not for a second understand that.

'I have my car,' Golkorn said. 'We could the three of us drive up to Luffnell Lodge now.'

Hugh shook his head.

'And you, Mrs Mansor?' Golkorn prompted.

'I would like to talk to my husband.'

'I was only hoping to save you petrol, madam.' He spoke as if, at a time like this, with such an issue, the saving of petrol was still important.

'Yes, we'd like to talk,' Hugh said.

'Indeed, sir. If I may only phone you from the hotel in an hour or so? To see how you've got on.'

They knew he would. They knew he would not rest now until he had dragged their consciences out of them and set them profitably to work. If they did not go to Luffnell Lodge he would return to argue further.

'You understand that if we do as you suggest we'd have to leave the village,' Hugh pointed out. 'We couldn't stay here.'

Golkorn frowned, seeming genuinely perplexed. He gestured with his hands. 'But why, sir? Why leave this village? With respect, I do not understand you?'

'We'd have been disloyal to our friends. We'd be letting everyone down.'

'You're not letting me down, sir. You're not letting two elderly persons down, nor women in need of care and love –'

'Yes, we're aware of that, Dr Golkorn.'

'Sir, may I say that the people of this village will see it our way in time? They'll observe the good work all around them, and understand.'

'In fact, they won't.'

'Well, I would argue that, sir. With respect –'

'We would like to be alone now, Dr Golkorn.'

He went away and they were left with the dying moments of the storm he had brought with him. They did not say much but in time they walked together from the house, through the garden, to the car. They waved at Colin Rhodes, out with his retrievers on the green, and at Miss Cogings hurrying to the post-box with a letter. It wasn't until the car drew up at Luffnell Lodge, until they stood with the Allenbys in the hall, that they were grateful they'd been exploited.

Beyond the Pale
and Other Stories

The Bedroom Eyes of Mrs Vansittart

'You couldn't trust those eyes,' people on Cap Ferrat say, for they find it hard to be charitable where Mrs Vansittart is concerned. 'The Wife Whom Nobody Cares For,' Joe-John remarks, attaching a tinselly jangle to the statement, which manages to suggest that Mrs Vansittart belongs in neon lights.

At fifty-four, so Joe-John has remarked as well, she remains a winner and a taker, for in St Jean and Monte Carlo young men still glance a second time when the slim body passes by, their attention lingering usually on the rhythmic hips. Years ago in Sicily – so the story is told – a peasant woman spat at her. Mrs Vansittart had gone to see the Greek ruins at Segesta, but what outraged the peasant woman was to observe Mrs Vansittart half undressed on the grass, permitting a local man to have his way with her. And then, as though nothing untoward had happened, she waited at the railway station for the next train to Catania. It was then that the woman spat at her.

Mrs Vansittart is American, but when she divides her perfect lips the voice that drawls is almost that of an English duchess. Few intonations betray her origins as a dentist's daughter from Holland Falls, Virginia; no phrase sounds out of place. Her husband, Harry, shares with her that polished Englishness – commanded to, so it is said on Cap Ferrat, as he is commanded in so much else. Early in their marriage the Vansittarts spent ten years in London, where Mrs Vansittart is reported to have had three affairs and sundry casual conjunctions. Harry, even then, was writing his cycle of songs.

The Vansittarts live now in the Villa Teresa just off the Avenue du Sémaphore, and they do not intend to move again. Their childless marriage has drifted all over Europe, from the hotels of Florence and Berlin to those of Château d'Oex and Paris and Seville. To the Villa Teresa the people from the other villas come to play tennis twice a week. In the evening there is bridge, in one villa or another.

Riches have brought these people to Cap Ferrat, riches maintain them. They have come from almost all the European countries, from America and other continents. They have come for the sun and the bougainvillaea, purchasing villas that were created to immortalize the personalities of previous owners – or building for themselves in the same whimsical manner. The varying styles of architecture have romance and nostalgia in common: a cluster of stone animals to remind their owners of somewhere else, a cupola added because a precious visitor once suggested it. Terracotta roofs slope decoratively, the eyes of emperors are sightless in their niches. Mimosa and pale wistaria add fairy-tale colour; cypresses cool the midday sun. Against the alien outside world a mesh of steel lurks within the boundary hedges; stern warnings abound, of a *Chien Méchant* and the ferocious *Sécurité du Cap*.

In her middle age Mrs Vansittart's life is one of swimming-pools that are bluer than the blue Mediterranean, and titles which recall forever a mistress or a lover, or someone else's road to success, or an obsession that remains mysterious: Villa Banana, Villa Magdalene, Morning Dew, Waikiki, Villa Glorietta, Villa Stephen, So What, My Way. The Daimlers and the Bentleys slide along the Boulevard Général de Gaulle, cocktails are taken on some special occasion in the green bar of the Grand-Hotel. The Blochs and the Cecils and the Borromeos, who play tennis on the court at the Villa Teresa, have never quarrelled with Mrs Vansittart, for quarrels would be a shame. Joe-John is her partner: her husband plays neither tennis nor bridge. He cooks instead, and helps old Pierre in the garden. Harry is originally of Holland Falls also, the inheritor of a paper-mill.

The Villa Teresa is as the Vansittarts wish it to be now; and as the years go by nothing much will change. In the large room which they call the salon there is the timeless sculptured wall, a variety of colours and ceramic shapes. There are the great Italian urns, the flowers in their vases changed every day; the Persian rugs, the Seurat, and the paper-weights which Harry has collected on his travels. Carola and Madame Spad come every day, to dust and clean and take in groceries. The Villa Teresa, like the other villas, is its own small island.

'Ruby, don't you think it's ridiculous?' Mrs Vansittart said a month or so ago. 'Don't you, Joe-John?'

Mrs Cecil inclined her head. Joe-John said:

'I think that sign they've put up is temporary.'

'If they spell it incorrectly now they'll do it again.'

Two tables of bridge were going, Mrs Cecil and Signor Borromeo with Joe-John and Mrs Vansittart at one, the Blochs, Signora Borromeo and Mr Cecil at the other. In the lull halfway through the evening, during which Harry served tea and little pâtisseries which he made himself, the conversation had turned to the honouring of Somerset Maugham: an avenue was to be named after him, a sign had gone up near the Villa Mauresque, on which, unfortunately, his surname had been incorrectly spelt.

'Then you must tell them, my dear,' urged Joe-John, who liked to make mischief when he could. 'You must go along and vigorously protest.'

'Oh, I have. I've talked to the most awful little prat.'

'Did he understand?'

'The stupid creature argued. Harry, that's a polished surface you've put your teapot on.'

Harry snatched up the offending teapot and at once looked apologetic, his eyes magnified behind his horn-rimmed spectacles. Harry isn't tall but has a certain bulkiness, especially around the waist. His hands and feet are tiny, his mouse-coloured hair neither greying nor receding. He has a ready smile, is nervous perhaps, so people think, not a great talker. Everyone who comes to the villa likes him, and sympathizes because his wife humiliates him so. To strangers he seems like a servant about the place, grubbily on his knees in the garden, emerging from the kitchen regions with flour on his face. Insult is constantly added to injury, strangers notice, but the regular tennis-companions and bridge-players have long since accepted that it goes rather further, that Harry is the creature of his wife. A saint, someone once said, a Swedish lady who lived in the Villa Glorietta until her death. Mrs Cecil and Mrs Bloch have often said so since.

'Oh, Harry, look, it *has* marked it.'

How could she tell? Mrs Cecil thought. How could it be even remotely possible to see halfway across the huge salon, to ascertain through the duskiness – beyond the pools of light demanded by the bridge tables – that the teapot had marked the top of an escritoire? Mrs Cecil was sitting closer to the escritoire than Mrs Vansittart and couldn't see a thing.

'I think it's all right,' Harry quietly said.

'Well, thank God for that, old thing.'

'Delicious, Harry,' Mrs Cecil murmured quickly, commenting upon the pâtisseries.

'Bravo! Bravo!' added Signor Borromeo, in whom a generous nature and obesity are matched. He sampled a second cherry tart, saying he should not.

'We were talking, Harry,' Mrs Vansittart said, 'of the Avenue Somerset Maugham.'

'Ah, yes.'

He pressed the silver tray of pâtisseries on Signora Borromeo and the Blochs, a wiry couple from South Africa. '*Al limone*?' Signora Borromeo questioned, an index finger poised. Signora Borromeo, though not as stout as her husband, is generously covered. She wears bright dresses that Mrs Vansittart regards with despair; and she has a way of becoming excited. Yes, that one was lemon, Harry said.

'I mean,' Mrs Vansittart went on, 'it wouldn't be the nicest thing in the world if someone decided to call an avenue after Harry and then got *his* name wrong.'

'If somebody –' Mr Cecil began, abruptly ceasing when his wife shook her head and frowned at him.

'No, no one's going to,' Mrs Vansittart continued in a dogged way, which is a characteristic of hers when her husband features in a conversation.

'No, no one's going to, but naturally it could happen. Harry being a creative person too.'

'Yes, of course,' said Mrs Cecil and Mrs Bloch swiftly and simultaneously.

'It's not outside the bounds of possibility,' added Mrs Vansittart, 'that Harry should become well known. His cycle is really most remarkable.'

'Indeed,' said Joe-John.

No one except Mrs Vansittart had been permitted to hear the cycle. It was through her, not its author, that the people of the villas knew what they did: that, for instance, the current composition concerned a Red Indian called Foontimo.

'No reason whatsoever,' said Joe-John, 'to suppose that there mightn't be an Avenue Harry Vansittart.'

He smiled encouragingly at Harry, as if urging him not to lose heart, or at least urging something. Joe-John wears a bangle with his name on it, and a toupé that most remarkably matches the remainder of his cleverly dyed hair. Sharply glancing at his lip-salve, Mrs Vansittart said:

'Don't be snide, Joe-John.'

'Someone's bought La Souco,' Mrs Cecil quickly intervened. 'Swiss, I hear.'

Harry gathered up the tea-cups, the bridge recommenced. While the cards at his table were being dealt, Joe-John placed a hand lightly on the back of one of Mrs Vansittart's. He had not meant to be snide, he protested, he was extremely sorry if he had sounded so. The apology was a formality, its effect that which Joe-John wished for: to make a little more of the incident. 'I wouldn't hurt poor Harry for the world,' he breathlessly whispered as he reached out for his cards.

It was then, as each hand of cards was being arranged and as Harry picked up his tray, that a bell sounded in the Villa Teresa. It was not the telephone; the ringing was caused by the agitating of a brass bell-pull, in the shape of a fish, by the gate of the villa.

'Good Lord!' said Mrs Vansittart, for unexpected visitors are not at all the thing at any of the villas.

'I would not answer,' advised Signor Borromeo. '*Un briccone!*'

The others laughed, as they always do when Signor Borromeo exaggerates. But when the bell sounded again, after only a pause of seconds, Signora Borromeo became excited. '*Un briccone!*' she cried. '*In nome di Dio! Un briccone!*'

Harry stood with his laden tray. His back was to the card-players. He did not move when the bell rang a third time, even though there was no servant to answer it. Old Pierre comes to the garden of the Villa Teresa every morning and leaves at midday. Carola and Madame Spad have gone by five.

'We'll go with you, Harry,' the wiry Mr Bloch suggested, already on his feet.

Mr Cecil stood up also, as did Joe-John. Signor Borromeo remained where he was.

Harry placed the tray on a table with a painted surface – beneath glass – of a hunting scene at the time of Louis XIV. Nervously, he shifted his spectacles on his nose. 'Yes, perhaps,' he said, accepting the offer of companionship on his way through the garden to the gate. Signora Borromeo fussily fanned her face with her splayed cards.

It was Joe-John who afterwards told of what happened next. Mr Bloch took charge. He said they should not talk in the garden just in case Signor Borromeo was right when he suggested that whoever sought entry was there with nefarious purpose. He'd had experience of intruders in South Africa. Each one caught was one less hazard to the whole community: the last thing they wanted was for a criminal to be frightened away, to bide his time for another attempt. So as the bell rang again in the villa the four marched stealthily, a hand occasionally raised to smack away a mosquito.

The man who stood at the gate was swarthy and very small. In the light that went on automatically when the gate was opened he looked from one face to the next, uncertain about which to address. His glance hovered longer on Harry's than on the others, Joe-John reported afterwards, and Harry frowned, as if trying to place the man. Neither of them appeared to be in the least alarmed.

'It is arranged,' the man said eventually. 'I search for Madame.'

'Madame Spad is not here,' Harry replied.

'Not Madame Spad. The Madame of the villa.'

'Look here, my old chap,' Mr Cecil put in, 'I doubt that Madame Vansittart is expecting you.' Mr Cecil is not one to make concessions when the nature of an occasion bewilders him, but it was Joe-John's opinion that the swarthy visitor did not look like anyone's old chap. He thought of saying so, *sotto voce*, to Mr Bloch, but changed his mind.

'Better,' he advised the man instead, 'to telephone in the morning.'

'My wife is playing bridge tonight,' Harry explained. 'It's no time to come calling.'

'It is arranged,' the man repeated.

In a troop, as though conveying a prisoner, they made their way back through the garden. The man, although questioned further by Mr Bloch, only shrugged his shoulders. No one spoke after that, but similar thoughts gathered in each man's mind. It was known that old Pierre would shortly be beyond it: after tennis one evening Mrs Vansittart had relayed that information to her friends, inquiring if any of them knew of a younger gardener. What would seem to have happened was that this present individual had telephoned the villa and been told by Mrs Vansittart to report for an interview, and had now arrived at ten o'clock in the evening instead of the morning. When they reached the villa Mr Cecil began to voice these conclusions, but the man did not appear to understand him.

He was placed in the hall, Joe-John and Mr Bloch guarding him just to be on the safe side. The others re-entered the salon and almost immediately Mrs Vansittart emerged. As she did so, Joe-John took advantage of the continuing interruption in order to go to the lavatory. Mr Bloch returned to the salon, where Harry picked up his tray of tea things and proceeded with it to the kitchen.

'I told you not to come here,' Mrs Vansittart furiously whispered. 'I had no idea it could possibly be you.'

'I tell a little lie, Madame. I say to the men there is arrangement.'

'My God!'

'This morning I wait, Madame, and you do not appear.'

'Will you kindly keep your voice down.'

'We go in your kitchen?'

'My husband is in the kitchen. I could not come this morning because I did not wake up.'

'I am by the lighthouse. It is time to fix the table-cloths but I stand by the lighthouse. How I know you ever come?'

'You could have telephoned, for God's sake,' whispered Mrs Vansittart, more furiously than before. 'All you had to do was to pick up the damn telephone. I was waiting in all day.'

'Yes, I pick up the damn telephone, Madame. You husband answer, I pick it down again. All the time Monsieur Jean watch me. "It is no good this time to fix the table-cloths!" he shout when I come running from the lighthouse. My hand make sweat on the table-cloths. I am no good, he shout, I am bad waiter, no good for Grand-Hotel –'

'I cannot talk to you here. I will meet you in the morning.'

'This at the lighthouse, Madame?'

'Of course at the lighthouse.'

All this Joe-John heard through the slightly open lavatory door. It was not, he recognized at once, a conversation that might normally occur between Mrs Vansittart and a prospective gardener. As he passed through the hall again his hostess was saying in a clenched voice that of course she would wake up. She would be at the lighthouse at half-past six.

'He's a waiter from the Grand-Hotel,' Joe-John reported softly in the salon, but not so softly that the information failed to reach anyone present. 'They're carrying on in the mornings at the lighthouse.'

Signor Borromeo won that night, and so did Mrs Cecil. At a quarter to twelve Harry carried in a tray with glasses on it, and another containing decanters of cognac and whisky, and bottles of Cointreau, cherry brandy and yellow Chartreuse. He drank some Cointreau himself, talking to Mrs Cecil and Mrs Bloch about azaleas.

'Harry dear, you've dribbled that stuff all over your jacket!' Mrs Vansittart cried. 'Oh, Harry, really!'

He went to the kitchen to wipe at the stain with a damp cloth. 'Hot water, Harry,' his wife called after him. 'Make sure it's really hot. And just a trace of soap.'

He'd had a bad day, she reported when he was out of earshot. In his Red Indian song Foontimo's child-wife – the wife who was not real but who appeared to Foontimo in dreams – continued to be elusive. Harry couldn't get her name right. He had written down upwards of four hundred names, but not one of them registered properly. For weeks poor Harry had been depressed over that.

While they listened they all of them in their different ways disliked Mrs Vansittart more than ever they had before. Even Joe-John, who had so enjoyed eavesdropping at the lavatory door, considered it extravagantly awful that Mrs Vansittart's seedy love life should have been displayed in front of everyone, while Harry washed up the dishes. Mrs Bloch several times tightened her lips during Mrs Vansittart's speech about the difficulties Harry was having with his creation of an Indian child-wife; her husband frowned and looked peppery. It was really too much, Mrs Cecil said to herself, and resolved that on the way home she'd suggest dropping the Vansittarts. There were all kinds of people in this world, Signor Borromeo said to himself, but found that this reflection caused him to like Mrs Vansittart no more. A *cornuto* was one thing, but a man humiliated *in pubblico* was an unforgivable shame. Harry was *buono*, Signora Borromeo said to herself, Harry was like a *bambino* sometimes. Mr Cecil did not say anything to himself, being confused.

At midnight the gathering broke up. The visitors remarked that the evening had been delightful. They smiled and thanked Mrs Vansittart.

'She has destroyed that man,' Mrs Cecil said with feeling as she and her husband entered their villa, the Villa Japhico.

Signora Borromeo wept in the Villa Good-Fun, and her husband, sustaining himself with a late-night sandwich and a glass of beer, sadly shook his head.

'She has destroyed that man,' Joe-John said to his friend in El Dorado, using the words precisely a minute after Mrs Cecil had used them in the Villa Japhico. In the Villa Hadrian the Blochs undressed in silence.

Mrs Vansittart lit a cigarette. She sat down at her dressing-table and removed her make-up, occasionally pausing to draw on her cigarette. Her mind contained few thoughts. Her mind was tired, afflicted with the same fatigue that deadened, just a little, the eyes that people are rude about.

Harry sat at the piano in the snug little room he called his den. It was full of things he liked, ornaments and pictures he'd picked up in Europe, bric-à-brac that was priceless or had a sentimental value only. The main lights of the room were not switched on; an ornate lamp lit his piano and the sheets of music paper on the small table beside him. He wore a cotton dressing-gown that was mainly orange, a Javanese pattern.

The child-wife who visited the dreams of Foontimo said her name was Soaring Cloud. She prepared a heaven for Foontimo. She would never leave him, nor would she ever grow old.

Harry smiled over that, his even white teeth moist with excitement. He had known she could not elude him for ever.

The following morning Joe-John watched from the rocks near the lighthouse. He carried with him a small pair of binoculars, necessary because the lie of the land would prevent him from getting close enough to observe his quarry profitably. He had to wait for some minutes before Mrs Vansittart appeared. She looked around her before descending a path that led to a gap among the rocks from which, later in the day, people bathed. She sat down and lit a cigarette. A moment later the swarthy waiter from the Grand-Hotel hurried to where she was.

Joe-John moved cautiously. He was slightly above the pair, but well obscured from their view. Unfortunately it would be impossible to overhear a word they said. Wedging himself uncomfortably, he raised his binoculars and adjusted them.

A conversation, apparently heated, took place. There were many gestures on the part of the swarthy man and at one point he began to go away but was recalled by Mrs Vansittart. She offered him a cigarette, which he accepted. Then Mrs Vansittart took a wallet from a pocket of her trousers and counted a large number of notes on the palm of her companion. 'My God,' said Joe-John, aloud, 'she pays for it!'

The couple parted, the waiter hurrying back towards the Grand-Hotel. Mrs Vansittart sat for a moment where he had left her and then clambered slowly back to the coastal path. She disappeared from Joe-John's view.

Privately, Mrs Vansittart keeps an account of her life. While Harry composes his songs she fills a number of hard-backed notebooks with the facts she does not wish to divulge to anyone now but which, one day after her death and after Harry's, she would like to be known. Of this particular day she wrote:

I paused now and again to watch the early-morning fishermen. I had paid ten thousand francs. At the end of the season the man might go and not return, as he had promised. But I could not be sure.

The morning was beautiful, not yet even faintly hot, the sky a perfect blue. The houses of Beaulieu seemed gracious across the glittering sea, yet the houses of Beaulieu are as ordinary as houses anywhere. A jogger glanced at me as I stood aside to let him pass, perspiration on his nose and chin. He did not speak or smile. I sometimes hate it on Cap Ferrat.

On the coastal path that morning I thought about Harry and myself when we were both eleven; I was in love with him even then. In Holland Falls he'd brought me to his mother's bedroom to show me the rings she crowded on to her plump fingers, her heavily-stoppered scent bottles, her garish silk stockings. But I wasn't interested in his mother's things. Harry told me to take my clothes off, which I shyly did, wanting to because he'd asked me and yet keeping my head averted. Everyone knew that Harry loathed his mother, but no one thought about it or blamed him particularly, she being huge and pink and doting on her only child in a shaming way. 'God!' he remarked, looking at my scrawny nakedness among his mother's frills. 'God, *Jesus*!' I had wires on my teeth, and freckles which I still have: I didn't have breasts of any size. I took off Harry's red windcheater, and after that the rest of his clothes and his shoes. We lay side by side between his mother's scented sheets, while two floors down she talked to Mrs Gilliland. 'Now, that's just a damned lie!' she afterwards shrieked at Rose when Rose said what she'd seen. I'll never forget poor Rose's pretty black face in the bedroom doorway, her eyes as round as tea-cups, bulging from her head. Harry's mother got rid of her because of it, but the story ran all over Holland Falls and someone told my own mother, who sat down and cried. My father bawled at me, his fury a single crimson explosion of lips and tongue, his dotted necktie gulping up and down. It wasn't Harry's fault, I said, I'd tempted Harry because I loved him. Besides, I added, nothing had happened. 'At eleven years of age?' my father yelled. 'It's not the point, for God's sake, that nothing happened!'

On the coastal path that morning I told myself it wasn't fair to remember my father in the moment of his greatest rage. He'd been a gentle man, at his gentlest when operating his high-speed dentist's drill, white-jacketed and happy. Even so, he never forgave me.

We ran away from Holland Falls when we were twenty-two. Harry had already inherited the paper-mill but it was run by a manager, by whom it has been run ever since. We drove about for a year, from town to town, motel to motel. We occupied different rooms because Harry had begun to compose his cycle and liked to be alone with it at night. I loved him more than I could ever tell him but never again, for Harry, did I take my clothes off. Harry has never kissed me, though I, in passing, cannot even now resist bending down to touch the side of his face with my lips. A mother's kiss, I dare say you would call it, and yet when I think of Harry and me I think as well of Héloïse and Abélard, Beatrice and Dante, and all the others. Absurd, of course.

I left the coastal path and went down to the rocks again, gazing into the depths of the clear blue water. 'You're never cross enough,' Harry said, with childish petulance in the City Hotel, Harrisburg, when we were still twenty-two. I had come into my room to find the girl lying on my bed, as I had lain on his mother's with him. In my presence he paid her forty dollars, but I knew he had not laid a finger on her, any more than he had on me when I was her age.

We went to England because Harry was frightened when a police patrol stopped our car one day and asked us if we'd ever been in Harrisburg. I denied it and they let us go, but that was why Harry thought of England, which he took to greatly as soon as we arrived. It became one of the games in our marriage to use only English phrases and to speak in the English way: Harry enjoyed that enormously, almost as much as working on his cycle. And loving him so, I naturally did my best to please him. Any distraction a harmless little game could provide, any compensation: that was how I saw my duty, if in the circumstances that is not too absurd a word. Anyway, the games and the distractions worked, sometimes for years on end. A great deal of time went by, for instance, between the incident in Harrisburg and the first of the two in England. 'It's all right,' the poor child cried out in London when I entered my room. 'Please don't tell, Mrs Vansittart.' Harry paid her the money he had promised her, and when she had gone I broke down and wept. I didn't even want to look at Harry, I didn't want to hear him speak. In an hour or so he brought me up a cup of tea.

It was, heaven knows, simple enough on the surface of things: I could not leave Harry because I loved him too much. I loved his chubby white hands and tranquil smile, and the weakness in his eyes when he took his spectacles off. If I'd left him, he would have ended up in prison because Harry needs to be loved. And then, besides, there has been so much happiness, at least for me: our travelling together, the pictures and the furniture we've so fondly collected, and of course the Villa Teresa. It's the strangest thing in the world, all that.

A fisherman brought his boat near to the rocks where I was sitting. I had lit a cigarette and put my sunglasses on because the glare of daytime was beginning. I watched the fisherman unloading his modest catch, his brown fingers expertly arranging nets and hooks. How different, I thought, marriage would have been with that stranger. And yet could I, with anyone else, have experienced such feelings of passion as I have known?

'I'm sorry,' Harry began to say, a catch-phrase almost, in the 1950s. He's always sorry when he comes in from the flowerbeds with clay on his shoes, or puts the teapot on a polished surface, or breaks the promises he makes. In a way that's hard to communicate Harry likes being sorry.

'*Bonjour, madame*,' the fisherman said, going by with his baskets of sole or whatever fish it was.

'*Bonjour*,' I replied, smiling at him.

Harry would be still in bed, having worked on his cycle until three or four in the morning. Old Pierre and Carola and Madame Spad would not arrive for another hour, and in any case I did not have to be there when they did. But at the back of my mind there's always the terror that when I return to the Villa Teresa Harry will be dead.

I clambered back to the coastal path and continued on my way. In England, after the first occasion, there was the convent girl in her red gymslip, who wasn't docile like the other ones but shouted at me that she loved Harry more than I did. Sometimes she was there when I returned from shopping in the afternoons, sometimes there was only the rumpling of my bed to remind me of her visit. We had to leave England because of the scenes she made, and after the awful melancholy that had seized him Harry promised that none of it would ever happen again.

My presence at the lighthouse that morning had to do with a German girl in Switzerland eleven years ago. The waiter who is at the Grand-Hotel for the season was at the Bon Accueil in Château d'Oex. The German girl was given wine at dinner-time and suddenly burst into tears, hysterically flinging her accusations about. I simply laughed. I said it was ridiculous.

We were gone by breakfast-time and Harry has kept his promise since, frightened for eleven years. Dear, gentle Harry, who never laid a finger on any of those girls, who never would.

Later that morning Joe-John's friend shopped in St Jean, with Joe-John's terrier on a lead. When he had finished he sat down to rest at the café by the bus stop to have a *jus d'abricot*. He watched the tourists and the young people from the yachts. The terrier, elderly now, crept beneath his chair in search of shade.

'Ah, Mrs Bloch!' Joe-John's friend called out after a little while, for the lean South African lady was shopping also. He persuaded her to join him – rather against her will, since Mrs Bloch does not at all care for Joe-John's friend. He then related what Joe-John had earlier related to him: that Mrs Vansittart now paid money for the intimate services she received from men. He described in detail, with some natural exaggeration, the transaction by the lighthouse. Repelled by the account, Mrs Bloch tightened her lips.

On the way back to the Villa Hadrian she called in at the Villa Japhico with two mouse-traps which she had promised last night she would purchase for Mrs Cecil. The Cecils, with neither gardener nor cleaning woman, do not easily find the time for daily shopping and the chandler's store in St Jean will not deliver mouse-traps. Mrs Bloch waited to be thanked and then began.

'To think that man came last night for money! With Harry there and everyone else!'

Mrs Cecil shook her head in horror. Joe-John was a trouble-maker and so was his rather unpleasant friend, yet neither would surely tell an outright lie. It was appalling to think of Mrs Vansittart conducting such business with a waiter. The satisfying of lust in a woman was most unpleasant.

'I really can't think why he doesn't leave her,' she said.

'Oh, he never would. That simply isn't Harry's style.'

'Yes, Harry's loyal.'

That morning the Cecils had discussed the dropping of the Vansittarts, but had in the end agreed that the result of such a course of action would be that Harry would suffer. So they had decided against it, a decision which Mrs Cecil now passed on to her friend.

Mrs Bloch gloomily agreed.

Mrs Vansittart plays an ace and wins the trick. It is autumn, the season is over, the swarthy waiter has gone.

Harry enters the salon with his tray of tea, and the pâtisseries he has made that morning. He is so quiet in the shadows of the room that Mrs Bloch recalls how strangers to the villa have occasionally taken him for a servant. Mrs Cecil throws a smile in his direction.

Mr Bloch and Mr Cecil and Signor Borromeo, all of whom know about the transaction that took place near the lighthouse, prefer not to think about it. Joe-John hopes that Mrs Vansittart will commit some further enormity shortly, so that the gossip it trails may while away the winter. It would be awfully dull, he often remarks to his friend, if Mrs Vansittart was like Mrs Bloch and Mrs Cecil and Signora Borromeo.

'Oh, my dear, don't pour it yet!' she cries across the room, and then with some asperity, 'We really aren't quite ready, old thing.'

Harry apologizes, enjoying the wave of sympathy her protest engenders. He waits until the hand is played, knowing that then her voice will again command him. He can feel the stifled irritation in the room, and then the sympathy.

He pours the tea and hands the cups around. She lights a cigarette. Once, at the beginning of their time in the Villa Teresa, she had a way of getting up and helping him with the tea-cups, but then she sensed that that was wrong. She senses things in a clumsy kind of way. She is not clever.

'Oh, look, you've made marzipan ones again! You *know* no one likes marzipan, dear.'

But Mrs Cecil and Mrs Bloch both select the marzipan ones, and Harry is apologetic. He is not aware that people have ever said his wife had three affairs and sundry casual conjunctions when they lived in England; nor does he know it is categorically stated that a peasant woman once spat in her face. It would not upset him to hear all this because it's only gossip and its falsity doesn't matter. It is a long time now since she sensed his modest wish, and in answer to it developed the rhythmic swing of her hips and the look in her eyes. Unconsciously, of course, she developed them; not quite in the way she allows the English intonations to creep into her voice. When he looks at her in the company of these people it's enjoyable to imagine the swarthy waiter undressing her among the rocks, even Signor Borromeo trying something on beneath the bridge table.

Harry smiles. He goes around with the teapot, refilling the cups. He wishes she would say again that an avenue on Cap Ferrat would be called after him. It's enjoyable, the feeling in the room then, the people thinking she shouldn't have said it. It's enjoyable when they think she shouldn't swing her hips so and when they come to conclusions about her made-up English voice. It's enjoyable when she listens to his saga of Soaring Cloud the child-wife, and when her face is worried because yet another song has a theme of self-inflicted death. Harry enjoys that most of all.

*

Mrs Vansittart loses, for her attention had briefly wandered, as it sometimes does just after he has brought the tea around. She tried not to love him when her father was so upset. She tried to forget him, but he was always there, wordlessly pleading from a distance, so passionately demanding the love she passionately felt. She'd felt it long before the day she took her clothes off for him, and she remembers perfectly how it was.

For a moment at the bridge table the thoughts that have slipped beneath her guard make her so light-headed that she wants to jump up and run after him to the kitchen. She sees herself, gazing at him from the doorway, enticing him with her eyes, as first of all she did in Holland Falls. He puts his arms around her, and she feels on hers the lips she never has felt.

'Diamonds,' someone says, for she has asked what trumps are. Her virginal longing still warms her as the daydream dissipates. From its fragments Harry thanks her for the companion she has been, and her love is calm again at the bridge table.

Cecilia's father would sit there, slowly eating oysters. Cecilia would tell him about school and about her half-brothers, and of course she'd have to mention her mother because it was impossible to have a conversation without doing that. She'd mention Ronan also, but because of her father's attitude to her stepfather this was never an embarrassment.

'Aren't they good today?' Tom, the waiter at Fitzgerald's, would remark, always at the same moment, when placing in front of Cecilia's father his second pint of jet-black stout.

'Great, Tom,' her father would unhesitatingly reply, and then Tom would ask Cecilia how her bit of steak was and if the chips were crisp. He'd mention the name of a racehorse and Cecilia's father would give his opinion of it, drawing a swift breath of disapproval or thoughtfully pursing his lips.

These occasions in Fitzgerald's Oyster Bar – downstairs at the counter – were like a thread of similar beads that ran through Cecilia's childhood, never afterwards to be forgotten. Dublin in the 1940s was a different city from the city it later became; she'd been different herself. Cecilia was five when her father first took her to Fitzgerald's, the year after her parents were divorced.

'And tell me,' he said some time later, when she was growing up a bit, 'have you an idea at all about what you'll do with yourself?'

'When I leave school, d'you mean?'

'Well, there's no hurry, I'm not saying there is. Still and all, you're nearly thirteen these days.'

'In June.'

'Ah, I know it's June, Cecilia.' He laughed, with his glass halfway to his lips. He looked at her over the rim, his light-blue eyes twinkling in a way she was fond of. He was a burly man with a brown bald head and freckles on the back of his hands and all over his forehead and his nose.

'I don't know what I'll do,' she said.

'Some fellow'll snap you up. Don't worry about that.' He swallowed another oyster and wiped his mouth with his napkin. 'How's your mother?'

'She's fine.'

He never spoke disparagingly of her mother, nor she of him. When Cecilia was younger he used to drive up the short avenue of the house in Chapelizod in his old sloping-backed Morris, and Cecilia would always be ready for him. Her mother would say hullo to him and they'd have a little chat, and if Ronan opened the door or happened to be in the garden her father would ask him how he was, as though nothing untoward had ever occurred between them. Cecilia couldn't understand any of it, but mistily there was the memory of her father living in the house in Chapelizod, and fragments from that time had lodged in her recollection. By the fire in the dining-room he read her a story she had now forgotten. 'Your jersey's inside out,' he said to her mother and then he laughed because it was April Fools' Day. Her father and Ronan had run a furniture-making business together, two large workshops in Chapelizod, not far from the house.

'Lucky,' he said in Fitzgerald's. 'Any fellow you'd accept.'

She blushed. At school a few of her friends talked of getting married, but in a way that wasn't serious. Maureen Finnegan was in love with James Stewart, Betsy Bloom with a boy called George O'Malley: silly, really, it all was.

'The hard case,' a man in a thick overcoat said to her father, pausing on his way to the other end of the bar. 'Would I chance money on Persian Gulf?'

Cecilia's father shook his head and the man, accepting this verdict, nodded his. He winked at Cecilia in the way her father's friends sometimes did after such an exchange, an acknowledgement of her father's race-track wisdom. When he had gone her father told her that he was a very decent person who had come down in the world due to heavy drinking. Her father often had such titbits to impart and when he did so his tone was matter-of-fact, neither malicious nor pitying. In return, Cecilia would relate another fact or two about school, about Miss O'Shaughnessy or Mr Horan or the way Maureen Finnegan went on about James Stewart. Her father always listened attentively.

He hadn't married again. He lived on his own in a flat in Waterloo Road, his income accumulating from a variety of sources, several of them to do with horse-racing. He'd explained that to her when she'd asked him once about this, wondering if he went to an office every day. She had never been to his flat, but he had described it to her because she'd wondered about that too.

'We'll take the trifle?' he suggested, the only alternative offered by Fitzgerald's being something called Bonanza Cream, over which Tom the waiter had years ago strenuously shaken his head.

'Yes, please,' she said.

When they'd finished it her father had a glass of whiskey and Cecilia another orange soda, and then he lit the third of his afternoon's cigarettes. They never had lunch upstairs at Fitzgerald's, where the restaurant proper was. 'Now come and I'll show you,' her father had offered a year or so ago, and they had stared through a glass door that had the word *Fitzgerald's* in elaborate letters running diagonally across it. Men and women sat at tables covered with pink tablecloths and with scarlet-shaded electric lamps on them, the lamps alight even though it was the afternoon. 'Ah no, it's nicer downstairs,' her father had insisted, but Cecilia hadn't entirely agreed, for downstairs in Fitzgerald's possessed none of that cosiness. There were green tiles instead of the pink peacock wallpaper of the upper room, and stark rows of gin and whiskey bottles, and a workmanlike mahogany food-lift that banged up and down loaded with plates of oysters. Tom the waiter was really a barman, and the customers were all men. Cecilia had never seen a woman downstairs in Fitzgerald's.

'Bedad, isn't her ladyship growing up,' Tom said when her father had finished his whiskey and they both stood up. 'Sure, it's hardly a day ago she was a chiseler.'

'Hardly a day,' Cecilia's father agreed, and Cecilia blushed again, glancing down at her wrists because she didn't know where else to look. She didn't like her wrists. They were the thinnest in Class Three, which was a fact she knew because a week ago one of the boys had measured everyone's wrists with a piece of string. She didn't like the black hair that hung down on either side of her face because it wasn't curly like her mother's. She didn't like her eyes and she didn't like the shape of her mouth, but the boy who had measured her wrists said she was the prettiest girl in Class Three. Other people said that too.

'She's a credit to yourself, sir,' Tom said, scooping up notes and coins from the bar. 'Thanks very much.'

Her father held her coat for her, taking it from a peg by the door. It and the hat he handed her were part of her school uniform, both of them green, the hat with a pale blue band. He didn't put on his own overcoat, saying that the afternoon wasn't chilly. He never wore a hat.

They walked past Christ Church Cathedral, towards Grafton Street. Their lunchtime encounters always took place on a Saturday, and sometimes in the middle of one Cecilia's father would reveal that he had tickets for a rugby international at Lansdowne Road, or a taxi-driver would arrive in Fitzgerald's to take them to the races at Phoenix Park. Sometimes they'd walk over to the Museum or the National Gallery. Cecilia's father no longer drove a car.

'Will we go to the pictures?' he said today. '*Reap the Wild Wind* at the Grafton?'

He didn't wait for an answer because he knew she'd want to go. He walked a little ahead of her, tidy in his darkish suit, his overcoat over his arm. On the steps of the cinema he gave her some money to go up to Noblett's to buy chocolate and when she returned he was waiting with the tickets in his hand. She smiled at him, thanking him. She often wondered if he was lonely in his flat, and at the back of her mind she had an idea that what she'd like best when she left school would be to look after him there. It gave her a warm feeling in her stomach when she imagined the flat he had described and thought about cooking meals for him in its tiny kitchen.

After the cinema they had tea in Roberts' and then he walked with her to the bus stop in the centre of the city. On the way he told her about an elderly couple in the café who'd addressed him by name, people who lived out in Greystones and bred Great Danes. 'Till next time then,' he said as the bus drew in, and kissed her shyly, in the manner of someone not used to kissing people.

She waved to him from her seat by the window and watched him turn and become lost in the crowded street. He would call in at a few public houses on his way back to the flat in Waterloo Road, places he often referred to by name, Toner's and O'Donoghue's and the upstairs lounge of Mooney's, places where he met his friends and talked about racing. She imagined him there, with men like the man who'd asked if he should chance his money on Persian Gulf. But again she wondered if he was lonely.

It was already dark and had begun to rain by the time Cecilia reached the white house in Chapelizod where her father had once lived but which was occupied now by her mother and Ronan, and by Cecilia and her two half-brothers. A stove, with baskets of logs on either side of it, burned in the square, lofty hall where she took her coat and hat off. The brass door-plates and handles gleamed in the electric light. From the drawing-room came the sound of the wireless. 'Ah, the wanderer's returned,' Ronan murmured when she entered, smiling, making her welcome.

Her half-brothers were constructing a windmill out of Meccano on the floor. Her mother and Ronan were sitting close together, he in an armchair, she on the hearthrug. They were going out that night, Cecilia could tell because her mother's face was already made up: cerise lipstick and mascara, smudges of shadow beneath her eyes that accentuated their brownness, the same brown as her own. Her mother was petite and dark-haired – like Claudette Colbert, as Maureen Finnegan had once said.

'Hullo,' her mother said. 'Nice time?'

'Yes, thanks.'

She didn't say anything else because they were listening to the wireless. Her father would be drinking more stout, she thought, his overcoat on a chair beside him, a fresh cigarette in his mouth. There wasn't a public house between Stephen's Green and Waterloo Road in which he wouldn't know somebody. Of course he wasn't lonely.

The voices on the wireless told jokes, a girl sang a song about a nightingale. Cecilia glanced at her mother and Ronan, she snuggling against his legs, his hand on her shoulder. Ronan was very thin, with a craggy face and a smile that came languidly on to his lips and died away languidly also. He was never cross: in the family, anger didn't play the part it did in the households of several of Cecilia's school friends, where there was fear of a father or a mother. Every Sunday she went with Ronan to the workshops where the furniture was made and he showed her what had been begun or completed during the week. She loved the smell of wood-shavings and glue and French polish.

When the programme on the wireless came to an end her mother rose to go upstairs, to finish getting ready. Ronan muttered lazily that he supposed he'd have to get himself into a suit. He stacked logs on to the fire and set the fireguard in place. 'Your tweed one's ironed,' Cecilia's mother reminded him sternly before she left the room. He grimaced at the boys, who were showing him their completed windmill. Then he grimaced at Cecilia. It was a joke in the family that Ronan never wanted to put on a suit.

Cecilia went to a school across the city from Chapelizod, in Ranelagh. It was an unusual place in the Dublin of that time, catering for both boys and girls, for Catholics and Protestants and Jews, and for Mohammedans when that rare need arose. Overflowing from a large suburban house into the huts and prefabricated buildings that served as extra classrooms, it was run by a headmaster, assisted by a staff of both sexes. There were sixty-eight pupils.

In spite of the superficially exotic nature of this establishment Cecilia was the only child whose parents had been divorced and in the kind of conversations she began to have when she was twelve the details of that were increasingly a subject of curiosity. Divorce had a whiff of Hollywood and wickedness. Betsy Bloom claimed to have observed her parents naked on their bed, engaged in the act of love; Enid Healy's father had run amok with a sofa leg. What had happened within the privacy of Cecilia's family belonged in that same realm, and Cecilia was questioned closely. Even though her parents' divorce had had to be obtained in England owing to the shortcomings of the Irish law, the events leading up to it must clearly have occurred in Chapelizod. Had Cecilia ever walked into a room and found her mother and her stepfather up to something? Was it true that her mother and her stepfather used to meet for cocktails in the Gresham Hotel? What exactly *were* cocktails? Had detectives been involved? Her mother and Ronan were glanced at with interest on the very few occasions when they put in an appearance at a school function, and it was agreed that they lived up to the roles they had been cast in. The clothes her mother wore were not like the all-purpose garments of Mrs O'Reilly-Hamilton or Kitty Benson's mother. 'Sophisticated,' Maureen Finnegan had pronounced. 'Chic.'

But in the end Cecilia was aware of her school-fellows' disappointment. There had been no detectives that she could recall, and she didn't know if there had been meetings in the Gresham Hotel. She had never walked into a room to find something untoward taking place and she could remember no quarrels – nothing that was even faintly in the same category as Enid Healy's father brandishing a sofa leg. In America, so the newspapers said, kidnappings occasionally took place when the estranged couples of divorce could not accept the dictates of the law where their children were concerned. 'Your daddy never try that?' Maureen Finnegan hopefully prompted, and Cecilia had to laugh at the absurdity of it. A satisfactory arrangement had been made, she explained for the umpteenth time, knowing it sounded dreary: everyone was content.

The headmaster of the school once spoke to her of the divorce also, though only in passing. He was a massively proportioned man known as the Bull, who shambled about the huts and prefabricated buildings calling out names in the middle of a lesson, ticking his way down the columns of his enormous roll-book. Often he would pause as if he had forgotten what he was about and for a moment or two would whistle through his breath 'The British Grenadiers', the marching song of the regiment in which he had once served with distinction. The only tasks he had ever been known to perform were the calling out of names and the issuing of an occasional vague announcement at the morning assemblies which were conducted by Mr Horan. Otherwise he remained lodged in his own cloudlands, a faint, blue-suited presence, benignly unaware of the feuds that stormed among his staff or the nature of the sixty-eight children whose immediate destinies had been placed in his care.

To Cecilia's considerable surprise the Bull sent for her one morning, the summons interrupting one of Miss O'Shaughnessy's science periods. Miss O'Shaughnessy was displaying how a piece of litmus paper had impressively changed colour, and when Mickey, the odd-job boy, entered the classroom and said that the headmaster wanted Cecilia an immediate whispering broke out. The substance of this was that a death must have taken place.

'Ah,' the Bull said when Cecilia entered the study where he ate all his meals, read the *Irish Times* and interviewed prospective parents. His breakfast tray was still on his desk, a paper-backed Sexton Blake adventure story beside it. 'Ah,' he said again, and did not continue. His bachelor existence was nicely expressed by the bleak furnishings of the room, the row of pipes above a damply smouldering fire, the insignia of the Grenadier Guards scattered on darkly panelled walls.

'Is anything the matter, sir?' Cecilia eventually enquired, for the suggestion that a death might have occurred still echoed as she stood there.

The headmaster regarded her without severity. The breathy whistling of the marching song began as he reached for a pipe and slowly filled it with tobacco. The whistling ceased. He said:

'The fees are sometimes a little tardy. The circumstances are unusual, since you are not regularly in touch with your father. But I would be obliged, when next you see him, if you would just say that the fees have of late been tardy.'

A match was struck, the tobacco ignited. Cecilia was not formally dismissed, but the headmaster's immense hand seized the Sexton Blake adventure story, indicating that the interview was over. It had never occurred to her before that it was her father, not her mother and Ronan, who paid her school fees. Her father had never in his life visited the school, as her mother and Ronan had. It was strange that he should be responsible for the fees, and Cecilia resolved to thank him when next she saw him. It was also embarrassing that they were sometimes late.

'Ah,' the Bull said when she had reached the door. 'You're – ah – all right, are you? The – ah – family trouble . . .?'

'Oh, that's all over, sir.'

'So it is. So it is. And everything . . .?'

'Everything's fine, sir.'

'Good. Good.'

Interest in the divorce had dwindled and might even have dissipated entirely had not the odd behaviour of a boy called Abrahamson begun. Quite out of the blue, about a month after the Saturday on which Cecilia and her father had gone to see *Reap the Wild Wind*, Abrahamson began to stare at her.

In the big classroom where Mr Horan's morning assemblies were held his eyes repeatedly darted over her features, and whenever they met in a corridor or by the tennis-courts he would glance at her sharply and then glance away again, trying to do so before she noticed. Abrahamson's father was the solicitor to the furniture-making business and because of that Abrahamson occasionally turned up in the house in Chapelizod. No one else from the school did so, Chapelizod being too distant from the neighbourhoods where most of the school's sixty-eight pupils lived. Abrahamson was younger than Cecilia, a small olive-skinned boy whom Cecilia had many times entertained in the nursery while his parents sat downstairs, having a drink. He was an only child, self-effacing and anxious not to be a nuisance: when he came to Chapelizod now he obligingly played with Cecilia's half-brothers, humping them about the garden on his back or acting the unimportant parts in the playlets they composed.

At school he was always called by his surname and was famous for his brains. He was neither popular nor unpopular, content to remain on the perimeter of things. Because of this, Cecilia found it difficult to approach him about his staring, and the cleverness that was reflected in the liquid depths of his eyes induced a certain apprehension. But since his interest in her showed no sign of diminishing she decided she'd have to point out that she found it discomfiting. One showery afternoon, on the way down the shrubbed avenue of the school, she questioned him.

Being taller than the boy and his voice being softly pitched, Cecilia had to bend over him to catch his replies. He had a way of smiling when he spoke – a smile, so everyone said, that had to do with his thoughts rather than with any conversation he happened to be having at the time.

'I'm sorry,' he said. 'I'm really sorry, Cecilia. I didn't know I was doing it.'

'You've been doing it for weeks, Abrahamson.'

He nodded, obligingly accepting the truth of the accusation. And since an explanation was required, he obligingly offered one.

'It's just that when you reach a certain age the features of your face aren't those of a child any more. I read it in a book: a child's face disguises its real features, but at a certain age the disguise falls off. D'you understand, Cecilia?'

'No, I don't. And I don't know why you've picked on me just because of something you read in a book.'

'It happens to everyone, Cecilia.'

'You don't go round staring at everyone.'

'I'm sorry. I'm terribly sorry, Cecilia.'

Abrahamson stopped and opened the black case in which he carried his school books. Cecilia thought that in some clever way he was going to produce from it an explanation that made more sense. She waited without pressing the matter. On the avenue boys kicked each other, throwing caps about. Miss O'Shaughnessy passed on her motorized bicycle. Mr Horan strode by with his violin.

'Like one?' Abrahamson had taken from his case a carton containing two small, garishly iced cakes. 'Go on, really.'

She took the raspberry-coloured one, after which Abrahamson meticulously closed the carton and returned it to his case. Every day he came to school with two of these cakes, supplied by his mother for consumption during the eleven o'clock break. He sold them to anyone who had a few pence to spare, and if he didn't sell them at school he did so to a girl in a newsagent's shop which he passed on his journey home.

'I don't want to tell you,' he said as they walked on. 'I'm sorry you noticed.'

'I couldn't help noticing.'

'Call it quits now, will we?' There was the slightest of gestures towards the remains of the cake, sticky in Cecilia's hand. Abrahamson's tone was softer than ever, his distant smile an echo from his private world. It was said that he played chess games in his head.

'I'd like to know, Abrahamson.'

His thin shoulders just perceptibly shifted up and down. He appeared to be stating that Cecilia was foolish to insist, and to be stating as well that if she continued to insist he did not intend to waste time and energy in argument. They had passed through the gates of the school and were standing on the street, waiting for a number 11 bus.

'It's odd,' he said, 'if you want to know. Your father and all that.'

'Odd?'

The bus drew up. They mounted to the upper deck. When they sat down Abrahamson stared out of the window. It was as if he had already said everything that was necessary, as if Cecilia should effortlessly be able to deduce the rest. She had to nudge him with her elbow, and then – politely and very swiftly – he glanced at her, silently apologizing for her inability to understand the obvious. A pity, his small face declared, a shame to have to carry this burden of stupidity.

'When people get divorced,' he said, carefully spacing the words, 'there's always a reason. You'll observe that in films. Or if you read in the paper about the divorce of, say, William Powell and Carole Lombard. They don't actually bother with divorce if they only dislike one another.'

The conductor came to take their fares. Again the conversation appeared to have reached its termination.

'But what on earth's that got to do with what we're talking about, Abrahamson?'

'Wouldn't there have been a reason why your parents got divorced? Wouldn't the reason be the man your mother married?'

She nodded vehemently, feeling hot and silly. Abrahamson said:

'They'd have had a love affair while your father was still around. In the end there would have been the divorce.'

'I know all that, Abrahamson.'

'Well, then.'

Impatiently, she began to protest again but broke off in the middle of a sentence and instead sat there frowning. She sensed that the last two words her companion had uttered contained some further declaration, but was unable to grasp it.

'Excuse me,' Abrahamson said, politely, before he went.

'Aren't you hungry?' her mother asked, looking across the lace-trimmed white cloth on the dining-room table. 'You haven't been gorging yourself, have you?'

Cecilia shook her head, and the hair she didn't like swung about. Her half-brothers giggled, a habit they had recently developed. They were years younger than Cecilia, yet the briskness in her mother's voice placed her in a category with them, and she suddenly wondered if her mother could somehow guess what had come into her mind and was telling her not to be silly. Her mother was wearing a red dress and her fingernails had been freshly tinted. Her black bobbed hair gleamed healthily in watery afternoon sunshine, her dimples came and went.

'How was the Latin?'

'All right.'

'Did you get the passive right?'

'More or less.'

'Why're you so grumpy, Cecilia?'

'I'm not.'

'Well, I think I'd disagree with that.'

Cecilia's cheeks had begun to burn, which caused her half-brothers to giggle again. She knew they were kicking one another beneath the table and to avoid their scrutiny she stared through the French windows, out the garden. She'd slept in a pram beneath the apple-tree and once had crawled about among the flowerbeds: she could just remember that, she could remember her father laughing as he picked her up.

Cecilia finished her cup of tea and rose, leaving half a piece of coffee cake on her plate. Her mother called after her when she reached the door.

'I'm going to do my homework,' Cecilia said.

'But you haven't eaten your cake.'

'I don't want it.'

'That's rude, you know.'

She didn't say anything. She opened the door and closed it softly behind her. Locked in the bathroom, she examined in the looking-glass the features Abrahamson had spoken of. She made herself smile. She squinted, trying to see her profile. She didn't want to think about any of it, yet she couldn't help herself. She hated being here, with the door locked at five o'clock in the evening, yet she couldn't help that either. She stared at herself for minutes on end, performing further contortions, glancing and grimacing, catching herself unawares. But she couldn't see anywhere a look of her stepfather.

'Well, you wouldn't,' Abrahamson explained. 'It's difficult to analyse your own face.'

They walked together slowly, on the cinder-track that ran around the tennis-courts and the school's single hockey pitch. She was wearing her summer uniform, a green and blue dress, short white socks. Abrahamson wore flannel shorts and the elaborate school blazer.

'Other people would have noticed, Abrahamson.'

He shook his head. Other people weren't so interested in things like that, he said. And other people weren't so familiar with her family.

'It isn't a likeness or anything, Cecilia. Not a strong resemblance, nothing startling. It's only a hint, Cecilia, an inkling you could call it.'

'I wish you hadn't told me.'

'You wanted me to.'

'Yes, I know.'

They had reached the end of the cinder-track. They turned and walked back towards the school buildings in silence. Girls were playing tennis. 'Love, forty,' called the elderly English master, No-teeth Carroll as he was known as.

'I've looked and looked,' Cecilia said. 'I spend hours in the bathroom.'

'Even if I hadn't read about the development of the features I think I'd have stumbled on it for myself. "Now, what on earth is it about that girl?" I kept saying to myself. "Why's her face so interesting all of a sudden?" '

'I think you're imagining it.'

'Well, maybe I am.'

They watched the tennis-players. He wasn't someone who made mistakes, or made things up; he wasn't like that at all. She wished she had her father's freckles, just a couple, anywhere, on her forehead or her nose. 'Deuce, No-teeth Carroll called. 'No, it's definitely deuce,' he insisted, but an argument continued. The poor old fellow was on a term's notice, Abrahamson said.

They walked on. She'd heard it too, she agreed, about the term's notice. Pity, because he wasn't bad, the way he let you do anything you liked provided you were quiet.

'Would you buy one of my cakes today?' Abrahamson asked.

'Please don't tell anyone, Abrahamson.'

'You could buy them *every* day, you know. I never eat them myself.'

A little time went by. On the fifteenth of June Cecilia became thirteen. A great fuss was made of the occasion, as was usual in the family whenever there was a birthday. Ronan gave her *A Tale of Two Cities*, her mother a dress which she had made herself, with rosebuds on it, and her half-brothers gave her a red bangle. There was chicken for her birthday lunch, with roast potatoes and peas, and then lemon meringue pie. All of them were favourites of hers.

'Happy birthday, darling,' Ronan whispered, finding a special moment to say it when everyone else was occupied. She knew he was fond of her, she knew that he enjoyed their Sunday mornings in the workshops. She liked him too. She'd never thought of not liking him.

'*Really* happy birthday,' he said and it was then, as he smiled and turned away, that something occurred to her which she hadn't thought of before, and which Abrahamson clearly hadn't thought of either: when you'd lived for most of your life in a house with the man whom your mother had married you could easily pick up some of his ways. You could pick them up without knowing it, like catching a cold, his smile or some other hint of himself. You might laugh the way he did, or say things with his voice. You'd never guess you were doing it.

'Oh, of course,' Abrahamson obligingly agreed when she put it to him. 'Of course, Cecilia.'

'But wouldn't that be it then? I mean, mightn't that account –'

'Indeed it might.'

His busy, unassuming eyes looked up into hers and then at the distant figure of No-teeth Carroll, who was standing dismally by the long-jump pit.

'Indeed,' Abrahamson said again.

'I'm *certain* that's it. I mean, I still can't see anything myself in my looks –'

'Oh, there's definitely something.' He interrupted sharply, his tone suggesting that it was illogical and ridiculous to question what had already been agreed upon. 'It's very interesting, what you're saying about growing like someone you live with and quite like. It's perfectly possible, just as the other is perfectly possible. If you asked your mother, Cecilia, she probably wouldn't know what's what any more than anyone else does. On account of the circumstances.'

He was bored by the subject. He had acceded to her request about not telling anyone. It was best to let the subject go.

'Chocolate and strawberry today,' he said, smiling again as he passed over the two small cakes.

There was another rendezvous in Fitzgerald's Oyster Bar. Cecilia wore her new rosebud dress and her red bangle. On her birthday a ten-shilling note had arrived from her father, which she now thanked him for.

'When I was thirteen myself,' he said, pulling the cellophane from a packet of Sweet Afton, 'I didn't know whether I was coming or going.'

Cecilia kept her head averted. At least the light wasn't strong. There was a certain amount of stained glass in the windows and only weak bulbs burned in the globe-topped brass lamps that were set at intervals along the mahogany bar. She tried not to smile in case the inkling in her face had something to do with that.

'Well, I see your man's going up in front of the stewards,' Tom the waiter remarked. 'Sure, isn't it time they laid down the law on that fellow?'

'Oh, a terrible chancer that fellow, Tom.'

Their order was taken, and shouted down the lift-shaft.

'We might indulge in a drop of wine, Tom. On account of her ladyship's birthday.'

'I have a great little French one, sir. Mâcon, sir.'

'That'll suit us fine, Tom.'

It was early, the bar was almost empty. Two men in camel-coloured coats were talking in low voices by the door. Cecilia had seen them before. They were bookies, her father had told her.

'Are you all right?' he enquired. 'You haven't got the toothache or anything?'

'No, I'm all right, thanks.'

The bar filled up. Men stopped to speak to her father and then sat at the small tables behind them or on stools by the bar itself. Her father lit another cigarette.

'I didn't realize you paid the fees,' she said.

'What fees do you mean?'

She told him in order to thank him, because she thought they could laugh over the business of the fees being late every term. But her father received the reprimand solemnly. He was at fault, he confessed: the headmaster was quite right, and must be apologized to on his behalf.

'He's not someone you talk to,' Cecilia explained, realizing that although she'd so often spoken about school to her father she'd never properly described the place, the huts and prefabricated buildings that were its classrooms, the Bull going round every morning with his huge roll-book.

She watched Tom drawing the cork from the bottle of red wine. She said that only yesterday Miss O'Shaughnessy's motorized bicycle had given up the ghost and she repeated the rumour that poor old No-teeth Carroll was on a term's notice. She couldn't say that she'd struck a silent bargain with a boy called Abrahamson, who brought to the school each day two dainty little cakes in a carton. She'd have liked just to tell about the cakes because her father would have appreciated the oddity of it. It was strange that she hadn't done so before.

'Now,' said Tom, placing the oysters in front of her father and her steak in front of her. He filled up their wine-glasses and drew a surplus of foam from the surface of someone else's stout.

'Is your mother well, Cecilia?'

'Oh, yes.'

'And everyone in Chapelizod?'

'They're all well.'

He looked at her. He had an oyster on the way to his mouth and he glanced at her and then he ate it. He took a mouthful of wine to wash it down.

'Well, that's great,' he said.

Slowly he continued to consume his oysters. 'If we felt like it,' he said, we could catch the races at the Park.'

He had been through all of it, just as she had. Ever since the divorce he must have wondered, looking at her as he had looked at her just now, for telltale signs. 'They'd have had a love affair while your father was still around,' came the echo of Abrahamson's confident voice, out of place in the oyster bar. Her father had seen Abrahamson's inkling and had felt as miserable as she had. He had probably even comforted himself with the theory about two people in the same house, she picking up her stepfather's characteristics. He had probably said all that to himself over and over again but the doubt had lingered, as it had lingered with her. Married to one man, her mother had performed with another the same act of passion which Betsy Bloom had witnessed in her parents' bedroom. As Abrahamson had fairly pointed out, in confused circumstances such as these no one would ever know what was what.

'We'll take the trifle, will we?' her father said.

'Two trifle,' Tom shouted down the lift-shaft.

'You're getting prettier all the time, girl.'

'I don't like my looks at all.'

'Nonsense, girl. You're lovely.'

His eyes, pinched a bit because he was laughing, twinkled. He was much older than her mother, Cecilia suddenly realized, something which had never struck her before. Were the fees not paid on time because he didn't always have the money? Was that why he had sold his car?

'Will we settle for the races, or something else? You're the birthday lady today.'

'The races would be lovely.'

'Could you ever put that on for me, sir?' Tom requested in a whisper, passing a pound note across the bar. 'Amazon Girl, the last race.'

'I will of course, Tom.'

His voice betrayed nothing of the pain which Cecilia now knew must mark these Saturday occasions for him. The car that was due to collect them was late, he said, and as he spoke the taximan entered.

'Step on it,' her father said, 'like a good man.'

He gave her money and advised her which horses to gamble on. He led her by the hand when they went to find a good place to watch from. It was a clear, sunny day, the sky without a cloud in it, and in the noise and bustle no one seemed unhappy.

'There's a boy at school,' she said, 'who brings two little cakes for the eleven o'clock lunch. He sells them to me every day.'

He wagged his head and smiled. But in a serious voice he said he hoped she didn't pay too much for the cakes, and she explained that she didn't.

It was odd the way Maureen Finnegan and all the others, even the Bull, had suspected the tidy settlement there'd been. It would be ridiculous, now, ever to look after him in his flat.

'I hate to lose poor Tom's money for him.'

'Won't Amazon Girl win?'

'Never a hope.'

Women in brightly coloured dresses passed by as Cecilia's father paused for a moment by a bookmaker's stand to examine the offered odds. He ran a hand over his jaw, considering. A woman with red hair and sunglasses came up. She said it was good to see him and then passed on.

'We'll take a small little flutter on Gillian's Choice,' he finally said. 'D'you like the sound of that, Cecilia?'

She said she did. She put some of the money he had given her on the horse and waited for him while he transacted with another bookmaker. He approached a third one with Tom's pound for Amazon Girl. It was a habit of his to bet with different bookmakers.

'That red-haired woman's from Carlow,' he said as they set off to their vantage point. 'The widow of the county surveyor.'

'Yes,' she said, not caring much about the red-haired woman.

'Gillian's Choice is the one with the golden hoops,' he said. 'Poor Tom's old nag is the grey one.'

The horses went under starter's orders and then, abruptly, were off. In the usual surprisingly short space of time the race was over.

'What did I tell you?' He laughed down at her as they went to collect the winnings from their two different bookmakers. He had won more than three hundred pounds, she fourteen and sixpence. They always counted at the end; they never lost when they went together. He said she brought him luck, but she knew it was the other way round.

'You'll find your way to the bus, Cecilia?'

'Yes, I will. Thanks very much.'

He nodded. He kissed her in his awkward way and then disappeared into the crowd, as he always seemed to do when they parted. It was standing about in the sun, she thought, that caused him to have so many freckles. She imagined him at other race-courses, idling between races without her, sunning himself while considering a race-card. She imagined him in his flat in Waterloo Road and wondered if he ever cried.

She walked slowly away, the money clenched in her hand because the rosebud dress had no pockets. He did cry, she thought: on the Saturdays when they met, when he was on his own again. It was easy to imagine him because she wanted to cry herself, because on all their occasions in the future there would be the doubt. Neither of them would ever really know what being together meant, downstairs at Fitzgerald's or anywhere else.

Mulvihill's Memorial

The man, naked himself, slowly removed the woman's clothes: a striped red and black dress, a petticoat, stockings, further underclothes. In an armchair he took the woman on to his knees, nuzzling her neck with his mouth.

A second man entered the room and divested himself of his clothes. A second woman, in a grey skirt and jersey, was divested of hers. The four sprawled together on the armchair and the floor. Complex sexual union took place.

The film ended; a square of bright light replaced the sexual antics on the sheet of cartridge paper which Mulvihill had attached to the back of his drawing-office door. He switched on a green-shaded desk-light, removed the cartridge paper and the drawing-pins that had held it in place. Packing away his projector in the bottom drawer of his filing-cabinet, he hummed beneath his breath an old tune from his childhood, 'I'll Be Around'. The projector and Mulvihill's films were naturally kept under lock and key. Some of his films he could project at home and often did; others he did not feel he could. 'Whatever are you doing, dear?' his sister sometimes called through the door of the garden shed where now and again he did a bit of carpentry, and of course it would be terrible if ever she discovered the stuff. So every Friday evening, when everyone else had left the Ygnis and Ygnis building – and before the West Indian cleaners arrived in the corridor where his office was – Mulvihill locked the door and turned the lights out. He'd been doing it for years.

He was a man with glasses, middle-aged, of medium height, neither fat nor thin. Given to wearing Harris tweed jackets and looking not unlike an advertisement for the Four Square tobacco he smoked, he travelled every day to the centre of London from the suburb of Purley, where his relationship with his slightly older sister was cemented by the presence in their lives of a sealyham called Pasco. By trade Mulvihill was a designer of labels – labels for soup-tins and coffee in plastic packets, for seed-packets and sachets of shampoo. The drawing-office he shared with a Hungarian display artist called Wilkinski reflected the work of both of them. The walls were covered with enlarged versions of designs that had in the past been used to assist in the selling of a variety of products; cardboard point-of-sale material stood on all the office's surfaces except the two sloping drawing-boards, each with its green-shaded light. Paint-brushes and pencils filled jam-jars, different-coloured papers were stored in a corner. In different colours also, sheaves of cellophane hung from bulldog-clips. Tins of Cow paper-adhesive were everywhere.

Being at the ordinary end of things, neither Mulvihill nor Wilkinski created the Ygnis and Ygnis glamour that appeared on the television screen and in the colour supplements: their labels and display material were merely echoes of people made marvellous with a red aperitif on the way to their lips, of women enriched by the lather of a scented soap, and men invigorated by the smooth operation of a razor-blade. From Ygnis and Ygnis came images lined always with a promise, of happiness or ecstasy. Girls stood aloof by castle walls, beautiful in silk. Children laughed as they played, full of the beans that did them good. Ygnis and Ygnis was of the present, but the past was never forgotten: the hot days of summer before the worst of the wars, brown bread and jam, and faded flowered dresses. The future was simple with plain white furniture and stainless steel and Japanese titbits. In the world of wonders that was Ygnis and Ygnis's, empresses ate Turkish Delight and men raced speedboats. For ever and for ever there was falling in love.

Mulvihill took his mackintosh from a peg on the wall, and picked up the two short pieces of timber he'd purchased during the lunch hour and with which, that weekend, he hoped to repair a bookcase. He didn't light his pipe, although while watching *Confessions of a Housewife* he had filled it with Four Square, ready to ignite it in the lift. 'Evening, Violet,' he said to the big West Indian lady who was just beginning to clean the offices of the corridor. He listened for a moment while she continued what she had been telling him last Friday, about a weakness her son had developed in his stomach. He nodded repeatedly and several times spoke sympathetically before moving on. He would call in at the Trumpet Major for a glass of red wine, as he did every Friday evening, and chat for a quarter of an hour to the usual people. It was all part of the weekend, but this time it wasn't to be. In the lift which Mulvihill always took – the one at the back of the building, which carried him to the garage and the mews – he died as he was lighting his pipe.

In the Trumpet Major nobody missed Mulvihill. His regular presence on Friday evenings was too brief to cause a vacuum when it did not occur. Insisting that a single glass of wine was all he required, he never became involved in rounds of drinks, and it was accepted that that was his way. H. H. Strathers was in the lounge bar, as always on Friday, with Tip Dainty and Capstick and Lilia. Other employees of Ygnis and Ygnis were there also, two of the post-boys in the public bar, Fred Stein the art buyer. At a quarter past eight Ox-Banham joined Strathers and his companions, who had made a place for themselves in a corner. Like Mulvihill, Ox-Banham was known to work late on Fridays, presumed to be finishing anything that had become outstanding during the week. In fact, like Mulvihill, he indulged a private hobby: the seduction, on the floor of his office, of his secretary, Rowena.

'Well, how are we all?' Ox-Banham demanded. 'And, more to the point, what are we having?'

Everyone was having the same as usual. Lilia, the firm's most important woman copywriter, was drunk, as she had been since lunchtime. H. H. Strathers, who had once almost played rugby for South Africa and was now the managing director of Ygnis and Ygnis, was hoping to be drunk shortly. Tip Dainty occasionally swayed.

Ox-Banham took a long gulp of his whisky and water and gave a little gasp of satisfaction. Rowena would be leaving the building about now, since the arrangement was that she stayed behind for ten minutes or so after he'd left her so that they wouldn't be seen together. In normal circumstances it didn't matter being seen together, an executive and his secretary, but just after sexual congress had taken place it might well be foolish: some telltale detail in their manner with one another might easily be still floating about on the surface. 'Point taken of course,' Rowena had said, being given to speaking in that masculine way. Hard as glass she was, in Ox-Banham's view.

'The confectionery boys first thing Monday,' he said now. 'Neat little campaign we've got for them, I think.'

Lilia, who was middle-aged and untidy, talked about shoes. She was clutching a bundle of papers in her left hand, pressing it tightly against her breast as if she feared someone might snatch it from her. Her grey hair had loosened, her eyes were glazed. 'How about Cliff Hangers?' she said to Tip Dainty, offering the term as a name for a new range of sandals.

Lilia's bundle of papers was full of such attempts to find a title for the new range. The sandals were well designed, so Ygnis and Ygnis had been told, with a definite no-nonsense look. Tip Dainty said Cliff Hangers sounded as if something dreadful might happen to you if you wore the things, and Lilia grinned extravagantly, her lean face opening until it seemed entirely composed of teeth. 'Hangers?' she suggested. 'Just Hangers?' But Tip Dainty said Hangers would make people think of death.

Ox-Banham talked to Capstick and H. H. Strathers about the confectionery people and the preparations that had been made by Ygnis and Ygnis to gain the advertising of a new chocolate bar. Again there had been the question of a name and Ygnis and Ygnis in the end had settled for Go. It was Mulvihill who had designed the wrapper and the various cartons in which the bar would be delivered to the shops, as well as window-stickers and other point-of-sale material.

'I like that Go idea,' Ox-Banham said, 'and I like the moody feel of that scene in the cornfield.' His back was a little painful because Rowena had a way of digging her fingernails into whatever flesh she could find, but of course it was worth it. Rowena had been foisted on him by her father, Bloody Smithson, the awful advertising manager of McCulloch Paints, and when Ox-Banham had first seduced her he'd imagined he was getting his own back for years of Smithson's awkwardness. But in no time at all he'd realized Rowena was using him as much as he was using her: she wanted him to get her into the copywriting department.

'How about Strollers?' Lilia was asking, and Tip Dainty pointed out that Clarke's were using it already. 'Cliff Hangers, Strath?' Lilia repeated, but in his blunt, rugby-playing way H. H. Strathers said Cliff Hangers was useless.

Mulvihill's sister, who was the manageress of an Express Dairy, was surprised when Mulvihill didn't put in an appearance at a quarter to nine, his usual time on Fridays. Every other evening he was back by ten past seven, in time for most of *The Archers*, but on Fridays, he liked to finish off his week's work so as to have a clean plate on Monday. He smelt a little of the wine he drank in the Trumpet Major, but since he always told her the gossip he'd picked up she never minded in the least having to keep their supper back. She knew it wasn't really for the gossip he went to the public house, but in order to pass a few moments with Ox-Banham and H. H. Strathers, to whom he owed his position at Ygnis and Ygnis. Not that either Ox-Banham or H. H. Strathers had employed him in the first place – neither had actually been at Ygnis and Ygnis in those days – but Ox-Banham had since become the executive to whom Mulvihill was mainly responsible and H. H. Strathers was naturally important, being the managing director. Miss Mulvihill had never met these men, but imagined them easily enough from the descriptions that had been passed on to her: Ox-Banham tight-faced in a striped dark suit, H. H. Strathers big, given to talking about rugby matches he had played in. Lilia was peculiar by the sound of her, and Capstick, who designed the best advertisements in Ygnis and Ygnis, was a bearded little creature with a tendency to become insulting when he reached a certain stage in drunkenness. Tip Dainty became genial.

Miss Mulvihill missed these people, her Friday people as she thought of them: she felt deprived as she impatiently waited, she even felt a little cross. Her brother had said he was going to pick up the timber pieces for the bookcase, but he'd have done that in his lunchtime. Never in a million years would he just stay on drinking, he didn't even like the taste. Shortly after ten o'clock the sealyham, Pasco, became agitated, and at eleven Miss Mulvihill noticed that her crossness had turned to fear. But it wasn't until the early hours of the morning that she telephoned the police.

On the following Monday morning the employees of Ygnis and Ygnis arrived at the office building variously refreshed after their weekend. The body had been removed from the back lift, no trace of the death remained. The Hungarian, Wilkinski, was surprised that Mulvihill was not already in the office they shared, for normally he was the first of the two to arrive. He was still pondering the cause of this when the tea-woman, Edith, told him she'd heard Mulvihill had died. She handed Wilkinski his tea, with two lumps of sugar in the saucer, and even while she released the news she poured from her huge, brown enamel teapot a cup for the deceased. 'Oh, stupid thing!' she chided herself.

'But however dead, Edith? However he die, my God?'

Edith shook her head. It was terrible, she said, placing the edge of the teapot on Mulvihill's drawing-board because it was heavy to hold. She still couldn't believe it, she said, laughing and joking he'd been Friday, right as rain. 'Well, it just goes to show,' she said. 'Poor man!'

'Are you sure of this, Edith?' The fat on Wilkinski's face was puckered in mystification, his thick spectacles magnifying the confusion in his eyes. 'Dead?' he said again.

'Definitely,' Edith added, and moved on to spread the news.

My God, dead! Wilkinski continued to reflect, for several minutes unable to drink his tea and finding it cold when he did so. Mulvihill had been the easiest man in the world to share an office with, neither broody nor a bore, a pleasant unassuming fellow, perhaps a little over-worried about the safety of his job, but then who doesn't have faults in this world? He'd been happy, as far as Wilkinski had ever made out, with his sister and their dog in Purley, a few friends in on a Saturday night to cheese and wine, old films on the television. Anything to do with films had interested him, photography being as much of a hobby as his do-it-yourself stuff. In 1971, when Wilkinski's elder daughter married, Mulvihill had recorded the occasion with the camera he'd just bought. He'd made an excellent job of it, with titles he'd lettered himself, and a really impressive shot of the happy couple coming down the steps of the reception place. Unfortunately the marriage had broken up a year ago, and the film was no longer of interest. As dead as poor old Mulvihill, Wilkinski thought sadly: my God, it just goes to show. Ernie Taplow, the art buyer's assistant, came in at that point, shaking his head over the shock of it. And then Len Billings came in, and Harry Plant, and Agnes Trotter the typographer.

Elsewhere in the building life continued normally that morning. The confectionery manufacturers arrived to see the proposals Ygnis and Ygnis had to put to them concerning the promotion of their new chocolate bar. Ox-Banham displayed posters and advertisements, and the labels and window-stickers Mulvihill had designed. 'Go,' one of the confectionery men said. 'Yes, I like that.' Ox-Banham took them down to the television theatre and showed them a series of commercials in which children were dressed up as cowboys and Indians. Afterwards his secretary Rowena, poured them all drinks in his office, smiling at them and murmuring because it was part of her duty to be charming. Just occasionally as she did so she recalled the conjunction that had taken place in the office on Friday evening, Ox-Banham's wiry body as brown as a nut in places, the smell of his underarm-odour preventive. She liked it to take place in the dark, but he preferred the lights on and had more than once mentioned mirrors, although there were no mirrors in the office. They took it in turns, his way one week, hers the next. The only trouble was that personally she didn't much care for him. 'I want you to fix it immediately,' she'd said in her no-nonsense voice on Friday, and this morning he'd arranged for her to be moved into the copy department at the end of the month. 'I'll need a new girl,' he'd said, meaning a secretary. 'I'll leave that to you.'

Ox-Banham introduced the confectionery men to H. H. Strathers, in whose office they had another drink. He then took them to lunch, referring in the taxi to the four times Strathers had been a reserve for the South African rugby team: often a would-be client was impressed by this fact. He didn't mention Mulvihill's death, even though there might have been a talking point in the fact that the chap who'd designed the wrapper for the Go bar had had a heart attack in a lift. But it might also have cast a gloom, you never could tell, so he concentrated instead on making sure that each of the confectionery men had precisely what he wished to have in the way of meat and vegetables, solicitously filling up the wine-glass of the one who drank more than the others. He saw that cigars and brandy were at hand when the moment came, and in the end the most important man said, 'I think we buy it.' All the others agreed: the image that had been devised for the chocolate bar was an apt one, its future safe in the skilful hands of Ygnis and Ygnis.

'Wednesday,' said Miss Mulvihill on the telephone to people who rang with messages of sympathy. 'Eleven-thirty, Putney Vale Crematorium.'

As the next few weeks went by so life continued smoothly in the Ygnis and Ygnis building. Happy in the copywriting department, Rowena practised the composition of slogans and thought up trade names for shoes, underwear and garden seeds. She wrote a television commercial for furniture polish, and explained to Ox-Banham that there would now be no more Friday evenings. She began to spend her lunchtimes with a new young man in market research. Unlike Ox-Banham, he was a bachelor.

Bloody Smithson telephoned Strathers to say he was dissatisfied with Ygnis and Ygnis's latest efforts for McCulloch Paints. Typical, Ox-Banham said when Strathers sent for him: as soon as little Rowena's home and dry the old bugger starts doing his nut again. 'Let us just look into all that,' he murmured delicately to Bloody Smithson on the telephone.

'There are private possessions,' Wilkinski said to Mulvihill's sister, on the telephone also. 'Maybe we send a messenger to your house with them?'

'That's very kind, Mr Wilkinski.'

'No, no. But the filing cabinet he had is locked. Maybe the key was on his person?'

'Yes, I have his bunch of keys. If I may, I'll post it to you, Mr Wilkinski.'

Everything else Wilkinski had tidied up: Mulvihill's paintbrushes and his pencils, his paints and his felt pens. Strictly speaking, they were the property of Ygnis and Ygnis, but Wilkinski thought Miss Mulvihill should have them. The filing-cabinet itself, the drawing-board and the green-shaded light, would pass on to Mulvihill's successor.

When the keys arrived, Wilkinski found that Mulvihill had retained samples of every label and sticker and wrapper, every packet and point-of-sale item he had ever designed. The samples were stuck on to sheets of white card, one to a sheet, and the sheets neatly documented and filed. Wilkinski decided that Mulvihill's sister would wish to have this collection, as well as the old Four Square tobacco tins containing drawing-pins and rubber bands, a pair of small brass hinges, several broken pipes, some dental fixative, and two pairs of spectacles. Mulvihill's camera was there, side by side with his projector. And in the bottom drawer, beneath ideas for the lettering on a toothpaste tube, were his films.

Pleased to have an excuse to walk about the building, Wilkinski made his way to the basement and asked Mr Betts, the office maintenance man, for a large, strong cardboard carton, explaining why he wanted it. Mr Betts did his best to supply what was necessary and Wilkinski returned to his office with it. He packed the projector and the camera with great care and when he came to the vast assortment of neatly titled films, all in metal containers, he looked out for one that Agnes Trotter wanted, to do with her father's retirement party. 'A Day in the Life of a Sealyham', he read, and then 'A Sealyham Has His Say' and 'A Sealyham at Three'. A note was attached to the label, 'Mr Trotter's Retirement Occasion', a reminder that the film still needed some editing. Wilkinski put it aside for Agnes Trotter and then, to his surprise, noticed that the label on the next tin said, 'Confessions of a Housewife'. He examined some of the others and was even more surprised to read, 'Virgins' Delight', 'Naughty Nell' and 'Bedtime with Bunny'.

Closer examination of the metal film-containers convinced Wilkinski that while most of the more exotic titles were not Mulvihill's own work, two or three of them were. 'Easy Lady', for instance, had a reminder stuck to it indicating that editing was necessary; 'Let's Go, Lover' and two untitled containers had a note about splicing. 'My God!' Wilkinski said.

He didn't know what to think. He imagined Mulvihill wandering about Soho in his lunch-hour, examining the pictures that advertised the strip joints, entering the pornographic shops where blue films were discreetly for sale. None of that fitted Mulvihill, none of it was like him. Quite often Wilkinski had accompanied him and his camera to Green Park, to catch the autumn, or the ducks in springtime.

Wilkinski sat down. He ran the tip of his tongue over his rather thick lips. They had shared an office since 1960, yet he had never known a thing about this man. Clearly Mulvihill had bought 'Virgins' Delight' and 'Bedtime with Bunny' to see how it was done, and then he had begun to make blue films himself. Being in terror of losing his job, he had every day passed humbly through the huge reception areas of Ygnis and Ygnis, its walls enriched by pictures of shoes and seed-packets and ironworks, and biscuits and whisky bottles. Humbly he had walked the corridors that rattled with the busyness of typewriters and voices in trivial conversation; humbly he had done his duty by the words and images that were daily created. Wilkinski recalled his saying that he'd always wanted to be a photographer: had he decided in the end to attempt to escape from his treadmill by becoming a pornographer instead? It was a sad thing to have happened to a man. It was an ugly thing as well.

Still, Wilkinski had a job to do and he knew that in the carton destined for Purley he must not include such items as 'Let's Go, Lover' and 'Confessions of a Housewife' because of the embarrassment they would cause. His first thought was that he should simply throw the pornographic films away, but even though he had emigrated from Hungary in 1955 Wilkinski was still aware that he had to be careful in a foreign country. Assiduously he avoided all trouble and was notably polite in tube trains and on the street: it seemed a doubtful procedure, to destroy the possessions of a dead man.

'Films?' Ox-Banham said on the telephone. 'You mean they're dirty?'

'Some you might call domestic. Others I think they could offend a lady.'

'I'll come and have a look.'

'Some are of a dog.'

Later that day Ox-Banham arrived in Wilkinski's small office and took charge of the films, including the ones of the dog. He locked them away in his own office, for he was personally not in the least interested in pornography and certainly not curious to investigate this private world of a label-designer who had remotely been in his charge. He didn't destroy the films because you never could tell: an occasion might quite easily arise when some client or would-be client would reveal, even without meaning to, an interest in such material. Topless waitresses, gambling clubs, or just getting drunk: where his clients were concerned, Ox-Banham was endlessly solicitous, a guide and a listener. It was unbecoming that Mulvihill should have titillated himself in this way, he reflected as he stood that evening in the Trumpet Major, getting more than a little drunk himself. Nasty he must have been, in spite of his pipe and his Harris tweed jackets.

In time the carton containing Mulvihill's effects was delivered to Purley. Miss Mulvihill returned from the Express Dairy one evening to find it on the doorstep. In the hall, where she opened it, she discovered that her brother's keys had been returned to her, Sellotaped on to one of the carton's flaps; only the key of the filing-cabinet had been removed, but Miss Mulvihill didn't even notice that. She looked through the white cards on which her brother had mounted the items he had designed at Ygnis and Ygnis; she wondered what to do with his old pipes. In the end she put everything back into the carton and hauled it into the cubbyhole beneath the stairs. Pasco bustled about at her feet, delighted to be able to make a foray into a cupboard that was normally kept locked.

An hour or so later, scrambling an egg for herself in the kitchen, Miss Mulvihill reflected that this was truly the end of her brother. The carton in the cubbyhole reminded her of the coffin that had slid away towards the fawn-coloured curtains in the chapel of the crematorium. She'd been through her brother's clothes, setting most of them aside for Help the Aged. She'd told the man next door that he could have the contents of the workshed in the garden, asking him to leave her only a screwdriver and a hammer and a pair of pliers.

She had always been fond of her brother; being the older one, she had looked after him as a child, taking him by the hand when they crossed the street together, answering his questions. Their mother had died when he was eight, and when their father died thirty years later it had seemed natural that they should continue to live together in the house in Purley. 'Let's have a dog,' her brother had said one Saturday morning nine years ago, and soon after that Pasco had entered their lives. The only animal the house had known before was Miss Muffin, their father's cat, but they'd agreed immediately about Pasco. Never once in their lives had they quarrelled, her brother being too nervous and she too even-tempered. Neither had ever wished to marry.

She'd put a rose in, she thought as she ate her scrambled egg, the way you could in the grounds of the crematorium, a living thing to remember him by.

A year went by in Ygnis and Ygnis. The new man who shared Wilkinski's office was young and given to whistling. On the telephone he addressed his wife as 'chick', which began to grate on Wilkinski's nerves. He possessed a 1951 Fiat, which he talked about; and a caravan, which he talked about also.

Established now in the copy department, Rowena Smithson was responsible for a slogan which won a prize. She had been put in charge of a frozen foods account and had devised a television campaign which displayed an ordinary family's preference for a packet of fish to a banquet. In Ygnis and Ygnis it was said more than once that Rowena Smithson was going places. Foolish in her dishevelled middle age, Lilia was said to be slipping.

During the course of that year Ox-Banham interested himself in one of Ygnis and Ygnis's three receptionists, a girl who wanted to get into the art department. The Trumpet Major continued to profit from the drinking requirements of Capstick, Lilia, Tip Dainty and H. H. Strathers. Several office parties took place during the year and at the end of it the Ygnis and Ygnis chairman was awarded an OBE.

'Well, I quite appreciate that of course,' Ox-Banham said on the telephone one morning after that year had passed. He was speaking to Bloody Smithson, who had not ceased to give him a bad time, forgetful of all that had been arranged in the matter of placing his daughter in her chosen career. Rowena was shortly to marry the man she'd begun to go out with, from the market research department. The man was welcome to her as far as Ox-Banham was concerned, but when her father was disagreeable it gave him no satisfaction whatsoever to recall how he'd repeatedly pleasured himself with her on the floor of his office. 'Let's iron it out over lunch,' he urged Bloody Smithson.

The lunch that took place was a sticky one, bitter with Bloody Smithson's acrimony. Only when coffee and glasses of Hine arrived on the table did the man from McCulloch Paints desist and Ox-Banham cease inwardly to swear. Then, quite unexpectedly, Bloody Smithson mentioned blue films. His mood was good by now, for he'd enjoyed being a bully for two hours; he described at length some material he'd been shown on a trip to Sweden. 'Awfully ripe,' he said, his large blood-red face inches from his companion's.

Until that moment Ox-Banham had forgotten about the metal containers he had locked away after Mulvihill's death. He didn't mention them, but that evening he read through their neatly labelled titles, and a week later he borrowed a projector. He found what he saw distasteful, as he'd known he would, but was aware that his own opinion didn't matter in the least. 'I've got hold of a few ripe ones that might interest you,' he said on the telephone to Bloody Smithson when he next had occasion to speak to him.

In the comfort of the television theatre they watched 'Confessions of a Housewife', 'Virgins' Delight' and 'Naughty Nell'. Bloody Smithson liked 'Virgins' Delight' best. Ox-Banham explained how the cache had fallen into his hands and how some of the films were apparently the late Mulvihill's own work. 'Let's try this "Day in the Life of a Sealyham",' he suggested. 'Goodness knows what all *that's* about.' But Bloody Smithson said he'd rather have another showing of 'Virgins' Delight'.

Ox-Banham told the story in the Trumpet Major. 'Not a word to my daughter, mind,' Bloody Smithson had insisted, chortling in a way that was quite unlike him. The next day all of it went around the Ygnis and Ygnis building, but it naturally never reached the ears of Rowena because no one liked to tell her that her father had a penchant for obscene films. Mulvihill's name was used again, his face and clothing recalled, a description supplied to newcomers at Ygnis and Ygnis. Wilkinski heard the story and it hurt him that Mulvihill should be remembered in this way. It was improper, Wilkinski considered, and it made him feel guilty himself: he should have thrown the films away, as his first instinct had been. 'Mulvihill's Memorial' the pornography came to be called, and the employees of Ygnis and Ygnis laughed when they thought of an overweight advertising manager being shown 'Virgins' Delight' in the television theatre. It seemed to Wilkinski that the dead face of Mulvihill was being rubbed in the dirt he had left behind him. It worried Wilkinski, and eventually he plucked up his courage and went to speak to Ox-Banham.

'We shared the office since 1960,' he said, and Ox-Banham looked at him in astonishment. 'It isn't very nice to call it "Mulvihill's Memorial".'

'Mulvihill's dead and gone. What d'you expect us to do with his goodies?'

'Maybe put them down Mr Betts' incinerator.'

Ox-Banham laughed and suggested that Wilkinski was being a bit Hungarian about the matter. The smile that appeared on his face was designed to be reassuring, but Wilkinski found this reference to his origins offensive. It seemed that if Mulvihill's wretched pornography brought solace to a recalcitrant advertising manager, then Mulvihill had not died in vain. The employees had to be paid, profits had to be made. 'It isn't very nice,' Wilkinski said again, quietly in the middle of one night. No one heard him, for though he addressed his wife she was dreaming at the time of something else.

Then two things happened at once. Wilkinski had a telephone call from Miss Mulvihill, and Ox-Banham made a mistake.

'It's just that I was wondering,' Miss Mulvihill said. 'I mean, he definitely made these little films and there's absolutely no trace of them.'

'About a dog maybe?'

'And a little one about the scouts. Then again one concerning Purley.'

'Leave the matter with me, Miss Mulvihill.'

The telephone call came late in the day, and when Wilkinski tried to see Ox-Banham it was suggested that he should try again in the morning. It pleased him that Miss Mulvihill had phoned, that she had sought to have returned to her what was rightfully hers. He'd considered it high-handed at the time that Ox-Banham hadn't bothered to divide the films into two groups, as he had done himself. 'Oh, let's not bother with all that,' Ox-Banham had said with a note of impatience in his voice.

Wilkinski hurried to catch his train on the evening of Miss Mulvihill's call; Ox-Banham entertained Bloody Smithson in the television theatre. 'No, no, no,' Bloody Smithson protested. 'We'll stick with our Virgins, Ox.'

But Ox-Banham was heartily sick of 'Virgins' Delight', which he had seen by now probably sixty times. He thought he'd die if he had to watch, yet again, the three schoolgirls putting down their hockey sticks and beginning to take off their gymslips. 'I thought we were maybe wearing it out,' he said. 'I thought I'd better have a copy made.'

'You mean it's not here?'

'Back in a week or so, Smithy.'

They began to go through the others. 'Let's try this "Day in the Life of a Sealyham",' Ox-Banham suggested, and shortly afterwards a dog appeared on the screen, ambling about a kitchen. Then the dog was put on a lead and taken for a walk around a suburb by a middle-aged woman. Back in the kitchen again, the dog begged with its head on one side and was given a titbit. There was another walk, a bus shelter, the dog smelling at bits of paper on the ground. 'Well, for God's sake!' Bloody Smithson protested when the animal was finally given a meal to eat and put to bed.

'Sorry, Smithy.'

'I thought she and the dog –'

'I know. So did I.'

'Some bloody nut made that one.'

Ox-Banham then showed 'Naughty Nell', followed by 'Country Fun', 'Oh Boy!' and 'Girlie'. But Bloody Smithson wasn't in the least impressed. He didn't care for 'Confessions of a Housewife' any more than he had the first time he'd seen it. He didn't care for 'Nothing on Tonight' and wasn't much impressed by anything else. Ox-Banham regretted that he'd said 'Virgins' Delight' was being copied. This tedious search for excitement could go on all night, for even though Smithson continued to say that everything was less good than 'Virgins' Delight' Ox-Banham had a feeling that some enjoyment at least was being derived from the continuous picture show.

'You're sure there isn't another reel or something to that dog stuff?' the advertising manager even enquired. 'I wouldn't mind seeing that dame with her undies off.' He gave a loud laugh, draining his glass of whisky and poking it out at Ox-Banham for a refill.

'I think that's the bloke's sister actually. I don't think she takes anything off.' Ox-Banham laughed himself, busy with glasses and ice. 'Call it a day after this one, shall we?'

'Might as well run through the lot, Ox.'

They saw 'Come and Get It', 'Girls on the Rampage', 'A Sealyham Has His Say', 'Street of Desire', a film of boy scouts camping, scenes on a golf course, 'Saturday Morning, Purley', and 'Flesh for Sale'. It was then, after a few moments of a film without a title, that Ox-Banham realized something was wrong. Unfortunately he realized it too late.

'Great God almighty,' said Bloody Smithson.

'You opened the filing-cabinet, Wilkinski, you took the films out. What did you do next?' Ox-Banham ground his teeth together, struggling with his impatience.

'I say myself it's not nice for the sister. The sister phoned up yesterday, I came down to see you –'

'You didn't project any of the films?'

'No, no. I think of Mulvihill lying dead and I think of the sister. What the sister wants is the ones about the dog, and anything else, maybe boy scouts, is there?'

'You are absolutely certain that you did not project any of the films? Not one called "Easy Lady" or another, "Let's Go, Lover"? Neither of the two untitled ones?'

'No, no. I have no interest in this. I get the box from Mr Betts –'

'Is it possible that someone else might have examined the films? Did you leave the filing-cabinet unlocked, for instance?'

'No, no. I get the box from Mr Betts, maybe ten minutes. The cabinet is closed and locked then. The property of a dead man, I say myself –'

'So no one could possibly have projected one of these films?'

'No, no. The sister rings me yesterday. She is anxious for the dog ones, also boy scouts, and others.'

'Oh, for God's sake, Wilkinski!'

'I promise I find –'

'They've all been destroyed. Everything's been destroyed.'

'Destroyed? But I thought –'

'I destroyed them myself last night.'

Returning to his office, Wilkinski paused for a moment in a corridor, removed his spectacles and polished them with his handkerchief. People hurried by him with proofs of new advertisements and typewritten pages of copy, but it was easier to think in the corridor than it would be in the office because of the whistling of Mulvihill's successor. Ox-Banham had looked almost ill, his voice had been shaky. Wilkinski shook his head and slowly padded back to his drawing-board, baffled by the turn of events. He didn't know what he was going to say to Mulvihill's sister.

What happened next was that Bloody Smithson removed the McCulloch Paints account from Ygnis and Ygnis. Then Rowena Smithson walked out. She didn't hand in her notice, she simply didn't return after lunch one day. The man in market research to whom she was engaged let it be known that the engagement had been broken off, and made it clear that it was he who had done the breaking. A rumour went round that the big shoe account – a Quaker concern and one of Ygnis and Ygnis's mainstays – was about to go, and a week later it did. Questions were asked by the men of the chocolate account which Ox-Banham had gained a year ago, and by the toiletries people, and by the men of Macclesfield Metals. Hasty lunches were arranged, explanations pressed home over afternoon brandy. *Ygnis and Ygnis in Trouble* a headline in a trade magazine was ready to state, but the headline – and the report that went with it – was abandoned at the eleventh hour because it appeared that Ygnis and Ygnis had weathered their storm.

Wilkinski tried to piece things together, and so did the other employees. In the Trumpet Major it was said that for reasons of his own Bloody Smithson had sworn to bring Ygnis and Ygnis to its knees, but neither Wilkinski nor anyone else knew why he had become so enraged. Then, making a rare appearance in the Trumpet Major, the market research man to whom Rowena Smithson had been engaged drank an extra couple of Carlsbergs while waiting for the rain to cease. Idling at the bar, he told Tip Dainty in the strictest confidence of a scene which had taken place at the time of the crisis in the Smithsons' house in Wimbledon: how he'd been about to leave, having driven Rowena home, when Bloody Smithson had thundered his way into the sitting-room, 'literally like a bull'. Mrs Smithson had been drinking a glass of Ovaltine at the time, Rowena had not yet taken off her coat. 'You filthy young prostitute!' Bloody Smithson had roared at her. 'You cheap whore!' It apparently hadn't concerned him that his daughter's fiancé was present, he hadn't even noticed when the cup of Ovaltine fell from his wife's grasp. He had just stood there shouting, oaths and obscenities bursting out of him, his face the colour of ripe strawberries.

By half past ten the following morning the story was known to every Ygnis and Ygnis employee: Mulvihill had made a film of Ox-Banham and Rowena Smithson banging away on the floor of Ox-Banham's office. Mulvihill had apparently hidden himself behind the long blue Dralon curtains, which in the circumstances had naturally been drawn. The lights in the room had been on and neither protagonist in the proceedings had been wearing a stitch.

At lunchtime that day, passing through the large, chic reception area, the people of Ygnis and Ygnis hardly noticed the images displayed on its walls. The messages that murmured at them were rich in sexual innuendo, but the hard facts of a dead pornographer briefly interested them more. 'Mulvihill!' some exclaimed in uneasy admiration, for to a few at least it seemed that Mulvihill had dealt in an honesty that just for a moment made the glamour of the images and the messages appear to be a little soiled. Wilkinski thought so, and longed to telephone Mulvihill's sister to tell her of what had occurred, but of course it was impossible to do that. He wrote a letter instead, apologizing for taking so long in replying to her query and informing her that the films she'd mentioned had been destroyed in error. It was not exactly a lie, and seemed less of one as the day wore on, as the glamour glittered again, undefeated when it came to the point.

Beyond the Pale

We always went to Ireland in June.

Ever since the four of us began to go on holidays together, in 1965 it must have been, we had spent the first fortnight of the month at Glencorn Lodge in Co. Antrim. Perfection, as Dekko put it once, and none of us disagreed. It's a Georgian house by the sea, not far from the village of Ardbeag. It's quite majestic in its rather elegant way, a garden running to the very edge of a cliff, its long rhododendron drive – or avenue, as they say in Ireland. The English couple who bought the house in the early sixties, the Malseeds, have had to build on quite a bit but it's all been discreetly done, the Georgian style preserved throughout. Figs grow in the sheltered gardens, and apricots, and peaches in the greenhouses which old Mr Saxton presides over. He's Mrs Malseed's father actually. They brought him with them from Surrey, and their Dalmatians, Charger and Snooze.

It was Strafe who found Glencorn for us. He'd come across an advertisement in the *Lady* in the days when the Malseeds still felt the need to advertise. 'How about this?' he said one evening at the end of the second rubber, and then read out the details. We had gone away together the summer before, to a hotel that had been recommended on the Costa del Sol, but it hadn't been a success because the food was so appalling. 'We could try this Irish one,' Dekko suggested cautiously, which is what eventually we did.

The four of us have been playing bridge together for ages, Dekko, Strafe, Cynthia and myself. They call me Milly, though strictly speaking my name is Dorothy Milson. Dekko picked up his nickname at school, Dekko Deakin sounding rather good, I dare say. He and Strafe were in fact at school together, which must be why we all call Strafe by his surname: Major R. B. Strafe he is, the initials standing for Robert Buchanan. We're of an age, the four of us, all in the early fifties: the prime of life, so Dekko insists. We live quite close to Leatherhead, where the Malseeds were before they decided to make the change from Surrey to Co. Antrim. Quite a coincidence, we always think.

'How *very* nice,' Mrs Malseed said, smiling her welcome again this year. Some instinct seems to tell her when guests are about to arrive, for she's rarely not waiting in the large low-ceilinged hall that always smells of flowers. She dresses beautifully, differently every day, and changing of course in the evening. Her blouse on this occasion was scarlet and silver, in stripes, her skirt black. This choice gave her a brisk look, which was fitting because being so busy she often has to be a little on the brisk side. She has smooth grey hair which she once told me she entirely looks after herself, and she almost always wears a black velvet band in it. Her face is well made up, and for one who arranges so many vases of flowers and otherwise has to use her hands she manages to keep them marvellously in condition. Her fingernails are varnished a soft pink, and a small gold bangle always adorns her right wrist, a wedding present from her husband.

'Arthur, take the party's luggage,' she commanded the old porter, who doubles as odd-job man. 'Rose, Geranium, Hydrangea, Fuchsia.' She referred to the titles of the rooms reserved for us: in winter, when no one much comes to Glencorn Lodge, pleasant little details like that are seen to. Mrs Malseed herself painted the flower-plaques that are attached to the doors of the hotel instead of numbers; her husband sees to redecoration and repairs.

'Well, well, well,' Mr Malseed said now, entering the hall through the door that leads to the kitchen regions. 'A hundred thousand welcomes,' he greeted us in the Irish manner. He's rather shorter than Mrs Malseed, who's handsomely tall. He wears Donegal tweed suits and is brown as a berry, including his head, which is bald. His dark brown eyes twinkle at you, making you feel rather more than just another hotel guest. They run the place like a country house, really.

'Good trip?' Mr Malseed enquired.

'Super,' Dekko said. 'Not a worry all the way.'

'Splendid.'

'The wretched boat sailed an hour early one day last week,' Mrs Malseed said. 'Quite a little band were left stranded at Stranraer.'

Strafe laughed. Typical of that steamship company, he said. 'Catching the tide, I dare say?'

'They caught a rocket from me,' Mrs Malseed replied good-humouredly. 'A couple of old dears were due with us on Tuesday and had to spend the night in some awful Scottish lodging-house. It nearly finished them.'

Everyone laughed, and I could feel the others thinking that our holiday had truly begun. Nothing had changed at Glencorn Lodge, all was well with its Irish world. Kitty from the dining-room came out to greet us, spotless in her uniform. 'Ach, you're looking younger,' she said, paying the compliment to all four of us, causing everyone in the hall to laugh again. Kitty's a bit of a card.

Arthur led the way to the rooms called Rose, Geranium, Hydrangea and Fuchsia, carrying as much of our luggage as he could manage and returning for the remainder. Arthur has a beaten, fisherman's face and short grey hair. He wears a green baize apron, and a white shirt with an imitation-silk scarf tucked into it at the neck. The scarf, in different swirling greens which blend nicely with the green of his apron, is an idea of Mrs Malseed's and one appreciates the effort, if not at a uniform, at least at tidiness.

'Thank you very much,' I said to Arthur in my room, smiling and finding him a coin.

We played a couple of rubbers after dinner as usual, but not of course going on for as long as we might have because we were still quite tired after the journey. In the lounge there was a French family, two girls and their parents, and a honeymoon couple – or so we had speculated during dinner – and a man on his own. There had been other people at dinner of course, because in June Glencorn Lodge is always full: from where we sat in the window we could see some of them strolling about the lawns, a few taking the cliff path down to the seashore. In the morning we'd do the same: we'd walk along the sands to Ardbeag and have coffee in the hotel there, back in time for lunch. In the afternoon we'd drive somewhere.

I knew all that because over the years this kind of pattern had developed. We had our walks and our drives, tweed to buy in Cushendall, Strafe's and Dekko's fishing day when Cynthia and I just sat on the beach, our visit to the Giant's Causeway and one to Donegal perhaps, though that meant an early start and taking pot-luck for dinner somewhere. We'd come to adore Co. Antrim, its glens and coastline, Rathlin Island and Tievebulliagh. Since first we got to know it, in 1965, we'd all four fallen hopelessly in love with every variation of this remarkable landscape. People in England thought us mad of course: they see so much of the troubles on television that it's naturally difficult for them to realize that most places are just as they've always been. Yet coming as we did, taking the road along the coast, dawdling through Ballygally, it was impossible to believe that somewhere else the unpleasantness was going on. We'd never seen a thing, nor even heard people talking about incidents that might have taken place. It's true that after a particularly nasty carry-on a few winters ago we did consider finding somewhere else, in Scotland perhaps, or Wales. But as Strafe put it at the time, we felt we owed a certain loyalty to the Malseeds and indeed to everyone we'd come to know round about, people who'd always been glad to welcome us back. It seemed silly to lose our heads, and when we returned the following summer we knew immediately we'd been right. Dekko said that nothing could be further away from all the violence than Glencorn Lodge, and though his remark could hardly be taken literally I think we all knew what he meant.

'Cynthia's tired,' I said because she'd been stifling yawns. 'I think we should call it a day.'

'Oh, not at all,' Cynthia protested. 'No, please.'

But Dekko agreed with me that she was tired, and Strafe said he didn't mind stopping now. He suggested a nightcap, as he always does; and as we always do also, Cynthia and I declined. Dekko said he'd like a Cointreau.

The conversation drifted about. Dekko told us an Irish joke about a drunk who couldn't find his way out of a telephone box, and then Strafe remembered an incident at school concerning his and Dekko's housemaster,

A. D. Cowley-Stubbs, and the house wag, Thrive Major. A. D. Cowley-Stubbs had been known as Cows and often featured in our after-bridge reminiscing. So did Thrive Major.

'Perhaps I *am* sleepy,' Cynthia said. 'I don't think I closed my eyes once last night.'

She never does on a sea crossing. Personally I'm out like a light the moment my head touches the pillow; I often think it must be the salt in the air because normally I'm an uneasy sleeper at the best of times.

'You run along, old girl,' Strafe advised.

'Brekky at nine,' Dekko said.

Cynthia said good-night and went, and we didn't remark on her tiredness because as a kind of unwritten rule we never comment on one another. We're four people who play bridge. The companionship it offers, and the holidays we have together, are all part of that. We share everything: the cost of petrol, the cups of coffee or drinks we have; we even each make a contribution towards the use of Strafe's car because it's always his we go on holiday in, a Rover it was on this occasion.

'Funny, being here on your own,' Strafe said, glancing across what the Malseeds call the After-Dinner Lounge at the man who didn't have a companion. He was a red-haired man of about thirty, not wearing a tie, his collar open at the neck and folded back over the jacket of his blue serge suit. He was uncouth-looking, though it's a hard thing to say, not at all the kind of person one usually sees at Glencorn Lodge. He sat in the After-Dinner Lounge as he had in the dining-room, lost in some concentration of his own, as if calculating sums in his mind. There had been a folded newspaper on his table in the dining-room. It now reposed tidily on the arm of his chair, still unopened.

'Commercial gent,' Dekko said. 'Fertilizers.'

'Good heavens, never. You wouldn't get a rep in here.'

I took no part in the argument. The lone man didn't much interest me, but I felt that Strafe was probably right: if there was anything dubious about the man's credentials he might have found it difficult to secure a room. In the hall of Glencorn Lodge there's a notice which reads: *We prefer not to feature in hotel guides, and we would be grateful to our guests if they did not seek to include Glencorn Lodge in the Good Food Guide, the Good Hotel Guide, the Michelin, Egon Ronay or any others. We have not advertised Glencorn since our early days, and prefer our recommendations to be by word of mouth.*

'Ah, thank you,' Strafe said when Kitty brought his whisky and Dekko's Cointreau. 'Sure you won't have something?' he said to me, although he knew I never did.

Strafe is on the stout side, I suppose you could say, with a gingery moustache and gingery hair, hardly touched at all by grey. He left the Army years ago, I suppose because of me in a sense, because he didn't want to be posted abroad again. He's in the Ministry of Defence now.

I'm still quite pretty in my way, though nothing like as striking as Mrs Malseed, for I've never been that kind of woman. I've put on weight, and wouldn't have allowed myself to do so if Strafe hadn't kept saying he can't stand a bag of bones. I'm careful about my hair and, unlike Mrs Malseed, I have it very regularly seen to because if I don't it gets a salt and pepper look, which I hate. My husband, Ralph, who died of food-poisoning when we were still quite young, used to say I wouldn't lose a single look in middle age, and to some extent that's true. We were still putting off having children when he died, which is why I haven't any. Then I met Strafe, which meant I didn't marry again.

Strafe is married himself, to Cynthia. She's small and ineffectual, I suppose you'd say without being untruthful or unkind. Not that Cynthia and I don't get on or anything like that, in fact we get on extremely well. It's Strafe and Cynthia who don't seem quite to hit it off, and I often think how much happier all round it would have been if Cynthia had married someone completely different, someone like Dekko in a way, except that that mightn't quite have worked out either. The Strafes have two sons, both very like their father, both of them in the Army. And the very sad thing is they think nothing of poor Cynthia.

'Who's that chap?' Dekko asked Mr Malseed, who'd come over to wish us good-night.

'Awfully sorry about that, Mr Deakin. My fault entirely, a booking that came over the phone.'

'Good heavens, not at all,' Strafe protested, and Dekko looked horrified in case it should be thought he was objecting to the locals. 'Splendid-looking fellow,' he said, overdoing it.

Mr Malseed murmured that the man had only booked in for a single night, and I smiled the whole thing away, reassuring him with a nod. It's one of the pleasantest of the traditions at Glencorn Lodge that every evening Mr Malseed makes the rounds of his guests just to say good-night. It's because of little touches like that that I, too, wished Dekko hadn't questioned Mr Malseed about the man because it's the kind of thing one doesn't do at Glencorn Lodge. But Dekko is a law unto himself, very tall and gangling, always immaculately suited, a beaky face beneath mousy hair in which flecks of grey add a certain distinction. Dekko has money of his own and though he takes out girls who are half his age he has never managed to get around to marriage. The uncharitable might say he has a rather gormless laugh; certainly it's sometimes on the loud side.

We watched while Mr Malseed bade the lone man good-night. The man didn't respond, but just sat gazing. It was ill-mannered, but this lack of courtesy didn't appear to be intentional: the man was clearly in a mood of some kind, miles away.

'Well, I'll go up,' I said. 'Good-night, you two.'

'Cheery-bye, Milly,' Dekko said. 'Brekky at nine, remember.'

'Good-night, Milly,' Strafe said.

The Strafes always occupy different rooms on holidays, and at home also. This time he was in Geranium and she in Fuchsia. I was in Rose, and in a little while Strafe would come to see me. He stays with her out of kindness, because he fears for her on her own. He's a sentimental, good-hearted man, easily moved to tears: he simply cannot bear the thought of Cynthia with no one to talk to in the evenings, with no one to make her life around. 'And besides,' he often says when he's being jocular, 'it would break up our bridge four.' Naturally we never discuss her shortcomings or in any way analyse the marriage. The unwritten rule that exists among the four of us seems to extend as far as that.

He slipped into my room after he'd had another drink or two, and I was waiting for him as he likes me to wait, in bed but not quite undressed. He has never said so, but I know that that is something Cynthia would not understand in him, or ever attempt to comply with. Ralph, of course, would not have understood either; poor old Ralph would have been shocked. Actually it's all rather sweet, Strafe and his little ways.

'I love you, dear,' I whispered to him in the darkness, but just then he didn't wish to speak of love and referred instead to my body.

If Cynthia hadn't decided to remain in the hotel the next morning instead of accompanying us on our walk to Ardbeag everything might have been different. As it happened, when she said at breakfast she thought she'd just potter about the garden and sit with her book out of the wind somewhere, I can't say I was displeased. For a moment I hoped Dekko might say he'd stay with her, allowing Strafe and myself to go off on our own, but Dekko – who doesn't go in for saying what you want him to say – didn't. 'Poor old sausage,' he said instead, examining Cynthia with a solicitude that suggested she was close to the grave, rather than just a little lowered by the change of life or whatever it was.

'I'll be perfectly all right,' Cynthia assured him. 'Honestly.'

'Cynthia likes to mooch, you know,' Strafe pointed out, which of course is only the truth. She reads too much, I always think. You often see her putting down a book with the most melancholy look in her eyes, which can't be good for her. She's an imaginative woman, I suppose you would say, and of course her habit of reading so much is often useful on our holidays: over the years she has read her way through dozens of Irish guide-books. 'That's where the garrison pushed the natives over the cliffs,' she once remarked on a drive. 'Those rocks are known as the Maidens,' she remarked on another occasion. She has led us to places of interest which we had no idea existed: Garron Tower on Garron Point, the mausoleum at Bonamargy, the Devil's Backbone. As well as which, Cynthia is extremely knowledgeable about all matters relating to Irish history. Again she has read endlessly: biographies and autobiographies, long accounts of the centuries of battling and politics there've been. There's hardly a town or village we ever pass through that hasn't some significance for Cynthia, although I'm afraid her impressive fund of information doesn't always receive the attention it deserves. Not that Cynthia ever minds; it doesn't seem to worry her when no one listens. My own opinion is that she'd have made a much better job of her relationship with Strafe and her sons if she could have somehow developed a bit more character.

We left her in the garden and proceeded down the cliff path to the shingle beneath. I was wearing slacks and a blouse, with the arms of a cardigan looped round my neck in case it turned chilly: the outfit was new, specially bought for the holiday, in shades of tangerine. Strafe never cares how he dresses and of course she doesn't keep him up to the mark: that morning, as far as I remember, he wore rather shapeless corduroy trousers, the kind men sometimes garden in, and a navy-blue fisherman's jersey. Dekko as usual was a fashion plate: a pale green linen suit with pleated jacket pockets, a maroon shirt open at the neck, revealing a medallion on a fine gold chain. We didn't converse as we crossed the rather difficult shingle, but when we reached the sand Dekko began to talk about some girl or other, someone called Juliet who had apparently proposed marriage to him just before we'd left Surrey. He'd told her, so he said, that he'd think about it while on holiday and he wondered now about dispatching a telegram from Ardbeag saying, *Still thinking*. Strafe, who has a simple sense of humour, considered this hugely funny and spent most of the walk persuading Dekko that the telegram must certainly be sent, and other telegrams later on, all with the same message. Dekko kept laughing, throwing his head back in a way that always reminds me of an Australian bird I once saw in a nature film on television. I could see this was going to become one of those jokes that would accompany us all through the holiday, a man's thing really, but of course I didn't mind. The girl called Juliet was nearly thirty years younger than Dekko. I supposed she knew what she was doing.

Since the subject of telegrams had come up, Strafe recalled the occasion when Thrive Major had sent one to A. D. Cowley-Stubbs: *Darling regret three months gone love Rowena*. Carefully timed, it had arrived during one of Cows' Thursday evening coffee sessions. Rowena was a maid, known as the Bicycle, who had been sacked the previous term, and old Cows had something of a reputation as a misogynist. When he read the message he apparently went white and collapsed into an armchair. Warrington P. J. managed to read it too, and after that the fat was in the fire. The consequences went on rather, but I never minded listening when Strafe and Dekko drifted back to their schooldays. I just wish I'd known Strafe then, before either of us had gone and got married.

We had our coffee at Ardbeag, the telegram was sent off, and then Strafe and Dekko wanted to see a man called Henry O'Reilly whom we'd met on previous holidays, who organizes mackerel-fishing trips. I waited on my own, picking out postcards in the village shop that sells almost everything, and then I wandered down towards the shore. I knew that they would be having a drink with the boatman because a year had passed since they'd seen him last. They joined me after about twenty minutes, Dekko apologizing but Strafe not seeming to be aware that I'd had to wait because Strafe is not a man who notices little things. It was almost one o'clock when we reached Glencorn Lodge and were told by Mr Malseed that Cynthia needed looking after.

The hotel, in fact, was in a turmoil. I have never seen anyone as ashen-faced as Mr Malseed; his wife, in a forget-me-not dress, was limp. It wasn't explained to us immediately what had happened, because in the middle of telling us that Cynthia needed looking after Mr Malseed was summoned to the telephone. I could see through the half-open door of their little office a glass of whisky or brandy on the desk and Mrs Malseed's bangled arm reaching out for it. Not for ages did we realize that it all had to do with the lone man whom we'd speculated about the night before.

'He just wanted to talk to me,' Cynthia kept repeating hysterically in the hall. 'He sat with me by the magnolias.'

I made her lie down. Strafe and I stood on either side of her bed as she lay there with her shoes off, her rather unattractively cut plain pink dress crumpled and actually damp from her tears. I wanted to make her take it off and to slip under the bed-clothes in her petticoat but somehow it seemed all wrong, in the circumstances, for Strafe's wife to do anything so intimate in my presence.

'I couldn't stop him,' Cynthia said, the rims of her eyes crimson by now, her nose beginning to run again. 'From half past ten till well after twelve. He had to talk to someone, he said.'

I could sense that Strafe was thinking precisely the same as I was: that the red-haired man had insinuated himself into Cynthia's company by talking about himself and had then put a hand on her knee. Instead of simply standing up and going away Cynthia would have stayed where she was, embarrassed or tongue-tied, at any rate unable to cope. And when the moment came she would have turned hysterical. I could picture her screaming in the garden, running across the lawn to the hotel, and then the pandemonium in the hall. I could sense Strafe picturing that also.

'My God, it's terrible,' Cynthia said.

'I think she should sleep,' I said quietly to Strafe. 'Try to sleep, dear,' I said to her, but she shook her head, tossing her jumble of hair about on the pillow.

'Milly's right,' Strafe urged. 'You'll feel much better after a little rest. We'll bring you a cup of tea later on.'

'My God!' she cried again. 'My God, how could I sleep?'

I went away to borrow a couple of mild sleeping pills from Dekko, who is never without them, relying on the things too much in my opinion. He

699 · BEYOND THE PALE

was tidying himself in his room, but found the pills immediately. Strangely enough, Dekko's always sound in a crisis.

I gave them to her with water and she took them without asking what they were. She was in a kind of daze, one moment making a fuss and weeping, the next just peering ahead of her, as if frightened. In a way she was like someone who'd just had a bad nightmare and hadn't yet completely returned to reality. I remarked as much to Strafe while we made our way down to lunch, and he said he quite agreed.

'Poor old Cynth!' Dekko said when we'd all ordered lobster bisque and entrecôte béarnaise. 'Poor old sausage.'

You could see that the little waitress, a new girl this year, was bubbling over with excitement; but Kitty, serving the other half of the dining-room, was grim, which was most unusual. Everyone was talking in hushed tones and when Dekko said, 'Poor old Cynth!' a couple of heads were turned in our direction because he can never keep his voice down. The little vases of roses with which Mrs Malseed must have decorated each table before the fracas had occurred seemed strangely out of place in the atmosphere which had developed.

The waitress had just taken away our soup-plates when Mr Malseed hurried into the dining-room and came straight to our table. The lobster bisque surprisingly hadn't been quite up to scratch, and in passing I couldn't help wondering if the fuss had caused the kitchen to go to pieces also.

'I wonder if I might have a word, Major Strafe,' Mr Malseed said, and Strafe rose at once and accompanied him from the dining-room. A total silence had fallen, everyone in the dining-room pretending to be intent on eating. I had an odd feeling that we had perhaps got it all wrong, that because we'd been out for our walk when it had happened all the other guests knew more of the details than Strafe and Dekko and I did. I began to wonder if poor Cynthia had been raped.

Afterwards Strafe told us what occurred in the Malseeds' office, how Mrs Malseed had been sitting there, slumped, as he put it, and how two policemen had questioned him. 'Look, what on earth's all this about?' he had demanded rather sharply.

'It concerns this incident that's taken place, sir,' one of the policemen explained in an unhurried voice. 'On account of your wife –'

'My wife's lying down. She must not be questioned or in any way disturbed.'

'Ach, we'd never do that, sir.'

Strafe does a good Co. Antrim brogue and in relating all this to us he couldn't resist making full use of it. The two policemen were in uniform and their natural slowness of intellect was rendered more noticeable by the lugubrious air the tragedy had inspired in the hotel. For tragedy was what it was; after talking to Cynthia for nearly two hours the lone man had walked down to the rocks and been drowned.

*

When Strafe finished speaking I placed my knife and fork together on my plate, unable to eat another mouthful. The facts appeared to be that the man, having left Cynthia by the magnolias, had clambered down the cliff to a place no one ever went to, on the other side of the hotel from the sands we had walked along to Ardbeag. No one had seen him except Cynthia, who from the cliff-top had apparently witnessed his battering by the treacherous waves. The tide had been coming in, but by the time old Arthur and Mr Malseed reached the rocks it had begun to turn, leaving behind it the fully dressed corpse. Mr Malseed's impression was that the man had lost his footing on the seaweed and accidentally stumbled into the depths, for the rocks were so slippery it was difficult to carry the corpse more than a matter of yards. But at least it had been placed out of view, while Mr Malseed hurried back to the hotel to telephone for assistance. He told Strafe that Cynthia had been most confused, insisting that the man had walked out among the rocks and then into the sea, knowing what he was doing.

Listening to it all, I no longer felt sorry for Cynthia. It was typical of her that she should so sillily have involved us in all this. Why on earth had she sat in the garden with a man of that kind instead of standing up and making a fuss the moment he'd begun to paw her? If she'd acted intelligently the whole unfortunate episode could clearly have been avoided. Since it hadn't, there was no point whatsoever in insisting that the man had committed suicide when at that distance no one could possibly be sure.

'It really does astonish me,' I said at the lunch table, unable to prevent myself from breaking our unwritten rule. 'Whatever came over her?'

'It can't be good for the hotel,' Dekko commented, and I was glad to see Strafe giving him a little glance of irritation.

'It's hardly the point,' I said coolly.

'What I meant was, hotels occasionally hush things like this up.'

'Well, they haven't this time.' It seemed an age since I had waited for them in Ardbeag, since we had been so happily laughing over the effect of Dekko's telegram. He'd included his address in it so that the girl could send a message back, and as we'd returned to the hotel along the seashore there'd been much speculation between the two men about the form this would take.

'I suppose what Cynthia's thinking,' Strafe said, 'is that after he'd tried something on with her he became depressed.'

'Oh, but he could just as easily have lost his footing. He'd have been on edge anyway, worried in case she reported him.'

'Dreadful kind of death,' Dekko said. His tone suggested that that was that, that the subject should now be closed, and so it was.

After lunch we went to our rooms, as we always do at Glencorn Lodge, to rest for an hour. I took my slacks and blouse off, hoping that Strafe would knock on my door, but he didn't and of course that was understandable. Oddly enough I found myself thinking of Dekko, picturing his long form stretched out in the room called Hydrangea, his beaky face in profile on his pillow. The precise nature of Dekko's relationship with these girls he picks up has always privately intrigued me: was it really possible that somewhere in London there was a girl called Juliet who was prepared to marry him for his not inconsiderable money?

I slept and briefly dreamed. Thrive Major and Warrington P. J. were running the post office in Ardbeag, sending telegrams to everyone they could think of, including Dekko's friend Juliet. Cynthia had been found dead beside the magnolias and people were waiting for Hercule Poirot to arrive. 'Promise me you didn't do it,' I whispered to Strafe, but when Strafe replied it was to say that Cynthia's body reminded him of a bag of old chicken bones.

Strafe and Dekko and I met for tea in the tea-lounge. Strafe had looked in to see if Cynthia had woken, but apparently she hadn't. The police officers had left the hotel, Dekko said, because he'd noticed their car wasn't parked at the front any more. None of the three of us said, but I think we presumed, that the man's body had been removed from the rocks during the quietness of the afternoon. From where we sat I caught a glimpse of Mrs Malseed passing quite briskly through the hall, seeming almost herself again. Certainly our holiday would be affected, but it might not be totally ruined. All that remained to hope for was Cynthia's recovery, and then everyone could set about forgetting the unpleasantness. The nicest thing would be if a jolly young couple turned up and occupied the man's room, exorcising the incident, as newcomers would.

The family from France – the two little girls and their parents – were chattering away in the tea-lounge, and an elderly trio who'd arrived that morning were speaking in American accents. The honeymoon couple appeared, looking rather shy, and began to whisper and giggle in a corner. People who occupied the table next to ours in the dining-room, a Wing-Commander Orfell and his wife, from Guildford, nodded and smiled as they passed. Everyone was making an effort, and I knew it would help matters further if Cynthia felt up to a rubber or two before dinner. That life should continue as normally as possible was essential for Glencorn Lodge, the example already set by Mrs Malseed.

Because of our interrupted lunch I felt quite hungry, and the Malseeds pride themselves on their teas. The chef, Mr McBride, whom of course we've met, has the lightest touch I know with sponge cakes and little curranty scones. I was, in fact, buttering a scone when Strafe said:

'Here she is.'

And there indeed she was. By the look of her she had simply pushed herself off her bed and come straight down. Her pink dress was even more crumpled than it had been. She hadn't so much as run a comb through her hair, her face was puffy and unpowdered. For a moment I really thought she was walking in her sleep.

Strafe and Dekko stood up. 'Feeling better, dear?' Strafe said, but she didn't answer.

'Sit down, Cynth,' Dekko urged, pushing back a chair to make room for her.

'He told me a story I can never forget. I've dreamed about it all over again.' Cynthia swayed in front of us, not even attempting to sit down. To tell the truth, she sounded inane.

'Story, dear?' Strafe enquired, humouring her.

She said it was the story of two children who had apparently ridden bicycles through the streets of Belfast, out into Co. Antrim. The bicycles were dilapidated, she said; she didn't know if they were stolen or not. She didn't know about the children's homes because the man hadn't spoken of them, but she claimed to know instinctively that they had ridden away from poverty and unhappiness. 'From the clatter and the quarrelling,' Cynthia said. 'Two children who later fell in love.'

'Horrid old dream,' Strafe said. 'Horrid for you, dear.'

She shook her head, and then sat down. I poured another cup of tea. 'I had the oddest dream myself,' I said. 'Thrive Major was running the post office in Ardbeag.'

Strafe smiled and Dekko gave his laugh, but Cynthia didn't in any way acknowledge what I'd said.

'A fragile thing the girl was, with depths of mystery in her wide brown eyes. Red-haired of course he was himself, thin as a rake in those days. Glencorn Lodge was derelict then.'

'You've had a bit of a shock, old thing,' Dekko said.

Strafe agreed, kindly adding, 'Look, dear, if the chap actually interfered with you –'

'Why on earth should he do that?' Her voice was shrill in the tea-lounge, edged with a note of hysteria. I glanced at Strafe, who was frowning into his tea-cup. Dekko began to say something, but broke off before his meaning emerged. Rather more calmly Cynthia said:

'It was summer when they came here. Honeysuckle he described. And mother of thyme. He didn't know the name of either.'

No one attempted any kind of reply, not that it was necessary, for Cynthia just continued.

'At school there were the facts of geography and arithmetic. And the legends of scholars and of heroes, of Queen Maeve and Finn MacCool. There was the coming of St Patrick to a heathen people. History was full of kings and high-kings, and Silken Thomas and Wolfe Tone, the Flight of the Earls, the Siege of Limerick.'

When Cynthia said that, it was impossible not to believe that the unfortunate events of the morning had touched her with some kind of madness. It seemed astonishing that she had walked into the tea-lounge without having combed her hair, and that she'd stood there swaying before sitting down, that out of the blue she had started on about two children.

None of it made an iota of sense, and surely she could see that the nasty experience she'd suffered should not be dwelt upon? I offered her the plate of scones, hoping that if she began to eat she would stop talking, but she took no notice of my gesture.

'Look, dear,' Strafe said, 'there's not one of us who knows what you're talking about.'

'I'm talking about a children's story, I'm talking about a girl and a boy who visited this place we visit also. He hadn't been here for years, but he returned last night, making one final effort to understand. And then he walked out into the sea.'

She had taken a piece of her dress and was agitatedly crumpling it between the finger and thumb of her left hand. It was dreadful really, having her so grubby-looking. For some odd reason I suddenly thought of her cooking, how she wasn't in the least interested in it or in anything about the house. She certainly hadn't succeeded in making a home for Strafe.

'They rode those worn-out bicycles through a hot afternoon. Can you feel all that? A newly surfaced road, the snap of chippings beneath their tyres, the smell of tar? Dust from a passing car, the city they left behind?'

'Cynthia dear,' I said, 'drink your tea, and why not have a scone?'

'They swam and sunbathed on the beach you walked along today. They went to a spring for water. There were no magnolias then. There was no garden, no neat little cliff paths to the beach. Surely you can see it clearly?'

'No,' Strafe said. 'No, we really cannot, dear.'

'This place that is an idyll for us was an idyll for them too: the trees, the ferns, the wild roses near the water spring, the very sea and sun they shared. There was a cottage lost in the middle of the woods: they sometimes looked for that. They played a game, a kind of hide and seek. People in a white farmhouse gave them milk.'

For the second time I offered Cynthia the plate of scones and for the second time she pointedly ignored me. Her cup of tea hadn't been touched. Dekko took a scone and cheerfully said:

'All's well that's over.'

But Cynthia appeared to have drifted back into a daze, and I wondered again if it could really be possible that the experience had unhinged her. Unable to help myself, I saw her being led away from the hotel, helped into the back of a blue van, something like an ambulance. She was talking about the children again, how they had planned to marry and keep a sweetshop.

'Take it easy, dear,' Strafe said, which I followed up by suggesting for the second time that she should make an effort to drink her tea.

'Has it to do with the streets they came from? Or the history they learnt, he from his Christian Brothers, she from her nuns? History is unfinished in this island; long since it has come to a stop in Surrey.'

Dekko said, and I really had to hand it to him:

'Cynth, we have to put it behind us.'

It didn't do any good. Cynthia just went rambling on, speaking again of the girl being taught by nuns, and the boy by Christian Brothers. She began to recite the history they might have learnt, the way she sometimes did when we were driving through an area that had historical connections. 'Can you imagine,' she embarrassingly asked, 'our very favourite places bitter with disaffection, with plotting and revenge? Can you imagine the treacherous murder of Shane O'Neill the Proud?'

Dekko made a little sideways gesture of his head, politely marvelling. Strafe seemed about to say something, but changed his mind. Confusion ran through Irish history, Cynthia said, like convolvulus in a hedgerow. On May 24th, 1487, a boy of ten called Lambert Simnel, brought to Dublin by a priest from Oxford, was declared Edward VI of all England and Ireland, crowned with a golden circlet taken from a statue of the Virgin Mary. On May 24th, 1798, here in Antrim, Presbyterian farmers fought for a common cause with their Catholic labourers. She paused and looked at Strafe. Chaos and contradiction, she informed him, were hidden everywhere beneath nice-sounding names. 'The Battle of the Yellow Ford,' she suddenly chanted in a sing-song way that sounded thoroughly peculiar, 'the Statutes of Kilkenny. The Battle of Glenmama, the Convention of Drumceat. The Act of Settlement, the Renunciation Act. The Act of Union, the Toleration Act. Just so much history it sounds like now, yet people starved or died while other people watched. A language was lost, a faith forbidden. Famine followed revolt, plantation followed that. But it was people who were stuck into the soil of other people's land, not forests of new trees; and it was greed and treachery that spread as a disease among them all. No wonder unease clings to these shreds of history and shots ring out in answer to the mockery of drums. No wonder the air is nervy with suspicion.'

There was an extremely awkward silence when she ceased to speak. Dekko nodded, doing his best to be companionable. Strafe nodded also. I simply examined the pattern of roses on our tea-time china, not knowing what else to do. Eventually Dekko said:

'What an awful lot you know, Cynth!'

'Cynthia's always been interested,' Strafe said. 'Always had a first-rate memory.'

'Those children of the streets are part of the battles and the Acts,' she went on, seeming quite unaware that her talk was literally almost crazy. 'They're part of the blood that flowed around those nice-sounding names.' She paused, and for a moment seemed disinclined to continue. Then she said:

'The second time they came here the house was being rebuilt. There were concrete-mixers, and lorries drawn up on the grass, noise and scaffolding everywhere. They watched all through another afternoon and then they went their different ways: their childhood was over, lost with their idyll. He became a dockyard clerk. She went to London, to work in a betting shop.'

'My dear,' Strafe said very gently, 'it's interesting, everything you say, but it really hardly concerns us.'

'No, of course not.' Quite emphatically Cynthia shook her head, appearing wholly to agree. 'They were degenerate, awful creatures. They must have been.'

'No one's saying that, my dear.'

'Their story should have ended there, he in the docklands of Belfast, she recording bets. Their complicated childhood love should just have dissipated, as such love often does. But somehow nothing was as neat as that.'

Dekko, in an effort to lighten the conversation, mentioned a boy called Gollsol who'd been at school with Strafe and himself, who'd formed a romantic attachment for the daughter of one of the groundsmen and had later actually married her. There was a silence for a moment, then Cynthia, without emotion, said:

'You none of you care. You sit there not caring that two people are dead.'

'Two people, Cynthia?' I said.

'For God's sake, I'm telling you!' she cried. 'That girl was murdered in a room in Maida Vale.'

Although there is something between Strafe and myself, I do try my best to be at peace about it. I go to church and take communion, and I know Strafe occasionally does too, though not as often as perhaps he might. Cynthia has no interest in that side of life, and it rankled with me now to hear her blaspheming so casually, and so casually speaking about death in Maida Vale on top of all this stuff about history and children. Strafe was shaking his head, clearly believing that Cynthia didn't know what she was talking about.

'Cynthia dear,' I began, 'are you sure you're not muddling something up here? You've been upset, you've had a nightmare: don't you think your imagination, or something you've been reading –'

'Bombs don't go off on their own. Death doesn't just happen to occur in Derry and Belfast, in London and Amsterdam and Dublin, in Berlin and Jerusalem. There are people who are murderers: that is what this children's story is about.'

A silence fell, no one knowing what to say. It didn't matter of course because without any prompting Cynthia continued.

'We drink our gin with Angostura bitters, there's lamb or chicken Kiev. Old Kitty's kind to us in the dining-room and old Arthur in the hall. Flowers are everywhere, we have our special table.'

'Please let us take you to your room now,' Strafe begged, and as he spoke I reached out a hand in friendship and placed it on her arm. 'Come on, old thing,' Dekko said.

'The limbless are left on the streets, blood spatters the car-parks. *Brits Out* it says on a rockface, but we know it doesn't mean us.'

I spoke quietly then, measuring my words, measuring the pause between each so that its effect might be registered. I felt the statement had to be made, whether it was my place to make it or not. I said:

'You are very confused, Cynthia.'

The French family left the tea-lounge. The two Dalmatians, Charger and Snooze, ambled in and sniffed and went away again. Kitty came to clear the French family's tea things. I could hear her speaking to the honeymoon couple, saying the weather forecast was good.

'Cynthia,' Strafe said, standing up, 'we've been very patient with you but this is now becoming silly.'

I nodded just a little. 'I really think,' I softly said, but Cynthia didn't permit me to go on.

'Someone told him about her. Someone mentioned her name, and he couldn't believe it. She sat alone in Maida Vale, putting together the mechanisms of her bombs: this girl who had laughed on the seashore, whom he had loved.'

'Cynthia,' Strafe began, but he wasn't permitted to continue either. Hopelessly, he just sat down again.

'Whenever he heard of bombs exploding he thought of her, and couldn't understand. He wept when he said that; her violence haunted him, he said. He couldn't work, he couldn't sleep at night. His mind filled up with images of her, their awkward childhood kisses, her fingers working neatly now. He saw her with a carrier-bag, hurrying it through a crowd, leaving it where it could cause most death. In front of the mouldering old house that had once been Glencorn Lodge they'd made a fire and cooked their food. They'd lain for ages on the grass. They'd cycled home to their city streets.'

It suddenly dawned on me that Cynthia was knitting this whole fantasy out of nothing. It all worked backwards from the moment when she'd had the misfortune to witness the man's death in the sea. A few minutes before he'd been chatting quite normally to her, he'd probably even mentioned a holiday in his childhood and some girl there'd been: all of it would have been natural in the circumstances, possibly even the holiday had taken place at Glencorn. He'd said goodbye and then unfortunately he'd had his accident. As she watched from the cliff edge, something had cracked in poor Cynthia's brain, she having always been a prey to melancholy. I suppose it must be hard having two sons who don't think much of you, and a marriage not offering you a great deal, bridge and holidays probably the best part of it. For some odd reason of her own she'd created her fantasy about a child turning into a terrorist. The violence of the man's death had clearly filled her imagination with Irish violence, so regularly seen on television. If we'd been on holiday in Suffolk I wondered how it would have seemed to the poor creature.

I could feel Strafe and Dekko beginning to put all that together also, beginning to realize that the whole story of the red-haired man and the girl was clearly Cynthia's invention. 'Poor creature,' I wanted to say, but did not do so.

'For months he searched for her, pushing his way among the people of London, the people who were her victims. When he found her she just looked at him, as if the past hadn't even existed. She didn't smile, as if incapable of smiling. He wanted to take her away, back to where they came from, but she didn't reply when he suggested that. Bitterness was like a disease in her, and when he left her he felt the bitterness in himself.'

Again Strafe and Dekko nodded, and I could feel Strafe thinking that there really was no point in protesting further. All we could hope for was that the end of the saga was in sight.

'He remained in London, working on the railways. But in the same way as before he was haunted by the person she'd become, and the haunting was more awful now. He bought a gun from a man he'd been told about and kept it hidden in a shoe-box in his rented room. Now and again he took it out and looked at it, then put it back. He hated the violence that possessed her, yet he was full of it himself: he knew he couldn't betray her with anything but death. Humanity had left both of them when he visited her again in Maida Vale.'

To my enormous relief and, I could feel, to Strafe's and Dekko's too, Mr and Mrs Malseed appeared beside us. Like his wife, Mr Malseed had considerably recovered. He spoke in an even voice, clearly wishing to dispose of the matter. It was just the diversion we needed.

'I must apologize, Mrs Strafe,' he said. 'I cannot say how sorry we are that you were bothered by that man.'

'My wife is still a little dicky,' Strafe explained, 'but after a decent night's rest I think we can say she'll be as right as rain again.'

'I only wish, Mrs Strafe, you had made contact with my wife or myself when he first approached you.' There was a spark of irritation in Mr Malseed's eyes, but his voice was still controlled. 'I mean, the unpleasantness you suffered might just have been averted.'

'Nothing would have been averted, Mr Malseed, and certainly not the horror we are left with. Can you see her as the girl she became, seated at a chipped white table, her wires and fuses spread around her? What were her thoughts in that room, Mr Malseed? What happens in the mind of anyone who wishes to destroy? In a back street he bought his gun for too much money. When did it first occur to him to kill her?'

'We really are a bit at sea,' Mr Malseed replied without the slightest hesitation. He humoured Cynthia by displaying no surprise, by speaking very quietly.

'All I am saying, Mr Malseed, is that we should root our heads out of the sand and wonder about two people who are beyond the pale.'

'My dear,' Strafe said, 'Mr Malseed is a busy man.'

Still quietly, still perfectly in control of every intonation, without a single glance around the tea-lounge to ascertain where his guests' attention was, Mr Malseed said:

'There is unrest here, Mrs Strafe, but we do our best to live with it.'

'All I am saying is that perhaps there can be regret when two children end like this.'

Mr Malseed did not reply. His wife did her best to smile away the awkwardness. Strafe murmured privately to Cynthia, no doubt beseeching her to come to her senses. Again I imagined a blue van drawn up in front of Glencorn Lodge, for it was quite understandable now that an imaginative woman should go mad, affected by the ugliness of death. The garbled speculation about the man and the girl, the jumble in the poor thing's mind – a children's story as she called it – all somehow hung together when you realized they didn't have to make any sense whatsoever.

'Murderers are beyond the pale, Mr Malseed, and England has always had its pales. The one in Ireland began in 1395.'

'Dear,' I said, 'what has happened has nothing whatsoever to do with calling people murderers and placing them beyond some pale or other. You witnessed a most unpleasant accident, dear, and it's only to be expected that you've become just a little lost. The man had a chat with you when you were sitting by the magnolias and then the shock of seeing him slip on the seaweed –'

'He didn't slip on the seaweed,' she suddenly screamed. 'My God, he didn't slip on the seaweed.'

Strafe closed his eyes. The other guests in the tea-lounge had fallen silent ages ago, openly listening. Arthur was standing near the door and was listening also. Kitty was waiting to clear away our tea things, but didn't like to because of what was happening.

'I must request you to take Mrs Strafe to her room, Major,' Mr Malseed said. 'And I must make it clear that we cannot tolerate further upset in Glencorn Lodge.'

Strafe reached for her arm, but Cynthia took no notice.

'An Irish joke,' she said, and then she stared at Mr and Mrs Malseed, her eyes passing over each feature of their faces. She stared at Dekko and Strafe, and last of all at me. She said eventually:

'An Irish joke, an unbecoming tale: of course it can't be true. Ridiculous, that a man returned here. Ridiculous, that he walked again by the seashore and through the woods, hoping to understand where a woman's cruelty had come from.'

'This talk is most offensive,' Mr Malseed protested, his calmness slipping just a little. The ashen look that had earlier been in his face returned. I could see he was beside himself with rage. 'You are trying to bring something to our doorstep which most certainly does not belong there.'

'On your doorstep they talked about a sweetshop: Cadbury's bars and different-flavoured creams, nut-milk toffee, Aero and Crunchie.'

'For God's sake pull yourself together,' I clearly heard Strafe whispering, and Mrs Malseed attempted to smile. 'Come along now, Mrs Strafe,' she said, making a gesture. 'Just to please us, dear. Kitty wants to clear away the dishes. Kitty!' she called out, endeavouring to bring matters down to earth.

Kitty crossed the lounge with her tray and gathered up the cups and saucers. The Malseeds, naturally still anxious, hovered. No one was surprised when Cynthia began all over again, by crazily asking Kitty what she thought of us.

'I think, dear,' Mrs Malseed began, 'Kitty's quite busy really.'

'Stop this at once,' Strafe quietly ordered.

'For fourteen years, Kitty, you've served us with food and cleared away the tea-cups we've drunk from. For fourteen years we've played our bridge and walked about the garden. We've gone for drives, we've bought our tweed, we've bathed as those children did.'

'Stop it,' Strafe said again, a little louder. Bewildered and getting red in the face, Kitty hastily bundled china on to her tray. I made a sign at Strafe because for some reason I felt that the end was really in sight. I wanted him to retain his patience, but what Cynthia said next was almost unbelievable.

'In Surrey we while away the time, we clip our hedges. On a bridge night there's coffee at nine o'clock, with macaroons or *petits fours*. Last thing of all we watch the late-night News, packing away our cards and scoring-pads, our sharpened pencils. There's been an incident in Armagh, one soldier's had his head shot off, another's run amok. Our lovely Glens of Antrim, we all four think, our coastal drives: we hope that nothing disturbs the peace. We think of Mr Malseed, still busy in Glencorn Lodge, and Mrs Malseed finishing her flower-plaques for the rooms of the completed annexe.'

'Will you for God's sake shut up?' Strafe suddenly shouted. I could see him struggling with himself, but it didn't do any good. He called Cynthia a bloody spectacle, sitting there talking rubbish. I don't believe she even heard him.

'Through honey-tinted glasses we love you and we love your island, Kitty. We love the lilt of your racy history, we love your earls and heroes. Yet we made a sensible pale here once, as civilized people create a garden, pretty as a picture.'

Strafe's outburst had been quite noisy and I could sense him being ashamed of it. He muttered that he was sorry, but Cynthia simply took advantage of his generosity, continuing about a pale.

'Beyond it lie the bleak untouchables, best kept as dots on the horizon, too terrible to contemplate. How can we be blamed if we make neither head nor tail of anything, Kitty, your past and your present, those battles and Acts of Parliament? We people of Surrey: how can we know? Yet I stupidly thought, you see, that the tragedy of two children could at least be understood. He didn't discover where her cruelty had come from because perhaps you never can: evil breeds evil in a mysterious way. That's the story the red-haired stranger passed on to me, the story you huddle away from.'

Poor Strafe was pulling at Cynthia, pleading with her, still saying he was sorry.

'Mrs Strafe,' Mr Malseed tried to say, but got no further. To my horror Cynthia abruptly pointed at me.

'That woman,' she said, 'is my husband's mistress, a fact I am supposed to be unaware of, Kitty.'

'My God!' Strafe said.

'My husband is perverted in his sexual desires. His friend, who shared his schooldays, has never quite recovered from that time. I myself am a pathetic creature who has closed her eyes to a husband's infidelity and his mistress's viciousness. I am dragged into the days of Thrive Major and A. D. Cowley-Stubbs: mechanically I smile. I hardly exist, Kitty.'

There was a most unpleasant silence, and then Strafe said:

'None of that's true. For God's sake, Cynthia,' he suddenly shouted, 'go and rest yourself.'

Cynthia shook her head and continued to address the waitress. She'd had a rest, she told her. 'But it didn't do any good, Kitty, because hell has invaded the paradise of Glencorn, as so often it has invaded your island. And we, who have so often brought it, pretend it isn't there. Who cares about children made into murderers?'

Strafe shouted again. 'You fleshless ugly bitch!' he cried. 'You bloody old fool!' He was on his feet, trying to get her to hers. The blood was thumping in his bronzed face, his eyes had a fury in them I'd never seen before. 'Fleshless!' he shouted at her, not caring that so many people were listening. He closed his eyes in misery and in shame again, and I wanted to reach out and take his hand but of course I could not. You could see the Malseeds didn't blame him, you could see them thinking that everything was ruined for us. I wanted to shout at Cynthia too, to batter the silliness out of her, but of course I could not do that. I could feel the tears behind my eyes, and I couldn't help noticing that Dekko's hands were shaking. He's quite sensitive behind his joky manner, and had quite obviously taken to heart her statement that he had never recovered from his schooldays. Nor had it been pleasant, hearing myself described as vicious.

'No one cares,' Cynthia said in the same unbalanced way, as if she hadn't just been called ugly and a bitch. 'No one cares, and on our journey home we shall all four be silent. Yet is the truth about ourselves at least a beginning? Will we wonder in the end about the hell that frightens us?'

Strafe still looked wretched, his face deliberately turned away from us. Mrs Malseed gave a little sigh and raised the fingers of her left hand to her cheek, as if something tickled it. Her husband breathed heavily. Dekko seemed on the point of tears.

Cynthia stumbled off, leaving a silence behind her. Before it was broken I knew she was right when she said we would just go home, away from this country we had come to love. And I knew as well that neither here nor at home would she be led to a blue van that was not quite an ambulance. Strafe would stay with her because Strafe is made like that, honourable in his own particular way. I felt a pain where perhaps my heart is, and again I wanted to cry. Why couldn't it have been she who had gone down to the rocks and slipped on the seaweed or just walked into the sea, it didn't matter which? Her awful rigmarole hung about us as the last of the tea things were gathered up – the earls who'd fled, the famine and the people planted. The children were there too, grown up into murdering riff-raff.

The Blue Dress

My cinder-grey room has a window, but I have never in all my time here looked out of it. It's easier to remember, to conjure up this scene or that, to eavesdrop. Americans give arms away, Russians promise tanks. In Brussels an English politician breakfasts with his mistress; a pornographer pretends he's selling Christmas cards. Carefully I listen, as in childhood I listened to the hushed conversation of my parents.

I stand in the cathedral at Vézelay, whose bishops once claimed it possessed the mortal remains of Mary Magdalene, a falseness which was exposed by Pope Boniface VIII. I wonder about that Pope, and then the scene is different.

I sit in the Piazza San Marco on the day when I discovered a sea of corruption among the local Communists. The music plays, visitors remark upon the pigeons.

Scenes coalesce: Miss MacNamara passes along the promenade, Major Trubstall lies, the blue dress flutters and is still. In Rotterdam I have a nameless woman. '*Feest wezen vieren*?' she says. '*Gedronken*?' In Corniglia the wine is purple, the path by the coast is marked as a lovers' lane. I am silly, Dorothea says, the dress is just a dress. She laughs, like water running over pebbles.

I must try, they tell me; it will help to write it down. I do not argue, I do precisely as they say. Carefully, I remember. Carefully, I write it down.

It was Bath, not Corniglia, not Rotterdam or Venice, not Vézelay: it was in Bath where Dorothea and I first met, by chance in the Pump Room. 'I'm sorry,' I said, actually bumping into her.

She shook her head, saying that of course I hadn't hurt her. She blamed the crowds, tourists pushing like mad things, always in a hurry. But nothing could keep her out of the Pump Room because of its Jane Austen associations.

'I've never been here before.'

'Goodness! You poor thing!'

'I was on the way to have some coffee. Would you like some?'

'I always have coffee when I come.'

She was small and very young – twenty-one or -two, I guessed – in a plain white dress without sleeves. She carried a basket, and had very fair hair, quite straight and cut quite short. Her oval face was perfect, her eyes intense, the blue of a washed-out sky. She smiled when she told me about herself, as though she found the subject a little absurd. She was studying the history of art but when she finished that she didn't know what on earth she was going to do next. I said I was in Bath because my ex-wife's mother, who'd only come to live there six months ago, had died. The funeral had taken place that morning and my ex-wife, Charlotte, had been furious that I'd attended it. But I'd always been fond of her mother, fonder in fact than Charlotte had ever been. I'd known of course that I would have to meet her at the funeral. She'd married again, a man who ran a wine business: he had been there too.

'Is it horrible, a divorce?' the girl asked me while we drank our weak, cool coffee. 'I can never think of my parents divorcing.'

'It's nice you can't. Yes, it's horrible.'

'Did you have children?'

'No.'

'There's that at least. But isn't it odd, to make such a very rudimentary mistake?'

'Extraordinary.'

I don't know what it was about her manner that first morning, but something seemed to tell me that this beautiful creature would not be outraged if I said – which I did – that we might go somewhere else in search of a better cup of coffee. And when I said, 'Let's have a drink,' I said it confidently. She telephoned her parents' house. We had lunch together in the Francis Hotel.

'I went to a boarding-school I didn't like,' she told me. 'Called after St Catherine but without her charity. I was bad at maths and French and geography. I didn't like a girl called Angela Tate and I didn't like the breakfasts. I missed my brothers. What about you? What was your wife like?'

'Fond of clothes. Very fine tweed, a certain shade of scarlet, scarves of every possible variation. She hated being abroad, trailing after me.' I didn't add that Charlotte had been unfaithful with anyone she had a fancy for; I didn't even want to think about that.

The waiter brought Dorothea veal *escalope* and steak *au poivre* for me. It was very like being in a dream. The funeral of my ex-mother-in-law had taken place at ten o'clock, there had been Charlotte's furious glances and her husband's disdain, my walking away when the ceremony was over without a word to anyone. I'd felt wound up, like a watch-spring, seeing vividly in my mind's eye an old, grey woman who'd always entertained me with her gossip, who'd written to me when Charlotte went to say how sorry she was, adding in a postscript that Charlotte had always been a handful. She and I had shared the truth about her daughter, and it was that that I'd honoured by making the journey to her funeral.

'They say I am compulsively naughty,' Dorothea said, as if guessing that I wondered what she had said to her parents on the telephone. I suspected she had not confessed the truth. There's been some excuse to account for her delay, and already that fitted in with what I knew of her. Certainly she would not have said that she'd been picked up by a middle-aged journalist who had come to Bath to attend a funeral. She spoke again of Jane Austen, of Elizabeth Bennet, and Emma and Elinor. She spoke as though these fictional characters were real. She almost loved them, she said, but that of course could not have been quite true.

'Who were encumbered with low connections and gave themselves airs? Who bestowed their consent with a most joyful alacrity?'

I laughed, and waited for her to tell me. I walked with her to a parked car, a white Mini that had collected a traffic warden's ticket. Formally we shook hands and all the way to London on the train I thought of her. I sat in the bar drinking one after another of those miniature bottles of whisky that trains go in for, while her face jumped about in my imagination, unnerving me. Again and again her white, even teeth smiled at me.

Within a day or two I was in Belfast, sending reports to a Washington newspaper and to a syndicate in Australia. As always, I posted photocopies of everything I wrote to Stoyckov, who operates a news bureau in Prague. Stoyckov used to pay me when he saw me, quite handsomely in a sense, but it was never the money that mattered: it was simply that I saw no reason why the truth about Northern Ireland should not be told behind the Iron Curtain as well as in Washington and Adelaide.

I had agreed to do a two-months stint – no longer, because from experience I knew that Belfast becomes depressing. Immediately afterwards I was to spend three days in Madrid, trying to discover if there was truth in the persistent rumour that the Pope was to visit Spain next year. 'Great Christ alive,' Charlotte used to scream at me, 'call this a marriage?'

In Belfast the army was doing its best to hush up a rape case. I interviewed a man called Ruairi O Baoill, whom I'd last seen drilling a gang of terrorists in the Syrian desert. 'My dear fellow, you can hardly call this rape,' a Major Trubstall insisted. 'The girl was yelling her head off for it.' But the girl had been doing no such thing; the girl was whey-faced, unable to stop crying; the girl was still in pain, she'd been rushed to hospital to have stitches. 'Listen,' Major Trubstall said, pushing a great crimson face into mine. 'If a girl goes out drinking with four soldiers, d'you think she isn't after something?' The Red Hand of Ulster meant what it said, O Baoill told me: the hand was waiting to grasp the hammer and the sickle. He didn't say it to his followers, and later he denied that he had said it at all.

Ruairi O Baoill is a sham, I wrote. *And so, it would appear, is a man called Major Trubstall. Fantasy rules*, I wrote, knowing it was the truth.

All the time in Northern Ireland and for three days in Spain Dorothea's voice continued about Emma and Elinor and Elizabeth Bennet, and Mrs Elton and Mr Woodhouse. I kept imagining us together in a clean, empty house that appeared to be our home. Like smoke evaporating, my failed marriage wasn't there any more. And my unhappy childhood slipped away also, as though by magic.

*

'Dorothea?'

'No, this is her mother. Please hold on. I'll fetch her.'

I waited for so long I began to fear that this was Mrs Lysarth's way of dealing with unwelcome telephone callers. I felt that perhaps the single word I'd spoken had been enough to convey an image of my unsuitableness, and my presumption.

'Yes?' Dorothea's voice said.

'It's Terris. Do you remember?'

'Of course I remember. Are you in Bath again?'

'No. But at least I've returned from Northern Ireland. I'm in London. How are you, Dorothea?'

'I'm very well. Are you well?'

'Yes.' I paused, not knowing how to put it.

'It's kind of you to ring, Terris.'

'D'you think we might meet?'

'Meet?'

'It would be nice to see you.'

She didn't answer. I felt I had proposed marriage already, that it was that she was considering. 'It doesn't matter,' I began to say.

'Of course we must meet. Would Thursday do? I have to be in London then.'

'We could have lunch again.'

'That would be lovely.'

And so it was. We sat in the bow window of an Italian restaurant in Romilly Street, and when anyone glanced in I felt inordinately proud. It was early September, a warm, clear day without a hint of autumn. Afterwards we strolled through Leicester Square and along Piccadilly. We were still in Green Park at six o'clock. 'I love you, Terris,' Dorothea said.

Her mother smiled a slanting smile at me, head a little on one side. She laid down an embroidery on a round, cane frame. She held a hand out.

'We've heard so much,' she said, still smiling, and then she introduced her sons. While we were drinking sherry Dorothea's father appeared, a thin, tall man, with spectacles on a length of leather, dancing on a tweed waistcoat.

'My dear fellow.' Vaguely he smiled and held a hand out: an amateur archaeologist, though by profession a medical doctor. That I was the divorced middle-aged man whom his young daughter wished to marry was not a fact that registered in his face. Dorothea had shown me a photograph of him, dusty in a crumpled linen suit, holding between finger and thumb a piece of glazed terracotta. 'A pleasure,' he continued as vaguely as before. 'A real pleasure.'

'A pleasure to meet *you*, Dr Lysarth.'

'Oh, not at all.'

'More sherry?' Dorothea suggested, pouring me whisky because she knew I probably needed it.

'That's whisky in that decanter, Dorothea,' her brother Adam pointed out and while I was saying it didn't matter, that whisky actually was what I preferred, her other brother, Jonathan, laughed.

'I'm sure Mr Terris knows what he wants,' Mrs Lysarth remarked, and Dorothea said:

'Terris is his Christian name.'

'Oh, I'm so sorry.'

'You must call him Terris, Mother. You cannot address a prospective son-in-law as Mister.'

'Please do,' I urged, feeling a word from me was necessary.

'Terris?' Adam said.

'Yes, it is an odd name.'

The brothers stood on either side of Dorothea's chair in that flowery drawing-room. There were pale blue delphiniums in two vases on the mantelpiece, and roses and sweet-peas in little vases everywhere. The mingled scent was delicious, and the room and the flowers seemed part of the family the Lysarths were, as did the way in which Adam and Jonathan stood, protectively, by their sister.

They were twins, both still at Cambridge. They had their mother's oval face, the pale blue eyes their parents shared, their father's languid tallness. I was aware that however protective they might seem they were not protecting Dorothea from me: I was not an interloper, they did not resent me. But their youth made me feel even older than I was, more knocked about and less suitable than ever for the role I wished to play.

'You've travelled a great deal,' Mrs Lysarth said. 'So Dorothea says.'

'Yes, I have.'

I didn't say I'd been an only child. I didn't mention the seaside town where I'd spent my childhood, or reveal that we'd lived in a kind of disgrace really, that my father worked ignominiously in the offices of the trawling business which the family had once owned. Our name remained on the warehouses and the fish-boxes, a daily reminder that we'd slipped down in the world. I'd told Dorothea, but I didn't really think all that would interest the other Lysarths.

'Fascinating, to travel so,' Mrs Lysarth remarked, politely smiling.

After dinner Dr Lysarth and I were left alone in the dining-room. We drank port in a manner which suggested that had I not been present Dr Lysarth would have sat there drinking it alone. He talked about a Roman pavement, twenty feet below the surface somewhere. Quite suddenly he said:

'Dorothea wants to marry you.'

'We both actually –'

'Yes, so she's told us.'

I hesitated. I said:

'I'm – I'm closer to your age, in a way, than to hers.'

'Yes, you probably are. I'm glad you like her.'

'I love her.'

'Of course.'

'I hope,' I began.

'My dear fellow, we're delighted.'

'I'm a correspondent, Dr Lysarth, as Dorothea, I think, has told you. I move about a bit, but for the next two years I'll be in Scandinavia.'

'Ah, yes.' He pushed the decanter towards me. 'She's a special girl, you know.'

'Yes, I do know, Dr Lysarth.'

'We're awfully fond of her. We're a tightly bound family – well, you may have noticed. We're very *much* a family.'

'Yes, indeed.'

'But of course we've always known that Dorothea would one day wish to marry.'

'I know I'm not what you must have imagined, Dr Lysarth, when you thought of Dorothea's husband. I assure you I'm aware of that.'

'It's just that she's more vulnerable than she seems to be: I just want to say that. She's really a very vulnerable girl.'

The decanter was again moved in my direction. The tone of voice closed the subject of Dr Lysarth's daughter. We returned to archaeological matters.

I spent that night at Wistaria Lodge and noticed at breakfast-time how right Dr Lysarth had been when he'd said that the family was a tightly bound one. Conversation drifted from one Lysarth to the next in a way that was almost artificial, as though the domestic scenes I witnessed belonged in the theatre. I formed the impression that the Lysarths invariably knew what was coming next, as though their lines had been learnt. My presence was accommodated through a telepathy that was certainly as impressive, another piece of practised theatre.

'Yes, we're like that,' Dorothea said in the garden after breakfast. 'We never seem to quarrel.'

She taught me how to play croquet and when we'd finished one game we were joined by her brothers. Adam was the best of the three and he, partnering Dorothea, easily beat Jonathan and myself. Mrs Lysarth brought a tray of drinks to a white table beside the lawn and we sat and sipped in the sunshine, while I was told of other games of croquet there had been, famous occasions when the tempers of visitors had become a little ragged.

'It's a perfect training for life,' Mrs Lysarth said, 'the game of croquet.'

'Cunning pays,' Adam continued. 'Generosity must know its place.'

'Not that we are against generosity, Terris,' Jonathan said. 'Not that we're on the side of cunning.'

'What a family poor Terris is marrying into!' Dorothea cried, and on cue her mother smiled and added:

'Terris is a natural croquet-player. He will one day put you all to shame.'

'I doubt that very much.' And as I spoke I felt I said precisely what was expected of me.

'You must teach the Scandinavians, Dorothea,' Adam said. 'Whatever else, you must flatten out a lawn in your little Scandinavian garden.'

'Oh yes, of course we shall. So there.'

After lunch Dorothea and I went for a walk. We had to say goodbye because that evening I was to go away; when I returned it would almost be the day we'd set for our wedding. We walked slowly through the village and out into the country. We left the road and passed along a track by the side of a cornfield. We rested by a stream which Dorothea had often told me about, a place she'd come to with her brothers as a child. We sat there, our backs against the same ivy-covered tree-stump. We talked about being married, of beginning our life together in Copenhagen. I made love to Dorothea by her stream, and it was afterwards that she told me the story of Agnes Kemp. She began it as we lay there, and continued while we washed and tidied ourselves and began the journey back to Wistaria Lodge.

'She was twelve at the time, staying with us while her parents were abroad. She fell from the beech-tree. Her neck was broken.'

I only nodded because there isn't much anyone can say when a fact like that is related.

'I had always wanted to climb that tree, I had been told I never must. "I dare you," she said. "I dare you, Dorothea." I was frightened, but when no one was looking we climbed it together, racing one another to the top.'

She spoke of the funeral of Agnes Kemp, how the dead child's parents had not been present because it had been impossible to contact them in time. 'We don't much hear of them now,' Dorothea said. 'A card at Christmas. Agnes was an only child.'

We walked a little in silence. Then I said:

'What was she like?'

'Oh, she was really awfully spoilt. The kind of person who made you furious.'

I suppose it was that last remark that started everything off, that and the feeling that Wistaria Lodge was a kind of theatre. The remark passed unnoticed at the time, for even as she made it Dorothea turned round, and smiled and kissed me. 'It's all forgotten now,' she said when that was over, 'but of course I had to tell you.'

It was certainly forgotten, for when we arrived in the garden the white table had been moved beneath the beech-tree out of the glare of the sun, and tea with scones and sandwiches and cake was spread all over it. I felt a dryness in my mouth that was not dispelled when I drank. I found it hard to eat, or even to smile in unison with the smiling faces around me. I kept seeing the spoilt child on the grass and Dr Lysarth bending over her, saying she was dead, as no doubt he must have. I kept thinking that the beech-tree should have been cut down years ago, no matter how beautiful it was.

*

'You're mad,' Charlotte shouted at me more than once. 'You're actually mad.' Her voice in its endless repetition is always a reminder of my parents' faces, that worry in their eyes. All I had wanted to know was the truth about ourselves: why did the offices and the warehouses still bear our name, what had my grandfather done? 'Best just left,' my mother said. 'Best not bothered with.' But in the end they told me because naturally I persisted – at eight and twelve and eighteen: naturally I persisted. My grandfather had been a criminal and that was that: a drunkard and an embezzler, a gambler who had run through a fortune in a handful of years: I'd guessed, of course, by the time they told me. I didn't know why they'd been so reluctant, or why they'd displayed concern when I persisted about Miss MacNamara: why did she weep when she walked along the promenade? I had to guess again, because all my childhood Miss MacNamara's tears possessed me so: she wept for the music teacher, who was married and had a family, and I did not forgive my parents for wishing to keep that covered up. Passionately I did not forgive them, although my mother begged me, saying I made myself unhappy. 'You sound so noble,' Charlotte snapped at me. 'Yet what's so marvellous about exposing a brothel-keeper for peddling drugs? Or a grimy pederast and a government minister?' Charlotte's mother called her 'a tricky kind of customer'. And tricky was just the word. Tricky, no doubt, with bank tellers and men met idly in bars. Tricky in beds all over the place, when I was so often away, having to be away.

I crossed the bedroom to the window. The beech-tree was lit by moonlight now. Gazing at it, I heard the voices that had haunted me ever since Dorothea told me the story.

'Then I dare you to,' Dorothea angrily shouts, stopping suddenly and confronting the other girl.

'You're frightened of it, Dorothea. You're frightened of a tree.'

'Of course I'm not.'

'Then I dare you to.'

In the garden the boys, delighted, listen. Their sister's cheeks have reddened. Agnes Kemp is standing on one foot and then the other, balancing in a way she has, a way that infuriates Dorothea.

'You're a horrid person,' Dorothea says. 'You aren't even pretty. You're stupid and spoilt and greedy. You always have two helpings. There's something the matter with your eyes.'

'There isn't, Dorothea Lysarth. You're jealous, that's all.'

'They're pig's eyes.'

'You're just afraid of a tree, Dorothea.'

They climb it, both at the same time, from different sides. There's a forked branch near the top, a sprawling knobbly crutch, easily distinguishable from the ground: they race to that.

The boys watch, expecting any moment that an adult voice will cry out in horror from the house, but no voice does. The blue dress of Agnes Kemp and the white one of Dorothea disappear into a mass of leaves, the boys stand further back, the dresses reappear. Agnes Kemp is in front, but their sister has chosen a different route to the top, a shorter one it seems. The boys long for their sister to win because if she does Agnes Kemp will at least be quiet for a day or two. They don't call out, although they want to: they want to advise Dorothea that in a moment she will have overtaken her challenger; they don't because their voices might attract attention from the house. From where they stand they can hear the grandfather clock in the hall striking ten. Most of the windows are open.

Dorothea slips and almost falls. Her shoes aren't right for climbing and when she glances to her left she can see that Agnes's are: Agnes has put on tennis shoes, knowing she will succeed that morning in goading Dorothea. This is typical of her, and when it is all over Dorothea will be blamed because of course Agnes will blurt it out, in triumph if she wins, in revenge if she doesn't.

The blue dress reaches the fork and then advances along one of its prongs, further than is necessary. Dorothea is a yard behind. She waits, crouched at the knobbly juncture, for Agnes Kemp's return. The boys don't understand that. They stare, wondering why their sister doesn't climb down again so that they can all three run away from Agnes Kemp, since it is running away from her that has been in their minds since breakfast-time. They watch while Agnes Kemp reaches a point at which to pose triumphantly. They watch while slowly she creeps backwards along the branch. Their sister's hand reaches out, pulling at the blue dress, at the child who has been such a nuisance all summer, who'll be worse than ever after her victory. There is a clattering among the leaves and branches. Like a stone, the body strikes the ground.

'Now what did anyone dream?' Mrs Lysarth enquired at breakfast. Knives rattled on plates, toast crackled, Dr Lysarth read *The Times*. It was a family thing to talk about dreams. I had been told that there were dreaming seasons, a period when dreams could be remembered easily and a time when they could not be. It was all another Lysarth game.

'I'd been skipping French classes again,' Adam said. 'For a year or even longer I'd been keeping so low a profile that Monsieur Bertain didn't even know I existed. And then some examination or other loomed.'

'Adam often has that dream,' Dorothea confided to me.

'I was in Istanbul,' Jonathan said, 'or at least it seemed like Istanbul. A man was selling me a stolen picture. A kind of goat, by Marc Chagall.'

'I had only a wisp of a thing,' Mrs Lysarth contributed. 'A bit out of Dorothea's birth.'

'I dreamed that Terris's wife was picking scallions in the garden,' Dorothea said. ' "You're wrong to think there's been a divorce," she said.'

'Did you dream, Terris?' Mrs Lysarth asked, buttering toast, but I was so confused about the night that had passed that I thought it better to say I hadn't.

'What's the criterion for *As You Like It*, ten letters, beginning with "T"?' Dr Lysarth asked.

'Touchstone,' Dorothea said, and another Lysarth game began. 'Lord of Eden End' was 'North', 'poet's black tie ruined by vulcanized rubber' was 'ebonite'. Within ten minutes the crossword puzzle was complete.

The faces laughed and smiled around the breakfast table, the conversation ran about. Especially for my benefit a description of Monsieur Bertain, Adam's French master, was engaged upon. His accent was imitated, his war wound designated as the cause of his short temper. Dr Lysarth looked forward to a dig in Derbyshire in the autumn; his wife was to accompany him and would, as always on archaeological occasions, spend her time walking and reading. Jonathan said he intended to visit us in Scandinavia. Dorothea pressed him and I found myself doing the same.

In the sunny room, while marmalade was passed and the flowered china had all the prettiness of a cottage garden, the horror was nonsensical. Mrs Lysarth's elegance, her perfect features and her burnished hair, would surely not be as they were. No wrinkles creased her face; the Doctor's eyes were honestly untroubled, forget-me-not blue, a darker shade than Dorothea's. And Dorothea's hands would surely be less beautiful. The fingers clawing at the blue dress would have acquired some sign, a joint arthritic, a single bitten nail. The faces of the boys could not have shed all traces of the awful ugliness. 'Dear, it isn't our affair, why Miss MacNamara is troubled,' my mother agitatedly protested. 'Senseless,' Charlotte shouted. 'You frighten me with your senseless talk.'

On Tuesday afternoon, three days away, we would marry and the car would take us to the station at Bath after the champagne on the lawn. Our flight to Paris was at five past seven, we would have dinner in the Chez les Anges. We would visit Versailles and Rouen, and the Jeu de Paume because Dorothea had never been there. I may for a moment have closed my eyes at the breakfast table, so lost was I in speculation and imaginings.

'Well, I have a surgery,' Dr Lysarth announced, folding the newspaper as he rose from the table.

'And I have Castlereagh to wonder about,' Adam said. 'That fascinating figure.'

For a moment in the sunny room the brothers again stood by Dorothea, an accidental conjunction or perhaps telepathy came into play: perhaps they guessed the contents of my mind. There was defiance in their stance, or so I thought, a reason for it now.

'When I was little I used to ride here on my ponies. On Jess first. Later on Adonis.'

We walked as we had on the day we'd made love, through a spinney, along the track by the cornfield. Poppies, not in bloom before, were everywhere now, cow-parsley whitened the hedges.

'The first thing I remember,' Dorothea said, 'is that bits of grass had got into my pram.'

I told myself that I should mention Agnes Kemp, but I did not do so. And when we reached the stream I did not embrace the girl who was to be my bride in a few days' time. We sat with our backs against the tree-trunk, watching the ripple of the water.

'I was lifted up,' Dorothea said, 'and there was a great tutting while the grass cuttings were removed. Years went by before I can remember anything else.'

Murder was not like stealing a pencil-sharpener at school, or spilling something. Agnes Kemp had been detested, a secret had afterwards become a way of life. Few words had perhaps been spoken within the family, Dr Lysarth's giving the cause of death as a broken neck being perhaps the only announcement as to how the future was to be. The faces of the boys on the lawn returned to me, and Dorothea's face as she looked down at the still body. Had she afterwards ridden her pony, Jess or Adonis, whichever it happened to be, by the cornfield and the poppies? 'I dreamed of Agnes,' was what she didn't say at breakfast any more, because the family had exorcized the ghost.

Alone, Miss MacNamara walks; the winter waves tumble about. 'Sea-spray,' my mother lies. 'Sea-spray on her cheeks, dear.' How can my father, morning after morning, leave our gaunt house in order to perform his ignominious work, pretending it is work like any other? How can he hope that I will not scratch away the falsehoods they tell? My father is caught like a creature in a trap, for ever paying back the debts his own father has incurred. It isn't nice, Miss MacNamara and a music teacher; it isn't nice, the truth in Northern Ireland. None of it is nice. 'No, no,' they tell me, 'you must be quiet, Terris.' But I am always quiet. I make no noise in the small grey room where I have to be alone because, so they say, it is better so. The room is full of falseness: then I must write it down, they tell me, quite triumphantly; it will be easier if I write it down.

Americans give arms away, Russians promise tanks. I stand again in the cathedral at Vézelay, pleased that Pope Boniface exposed the pretence about Mary Magdalene. Charlotte passes me a drink, smiling with *ersatz* affection. Our fingers touch, I know how she has spent that afternoon. 'Poor Dorothea,' Mrs Lysarth comforts, and the boys are angry because Dorothea has always needed looking after, ever since the day of the accident, the wretched death of a nuisance. I know I am right, as that Pope knew also. They hold me and buckle the thing on to me, but still I know I am right. Flowers are arranged in vases, croquet played beneath the beech-tree. Ruairi O Baoill adopts a hero's voice to proclaim his pretence of a cause, Major Trubstall's smile is loaded with hypocrisy. The blue dress flutters and is still, telling me again that I am right.

The Time of Year

All that autumn, when they were both fourteen, they had talked about their Christmas swim. She'd had the idea: that on Christmas morning when everyone was still asleep they would meet by the boats on the strand at Ballyquin and afterwards quite casually say that they had been for a swim on Christmas Day. Whenever they met during that stormy October and November they wondered how fine the day might be, how cold or wet, and if the sea could possibly be frozen. They walked together on the cliffs, looking down at the breaking waves of the Atlantic, shivering in anticipation. They walked through the misty dusk of the town, lingering over the first signs of Christmas in the shops: coloured lights strung up, holly and Christmas trees and tinsel. They wondered if people guessed about them. They didn't want them to, they wanted it to be a secret. People would laugh because they were children. They were in love that autumn.

Six years later Valerie still remembered, poignantly, in November. Dublin, so different from Ballyquin, stirred up the past as autumn drifted into winter and winds bustled around the grey buildings of Trinity College, where she was now a student. The city's trees were bleakly bare, it seemed to Valerie; there was sadness, even, on the lawns of her hall of residence, scattered with finished leaves. In her small room, preparing herself one Friday evening for the Skullys' end-of-term party, she sensed quite easily the Christmas chill of the sea, the chilliness creeping slowly over her calves and knees. She paused with the memory, gazing at herself in the looking-glass attached to the inside of her cupboard door. She was a tall girl, standing now in a white silk petticoat, with a thin face and thin long fingers and an almost classical nose. Her black hair was as straight as a die, falling to her shoulders. She was pretty when she smiled and she did so at her reflection, endeavouring to overcome the melancholy that visited her at this time of year. She turned away and picked up a green corduroy dress which she had laid out on her bed. She was going to be late if she dawdled like this.

The parties given by Professor and Mrs Skully were renowned neither for the entertainment they provided nor for their elegance. They were, unfortunately, difficult to avoid, the Professor being persistent in the face of repeated excuses – a persistence it was deemed unwise to strain.

Bidden for half past seven, his History students came on bicycles, a few in Kilroy's Mini, Ruth Cusper on her motor-cycle, Bewley Joal on foot.

Woodward, Whipp and Woolmer-Mills came cheerfully, being kindred spirits of the Professor's and in no way dismayed by the immediate prospect. Others were apprehensive or cross, trying not to let it show as smilingly they entered the Skullys' house in Rathgar.

'How very nice!' Mrs Skully murmured in a familiar manner in the hall. 'How jolly good of you to come.'

The hall was not yet decorated for Christmas, but the Professor had found the remains of last year's crackers and had stuck half a dozen behind the heavily framed scenes of Hanover that had been established in the hall since the early days of the Skullys' marriage. The gaudy crêpe paper protruded above the pictures in splurges of green, red and yellow, and cheered up the hall to a small extent. The coloured scarves and overcoats of the History students, already accumulating on the hall-stand, did so more effectively.

In the Skullys' sitting-room the Professor's record-player, old and in some way special, was in its usual place: on a mahogany table in front of the French windows, which were now obscured by brown curtains. Four identical rugs, their colour approximately matching that of the curtains, were precisely arranged on darker brown linoleum. Rexine-seated dining-chairs lined brownish walls.

The Professor's History students lent temporary character to this room, as their coats and scarves did to the hall. Kilroy was plump in a royal-blue suit. The O'Neill sisters' cluster of followers, jostling even now for promises of favours, wore carefully pressed denim or tweed. The O'Neill sisters themselves exuded a raffish, cocktail-time air. They were twins, from Lurgan, both of them blonde and both favouring an excess of eye-shadow, with lipstick that wetly gleamed, the same shade of pink as the trouser suits that nudgingly hugged the protuberances of their bodies. Not far from where they now held court, the rimless spectacles of Bewley Joal had a busy look in the room's harsh light; the complexion of Yvonne Smith was displayed to disadvantage. So was the troublesome fair hair of Honor Hitchcock, who was engaged to a student known as the Reverend because of his declared intention one day to claim the title. Cosily in a corner she linked her arm with his, both of them seeming middle-aged before their time, inmates already of a draughty rectory in Co. Cork or Clare. 'I'll be the first,' Ruth Cusper vowed, 'to visit you in your parish. Wherever it is.' Ruth Cusper was a statuesque English girl, not yet divested of her motor-cycling gear.

The colours worn by the girls, and the denim and tweed, and the royal blue of Kilroy, contrasted sharply with the uncared-for garb of Woodward, Whipp and Woolmer-Mills, all of whom were expected to take Firsts. Stained and frayed, these three hung together without speaking, Woodward very tall, giving the impression of an etiolated newt, Whipp small, his glasses repaired with Sellotape, Woolmer-Mills for ever launching himself back and forth on the balls of his feet.

In a pocket of Kilroy's suit there was a miniature bottle of vodka, for only tea and what the Professor described as 'cup' were served in the course of the evening. Kilroy fingered it, smiling across the room at the Professor, endeavouring to give the impression that he was delighted to be present. He was a student who was fearful of academic failure, his terror being that he would not get a Third: he had set his sights on a Third, well aware that to have set them higher would not be wise. He brought his little bottles of vodka to the Professor's parties as an act of bravado, a gesture designed to display jauntiness, to show that he could take a chance. But the chances he took with his vodka were not great.

Bewley Joal, who would end up with a respectable Second, was laying down the law to Yvonne Smith, who would be grateful to end up with anything at all. Her natural urge to chatter was stifled, for no one could get a word in when the clanking voice of Bewley Joal was in full flow. 'Oh, it's far more than just a solution, dear girl,' he breezily pronounced, speaking of Moral Rearmament. Yvonne Smith nodded and agreed, trying to say that an aunt of hers thought most highly of Moral Rearmament, that she herself had always been meaning to look into it. But the voice of Bewley Joal cut all her sentences in half.

'I thought we'd start,' the Professor announced, having coughed and cleared his throat, 'with the *Pathétique*.' He fiddled with the record-player while everyone sat down, Ruth Cusper on the floor. He was a biggish man in a grey suit that faintly recalled the clothes of Woodward, Whipp and Woolmer-Mills. On a large head hair was still in plentiful supply even though the Professor was fifty-eight. The hair was grey also, bushing out around his head in a manner that suggested professorial vagueness rather than a gesture in the direction of current fashion. His wife, who stood by his side while he placed a record on the turntable, wore a magenta skirt and twin-set, and a string of jade beads. In almost every way – including this lively choice of dress – she seemed naturally to complement her husband, to fill the gaps his personality couldn't be bothered with. Her nervous manner was the opposite of his confident one. He gave his parties out of duty, and having done so found it hard to take an interest in any students except those who had already proved themselves academically sound. Mrs Skully preferred to strike a lighter note. Now and again she made offers to entice a few of the girls to join her on Saturday evenings, offering the suggestion that they might listen together to Saturday Night Theatre and afterwards sit around and discuss it. Because the Professor saw no point in television there was none in the Skullys' house.

Tchaikovsky filled the sitting-room. The Professor sat down and then Mrs Skully did. The doorbell rang.

'Ah, of course,' Mrs Skully said.
'Valerie Upcott,' Valerie said. 'Good evening, Mrs Skully.'
'Come in, come in, dear. The *Pathétique*'s just started.' She remarked in

the hall on the green corduroy dress that was revealed when Valerie took off her coat. The green was of so dark a shade that it might almost have been black. It had large green buttons all down the front. 'Oh, how really nice!' Mrs Skully said.

The crackers that decorated the scenes of Hanover looked sinister, Valerie thought: Christmas was on the way, soon there'd be the coloured lights and imitation snow. She smiled at Mrs Skully. She wondered about saying that her magenta outfit was nice also, but decided against it. 'We'll slip in quietly,' Mrs Skully said.

Valerie tried to forget the crackers as she entered the sitting-room and took her place on a chair, but in her mind the brash images remained. They did so while she acknowledged Kilroy's winking smile and while she glanced towards the Professor in case he chose to greet her. But the Professor, his head bent over clasped hands, did not look up.

Among the History students Valerie was an unknown quantity. During the two years they'd all known one another she'd established herself as a person who was particularly quiet. She had a private look even when she smiled, when the thin features of her face were startled out of tranquillity, as if an electric light had suddenly been turned on. Kilroy still tried to take her out, Ruth Cusper was pally. But Valerie's privacy, softened by her sudden smile, unfussily repelled these attentions.

For her part she was aware of the students' curiosity, and yet she could not have said to any one of them that a tragedy which had occurred was not properly in the past yet. She could not mention the tragedy to people who didn't know about it already. She couldn't tell it as a story because to her it didn't seem in the least like that. It was a fact you had to live with, half wanting to forget it, half feeling you could not. This time of year and the first faint signs of Christmas were enough to tease it brightly into life.

The second movement of the *Pathétique* came to an end, the Professor rose to turn the record over, the students murmured. Mrs Skully slipped away, as she always did at this point, to attend to matters in the kitchen. While the Professor was bent over the record-player Kilroy waved his bottle of vodka about and then raised it to his lips. 'Hullo, Valerie,' Yvonne Smith whispered across the distance that separated them. She endeavoured to continue her communication by shaping words with her lips. Valerie smiled at her and at Ruth Cusper, who had turned her head when she'd heard Yvonne Smith's greeting. 'Hi,' Ruth Cusper said.

The music began again. The mouthing of Yvonne Smith continued for a moment and then ceased. Valerie didn't notice that, because in the room the students and the Professor were shadows of a kind, the music a distant piping. The swish of wind was in the room, and the shingle cold on her bare feet; so were the two flat stones they'd placed on their clothes to keep them from blowing away. White flecks in the air were snow, she said: Christmas snow, what everyone wanted. But he said the flecks were flecks of foam.

He took her hand, dragging her a bit because the shingle hurt the soles of her feet and slowed her down. He hurried on the sand, calling back to her, reminding her that it was her idea, laughing at her hesitation. He called out something else as he ran into the breakers, but she couldn't hear because of the roar of the sea. She stood in the icy shallows and when she heard him shouting again she imagined he was still mocking her. She didn't even know he was struggling, she wasn't in the least aware of his death. It was his not being there she noticed, the feeling of being alone on the strand at Ballyquin.

'Cup, Miss Upcott?' the Professor offered in the dining-room. Poised above a glass, a jug contained a yellowish liquid. She said she'd rather have tea.

There were egg sandwiches and cakes, plates of crisps, biscuits and Twiglets. Mrs Skully poured tea, Ruth Cusper handed round the cups and saucers. The O'Neill sisters and their followers shared an obscene joke, which was a game that had grown up at the Skullys' parties: one student doing his best to make the others giggle too noisily. A point was gained if the Professor demanded to share the fun.

'Oh, but of course there isn't any argument,' Bewley Joal was insisting, still talking to Yvonne Smith about Moral Rearmament. Words had ceased to dribble from her lips. Instead she kept nodding her head. 'We live in times of decadence,' Bewley Joal pronounced.

Woodward, Whipp and Woolmer-Mills were still together, Woolmer-Mills launching himself endlessly on to the balls of his feet, Whipp sucking at his cheeks. No conversation was taking place among them: when the Professor finished going round with his jug of cup, talk of some kind would begin, probably about a mediaeval document Woodward had earlier mentioned. Or about a reference to *panni streit sine grano* which had puzzled Woolmer-Mills.

'Soon be Christmas,' Honor Hitchcock remarked to Valerie.

'Yes, it will.'

'I love it. I love the way you can imagine everyone doing just the same things on Christmas Eve, tying up presents, running around with holly, listening to the carols. And Christmas Day: that same meal in millions of houses, and the same prayers. All over the world.'

'Yes, there's that.'

'Oh, I think it's marvellous.'

'Christmas?' Kilroy said, suddenly beside them. He laughed, the fat on his face shaking a bit. 'Much overrated in my small view.' He glanced as he spoke at the Professor's profile, preparing himself in case the Professor should look in his direction. His expression changed, becoming solemn.

There were specks of dandruff, Valerie noticed, on the shoulders of the Professor's grey suit. She thought it odd that Mrs Skully hadn't drawn his attention to them. She thought it odd that Kilroy was so determined about his Third. And that Yvonne Smith didn't just walk away from the clanking voice of Bewley Joal.

'Orange or coffee?' Ruth Cusper proffered two cakes that had been cut into slices. The fillings in Mrs Skully's cakes were famous, made with Trex and castor sugar. The cakes themselves had a flat appearance, like large biscuits.

'I wouldn't touch any of that stuff,' Kilroy advised, jocular again. 'I was up all night after it last year.'

'Oh, nonsense!' Ruth Cusper placed a slice of orange cake on Valerie's plate, making a noise that indicated she found Kilroy's attempt at wit a failure. She passed on, and Kilroy without reason began to laugh.

Valerie looked at them, her eyes pausing on each face in the room. She was different from these people of her own age because of her autumn melancholy and the bitterness of Christmas. A solitude had been made for her, while they belonged to each other, separate yet part of a whole.

She thought about them, envying them their ordinary normality, the good fortune they accepted as their due. They trailed no horror, no ghosts or images that wouldn't go away: you could tell that by looking at them. Had she herself already been made peculiar by all of it, eccentric and strange and edgy? And would it never slip away, into the past where it belonged? Each year it was the same, no different from the year before, intent on hanging on to her. Each year she smiled and made an effort. She was brisk with it, she did her best. She told herself she had to live with it, agreeing with herself that of course she had to, as if wishing to be overheard. And yet to die so young, so pointlessly and so casually, seemed to be something you had to feel unhappy about. It dragged out tears from you; it made you hesitate again, standing in the icy water. Your idea it had been.

'Tea, you people?' Mrs Skully offered.

'Awfully kind of you, Mrs Skully,' Kilroy said. 'Splendid tea this is.'

'I should have thought you'd be keener on the Professor's cup, Mr Kilroy.'

'No, I'm not a cup man, Mrs Skully.'

Valerie wondered what it would be like to be Kilroy. She wondered about his private thoughts, even what he was thinking now as he said he wasn't a cup man. She imagined him in his bedroom, removing his royal-blue suit and meticulously placing it on a hanger, talking to himself about the party, wondering if he had done himself any damage in the Professor's eyes. She imagined him as a child, plump in bathing-trunks, building a sandcastle. She saw him in a kitchen, standing on a chair by an open cupboard, nibbling the corner of a Chivers' jelly.

She saw Ruth Cusper too, bossy at a children's party, friendlily bossy, towering over other children. She made them play a game and wasn't disappointed when they didn't like it. You couldn't hurt Ruth Cusper;

she'd grown an extra skin beneath her motor-cycling gear. At night, she often said, she fell asleep as soon as her head touched the pillow.

You couldn't hurt Bewley Joal, either: a grasping child Valerie saw him as, watchful and charmless. Once he'd been hurt, she speculated: another child had told him that no one enjoyed playing with him, and he'd resolved from that moment not to care about stuff like that, to push his way through other people's opinion of him, not wishing to know it.

As children, the O'Neill sisters teased; their faithful tormentors pulled their hair. Woodward, Whipp and Woolmer-Mills read the *Children's Encyclopaedia*. Honor Hitchcock and the Reverend played mummies and daddies. 'Oh, listen to that chatterbox!' Yvonne Smith's father dotingly cried, affection that Yvonne Smith had missed ever since.

In the room the clanking of Bewley Joal punctuated the giggling in the corner where the O'Neill sisters were. More tea was poured and more of the Professor's cup, more cake was handed round. 'Ah, yes,' the Professor began. '*Panni streit sine grano.*' Woodward, Whipp and Woolmer-Mills bent their heads to listen.

The Professor, while waiting on his upstairs landing for Woolmer-Mills to use the lavatory, spoke of the tomatoes he grew. Similarly delayed downstairs, Mrs Skully suggested to the O'Neill sisters that they might like, one Saturday night next term, to listen to Saturday Night Theatre with her. It was something she enjoyed, she said, especially the discussion afterwards. 'Or you, Miss Upcott,' she said. 'You've never been to one of my evenings either.'

Valerie smiled politely, moving with Mrs Skully towards the sitting-room, where Tchaikovsky once more resounded powerfully. Again she examined the arrayed faces. Some eyes were closed in sleep, others were weary beneath a weight of tedium. Woodward's newt-like countenance had not altered, nor had Kilroy's fear dissipated. Frustration still tugged at Yvonne Smith. Nothing much was happening in the face of Mrs Skully.

Valerie continued to regard Mrs Skully's face and suddenly she found herself shivering. How could that mouth open and close, issuing invitations without knowing they were the subject of derision? How could this woman, in her late middle age, officiate at student parties in magenta and jade, or bake inedible cakes without knowing it? How could she daily permit herself to be taken for granted by a man who cared only for students with academic success behind them? How could she have married his pomposity in the first place? There was something wrong with Mrs Skully, there was something missing, as if some part of her had never come to life. The more Valerie examined her the more extraordinary Mrs Skully seemed, and then it seemed extraordinary that the Professor should be unaware that no one liked his parties. It was as if some part of him hadn't come to life either, as if they lived together in the dead wood of a relationship, together in this house because it was convenient.

She wondered if the other students had ever thought that, or if they'd be bothered to survey in any way whatsoever the Professor and his wife. She wondered if they saw a reflection of the Skullys' marriage in the brownness of the room they all sat in, or in the crunchy fillings of Mrs Skully's cakes, or in the Rexine-seated dining-chairs that were not comfortable. You couldn't blame them for not wanting to think about the Skullys' marriage: what good could come of it? The other students were busy and more organized than she. They had aims in life. They had futures she could sense, as she had sensed their pasts. Honor Hitchcock and the Reverend would settle down as right as rain in a provincial rectory, the followers of the O'Neill sisters would enter various business worlds. Woodward, Whipp and Woolmer-Mills would be the same as the Professor, dandruff on the shoulders of three grey suits. Bewley Joal would rise to heights, Kilroy would not. Ruth Cusper would run a hall of residence, the O'Neill sisters would give two husbands hell in Lurgan. Yvonne Smith would live in hopes.

The music of Tchaikovsky gushed over these reflections, as if to soften some harshness in them. But to Valerie there was no harshness in her contemplation of these people's lives, only fact and a lacing of speculation. The Skullys would go on ageing and he might never turn to his wife and say he was sorry. The O'Neill sisters would lose their beauty and Bewley Joal his vigour. One day Woolmer-Mills would find that he could no longer launch himself on to the balls of his feet. Kilroy would enter a home for the senile. Death would shatter the cotton-wool cosiness of Honor Hitchcock and the Reverend.

She wondered what would happen if she revealed what she had thought, if she told them that in order to keep her melancholy in control she had played about with their lives, seeing them in childhood, visiting them with old age and death. Which of them would seek to stop her while she cited the arrogance of the Professor and the pusillanimity of his wife? She heard her own voice echoing in a silence, telling them finally, in explanation, of the tragedy in her own life.

'Please all have a jolly Christmas,' Mrs Skully urged in the hall as scarves and coats were lifted from the hall-stand. 'Please now.'

'We shall endeavour,' Kilroy promised, and the others made similar remarks, wishing Mrs Skully a happy Christmas herself, thanking her and the Professor for the party, Kilroy adding that it had been most enjoyable. There'd be another, the Professor promised, in May.

There was the roar of Ruth Cusper's motor-cycle, and the overloading of Kilroy's Mini, and the striding into the night of Bewley Joal, and others making off on bicycles. Valerie walked with Yvonne Smith through the suburban roads. 'I quite like Joal,' Yvonne Smith confided, releasing the first burst of her pent-up chatter. 'He's all right, isn't he? Quite nice, really, quite clever. I mean, if you care for a clever kind of person. I mean, I wouldn't mind going out with him if he asked me.'

Valerie agreed that Bewley Joal was all right if you cared for that kind of person. It was pleasant in the cold night air. It was good that the party was over.

Yvonne Smith said good-night, still chattering about Bewley Joal as she turned into the house where her lodgings were. Valerie walked on alone, a thin shadow in the gloom. Compulsively now, she thought about the party, seeing again the face of Mrs Skully and the Professor's face and the faces of the others. They formed, like a backdrop in her mind, an assembly as vivid as the tragedy that more grimly visited it. They seemed like the other side of the tragedy, as if she had for the first time managed to peer round a corner. The feeling puzzled her. It was odd to be left with it after the Skullys' end-of-term party.

In the garden of the hall of residence the fallen leaves were sodden beneath her feet as she crossed a lawn to shorten her journey. The bewilderment she felt lifted a little. She had been wrong to imagine she envied other people their normality and good fortune. She was as she wished to be. She paused in faint moonlight, repeating that to herself and then repeating it again. She did not quite add that the tragedy had made her what she was, that without it she would not possess her reflective introspection, or be sensitive to more than just the time of year. But the thought hovered with her as she moved towards the lights of the house, offering what appeared to be a hint of comfort.

The Teddy-bears' Picnic

'I simply don't believe it,' Edwin said. 'Grown-up people?'

'Well, grown-up now, darling. We weren't always grown-up.'

'But *teddy-bears*, Deborah?'

'I'm sure I've told you dozens of times before.'

Edwin shook his head, frowning and staring at his wife. They'd been married six months: he was twenty-nine, swiftly making his way in a stockbroker's office, Deborah was twenty-six and intended to continue being Mr Harridance's secretary until a family began to come along. They lived in Wimbledon, in a block of flats called The Zodiac. 23 The Zodiac their address was and friends thought the title amusing and lively, making jokes about Gemini and Taurus and Capricorn when they came to drinks. A Dane had designed The Zodiac in 1968.

'I'll absolutely tell you this,' Edwin said, 'I'm not attending this thing.'

'But darling –'

'Oh, don't be bloody silly, Deborah.'

Edwin's mother had called Deborah 'a pretty little thing', implying for those who cared to be perceptive a certain reservation. She'd been more direct with Edwin himself, in a private conversation they'd had after Edwin had said he and Deborah wanted to get married. 'Remember, dear,' was how Mrs Chalm had put it then, 'she's not always going to be a pretty little thing. This really isn't a very sensible marriage, Edwin.' Mrs Chalm was known to be a woman who didn't go in for cant when dealing with the lives of the children she had borne and brought up; she made no bones about it and often said so. Her husband, on the other hand, kept out of things.

Yet in the end Edwin and Deborah had married, one Tuesday afternoon in December, and Mrs Chalm resolved to make the best of it. She advised Deborah about this and that, she gave her potted plants for 23 The Zodiac, and in fact was kind. If Deborah had known about her mother-in-law's doubts she'd have been surprised.

'But we've always done it, Edwin. All of us.'

'All of who, for heaven's sake?'

'Well, Angela for one. And Holly and Jeremy of course.'

'*Jeremy*? My God!'

'And Peter. And Enid and Charlotte and Harriet.'

'You've never told me a word about this, Deborah.'

'I'm really sure I have.'

The sitting-room where this argument took place had a single huge window with a distant view of Wimbledon Common. The walls were covered with rust-coloured hessian, the floor with a rust-coloured carpet. The Chalms were still acquiring furniture: what there was, reflecting the style of The Zodiac's architecture, was in bent steel and glass. There was a single picture, of a field of thistles, revealed to be a photograph on closer examination. Bottles of alcohol stood on a glass-topped table, their colourful labels cheering that corner up. Had the Chalms lived in a Victorian flat, or a cottage in a mews, their sitting-room would have been different, fussier and more ornate, dictated by the architectural environment. Their choice of decor and furniture was the choice of newly-weds who hadn't yet discovered a confidence of their own.

'You mean you all sit round with your teddies,' Edwin said, 'having a picnic? And you'll still be doing that at eighty?'

'What d'you mean, eighty?'

'When you're eighty years of age, for God's sake. You're trying to tell me you'll still be going to this garden when you're stumbling about and hard of hearing, a gang of O.A.P.s squatting out on the grass with teddy-bears?'

'I didn't say anything about when we're old.'

'You said it's a tradition, for God's sake.'

He poured some whisky into a glass and added a squirt of soda from a Sparklets syphon. Normally he would have poured a gin and dry vermouth for his wife, but this evening he felt too cross to bother. He hadn't had the easiest of days. There'd been an error in the office about the B.A.T. shares a client had wished to buy, and he hadn't managed to have any lunch because as soon as the B.A.T. thing was sorted out a crisis had blown up over sugar speculation. It was almost eight o'clock when he'd got back to The Zodiac and instead of preparing a meal Deborah had been on the telephone to her friend Angela, talking about teddy-bears.

Edwin was an agile young man with shortish black hair and a face that had a very slight look of a greyhound about it. He was vigorous and athletic, sound on the tennis court, fond of squash and recently of golf. His mother had once stated that Edwin could not bear to lose and would go to ruthless lengths to ensure that he never did. She had even remarked to her husband that she hoped this quality would not one day cause trouble, but her husband replied it was probably just what a stockbroker needed. Mrs Chalm had been thinking more of personal relationships, where losing couldn't be avoided. It was that she'd had on her mind when she'd had doubts about the marriage, for the doubts were not there simply because Deborah was a pretty little thing: it was the conjunction Mrs Chalm was alarmed about.

'I didn't happen to get any lunch,' Edwin snappishly said now. 'I've had a long unpleasant day and when I get back here –'

'I'm sorry, dear.'

Deborah immediately rose from among the rust-coloured cushions of the sofa and went to the kitchen, where she took two pork chops from a Marks and Spencer's carrier-bag and placed them under the grill of the electric cooker. She took a packet of frozen broccoli spears from the carrier-bag as well, and two Marks and Spencer's trifles. While typing letters that afternoon she'd planned to have fried noodles with the chops and broccoli spears, just for a change. A week ago they'd had fried noodles in the new Mexican place they'd found and Edwin said they were lovely. Deborah had kicked off her shoes as soon as she'd come into the flat and hadn't put them on since. She was wearing a dress with scarlet petunias on it. Dark-haired, with a heart-shaped face and blue eyes that occasionally acquired a bewildered look, she seemed several years younger than twenty-six, more like eighteen.

She put on water to boil for the broccoli spears even though the chops would not be ready for some time. She prepared a saucepan of oil for the noodles, hoping that this was the way to go about frying them. She couldn't understand why Edwin was making such a fuss just because Angela had telephoned, and put it down to his not having managed to get any lunch.

In the sitting-room Edwin stood by the huge window, surveying the tops of trees and, in the distance, Wimbledon Common. She must have been on the phone to Angela for an hour and a half, probably longer. He'd tried to ring himself to say he'd be late but each time the line had been engaged. He searched his mind carefully, going back through the three years he'd known Deborah, but no reference to a teddy-bears' picnic came to him. He'd said very positively that she had never mentioned it, but he'd said that in anger, just to make his point: reviewing their many conversations now, he saw he had been right and felt triumphant. Of course he'd have remembered such a thing, any man would.

Far down below, a car turned into the wide courtyard of The Zodiac, a Rover it looked like, a discreet shade of green. It wouldn't be all that long before they had a Rover themselves, even allowing for the fact that the children they hoped for would be arriving any time now. Edwin had not objected to Deborah continuing her work after their marriage, but family life would naturally be much tidier when she no longer could, when the children were born. Eventually they'd have to move into a house with a garden because it was natural that Deborah would want that, and he had no intention of disagreeing with her.

'Another thing is,' he said, moving from the window to the open doorway of the kitchen, 'how come you haven't had a reunion all the years I've known you? If it's an annual thing –'

'It isn't an annual thing, Edwin. We haven't had a picnic since 1975 and before that 1971. It's just when someone feels like it, I suppose. It's just a bit of fun, darling.'

'You call sitting down with teddy-bears a bit of fun? Grown-up people?'

'I wish you wouldn't keep on about grown-ups. I know we're grown-ups. That's the whole point. When we were little we all vowed –'

'Jesus Christ!'

He turned and went to pour himself another drink. She'd never mentioned it because she knew it was silly. She was ashamed of it, which was something she would discover when she grew up a bit.

'You know I've got Binky,' she said, following him to where the drinks were and pouring herself some gin. 'I've told you hundreds of times how I took him everywhere. If you don't like him in the bedroom I'll put him away. I didn't know you didn't like him.'

'I didn't say that, Deborah. It's completely different, what you're saying. It's private for a start. I mean, it's your teddy-bear and you've told me how fond you were of it. That's completely different from sitting down with a crowd of idiots –'

'They're not idiots, Edwin, actually.'

'Well, they certainly don't sound like anything else. D'you mean Jeremy and Peter are going to arrive clutching teddy-bears and then sit down on the grass pretending to feed them biscuit crumbs? For God's sake, Jeremy's a medical *doctor*!'

'Actually, nobody'll sit on the grass because the grass will probably be damp. Everyone brought rugs last time. It's really because of the garden, you know. It's probably the nicest garden in South Bucks, and then there're the Ainley-Foxletons. I mean, they do so love it all.'

He'd actually been in the garden, and he'd once actually met the Ainley-Foxletons. One Saturday afternoon during his engagement to Deborah there had been tea on a raised lawn. Laburnum and broom were out, a mass of yellow everywhere. Quite pleasant old sticks the Ainley-Foxletons had been, but neither of them had mentioned a teddy-bears' picnic.

'I think she did as a matter of fact,' Deborah mildly insisted. 'I remember because I said it hadn't really been so long since the last one – eighteen months ago would it be when I took you to see them? Well, 1975 wasn't all that long before that, and she said it seemed like aeons. I remember her saying that, I remember "aeons" and thinking it just like her to come out with a word people don't use any more.'

'And you never thought to point out the famous picnic site? For hours we walked round and round that garden and yet it never occurred to you –'

'We didn't walk round and round. I'm sorry you were bored, Edwin.'

'I didn't say I was bored.'

'I know the Ainley-Foxletons can't hear properly and it's a strain, but you said you wanted to meet them –'

'I didn't say anything of the kind. You kept telling me about these people and their house and garden, but I can assure you I wasn't crying out to meet them in any way whatsoever. In fact, I rather wanted to play tennis that afternoon.'

'You didn't say so at the time.'

'Of course I didn't say so.'

'Well, then.'

'What I'm trying to get through to you is that we walked round and round that garden even though it had begun to rain. And not once did you say, "That's where we used to have our famous teddy-bears' picnic." '

'As a matter of fact I think I did. And it isn't famous. I wish you wouldn't keep on about it being famous.'

Deborah poured herself more gin and added the same amount of dry vermouth to the glass. She considered it rude of Edwin to stalk about the room just because he'd had a bad day, drinking himself and not bothering about her. If he hadn't liked the poor old Ainley-Foxletons he should have said so. If he'd wanted to play tennis that afternoon he should have said so too.

'Well, be all that as it may,' he was saying now, rather pompously in Deborah's opinion, 'I do not intend to take part in any of this nonsense.'

'But everybody's husband will, and the wives too. It's only fun, darling.'

'Oh, do stop saying it's fun. You sound like a half-wit. And something's smelling in the kitchen.'

'I don't think that's very nice, Edwin. I don't see why you should call me a half-wit.'

'Listen, I've had an extremely unpleasant day –'

'Oh, do stop about your stupid old day.'

She carried her glass to the kitchen with her and removed the chops from beneath the grill. They were fairly black, and serve him right for upsetting her. Why on earth did he have to make such a fuss, why couldn't he be like everyone else? It was something to giggle over, not take so seriously, a single Sunday afternoon when they wouldn't be doing anything anyway. She dropped a handful of noodles into the hot oil, and then a second handful.

In the sitting-room the telephone rang just as Edwin was squirting soda into another drink. 'Yes?' he said, and Angela's voice came lilting over the line, saying she didn't want to bother Debbie but the date had just been fixed: June 17th. 'Honestly, you'll split your sides, Edwin.'

'Yes, all right, I'll tell her,' he said as coldly as he could. He replaced the receiver without saying goodbye. He'd never cared for Angela, patronizing kind of creature.

Deborah knew it had been Angela on the telephone and she knew she would have given Edwin the date she had arranged with Charlotte and Peter, who'd been the doubtful ones about the first date, suggested by Jeremy. Angela had said she was going to ring back with this information, but when the Chalms sat down to their chops and broccoli spears and noodles Edwin hadn't yet passed the information on.

'Christ, what are these?' he said, poking at a brown noodle with his fork and then poking at the burnt chop.

'The little things are fried noodles, which you enjoyed so much the other night. The larger thing is a pork chop, which wouldn't have got overcooked if you hadn't started an argument.'

'Oh, for God's sake!'

He pushed his chair back and stood up. He returned to the sitting-room and Deborah heard the squirting of the soda syphon. She stood up herself, followed him to the sitting-room and poured herself another gin and vermouth. Neither of them spoke. Deborah returned to the kitchen and ate her share of the broccoli spears. The sound of television came from the sitting-room. 'Listen, buster, you give this bread to the hit or don't you?' a voice demanded. 'O.K., I give the bread,' a second voice replied.

They'd had quarrels before. They'd quarrelled on their honeymoon in Greece for no reason whatsoever. They'd quarrelled because she'd once left the ignition of the car turned on, causing a flat battery. They'd quarrelled because of Enid's boring party just before Christmas. The present quarrel was just the same kind of thing, Deborah knew: Edwin would sit and sulk, she'd wash the dishes up feeling miserable, and he'd probably eat the chop and the broccoli when they were cold. She couldn't blame him for not wanting the noodles because she didn't seem to have cooked them correctly. Then she thought: what if he doesn't come to the picnic, what if he just goes on being stubborn, which he could be when he wanted to? Everyone would know. 'Where's Edwin?' they would ask, and she'd tell some lie and everyone would know it was a lie, and everyone would know they weren't getting on. Only six months had passed, everyone would say, and he wouldn't join in a bit of fun.

But to Deborah's relief that didn't happen. Later that night Edwin ate the cold pork chop, eating it from his fingers because he couldn't manage to stick a fork into it. He ate the cold broccoli spears as well, but he left the noodles. She made him tea and gave him a Danish pastry and in the morning he said he was sorry.

'So if we could it would be lovely,' Deborah said on her office telephone. She'd told her mother there was to be another teddy-bears' picnic, Angela and Jeremy had arranged it mainly, and the Ainley-Foxletons would love it of course, possibly the last they'd see.

'My dear, you're always welcome, as you know.' The voice of Deborah's mother came all the way from South Bucks, from the village where the Ainley-Foxletons' house and garden were, where Deborah and Angela, Jeremy, Charlotte, Harriet, Enid, Peter and Holly had been children together. The plan was that Edwin and Deborah should spend the weekend of June 17th with Deborah's parents, and Deborah's mother had even promised to lay on some tennis for Edwin on the Saturday. Deborah herself wasn't much good at tennis.

'Thanks, Mummy,' she managed to say just as Mr Harridance returned from lunch.

'No, spending the whole weekend actually,' Edwin informed his mother. 'There's this teddy-bear thing Deborah has to go to.'

'What teddy-bear thing?'

Edwin went into details, explaining how the children who'd been friends in a South Bucks village nearly twenty years ago met from time to time to have a teddy-bears' picnic because that was what they'd done then.

'But they're adults surely now,' Mrs Chalm pointed out.

'Yes, I know.'

'Well, I hope you have a lovely time, dear.'

'Delightful, I'm sure.'

'It's odd when they're adults, I'd have thought.'

Between themselves, Edwin and Deborah did not again discuss the subject of the teddy-bears' picnic. During the quarrel Edwin had felt bewildered, never quite knowing how to proceed, and he hoped that on some future occasion he would be better able to cope. It made him angry when he wasn't able to cope, and the anger still hung about him. On the other hand, six months wasn't long in a marriage which he hoped would go on for ever: the marriage hadn't had a chance to settle into the shape that suited it, any more than he and Deborah had had time to develop their own taste in furniture and decoration. It was only to be expected that there should be problems and uncertainty.

As for Deborah, she knew nothing about marriages settling into shape: she wasn't aware that rules and tacit understandings, arrangements of give and take, were what made marriage possible when the first gloss had worn off. Marriage for Deborah was the continuation of a love affair, and as yet she had few complaints. She knew that of course they had to have quarrels.

They had met at a party. Edwin had left a group of people he was listening to and had crossed to the corner where she was being bored by a man in computers. 'Hello,' Edwin just said. All three of them were eating plates of paella.

Finding a consideration of the past pleasanter than speculation about the future, Deborah often recalled that moment: Edwin's sharp face smiling at her, the computer man discomfited, a sour taste in the paella. 'You're not Fiona's sister?' Edwin said, and when ages afterwards she'd asked him who Fiona was he confessed he'd made her up. 'I shouldn't eat much more of this stuff,' he said, taking the paella away from her. Deborah had been impressed by that: she and the computer man had been fiddling at the paella with their forks, both of them too polite to say that there was something the matter with it. 'What do you do?' Edwin said a few minutes later, which was more than the computer man had asked.

In the weeks that followed they told one another all about themselves, about their parents and the houses they'd lived in as children, the schools they'd gone to, the friends they'd made. Edwin was a daring person, he was successful, he liked to be in charge of things. Without in any way sounding boastful, he told her of episodes in his childhood, or risks taken at school. Once he'd dismantled the elderly music master's bed, causing it to collapse when the music master later lay down on it. He'd removed the carburettor from some other master's car, he'd stolen an egg-beater from an ironmonger's shop. All of them were dares, and by the end of his schooldays he had acquired the reputation of being fearless: there was nothing, people said, he wouldn't do.

It was easy for Deborah to love him, and everything he told her, self-deprecatingly couched, was clearly the truth. But Deborah in love naturally didn't wonder how this side of Edwin would seem in marriage, nor how it might develop as Edwin moved into middle age. She couldn't think of anything nicer than having him there every day, and in no way did she feel let down on their honeymoon in Greece or by the couple of false starts they made with flats before they eventually ended up in 23 The Zodiac. Edwin went to his office every day and Deborah went to hers. That he told her more about share prices than she told him about the letters she typed for Mr Harridance was because share prices were more important. It was true that she would often have quite liked to pass on details of this or that, for instance of the correspondence with Flitts, Hay and Co. concerning nearly eighteen thousand defective chair castors. The correspondence was interesting because it had continued for two years and had become vituperative. But when she mentioned it Edwin just agreeably nodded. There was also the business about Miss Royal's scratches, which everyone in the office had been conjecturing about: how on earth had a woman like Miss Royal acquired four long scratches on her face and neck between five-thirty one Monday evening and nine-thirty the following morning? 'Oh yes?' Edwin had said, and gone on to talk about the Mercantile Investment Trust.

Deborah did not recognize these telltale signs. She did not remember that when first she and Edwin exchanged information about one another's childhoods Edwin had sometimes just smiled, as if his mind had drifted away. It was only a slight disappointment that he didn't wish to hear about Flitts, Hay and Co., and Miss Royal's scratches: no one could possibly get into a state about things like that. Deborah saw little significance in the silly quarrel they'd had about the teddy-bears' picnic, which was silly itself of course. She didn't see that it had had to do with friends who were hers and not Edwin's; nor did it occur to her that when they really began to think about the decoration of 23 The Zodiac it would be Edwin who would make the decisions. They shared things, Deborah would have said: after all, in spite of the quarrel they were going to go to the teddy-bears' picnic. Edwin loved her and was kind and really rather marvellous. It was purely for her sake that he'd agreed to give up a whole weekend.

So on a warm Friday afternoon, as they drove from London in their Saab, Deborah was feeling happy. She listened while Edwin talked about a killing a man called Dupree had made by selling out his International Asphalt holding. 'James James Morrison Morrison Weatherby George Dupree,' she said.

'What on earth's that?'

'It's by A. A. Milne, the man who wrote about Pooh Bear. Poor Pooh!'

Edwin didn't say anything.

'Jeremy's is called Pooh.'

'I see.'

In the back of the car, propped up in a corner, was the blue teddy-bear called Binky which Deborah had had since she was one.

The rhododendrons were in bloom in the Ainley-Foxletons' garden, late that year because of the bad winter. So was the laburnum Edwin remembered, and the broom, and some yellow azaleas. 'My dear, we're so awfully glad,' old Mrs Ainley-Foxleton said, kissing him because she imagined he must be one of the children in her past. Her husband, tottering about on the raised lawn which Edwin also remembered from his previous visit, had developed the shakes. 'Darlings, Mrs Bright has ironed our tablecloth for us!' Mrs Ainley-Foxleton announced with a flourish.

She imparted this fact because Mrs Bright, the Ainley-Foxletons' charwoman, was emerging at that moment from the house, with the ironed tablecloth over one arm. She carried a tray on which there were glass jugs of orange squash and lemon squash, a jug of milk, mugs with Beatrix Potter characters on them, and two plates of sandwiches that weren't much larger than postage stamps. She made her way down stone steps from the raised lawn, crossed a more extensive lawn and disappeared into a shrubbery. While everyone remained chatting to the Ainley-Foxletons – nobody helping to lay the picnic out because that had never been part of the proceedings – Mrs Bright reappeared from the shrubbery, returned to the house and then made a second journey, her tray laden this time with cakes and biscuits.

Before lunch Edwin had sat for a long time with Deborah's father in the summerhouse, drinking. This was something Deborah's father enjoyed on Sunday mornings, permitting himself a degree of dozy inebriation which only became noticeable when two bottles of claret were consumed at lunch. Today Edwin had followed his example, twice getting to his feet to refill their glasses and during the course of lunch managing to slip out to the summerhouse for a fairly heavy tot of whisky, which mixed nicely with the claret. He could think of no other condition in which to present himself – with a teddy-bear Deborah's mother had pressed upon him – in the Ainley-Foxletons' garden. 'Rather you than me, old chap,' Deborah's father had said after lunch, subsiding into an armchair with a gurgle. At the last moment Edwin had quickly returned to the summerhouse and had helped himself to a further intake of whisky, drinking from the cap of the Teacher's bottle because the glasses had been collected up. He reckoned that when Mrs Ainley-Foxleton had kissed him he must have smelt like a distillery, and he was glad of that.

'Well, here we are,' Jeremy said in the glade where the picnic had first taken place in 1957. He sat at the head of the tablecloth, cross-legged on a tartan rug. He had glasses and was stout. Peter at the other end of the tablecloth didn't seem to have grown much in the intervening years, but Angela had shot up like a hollyhock and in fact resembled one. Enid was dumpy, Charlotte almost beautiful; Harriet had protruding teeth, Holly was bouncy. Jeremy's wife and Peter's wife, and Charlotte's husband – a man in Shell – all entered into the spirit of the occasion. So did Angela's husband, who came from Czechoslovakia and must have found the proceedings peculiar, everyone sitting there with a teddy-bear that had a name. Angela put a record on Mrs Ainley-Foxleton's old wind-up gramophone. 'Oh, don't go down to the woods today,' a voice screeched, 'without consulting me.' Mr and Mrs Ainley-Foxleton were due to arrive at the scene later, as was the tradition. They came with chocolates apparently, and bunches of buttercups for the teddy-bears.

'Thank you, Edwin,' Deborah whispered while the music and the song continued. She wanted him to remember the quarrel they'd had about the picnic; she wanted him to know that she now truly forgave him, and appreciated that in the end he'd seen the fun of it all.

'Listen, I have to go to the lav,' Edwin said. 'Excuse me for a minute.' Nobody except Deborah seemed to notice when he ambled off because everyone was talking so, exchanging news.

The anger which had hung about Edwin after the quarrel had never evaporated. It was in anger that he had telephoned his mother, and further anger had smacked at him when she'd said she hoped he would have a lovely time. What she had meant was that she'd told him so: marry a pretty little thing and before you can blink you're sitting down to tea with teddy-bears. You're a fool to put up with rubbish like this was what Deborah's father had meant when he'd said rather you than me.

Edwin did not lack brains and he had always been aware of it. It was his cleverness that was still offended by what he considered to be an embarrassment, a kind of gooey awfulness in an elderly couple's garden. At school he had always hated anything to do with dressing up, he'd even felt awkward when he'd had to read poetry aloud. What Edwin admired was solidity: he liked Westminster and the City, he liked trains moving smoothly, suits and clean shirts. When he'd married Deborah he'd known – without having to be told by his mother – that she was not a clever person, but in Edwin's view a clever wife was far from necessary. He had seen a future in which children were born and educated, in which Deborah developed various cooking and housekeeping skills, in which together they gave nice dinner parties. Yet instead of that, after only six months, there was this grotesque absurdity. Getting drunk wasn't a regular occurrence with Edwin: he drank when he was angry, as he had on the night of the quarrel.

Mr Ainley-Foxleton was pottering about with his stick on the raised lawn, but Edwin took no notice of him. The old man appeared to be looking for something, his head poked forward on his scrawny neck, bespectacled eyes examining the grass. Edwin passed into the house. From behind a closed door he could hear the voices of Mrs Ainley-Foxleton and Mrs Bright, talking about buttercups. He opened another door and entered the Ainley-Foxletons' dining-room. On the sideboard there was a row of decanters.

Edwin discovered that it wasn't easy to drink from a decanter, but he managed it none the less. Anger spurted in him all over again. It seemed incredible that he had married a girl who hadn't properly grown up. None of them had grown up, none of them desired to belong in the adult world, not even the husbands and wives who hadn't been involved in the first place. If Deborah had told him about any of it on that Sunday afternoon when they'd visited this house he wondered even if he would have married her.

Yet replacing the stopper of the decanter between mouthfuls in case anyone came in, Edwin found it impossible to admit that he had made a mistake in marrying Deborah: he loved her, he had never loved anyone else, and he doubted if he would ever love anyone else in the future. Often in an idle moment, between selling and buying in the office, he thought of her, seeing her in her different clothes and sometimes without any clothes at all. When he returned to 23 The Zodiac he sometimes put his arms around her and would not let her go until he had laid her gently down on their bed. Deborah thought the world of him, which was something she often said.

In spite of all that it was extremely annoying that the quarrel had caused him to feel out of his depth. He should have been able to sort out such nonsense within a few minutes; he deserved his mother's jibe and his father-in-law's as well. Even though they'd only been married six months, it was absurd that since Deborah loved him so he hadn't been able to make her see how foolish she was being. It was absurd to be standing here drunk.

The Ainley-Foxletons' dining-room, full of silver and polished furniture and dim oil paintings, shifted out of focus. The row of decanters became two rows and then one again. The heavily carpeted floor tilted beneath him, falling away to the left and then to the right. Deborah had let him down. She had brought him here so that he could be displayed in front of Angela and Jeremy and Charlotte, Harriet, Holly, Enid, Peter, and the husbands and the wives. She was making the point that she had only to lift her little finger, that his cleverness was nothing compared with his love for her. The anger hammered at him now, hurting him almost. He wanted to walk away, to drive the Saab back to London and when Deborah followed him to state quite categorically that if she intended to be a fool there would have to be a divorce. But some part of Edwin's anger insisted that such a course of action would be an admission of failure and defeat. It was absurd that the marriage he had chosen to make should end before it had properly begun, due to silliness.

Edwin took a last mouthful of whisky and replaced the glass stopper. He remembered another social occasion, years ago, and he was struck by certain similarities with the present one. People had given a garden party in aid of some charity or other which his mother liked to support, to which he and his brother and sister, and his father, had been dragged along. It had been an excruciatingly boring afternoon, in the middle of a heatwave. He'd had to wear his floppy cotton hat, which he hated, and an awful tan-coloured summer suit, made of cotton also. There had been hours and hours of just standing while his mother talked to people, sometimes slowly giving them recipes, which they wrote down. Edwin's brother and sister didn't seem to mind that; his father did as he was told. So Edwin had wandered off, into a house that was larger and more handsome than the Ainley-Foxletons'. He had poked about in the downstairs rooms, eaten some jam he found in the kitchen, and then gone upstairs to the bedrooms. He'd rooted around for a while, opening drawers and wardrobes, and then he'd climbed a flight of uncarpeted stairs to a loft. From here he'd made his way out on to the roof. Edwin had almost forgotten this incident and certainly never dwelt on it, but with a vividness that surprised him it now returned.

He left the dining-room. In the hall he could still hear the voices of Mrs Ainley-Foxleton and Mrs Bright. Nobody had bothered with him that day; his mother, whose favourite he had always been, was even impatient when he said he had a toothache. Nobody had noticed when he'd slipped away. But from the parapet of the roof everything had been different. The faces of the people were pale, similar dots, all gazing up at him. The colours of the women's dresses were confused among the flowers. Arms waved frantically at him; someone shouted, ordering him to come down.

On the raised lawn the old man was still examining the grass, his head still poked down towards it, his stick prodding at it. From the glade where the picnic was taking place came a brief burst of applause, as if someone had just made a speech. '. . . today's the day the teddy-bears have their picnic,' sang the screeching voice, faintly.

A breeze had cooled Edwin's sunburnt arms as he crept along the parapet. He'd sensed his mother's first realization that it was he, and noticed his brother's and his sister's weeping. He had seen his father summoned from the car where he'd been dozing. Edwin had stretched his arms out, balancing like a tightrope performer. All the boredom, the tiresome heat, the cotton hat and suit, were easily made up for. Within minutes it had become his day.

'Well, it's certainly the weather for it,' Edwin said to the old man.

'Eh?'

'The weather's nice,' he shouted. 'It's a fine day.'

'There's fungus in this lawn, you know. Eaten up with it.' Mr Ainley-Foxleton investigated small black patches with his stick. 'Never knew there was fungus here,' he said.

They were close to the edge of the lawn. Below them there was a rockery full of veronica and sea-pinks and saponaria. The rockery was arranged in a semicircle, around a sundial.

'Looks like fungus there too,' Edwin said, pointing at the larger lawn that stretched away beyond this rockery.

'Eh?' The old man peered over the edge, not knowing what he was looking for because he hadn't properly heard. 'Eh?' he said again, and Edwin nudged him with his elbow. The stick went flying off at an angle, the old man's head struck the edge of the sundial with a sharp, clean crack. 'Oh, don't go down to the woods today,' the voice began again, drifting through the sunshine over the scented garden. Edwin glanced quickly over the windows of the house in case there should be a face at one of them. Not that it would matter: at that distance no one could see such a slight movement of an elbow.

They ate banana sandwiches and egg sandwiches, and biscuits with icing on them, chocolate cake and coffee cake. The teddy-bears' snouts were pressed over the Beatrix Potter mugs, each teddy-bear addressed by name. Edwin's was called Tomkin.

'Remember the day of the thunderstorm?' Enid said, screwing up her features in a way she had – like a twitch really, Edwin considered. The day he had walked along the parapet might even have been the day of the thunderstorm, and he smiled because somehow that was amusing. Angela was smiling too, and so were Jeremy and Enid, Charlotte, Harriet and Holly, Peter and the husbands and the wives. Deborah in particular was smiling. When Edwin glanced from face to face he was reminded of the faces that had gazed up at him from so far below, except that there'd been panic instead of smiles.

'Remember the syrup?' Angela said. 'Poor Algernon had to be given a horrid bath.'

'Wasn't it Horatio, surely?' Deborah said.

'Yes, it was Horatio,' Enid confirmed, amusingly balancing Horatio on her shoulder.

'Today's the day the teddy-bears have their picnic,' suddenly sang everyone, taking a lead from the voice on the gramophone. Edwin smiled and even began to sing himself. When they returned to Deborah's parents' house the atmosphere would be sombre. 'Poor old chap was overlooked,' he'd probably be the one to explain, 'due to all that fuss.' And in 23 The Zodiac the atmosphere would be sombre also. 'I'm afraid you should get rid of it,' he'd suggest, arguing that the blue teddy-bear would be for ever a reminder. Grown up a bit because of what had happened, Deborah would of course agree. Like everything else, marriage had to settle into shape.

Charlotte told a story of an adventure her Mikey had had when she'd taken him back to boarding-school, how a repulsive girl called Agnes Thorpe had stuck a skewer in him. Holly told of how she'd had to rescue her Percival from drowning when he'd toppled out of a motor-boat. Jeremy wound up the gramophone and the chatter jollily continued, the husbands and wives appearing to be as delighted as anyone. Harriet said how she'd only wanted to marry Peter and Peter how he'd determined to marry Deborah. 'Oh, don't go down to the woods today,' the voice began again, and then came Mrs Ainley-Foxleton's scream.

Everyone rushed, leaving the teddy-bears just anywhere and the gramophone still playing. Edwin was the first to bend over the splayed figure of the old man. He declared that Mr Ainley-Foxleton was dead, and then took charge of the proceedings.

Being Stolen From

'I mean I'm not like I used to be.'

She had married, Norma continued, she had settled down. A young man, sitting beside her on the sofa, agreed that this was so. He was soberly dressed, jolly of manner, not quite fat. His smiling blue eyes suggested that if Norma had ever been flighty and irresponsible she no longer was, due to the influence he had brought into her life.

'I mean in a way,' Norma said, 'things have changed for you too, Mrs Lacy.'

Bridget became flustered. Ever since childhood she had been embarrassed when she found herself the centre of attention, and even though she was forty-nine now none of that had improved. She was plump and black-haired, her manner affected by her dislike of being in the limelight. It was true that things had changed for her also in the last six years, but how had Norma discovered it? Had neighbours been questioned?

'Yes, things have changed,' she said, quite cheerfully because she'd become used to the change.

Norma nodded, and so did her husband. Bridget could tell from their faces that although they might not know the details they certainly knew the truth of the matter. And the details weren't important because strangers wouldn't be interested in the countryside of Co. Cork where she and Liam had come from, or in the disappointment of their childless marriage. London had become their home, a small house in a terrace, with the *Cork Weekly Examiner* to keep them in touch. Liam had found a job in a newsagent's, the same shop he and the woman now owned between them.

'Your husband didn't seem the kind,' Norma began. 'I mean, not that I knew him.'

'No, he didn't seem like that.'

'I know what it feels like to be left, Mrs Lacy.'

'It feels like nothing now.'

She smiled again, but her cheeks had become hot because the conversation was about her. When Norma had phoned a week ago, to ask if they could have a chat, she hadn't known what to say. It would have been unpleasant simply to say no, nor was there any reason why she should take that attitude, but even so she'd been dreading their visit ever since. She'd felt cross with herself for not managing to explain that Betty could easily be upset, which was why Betty wasn't in the house that afternoon. It was the first thing she'd said to them when she'd opened the hall-door, not knowing if they were expecting to see the child or not. She'd sounded apologetic and was cross with herself for that, too.

All three of them drank tea while they talked. Bridget, who didn't make cakes because Liam hadn't liked them and she'd never since got into the way of it, had bought two kinds of biscuits and a Battenburg in Victor Value's. Alarmed at the last moment in case there wouldn't be enough and she'd be thought inhospitable, she had buttered some bread and put out a jar of apricot jam. She was glad she had because Norma's husband made quite a meal of it, taking most of the gingersnaps and folding the sliced bread into sandwiches. Norma didn't eat anything.

'I can't have another baby, Mrs Lacy. That's the point, if you get what I mean? Like after Betty I had to have an abortion and then two more, horrible they were, the last one a bit of trouble really. I mean, it left my insides like this.'

'Oh dear, I'm sorry.'

Nodding, as if in gratitude for this sympathy, Norma's husband reached for a gingersnap. He said they had a nice flat and there were other children living near by for Betty to play with. He glanced around the small living-room, which was choked with pieces of furniture and ornaments which Bridget was always resolving to weed out. In what he said, and in the way he looked, there was the implication that this room in a cramped house was an unsuitable habitat for a spirited four-year-old. There was also the implication that Bridget at forty-nine, and without a husband, belonged more naturally among the sacred pictures on the walls than she possibly could in a world of toys and children. It was Betty they had to think of, the young man's concerned expression insisted; it was Betty's well-being.

'We signed the papers at the time.' Bridget endeavoured, not successfully, to make her protest sound different from an apology. 'When a baby's adopted that's meant to be that.'

Norma's husband nodded, as if agreeing that that was a reasonable point of view also. Norma said:

'You were kindness itself to me, Mrs Lacy, you and your husband. Didn't I say so?' she added, turning to her companion, who nodded again.

The baby had been born when Norma was nineteen. There'd been an effort on her part to look after it, but within a month she'd found the task impossible. She'd been living at the time in the house across the road from the Lacys', in a bed-sitting-room. She'd had a bad reputation in the neighbourhood, even reputed to be a prostitute, which wasn't in fact true. Bridget had always nodded to her in the street, and she'd always smiled back. Remembering all that when Norma had telephoned a day or two ago, Bridget found she had retained an impression of chipped red varnish on the girl's fingernails and her shrunken whey-white face. There'd been a prettiness about her too, though, and there still was. 'I don't know what to do,' she'd said four years ago. 'I don't know why I've had this kid.' She'd said it quite out of the blue, crossing the street to where Bridget had paused for a moment on the pavement to change the shopping she was carrying from one hand to the other. 'I often see you,' Norma had added, and Bridget, who noticed that she had recently been weeping and indeed looked quite ill, had invited her in for a cup of tea. Once or twice the sound of the baby's crying had drifted across the street, and of course she'd been quite interested to watch the progress of the pregnancy. Local opinion decreed that the pregnancy was what you'd expect of this girl, but Bridget didn't easily pass judgement. As Irish people in London, there was a politeness about the Lacys, a reluctance to condemn anyone who was English since they themselves were not. 'I've been a fool about this kid,' the girl had said: the father had let her down, as simple as that. He'd seemed as steady as a rock, but one night he hadn't been in the Queen's Arms and he hadn't been there the next night either, in fact not ever again.

'I couldn't let Betty go,' Bridget said, her face becoming hot again. 'I couldn't possibly. That's quite out of the question.'

A silence hung in the living-room for a moment. The air seemed heavier and stuffier, and Bridget wanted to open a window but did not. Betty was spending the afternoon with Mrs Grounds, who was always good about having her on the rare occasions when it was necessary.

'No, it's not a question of letting her go,' the young man said. 'No one would think of it like that, Mrs Lacy.'

'We'd always like her to see you,' Norma explained. 'I mean, it stands to reason she'll have got fond of you.'

The young man again nodded, his features good-humouredly crinkled. There was no question, he repeated, of the relationship between the child and her adoptive mother being broken off. An arrangement that was suitable all round could easily be made, and any offer of babysitting would always be more than welcome. 'What's needed, Mrs Lacy, is for mother and child to be together. Now that the circumstances have altered.'

'It's two years since my husband left me.'

'I'm thinking of Norma's circumstances, Mrs Lacy.'

'I can't help wanting her,' Norma said, her lean cheeks working beneath her make-up. Her legs were crossed, the right one over the left. Her shoes, in soft pale leather, were a lot smarter than the shoes Bridget remembered from the past. So was her navy-blue shirt and her navy-blue corduroy jacket that zipped up the front. Her fingers were marked with nicotine, and Bridget knew she wanted to light a cigarette now, the way she had repeatedly done the first day she'd come to the sitting-room, six years ago.

'We made it all legal,' Bridget said, putting into different words what she had stated already. 'Everything was legal, Norma.'

'Yes, we do know that,' the young man replied, still patiently smiling, making her feel foolish. 'But there's the human side too, you see. Perhaps more important than legalities.'

He was better educated than Norma, Bridget noticed; and there was an honest niceness in his eyes when he referred to the human side. There was justice above the ordinary justice of solicitors' documents and law courts, his niceness insisted: Norma had been the victim of an unfair society and all they could do now was to see that the unfairness should not be perpetuated.

'I'm sorry,' Bridget said. 'I'm sorry I can't see it like that.'

Soon after that the visitors left, leaving behind them the feeling that they and Bridget would naturally be meeting again. She went to collect Betty from Mrs Grounds and after tea they settled down to a familiar routine: Betty's bath and then bed, a few minutes of *The Tailor of Gloucester*. The rest of the evening stretched emptily ahead, with *Dallas* on the television, and a cardigan she was knitting. She quite liked *Dallas*, J.R. in particular, the most villainous TV figure she could think of, but while she watched his villainy now the conversation she'd had with her afternoon visitors kept recurring. Betty's round face, and the black hair that curved in smoothly on either side of it, appeared in her mind, and there was also the leanness of Norma and the sincerity of the man who wanted to become Betty's stepfather. The three faces went together as if they belonged, for though Betty's was differently shaped from the face of the woman who had given birth to her she had the same wide mouth and the same brown eyes.

At half past nine Miss Custle came into the house. She was an oldish woman who worked on the Underground and often had to keep odd hours, some days leaving the house shortly after dawn and on other days not until the late afternoon. 'Cup of tea, Miss Custle?' Bridget called out above the noise of the television.

'Well, thanks, Mrs Lacy,' Miss Custle replied, as she always did when this invitation came. She had a gas stove and a sink in her room and did all her cooking there, but whenever Bridget heard her coming in as late as this she offered her a cup of tea. She'd been a lodger in the house ever since the break-up of the marriage, a help in making ends meet.

'Those people came,' Bridget said, offering Miss Custle what remained of the gingersnaps. 'You know: Norma.'

'I told you to beware of them. Upset you, did they?'

'Well, talking about Betty like that. You know, Betty didn't even have a name when we adopted her. It was we thought of Betty.'

'You told me.'

Miss Custle was a powerful, grey-haired woman in a London Transport uniform which smelt of other people's cigarettes. Earlier in her life there'd been a romance with someone else on the Underground, but without warning the man had died. Shocked by the unexpectedness of it, Miss Custle had remained on her own for the next thirty years, and was given to gloom when she recalled the time of her loss. Among her colleagues on the Underground she was known for her gruffness and her devotion to the tasks she had performed for so much of her life. The London Underground, she occasionally stated in Bridget's living-room, had become her life, a substitute for what might have been. But tonight her mood was brisk.

'When a child's adopted, Mrs Lacy, there's no way it can be reversed. As I told you last evening, dear.'

'Yes, I do know that. I said it to them.'

'Trying it on, they was.'

With that, Miss Custle rose to her feet, and said good-night. She never stayed long when she looked in for a cup of tea and a biscuit because she was usually tired. Her face took on a crumpled look, matching her crumpled uniform. She would iron her uniform before her next turn of duty, taking ages over it.

'Good-night, Miss Custle,' Bridget said, observing the weary passage of her lodger across the living-room and wondering just for a moment what the man who'd died had been like. One night, a year or so ago, she had told Miss Custle all about her own loss, not of course that it could be compared with death, although it had felt like it at the time. 'Horrible type of woman, that is,' Miss Custle had said.

Bridget cleared up the tea things and unplugged the television lead. She knew she wouldn't sleep properly: the visit of Norma and her husband had stirred everything up again, forcing her to travel backwards in time, to survey again all she had come to terms with. It was extraordinary that they'd thought she'd even consider handing Betty over to them.

In her bedroom she undressed and tidily arranged her clothes on a chair. She could hear Miss Custle moving about in her room next door, undressing also. Betty had murmured in her sleep when she'd kissed her good-night, and Bridget tried to imagine what life would be like not having Betty there to tuck up last thing, not having Betty's belongings about the house, her clothes to wash, toys to pick up. Sometimes Betty made her cross, but that was part of it too.

She lay in the darkness, her mind going back again. In the countryside of Co. Cork she had been one of a family of ten, and Liam had come from a large family also. It had astonished them when years later they had failed to have children of their own, but in no way had the disappointment impaired their marriage; and then Betty's presence had drawn them even closer together. 'I'm sorry,' Liam had said in the end, though, the greatest shock she'd ever had. 'I'm sorry, dear.'

Bridget had never seen the woman, but had imagined her: younger than she was, a Londoner, black hair like silk, predatory lips, and eyes that looked away from you. This woman and her mother had bought the newsagent's where Liam had worked for all his years in London, the manager more or less, under old Mr Vanish. The woman had been married before, an unhappy marriage according to Liam, a relationship that had left her wounded. 'Dear, it's serious,' he had said, trying to keep out of his voice a lightness that was natural in it, not realizing that he was opening a wound himself. In everything he said there was the implication that the love he'd felt for Bridget, though in no way false, hadn't been touched by the same kind of excitement.

The newsagent's shop was in another neighbourhood, miles across London, but in the days of old Mr Vanish Bridget would just occasionally take Betty on a number 9 bus. When the woman and her mother took over the business some kind of shyness prevented the continuation of this habit, and after that some kind of fear. She had been ready to forgive Liam, to live in the hope that his infatuation would be washed away by time. She pleaded, but did not make scenes. She didn't scream at him or parade his treachery, or call the woman names. None of that came easily to Bridget, and all she could wonder was what life would be like if Liam stayed with her and went on loving the woman. It wasn't hard to imagine the bitterness that would develop in him, the hatred there would be in the end, yet she had continued to plead. Six weeks later he was gone.

For a moment in the darkness she wept. It was true what she'd said to her visitors that afternoon: that she felt nothing now. It was true, yet sometimes she wept when she remembered how together they had weathered the strangeness of their emigration or when she thought of Liam now, living in mortal sin with the woman and her mother above the newsagent's, not going to Confession or Mass any more. Every month money arrived from him, which with Miss Custle's rent and what she earned herself from cleaning the Winnards' flat three times a week was enough to manage on. But Liam never came back, to see her or to see Betty, which implied the greatest change of all in him.

Memories were always difficult for her. Alone now, she too easily remembered the countryside she had grown up in, and the face of the Reverend Mother at the Presentation Convent, and Mrs Lynch's squat public house and grocery at a crossroads. Maureen Ryall had stolen her Phillips' atlas, putting ink blots over her name and substituting her own. Madge Foley had curled her hair for her. Liam had always been in the neighbouring farm, but until after they'd both left school she'd hardly noticed him. He'd asked her to go for a walk with him, and in a field that was yellow with buttercups he had taken her hand and kissed her, causing her to blush. He'd laughed at her, saying the pink in her cheeks was lovely. He was the first person she'd ever danced with, in a nameless roadside dance-hall, ten miles away.

It was then, while she was still a round-faced girl, that Bridget had first become aware of fate. It was what you had to accept, what you couldn't kick against: God's will, the Reverend Mother or Father Keogh would have said, but for Bridget it began with the kind of person you were. Out of that, the circumstances of your life emerged: Bridget's shyness and her tendency to blush, her prettiness and her modesty, were the fate which had been waiting for her before she was born, and often she felt that Liam had been waiting for her also, that they were fated to fall in love because they complemented each other so well, he so bouncy and amusing, she so fond of the shadows. In those days it would have been impossible to imagine that he would ever go off with a woman in a newsagent's.

They were married on a Saturday in June, in a year when the foxgloves were profuse. She wore a veil of Limerick lace, borrowed from her grandmother. She carried scarlet roses. Liam was handsome, dark as a Spaniard in the Church of the Holy Virgin, his blue eyes jokily darting about. She had been glad when all of it was over, the reception in Kelly's Hotel, the car bedecked with ribbons. They'd gone away for three days, and soon after they'd returned they had had to emigrate to England because the sawmills where Liam had a job closed down. They'd been in London for more than twenty years when the woman came into his life.

Eventually Bridget slept, and dreamed of the countryside of her childhood. She sat on a cart beside her father, permitted to hold the reins of the horse while empty milk churns were rattled back from the creamery at the crossroads. Liam was suddenly there, trudging along in the dust, and her father drew up the reins in order to give him a lift. Liam was ten or eleven, a patch of sunburn on the back of his neck where his hair had been cut very short. It wasn't really a dream, because all of it had happened in the days when Liam hadn't been important.

Norma's husband came on his own. 'I hope you've no objection, Mrs Lacy,' he said, smiling in his wide-eyed way. There was a wave in his fairish hair, she noticed, a couple of curls hanging over his forehead. Everything about him was agreeable.

'Well, really I don't know.' She faltered, immediately feeling hot. 'I really think it's better if we don't go on about it.'

'I won't keep you ten minutes, Mrs Lacy. I promise.'

She held the hall-door open and he walked into the hall. He stepped over a Weetabix packet which Betty had thrown down and strode away from. In the kitchen Betty was unpacking the rest of the shopping, making a kind of singing noise, which she often did.

'Sit down,' Bridget said in the living-room, as she would to any visitor.

'Thanks, Mrs Lacy,' he said politely.

'I won't be a minute.'

She had to see to Betty in the kitchen. There was flour among the shopping, and eggs, and other items in bags that might become perforated or would break when dropped from the kitchen table to the floor. Betty wasn't naughtier than any other child, but only a week ago, left on her own, she'd tried to make a cake.

'You go and get the Weetabix,' Bridget said, and Betty obediently marched into the hall to do so. Bridget hastily put the rest of the shopping out of reach. She took coloured pencils and a new colouring-book from a drawer and laid them out on the table. Betty didn't much care for filling already-drawn outlines with colour and generally just scrawled her name all over them: *Betty Lacy* in red, and again in blue and orange and green.

'Be a good big girl now,' Bridget said.

'Big,' Betty repeated.

In the sitting-room Norma's husband had picked up the *Cork Weekly Examiner*. As she entered, he replaced it on the pile of magazines near his armchair, saying that it appeared to be interesting.

'It's hard to know how to put this to you, Mrs Lacy.' He paused, his smile beginning to fade. Seriousness invaded his face as his eyes passed over the contents of the living-room, over the sacred pictures and the odds and ends that Bridget had been meaning to throw out. He said:

'Norma was in a bad way when I met up with her, Mrs Lacy. She'd been to the Samaritans; it was from them I heard about her. I'm employed by the council, actually. Social Services, counselling. That's my job, see.'

'Yes, I understand.'

'Norma was suffering from depression. Unhappiness, Mrs Lacy. She got in touch with the Samaritans and later she came round to us. I was able to help her. I won her confidence through the counselling I could give her. I love Norma now, Mrs Lacy.'

'Of course.'

'It doesn't often happen that way. A counsellor and a client.'

'No, I'm sure not.' She interrupted because she knew he was going to continue with that theme, to tell her more about a relationship that wasn't her business. She said that to herself. She said to herself that six years ago Norma had drifted into her life, leaving behind a child. She said to herself that the adoption of Betty had been at Norma's request. 'You're a lovely person, Mrs Lacy,' Norma had said at the time.

'I can't get to her at the moment,' Norma's husband explained. 'Ever since the other day she's hiding within herself. All the good that's been done, Mrs Lacy, all the care of our own relationship: it's going for nothing, you see.'

'I'm sorry.'

'She went to the Samaritans because she was suicidal. There was nothing left of the poor thing, Mrs Lacy. She was hardly a human person.'

'But Betty, you see – Betty has become my child.'

'I know, I know, Mrs Lacy.' He nodded earnestly, understandingly. 'The Samaritans gave Norma back her humanity, and then the council housed her. When she was making the recovery we fell in love. You understand, Mrs Lacy? Norma and I fell in love.'

'Yes, I do understand that.'

'We painted the flat out together. Saturdays we spent buying bits of furniture, month by month, what we could afford. We made a home because a home was what Norma had never had. She never knew her parents: I don't know if you were aware of that? Norma comes of a deprived background, she had no education, not to speak of. When I first met her, I had to help her read a newspaper.' Suddenly he smiled. 'She's much better now, of course.'

Bridget felt a silence gathering, the kind there'd been several of the other afternoon. She broke it herself, speaking as calmly as she could, trying to hold her visitor's eye but not succeeding because he was glancing round the living-room again.

'I'm sorry for Norma,' she said. 'I was sorry for her at the time, that is why I took in Betty. Only my husband and I insisted that it had to be legal and through the proper channels. We were advised about that, in case there was trouble later.'

'Trouble? Who advised you, Mrs Lacy?' He blinked and frowned. His voice sounded almost dense.

'We went to a solicitor,' she said, remembering that solicitor, small and moustached, recommended by Father Gogarty. He'd been very helpful; he'd explained everything.

'Mrs Lacy, I don't want to sound rude but there are two angles we can examine this case from. There is Norma's and there is your own. You've seen the change in Norma; you must take my word for it that she could easily revert. Then consider yourself, Mrs Lacy, as another person might see you, a person like myself for instance, a case-worker if you like, an outsider.'

'I don't think of it as a case, with angles or anything else. I really don't want to go on like this. Please.'

'I know it's difficult, and I'm sorry. But when the baby has become an adolescent you could find it hard to cope, Mrs Lacy. I see a lot of that in my work, a woman on her own, no father figure in the home. I know you have a caring relationship with Betty, Mrs Lacy, but the fact can't be altered that you're alone in this house with her, day in day out. All I'm saying is that another case-worker might comment on that.'

'There's Miss Custle too.'

'I beg your pardon, Mrs Lacy?'

'There's a lodger, Miss Custle.'

'You have a lodger? Another woman on her own?'

'Yes.'

'Young, is she?'

'No, Miss Custle isn't young.'

'An elderly woman, Mrs Lacy?'

'Miss Custle still works on the Underground.'

'The Underground?'

'Yes.'

'You see, Mrs Lacy, what might be commented upon is the lack of playmates. Just yourself, and a woman who is employed on the Underground. Again, Mrs Lacy, I'm not saying there isn't caring. I'm not saying that for an instant.'

'Betty is happy. Look, I'm afraid I'd rather you didn't come here again. I have things to do now —'

'I'm sorry to offend you, Mrs Lacy.'

She had stood up, making him stand up also. He nodded and smiled at her in his patient manner, which she now realized was professional, he being a counsellor. He said again he was sorry he'd offended her.

'I just thought you'd want to hear about Norma,' he said before he left, and on the doorstep he suddenly became awkward. The smile and the niceness vanished: solemnity replaced them. 'It's like putting a person together again. If you know what I mean, Mrs Lacy.'

In the kitchen Betty printed her name across the stomach of a whale. She heard voices in the hall, but paid them no attention. A moment later the door banged and then her mother came into the kitchen.

'Look,' Betty said, but to her surprise her mother didn't. Her mother hugged her, whispering her name. 'You've been washing your face,' Betty said. 'It's all cold.'

That afternoon Bridget cleaned the Winnards' flat, taking Betty with her, as she always did. She wondered about mentioning the trouble she was having with Norma and her husband to Mrs Winnard, who might suggest something for her to say so that the matter could be ended. Mrs Winnard was pretty and bespectacled, a kind young woman, full of sympathy, but that afternoon her two obstreperous boys, twins of two and a half, were giving her quite a time so Bridget didn't say anything. She hoovered the hallway and the bathroom and the four bedrooms, looking into the kitchen from time to time, where Betty was playing with the Winnard boys' bricks. She still hadn't said anything when the time came to pack up to go, and suddenly she was glad she hadn't because quite out of the blue she found herself imagining a look on Mrs Winnard's sympathetic face which suggested that the argument of Norma and her husband could not in all humanity be just dismissed. Bridget couldn't imagine Mrs Winnard actually saying so, but her intuition about the reaction remained.

In the park, watching Betty on a slide, she worried about that. Would the same thing happen if she talked to Father Gogarty? Would an instant of hesitation be reflected in his bony grey features as he, too, considered that Norma should not be passed by? Not everyone had experienced as awful a life as Norma had. On top of that, the regret of giving away the only child you had been able to have was probably a million times worse than simply being childless.

Not really wishing to, Bridget remembered how fate had seemed to her when she was a girl: that it began with the kind of person you were. 'We're greedy,' Liam had confessed, speaking of himself and the woman. 'I suppose we're made like that, we can't help it.' The woman was greedy, he had meant, making it cosier by saying he was too.

She watched Betty on the slide. She waved at her and Betty waved back. You couldn't call Norma greedy, not in the same way. Norma made a mess of things and then looked around for other people: someone to look after a child that had been carelessly born, the Samaritans, the man she'd married. In the end Norma was lucky because she'd survived, because all the good in her had been allowed to surface. It was the man's love that had done that, his gentleness and his sincerity. You couldn't begrudge her anything. Like Liam and the woman, fate had come up trumps for her because of the person she was.

'Watch, Mummy,' Betty shouted from the top of the slide, and again Betty watched her sliding down it.

Eventually Bridget did speak to Mrs Winnard and to Father Gogarty because it was hard to keep the upset to herself, and because it worried her even more when she kept telling herself that she was being imaginative about what their reaction would be. Mrs Winnard said the couple's presumption was almost a matter for the police; Father Gogarty offered to go and see them, if they could easily be found. But before either Mrs Winnard or the priest spoke Bridget was certain that the brief flicker she'd been dreading had come into their faces. There had been the hesitation and the doubt and – far quicker than thought – the feeling that a child belonged more suitably with a young married couple than with a lone middle-aged woman and an ageing employee of the London Underground. In continuing to talk about it to Miss Custle herself, Bridget could swear she experienced the same intuition: beneath all Miss Custle's outrage and fury there was the same reasonable doubt.

The telephone rang one evening and the young man's voice said:

'Norma hasn't done anything silly. I just thought you'd like to know that, Mrs Lacy.'

'Yes, of course. I'm glad she's all right.'

'Well, she's not really all right of course. But she does take heart from your caring in the past.'

'I did what a lot of people would have done.'

'You did what was necessary, Mrs Lacy. You understood a cry for help. It's an unpleasant fact, but neither she nor Betty might be alive today if it hadn't been for you.'

'Oh, I can't believe that for an instant.'

'I think you have to, you know. There's only one small point, Mrs Lacy, if you could bear with me. I spoke to a colleague about this case – well, having a personal interest, I thought I better. You may remember I mentioned an outsider? Well, strangely enough my colleague raised an interesting question.'

'Look, I don't want to go on talking about any of this. I've told you I couldn't even begin to contemplate what you're suggesting.'

'My colleague pointed out that it isn't just Norma's circumstances which have changed, nor indeed your own. There's a third factor in all this, my colleague pointed out: this child is being brought up as the child of Irish parents. Well, fair enough you may say, Mrs Lacy, until you remember that the Irish are a different kettle of fish today from what they were ten years ago. How easy is it, you have to ask yourself, to be a child of Irish parents today, to bear an Irish name, to be a member of the Roman Catholic Church? That child will have to attend a London school, for instance, where there could easily be hostility. Increasingly we come across this in our work, Mrs Lacy.'

'Betty is my child –'

'Of course. That's quite understood, Mrs Lacy. But what my colleague pointed out is that sooner or later Norma is going to worry about the Irish thing as well. What will go through her mind is that it's not just a question of her baby being affected by a broken marriage, but of her baby being brought up in an atmosphere that isn't always pleasant. I'm sorry to mention it, Mrs Lacy, but, as my colleague says, no mother on earth would care to lie awake at night and worry about that.'

Her hand felt hot and damp on the telephone receiver. She imagined the young man sitting in an office, concerned and serious, and then smiling as he tried to find a bright side. She imagined Norma in their newly decorated flat, needing her child because everything was different now, hoping.

'I can't go on talking to you. I'm sorry.'

She replaced the receiver, and immediately found herself thinking about Liam. It was Liam's fault as well as hers that Betty had been adopted and was now to be regarded as the child of Irish parents. Liam had always firmly regarded himself as Betty's father, even if he never came near her now.

She didn't want to go and see him. She didn't want to make the journey on a number 9 bus, she didn't want to have to see the woman's predatory lips. But even as she thought that, she could hear herself asking Mrs Grounds to have Betty for a couple of hours one afternoon. 'Hullo, Liam,' she said a few days later in the newsagent's.

She'd waited until there were no customers, and to her relief the woman wasn't there. The woman's old mother, very fat and dressed all in brown, was resting in an armchair in a little room behind the shop itself, a kind of storeroom it seemed to be, with stacks of magazines tied with string, just as they'd come off the van.

'Heavens above!' Liam said.

'Liam, could I have a word?'

The old woman appeared to be asleep. She hadn't moved when Bridget had spoken. She was wearing a hat, and seemed a bit eccentric, sleeping there among the bundles of magazines.

'Of course you could, dear. How are you, Bridget?'

'I'm fine, Liam. And yourself?'

'I'm fine too, dear.'

She told him quickly. Customers hurried in for the *Evening Standard* or *Dalton's Weekly*, children paused on their way home from school. Liam looked for rubbers and ink cartridges, Yorkie bars and tubes of fruit pastilles. Twice he said that the *New Musical Express* didn't come out till Thursday. 'Extraordinary, how some of them forget that,' he said.

He listened to her carefully, picking up the thread of what she told him after each interruption. Because once they'd known one another so well, she mentioned the intuition she felt where Father Gogarty and Mrs Winnard and Miss Custle were concerned. She watched the expressions changing on his face, and she could feel him nodding inwardly: she felt him thinking that she was the same as she'd always been, nervous where other people were concerned, too modest and unsure of herself.

'I'll never forget how pretty you looked,' he said suddenly, and for no reason that Bridget could see. 'Wasn't everything great long ago, Bridie?'

'It's Betty we have to think of, Liam. The old days are over and done with.'

'I often go back to them. I'll never forget them, dear.'

He was trying to be nice, but it seemed to Bridget that he was saying she still belonged to the time he spoke of, that she had not managed to come to terms with life as it had been since. You had to be tougher to come to terms with a world that was tough itself, you had to get over being embarrassed when you were pulled out of the background. All that hadn't mattered long ago; when Maureen Ryall had stolen her atlas she hadn't even complained. Being stolen from, she suddenly thought.

'I don't know what to say to them,' she said. 'The man keeps telephoning me.'

'Tell him to leave you alone, Bridget. Tell him he has no business bothering you.'

'I've tried saying that.'

'Tell him the thing was legally done and he hasn't a foot to stand on. Tell him he can be up for harassment.'

A child came into the shop and Liam had to look for drawing-pins. 'I'm afraid I have to shut up now,' he said when the child had gone, and as he spoke the old woman in the armchair stirred. She spoke his name. She said she'd fancy peaches for tea. 'There's a tin set aside for you, dear,' Liam said, winking at Bridget. He had raised his voice to address the old woman. He lowered it again to say goodbye. 'The best of luck with it,' he said, and Bridget knew he meant it.

'Thanks, Liam.' She tried to smile, and realized that she hadn't repeated the young man's remarks about Betty being brought up in a hostile atmosphere. She almost did so, standing at the door of the shop, imagining Liam angrily saying that the man needed putting in his place and offering to meet him. But as she walked away she knew all that was make-belief. Liam had his own life to live, peaches and a sort of mother-in-law. He couldn't be blamed for only wishing her luck.

She collected Betty from Mrs Grounds and later in the evening, when she was watching television, the telephone rang. The young man said:

'I'm sorry, Mrs Lacy, I didn't mean to bring up that thing about your nationality. It's not your fault, Mrs Lacy, and please forget I mentioned it. I'm sorry.'

'Please don't telephone me again. That's all I ask. I've given you the only answer I can.'

'I know you have, Mrs Lacy. You've been kind to listen to me, and I know you're concerned for Norma, don't think I'm not aware of that. I love Norma, Mrs Lacy, which has made me a little unprofessional in my conversations with you, but I promise we'll neither of us bother you again. It was just that she felt she'd made a terrible mistake and all the poor thing wanted was to rectify it. But as my work so often shows me, Mrs Lacy, that is hardly ever possible. Are you there, Mrs Lacy?'

'Yes, I'm here.'

'I'll never stop loving Norma, Mrs Lacy. I promise you that also. No matter what happens to her now.'

She sat alone in her living-room watching the ten o'clock news, and when she heard Miss Custle in the hall she didn't offer her a cup of tea. Instead of Betty's rattling feet on the stairs there would be Miss Custle's aged panting as she propelled her bulk to her upstairs room. Instead of Betty's wondering questions there would be Miss Custle's gloom as still she mourned her long departed lover.

The television news came to an end, an advertisement for Australian margarine began. Soon after that the programmes ceased altogether, but Bridget continued to sit in her living-room, weeping without making a noise. Several times she went upstairs and stood with the light on by Betty's bed, gazing at the child, not wiping away her tears. For Betty's well-being, and for Norma's too, in all humanity the law would be reversed. No longer would she search the faces of Father Gogarty and Mrs Winnard and Miss Custle for the signs of what they really believed. They would put that into words by saying she was good and had courage.

In the countryside of long ago her failure in marriage and motherhood might be easier to bear, but she would be a stranger there now. She belonged among her accumulated odds and ends, as Betty belonged with her mother, and Liam with the woman he loved. She would look after Miss Custle when Miss Custle retired from the Underground, as fate dictated.

Mr Tennyson

He had, romantically, a bad reputation. He had a wife and several children. His carry-on with Sarah Spence was a legend among a generation of girls, and the story was that none of it had stopped with Sarah Spence. His old red Ford Escort had been reported drawn up in quiet lay-bys; often he spent weekends away from home; Annie Green had come across him going somewhere on a train once, alone and morose in the buffet car. Nobody's parents were aware of the facts about him, nor were the other staff, nor even the boys at the school. His carry-on with Sarah Spence, and coming across him or his car, were a little tapestry of secrets that suddenly was yours when you became fifteen and a senior, a member of 2A. For the rest of your time at Foxfield Comprehensive – for the rest of your life, preferably – you didn't breathe a word to people whose business it wasn't.

It was understandable when you looked at him that parents and staff didn't guess. It was also understandable that his activities were protected by the senior girls. He was forty years old. He had dark hair with a little grey in it, and a face that was boyish – like a French boy's, someone had once said, and the description had stuck, often to be repeated. There was a kind of ragamuffin innocence about his eyes. The cast of his lips suggested a melancholy nature and his smile, when it came, had sadness in it too. His name was Mr Tennyson. His subject was English.

Jenny, arriving one September in 2A, learnt all about him. She remembered Sarah Spence, a girl at the top of the school when she had been at the bottom, tall and beautiful. He carried on because he was unhappily married, she was informed. Consider where he lived even: trapped in a tiny gate-lodge on the Ilminster road because he couldn't afford anything better, trapped with a wife and children when he deserved freedom. Would he one day publish poetry as profound as his famous namesake's, though of course more up-to-date? Or was his talent lost for ever? One way or the other he was made for love.

It seemed to Jenny that the girls of 2A eyed one another, wondering which among them would become a successor to Sarah Spence. They eyed the older girls, of Class 1, 1A and 1B, wondering which of them was already her successor, discreetly taking her place in the red Ford Escort on dusky afternoons. He would never be coarse, you couldn't imagine coarseness in him. He'd never try anything unpleasant, he'd never in a million years fumble at you. He'd just be there, being himself, smelling faintly of fresh tobacco, the fingers of a hand perhaps brushing your arm by accident.

'Within the play,' he suggested in his soft voice, almost a whisper, 'order is represented by the royal house of Scotland. We must try and remember Shakespeare's point of view, how Shakespeare saw these things.'

They were studying *Macbeth* and *Huckleberry Finn* with him, but when he talked about Shakespeare it seemed more natural and suited to him than when he talked about Mark Twain.

'On Duncan's death,' he said, 'should the natural order continue, his son Malcolm would become king. Already Duncan has indicated – by making Malcolm Prince of Cumberland – that he considers him capable of ruling.'

Jenny had pale fair hair, the colour of ripened wheat. It fell from a divide at the centre of her head, two straight lines on either side of a thin face. Her eyes were large and of a faded blue. She was lanky, with legs which she considered to be too long but which her mother said she'd be thankful for one day.

'Disruption is everywhere, remember,' he said. 'Disruption in nature as well as in the royal house. Shakespeare insinuates a comparison between what is happening in human terms and in terms of nature. On the night of Duncan's death there is a sudden storm in which chimneys are blown off and houses shaken. Mysterious screams are heard. Horses go wild. A falcon is killed by a mousing owl.'

Listening to him, it seemed to Jenny that she could listen for ever, no matter what he said. At night, lying in bed with her eyes closed, she delighted in leisurely fantasies, of having breakfast with him and ironing his clothes, of walking beside him on a seashore or sitting beside him in his old Ford Escort. There was a particular story she repeated to herself: that she was on the promenade at Lyme Regis and that he came up to her and asked her if she'd like to go for a walk. They walked up to the cliffs and then along the cliff-path, and everything was different from Foxfield Comprehensive because they were alone together. His wife and he had been divorced, he told her, having agreed between themselves that they were incompatible. He was leaving Foxfield Comprehensive because a play he'd written was going to be done on the radio and another one on the London stage. 'Oh, darling,' she said, daring to say it. 'Oh, Jenny,' he said.

Terms and holidays went by. Once, just before the Easter of that year, she met him with his wife, shopping in the International Stores in Ilminster. They had two of their four children with them, little boys with freckles. His wife had freckles also. She was a woman like a sack of something, Jenny considered, with thick, unhealthy-looking legs. He was pushing a trolley full of breakfast cereals and wrapped bread, and tins. Although he didn't speak to her or even appear to see her, it was a stroke of luck to come across him in the town because he didn't often come into the village. Foxfield had only half a dozen shops and the Bow and Arrow public house, even though it was enormous, a sprawling dormitory village that had had the new Comprehensive added to all the other new building in 1969.

Because of the position of the Tennysons' gate-lodge it was clearly more convenient for them to shop in Ilminster.

'Hullo, Mr Tennyson,' she said in the International Stores, and he turned and looked at her. He nodded and smiled.

Jenny moved into 1A at the end of that school year. She wondered if he'd noticed how her breasts had become bigger during the time she'd been in 2A, and how her complexion had definitely improved. Her breasts were quite presentable now, which was a relief because she'd had a fear that they weren't going to develop at all. She wondered if he'd noticed her Green Magic eye-shadow. Everyone said it suited her, except her father, who always blew up over things like that. Once she heard one of the new kids saying she was the prettiest girl in the school. Adam Swann and Chinny Martin from 1B kept hanging about, trying to chat her up. Chinny Martin even wrote her notes.

'You're mooning,' her father said. 'You don't take a pick of notice these days.'

'Exams,' her mother hastily interjected and afterwards, when Jenny was out of the room, quite sharply reminded her husband that adolescence was a difficult time for girls. It was best not to remark on things.

'I didn't mean a criticism, Ellie,' Jenny's father protested, aggrieved.

'They take it as a criticism. Every word. They're edgy, see.'

He sighed. He was a painter and decorator, with his own business. Jenny was their only child. There'd been four miscarriages, all of which might have been boys, which naturally were what he'd wanted, with the business. He'd have to sell it one day, but it didn't matter all that much when you thought about it. Having miscarriages was worse than selling a business, more depressing really. A woman's lot was harder than a man's, he'd decided long ago.

'Broody,' his wife diagnosed. 'Just normal broody. She'll see her way through it.'

Every evening her parents sat in their clean, neat sitting-room watching television. Her mother made tea at nine o'clock because it was nice to have a cup with the News. She always called upstairs to Jenny, but Jenny never wanted to have tea or see the News. She did her homework in her bedroom, a small room that was clean and neat also, with a pebbly cream wallpaper expertly hung by her father. At half-past ten she usually went down to the kitchen and made herself some Ovaltine. She drank it at the table with the cat, Tinkle, on her lap. Her mother usually came in with the tea things to wash up, and they might chat, the conversation consisting mainly of gossip from Foxfield Comprehensive, although never of course containing a reference to Mr Tennyson. Sometimes Jenny didn't feel like chatting and wouldn't, feigning sleepiness. If she sat there long enough her father would come in to fetch himself a cup of water because he always liked to have one near him in the night. He couldn't help glancing at her eye-shadow when he said good-night and she could see him making an effort not to mention it, having doubtless been told not to by her mother. They did their best. She liked them very much. She loved them, she supposed.

But not in the way she loved Mr Tennyson. 'Robert Tennyson,' she murmured to herself in bed. 'Oh, Robert dear.' Softly his lips were there, and the smell of fresh tobacco made her swoon, forcing her to close her eyes. 'Oh, yes,' she said. 'Oh, yes, yes.' He lifted the dress over her head. His hands were taut, charged with their shared passion. 'My love,' he said in his soft voice, almost a whisper. Every night before she went to sleep his was the face that entirely filled her mind. Had it once not been there she would have thought herself faithless. And every morning, in a ceremonial way, she conjured it up again, first thing, pride of place.

Coming out of Harper's the newsagent's one Saturday afternoon, she found waiting for her, not Mr Tennyson, but Chinny Martin, with his motor-cycle on its pedestal in the street. He asked her if she'd like to go for a spin into the country and offered to supply her with a crash helmet. He was wearing a crash helmet himself, a bulbous red object with a peak and a windshield that fitted over his eyes. He was also wearing heavy plastic gloves, red also, and a red windcheater. He was smiling at her, the spots on his pronounced chin more noticeable after exposure to the weather on his motor-cycle. His eyes were serious, closely fixed on hers.

She shook her head at him. There was hardly anything she'd have disliked more than a ride into the country with Chinny Martin, her arms half round his waist, a borrowed crash helmet making her feel silly. He'd stop the motor-cycle in a suitable place and he'd suggest something like a walk to the river or to some old ruin or into a wood. He'd suggest sitting down and then he'd begin to fumble at her, and his chin would be sticking into her face, cold and unpleasant. His fingernails would be ingrained, as the fingernails of boys who owned motor-cycles always were.

'Thanks all the same,' she said.

'Come on, Jenny.'

'No, I'm busy. Honestly. I'm working at home.'

It couldn't have been pleasant, being called Chinny just because you had a jutting chin. Nicknames were horrible: there was a boy called Nut Adams and another called Wet Small and a girl called Kisses. Chinny Martin's name was Clive, but she'd never heard anyone calling him that. She felt sorry for him, standing there in his crash helmet and his special clothes. He'd probably planned it all, working it out that she'd be impressed by his gear and his motor-cycle. But of course she wasn't. *Yamaha* it said on the petrol tank of the motor-cycle, and there was a girl in a swimsuit which he had presumably stuck on to the tank himself. The girl's swimsuit was yellow and so was her hair, which was streaming out behind her, as if caught in a wind. The petrol tank was black.

'Jenny,' he said, lowering his voice so that it became almost croaky. 'Listen, Jenny –'

'Sorry.'

She began to walk away, up the village street, but he walked beside her, pushing the Yamaha.

'I love you, Jenny,' he said.

She laughed because she felt embarrassed.

'I can't bear not seeing you, Jenny.'

'Oh, well –'

'Jenny.'

They were passing the petrol-pumps, the Orchard Garage. Mr Batten was on the pavement, wiping oil from his hands with a rag. 'How's he running?' he called out to Chinny Martin, referring to the Yamaha, but Chinny Martin ignored the question.

'I think of you all the time, Jenny.'

'Oh, Clive, don't be silly.' She felt silly herself, calling him by his proper name.

'D'you like me, Jenny?'

'Of course I like you.' She smiled at him, trying to cover up the lie: she didn't particularly like him, she didn't particularly not. She just felt sorry for him, with his noticeable chin and the nickname it had given him. His father worked in the powdered milk factory. He'd do the same: you could guess that all too easily.

'Come for a ride with me, Jenny.'

'No, honestly.'

'Why not then?'

'It's better not to start anything, Clive. Look, don't write me notes.'

'Don't you like my notes?'

'I don't want to start anything.'

'There's someone else, is there, Jenny? Adam Swann? Rick Hayes?'

He sounded like a character in a television serial; he sounded sloppy and stupid.

'If you knew how I feel about you,' he said, lowering his voice even more. 'I love you like anything. It's the real thing.'

'I like you too, Clive. Only not in that way,' she hastily added.

'Wouldn't you ever? Wouldn't you even try?'

'I've told you.'

'Rick Hayes is only after sex.'

'I don't like Rick Hayes.'

'Any girl with legs on her is all he wants.'

'Yes, I know.'

'I can't concentrate on things, Jenny. I think of you the entire time.'

'I'm sorry.'

'Oh God, Jenny.'

She turned into the Mace shop just to escape. She picked up a wire basket and pretended to be looking at tins of cat food. She heard the roar of the Yamaha as her admirer rode away, and it seemed all wrong that he should have gone like that, so noisily when he was so upset.

At home she thought about the incident. It didn't in the least displease her that a boy had passionately proclaimed love for her. It even made her feel quite elated. She felt pleasantly warm when she thought about it, and the feeling bewildered her. That she, so much in love with someone else, should be moved in the very least by the immature protestations of a youth from 1B was a mystery. She even considered telling her mother about the incident, but in the end decided not to. 'Quite sprightly, she seems,' she heard her father murmuring.

'In every line of that sonnet,' Mr Tennyson said the following Monday afternoon, 'there is evidence of the richness that makes Shakespeare not just our own greatest writer but the world's as well.'

She listened, enthralled, physically pleasured by the utterance of each syllable. There was a tiredness about his boyish eyes, as if he hadn't slept. His wife had probably been bothering him, wanting him to do jobs around the house when he should have been writing sonnets of his own. She imagined him unable to sleep, lying there worrying about things, about his life. She imagined his wife like a grampus beside him, her mouth open, her upper lip as coarse as a man's.

'When forty winters shall besiege thy brow,' he said, 'And dig deep trenches in thy beauty's field.'

Dear Jenny, a note that morning from Chinny Martin had protested. *I just want to be with you. I just want to talk to you. Please come out with me.*

'Jenny, stay a minute,' Mr Tennyson said when the bell went. 'Your essay.'

Immediately there was tension among the girls of 1A, as if the English master had caused threads all over the classroom to become taut. Unaware, the boys proceeded as they always did, throwing books into their briefcases and sauntering into the corridor. The girls lingered over anything they could think of. Jenny approached Mr Tennyson's desk.

'It's very good,' he said, opening her essay book. 'But you're getting too fond of using three little dots at the end of a sentence. The sentence should imply the dots. It's like underlining to suggest emphasis, a bad habit also.'

One by one the girls dribbled from the classroom, leaving behind them the shreds of their reluctance. Out of all of them he had chosen her: was she to be another Sarah Spence, or just some kind of stop-gap, like other girls since Sarah Spence were rumoured to have been? But as he continued to talk about her essay – called *Belief in Ghosts* – she wondered if she'd even be a stop-gap. His fingers didn't once brush the back of her hand. His French boy's eyes didn't linger once on hers.

'I've kept you late,' he said in the end.

'That's all right, sir.'

'You will try to keep your sentences short? Your descriptions have a way of becoming too complicated.'

'I'll try, sir.'

'I really enjoyed that essay.'

He handed her the exercise book and then, without any doubt whatso-ever, he smiled meaningfully into her eyes. She felt herself going hot. Her hands became clammy. She just stood there while his glance passed over her eye-shadow, over her nose and cheeks, over her mouth.

'You're very pretty,' he said.

'Thank you, sir.'

Her voice reminded her of the croak in Chinny Martin's when he'd been telling her he loved her. She tried to smile, but could not. She wanted his hand to reach out and push her gently away from him so that he could see her properly. But it didn't. He stared into her eyes again, as if endeavouring to ascertain their precise shade of blue.

'You look like a girl we had here once,' he said. 'Called Sarah Spence.'

'I remember Sarah Spence.'

'She was good at English too.'

She wanted something to happen, thunder to begin, or a torrent of rain, anything that would keep them in the classroom. She couldn't even bear the thought of walking to her desk and putting her essay book in her briefcase.

'Sarah went to Warwick University,' he said.

She nodded. She tried to smile again and this time the smile came. She said to herself that it was a brazen smile and she didn't care. She hoped it made her seem more than ever like Sarah Spence, sophisticated and able for anything. She wondered if he said to all the girls who were stop-gaps that they looked like Sarah Spence. She didn't care. His carry-on with Sarah Spence was over and done with, he didn't even see her any more. By all accounts Sarah Spence had let him down, but never in a million years would she. She would wait for him for ever, or until the divorce came through. When he was old she would look after him.

'You'd better be getting home, Jenny.'

'I don't want to, sir.'

She continued to stand there, the exercise book in her left hand. She watched while some kind of shadow passed over his face. For a moment his eyes closed.

'Why don't you want to go?' he said.

'Because I'm in love with you, sir.'

'You mustn't be, Jenny.'

'Why not?'

'You know why not.'

'What about Sarah Spence?'

'Sarah was different.'

'I don't care how many stop-gaps you've had. I don't care. I don't love you any less.'

'Stop-gaps, Jenny?'

'The ones you made do with.'

'Made do?' He was suddenly frowning at her, his face screwed up a little. 'Made do?' he said again.

'The other girls. The ones who reminded you of her.'

'There weren't any other girls.'

'You were seen, sir –'

'Only Sarah and I were seen.'

'Your car –'

'Give a dog a bad name, Jenny. There weren't any others.'

She felt iciness inside her, somewhere in her stomach. Other girls had formed an attachment for him, as she had. Other girls had probably stood on this very spot, telling him. It was that, and the reality of Sarah Spence, that had turned him into a schoolgirls' legend. Only Sarah Spence had gone with him in his old Ford Escort to quiet lay-bys, only Sarah Spence had felt his arms around her. Why shouldn't he be seen in the buffet-car of a train, alone? The weekends he'd spent away from home were probably with a sick mother.

'I'm no Casanova, Jenny.'

'I had to tell you I'm in love with you, sir. I couldn't not.'

'It's no good loving me, I'm afraid.'

'You're the nicest person I'll ever know.'

'No, I'm not, Jenny. I'm just an English teacher who took advantage of a young girl's infatuation. Shabby, people would say.'

'You're not shabby. Oh God, you're not shabby.' She heard her own voice crying out shrilly, close to tears. It astonished her. It was unbelievable that she should be so violently protesting. It was unbelievable that he should have called himself shabby.

'She had an abortion in Warwick,' he said, 'after a weekend we spent in an hotel. I let that happen, Jenny.'

'You couldn't help it.'

'Of course I could have helped it.'

Without wanting to, she imagined them in the hotel he spoke of. She imagined them having a meal, sitting opposite each other at a table, and a waiter placing plates in front of them. She imagined them in their bedroom, a grimy room with a lace curtain drawn across the lower part of the single window and a washbasin in a corner. The bedroom had featured in a film she'd seen, and Sarah Spence was even like the actress who had played the part of a shopgirl. She stood there in her underclothes just as the shopgirl had, awkwardly waiting while he smiled his love at her. 'Then let not winter's ragged hand deface,' he whispered, 'In thee thy summer, ere thou be distilled. Oh Sarah, love.' He took the underclothes from her body, as the actor in the film had, all the time whispering sonnets.

'It was messy and horrible,' he said. 'That's how it ended, Jenny.'

'I don't care how it ended. I'd go with you anywhere. I'd go to a thousand hotels.'

'No, no, Jenny.'

'I love you terribly.'

She wept, still standing there. He got down from the stool in front of his desk and came and put his arms about her, telling her to cry. He said that tears were good, not bad. He made her sit down at a desk and then he sat down beside her. His love affair with Sarah Spence sounded romantic, he said, and because of its romantic sheen girls fell in love with him. They fell in love with the unhappiness they sensed in him. He found it hard to stop them.

'I should move away from here,' he said, 'but I can't bring myself to do it. Because she'll always come back to see her family and whenever she does I can catch a glimpse of her.'

It was the same as she felt about him, like the glimpse that day in the International Stores. It was the same as Chinny Martin hanging about outside Harper's. And yet of course it wasn't the same as Chinny Martin. How could it possibly be? Chinny Martin was stupid and unprepossessing and ordinary.

'I'd be better to you,' she cried out in sudden desperation, unable to prevent herself. Clumsily she put a hand on his shoulder, and clumsily took it away again. 'I would wait for ever,' she said, sobbing, knowing she looked ugly.

He waited for her to calm down. He stood up and after a moment so did she. She walked with him from the classroom, down the corridor and out of the door that led to the car park.

'You can't just leave,' he said, 'a wife and four children. It was hard to explain that to Sarah. She hates me now.'

He unlocked the driver's door of the Ford Escort. He smiled at her. He said:

'There's no one else I can talk to about her. Except girls like you. You mustn't feel embarrassed in class, Jenny.'

He drove away, not offering her a lift, which he might have done, for their direction was the same. She didn't in the least look like Sarah Spence: he'd probably said the same thing to all the others, the infatuated girls he could talk to about the girl he loved. The little scenes in the classroom, the tears, the talk: all that brought him closer to Sarah Spence. The love of a girl he didn't care about warmed him, as Chinny Martin's love had warmed her too, even though Chinny Martin was ridiculous.

She walked across the car park, imagining him driving back to his gate-lodge with Sarah Spence alive again in his mind, loving her more than ever. 'Jenny,' the voice of Chinny Martin called out, coming from nowhere.

He was there, standing by his Yamaha, beside a car. She shook her head at him, and began to run. At home she would sit and eat in the kitchen with her parents, who wouldn't be any different. She would escape and lie on her bed in her small neat bedroom, longing to be where she'd never be now, beside him in his car, or on a train, or anywhere. 'Jenny,' the voice of Chinny Martin called out again, silly with his silly love.

Autumn Sunshine

The rectory was in County Wexford, eight miles from Enniscorthy. It was a handsome eighteenth-century house with Virginia creeper covering three sides and a tangled garden full of buddleia and struggling japonica which had always been too much for its incumbents. It stood alone, seeming lonely even, approximately at the centre of the country parish it served. Its church – St Michael's Church of Ireland – was two miles away, in the village of Boharbawn.

For twenty-six years the Morans had lived there, not wishing to live anywhere else. Canon Moran had never been an ambitious man; his wife, Frances, had found contentment easy to attain in her lifetime. Their four girls had been born in the rectory, and had become a happy family there. They were grown up now, Frances's death was still recent: like the rectory itself, its remaining occupant was alone in the countryside. The death had occurred in the spring of the year, and the summer had somehow been bearable. The clergyman's eldest daughter had spent May and part of June at the rectory with her children. Another one had brought her family for most of August, and a third was to bring her newly married husband in the winter. At Christmas nearly all of them would gather at the rectory and some would come at Easter. But that September, as the days drew in, the season was melancholy.

Then, one Tuesday morning, Slattery brought a letter from Canon Moran's youngest daughter. There were two other letters as well, in unsealed buff envelopes which meant that they were either bills or receipts. Frail and grey-haired in his elderliness, Canon Moran had been wondering if he should give the lawn in front of the house a last cut when he heard the approach of Slattery's van. The lawnmower was the kind that had to be pushed, and in the spring the job was always easier if the grass had been cropped close at the end of the previous summer.

'Isn't that a great bit of weather, Canon?' Slattery remarked, winding down the window of the van and passing out the three envelopes. 'We're set for a while, would you say?'

'I hope so, certainly.'

'Ah, we surely are, sir.'

The conversation continued for a few moments longer, as it did whenever Slattery came to the rectory. The postman was young and easy-going, not long the successor to old Mr O'Brien, who'd been making the round on a bicycle when the Morans first came to the rectory in 1952. Mr O'Brien used to talk about his garden; Slattery talked about fishing, and often brought a share of his catch to the rectory.

'It's a great time of year for it,' he said now, 'except for the darkness coming in.'

Canon Moran smiled and nodded; the van turned round on the gravel, dust rising behind it as it moved swiftly down the avenue to the road. Everyone said Slattery drove too fast.

He carried the letters to a wooden seat on the edge of the lawn he'd been wondering about cutting. Deirdre's handwriting hadn't changed since she'd been a child; it was round and neat, not at all a reflection of the girl she was. The blue English stamp, the Queen in profile blotched a bit by the London postmark, wasn't on its side or half upside down, as you might possibly expect with Deirdre. Of all the Moran children, she'd grown up to be the only difficult one. She hadn't come to the funeral and hadn't written about her mother's death. She hadn't been to the rectory for three years.

'*I'm sorry,*' she wrote now. '*I couldn't stop crying actually. I've never known anyone as nice or as generous as she was. For ages I didn't even want to believe she was dead. I went on imagining her in the rectory and doing the flowers in church and shopping in Enniscorthy.*'

Deirdre was twenty-one now. He and Frances had hoped she'd go to Trinity and settle down, but although at school she'd seemed to be the cleverest of their children she'd had no desire to become a student. She'd taken the Rosslare boat to Fishguard one night, having said she was going to spend a week with her friend Maeve Coles in Cork. They hadn't known she'd gone to England until they received a picture postcard from London telling them not to worry, saying she'd found work in an egg-packing factory.

'*Well, I'm coming back for a little while now,*' she wrote, '*if you could put up with me and if you wouldn't find it too much. I'll cross over to Rosslare on the twenty-ninth, the morning crossing, and then I'll come on to Enniscorthy on the bus. I don't know what time it will be but there's a pub just by where the bus drops you so could we meet in the small bar there at six o'clock and then I won't have to lug my cases too far? I hope you won't mind going into such a place. If you can't make it, or don't want to see me, it's understandable, so if you don't turn up by half six I'll see if I can get a bus on up to Dublin. Only I need to get back to Ireland for a while.*'

It was, as he and Slattery had agreed, a lovely autumn. Gentle sunshine mellowed the old garden, casting an extra sheen of gold on leaves that were gold already. Roses that had been ebullient in June and July bloomed modestly now. Michaelmas daisies were just beginning to bud. Already the crab-apples were falling, hydrangeas had a forgotten look. Canon Moran carried the letter from his daughter into the walled vegetable-garden and leaned against the side of the greenhouse, half sitting on a protruding ledge, reading the letter again. Panes of glass were broken in the greenhouse, white paint and putty needed to be renewed, but inside a vine still thrived, and was heavy now with black ripe fruit. Later that morning he would pick some and drive into Enniscorthy, to sell the grapes to Mrs Roche in Slaney Street.

'*Love, Deirdre*': the letter was marvellous. Beyond the rectory the fields of wheat had been harvested, and the remaining stubble had the same tinge of gold in the autumn light; the beech-trees and the chestnuts were triumphantly magnificent. But decay and rotting were only weeks away, and the letter from Deirdre was full of life. '*Love, Deirdre*' were words more beautiful than all the season's glories. He prayed as he leaned against the sunny greenhouse, thanking God for this salvation.

For all the years of their marriage Frances had been a help. As a younger man, Canon Moran hadn't known quite what to do. He'd been at a loss among his parishioners, hesitating in the face of this weakness or that: the pregnancy of Alice Pratt in 1954, the argument about grazing rights between Mr Willoughby and Eugene Ryan in 1960, the theft of an altar cloth from St Michael's and reports that Mrs Tobin had been seen wearing it as a skirt. Alice Pratt had been going out with a Catholic boy, one of Father Hayes's flock, which made the matter more difficult than ever. Eugene Ryan was one of Father Hayes's also, and so was Mrs Tobin.

'Father Hayes and I had a chat,' Frances had said, and she'd had a chat as well with Alice Pratt's mother. A month later Alice Pratt married the Catholic boy, but to this day attended St Michael's every Sunday, the children going to Father Hayes. Mrs Tobin was given Hail Marys to say by the priest; Mr Willoughby agreed that his father had years ago granted Eugene Ryan the grazing rights. Everything, in these cases and in many others, had come out all right in the end: order emerged from the confusion that Canon Moran so disliked, and it was Frances who had always begun the process, though no one ever said in the rectory that she understood the mystery of people as well as he understood the teachings of the New Testament. She'd been a freckle-faced girl when he'd married her, pretty in her way. He was the one with the brains.

Frances had seen human frailty everywhere: it was weakness in people, she said, that made them what they were as much as strength did. And she herself had her own share of such frailty, falling short in all sorts of ways of the God's image her husband preached about. With the small amount of housekeeping money she could be allowed she was a spendthrift, and she said she was lazy. She loved clothes and often overreached herself on visits to Dublin; she sat in the sun while the rectory gathered dust and the garden became rank; it was only where people were concerned that she was practical. But for what she was her husband had loved her with unobtrusive passion for fifty years, appreciating her conversation and the help she'd given him because she could so easily sense the truth. When he'd found her dead in the garden one morning he'd felt he had lost some part of himself.

Though many months had passed since then, the trouble was that

Frances hadn't yet become a ghost. Her being alive was still too recent, the shock of her death too raw. He couldn't distance himself; the past refused to be the past. Often he thought that her fingerprints were still in the rectory, and when he picked the grapes or cut the grass of the lawn it was impossible not to pause and remember other years. Autumn had been her favourite time.

'Of course I'd come,' he said. 'Of course, dear. Of course.'

'I haven't treated you very well.'

'It's over and done with, Deirdre.'

She smiled, and it was nice to see her smile again, although it was strange to be sitting in the back bar of a public house in Enniscorthy. He saw her looking at him, her eyes passing over his clerical collar and black clothes, and his thin quiet face. He could feel her thinking that he had aged, and putting it down to the death of the wife he'd been so fond of.

'I'm sorry I didn't write,' she said.

'You explained in your letter, Deirdre.'

'It was ages before I knew about it. That was an old address you wrote to.'

'I guessed.'

In turn he examined her. Years ago she'd had her long hair cut. It was short now, like a neat black cap on her head. And her face had lost its chubbiness; hollows where her cheeks had been made her eyes more dominant, pools of seaweed green. He remembered her child's stocky body, and the uneasy adolescence that had spoilt the family's serenity. Her voice had lost its Irish intonation.

'I'd have met you off the boat, you know.'

'I didn't want to bother you with that.'

'Oh, now, it isn't far, Deirdre.'

She drank Irish whiskey, and smoked a brand of cigarettes called Three Castles. He'd asked for a mineral himself, and the woman serving them had brought him a bottle of something that looked like water but which fizzed up when she'd poured it. A kind of lemonade he imagined it was, and didn't much care for it.

'I have grapes for Mrs Roche,' he said.

'Who's that?'

'She has a shop in Slaney Street. We always sold her the grapes. You remember?'

She didn't, and he reminded her of the vine in the greenhouse. A shop surely wouldn't be open at this hour of the evening, she said, forgetting that in a country town of course it would be. She asked if the cinema was still the same in Enniscorthy, a cement building halfway up a hill. She said she remembered bicycling home from it at night with her sisters, not being able to keep up with them. She asked after her sisters and he told her about the two marriages that had taken place since she'd left: she had in-laws she'd never met, and nephews and a niece.

They left the bar, and he drove his dusty black Vauxhall straight to the small shop he'd spoken of. She remained in the car while he carried into the shop two large chip-baskets full of grapes. Afterwards Mrs Roche came to the door with him.

'Well, is that Deirdre?' she said as Deirdre wound down the window of the car. 'I'd never know you, Deirdre.'

'She's come back for a little while,' Canon Moran explained, raising his voice a little because he was walking round the car to the driver's seat as he spoke.

'Well, isn't that grand?' said Mrs Roche.

Everyone in Enniscorthy knew Deirdre had just gone off, but it didn't matter now. Mrs Roche's husband, who was a red-cheeked man with a cap, much smaller than his wife, appeared beside her in the shop doorway. He inclined his head in greeting, and Deirdre smiled and waved at both of them. Canon Moran thought it was pleasant when she went on waving while he drove off.

In the rectory he lay wakeful that night, his mind excited by Deirdre's presence. He would have loved Frances to know, and guessed that she probably did. He fell asleep at half past two and dreamed that he and Frances were young again, that Deirdre was still a baby. The freckles on Frances's face were out in profusion, for they were sitting in the sunshine in the garden, tea things spread about them, the children playing some game among the shrubs. It was autumn then also, the last of the September heat. But because he was younger in his dream he didn't feel part of the season himself, or sense its melancholy.

A week went by. The time passed slowly because a lot was happening, or so it seemed. Deirdre insisted on cooking all the meals and on doing the shopping in Boharbawn's single shop or in Enniscorthy. She still smoked her endless cigarettes, but the peakiness there had been in her face when she'd first arrived wasn't quite so pronounced – or perhaps, he thought, he'd become used to it. She told him about the different jobs she'd had in London and the different places she'd lived in, because on the postcards she'd occasionally sent there hadn't been room to go into detail. In the rectory they had always hoped she'd managed to get a training of some sort, though guessing she hadn't. In fact, her jobs had been of the most rudimentary kind: as well as her spell in the egg-packing factory, there'd been a factory that made plastic earphones, a cleaning job in a hotel near Euston, and a year working for the Use-Us Office Cleansing Service. 'But you can't have liked any of that work, Deirdre?' he suggested, and she agreed she hadn't.

From the way she spoke he felt that that period of her life was over: adolescence was done with, she had steadied and taken stock. He didn't suggest to her that any of this might be so, not wishing to seem either too anxious or too pleased, but he felt she had returned to the rectory in a very different frame of mind from the one in which she'd left it. He imagined she would remain for quite a while, still taking stock, and in a sense occupying her mother's place. He thought he recognized in her a loneliness that matched his own, and he wondered if it was a feeling that their loneliness might be shared which had brought her back at this particular time. Sitting in the drawing-room while she cooked or washed up, or gathering grapes in the greenhouse while she did the shopping, he warmed delightedly to this theme. It seemed like an act of God that their circumstances should interlace this autumn. By Christmas she would know what she wanted to do with her life, and in the spring that followed she would perhaps be ready to set forth again. A year would have passed since the death of Frances.

'I have a friend,' Deirdre said when they were having a cup of coffee together in the middle of one morning. 'Someone who's been good to me.'

She had carried a tray to where he was composing next week's sermon, sitting on the wooden seat by the lawn at the front of the house. He laid aside his exercise book, and a pencil and a rubber. 'Who's that?' he enquired.

'Someone called Harold.'

He nodded, stirring sugar into his coffee.

'I want to tell you about Harold, Father. I want you to meet him.'

'Yes, of course.'

She lit a cigarette. She said, 'We have a lot in common. I mean, he's the only person . . .'

She faltered and then hesitated. She lifted her cigarette to her lips and drew on it.

He said, 'Are you fond of him, Deirdre?'

'Yes, I am.'

Another silence gathered. She smoked and drank her coffee. He added more sugar to his.

'Of course I'd like to meet him,' he said.

'Could he come to stay with us, Father? Would you mind? Would it be all right?'

'Of course I wouldn't mind. I'd be delighted.'

Harold was summoned, and arrived at Rosslare a few days later. In the meantime Deirdre had explained to her father that her friend was an electrician by trade and had let it fall that he was an intellectual kind of person. She borrowed the old Vauxhall and drove it to Rosslare to meet him, returning to the rectory in the early evening.

'How d'you do?' Canon Moran said, stretching out a hand in the direction of an excessively thin youth with a birthmark on his face. His dark hair was cut very short, cropped almost. He was wearing a black leather jacket.

'I'm fine,' Harold said.

'You've had a good journey?'

'Lousy,'smatter of fact, Mr Moran.'

Harold's voice was strongly Cockney, and Canon Moran wondered if Deirdre had perhaps picked up some of her English vowel sounds from it. But then he realized that most people in London would speak like that, as people did on the television and the wireless. It was just a little surprising that Harold and Deirdre should have so much in common, as they clearly had from the affectionate way they held one another's hand. None of the other Moran girls had gone in so much for holding hands in front of the family.

He was to sit in the drawing-room, they insisted, while they made supper in the kitchen, so he picked up the *Irish Times* and did as he was bidden. Half an hour later Harold appeared and said that the meal was ready: fried eggs and sausages and bacon, and some tinned beans. Canon Moran said grace.

Having stated that Co. Wexford looked great, Harold didn't say much else. He didn't smile much, either. His afflicted face bore an edgy look, as if he'd never become wholly reconciled to his birthmark. It was like a scarlet map on his left cheek, a shape that reminded Canon Moran of the toe of Italy. Poor fellow, he thought. And yet a birthmark was so much less to bear than other afflictions there could be.

'Harold's fascinated actually,' Deirdre said, 'by Ireland.'

Her friend didn't add anything to that remark for a moment, even though Canon Moran smiled and nodded interestedly. Eventually Harold said, 'The struggle of the Irish people.'

'I didn't know a thing about Irish history,' Deirdre said. 'I mean, not anything that made sense.'

The conversation lapsed at this point, leaving Canon Moran greatly puzzled. He began to say that Irish history had always been of considerable interest to him also, that it had a good story to it, its tragedy uncomplicated. But the other two didn't appear to understand what he was talking about and so he changed the subject. It was a particularly splendid autumn, he pointed out.

'Harold doesn't go in for anything like that,' Deirdre replied.

During the days that followed Harold began to talk more, surprising Canon Moran with almost everything he said. Deirdre had been right to say he was fascinated by Ireland, and it wasn't just a tourist's fascination. Harold had read widely: he spoke of ancient battles, and of the plantations of James I and Elizabeth, of Robert Emmet and the Mitchelstown martyrs, of Pearse and de Valera. 'The struggle of the Irish people' was the expression he most regularly employed. It seemed to Canon Moran that the relationship between Harold and Deirdre had a lot to do with Harold's fascination, as though his interest in Deirdre's native land had somehow caused him to become interested in Deirdre herself.

There was something else as well. Fascinated by Ireland, Harold hated his own country. A sneer whispered through his voice when he spoke of England: a degenerate place, he called it, destroyed by class-consciousness and the unjust distribution of wealth. He described in detail the city of Nottingham, to which he appeared to have a particular aversion. He spoke of unnecessary motorways and the stupidity of bureaucracy, the stifling presence of a Royal family. 'You could keep an Indian village,' he claimed, 'on what those corgis eat. You could house five hundred homeless in Buckingham Palace.' There was brainwashing by television and the newspaper barons. No ordinary person had a chance because pap was fed to the ordinary person, a deliberate policy going back into Victorian times when education and religion had been geared to the enslavement of minds. The English people had brought it on themselves, having lost their spunk, settling instead for consumer durables. 'What better can you expect,' Harold demanded, 'after the hypocrisy of that empire the bosses ran?'

Deirdre didn't appear to find anything specious in this line of talk, which surprised her father. 'Oh, I wonder about that,' he said himself from time to time, but he said it mildly, not wishing to cause an argument, and in any case his interjections were not acknowledged. Quite a few of the criticisms Harold levelled at his own country could be levelled at Ireland also and, Canon Moran guessed, at many countries throughout the world. It was strange that the two neighbouring islands had been so picked out, although once Germany was mentioned and the point made that developments beneath the surface there were a hopeful sign, that a big upset was on the way.

'We're taking a walk,' Harold said one afternoon. 'She's going to show me Kinsella's Barn.'

Canon Moran nodded, saying to himself that he disliked Harold. It was the first time he had admitted it, but the feeling was familiar. The less generous side of his nature had always emerged when his daughters brought to the rectory the men they'd become friendly with or even proposed to marry. Emma, the eldest girl, had brought several before settling in the end for Thomas. Linda had brought only John, already engaged to him. Una had married Carley not long after the death, and Carley had not yet visited the rectory: Canon Moran had met him in Dublin, where the wedding had taken place, for in the circumstances Una had not been married from home. Carley was an older man, an importer of tea and wine, stout and flushed, certainly not someone Canon Moran would have chosen for his second-youngest daughter. But, then, he had thought the same about Emma's Thomas and about Linda's John.

Thomas was a farmer, sharing a sizeable acreage with his father in Co. Meath. He always brought to mind the sarcasm of an old schoolmaster who in Canon Moran's distant schooldays used to refer to a gang of boys at the back of the classroom as 'farmers' sons', meaning that not much could be expected of them. It was an inaccurate assumption but even now, whenever Canon Moran found himself in the company of Thomas, he couldn't help recalling it. Thomas was mostly silent, with a good-natured smile that came slowly and lingered too long. According to his father, and there was no reason to doubt the claim, he was a good judge of beef cattle

Linda's John was the opposite. Wiry and suave, he was making his way in the Bank of Ireland, at present stationed in Waterford. He had a tiny orange-coloured moustache and was good at golf. Linda's ambition for him was that he should become the Bank of Ireland's manager in Limerick or Galway, where the insurances that went with the position were particularly lucrative. Unlike Thomas, John talked all the time, telling jokes and stories about the Bank of Ireland's customers.

'Nothing is perfect,' Frances used to say, chiding her husband for an uncharitableness he did his best to combat. He disliked being so particular about the men his daughters chose, and he was aware that other people saw them differently: Thomas would do anything for you, John was fun, the middle-aged Carley laid his success at Una's feet. But whoever the husbands of his daughters had been, Canon Moran knew he'd have felt the same. He was jealous of the husbands because ever since his daughters had been born he had loved them unstintingly. When he had prayed after Frances's death he'd felt jealous of God, who had taken her from him.

'There's nothing much to see,' he pointed out when Harold announced that Deirdre was going to show him Kinsella's Barn. 'Just the ruin of a wall is all that's left.'

'Harold's interested, Father.'

They set off on their walk, leaving the old clergyman ashamed that he could not like Harold more. It wasn't just his griminess: there was something sinister about Harold, something furtive about the way he looked at you, peering at you cruelly out of his afflicted face, not meeting your eye. Why was he so fascinated about a country that wasn't his own? Why did he refer so often to 'Ireland's struggle' as if that struggle particularly concerned him? He hated walking, he had said, yet he'd just set out to walk six miles through woods and fields to examine a ruined wall.

Canon Moran had wondered as suspiciously about Thomas and John and Carley, privately questioning every statement they made, finding hidden motives everywhere. He'd hated the thought of his daughters being embraced or even touched, and had forced himself not to think about that. He'd prayed, ashamed of himself then, too. 'It's just a frailty in you,' Frances had said, her favourite way of cutting things down to size.

He sat for a while in the afternoon sunshine, letting all of it hang in his mind. It would be nice if they quarrelled on their walk. It would be nice if they didn't speak when they returned, if Harold simply went away. But that wouldn't happen, because they had come to the rectory with a purpose. He didn't know why he thought that, but he knew it was true: they had come for a reason, something that was all tied up with Harold's fascination and with the kind of person Harold was, with his cold eyes and his afflicted face.

In March 1798 an incident had taken place in Kinsella's Barn, which at that time had just been a barn. Twelve men and women, accused of harbouring insurgents, had been tied together with ropes at the command of a Sergeant James. They had been led through the village of Boharbawn, the Sergeant's soldiers on horseback on either side of the procession, the Sergeant himself bringing up the rear. Designed as an act of education, an example to the inhabitants of Boharbawn and the country people around, the twelve had been herded into a barn owned by a farmer called Kinsella and there burned to death. Kinsella, who had played no part either in the harbouring of insurgents or in the execution of the twelve, was afterwards murdered by his own farm labourers.

'Sergeant James was a Nottingham man,' Harold said that evening at supper. 'A soldier of fortune who didn't care what he did. Did you know he acquired great wealth, Mr Moran?'

'No, I wasn't at all aware of that,' Canon Moran replied.

'Harold found out about him,' Deirdre said.

'He used to boast he was responsible for the death of a thousand Irish people. It was in Boharbawn he reached the thousand. They rewarded him well for that.'

'Not much is known about Sergeant James locally. Just the legend of Kinsella's Barn.'

'No way it's a legend.'

Deirdre nodded; Canon Moran did not say anything. They were eating cooked ham and salad. On the table there was a cake which Deirdre had bought in Murphy Flood's in Enniscorthy, and a pot of tea. There were several bunches of grapes from the greenhouse, and a plate of wafer biscuits. Harold was fond of salad cream, Canon Moran had noticed; he had a way of hitting the base of the jar with his hand, causing large dollops to spurt all over his ham. He didn't place his knife and fork together on the plate when he'd finished, but just left them anyhow. His fingernails were edged with black.

'You'd feel sick,' he was saying now, working the salad cream again. 'You'd stand there looking at that wall and you'd feel a revulsion in your stomach.'

'What I meant,' Canon Moran said, 'is that it has passed into local legend. No one doubts it took place; there's no question about that. But two centuries have almost passed.'

'And nothing has changed,' Harold interjected. 'The Irish people still share their bondage with the twelve in Kinsella's Barn.'

'Round here of course –'

'It's not round here that matters, Mr Moran. The struggle's world-wide; the sickness is everywhere actually.'

Again Deirdre nodded. She was like a zombie, her father thought. She was being used because she was an Irish girl; she was Harold's Irish connection, and in some almost frightening way she believed herself in love with him. Frances had once said they'd made a mistake with her. She had wondered if Deirdre had perhaps found all the love they'd offered her too much to bear. They were quite old when Deirdre was a child, the last expression of their own love. She was special because of that.

'At least Kinsella got his chips,' Harold pursued, his voice relentless. 'At least that's something.'

Canon Moran protested. The owner of the barn had been an innocent man, he pointed out. The barn had simply been a convenient one, large enough for the purpose, with heavy stones near it that could be piled up against the door before the conflagration. Kinsella, that day, had been miles away, ditching a field.

'It's too long ago to say where he was,' Harold retorted swiftly. 'And if he was keeping a low profile in a ditch it would have been by arrangement with the imperial forces.'

When Harold said that, there occurred in Canon Moran's mind a flash of what appeared to be the simple truth. Harold was an Englishman who had espoused a cause because it was one through which the status quo in his own country might be damaged. Similar such Englishmen, read about in newspapers, stirred in the clergyman's mind: men from Ealing and Liverpool and Wolverhampton who had changed their names to Irish names, who had even learned the Irish language, in order to ingratiate themselves with the new Irish revolutionaries. Such men dealt out death and chaos, announcing that their conscience insisted on it.

'Well, we'd better wash the dishes,' Deirdre said, and Harold rose obediently to help her.

The walk to Kinsella's Barn had taken place on a Saturday afternoon. The following morning Canon Moran conducted his services in St Michael's, addressing his small Protestant congregation, twelve at Holy Communion, eighteen at morning service. He had prepared a sermon about repentance, taking as his text St Luke, 15:32: '. . . *for this thy brother was dead, and is alive again; and was lost, and is found.*' But at the last moment he changed his mind and spoke instead of the incident in Kinsella's Barn nearly two centuries ago. He tried to make the point that one horror should not fuel another, that passing time contained its own forgiveness. Deirdre and Harold were naturally not in the church, but they'd been present at breakfast, Harold frying eggs on the kitchen stove, Deirdre pouring tea. He had looked at them and tried to think of them as two young people on holiday. He had tried to tell himself they'd come to the rectory for a rest and for his blessing, that he should be grateful instead of fanciful. It was for his blessing that Emma had brought Thomas to the rectory, that Linda had brought John. Una would bring Carley in November. 'Now, don't be silly,' Frances would have said.

'The man Kinsella was innocent of everything,' he heard his voice insisting in his church. 'He should never have been murdered also.'

Harold would have delighted in the vengeance exacted on an innocent man. Harold wanted to inflict pain, to cause suffering and destruction. The

780 · AUTUMN SUNSHINE

end justified the means for Harold, even if the end was an artificial one, a pettiness grandly dressed up. In his sermon Canon Moran spoke of such matters without mentioning Harold's name. He spoke of how evil drained people of their humour and compassion, how people pretended even to themselves. It was worse than Frances's death, he thought as his voice continued in the church: it was worse that Deirdre should be part of wickedness.

He could tell that his parishioners found his sermon odd, and he didn't blame them. He was confused, and naturally distressed. In the rectory Deirdre and Harold would be waiting for him. They would all sit down to Sunday lunch while plans for atrocities filled Harold's mind, while Deirdre loved him.

'Are you well again, Mrs Davis?' he enquired at the church door of a woman who suffered from asthma.

'Not too bad, Canon. Not too bad, thank you.'

He spoke to all the others, enquiring about health, remarking on the beautiful autumn. They were farmers mostly and displayed a farmer's gratitude for the satisfactory season. He wondered suddenly who'd replace him among them when he retired or died. Father Hayes had had to give up a year ago. The young man, Father White, was always in a hurry.

'Goodbye so, Canon,' Mr Willoughby said, shaking hands as he always did, every Sunday. It was a long time since there'd been the trouble about Eugene Ryan's grazing rights; three years ago Mr Willoughby had been left a widower himself. 'You're managing all right, Canon?' he asked, as he also always did.

'Yes, I'm all right, thank you, Mr Willoughby.'

Someone else enquired if Deirdre was still at the rectory, and he said she was. Heads nodded, the unspoken thought being that that was nice for him, his youngest daughter at home again after all these years. There was forgiveness in several faces, forgiveness of Deirdre, who had been thoughtless to go off to an egg-packing factory. There was the feeling, also unexpressed, that the young were a bit like that.

'Goodbye,' he said in a general way. Car doors banged, engines started. In the vestry he removed his surplice and his cassock and hung them in a cupboard.

'We'll probably go tomorrow,' Deirdre said during lunch.

'Go?'

'We'll probably take the Dublin bus.'

'I'd like to see Dublin,' Harold said.

'And then you're returning to London?'

'We're easy about that,' Harold interjected before Deirdre could reply. 'I'm a tradesman, Mr Moran, an electrician.'

'I know you're an electrician, Harold.'

'What I mean is, I'm on my own; I'm not answerable to the bosses. There's always a bob or two waiting in London.'

For some reason Canon Moran felt that Harold was lying. There was a quickness about the way he'd said they were easy about their plans, and it didn't seem quite to make sense, the logic of not being answerable to bosses and a bob or two always waiting for him. Harold was being evasive about their movements, hiding the fact that they would probably remain in Dublin for longer than he implied, meeting other people like himself.

'It was good of you to have us,' Deirdre said that evening, all three of them sitting around the fire in the drawing-room because the evenings had just begun to get chilly. Harold was reading a book about Che Guevara and hadn't spoken for several hours. 'We've enjoyed it, Father.'

'It's been nice having you, Deirdre.'

'I'll write to you from London.'

It was safe to say that: he knew she wouldn't because she hadn't before, until she'd wanted something. She wouldn't write to thank him for the rectory's hospitality, and that would be quite in keeping. Harold was the same kind of man as Sergeant James had been: it didn't matter that they were on different sides. Sergeant James had maybe borne an affliction also, a humped back or a withered arm. He had ravaged a country that existed then for its spoils, and his most celebrated crime was neatly at hand so that another Englishman could make matters worse by attempting to make amends. In Harold's view the trouble had always been that these acts of war and murder died beneath the weight of print in history books, and were forgotten. But history could be rewritten, and for that Kinsella's Barn was an inspiration: Harold had journeyed to it as people make journeys to holy places.

'Yes?' Deirdre said, for while these reflections had passed through his mind he had spoken her name, wanting to ask her to tell him the truth about her friend.

He shook his head. 'I wish you could have seen your mother again,' he said instead. 'I wish she were here now.'

The faces of his three sons-in-law irrelevantly appeared in his mind: Carley's flushed cheeks, Thomas's slow good-natured smile, John's little moustache. It astonished him that he'd ever felt suspicious of their natures, for they would never let his daughters down. But Deirdre had turned her back on the rectory, and what could be expected when she came back with a man? She had never been like Emma or Linda or Una, none of whom smoked Three Castles cigarettes and wore clothes that didn't seem quite clean. It was impossible to imagine any of them becoming involved with a revolutionary, a man who wanted to commit atrocities.

'He was just a farmer, you know,' he heard himself saying. 'Kinsella.'

Surprise showed in Deirdre's face. 'It was Mother we were talking about,' she reminded him, and he could see her trying to connect her mother with a farmer who had died two hundred years ago, and not being able to. Elderliness, he could see her thinking. 'Only time he wandered,' she would probably say to her friend.

'It was good of you to come, Deirdre.'

He looked at her, far into her eyes, admitting to himself that she had always been his favourite. When the other girls were busily growing up she had still wanted to sit on his knee. She'd had a way of interrupting him no matter what he was doing, arriving beside him with a book she wanted him to read to her.

'Goodbye, Father,' she said the next morning while they waited in Enniscorthy for the Dublin bus. 'Thank you for everything.'

'Yeah, thanks a ton, Mr Moran,' Harold said.

'Goodbye, Harold. Goodbye, my dear.'

He watched them finding their seats when the bus arrived and then he drove the old Vauxhall back to Boharbawn, meeting Slattery in his postman's van and returning his salute. There was shopping he should have done, meat and potatoes, and tins of things to keep him going. But his mind was full of Harold's afflicted face and his black-rimmed fingernails, and Deirdre's hand in his. And then flames burst from the straw that had been packed around living people in Kinsella's Barn. They burned through the wood of the barn itself, revealing the writhing bodies. On his horse the man called Sergeant James laughed.

Canon Moran drove the car into the rectory's ramshackle garage, and walked around the house to the wooden seat on the front lawn. Frances should come now with two cups of coffee, appearing at the front door with the tray and then crossing the gravel and the lawn. He saw her as she had been when they first came to the rectory, when only Emma had been born; but the grey-haired Frances was somehow there as well, shadowing her youth. 'Funny little Deirdre,' she said, placing the tray on the seat between them.

It seemed to him that everything that had just happened in the rectory had to do with Frances, with meeting her for the first time when she was eighteen, with loving her and marrying her. He knew it was a trick of the autumn sunshine that again she crossed the gravel and the lawn, no more than pretence that she handed him a cup and saucer. 'Harold's just a talker,' she said. 'Not at all like Sergeant James.'

He sat for a while longer on the wooden seat, clinging to these words, knowing they were true. Of course it was cowardice that ran through Harold, inspiring the whisper of his sneer when he spoke of the England he hated so. In the presence of a befuddled girl and an old Irish clergyman England was an easy target, and Ireland's troubles a kind of target also.

Frances laughed, and for the first time her death seemed far away, as her life did too. In the rectory the visitors had blurred her fingerprints to nothing, and had made of her a ghost that could come back. The sunshine warmed him as he sat there, the garden was less melancholy than it had been.

Sunday Drinks

There was no one else about, not even a cat on the whole extent of the common. The early morning air hadn't yet been infected by the smell of London, houses were as silent as the houses of the dead. It was half-past seven, a Sunday morning in June: on a weekday at this time voices would be calling out, figures already hurrying across the common to Barnes station; the buses would have started. On a weekday Malcolm would be lying for a last five minutes in bed, conserving his energy.

Not yet shaven, a fawn dressing-gown over striped red and blue pyjamas, he strolled on the cricket pitch, past the sight-screens and a small pavilion. He was middle-aged and balding, with glasses. Though no eccentric in other ways, he often walked on fine Sunday mornings across the common in his dressing-gown, as far as the poplars which grew in a line along one boundary.

Reaching them now, he turned and slowly made his way back to the house where he lived with Jessica, who was his wife. They'd lived there since he'd begun to be prosperous as a solicitor: an Edwardian house of pleasant brown brick, with some Virginia creeper on it, and bay trees in tubs on either side of the front door. They were a small family: quietly occupying an upstairs room, in many ways no trouble to anyone, there was Malcolm and Jessica's son.

In the kitchen Malcolm finished chapter eight of *Edwin Drood* and eventually heard the Sunday papers arrive. He went to fetch them, glanced through them, and then made coffee and toast. He took a tray and the newspapers up to his wife.

'I've brought you a cup of tea,' Jessica said later that morning, in their son's room. Sometimes he drank it, but often it was still there on the bedside table when she returned at lunchtime. He never carried the cup and saucer down to the kitchen himself and would apologize for that, wagging his head in irritation at his shortcomings.

He didn't reply when she spoke about the tea. He stared at her and smiled. One hand was clenched close to his bearded face, the fingernails bitten, the fingers gnawed here and there. The room smelt of his sweat because he couldn't bear to have the window open, nor indeed to have the blind up. He made his models with the electric light on, preferring that to daylight. In the room the models were everywhere: Hurricanes and Spitfires, sea-planes and Heinkel 178s, none of them finished. A month ago, on 25th May, they'd made an attempt to celebrate his twenty-fourth birthday.

She closed the door behind her. On the landing walls there was a wallpaper splashed with poppies and cornflowers, which ran down through the house. People often remarked on its pastoral freshness when Jessica opened the hall-door to them, though others sometimes blinked. The hall had had a gloomy look before, the paintwork a shade of gravy. Doors and skirting-boards were brightly white now.

'Let's not go to the Morrishes',' Malcolm suggested in the kitchen, even though he'd put on his Sunday-morning-drinks clothes.

'Of course we must,' she said, not wanting to go to the Morrishes' either. 'I won't be a minute.'

In the downstairs lavatory she applied eye-shadow. Her thin face had a shallow look if she didn't make an effort with make-up; a bit of colour suited her, she reckoned, as it did the hall. She smeared on lipstick and pressed a tissue between her lips to clear away the surplus, continuing to examine her application of eye-shadow in the mirror above the washbasin. Dark hair, greying now, curved around her face. Her deep blue eyes still managed a sparkle that spread beauty into her features, transforming her: nondescript little thing, someone once had said, catching her in a tired moment.

In the kitchen she turned on the extractor fan above the electric cooker; pork chops were cooking slowly in the oven. 'All right?' she said, and Malcolm, idling over an advertisement for photochromic lenses, nodded and stood up.

Their son was dreaming now: he was there, on the bank of the river. Birds with blue plumage swooped over the water; through the foliage came the strum of a guitar. All the friends there'd been were there, in different coloured sleeping-bags, lying as he was. They were happy by the river because India was where the truth was, wrapped up in gentleness and beauty. Someone said that, and everyone else agreed.

Anthea Chalmers was at the Morrishes', tall and elegant in green, long since divorced. She had a look of Bette Davis, eyes like soup-plates, that kind of mouth. The Livingstons were there also, and Susanna and David Maidstone, and the Unwins. So was Mr Fulmer, a sandy-complexioned man whom people were sorry for because his wife was a stick-in-the-mud and wouldn't go to parties. June and Tom Highband were there, and the Taylor-Deeths, and Marcus Stire and his friend. There was a handful of faces that were unfamiliar to Jessica and Malcolm.

'Hullo, hullo,' their host called out, welcoming them with party joviality. The guests were passing from the sitting-room, through the French windows to the garden, all of them with glasses in their hands. The Morrishes – he pink and bluff, she pretty in a faded way – were busily making certain that these glasses contained precisely what people wanted. In the garden their French *au pair* boy was handing round bowls of nuts and shiny little biscuits from Japan. Children – the Morrishes' and others' – had congregated in a distant corner, by a tool-shed.

Jessica and Malcolm both asked for white wine, since chilled bottles of it stood there, inviting on a warm morning. They didn't say much to the Morrishes, who clearly wanted to get things going before indulging in chat. They stepped out into the garden, where a mass of flowers spectacularly bloomed and the lawns were closely shorn.

'Hi, Jessica,' Marcus Stire's friend said, a short, stout young man in a blue blazer. He'd made her black-bottom pie, he reported. He shook his head, implying disappointment with his version of the dish.

'Hullo, stranger,' Anthea Chalmers said to Malcolm.

She always seemed to pick him out. Ages ago he'd rejected the idea that a balding solicitor with glasses might possibly have some sensual attraction for her, even though all she ever talked to him about were sensual matters. She liked to get him into a corner, as she had done now, and had a way of turning interlopers away with a snakelike shift of her shoulders. She'd placed him with his back to the wall of the house, along which a creamy honeysuckle had been trained. A trellis to his right continued to support it; to his left, two old water-butts were swathed with purple clematis.

'A pig,' she said, referring to the man she'd once been married to. 'And I told him, Malcolm. I'd sooner share a bed with a farmyard pig was precisely what I said. Needless to say, he became violent.'

Jessica, having discussed the preparation of black-bottom pie with Marcus Stire's friend, smiled at the stout young man and passed on. The *au pair* boy offered her a Japanese biscuit and then a man she didn't know remarked upon the weather. Could anything be nicer, he asked her, than a drink or two on a Sunday morning in a sunny London garden? He was a man in brown suede, expensively cut to disguise a certain paunchiness. He had damp eyes and a damp-looking moustache. He had well-packed jowls, and a sun-browned head that matched the shade of his clothes. A businessman, Jessica speculated, excessively rich, a tough performer in his business world. He began to talk about a house he owned near Estepona.

On the surface of the tea which Jessica had earlier brought her son a skin had formed, in which a small fly now struggled. Nothing else was happening in the room. The sound of breathing could hardly be heard, the dream about birds with blue plumage had abruptly ceased. Then – in that same abrupt manner, a repetition of the suddenness that in different ways affected this boy's life – his eyes snapped open.

Through the gloom, and seeming larger than reality, the Spitfires and the Heinkels greeted his consciousness. He was in a room with aeroplanes, he told himself, and while he lay there nothing more impinged on his mind. Eventually he rose and began to dress, his youthful beard scanty and soft, quite like a bearded lady's. Tears ran into it while slowly he pulled his clothes over his white flesh.

His T-shirt was pale blue, the paler message it bore almost washed away. *Wham!* it had said, the word noisily proclaimed against lightning flashes and the hooded figures of Batman and Robin. A joke all of it had been: those years had been full of jokes, with no one wanting to grow up, with that longing to be children for ever. Tears dripped from his beard to the T-shirt now; some fell on to his jeans. He turned the electric light on and then noticed the cup of tea by his bed. He drank it, swallowing the skin and the fly that had died in it. His tears did not distress him.

'Well, that was it, Malcolm,' Anthea Chalmers said. 'I mean, no one enjoys a bedroom more than I do, but for God's sake!'

Her soup-plate eyes rapidly blinked, her lips were held for a moment in a little knot. The man she'd married, she yet again revealed, had not been able to give her what she'd wanted and needed. Instead, intoxicated, he would return to their house at night and roar about from room to room. Often he armed himself with a bamboo cane. 'Which he bought,' she reminded Malcolm, 'quite openly in a garden shop.'

In the honeysuckle, suburban bees paused between moments of buzzing. A white butterfly fluttered beside Malcolm's face. 'You must be awfully glad to be rid of him,' he politely said.

'One's alone, Malcolm. It isn't easy, being alone.'

She went into details about how difficult it was, and how various frustrations could be eased. She lowered her voice, she said she spoke in confidence. Sexual fantasy flooded from her, tired and seeming soiled in the bright sunshine, with the scent of the honeysuckle so close to both of them. Malcolm listened, not moving away, not trying to think of other things. It was nearly two years since Anthea Chalmers had discovered that he would always listen at a party.

In the garden the voices had become louder as more alcohol was consumed. Laughter was shriller, cigarette smoke hung about. By the tool-shed in the far distance the children, organized by a girl who was a little older than the others, played a variation of Grandmother's Footsteps.

Tom Highband, who wrote under another name a column for the *Daily Telegraph*, told a joke that caused a burst of laughter. Sandy Mr Fulmer, whom nobody knew very well, listened to the Unwins exchanging gossip with Susanna Maidstone about the school their children all attended. 'Just a little slower,' Marcus Stire's friend pleaded, writing down a recipe for prune jelly on the back of a cheque-book. Taylor-Deeth was getting drunk.

'It has its own little beach of course,' the man with the damp-looking moustache informed Jessica. You went down a flight of steps and there you were. They adored the Spaniards, he added, Joan especially did.

And then Joan, who was his wife, was there beside them, in shades of pink. She was bulky, like her husband, with a smile so widely beaming that it seemed to run off her face into her smooth grey hair. She had always had a thing about the Spanish, she agreed, the quality of Spanish life, their little churches. 'We have a maid of course,' her husband said, 'who keeps an eye on things. Old Violetta.'

Glasses were again refilled, the Morrishes together attending to that, as was their way at their parties. She did so quietly, he with more dash. People often remarked that they were like good servants, the way they complemented one another in this way. As well, they were said to be happily married.

Glancing between the couple who were talking to her, Jessica could see that Malcolm was still trapped. The Livingstons tried to cut in on the tête-à-tête but Anthea Chalmers's shoulder sharply edged them away. Together again after their separation, the Livingstons looked miserable.

'Violetta mothers us,' the man with the damp moustache said. 'We could never manage without old Violetta.'

'Another thing is Spanish dignity,' his wife continued, and the man added that old Violetta certainly had her share of that.

'Oh yes, indeed,' his wife agreed.

Marcus Stire arrived then, lanky and malicious. The couple with the house in Spain immediately moved away, as if they didn't like the look of him. He laughed. They were embarrassed, he explained, because at another party recently they'd all of a sudden quarrelled most violently in his presence. The man had even raised an arm to strike his wife, and Marcus Stire had had to restrain him.

'You'd never think it, would you, Jessica? All that guff about cosiness in Spain when more likely that smile of hers covers a multitude of sins. What awful frauds people are!' He laughed again and then continued, his soft voice drawling, a cigarette between the rings on his fingers.

He ran through all the people in the garden. Susanna Maidstone had been seen with Taylor-Deeth in the Trat-West. The Livingstons' patched-up arrangement wouldn't of course last. The Unwins were edgy, frigidity was Anthea Chalmers's problem. 'Suburban middle age,' he said in his drawl. 'It's like a minefield.' The Morrishes had had a ghastly upset a month ago when a girl from his office had pursued him home one night, messily spilling the beans.

Jessica looked at the Morrishes, so neatly together as they saw to people's drinks, attending now to Mr Fulmer. It seemed astonishing that they, too, weren't quite as they appeared to be. 'Oh, heavens, yes,' Marcus Stire said, guessing at this doubt in her mind.

His malice was perceptive, and he didn't much exaggerate. He had a way of detecting trouble, and of accurately piecing together the fragments that came his way. Caught off her guard, she wondered what he said to other people about Malcolm and herself. She wondered just how he saw them and then immediately struggled to regain her concentration, knowing she should not wonder that.

He was commenting now on the girl who had persuaded the other children to play her version of Grandmother's Footsteps, a bossy handful he called her. How dreadful she'd be at forty-eight, her looks three-quarters gone, famous in some other suburb as a nagging wife. Jessica smiled, as if he had related a pleasant joke. Again she made the effort to concentrate.

You had to do that: to concentrate and to listen properly, as Malcolm was listening, as she had listened herself to the talk about a house in Spain. You had to have a bouncy wallpaper all over the house, and fresh white paint instead of gravy-brown. You mustn't forget your plan to get the garden as colourful as this one; you mustn't let your mind wander. Busily you must note the damp appearance of a man's moustache and the smooth greyness of a woman's hair, and the malevolence in the eyes that were piercing into you now.

'I've written off those years, Malcolm,' Anthea Chalmers said, and across the garden Malcolm saw that his wife had collapsed. He could tell at once, as if she'd fallen to the grass and was lying there in a heap. Occasionally one or the other of them went under; impossible to anticipate which, or how it would happen.

He watched her face and saw that she was back in 1954, her pains developing a rhythm, a sweltering summer afternoon. A message had come to him in court, and when he'd returned to the house the midwife was smoking a cigarette in the hall. The midwife and the nurse had been up all night with a difficult delivery in Sheen. Afterwards, when the child had been born and everything tidied up, he'd given them a glass of whisky each.

Like an infection, all of it slipped across the garden, through the cigarette smoke and the people and the smartly casual Sunday clothes, from Jessica to Malcolm. Down their treacherous Memory Lane it dragged them, one after the other. The first day at the primary school, tears at the gate, the kindly dinner lady. The gang of four, their child and three others, at daggers drawn with other gangs. The winning of the high jump.

'Excuse me,' Malcolm said. It was worse for Jessica, he thought in a familiar way as he made his way to her. It was worse because after the birth she'd been told she must not have other babies: she blamed herself now for being obedient.

They left the party suddenly, while the children still played a version of Grandmother's Footsteps by the toolshed, and the adults drank and went on talking to one another. People who knew them guessed that their abrupt departure might somehow have to do with their son, whom no one much mentioned these days, he being a registered drug addict. The couple who had spoken to Jessica about their Spanish house spoke of it now to their hosts, who did not listen as well as she had. Anthea Chalmers tried to explain to Marcus Stire's friend, but that was hopeless. Marcus Stire again surveyed the people in the garden.

*

Anger possessed Malcolm as they walked across the common that had been peaceful in the early morning. It was less so now. Cricket would be played that afternoon and preparations were being made, the square marked, the sight-screens wheeled into position. An ice-cream van was already trading briskly. People lay on the grass, youths kicked a football.

'I'm sorry,' Jessica said. Her voice was nervous; she felt ashamed of herself.

'It isn't you, Jessica.'

'Let's have a drink on our own, shall we?'

Neither of them wishing to return immediately to their house, they went to the Red Rover and sat outside. She guessed his thoughts, as earlier he had seen hers in her face. When people wondered where all of it had gone, all that love and all those flowers, he would like to have shown them their darkened upstairs room. The jolly Sixties and those trips to wonderland were there, he'd once cried out, with half-made aeroplanes gathering a dust. Their son had a name, which was used when they addressed him; but when they thought of him he was nameless in their minds. Years ago they'd discovered that that was the same for both of them.

'Maybe,' she said, referring to the future, trying to cheer him up.

He made a gesture, half a nod: the speculation was impossible. And the consolation that families had always had children who were locked away and looked after wasn't a consolation in the least. They didn't have to live with a monstrous fact of nature, but with a form of accidental suicide, and that was worse.

They sat a little longer in the sunshine, both of them thinking about the house they'd left an hour or so ago. It would be as silent as if they'd never had a child, and then little noises would begin, like the noises of a ghost. The quiet descent of the stairs, the shuffling through the hall. He would be there in the kitchen, patiently sitting, when they returned. He would smile at them and during lunch a kind of conversation might develop, or it might not. A week ago he'd said, quite suddenly, that soon he intended to work in a garden somewhere, or a park. Occasionally he said things like that.

They didn't mention him as they sat there; they never did now. And it was easier for both of them to keep away from Memory Lane when they were together and alone. Instead of all that there was the gossip of Marcus Stire: Susanna Maidstone in the Trat-West, the girl from the office arriving in the Morrishes' house, the quarrel between the smiling woman and her suede-clad husband, Anthea Chalmers, lone Mr Fulmer, the Livingstons endeavouring to make a go of it. Easily, Malcolm imagined Marcus Stire's drawling tones and the sharpness of his eye, like a splinter of glass. He knew now how Jessica had been upset: a pair of shadows Marcus Stire would have called them, clinging to the periphery of life because that was where they felt safe, both of them a little destroyed.

They went on discussing the people they'd just left, wondering if some fresh drama had broken out, another explosion in the landscape of marriage that Marcus Stire had likened to a minefield. Finishing their drinks, they agreed that he'd certainly tell them if it had. They talked about him for a moment, and then the subject of the party drifted away from them and they talked of other things. Malcolm told her what was happening in *Edwin Drood*, because it was a book she would never read. His voice continued while they left the Red Rover and walked across the common, back to their house. It was odd, she reflected as she listened to it, that companionship had developed in their middle age, when luckier people trailed from their marriages such tales of woe.

The Paradise Lounge

On her high stool by the bar the old woman was as still as a statue. Perhaps her face is expressionless, Beatrice thought, because in repose it does not betray the extent of her years. The face itself was lavishly made up, eyes and mouth, rouge softening the wrinkles, a dusting of perfumed powder. The chin was held more than a little high, at an angle that tightened the loops of flesh beneath it. Grey hair was short beneath a black cloche hat that suggested a fashion of the past, as did the tight black skirt and black velvet coat. Eighty she'd be, Beatrice deduced, or eighty-two or -three.

'We can surely enjoy ourselves,' Beatrice's friend said, interrupting her scrutiny of the old woman. 'Surely we can, Bea?'

She turned her head. The closeness of his brick-coloured flesh and of the smile in his eyes caused her lips to tremble. She appeared to smile also, but what might have been taken for pleasure was a checking of her tears.

'Yes,' she said. 'Of course.'

They were married, though not to one another. Beatrice's friend, casually dressed for a summer weekend, was in early middle age, no longer slim yet far from bulky. Beatrice was thirty-two, petite and black-haired in a blue denim dress. Sunglasses disguised her deep-rust eyes, which was how – a long time ago now – her father had described them. She had wanted to be an actress then.

'It's best,' her friend said, repeating the brief statement for what might have been the hundredth time since they had settled into his car earlier that afternoon. The affair was over, the threat to their families averted. They had come away to say goodbye.

'Yes, I know it's best,' she said, a repetition also.

At the bar the old woman slowly raised a hand to her hat and touched it delicately with her fingers. Slowly the hand descended, and then lifted her cocktail glass. Her scarlet mouth was not quite misshapen, but age had harshly scored what once had been a perfect outline, lips pressed together like a rosebud on its side. Failure, Beatrice thought as casually she observed all this: in the end the affair was a failure. She didn't even love him any more, and long ago he'd ceased to love her. It was euphemism to call it saying goodbye: they were having a dirty weekend, there was nothing left to lift it higher than that.

'I'm sorry we couldn't manage longer,' he said. 'I'm sorry about Glengarriff.'

'It doesn't matter.'

'Even so.'

She ceased to watch the old woman at the bar. She smiled at him, again disguising tears but also wanting him to know that there were no hard feelings, for why on earth should there be?

'After all, we've been to Glengarriff,' she said, a joke because on the one occasion they'd visited the place they had nearly been discovered in their deceptions. She'd used her sister as an excuse for her absences from home: for a long time now her sister had been genuinely unwell in a farmhouse in Co. Meath, a house that fortunately for Beatrice's purpose didn't have a telephone.

'I'll never forget you,' he said, his large tanned hand suddenly on one of hers, the vein throbbing in his forehead. A line of freckles ran down beside the vein, five smudges on the redbrick skin. In winter you hardly noticed them.

'Nor I you.'

'Darling old Bea,' he said, as if they were back at the beginning.

The bar was a dim, square lounge with a scattering of small tables, one of which they occupied. Ashtrays advertised Guinness, beer-mats Heineken. Sunlight touched the darkened glass in one of two windows, drawing from it a glow that was not unlike the amber gleam of whiskey. Behind the bar itself the rows of bottles, spirits upside down above their global measures, glittered pleasantly as a centre-piece, their reflections gaudy in a cluttered mirror. The floor had a patterned carpet, further patterned with cigarette burns and a diversity of stains. The Paradise Lounge the bar had been titled in a moment of hyperbole by the grandfather of the present proprietor, a sign still proclaiming as much on the door that opened from the hotel's mahogany hall. Beatrice's friend had hesitated, for the place seemed hardly promising: Keegan's Railway Hotel in a town neither of them knew. They might have driven on, but he was tired and the sun had been in his eyes. 'It's all right,' she had reassured him.

He took their glasses to the bar and had to ring a bell because the man in charge had disappeared ten minutes ago. 'Nice evening,' he said to the old woman on the barstool, and she managed to indicate agreement without moving a muscle of her carefully held head. 'We'll have the same again,' he said to the barman, who apologized for his absence, saying he'd been mending a tap.

Left on her own, Beatrice sighed a little and took off her sunglasses. There was no need for this farewell, no need to see him for the last time in his pyjamas or to sit across a table from him at dinner and at breakfast, making conversation that once had come naturally. 'A final fling,' he'd put it, and she'd thought of someone beating a cracked drum, trying to extract a sound that wasn't there any more. How could it have come to this? The Paradise Lounge of Keegan's Railway Hotel, Saturday night in a hilly provincial town, litter caught in the railings of the Christian Brothers':

how *could* this be the end of what they once had had? Saying goodbye to her, he was just somebody else's husband: the lover had slipped away.

'Well, it's a terrible bloody tap we have,' the barman was saying. 'Come hell or high water, I can't get a washer into it.'

'It can be a difficult job.'

'You could come in and say that to the wife for me, sir.'

The drinks were paid for, the transaction terminated. Further gin and Martini were poured into the old woman's glass, and Beatrice watched again while like a zombie the old woman lit a cigarette.

Miss Doheny her name was: though beautiful once, she had never married. Every Saturday evening she met the Meldrums in the Paradise Lounge, where they spent a few hours going through the week that had passed, exchanging gossip and commenting on the world. Miss Doheny was always early and would sit up at the bar for twenty minutes on her own, having the extra couple of drinks that, for her, were always necessary. Before the Meldrums arrived she would make her way to a table in a corner, for that was where Mrs Meldrum liked to be.

It wasn't usual that other people were in the bar then. Occasionally it filled up later but at six o'clock, before her friends arrived, she nearly always had it to herself. Francis Keegan – the hotel's inheritor, who also acted as barman – spent a lot of time out in the back somewhere, attending to this or that. It didn't matter because after their initial greeting of one another, and a few remarks about the weather, there wasn't much conversation that Miss Doheny and he had to exchange. She enjoyed sitting up at the bar on her own, glancing at the reflections in the long mirror behind the bottles, provided the reflections were never of herself. On the other hand it was a pleasant enough diversion, having visitors.

Miss Doheny, who had looked twice at Beatrice and once at her companion, guessed at their wrong-doing. Tail-ends of conversation had drifted across the lounge, no effort being made to lower voices since more often than not the old turn out to be deaf. They were people from Dublin whose relationship was not that recorded in Francis Keegan's register in the hall. Without much comment, modern life permitted their sin; the light-brown motor-car parked in front of the hotel made their self-indulgence a simple matter.

How different it had been, Miss Doheny reflected, in 1933! Correctly she estimated that that would have been the year when she herself was the age the dark-haired girl was now. In 1933 adultery and divorce and light-brown motor-cars had belonged more in America and England, read about and alien to what already was being called the Irish way of life. 'Catholic Ireland,' Father Horan used to say. 'Decent Catholic Ireland.' The term was vague and yet had meaning: the emergent nation, seeking pillars on which to build itself, had plumped for holiness and the Irish language – natural choices in the circumstances. 'A certain class of woman,' old Father

Horan used to say, 'constitutes an abhorrence.' The painted women of Clancy's Picture House – sound introduced in 1936 – were creatures who carried a terrible warning. Jezebel women, Father Horan called them, adding that the picture house should never have been permitted to exist. In his grave for a quarter of a century, he would hardly have believed his senses if he'd walked into the Paradise Lounge in Keegan's Railway Hotel to discover two adulterers, and one of his flock who had failed to heed his castigation of painted women. Yet for thirty-five years Miss Doheny had strolled through the town on Saturday evenings to this same lounge, past the statue of the 1798 rebels, down the sharp incline of Castle Street. On Sundays she covered the same ground again, on the way to and from Mass. Neither rain nor cold prevented her from making the journey to the Church of the Immaculate Conception or to the hotel, and illness did not often afflict her. That she had become more painted as the years piled up seemed to Miss Doheny to be natural in the circumstances.

In the Paradise Lounge she felt particularly at home. In spring and summer the Meldrums brought plants for her, or bunches of chives or parsley, sometimes flowers. Not because she wished to balance the gesture with one of her own but because it simply pleased her to do so she brought for them a pot of jam if she had just made some, or pieces of shortbread. At Christmas, more formally, they exchanged gifts of a different kind. At Christmas the lounge was decorated by Francis Keegan, as was the hall of the hotel and the dining-room. Once a year, in April, a dance was held in the dining-room, in connection with a local point-to-point, and it was said in the town that Francis Keegan made enough in the bar during the course of that long night to last him for the next twelve months. The hotel ticked over from April to April, the Paradise Lounge becoming quite brisk with business when an occasional function was held in the dining-room, though never achieving the abandoned spending that distinguished the night of the point-to-point. Commercial travellers sometimes stayed briefly, taking pot-luck with Mrs Keegan's cooking, which at the best of times was modest in ambition and achievement. After dinner these men would sit on one of the high stools in the Paradise Lounge, conversing with Francis Keegan and drinking bottles of stout. Mrs Keegan would sometimes put in a late appearance and sip a glass of gin and water. She was a woman of slatternly appearance, with loose grey hair and slippers. Her husband complemented her in style and manner, his purplish complexion reflecting a dedication to the wares he traded in across his bar. They were an undemanding couple, charitable in their opinions, regarded as unfortunate in the town since their union had not produced children. Because of that, Keegan's Railway Hotel was nearing the end of its days as a family concern and in a sense it was fitting that that should be so, for the railway that gave it its title had been closed in 1951.

How I envy her! Miss Doheny thought. How fortunate she is to find herself in these easy times, not condemned because she loves a man! It seemed right to Miss Doheny that a real love affair was taking place in the Paradise Lounge and that no one questioned it. Francis Keegan knew perfectly well that the couple were not man and wife, the strictures of old Father Horan were as fusty by now as neglected mice droppings. The holiness that had accompanied the birth of a nation had at last begun to shed its first tight skin: liberation, Miss Doheny said to herself, marvelling over the word.

They walked about the town because it was too soon for dinner. Many shops were still open, greengrocers anxious to rid themselves of cabbage that had been limp for days and could not yet again be offered for sale after the weekend, chemists and sweetshops. Kevin Ryan, Your Best for Hi-Fi, had arranged a loudspeaker in a window above his premises: Saturday-night music blared forth, punk harmonies and a tenor rendering of 'Kelly the Boy from Killann'. All tastes were catered for.

The streets were narrow, the traffic congested. Women picked over the greengrocers' offerings, having waited until this hour because prices would be reduced. Newly shaved men slipped into the public houses, youths and girls loitered outside Redmond's Café and on the steps of the 1798 statue. Two dogs half-heartedly fought outside the Bank of Ireland.

The visitors to the town enquired where the castle was, and then made their way up Castle Hill. 'Opposite Castle Motors,' the child they'd asked had said, and there it was: an ivy-covered ruin, more like the remains of a cowshed. Corrugated iron sealed off an archway, its torn bill-posters advertising Calor Gas and a rock group, Duffy's Circus and Fine Gael, and the annual point-to-point that kept Keegan's Railway Hotel going. Houses had been demolished in this deserted area, concrete replacements only just begun. The graveyard of the Protestant church was unkempt; *New Premises in Wolfe Tone Street*, said a placard in the window of Castle Motors. Litter was everywhere.

'Not exactly camera fodder,' he said with his easy laugh. 'A bloody disgrace, some of these towns are.'

'The people don't notice, I suppose.'

'They should maybe wake themselves up.'

The first time he'd seen her, he'd afterwards said, he had heard himself whispering that it was she he should have married. They'd sat together, talking over after-dinner coffee in someone else's house. He'd told her, lightly, that he was in the Irish rope business, almost making a joke of it because that was his way. A week later his car had drawn up beside her in Rathgar Road, where she'd lived since her marriage. 'I thought I recognized you,' he said, afterwards confessing that he'd looked up her husband's name in the telephone directory. 'Come in for a drink,' she invited, and of course he had. Her two children had been there, her husband had come in.

They made their way back to the town, she taking his arm as they descended the steep hill they'd climbed. A wind had gathered, cooling the evening air.

'It feels so long ago,' she said. 'The greater part of my life appears to have occurred since that day when you first came to the house.'

'I know, Bea.'

He'd seemed extraordinary and nice, and once when he'd smiled at her she'd found herself looking away. She wasn't unhappy in her marriage, only bored by the monotony of preparing food and seeing to the house and the children. She had, as well, a reluctant feeling that she wasn't appreciated, that she hadn't been properly loved for years.

'You don't regret it happened?' he said, stepping out into the street because the pavement was still crowded outside Redmond's Café.

She pitched her voice low so that he wouldn't hear her saying she wasn't sure. She didn't want to tell a lie, she wasn't certain of the truth.

He nodded, assuming her reassurance. Once, of course, he would never have let a mumbled reply slip by.

Miss Doheny had moved from the bar and was sitting at a table with the Meldrums when Beatrice and her friend returned to the Paradise Lounge after dinner. Mrs Meldrum was telling all about the visit last Sunday afternoon of her niece, Kathleen. 'Stones she's put on,' she reported, and then recalled that Kathleen's newly acquired husband had sat there for three hours hardly saying a word. Making a fortune he was, in the dry goods business, dull but good-hearted.

Miss Doheny listened. Strangely, her mind was still on the visitors who had returned to the lounge. She'd heard the girl saying that a walk about the town would be nice, and as the Meldrums had entered the lounge an hour or so ago she'd heard the man's voice in the hall and had guessed they were then on their way to the dining-room. The dinner would not have been good, for Miss Doheny had often heard complaints about the nature of Mrs Keegan's cooking. And yet the dinner, naturally, would not have mattered in the least.

Mrs Meldrum's voice continued: Kathleen's four children by her first marriage were all grown up and off her hands, she was lucky to have married so late in life into a prosperous dry goods business. Mr Meldrum inclined his head or nodded, but from time to time he would also issue a mild contradiction, setting the facts straight, regulating his wife's memory. He was a grey-haired man in a tweed jacket, very tall and thin, his face as sharp as a blade, his grey moustache well cared-for. He smoked while he drank, allowing a precise ten minutes to elapse between the end of one cigarette and the lighting of the next. Mrs Meldrum was smaller than her companions by quite some inches, round and plump, with glasses and a black hat.

The strangers were drinking Drambuie now, Miss Doheny noticed. The man made a joke, probably about the food they'd eaten; the girl smiled.

It was difficult to understand why it was that they were so clearly not man and wife. There was a wistfulness in the girl's face, but the wistfulness said nothing very much. In a surprising way Miss Doheny imagined herself crossing the lounge to where they were. 'You're lucky, you know,' she heard herself saying. 'Honestly, you're lucky, child.' She glanced again in the girl's direction and for a moment caught her eye. She almost mouthed the words, but changed her mind because as much as possible she liked to keep her face in repose.

Beatrice listened to her companion's efforts to cheer the occasion up. The town and the hotel – especially the meal they'd just consumed – combined to reflect the mood that the end of the affair had already generated. They were here, Beatrice informed herself again, not really to say goodbye to one another but to commit adultery for the last time. They would enjoy it as they always had, but the enjoyment would not be the same as that inspired by the love there had been. They might not have come, they might more elegantly have said goodbye, yet their presence in a bar ridiculously named the Paradise Lounge seemed suddenly apt. The bedroom where acts of mechanical passion would take place had a dingy wallpaper, its flattened pink soap already used by someone else. Dirty weekend, Beatrice thought again, for stripped of love all that was left was the mess of deception and lies there had been, of theft and this remaining, too ordinary desire. Her sister, slowly dying in the farmhouse, had been a bitter confidante and would never forgive her now. Tonight in a provincial bedroom a manufacturer of rope would have his way with her and she would have her way with him. There would be their nakedness and their mingled sweat.

'I thought that steak would walk away,' he spiritedly was continuing now. 'Being somebody's shoe-leather.'

She suddenly felt drunk, and wanted to be drunker. She held her glass toward him. 'Let's just drink,' she said.

She caught the eye of the old woman at the other table and for a moment sensed Miss Doheny's desire to communicate with her. It puzzled her that an elderly woman whom she did not know should wish to say something, yet she strongly felt that this was so. Then Miss Doheny returned her attention to what the other old woman was saying.

When they'd finished the drinks that Beatrice's companion had just fetched they moved from the table they were at and sat on two barstools, listening to Francis Keegan telling them about the annual liveliness in the hotel on the night of the April point-to-point. Mrs Keegan appeared at his side and recalled an occasion when two crates of day-old chicks, deposited in the hall of the hotel for a couple of hours, had been released by some of the wilder spirits and how old Packy O'Brien had imagined he'd caught the d.t.s when he saw them fluttering up the stairs. And there was the story – before Mrs Keegan's time, as she was swift to point out – when Jack

Doyle and Movita had stayed in Keegan's, when just for the hell of it Jack Doyle had chased a honeymoon couple up Castle Hill, half naked from their bed. After several further drinks, Beatrice began to laugh. She felt much less forlorn now that the faces of Francis Keegan and his wife were beginning to float agreeably in her vision. When she looked at the elderly trio in the corner, the only other people in the lounge, their faces floated also.

The thin old man came to the bar for more drinks and cigarettes. He nodded and smiled at Beatrice; he remarked upon the weather. 'Mr Meldrum,' said Francis Keegan by way of introduction. 'How d'you do,' Beatrice said.

Her companion yawned and appeared to be suggesting that they should go to bed. Beatrice took no notice. She pushed her glass at Francis Keegan, reaching for her hand-bag and announcing that it was her round. 'A drink for everyone,' she said, aware that when she gestured towards the Keegans and the elderly trio she almost lost her balance. She giggled. 'Definitely my round,' she slurred, giggling again.

Mrs Keegan told another story, about a commercial traveller called Artie Logan who had become drunk in his room and had sent down for so many trays of tea and buttered bread that every cup and saucer in the hotel had been carried up to him. 'They said to thank you,' her husband passed on, returning from the elderly trio's table. Beatrice turned her head. All three of them were looking at her, their faces still slipping about a bit. Their glasses were raised in her direction. 'Good luck,' the old man called out.

It was then that Beatrice realized. She looked from face to face, making herself smile to acknowledge the good wishes she was being offered, the truth she sensed seeming to emerge from a blur of features and clothes and three raised glasses. She nodded, and saw the heads turn away again. It had remained unstated: the love that was there had never in any way been exposed. In this claustrophobic town, in this very lounge, there had been the endless lingering of a silent passion, startlingly different from the instant requiting of her own.

Through the muzziness of inebriation Beatrice glanced again across the bar. Behind her the Keegans were laughing, and the man she'd once so intensely loved was loudly laughing also. She heard the sound of the laughter strangely, as if it echoed from a distance, and she thought for a moment that it did not belong in the Paradise Lounge, that only the two old women and the old man belonged there. He was loved, and in silence he returned that love. His plump, bespectacled wife had never had reason to feel betrayed; no shame or guilt attached. In all the years a sister's dying had never been made use of. Nor had there been hasty afternoons in Rathgar Road, blinds drawn against neighbours who might guess, a bedroom set to rights before children came in from school. There hadn't been a single embrace.

Yet the love that had continued for so long would go on now until the grave: without even thinking, Beatrice knew that that was so. The old woman paraded for a purpose the remnants of her beauty, the man was elegant in his tweed. How lovely that was! Beatrice thought, still muzzily surveying the people at the table, the wife who had not been deceived quite contentedly chatting, the two who belonged together occupying their magic worlds.

How lovely that nothing had been destroyed: Beatrice wanted to tell someone that, but there was no one to tell. In Rathgar Road her children would be watching the television, their father sitting with them. Her sister would die before the year was finished. What cruelty there seemed to be, and more sharply now she recalled the afternoon bedroom set to rights and her sister's wasted face. She wanted to run away, to go backwards into time so that she might shake her head at her lover on the night they'd first met.

Miss Doheny passed through the darkened town, a familiar figure on a Saturday night. It had been the same as always, sitting there, close to him, the smoke drifting from the cigarette that lolled between his fingers. The girl by now would be close in a different way to the man who was somebody else's husband also. As in a film, their clothes would be scattered about the room that had been hired for love, their murmurs would break a silence. Tears ran through Miss Doheny's meticulous make-up, as often they did when she walked away from the Paradise Lounge on a Saturday night. It was difficult sometimes not to weep when she thought about the easy times that had come about in her lifetime, mocking the agony of her stifled love.